EDNA FERBER

FIVE COMPLETE NOVELS

EDNA FERBER

FIVE COMPLETE NOVELS

So Big

❧

Show Boat

❧

Cimarron

❧

Saratoga Trunk

❧

Giant

AVENEL BOOKS · NEW YORK

CONTENTS

So Big

1

UNTIL HE WAS almost ten the name stuck to him. He had literally to fight his way free of it. From So Big (of fond and infantile derivation) it had been condensed into Sobig. And Sobig DeJong, in all its consonantal disharmony, he had remained until he was a ten-year-old schoolboy in that incredibly Dutch district southwest of Chicago known first as New Holland and later as High Prairie. At ten, by dint of fists, teeth, copper-toed boots, and temper, he earned the right to be called by his real name, Dirk DeJong. Now and then, of course, the nickname bobbed up and had to be subdued in a brief and bitter skirmish. His mother, with whom the name had originated, was the worst offender. When she lapsed he did not, naturally, use schoolyard tactics on her. But he sulked and glowered portentously and refused to answer, though her tone, when she called him So Big, would have melted the heart of any but that natural savage, a boy of ten.

The nickname had sprung from the early and idiotic question invariably put to babies and answered by them, with infinite patience, through the years of their infancy.

Selina DeJong, darting expertly about her kitchen, from washtub to baking board, from stove to table, or, if at work in the fields of the truck farm, straightening the numbed back for a moment's respite from the close-set rows of carrots, turnips, spinach, or beets over which she was labouring, would wipe the sweat beads from nose and forehead with a quick duck of her head in the crook of her bent arm. Those great fine dark eyes of hers would regard the child perched impermanently on a little heap of empty potato sacks, one of which comprised his costume. He was constantly detaching himself from the parent sack heap to dig and burrow in the rich warm black loam of the truck garden. Selina DeJong had little time for the expression of affection. The work was always hot at her heels. You saw a young woman in a blue calico dress, faded and earth-grimed. Between her eyes was a driven look as of one who walks always a little ahead of herself in her haste. Her dark abundant hair was skewered into a utilitarian knob from which soft loops and strands were constantly escaping, to be pushed back by that same harried ducking gesture of head and bent arm. Her hands, for such use, were usually too crusted and inground with the soil into which she was delving. You saw a child of perhaps two years, dirt-streaked, sunburned, and generally otherwise defaced by those bumps, bites, scratches, and contusions that are the common lot of the farm child of a mother harried by work. Yet, in that moment, as the woman looked at the child there in the warm moist spring of the Illinois prairie land, or in the cluttered kitchen of the farmhouse, there quivered and vibrated between them and all about them an aura, a glow, that imparted to them and their surroundings a mystery, a beauty, a radiance.

"How big is baby?" Selina would demand, senselessly. "How big is my man?".

The child would momentarily cease to poke plump fingers into the rich black loam. He would smile a gummy though slightly weary smile and stretch wide his arms. She, too, would open her tired arms wide, wide. Then they would say in a duet, his mouth a puckered pink petal, hers quivering with tenderness and a certain amusement, "*So-o-o-o* big!" with the voice soaring on the prolonged vowel and dropping suddenly with the second word. Part of the game. The child became so habituated to this question that sometimes, if Selina happened to glance round at him suddenly in the midst of her task, he would take his cue without the familiar question being put and would squeal his "So-o-o-o big!" rather absently, in dutiful solo. Then he would throw back his head and laugh a triumphant laugh, his open mouth a coral orifice. She would run to him, and swoop down upon him, and bury her flushed face in the warm moist creases of his neck, and make as though to devour him. "So big!"

But of course he wasn't. He wasn't as big as that. In fact, he never became as big as the wide-stretched arms of her love and imagination would have had him. You would have thought she should have been satisfied when, in later years, he was the Dirk DeJong whose name you saw (engraved) at the top of heavy cream linen paper, so rich and thick and stiff as to have the effect of being starched and ironed by some costly American business process; whose clothes were made by Peter Peel, the English tailor; whose roadster ran on a French chassis; whose cabinet held mellow Italian vermouth and Spanish sherry; whose wants were served by a Japanese houseman; whose life, in short, was that of the successful citizen of the Republic. But she wasn't. Not only was she dissatisfied: she was at once remorseful and indignant, as though she, Selina DeJong, the vegetable pedler, had been partly to blame for this success of his, and partly cheated by it.

When Selina DeJong had been Selina Peake she had lived in Chicago with her father. They had lived in many other cities as well. In Denver during the rampant '80s. In New York when Selina was twelve. In Milwaukee briefly. There was even a San Francisco interlude which was always a little sketchy in Selina's mind and which had ended in a departure so hurried as to bewilder even Selina who had learned to accept sudden comings and abrupt goings without question. "Business," her father always said. "Little deal." She never knew until the day of his death how literally the word deal was applicable to his business transactions. Simeon Peake, travelling the country with his little daughter, was a gambler by profession, temperament, and natural talents. When in luck they lived royally, stopping at the best hotels, eating strange, succulent sea-viands, going to the play, driving in hired rigs (always with two horses. If Simeon Peake had not enough money for a two-horse equipage he walked). When fortune hid her face they lived in boarding houses, ate boarding-house meals, wore the clothes bought when Fortune's breath was balmy. During all this time Selina attended schools, good, bad, private, public, with surprising regularity considering her nomadic existence. Deep-bosomed matrons, seeing this dark-eyed serious child seated alone in a hotel lobby or boarding-house parlour, would bend over her in solicitous questioning.

"Where is your mamma, little girl?"

"She is dead," Selina would reply, politely and composedly.

"Oh, my poor little dear!" Then, with a warm rush, "Don't you want to come and play with my little girl? She loves little girls to play with. H'm?" The "m" of the interrogation held hummingly, tenderly.

"No, thank you very much. I'm waiting for my father. He would be disappointed not to find me here."

These good ladies wasted their sympathy. Selina had a beautiful time. Except for three years, to recall which was to her like entering a sombre icy room on leaving a warm and glowing one, her life was free, interesting, varied. She made decisions usually devolving upon the adult mind. She selected clothes. She ruled her father. She read absorbedly books found in boarding-house parlours, in hotels, in such public libraries as the times afforded. She was alone for hours a day, daily. Frequently her father, fearful of loneliness for her, brought her an armful of books and she had an orgy, dipping and swooping about among them in a sort of gourmand's ecstasy of indecision. In this way, at fifteen, she knew the writings of Byron, Jane Austen, Dickens, Charlotte Brontë, Felicia Hemans. Not to speak of Mrs. E. D. E. N. Southworth, Bertha M. Clay, and that good fairy of the scullery, the *Fireside Companion,* in whose pages factory girls and dukes were brought together as inevitably as steak and onions. These last were, of course, the result of Selina's mode of living, and were loaned her by kind-hearted landladies, chambermaids, and waitresses all the way from California to New York.

Her three dark years—from nine to twelve—were spent with her two maiden aunts, the Misses Sarah and Abbie Peake, in the dim, prim Vermont Peake house from which her father, the black sheep, had run away when a boy. After her mother's death Simeon Peake had sent his little daughter back east in a fit of remorse and temporary helplessness on his part and a spurt of forgiveness and churchly charity on the part of his two sisters. The two women were incredibly drawn in the pattern of the New England spinster of fiction. Mitts, preserves, Bible, chilly best room, solemn and kittenless cat, order, little-girls-mustn't. They smelled of apples—of withered apples that have rotted at the core. Selina had once found such an apple in a corner of a disorderly school-desk, had sniffed it, regarded its wrinkled, sapless pink cheek, and had bitten into it adventuresomely, only to spit out the mouthful in an explosive and unladylike spray. It had been all black and mouldy at its heart.

Something of this she must have conveyed, in her desperation, to her father in an uncensored letter. Without warning he had come for her, and at sight of him she had been guilty of the only fit of hysteria that marked her life, before or after the episode.

So, then, from twelve to nineteen she was happy. They had come to Chicago in 1885, when she was sixteen. There they remained. Selina attended Miss Fister's Select School for Young Ladies. When her father brought her there he had raised quite a flutter in the Fister breast—so soft-spoken was he, so gentle, so sad-appearing, so winning as to smile. In the investment business, he explained. Stocks and that kind of thing. A widower. Miss Fister said, yes, she understood.

Simeon Peake had had nothing of the look of the professional gambler of the day. The wide slouch hat, the flowing mustache, the glittering eye, the too-bright boots, the gay cravat, all were missing in Simeon Peake's makeup. True, he did sport a singularly clear white diamond pin in his shirt front; and his hat he wore just a little on one side. But then, these both were in the male mode and quite commonly seen. For the rest he seemed a mild and suave man, slim, a trifle diffident, speaking seldom and then with a New England drawl by which he had come honestly enough, Vermont Peake that he was.

Chicago was his meat. It was booming, prosperous. Jeff Hankins's red plush and mirrored gambling house, and Mike McDonald's, too, both on

Clark Street, knew him daily. He played in good luck and bad, but he managed somehow to see to it that there was always the money to pay for the Fister schooling. His was the ideal poker face—bland, emotionless, immobile. When he was flush they ate at the Palmer House, dining off chicken or quail and thick rich soup and the apple pie for which the hostelry was famous. Waiters hovered solicitously about Simeon Peake, though he rarely addressed them and never looked at them. Selina was happy. She knew only such young people—girls—as she met at Miss Fister's school. Of men, other than her father, she knew as little as a nun—less. For those cloistered creatures must, if only in the conning of their Bible, learn much of the moods and passions that sway the male. The Songs of Solomon alone are a glorious sex education. But the Bible was not included in Selina's haphazard reading, and the Gideonite was not then a force in the hotel world.

Her chum was Julie Hempel, daughter of August Hempel, the Clark Street butcher. You probably now own some Hempel stock, if you're lucky; and eat Hempel bacon and Hempel hams cured in the hickory, for in Chicago the distance from butcher of 1885 to packer of 1890 was only a five-year leap.

Being so much alone developed in her a gift for the make-believe. In a comfortable, well-dressed way she was a sort of mixture of Dick Swiveller's Marchioness and Sarah Crewe. Even in her childhood she extracted from life the double enjoyment that comes usually only to the creative mind. "Now I'm doing this. Now I'm doing that," she told herself while she was doing it. Looking on while she participated. Perhaps her theatre-going had something to do with this. At an age when most little girls were not only unheard but practically unseen, she occupied a grown-up seat at the play, her rapt face, with its dark serious eyes, glowing in a sort of luminous pallor as she sat proudly next her father. Simeon Peake had the gambler's love of the theatre, himself possessing the dramatic quality necessary to the successful following of his profession.

In this way Selina, half-hidden in the depths of an orchestra seat, wriggled in ecstatic anticipation when the curtain ascended on the grotesque rows of Haverly's minstrels. She wept (as did Simeon) over the agonies of The Two Orphans when Kitty Blanchard and McKee Rankin came to Chicago with the Union Square Stock Company. She witnessed that startling innovation, a Jewish play, called Samuel of Posen. She saw Fanny Davenport in Pique. Simeon even took her to a performance of that shocking and delightful form of new entertainment, the Extravaganza. She thought the plump creature in tights and spangles, descending the long stairway, the most beautiful being she had ever seen.

"The thing I like about plays and books is that anything can happen. Anything! You never know," Selina said, after one of these evenings.

"No different from life," Simeon Peake assured her. "You've no idea the things that happen to you if you just relax and take them as they come."

Curiously enough, Simeon Peake said this, not though ignorance, but deliberately and with reason. In his way and day he was a very modern father. "I want you to see all kinds," he would say to her. "I want you to realize that this whole thing is just a grand adventure. A fine show. The trick is to play in it and look at it at the same time."

"What whole thing?"

"Living. All mixed up. The more kinds of people you see, and the more things you do, and the more things that happen to you, the richer you are. Even if they're not pleasant things. That's living. Remember, no matter what happens, good or bad, it's just so much"—he used the gambler's term, unconsciously—"just so much velvet."

But Selina, somehow, understood. "You mean that anything's better than being Aunt Sarah and Aunt Abbie."

"Well—yes. There are only two kinds of people in the world that really count. One kind's wheat and the other kind's emeralds."

"Fanny Davenport's an emerald," said Selina, quickly, and rather surprised to find herself saying it.

"Yes. That's it."

"And—and Julie Hempel's father—he's wheat."

"By golly, Sele!" shouted Simeon Peake. "You're a shrewd little tyke!"

It was after reading "Pride and Prejudice" that she decided to be the Jane Austen of her time. She became very mysterious and enjoyed a brief period of unpopularity at Miss Fister's owing to her veiled allusions to her "work"; and an annoying way of smiling to herself and tapping a ruminative toe as though engaged in visions far too exquisite for the common eye. Her chum Julie Hempel, properly enough, became enraged at this and gave Selina to understand that she must make her choice between revealing her secret or being cast out of the Hempel heart. Selina swore her to secrecy.

"Very well, then. Now I'll tell you. I'm going to be a novelist." Julie was palpably disappointed, though she said, "Selina!" as though properly impressed, but followed it up with: "Still, I don't see why you had to be so mysterious about it."

"You just don't understand, Julie. Writers have to study life at first hand. And if people know you're studying them they don't act natural. Now, that day you were telling me about the young man in your father's shop who looked at you and said————"

"Selina Peake, if you dare to put that in your book I'll never speak————"

"All right. I won't. But that's what I mean. You see!"

Julie Hempel and Selina Peake, both finished products of Miss Fister's school, were of an age—nineteen. Selina, on this September day, had been spending the afternoon with Julie, and now, adjusting her hat preparatory to leaving, she clapped her hands over her ears to shut out the sounds of Julie's importunings that she stay to supper. Certainly the prospect of the usual Monday evening meal in Mrs. Tebbitt's boarding house (the Peake luck was momentarily low) did not present sufficient excuse for Selina's refusal. Indeed, the Hempel supper as sketched dish for dish by the urgent Julie brought little greedy groans from Selina.

"It's prairie chickens—three of them—that a farmer west of town brought Father. Mother fixes them with stuffing, and there's currant jell. Creamed onions and baked tomatoes. And for dessert, apple roll."

Selina snapped the elastic holding her high-crowned hat under her chignon of hair in the back. She uttered a final and quavering groan. "On Monday nights we have cold mutton and cabbage at Mrs. Tebbitt's. This is Monday."

"Well then, silly, why not stay!"

"Father comes home at six. If I'm not there he's disappointed."

Julie, plump, blonde, placid, forsook her soft white blandishments and tried steel against the steel of Selina's decision.

"He leaves you right after supper. And you're alone every night until twelve and after."

"I don't see what that has to do with it," Selina said, stiffly.

Julie's steel, being low-grade, melted at once and ran off her in rivulets. "Of course it hasn't, Selie dear. Only I thought you might leave him just this once."

"If I'm not there he's disappointed. And that terrible Mrs. Tebbitt makes eyes at him. He hates it there."

"Then I don't see why you stay. I never could see. You've been there four months now, and I think it's horrid and stuffy; and oilcloth on the stairs."

"Father has had some temporary business setbacks."

Selina's costume testified to that. True, it was modish, and bustled, and basqued, and flounced; and her high-crowned, short-rimmed hat, with its trimming of feathers and flowers and ribbons had come from New York. But both were of last spring's purchasing, and this was September.

In the course of the afternoon they had been looking over the pages of Godey's *Ladies' Book* for that month. The disparity between Selina's costume and the creations pictured there was much as the difference between the Tebbitt meal and that outlined by Julie. Now Julie, fond though defeated, kissed her friend goodbye.

Selina walked quickly the short distance from the Hempel house to Tebbitt's, on Dearborn Avenue. Up in her second-floor room she took off her hat and called to her father, but he had not yet come in. She was glad of that. She had been fearful of being late. She regarded her hat now with some distaste, decided to rip off the faded spring roses, did rip a stitch or two, only to discover that the hat material was more faded than the roses, and that the uncovered surface showed up a dark splotch like a wall-spot when a picture, long hung, is removed. So she got a needle and prepared to tack the offending rose in its accustomed place.

Perched on the arm of a chair near the window, taking quick deft stitches, she heard a sound. She had never heard that sound before—that peculiar sound—the slow, ominous tread of men laden with a heavy inert burden; bearing with infinite care that which was well beyond hurting. Selina had never heard that sound before, and yet, hearing it, she recognized it by one of those pangs, centuries old, called woman's instinct. Thud—shuffle—thud—shuffle—up the narrow stairway, along the passage. She stood up, the needle poised in her hand. The hat fell to the floor. Her eyes were wide, fixed. Her lips slightly parted. The listening look. She knew.

She knew even before she heard the hoarse man's voice saying, "Lift 'er up there a little on the corner, now. Easy—e-e-easy." And Mrs. Tebbitt's high shrill clamour: "You can't bring it in there! You hadn't ought to bring it in here like this!"

Selina's suspended breath came back. She was panting now. She had flung open the door. A flat still burden partially covered with an overcoat carelessly flung over the face. The feet, in their square-toed boots, wobbled listlessly. Selina noticed how shiny the boots were. He was always very finicking about such things.

Simeon Peake had been shot in Jeff Hankins's place at five in the afternoon. The irony of it was that the bullet had not been intended for him at all. Its derelict course had been due to feminine aim. Sped by one of those over-dramatic ladies who, armed with horsewhip or pistol in tardy defence of their honour, spangled Chicago's dull '80s with their doings, it had been meant for a well-known newspaper publisher usually mentioned (in papers other than his own) as a bon vivant. The lady's leaden remonstrance was to have been proof of the fact that he had been more vivacious than bon.

It was, perhaps, because of this that the matter was pretty well hushed up. The publisher's paper—which was Chicago's foremost—scarcely mentioned the incident and purposely misspelled the name. The lady, thinking her task accomplished, had taken truer aim with her second bullet, and had saved herself the trouble of trial by human jury.

Simeon Peake left his daughter Selina a legacy of two fine clear blue-white diamonds (he had had the gambler's love of them) and the sum of four hundred and ninety-seven dollars in cash. Just how he had managed to have a sum like this put by was a mystery. The envelope containing it had evidently once held a larger sum. It had been sealed, and then slit. On the outside was written, in Simeon Peake's fine, almost feminine hand: "For my little daughter Selina Peake in case anything should happen to me." It bore a date seven years old. What the original sum had been no one ever knew. That any sum remained was evidence of the almost heroic self-control practised by one to whom money—ready money in any sum at all—meant only fuel to feed the flames of his gaming fever.

To Selina fell the choice of earning her own living or of returning to the Vermont village and becoming a withered and sapless dried apple, with black fuzz and mould at her heart, like her aunts, the Misses Sarah and Abbie Peake. She did not hesitate.

"But what kind of work?" Julie Hempel demanded. "What kind of work can you do?" Women—that is, the Selina Peakes—did not work.

"I—well, I can teach."

"Teach what?"

"The things I learned at Miss Fister's."

Julie's expression weighed and discredited Miss Fister. "Who to?" Which certainly justified her expression.

"To children. People's children. Or in the public schools."

"You have to do something first—go to Normal, or teach in the country, don't you?—before you can teach in the public schools. They're mostly old. Twenty-five or even thirty—or more!" with nineteen's incapacity to imagine an age beyond thirty.

That Julie was taking the offensive in this conversation, and Selina the defensive, was indicative of the girl's numbed state. Selina did not then know the iron qualities her friend was displaying in being with her at all. Mrs. Hempel had quite properly forbidden Julie ever to see the dead dissolute gambler's daughter again. She had even sent a note to Miss Fister expressing her opinion of a school which would, by admitting such unselected ladies to its select circle, expose other pupils to contamination.

Selina rallied to Julie's onslaught. "Then I'll just teach a country school. I'm good at arithmetic. You know that." Julie should have known it, having had all her Fister sums solved by Selina. "Country schools are just arithmetic and grammar and geography."

"You! Teaching a country school!"

She looked at Selina.

She saw a misleadingly delicate face, the skull small and exquisitely formed. The cheek bones rather high—or perhaps they looked so because of the fact that the eyes, dark, soft, and luminous, were unusually deep-set in their sockets. The face, instead of narrowing to a soft curve at the chin, developed unexpected strength in the jaw-line. That line, fine, steel-strong, sharp and clear, was of the stuff of which pioneer women are made. Julie, inexperienced in the art of reading the human physiognomy, did not decipher the meaning of it. Selina's hair was thick, long, and fine, so that she piled it easily in the loops, coils, and knots that fashion demanded. Her nose, slightly pinched at the nostrils, was exquisite. When she laughed it had the trick of wrinkling just a little across the narrow bridge; very engaging, and mischievous. She was thought a rather plain little thing, which she wasn't. But the eyes were what you marked and remembered. People to whom she was speaking had a way of looking into them deeply. Selina was often embarrassed to discover that they were not hearing what she had to say. Perhaps it was this velvety softness of the eyes that caused one to overlook the firmness of the lower face. When the next ten years had done their worst to her, and Julie had suddenly come upon her stepping agilely out of a truck gardener's wagon on Prairie Avenue, a tanned, weather-beaten, toil-worn woman, her abundant hair skewered into a knob and held by a long gray hairpin, her full calico skirt grimed with the mud of the wagon wheel, a pair of men's old side-boots on her slim feet, a grotesquely battered old felt hat (her husband's) on her head, her arms full of ears of sweet corn, and carrots, and radishes, and bunches of beets; a woman with bad teeth, flat breasts, a sagging pocket in her capacious skirt—even then Julie, staring, had known her by her eyes. And she had run to her in her silk suit and her fine silk shirtwaist and her hat with the plume and had cried, "Oh, Selina! My dear! My dear!"—with a sob of horror and pity—"My dear." And had taken Selina, carrots, beets, corn, and radishes, in her arms. The vegetables lay scattered all about them on the sidewalk in front of Julie Hempel Arnold's great stone house on Prairie Avenue. But strangely enough it had been Selina who had done the comforting, patting Julie's silken shoulder and saying, over and over, "There, there! It's all right, Julie. It's all right. Don't cry. What's there to cry for! Sh! . . . It's all right."

2

SELINA HAD THOUGHT herself lucky to get the Dutch school at High Prairie, ten miles outside Chicago. Thirty dollars a month! She was to board at the house of Klaas Pool, the truck farmer. It was August Hempel who had brought it all about; or Julie, urging him. Now, at forty-five, August Hempel, the Clark Street butcher, knew every farmer and stockman for miles around, and hundreds besides scattered throughout Cook County and the State of Illinois.

To get the Dutch school for Selina Peake was a simple enough matter for him. The High Prairie district school teacher had always, heretofore, been a man. A more advantageous position presenting itself, this year's prospective teacher had withdrawn before the school term had begun. This was in September. High Prairie school did not open until the first week in November. In that region of truck farms every boy and girl over six was busy in the fields throughout the early autumn. Two years of this, and Selina would be qualified for a city grade. August Hempel indicated that he could arrange that, too, when the time came. Selina thought this shrewd red-faced butcher a wonderful man, indeed. Which he was.

At forty-seven, single-handed, he was to establish the famous Hempel Packing Company. At fifty he was the power in the yards, and there were Hempel branches in Kansas City, Omaha, Denver. At sixty you saw the name of Hempel plastered over packing sheds, factories, and canning plants all the way from Honolulu to Portland. You read:

Don't Say Ham: Say Hempel's.

Hempel products ranged incredibly from pork to pineapple; from grease to grape-juice. An indictment meant no more to Hempel, the packer, than an injunction for speeding to you. Something of his character may be gleaned from the fact that farmers who had known the butcher at forty still addressed this millionaire, at sixty, as Aug. At sixty-five he took up golf and beat his son-in-law, Michael Arnold, at it. A magnificent old pirate, sailing the perilous commercial seas of the American '90s before commissions, investigations, and inquisitive senates insisted on applying whitewash to the black flag of trade.

Selina went about her preparations in a singularly clear-headed fashion, considering her youth and inexperience. She sold one of the blue-white diamonds, and kept one. She placed her inheritance of four hundred and ninety-seven dollars, complete, in the bank. She bought stout sensible boots, two dresses, one a brown lady's-cloth which she made herself, finished with white collars and cuffs, very neat (the cuffs to be protected by black sateen sleevelets, of course, while teaching); and a wine-red cashmere (mad, but she couldn't resist it) for best.

She eagerly learned what she could of this region once known as New Holland. Its people were all truck gardeners, and as Dutch as the Netherlands from which they or their fathers had come. She heard stories of wooden shoes worn in the wet prairie fields; of a red-faced plodding Cornelius Van der Bilt living in placid ignorance of the existence of his distinguished New York patronymic connection; of sturdy, phlegmatic, industrious farmers in squat, many-windowed houses patterned after the north Holland houses of their European memories. Many of them had come from the town of Schoorl, or near it. Others from the lowlands outside Amsterdam. Selina pictured it another Sleepy Hollow, a replica of the quaint settlement in Washington Irving's delightful tale. The deserting schoolmaster had been a second Ichabod Crane, naturally; the farmer at whose house she was to live a modern Mynheer Van Tassel, pipe, chuckle, and all. She and Julie Hempel read the tale over together on an afternoon when Julie managed to evade the maternal edict. Selina, picturing mellow golden corn fields; crusty crullers, crumbling oly-koeks, toothsome wild ducks, sides of smoked beef, pumpkin pies; country dances, apple-cheeked farmer girls, felt sorry for poor Julie staying on in the dull gray commmonplaceness of Chicago.

The last week in October found her on the way to High Prairie, seated beside Klaas Pool in the two-horse wagon with which he brought his garden stuff to the Chicago market. She sat perched next him on the high seat like a saucy wren beside a ruminant Holstein. So they jolted up the long Halsted road through the late October sunset. The prairie land just outside Chicago had not then been made a terrifying and epic thing of slag-heaps, smoke-stacks, and blast furnaces like a Pennell drawing. To-day it stretched away and away in the last rays of the late autumn sunlight over which the lake mist was begging to creep like chiffon covering gold. Mile after mile of cabbage fields, jade-green against the earth. Mile after mile of red cabbage, a rich plummy Burgundy veined with black. Between these, heaps of corn were piled-up sunshine. Against the horizon an occasional patch of woods showed the last russet and bronze of oak and maple. These things Selina saw with her beauty-loving eye, and she clasped her hands in their black cotton gloves.

"Oh, Mr. Pool!" she cried. "Mr. Pool. How beautiful it is here!"

Klaas Pool, driving his team of horses down the muddy Halsted road, was looking straight ahead, his eyes fastened seemingly on an invisible spot between the off-horse's ears. His was not the kind of brain that acts quickly, nor was his body's mechanism the sort that quickly responds to that brain's message. His eyes were china-blue in a round red face that was covered with a stubble of stiff golden hairs. His round moon of a head was set low and solidly between his great shoulders, so that as he began to turn it now, slowly, you marvelled at the process and waited fearfully to hear a creak. He was turning his head toward Selina, but keeping his gaze on the spot between his horse's ears. Evidently the head and the eyes revolved by quite distinct processes. Now he faced Selina almost directly. Then he brought his eyes around, slowly, until they focused on her cameolike face all alight now with her enjoyment of the scene around her; with a certain elation at this new venture into which she was entering; and with excitement such as she used to feel when the curtain rose with tantalizing deliberateness on the first act of a play which she was seeing with her father. She was well bundled up against the sharp October air in her cloak and muffler, with a shawl tucked about her knees and waist. The usual creamy pallor of her fine clear skin showed an unwonted pink, and her eyes were wide, dark, and bright. Beside this sparkling delicate girl's face Klaas Pool's heavy features seemed carved from the stuff of another clay and race. His pale blue eyes showed incomprehension.

"Beautiful?" he echoed, in puzzled interrogation. "What is beautiful?"

Selina's slim arms flashed out from the swathings of cloak, shawl, and muffler and were flung wide in a gesture that embraced the landscape on which the late afternoon sun was casting a glow peculiar to that lake region, all rose and golden and mistshimmering.

"This! The—the cabbages."

A slow-dawning film of fun crept over the blue of Klaas Pool's stare. This film spread almost imperceptibly so that it fluted his broad nostrils, met and widened his full lips, reached and agitated his massive shoulders, tickled the round belly, so that all Klaas Pool, from his eyes to his waist, was rippling and shaking with slow, solemn, heavy Dutch mirth.

"Cabbages is beautiful!" his round pop eyes staring at her in a fixity of glee. "Cabbages is beautiful!" His silent laughter now rose and became audible in a rich throaty chortle. It was plain that laughter, with Klaas Pool, was not a thing to be lightly dismissed, once raised. "Cabbages——" he choked a little, and spluttered, overcome. Now he began to shift his gaze back to his horses and the road, by the same process of turning his head first and then his eyes, so that to Selina the mirthful tail of his right eye and his round red cheek with the golden fuzz on it gave him an incredibly roguish brownie look.

Selina laughed, too, even while she protested his laughter. "But they are!" she insisted. "They *are* beautiful. Like jade and Burgundy. No, like—uh—like—what's that in—like chrysoprase and porphyry. All those fields of cabbages and the corn and the beet-tops together look like Persian patches."

Which was, certainly, no way for a new school teacher to talk to a Holland truck gardener driving his team along the dirt road on his way to High Prairie. But then, Selina, remember, had read Byron at seventeen.

Klaas Pool knew nothing of chrysoprase and porphyry. Nor of Byron. Nor, for that matter, of jade and Burgundy. But he did know cabbages, both green and red. He knew cabbage from seed to sauerkraut; he knew and grew varieties from the sturdy Flat Dutch to the early Wakefield. But that they were beautiful; that they looked like jewels; that they lay like Persian patches, had never entered his head, and rightly. What has the head of a cabbage, or, for that matter, of a robust, soil-stained, toiling Dutch truck farmer to do with nonsense like chrysoprase, with jade, with Burgundy, with Persian patterns!

The horses clopped down the heavy country road. Now and again the bulk beside Selina was agitated silently, as before. And from between the golden fuzz of stubble beard she would hear, "Cabbages! Cabbages is——" But she did not feel offended. She could not have been offended at anything to-day. For in spite of her recent tragedy, her nineteen years, her loneliness, the terrifying thought of this new home to which she was going, among strangers, she was conscious of a warm little thrill of elation, of excitement—of adventure! That was it. "The whole thing's just a grand adventure," Simeon Peake had said. Selina gave a little bounce of anticipation. She was doing a revolutionary and daring thing; a thing that the Vermont and now, fortunately, inaccessible Peakes would have regarded with horror. For equipment she had youth, curiosity, a steel-strong frame; one brown lady's-cloth, one wine-red cashmere; four hundred and ninety-seven dollars; and a gay, adventuresome spirit that was never to die, though it led her into curious places and she often found, at the end, only a trackless waste from which she had to retrace her steps, painfully. But always, to her, red and green cabbages were to be jade and Burgundy, chrysoprase and porphyry. Life has no weapons against a woman like that.

So now, as they bumped and jolted along the road Selina thought herself lucky, though she was a little terrified. She turned her gaze from the flat prairie land to the silent figure beside her. Hers was a lively, volatile nature, and his uncommunicativeness made her vaguely uncomfortable. Yet there was nothing glum about his face. Upon it there even lingered, in the corners of his eyes and about his mouth, faint shadows of merriment.

Klaas Pool was a school director. She was to live at his house. Perhaps she should not have said that about the cabbages. So now she drew herself up primly and tried to appear the school teacher, and succeeded in looking as severe as a white pansy.

"Ahem!" (or nearly that). "You have three children, haven't you, Mr. Pool? They'll all be my pupils?"

Klaas Pool ruminated on this. He concentrated so that a slight frown marred the serenity of his brow. In this double question of hers, an attempt to give the conversation a dignified turn, she had apparently created some difficulty for her host. He was trying to shake his head two ways at the same time. This gave it a rotary motion. Selina saw, with amazement, that he was attempting to nod negation and confirmation at once.

"You mean you haven't—or they're not?—or———?"

"I have got three children. All will not be your pupils." There was something final, unshakable in his delivery of this.

"Dear me! Why not? Which ones won't?"

This fusillade proved fatal. It served permanently to check the slight trickle of conversation which had begun to issue from his lips. They jogged on for perhaps a matter of three miles, in silence. Selina told herself then, sternly, that she must not laugh. Having told herself this, sternly, she began to laugh because she could not help it; a gay little sound that flew out like the whir of a bird's wing on the crisp autumnal sunset air. And suddenly this light sound was joined by a slow rumbling that swelled and bubbled a good deal in the manner of the rich glubby sounds that issue from a kettle that has been simmmering for a long time. So they laughed together, these two; the rather scared young thing who was trying to be prim, and the dull, unimaginative truck farmer because this alert, great-eyed, slim white creature perched birdlike on the wagon seat beside him had tickled his slow humour-sense.

Selina felt suddenly friendly and happy. "Do tell me which ones will and which won't."

"Geertje goes to school. Jozina goes to school. Roelf works by the farm."

"How old is Roelf?" She was being school teacherly again.

"Roelf is twelve."

"Twelve! And no longer at school! But why not!"

"Roelf he works by the farm."

"Doesn't Roelf like school?"

"But sure."

"Don't you think he ought to go to school?"

"But sure."

Having begun, she could not go back. "Doesn't your wife want Roelf to go to school any more?"

"Maartje? But sure."

She gathered herself together; hurled herself behind the next question. "Then why *doesn't* he go to school, for pity's sake!"

Klaas Pool's pale blue eyes were fixed on the spot between the horse's ears. His face was serene, placid, patient.

"Roelf he works by the farm."

Selina subsided, beaten.

She wondered about Roelf. Would he be a furtive, slinking boy, like Smike? Geertje and Jozina. Geertje—Gertrude, of course. Jozina? Josephine. Maartje?—m-m-m-m—Martha, probably. At any rate, it was going to be interesting. It was going to be wonderful! Suppose she had gone to Vermont and become a dried apple!

Dusk was coming on. The lake mist came drifting across the prairie and hung, a pearly haze, over the frost-nipped stubble and the leafless trees. It caught the last light in the sky, and held it, giving to fields, trees, black earth, to the man seated stolidly beside the girl, and to the face of the girl herself an opalescent glow very wonderful to see. Selina, seeing it, opened her lips to exclaim again; and then, remembering, closed them. She had learned her first lesson in High Prairie.

3

THE KLAAS POOLS lived in a typical High Prairie house. They had passed a score like it in the dusk. These sturdy Holland-Americans had built here in Illinois after the pattern of the squat houses that dot the lowlands about Amsterdam, Haarlem, and Rotterdam. A row of pollards stood stiffly by the roadside. As they turned in at the yard Selina's eye was caught by the glitter of glass. The house was many-windowed, the panes the size of pocket-handkerchiefs. Even in the dusk Selina thought she had never seen windows sparkle so. She did not then know that spotless window-panes were a mark of social standing in High Prairie. Yard and dwelling had a geometrical neatness like that of a toy house in a set of playthings. The effect was marred by a clothesline hung with a dado of miscellaneous wash—a pair of faded overalls, a shirt, socks, a man's drawers carefully patched and now bellying grotesquely in the breeze like a comic tramp turned bacchanal. Selina was to know this frieze of nether garments as a daily decoration in the farm-wife's yard.

Peering down over the high wheel she waited for Klaas Pool to assist her in alighting. He seemed to have no such thought. Having jumped down, he was throwing empty crates and boxes out of the back of the wagon. So Selina, gathering her shawls and cloak about her, clambered down the side of the wheel and stood looking about her in the dim light, a very small figure in a very large world. Klaas had opened the barn door. Now he returned and slapped one of the horses smartly on the flank. The team trotted obediently off to the barn. He picked up her little hide-bound trunk. She took her satchel. The yard was quite dark now. As Klaas Pool opened the kitchen door the red mouth that was the open draught in the kitchen stove grinned a toothy welcome at them.

A woman stood over the stove, a fork in her hand. The kitchen was clean, but disorderly, with the disorder that comes of pressure of work, There was a not unpleasant smell of cooking. Selina sniffed it hungrily. The woman turned to face them. Selina stared.

This, she thought, must be some other—an old woman—his mother perhaps. But: "Maartje, here is school teacher," said Klaas Pool. Selina put out her hand to meet the other woman's hand, rough, hard, calloused. Her own, touching it, was like satin against a pine board. Maartje smiled, and you saw her broken discoloured teeth. She pushed back the sparse hair from her high forehead, fumbled a little, shyly, at the collar of her clean blue calico dress.

"Pleased to meet you," Maartje said, primly. "Make you welcome." Then, as Pool stamped out to the yard, slamming the door behind him, "Pool he could have come with you by the front way, too. Lay off your things." Selina began to remove the wrappings that swathed her—the muffler, the shawl, the cloak. Now she stood, a slim, incongruously elegant little figure in that kitchen. The brown lady's-cloth was very tight and basqued above, very flounced and bustled below. "My, how you are young!" cried Maartje. She moved nearer, as if impelled, and fingered the stuff of Selina's gown. And as she did this Selina suddenly saw that she, too, was young. The bad teeth, the thin hair, the careless dress, the littered kitchen, the harassed frown—above all these, standing out clearly, appeared the look of a girl.

"Why, I do believe she's not more than twenty-eight!" Selina said to herself in a kind of panic. "I do believe she's not more than twenty-eight."

She had been aware of the two pigtailed heads appearing and vanishing in the doorway of the next room. Now Maartje was shooing her into this room. Evidently her hostess was distressed because the school teacher's formal entrance had not been made by way of parlour instead of kitchen. She followed Maartje Pool into the front room. Behind the stove, tittering, were two yellow-haired little girls. Geertje and Jozina, of course. Selina went over to them, smiling. "Which is Geertje?" she asked. "And which Jozina?" But at this the titters became squeals. They retired behind the round black bulwark of the wood burner, overcome. There was no fire in this shining ebon structure, though the evening was sharp. Above the stove a length of pipe, glittering with polish as was the stove itself, crossed the width of the room and vanished through a queer little perforated grating in the ceiling. Selina's quick glance encompassed the room. In the window were a few hardy plants in pots on a green-painted wooden rack. There were geraniums, blossomless; a cactus with its thick slabs of petals like slices of gangrenous ham set up for beauty in a parlour; a plant called Jacob's ladder, on a spindling trellis. The bony scaffolding of the green-painted wooden stand was turned toward the room. The flowers blindly faced the dark square of the window. There was a sofa with a wrinkled calico cover; three rocking chairs; some stark crayons of incredibly hard-featured Dutch ancients on the wall. It was all neat, stiff, unlovely. But Selina had known too many years of boarding-house ugliness to be offended at this.

Maartje had lighted a small glass-bowled lamp. The chimney of this sparkled as had the window-panes. A steep, uncarpeted stairway, enclosed, led off the sitting room. Up this Maartje Pool, talking, led the way to Selina's bedroom. Selina was to learn that the farm woman, often inarticulate through lack of companionship, becomes a torrent of talk when opportunity presents itself. They made quite a little procession. First, Mrs. Pool with the lamp; then Selina with the satchel; then, tap-tap, tap-tap, Jozina and Geertje, their heavy hob-nailed shoes creating a great clatter on the wooden stairs, though they were tiptoeing in an effort to make themselves unheard by their mother. There evidently had been an arrangement on the subject of their invisibility. The procession moved to the accompaniment of Maartje's, "Now you stay downstairs didn't I tell you!" There was in her tone a warning; a menace. The two pigtails would hang back a moment, only to come tap-tapping on again, their saucer eyes at once fearful and mischievous.

A narrow, dim, close-smelling hallway, uncarpeted. At the end of it a door opening into the room that was to be Selina's. As its chill struck her to the marrow three objects caught her eye. The bed, a huge and not unhandsome walnut mausoleum, reared its sombre height almost to the room's top. Indeed, its apex of grapes did actually seem to achieve a meeting with the whitewashed ceiling. The mattress of straw and cornhusks was unworthy of this edifice, but over it Mrs. Pool had mercifully placed a feather bed, stitched and quilted, so that Selina lay soft and warm through the winter. Along one wall stood a low chest so richly brown as to appear black. The front panel of this was curiously carved. Selina stooped before it and for the second time that day said: "How beautiful!" then looked quickly round at Maartje Pool as though fearful of finding her laughing as Klaas Pool had laughed. But Mrs. Pool's face reflected the glow in her own. She came over to Selina and stooped with her over the chest, holding the lamp so that its yellow flame lighted up the scrolls and tendrils of the carved surface. With one discoloured forefinger she traced the bold flourishes on the panel. "See? How it makes out letters?"

Selina peered closer. "Why, sure enough! This first one's an S!"

Maartje was kneeling before the chest now. "Sure an S. For Sophia. It is a Holland bride's chest. And here is K. And here is big D. It makes Sophia Kroon DeVries. It is anyways two hundred years. My mother she gave it to me when I was married, and her mother she gave it to her when she was married, and her mother gave it to her when she was married, and her——"

"I should think so!" exclaimed Selina, rather meaninglessly; but stemming the torrent. "What's in it? Anything? There ought to be bride's clothes in it, yellow with age."

"It is!" cried Maartje Pool and gave a little bounce that imperilled the lamp.

"No!" The two on their knees sat smiling at each other, wide-eyed, like schoolgirls. The pigtails, emboldened, had come taptapping nearer and were peering over the shoulders of the women before the chest.

"Here—wait." Maartje Pool thrust the lamp into Selina's hand, raised the lid of the chest, dived expertly into its depths amidst a great rustling of old newspapers and emerged red-faced with a Dutch basque and voluminous skirt of silk; an age-yellow cap whose wings, stiff with embroidery, stood out grandly on either side; a pair of wooden shoes, stained terra-cotta like the sails of the Vollendam fishing boats, and carved from toe to heel in a delicate and intricate pattern. A bridal gown, a bridal cap, bridal shoes.

"Well!" said Selina, with the feeling of a little girl in a rich attic on a rainy day. She clasped her hands. "May I dress up in it some time?"

Maartje Pool, folding the garments hastily, looked shocked and horrified. "Never must anybody dress up in a bride's dress only to get married. It brings bad luck." Then, as Selina stroked the stiff silken folds of the skirt with a slim and caressing forefinger: "So you get married to a High Prairie Dutchman I let you wear it." At this absurdity they both laughed again. Selina thought that this school-teaching venture was starting out very well. She would have *such* things to tell her father—then she remembered. She shivered a little as she stood up now. She raised her arms to take off her hat, feeling suddenly tired, cold, strange in this house with this farm woman, and the two staring little girls, and the great red-faced man. There surged over her a great wave of longing for her father—for the gay little dinners, for the theatre treats, for his humorous philosophical drawl, for the Chicago streets, and the ugly Chicago houses; for Julie; for Miss Fister's school; for anything and any one that was accustomed, known, and therefore dear.

Even Aunt Abbie and Aunt Sarah had a not unlovely aspect, viewed from this chill farmhouse bedroom that had suddenly become her home. She had a horrible premonition that she was going to cry, began to blink very fast, turned a little blindly in the dim light and caught sight of the room's third arresting object. A blue-black cylinder of tin sheeting, like a stove and yet unlike. It was polished like the length of pipe in the sitting room below. Indeed, it was evidently a giant flower of this stem.

"What's that?" demanded Selina, pointing.

Maartje Pool, depositing the lamp on the little wash-stand preparatory to leaving, smiled pridefully. "Drum."

"Drum?"

"For heat your room." Selina touched it. It was icy. "When there is fire," Mrs. Pool added, hastily. In her mind's eye Selina traced the tin tube below running along the ceiling in the peaceful and orderly path of a stove-pipe, thrusting its way through the cylindrical hole in the ceiling and here bursting suddenly into swollen and monstrous bloom like an unthinkable goitre on a black neck. Selina was to learn that its heating powers were mythical. Even when the stove in the sitting room was blazing away with a cheerful roar none of the glow communicated itself to the drum. It remained as coolly indifferent to the blasts breathed upon it as a girl hotly besieged by an unwelcome lover. This was to influence a number of Selina's habits, including nocturnal reading and matutinal bathing. Selina was a daily morning bather in a period which looked upon the daily bath as an eccentricity, or, at best, an affectation. It would be charming to be able to record that she continued the practice in the Pool household; but a morning bath in the arctic atmosphere of an Illinois prairie farmhouse would not have been eccentric merely, but mad, even if there had been an available kettle of hot water at 6.30 A.M., which there emphatically was not. Selina was grateful for an occasional steaming basin of water at night and a hurried piecemeal bath by the mythical heat of the drum.

"Maartje!" roared a voice from belowstairs. The voice of the hungry male. There was wafted up, too, a faint smell of scorching. Then came sounds of a bumping and thumping along the narrow stairway.

"Og heden!" cried Maartje, in a panic, her hands high in air. She was off, sweeping the two pigtails with her in her flight. There were sounds of scuffling on the stairway, and Maartje's voice calling something that sounded like hookendunk to Selina. But she decided that that couldn't be. The bumping now sounded along the passage outside her room. Selina turned from her satchel to behold a gnome in the doorway. Below, she saw a pair of bowlegs; above, her own little hide-bound trunk; between, a broad face, a grizzled beard, a lack-lustre eye in a weather-beaten countenance.

"Jakob Hoogendunk," the gnome announced, briefly, peering up at her from beneath the trunk balanced on his back.

Selina laughed delightedly. "Not really! Do come in. This is a good place, don't you think? Along the wall? Mr.—Mr. Hoogendunk?"

Jakob Hoogendunk grunted and plodded across the room, the trunk lurching perilously above his bowlegged stride. He set it down with a final thump, wiped his nose with the back of his hand —sign of a task completed—and surveyed the trunk largely, as if he had made it. "Thank you, Mr. Hoogendunk," said Selina, and put out her hand. "I'm Selina Peake. How"—she couldn't resist it—"how did you leave Rip?"

It was characteristic of her that in this grizzled hired man, twisted with rheumatism, reeking of mould and manure, she should see a direct descendant of those gnarled and bearded bowlers so mysteriously encountered by Rip Van Winkle on that fatal day in the Kaatskills. The name, too, appealed to her in its comic ugliness. So she laughed a soft little laugh; held out her hand. The man was not offended. He knew that people laughed when they were introduced. So he laughed, too, in a mixture of embarrassment and attempted ease, looking down at the small hand extended to him. He blinked at it curiously. He wiped his two hands down his thighs, hard; then shook his great grizzled head. "My hand is all muck. I ain't washed up yet," and lurched off, leaving Selina looking rather helplessly down at her own extended hand. His clatter on the wooden stairway sounded like cavalry on a frozen road.

Left alone in her room Selina unlocked her trunk and took from it two photographs—one of a mild-looking man with his hat a little on one side, the other of a woman who might have been a twenty-five-year-old Selina, minus the courageous jaw-line. Looking about for a fitting place on which to stand these leather-framed treasures she considered the top of the chill drum, humorously, then actually placed them there, for lack of better refuge, from which vantage point they regarded her with politely interested eyes. Perhaps Jakob Hoogendunk would put up a shelf for her. That would serve for her little stock of books and for the pictures as well. She was enjoying that little flush of exhilaration that comes to a woman, unpacking. There was about her trunk, even though closed but this very day, the element of surprise that gilds familiar objects when disclosed for the first time in unfamiliar surroundings. She took out her neat pile of warm woollen underwear, her stout shoes. She shook out the crushed folds of the wine-coloured cashmere. Now, if ever, she should have regretted its purchase. But she didn't. No one, she reflected, as she spread it rosily on the bed, possessing a wine-coloured cashmere could be altogether downcast.

The wine cashmere on the bed, the photographs on the drum, her clothes hanging comfortably on wall-hooks with a calico curtain on a cord protecting them, her stock of books on the closed trunk. Already the room wore the aspect of familiarity.

From belowstairs came the hiss of frying. Selina washed in the chill water of the basin, took down her hair and coiled it again before the swimmy little mirror over the wash-stand. She adjusted the stitched white bands of the severe collar and patted the cuffs of the brown lady's-cloth. The tight basque was fastened with buttons from throat to waist. Her fine long head rose above this trying base with such grace and dignity as to render the stiff garment beautiful. The skirt billowed and puffed out behind, and was drawn in folds across the front. It was a day of appalling bunchiness and equally appalling tightness in dress; of panniers, galloons, plastrons, reveres, bustles, and all manner of lumpy bedevilment. That Selina could appear in this disfiguring garment a creature still graceful, slim, and pliant was a sheer triumph of spirit over matter.

She blew out the light now and descended the steep wooden stairway to the unlighted parlour. The door between parlour and kitchen was closed. Selina sniffed sensitively. There was pork for supper. She was to learn that there always was pork for supper. As the winter wore on she developed a horror of this porcine fare, remembering to have read somewhere that one's diet was in time reflected in one's face; that gross eating made one gross looking. She would examine her features fearfully in the swimmy mirror—the lovely little white nose—was it coarsening? The deep-set dark eyes—were they squinting? The firm sweet lips—were they broadening? But the reflection in the glass reassured her.

She hesitated a moment there in the darkness. Then she opened the kitchen door. There swam out at her a haze of smoke, from which emerged round blue eyes, guttural talk, the smell of frying grease, of stable, of loam, and of woollen wash freshly brought in from the line. With an inrush of cold air that sent the blue haze into swirls the outer kitchen door opened. A boy, his arm piled high with stove-wood, entered; a dark, handsome sullen boy who stared at Selina over the armload of wood. Selina stared back at him. There sprang to life between the boy of twelve and the woman of nineteen an electric current of feeling.

"Roelf," thought Selina; and even took a step toward him, inexplicably drawn.

"Hurry then with that wood there!" fretted Maartje at the stove. The boy flung the armful into the box, brushed his sleeve and coat-front mechanically, still looking at Selina. A slave to the insatiable maw of the wood-box.

Klaas Pool, already at table, thumped with his knife. "Sit down! Sit down, teacher." Selina hesitated, looked at Maartje. Maartje was holding a frying pan aloft in one hand while with the other she thrust and poked a fresh stick of wood into the open-lidded stove. The two pigtails seated themselves at the table, set with its red-checked cloth and bone-handled cutlery. Jakob Hoogendunk, who had been splashing, snorting, and puffing porpoise-fashion in a corner over a hand-basin whose cubic contents were out of all proportion to the sounds extracted therefrom, now seated himself. Roelf flung his cap on a wall-hook and sat down. Only Selina and Maartje remained standing. "Sit down! Sit down!" Klaas Pool said again, jovially. "Well, how is cabbages?" He chuckled and winked. Jakob Hoogendunk snorted. A duet of titters from the pigtails. Maartje at the stove smiled; but a trifle grimly, one might have thought, watching her. Evidently Klaas had not hugged his joke in secret. Only the boy Roelf remained unsmiling. Even Selina, feeling the red mounting her cheeks, smiled a little, nervously, and sat down with some suddenness.

Maartje Pool now thumped down on the table a great bowl of potatoes fried in grease; a platter of ham. There was bread cut in chunks. The coffee was rye, roasted in the oven, ground, and taken without sugar or cream. Of this food there was plenty. It made Mrs. Tebbitt's Monday night meal seem ambrosial. Selina's visions of chickens, oly-koeks, wild ducks, crusty crullers, and pumpkin pies vanished, never to return. She had been very hungry, but now, as she talked, nodded, smiled, she cut her food into infinitesimal bites, did not chew them so very well, and despised herself for being dainty. A slight, distinctive little figure there in the yellow lamplight, eating this coarse fare bravely, turning her soft dark glance on the woman who was making countless trips from stove to table, from table to stove; on the sullen handsome boy with his purplish chapped hands and his sombre eyes; on the two round-eyed, red-cheeked little girls; on the great red-faced full-lipped man eating his supper noisily and with relish; on Jakob Hoogendunk, grazing greedily. . . .

"Well," she thought, "it's going to be different enough, that's certain. . . . This is a vegetable farm, and they don't eat vegetables. I wonder why. . . . What a pity that she lets herself look like that, just because she's a farm woman. Her hair screwed into that knob, her skin rough and neglected. That hideous dress. Shapeless. She's not bad looking, either. A red spot on either cheek, now; and her eyes so blue. A little like those women in the Dutch pictures Father took me to see in—where?—where?—New York, years ago?—yes. A woman in a kitchen, a dark sort of room with pots of brass on a shelf; a high mullioned window. But that woman's face was placid. This one's strained. Why need she look like that, frowsy, harried, old! . . . The boy is, somehow, foreign looking—Italian. Queer. . . . They talk a good deal like some German neighbours we had in Milwaukee. They twist sentences. Literal translations from the Dutch, I suppose." . . .

Jakob Hoogendunk was talking. Supper over, the men sat relaxed, pipe in mouth. Maartje was clearing the supper things, with Geertje and Jozina making a great pretense at helping. If they giggled like that in school, Selina thought, she would, in time, go mad, and knock their pigtailed heads together.

"You got to have rich bottom land," Hoogendunk was saying, "else you get little tough stringy stuff. I seen it in market Friday, laying. Stick to vegetables that is vegetables and not new-fangled stuff. Celery! What is celery! It ain't rightly a vegetable, and it ain't a yerb. Look how Voorhees he used as much as one hundred fifty pounds nitrate of sody, let alone regular fertilizer, and what comes from it? Little stringy stuff. You got to have rich bottom land."

Selina was interested. She had always thought that vegetables grew. You put them in the ground—seeds or something—and pretty soon things came popping up—potatoes, cabbages, onions, carrots, beets. But what was this thing called nitrate of soda? It must have had something to do with the creamed cabbage at Mrs. Tebbitt's. And she had never known it. And what was regular fertilizer? She leaned forward.

"What's a regular fertilizer?"

Klaas Pool and Jakob Hoogendunk looked at her. She looked at them, her fine intelligent eyes alight with interest. Pool then tipped back his chair, lifted a stove-lid, spat into the embers, replaced the lid and rolled his eyes in the direction of Jakob Hoogendunk. Hoogendunk rolled his slow gaze in the direction of Klaas Pool. Then both turned to look at this audacious female who thus interrupted men's conversation.

Pool took his pipe from his mouth, blew a thin spiral, wiped his mouth with the back of his hand. "Regular fertilizer is—regular fertilizer."

Jakob Hoogendunk nodded his solemn confirmation of this.

"What's in it?" persisted Selina.

Pool waved a huge red hand as though to waft away this troublesome insect. He looked at Maartje. But Maartje was slamming about her work. Geertje and Jozina were absorbed in some game of their own behind the stove. Roelf, at the table, sat reading, one slim hand, chapped and gritty with rough work, outspread on the cloth. Selina noticed, without knowing she noticed, that the fingers were long, slim, and the broken nails thin and fine. "But what's in it?" she said again. Suddenly life in the kitchen hung suspended. The two men frowned. Maartje half turned from her dishpan. The two little girls peered out from behind the stove. Roelf looked up from his book. Even the collie, lying in front of the stove half asleep, suddenly ran his tongue out, winked one eye. But Selina, all sociability, awaited her answer. She could not know that in High Prairie women did not brazenly intrude thus on men's weighty conversation. The men looked at her, unanswering. She began to feel a little uncomfortable. The boy Roelf rose and went to the cupboard in the kitchen corner. He took down a large green-bound book, and placed it in Selina's hand. The book smelled terribly. Its covers were greasy with handling. On the page margins a brown stain showed the imprint of fingers. Roelf pointed at a page. Selina followed the line with her eye.

Good Basic Fertilizer for Market-Garden Crops.
Then, below:

Nitrate of soda.
Ammonium sulfate.
Dried blood.

Selina shut the book and handed it back to Roelf, gingerly. Dried blood! She stared at the two men. "What does it mean by dried blood?"

Klaas answered stubbornly, "Dried blood is dried blood. You put in the field dried blood and it makes grow. Cabbages, onions, squash." At sight of her horrified face he grinned. "Well, cabbages is anyway beautiful, huh?" He rolled a facetious eye around at Jakob. Evidently this joke was going to last him the winter.

Selina stood up. She wasn't annoyed; but she wanted, suddenly, to be alone in her room—in the room that but an hour before had been a strange and terrifying chamber with its towering bed, its chill drum, its ghostly bride's chest. Now it had become a refuge, snug, safe, infinitely desirable. She turned to Mrs. Pool. "I—I think I'll go up to my room. I'm very tired. The ride, I suppose. I'm not used . . ." Her voice trailed off.

"Sure," said Maartje, briskly. She had finished the supper dishes and was busy with a huge bowl, flour, a baking board. "Sure go up. I got my bread to set yet and what all.

"If I could have some hot water———"

"Roelf! Stop once that reading and show school teacher where is hot water. Geertje! Jozina! Never in my world did I see such." She cuffed a convenient pigtail by way of emphasis. A wail arose.

"Never mind. It doesn't matter. Don't bother." Selina was in a sort of panic now. She wanted to be out of the room. But the boy Roelf, with quiet swiftness, had taken a battered tin pail from its hook on the wall, had lifted an iron slab at the back of the kitchen stove. A mist of steam arose. He dipped the pail into the tiny reservoir thus revealed. Then, as Selina made as though to take it, he walked past her. She heard him ascending the wooden stairway. She wanted to be after him. But first she must know that name of the book over which he had been poring. But between her and the book outspread on the table were Pool, Hoogendunk, dog, pigtails, Maartje. She pointed with a determined forefinger. "What's that book Roelf was reading?"

Maartje thumpd a great ball of dough on the baking board. Her arms were white with flour. She kneaded and pummmelled expertly. "Woorden boek."

Well. That meant nothing. Woorden boek. Woorden b——— Dimly the meaning of the Dutch words began to come to her. But it couldn't be. She brushed past the men in the tipped-back chairs, stepped over the collie, reached across the table. Woorden—word. Boek—book. Word book. "He's reading the dictionary!" Selina said, aloud. "He's reading the dictionary!" She had the horrible feeling that she was going to laugh and cry at once; hysteria.

Mrs. Pool glanced around. "School teacher he gave it to Roelf time he quit last year for spring planting. A word book. In it is more as a hundred thousand words, all different."

Selina flung a good-night over her shoulder and made for the stairway. He should have all her books. She would send to Chicago for books. She would spend her thirty dollars a month buying books for him. He had been reading the dictionary!

Roelf had placed the pail of hot water on the little wash-stand, and had lighted the glass lamp. He was intent on replacing the glass chimney within the four prongs that held it firm. Downstairs, in the crowded kitchen, he had seemed quite the man. Now, in the yellow lamplight, his profile sharply outlined, she saw that he was just a small boy with tousled hair. About his cheeks, his mouth, his chin one could even see the last faint traces of soft infantile roundness. His trousers, absurdly cut down from a man's pair by inexpert hands, hung grotesquely about his slim shanks.

"He's just a little boy," thought Selina, with a quick pang. He was about to pass her now, without glancing at her, his head down. She put out her hand; touched his shoulder. He looked up at her, his face startlingly alive, his eyes blazing. It came to Selina that until now she had not heard him speak. Her hand pressed the thin stuff of his coat sleeve.

"Cabbages—fields of cabbages—what you said—they *are* beautiful," he stammered. He was terribly in earnest. Before she could reply he was out of the room, clattering down the stairs.

Selina stood, blinking a little.

The glow that warmed her now endured while she splashed about in the inadequate basin; took down the dark soft masses of her hair; put on the voluminous long-sleeved, high-necked nightgown. Just before she blew out the lamp her last glimpse was of the black drum stationed like a patient eunuch in the corner; and she could smile at that; even giggle a little, what with weariness, excitement, and a general feeling of being awake in a dream. But once in the vast bed she lay there utterly lost in the waves of terror and loneliness that envelop one at night in a strange house amongst strange people. She lay there, tensed and tight, her toes curled with nervousness, her spine hunched with it, her leg muscles taut. She peeked over the edge of the covers looking a good deal like a frightened brownie, if one could have seen her; her eyes very wide, the pupils turned well toward the corners with the look of listening and distrust. The sharp November air cut in from the fields that were fertilized with dried blood. She shivered, and wrinkled up her lovely little nose and seemed to sniff this loathsome taint in the air. She listened to the noises that came from belowstairs; voices gruff, unaccustomed; shrill, high. These ceased and gave place to others less accustomed to her city-bred ears; a dog's bark and an answering one; a far-off train whistle; the dull thud of hoofs stamping on the barn floor; the wind in the bare tree branches outside the window.

Her watch—a gift from Simeon Peake on her eighteenth birthday—with the gold case all beautifully engraved with a likeness of a gate, and a church, and a waterfall and a bird, linked together with spirals and flourishes of the most graceful description, was ticking away companionably under her pillow. She felt for it, took it out and held it in her palm, under her cheek, for comfort.

She knew she would not sleep that night. She knew she would not sleep——

She awoke to a clear, cold November dawn; children's voices; the neighing of horses; a great sizzling and hissing, and scent of frying bacon; a clucking and squawking in the barnyard. It was six o'clock. Selina's first day as a school teacher. In a little more than two hours she would be facing a whole roomful of round-eyed Geertjes and Jozinas and Roelfs. The bedroom was cruelly cold. As she threw the bedclothes heroically aside Selina decided that it took an appalling amount of courage—this life that Simeon Peake had called a great adventure.

4

EVERY MORNING THROUGHOUT November it was the same. At six o'clock: "Miss Peake! *Oh,* Miss Peake!"

"I'm up!" Selina would call in what she meant to be a gay voice, through chattering teeth.

"You better come down and dress where is warm here by the stove."

Peering down the perforations in the floor-hole through which the parlour chimney swelled so proudly into the drum, Selina could vaguely descry Mrs. Pool stationed just below, her gaze upturned.

That first morning, on hearing this invitation Selina had been rocked between horror and mirth. "I'm not cold, really. I'm almost dressed. I'll be down directly."

Maartje Pool must have sensed some of the shock in the girl's voice; or, perhaps, even some of the laughter. "Pool and Jakob are long out already cutting. Here back of the stove you can dress warm."

Shivering and tempted though she was, Selina had set her will against it. A little hardening of the muscles around her jaw so that they stood out whitely beneath the fine-grained skin. "I won't go down," she said to herself, shaking with the cold. "I won't come down to dressing behind the kitchen stove like a—like a peasant in one of those dreadful Russian novels. . . . That sounds stuck up and horrid. . . . The Pools are good and kind and decent. . . . But I *won't* come down to huddling behind the stove with a bundle of underwear in my arms. Oh, *dear,* this corset's like a casing of ice."

Geertje and Jozina had no such maidenly scruples. Each morning they gathered their small woollen garments in a bundle and scudded briskly to the kitchen for warmth, though their bedroom just off the parlour had by no means the degree of refrigeration possessed by Selina's clammy chamber. Not only that, the Misses Pool slept snugly in the woollen nether garments that invested them by day and so had only mounds of woollen petticoats, woollen stockings, and mysterious grimy straps, bands, and fastenings with which to struggle. Their intimate flannels had a cactus quality that made the early martyrs' hair shirts seem, in comparison, but a fleece-lined cloud. Dressing behind the kitchen stove was a natural and universal custom in High Prairie.

By the middle of December as Selina stuck her nose cautiously out of the covers into the midnight blackness of early morning you might have observed, if it had been at all light, that the tip of that elegant and erstwhile alabaster feature had been encarmined during the night by a mischievous brush wielded by that same wight who had been busy painting fronds and lacy ferns and gorgeous blossoms of silver all over the bedroom window. Slowly, inch by inch, that bedroom window crept down, down. Then, too, the Pools objected to the icy blasts which swept the open stairway and penetrated their hermetically sealed bedrooms below. Often the water in the pitcher on her wash-stand was frozen when Selina awoke. Her garments, laid out the night before so that their donning next morning might occupy a minimum of time, were mortuary to the touch. Worst of all were the steel-stiffened, unwieldy, and ridiculous stays that encased the female form of that day. As Selina's numbed fingers struggled with the fastenings of this iciest of garments her ribs shrank from its arctic embrace.

"But I won't dress behind the kitchen stove!" declared Selina, glaring meanwhile at that hollow pretense, the drum. She even stuck her tongue out at it (only nineteen, remember!). For that matter, it may as well be known that she brought home a piece of chalk from school and sketched a demon face on the drum's bulging front, giving it a personal and horrid aspect that afforded her much satisfaction.

When she thought back, years later, on that period of her High Prairie experience, stoves seemed to figure with absurd prominence in her memory. That might well be. A stove changed the whole course of her life.

From the first, the schoolhouse stove was her bête noir. Out of the welter of that first year it stood, huge and menacing, a black tyrant. The High

Prairie schoolhouse in which Selina taught was a little more than a mile up the road beyond the Pool farm. She came to know that road in all its moods—ice-locked, drifted with snow, wallowing in mud. School began at half-past eight. After her first week Selina had the mathematics of her early morning reduced to the least common denominator. Up at six. A plunge into the frigid garments; breakfast of bread, cheese, sometimes bacon, always rye coffee without cream or sugar. On with the cloak, muffler, hood, mittens, galoshes. The lunch box in bad weather. Up the road to the schoolhouse, battling the prairie wind that whipped the tears into the eyes, ploughing the drifts, slipping on the hard ruts and icy ridges in dry weather. Excellent at nineteen. As she flew down the road in sun or rain, in wind or snow, her mind's eye was fixed on the stove. The schoolhouse reached, her numbed fingers wrestled with the rusty lock. The door opened, there smote her the schoolroom smell—a mingling of dead ashes, kerosene, unwashed bodies, dust, mice, chalk, stove-wood, lunch crumbs, mould, slate that has been washed with saliva. Into this Selina rushed, untying her muffler as she entered. In the little vestibule there was a box piled with chunks of stove-wood and another heaped with dried corn-cobs. Alongside this a can of kerosene. The cobs served as kindling. A dozen or more of these you soaked with kerosene and stuffed into the maw of the rusty iron pot-bellied stove. A match. Up flared the corn-cobs. Now was the moment for a small stick of wood; another to keep it company. Shut the door. Draughts. Dampers. Smoke. Suspense. A blaze, then a crackle. The wood has caught. In with a chunk now. A wait. Another chunk. Slam the door. The schoolhouse fire is started for the day. As the room thawed gradually Selina removed layers of outer garments. By the time the children arrived the room was livable.

Naturally, those who sat near this monster baked; those near the windows froze. Sometimes Selina felt she must go mad beholding the writhings and contortions of a roomful of wriggling bodies scratching at backs, legs, and sides as the stove grew hotter and flesh rebelled against the harsh contact with the prickling undergarments of an over-cautious day.

Selina had seen herself, dignified, yet gentle, instructing a roomful of Dutch cherubs in the simpler elements of learning. But it is difficult to be dignified and gracious when you are suffering from chilblains. Selina fell victim to this sordid discomfort, as did every child in the room. She sat at the battered pine desk or moved about, a little ice-wool shawl around her shoulders when the wind was wrong and the stove balky. Her white little face seemed whiter in contrast with the black folds of this sombre garment. Her slim hands were rough and chapped. The oldest child in the room was thirteen, the youngest four and a half. From eight-thirty until four Selina ruled this grubby domain; a hot-and-cold roomful of sneezing, coughing, wriggling, shuffling, dozing children, toe scuffling on agonized heel, and heel scrunching on agonized toe, in a frenzy of itching.

"Aggie Vander Sijde, parse this sentence: The ground is wet because it has rained."

Miss Vander Sijde, eleven, arises with a switching of skirts and a tossing of pigtail. " 'Ground' the subject; 'is wet' the predicate 'because' . . ."

Selina is listening with school-teacherly expression indicative of encouragement and approval. "Jan Snip, parse this sentence: The flower will wither if it is picked."

Brown lady's-cloth; ice-wool shawl; chalk in hand. Just a phase; a brief chapter in the adventure. Something to remember and look back on with a mingling of amusement and wonder. Things were going to happen. Such things, with life and life and life stretching ahead of her! In five years—two—even one, perhaps, who knows but that she might be lying on lacy pillows

on just such a bleak winter morning, a satin coverlet over her, the morning
light shaded by soft rose-coloured hangings. (Early influence of the *Fireside
Companion*.)

"What time is it, Celeste?"

"It is now eleven o'clock, madame."

"Is that all!"

"Would madame like that I prepare her bath now, or later?"

"Later, Celeste. My chocolate now. My letters."

". . . and if is the conjunction modifying . . ."

Early in the winter Selina had had the unfortunate idea of opening the ice-
locked windows at intervals and giving the children five minutes of exercise
while the fresh cold air cleared brains and room at once. Arms waved wildly,
heads wobbled, short legs worked vigorously. At the end of the week twenty
High Prairie parents sent protests by note or word of mouth. Jan and Cornelius, Katrina and Aggie went to school to learn reading and writing and
numbers, not to stand with open windows in the winter.

On the Pool farm the winter work had set in. Klaas drove into Chicago
with winter vegetables only once a week now. He and Jakob and Roelf were
storing potatoes and cabbages underground; repairing fences; preparing
frames for the early spring planting; sorting seedlings. It had been Roelf who
had taught Selina to build the schoolhouse fire. He had gone with her on
that first morning, had started the fire, filled the water pail, initiated her in
the rites of corn-cobs, kerosene, and dampers. A shy, dark, silent boy. She
set out deliberately to woo him to friendship.

"Roelf, I have a book called 'Ivanhoe.' Would you like to read it?"

"Well, I don't get much time."

"You wouldn't have to hurry. Right there in the house. And there's another called 'The Three Musketeers'."

He was trying not to look pleased; to appear stolid and Dutch, like the
people from whom he had sprung. Some Dutch sailor ancestor, Selina
thought, or fisherman, must have touched at an Italian port or Spanish and
brought back a wife whose eyes and skin and feeling for beauty had skipped
layer on layer of placid Netherlanders to crop out now in this wistful sensitive
boy.

Selina had spoken to Jakob Hoogendunk about a shelf for her books and
her photographs. He had put up a rough bit of board, very crude and ugly,
but it had served. She had come home one snowy afternoon to find this shelf
gone and in its place a smooth and polished one, with brackets intricately
carved. Roelf had cut, planed, polished, and carved it in many hours of work
in the cold little shed off the kitchen. He had there a workshop of sorts,
fitted with such tools and implements as he could devise. He did man's work
on the farm, yet often at night Selina could faintly hear the rasp of his
handsaw after she had gone to bed. He had built a doll's house for Geertje
and Jozina that was the black envy of every pigtail in High Prairie. This sort
of thing was looked upon by Klaas Pool as foolishness. Roelf's real work
in the shed was the making and mending of coldframes and hotbeds for the
early spring plants. Whenever possible Roelf neglected this dull work for
some fancy of his own. To this Klaas Pool objected as being "dumb." For
that matter, High Prairie considered Pool's boy "dumb like." He said such
things. When the new Dutch Reformed church was completed after gigantic
effort—red brick, and the first brick church in High Prairie—bright yellow
painted pews—a red and yellow glass window, most handsome—the Reverend Vaarwerk brought from New Haarlem to preach the first sermon —
Pool's Roelf was heard to hint darkly to a group of High Prairie boys that

some night he was going to burn the church down. It was ugly. It hurt you to look at it, just.

Certainly, the boy was different. Selina, none too knowledgeous herself, still recognized that here was something rare, something precious to be fostered, shielded, encouraged.

"Roelf, stop that foolishness, get your ma once some wood. Carving on that box again instead finishing them coldframes. Some day, by golly, I show you. I break every stick . . . dumb as a Groningen . . ."

Roelf did not sulk. He seemed not to mind, particularly, but he came back to the carved box as soon as chance presented itself. Maartje and Klaas Pool were not cruel people, nor unkind. They were a little bewildered by this odd creature that they, inexplicably enough, had produced. It was not a family given to demonstration of affection. Life was too grim for the flowering of this softer side. Then, too, they had sprung from a phlegmatic and unemotional people. Klaas toiled like a slave in the fields and barn; Maartje's day was a treadmill of cooking, scrubbing, washing, mending from the moment she arose (four in the summer, five in the winter) until she dropped with a groan in her bed often long after the others were asleep. Selina had never seen her kiss Geertje or Jozina. But once she had been a little startled to see Maartje, on one of her countless trips between stove and table, run her hand through the boy's shock of black hair, down the side of his face to his chin which she tipped up with an indescribably tender gesture as she looked down into his eyes. It was a movement fleeting, vague, yet infinitely compassionate. Sometimes she even remonstrated when Klaas berated Roelf. "Leave the boy be, then, Klaas. Leave him be, once."

"She loves him best," Selina thought. "She'd even try to understand him if she had time."

He was reading her books with such hunger as to cause her to wonder if her stock would last him the winter. Sometimes, after supper, when he was hammering and sawing away in the little shed Selina would snatch Maartje's old shawl off the hook, and swathed in this against draughty chinks, she would read aloud to him while he carved, or talk to him above the noise of his tools. Selina was a gay and volatile person. She loved to make this boy laugh. His dark face would flash into almost dazzling animation. Sometimes Maartje, hearing their young laughter, would come to the shed door and stand there a moment, hugging her arms in her rolled apron and smiling at them, uncomprehending but companionable.

"You make fun, h'm?"

"Come in, Mrs. Pool. Sit down on my box and make fun, too. Here, you may have half the shawl."

"Og heden! I got no time to sit down." She was off.

Roelf slid his plane slowly, more slowly, over the surface of a satin-smooth oak board. He stopped, twined a curl of shaving about his finger. "When I am a man, and earning, I am going to buy my mother a silk dress like I saw in a store in Chicago and she should put it on every day, not only for Sunday; and sit in a chair and make little fine stitches like Widow Paarlenberg."

"What else are you going to do when you grow up?" She waited, certain that he would say something delightful.

"Drive the team to town alone to market."

"Oh, Roelf!"

"Sure. Already I have gone five times—twice with Jakob and three times with Pop. Pretty soon, when I am seventeen or eighteen, I can go alone. At five in the afternoon you start and at nine you are in the Haymarket. There all night you sleep on the wagon. There are gas lights. The men play dice and cards. At four in the morning you are ready when they come, the commission men and the pedlers and the grocery men. Oh, it's fine, I tell you!''

"Roelf!" She was bitterly disappointed.

"Here. Look." He rummaged around in a dusty box in a corner and, suddenly shy again, laid before her a torn sheet of coarse brown paper on which he had sketched crudely, effectively, a mêlée of great-haunched horses; wagons piled high with garden truck; men in overalls and corduroys; flaring gas torches. He had drawn it with a stub of pencil exactly as it looked to him. The result was as startling as that achieved by the present-day disciple of the impressionistic school.

Selina was enchanted.

Many of her evenings during November were spent thus. The family life was lived in a kitchen blue with pipe smoke, heavy with the smell of cooking. Sometimes—though rarely—a fire was lighted in the parlour stove. Often she had school papers to correct—grubby sheaves of arithimetic, grammar, or spelling lessons. Often she longed to read; wanted to sew. Her bedroom was too cold. The men sat in the kitchen or tramped in and out. Geertje and Jozina scuffled and played. Maartje scuttled about like a harried animal, heavy-footed but incredibly swift. The floor was always gritty with the sandy loam tracked in by the men's heavy boots.

Once, early in December, Selina went into town. The trip was born of sudden revolt against her surroundings and a great wave of nostalgia for the dirt and clamour and crowds of Chicago. Early Saturday morning Klaas drove her to the railway station five miles distant. She was to stay until Sunday. A letter had been written Julie Hempel ten days before, but there had been no answer. Once in town she went straight to the Hempel house. Mrs. Hempel, thin-lipped, met her in the hall and said that Julie was out of town. She was visiting her friend Miss Arnold, in Kansas City. Selina was not asked to stay to dinner. She was not asked to sit down. When she left the house her great fine eyes seemed larger and more deep-set than ever, and her jaw-line was set hard against the invasion of tears. Suddenly she hated this Chicago that wanted none of her; that brushed past her, bumping her elbow and offering no apology; that clanged, and shrieked, and whistled, and roared in her ears now grown accustomed to the prairie silence.

"I don't care," she said, which meant she did. "I don't care. Just you wait. Some day I'm going to be—oh, terribly important. And people will say, "Do you know that wonderful Selina Peake? Well, they say she used to be a country school teacher and slept in an ice-cold room and ate pork three times a . . .' There! I know what I'm going to do. I'm going to have luncheon and I'll order the most delicious things. I think I'll go to the Palmer House where Father and I . . . no, I couldn't stand that. I'll go to the Auditorium Hotel restaurant and have ice cream; and chicken broth in a silver cup; and cream puffs, and all kinds of vegetables and little lamb chops in paper panties. And orange pekoe tea."

She actually did order all these things and had a group of amazed waiters hovering about her table waiting to see her devour this meal, much as a similar group had stared at David Copperfield when he was innocent of having bolted the huge dinner ordered in the inn on his way to London.

She ate the ice cream and drank the orange pekoe (mainly because she loved the sound of its name; it made her think of chrysanthemums and cherry blossoms, spices, fans, and slant-eyed maidens). She devoured a crisp salad with the avidity of a canary pecking at a lettuce leaf. She flirted with the lamb chops. She remembered the size of her father's generous tips and left a sum on the table that temporarily dulled the edge of the waiter's hatred of women diners. But the luncheon could not be said to have been a success. She thought of dinner, and her spirit quailed, She spent the time between one and three buying portable presents for the entire Pool household—including bananas for Geertje and Jozina, for whom that farinaceous fruit had the fascination always held for the farm child. She caught a train at four thirty-five and actually trudged the five miles from the station to the farm, arriving half frozen, weary, with aching arms and nipped toes, to a great welcome of the squeals, grunts, barks, and gutturals that formed the expression of the Pool household. She was astonished to find how happy she was to return to the kitchen stove, to the smell of frying pork, to her own room with the walnut bed and the book shelf. Even the grim drum had taken on the dear and comforting aspect of the accustomed.

5

HIGH PRAIRIE SWAINS failed to find Selina alluring. She was too small, too pale and fragile for their robust taste. Naturally, her coming had been an event in this isolated community. She would have been surprised to know with what eagerness and curiosity High Prairie gathered crumbs of news about her; her appearance, her manner, her dress. Was she stuck up? Was she new fangled? She failed to notice the agitation of the parlour curtains behind the glittering windows of the farmhouses she passed on her way to school. With no visible means of communication news of her leaped from farm to farm as flame leaps the gaps in a forest fire. She would have been aghast to learn that High Prairie, inexplicably enough, knew all about her from the colour of the ribbon that threaded her neat little white corset covers to the number of books on her shelf. She thought cabbage fields beautiful; she read books to that dumb-acting Roelf Pool; she was making over a dress for Maartje after the pattern of the stylish brown lady's cloth she wore (foolishly) to school. Now and then she encountered a team on the road. She would call a good-day. Sometimes the driver answered, tardily, as though surprised. Sometimes he only stared. She almost never saw the High Prairie farm women, busy in their kitchens.

On her fifth Sunday in the district she accompanied the Pools to the morning service at the Dutch Reformed church. Maartje seldom had the time for such frivolity. But on this morning Klaas hitched up the big farm wagon with the double seat and took the family complete—Maartje, Selina, Roelf, and the pigtails. Maartje, out of her kitchen calico and dressed in her best black, with a funereal bonnet made sadder by a sparse and drooping feather whose listless fronds emerged surprisingly from a faded red cotton rose wore a new strange aspect to Selina's eyes, as did Klaas in his clumsy sabbaticals. Roelf had rebelled against going, had been cuffed for it, and had sat very still all through the service, gazing at the red and yellow glass church window. Later he confided to Selina that the sunlight filtering through the crude yellow panes had imparted a bilious look to the unfortunates seated within its range, affording him much secret satisfaction.

Selina's appearance had made quite a stir, of which she was entirely unaware. As the congregation entered by twos and threes she thought they resembled startlingly a woodcut in an old illustrated book she once had seen. The men's Sunday trousers and coats had a square stiff angularity, as though chopped out of a block. The women, in shawls and bonnets of rusty black, were incredibly cut in the same pattern. The unmarried girls, though, were plump, red-cheeked, and not uncomely, with high round cheek bones on which sat a spot of brick-red which imparted no glow to the face. Their foreheads were prominent and meaningless.

In the midst of this drab assemblage there entered late and rustlingly a tall, slow-moving woman in a city-bought cloak and a bonnet quite unlike the vintage millinery of High Prairie. As she came down the aisle Selina thought she was like a full-sailed frigate. An ample woman, with a fine fair skin and a ripe red mouth; a high firm bosom and great thighs that moved rhythmically, slowly. She had thick, insolent eyelids. Her hands, as she turned the leaves of her hymn book, were smooth and white. As she entered there was a little rustle thoughout the congregation; a craning of necks. Though she was bustled and flounced and panniered, you thought, curiously enough, of those lolling white-fleshed and unconventional ladies whom the sixteenth century painters were always portraying as having their toe nails cut with nothing on.

"Who's that?" whispered Selina to Maartje.

"Widow Paarlenberg. She is rich like anything."

"Yes?" Selina was fascinated.

"Look once how she makes eyes at him."

"At him? Who? Who?"

"Pervus DeJong. By Gerrit Pon he is sitting with the blue shirt and sad looking so."

Selina craned, peered. "The—oh—he's very good looking, isn't he?"

"Sure. Widow Paarlenberg is stuck on him. See how she—Sh-sh-sh!— Reverend Dekker looks at us. I tell you after."

Selina decided she'd come to church oftener. The service went on, dull, heavy. It was in English and Dutch. She heard scarcely a word of it. The Widow Paarlenberg and this Pervus DeJong occupied her thoughts. She decided, without malice, that the widow resembled one of the sleekest of the pink porkers rooting in Klaas Pool's barnyard, waiting to be cut into Christmas meat.

The Widow Paarlenberg turned and smiled. Her eyes were slippery (Selina's term). Her mouth became loose and wide with one corner sliding down a trifle into something very like a leer.

With one surge the Dutch Reformed congregation leaned forward to see how Pervus DeJong would respond to this public mark of favour. His gaze was stern, unsmiling. His eyes were fixed on that extremely dull gentleman, the Reverend Dekker.

"He's annoyed," thought Selina, and was pleased at the thought. "Well, I may not be a widow, but I'm sure that's not the way." And then: "Now I wonder what it's like when *he* smiles."

According to fiction as Selina had found it in the *Fireside Companion* and elsewhere, he should have turned at this moment, irresistibly drawn by the magnetism of her gaze, and smiled a rare sweet smile that lighted up his stern young face. But he did not. He yawned suddenly and capaciously. The Dutch Reformed congregation leaned back feeling cheated. Handsome, certainly, Selina reflected. But then, probably Klaas Pool, too, had been handsome a few years ago.

The service ended, there was much talk of the weather, seedlings, stock, the approaching holiday season. Maartje, her Sunday dinner heavy on her mind, was elbowing her way up the aisle. Here and there she introduced Selina briefly to a woman friend. "Mrs. Vander Sijde, meet school teacher."

"Aggie's mother?" Selina would begin, primly, only to be swept along by Maartje on her way to the door. "Mrs. Von Mijnen, meet school teacher. Is Mrs. Von Mijnen." They regarded her with a grim gaze. Selina would smile and nod rather nervously, feeling young, frivolous, and somehow guilty.

When, with Maartje, she reached the church porch Pervus DeJong was unhitching the dejected horse that was harnessed to his battered and lopsided cart. The animal stood with four feet bunched together in a drooping and pathetic attitude and seemed inevitably meant for mating with this decrepit vehicle. DeJong untied the reins quickly, and was about to step into the sagging conveyance when the Widow Paarlenberg sailed down the church steps with admirable speed for one so amply proportioned. She made straight for him, skirts billowing, flounces flying, plumes waving. Maartje clutched Selina's arm. "Look how she makes! She asks him to eat Sunday dinner I bet you! See once how he makes with his head no."

Selina—and the whole congregation unashamedly watching—could indeed see how he made with his head no. His whole body seemed set in negation—the fine head, the broad patient shoulders, the muscular powerful legs in their ill-fitting Sunday blacks. He shook his head, gathered up the reins, and drove away, leaving the Widow Paarlenberg to carry off with such bravado as she could muster this public outing in full sight of the Dutch Reformed congregation of High Prairie. It must be said that she actually achieved this feat with a rather magnificent composure. Her round pink face, as she turned away, was placid; her great cowlike eyes mild. Selina abandoned the pink porker simile for that of a great Persian cat, full-fed and treacherous, its claws all sheathed in velvet. The widow stepped agilely into her own neat phaeton with its sleek horse and was off down the hard snowless road, her head high.

"Well!" exclaimed Selina, feeling as though she had witnessed the first act of an exciting play. And breathed deeply. So, too, did the watching congregation, so that the widow could be said to have driven off in quite a gust.

As they jogged home in the Pool farm wagon Maartje told her tale with a good deal of savour.

Pervus DeJong had been left a widower two years before. Within a month of that time Leendert Paarlenberg had died, leaving to his widow the richest and most profitable farm in the whole community. Pervus DeJong, on the contrary, through inheritance from his father, old Johannes, possessed a scant twenty-five acres of the worst lowland—practically the only lowland—in all High Prairie. The acreage was notoriously barren. In spring, the critical time for seedlings and early vegetable crops, sixteen of the twenty-five were likely to be under water. Pervus DeJong patiently planted, sowed, gathered crops, hauled them to market; seemed still never to get on in this thrifty Dutch community where getting on was so common a trait as to be no longer thought a virtue. Luck and nature seemed to work against him. His seedlings proved unfertile; his stock was always ailing; his cabbages were worm-infested; snout-beetle bored his rhubarb. When he planted largely of spinach, hoping for a wet spring, the season was dry. Did he turn the following year to sweet potatoes, all auguries pointing to a dry spring and summer, the summer proved the wettest in a decade. Insects and fungi seemed drawn to his fields as by a malevolent force. Had he been small, puny, and insignificant his bad luck would have called forth contemptuous pity. But there was about him the lovableness and splendour of the stricken giant. To complete his discomfort, his household was inadequately ministered by an elderly and rheumatic female connection whose pies and bread were the scandal of the neighbouring housewives.

It was on this Pervus DeJong, then, that the Widow Paarlenberg of the rich acres, the comfortable farmhouse, the gold neck chain, the silk gowns, the soft white hands and the cooking talents, had set her affections. She wooed him openly, notoriously, and with a Dutch vehemence that would have swept another man off his feet. It was known that she sent him a weekly baking of cakes, pies, and bread. She urged upon him choice seeds from her thriving fields; seedlings from her hotbeds; plants, all of which he steadfastly refused. She tricked, cajoled, or nagged him into eating her ample meals. She even asked his advice—that subtlest form of flattery. She asked him about sub-soiling, humus, rotation—she whose rich land yielded, under her shrewd management, more profitably to the single acre than to any ten of Pervus's. One Jan Bras managed her farm admirably under her supervision.

DeJong's was a simple mind. In the beginning, when she said to him, in her deep, caressing voice, "Mr. DeJong, could I ask you a little advice about something? I'm a woman alone since I haven't got Leendert any more, and strangers what do they care how they run the land! It's about my radishes, lettuce, spinach, and turnips. Last yearrr, instead of tender, they were stringy and full of fibre on account that Jan Bras. He's for slow growing. Those vegetables you've got to grow quick. Bras says my fertilizer is the fault, but I know different. What you think?"

Jan Bras, getting wind of this, told it abroad with grim humour. Masculine High Prairie, meeting Pervus DeJong on the road, greeted him with: "Well, DeJong, you been giving the Widow Paarlenberg any good advice here lately about growing?"

It had been a particularly bad season for his fields. As High Prairie poked a sly thumb into his ribs thus he realized that he had been duped by the wily widow. A slow Dutch wrath rose in him against her; a male resentment at being manipulated by a woman. When next she approached him, cajolery in her voice, seeking guidance about tillage, drainage, or crops, he said, bluntly: "Better you ask Harm Tien his advice." Harm Tien was the district idiot, a poor witless creature of thirty with the mind of a child.

Knowing well that the entire community was urging him toward this profitable match with the plump, rich, red-lipped widow, Pervus set his will like a stubborn steer and would have none of her. He was uncomfortable in his untidy house; he was lonely, he was unhappy. But he would have none of her. Vanity, pride, resentment were all mixed up in it.

The very first time that Pervus DeJong met Selina he had a chance to protect her. With such a start, the end was inevitable. Then, too, Selina had on the wine-coloured cashmere and was trying hard to keep the tears back in full view of the whole of High Prairie. Urged by Maartje (and rather fancying the idea) Selina had attended the great meeting and dance at Adam Ooms's hall above the general store near the High Prairie station. Farmer families for miles around were there. The new church organ—that time-hallowed pretext for sociability—was the excuse for this gathering. There was a small admission charge. Adam Ooms had given them the hall. The three musicians were playing without fee. The women were to bring supper packed in boxes or baskets, these to be raffled off to the highest bidder whose privilege it then was to sup with the fair whose basket he had bought. Hot coffee could be had at so much the cup. All the proceeds were to be devoted to the organ. It was understood, of course, that there was to be no lively bidding against husbands. Each farm woman knew her own basket as she knew the countenance of her children, and each farmer, as that basket came up at auction, named a cautious sum which automatically made him the basket's possessor. The larger freedom had not come to High Prairie in 1890. The baskets and boxes of the unwed women were to be the fought-for prizes. Maartje had packed her own basket at noon and had driven off at four with Klaas and the children. She was to serve on one of those bustling committees whose duties ranged from coffee making to dish washing. Klaas and Roelf were to be pressed into service. The pigtails would slide up and down the waxed floor of Ooms's hall with other shrieking pigtails of the neighbourhood until the crowd began to arrive for the auction and supper. Jakob Hoogendunk would convey Selina to the festivities when his chores were done. Selina's lunch basket was to be a separate and distinct affair, offered at auction with those of the Katrinas and Linas and Sophias of High Prairie. Not a little apprehensive, she was to pack this basket herself. Maartje, departing, had left copious but disjointed instructions.

"Ham . . . them big cookies in the crock . . . pickles . . . watch how you don't spill . . . plum preserves . . ."

Maartje's own basket was of gigantic proportions and staggering content. Her sandwiches were cubic blocks; her pickles clubs of cucumber; her pies vast plateaus.

The basket provided for Selina, while not quite so large, still was of appalling size as Selina contemplated it. She decided, suddenly, that she would have none of it. In her trunk she had a cardboard box such as shoes come in. Certainly this should hold enough lunch for two, she thought. She and Julie Hempel had used such boxes for picnic lunches on their Saturday holidays. She was a little nervous about the whole thing; rather dreaded the prospect of eating her supper with a High Prairie swain unknown to her. Suppose no one should bid for her box! She resolved to fill it after her own pattern, disregarding Maartje's heavy provender.

She had the kitchen to herself. Jakob was in the fields or outhouses. The house was deliciously quiet. Selina rummaged for the shoe box, lined it with a sheet of tissue paper, rolled up her sleeves, got out mixing bowl, flour, pans. Cup cakes were her ambition. She baked six of them. They came out a beautiful brown but somewhat leaden. Still, anything was better than a wedge of soggy pie, she told herself. She boiled eggs very hard, halved them, devilled their yolks, filled the whites neatly with this mixture and clapped the halves together again, skewering them with a toothpick. Then she rolled each egg separately in tissue paper twisted at the ends. Daintiness, she had decided, should be the keynote of her supper box. She cut bread paper-thin and made jelly sandwiches, scorning the ubiquitous pork. Bananas, she knew, belonged in a lunch box, but these were unobtainable. She substituted two juicy pippins, polished until their cheeks glittered. The food neatly packed, she wrapped the box in paper and tied it with a gay red ribbon yielded by her trunk. At the last moment she whipped into the yard, twisted a brush of evergreen from the tree at the side of the house, and tucked this into the knot of ribbon atop the box. She stepped back and thought the effect enchanting.

She was waiting in her red cashmere and her cloak and hood when Hoogendunk called for her. They were late arrivals, for outside Ooms's hall were hitched all manner of vehicles. There had been a heavy snowfall two days before. This had brought out bobsleds, cutters, sleighs. The horse sheds were not large enough to shelter all. Late comers had to hitch where they could. There was a great jangling of bells as the horses stamped in the snow.

Selina, balancing her box carefully, opened the door that led to the wooden stairway. The hall was on the second floor. The clamour that struck her ears had the effect of a physical blow. She hesitated a moment, and if there had been any means of returning to the Pool farm, short of walking five miles in the snow, she would have taken it. Up the stairs and into the din. Evidently the auctioning of supper baskets was even now in progress. The roar of voices had broken out after the sale of a basket and now was subsiding under the ear-splitting cracks of the auctioneer's hammer. Through the crowded doorway Selina could catch a glimpse of him as he stood on a chair, the baskets piled before him. He used a barrel elevated on a box as his pulpit. The auctioneer was Adam Ooms who himself had once been the High Prairie school teacher. A fox-faced little man, bald, falsetto, the village clown with a solid foundation of shrewdness under his clowning and a tart layer of malice over it.

High and shrill came his voice. "What am I bid! What am I bid! Thirty cents! Thirty-five! Shame on you, gentlemen. What am I bid! Who'll make it forty!"

Selina felt a little thrill of excitement. She looked about for a place on which to lay her wraps. Every table, chair, hook, and rack in the hallway was piled with clothing. She espied a box that appeared empty, rolled her cloak, muffler, and hood into a neat bundle and, about to cast it into the box, saw, upturned to her from its depths, the round pink faces of the sleeping Kuyper twins, aged six months. From the big hall now came a great shouting, clapping of hands, stamping, cat-calls. Another basket had been disposed of. Oh, dear! In desperation Selina placed her bundle on the floor in a corner, smoothed down the red cashmere, snatched up her lunch box and made for the doorway with the childish eagerness of one out of the crowd to be in it. She wondered where Maartje and Klaas Pool were in this close-packed roomful; and Roelf. In the doorway she found that broad black-coated backs shut off sight and ingress. She had written her name neatly on her lunch box. Now she was at a loss to find a way to reach Adam Ooms. She eyed the great-shouldered expanse just ahead of her. In desperation she decided to dig into it with a corner of her box. She dug, viciously. The back winced. Its owner turned. "Here! What———!''

Selina looked up into the wrathful face of Pervus DeJong, Pervus DeJong looked down into the startled eyes of Selina Peake. Large enough eyes at any time; enormous now in her fright at what she had done.

"I'm sorry! I'm—sorry. I thought if I could—there's no way of getting my lunch box up there—such a crowd———"

A slim, appealing, lovely little figure in the wine-red cashmere, amidst all those buxom bosoms, and overheated bodies, and flushed faces. His gaze left her reluctantly, settled on the lunch box, became, if possible, more bewildered. "That? Lunch box?"

"Yes. For the raffle. I'm the school teacher. Selina Peake."

He nodded. "I saw you in church Sunday."

"You did! I didn't think you. . . . Did you?"

"Wait here. I'll come back. Wait here."

He took the shoe box. She waited. He ploughed his way through the crowd like a Juggernaut, reached Adam Ooms's platform and placed the box inconspicuously next a colossal hamper that was one of a dozen grouped awaiting Adam's attention. When he had made his way back to Selina he again said, "Wait," and plunged down the wooden stairway. Selina waited. She had ceased to feel distressed at her inability to find the Pools in the crowd, a-tiptoe though she was. When presently he came back he had in his hand an empty wooden soap-box. This he up-ended in the doorway just behind the crowd stationed there. Selina mounted it; found her head a little above the level of his. She could survey the room from end to end. There were the Pools. She waved to Maartje; smiled at Roelf. He made as though to come toward her; did come part way, and was restrained by Maartje catching at his coat tail.

Selina wished she could think of something to say. She looked down at Pervus DeJong. The back of his neck was pink, as though with effort. She thought, instinctively, "My goodness, he's trying to think of something to say, too." That, somehow, put her at her ease. She would wait until he spoke. His neck was now a deep red. The crowd surged back at some disturbance around Adam Ooms's elevation. Selina teetered perilously on her box, put out a hand blindly, felt his great hard hand on her arm, steadying her.

"Quite a crowd, ain't it?" The effort had reached its apex. The red of his neck began to recede.

"Oh, quite!"

"They ain't all High Prairie. Some of 'em's from Low Prairie way. New Haarlem, even."

"Really!"

A pause. Another effort.

"How goes it school teaching?"

"Oh—it goes pretty well."

"You are little to be school teacher, anyway, ain't you?"

"Little!" She drew herself up from her vantage point of the soap-box. "I'm bigger than you are."

They laughed at that as at an exquisite piece of repartee.

Adam Ooms's gavel (a wooden potato masher) crashed for silence. "Ladies!" [Crash!] "And gents!" [Crash!] "Gents! Look what basket we've got here!"

Look indeed. A great hamper, grown so plethoric that it could no longer wear its cover. Its contents bellied into a mound smoothly covered with a fine white cloth whose glistening surface proclaimed it damask. A Himalaya among hampers. You knew that under that snowy crust lay gold that was fowl done crisply, succulently; emeralds in the form of gherkins; rubies that melted into strawberry preserves; cakes frosted like diamonds; to say nothing of such semi-precious jewels as potato salad; cheeses; sour cream to be spread on rye bread and butter; coffee cakes; crullers.

Crash! "The Widow Paarlenberg's basket, ladies—*and* gents! The Widow Paarlenberg! I don't know what's in it. You don't know what's in it. We don't have to know what's in it. Who has eaten Widow Paarlenberg's chicken once don't have to know. Who has eaten Widow Paarlenberg's cake once don't have to know. What am I bid on Widow Paarlenberg's basket! What am I bid! WhatmIbidwhatmIbidwhatmIbid!" [Crash!]

The widow herself, very handsome in black silk, her gold neck chain rising and falling richly with the little flurry that now agitated her broad bosom, was seated in a chair against the wall not five feet from the auctioneer's stand. She bridled now, blushed, cast down her eyes, cast up her eyes, succeeded in looking as unconscious as a complaisant Turkish slave girl on the block.

Adam Ooms's glance swept the hall. He leaned forward, his fox-like face fixed in a smile. From the widow herself, seated so prominently at his right, his gaze marked the young blades of the village; the old bucks; youths and widowers and bachelors. Here was the prize of the evening. Around, in a semi-circle, went his keen glance until it reached the tall figure towering in the doorway—reached it, and rested there. His gimlet eyes seemed to bore their way into Pervus DeJong's steady stare. He raised his right arm aloft, brandishing the potato masher. The whole room fixed its gaze on the blond head in the doorway. "Speak up! Young men of High Prairie! Heh, you, Pervus DeJong! WhatmIbidwhatmIbidwhatmIbid!"

"Fifty cents!" The bid came from Gerrit Pon at the other end of the hall. A dashing offer, as a start, in this district where one dollar often represented the profits on a whole load of market truck brought to the city.

Crash! went the potato masher. "Fifty cents I'm bid. Who'll make it seventy-five? Who'll make it seventy-five?"

"Sixty!" Johannes Ambuul, a widower, his age more than the sum of his bid.

"Seventy!" Gerrit Pon.

Adam Ooms whispered it—hissed it. "S-s-s-seventy. Ladies and gents, I wouldn't repeat out loud sucha figger. I would be ashamed. Look at this basket, gents, and then you can say . . . s-s-seventy!"

"Seventy-five!" the cautious Ambuul.

Scarlet, flooding her face, belied the widow's outward air of composure. Pervus DeJong, standing beside Selina, viewed the proceedings with an air of detachment. High Prairie was looking at him expectantly, openly. The widow bit her red lip, tossed her head. Pervus DeJong returned the auctioneer's meaning smirk with the mild gaze of a disinterested outsider. High Prairie, Low Prairie, and New Haarlem sat tense, like an audience at a play. Here, indeed, was drama being enacted in a community whose thrills were all too rare.

"Gents!" Adam Ooms's voice took on a tearful note—the tone of one who is more hurt than angry. "Gents!" Slowly, with infinite reverence, he lifted one corner of the damask cloth that concealed the hamper's contents— lifted it and peered within as at a treasure. At what he saw there he started back dramatically, at once rapturous, despairing, amazed. He rolled his eyes. He smacked his lips. He rubbed his stomach. The sort of dumb show that, since the days of the Greek drama, has been used to denote gastronomic delight.

"Eighty!" was wrenched suddenly from Goris Von Vuuren, the nineteen-year-old fat and gluttonous son of a prosperous New Haarlem farmer.

Adam Ooms rubbed brisk palms together. "Now then! A dollar! A dollar! It's an insult to this basket to make it less than a dollar." He lifted the cover again, sniffed, appeared overcome. "Gents, if it wasn't for Mrs. Ooms sitting there I'd make it a dollar myself and a bargain. A dollar! Am I bid a dollar!" He leaned far forward over his improvised pulpit. "Did I hear you say a dollar, Pervus DeJong?" DeJong stared, immovable, unabashed. His very indifference was contagious. The widow's bountiful basket seemed to shrink before one's eyes. "Eighty-eighty-eighty-eighty—gents! I'm going to tell you something. I'm going to whisper a secret." His lean face was veined with craftiness. "Gents. Listen. It isn't chicken in this beautiful basket. It isn't chicken. It's"—a dramatic pause—"it's *roast duck!*" He swayed back, mopped his brow with his red handkerchief, held one hand high in the air. His last card.

"Eighty-five!" groaned the fat Goris Von Vuuren.

"Eighty-five! Eighty-five! Eightyfiveeightyfiveeightyfive eighty-five! Gents! Gen-tle-men! Eighty-five once! Eighty-five—twice!" [Crash!] "Gone to Goris Von Vuuren for eighty-five."

A sigh went up from the assemblage; a sigh that was the wind before the storm. There followed a tornado of talk. It crackled and thundered. The rich Widow Paarlenberg would have to eat her supper with Von Vuuren's boy, the great thick Goris. And there in the doorway, talking to teacher as if they had known each other for years, was Pervus DeJong with his money in his pocket. It was as good as a play.

Adam Ooms was angry. His lean, fox-like face became pinched with spite. He prided himself on his antics as auctioneer; and his chef d'œuvre had brought a meagre eighty-five cents, besides doubtless winning him the enmity of that profitable store customer, the Widow Paarlenberg. Goris Von Vuuren came forward to claim his prize amidst shouting, clapping, laughter. The great hamper was handed down to him; an ample, rich-looking burden, its handle folded comfortably over its round stomach, its white cover so glistening with starch and ironing that it gave back the light from the big lamp above the auctioneer's stand. As Goris Von Vuuren lifted it his great shoulders actually sagged. Its contents promised satiety even to such a feeder as he. A grin, half sheepish, half triumphant, creased his plump pink face.

Adam Ooms scuffled about among the many baskets at his feet. His nostrils looked pinched and his skinny hands shook a little as he searched for one small object.

When he stood upright once more he was smiling. His little eyes gleamed. His wooden sceptre pounded for silence. High in one hand, balanced daintily on his finger tips, he held Selina's little white shoe box, with its red ribbon binding it, and the plume of evergreen stuck in the ribbon. Affecting great solicitude he brought it down then to read the name written on it; held it aloft again, smirking.

He said nothing. Grinning, he held it high. He turned his body at the waist from side to side, so that all might see. The eyes of those before him still held a mental picture of the huge hamper, food-packed, that had just been handed down. The contrast was too absurd, too cruel. A ripple of laughter swept the room; rose; swelled to a roar. Adam Ooms drew his mouth down solemnly. His little finger elegantly crooked, he pendulumed the box to right and left. He swerved his beady eyes from side to side. He waited with a nice sense of the dramatic until the laughter had reached its height, then held up a hand for silence. A great scraping "Ahem!", as he cleared his throat threatened to send the crowd off again.

"Ladies—*and* gents! Here's a dainty little tidbit. Here's something not only for the inner man, but a feast for the eye. Well, boys, if the last lot was too much for you this lot ought to be just about right. If the food ain't quite enough for you, you can tie the ribbon in the lady's hair and put the posy in your buttonhole and there you are. *There* you are! What's more, the lady herself goes with it. You don't get a country girl with this here box, gents. A city girl, you can tell by looking at it, just. And who is she? Who did up this dainty little box just big enough for two?" He inspected it again, solemnly, and added, as an afterthought, "If you ain't feeling specially hungry. Who?———" He looked about, apishly.

Selina's cheeks matched her gown. Her eyes were wide and dark with the effort she was making to force back the hot haze threatening them. Why had she mounted this wretched soap-box! Why had she come to this hideous party! Why had she come to High Prairie! Why! . . .

"Miss Selina Peake, that's who. Miss Se-li-na Peake!"

A hundred balloon faces pulled by a single cord turned toward her as she stood there on the box for all to see. They swam toward her. She put up a hand to push them back.

"What'm I bid! What'm I bid! What'm I bid for this here lovely little toothful, gents! Start her up!"

"Five cents!" piped up old Johannes Ambuul, with a snicker. The tittering crowd broke into a guffaw. Selina was conscious of a little sick feeling at the pit of her stomach. Through the haze she saw the widow's face, no longer sulky, but smiling now. She saw Roelf's dear dark head. His face was set, like a man's. He was coming toward her, or trying to, but the crowd wedged him in, small as he was among those great bodies. She lost sight of him. How hot it was! how hot . . . An arm at her waist. Some one had mounted the little box and stood teetering there beside her, pressed against her slightly, reassuringly. Pervus DeJong. Her head was on a level with his great shoulder now. They stood together in the doorway, on the soap-box, for all High Prairie to see.

"Five cents I'm bid for this lovely little mouthful put up by the school teacher's own fair hands. Five cents! Five————"

"One dollar!" Pervus DeJong.

The balloon faces were suddenly punctured with holes. High Prairie's jaw dropped with astonishment. Its mouth stood open.

There was nothing plain about Selina now. Her dark head was held high, and his fair one beside it made a vivid foil. The purchase of the wine-coloured cashmere was at last justified.

"And ten!" cackled old Johannes Ambuul, his rheumy eyes on Selina.

Art and human spitefulness struggled visibly for mastery in Adam Ooms's face—and art won. The auctioneer triumphed over the man. The term "crowd psychology" was unknown to him, but he was artist enough to sense that some curious magic process, working through this roomful of people, had transformed the little white box, from a thing despised and ridiculed, into an object of beauty, of value, of infinite desirability. He now eyed it in a catalepsy of admiration.

"One-ten I'm bid for this box all tied with a ribbon to match the gown of the girl who brought it. Gents, you get the ribbon, the lunch, *and* the girl. And only one-ten bid for all that. Gents! Gents! Remember, it ain't only a lunch—it's a picture. It pleases the eye. Do I hear one————"

"Five bits!" Barend DeRoo, of Low Prairie, in the lists. A strapping young Dutchman, the Brom Bones of the district. Aaltje Huff, in a fit of pique at his indifference, had married to spite him. Cornelia Vinke, belle of New Haarlem, was said to be languishing for love of him. He drove to the Haymarket with his load of produce and played cards all night on the wagon under the gas torches while the street girls of the neighbourhood assailed him in vain. Six feet three, his red face shone now like a harvest moon above the crowd. A merry, mischievous eye that laughed at Pervus DeJong and his dollar bid.

"Dollar and a half!" A high clear voice—a boy's voice. Roelf.

"Oh, no!" said Selina aloud. But she was unheard in the gabble. Roelf had once confided to her that he had saved three dollars and fifty cents in the last three years. Five dollars would purchase a set of tools that his mind had been fixed on for months past. Selina saw Klaas Pool's look of astonishment changing to anger. Saw Maartje Pool's quick hand on his arm, restraining him.

"Two dollars!" Pervus DeJong.

"Twotwotwotwotwotwo!" Adam Ooms in a frenzy of salesmanship.

"And ten." Johannes Ambuul's cautious bid.

"Two and a quarter." Barend DeRoo.

"Two-fifty!" Pervus DeJong.

"Three dollars!" The high voice of the boy. It cracked a little on the last syllable, and the crowd laughed.

"Three-three-three-three-threetheethree. Three once————"

"And a half." Pervus DeJong.

"Three sixty."

"Four!" DeRoo.

"And ten."

The boy's voice was heard no more.

"I wish they'd stop," whispered Selina.

"Five!" Pervus DeJong.

"Six!" DeRoo, his face very red.

"And ten."

"Seven!"

"It's only jelly sandwiches," said Selina to DeJong, in a panic.

"Eight!" Johannes Ambuul, gone mad.

"Nine!" DeRoo.

"Nine! Nine I'm bid! Nine-nine-nine! Who'll make it————"

"Let him have it. The cup cakes fell a little. Don't————"

"Ten!" said Pervus DeJong.

Barend DeRoo shrugged his great shoulders.

"Ten-ten-ten. Do I hear eleven? Do I hear ten-fifty! Ten-ten-ten tenten-tentententententen! Gents! Ten once. Ten twice. Gone!—for ten dollars to Pervus DeJong. And a bargain." Adam Ooms mopped his bald head and his cheeks and the damp spot under his chin.

Ten dollars. Adam Ooms knew, as did all the countryside, this was not the sum of ten dollars merely. No basket of food, though it contained night-ingales' tongues, the golden apple of Atalanta, wines of rare vintage, could have been adequate recompense for these ten dollars. They represented sweat and blood; toil and hardship; hours under the burning prairie sun at mid-day; work doggedly carried on through the drenching showers of spring; nights of restless sleep snatched an hour at a time under the sky in the Chicago market place; miles of weary travel down the rude corduroy road between High Prairie and Chicago, now up to the hubs in mud, now blinded by dust and blowing sand.

A sale at Christie's, with a miniature going for a million, could not have met with a deeper hush, a more dramatic babble following the hush.

They ate their lunch together in one corner of Adam Ooms's hall. Selina opened the box and took out the devilled eggs, and the cup cakes that had fallen a little, and the apples, and the sandwiches sliced very, very thin. The coldly appraising eye of all High Prairie, Low Prairie, and New Haarlem watched this sparse provender emerge from the ribbon-tied shoe box. She offered him a sandwich, It looked infinitesimal in his great paw. Suddenly all Selina's agony of embarrassment was swept away, and she was laughing, not wildly or hysterically, but joyously and girlishly. She sank her little white teeth into one of the absurd sandwiches and looked at him, expecting to find him laughing, too. But he wasn't laughing. He looked very earnest and his blue eyes were fixed hard on the bit of bread in his hand, and his face was very red and clean-shaven. He bit into the sandwich and chewed it solemnly. And Selina thought: "Why, the dear thing! The great big dear thing! And he might have been eating breast of duck . . . Ten dollars!" Aloud she said, "What made you do it?"

"I don't know. I don't know." Then, "You looked so little. And they were making fun. Laughing." He looked very earnest, and his blue eyes were fixed hard on the sandwich, and his face was very red.

"That's a very foolish reason for throwing away ten dollars," Selina said, severely.

He seemed not to hear her; bit ruminantly into one of the cup cakes. Suddenly: "I can't hardly write at all, only to sign my name and like that."

"Read?"

"Only to spell out the words. Anyways I don't get time for reading. But figuring I wish I knew. 'Rithmetic. I can figger some, but those fellows in Haymarket they are too sharp for me. They do numbers in their head—like that, so quick."

Selina leaned toward him. "I'll teach you. I'll teach you."

"How do you mean, teach me?"

"Evenings."

He looked down at his great calloused palms, then up at her. "What would you take for pay?"

"Pay! I don't want any pay." She was genuinely shocked.

His face lighted up with a sudden thought. "Tell you what. My place is just this side the school, next to Bouts's place. I could start for you the fire, mornings, in the school. And thaw the pump and bring in a pail of water. This month, and January and February and part of March, even, now I don't go to market on account it's winter, I could start you the fire. Till spring. And I could come maybe three times a week, evenings, to Pool's place, for lessons." He looked so helpless, so humble, so huge; and the more pathetic for his hugeness.

She felt a little rush of warmth toward him that was at once impersonal and maternal. She thought again, "Why, the dear thing! The great helpless big thing! How serious he is! And funny." He was indeed both serious and funny, with the ridiculous cup cake in his great hand, his eyes wide and ruminant, his face ruddier than ever, his forehead knotted with earnestness. She laughed, suddenly, a gay little laugh, and he, after a puzzled pause, joined her companionably.

"Three evenings a week," repeated Selina, then, from the depths of her ignorance. "Why, I'd love to. I'd—love to."

6

THE EVENINGS TURNED out to be Tuesdays, Thursdays, and Saturdays. Supper was over by six-thirty in the Pool household. Pervus was there by seven, very clean as to shirt, his hair brushed till it shone; shy, and given to dropping his hat and bumping against chairs, and looking solemn. Selina was torn between pity and mirth. If only he had blustered. A blustering big man puts the world on the defensive. A gentle giant disarms it.

Selina got out her McBride's Grammar and Duffy's Arithmetic, and together they started to parse verbs, paper walls, dig cisterns, and extract square roots. They found study impossible at the oilcloth-covered kitchen table, with the Pool household eddying about it. Jakob built a fire in the parlour stove and there they sat, teacher and pupil, their feet resting cosily on the gleaming nickel railing that encircled the wood burner.

On the evening of the first lesson Roelf had glowered throughout supper and had disappeared into the work-shed, whence issued a great sound of hammering, sawing, and general clatter. He and Selina had got into the way of spending much time together, in or out of doors. They skated on Vander Sijde's pond; together with the shrieking pigtails they coasted on the little slope that led down from Kuyper's woods to the main road, using sleds that had been put together by Roelf. On bad days they read or studied. Not Sundays merely, but many week-day evenings were spent thus. Selina was determined that Roelf should break away from the uncouth speech of the countryside; that he should at least share with her the somewhat sketchy knowledge gained at Miss Fister's select school. She, the woman of almost twenty, never talked down to this boy of twelve. The boy worshipped her inarticulately. She had early discovered that he had a feeling for beauty— beauty of line, texture, colour, and grouping—that was rare in one of his years. The feel of a satin ribbon in his fingers; the orange and rose of a sunset; the folds of the wine-red cashmere dress; the cadence of a spoken line, brought a look to his face that startled her. She had a battered volume of Tennyson. When first she read him the line begnning, "Elaine the fair,

Elaine the lovable, Elaine, the lily maid of Astolat————" he had uttered
a little exclamation. She, glancing up from her book, had found his eyes
wide, bright, and luminous in his lean dark face.

"What is it, Roelf?"

He had flushed. "I didn't say nothing—anything. Start over again how it
goes, 'Elaine————' "

She had begun again the fragrant lines, "Elaine the fair, Elaine the lovable . . ."

Since the gathering at Ooms's hall he had been moody and sullen; had
refused to answer when she spoke to him of his bid for her basket. Urged,
he would only say, "Oh, it was just fun to make old Ooms mad."

Now, with the advent of Pervus DeJong, Roelf presented that most touching and miserable of spectacles, a small boy jealous and helpless in his
jealousy. Selina had asked him to join the tri-weekly evening lessons; had,
indeed, insisted that he be a pupil in the class round the parlour stove.
Maartje had said, on the night of Pervus DeJong's first visit, "Roelf, you
sit, too, and learn. Is good for you to learn out of books the way teacher
says." Klaas Pool, too, had approved the plan, since it would cost nothing
and, furthermore, would in no way interfere with Roelf's farm work. "Sure;
learn," he said, with a large gesture.

Roelf would not. He behaved very badly; slammed doors, whistled,
scuffled on the kitchen floor, made many mysterious trips through the parlour
up the stairs that led off that room, ascending with a clatter; incited Geertje
and Jozina to quarrels and tears; had the household in a hubbub; stumbled
over Dunder, the dog, so that that anguished animal's yelps were added to
the din.

Selina was frantic. Lessons were impossible amidst this uproar. "It has
never been like this before," she assured Pervus, almost tearfully. "I don't
know what's the matter. It's awful."

Pervus had looked up from his slate. His eyes were calm, his lips smiling.
"Is all right. In my house is too still, evenings. Next time it goes better.
You see."

Next time it did go better. Roelf disappeared into his work-shed after
supper; did not emerge until after DeJong's departure.

There was something about the sight of this great creature bent laboriously
over a slate, the pencil held clumsily in his huge fingers, that moved Selina
strangely. Pity wracked her. If she had known to what emotion this pity was
akin she might have taken away the slate and given him a tablet, and the
whole course of her life would have been different. "Poor lad," she thought.
"Poor lad." Chided herself for being amused at his childlike earnestness.

He did not make an apt pupil, though painstaking. Usually the top draught
of the stove was open, and the glow of the fire imparted to his face and head
a certain roseate glory. He was very grave. His brow wore a troubled frown.
Selina would go over a problem or a sentence again and again, patiently,
patiently. Then, suddenly, like a hand passed over his face, his smile would
come, transforming it. He had white strong teeth, too small, and perhaps
not so white as they seemed because of his russet blondeur. He would smile
like a child, and Selina should have been warned by the warm rush of joy
that his smile gave her. She would smile, too. He was as pleased as though
he had made a fresh and wonderful discovery.

"It's easy," he would say, "when you know it once." Like a boy.

He usually went home by eight-thirty or nine. Often the Pools went to
bed before he left. After he had gone Selina was wakeful. She would heat
water and wash; brush her hair vigorously; feeling at once buoyant and
depressed.

Sometimes they fell to talking. His wife had died in the second year of their marriage, when the child was born. The child, too, had died. A girl. He was unlucky, like that. It was the same with the farm.

"Spring, half of the land is under water. My piece, just. Bouts's place, next to me, is high and rich. Bouts, he don't even need deep ploughing. His land is quick land. It warms up in the spring early. After rain it works easy. He puts in fertilizer, any kind, and his plants jump, like. My place is bad for garden truck. Wet. All the time, wet; or in summer baked before I can loosen it again. Muckland."

Selina thought a moment. She had heard much talk between Klaas and Jakob, winter evenings. "Can't you do something to it—fix it—so that the water will run off? Raise it, or dig a ditch or something?"

"We-e-ell, maybe. Maybe you could. But it costs money, draining."

"It costs money not to, doesn't it?"

He considered this, ruminatively. "Guess it does. But you don't have to have ready cash to let the land lay. To drain it you do."

Selina shook her head impatiently. "That's a very foolish, shortsighted way to reason."

He looked helpless as only the strong and powerful can look. Selina's heart melted in pity. He would look down at the great calloused hands; up at her. One of the charms of Pervus DeJong lay in the things that his eyes said and his tongue did not. Women always imagined he was about to say what he looked, but he never did. It made otherwise dull conversation with him most exciting.

His was in no way a shrewd mind. His respect for Selina was almost reverence. But he had this advantage: he had married a woman, had lived with her for two years. She had borne him a child. Selina was a girl in experience. She was a woman capable of a great deal of passion, but she did not know that. Passion was a thing no woman possessed, much less talked about. It simply did not exist, except in men, and then was something to be ashamed of, like a violent temper, or a weak stomach.

By the first of March he could speak a slow, careful, and fairly grammatical English. He could master simple sums. By the middle of March the lessons would cease. There was too much work to do about the farm—night work as well as day. She found herself trying not to think about the time when the lessons should cease. She refused to look ahead to April.

One night, late in February, Selina was conscious that she was trying to control something. She was trying to keep her eyes away from something. She realized that she was trying not to look at his hands. She wanted, crazily, to touch them. She wanted to feel them about her throat. She wanted to put her lips on his hands—brush the backs of them, slowly, moistly, with her mouth, lingeringly. She was terribly frightened. She thought to herself: "I am going crazy. I am losing my mind. There is something the matter with me. I wonder how I look. I must look queer."

She said something to make him look up at her. His glance was mild, undismayed. So this hideous thing did not show in her face. She kept her eyes resolutely on the book. At half-past eight she closed her book suddenly. "I'm tired. I think it's the spring coming on." She smiled a little wavering smile. He rose and stretched himself, his great arms high above his head. Selina shivered.

"Two more weeks," he said, "is the last lesson. Well, do you think I have done pretty good—well?"

"Very well," Selina replied, evenly. She felt very tired.

The first week in March he was ill, and did not come. A rheumatic affliction to which he was subject. His father, old Johannes DeJong, had had it before him. Working in the wet fields did it, they said. It was the curse of the truck farmer. Selina's evenings were free to devote to Roelf, who glowed again. She sewed, too; read; helped Mrs. Pool with the housework in a gust of sympathy and found strange relief therein; made over an old dress; studied; wrote all her letters (few enough), even one to the dried-apple aunts in Vermont. She no longer wrote to Julie Hempel. She had heard that Julie was to be married to a Kansas man named Arnold. Julie herself had not written. The first week in March passed. He did not come. Nor did he come the following Tuesday or Thursday. After a terrific battle with herself Selina, after school on Thursday, walked past his house, busily, as though bent on an errand. Despised herself for doing it, could not help herself, found a horrible and tortuous satisfaction in not looking at the house as she passed it.

She was bewildered, frightened. All that week she had a curious feeling— or succession of feelings. There was the sensation of suffocation followed by that of emptiness—of being hollow—boneless—bloodless. Then, at times, there was a feeling of physical pain; at others a sense of being disembowelled. She was restless, listless, by turns. Period of furious activity followed by days of inertia. It was the spring, Maartje said. Selina hoped she wasn't going to be ill. She had never felt like that before. She wanted to cry. She was irritable to the point of waspishness with the children in the schoolroom.

On Saturday—the fourteenth of March—he walked in at seven. Klaas, Maartje, and Roelf had driven off to a gathering at Low Prairie, leaving Selina with the pigtails and old Jakob. She had promised to make taffy for them, and was in the midst of it when his knock sounded at the kitchen door. All the blood in her body rushed to her head; pounded there hotly. He entered. There slipped down over her a complete armour of calmness, of self-possession; of glib how do you do Mr. DeJong and how are you feeling and won't you sit down and there's no fire in the parlour we'll have to sit here.

He took part in the taffy pulling. Selina wondered if Geertje and Jozina would ever have done squealing. It was half-past eight before she bundled them off to bed with a plate of clipped taffy lozenges between them. She heard them scuffling and scrimmaging about in the rare freedom of their parents' absence.

"Now, children!" she called. "You know what you promised your mother and father."

She heard Geertje's tones mimicking her mincingly, "You know what you promised your mother and father." Then a cascade of smothered giggles.

Pervus had been to town, evidently, for he now took from his coat pocket a bag containing half a dozen bananas—that delicacy of delicacies to the farm palate. She half peeled two and brought them in to the pigtails. They ate them thickly rapturous, and dropped off to sleep immediately, surfeited.

Pervus DeJong and Selina sat at the kitchen table, their books spread out before them on the oilcloth. The sweet heavy scent of the fruit filled the room. Selina brought the parlour lamp into the kitchen, the better to see. It was a nickel-bellied lamp with a yellow glass shade that cast a mellow golden glow.

"You didn't go to the meeting," primly. "Mr. and Mrs. Pool went."

"No. No, I didn't go."

"Why not?"

She saw him swallow. "I got through too late. I went to town, and I got through too late. We're fixing to sow tomato seeds in the hotbeds to-morrow."

Selina opened McBride's Grammar. "Ahem!" a school-teacherly cough.

"Now, then, we'll parse this sentence: Blucher arrived on the field of Waterloo just as Wellington was receiving the last onslaught of Napoleon. 'Just' may be treated as a modifier of the dependent clause. That is: 'Just' means: at the time *at which*. Well. *Just* here modified *at the time*. And Wellington is the . . ."

This for half an hour. Selina kept her eyes resolutely on the book. His voice went on with the dry business of parsing and its deep resonance struck a response from her as a harp responds when a hand is swept over its strings. Upstairs she could hear old Jakob clumping about in his preparations for bed. Then there was only stillness overhead. Selina kept her eyes resolutely on the book. Yet she saw, as though her eyes rested on them, his large, strong hands. On the backs of them was a fine golden down that deepened at his wrists. Heavier and darker at the wrists. She found herself praying a little for strength—for strength against this horror and wickedness. This sin, this abomination that held her. A terrible, stark, and pitiful prayer, couched in the idiom of the Bible.

Oh, God, keep my eyes and my thoughts away from him. Away from his hands. Let me keep my eyes and my thoughts away from the golden hairs on his wrists. Let me not think of his wrists. . . . "The owner of the southwest ¼ sells a strip 20 rods wide along the south side of his farm. How much does he receive at $150 per acre?"

He triumphed in this transaction, began the struggle with the square root of 576. Square roots agonized him. She washed the slate clean with her little sponge. He was leaning close in his effort to comprehend the fiendish little figures that marched so tractably under Selina's masterly pencil.

She took it up, glibly. "The remainder must contain twice the product of the tens by the units plus the square of the units." He blinked. Utterly bewildered. *"And"*, went on Selina, blithely, "twice the tens, times the units, plus the square of the units, is the same as the sum of twice the tens, and the units, times the units. *Therefore"*—with a flourish—"add 4 units to the 40 and multiply the result by 4. *Therefore"*—in final triumph—"the square root of 576 is 24."

She was breathing rather fast. The fire in the kitchen stove snapped and cracked. "Now, then, suppose you do that for me. We'll wipe it out. There! What must the remainder contain?"

He took it up, slowly, haltingly. The house was terribly still except for the man's voice. "The remainder . . . twice . . . product . . . tens . . . units . . ." A something in his voice—a note—a timbre. She felt herself swaying queerly, as though the whole house were gently rocking. Little delicious agonizing shivers chased each other, hot and cold, up her arms, down her legs, over her spine. . . . "plus the square of the units is the same as the sum twice the tens . . . twice . . . the tens . . . the tens . . ." His voice stopped.

Selina's eyes leaped from the book to his hands, uncontrollably. Something about them startled her. They were clenched into fists. Her eyes now leaped from those clenched fists to the face of the man beside her. Her head came up, and back. Her wide startled eyes met his. His were a blaze of blinding blue in his tanned face. Some corner of her mind that was still working clearly noted this. Then his hands unclenched. The blue blaze scorched her, enveloped her. Her cheek knew the harsh cool feel of a man's cheek. She sensed the potent, terrifying, pungent odour of close contact—a mixture of tobacco smoke, his hair, freshly laundered linen, an indefinable body smell. It was a mingling that disgusted and attracted her. She was at once repelled and drawn. Then she felt his lips on hers and her own, incredibly, responding eagerly, wholly to that pressure.

7

THEY WERE MARRIED the following May, just two months later. The High Prairie school year practically ended with the appearance of the first tender shoots of green that meant onions, radishes, and spinach above the rich sandy loam. Selina's classes broke, dwindled, shrank to almost nothing. The school became a kindergarten of five-year-old babies who wriggled and shifted and scratched in the warm spring air that came from the teeming prairie through the open windows. The schoolhouse stove stood rusty-red and cold. The drum in Selina's bedroom was a black genie deprived of his power now to taunt her.

Selina was at once bewildered and calm; rebellious and content. Overlaying these emotions was something like grim amusement. Beneath them, something like fright. High Prairie, in May, was green and gold and rose and blue. The spring flowers painted the fields and the roadside with splashes of yellow, of pink, of mauve, and purple. Violets, buttercups, mandrakes, marsh-marigolds, hepatica. The air was soft and cool from the lake. Selina had never known spring in the country before. It made her ache with an actual physical ache. She moved with a strange air of fatality. It was as if she were being drawn inexorably, against her will, her judgment, her plans, into something sweet and terrible. When with Pervus she was elated, gay, voluble. He talked little; looked at her dumbly, worshippingly. When he brought her a withered bunch of trilliums, the tears came to her eyes. He had walked to Updike's woods to get them because he had heard her say she loved them, and there were none nearer. They were limp and listless from the heat, and from being held in his hand. He looked up at her from where he stood on the kitchen steps, she in the doorway. She took them, laid her hand on his head. It was as when some great gentle dog brings in a limp and bedraggled prize dug from the yard and, laying it at one's feet, looks up at one with soft asking eyes.

There were days when the feeling of unreality possessed her. She, a truck farmer's wife, living in High Prairie the rest of her days! Why, no! No! Was this the great adventure that her father had always spoken of? She, who was going to be a happy wayfarer down the path of life—any one of a dozen things. This High Prairie winter was to have been only an episode. Not her life! She looked at Maartje. Oh, but she'd never be like that. That was stupid, unnecessary. Pink and blue dresses in the house, for her. Frills on the window curtains. Flowers in bowls.

Some of the pangs and terrors with which most prospective brides are assailed she confided to Mrs. Pool while that active lady was slamming about the kitchen.

"Did you ever feel scared and—and sort of—scared when you thought about marriage, Mrs. Pool?"

Maartje Pool's hands were in a great batch of bread dough which she pummelled and slapped and kneaded vigorously. She shook out a handful of flour on the baking board while she held the dough mass in the other hand, then plumped it down and again began to knead, both hands doubled into fists.

She laughed a short little laugh. "I ran away."

"You did! You mean you really ran—but why? Didn't you lo—like Klaas?"

Maartje Pool kneaded briskly, the colour high in her cheeks, what with the vigorous pummelling and rolling, and something else that made her look strangely young for the moment—girlish, almost. "Sure I liked him. I liked him."

"But you ran away?"

"Not far. I came back. Nobody ever knew I ran, even. But I ran. I knew."

"Why did you come back?"

Maartje elucidated her philosophy without being in the least aware that it could be called by any such high-sounding name. "You can't run away far enough. Except you stop living you can't run away from life."

The girlish look had fled. She was world-old. Her strong arms ceased their pounding and thumping for a moment. On the steps just outside Klaas and Jakob were scanning the weekly reports preparatory to going into the city late that afternoon.

Selina had the difficult task of winning Roelf to her all over again. He was like a trusting little animal, who, wounded by the hand he has trusted, is shy of it. She used blandishments on this boy of thirteen such as she had never vouchsafed the man she was going to marry. He had asked her, bluntly, one day: "Why are you going to marry with him?" He never spoke the name.

She thought deeply. What to say? The answer ready on her tongue would have little meaning for this boy. There came to her a line from Lancelot and Elaine. She answered, "To serve him, and to follow him through the world." She thought that rather fine-sounding until Roelf promptly rejected it. "That's no reason. An answer out of a book. Anyway, to follow him through the world is dumb. He stays right here in High Prairie all his life."

"How do you know!" Selina retorted, almost angrily. Startled, too.

"I know. He stays."

Still, he could not withstand her long. Together they dug and planted flower beds in Pervus's dingy front yard. It was too late for tulips now. Pervus had brought her some seeds from town. They ranged all the way from poppies to asters; from purple iris to morning glories. The last named were to form the back-porch vine, of course, because they grew quickly. Selina, city-bred, was ignorant of varieties, but insisted she wanted an old-fashioned garden—marigolds, pinks, mignonette, phlox. She and Roelf dug, spaded, planted. The DeJong place was markedly ugly even in that community of squat houses. It lacked the air of sparkling cleanliness that saved the other places from sordidness. The house, even then, was thirty years old—a gray, weather-beaten frame box with a mansard roof and a flat face staring out at the dense willows by the roadside. It needed paint; the fences sagged; the window curtains were awry. The parlour was damp, funereal. The old woman who tended the house for Pervus slopped about all day with a pail and a wet gray rag. There was always a crazy campanile of dirty dishes stacked on the table, and the last meal seemed never to catch up with the next. About the whole house there was a starkness, a bareness that proclaimed no woman who loved it dwelt therein.

Selina told herself (and Pervus) that she would change all that. She saw herself going about with a brush and a can of white paint, leaving beauty in her wake, where ugliness had been.

Her trousseau was of the scantiest. Pervus's household was already equipped with such linens as they would need. The question of a wedding gown troubled her until Maartje suggested that she be married in the old Dutch wedding dress that lay in the bride's chest in Selina's bedroom.

"A real Dutch bride," Maartje said. "Your man will think that is fine." Pervus was delighted. Selina basked in his love like a kitten in the sun. She was, after all, a very lonely little bride with only two photographs on the shelf in her bedroom to give her courage and counsel. The old Dutch wedding gown was many inches too large for her. The skirt-band overlapped her slim waist; her slender little bosom did not fill out the generous width of the bodice; but the effect of the whole was amazingly quaint as well as pathetic. The wings of the stiffly embroidered coif framed the white face from which the eyes looked out, large and dark. She had even tried to wear the hand-carved shoes, but had to give that up. In them her feet were as lost as minnows in a rowboat. She had much difficulty with the queer old buttons and fastenings. It was as though the dead and gone Sophia Kroon were trying, with futile ghostly fingers, to prevent this young thing from meeting the fate that was to be hers.

They were married at the Pools'. Klaas and Maartje had insisted on furnishing the wedding supper—ham, chickens, sausages, cakes, pickles, beer. The Reverend Dekker married them and all through the ceremony Selina chided herself because she could not keep her mind on his words in the fascination of watching his short stubby beard as it waggled with every motion of his jaw. Pervus looked stiff, solemn, and uncomfortable in his wedding blacks—not at all the handsome giant of the everyday corduroys and blue shirt. In the midst of the ceremony Selina had her moment of panic when she actually saw herself running shrieking from this company, this man, this house, down the road, on, on toward—toward what? The feeling was so strong that she was surprised to find herself still standing there in the Dutch wedding gown answering "I do" in the proper place.

The wedding gifts were few. The Pools had given them a "hanging lamp," coveted of the farmer's wife; a hideous atrocity in yellow, with pink roses on its shade and prisms dangling and tinkling all around the edge. It was intended to hang suspended from the parlour ceiling, and worked up and down on a sort of pulley chain. From the Widow Paarlenberg came a water set in red frosted glass shading to pink—a fat pitcher and six tumblers. Roelf's gift, the result of many weeks' labour in the work-shed, was a bride's chest copied from the fine old piece that had saved Selina's room from sheer ugliness. He had stained the wood, polished it. Had carved the front of it with her initials—very like those that stood out so boldly on the old chest upstairs—S. P. D. And the year—1890. The whole was a fine piece of craftsmanship for a boy of thirteen—would not have discredited a man of any age. It was the one beautiful gift among Selina's clumsy crude wedding things. She had thanked him with tears in her eyes. "Roelf, you'll come to see me often, won't you? Often!" Then, as he had hesitated, "I'll need you so. You're all I've got." A strange thing for a bride to say.

"I'll come," the boy had said, trying to make his voice casual, his tone careless. "Sure, I'll come oncet in a while."

"Once, Roelf. *Once* in a while."

He repeated it after her, dutifully.

After the wedding they went straight to DeJong's house. In May the vegetable farmer cannot neglect his garden even for a day. The house had been made ready for them. The sway of the old housekeeper was over. Her kitchen bedroom was empty.

Throughout the supper Selina had had thoughts which were so foolish and detached as almost to alarm her.

"Now I am married. I am Mrs. Pervus DeJong. That's a pretty name. It would look quite distinguished on a calling card, very spidery and fine:

MRS. PERVUS DEJONG

At Home Fridays.

She recalled this later, grimly, when she was Mrs. Pervus DeJong, at home not only Fridays, but Saturdays, Sundays, Mondays, Tuesdays, Wednesdays, and Thursdays.

They drove down the road to DeJong's place. Selina thought, "Now I am driving home with my husband. I feel his shoulder against mine. I wish he would talk. I wish he would say something. Still, I'm not frightened."

Pervus's market wagon was standing in the yard, shafts down. He should have gone to market to-day; would certainly have to go to-morrow, starting early in the afternoon so as to get a good stand in the Haymarket. By the light of his lantern the wagon seemed to Selina to be a symbol. She had often seen it before, but now that it was to be a part of her life—this the DeJong market wagon and she Mrs. DeJong—she saw clearly what a crazy, disreputable, and poverty-proclaiming old vehicle it was, in contrast with the neat strong wagon in Klaas Pool's yard, smart with green paint and red lettering that announced, "Klaas Pool, Garden produce." With the two sleek farm horses the turnout looked as prosperous and comfortable as Klaas himself.

Pervus swung her down from the seat of the buggy, his hand about her waist, and held her so for a moment, close. Selina said, "You must have that wagon painted, Pervus. And the seat-springs fixed and the sideboard mended."

He stared. "Wagon!"

"Yes. It looks a sight."

The house was tidy enough, but none too clean. Old Mrs. Voorhees had not been minded to keep house too scrupulously for a man who would be unlikely to know whether or not it was clean. Pervus lighted the lamps. There was a fire in the kitchen stove. It made the house seem stuffy on this mild May night. Selina thought that her own little bedroom at the Pools', no longer hers, must be deliciously cool and still with the breeze fanning fresh from the west. Pervus was putting the horse into the barn. The bedroom was off the sitting room. The window was shut. This last year had taught Selina to prepare the night before for next morning's rising, so as to lose the least possible time. She did this now, unconsciously. She took off her white muslin underwear with its frills and embroidery—the three stiff petticoats, and the stiffly starched corset-cover, and the high-bosomed corset and put them into the bureau drawer that she herself had cleaned and papered neatly the week before. She brushed her hair, laid out to-morrow's garments, put on her high-necked, long-sleeved nightgown and got into this strange bed. She heard Pervus DeJong shut the kitchen door; the latch clicked, the lock turned. Heavy quick footsteps across the bare kitchen floor. This man was coming into her room . . . "You can't run far enough," Maartje Pool had said. "Except you stop living you can't run away from life."

Next morning it was dark when he awakened her at four. She started up with a little cry and sat up, straining her ears, her eyes. "Is that you, Father?" She was little Selina Peake again, and Simeon Peake had come in, gay, debonair, from a night's gaming.

Pervus DeJong was already padding about the room in stocking feet. "What—what time is it? What's the matter, Father? Why are you up? Haven't you gone to bed . . ." Then she remembered.

Pervus DeJong laughed and came toward her. "Get up, little lazy bones. It's after four. All yesterday's work I've got to do, and all to-day's. Breakfast, little Lina, breakfast. You are a farmer's wife now."

8

BY OCTOBER HIGH Prairie housewives told each other that Mrs. Pervus DeJong was "expecting." Dirk DeJong was born in the bedroom off the sitting room on the fifteenth day of March, of a bewildered, somewhat resentful, but deeply interested mother; and a proud, foolish, and vainglorious father whose air of achievement, considering the really slight part he had played in the long, tedious, and racking business, was disproportionate. The name Dirk had sounded to Selina like something tall, straight, and slim. Pervus had chosen it. It had been his grandfather's name.

Sometimes, during those months, Selina would look back on her first winter in High Prairie—that winter of the icy bedroom, the chill black drum, the schoolhouse fire, the chilblains, the Pool pork—and it seemed a lovely dream; a time of ease, of freedom, of careless happiness. That icy room had been her room; that mile of road traversed on bitter winter mornings a mere jaunt; the schoolhouse stove a toy, fractious but fascinating.

Pervus DeJong loved his pretty young wife, and she him. But young love thrives on colour, warmth, beauty. It becomes prosaic and inarticulate when forced to begin its day at four in the morning by reaching blindly, dazedly, for limp and obscure garments dangling from bedpost or chair, and to end that day at nine, numb and sodden with weariness, after seventeen hours of physical labour.

It was a wet summer. Pervus's choice tomato plants, so carefully set out in the hope of a dry season, became draggled gray spectres in a waste of mire. Of fruit the field bore one tomato the size of a marble.

For the rest, the crops were moderately successful on the DeJong place. But the work necessary to make this so was heartbreaking. Pervus and his hired helper, Jan Steen, used the hand sower and hand cultivator. It seemed to Selina that they were slaves to these buds, shoots, and roots that clamoured with a hundred thousand voices, "Let me out! Let me out!" She had known, during her winter at the Pools', that Klaas, Roelf, and old Jakob worked early and late, but her months there had encompassed what is really the truck farmer's leisure period. She had arrived in November. She had married in May. From May until October it was necessary to tend the fields with a concentration amounting to fury. Selina had never dreamed that human beings toiled like that for sustenance. Toil was a thing she had never encountered until coming to High Prairie. Now she saw her husband wrenching a living out of the earth by sheer muscle, sweat, and pain. During June, July, August, and September the good black prairie soil for miles around was teeming, a hotbed of plenty. There was born in Selina at this time a feeling for the land that she was never to lose. Perhaps the child within her had something to do with this. She was aware of a feeling of kinship with the earth; an illusion of splendour, of fulfilment. Sometimes, in a moment's respite from her work about the house, she would stand in the kitchen doorway, her flushed face turned toward the fields. Wave on wave of green, wave on wave, until the waves melted into each other and became a verdant sea.

As cabbages had been cabbages, and no more, to Klaas Pool, so, to Pervus, these carrots, beets, onions, turnips, and radishes were just so much produce, to be planted, tended, gathered, marketed. But to Selina, during that summer, they became a vital part in the vast mechanism of a living world. Pervus, earth, sun, rain, all elemental forces that laboured to produce the food for millions of humans. The sordid, grubby little acreage became a kingdom; the phlegmatic Dutch-American truck farmers of the region were high priests consecrated to the service of the divinity, Earth. She thought of Chicago's children. If they had red cheeks, clear eyes, nimble brains it was because Pervus brought them the food that made them so. It was before the day when glib talk of irons, vitamines, arsenic entered into all discussion pertaining to food. Yet Selina sensed something of the meaning behind these toiling, patient figures, all unconscious of meaning, bent double in the fields for miles throughout High Prairie. Something of this she tried to convey to Pervus. He only stared, his blue eyes wide and unresponsive.

"Farm work grand! Farm work is slave work. Yesterday, from the load of carrots in town I didn't make enough to bring you the goods for the child so when it comes you should have clothes for it. It's better I feed them to the livestock."

Pervus drove into the Chicago market every other day. During July and August he sometimes did not have his clothes off for a week. Together he and Jan Steen would load the wagon with the day's garnering. At four he would start on the tedious trip into town. The historic old Haymarket on West Randolph Street had become the stand for market gardeners for miles around Chicago. Here they stationed their wagons in preparation for the next day's selling. The wagons stood, close packed, in triple rows, down both sides of the curb and in the middle of the street. The early comer got the advantageous stand. There was no regular allotment of space. Pervus tried to reach the Haymarket by nine at night. Often bad roads made a detour necessary and he was late. That usually meant bad business next day. The men, for the most part, slept on their wagons, curled up on the wagon seat or stretched out on the sacks. Their horses were stabled and fed in near-by sheds, with more actual comfort than the men themselves. One could get a room for twenty-five cents in one of the ramshackle rooming houses that faced the street. But the rooms were small, stuffy, none too clean; the beds little more comfortable than the wagons. Besides, twenty-five cents! You got twenty-five cents for half a barrel of tomatoes. You got twenty-five cents for a sack of potatoes. Onions brought seventy-five cents a sack. Cabbages went a hundred heads for two dollars, and they were five-pound heads. If you drove home with ten dollars in your pocket it represented a profit of exactly zero. The sum must go above that. No; one did not pay out twenty-five cents for the mere privilege of sleeping in a bed.

One June day, a month or more after their marriage, Selina drove into Chicago with Pervus, an incongruous little figure in her bride's finery perched on the seat of the vegetable wagon piled high with early garden stuff. They had started before four that afternoon, and reached the city at nine, though the roads were still heavy from the late May rains. It was, in a way, their wedding trip, for Selina had not been away from the farm since her marriage. The sun was bright and hot. Selina held an umbrella to shield herself from the heat and looked about her with enjoyment and interest. She chattered, turned her head this way and that, exclaimed, questioned. Sometimes she wished that Pervus would respond more quickly to her mood. A gay, volatile creature, she frisked about him like a friendly bright-eyed terrier about a stolid, ponderous St. Bernard.

As they jogged along now she revealed magnificent plans that had been forming in her imagination during the past four weeks. It had not taken her four weeks—or days—to discover that this great broad-shouldered man she had married was a kindly creature, tender and good, but lacking any vestige of initiative, of spirit. She marvelled, sometimes, at the memory of his boldness in bidding for her lunch box that evening of the raffle. It seemed incredible now, though he frequently referred to it, wagging his head doggishly and grinning the broadly complacent grin of the conquering male. But he was, after all, a dull fellow, and there was in Selina a dash of fire, of wholesome wickedness, of adventure, that he never quite understood. For her flashes of flame he had a mingled feeling of uneasiness and pride.

In the manner of all young brides, Selina started bravely out to make her husband over. He was handsome, strong, gentle; slow, conservative, morose. She would make him keen, daring, successful, buoyant. Now, bumping down the Halsted road, she sketched some of her plans in large dashing strokes.

"Pervus, we must paint the house in October, before the frost sets in, and after the summer work is over. White would be nice, with green trimmings. Though perhaps white isn't practical. Or maybe green with darker green trimmings. A lovely background for the hollyhocks." (Those that she and Roelf had planted showed no signs of coming up.) "Then that west sixteen. We'll drain it."

"Yeh, drain," Pervus muttered. "It's clay land. Drain and you have got yet clay. Hard clay soil."

Selina had the answer to that. "I know it. You've got to use tile drainage. And—wait a minute—humus. I know what humus is. It's decayed vegetables. There's always a pile by the side of the barn; and you've been using it on the quick land. All the west sixteen isn't clay. Part of it's muckland. All it needs is draining and manure. With potash, too, and phosphoric acid."

Pervus laughed a great hearty laugh that Selina found surprisingly infuriating. He put one great brown hand patronizingly on her flushed cheek; pinched it gently.

"Don't!" said Selina, and jerked her head away. It was the first time she had ever resented a caress from him.

Pervus laughed again. "Well, well, well! School teacher is a farmer now, huh? I bet even Widow Paarlenberg don't know as much as my little farmer about"—he exploded again—"about this, now, potash and—what kind of acid? Tell me, little Lina, from where did you learn all this about truck farming?"

"Out of a book," Selina said, almost snappishly. "I sent to Chicago for it."

"A book! A book!" He slapped his knee. "A vegetable farmer out of a book."

"Why not! The man who wrote it knows more about vegetable farming than anybody in all High Prairie. He knows about new ways. You're running the farm just the way your father ran it."

"What was good enough for my father is good enough for me."

"It isn't!" cried Selina. "It isn't! The book says clay loam is all right for cabbages, peas, and beans. It tells you how. It tells you how!" She was like a frantic little fly darting and pricking him on to accelerate the stolid sluggishness of his slow plodding gait.

Having begun, she plunged on. "We ought to have two horses to haul the wagon to market. It would save you hours of time that you could spend on the place. Two horses, and a new wagon, green and red, like Klaas Pool's."

Pervus stared straight ahead down the road between his horse's ears much as Klaas Pool had done so maddeningly on Selina's first ride on the Halsted road. "Fine talk. Fine talk."

"It isn't talk. It's plans. You've got to plan."

"Fine talk. Fine talk.'

"Oh!" Selina beat her knee with an impotent fist.

It was the nearest they had ever come to quarrelling. It would seem that Pervus had the best of the argument, for when two years had passed the west sixteen was still a boggy clay mass, and unprolific; and the old house stared out shabby and paintless, at the dense willows by the roadside.

They slept that night in one of the twenty-five-cent rooming houses. Rather, Pervus slept. The woman lay awake, listening to the city noises that had become strange in her ears; staring out into the purple-black oblong that was the open window, until that oblong became gray, She wept a little, perhaps. But in the morning Pervus might have noted (if he had been a man given to noting) that the fine jaw-line was set as determinedly as ever with an angle that spelled inevitably paint, drainage, humus, potash, phosphoric acid, and a horse team.

She rose before four with Pervus, glad to be out of the stuffy little room with its spotted and scaly green wall paper, its rickety bed and chair. They had a cup of coffee and a slice of bread in the eating house on the first floor. Selina waited while he tended the horse. The night-watchman had been paid another twenty-five cents for watching the wagonload through the night as it stood in a row with the hundreds of others in the Haymarket. It was scarcely dawn when the trading began. Selina, watching it from the wagon seat, thought that this was a ridiculously haphazard and perilous method of distributing the food for whose fruition Pervus had toiled with aching back and tired arms. But she said nothing.

She kept, perforce, to the house that first year, and the second. Pervus declared that his woman should never work in the fields as did many of the High Prairie wives and daughters. Of ready cash there was almost none. Pervus was hard put to it to pay Jan Steen his monthly wage during May, June, July, and August, when he was employed on the DeJong place, though Steen got but a pittance, being known as a poor hand, and "dumb." Selina learned much that first year, and the second, but she said little. She kept the house in order—rough work, and endless—and she managed, miraculously, to keep herself looking fresh and neat. She understood now Maartje Pool's drab garments, harassed face, heavily swift feet, never at rest. The idea of flowers in bowls was abandoned by July. Had it not been for Roelf's faithful tending, the flower beds themselves, planted with such hopes, would have perished for lack of care.

Roelf came often to the house. He found there a tranquillity and peace never known in the Pool place, with its hubbub and clatter. In order to make her house attractive Selina had actually rifled her precious little bank hoard— the four hundred and ninety-seven dollars left her by her father. She still had one of the clear white diamonds. She kept it sewed in the hem of an old flannel petticoat. Once she had shown it to Pervus.

"If I sell this maybe we could get enough money to drain and tile."

Pervus took the stone, weighed it in his great palm, blinked as he always did when discussing a subject of which he was ignorant. "How much could you get for it? Fifty dollars, maybe. Five hundred is what I would need."

"I've got that. I've got it in the bank!"

"Well, maybe next spring. Right now I got my hands full, and more."

To Selina that seemed a short-sighted argument. But she was too newly married to stand her ground; too much in love; too ignorant still of farm conditions.

The can of white paint and the brush actually did materialize. For weeks·

it was dangerous to sit, lean, or tread upon any paintable thing in the DeJong farmhouse without eliciting a cry of warning from Selina. She would actually have tried her hand at the outside of the house with a quart can and three-inch brush if Pervus hadn't intervened. She hemmed dimity curtains, made slip-covers for the hideous parlour sofa and the ugliest of the chairs. Subscribed for a magazine called *House and Garden*. Together she and Roelf used to pore over this fascinating periodical. Terraces, lily-pools, leaded casements, cretonne, fireplaces, yew trees, pergolas, fountains—they absorbed them all, exclaimed, admired, actually criticized. Selina was torn between an English cottage with timbered porch, bay window, stone flagging, and an Italian villa with a broad terrace on which she would stand in trailing white with a Russian wolf-hound. If High Prairie had ever overheard one of these conversations between the farm woman who would always be a girl and the farm boy who had never been quite a child, it would have raised palms high in an "Og heden!" of horror. But High Prairie never heard, and wouldn't have understood if it had. She did another strange thing: She placed the fine hand-carved oak chest Roelf had given her in a position so that her child should see it as soon as he opened his eyes in the morning. It was the most beautiful thing she possessed. She had, too, an incomplete set of old Dutch lustre ware. It had belonged to Pervus's mother, and to her mother before her. On Sunday nights Selina used this set for supper, though Pervus protested. And she always insisted that Dirk drink his milk out of one of the lovely jewel-like cups. Pervus thought this a piece of madness.

Selina was up daily at four. Dressing was a swift and mechanical covering of the body. Breakfast must be ready for Pervus and Jan when they came in from the barn. The house to clean, the chickens to tend, sewing, washing, ironing, cooking. She contrived ways of minimizing her steps, of lightening her labour. And she saw clearly how the little farm was mismanaged through lack of foresight, imagination, and—she faced it squarely—through stupidity. She was fond of this great, kindly, blundering, stubborn boy who was her husband. But she saw him with amazing clearness through the mists of her love. There was something prophetic about the way she began to absorb knowledge of the farm work, of vegetable culture, of marketing. Listening, seeing, she learned about soil, planting, weather, selling. The daily talk of the house and fields was of nothing else. About this little twenty-five-acre garden patch there was nothing of the majesty of the Iowa, Illinois, and Kansas grain farms, with their endless billows of wheat and corn, rye, alfalfa, and barley rolling away to the horizon. Everything was done in diminutive here. An acre of this. Two acres of that. A score of chickens. One cow. One horse. Two pigs. Here was all the drudgery of farm life with none of its bounteousness, fine sweep, or splendour. Selina sensed that every inch of soil should have been made to yield to the utmost. Yet there lay the west sixteen, useless during most of the year; reliable never. And there was no money to drain it or enrich it; no ready cash for the purchase of profitable neighbouring acreage. She did not know the term intensive farming, but this was what she meant. Artificial protection against the treacherous climate of the Great Lakes region was pitifully lacking in Pervus's plans. Now it would be hot with the humid, withering, sticky heat of the district. The ground was teeming, smoking, and the green things seemed actually to be pushing their way out of the earth so that one could almost see them growing, as in some absurd optical illusion. Then, without warning, would come the icy Lake Michigan wind, nipping the tender shoots with fiendish fingers. There should have been hotbeds and coldframes, forcing-hills, hand-boxes. There were almost none.

These things Selina saw, but not quite clearly. She went about her housework, now dreamily, now happily. Her physical condition swayed her mood.

Sometimes, in the early autumn, when the days became cooler, she would go to where Pervus and Jan were working in the fields in the late afternoon gathering the produce for that night's trip to market. She would stand there, a bit of sewing in her hand, perhaps, the wind ruffling her hair, whipping her skirt, her face no longer pale, tilted a little toward the good sun like a lovely tawny flower. Sometimes she sat perched on a pile of empty sacks, or on an up-ended crate, her sewing in her hand. She was happiest at such times—most content—except for the pang she felt at sight of the great dark splotch on the blue of Pervus's work-shirt where the sweat stained it.

She had come out so one autumn afternoon. She was feeling particularly gay, buoyant. In one of his rare hours of leisure Roelf Pool had come to help her with her peony roots which Pervus had brought her from Chicago for fall planting. Roelf had dug the trench, deep and wide, mulched it with cow-manure, banked it. They were to form a double row up the path to the front of the house, and in her mind's eye Selina already saw them blooming when spring should come, shaggy balls of luscious pink. Now Roelf was lending a hand to Pervus and Jan as they bent over the late beets and radishes. It was a day all gold and blue and scarlet; warm for the season with a ripe mellow warmth like yellow chartreuse. There were stretches of seal-black loam where the vegetables had been uprooted. Bunches of them, string-tied, lay ready for gathering into baskets. Selina's eye was gladdened by the clear coral of radishes flung against the rich black loam.

"A jewel, Pervus!" she cried. "A jewel in an Ethiop's ear!"

"What?" said Pervus, looking up, amiable but uncomprehending. But the boy smiled. Selina had left him that book for his own when she went away. Suddenly Selina stooped and picked up one of the scarlet and green clusters tied with its bit of string. Laughing, she whipped out a hairpin and fastened the bunch in her hair just behind her ear. An absurd thing to do, and childish. It should have looked as absurd as it was, but it didn't. Instead it was like a great crimson flower there. Her cheeks were flushed with the hot sun. Her fine dark hair was wind-blown and a little loosened, her dress open at the throat. Her figure was fuller, her breast had a richer curve, for the child was four months on the way. She was laughing. At a little exclamation from Roelf, Pervus looked up, as did Jan. Selina took a slow rhythmic step, and another, her arms upraised, a provocative lovely bacchic little figure there in the fields under the hot blue sky. Jan Steen wiped the sweat from his brown face, a glow in his eyes.

"You are like the calendar!" cried Roelf, "on the wall in the parlour." A cheap but vivid and not unlovely picture of a girl with cherries in her hair. It hung in the Pool farmhouse.

Pervus DeJong showed one of his rare storms of passion. Selina had not seen that blaze of blue in his eyes since the night months ago, in the Pools' kitchen. But that blaze had been a hot and burning blue, like the sky of to-day. This was a bitter blue, a chill and freezing thing, like the steel-blue of ice in the sun.

"Take them things out of your hair now! Take shame to yourself!" He strode over to her and snatched the things from her hair and threw them down and ground them into the soft earth with his heavy heel. A long coil of her fine dark hair came rippling over her shoulder as he did so. She stood looking at him, her eyes wide, dark, enormous in her face now suddenly white.

His wrath was born of the narrow insular mind that fears gossip. He knew that the hired man would tell through the length and width of High Prairie how Pervus DeJong's wife pinned red radishes in her hair and danced in the fields like a loose woman.

Selina had turned, fled to the house. It was their first serious quarrel. For days she was hurt, ashamed, moody. They made it up, of course. Pervus was contrite, abject almost. But something that belonged to her girlhood had left her that day.

During that winter she was often hideously lonely. She never got over her hunger for companionship. Here she was, a gregarious and fun-loving creature, buried in a snow-bound Illinois prairie farmhouse with a husband who looked upon conversation as a convenience, not a pastime. She learned much that winter about the utter sordidness of farm life. She rarely saw the Pools; she rarely saw any one outside her own little household. The front room—the parlour—was usually bitterly cold but sometimes she used to slip in there, a shawl over her shoulders, and sit at the frosty window to watch for a wagon to go by, or a chance pedestrian up the road. She did not pity herself, nor regret her step. She felt, physically, pretty well for a child-bearing woman; and Pervus was tender, kindly, sympathetic, if not always understanding. She struggled gallantly to keep up the small decencies of existence. She loved the glow in Pervus's eyes when she appeared with a bright ribbon, a fresh collar, though he said nothing and perhaps she only fancied that he noticed. Once or twice she had walked the mile and a half of slippery road to the Pools', and had sat in Maartje's warm bright bustling kitchen for comfort. It seemed to her incredible that a little more than a year ago she had first stepped into this kitchen in her modish brown lady's-cloth dress, muffled in wraps, cold but elated, interested, ready for adventure, surprise, discomfort—anything. And now here she was in that same kitchen, amazingly, unbelievably Mrs. Pervus DeJong, truck farmer's wife, with a child soon to be born. And where was adventure now? And where was life? And where the love of chance bred in her by her father?

The two years following Dirk's birth were always somewhat vague in Selina's mind, like a dream in which horror and happiness are inextricably blended. The boy was a plump hardy infant who employed himself cheerfully in whatever spot Selina happened to deposit him. He had his father's blond exterior, his mother's brunette vivacity. At two he was a child of average intelligence, sturdy physique, and marked good humour. He almost never cried.

He was just twelve months old when Selina's second child—a girl—was born dead. Twice during those two years Pervus fell victim to his so-called rheumatic attacks following the early spring planting when he was often forced to stand in water up to his ankles. He suffered intensely and during his illness was as tractable as a goaded bull. Selina understood why half of High Prairie was bent and twisted with rheumatism—why the little Dutch Reformed church on Sunday mornings resembled a shrine to which sick and crippled pilgrims creep.

High Prairie was kind to the harried household. The farm women sent Dutch dainties. The men lent a hand in the fields, though they were hard put to it to tend their own crops at this season. The Widow Paarlenberg's neat smart rig was frequently to be seen waiting under the willows in the DeJong yard. The Paarlenberg, still widow, still Paarlenberg, brought soups and chickens and cakes which never stuck in Selina's throat because she refused to touch them. The Widow Paarlenberg was what is known as goodhearted. She was happiest when some one else was in trouble. Hearing of an illness, a catastrophe, "Og heden!" she would cry, and rush off to the scene with sustaining soup. She was the sort of lady bountiful who likes to see her beneficiaries benefit before her very eyes. If she brought them soup at ten in the morning she wanted to see that soup consumed.

"Eat it all," she would urge. "Take it now, while it is hot. See, you are looking better already. Just another spoonful."

In the DeJongs' plight she found a grisly satisfaction, cloaked by commiseration. Selina, white and weak following her tragic second confinement, still found strength to refuse the widow's sustaining potions. The widow, her silks making a gentle susurrus in the bare little bedroom, regarded Selina with eyes in which pity and triumph made horrid conflict. Selina's eyes, enormous now in her white face, were twin pools of Peake pride.

"It's most kind of you, Mrs. Paarlenberg, but I don't like soup."

"A whole chicken boiled in it."

"Especially chicken soup. Neither does Pervus. But I'm sure Mrs. Voorhees will enjoy it." This being Pervus's old housekeeper pressed now into temporary emergency service.

It was easy to see why the DeJong house still was unpainted two years after Selina's rosy plans began to form; why the fences still sagged, the wagon creaked, the single horse hauled the produce to market.

Selina had been married almost three years when there came to her a letter from Julie Hempel, now married. The letter had been sent to the Klaas Pool farm and Jozina had brought it to her. Though she had not seen it since her days at Miss Fister's school, Selina recognized with a little hastening heart-beat the spidery handwriting with the shading and curleycues. Seated on her kitchen steps in her calico dress she read it.

DARLING SELINA:—

I thought it was so queer that you didn't answer my letter and now I know you must have thought it queer that I did not answer yours. I found your letter to me, written long ago, when I was going over Mother's things last week. It was the letter you must have written when I was in Kansas City. Mother had never given it to me. I am not reproaching her. You see, I had written you from Kansas City, but had sent my letter to Mamma to mail because I never could remember that funny address of yours in the country.

Mamma died three weeks ago. Last week I was going over her things—a trying task, you may imagine—and there were your two letters addressed to me. She had never destroyed them. Poor Mamma . . .

Well, dear Selina, I suppose you don't even know that I am married. I married Michael Arnold of Kansas City. The Arnolds were in the packing business there, you know. Michael has gone into business with Pa here in Chicago and I suppose you have heard of Pa's success. Just all of a sudden he began to make a great deal of money after he left the butcher business and went into the yards—the stockyards, you know. Poor Mamma was so happy these last few years, and had everything that was beautiful. I have two children. Eugene and Pauline.

I am getting to be quite a society person. You would laugh to see me. I am on the Ladies' Entertainment Committee of the World's Fair. We are supposed to entertain all the visiting big bugs—that is the lady bugs, There! How is that for a joke?

I suppose you know about the Infanta Eulalie. Of Spain, you know. And what she did about the Potter Palmer ball. . . .

Selina, holding the letter in her work-stained hand, looked up and across the fields and away to where the prairie met the sky and closed in on

her; her world. The Infanta Eulalie of Spain. . . . She went back to the
letter.

> Well, she came to Chicago for the Fair and Mrs. Potter
> Palmer was to give a huge reception and ball for her. Mrs.
> P. is head of the whole committee, you know, and I must
> say she looks queenly with her white hair so beautifully
> dressed and her diamond dog-collar and her black velvet
> and all. Well, at the very last minute the Infanta refused to
> attend the ball because she had just heard that Mrs. P. was
> an innkeeper's wife. Imagine! The Palmer House, of course.

Selina, holding the letter in her hand, imagined.

It was in the third year of Selina's marriage that she first went into the
fields to work. Pervus had protested miserably, though the vegetables were
spoiling in the ground.

"Let them rot," he said. "Better the stuff rots in the ground. DeJong
women folks they never worked in the fields. Not even in Holland. Not my
mother or my grandmother. It isn't for women."

Selina had regained health and vigour after two years of wretchedness.
She felt steel-strong and even hopeful again, sure sign of physical well-being.
Long before now she had realized that this time must inevitably come. So
she answered briskly, "Nonsense, Pervus. Working in the field's no harder
than washing or ironing or scrubbing or standing over a hot stove in August.
Women's work! Housework's the hardest work in the world. That's why
men won't do it."

She would often take the boy Dirk with her into the fields, placing him
on a heap of empty sacks in the shade. He invariably crawled off this lowly
throne to dig and burrow in the warm black dirt. He even made as though
to help his mother, pulling at the rooted things with futile fingers, and sitting
back with a bump when a shallow root did unexpectedly yield to his tugging.

"Look! He's a farmer already," Pervus would say.

But within Selina something would cry, "No! No!"

During May, June, and July Pervus worked not only from morning until
night, but by moonlight as well, and Selina worked with him. Often their
sleep was a matter of three hours only, or four.

So two years went—three years—four. In the fourth year of Selina's
marriage she suffered the loss of her one woman friend in all High Prairie.
Maartje Pool died in childbirth, as was so often the case in this region where
a Gampish midwife acted as obstetrician. The child, too, had not lived.
Death had not been kind to Maartje Pool. It had brought neither peace nor
youth to her face, as it so often does. Selina, looking down at the strangely
still figure that had been so active, so bustling, realized that for the first time
in the years she had known her she was seeing Maartje Pool at rest. It
seemed incredible that she could lie there, the infant in her arms, while the
house was filled with people and there were chairs to be handed, space to
be cleared, food to be cooked and served. Sitting there with the other High
Prairie women Selina had a hideous feeling that Maartje would suddenly rise
up and take things in charge; rub and scratch with capable fingers the spatters
of dried mud on Klaas Pool's black trousers (he had been in the yard to see
to the horses); quiet the loud wailing of Geertje and Jozina; pass her gnarled
hand over Roelf's wide-staring tearless eyes; wipe the film of dust from the
parlour table that had never known a speck during her régime.

"You can't run far enough," Maartje had said. "Except you stop living
you can't run away from life."

Well, she had run far enough this time.

Roelf was sixteen now, Geertje twelve, Jozina eleven. What would this household do now, Selina wondered, without the woman who had been so faithful a slave to it? Who would keep the pigtails—no longer giggling—in clean ginghams and decent square-toed shoes? Who, when Klaas broke out in rumbling Dutch wrath against what he termed Roelf's "dumb" ways, would say, "Og, Pool, leave the boy alone once. He does nothing." Who would keep Klaas himself in order; cook his meals, wash his clothes, iron his shirts, take pride in the great ruddy childlike giant?

Klaas answered these questions just nine months later by marrying the Widow Paarlenberg. High Prairie was rocked with surprise. For months this marriage was the talk of the district. They had gone to Niagara Falls on a wedding trip; Pool's place was going to have this improvement and that; no, they were going to move to the Widow Paarlenberg's large farmhouse (they would always call her that); no, Pool was putting in a bathroom with a bathtub and running water; no, they were going to buy the Stikker place between Pool's and Paarlenberg's and make one farm of it, the largest in all High Prairie, Low Prairie, or New Haarlem. Well, no fool like an old fool.

So insatiable was High Prairie's curiosity that every scrap of fresh news was swallowed at a gulp. When the word went round of Roelf's flight from the farm, no one knew where, it served only as sauce to the great dish of gossip.

Selina had known. Pervus was away at the market when Roelf had knocked at the farmhouse door one night at eight, had turned the knob and entered, as usual. But there was nothing of the usual about his appearance. He wore his best suit—his first suit of store clothes, bought at the time of his mother's funeral. It never had fitted him; now was grotesquely small for him, He had shot up amazingly in the last eight or nine months. Yet there was nothing of the ridiculous about him as he stood before her now, tall, lean, dark. He put down his cheap yellow suitcase.

"Well, Roelf."

"I am going away. I couldn't stay."

She nodded. "Where?"

"Away. Chicago maybe." He was terribly moved, so he made his tone casual. "They came home last night. I have got some books that belong to you." He made as though to open the suitcase.

"No, no! Keep them."

"Good-bye."

"Good-bye, Roelf." She took the boy's dark head in her two hands and, standing on tiptoe, kissed him. He turned to go. "Wait a minute. Wait a minute." She had a few dollars—in quarters, dimes, half dollars—perhaps ten dollars in all—hidden away in a canister on the shelf. She reached for it. But when she came back with the box in her hand he was gone.

9

DIRK WAS EIGHT; Little Sobig DeJong, in a suit made of bean-sacking sewed together by his mother. A brown blond boy with mosquito bites on his legs and his legs never still. Nothing of the dreamer about this lad. The one-room schoolhouse of Selina's day had been replaced by a two-story brick structure, very fine, of which High Prairie was vastly proud. The rusty iron stove had been dethroned by a central heater. Dirk went to school from October until June. Pervus protested that this was foolish. The boy could be of great help in the fields from the beginning of April to the first of November, but Selina fought savagely for his schooling, and won.

"Reading and writing and figgering is what a farmer is got to know," Pervus argued. "The rest is all foolishness. Constantinople is the capital of Turkey he studies last night and uses good oil in the lamp. What good does it do a truck farmer when he knows Constantinople is the capital of Turkey? That don't help him raise turnips."

"Sobig isn't a truck farmer."

"Well, he will be pretty soon. Time I was fifteen I was running our place."

Verbally Selina did not combat this. But within her every force was gathering to fight it when the time should come. Her Sobig a truck farmer, a slave to the soil, bent by it, beaten by it, blasted by it, so that he, in time, like the other men of High Prairie, would take on the very look of the rocks and earth among which they toiled!

Dirk, at eight, was a none too handsome child, considering his father and mother—or his father and mother as they had been. He had, though, a "different" look, His eyelashes were too long for a boy. Wasted, Selina said as she touched them with a fond forefinger, when a girl would have been so glad of them. He had developed, too, a slightly aquiline nose, probably a long-jump inheritance from some Cromwellian rapscallion of the English Peakes of a past century. It was not until he was seventeen or eighteen that he was to metamorphose suddenly into a graceful and aristocratic youngster with an indefinable look about him of distinction and actual elegance. It was when Dirk was thirty that Peter Peel the English tailor (of Michigan Avenue north) said he was the only man in Chicago who could wear English clothes without having them look like Halsted Street. Dirk probably appeared a little startled at that, as well he might, West Halsted Street having loomed up so large in his background.

Selina was a farm woman now, nearing thirty. The work rode her as it had ridden Maartje Pool. In the DeJong yard there was always a dado of washing, identical with the one that had greeted Selina's eye when first she drove into the Pool yard years before. Faded overalls, a shirt, socks, a boy's drawers grotesquely patched and mended, towels of rough sacking. She, too, rose at four, snatched up shapeless garments, invested herself with them, seized her great coil of fine cloudy hair, twisted it into a utilitarian knob and skewered it with a hairpin from which the varnish had long departed, leaving it a dull gray; thrust her slim feet into shapeless shoes, dabbed her face with cold water, hurried to the kitchen stove. The work was always at her heels, its breath hot on her neck. Baskets of mending piled up, threatened to overwhelm her. Overalls, woollen shirts, drawers, socks. Socks! They lay coiled and twisted in an old market basket. Sometimes as she sat late at night mending them, in and out, in and out, with quick fierce stabs of the needle in her work-scarred hand, they seemed to writhe and squirm and wriggle horribly, like snakes. One of her bad dreams was that in which she saw herself overwhelmed, drowned, swallowed up by a huge welter and boiling of undarned, unmended nightshirts, drawers, socks, aprons, overalls.

Seeing her thus one would have thought that the Selina Peake of the wine-red cashmere, the fun-loving disposition, the high-spirited courage, had departed forever. But these things still persisted. For that matter, even the wine-red cashmere clung to existence. So hopelessly old-fashioned now as to be almost picturesque, it hung in Selina's closet like a rosy memory. Sometimes when she came upon it in an orgy of cleaning she would pass her rough hands over its soft folds and by that magic process Mrs. Pervus DeJong vanished in a pouf and in her place was the girl Selina Peake perched a-tiptoe on a soap-box in Adam Ooms's hall while all High Prairie, open-mouthed, looked on as the impecunious Pervus DeJong threw ten hard-earned dollars at her feet. In thrifty moments she had often thought of cutting the wine-red cashmere into rag-rug strips; of dyeing it a sedate brown or black and remodelling it for a much-needed best dress; of fashioning it into shirts for Dirk. But she never did.

It would be gratifying to be able to record that in these eight or nine years Selina had been able to work wonders on the DeJong farm; that the house glittered, the crops thrived richly, the barn housed sleek cattle. But it could not be truthfully said. True, she had achieved some changes, but at the cost of terrific effort. A less indomitable woman would have sunk into apathy years before. The house had a coat of paint—lead-gray, because it was cheapest. There were two horses—the second a broken-down old mare, blind in one eye, that they had picked up for five dollars after it had been turned out to pasture for future sale as horse-carcass. Piet Pon, the mare's owner who drove a milk route, had hoped to get three dollars for the animal, dead. A month of rest and pasturage restored the mare to usefulness. Selina had made the bargain, and Pervus had scolded her roundly for it. Now he drove the mare to market, saw that she pulled more sturdily than the other horse, but had never retracted. It was no quality of meanness in him. Pervus merely was like that.

But the west sixteen! That had been Selina's most heroic achievement. Her plan, spoken of to Pervus in the first month of her marriage, had taken years to mature; even now was but a partial triumph. She had even descended to nagging.

"Why don't we put in asparagus?"

"Asparagus!" considered something of a luxury, and rarely included in the High Prairie truck farmer's products. "And wait three years for a crop!"

"Yes, but then we'd have it. And a plantation's good for ten years, once it's started."

"Plantation! What is that? An asparagus plantation? Asparagus I've always heard of in beds."

"That's the old idea. I've been reading up on it. The new way is to plant asparagus in rows, the way you would rhubarb or corn. Plant six feet apart, and four acres anyway."

He was not even sufficiently interested to be amused. "Yeh, four acres where? In the clay land, maybe." He did laugh then, if the short bitter sound he made could be construed as indicating mirth. "Out of a book."

"In the clay land," Selina urged, crisply. "And out of a book. Every farmer in High Prairie raises cabbages, turnips, carrots, beets, beans, onions, and they're better quality than ours. That west sixteen isn't bringing you anything, so what difference does it make if I am wrong! Let me put my own money into it, I've thought it all out, Pervus. Please. We'll underdrain the clay soil. Just five or six acres, to start, We'll manure it heavily—as much as we can afford—and then for two years we'll plant potatoes there. We'll put in our asparagus plants the third spring—one-year-old seedlings. I'll promise to keep it weeded—Dirk and I. He'll be a big boy by that time."

"How much manure?"

"Oh, twenty to forty tons to the acre————"

He shook his head in slow Dutch opposition.

"—but if you'll let me use humus I won't need that much. Let me try it, Pervus. Let me try."

In the end she had her way, partly because Pervus was too occupied with his own endless work to oppose her; and partly because he was, in his undemonstrative way, still in love with his vivacious, nimble-witted, high-spirited wife, though to her frantic goadings and proddings he was as phlegmatically oblivious as an elephant to a pin prick. Year in, year out, he maintained his slowplodding gait, content to do as his father had done before him; content to let the rest of High Prairie pass him on the road. He rarely showed temper. Selina often wished he would. Sometimes, in a sort of hysteria of hopelessness, she would rush at him, ruffle up his thick coarse hair, now beginning to be threaded with gray; shake his great impassive shoulders.

"Pervus! Pervus! if you'd only get mad—real mad! Fly into a rage. Break things! Beat me! Sell the farm! Run away!" She didn't mean it, of course. It was the vital and constructive force in her resenting his apathy, his acceptance of things as they were.

"What is that for dumb talk?" He would regard her solemnly through a haze of smoke, his pipe making a maddening putt-putt of sleepy content.

Though she worked as hard as any woman in High Prairie, had as little, dressed as badly, he still regarded her as a luxury; an exquisite toy which, in a moment of madness, he had taken for himself. "Little Lina"—tolerantly, fondly. You would have thought that he spoiled her, pampered her. Perhaps he even thought he did.

When she spoke of modern farming, of books on vegetable gardening, he came very near to angry impatience, though his amusement at the idea saved him from it. College agricultural courses he designated as foolishness. Of Linnæus he had never heard. Burbank was, for him, non-existent, and he thought head-lettuce a silly fad. Selina sometimes talked of raising this last named green as a salad, with marketing value. Everyone knew that regular lettuce was leaf lettuce which you ate with vinegar and a sprinkling of sugar, or with hot bacon and fat sopping its wilted leaves.

He said, too, she spoiled the boy. Back of this may have been a lurking jealousy. "Always the boy; always the boy," he would mutter when Selina planned for the child; shielded him; took his part (sometimes unjustly). "You will make a softy of him with your always babying." So from time to time he undertook to harden Dirk. The result was generally disastrous. In one case the process terminated in what was perilously near to tragedy. It was during the midsummer school vacation. Dirk was eight. The woody slopes about High Prairie and the sand hills beyond were covered with the rich blue of huckleberries. They were dead ripe. One shower would spoil them. Geertje and Jozina Pool were going huckleberrying and had consented to take Dirk— a concession, for he was only eight and considered, at their advanced age, a tagger. But the last of the tomatoes on the DeJong place were also ripe and ready for picking. They hung, firm, juicy scarlet globes, prime for the Chicago market. Pervus meant to haul them to town that day. And this was work in which the boy could help. To Dirk's, "Can I go berrying? The huckleberries are ripe. Geert and Jozina are going," his father shook a negative head.

"Yes, well tomatoes are ripe, too, and that comes before huckleberries. There's the whole patch to clean up this afternoon by four."

Selina looked up, glanced at Pervus's face, at the boy's, said nothing. The look said, "He's a child. Let him go, Pervus."

Dirk flushed with disappointment. They were at breakfast. It was barely daybreak. He looked down at his plate, his lip quivered, his long lashes lay heavy on his cheeks. Pervus got up, wiped his mouth with the back of his hand. There was a hard day ahead of him. "Time I was your age, Sobig, I would think it was an easy day when all I had to do was pick a tomato patch clean."

Dirk looked up then, quickly. "If I get it all picked can I go?"

"It's a day's job."

"But if I do pick the patch—if I get through early enough—can I go?"

In his mind's eye Pervus saw the tomato patch, more scarlet than green, so thick hung the fruit upon the bushes. He smiled. "Yes. You pick them tomatoes and you can go. But no throwing into the baskets and getting 'em all softed up."

Secretly Selina resolved to help him, but she knew that this could not be until afternoon. The berry patches were fully three miles from the DeJong farm. Dirk would have to finish by three o'clock, at the latest, to get there. Selina had her morning full with the housework.

He was in the patch before six; fell to work feverishly. He picked, heaped the fruit into hillocks. The scarlet patches glowed, blood-red, in the sun. The child worked like a machine, with an economy of gesture calculated to the fraction of an inch. He picked, stooped, heaped the mounds in the sultry heat of the August morning. The sweat stood out on his forehead, darkened his blond hair, slid down his cheeks that were pink, then red, then tinged with a purplish tone beneath the summer tan. When dinner time came he gulped a dozen alarming mouthfuls and was out again in the broiling noonday glare. Selina left her dinner dishes unwashed on the table to help him, but Pervus intervened. "The boy's got to do it alone," he insisted.

"He'll never do it, Pervus. He's only eight."

"Time I was eight————"

He actually had cleared the patch by three. He went to the well and took a huge draught of water; drank two great dipperfuls, lipping it down thirstily, like a colt. It was cool and delicious beyond belief. Then he sloshed a third and a fourth dipperful over his hot head and neck, took an empty lard pail for berries and was off down the dusty road and across the fields, running fleetly in spite of the quivering heat waves that seemed to dance between fiery heaven and parched earth. Selina stood in the kitchen doorway a moment, watching him. He looked very small and determined.

He found Geertje and Jozina, surfeited with fruit, berry stained and bramble torn, lolling languidly in Kuyper's woods. He began to pick the plump blue balls but he ate them listlessly, though thriftily, because that was what he had come for and his father was Dutch. When Geertje and Jozina prepared to leave not an hour after he had come he was ready to go, yet curiously loath to move. His lard pail was half filled. He trotted home laboriously through the late afternoon, feeling giddy and sick, with horrid pains in his head. That night he tossed in delirium, begged not to be made lie down, came perilously near to death.

Selina's heart was an engine pumping terror, hate, agony through her veins. Hate for her husband who had done this to the boy.

"You did it! You did it! He's a baby and you made him work like a man. If anything happens to him! If anything happens to him!————"

"Well, I didn't think the kid would go for to do it. I didn't ask him to pick and then go berrying. He said could he and I said yes. If I had said no it would have been wrong, too, maybe."

"You're all alike. Look at Roelf Pool! They tried to make a farmer of him, too. And ruined him."

"What's the matter with farming? What's the matter with a farmer? You said farm work was grand work, once."

"Oh, I did. It is. It could be. It———— Oh, what's the use of talking like that now! Look at him! Don't, Sobig! Don't, baby. How hot his head is! Listen! Is that Jan with the doctor? No. No, it isn't. Mustard plasters. Are you sure that's the right thing?"

It was before the day of the omnipresent farmhouse telephone and the farmhouse Ford. Jan's trip to High Prairie village for the doctor and back to the farm meant a delay of hours. But within two days the boy was again about, rather pale, but otherwise seeming none the worse for his experience.

That was Pervus. Thrifty, like his kind, but unlike them in shrewdness. Penny wise, pound foolish; a characteristic that brought him his death. September, usually a succession of golden days and hazy opalescent evenings on the Illinois prairie land, was disastrously cold and rainy that year.

Pervus's great frame was racked by rheumatism. He was forty now, and over, still of magnificent physique, so that to see him suffering gave Selina the pangs of pity that one has at sight of the very strong or the very weak in pain. He drove the weary miles to market three times a week, for September was the last big month of the truck farmer's season. After that only the hardier plants survived the frosts—the cabbages, beets, turnips, carrots, pumpkins, squash. The roads in places were morasses of mud into which the wheels were likely to sink to the hubs. Once stuck you had often to wait for a friendly passing team to haul you out. Pervus would start early, detour for miles in order to avoid the worst places. Jan was too stupid, too old, too inexpert to be trusted with the Haymarket trading. Selina would watch Pervus drive off down the road in the creaking old market wagon, the green stuff protected by canvas, but Pervus wet before ever he climbed into the seat. There never seemed to be enough waterproof canvas for both.

"Pervus, take it off those sacks and put it over your shoulders."

"That's them white globe onions. The last of 'em. I can get a fancy price for them but not if they're all wetted down."

"Don't sleep on the wagon to-night, Pervus. Sleep in. Be sure. It saves in the end. You know the last time you were laid up for a week."

"It'll clear. Breaking now over there in the west."

The clouds did break late in the afternoon; the false sun came out hot and bright. Pervus slept out in the Haymarket, for the night was close and humid. At midnight the lake wind sprang up, cold and treacherous, and with it came the rain again. Pervus was drenched by morning, chilled, thoroughly miserable. A hot cup of coffee at four and another at ten when the rush of trading was over stimulated him but little. When he reached home it was mid-afternoon. Beneath the bronze wrought by the wind and sun of many years the gray-white of sickness shone dully, like silver under enamel. Selina put him to bed against his half-hearted protests. Banked him with hot water jars, a hot iron wrapped in flannel at his feet. But later came fever instead of the expected relief of perspiration. Ill though he was he looked more ruddy and hale than most men in health; but suddenly Selina, startled, saw black lines like gashes etched under his eyes, about his mouth, in his cheeks.

In a day when pneumonia was known as lung fever and in a locality that advised closed windows and hot air as a remedy, Pervus's battle was lost before the doctor's hooded buggy was seen standing in the yard for long hours through the night. Toward morning the doctor had Jan Steen stable the horse. It was a sultry night, with flashes of heat lightning in the west.

"I should think if you opened the windows," Selina said to the old High Prairie doctor over and over, emboldened by terror, "it would help him to breathe. He—he's breathing so—he's breathing so———" She could not bring herself to say so terribly. The sound of the words wrung her as did the sound of his terrible breathing.

10

PERHAPS THE MOST poignant and touching feature of the days that followed was not the sight of this stricken giant, lying majestic and aloof in his unwonted black; nor of the boy Dirk, mystified but elated, too, with the unaccustomed stir and excitement; nor of the shabby little farm that seemed to shrink and dwindle into further insignficance beneath the sudden publicity turned upon it. No; it was the sight of Selina, widowed, but having no time for decent tears. The farm was there; it must be tended. Illness, death, sorrow—the garden must be tended, the vegetables pulled, hauled to market, sold. Upon the garden depended the boy's future, and hers.

For the first few days following the funeral one or another of the neighbouring farmers drove the DeJong team to market, aided the blundering Jan in the fields. But each had his hands full with his own farm work. On the fifth day Jan Steen had to take the garden truck to Chicago, though not without many misgivings on Selina's part, all of which were realized when he returned late next day with half the load still on his wagon and a sum of money representing exactly zero in profits. The wilted left-over vegetables were dumped behind the barn to be used later as fertilizer.

"I didn't do so good this time," Jan explained, "on account I didn't get no right place in the market."

"You started early enough."

"Well, they kind of crowded me out, like. They see I was a new hand and time I got the animals stabled and come back they had the wagon crowded out, like."

Selina was standing in the kitchen doorway, Jan in the yard with the team. She turned her face toward the fields. An observant person (Jan Steen was not one of these) would have noted the singularly determined and clear-cut jaw-line of this drably calicoed farm woman.

"I'll go myself Monday."

Jan stared. "Go? Go where, Monday?"

"To market."

At this seeming pleasantry Jan Steen smiled uncertainly, shrugged his shoulders, and was off to the barn. She was always saying things that didn't make sense. His horror and unbelief were shared by the rest of High Prairie when on Monday Selina literally took the reins in her own slim work-scarred hands.

"To market!" argued Jan as excitedly as his phlegmatic nature would permit. "A woman she don't go to market. A woman———"

"This woman does." Selina had risen at three in the morning. Not only that, she had got Jan up, grumbling. Dirk had joined them in the fields at five. Together the three of them had pulled and bunched a wagon load. "Size them," Selina ordered, as they started to bunch radishes, beets, turnips, carrots. "And don't leave them loose like that. Tie them tight at the heads, like this. Twice around with the string, and through. Make bouquets of them, not bunches. And we're going to scrub them."

High Prairie washed its vegetables desultorily; sometimes not at all. Higgledy-piggledy, large and small, they were bunched and sold as vegetables, not objets d'art. Generally there was a tan crust of good earth coating them which the housewife could scrub off at her own kitchen sink. What else had housewives to do!

Selina, scrubbing the carrots vigorously under the pump, thought they emerged from their unaccustomed bath looking like clustered spears of pure gold. She knew better, though, than to say this in Jan's hearing. Jan, by now, was sullen with bewilderment. He refused to believe that she actually intended to carry out her plan. A woman—a High Prairie farmer's wife—driving to market like a man! Alone at night in the market place—or at best in one of the cheap rooming houses! By Sunday somehow, mysteriously, the news had filtered through the district. High Prairie attended the Dutch Reformed church with a question hot on its tongue and Selina did not attend the morning services. A fine state of things, and she a widow of a week! High Prairie called at the DeJong farm on Sunday afternoon and was told that the widow was over in the wet west sixteen, poking about with the boy Dirk at her heels.

The Reverend Dekker appeared late Sunday afternoon on his way to evening service. A dour dominie, the Reverend Dekker, and one whose talents were anachronistic. He would have been invaluable in the days when New York was New Amsterdam. But the second and third generations of High Prairie Dutch were beginning to chafe under his old-world régime. A hard blue eye, had the Reverend Dekker, and a fanatic one.

"What is this talk I hear, Mrs. DeJong, that you are going to the Haymarket with the garden stuff, a woman alone?"

"Dirk goes with me."

"You don't know what you are doing, Mrs. DeJong. The Haymarket is no place for a decent woman. As for the boy! There is card-playing, drinking—all manner of wickedness—daughters of Jezebel on the street, going among the wagons."

"Really!" said Selina. It sounded thrilling, after twelve years on the farm.

"You must not go."

"The vegetables are rotting in the ground. And Dirk and I must live."

"Remember the two sparrows. 'One of them shall not fall on the ground without'—Matthew X-29."

"I don't see," replied Selina, simply, "what good that does the sparrow, once it's fallen."

By Monday afternoon the parlour curtains of every High Prairie farmhouse that faced the Halsted road were agitated as though by a brisk wind between the hours of three and five, when the market wagons were to be seen moving toward Chicago. Klaas Pool at dinner that noon had spoken of Selina's contemplated trip with a mingling of pity and disapproval.

"It ain't decent a woman should drive to market."

Mrs. Klaas Pool (they still spoke of her as the Widow Paarlenberg) smiled her slippery crooked smile. "What could you expect! Look how she's always acted."

Klaas did not follow this. He was busy with his own train of thought. "It don't seem hardly possible. Time she come here school teacher I drove her out and she was like a little robin or what, set up on the seat. She says, I remember like yesterday, cabbages was beautiful. I bet she learned different by this time."

But she hadn't. So little had Selina learned in these past twelve years that now, having loaded the wagon in the yard she surveyed it with more sparkle in her eye than High Prairie would have approved in a widow of little more than a week. They had picked and bunched only the best of the late crop— the firmest reddest radishes, the roundest juiciest beets; the carrots that tapered a good seven inches from base to tip; kraut cabbages of the drumhead variety that were flawless green balls; firm juicy spears of cucumber; cauliflower (of her own planting; Pervus had opposed it) that looked like a bride's bouquet. Selina stepped back now and regarded this riot of crimson and green, of white and gold and purple.

"Aren't they beautiful! Dirk, aren't they beautiful!"

Dirk, capering in his excitement at the prospect of the trip before him, shook his head impatiently. "What? I don't see anything beautiful. What's beautiful?"

Selina flung out her arms. "The—the whole wagon load. The cabbages."

"I don't know what you mean," said Dirk. "Let's go, Mother. Aren't we going now? You said as soon as the load was on."

"Oh, Sobig, you're just exactly like your———" She stopped.

"Like my what?"

"We'll go now, son, There's cold meat for your supper, Jan, and potatoes all sliced for frying and half an apple pie left from noon. Wash your dishes— don't leave them cluttering around the kitchen. You ought to get in the rest of the squash and pumpkins by evening. Maybe I can sell the lot instead of taking them in by the load. I'll see a commission man. Take less, if I have to.''

She had dressed the boy in his home-made suit cut down from one of his father's. He wore a wide-brimmed straw hat which he hated. Selina had made him an overcoat of stout bean-sacking and this she tucked under the wagon seat, together with an old black fascinator, for though the September afternoon was white-hot she knew that the evenings were likely to be chilly, once the sun, a great crimson Chinese balloon, had burned itself out in a blaze of flame across the prairie horizon. Selina herself, in a fullskirted black-stuff dress, mounted the wagon agilely, took up the reins, looked down at the boy seated beside her, clucked to the horses. Jan Steen gave vent to a final outraged bellow.

"Never in my life did I hear of such a thing!"

Selina turned the horses' heads toward the city. "You'd be surprised, Jan, to know of all the things you're going to hear of some day that you've never heard of before." Still, when twenty years had passed and the Ford, the phonograph, the radio, and the rural mail delivery had dumped the world at Jan's plodding feet he liked to tell of that momentous day when Selina DeJong had driven off to market like a man with a wagon load of hand-scrubbed garden truck and the boy Dirk perched beside her on the seat.

If, then, you had been traveling the Halsted road, you would have seen a decrepit wagon, vegetable-laden, driven by a too-thin woman sallow, bright-eyed, in a shapeless black dress, a battered black felt hat that looked like a man's old "fedora" and probably was. Her hair was unbecomingly strained away from the face with its high cheek bones, so that unless you were really observant you failed to notice the exquisite little nose or the really fine eyes so unnaturally large now in the anxious face. On the seat beside her you would have seen a farm boy of nine or thereabouts—a brown freckle-faced lad in a comically home-made suit of clothes and a straw hat with a broken and flopping brim which he was forever jerking off only to have it set firmly on again by the woman who seemed to fear the effects of the hot afternoon sun on his close-cropped head. But in the brief intervals when the hat was off you must have noted how the boy's eyes were shining.

At their feet was the dog Pom, a mongrel whose tail bore no relation to his head, whose ill-assorted legs appeared wholly at variance with his sturdy barrel of a body. He dozed now, for it had been his duty to watch the wagon load at night, while Pervus slept.

A shabby enough little outfit, but magnificent, too. Here was Selina DeJong driving up the Halsted road toward the city instead of sitting, black-robed, in the farm parlour while High Prairie came to condole. In Selina, as they jogged along the hot dusty way, there welled up a feeling very like elation. Conscious of this, the New England strain in her took her to task. "Selina Peake, aren't you ashamed of yourself! You're a wicked woman! Feeling almost gay when you ought to be sad. . . . Poor Pervus . . . the farm . . . Dirk . . . and you can feel almost gay! You ought to be ashamed of yourself!''

But she wasn't, and knew it. For even as she thought this the little wave of elation came flooding over her again. More than ten years ago she had driven with Klaas Pool up that same road for the first time, and in spite of the recent tragedy of her father's death, her youth, her loneliness, the terrifying thought of the new home to which she was going, a stranger among strangers, she had been conscious of a warm little thrill of elation, of excitement—of adventure! That was it. "The whole thing's just a grand adventure," her father, Simeon Peake, had said. And now the sensations of that day were repeating themselves. Now, as then, she was doing what was considered a revolutionary and daring thing; a thing that High Prairie regarded with horror. And now, as then, she took stock. Youth was gone, but she had health, courage; a boy of nine; twenty-five acres of worn-out farm land; dwelling and out-houses in a bad state of repair; and a gay adventure-some spirit that was never to die, though it led her into curious places and she often found, at the end, only a trackless waste from which she had to retrace her steps painfully. But always, to her, red and green cabbages were to be jade and Burgundy, chrysoprase and porphyry. Life has no weapons against a woman like that.

And the wine-red cashmere. She laughed aloud.

"What are you laughing at, Mom?"

That sobered her. "Oh, nothing, Sobig. I didn't know I was laughing. I was just thinking about a red dress I had when I first came to High Prairie a girl. I've got it yet."

"What's that to laugh at?" He was following a yellow-hammer with his eyes.

"Nothing. Mother said it was nothing."

"Wisht I'd brought my sling-shot." The yellow-hammer was perched on the fence by the roadside not ten feet away.

"Sobig, you promised me you wouldn't throw at any more birds, ever."

"Oh, I wouldn't hit it. I would just like to aim at it."

Down the hot dusty country road. She was serious enough now. The cost of the funeral to be paid. The doctor's bills. Jan's wage. All the expenses, large and small, of the poor little farm holding. Nothing to laugh at, certainly. The boy was wiser than she.

"There's Mrs. Pool on her porch, Mom. Rocking."

There, indeed, was the erstwhile Widow Paarlenberg on her porch, rocking. A pleasant place to be in mid-afternoon of a hot September day. She stared at the creaking farm wagon, vegetable-laden; at the boy perched on the high seat; at the sallow shabby woman who was charioteer for the whole crazy outfit. Mrs. Klaas Pool's pink face creased in a smile. She sat forward in her chair and ceased to rock.

"Where you going this hot day, Mis' DeJong?"

Selina sat up very straight. "To Bagdad, Mrs. Pool."

"To—Where's that? What for?"

"To sell my jewels, Mrs. Pool. And to see Aladdin, and Harunal-Rashid and Ali Baba. And the Forty Thieves."

Mrs. Pool had left her rocker and had come down the steps. The wagon creaked on past her gate. She took a step or two down the path, and called after them. "I never heard of it. Bag—How do you get there?"

Over her shoulder Selina called out from the wagon seat. "You just go until you come to a closed door. And you say 'Open Sesame!' and there you are."

Bewilderment shadowed Mrs. Pool's placid face. As the wagon lurched on down the road it was Selina who was smiling and Mrs. Pool who was serious.

The boy, round-eyed, was looking up at his mother. "That's out of *Arabian Nights*, what you said. Why did you say that?" Suddenly excitement tinged his voice. "That's out of the book. Isn't it? Isn't it! We're not really—"

She was a little contrite, but not very. "Well, not really, perhaps. But 'most any place is Bagdad if you don't know what will happen in it. And this is an adventure, isn't it, that we're going on? How can you tell! All kinds of things can happen. All kinds of people. People in disguise in the Haymarket. Caliphs, and princes, and slaves, and thieves, and good fairies, and witches."

"In the Haymarket! That Pop went to all the time! That is just dumb talk."

Within Selina something cried out. "Don't say that, Sobig! Don't say that!"

On down the road. Here a head at a front room window. There a woman's calicoed figure standing in the doorway. Mrs. Vander Sijde on the porch, fanning her flushed face with her apron; Cornelia Snip in the yard pretending to tie up the drooping stalks of the golden-glow and eyeing the approaching team with the avid gossip's gaze. To these Selina waved, bowed, called.

"How d'you do, Mrs. Vander Sijde!"

A prim reply to this salutation. Disapproval writ large on the farm-wife's flushed face.

"Hello, Cornelia!"

A pretended start, notable for its bad acting. "Oh, is it you, Mrs. DeJong! Sun's in my eyes. I couldn't think it was you like that."

Women's eyes, hostile, cold, peering.

Five o'clock. Six. The boy climbed over the wheel, filled a tin pail with water at a farmhouse well. They ate and drank as they rode along, for there was no time to lose. Bread and meat and pickles and pie. There were vegetables in the wagon, ripe for eating. There were other varieties that Selina might have cooked at home in preparation for this meal—German celery root boiled tender and soaked in vinegar; red beets, pickled; onions; coleslaw; beans. They would have regarded these with an apathetic eye all too familiar with the sight of them. Selina knew now why the Pools' table, in her school-teacher days, had been so lacking in the green stuff she had craved. The thought of cooking the spinach which she had planted, weeded, spaded, tended, picked, washed, bunched, filled her with a nausea of distaste such as she might have experienced at the contemplation of cannibalism.

The boy had started out bravely enough in the heat of the day, sitting up very straight beside his mother, calling to the horses, shrieking and waving his arms at chickens that flew squawking across the road. Now he began to droop. Evening was coming on. A cool blanket of air from the lake on the east enveloped them with the suddenness characteristic of the region, and the mist began to drift across the prairie, softening the autumn stubble, cooling the dusty road, misting the parched willows by the roadside, hazing the shabby squat farmhouses.

She brushed away the crumbs, packed the remaining bread and meat thriftily into the basket and covered it with a napkin against the boy's future hunger should he waken in the night.

"Sleepy, Sobig?"

"No. Should say not." His lids were heavy. His face and body, relaxed, took on the soft baby contours that come with weariness. The sun was low. Sunset gloried the west in a final flare of orange and crimson. Dusk. The boy drooped against her heavy, sagging. She wrapped the old black fascinator about him. He opened his eyes, tugged at the wrapping about his shoulders. "Don't want the old thing . . . fas'nator . . . like a girl . . ." drooped again with a sigh and found the soft curve where her side just cushioned his head. In the twilight the dust gleamed white on weeds, and brush, and grass. The far-off mellow sonance of a cowbell. Horses' hoofs clopping up behind them, a wagon passing in a cloud of dust, a curious backward glance, or a greeting exchanged.

One of the Ooms boys, or Jakob Boomsma. "You're never going to market, Mis' DeJong!" staring with china-blue eyes at her load.

"Yes, I am, Mr. Boomsma."

"That ain't work for a woman, Mis' DeJong. You better stay home and let the men folks go."

Selina's men folks looked up at her—one with the asking eyes of a child, one with the trusting eyes of a dog. "My men folks are going," answered Selina. But then, they had always thought her a little queer, so it didn't matter much.

She urged the horses on, refusing to confess to herself her dread of the destination which they were approaching. Lights now, in the houses along the way, and those houses closer together. She wrapped the reins around the whip, and holding the sleeping boy with one hand reached beneath the seat with the other for the coat of sacking. This she placed around him snugly, folded an empty sack for a pillow, and lifting the boy in her arms laid him gently on the lumpy bed formed by the bags of potatoes piled up just behind the seat in the back of the wagon. So the boy slept. Night had come on.

The figure of the woman drooped a little now as the old wagon creaked on toward Chicago. A very small figure in the black dress and a shawl over her shoulders. She had taken off her old black felt hat. The breeze ruffled her hair that was fine and soft, and it made a little halo about the white face that gleamed almost luminously in the darkness as she turned it up toward the sky.

"I'll sleep out with Sobig in the wagon. It won't hurt either of us. It will be warm in town, there in the Haymarket. Twenty-five cents—maybe fifty for the two of us, in the rooming house. Fifty cents just to sleep. It takes hours of work in the fields to make fifty cents."

She was sleepy now. The night air was deliciously soft and soothing. In her nostrils was the smell of the fields, of grass dew-wet, of damp dust, of cattle; the pungent prick of goldenrod, and occasionally a scented wave that meant wild phlox in a near-by ditch. She sniffed all this gratefully, her mind and body curiously alert to sounds, scents, forms even, in the darkness. She had suffered much in the past week; had eaten and slept but little. Had known terror, bewilderment, agony, shock. Now she was relaxed, receptive, a little light-headed perhaps, what with under-feeding and tears and over-work. The racking process had cleared brain and bowels; had washed her spiritually clean; had quickened her perceptions abnormally. Now she was like a delicate and sensitive electric instrument keyed to receive and register; vibrating to every ether wave.

She drove along in the dark, a dowdy farm woman in shapeless garments; just a bundle on the rickety seat of a decrepit truck wagon. The boy slept on his hard lumpy bed like the little vegetable that he was. The farm lights went out. The houses were blurs in the black. The lights of the city came nearer. She was thinking clearly, if disconnectedly, without bitterness, without reproach.

"My father was wrong. He said that life was a great adventure—a fine show. He said the more things that happen to you the richer you are, even if they're not pleasant things. That's living, he said. No matter what happens to you, good or bad, it's just so much—what was that word he used?—so much—oh, yes—'velvet.' Just so much velvet. Well, it isn't true. He had brains, and charm, and knowledge and he died in a gambling house, shot while looking on at some one else who was to have been killed. . . . Now we're on the cobblestones. Will Dirk wake up? My little So Big. . . . No, he's asleep. Asleep on a pile of potato sacks because his mother thought that life was a grand adventure—a fine show—and that you took it as it came. A lie! I've taken it as it came and made the best of it. That isn't the way. You take the best, and make the most of it . . . Thirty-fifth Street, that was. Another hour and a half to reach the Haymarket. . . . I'm not afraid. After all, you just sell your vegetables for what you can get. . . . Well, it's going to be different with him. I mustn't call him Sobig any more.

He doesn't like it. Dirk. That's a fine name. Dirk DeJong. . . . No drifting along for him. I'll see that he starts with a plan, and follows it. He'll have every chance. Every chance. Too late for me, now, but he'll be different. . . . Twenty-second Street . . . Twelfth . . . Look at all the people! . . . I'm enjoying this. No use denying it. I'm enjoying this. Just as I enjoyed driving along with Klaas Pool that evening, years and years ago. Scared, but enjoying it. Perhaps I oughtn't to be—but that's hypocritical and sneaking. Why not, if I really do enjoy it! I'll wake him. . . . Dirk! Dirk, we're almost there. Look at all the people, and the lights. We're almost there."

The boy awoke, raised himself from his bed of sacking, looked about, blinked, sank back again and curled into a ball. "Don't want to see the lights . . . people . . ."

He was asleep again. Selina guided the horses skilfully through the downtown streets. She looked about with wide ambient eyes. Other wagons passed her. There was a line of them ahead of her. The men looked at her curiously. They called to one another, and jerked a thumb in her direction, but she paid no heed. She decided, though, to have the boy on the seat beside her. They were within two blocks of the Haymarket, on Randolph Street.

"Dirk! Come, now. Come up here with mother." Grumbling, he climbed to the seat, yawned, smacked his lips, rubbed his knuckles into his eyes.

"What are we here for?"

"So we can sell the garden truck and earn money."

"What for?"

"To send you to school to learn things."

"That's funny. I go to school already."

"A different school. A big school."

He was fully awake now, and looking about him interestedly. They turned into the Haymarket. It was a tangle of horses, carts, men. The wagons were streaming in from the German truck farms that lay to the north of Chicago as well as from the Dutch farms that lay to the southwest, whence Selina came. Fruits and vegetables—tons of it—acres of it—piled in the wagons that blocked the historic square. An unarmed army bringing food to feed a great city. Through this little section, and South Water Street that lay to the east, passed all the verdant growing things that fed Chicago's millions. Something of this came to Selina as she manœuvred her way through the throng. She felt a little thrill of significance, of achievement. She knew the spot she wanted for her own. Since that first trip to Chicago with Pervus in the early days of her marriage she had made the journey into town perhaps not more than a dozen times, but she had seen, and heard, and remembered. A place near the corner of Des Plaines, not at the curb, but rather in the double line of wagons that extended down the middle of the road. Here the purchasing pedlers and grocers had easy access to the wagons. Here Selina could display her wares to the best advantage. It was just across the way from Chris Spanknoebel's restaurant, rooming house, and saloon. Chris knew her; had known Pervus for years and his father before him; would be kind to her and the boy in case of need.

Dirk was wide awake now; eager, excited. The lights, the men, the horses, the sound of talk, and laughter, and clinking glasses from the eating houses along the street were bewilderingly strange to his country-bred eyes and ears. He called to the horses; stood up in the wagon; but clung closer to her as they found themselves in the thick of the mêlée.

On the street corners where the lights were brightest there were stands at which men sold chocolate, cigars, collar buttons, suspenders, shoe strings, patent contrivances. It was like a fair. Farther down the men's faces loomed mysteriously out of the half light. Stolid, sunburned faces now looked dark, terrifying, the whites of the eyes very white, the mustaches very black, their shoulders enormous. Here was a crap game beneath the street light. There stood two girls laughing and chatting with a policeman.

"Here's a good place, Mother. Here! There's a dog on that wagon like Pom."

Pom, hearing his name, stood up, looked into the boy's face, quivered, wagged a nervous tail, barked sharply. The Haymarket night life was an old story to Pom, but it never failed to stimulate him. Often he had guarded the wagon when Pervus was absent for a short time. He would stand on the seat ready to growl at any one who so much as fingered a radish in Pervus's absence.

"Down, Pom! Quiet, Pom!" She did not want to attract attention to herself and the boy. It was still early. She had made excellent time. Pervus had often slept in snatches as he drove into town and the horses had lagged, but Selina had urged them on to-night. They had gained a good half hour over the usual time. Halfway down the block Selina espied the place she wanted. From the opposite direction came a truck farmer's cart obviously making for the same stand. For the first time that night Selina drew the whip out of its socket and clipped sharply her surprised nags. With a start and a shuffle they broke into an awkward lope. Ten seconds too late the German farmer perceived her intention, whipped up his own tired team, arrived at the spot just as Selina, blocking the way, prepared to back into the vacant space.

"Heh, get out of there you———" he roared; then, for the first time, perceived in the dim light of the street that his rival was a woman. He faltered, stared open-mouthed, tried other tactics. "You can't go in there, missus."

"Oh, yes, I can." She backed her team dexterously.

"Yes, we can!" shouted Dirk in an attitude of fierce belligerence.

From the wagons on either side heads were lifted. "Where's your man?" demanded the defeated driver, glaring.

"Here," replied Selina; put her hand on Dirk's head.

The other, preparing to drive on, received this with incredulity. He assumed the existence of a husband in the neighbourhood —at Chris Spanknoebel's probably, or talking prices with a friend at another wagon when he should be here attending to his own. In the absence of this, her natural protector, he relieved his disgruntled feelings as he gathered up the reins. "Woman ain't got no business here in Haymarket, anyway. Better you're home night time in your kitchen where you belong."

This admonition, so glibly mouthed by so many people in the past few days, now was uttered once too often. Selina's nerves snapped. A surprised German truck farmer found himself being harangued from the driver's seat of a vegetable wagon by an irate and fluent woman in a mashed black hat.

"Don't talk to me like that, you great stupid! What good does it do a woman to stay home in her kitchen if she's going to starve there, and her boy with her! Staying home in my kitchen won't earn me any money. I'm here to sell the vegetables I helped raise and I'm going to do it. Get out of my way, you. Go along about your business or I'll report you to Mike, the street policeman."

Now she clambered over the wagon wheel to unhitch the tired horses. It is impossible to tell what interpretation the dumfounded north-sider put upon her movements. Certainly he had nothing to fear from this small gaunt creature with the blazing eyes. Nevertheless as he gathered up his reins terror was writ large on his rubicund face.

"*Tuefel!* What a woman!" Was off in a clatter of wheels and hoofs on the cobblestones.

Selina unharnessed swiftly. "You stay here, Dirk, with Pom. Mother'll be back in a minute." She marched down the street driving the horses to the barns where, for twenty-five cents, the animals were to be housed in more comfort than their owner. She returned to find Dirk deep in conversation with two young women in red shirtwaists, plaid skirts that swept the ground, and sailor hats tipped at a saucy angle over pyramidal pompadours.

"I can't make any sense out of it, can you, Elsie? Sounds like Dirt to me, but nobody's going to name a kid that, are they? Stands to reason."

"Oh, come on. Your name'll be mud first thing you know. Here it's after nine already and not a———" she turned and saw Selina's white face.

"There's my mother," said Dirk, triumphantly, pointing. The three women looked at each other. Two saw the pathetic hat and the dowdy clothes, and knew. One saw the red shirtwaists and the loose red lips, and knew.

"We was just talking to the kid," said the girl who had been puzzled by Dirk's name. Her tone was defensive. "Just asking him his name, and like that."

"His name is Dirk," said Selina, mildly. "It's a Dutch name—Holland, you know. We're from out High Prairie way, south. Dirk DeJong. I'm Mrs. DeJong."

"Yeh?" said the other girl. "I'm Elsie. Elsie from Chelsea, that's me. Come on, Mabel. Stand gabbin' all night." She was blonde and shrill. The other was older, dark-haired. There was about her a paradoxical wholesomeness.

Mabel, the older one, looked at Selina sharply. From the next wagon came loud snores issuing from beneath the seat. From down the line where a lantern swung from the tailboard of a cart came the rattle of dice. "What you doing down here, anyway?"

"I'm here to sell my stuff to-morrow morning. Vegetables. From the farm."

Mabel looked around. Hers was not a quick mind. "Where's your man?"

"My husband died a week ago." Selina was making up their bed for the night. From beneath the seat she took a sack of hay, tight-packed, shook out its contents, spread them evenly on the floor of the wagon, at the front, first having unhinged the seat and clapped it against the wagon side as a headboard. Over the hay she spread empty sacking. She shook out her shawl, which would serve as cover. The girl Mabel beheld these preparations. Her dull eyes showed a gleam of interest which deepened to horror.

"Say, you ain't never going to sleep out here, are you? You and the kid. Like that!"

"Yes."

"Well, for———" She stared, turned to go, came back. From her belt that dipped so stylishly in the front hung an arsenal of jangling metal articles—purse, pencil, mirror, comb—a chatelaine, they called it. She opened the purse now and took from it a silver dollar. This she tendered Selina, almost roughly. "Here. Get the kid a decent roost for the night. You and the kid, see."

Selina stared at the shining round dollar; at Mabel's face. The quick sting of tears came to her eyes. She shook her head, smiled.

"We don't mind sleeping out here. Thank you just the same—Mabel."

The girl put her dollar plumply back into her purse. "Well, takes all kinds, I always say. I thought I had a bum deal but, say, alongside of what you got I ain't got it so worse. Place to sleep in, anyways, even if it is—well, goodnight. Listen to that Elsie, hollering for me. I'm comin'! Shut up!"

You heard the two on their way up the street, arm in arm, laughing.

"Come Dirk."

"Are we going to sleep here!" He was delighted.

"Right here, all snug in the hay, like campers."

The boy lay down, wriggling, laughing. "Like gypsies. Ain't it, Mom?"

" 'Isn't it,' Dirk—not 'ain't it'." The school teacher.

She lay down beside him. The boy seemed terribly wide awake. "I liked the Mabel one best, didn't you? She was the nicest, h'm?"

"Oh, much the nicest," said Selina, and put one arm around him and drew him to her, close. And suddenly he was asleep, deeply. The street became quieter. The talking and laughter ceased. The lights were dim at Chris Spanknoebel's. Now and then the clatter of wheels and horses' hoofs proclaimed a late comer seeking a place, but the sound was not near by, for this block and those to east and west were filled by now. These men had been up at four that morning, must be up before four the next.

The night was cool, but not cold. Overhead you saw the wide strip of sky between the brick buildings on either side of the street. Two men came along singing. "Shut up!" growled a voice from a wagon along the curb. The singers subsided. It must be ten o'clock and after, Selina thought. She had with her Pervus's nickel watch, but it was too dark to see its face, and she did not want to risk a match. Measured footsteps that passed and repassed at regular intervals. The night policeman.

She lay looking up at the sky. There were no tears in her eyes. She was past tears. She thought, "Here I am, Selina Peake, sleeping in a wagon, in the straw, like a bitch with my puppy snuggled beside me. I was going to be like Jo in Louisa Alcott's book. On my feet are boots and on my body a dyed dress. How terribly long it is going to be until morning . . . I must try to sleep. . . . I must try to sleep . . ."

She did sleep, miraculously. The September stars twinkled brightly down on them, As she lay there, the child in her arms, asleep, peace came to the haggard face, relaxed the tired limbs. Much like another woman who had lain in the straw with her child in her arms almost two thousand years before.

11

IT WOULD BE enchanting to be able to record that Selina next day, had phenomenal success, disposing of her carefully bunched wares to great advantage, driving smartly off up Halsted Street toward High Prairie with a goodly profit jingling in her scuffed leather purse. The truth is that she had a day so devastating, so catastrophic, as would have discouraged most men and certainly any woman less desperate and determined.

She had awakened, not to daylight, but to the three o'clock blackness. The street was already astir. Selina brushed her skirt to rid it of the clinging hay, tidied herself as best she could. Leaving Dirk still asleep, she called Pom from beneath the wagon to act as sentinel at the dashboard, and crossed the street to Chris Spanknoebel's. She knew Chris, and he her. He would let her wash at the faucet at the rear of the eating house. She would buy hot coffee for herself and Dirk to warm and revivify them. They would eat the sandwiches left from the night before.

Chris himself, a pot-paunched Austrian, blond, benevolent, was standing behind his bar, wiping the slab with a large moist cloth. With the other hand he swept the surface with a rubber-tipped board about the size of a shingle. This contrivance gathered up such beads of moisture as might be left by the cloth. Two sweeps of it rendered the counter dry and shining. Later Chris allowed Dirk to wield this rubber-tipped contrivance—a most satisfactory thing to do, leaving one with a feeling of perfect achievement.

Spanknoebel seemed never to sleep, yet his colour was ruddy, his blue eyes clear. The last truckster coming in at night for a beer or a cup of coffee and a sandwich was greeted by Chris, white-aproned, pink-cheeked, wide awake, swabbing the bar's shining surface with the thirsty cloth, swishing it with the sly rubber-tipped board. "Well, how goes it all the while?" said Chris. The earliest morning trader found Chris in a fresh white apron crackling with starch and ironing. He would swab the bar with a gesture of welcome, of greeting. "Well, how goes it all the while?"

"As Selina entered the long room now there was something heartening, reassuring about Chris's clean white apron, his ruddy colour, the very sweep of his shirt-sleeved arm as it encompassed the bar-slab. From the kitchen at the rear came the sounds of sizzling and frying, and the gracious scent of coffee and of frying pork and potatoes. Already the market men were seated at the tables eating huge and hurried breakfasts: hunks of ham; eggs in pairs; potatoes cut in great cubes; cups of steaming coffee and chunks of bread that they plastered liberally with butter.

Selina approached Chris. His round face loomed out through the smoke like the sun in a fog. "Well, how goes it all the while?" Then he recognized her. *"Um Gottes!*—why, it's Mis' DeJong!" He wiped his great hand on a convenient towel, extended it in sympathy to the widow. "I heerd," he said, "I heerd." His inarticulateness made his words doubly effective.

"I've come in with the load, Mr. Spanknoebel. The boy and I. He's still asleep in the wagon. May I bring him over here to clean him up a little before breakfast?"

"Sure! Sure!" A sudden suspicion struck him. "You ain't slept in the wagon, Mis' DeJong! *Um Gottes!—*"

"Yes. It wasn't bad. The boy slept the night through. I slept, too, quite a little."

"Why you didn't come here! Why———" At the look in Selina's face he knew then. "For nothing you and the boy could sleep here."

"I knew that! That's why."

"Don't talk dumb, Mrs. DeJong. Half the time the rooms is vacant. You and the boy chust as well—twenty cents, then, and pay me when you got it. But any way you don't come in reg'lar with the load, do you? That ain't for womans."

"There's no one to do it for me, except Jan. And he's worse than nobody. Just through September and October. After that, maybe———" Her voice trailed off. It is hard to be hopeful at three in the morning, before breakfast.

She went to the little wash room at the rear, felt better immediately she had washed vigorously, combed her hair. She returned to the wagon to find a panic-stricken Dirk sure of nothing but that he had been deserted by his mother. Fifteen minutes later the two were seated at a table on which was spread what Chris Spanknoebel considered an adequate breakfast. A heartening enough beginning for the day, and a deceptive.

The Haymarket buyers did not want to purchase its vegetables from Selina DeJong. It wasn't used to buying of women, but to selling to them. Pedlers and small grocers swarmed in at four—Greeks, Italians, Jews. They bought shrewdly, craftily, often dishonestly. They sold their wares to the housewives. Their tricks were many. They would change a box of tomatoes while your back was turned; filch a head of cauliflower. There was little system or organization.

Take Luigi. Luigi peddled on the north side. He called his wares through the alleys and side streets of Chicago, adding his raucous voice to the din of an inchoate city. A swarthy face had Luigi, a swift brilliant smile, a crafty eye. The Haymarket called him Loogy. When prices did not please Luigi he pretended not to understand. Then the Haymarket would yell, unde-ceived, "Heh, Loogy, what de mattah! Spika da Engleesh!" They knew him.

Selina had taken the covers off her vegetables. They were revealed crisp, fresh, colourful. But Selina knew they must be sold now, quickly. When the leaves began to wilt, when the edges of the cauliflower heads curled ever so slightly, turned brown and limp, their value decreased by half, even though the heads themselves remained white and firm.

Down the street came the buyers—little black-eyed swarthy men; plump, shirt-sleeved, greasy men; shrewd, tobacco-chewing men in overalls. Stolid red Dutch faces, sunburned. Lean dark foreign faces. Shouting, clatter, turmoil.

"Heh! Get your horse outta here! What the hell!"

"How much for the whole barrel?"

"Got any beans? No, don't want no cauliflower. Beans!"

"Tough!"

"Well, keep 'em. I don't want 'em."

"Quarter for the sack."

"G'wan, them ain't five-pound heads. Bet they don't come four pounds to the head."

"Who says they don't!"

"Gimme five bushels them."

Food for Chicago's millions. In and out of the wagons. Under horses' hoofs. Bare-footed children, baskets on their arms, snatching bits of fallen vegetables from the cobbles. Gutter Annie, a shawl pinned across her pen-dulous breasts, scavengering a potato there, an onion fallen to the street, scraps of fruit and green stuff in the ditch. Big Kate buying carrots, parsley, turnips, beets, all slightly wilted and cheap, which she would tie into bunches with her bit of string and sell to the real grocers for soup greens.

The day broke warm. The sun rose red. It would be a humid September day such as frequently came in the autumn to this lake region. Garden stuff would have to move quickly this morning. Afternoon would find it worthless.

Selina stationed herself by her wagon. She saw the familiar faces of a half dozen or more High Prairie neighbours. These called to her, or came over briefly to her wagon, eyeing her wares with a calculating glance. "How you making out, Mis' DeJong? Well, you got a good load there. Move it along quick this morning. It's going to be hot I betcha." Their tone was kindly, but disapproving, too. Their look said, "No place for a woman. No place for a woman."

The pedlers looked at her bunched bouquets, glanced at her, passed her by. It was not unkindness that prompted them, but a certain shyness, a fear of the unaccustomed. They saw her pale fine face with its great sombre eyes; the slight figure in the decent black dress; the slim brown hands clasped so anxiously together. Her wares were tempting but they passed her by with the instinct that the ignorant have against that which is unusual.

By nine o'clock trading began to fall off. In a panic Selina realized that the sales she had made amounted to little more than two dollars. If she stayed there until noon she might double that, but no more. In desperation she harnessed the horses, threaded her way out of the swarming street, and made for South Water Street farther east. Here were the commission houses. The district was jammed with laden carts and wagons exactly as the Hay-market had been, but trading was done on a different scale. She knew that Pervus had sometimes left his entire load with an established dealer here, to be sold on commission. She remembered the name—Talcott—though she did not know the exact location.

"Where we going now, Mom?" The boy had been almost incredibly patient and good. He had accepted his bewildering new surroundings with the adaptability of childhood. He had revelled richly in Chris Spanknoebel's generous breakfast. He had thought the four dusty artificial palms that graced Chris's back room luxuriantly tropical. He had been fascinated by the kitchen with its long glowing range, its great tables for slicing, paring, cutting. He liked the ruddy cheer of it, the bustle, the mouth-watering smells. At the wagon he had stood sturdily next his mother, had busied himself vastly assisting her in her few pitiful sales; had plucked wilted leaves, brought forward the freshest and crispest vegetables. But now she saw that he was drooping a little as were her wares, with the heat and the absence from accustomed soil. "Where we going now, Mom?"

"To another street, Sobig————"

"Dirk!"

"—Dirk, where there's a man who'll buy all our stuff at once—maybe. Won't that be fine! Then we'll go home. You help mother find his name over the store. Talcott—T-a-l-c-o-double t."

South Water Street was changing with the city's growth. Yankee names they used to be—Flint—Keen—Rusk—Lane. Now you saw Cuneo—Meleges—Garibaldi—Campagna. There it was: William Talcott. Fruits and Vegetables.

William Talcott, standing in the cool doorway of his great deep shed-like store, was the antithesis of the feverish crowded street which he so calmly surveyed. He had dealt for forty years in provender. His was the unruffled demeanour of a man who knows the world must have what he has to sell. Every week-day morning at six his dim shaded cavern of a store was packed with sacks, crates, boxes, barrels from which peeped ruffles and sprigs of green; flashes of scarlet, plum-colour, orange. He bought the best only; sold at high prices. He had known Pervus, and Pervus's father before him, and had adjudged them honest, admirable men. But of their garden truck he had small opinion. The Great Lakes boats brought him choice Michigan peaches and grapes; refrigerator cars brought him the products of California's soil in a day when out-of-season food was a rare luxury. He wore neat pepper-and-salt pants and vest; shirt sleeves a startling white in that blue-shirted overalled world; a massive gold watch chain spanning his middle; square-toed boots; a straw fedora set well back; a pretty good cigar, unlighted, in his mouth. Shrewd blue eyes he had; sparse hair much the colour of his suit. Like a lean laconic god he stood in his doorway niche while toilers offered for his inspection the fruits of the earth.

"Nope. Can't use that lot, Jake. Runty. H'm. Wa-a-al, guess you'd better take them farther up the street, Tunis. Edges look kind of brown. Wilty."

Stewards from the best Chicago hotels of that day—the Sherman House, the Auditorium, the Palmer House, the Wellington, the Stratford—came to Will Talcott for their daily supplies. The grocers who catered to the well-to-do north-side families and those in the neighbourhood of fashionable Prairie Avenue on the south bought of him.

Now, in his doorway, he eyed the spare little figure that appeared before him all in rusty black, with its strained anxious face, its great deep-sunk eyes.

"DeJong, eh? Sorry to hear about your loss, ma'am. Pervus was a fine lad. No great shakes at truck farming, though. His widow, h'm? H'm." Here, he saw, was no dull-witted farm woman; no stolid Dutch woman truckster. He went out to her wagon, tweaked the boy's brown cheek. "Wa-al now, Mis' DeJong, you got a right smart lot of garden stuff here and it looks pretty good. Yessir, pretty good. But you're too late. Ten, pret' near.''

"Oh, no!" cried Selina. "Oh, no! Not too late!" And at the agony in her voice he looked at her sharply.

"Tell you what, mebbe I can move half of 'em along for you. But stuff don't keep this weather. Turns wilty and my trade won't touch it . . . First trip in?"

She wiped her face that was damp and yet cold to the touch. "First—trip in." Suddenly she was finding it absurdly hard to breathe.

He called from the sidewalk to the men within: "George! Ben! Hustle this stuff in. Half of it. The best. Send you check tomorrow, Mis' DeJong. Picked a bad day, didn't you, for your first day?"

"Hot, you mean?"

"Wa-al, hot, yes. But I mean a holiday like this pedlers mostly ain't buying."

"Holiday?"

"You knew it was a Jew holiday, didn't you? Didn't!—Wa-al, my sakes! Worst day in the year. Jew pedlers all at church to-day and all the others not pedlers bought in Saturday for two days. Chicken men down the street got empty coops and will have till to-morrow, Yessir. Biggest chicken eaters, Jews are, in the world . . . H'm . . . Better just drive along home and just dump the rest that stuff, my good woman."

One hand on the seat she prepared to climb up again—did step to the hub. You saw her shabby, absurd side-boots that were so much too big for the slim little feet. "If you're just buying my stuff because you're sorry for ———" The Peake pride.

"Don't do business that way. Can't afford to, ma'am. My da'ter she's studying to be a singer. In Italy now, Car'line is, and costs like all get-out. Takes all the money I can scrape together, just about."

There was a little colour in Selina's face now. "Italy! Oh, Mr. Talcott!" You'd have thought she had seen it, from her face. She began to thank him, gravely.

"Now, that's all right, Mis' DeJong. I notice your stuff's bunched kind of extry, and all of a size. Fixin' to do that way right along?"

"Yes. I thought—they looked prettier that way—of course vegetables aren't supposed to look pretty, I expect———" she stammered, stopped.

"You fix 'em pretty like that and bring 'em in to me first thing, or send 'em. My trade, they like their stuff kind of special. Yessir."

As she gathered up the reins he stood again in his doorway, cool, remote, his unlighted cigar in his mouth, while hand-trucks rattled past him, barrels and boxes thumped to the sidewalk in front of him, wheels and hoofs and shouts made a great clamour all about him.

"We going home now?" demanded Dirk. "We going home now? I'm hungry."

"Yes, lamb." Two dollars in her pocket. All yesterday's grim toil, and all to-day's, and months of labour behind those two days. Two dollars in the pocket of her black calico petticoat. "We'll get something to eat whcn we drive out a ways. Some milk and bread and cheese."

The sun was very hot. She took the boy's hat off, passed her tender work-calloused hand over the damp hair that clung to his forehead. "It's been fun, hasn't it, she said." "Like an adventure. Look at the kind of people we've met. Mr. Spanknoebel, and Mr. Talcott———"

"And Mabel."

Startled, "And Mabel."

She wanted suddenly to kiss him, knew he would hate it with all the boy and all the Holland Dutch in him, and did not.

She made up her mind to drive east and then south. Pervus had sometimes achieved a late sale to outlying grocers. Jan's face if she came home with half the load still on the wagon! And what of the unpaid bills? She had, perhaps, thirty dollars, all told. She owed four hundred. More than that. There were seedlings that Pervus had bought in April to be paid for at the end of the growing season, in the fall. And now fall was here.

Fear shook her. She told herself she was tired, nervous. That terrible week. And now this. The heat. Soon they'd he home, she and Dirk. How cool and quiet the house would seem. The squares of the kitchen tablecloth. Her own neat bedroom with the black walnut bed and dresser. The sofa in the parlour with the ruffled calico cover. The old chair on the porch with the cane seat sagging where warp and woof had become loosened with much use and stuck out in ragged tufts. It seemed years since she had seen all this. The comfort of it, the peace of it. Safe, desirable, suddenly dear. No work for a woman, this. Well, perhaps they were right.

Down Wabash Avenue, with the L trains thundering overhead and her horses, frightened and uneasy with the unaccustomed roar and clangour of traffic, stepping high and swerving, stiffly grotesque and angular in their movements. A dowdy farm woman and a sunburned boy in a rickety vegetable wagon absurdly out of place in this canyon of cobblestones, shops, street cars, drays, carriages, bicycles, pedestrians. It was terribly hot.

The boy's eyes popped with excitement and bewilderment.

"Pretty soon," Selina said. The muscles showed white beneath the skin of her jaw. "Pretty soon. Prairie Avenue. Great big houses, and lawns, all quiet." She even managed a smile.

"I like it better home."

Prairie Avenue at last, turning in at Sixteenth Street. It was like calm after a storm. Selina felt battered, spent.

There were groceries near Eighteenth, and at the other cross-streets— Twenty-second, Twenty-sixth, Thirty-first, Thirty-fifth. They were passing the great stone houses of Prairie Avenue of the '90s. Turrets and towers, cornices and cupolas, humpbacked conservatories, porte-cochères, bow windows—here lived Chicago's rich that had made their riches in pork and wheat and dry goods; the selling of necessities to a city that clamoured for them.

"Just like me," Selina thought, humorously. Then another thought came to her. Her vegetables, canvas covered, were fresher than those in the nearby markets. Why not try to sell some of them here, in these big houses? In an hour she might earn a few dollars this way at retail prices slightly less than those asked by the grocers of the neighbourhood.

She stopped her wagon in the middle of the block on Twenty-fourth Street. Agilely she stepped down the wheel, gave the reins to Dirk. The horses were no more minded to run than the wooden steeds on a carrousel. She filled a large market basket with the finest and freshest of her stock and with this on her arm looked up a moment at the house in front of which she had stopped. It was a four-story brownstone, with a hideous high stoop. Beneath the steps were a little vestibule and a door that was the tradesmen's entrance. The kitchen entrance, she knew, was by way of the alley at the back, but this she would not take. Across the sidewalk, down a little flight of stone steps, into the vestibule under the porch. She looked at the bell—a brass knob. You pulled it out, shoved it in, and there sounded a jangling down the dim hallway beyond. Simple enough Her hand was on the bell. "Pull it!" said the desperate Selina. "I can't! I can't!" cried all the prim dim Vermont

Peakes, in chorus. "All right. Starve to death and let them take the farm and Dirk, then."

At that she pulled the knob hard. Jangle went the bell in the hall. Again. Again.

Footsteps up the hall. The door opened to disclose a large woman, high cheek-boned, in a work apron; a cook, apparently.

"Good morning," said Selina. "Would you like some fresh country vegetables?"

"No." She half shut the door, opening it again to ask, "Got any fresh eggs or butter?" At Selina's negative she closed the door, bolted it. Selina, standing there, basket on arm, could hear her heavy tread down the passageway toward the kitchen. Well, that was all right. Nothing so terrible about that, Selina told herself. Simply hadn't wanted any vegetables. The next house. The next house, and the next, and the next. Up one side of the street, and down the other. Four times she refilled her basket. At one house she sold a quarter's worth. Fifteen at another. Twenty cents here. Almost fifty there. "Good morning," she always said at the door in her clear, distinct way. They stared, usually. But they were curious, too, and did not often shut the door in her face.

"Do you know of a good place?" one kitchen maid said. "This place ain't so good. She only pays me three dollars. You can get four now. Maybe you know a lady wants a good girl."

"No," Selina answered. "No."

At another house the cook had offered her a cup of coffee, noting the white face, the look of weariness. Selina refused it, politely. Twenty-first Street—Twenty-fifth—Twenty-eighth. She had over four dollars in her purse. Dirk was weary now and hungry to the point of tears. "The last house," Selina promised him, "the very last one. After this one we'll go home." She filled her basket again. "We'll have something to eat on the way, and maybe you'll go to sleep with the canvas over you, high, fastened to the seat like a tent. And we'll be home in a jiffy."

The last house was a new gray stone one, already beginning to turn dingy from the smoke of the Illinois Central suburban trains that puffed along the lake front a block to the east. The house had large bow windows, plump and shining. There was a lawn, with statues, and a conservatory in the rear. Real lace curtains at the downstairs windows with plush hangings behind them. A high iron grille ran all about the property giving it an air of aloofness, of security. Selina glanced at this wrought-iron fence. And it seemed to bar her out. There was something forbidding about it—menacing. She was tired, that was it. The last house. She had almost five dollars, earued in the last hour. "Just five minutes," she said to Dirk, trying to make her tone bright, her voice gay. Her arms full of vegetables which she was about to place in the basket at her feet, she heard at her elbow:

"Now, then, where's your license?"

She turned. A policeman at her side. She stared up at him. How enormously tall, she thought; and how red his face. "License?"

"Yeh, you heard me. License. Where's your pedler's license? You got one, I s'pose."

"Why, no. No." She stared at him, still.

His face grew redder. Selina was a little worried about him. She thought, stupidly, that if it grew any redder——

"Well, say, where d'ye think you are, peddlin' without a license! A good mind to run you in. Get along out of here, you and the kid. Leave me ketch you around here again!"

"What's the trouble, Officer?" said a woman's voice. A smart open carriage of the type known as a victoria, with two chestnut horses whose harness shone with metal. Spanking, was the word that came to Selina's mind, which was acting perversely certainly; crazily. A spanking team. The spankers disdainfully faced Selina's comic bony nags which were grazing the close-cropped grass that grew in the neat little lawn-squares between curb and sidewalk. "What's the trouble, Reilly?"

The woman stepped out of the victoria. She wore a black silk Eton suit, very modish, and a black hat with a plume.

"Woman peddling without a license, Mrs. Arnold. You got to watch 'em like a hawk. . . . Get along wid you, then." He put a hand on Selina's shoulder and gave her a gentle push.

There shook Selina from head to foot such a passion, such a storm of outraged sensibilities, as to cause street, victoria, silk-clad woman, horses, and policeman to swim and shiver in a haze before her eyes. The rage of a fastidious woman who had had an alien male hand put upon her. Her face was white. Her eyes glowed black, enormous. She seemed tall, majestic even.

"Take your hand off me!" Her speech was clipped, vibrant. "How dare you touch me! How dare you! Take your hand!—" The blazing eyes in the white mask. He took his hand from her shoulder. The red surged into her face. A tanned weather-beaten toil-worn woman, her abundant hair skewered into a knob and held by a long gray-black hairpin, her full skirt grimed with the mud of the wagon wheel, a pair of old side-boots on her slim feet, a grotesquely battered old felt hat (her husband's) on her head, her arms full of ears of sweet corn, and carrots, and radishes and bunches of beets; a woman with bad teeth, flat breasts—even then Julie had known her by her eyes. And she had stared and then run to her in her silk dress and her plumed hat, crying, "Oh, Selina! My dear! My dear!" with a sob of horror and pity. "My dear!" And had taken Selina, carrots, beets, corn, and radishes in her arms. The vegetables lay scattered all about them on the sidewalk in front of Julie Hempel Arnold's great stone house on Prairie Avenue. But strangely enough it had been Selina who had done the comforting, patting Julie's plump silken shoulder and saying, over and over, soothingly, as to a child, "There, there! It's all right, Julie. It's all right. Don't cry. What's there to cry for! Sh-sh! It's all right."

Julie lifted her head in its modish black plumed hat, wiped her eyes, blew her nose. "Get along with you, do," she said to Reilly, the policeman, using his very words to Selina. "I'm going to report you to Mr. Arnold, see if I don't. And you know what that means."

"Well, now, Mrs. Arnold, ma'am, I was only doing my duty. How cud I know the lady was a friend of yours. Sure, I———" He surveyed Selina, cart, jaded horses, wilted vegetables. "Well, how *cud* I, now, Mrs. Arnold, ma'am!"

"And why not!" demanded Julie with superb unreasonableness, "Why not, I'd like to know. Do get along with you."

He got along, a defeated officer of the law, and a bitter. And now it was Julie who surveyed Selina, cart, Dirk, jaded horses, wilted left-over vegetables. "Selina, whatever in the world! What are you doing with———" She caught sight of Selina's absurd boots then and she began to cry again. At that Selina's overwrought nerves snapped and she began to laugh, hysterically. It frightened Julie, that laughter. "Selina, don't! Come in the house with me. What are you laughing at! Selina!"

With shaking finger Selina was pointing at the vegetables that lay tumbled at her feet. "Do you see that cabbage, Julie? Do you remember how I used to despise Mrs. Tebbitt's because she used to have boiled cabbage on Monday nights?''

"That's nothing to laugh at, is it? Stop laughing this minute, Selina Peake!''

"I'll stop. I've stopped now. I was just laughing at my ignorance. Sweat and blood and health and youth go into every cabbage. Did you know that, Julie? One doesn't despise them as food, knowing that. . . . Come, climb down, Dirk. Here's a lady mother used to know—oh, years and years ago, when she was a girl. Thousands of years ago.''

12

THE BEST THING for Dirk. The best thing for Dirk. It was the phrase that repeated itself over and over in Selina's speech during the days that followed. Julie Arnold was all for taking him into her gray stone house, dressing him like Lord Fauntleroy and sending him to the north-side private school attended by Eugene, her boy, and Pauline, her girl. In this period of bewilderment and fatigue Julie had attempted to take charge of Selina much as she had done a dozen years before at the time of Simeon Peake's dramatic death. And now, as then, she pressed into service her wonder-working father and bounden slave, August Hempel. Her husband she dismissed with affectionate disregard.

"Michael's all right,'' she had said on that day of their first meeting, "if you tell him what's to be done. He'll always do it. But Pa's the one that thinks of things. He's like a general, and Michael's the captain. Well, now, Pa'll be out to-morrow and I'll probably come with him. I've got a committee meeting, but I can easily————''

"You said—did you say your father would be out to-morrow! Out where?''

"To your place. Farm.''

"But why should he? It's a little twenty-five-acre truck farm, and half of it under water a good deal of the time.''

"Pa'll find a use for it, never fear. He won't say much, but he'll think of things. And then everything will be all right.''

"It's miles. Miles. Way out in High Prairie.''

"Well, if you could make it with those horses, Selina, I guess we can with Pa's two grays that hold a record for a mile in three minutes or three miles in a minute, I forget which. Or in the auto, though Pa hates it. Michael is the only one in the family who likes it.''

A species of ugly pride now possessed Selina. "I don't need help. Really I don't, Julie dear. It's never been like to-day. Never before. We were getting on very well, Pervus and I. Then after Pervus's death so suddenly like that I was frightened. Terribly frightened. About Dirk. I wanted him to have everything. Beautiful things. I wanted his life to be beautiful. Life can be so ugly, Julie. You don't know. You don't know.''

"Well, now, that's why I say. We'll be out to-morrow, Pa and I. Dirk's going to have everything beautiful. We'll see to that.''

It was then that Selina had said, "But that's just it. I want to do it myself, for him. I can. I want to give him all these things myself.''

"But that's selfish.''

"I don't mean to be. I just want to do the best thing for Dirk.''

It was shortly after noon that High Prairie, hearing the unaccustomed chug of a motor, rushed to its windows or porches to behold Selina DeJong in her mashed black felt hat and Dirk waving his battered straw wildly, riding up the Halsted road toward the DeJong farm in a bright red automobile that had shattered the nerves of every farmer's team it had met on the way. Of the DeJong team and the DeJong dog Pom, and the DeJong vegetable wagon there was absolutely no sign. High Prairie was rendered unfit for work throughout the next twenty-four hours.

The idea had been Julie's, and Selina had submitted rather than acquiesced, for by now she was too tired to combat anything or any one. If Julie had proposed her entering High Prairie on the back of an elephant with a mahout perched between his ears Selina would have agreed—rather, would have been unable to object.

"It'll get you home in no time," Julie had said, energetically. "You look like a ghost and the boy's half asleep. I'll telephone Pa and he'll have one of the men from the barns drive your team out so it'll be there by six. Just you leave it all to me. Haven't you ever ridden in one! Why, there's nothing to be scared of. I like the horses best, myself. I'm like Pa. He says if you use horses you get there."

Dirk had accepted the new conveyance with the adaptability of childhood, had even predicted, grandly, "I'm going to have one when I grow up that'll go faster 'n this, even."

"Oh, you wouldn't want to go faster than this, Dirk," Selina had protested breathlessly as they chugged along at the alarming rate of almost fifteen miles an hour.

Jan Steen had been rendered speechless. Until the actual arrival of the team and wagon at six he counted them as mysteriously lost and DeJong's widow clearly gone mad. August Hempel's arrival next day with Julie seated beside him in the light spider-phaeton drawn by two slim wild-eyed quivering grays made little tumult in Jan's stunned mind by now incapable of absorbing any fresh surprises.

In the twelve years' transition from butcher to packer Aug Hempel had taken on a certain authority and distinction. Now, at fifty-five, his hair was gray, relieving the too-ruddy colour of his face. He talked almost without an accent; used the idiomatic American speech he heard about the yards, where the Hempel packing plant was situated. Only his d's were likely to sound like t's. The letter j had a slightly ch sound. In the last few years he had grown very deaf in one ear, so that when you spoke to him he looked at you intently. This had given him a reputation for keenness and great character insight, when it was merely the protective trick of a man who does not want to confess that he is hard of hearing. He wore square-toed shoes with soft tips and square-cut gray clothes and a large gray hat with a chronically inadequate sweat-band. The square-cut boots were expensive, and the square-cut gray clothes and the large gray hat, but in them he always gave the effect of being dressed in the discarded garments of a much larger man.

Selina's domain he surveyed with a keen and comprehensive eye.

"You want to sell?"

"No."

"That's good." (It was nearly goot as he said it.) "Few years from now this land will be worth money." He had spent a bare fifteen minutes taking shrewd valuation of the property from fields to barn, from barn to house. "Well, what *do* you want to do, heh, Selina?"

They were seated in the cool and unexpectedly pleasing little parlour, with its old Dutch lustre set gleaming softly in the cabinet, its three rows of books, its air of comfort and usage.

Dirk was in the yard with one of the Van Ruys boys, surveying the grays proprietorially. Jan was rooting in the fields. Selina clasped her hands tightly in her lap—those hands that, from much grubbing in the soil, had taken on something of the look of the gnarled things they tended. The nails were short, discoloured, broken. The palms rough, calloused. The whole story of the last twelve years of Selina's life was written in her two hands.

"I want to stay here, and work the farm, and make it pay. I can. By next spring my asparagus is going to begin to bring in money. I'm not going to grow just the common garden stuff any more—not much, anyway. I'm going to specialize in the fine things—the kind the South Water Street commission men want. I want to drain the low land. Tile it. That land hasn't been used for years. It ought to be rich growing land by now, if once it's properly drained. And I want Dirk to go to school. Good schools. I never want my son to go to the Haymarket. Never. Never."

Julie stirred with a little rustle and click of silk and beads. Her gentle amiability was vaguely alarmed by the iron quality of determination in the other's tone.

"Yes, but what about you, Selina?"

"Me?"

"Yes, of course. You talk as though you didn't count. Your life. Things to make you happy."

"My life doesn't count, except as something for Dirk to use. I'm done with anything else. Oh, I don't mean that I'm discouraged, or disappointed in life, or anything like that. I mean I started out with the wrong idea. I know better now. I'm here to keep Dirk from making the mistakes I made."

Here Aug Hempel, lounging largely in his chair and eyeing Selina intently, turned his gaze absently through the window to where the grays, a living equine statue, stood before the house. His tone was one of meditation, not of argument. "It don't work out that way, seems. About mistakes it's funny. You got to make your own; and not only that, if you try to keep people from making theirs they get mad." He whistled softly through his teeth following this utterance and tapped the chair seat with his finger nails.

"It's beauty!" Selina said then, almost passionately. Aug Hempel and Julie plainly could make nothing of this remark so she went on, eager, explanatory. "I used to think that if you wanted beauty—if you wanted it hard enough and hopefully enough—it came to you. You just waited, and lived your life as best you could, knowing that beauty might be just around the corner. You just waited, and then it came."

"Beauty!" exclaimed Julie, weakly. She stared at Selina in the evident belief that this work-worn haggard woman was bemoaning her lack of personal pulchritude.

"Yes. All the worth-while things in life. All mixed up. Rooms in candlelight. Leisure. Colour. Travel. Books. Music. Pictures. People—all kinds of people. Work that you love. And growth—growth and watching people grow. Feeling very strongly about things and then developing that feeling to—to make something fine come of it." The word self-expression was not in cant use then, and Selina hadn't it to offer them. They would not have known what she meant if she had. She threw out her hands now in a futile gesture. "That's what I mean by beauty. I want Dirk to have it."

Julie blinked and nodded with the wise amiable look of comprehension assumed by one who has understood no single word of what has been said. August Hempel cleared his throat.

"I guess I know what you're driving at Selina, maybe. About Julie I felt just like that. She should have everything fine. I wanted her to have everything. And she did, too. Cried for the moon she had it."

"I never did have it Pa, any such thing!"

"Never cried for it, I know of."

"For pity's sake!" pleaded Julie, the literal, "let's stop talking and do something. My goodness, anybody with a little money can have books and candles and travel around and look at pictures, if that's all. So let's *do* something. Pa, you've probably got it all fixed in your mind long ago. It's time we heard it. Here Selina was one of the most popular girls in Miss Fister's school, and lots of people thought the prettiest. And now just look at her!''

A flicker of the old flame leaped up in Selina. "Flatterer!" she murmured.

Aug Hempel stood up. "If you think giving your whole life to making the boy happy is going to make him happy you ain't so smart as I took you for. You go trying to live somebody's else's life for them."

"I'm not going to live his life for him. I want to show him how to live it so that he'll get full value out of it."

"Keeping him out of the Haymarket if the Haymarket's the natural place for him to be won't do that. How can you tell! Monkeying with what's to be. I'm out at the yards every day, in and out of the cattle pens, talking to the drovers and herders, mixing in with the buyers. I can tell the weight of a hog and what he's worth just by a look at him, and a steer, too. My son-in-law Michael Arnold sits up in the office all day in our plant, dictating letters. His clothes they never stink of the pens like mine do. . . . Now I ain't saying anything against him, Julie. But I bet my grandson Eugene''— he repeated it, stressing the name so that you sensed his dislike of it— "Eugene, if he comes into the business at all when he grows up, won't go within smelling distance of the yards. His office I bet will be in a new office building on, say Madison Street, with a view of the lake. Life! You'll be hoggin' it all yourself and not know it."

"Don't pay any attention to him," Julie interposed. "He goes on like that. Old yards!"

August Hempel bit off the end of a cigar, was about to spit out the speck explosively, thought better of it and tucked it in his vest pocket. "I wouldn't change places with Mike, not————"

"Please don't call him Mike, Pa."

"Michael, then. Not for ten million. And I need ten million right now."

"And I suppose," retorted Selina, spiritedly, "that when your son-in-law Michael Arnold is your age he'll be telling Eugene how he roughed it in an office over at the yards in the old days. These will be the old days."

August Hempel laughed good humouredly. "That can be, Selina. That can be." He chewed his cigar and settled to the business at hand.

"You want to drain and tile. Plant high-grade stuff. You got to have a man on the place that knows what's what, not this Rip Van Winkle we saw in the cabbage field. New horses. A wagon." His eyes narrowed speculatively. Shrewd wrinkles radiated from their corners. "I betcha we'll see the day when you truck farmers will run into town with your stuff in big automobile wagons that will get you there in under an hour. It's bound to come. The horse is doomed, that's chust what." Then, abruptly, "I will get you the horses, a bargain, at the yards." He took out a long flat check book. He began writing in it with a pen that he took from his pocket—some sort of marvellous pen that seemed already filled with ink and that you unscrewed at the top and then screwed at the bottom. He squinted through his cigar smoke, the check book propped on his knee. He tore off the check with a clean rip. "For a starter," he said. He held it out to Selina.

"There now!" exclaimed Julie, in triumphant satisfaction. That was more like it. Doing something.

But Selina did not take the check. She sat very still in her chair, her hands folded. "That isn't the regular way," she said.

August Hempel was screwing the top on his fountain pen again. "Regular way? for what?"

"I'm borrowing this money, not taking it. Oh, yes, I am! I couldn't get along without it. I realize that now, after yesterday. Yesterday! But in five years—seven—I'll pay it back." Then, at a half-uttered protest from Julie, "That's the only way I'll take it. It's for Dirk. But I'm going to earn it—and pay it back. I want a————" she was being enormously businesslike, and unconsciously enjoying it— "a—an I. O. U. A promise to pay you back just as—as soon as I can. That's business, isn't it? And I'll sign it."

"Sure," said Aug Hempel, and unscrewed his fountain pen again. "Sure that's business." Very serious, he scribbled again, busily, on a piece of paper. A year later, when Selina had learned many things, among them that simple and compound interest on money loaned are not mere problems devised to fill Duffy's Arithmetic in her school-teaching days, she went to August Hempel between laughter and tears.

"You didn't say one word about interest, that day. Not a word. What a little fool you must have thought me."

"Between friends," protested August Hempel.

But— "No," Selina insisted. "Interest."

"I guess I better start me a bank pretty soon if you keep on so businesslike."

Ten years later he was actually the controlling power in the Yards & Rangers' Bank. And Selina had that original I. O. U. with its "Paid In Full. Aug Hempel," carefully tucked away in the carved oak chest together with other keepsakes that she foolishly treasured—ridiculous scraps that no one but she would have understood or valued—a small school slate such as little children use (the one on which she had taught Pervus to figure and parse); a dried bunch of trilliums; a bustled and panniered wine-red cashmere chess, absurdly old-fashioned; a letter telling about the Infanta Eulalie of Spain, and signed Julie Hempel Arnold; a pair of men's old side-boots with mud caked on them; a crude sketch, almost obliterated now, done on a torn scrap of brown paper and showing the Haymarket with the wagons vegetable-laden and the men gathered beneath the street-flares, and the patient farm horses—Roelf's childish sketch.

Among this rubbish she rummaged periodically in the years that followed. Indeed, twenty years later Dirk, coming upon her smoothing out the wrinkled yellow creases of the I. O. U. or shaking the camphor-laden folds of the wine-red cashmere, would say, "At it again! What a sentimental generation yours was, Mother. Pressed flowers! They went out with the attic, didn't they? If the house caught fire you'd probably run for the junk in that chest. It isn't worth two cents, the lot of it."

"Perhaps not," Selina said, slowly. "Still, there'd be some money value, I suppose, in an early original signed sketch by Rodin."

"Rodin! You haven't got a————"

"No, but here's one by Pool—Roelf Pool—signed. At a sale in New York last week one of his sketches—not a finished thing at all—just a rough drawing that he'd made of some figures in a group that went into the Dough-boy statue—brought one thous————"

"Oh, well, that—yes. But the rest of the stuff you've got there—funny how people will treasure old stuff like that. Useless stuff. It isn't even beautiful."

"Beautiful," said Selina, and shut the lid of the old chest. "Why, Dirk—Dirk! You don't even know what beauty is. You never will know."

13

IF THOSE VAGUE characteristics called (variously) magnetism, manner, grace, distinction, attractiveness, fascination, go to make up that nebulous quality known as charm; and if the possessor of that quality is accounted fortunate in his equipment for that which the class-day orators style the battle of life, then Dirk DeJong was a lucky lad and life lay promisingly before him. Undoubtedly he had it; and undoubtedly it did. People said that things "came easy" for Dirk. He said so himself, not boastfully, but rather shyly. He was not one to talk a great deal. Perhaps that was one of his most charming qualities. He listened so well. And he was so quietly effortless. He listened while other people talked, his fine head inclined just a little to one side and bent toward you. Intent on what you were saying, and evidently impressed by it. You felt him immensely intelligent, appreciative. It was a gift more valuable than any other social talent he might have possessed. He himself did not know how precious an attribute this was to prove in a later day when to be allowed to finish a sentence was an experience all too rare. Older men especially said he was a smart young feller and would make his mark. This, surprisingly enough, after a conversation to which he had contributed not a word other than "Yes," or "No," or, "Perhaps you're right, sir," in the proper places.

Selina thought constantly of Dirk's future. A thousand other thoughts might be racing through her mind during the day—plans for the farm, for the house—but always, over and above and through all these, like the steady beat of a drum penetrating sharper and more urgent sounds—was the thought of Dirk. He did well enough at high school. Not a brilliant student, nor even a very good one. But good enough. Average. And well liked.

It was during those careless years of Dirk's boyhood between nine and fifteen that Selina changed the DeJong acres from a worn-out and down-at-heel truck farm whose scant products brought a seond-rate price in a second-rate market to a prosperous and blooming vegetable garden whose output was sought a year in advance by the South Water Street commission merchants. DeJong asparagus with firm white thick stalk bases tapering to a rich green streaked with lavender at the tips. DeJong hothouse tomatoes in February, plump, scarlet, juicy. You paid for a pound a sum Pervus had been glad to get for a bushel.

These six or seven years of relentless labour had been no showy success with Selina posing grandly as the New Woman in Business. No, it had been a painful, grubbing, heart-breaking process as is any project that depends on the actual soil for its realization. She drove herself pitilessly. She literally tore a living out of the earth with her two bare hands. Yet there was nothing pitiable about this small energetic woman of thirty-five or forty with her fine soft dark eyes, her clean-cut jaw-line, her shabby decent clothes that were so likely to be spattered with the mud of the road or fields, her exquisite nose with the funny little wrinkle across the bridge when she laughed. Rather, there was something splendid about her; something rich, prophetic. It was the splendour and richness that achievement imparts.

It is doubtful that she ever could have succeeded without the money borrowed from August Hempel; without his shrewd counsel. She told him this, sometimes. He denied it. "Easier, yes. But you would have found a way, Selina. Some way. Julie, no. But you, yes. You are like that. Me, too. Say, plenty fellers that was butchers with me twenty years ago over on North Clark Street are butchers yet, cutting off a steak or a chop. 'Good morning, Mrs. Kruger. What'll it be to-day?' "

The Hempel Packing Company was a vast monster now stretching great arms into Europe, into South America. In some of the yellow journals that had cropped up in the last few years you even saw old Aug himself portrayed in cartoons as an octopus with cold slimy eyes and a hundred writhing reaching tentacles. These bothered Aug a little, though he pretended to laugh at them. "What do they want to go to work and make me out like that for? I sell good meat for all I can get for it. That's business, ain't it?"

Dirk had his tasks on the farm. Selina saw to that. But they were not heavy. He left for school at eight in the morning, driving, for the distance was too great for walking. Often it was dark on his return in the late afternoon. Between these hours Selina had accomplished the work of two men. She had two field-helpers on the place now during the busy season and a woman in the house, the wife of Adam Bras, one of the labourers. Jan Steen, too, still worked about the place in the barn, the sheds, tending the cold-frames and hothouses, doing odd jobs of carpentering. He distrusted Selina's new-fangled methods, glowered at any modern piece of machinery, predicted dire things when Selina bought the twenty acres that comprised the old Bouts place adjoining the DeJong farm.

"You bit off more as you can chaw," he told her. "You choke yet. You see."

By the time Dirk returned from school the rough work of the day was over. His food was always hot, appetizing, plentiful. The house was neat, comfortable. Selina had installed a bathroom—one of the two bathrooms in High Prairie. The neighbourhood was still rocking with the shock of this when it was informed by Jan that Selina and Dirk ate with candles lighted on the supper table. High Prairie slapped its thigh and howled with mirth. "Cabbages is beautiful," said old Klaas Pool when he heard this. "Cabbages is beautiful I betcha."

Selina, during the years of the boy's adolescence, had never urged him to a decision about his future. That, she decided, would come. As the farm prospered and the pressure of necessity lifted she tried, in various ingenious ways, to extract from him some unconscious sign of definite preference for this calling, that profession. As in her leanest days she had bought an occasional book at the cost of much-needed shoes for herself so now she bought many of them with money that another woman would have used for luxury or adornments. Years of personal privation had not killed her love of fine soft silken things, mellow colouring, exquisite workmanship. But they had made it impossible for her to covet these things for herself. She loved to see them, to feel them. Could not wear them. Years later, when she could well afford a French hat in one of the Michigan Avenue millinery shops, she would look at the silk and satin trifles blooming in the windows like gay brilliant flowers in a conservatory—and would buy an untrimmed "shape" for $2.95 in Field's basement. The habit of a lifetime is strong. Just once she made herself buy one of these costly silk-and-feather extravagances, going about the purchase deliberately and coldly as a man gets drunk once for the experience. The hat had cost twenty-two dollars. She never had worn it.

Until Dirk was sixteen she had been content to let him develop as naturally as possible, and to absorb impressions unconsciously from the traps she so guilefully left about him. Books on the lives of great men—lives of Lincoln, of Washington, Gladstone, Disraeli, Voltaire. History. Books on painting, charmingly illustrated. Books on architecture; law; medicine, even. She subscribed to two of the best engineering magazines. There was a shed which he was free to use as a workshop, fitted up with all sorts of tools. He did not use it much after the first few weeks. He was pleasantly and mildly interested in all these things; held by none of them. Selina had thought of

Roelf when they were fitting up the workshop. The Pools had heard from
Roelf just once since his flight from the farm. A letter had come from France.
In it was a sum of money for Geertje and Jozina—a small sum to take the
trouble to send all the way from an outlandish country, the well-to-do Pool
household thought. Geertje was married now to Vander Sijde's son Gerrit
and living on a farm out Low Prairie way. Jozina had a crazy idea that she
wanted to go into the city as a nurse. Roelf's small gift of money made little
difference in their day. They never knew the struggle that the impecunious
young Paris art student had had to save it sou by sou. Selina had never heard
from him. But one day years later she had come runinng to Dirk with an
illustrated magazine in her hand.

"Look!" she had cried, and pointed to a picture. He had rarely seen her
so excited, so stirred. The illustration showed a photographic reproduction
of a piece of sculpture—a woman's figure. It was called The Seine. A figure
sinuous, snake-like, graceful, revolting, beautiful, terrible. The face alluring,
insatiable, generous, treacherous, all at once. It was the Seine that fed the
fertile valley land; the Seine that claimed a thousand bloated lifeless floating
Things; the red-eyed hag of 1793; the dimpling coquette of 1650. Beneath
the illustration a line or two—Roelf Pool . . . Salon . . . American . . .
future . . .

"It's Roelf!" Selina had cried. "Roelf. Little Roelf Pool!" Tears in her
eyes. Dirk had been politely interested. But then he had never known him,
really. He had heard his mother speak of him, but———

Selina showed the picture to the Pools, driving over there one evening to
surprise them with it. Mrs. Klaas Pool had been horrified at the picture of
a nude woman's figure; had cried "Og heden!" in disgust, and had seemed
to think that Selina had brought it over in a spirit of spite. Was she going
to show it to the rest of High Prairie!

Selina understood High Prairie folk better now, though not altogether,
even after almost twenty years of living amongst them. A cold people, yet
kindly. Suspicious, yet generous. Distrustful of all change, yet progressing
by sheer force of thrift and unceasing labour. Uminaginative for generations,
only to produce—a Roelf Pool.

She tried now to explain the meaning of the figure Roelf had moulded so
masterfully. "You see, it's supposed to represent the Seine. The River Seine
that flows through Paris into the countryside beyond. The whole history of
Paris—of France—is bound up in the Seine; intertwined with it. Terrible
things, and magnificent things. It flows just beneath the Louvre. You can
see it from the Bastille. On its largest island stands Notre Dame. The Seine
has seen such things, Mrs. Pool!———"

"What *dom* talk!" interrupted the late widow. "A river can't see. Anybody
knows that."

At seventeen Dirk and Selina talked of the year to come. He was going
to a university. But to what university? And what did he want to study?
We-e-ll, hard to say. Kind of a general course, wasn't there? Some languages—little French or something—and political economy, and some literature and maybe history.

"Oh," Selina had said. "Yes. General. Of course, if a person wanted to
be an architect, why, I suppose Cornell would be the place. Or Harvard for
law. Or Boston Tech for engineering, or———"

Oh, yeh, if a fellow wanted any of those things. Good idea, though, to
take a kind of general course until you found out exactly what you wanted
to do. Languages and literature and that kind of thing.

Selina was rather delighted than otherwise. That, she knew, was the way
they did it in England. You sent your son to a university not to cram some

technical course into him, or to railroad him through a book-knowledge of some profession. You sent him so that he might develop in an atmosphere of books, of learning; spending relaxed hours in the companionship of men who taught for the love of teaching; whose informal talks before a study fire were more richly valuable than whole courses of classroom lectures. She had read of these things in English novels. Oxford. Cambridge. Dons. Ivy. Punting. Prints. Mullioned windows. Books. Discussion. Literary clubs.

This was England. An older civilization, of course. But there must be something of that in American universities. And if that was what Dirk wanted she was glad. Glad! A reaching after true beauty.

You heard such wonderful things about Midwest University, in Chicago. On the south side. It was new, yes. But those Gothic buildings gave an effect, somehow, of age and permanence (the smoke and cinders from the Illinois Central suburban trains were largely responsible for that, as well as the soft coal from a thousand neighbouring chimneys). And there actually was ivy. Undeniable ivy, and mullioned windows.

Dirk had suggested it, not she. The entrance requirements were quite mild. Harvard? Yale? Oh, those fellows all had wads of money. Eugene Arnold had his own car at New Haven.

In that case, they decided, Midwest University, in Chicago, on the south side near the lake, would do splendidly. For a general course, sort of. The world lay ahead of Dirk. It was like the childhood game of counting buttons.

> Rich man, poor man, beggar-man, thief,
> Doctor, lawyer, merchant, chief.

Together they counted Dirk's mental buttons but it never came out twice the same. It depended on the suit you happened to be wearing, of course. Eugene Arnold was going to take law at Yale. He said it would be necessary if he was going into the business. He didn't put it just that way, when talking to Dirk. He said the damned old hog business. Pauline (she insisted that they call her Paula now) was at a girls' school up the Hudson—one of those schools that never advertise even in the front of the thirty-five-cent magazines.

So, at eighteen, it had been Midwest University for Dirk. It was a much more economical plan than would have resulted from the choice of an eastern college. High Prairie heard that Dirk DeJong was going away to college. A neighbour's son said, "Going to Wisconsin? Agricultural course there?"

"My gosh no!" Dirk had answered. He told this to Selina, laughing. But she had not laughed.

"I'd like to take that course myself, if you must know. They say it's wonderful." She looked at him, suddenly. "Dirk, you wouldn't like to take it, would you? To go to Madison, I mean. Is that what you'd like?"

He stared. "Me! No! . . . Unless you want me to, Mother. Then I would, gladly. I hate your working like this, on the farm, while I go off to school. It makes me feel kind of rotten, having my mother working for me. The other fellows——"

"I'm doing the work I'm interested in, for the person I love best in the world. I'd be lost—unhappy—without the farm. If the city creeps up on me here, as they predict it will, I don't know what I shall do."

But Dirk had a prediction of his own to make. "Chicago'll never grow this way, with all those steel mills and hunkies to the south of us. The north side is going to be the place to live. It is already."

"The place for whom?"

"For the people with money."

She smiled then so that you saw the funny little wrinkle across her nose. "Well, then the south section of Chicago is going to be all right for us yet a while."

"Just you wait till I'm successful. Then there'll be no more working for you."

"What do you mean by 'successful', Sobig?" She had not called him that in years. But now the old nickname came to her tongue perhaps because they were speaking of his future, his success. "What do you mean by 'successful', Sobig?"

"Rich. Lots of money."

"Oh, no, Dirk! No! That's not success. Roelf—the thing Roelf does— that's success."

"Oh, well, if you have money enough you can buy the things he makes, and have 'em. That's almost as good, isn't it?"

Midwest University had sprung up almost literally overnight on the property that had been the site of the Midway Plaisance during the World's Fair in Chicago in '93. One man's millions had been the magic wand that, waved over a bare stretch of prairie land, had produced a seat of learning. The university guide book spoke of him reverently as the Founder, capitalizing the word as one does the Deity. The student body spoke of him with somewhat less veneration. They called him Coal-Oil Johnny. He had already given thirty millions to the university and still the insatiable maw of this institute of learning yawned for more. When oil went up a fraction of a cent they said, "Guess Coal-Oil Johnny's fixing to feed us another million."

Dirk commenced his studies at Midwest University in the autumn of 1909. His first year was none too agreeable, as is usually the case in first years. He got on well, though. A large proportion of the men students were taking law, which accounts for the great number of real-estate salesmen and insurance agents now doing business in and about Chicago. Before the end of the first semester he was popular. He was a natural-born floor committeeman and badges bloomed in his buttonhole. Merely by donning a ready-made dress suit he could give it a made-to-order air. He had great natural charm of manner. The men liked him, and the girls, too. He learned to say, "Got Pol Econ at ten," which meant that he took Political Economy at that hour; and "I'd like to cut Psyk," meant that he was not up on his approaching lesson in Applied Psychology. He rarely "cut" a class. He would have felt that this was unfair and disloyal to his mother. Some of his fellow students joked about this faithfulness to his classes. "Person would think you were an Unclassified," they said.

The Unclassifieds were made up, for the most part, of earnest and rather middle-aged students whose education was a delayed blooming. They usually were not enrolled for a full course, or were taking double work feverishly. The Classifieds, on the other hand, were the regularly enrolled students, pretty well of an age (between seventeen and twenty-three) who took their education with a sprinkling of sugar. Of the Unclassified students the university catalogue said:

> Persons at least twenty-one years of age, not seeking a degree, may be admitted through the office of the University Examiner to the courses of instruction offered in the University, as unclassified students. They shall present evidence of successful experience as a teacher or *other valuable educative experience in practical life*. . . . They are ineligible for public appearance . . .

You saw them the Cinderellas and the Smikes of this temple of learning.

The Classifieds and the Unclassifieds rarely mixed. Not age alone, but purpose separated them. The Classifieds, boys and girls, were, for the most part, slim young lads with caps and pipes and sweaters, their talk of football, baseball, girls; slim young girls in sheer shirtwaists with pink ribbons run through the corset covers showing beneath, pleated skirts that switched delightfuly as they strolled across the campus arm in arm, their talk of football games, fudge, clothes, boys. They cut classes whenever possible. The Student Body. Midwest turned them out by the hundreds—almost by the link, one might say, as Aug Hempel's sausage factory turned out its fine plump sausages, each one exactly like the one behind and the one ahead of it. So many hundreds graduated in this year's class. So many more hundreds to be graduated in next year's class. Occasionally an unruly sausage burst its skin and was discarded. They attended a university because their parents—thrifty shop-keepers, manufacturers, merchants, or professional men and their good wives—wanted their children to have an education. Were ambitious for them. "I couldn't have it myself, and alway regretted it. Now I want my boy (or girl) to have a good education that'll fit 'em for the battle of life. This is an age of specialization, let me tell you."

Football, fudge, I-said-to-Jim, I-said-to-Bessie.

The Unclassifieds would no more have deliberately cut a class than they would have thrown their sparse weekly budget-allowance into the gutter. If it had been physically possible they would have attended two classes at once, listened to two lectures, prepared two papers simultaneously. Drab and earnest women between thirty and forty-eight, their hair not an ornament but something to be pinned up quickly out of the way, their clothes a covering, their shoes not even smartly "sensible," but just shoes, scuffed, patched, utilitarian. The men were serious, shabby, often spectacled; dandruff on their coat collars; their lined, anxious faces in curious contrast to the fresh, boyish, care-free countenances of the Classifieds. They said, carefully, almost sonorously, "Political Economy. Applied Psychology." Most of them had worked ten years, fifteen years for this deferred schooling. This one had had to support a mother; that one a family of younger brothers and sisters. This plump woman of thirty-nine, with the jolly kindly face, had had a paralyzed father. Another had known merely poverty, grinding, sordid poverty, with fifteen years of painful penny savings to bring true this gloriously realized dream of a university education. Here was one studying to be a trained Social Service Worker. She had done everything from housework as a servant girl to clerking in a 5- and 10-cent store. She had studied evenings; saved pennies, nickels, dimes, quarters. *Other valuable educative experience in practical life.* They had had it, God knows.

They regarded the university at first with the love-blind eyes of a bridegroom who looks with the passionate tenderness of possession upon his mistress for whom he has worked and waited through the years of his youth. The university was to bring back that vanished youth—and something more. Wisdom. Knowledge. Power. Understanding. They would have died for it— they almost had, what with privation, self-denial, work.

They came with love clasped close in their two hands, an offertory. "Take me!" they cried. "I come with all I have. Devotion, hope, desire to learn, a promise to be a credit to you. I have had experience, bitter-sweet experience. I have known the battle. See, here are my scars. I can bring to your classrooms much that is valuable. I ask only for bread—the bread of knowledge."

And the university gave them a stone.

"Get on to the hat!" said the Classifieds, humorously, crossing the campus. "A fright!"

The professors found them a shade too eager, perhaps; too inquiring; demanding too much. They stayed after class and asked innumerable questions. They bristled with interrogation. They were prone to hold forth in the classroom, "Well, I have found it to be the case in my experience that————"

But the professor preferred to do the lecturing himself. If there was to be any experience related it should come from the teacher's platform, not the student's chair. Besides, this sort of thing interfered with the routine; kept you from covering ground fast enough. The period bell rang, and there you were, halfway through the day's prescribed lesson.

In his first year Dirk made the almost fatal mistake of being rather friendly with one of these Unclassifieds—a female Unclassified. She was in his Pol Econ class and sat next to him. A large, good-humoured, plump girl, about thirty-eight, with a shiny skin which she never powdered and thick hair that exuded a disagreeable odour of oil. She was sympathetic and jolly, but her clothes were a fright, the Classifieds would have told you, and no matter how cold the day there was always a half-moon of stain showing under her armpits. She had a really fine mind, quick, eager, balanced, almost judicial. She knew just which references were valuable, which useless. Just how to go about getting information for next day's class; for the weekly paper to be prepared. Her name was Schwengauer—Mattie Schwengauer. Terrible!

"Here," she would say good-naturedly, to Dirk. "You don't need to read all those. My, no! I'll tell you. You'll get exactly what you want by reading pages 256 to 273 in Blaine's; 549 to 567 in Jaeckel; and the first eleven—no, twelve—pages of Trowbridge's report. That'll give you practically everything you need."

Dirk was grateful. Her notes were always copious, perfect. She never hesitated to let him copy them. They got in the way of walking out of the classroom together, across the campus. She told him something of herself.

"Your people farmers!" Surprised, she looked at his well-cut clothes, his slim, strong, unmarked hands, his smart shoes and cap. "Why, so are mine. Iowa." She pronounced it Ioway. "I lived on the farm all my life till I was twenty-seven. I always wanted to go away to school, but we never had the money and I couldn't come to town to earn because I was the oldest, and Ma was sickly after Emma—that's the youngest—there are nine of us—was born. Ma was anxious I should go and Pa was willing, but it couldn't be. No fault of theirs. One year the summer would be so hot, with no rain hardly from spring till fall, and the corn would just dry up on the stalks, like paper. The next year it would be so wet the seed would rot in the ground. Ma died when I was twenty-six. The kids were all pretty well grown up by that time. Pa married again in a year and I went to Des Moines to work. I stayed there six years but I didn't save much on account of my brother. He was kind of wild. He had come to Des Moines, too, after Pa married. He and Aggie— that's the second wife—didn't get along. I came to Chicago about five years ago. . . . I've done all kinds of work, I guess, except digging in a coal mine. I'd have done that if I'd had to."

She told him all this ingenuously, simply. Dirk felt drawn toward her, sorry for her. His was a nature quick to sympathy. Something she said now stirred him while it bewildered him a little, too.

"You can't have any idea what it means to me to be here . . . All those years! I used to dream about it. Even now it seems to me it can't be true. I'm conscious of my surroundings all the time and yet I can't believe them. You know, like when you are asleep and dream about something beautiful, and then wake up and find it's actually true. I get a thrill out of just being here. 'I'm crossing the campus,' I say to myself, 'I'm a student—a girl student—in Midwest University and now I'm crossing the campus of my university to go to a class.' "

Her face was very greasy and earnest and fine.

"Well, that's great," Dirk replied, weakly. "That's cer'nly great."

He told his mother about her. Usually he went home on Friday nights to stay until Monday morning. His first Monday-morning class was not until ten. Selina was deeply interested and stirred. "Do you think she'd spend some Saturday and Sunday here with us on the farm? She could come with you on Friday and go back Sunday night if she wanted to. Or stay until Monday morning and go back with you. There's the spare room, all quiet and cool. She could do as she liked. I'd give her cream and all the fresh fruit and vegetables she wanted. And Meena would bake one of her fresh cocoanut cakes. I'd have Adam bring a fresh cocoanut from South Water Street."

Mattie came one Friday night. It was the end of October, and Indian summer, the most beautiful time of the year on the Illinois prairie. A mellow golden light seemed to suffuse everything. It was as if the very air were liquid gold, and tonic. The squash and pumpkins next the good brown earth gave back the glow, and the frost-turned leaves of the maples in the sun. About the countryside for miles was the look of bounteousness, of plenty, of prophecy fulfilled as when a beautiful and fertile woman having borne her children and found them good, now sits serene-eyed, gracious, ample-bosomed, satisfied.

Into the face of Mattie Schwengauer there came a certain glory. When she and Selina clasped hands Selina stared at her rather curiously, as though startled. Afterward she said to Dirk, aside, "But I thought you said she was ugly!"

"Well, she is, or—well, isn't she?"

"Look at her!"

Mattie Schwengauer was talking to Meena Bras, the houseworker. She was standing with her hands on her ample hips, her fine head thrown back, her eyes alight, her lips smiling so that you saw her strong square teeth. A new cream separator was the subject of their conversation. Something had amused Mattie. She laughed. It was the laugh of a young girl, care-free, relaxed, at ease.

For two days Matrie did as she pleased, which meant she helped pull vegetables in the garden, milk the cows, saddle the horses; rode them without a saddle in the pasture. She tramped the road. She scuffled through the leaves in the woods, wore a scarlet maple leaf in her hair, slept like one gloriously dead from ten until six; ate prodigiously of cream, fruits, vegetables, eggs, sausage, cake.

"It got so I hated to do all those things on the farm," she said, laughing a little shamefacedly. "I guess it was because I had to. But now it comes back to me and I enjoy it because it's natural to me, I suppose. Anyway, I'm having a grand time, Mrs. DeJong. The grandest time I ever had in my life." Her face was radiant and almost beautiful.

"If you want me to believe that," said Selina, "you'll come again."

But Mattie Schwengauer never did come again.

Early the next week one of the university students approached Dirk. He was a Junior, very influential in his class, and a member of the fraternity to which Dirk was practically pledged. A decidedly desirable frat.

"Say, look here, DeJong, I want to talk to you a minute. Uh, you've got to cut out that girl—Swinegour or whatever her name is—or it's all off with the fellows in the frat."

"What d'you mean! Cut out! What's the matter with her!"

"Matter! She's Unclassified, isn't she! And do you know what the story is? She told it herself as an economy hint to a girl who was working her way through. She bathes with her union suit and white stockings on to save laundry soap. Scrubs 'em on her! 'S the God's truth."

Into Dirk's mind there flashed a picture of this large girl in her tight knitted union suit and her white stockings sitting in a tub half full of water and scrubbing them and herself simultaneously. A comic picture, and a revolting one. Pathetic, too, but he would not admit that.

"Imagine!" the frat brother-to-be was saying. "Well, we can't have a fellow who goes around with a girl like that. You got to cut her out, see! Completely. The fellahs won't stand for it."

Dirk had a mental picture of himself striking a noble attitude and saying, "Won't stand for it, huh! She's worth more than the whole caboodle of you put together. And you can all go to hell!"

Instead he said, vaguely, "Oh. Well. Uh————"

Dirk changed his seat in the classroom, avoided Mattie's eye, shot out of the door the minute class was over. One day he saw her coming toward him on the campus and he sensed that she intended to stop and speak to him—chide him laughingly, perhaps. He quickened his pace, swerved a little to one side, and as he passed lifted his cap and nodded, keeping his eyes straight ahead. Out of the tail of his eye he could see her standing a moment irresolutely in the path.

He got into the fraternity. The fellahs liked him from the first. Selina said once or twice, "Why don't you bring that nice Mattie home with you again some time soon? Such a nice girl—woman, rather. But she seemed so young and care-free while she was here, didn't she? A fine mind, too, that girl. She'll make something of herself. You'll see. Bring her next week, h'm?"

Dirk shuffled, coughed, looked away. "Oh, I dunno. Haven't seen her lately. Guess she's busy with another crowd, or something."

He tried not to think of what he had done, for he was honestly ashamed. Terribly ashamed. So he said to himself, "Oh, what of it!" and hid his shame. A month later Selina again said, "I wish you'd invite Mattie for Thanksgiving dinner. Unless she's going home, which I doubt. We'll have turkey and pumpkin pie and all the rest of it. She'll love it."

"Mattie?" He had actually forgotten her name.

"Yes, of course. Isn't that right? Mattie Schwengauer?"

"Oh, her. Uh—well—I haven't been seeing her lately."

"Oh, Dirk you haven't quarrelled with that nice girl!"

He decided to have it out. "Listen, Mother. There are a lot of different crowds at the U, see? And Mattie doesn't belong to any of 'em. You wouldn't understand, but it's like this. She—she's smart and jolly and everything but she just doesn't belong. Being friends with a girl like that doesn't get you anywhere. Besides, she isn't a girl. She's a middle-aged woman, when you come to think of it."

"Doesn't get you anywhere!" Selina's tone was cool and even. Then, as the boy's gaze did not meet hers: "Why, Dirk DeJong, Mattie Schwengauer is one of my reasons for sending you to a university. She's what I call part of a university education. Just talking to her is learning something valuable. I don't mean that you wouldn't naturally prefer pretty young girls of your own age to go around with, and all. It would be queer if you didn't. But this Mattie—why, she's life. Do you remember that story of when she washed dishes in the kosher restaurant over on Twelfth Street and the proprietor used to rent out dishes and cutlery for Irish and Italian neighbourhood weddings where they had pork and goodness knows what all, and then use them next day in the restaurant again for the kosher customers?''

Yes, Dirk remembered. Selina wrote Mattie, inviting her to the farm for Thanksgiving, and Mattie answered gratefully, declining. "I shall always remember you," she wrote in that letter, "with love.''

14

THROUGHOUT DIRK'S FRESHMAN year there were, for him, no heartening, informal, mellow talks before the wood-fire in the book-lined study of some professor whose wisdom was such a mixture of classic lore and modernism as to be an inspiration to his listeners. Midwest professors delivered their lectures in the classroom as they had been delivering them in the past ten or twenty years and as they would deliver them until death or a trustees' meeting should remove them. The younger professors and instructors in natty gray suits and bright-coloured ties made a point of being unpedantic in the classroom and rather overdid it. They posed as being one of the fellows; would dashingly use a bit of slang to create a laugh from the boys and an adoring titter from the girls. Dirk somehow preferred the pedants to these. When these had to give an informal talk to the men before some university event they would start by saying, "Now listen, fellahs————" At the dances they were not above "rushing" the pretty co-eds.

Two of Dirk's classes were conducted by women professors. They were well on toward middle age, or past it; desiccated women. Only their eyes were alive. Their clothes were of some indefinite dark stuff, brown or drab-gray; their hair lifeless; their hands long, bony, unvital. They had seen classes and classes and classes. A roomful of fresh young faces that appeared briefly only to be replaced by another roomful of fresh young faces like round white pencil marks manipulated momentarily on a slate, only to be sponged off to give way to other round white marks. Of the two women one—the elder—was occasionally likely to flare into sudden life; a flame in the ashes of a burned-out grate. She had humour and a certain caustic wit, qualities that had managed miraculously to survive even the deadly and numbing effects of thirty years in the classroom. A fine mind, and iconoclastic, hampered by the restrictions of a conventional community and the soul of a congenital spinster.

Under the guidance of these Dirk chafed and grew restless. Miss Euphemia Hollingswood had a way of emphasizing every third or fifth syllable, bringing her voice down hard on it, thus:

"In the *con*sideration of *all* the facts in the *case* presented be*fore* us we must *first* review the *his*tory and at*tempt* to analyze the *out*standing————''

He found himself waiting for that emphasis and shrinking from it as from a sledge-hammer blow. It hurt his head.

Miss Lodge droned. She approached a word with a maddening uh-uh-uh-uh. In the uh-uh-uh face of the uh-uh-uh-uh geometrical situation of the uh-uh-uh-uh————

He shifted restlessly in his chair, found his hands clenched into fists, and took refuge in watching the shadow cast by an oak branch outside the window on a patch of sunlight against the blackboard behind her.

During the early spring Dirk and Selina talked things over again, seated before their own fireplace in the High Prairie farmhouse. Selina had had that fireplace built five years before and her love of it amounted to fire-worship.

She had it lighted always on winter evenings and in the spring when the nights were sharp. In Dirk's absence she would sit before it at night long after the rest of the weary household had gone to bed. Old Pom, the mongrel, lay stretched at her feet enjoying such luxury in old age as he had never dreamed of in his bastard youth. High Prairie, driving by from some rare social gathering or making a late trip to market as they sometimes were forced to do, saw the rosy flicker of Mrs. DeJong's fire dancing on the wall and warmed themselves by it even while they resented it.

"A good heater in there and yet anyway she's got to have a fire going in a grate. Always she does something funny like that. I should think she'd be lonesome sitting there like that with her dog only."

They never knew how many guests Selina entertained there before her fire those winter evenings—old friends and new. Sobig was there, the plump earth-grimed baby who rolled and tumbled in the fields while his young mother wiped the sweat from her face to look at him with fond eyes. Dirk DeJong of ten years hence was there. Simeon Peake, dapper, soft-spoken, ironic, in his shiny boots and his hat always a little on one side. Pervus DeJong, a blue-shirted giant with strong tender hands and little fine golden hairs on the backs of them. Fanny Davenport, the actress-idol of her girlhood came back to her, smiling, bowing; and the gorgeous spangled creatures in the tights and bodices of the old Extravaganzas. In strange contrast to these was the patient tireless figure of Maartje Pool standing in the doorway of Roelf's little shed, her arms tucked in her apron for warmth. "You make fun, huh?" she said, wistfully, "you and Roelf. You make fun." And Roelf, the dark vivid boy, misunderstood. Roelf, the genius. He was always one of the company.

Oh, Selina DeJong never was lonely on these winter evenings before her fire.

She and Dirk sat there one fine sharp evening in early April. It was Saturday. Of late Dirk had not always come to the farm for the week-end. Eugene and Paula Arnold had been home for the Easter holidays. Julie Arnold had invited Dirk to the gay parties at the Prairie Avenue house. He had even spent two entire week-ends there. After the brocaded luxury of the Prairie Avenue house his farm bedroom seemed almost startlingly stark and bare. Selina frankly enjoyed Dirk's somewhat fragmentary accounts of these visits; extracted from them as much vicarious pleasure as he had had in the reality—more, probably.

"Now tell me what you had to eat," she would say, sociably, like a child. "What did you have for dinner, for example? Was it grand? Julie tells me they have a butler now. Well! I can't wait till I hear Aug Hempel on the subject."

He would tell her of the grandeurs of the Arnold ménage. She would interrupt and exclaim: "Mayonnaise! On fruit! Oh, I don't believe I'd like *that*. You did! Well, I'll have it for you next week when you come home. I'll get the recipe from Julie."

He didn't think he'd be home next week. One of the fellows he'd met at the Arnolds' had invited him to their place out north, on the lake. He had a boat.

"That'll be lovely!" Selina exclaimed, after an almost unnoticeable moment of silence—silence with panic in it. "I'll try not to fuss and be worried like an old hen every minute of the time I think you're on the water. . . . Now do go on, Sobig. First fruit with mayonnaise, h'm? What kind of soup?"

He was not a naturally talkative person. There was nothing surly about his silence. It was a taciturn streak inherited from his Dutch ancestry. This time, though, he was more voluble than usual. "Paula . . ." came again

and again into his conversation. "Paula . . . Paula . . ." and again
". . . Paula." He did not seem conscious of the repetition, but Selina's
quick ear caught it.

"I haven't seen her," Selina said, "since she went away to school the
first year. She must be—let's see—she's a year older than you are. She's
nineteen going on twenty. Last time I saw her I thought she was a dark
scrawny little thing. Too bad she didn't inherit Julie's lovely gold colouring
and good looks, instead of Eugene, who doesn't need 'em."

"She isn't!" said Dirk, hotly. "She's dark and slim and sort of—uh—
sensuous"—Selina started visibly, and raised her hand quickly to her mouth
to hide a smile— "like Cleopatra. Her eyes are high and kind of slanting—
not squinty I don't mean, but slanting up a little at the corners. Cut out kind
of, so that they look bigger than most people's."

"My eyes used to be considered rather fine," said Selina, mischievously;
but he did not hear.

"She makes all the other girls look sort of blowzy." He was silent a
moment. Selina was silent, too, and it was not a happy silence. Dirk spoke
again, suddenly, as though continuing aloud a train of thought, "—all but
her hands."

Selina made her voice sound natural, not sharply inquisitive. "What's the
matter with her hands, Dirk?"

He pondered a moment, his brows knitted. At last, slowly, "Well, I don't
know. They're brown, and awfully thin and sort of—grabby. I mean it makes
me nervous to watch them. And when the rest of her is cool they're hot
when you touch them."

He looked at his mother's hands that were busy with some sewing. The
stuff on which she was working was a bit of satin ribbon; part of a hood
intended to grace the head of Geertje Pool Vander Sijde's second baby. She
had difficulty in keeping her rough fingers from catching on the soft surface
of the satin. Manual work, water, sun, and wind had tanned those hands,
hardened them, enlarged the knuckles, spread them, roughened them. Yet
how sure they were, and strong, and cool and reliable—and tender. Suddenly, looking at them, Dirk said, "Now your hands. I love your hands,
Mother."

She put down her work hastily, yet quietly, so that the sudden rush of
happy grateful tears in her eyes should not sully the pink satin ribbon. She
was flushed, like a girl. "Do you, Sobig?" she said.

After a moment she took up her sewing again. Her face looked young,
eager, fresh, like the face of the girl who had found cabbages so beautiful
that night when she bounced along the rutty Halsted road with Klaas Pool,
many years ago. It came into her face, that look, when she was happy,
exhilarated, excited. That was why those who loved her and brought that
look into her face thought her beautiful, while those who did not love her
never saw the look and consequently considered her a plain woman.

There was another silence between the two. Then: "Mother, what would
you think of my going East next fall, to take a course in architecture?"

"Would you like that, Dirk?"

"Yes, I think so—yes."

"Then I'd like it better than anything in the world. I—it makes me happy
just to think of it."

"It would—cost an awful lot."

"I'll manage. I'll manage. . . . What made you decide on architecture?"

"I don't know, exactly. The new buildings at the university—Gothic, you
know—are such a contrast to the old. Then Paula and I were talking the
other day. She hates their house on Prairie—terrible old lumpy gray stone

pile, with the black of the I. C. trains all over it. She wants her father to build north—an Italian villa or French château. Something of that sort. So many of her friends are moving to the north shore, away from these hideous south-side and north-side Chicago houses with their stoops, and their bay windows, and their terrible turrets. Ugh!''

"Well, now, do you know," Selina remonstrated mildly, "I like 'em. I suppose I'm wrong, but to me they seem sort of natural and solid and unpretentious, like the clothes that old August Hempel wears, so square-cut and baggy. Those houses look dignified to me, and fitting. They may be ugly—probably are—but anyway they're not ridiculous. They have a certain rugged grandeur. They're Chicago. Those French and Italian gimcracky things they—they're incongruous. It's as if Abraham Lincoln were to appear suddenly in pink satin knee breeches and buckled shoes, and lace ruffles at his wrists.''

Dirk could laugh at that picture. But he protested, too. "But there's no native architecture, so what's to be done! You wouldn't call those smoke-blackened old stone and brick piles with their iron fences and their conservatories and cupolas and gingerbread exactly native, would you?''

"No," Selina admitted, "but those Italian villas and French châteaux in north Chicago suburbs are a good deal like a lace evening gown in the Arizona desert. It wouldn't keep you cool in the daytime, and it wouldn't be warm enough at night. I suppose a native architecture is evolved from building for the local climate and the needs of the community, keeping beauty in mind as you go. We don't need turrets and towers any more than we need drawbridges and moats. It's all right to keep them, I suppose, where they grew up, in a country where the feudal system meant that any day your next-door neighbour might take it into his head to call his gang around him and sneak up to steal your wife and tapestries and gold drinking cups.''

Dirk was interested and amused. Talks with his mother were likely to affect him thus. "What's your idea of a real Chicago house, Mother?''

Selina answered quickly, as if she had thought often about it; as if she would have liked just such a dwelling on the site of the old DeJong farmhouse in which they now were seated so comfortably. "Well, it would need big porches for the hot days and nights so's to catch the prevailing southwest winds from the prairies in the summer—a porch that would be swung clear around to the east, too—or a terrace or another porch east so that if the precious old lake breeze should come up just when you think you're dying of the heat, as it sometimes does, you could catch that, too. It ought to be built—the house, I mean—rather squarish and tight and solid against our cold winters and northeasters. Then sleeping porches, of course. There's a grand American institution for you! England may have its afternoon tea on the terrace, and Spain may have its patio, and France its courtyard, and Italy its pergola, vine-covered; but America's got the sleeping porch—the screened-in open-air sleeping porch, and I shouldn't wonder if the man who first thought of that would get precedence, on Judgment Day, over the men who invented the aeroplane, the talking machine, and the telephone. After all, he had nothing in mind but the health of the human race.'' After which grand period Selina grinned at Dirk, and Dirk grinned at Selina and the two giggled together there by the fireplace, companionably.

"Mother, you're simply wonderful!—only your native Chicago dwelling seems to be mostly porch.''

Selina waved such carping criticism away with a careless hand. "Oh, well, any house that has enough porches, and two or three bathrooms and at least eight closets can be lived in comfortably, no matter what else it has or hasn't got.''

Next day they were more serious. The eastern college and the architectural career seemed to be settled things. Selina was content, happy. Dirk was troubled about the expense. He spoke of it at breakfast next morning (Dirk's breakfast; his mother had had hers hours before and now as he drank his coffee, was sitting with him a moment and glancing at the paper that had come in the rural mail delivery). She had been out in the fields overseeing the transplanting of young tomato seedlings from hotbed to field. She wore an old gray sweater buttoned up tight, for the air was still sharp. On her head was a battered black felt soft hat (an old one of Dirk's) much like the one she had worn to the Haymarket that day ten years ago. Selina's cheeks were faintly pink from her walk across the fields in the brisk morning air.

She sniffed. "That coffee smells wonderful. I think I'll just————" She poured herself a half cup with the air of virtue worn by one who really longs for a whole cup and doesn't take it.

"I've been thinking," he began, "the expense————"

"Pigs," said Selina, serenely.

"Pigs!" He looked around, bewildered; stared at his mother.

"Pigs'll do it," Selina explained, calmly. "I've been wanting to put them in for three or four years. It's August Hempel's idea. Hogs, I should have said."

Again, as before, he echoed, "Hogs!" rather faintly.

"High-bred hogs. They're worth their weight in silver this minute, and will be for years to come. I won't go in for them extensively. Just enough to make an architect out of Mr. Dirk DeJong." Then, at the expression in his face: "Don't look so pained, son. There's nothing revolting about a hog— not my kind, brought up in a pen as sanitary as a tiled bathroom and fed on corn. He's a handsome, impressive-looking animal, the hog, when he isn't treated like one."

He looked dejected. "I'd rather not go to school on—hogs."

She took off the felt hat and tossed it over to the old couch by the window; smoothed her hair back with the flat of her palm. You saw that the soft dark hair was liberally sprinkled with gray now, but the eyes were bright and clear as ever.

"You know, Sobig, this is what they call a paying farm—as vegetable farms go. We're out of debt, the land's in good shape, the crop promises well if we don't have another rainy cold spring like last year's. But no truck garden is going to make its owner rich these days, with labour so high and the market what it is, and the expense of hauling and all. Any truck farmer who comes out even thinks he's come out ahead."

"I know it." Rather miserably.

"Well. I'm not complaining, son. I'm just telling you. I'm having a grand time. When I see the asparagus plantation actually yielding, that I planted ten years ago, I'm as happy as if I'd stumbled on a gold mine. I think, sometimes, of the way your father objected to my planting the first one. April, like this, in the country, with everything coming up green and new in the rich black loam—I can't tell you. And when I know that it goes to market as food—the best kind of food, that keeps people's bodies clean and clear and flexible and strong! I like to think of babies' mothers saying: 'Now eat your spinach, every scrap, or you can't have any dessert! . . . Carrots make your eyes bright. . . . Finish your potato. Potatoes make you strong!' "

Selina laughed, flushed a little.

"Yes, but how about hogs? Do you feel that way about hogs?"

"Certainly!" said Selina, briskly. She pushed toward him a little blue-

and-white platter that lay on the white cloth near her elbow. "Have a bit more bacon, Dirk. One of these nice curly slivers that are so crisp."

"I've finished my breakfast, Mother." He rose.

The following autumn saw him a student of architecture at Cornell. He worked hard, studied even during his vacations. He would come home to the heat and humidity of the Illinois summers and spend hours each day in his own room that he had fitted up with a long work table and a drawing board. His T-square was at hand; two triangles—a 45 and a 60; his compass; a pair of dividers. Selina sometimes stood behind him watching him as he carefully worked on the tracing paper. His contempt for the local architecture was now complete. Especially did he hold forth on the subject of the apartment-houses that were mushrooming on every street in Chicago from Hyde Park on the south to Evanston on the north. Chicago was very elegant in speaking of these; never called them "flats"; always apartments. In front of each of these (there were usually six to a building) was stuck a little glass-enclosed cubicle known as a sun-parlour. In these (sometimes you heard them spoken of, grandly, as solariums) Chicago dwellers took refuge from the leaden skies, the heavy lake atmosphere, the gray mist and fog and smoke that so frequently swathed the city in gloom. They were done in yellow or rose cretonnes. Silk lamp shades glowed therein, and flower-laden boxes. In these frank little boxes Chicago read its paper, sewed, played bridge, even ate its breakfast. It never pulled down the shades.

"Terrible!" Dirk fumed. "Not only are they hideous in themselves, stuck on the front of those houses like three pairs of spectacles; but the lack of decent privacy! They do everything but bathe in 'em. Have they never heard the advice given people who live in glass houses!"

By his junior year he was talking in a large way about the Beaux Arts. But Selina did not laugh at this. "Perhaps," she thought. "Who can tell! After a year or two in an office here, why not another year of study in Paris if he needs it."

Though it was her busiest time on the farm Selina went to Ithaca for his graduation in 1913. He was twenty-two and, she was calmly sure, the best-looking man in his class. Undeniably he was a figure to please the eye; tall, well-built, as his father had been, and blond, too, like his father, except for his eyes. These were brown—not so dark as Selina's, but with some of the soft liquid quality of her glance. They strengthened his face, somehow; gave him an ardent look of which he was not conscious. Women, feeling the ardour of that dark glance turned upon them, were likely to credit him with feelings toward themselves of which he was quite innocent. They did not know that the glance and its effect were mere matters of pigmentation and eye-conformation. Then, too, the gaze of a man who talks little is always more effective than that of one who is loquacious.

Selina, in her black silk dress, and her plain black hat, and her sensible shoes was rather a quaint little figure amongst all those vivacious, bevoiled, and beribboned mammas. But a distinctive little figure, too. Dirk need not be ashamed of her. She eyed the rather paunchy, prosperous, middle-aged fathers and thought, with a pang, how much handsomer Pervus would have been than any of these, if only he could have lived to see this day. Then, involuntarily, she wondered if this day would ever have occurred, had Pervus lived. Chided herself for thinking thus.

When he returned to Chicago, Dirk went into the office of Hollis & Sprague, Architects. He thought himself lucky to work with this firm, for it was doing much to guide Chicago's taste in architecture away from the box car. Already Michigan Boulevard's skyline soared somewhat above the grimly horizontal. But his work there was little more than that of draughtsman, and his weekly stipend could hardly be dignified by the term of salary. But he had large ideas about architecture and he found expression for his suppressed feelings on his week-ends spent with Selina at the farm. "Baroque" was the word with which he dismissed the new Beachside Hotel, north. He said the new Lincoln Park band-stand looked like an igloo. He said that the city council ought to order the Potter Palmer mansion destroyed as a blot on the landscape, and waxed profane on the subject of the east face of the Public Library Building, downtown.

"Never mind," Selina assured him, happily. "It was all thrown up so hastily. Remember that just yesterday, or the day before, Chicago was an Indian fort, with tepees where towers are now, and mud wallows in place of asphalt. Beauty needs time to perfect it. Perhaps we've been waiting all these years for just such youngsters as you. And maybe some day I'll be driving down Michigan Boulevard with a distinguished visitor—Roelf Pool, perhaps. Why not? Let's say Roelf Pool, the famous sculptor. And he'll say, 'Who designed that building—the one that is so strong and yet so light? So gay and graceful, and yet so reticent!' And I'll say, 'Oh, that! That's one of the earlier efforts of my son, Dirk DeJong.' "

But Dirk pulled at his pipe moodily; shook his head. "Oh, you don't know, Mother. It's so damned slow. First thing you know I'll be thirty. And what am I! An office boy—or little more than that—at Hollis's."

During his university years Dirk had seen much of the Arnolds, Eugene and Paula, but it sometimes seemed to Selina that he avoided these meetings—these parties and week-ends. She was content that this should be so, for she guessed that the matter of money held him back. She thought it was well that he should realize the difference now. Eugene had his own car—one of five in the Arnold garage. Paula, too, had hers. She had been one of the first Chicago girls to drive a gas car; had breezed about Chicago's boulevards in one when she had been little more than a child in short skirts. At the wheel she was dexterous, dare-devil, incredibly relaxed. Her fascination for Dirk was strong. Selina knew that, too. In the last year or two he had talked very little of Paula and that, Selina knew, meant that he was hard hit.

Sometimes Paula and Eugene drove out to the farm, making the distance from their new north-shore house to the DeJong place far south in some breath-taking number of minutes. Eugene would appear in rakish cap, loose London coat, knickers, queer brogans with an English look about them, a carefully careless looseness about the hang and fit of his jacket. Paula did not affect sports clothes for herself. She was not the type, she said. Slim, dark, vivacious, she wore slinky clothes—crêpes, chiffons. Her feet were slim in sheer silk stockings and slippers with buckles. Her eyes were languorous, lovely. She worshipped luxury and said so.

"I'll have to marry money," she declared. "Now that they've finished calling poor Grandpa a beef-baron and taken I don't know how many millions away from him, we're practically on the streets."

"You look it!" from Dirk; and there was bitterness beneath his light tone.

"Well, it's true. All this silly muckraking in the past ten years or more. Poor Father! Of course Grand-dad was pur-ty rough, let me tell you. I read some of the accounts of that last indictment—the 1910 one—and I must say I gathered that dear old Aug made Jesse James look like a philanthropist. I should think, at his age, he'd be a little scared. After all, when you're over seventy you're likely to have some doubts and fears about punishment in the next world. But not a grand old pirate like Grandfather. He'll sack and burn and plunder until he goes down with the ship. And it looks to me as if the old boat had a pretty strong list to starboard right now. Father says himself that unless a war breaks, or something, which isn't at all likely, the packing industry is going to spring a leak.''

"Elaborate figure of speech," murmured Eugene. The four of them—Paula, Dirk, Eugene, and Selina—were sitting on the wide screened porch that Selina had had built at the southwest corner of the house. Paula was, of course, in the couch-swing. Occasionally she touched one slim languid foot to the floor and gave indolent impetus to the couch.

"It is, rather, isn't it? Might as well finish it, then. Darling Aug's been the grand old captain right through the vi'age. Dad's never been more than a pretty bum second mate. And as for you, Gene my love, cabin boy would be, y'understand me, big." Eugene had gone into the business a year before.

"What can you expect," retorted Eugene, "of a lad that hates salt pork? And every other kind of pig meat?" He despised the yards and all that went with it.

Selina now got up and walked to the end of the porch. She looked out across the fields, shading her eyes with her hand. "There's Adam coming in with the last load for the day. He'll be driving into town now. Cornelius started an hour ago." The DeJong farm sent two great loads to the city now. Selina was contemplating the purchase of one of the large automobile trucks that would do away with the plodding horses and save hours of time on the trip. She went down the steps now on her way to oversee the loading of Adam Bras's wagon. At the bottom of the steps she turned. "Why can't you two stay to supper? You can quarrel comfortably right through the meal and drive home in the cool of the evening."

"I'll stay," said Paula, "thanks. If you'll have all kinds of vegetables, cooked and uncooked. The cooked ones smothered in cream and oozing butter. And let me go out into the fields and pick 'em myself like Maud Muller or Marie Antoinette or any of those make-believe rustic gals."

In her French-heeled slippers and her filmy silk stockings she went out into the rich black furrows of the fields, Dirk carrying the basket.

"Asparagus," she ordered first. Then, "But where is it? Is *that* it!"

"You dig for it, idiot," said Dirk, stooping, and taking from his basket the queerly curved sharp knife or spud used for cutting the asparagus shoots. "Cut the shoots three or four inches below the surface."

"Oh, let me do it!" She was down on her silken knees in the dirt, ruined a goodly patch of the fine tender shoots, gave it up and sat watching Dirk's expert manipulation of the knife. "Let's have radishes, and corn, and tomatoes and lettuce and peas and artichokes and————"

"Artichokes grow in California, not Illinois." He was more than usually uncommunicative, and noticeably moody.

Paula remarked it. "Why the Othello brow?"

"You didn't mean that rot, did you? about marrying a rich man."

"Of course I meant it. What other sort of man do you think I ought to marry?" He looked at her, silently. She smiled. "Yes, wouldn't I make an ideal bride for a farmer!"

"I'm not a farmer."

"Well, architect then. Your job as draughtsman at Hollis & Sprague's must pay you all of twenty-five a week."

"Thirty-five," said Dirk, grimly. "What's that got to do with it!"

"Not a thing, darling." She stuck out one foot. "These slippers cost thirty."

"I won't be getting thirty-five a week all my life. You've got brains enough to know that. Eugene wouldn't be getting that much if he weren't the son of his father."

"The grandson of his grandfather," Paula corrected him. "And I'm not

so sure he wouldn't. Gene's a born mechanic if they'd just let him work at
it. He's crazy about engines and all that junk. But no—'Millionaire Packer's
Son Learns Business from Bottom Rung of Ladder.' Picture of Gene in
workman's overalls and cap in the Sunday papers. He drives to the office
on Michigan at ten and leaves at four and he doesn't know a steer from a
cow when he sees it.''

"I don't care a damn about Gene. I'm talking about you. You were joking,
weren't you?''

"I wasn't. I'd hate being poor, or even just moderately rich. I'm used to
money—loads of it. I'm twenty-four. And I'm looking around.''

He kicked an innocent beet-top with his boot. "You like me better than
any man you know.''

"Of course I do. Just my luck.''

"Well, then!''

"Well, then, let's take these weggibles in and have 'em cooked in cream,
as ordered.''

She made a pretense of lifting the heavy basket. Dirk snatched it roughly
out of her hand so that she gave a little cry and looked ruefully down at the
red mark on her palm. He caught her by the shoulder—even shook her a
little. "Look here, Paula. Do you mean to tell me you'd marry a man simply
because he happened to have a lot of money!''

"Perhaps not simply because he had a lot of money. But it certainly would
be a factor, among other things. Certainly he would be preferable to a man
who knocked me about the fields as if I were a bag of potatoes.''

"Oh, forgive me. But—listen, Paula—you know I'm—gosh!—— And
there I am stuck in an architect's office and it'll be years before I——''

"Yes, but it'll probably be years before I meet the millions I require, too.
So why bother? And even if I do, you and I can be just as good friends.''

"Oh, shut up. Don't pull that ingénue stuff on me, please. Remember I've
known you since you were ten years old.''

"And you know just how black my heart is, don't you, what? You want,
really, some nice hearty lass who can tell asparagus from peas when she
sees 'em, and who'll offer to race you from here to the kitchen.''

"God forbid!''

Six months later Paula Arnold was married to Theodore A. Storm, a man
of fifty, a friend of her father's, head of so many companies, stockholder in
so many banks, director of so many corporations that even old Aug Hempel
seemed a recluse from business in comparison. She never called him Teddy.
No one ever did. Theodore Storm was a large man—not exactly stout,
perhaps, but flabby. His inches saved him from grossness. He had a large
white serious face, fine thick dark hair, graying at the temples, and he dressed
very well except for a leaning toward rather effeminate ties. He built for
Paula a town house on the Lake Shore Drive in the region known as the
Gold Coast. The house looked like a restrained public library. There was
a country place beyond Lake Forest far out on the north shore, sloping down
to the lake and surrounded by acres and acres of fine woodland, expertly
parked. There were drives, ravines, brooks, bridges, hothouses, stables, a
race-track, gardens, dairies, fountains, bosky paths, keeper's cottage (twice
the size of Selina's farmhouse). Within three years Paula had two children,
a boy and a girl. "There! That's done," she said. Her marriage was a great
mistake and she knew it. For the war, coming in 1914, a few months after
her wedding, sent the Hempel-Arnold interests sky-rocketing. Millions of
pounds of American beef and pork were shipped to Europe. In two years
the Hempel fortune was greater than it ever had been. Paula was up to her
eyes in relief work for Bleeding Belgium. All the Gold Coast was. The

Beautiful Mrs. Theodore A. Storm in her Gift Shop Conducted for the Relief of Bleeding Belgium.

Dirk had not seen her in months. She telephoned him unexpectedly one Friday afternoon in his office at Hollis & Sprague's.

"Come out and spend Saturday and Sunday with us, won't you? We're running away to the country this afternoon. I'm so sick of Bleeding Belgium, you can't imagine. I'm sending the children out this morning. I can't get away so early. I'll call for you in the roadster this afternoon at four and drive you out myself."

"I am going to spend the week-end with Mother. She's expecting me."

"Bring her along."

"She wouldn't come. You know she doesn't enjoy all that velvet-footed servitor stuff."

"Oh, but we live quite simply out there, really. Just sort of rough it. Do come, Dirk. I've got some plans to talk over with you . . . How's the job?"

"Oh, good enough. There's very little building going on, you know."

"Will you come?"

"I don't think I———"

"I'll call for you at four. I'll be at the curb. Don't keep me waiting, will you? The cops fuss so if you park in the Loop after four."

15

"Run along!" said Selina, when he called her on the farm telephone. "It'll do you good. You've been as grumpy as a gander for weeks. How about shirts? And you left one pair of flannel tennis pants out here last fall—clean ones. Won't you need . . ."

In town he lived in a large front room and alcove on the third floor of a handsome old-fashioned three-story-and-basement house in Deming Place. He used the front room as a living room, the alcove as a bedroom. He and Selina had furnished it together, discarding all of the room's original belongings except the bed, a table, and one fat comfortable faded old armchair whose brocade surface hinted a past grandeur. When he had got his books ranged in open shelves along one wall, soft-shaded lamps on table and desk, the place looked more than livable; lived in. During the process of furnishing Selina got into the way of coming into town for a day or two to prowl the auction rooms and the second-hand stores. She had a genius for this sort of thing; hated the spick-and-span varnish and veneer of the new furniture to be got in the regular way.

"Any piece of furniture, I don't care how beautiful it is, has got to be lived with, and kicked about, and rubbed down, and mistreated by servants, and repolished, and knocked around and dusted and sat on or slept in or eaten off of before it develops its real character," Selina said. "A good deal like human beings. I'd rather have my old maple table, mellow with age and rubbing, that Pervus's father put together himself by hand seventy years ago, than all the mahogany library slabs on Wabash Avenue."

She enjoyed these rare trips into town; made a holiday of them. Dirk would take her to the theatre and she would sit entranced. Her feeling for this form of entertainment was as fresh and eager as it had been in the days of the Daly Stock Company when she, a little girl, had been seated in the parquet with her father, Simeon Peake. Strangely enough, considering the lack of what the world calls romance and adventure in her life, she did not like the motion pictures. "All the difference in the world," she would say, "between the movies and the thrill I get out of a play at the theatre. My, yes! Like fooling with paper dolls when you could be playing with a real live baby."

She developed a mania for nosing into strange corners of the huge sprawling city; seemed to discover a fresh wonder on each visit. In a short time she was more familiar with Chicago than was Dirk—for that matter, than old Aug Hempel who had lived in it for over half a century but who never had gone far afield in his pendulum path between the yards and his house, his house and the yards.

The things that excited her about Chicago did not seem to interest Dirk at all. Sometimes she took a vacant room for a day or two in Dirk's boarding house. "What do you think!" she would say to him, breathlessly, when he returned from the office in the evening. "I've been way over on the northwest side. It's another world. It's—it's Poland. Cathedrals and shops and men sitting in restaurants all day long reading papers and drinking coffee and playing dominoes or something like it. And what do you think I found out! Chicago's got the second largest Polish population of any city in the world. In the *world!*

"Yeh?" Dirk would reply, absently.

There was nothing absent-minded about his tone this afternoon as he talked to his mother on the telephone. "Sure you don't mind? Then I'll be out next Saturday. Or I may run out in the middle of the week to stay over night . . . Are you all right?"

"I'm fine. Be sure and remember all about Paula's new house so's you can tell me about it. Julie says it's like the kind you read of in the novels. She says old Aug saw it just once and now won't go near it even to visit his grandchildren."

The day was marvellously mild for March in Chicago. Spring, usually so coy in this region, had flung herself at them head first. As the massive revolving door of Dirk's office building fanned him into the street he saw Paula in her long low sporting roadster at the curb. She was dressed in black. All feminine fashionable and middle-class Chicago was dressed in black. All feminine fashionable and middle-class America was dressed in black. Two years of war had robbed Paris of its husbands, brothers, sons. All Paris walked in black. America, untouched, gayly borrowed the smart habiliments of mourning and now Michigan Boulevard and Fifth Avenue walked demurely in the gloom of crêpe and chiffon; black hats, black gloves, black slippers. Only black was "good" this year.

Paula did not wear black well. She was a shade too sallow for these sombre swathings even though relieved by a pearl strand of exquisite colour, flawlessly matched; and a new sly face-powder. Paula smiled up at him, patted the leather seat beside her with one hand that was absurdly thick-fingered in its fur-lined glove.

"It's cold driving. Button up tight. Where'll we stop for your bag? Are you still in Deming Place?"

He was still in Deming Place. He climbed into the seat beside her—a feat for the young and nimble. Theodore Storm never tried to double his bulk into the jack-knife position necessary to riding in his wife's roadster. The car was built for speed, not comfort. One sat flat with the length of one's legs stretched out. Paula's feet, pedalling brake and clutch so expertly, were inadequately clothed in sheer black silk stockings and slim buckled patent-leather slippers.

"You're not dressed warmly enough," her husband would have said. "Those shoes are idiotic for driving." And he would have been right.

Dirk said nothing.

Her manipulation of the wheel was witchcraft. The roadster slid in and out of traffic like a fluid thing, an enamel stream, silent as a swift current in a river. "Can't let her out here," said Paula. "Wait till we get past Lincoln Park. Do you suppose they'll ever really get rid of this terrible Rush Street bridge?" When his house was reached, "I'm coming up," she said. "I suppose you haven't any tea?"

"Gosh, no! What do you think I am! A young man in an English novel!"

"Now, don't be provincial and Chicago-ish, Dirk." They climbed the three flights of stairs. She looked about. Her glance was not disapproving. "This isn't so bad. Who did it? She did! Very nice. But of course you ought to have your own smart little apartment, with a Jap to do you up. To do that for you, for example."

"Yes," grimly. He was packing his bag—not throwing clothes into it, but folding them deftly, neatly, as the son of a wise mother packs. "My salary'd just about keep him in white linen housecoats."

She was walking about the living room, picking up a book, putting it down, fingering an ash tray, gazing out of the window, examining a photograph, smoking a cigarette from the box on his table. Restless, nervously alive, catlike. "I'm going to send you some things for your room, Dirk."

"For God's sake don't!"

"Why not?"

"Two kinds of women in the world. I learned that at college. Those who send men things for their rooms and those that don't."

"You're very rude."

"You asked me. There! I'm all set." He snapped the lock of his bag. "I'm sorry I can't give you anything. I haven't a thing. Not even a glass of wine and a—what is it they say in books?—oh, yeh—a biscuit."

In the roadster again they slid smoothly out along the drive, along Sheridan Road, swung sharply around the cemetery curve into Evanston, past the smug middle-class suburban neatness of Wilmette and Winnetka. She negotiated expertly the nerveracking curves of the Hubbard Woods hills, then maintained a fierce and steady speed for the remainder of the drive.

"We call the place Stormwood," Paula told him. "And nobody outside the dear family knows how fitting that is. Don't scowl. I'm not going to tell you my marital woes. And don't you say I asked for it. . . . How's the job?"

"Rotten."

"You don't like it? The work?"

"I like it well enough, only—well, you see we leave the university architectural course thinking we're all going to be Stanford Whites or Cass Gilberts, tossing off a Woolworth building and making ourselves famous overnight. I've spent all yesterday and to-day planning how to work in space for toilets on every floor of the new office building, six stories high and shaped like a drygoods box, that's going up on the corner of Milwaukee Avenue and Ashland, west."

"And ten years from now?"

"Ten years from now maybe they'll let me do the plans for the drygoods box all alone."

"Why don't you drop it!"

He was startled. "Drop it! How do you mean?"

"Chuck it. Do something that will bring you quick results. This isn't an age of waiting. Suppose, twenty years from now, you do plan a grand Gothic office building to grace this new and glorified Michigan Boulevard they're always shouting about! You'll be a middle-aged man living in a middle-class house in a middle-class suburb with a middle-class wife."

"Maybe"—slightly nettled. "And maybe I'll be the Sir Christopher Wren of Chicago."

"Who's he?"

"Good G———, how often have you been in London?"

"Three times."

"Next time you find yourself there you might cast your eye over a very nice little structure called St. Paul's Cathedral. I've never seen it but it has been very well spoken of."

They turned in at the gates of Stormwood. Though the trees and bushes were gaunt and bare the grass already showed stretches of vivid green. In the fading light one caught glimpses through the shrubbery of the lake beyond. It was a dazzling sapphire blue in the sunset. A final turn of the drive. An avenue of trees. A house, massive, pillared, porticoed. The door opened as they drew up at the entrance. A maid in cap and apron stood in the doorway. A man appeared at the side of the car, coming seemingly from nowhere, greeted Paula civilly and drove the car off. The glow of an open fire in the hall welcomed them. "He'll bring up your bag," said Paula. "How're the babies, Anna? Has Mr. Storm got here?"

"He telephoned, Mrs. Storm. He says he won't be out till late—maybe ten or after. Anyway, you're not to wait dinner."

Paula, from being the limp, expert, fearless driver of the high-powered roadster was now suddenly very much the mistress of the house, quietly observant, giving an order with a lift of the eyebrow or a nod of the head. Would Dirk like to go to his room at once? Perhaps he'd like to look at the babies before they went to sleep for the night, though the nurse would probably throw him out. One of those stern British females. Dinner at seven-thirty. He needn't dress. Just as he liked. Everything was very informal here. They roughed it. (Dirk had counted thirteen servants by noon next day and hadn't been near the kitchen, laundry, or dairy.)

His room, when he reached it, he thought pretty awful. A great square chamber with narrow leaded windows, deep-set, on either side. From one he could get a glimpse of the lake, but only a glimpse. Evidently the family bedrooms were the lake rooms. In the DeJong code and class the guest had the best but evidently among these moneyed ones the family had the best and the guest was made comfortable, but was not pampered. It was a new angle for Dirk. He thought it startling but rather sensible. His bag had been brought up, unpacked, and stowed away in a closet before he reached his room. "Have to tell that to Selina," he thought, grinning. He looked about the room, critically. It was done in a style that he vaguely defined as French. It gave him the feeling that he had stumbled accidentally into the chamber of a Récamier and couldn't get out. Rose brocade with gold net and cream lace and rosebuds. "Swell place for a man," he thought, and kicked a footstool—a *fauteuil* he supposed it was called, and was secretly glad that he could pronounce it faultlessly. Long mirrors, silken hangings, cream walls. The bed was lace hung. The coverlet was rose satin, feather-light. He explored his bathroom. It actually was a room, much larger than his alcove bedroom on Deming Place —as large as his own bedroom at home on the farm. The bath was done dazzlingly in blue and white. The tub was enormous and as solid as if the house had been built around it. There were towels and towels and towels in blue and white, ranging in size all the way from tiny embroidered wisps to fuzzy all-enveloping bath towels as big as a carpet.

He was much impressed.

He decided to bathe and change into dinner clothes and was glad of this when he found Paula in black chiffon before the fire in the great beamed room she had called the library. Dirk thought she looked very beautiful in that diaphanous stuff, with the pearls. Her heart-shaped face, with its large eyes that slanted a little at the corners; her long slim throat; her dark hair piled high and away from her little ears. He decided not to mention it.

"You look extremely dangerous," said Paula.

"I am," replied Dirk, "but it's hunger that brings this look of the beast to my usually mild Dutch features. Also, why do you call this the library?" Empty shelves gaped from the wall on all sides. The room was meant to hold hundreds of volumes. Perhaps fifty or sixty in all now leaned limply against each other or lay supine.

Paula laughed. "They do look sort of sparse, don't they? Theodore bought this place, you know, as is. We've books enough in town, of course. But I don't read much out here. And Theodore!—I don't believe he ever in his life read anything but detective stories and the newspapers."

Dirk told himself that Paula had known her husband would not be home until ten and had deliberately planned a tête-à-tête meal. He would not, therefore, confess himself a little nettled when Paula said, "I've asked the Emerys in for dinner; and we'll have a game of bridge afterward. Phil Emery, you know, the Third. He used to have it on his visiting card, like royalty."

The Emerys were drygoods; had been drygoods for sixty years; were accounted Chicago aristocracy; preferred England; rode to hounds in pink coats along Chicago's prim and startled suburban prairies. They had a vast estate on the lake near Stormwood. They arrived a trifle late. Dirk had seen pictures of old Phillip Emery ("Phillip the First," he thought, with an inward grin) and decided, looking at the rather anæmic third edition, that the stock was running a little thin. Mrs. Emery was blonde, statuesque, and unmagnetic. In contrast Paula seemed to glow like a sombre jewel. The dinner was delicious but surprisingly simple; little more than Selina would have given him, Dirk thought, had he come home to the farm this week-end. The talk was desultory and rather dull. And this chap had millions, Dirk said to himself. Millions. No scratching in an architect's office for this lad. Mrs. Emery was interested in the correct pronunciation of Chicago street names.

"It's terrible," she said. "I think there ought to be a Movement for the proper pronunciation. The people ought to be taught; and the children in the schools. They call Goethe Street 'Gerly'; and pronounce all the s's in Des Plaines. Even Illinois they call Illi*noise*.' " She was very much in earnest. Her breast rose and fell. She ate her salad rapidly. Dirk thought that large blondes oughn't to get excited. It made their faces red.

At bridge after dinner Phillip the Third proved to be sufficiently the son of his father to win from Dirk more money than he could conveniently afford to lose. Though Mrs. Phil had much to do with this, as Dirk's partner. Paula played with Emery, a bold shrewd game.

Theodore Storm came in at ten and stood watching them. When the guests had left the three sat before the fire. "Something to drink?" Storm asked Dirk. Dirk refused but Storm mixed a stiff highball for himself, and then another. The whiskey brought no flush to his large white impassive face. He talked almost not at all. Dirk, naturally silent, was loquacious by comparison. But while there was nothing heavy, unvital about Dirk's silence this man's was oppressive, irritating. His paunch, his large white hands, his great white face gave the effect of bleached bloodless bulk. "I don't see how she stands him," Dirk thought. Husband and wife seemed to be on terms of polite friendliness. Storm excused himself and took himself off with a word about being tired, and seeing them in the morning.

After he had gone: "He likes you," said Paula.

"Important," said Dirk, "if true."

"But it is important. He can help you a lot."

"Help me how? I don't want————"

"But I do. I want you to be successful. I want you to be. You can be. You've got it written all over you. In the way you stand, and talk, and don't talk. In the way you look at people. In something in the way you carry yourself. It's what they call force, I suppose. Anyway, you've got it."

"Has your husband got it?"

"Theodore! No! That is————"

"There you are. I've got the force, but he's got the money."

"You can have both." She was leaning forward. Her eyes were bright, enormous. Her hands—those thin dark hot hands—were twisted in her lap. He looked at her quietly. Suddenly there were tears in her eyes. "Don't look at me that way, Dirk." She huddled back in her chair, limp. She looked a little haggard and older, somehow. "My marriage is a mess, of course. You can see that."

"You knew it would be, didn't you?"

"No. Yes. Oh, I don't know. Anyway, what's the difference, now? I'm not trying to be what they call an Influence in your life. I'm just fond of you—you know that—and I want you to be great and successful. It's maternal, I suppose."

"I should think two babies would satisfy that urge."

"Oh, I can't get excited about two pink healthy lumps of babies. I love them and all that, but all they need is to have a bottle stuffed into their mouths at proper intervals and to be bathed, and dressed and aired and slept. It's a mechanical routine and about as exciting as a treadmill. I can't go round being maternal and beating my breast over two nice firm lumps of flesh."

"Just what do you want me to do, Paula?"

She was eager again, vitally concerned in him. "It's all so ridiculous. All these men whose incomes are thirty—forty—sixty—a hundred thousand a year usually haven't any qualities, really, that the five-thousand-a-year man hasn't. The doctor who sent Theodore a bill for four thousand dollars when each of my babies was born didn't do a thing that a country doctor with a Ford wouldn't do. But he knew he could get it and he asked it. Somebody has to get the fifty-thousand-dollar salaries—some advertising man, or bond salesman or—why, look at Phil Emery! He probably couldn't sell a yard of pink ribbon to a schoolgirl if he had to. Look at Theodore! He just sits and blinks and says nothing. But when the time comes he doubles up his fat white fist and mumbles, 'Ten million,' or 'Fifteen million,' and that settles it."

Dirk laughed to hide his own little mounting sensation of excitement. "It isn't quite as simple as that, I imagine. There's more to it than meets the eye."

"There isn't! I tell you I know the whole crowd of them. I've been brought up with this moneyed pack all my life, haven't I? Pork packers and wheat grabbers and pedlers of gas and electric light and drygoods. Grandfather's the only one of the crowd that I respect. He has stayed the same. They can't fool him. He knows he just happened to go into wholesale beef and pork when wholesale beef and pork was a new game in Chicago. Now look at him!"

"Still, you will admit there's something in knowing when," he argued.

Paula stood up. "If you don't know I'll tell you. Now is when. I've got Grandfather and Dad and Theodore to work with. You can go on being an architect if you want to. It's a fine enough profession. But unless you're a genius where'll it get you! Go in with them, and Dirk, in five years————"

"What!" They were both standing, facing each other, she tense, eager; he relaxed but stimulated.

"Try it and see what, will you? Will you, Dirk?"

"I don't know, Paula. I should say my mother wouldn't think much of it."

"What does she know! Oh, I don't mean that she isn't a fine, wonderful person. She is. I love her. But success! She thinks success is another acre of asparagus or cabbage; or a new stove in the kitchen now that they've brought gas out as far as High Prairie."

He had a feeling that she possessed him; that her hot eager hands held him though they stood apart and eyed each other almost hostilely.

As he undressed that night in his rose and satin room he thought, "Now what's her game? What's she up to? Be careful, Dirk, old boy." On coming into the room he had gone immediately to the long mirror and had looked at himself carefully, searchingly, not knowing that Paula, in her room, had done the same. He ran a hand over his close-shaved chin, looked at the fit of his dinner coat. He wished he had had it made at Peter Peel's, the English tailor on Michigan Boulevard. But Peel was so damned expensive. Perhaps next time . . .

As he lay in the soft bed with the satin coverlet over him he thought, "Now what's her lit-tle game!"

He awoke at eight, enormously hungry. He wondered, uneasily, just how he was going to get his breakfast. She had said his breakfast would be brought him in his room. He stretched luxuriously, sprang up, turned on his bath water, bathed. When he emerged in dressing gown and slippers his breakfast tray had been brought him mysteriously and its contents lay appetizingly on a little portable table. There were flocks of small covered dishes and a charming individual coffee service. The morning papers, folded and virgin, lay next this. A little note from Paula: "Would you like to take a walk at about half-past nine? Stroll down to the stables. I want to show you my new horse."

The distance from the house to the stables was actually quite a brisk little walk in itself. Paula, in riding clothes, was waiting for him. She looked boyish and young standing beside the sturdy bulk of Pat, the head stableman. She wore tan whipcord breeches, a coat of darker stuff, a little round felt hat whose brim curved away from her face.

She greeted him. "I've been out two hours. Had my ride."

"I hate people who tell you, first thing in the morning, that they've been out two hours."

"If that's the kind of mood you're in we won't show him the horse, will we, Pat?"

Pat thought they would. Pat showed him the new saddle mare as a mother exhibits her latest offspring, tenderly, proudly. "Look at her back," said Pat. "That's the way you tell a horse, sir. By the length of this here line. Lookut it! There's a picture for you, now!"

Paula looked up at Dirk. "You ride, don't you?"

"I used to ride the old nags, bareback, on the farm."

"You'll have to learn. We'll teach him, won't we, Pat?"

Pat surveyed Dirk's lean, flexible figure. "Easy."

"Oh, say!" protested Dirk.

"Then I'll have some one to ride with me. Theodore never rides. He never takes any sort of exercise. Sits in that great fat car of his."

They went into the coach house, a great airy whitewashed place with glittering harness and spurs and bridles like jewels in glass cases. There were ribbons, too, red and yellow and blue in a rack on the wall; and trophy cups.

The coach house gave Dirk a little hopeless feeling. He had never before seen anything like it. In the first place, there were no motors in it. He had forgotten that people rode in anything but motors. A horse on Chicago's boulevards raised a laugh. The sight of a shining brougham with two sleek chestnuts driving down Michigan Avenue would have set that street to staring and sniggering as a Roman chariot drawn by zebras might have done. Yet here was such a brougham, glittering, spotless. Here was a smart cream surrey with a cream-coloured top hung with fringe. There were two-wheeled carts high and slim and chic. A victoria. Two pony carts. One would have thought, seeing this room, that the motor vehicle had never been invented. And towering over all, dwarfing the rest, outglittering them, stood a tally-ho, a sheer piece of wanton insolence. It was in perfect order. Its cushions were immaculate. Its sides shone. Its steps glistened. Dirk, looking up at it, laughed outright. It seemed too splendid, too absurd. With a sudden boyish impulse he swung himself up the three steps that led to the box and perched himself on the fawn cushioned seat. He looked very handsome there. "A coach and four—isn't that what they call it? Got any Roman juggeruauts?"

"Do you want to drive it?" asked Paula. "This afternoon? Do you think you can? Four horses, you know." She laughed up at him, her dark face upturned to his.

Dirk looked down at her. "No." He climbed down. "I suppose that at about the time they drove this hereabouts my father was taking the farm plugs into the Haymarket."

Something had annoyed him, she saw. Would he wait while she changed to walking things? Or perhaps he'd rather drive in the roadster. They walked up to the house together. He wished that she would not consult his wishes so anxiously. It made him sulky, impatient.

She put a hand on his arm. "Dirk, are you annoyed at me for what I said last night?"

"No."

"What did you think when you went to your room last night? Tell me. What did you think?"

"I thought: "She's bored with her husband and she's trying to vamp me. I'll have to be careful.""

Paula laughed delightedly. "That's nice and frank . . . What else?"

"I thought my coat didn't fit very well and I wished I could afford to have Peel make my next one."

"You can," said Paula.

16

AS IT TURNED out, Dirk was spared the necessity of worrying about the fit of his next dinner coat for the following year and a half. His coat, during that period, was a neat olive drab as was that of some millions of young men of his age, or thereabouts. He wore it very well, and with the calm assurance of one who knows that his shoulders are broad, his waist slim, his stomach flat, his flanks lean, and his legs straight. Most of that time he spent at Fort Sheridan, first as an officer in training, then as an officer training others to be officers. He was excellent at this job. Influence put him there and kept him there even after he began to chafe at the restraint. Fort Sheridan is a few miles outside Chicago, north. No smart North Shore dinner was considered complete without at least a major, a colonel, two captains, and a sprinkling of first lieutenants. Their boots shone so delightfully while dancing.

In the last six months of it (though he did not, of course, know that it was to be the last six months) Dirk tried desperately to get to France. He was suddenly sick of the neat job at home; of the dinners; of the smug routine; of the olive-drab motor car that whisked him wherever he wanted to go (he had a captaincy); of making them "snap into it"; of Paula; of his mother, even. Two months before the war's close he succeeded in getting over; but Paris was his headquarters.

Between Dirk and his mother the first rift had appeared.

"If I were a man," Selina said, "I'd make up my mind straight about this war and then I'd do one of two things. I'd go into it the way Jan Steen goes at forking the manure pile—a dirty job that's got to be cleaned up; or I'd refuse to do it altogether if I didn't believe in it as a job for me. I'd fight or I'd be a conscientious objector. There's nothing in between for any one who isn't old or crippled, or sick."

Paula was aghast when she heard this. So was Julie whose wailings had been loud when Eugene had gone into the air service. He was in France now, thoroughly happy. "Do you mean," demanded Paula, "that you actually want Dirk to go over there and be wounded or killed!"

"No. If Dirk were killed my life would stop. I'd go on living, I suppose, but my life would have stopped."

They all were doing some share in the work to be done.

Selina had thought about her own place in this war welter. She had wanted to do canteen work in France but had decided against this as being selfish. "The thing for me to do," she said, "is to go on raising vegetables and hogs as fast as I can." She supplied countless households with free food while their men were gone. She herself worked like a man, taking the place of the able-bodied helper who had been employed on her farm.

Paula was lovely in her Red Cross uniform. She persuaded Dirk to go into the Liberty Bond selling drive and he was unexpectedly effective in his quiet, serious way; most convincing and undeniably thrilling to look at in uniform. Paula's little air of possession had grown until now it enveloped him. She wasn't playing now; was deeply and terribly in love with him.

When, in 1918, Dirk took off his uniform he went into the bond department of the Great Lakes Trust Company in which Theodore Storm had a large interest. He said that the war had disillusioned him. It was a word you often heard uttered as a reason or an excuse for abandoning the normal. "Disillusioned."

"What did you think war was going to do?" said Selina. "Purify! It never has yet."

It was understood, by Selina at least, that Dirk's abandoning of his profession was a temporary thing. Quick as she usually was to arrive at conclusions, she did not realize until too late that this son of hers had definitely deserted building for bonds; that the only structures he would rear were her own castles in Spain. His first two months as a bond salesman netted him more than a year's salary at his old post at Hollis & Sprague's. When he told this to Selina, in triumph, she said, "Yes, but there isn't much fun in it, is there? This selling things on paper? Now architecture, that must be thrilling. Next to writing a play and seeing it acted by real people—seeing it actually come alive before your eyes—architecture must be the next most fun. Putting a building down on paper—little marks here, straight lines there, figures, calculations, blueprints, measurements—and then, suddenly one day, the actual building itself. Steel and stone and brick, with engines throbbing inside it like a heart, and people flowing in and out. Part of a city. A piece of actual beauty conceived by you! Oh, Dirk!'' To see her face then must have given him a pang, it was so alive, so eager.

He found excuses for himself. ''Selling bonds that make that building possible isn't so dull, either.''

But she waved that aside almost contemptuously. ''What nonsense, Dirk. It's like selling seats at the box office of a theatre for the play inside.''

Dirk had made many new friends in the last year and a half. More than that, he had acquired a new manner; an air of quiet authority, of assurance. The profession of architecture was put definitely behind him. There had been no building in all the months of the war; probably would be none in years. Materials were prohibitive, labour exorbitant. He did not say to Selina that he had put the other work from him. But after six months in his new position he knew that he would never go back.

From the start he was a success. Within one year he was so successful that you could hardly distinguish him from a hundred other successful young Chicago business and professional men whose clothes were made at Peel's; who kept their collars miraculously clean in the soot-laden atmosphere of the Loop; whose shoes were bench-made; who lunched at the Noon Club on the roof of the First National Bank where Chicago's millionaires ate corned-beef hash whenever that plebeian dish appeared on the bill of fare. He had had a little thrill out of his first meal at this club whose membership was made up of the ''big men'' of the city's financial circle. Now he could even feel a little flicker of contempt for them. He had known old Aug Hempel, of course, for years, as well as Michael Arnold, and, later, Phillip Emery, Theodore Storm, and others. But he had expected these men to be different.

Paula had said, ''Theodore, why don't you take Dirk up to the Noon Club some day? There are a lot of big men he ought to meet.''

Dirk went in some trepidation. The great grilled elevator, as large as a room, whisked them up to the roof of the fortress of gold. The club lounge furnished his first disappointment. It looked like a Pullman smoker. The chairs were upholstered in black leather or red plush. The woodwork was shiny red imitation mahogany. The carpet was green. There were bright shining brass cuspidors in the hall near the cigar counter. The food was well cooked. Man's food. Nine out of every ten of these men possessed millions. Whenever corned beef and cabbage appeared on the luncheon menu nine out of ten took it. These were not at all the American Big Business Man of the comic papers and of fiction—that yellow, nervous, dyspeptic creature who lunches off milk and pie. They were divided into two definite types. The older men of between fifty and sixty were great high-coloured fellows of full habit. Many of them had had a physician's warning of high blood pressure, hardening arteries, overworked heart, rebellious kidneys. So now they waxed cautious, taking time over their substantial lunches, smoking and talking. Their faces were impassive, their eyes shrewd, hard. Their talk was colloquial and frequently illiterate. They often said ''was'' for ''were.'' ''Was you going to see Baldwin about that South American stuff or is he going to ship it through without?'' Most of them had known little of play in their youth and now they played ponderously and a little sadly and yet eagerly as does one to whom the gift of leisure had come too late. On Saturday afternoon you saw them in imported heather green golf stockings and Scotch tweed suits making for the links or the lake. They ruined their palates and livers with strong cigars, thinking cigarette smoking undignified and pipes common. ''Have a cigar!'' was their greeting, their password, their open sesame. ''Have a cigar.'' Only a few were so rich, so assured as to smoke cheap light panatellas. Old Aug Hempel was one of these. Dirk noticed that when he made one of his rare visits to the Noon Club his entrance was met with a little stir, a deference. He was nearing seventy-five now; was still straight, strong, zestful of life; a magnificent old buccaneer among the pettier crew. His had been the direct and brutal method—swish! swash! and his enemies walked the plank. The younger men eyed him with a certain amusement and respect.

These younger men whose ages ranged from twenty-eight to forty-five were disciples of the new system in business. They were graduates of universities. They had known luxury all their lives. They were the second or third generation. They used the word "psychology." They practised restraint. They knew the power of suggestion. Where old Aug Hempel had flown the black flag they resorted to the periscope. Dirk learned that these men did not talk business during meal time except when they had met definitely for that purpose. They wasted a good deal of time, Dirk thought, and often, when they were supposed to be "in conference" or when their secretaries said primly that they were very busy and not to be disturbed until three, they were dozing off for a comfortable half hour in their private offices. They were the sons or grandsons of those bearded, rugged, and rather terrible old boys who, in 1835 or 1840, had come out of County Limerick or County Kilkenny or out of Scotland or the Rhineland to mould this new country in their strong hairy hands; those hands whose work had made possible the symphony orchestras, the yacht clubs, the golf clubs through which their descendants now found amusement and relaxation.

Dirk listened to the talk of the Noon Club.

"I made it in eighty-six. That isn't so bad for the Tippecanoe course."

". . . boxes are going pretty well but the Metropolitan grabs up all the big ones and the house wants names. Garden doesn't draw the way she used to, even in Chicago. It's the popular subscription that counts."

". . . grabbed the Century out of New York at two-forty-five and got back here in time to try out my new horse in the park. She's a little nervous for city riding but we're opening the house at Lake Forest next week————"

". . . pretty good show but they don't send the original companies here, that's the trouble . . ."

". . . in London. It's a neat shade of green, isn't it? You can't get ties like this over here, I don't know why. Got a dozen last time I was over. Yeh, Plumbridge in Bond Street."

Well, Dirk could talk like that easily enough. He listened quietly, nodded, smiled, agreed or disagreed. He looked about him carefully, appraisingly. Waist lines well kept in; carefully tailored clothes; shrewd wrinkles of experience radiating in fine sprays in the skin around the corners of their eyes. The president of an advertising firm lunching with a banker; a bond salesman talking to a rare book collector; a packer seated at a small table with Horatio Craft, the sculptor.

Two years and Dirk, too, had learned to "grab the Century" in order to save an hour or so of time between Chicago and New York. Peel said it was a pleasure to fit a coat to his broad, flat tapering back, and trousers to his strong sturdy legs. His colour, inherited from his red-cheeked Dutch ancestors brought up in the fresh sea-laden air of the Holland flats, was fine and clear. Sometimes Selina, in pure sensuous delight, passed her gnarled, work-worn hand over his shoulders and down his fine, strong, straight back. He had been abroad twice. He learned to call it "running over to Europe for a few days." It had all come about in a scant two years, as is the theatrical way in which life speeds in America.

Selina was a little bewildered now at this new Dirk whose life was so full without her. Sometimes she did not see him for two weeks, or three. He

sent her gifts which she smoothed and touched delightedly and put away;
fine soft silken things, handmade—which she could not wear. The habit of
years was too strong upon her. Though she had always been a woman of
dainty habits and fastidious tastes the grind of her early married life had left
its indelible mark. Now, as she dressed, you might have seen that her petticoat was likely to be black sateen and her plain, durable corset cover neatly
patched where it had worn under the arms. She employed none of the artifices
of a youth-mad day. Sun and wind and rain and the cold and heat of the
open prairie had wreaked their vengeance on her flouting of them. Her skin
was tanned, weather-beaten; her hair rough and dry. Her eyes, in that frame,
startled you by their unexpectedness, they were so calm, so serene, yet so
alive. They were the beautiful eyes of a wise young girl in the face of a
middle-aged woman. Life was still so fresh to her.

She had almost poignantly few personal belongings. Her bureau drawers
were like a nun's; her brush and comb, a scant stock of plain white underwear. On the bathroom shelf her toothbrush, some vaseline, a box of talcum
powder. None of those aids to artifice with which the elderly woman deludes
herself into thinking that she is hoodwinking the world. She wore well-made
walking oxfords now, with sensible heels—the kind known as Field's special;
plain shirtwaists and neat dark suits, or a blue cloth dress. A middle-aged
woman approaching elderliness; a woman who walked and carried herself
well; who looked at you with a glance that was direct but never hard. That
was all. Yet there was about her something arresting, something compelling.
You felt it.

"I don't see how you do it!" Julie Arnold complained one day as Selina
was paying her one of her rare visits in town. "Your eyes are as bright as
a baby's and mine look like dead oysters." They were up in Julie's dressing
room in the new house on the north side—the new house that was now the
old house. Julie's dressing table was a bewildering thing. Selina DeJong, in
her neat black suit and her plain black hat, sat regarding it and Julie seated
before it, with a grim and lively interest.

"It looks," Selina said, "like Mandel's toilette section, or a hospital op-
erating room just before a major operation." There were great glass jars that
contained meal, white and gold. There were rows and rows of cream pots
holding massage cream, vanishing cream, cleansing cream. There were little
china bowls of scarlet and white and yellowish pastes. A perforated container
spouted a wisp of cotton. You saw toilet waters, perfumes, atomizers, French
soaps, unguents, tubes. It wasn't a dressing table merely, but a laboratory.

"This!" exclaimed Julie. "You ought to see Paula's. Compared to her
toilette ceremony mine is just a splash at the kitchen sink." She rubbed cold
cream now around her eyes with her two forefingers, using a practised
upward stroke.

"It looks fascinating," Selina exclaimed. "Some day I'm going to try it.
There are so many things I'm going to try some day. So many things I've
never done that I'm going to do for the fun of it. Think of it, Julie! I've never
had a manicure! Some day I'm going to have one. I'll tell the girl to paint
my nails a beautiful bright vermilion. And I'll tip her twenty-five cents.
They're so pretty with their bobbed hair and their queer bright eyes. I s'pose
you'll think I'm crazy if I tell you they make me feel young."

Julie was massaging. Her eyes had an absent look. Suddenly: "Listen,
Selina. Dirk and Paula are together too much. People are talking."

"Talking?" The smile faded from Selina's face.

"Goodness knows I'm not strait-laced. You can't be in this day and age.
If I had ever thought I'd live to see the time when——— Well, since the
war of course anything's all right, seems. But Paula has no sense. Everybody

knows she's insane about Dirk. That's all right for Dirk, but how about Paula! She won't go anywhere unless he's invited. Of course Dirk is awfully popular. Goodness knows there are few enough young men like him in Chicago—handsome and successful and polished and all. Most of them dash off East just as soon as they can get their fathers to establish an Eastern branch or something. . . . They're together all the time, everywhere. I asked her if she was going to divorce Storm and she said no, she hadn't enough money of her own and Dirk wasn't earning enough. His salary's thousands, but she's used to millions. Well!"

"They were boy and girl together," Selina interrupted feebly.

"They're not any more. Don't be silly, Selina. You're not as young as that."

No, she was not as young as that. When Dirk next paid one of his rare visits to the farm she called him into her bedroom—the cool, dim shabby bedroom with the old black walnut bed in which she had lain as Pervus DeJong's bride more than thirty years ago. She had on a little knitted jacket over her severe white nightgown. Her abundant hair was neatly braided in two long plaits. She looked somehow girlish there in the dim light, her great soft eyes gazing up at him.

"Dirk, sit down here at the side of my bed the way you used to."

"I'm dead tired, Mother. Twenty-seven holes of golf before I came out."

"I know. You ache all over—a nice kind of ache. I used to feel like that when I'd worked in the fields all day, pulling vegetables, or planting." He was silent. She caught his hand. "You didn't like that. My saying that. I'm sorry. I didn't say it to make you feel bad, dear."

"I know you didn't, Mother."

"Dirk, do you know what that woman who writes the society news in the Sunday *Tribune* called you to-day?"

"No. What? I never read it."

"She said you were one of the *jeunesse dorée*."

Dirk grinned. "Gosh!"

"I remember enough of my French at Miss Fister's school to know that that means gilded youth."

"Me! That's good! I'm not even spangled."

"Dirk!" her voice was low, vibrant. "Dirk, I don't want you to be a gilded youth, I don't care how thick the gilding. Dirk, that isn't what I worked in the sun and cold for. I'm not reproaching you; I didn't mind the work. Forgive me for even mentioning it. But, Dirk, I don't want my son to be known as one of the *jeunesse dorée*. No! Not my son!"

"Now, listen, Mother. That's foolish. If you're going to talk like that. Like a mother in a melodrama whose son's gone wrong. . . . I work like a dog. You know that. You get the wrong angle on things, stuck out here on this little farm. Why don't you come into town and take a little place and sell the farm?"

"Live with you, you mean?" Pure mischievousness.

"Oh, no. You wouldn't like that," hastily. "Besides, I'd never be there. At the office all day, and out somewhere in the evening."

"When do you do your reading, Dirk?"

"Why—uh———"

She sat up in bed, looking down at the thin end of her braid as she twined it round and round her finger. "Dirk, what is this you sell in that mahogany office of yours? I never did get the hang of it."

"Bonds, Mother. You know that perfectly well."

"Bonds." She considered this a moment. "Are they hard to sell? Who buys them?"

"That depends. Everybody buys them—that is . . ."

"I don't. I suppose because whenever I had any money it went back into the farm for implements, or repairs, or seed, or stock, or improvements. That's always the way with a farmer—even on a little truck farm like this." She pondered again a moment. He fidgeted, yawned. "Dirk DeJong—Bond Salesman."

"The way you say it, Mother, it sounds like a low criminal pursuit."

"Dirk, do you know sometimes I actually think that if you had stayed here on the farm————"

"Good God, Mother! What for!"

"Oh, I don't know. Time to dream. Time to—no, I suppose that isn't true any more. I suppose the day is past when the genius came from the farm. Machinery has cut into his dreams. He used to sit for hours on the wagon seat, the reins slack in his hands, while the horses plodded into town. Now he whizzes by in a jitney. Patent binders, ploughs, reapers—he's a mechanic. He hasn't time to dream. I guess if Lincoln had lived to-day he'd have split his rails to the tune of a humming, snarling patent wood cutter, and in the evening he'd have whirled into town to get his books at the public library, and he'd have read them under the glare of the electric light bulb instead of lying flat in front of the flickering wood-fire. . . . Well. . . ."

She lay back, looked up at him. "Dirk, why don't you marry?"

"Why—there's no one I want to marry."

"No one who's free, you mean?"

He stood up. "I mean no one." He stooped and kissed her lightly. Her arms went round him close. Her hand with the thick gold wedding band on it pressed his head to her hard. "Sobig!" He was a baby again.

"You haven't called me that in years." He was laughing.

She reverted to the old game they had played when he was a child. "How big is my son! How big?" She was smiling, but her eyes were sombre.

"So big!" answered Dirk, and measured a very tiny space between thumb and forefinger. "So big."

She faced him, sitting up very straight in bed, the little wool shawl hunched about her shoulders. "Dirk, are you ever going back to architecture? The war is history. It's now or never with you. Pretty soon it will be too late. Are you ever going back to architecture? To your profession?"

A clean amputation. "No, Mother."

She gave an actual gasp, as though icy water had been thrown full in her face. She looked suddenly old, tired. Her shoulders sagged. He stood in the doorway, braced for her reproaches. But when she spoke it was to reproach herself. "Then I'm a failure."

"Oh, what nonsense, Mother. I'm happy. You can't live somebody else's life. You used to tell me, when I was a kid I remember, that life wasn't just an adventure, to be taken as it came, with the hope that something glorious was always hidden just around the corner. You said you had lived that way and it hadn't worked. You said————"

She interrupted him with a little cry. "I know I did. I know I did." Suddenly she raised a warning finger. Her eyes were luminous, prophetic. "Dirk, you can't desert her like that!"

"Desert who?" He was startled.

"Beauty! Self-expression. Whatever you want to call it. You wait! She'll turn on you some day. Some day you'll want her, and she won't be there."

Inwardly he had been resentful of this bedside conversation with his mother. She made little of him, he thought, while outsiders appreciated his success. He had said, "So big," measuring a tiny space between thumb and forefinger in answer to her half-playful question, but he had not honestly meant it. He thought her ridiculously old-fashioned now in her viewpoint, and certainly unreasonable, But he would not quarrel with her.

"You wait, too, Mother," he said now, smiling. "Some day your wayward son will be a real success. Wait till the millions roll in. Then we'll see."

She lay down, turned her back deliberately upon him, pulled the covers up about her.

"Shall I turn out your light, Mother, and open the windows?"

"Meena'll do it. She always does. Just call her. . . . Good-night."

He knew that he had come to be a rather big man in his world. Influence had helped. He knew that, too. But he shut his mind to much of Paula's manoeuvring and wise pulling—refused to acknowledge that her lean, dark, eager fingers had manipulated the mechanism that ordered his career. Paula herself was wise enough to know that to hold him she must not let him feel indebted to her. She knew that the debtor hates his creditor. She lay awake at night planning for him, scheming for his advancement, then suggested these schemes to him so deftly as to make him think he himself had devised them. She had even realized of late that their growing intimacy might handicap him if openly commented on. But now she must see him daily, or speak to him. In the huge house on Lake Shore Drive her own rooms—sitting room, bedroom, dressing room, bath—were as detached as though she occupied a separate apartment. Her telephone was a private wire leading only to her own bedroom. She called him the first thing in the morning; the last thing at night. Her voice, when she spoke to him, was an organ transformed; low, vibrant, with a timbre in its tone that would have made it unrecognizable to an outsider. Her words were commonplace enough, but pregnant and meaningful for her.

"What did you do to-day? Did you have a good day? . . . Why didn't you call me? . . . Did you follow up that suggestion you made about Kennedy? I think it's a wonderful idea, don't you? You're a wonderful man, Dirk; did you know that? . . . I miss you. . . . Do you? . . . When? . . . Why not lunch? . . . Oh, not if you have a business appointment . . . How about five o'clock? . . . No, not there . . . Oh, I don't know. It's so public . . . Yes . . . Good-bye. . . . Good-night. . . . Good-night. . . ."

They began to meet rather furtively, in out-of-the-way places. They would lunch in department store restaurants where none of their friends ever came. They spent off afternoon hours in the dim, close atmosphere of the motion picture palaces, sitting in the back row, seeing nothing of the film, talking in eager whispers that failed to annoy the scattered devotees in the middle of the house. When they drove it was on obscure streets of the south side, as secure there from observation as though they had been in Africa, for to the north sider the south side of Chicago is the hinterland of civilization.

Paula had grown very beautiful, her world thought. There was about her the aura, the glow, the roseate exhalation that surrounds the woman in love.

Frequently she irritated Dirk. At such times he grew quieter than ever; more reserved. As he involuntarily withdrew she advanced. Sometimes he thought he hated her—her hot eager hands, her glowing asking eyes, her thin red mouth, her sallow heart-shaped exquisite face, her perfumed clothing, her air of ownership. That was it! Her possessiveness. She clutched him so with her every look and gesture, even when she did not touch him. There was about her something avid, sultry. It was like the hot wind that sometimes blew over the prairie—blowing, blowing, but never refreshing. It made you feel dry, arid, irritated, parched. Sometimes Dirk wondered what Theodore Storm thought and knew behind that impassive flabby white mask of his.

Dirk met plenty of other girls. Paula was clever enough to see to that. She asked them to share her box at the opera. She had them at her dinners. She affected great indifference to their effect on him. She suffered when he talked to one of them.

"Dirk, why don't you take out that nice Farnham girl?"

"Is she nice?"

"Well, isn't she! You were talking to her long enough at the Kirks' dance. What were you talking about?"

"Books."

"Oh. Books. She's awfully nice and intelligent, isn't she? A lovely girl." She was suddenly happy. Books.

The Farnham girl was a nice girl, She was the kind of girl one should fall in love with and doesn't. The Farnham girl was one of many well-bred Chicago girls of her day and class. Fine, honest, clear-headed, frank, capable, good-looking in an indefinite and unarresting sort of way. Hair-coloured hair, good teeth, good enough eyes, clear skin, sensible medium hands and feet; skated well, danced well, talked well. Read the books you had read. A companionable girl. Loads of money but never spoke of it. Travelled. Her hand met yours firmly—and it was just a hand. At the contract no current darted through you, sending its shaft with a little zing to your heart.

But when Paula showed you a book her arm, as she stood next you, would somehow fit into the curve of yours and you were conscious of the feel of her soft slim side against you.

He knew many girls. There was a distinct type known as the North Shore Girl. Slim, tall, exquisite; a little fine nose, a high, sweet, slightly nasal voice, earrings, a cigarette, luncheon at Huyler's. All these girls looked amazingly alike, Dirk thought; talked very much alike. They all spoke French with a pretty good accent; danced intricate symbolic dances; read the new books; had the same patter. They prefaced, interlarded, concluded their remarks to each other with, "My deah!" It expressed, for them, surprise, sympathy, amusement, ridicule, horror, resignation. "My *deah!* You should have seen her! My *deah!*"—horror. Their slang was almost identical with that used by the girls working in his office. "She's a good kid," they said, speaking in admiration of another girl. They made a fetish of frankness. In a day when everyone talked in screaming headlines they knew it was necessary to red-ink their remarks in order to get them noticed at all. The word rot was replaced by garbage and garbage gave way to the ultimate swill. One no longer said "How shocking!" but, "How perfectly obscene!" The words, spoken in their sweet clear voices, fell nonchalantly from their pretty lips. All very fearless and uninhibited and free. That, they told you, was the main thing. Sometimes Dirk wished they wouldn't work so hard at their play. They were forever getting up pageants and plays and large festivals for charity; Venetian fêtes, Oriental bazaars, charity balls, In the programme performance of these many of them sang better, acted better, danced better than most professional performers, but the whole thing always lacked the flavour, somehow, of professional performance. On these affairs they lavished thousands in costumes and decorations, receiving in return other thousands which they soberly turned over to the Cause. They found nothing ludicrous in this. Spasmodically they went into business or semi-professional ventures, defying the conventions. Paula did this too. She or one of her friends were forever opening blouse shops; starting Gifte Shoppes; burgeoning into tea rooms decorated in crude green and vermilion and orange and black; announcing their affiliation with an advertising agency. These adventures blossomed, withered, died. They were the result of post-war restlessness. Many of these girls had worked indefatigably during the 1917-

1918 period; had driven service cars, managed ambulances, nursed, scrubbed, conducted canteens. They missed the excitement, the satisfaction of achievement.

They found Dirk fair game, resented Paula's proprietorship. Susans and Janes and Kates and Bettys and Sallys—plain old-fashioned names for modern, erotic misses—they talked to Dirk, danced with him, rode with him, flirted with him. His very unattainableness gave him piquancy. That Paula Storm had him fast. He didn't care a hoot about girls.

"Oh, Mr. DeJong," they said, "your name's Dirk, isn't it? What a slick name! What does it mean?"

"Nothing, I suppose. It's a Dutch name. My people—my father's people—were Dutch, you know."

"A dirk's a sort of sword, isn't it, or poniard? Anyway, it sounds very keen and cruel and fatal—Dirk."

He would flush a little (one of his assets) and smile, and look at them, and say nothing. He found that to be all that was necessary.

He got on enormously.

17

BETWEEN THESE GIRLS and the girls that worked in his office there existed a similarity that struck and amused Dirk. He said, "Take a letter, Miss Roach," to a slim young creature as exquisite as the girl with whom he had danced the day before; or ridden or played tennis or bridge. Their very clothes were faultless imitations. They even used the same perfume. He wondered, idly, how they did it. They were eighteen, nineteen, twenty, and their faces and bodies and desires and natural equipment made their presence in a business office a paradox, an absurdity. Yet they were capable, too, in a mechanical sort of way. Theirs were mechanical jobs. They answered telephones, pressed levers, clicked buttons, tapped typewriters, jotted down names. They were lovely creatures with the minds of fourteen-year-old children. Their hair was shining, perfectly undulated, as fine and glossy and tenderly curling as a young child's. Their breasts were flat, their figures singularly sexless like that of a very young boy. They were wise with the wisdom of the serpent. They wore wonderful little sweaters and flat babyish collars and ridiculously sensible stockings and oxfords. Their legs were slim and sturdy. Their mouths were pouting, soft pink, the lower lip a little curled back, petalwise, like the moist mouth of a baby that has just finished nursing. Their eyes were wide apart, empty, knowledgeous. They managed their private affairs like generals. They were cool, remote, disdainful. They reduced their boys to desperation. They were brigands, desperadoes, pirates, taking all, giving little. They came, for the most part, from sordid homes, yet they knew, in some miraculous way, all the fine arts that Paula knew and practised. They were corsetless, pliant, bewildering, lovely, dangerous. They ate lunches that were horrible mixtures of cloying sweets and biting acids yet their skin was like velvet and cream. Their voices were thin, nasal, vulgar; their faces like those in a Greuze or a Fragonard. They said, with a twang that racked the listener, "I wouldn't of went if I got an invite but he could of give me a ring, anyways. I called him right. I was sore."

"Yeh? Wha'd he say?"

"Oh, he laffed."

"Didja go?"

"Me! No! Whatcha think I yam, anyway?"

"Oh, he's a good kid."

Among these Dirk worked immune, aloof, untouched. He would have been surprised to learn that he was known among them as Frosty. They approved his socks, his scarfs, his nails, his features, his legs in their well-fitting pants, his flat strong back in the Peel coat. They admired and resented him. Not one that did not secretly dream of the day when he would call her into his office, shut the door, and say, "Loretta" (their names were burbankian monstrosities, born of grafting the original appellation onto their own idea of beauty in nomenclature—hence Loretta, Imogene, Nadine, Natalie, Ardella), "Loretta, I have watched you for a long, long time and you must have noticed how deeply I admire you."

It wasn't impossible. Those things happen. The movies had taught them that.

Dirk, all unconscious of their pitiless, all-absorbing scrutiny, would have been still further appalled to learn how fully aware they were of his personal and private affairs. They knew about Paula, for example. They admired and resented her, too. They were fair in granting her the perfection of her clothes, drew immense satisfaction from the knowledge of their own superiority in the matters of youth and colouring; despised her for the way in which she openly displayed her feeling for him (how they knew this was a miracle and a mystery, for she almost never came into the office and disguised all her telephone talks with him). They thought he was grand to his mother. Selina had been in his office twice, perhaps. On one of these occasions she had spent five minutes chatting sociably with Ethelinda Quinn who had the face of a Da Vinci cherub and the soul of a man-eating shark. Selina always talked to everyone. She enjoyed listening to street car conductors, washwomen, janitors, landladies, clerks, doormen, chauffeurs, policemen. Something about her made them talk. They opened to her as flowers to the sun. They sensed her interest, her king. As they talked Selina would exclaim, "You don't say! Well, that's terrible!" Her eyes would be bright with sympathy.

Selina had said, on entering Dirk's office, "My land! I don't see how you can work among those pretty creatures and not be a sultan. I'm going to ask some of them down to the farm over Sunday."

"Don't, Mother! They wouldn't understand. I scarcely see them. They're just part of the office equipment."

Afterward, Ethelinda Quinn had passed expert opinion. "Say, she's got ten times the guts that Frosty's got. I like her fine. Did you see her terrible hat! But say, it didn't look funny on her, did it? Anybody else in that getup would look comical, but she's the kind that could walk off with anything. I don't know. She's got what I call an air. It beats style. Nice, too. She said I was a pretty little thing. Can you beat it! At that she's right. I cer'nly yam."

All unconscious, "Take a letter, Miss Quinn," said Dirk half an hour later.

In the midst, then, of this fiery furnace of femininity Dirk walked unscorched. Paula, the North Shore girls, well-bred business and professional women he occasionally met in the course of business, the enticing little nymphs he encountered in his own office, all practised on him their warm and perfumed smiles. He moved among them cool and serene. Perhaps his sudden success had had something to do with this; and his quiet ambition for further success. For he really was accounted successful now, even in the spectacular whirl of Chicago's meteoric financial constellation. Northside mammas regarded his income, his career, and his future with eyes of respect and wily speculation. There was always a neat little pile of invitations in the mail that lay on the correct little console in the correct little apartment ministered by the correct little Jap on the correct north-side street near (but not too near) the lake, and overlooking it.

The apartment had been furnished with Paula's aid. Together she and Dirk had gone to interior decorators. "But you've got to use your own taste, too," Paula had said, "to give it the individual touch." The apartment was furnished in a good deal of Italian furniture, the finish a dark oak or walnut, the whole massive and yet somehow unconvincing. The effect was sombre without being impressive. There were long carved tables on which an ash tray seemed a desecration; great chairs roomy enough for lolling, yet in which you did not relax; dull silver candlesticks; vestments; Dante's saturnine features sneering down upon you from a correct cabinet. There were not many books. Tiny foyer, large living room, bedroom, dining room, kitchen, and a cubby-hole for the Jap. Dirk did not spend much time in the place. Sometimes he did not sit in a chair in the sitting room for days at a time, using the room only as a short cut in his rush for the bedroom to change from office to dinner clothes. His upward climb was a treadmill, really. His office, the apartment, a dinner, a dance. His contacts were monotonous, and too few. His office was a great splendid office in a great splendid office building in LaSalle Street. He drove back and forth in a motor car along the boulevards. His social engagements lay north. LaSalle Street bounded him on the west, Lake Michigan on the east, Jackson Boulevard on the south, Lake Forest on the north. He might have lived a thousand miles away for all he knew of the rest of Chicago—the mighty, roaring, sweltering, pushing, screaming, magnificent hideous steel giant that was Chicago.

Selina had had no hand in the furnishing of his apartment. When it was finished Dirk had brought her in triumph to see it. "Well," he had said, "what do you think of it, Mother?"

She had stood in the centre of the room, a small plain figure in the midst of these massive sombre carved tables, chairs, chests. A little smile had quirked the corner of her mouth. "I think it's as cosy as a cathedral."

Sometimes Selina remonstrated with him, though of late she had taken on a strange reticence. She no longer asked him about the furnishings of the houses he visited (Italian villas on Ohio Street), or the exotic food he ate at splendid dinners. The farm flourished. The great steel mills and factories to the south were closing in upon her but had not yet set iron foot on her rich green acres. She was rather famous now for the quality of her farm products and her pens. You saw "DeJong asparagus" on the menu at the Blackstone and the Drake hotels. Sometimes Dirk's friends twitted him about this and he did not always acknowledge that the similarity of names was not a coincidence.

"Dirk, you seem to see no one but just these people," Selina told him in one of her infrequent rebukes. "You don't get the full flavour of life. You've got to have a vulgar curiosity about people and things. All kinds of people. All kinds of things. You revolve in the same little circle, over and over and over."

"Haven't time. Can't afford to take the time."

"You can't afford not to."

Sometimes Selina came into town for a week or ten days at a stretch, and indulged in what she called an orgy. At such times Julie Arnold would invite her to occupy one of the guest rooms at the Arnold house, or Dirk would offer her his bedroom and tell her that he would be comfortable on the big couch in the living room, or that he would take a room at the University Club. She always declined. She would take a room in a hotel, sometimes

north, sometimes south. Her holiday before her she would go off roaming
gaily as a small boy on a Saturday morning, with the day stretching gor-
geously and adventuresomely ahead of him, sallies down the street without
plan or appointment, knowing that richness in one form or another lies before
him for the choosing. She loved the Michigan Boulevard and State Street
shop windows in which haughty waxed ladies in glittering evening gowns
postured, fingers elegantly crooked as they held a fan, a rose, a programme,
meanwhile smiling condescendingly out upon an envious world flattening its
nose against the plate glass barrier. A sociable woman, Selina, savouring
life, she liked the lights, the colour, the rush, the noise. Her years of grinding
work, with her face pressed down to the very soil itself, had failed to kill
her zest for living. She prowled into the city's foreign quarters—Italian,
Greek, Chinese, Jewish. She penetrated the Black Belt, where Chicago's
vast and growing Negro population shifted and moved and stretched its great
limbs ominously, reaching out and out in protest and overflowing the bounds
that irked it. Her serene face and her quiet manner, her bland interest and
friendly look protected her. They thought her a social worker, perhaps; one
of the uplifters. She bought and read the *Independent,* the Negro newspaper
in which herb doctors advertised magic roots. She even sent the twenty-five
cents required for a box of these, charmed by their names—Adam and Eve
roots, Master of the Woods, Dragon's Blood, High John the Conqueror,
Jezebel Roots, Grains of Paradise.

"Look here, Mother," Dirk would protest, "you can't wander around
like that. It isn't safe. This isn't High Prairie, you know. If you want to go
round I'll get Saki to drive you."

"That would be nice," she said, mildly. But she never availed herself of
this offer. Sometimes she went over to South Water Street, changed now,
and swollen to such proportions that it threatened to burst its confines. She
liked to stroll along the crowded sidewalks, lined with crates and boxes and
barrels of fruits, vegetables, poultry. Swarthy foreign faces predominated
now. Where the red-faced overalled men had been she now saw lean muscular lads in old army shirts and khaki pants and scuffed puttees wheeling
trucks, loading boxes, charging down the street in huge rumbling auto vans,
Their faces were hard, their talk terse. They moved gracefully, with an
economy of gesture. Any one of these, she reflected, was more vital, more
native, functioned more usefully and honestly than her successful son, Dirk
DeJong.

"Where 'r' beans?"

"In th' ol' beanery."

"Tough."

"Best you can get."

"Keep 'em."

Many of the older men knew her, shook hands with her, chatted a moment
friendlily. William Talcott, a little more dried up, more wrinkled, his sparse
hair quite gray now, still leaned up against the side of his doorway in his
shirt sleeves and his neat pepper-and-salt pants and vest, a pretty good cigar,
unlighted, in his mouth, the heavy gold watch chain spanning his middle.

"Well, you certainly made good, Mrs. DeJong. Remember the day you
come here with your first load?"

Oh, yes. She remembered.

"That boy of yours has made his mark, too, I see. Doing grand, ain't he?
Wa-al, great satisfaction having a son turn out well like that. Yes, sirree!
Why, look at my da'ter Car'line———"

Life at High Prairie had its savour, too. Frequently you saw strange visitors
there for a week or ten days at a time—boys and girls whose city pallor gave

way to a rich tan; tired-looking women with sagging figures who drank Selina's cream and ate her abundant vegetables and tender chickens as though they expected these viands to be momentarily snatched from them. Selina picked these up in odd corners of the city. Dirk protested against this, too. Selina was a member of the High Prairie school board now. She often drove about the roads and into town in a disreputable Ford which she manipulated with imagination and skill. She was on the Good Roads Committee and the Truck Farmers' Association valued her opinion. Her life was full, pleasant, prolific.

18

PAULA HAD A scheme for interesting women in bond buying. It was a good scheme. She suggested it so that Dirk thought he had thought of it. Dirk was head now of the bond department in the Great Lakes Trust Company's magnificent new white building on Michigan Boulevard north. Its white towers gleamed pink in the lake mists. Dirk said it was a terrible building, badly proportioned, and that it looked like a vast vanilla sundae. His new private domain was more like a splendid bookless library than a business office. It was finished in rich dull walnut and there were great upholstered chairs, soft rugs, shaded lights. Special attention was paid to women clients. There was a room for their convenience fitted with low restful chairs and couches, lamps, writing desks, in mauve and rose. Paula had selected the furnishings for this room. Ten years earlier it would have been considered absurd in a suite of business offices. Now it was a routine part of the equipment.

Dirk's private office was almost as difficult of access as that of the nation's executive. Cards, telephones, office boys, secretaries stood between the caller and Dirk DeJong, head of the bond department. You asked for him, uttering his name in the ear of the six-foot statuesque detective who, in the guise of usher, stood in the centre of the marble rotunda eyeing each visitor with a coldly appraising gaze. This one padded softly ahead of you on rubber heels, only to give you over to the care of a glorified office boy who took your name. You waited. He returned. You waited. Presently there appeared a young woman with inquiring eyebrows. She conversed with you. She vanished. You waited. She reappeared. You were ushered into Dirk DeJong's large and luxurious inner office. And there formality fled.

Dirk was glad to see you; quietly, interestedly glad to see you. As you stated your business he listened attentively, as was his charming way. The volume of business done with women clients by the Great Lakes Trust Company was enormous. Dirk was conservative, helpful—and he always got the business. He talked little. He was amazingly effective. Ladies in the modish black of recent bereavement made quite a sombre procession to his door. His suggestions (often originating with Paula) made the Great Lakes Trust Company's discreet advertising rich in results. Neat little pamphlets written for women on the subjects of saving, investments. "You are not dealing with a soulless corporation," said these brochures. "May we serve you? You need more than friends. Before acting, you should have your judgment vindicated by an organization of investment specialists. You may have relatives and friends, some of whom would gladly advise you on investments. But perhaps you rightly feel that the less they know about your financial affairs, the better. To handle trusts, and to care for the securities of widows and orphans, is our business."

It was startling to note how this sort of thing mounted into millions. "Women are becoming more and more used to the handling of money," Paula said, shrewdly. "Pretty soon their patronage is going to be as valuable as that of men. The average woman doesn't know about bonds—about bond buying. They think they're something mysterious and risky. They ought to be educated up to it. Didn't you say something, Dirk, about classes in finance for women? You could make a sort of semi-social affair of it. Send out invitations and get various bankers—big men, whose names are known—to talk to these women."

"But would the women come?"

"Of course they'd come. Women will accept any invitation that's engraved on heavy cream paper."

The Great Lakes Trust had a branch in Cleveland now, and one in New York, on Fifth Avenue. The drive to interest women in bond buying and to instruct them in finance was to take on almost national proportions. There was to be newspaper and magazine advertising.

The Talks for Women on the Subject of Finance were held every two weeks in the crystal room of the Blackstone and were a great success. Paula was right. Much of old Aug Hempel's shrewdness and business foresight had descended to her. The women came—widows with money to invest; business women who had thriftily saved a portion of their salaries; moneyed women who wanted to manage their own property, or who resented a husband's interference. Some came out of curiosity. Others for lack of anything better to do. Others to gaze on the well-known banker or lawyer or business man who was scheduled to address the meeting. Dirk spoke three or four times during the winter and was markedly a favourite. The women, in smart crêpe gowns and tailored suits and small chic hats, twittered and murmured about him, even while they sensibly digested his well-thought-out remarks. He looked very handsome, clean-cut, and distinguished there on the platform in his admirably tailored clothes, a small white flower in his buttonhole. He talked easily, clearly, fluently; answered the questions put to him afterward with just the right mixture of thoughtful hesitation and confidence.

It was decided that for the national advertising there must be an illustration that would catch the eye of women, and interest them. The person to do it, Dirk thought, was this Dallas O'Mara whose queer hen-track signature you saw scrawled on half the advertising illustrations that caught your eye. Paula had not been enthusiastic about this idea.

"M-m-m', she's very good," Paula had said, guardedly, "but aren't there others who are better?"

"She!" Dirk had exclaimed. "Is it a woman? I didn't know. That name might be anything."

"Oh, yes, she's a woman. She's said to be very—very attractive."

Dirk sent for Dallas O'Mara. She replied, suggesting an appointment two weeks from that date. Dirk decided not to wait, consulted other commercial artists, looked at their work, heard their plans outlined, and was satisfied with none of them. The time was short. Ten days had passed. He had his secretary call Dallas O'Mara on the telephone. Could she come down to see him that day at eleven?

No: she worked until four daily at her studio.

Could she come to his office at four-thirty, then?

Yes, but wouldn't it be better if he could come to her studio where he could see something of the various types of drawings—oils; or black-and-white, or crayons. She was working mostly in crayons now.

All this relayed by his secretary at the telephone to Dirk at his desk. He jammed his cigarette-end viciously into a tray, blew a final infuriated wraith of smoke, and picked up the telephone connection on his own desk. "One of those damned temperamental near-artists trying to be grand," he muttered, his hand over the mouthpiece. "Here, Miss Rawlings—I'll talk to her. Switch her over."

"Hello, Miss—uh—O'Mara. This is Mr. DeJong talking. I much prefer that you come to my office and talk to me." (No more of this nonsense.)

Her voice: "Certainly, if you prefer it. I thought the other would save us both some time. I'll be there at four-thirty." Her voice was leisurely, low, rounded. An admirable voice. Restful.

"Very well. Four-thirty," said Dirk, crisply. Jerked the receiver onto the hook. That was the way to handle 'em. These females of forty with straggling hair and a bundle of drawings under their arm.

The female of forty with straggling hair and a bundle of drawings under her arm was announced at four-thirty to the dot. Dirk let her wait five minutes in the outer office, being still a little annoyed. At four-thirty-five there entered his private office a tall slim girl in a smart little broadtail jacket, fur-trimmed skirt, and a black hat at once so daring and so simple that even a man must recognize its French nativity. She carried no portfolio of drawings under her arms.

Through the man's mind flashed a series of unbusinesslike thoughts such as: "Gosh! . . . Eyes! . . . That's way I like to see girls dress . . . Tired looking . . . No, guess it's her eyes—sort of fatigued. . . . Pretty . . . No, she isn't . . . yes, she . . ." Aloud he said, "This is very kind of you, Miss O'Mara." Then he thought that sounded pompous and said, curtly, "Sit down."

Miss O'Mara sat down. Miss O'Mara looked at him with her tired deep blue eyes. Miss O'Mara said nothing. She regarded him pleasantly, quietly, composedly. He waited for her to say that usually she did not come to business offices; that she had only twenty minutes to give him; that the day was warm, or cold; his office handsome; the view over the river magnificent. Miss O'Mara said nothing, pleasantly. So Dirk began to talk, rather hurriedly.

Now, this was a new experience for Dirk DeJong. Usually women spoke to him first and fluently. Quiet women waxed voluble under his silence; voluble women chattered. Paula always spoke a hundred words to his one. But here was a woman more silent than he; not sullenly silent, nor heavily silent, but quietly, composedly, restfully silent.

"I'll tell you the sort of thing we want, Miss O'Mara." He told her. When he had finished she probably would burst out with three or four plans. The others had done that.

When he had finished she said, "I'll think about it for a couple of days while I'm working on something else. I always do. I'm doing an olive soap picture now. I can begin work on yours Wednesday."

"But I'd like to see it—that is, I'd like to have an idea of what you're planning to do with it." Did she think he was going to let her go ahead without consulting his judgment!

"Oh, it will be all right. But drop into the studio if you like. It will take me about a week, I suppose. I'm over on Ontario in that old studio building. You'll know it by the way most of the bricks have fallen out of the building and are scattered over the sidewalk." She smiled a slow wide smile. Her teeth were good but her mouth was too big, he thought. Nice big warm kind of smile, though. He found himself smiling, too, sociably. Then he became businesslike again. Very businesslike.

"How much do you—what is your—what would you expect to get for a drawing such as that?"

"Fifteen hundred dollars," said Miss O'Mara.

"Nonsense." He looked at her then. Perhaps that had been humour. But she was not smiling. "You mean fifteen hundred for a single drawing?"

"For that sort of thing, yes."

"I'm afraid we can't pay that, Miss O'Mara."

Miss O'Mara stood up. "That is my price." She was not at all embarrassed. He realized that he had never seen such effortless composure. It was he who was fumbling with the objects on his flat-topped desk—a pen, a sheet of paper, a blotter. "Good-bye, Mr.—DeJong." She held out a friendly hand. He took it. Her hair was gold—dull gold, not bright—and coiled in a single great knot at the back of her head, low. He took her hand. The tired eyes looked up at him.

"Well, if that's your price, Miss O'Mara. I wasn't prepared to pay any such—but of course I suppose you top-notchers do get crazy prices for your work."

"Not any crazier than the prices you top-notchers get."

"Still, fifteen hundred dollars is quite a lot of money." I think so, too. But then, I'll always think anything over nine dollars is quite a lot of money. You see, I used to get twenty-five cents apiece for sketching hats for Gage's."

She was undeniably attractive. "And now you've arrived. You're successful."

"Arrived! Heavens, no! I've started."

"Who gets more money than you do for a drawing?"

"Nobody, I suppose."

"Well, then?"

"Well, then, in another minute I'll be telling you the story of my life."

She smiled again her slow wide smile; turned to leave. Dirk decided that while most women's mouths were merely features this girl's was a decoration.

She was gone. Miss Ethelinda Quinn *et al.*, in the outer office, appraised the costume of Miss Dallas O'Mara from her made-to-order footgear to her made-in-France millinery and achieved a lightning mental reconstruction of their own costumes. Dirk DeJong in the inner office realized that he had ordered a fifteen-hundred-dollar drawing, sight unseen, and that Paula was going to ask questions about it.

"Make a note, Miss Rawlings, to call Miss O'Mara's studio on Thursday."

In the next few days he learned that a surprising lot of people knew a surprisingly good deal about this Dallas O'Mara. She hailed from Texas, hence the absurd name. She was twenty-eight—twenty-five—thirty-two—thirty-six. She was beautiful. She was ugly. She was an orphan. She had worked her way through art school. She had no sense of the value of money. Two years ago she had achieved sudden success with her drawings. Her ambition was to work in oils. She toiled like a galley-slave; played like a child; had twenty beaux and no lover; her friends, men and women, were legion and wandered in and out of her studio as though it were a public thoroughfare. You were likely to find there at any hour any one from Bert Colson, the blackface musical comedy star, to Mrs. Robinson Gilman of Lake Forest and Paris; from Leo Mahler, first violin with the Chicago Symphony Orchestra, to Fanny Whipple who designed dresses for Carson's. She supported an assortment of unlucky brothers and spineless sisters in Texas and points west.

Miss Rawlings made an appointment for Thursday at three. Paula said she'd go with him and went. She dressed for Dallas O'Mara and the result was undeniably enchanting. Dallas sometimes did a crayon portrait, or even attempted one in oils. Had got a prize for her portrait of Mrs. Robinson Gilman at last spring's portrait exhibit at the Chicago Art Institute. It was considered something of an achievement to be asked to pose for her. Paula's hat had been chosen in deference to her hair and profile, and the neck line of her gown in deference to hat, hair, and profile, and her pearls with an eye to all four. The whole defied competition on the part of Miss Dallas O'Mara.

Miss Dallas O'Mara, in her studio, was perched on a high stool before an easel with a large tray of assorted crayons at her side. She looked a sight and didn't care at all. She greeted Dirk and Paula with a cheerful friendliness and went right on working. A model, very smartly gowned, was sitting for her.

"Hello!" said Dallas O'Mara. "This is it. Do you think you're going to like it?"

"Oh," said Dirk. "Is that it?" It was merely the beginning of a drawing of the smartly gowned model. "Oh, that's it, is it?" Fifteen hundred dollars!

"I hope you didn't think it was going to be a picture of a woman buying bonds." She went on working. She squinted one eye, picked up a funny little mirror thing which she held to one side, looked into, and put down. She made a black mark on the board with a piece of crayon then smeared the mark with her thumb. She had on a faded all-enveloping smock over which French ink, rubber cement, pencil marks, crayon dust and wash were so impartially distributed that the whole blended and mixed in a rich mellow haze like the Chicago atmosphere itself. The collar of a white silk blouse, not especially clean, showed above this. On her feet were soft kid bedroom slippers, scuffed, with pompons on them. Her dull gold hair was carelessly rolled into that great loose knot at the back. Across one cheek was a swipe of black.

"Well," thought Dirk, "she looks a sight."

Dallas O'Mara waved a friendly hand toward some chairs on which were piled hats, odd garments, bristol board and (on the broad arm of one) a piece of yellow cake. "Sit down." She called to the girl who had opened the door to them: "Gilda, will you dump some of those things. This is Mrs. Storm, Mr. DeJong—Gilda Hanan." Her secretary, Dirk later learned.

The place was disorderly, comfortable, shabby. A battered grand piano stood in one corner. A great skylight formed half the ceiling and sloped down at the north end of the room. A man and a girl sat talking earnestly on the couch in another corner. A swarthy foreign-looking chap, vaguely familiar to Dirk, was playing softly at the piano. The telephone rang. Miss Hanan took the message, transmitted it to Dallas O'Mara, received the answer, repeated it. Perched atop the stool, one slippered foot screwed in a rung, Dallas worked on concentratedly, calmly, earnestly. A lock of hair straggled over her eyes. She pushed it back with her wrist and left another dark splotch on her forehead. There was something splendid, something impressive, something magnificent about her absorption, her indifference to appearance, her unawareness of outsiders, her concentration on the work before her. Her nose was shiny. Dirk hadn't seen a girl with a shiny nose in years. They were always taking out those little boxes and things and plastering themselves with the stuff in 'em.

"How can you work with all this crowd around?"

"Oh," said Dallas in that deep restful leisurely voice of hers, "there are always between twenty and thirty"—she slapped a quick scarlet line on the board, rubbed it out at once— "thousand people in and out of here every hour, just about. I like it. Friends around me while I'm slaving."

"Gosh!" he thought, "she's——— I don't know—she's———"

"Shall we go?" said Paula.

He had forgotten all about her. "Yes. Yes, I'm ready if you are."

Outside, "Do you think you're going to like the picture?" Paula asked. They stepped into her car.

"Oh, I don't know. Can't tell much about it at this stage, I suppose."

"Back to your office?"

"Sure."

"Attractive, isn't she?"

"Think so?"

So he was going to be on his guard, was he! Paula threw in the clutch viciously, jerked the lever into second speed. "Her neck was dirty."

"Crayon dust," said Dirk.

"Not necessarily," replied Paula.

Dirk turned sideways to look at her. It was as though he saw her for the first time. She looked brittle, hard, artificial—small, somehow. Not in physique but in personality.

The picture was finished and delivered within ten days. In that time Dirk went twice to the studio in Ontario Street. Dallas did not seem to mind. Neither did she appear particularly interested. She was working hard both times. Once she looked as he had seen her on her first visit. The second time she had on a fresh crisp smock of faded yellow that was glorious with her hair; and high-heeled beige kid slippers, very smart. She was like a little girl who has just been freshly scrubbed and dressed in a clean pinafore, Dirk thought.

He thought a good deal about Dallas O'Mara. He found himself talking about her in what he assumed to be a careless offhand manner. He liked to talk about her. He told his mother of her. He could let himself go with Selina and he must have taken advantage of this for she looked at him intently and said: "I'd like to meet her. I've never met a girl like that."

"I'll ask her if she'll let me bring you up to the studio some time when you're in town."

It was practically impossible to get a minute with her alone. That irritated him. People were always drifting in and out of the studio—queer, important, startling people; little, dejected, shabby people, An impecunious girl art student, red-haired and wistful, that Dallas was taking in until the girl got some money from home; a pearl-hung grand-opera singer who was condescending to the Chicago Opera for a fortnight. He did not know that Dallas played until he came upon her late one afternoon sitting at the piano in the twilight with Bert Colson, the blackface comedian. Colson sang those terrible songs about April showers bringing violets, and about mah Ma-ha-ha-ha-ha-ha-ha-my but they didn't seem terrible when he sang them. There was about this lean, hollow-chested, sombre-eyed comedian a poignant pathos, a gorgeous sense of rhythm—a something unnameable that bound you to him, made you love him. In the theatre he came out to the edge of the runway and took the audience in his arms. He talked like a bootblack and sang like an angel. Dallas at the piano, he leaning over it, were doing "blues." The two were rapt, ecstatic. I got the blues—I said the blues—I got the this or that—the somethingorother—blue—hoo-hoos. They scarcely noticed Dirk. Dallas had nodded when he came in, and had gone on playing, Colson sang the cheaply sentimental ballad as though it were the folk-song of a tragic race. His arms were extended, his face rapt. As Dallas played the tears stood in her eyes. When they had finished, "Isn't it a terrible song?" she said. "I'm crazy about it. Bert's going to try it out to-night."

"Who—uh—wrote it?" asked Dirk politely.

Dallas began to play again. "H'm? Oh, I did." They were off once more. They paid no more attention to Dirk. Yet there was nothing rude about their indifference. They simply were more interested in what they were doing.

He left telling himself that he wouldn't go there again. Hanging around a studio. But next day he was back.

"Look here, Miss O'Mara," he had got her alone for a second. "Look here, will you come out to dinner with me some time? And the theatre?"

"Love to."

"When?" He was actually trembling.

"To-night." He had an important engagement. He cast it out of his life.

"To-night! That's grand. Where do you want to dine? The Casino?" The smartest club in Chicago; a little pink stucco Italian box of a place on the Lake Shore Drive. He was rather proud of being in a position to take her there as his guest.

"Oh, no, I hate those arty little places. I like dining in a hotel full of all sorts of people. Dining in a club means you're surrounded by people who're pretty much alike. Their membership in the club means they're there because they are all interested in golf, or because they're university graduates, or belong to the same political party or write, or paint, or have incomes of over fifty thousand a year, or something. I like 'em mixed up, higgledy-piggledy. A dining room full of gamblers, and insurance agents, and actors, and merchants, thieves, bootleggers, lawyers, kept ladies, wives, flaps, travelling men, millionaires—everything. That's what I call dining out. Unless one is dining at a friend's house, of course." A rarely long speech for her.

"Perhaps," eagerly, "you'll dine at my little apartment some time. Just four or six of us, or even————"

"Perhaps."

"Would you like the Drake to-night?"

"It looks too much like a Roman bath. The pillars scare me. Let's go to the Blackstone. I'll always be sufficiently from Texas to think the Blackstone French room the last word in elegance."

They went to the Blackstone. The head waiter knew him. "Good evening, Mr. DeJong." Dirk was secretly gratified. Then, with a shock, he realized that the head waiter was grinning at Dallas and Dallas was grinning at the head waiter. "Hello, André," said Dallas.

"Good evening, Miss O'Mara." The text of his greeting was correct and befitting the head waiter of the French room at the Blackstone. But his voice was lyric and his eyes glowed. His manner of seating her at a table was an enthronement.

At the look in Dirk's eyes, "I met him in the army," Dallas explained, "when I was in France. He's a grand lad."

"Were you in—what did you do in France?"

"Oh, odd jobs."

Her dinner gown was very smart, but the pink ribbon strap of an undergarment showed untidily at one side. Her silk brassiere, probably. Paula would have—but then, a thing like that was impossible in Paula's perfection of toilette. He loved the way the gown cut sharply away at the shoulder to show her firm white arms. It was dull gold, the colour of her hair. This was one Dallas. There were a dozen—a hundred. Yet she was always the same. You never knew whether you were going to meet the gamin of the rumpled smock and the smudged face or the beauty of the little fur jacket. Sometimes Dirk thought she looked like a Swede hired girl with those high cheek bones of hers and her deep-set eyes and her large capable hands. Sometimes he thought she looked like the splendid goddesses you saw in paintings—the kind with high pointed breasts and gracious gentle pose—holding out a horn of plenty. There was about her something genuine and earthy and elemental. He noticed that her nails were short and not well cared for—not glittering and pointed and cruelly sharp and horridly vermilon, like Paula's. That pleased him, too, somehow.

"Some oysters?" he suggested. "They're perfectly safe here. Or fruit cocktail? Then breast of guinea hen under glass and an artichoke————"

She looked a little worried. "If you—suppose you take that. Me, I'd like a steak and some potatoes au gratin and a salad with Russian————"

"That's fine!" He was delighted. He doubled that order and they consumed it with devastating thoroughness. She ate rolls. She ate butter. She made no remarks about the food except to say, once, that it was good and that she had forgotten to eat lunch because she had been so busy working. All this Dirk found most restful and refreshing. Usually, when you dined in a restaurant with a woman she said, "Oh, I'd love to eat one of those crisp little rolls!"

You said, "Why not?"

Invariably the answer to this was, "I daren't! Goodness! A half pound at least. I haven't eaten a roll with butter in a year."

Again you said, "Why not?"

"Afraid I'll get fat."

Automatically, "You! Nonsense. You're just right."

He was bored with these women who talked about their weight, figure, lines. He thought it in bad taste. Paula was always rigidly refraining from this or that. It made him uncomfortable to sit at the table facing her; eating his thorough meal while she nibbled fragile curls of Melba toast, a lettuce leaf, and half a sugarless grapefruit. It lessened his enjoyment of his own oysters, steak, coffee. He thought that she always eyed his food a little avidly, for all her expressed indifference to it. She was looking a little haggard, too.

"The theatre's next door," he said. "Just a step. We don't have to leave here until after eight."

"That's nice." She had her cigarette with her coffee in a mellow sensuous atmosphere of enjoyment. He was talking about himself a good deal. He felt relaxed, at ease, happy.

"You know I'm an architect—at least, I was one. Perhaps that's why I like to hang around your shop so. I get sort of homesick for the pencils and the drawing board—the whole thing."

"Why did you give it up, then?"

"Nothing in it."

"How do you mean—nothing in it?"

"No money. After the war nobody was building. Oh, I suppose if I'd hung————"

"And then you became a banker, h'm? Well, there ought to be money enough in a bank."

He was a little nettled. "I wasn't a banker—at first. I was a bond salesman."

Her brows met in a little frown. Her eyebrows were thick and strongly marked and a little uneven and inclined to meet over her nose. Paula's brows were a mere line of black—a carefully traced half-parenthesis above her unmysterious dark eyes. "I'd rather," Dallas said, slowly, "plan one back door of a building that's going to help make this town beautiful and significant than sell all the bonds that ever floated a—whatever it is that bonds are supposed to float."

He defended himself. "I felt that way, too. But you see my mother had given me my education, really. She worked for it. I couldn't go dubbing along, earning just enough to keep me. I wanted to give her things. I wanted————"

"Did she want those things? Did she want you to give up architechire and go into bonds?"

"Well—she—I don't know that she exactly—" He was too decent—still too much the son of Selina DeJong—to be able to lie about that.

"You said you were going to let me meet her."

"Would you let me bring her in? Or perhaps you'd even—would you drive out to the farm with me some day. She'd like that so much."

"So would I."

He leaned toward her, suddenly. "Listen, Dallas. What do you think of me, anway?" He wanted to know. He couldn't stand not knowing any longer.

"I think you're a nice young man."

That was terrible. "But I don't want you to think I'm a nice young man. I want you to like me—a lot. Tell me, what haven't I got that you think I ought to have? Why do you put me off so many times? I never feel that I'm really near you. What is it I lack?" He was abject.

"Well, if you're asking for it. I do demand of the people I see often that they possess at least a splash of splendour in their makeup. Some people are nine tenths splendour and one tenth tawdriness, like Gene Meran. And some are nine tenths tawdriness and one tenth splendour, like Sam Huebch. But some people are all just a nice even pink without a single patch of royal purple."

"And that's me, h'm?"

He was horribly disappointed, hurt, wretched. But a little angry, too. His pride. Why, he was Dirk DeJong, the most successful of Chicago's younger men; the most promising; the most popular. After all, what did she do but paint commercial pictures for fifteen hundred dollars apiece?

"What happens to the men who fall in love with you? What do they do?"

Dallas stirred her coffee thoughtfully. "They usually tell me about it."

"And then what?"

"Then they seem to feel better and we become great friends."

"But don't you ever fall in love with them?" Pretty damned sure of herself. "Don't you ever fall in love with them?"

"I almost always do," said Dallas.

He plunged. "I could give you a lot of things you haven't got, purple or no purple."

"I'm going to France in April. Paris."

"What d'you mean! Paris. What for?"

"Study. I want to do portraits. Oils."

He was terrified. "Can't you do them here?"

"Oh, no. Not what I need. I have been studying here. I've been taking life-work three nights a week at the Art Institute, just to keep my hand in."

"So that's where you are, evenings." He was strangely relieved. "Let me go with you some time, will you?" Anything, Anything.

She took him with her one evening, steering him successfully past the stern Irishman who guarded the entrance to the basement classrooms; to her locker, got into her smock, grabbed her brushes. She rushed down the hall. "Don't talk," she cautioned him.? "It bothers them. I wonder what they'd think of my shop." She turned into a small, cruelly bright, breathlessly hot little room, its walls whitewashed. Every inch of the floor space was covered with easels. Before them stood men and women, brushes in hand, intent. Dallas went directly to her place, fell to work at once. Dirk blinked in the strong light. He glanced at the dais toward which they were all gazing from time to time as they worked. On it lay a nude woman.

To himself Dirk said in a sort of panic: "Why, say, she hasn't got any clothes on! My gosh! this is fierce. She hasn't got anything on!" He tried, meanwhile, to look easy, careless, critical. Strangely enough he succeeded, after the first shock, not only in looking at ease, but feeling so. The class was doing the whole figure in oils.

The model was a moron with a skin like velvet and rose petals. She fell into poses that flowed like cream. Her hair was waved in wooden undulations and her nose was pure vulgarity and her earrings were drug-store pearls in triple strands but her back was probably finer than Helen's and her breasts twin snowdrifts peaked with coral. In twenty minutes Dirk found himself impersonally interested in tone, shadows, colours, line. He listened to the low-voiced instructor and squinted carefully to ascertain whether that shadow on the model's stomach really should be painted blue or brown. Even he could see that Dallas's canvas was almost insultingly superior to that of the men and women about her. Beneath the flesh on her canvas there were muscles, and beneath those muscles blood and bone. You felt she had a surgeon's knowledge of anatomy. That, Dirk decided, was what made her commercial pictures so attractive. The drawing she had done for the Great Lakes Trust Company's bond department had been conventional enough in theme. The treatment, the technique, had made it arresting. He thought that if she ever did portraits in oils they would be vital and compelling portraits. But oh, he wished she didn't want to do portraits in oils. He wished———

It was after eleven when they emerged from the Art Institute doorway and stood a moment together at the top of the broad steps surveying the world that lay before them. Dallas said nothing. Suddenly the beauty of the night rushed up and overwhelmed Dirk. Gorgeousness and tawdriness; colour and gloom. At the right the white tower of the Wrigley building rose wraithlike against a background of purple sky. Just this side of it a swarm of impish electric lights grinned their message in scarlet and white. In white:

TRADE AT

then blackness, while you waited against your will. In red:

THE FAIR

Blackness again. Then, in a burst of both colours, in bigger letters, and in a blaze that hurled itself at your eyeballs, momentarily shutting out tower, sky, and street:

SAVE MONEY

Straight ahead the hut of the Adams Street L station in midair was a Venetian bridge with the black canal of asphalt flowing sluggishly beneath. The reflection of cafeteria and cigar-shop windows on either side were slender shafts of light along the canal. An enchanting sight. Dirk thought suddenly that Dallas was a good deal like that—like Chicago. A mixture of grandeur and cheapness; of tawdriness and magnificence; of splendour and ugliness.

"Nice" said Dallas A long breath. She was a part of all this.

"Yes." He felt an outsider. "Want a sandwich? Are you hungry?"

"I'm starved."

They had sandwiches and coffee at an all-night one-arm lunch room because Dallas said her face was too dirty for a restaurant and she didn't want to bother to wash it. She was more than ordinarily companionable that night; a little tired; less buoyant and independent than usual. This gave her a little air of helplessness—of fatigue—that aroused all his tenderness. Her smile gave him a warm rush of pure happiness—until he saw her smile in exactly the same way at the pimply young man who lorded it over the shining nickel coffee container, as she told him that his coffee was grand.

19

THE THINGS THAT had mattered so vitally didn't seem to be important somehow, now. The people who had seemed so desirable had become suddenly insignificant. The games he had played appeared silly games. He was seeing things through Dallas O'Mara's wise, beauty-loving eyes. Strangely enough, he did not realize that this girl saw life from much the same angle as that at which his mother regarded it. In the last few years his mother had often offended him by her attitude toward these rich and powerful friends of his— their ways, their games, their amusements, their manners. And her way of living in turn offended him. On his rare visits to the farm it seemed to him there was always some drab dejected female in the kitchen or living room or on the porch—a woman with broken teeth and comic shoes and tragic eyes—drinking great draughts of coffee and telling her woes to Selina— Sairey Gampish ladies smelling unpleasantly of peppermint and perspiration and poverty. "And he ain't had a lick of work since November————"

"You don't say! That's terrible!"

He wished she wouldn't.

Sometimes old Aug Hempel drove out there and Dirk would come upon the two snickering wickedly together about something that he knew concerned the North Shore crowd.

It had been years since Selina had said, sociably, "What did they have for dinner, Dirk? H'm?"

"Well—soup————"

"Nothing before the soup?"

"Oh, yeh. Some kind of a—one of those canape things, you know. Caviare."

"My! Caviare!"

Sometimes Selina giggled like a naughty girl at things that Dirk had taken quite seriously. The fox hunts, for example. Lake Forest had taken to fox hunting, and the Tippecanoe crowd kept kennels. Dirk had learned to ride— pretty well. An Englishman—a certain Captain Stokes-Beatty—had initiated the North Shore into the mysteries of fox hunting. Huntin'. The North Shore learned to say nec's'ry and conservat'ry. Captain Stokes-Beatty was a tall, bow-legged, and somewhat horse-faced young man, remote in manner. The nice Farnham girl seemed fated to marry him. Paula had had a hunt breakfast at Stormwood and it had been very successful, though the American men had balked a little at the devilled kidneys. The food had been patterned as far as possible after the pale flabby viands served at English hunt breakfasts and ruined in an atmosphere of lukewarm steam. The women were slim and perfectly tailored but wore their hunting clothes a trifle uneasily and self-consciously like girls in their first low-cut party dresses. Most of the men had turned stubborn on the subject of pink coats, but Captain Stokes-Beatty wore his handsomely. The fox—a worried and somewhat dejected-looking animal—had been shipped in a crate from the south and on being released had a way of sitting sociably in an Illinois corn field instead of leaping fleetly to cover. At the finish you had a feeling of guilt, as though you had killed a cockroach.

Dirk had told Selina about it, feeling rather magnificent. A fox hunt.

"A fox hunt! What for?"

"For! Why, what's any fox hunt for?"

"I can't imagine. They used to be for the purpose of ridding a fox-infested country of a nuisance. Have the foxes been bothering 'em out in Lake Forest?"

"Now, Mother, don't be funny." He told her about the breakfast.

"Well, but it's so silly, Dirk. It's smart to copy from another country the things that that country does better than we do. England does gardens and wood-fires and dogs and tweeds and walking shoes and pipes and leisure better than we do. But those lukewarm steamy breakfasts of theirs! It's because they haven't gas, most of them. No Kansas or Nebraska farmer's wife would stand for one of their kitchens—not for a minute. And the hired man would balk at such bacon." She giggled.

"Oh, well, if you're going to talk like that."

But Dallas O'Mara felt much the same about these things. Dallas, it appeared, had been something of a fad with the North Shore society crowd after she had painted Mrs. Robinson Gilman's portrait. She had been invited to dinners and luncheons and dances, but their doings, she told Dirk, had bored her.

"They're nice," she said, "but they don't have much fun. They're all trying to be something they're not. And that's such hard work. The women were always explaining that they lived in Chicago because their husband's business was here. They all do things pretty well—dance or paint or ride or write or sing—but not well enough. They're professional amateurs, trying to express something they don't feel; or that they don't feel strongly enough to make it worth while expressing."

She admitted, though, that they did appreciate the things that other people did well. Visiting and acknowledged writers, painters, lecturers, heroes, they entertained lavishly and hospitably in their Florentine or English or Spanish or French palaces on the north side of Chicago, Illinois. Especially foreign notables of this description. Since 1918 these had descended upon Chicago (and all America) like a plague of locusts, starting usually in New York and sweeping westward, devouring the pleasant verdure of greenbacks and chirping as they came. Returning to Europe, bursting with profits and spleen, they thriftily wrote of what they had seen and the result was more clever than amiable; bearing, too, the taint of bad taste.

North Shore hostesses vied for the honour of entertaining these notables. Paula—pretty, clever, moneyed, shrewd—often emerged from these contests the winner. Her latest catch was Emile Goguet—General Emile Goguet, hero of Champagne—Goguet of the stiff white beard, the empty left coat-sleeve, and the score of medals. He was coming to America ostensibly to be the guest of the American Division which, with Goguet's French troops, had turned the German onslaught at Champagne, but really, it was whispered, to cement friendly relations between his country and a somewhat diffident United States.

"And guess," trilled Paula, "guess who's coming with him, Dirk! That wonderful Roelf Pool, the French sculptor! Goguet's going to be my guest. Pool's going to do a bust, you know, of young Quentin Roosevelt from a photograph that Mrs. Theodore Roosevelt——"

"What d'you mean—French sculptor! He's no more French than I am. He was born within a couple of miles of my mother's farm. His people were Dutch truck farmers. His father lived in High Prairie until a year ago, when he died of a stroke."

When he told Selina she flushed like a girl, as she sometimes still did when she was much excited. "Yes, I saw it in the paper. I wonder," she added, quietly, "if I shall see him."

That evening you might have seen her sitting, cross-legged, before the old carved chest, fingering the faded shabby time-worn objects the saving of which Dirk had denounced as sentimental. The crude drawing of the Haymarket; the wine-red cashmere dress; some faded brittle flowers.

Paula was giving a large—but not too large—dinner on the second night. She was very animated about it, excited, gay. "They say," she told Dirk, "that Goguet doesn't eat anything but hard-boiled eggs and rusks. Oh, well, the others won't object to squabs and mushrooms and things, And his hobby is his farm in Brittany. Pool's stunning—dark and sombre and very white teeth."

Paula was very gay these days. Too gay. It seemed to Dirk that her nervous energy was inexhaustible—and exhausting. Dirk refused to admit to himself how irked he was by the sallow heart-shaped exquisite face, the lean brown clutching fingers, the air of ownership. He had begun to dislike things about her as an unfaithful spouse is irritated by quite innocent mannerisms of his unconscious mate. She scuffed her heels a little when she walked, for example. It maddened him. She had a way of biting the rough skin around her carefully tended nails when she was nervous. "Don't *do* that!" he said.

Dallas never irritated him. She rested him, he told himself. He would arm himself against her, but one minute after meeting her he would sink gratefully and resistlessly into her quiet depths. Sometimes he thought all this was an assumed manner in her.

"This calm of yours—this effortlessness," he said to her one day, "is a pose, isn't it?" Anything to get her notice.

"Partly," Dallas had replied, amiably. "It's a nice pose though, don't you think?"

What are you going to do with a girl like that!

Here was the woman who could hold him entirely, and who never held out a finger to hold him. He tore at the smooth wall of her indifference, though he only cut and bruised his own hands in doing it.

"Is it because I'm a successful business man that you don't like me?"

"But I do like you."

"That you don't find me attractive, then."

"But I think you're an awfully attractive man. Dangerous, that's wot."

"Oh, don't be the wide-eyed ingénue. You know damned well what I mean. You've got me and you don't want me. If I had been a successful architect instead of a successful business man would that have made any difference?" He was thinking of what his mother had said just a few years back, that night when they had talked at her bedside. "Is that it? He's got to be an artist, I suppose, to interest you."

"Good Lord, no! Some day I'll probably marry a horny-handed son of toil, and if I do it'll be the horny hands that will win me. If you want to know, I like 'em with their scars on them. There's something about a man who has fought for it—I don't know what it is—a look in his eye—the feel of his hand. He needn't have been successful—though he probably would be. I don't know. I'm not very good at this analysis stuff. I only know he—well, you haven't a mark on you. Not a mark. You quit being an architect, or whatever it was, because architecture was an uphill disheartening job at the time. I don't say that you should have kept on. For all I know you were a bum architect. But if you had kept on—if you had loved it enough to keep on—fighting, and struggling, and sticking it out—why, that fight would show in your face to-day—in your eyes and your jaw and your hands and in your way of standing and walking and sitting and talking. Listen. I'm not criticizing you. But you're all smooth. I like 'em bumpy. That sounds terrible. It isn't what I mean at all. It isn't———"

"Oh, never mind," Dirk said, wearily, "I think I know what you mean." He sat looking down at his hands—his fine strong unscarred hands. Suddenly and unreasonably he thought of another pair of hands—his mother's—with the knuckles enlarged, the skin broken—expressive—her life written on them. Scars. She had them. "Listen, Dallas. If I thought—I'd go back to Hollis & Sprague's and begin all over again at forty a week if I thought you'd———"

"Don't."

20

GENERAL GOGUET AND Roelf Pool had been in Chicago one night and part of a day. Dirk had not met them—was to meet them at Paula's dinner that evening. He was curious about Pool but not particularly interested in the warrior. Restless, unhappy, wanting to see Dallas (he admitted it, bitterly), he dropped into her studio at an unaccustomed hour almost immediately after lunch and heard gay voices and laughter. Why couldn't she work alone once in a while without that rabble around her!

Dallas in a grimy smock and the scuffed kid slippers was entertaining two truants from Chicago society—General Emile Goguet and Roelf Pool. They seemed to be enjoying themselves immensely. She introduced Dirk as casually as though their presence were a natural and expected thing—which it was. She had never mentioned them to him. Yet now: "This is Dirk DeJong— General Emile Goguet. We were campaigners together in France. Roelf Pool. So were we, weren't we, Roelf?"

General Emile Goguet bowed formally, but his eyes were twinkling. He appeared to be having a very good time. Roelf Pool's dark face had lighted up with such a glow of surprise and pleasure as to transform it. He strode over to Dirk, clasped his hand. "Dirk DeJong! Not—why, say, don't you know me? I'm Roelf Pool!"

"I ought to know you," said Dirk.

"Oh, but I mean I'm—I knew you when you were a kid. You're Selina's Dirk. Aren't you? My Selina. I'm driving out to see her this afternoon. She's one of my reasons for being here. Why, I'm—" He was laughing, talking excitedly, like a boy. Dallas, all agrin, was enjoying it immensely.

"They've run away," she explained to Dirk, "from the elaborate programme that was arranged for them this afternoon. I don't know where the French got their reputation for being polite. The General is a perfect boor, aren't you? And scared to death of women. He's the only French general in captivity who ever took the trouble to learn English."

General Goguet nodded violently and roared. "And you?" he said to Dirk in his careful and perfect English. "You, too, are an artist?"

"No," Dirk said, "not an artist."

"What, then?"

"Why—uh—bonds. That is, the banking business. Bonds."

"Ah, yes," said General Goguet, politely. "Bonds. A very good thing, bonds. We French are very fond of them, We have great respect for American bonds, we French." He nodded and twinkled and turned away to Dallas.

"We're all going," announced Dallas, and made a dash for the stuffy little bedroom off the studio.

Well, this was a bit too informal. "Going where?" inquired Dirk. The General, too, appeared bewildered.

Roelf explained, delightedly. "It's a plot. We're all going to drive out to your mother's. You'll go, won't you? You simply must."

"Go?" now put in General Goguet. "Where is it that we go? I thought we stayed here, quietly. It is quiet here, and no reception committees." His tone was wistful.

Roelf attempted to make it clear. "Mr. DeJong's mother is a farmer. You remember I told you all about her in the ship coming over. She was wonderful to me when I was a kid. She was the first person to tell me what beauty was—is. She's magnificent. She raises vegetables."

"Ah! A farm! But yes! I, too, am a farmer. Well!" He shook Dirk's hand again. He appeared now for the first time to find him interesting.

"Of course I'll go. Does Mother know you're coming? She has been hoping she'd see you but she thought you'd grown so grand————"

"Wait until I tell her about the day I landed in Paris with five francs in my pocket. No, she doesn't know we're coming, but she'll be there, won't she? I've a feeling she'll be there, exactly the same. She will, won't she?"

"She'll be there." It was early spring; the busiest of seasons on the farm.

Dallas emerged in greatcoat and a new spring hat. She waved a hand to the faithful Gilda Hanan. "Tell any one who inquires for me that I've felt the call of spring. And if the boy comes for that clay pack picture tell him to-morrow was the day."

They were down the stairs and off in the powerful car that seemed to be at the visitors' disposal. Through the Loop, up Michigan Avenue, into the south side. Chicago, often lowering and gray in April, was wearing gold and blue to-day. The air was sharp but beneath the brusqueness of it was a gentle promise. Dallas and Pool were very much absorbed in Paris plans, Paris reminiscences. "And do you remember the time we . . . only seven francs among the lot of us and the dinner was . . . you're surely coming over in June, then . . . oils . . . you've got the thing, I tell you . . . you'll be great, Dallas . . . remember what Vibray said . . . study . . . work . . ."

Dirk was wretched. He pointed out objects of interest to General Goguet. Sixty miles of boulevard. Park system. Finest in the country. Grand Boulevard. Drexel Boulevard. Jackson Park. Illinois Central trains. Terrible, yes, but they were electrifying. Going to make 'em run by electricity, you know. Things wouldn't look so dirty, after that. Halsted Street. Longest street in the world.

And, "Ah, yes," said the General, politely. "Ah, yes. Quite so. Most interesting."

The rich black loam of High Prairie. A hint of fresh green things just peeping out of the earth. Hothouses. Coldframes. The farm.

It looked very trim and neat. The house, white with green shutters (Selina's dream realized), smiled at them from among the willows that were already burgeoning hazily under the wooing of a mild and early spring.

"But I thought you said it was a small farm!" said General Goguet, as they descended from the car. He looked about at the acreage.

"It is small," Dirk assured him. "Only about forty acres."

"Ah, well, you Americans. In France we farm on a very small scale, you understand. We have not the land. The great vast country." He waved his right arm. You felt that if the left sleeve had not been empty he would have made a large and sweeping gesture with both arms.

Selina was not in the neat quiet house. She was not on the porch, or in the yard. Meena Bras, phlegmatic and unflustered, came in from the kitchen. Mis' DeJong was in the fields. She would call her. This she proceeded to do by blowing three powerful blasts and again three on a horn which she took from a hook on the wall. She stood in the kitchen doorway facing the fields, blowing, her red cheeks puffed outrageously. "That brings her," Meena assured them; and went back to her work. They came out on the porch to await Selina. She was out on the west sixteen—the west sixteen that used to be unprolific, half-drowned muckland. Dirk felt a little uneasy, and ashamed that he should feel so.

Then they saw her coming, a small dark figure against the background of sun and sky and fields. She came swiftly yet ploddingly, for the ground was heavy. They stood facing her, the four of them. As she came nearer they saw that she was wearing a dark skirt pinned up about her ankles to protect it from the wet spring earth and yet it was spattered with a border of mud spots. A rough heavy gray sweater was buttoned closely about the straight slim body. On her head was a battered soft black hat. Her feet, in broad-toed sensible boots, she lifted high out of the soft clinging soil. As she came nearer she took off her hat and holding it a little to one side against the sun, shaded her eyes with it. Her hair blew a little in the gentle spring breeze. Her cheeks were faintly pink. She was coming up the path now. She could distinguish their faces. She saw Dirk; smiled, waved. Her glance went inquiringly to the others—the bearded man in uniform, the tall girl, the man with the dark vivid face. Then she stopped, suddenly, and her hand went to her heart as though she had felt a great pang, and her lips were parted, and her eyes enormous. As Roelf came forward swiftly she took a few quick running steps toward him like a young girl. He took the slight figure in the mud-spattered skirt, the rough gray sweater, and the battered old hat into his arms.

21

THEY HAD HAD tea in the farm sitting room and Dallas made a little moaning over the beauty of the Dutch lustre set. Selina had entertained them with the shining air of one who is robed in silk and fine linen. She and General Goguet had got on famously from the start, meeting on the common ground of asparagus culture.

"But how thick?" he had demanded, for he, too, had his pet asparagus beds on the farm in Brittany. "How thick at the base?"

Selina made a circle with thumb and forefinger. The General groaned with envy and despair. He was very comfortable, the General. He partook largely of tea and cakes. He flattered Selina with his eyes. She actually dimpled, flushed, laughed like a girl. But it was to Roelf she turned; it was on Roelf that her eyes dwelt and rested. It was with him she walked when she was silent and the others talked. It was as though he were her one son, and had come home. Her face was radiant, beautiful.

Seated next to Dirk, Dallas said, in a low voice: "There, that's what I mean. That's what I mean when I say I want to do portraits. Not portraits of ladies with a string of pearls and one lily hand half hidden in the folds of a satin skirt. I mean character portraits of men and women who are really distinguished looking—distinguishedly American, for example—like your mother."

Dirk looked up at her quickly, half smiling, as though expecting to find her smiling, too. But she was not smiling. "My mother!"

"Yes, if she'd let me. With that fine splendid face all lit up with the light that comes from inside; and the jaw-line like that of the women who came over in the *Mayflower;* or crossed the continent in a covered wagon; and her eyes! And that battered funny gorgeous bum old hat and the white shirtwaist—and her hands! She's beautiful. She'd make me famous at one leap. You'd see!''

Dirk stared at her. It was as though he could not comprehend. Then he turned in his chair to stare at his mother. Selina was talking to Roelf.

"And you've done all the famous men of Europe, haven't you, Roelf! To think of it! You've seen the world, and you've got it in your hand. Little Roelf Pool. And you did it all alone. In spite of everything.''

Roelf leaned toward her. He put his hand over her rough one. "Cabbages are beautiful,'' he said. Then they both laughed as at some exquisite joke. Then, seriously: "What a fine life you've had, too, Selina. A full life, and a rich one and successful.''

"I!'' exclaimed Selina. "Why, Roelf, I've been here all these years, just where you left me when you were a boy. I think the very hat and dress I'm wearing might be the same I wore then. I've been nowhere, done nothing, seen nothing. When I think of all the places I was going to see! All the things I was going to do!''

"You've been everywhere in the world,'' said Roelf. "You've seen all the places of great beauty and light. You remember you told me that your father had once said, when you were a little girl, that there were only two kinds of people who really mattered in the world. One kind was wheat and the other kind emeralds. You're wheat, Selina.''

"And you're emerald,'' said Selina, quickly.

The General was interested but uncomprehending. He glanced now at the watch on his wrist and gave a little exclamation. "But the dinner! Our hostess, Madame Storm! It is very fine to run away but one must come back. Our so beautiful hostess.'' He had sprung to his feet.

"She is beautiful, isn't she?'' said Selina.

"No,'' Roelf replied, abruptly. "The mouth is smaller than the eyes. With Mrs. Storm from here to here''—he illustrated by turning to Dallas, touching her lips, her eyes, lightly with his slender powerful brown fingers—"is smaller than from here to here. When the mouth is smaller than the eyes there is no real beauty. Now Dallas here————''

"Yes, me,'' scoffed Dallas, all agrin. "There's a grand mouth for you. If a large mouth is your notion of beauty then I must look like Helen of Troy to you, Roelf.''

"You do,'' said Roelf, simply.

Inside Dirk something was saying, over and over, "You're nothing but a rubber stamp, Dirk DeJong. You're nothing but a rubber stamp.'' Over and over.

"These dinners!'' exclaimed the General. "I do not wish to seem ungracious, but these dinners! Much rather would I remain here on this quiet and beautiful farm.''

At the porch steps he turned, brought his heels together with a sharp smack, bent from the waist, picked up Selina's rough work-worn hand and kissed it. And then, as she smiled a little, uncertainly, her left hand at her breast, her cheeks pink, Roelf, too, kissed her hand tenderly.

"Why,'' said Selina, and laughed a soft tremulous little laugh, "why, I've never had my hand kissed before.''

She stood on the porch steps and waved at them as they were whirled swiftly away, the four of them. A slight straight little figure in the plain white blouse and the skirt spattered with the soil of the farm.

"You'll come out again?'' she had said to Dallas. And Dallas had said yes, but that she was leaving soon for Paris, to study and work.

"When I come back you'll let me do your portrait?"

"*My* portrait!" Selina had exclaimed, wonderingly.

Now as the four were whirled back to Chicago over the asphalted Halsted road they were relaxed, a little tired. They yielded to the narcotic of spring that was in the air.

Roelf Pool took off his hat. In the cruel spring sunshine you saw that the black hair was sprinkled with gray. "On days like this I refuse to believe that I'm forty-five. Dallas, tell me I'm not forty-five."

"You're not forty-five," said Dallas in her leisurely caressing voice.

Roelf's lean brown hand reached over frankly and clasped her strong white one. "When you say it like that, Dallas, it sounds true."

"It is true," said Dallas.

They dropped Dallas first at the shabby old Ontario Street studio, then Dirk at his smart little apartment, and went on.

Dirk turned his key in the lock. Saki, the Japanese houseman, slid silently into the hall making little hissing noises of greeting. On the correct little console in the hall there was a correct little pile of letters and invitations. He went through the Italian living room and into his bedroom. The Jap followed him. Dirk's correct evening clothes (made by Peel the English tailor on Michigan Boulevard) were laid correctly on his bed—trousers, vest, shirt, coat; fine, immaculate.

"Messages, Saki?"

"Missy Stlom telephone."

"Oh. Leave any message?"

"No. Say s'e call 'gain."

"All right, Saki." He waved him away and out of the room. The man went and closed the door softly behind him as a correct Jap servant should. Dirk took off his coat, his vest, threw them on a chair near the bed. He stood at the bedside looking down at his Peel evening clothes, at the glossy shirt-front that never bulged. A bath, he thought, dully, automatically. Then, quite suddenly, he flung himself on the fine silk-covered bed, face down, and lay there, his head in his arms, very still, He was lying there half an hour later when he heard the telephone's shrill insistence and Saki's gentle deferential rap at the bedroom door.

Show Boat

INTRODUCTION

"SHOW BOAT" is neither history nor biography, but fiction. This statement is made in the hope that it will forestall such protest as may be registered by demon statisticians against certain liberties taken with characters, places, and events. In the Chicago portion of the book, for example, a character occasionally appears some three or four years after the actual date of his death. Now and then a restaurant or gambling resort is described as running full blast at at time when it had vanished at the frown of civic virtue. This, then, was done, not through negligence in research, but because, in the attempt to give a picture of the time, it was necessary slightly to condense a period of fifteen or twenty years.

E. F.

1

BIZARRE AS WAS the name she bore, Kim Ravenal always said she was thankful it had been no worse. She knew whereof she spoke, for it was literally by a breath that she had escaped being called Mississippi.

"Imagine Mississippi Ravenal!" she often said, in later years. "They'd have cut it to Missy, I suppose, or even Sippy, if you can bear to think of anything so horrible. And then I'd have had to change my name or give up the stage altogether. Because who'd go to see—seriously, I mean—an actress named Sippy? It sounds half-witted, for some reason. Kim's bad enough, God knows."

And as Kim Ravenal you doubtless are familiar with her. It is no secret that the absurd monosyllable which comprises her given name is made up of the first letters of three states—Kentucky, Illinois, and Missouri—in all of which she was, incredibly enough, born—if she can be said to have been born in any state at all. Her mother insists that she wasn't. If you were an habitué of old South Clark Street in Chicago's naughty '90s you may even remember her mother, Magnolia Ravenal, as Nola Ravenal, soubrette—though Nola Ravenal never achieved the doubtful distinction of cigarette pictures. In a day when the stage measured feminine pulchritude in terms of hips, thighs, and calves, she was considered much too thin for beauty, let alone for tights.

It had been this Magnolia Ravenal's respiratory lack that had saved the new-born girl from being cursed through life with a name boasting more quadruple vowels and consonants than any other in the language. She had meant to call the child Mississippi after the tawny untamed river on which she had spent so much of her girlhood, and which had stirred and fascinated her always. Her accouchement had been an ordeal even more terrifying than is ordinarily the case, for Kim Ravenal had actually been born on the raging turgid bosom of the Mississippi River itself, when that rampageous stream was flooding its banks and inundating towns for miles around, at five o'clock of a storm-racked April morning in 1889. It was at a point just below Cairo, Illinois; that region known as Little Egypt, where the yellow waters of the Mississippi and the olive-green waters of the Ohio so disdainfully meet and refuse, with bull-necked pride, to mingle.

From her cabin window on the second deck of the Cotton Blossom Floating Palace Theatre, Magnolia Ravenal could have seen the misty shores of three states—if any earthly shores had interested her at the moment. Just here was Illinois, to whose crumbling clay banks the show boat was so perilously pinioned. Beyond, almost hidden by the rain veil, was Missouri; and there, Kentucky. But Magnolia Ravenal lay with her eyes shut because the effort of lifting her lids was beyond her. Seeing her, you would have said that if any shores filled her vision at the moment they were heavenly ones, and those dangerously near. So white, so limp, so spent was she that her face on the pillow was startlingly like one of the waxen blossoms whose name she bore. Her slimness made almost no outline beneath the bedclothes. The coverlet was drawn up to her chin. There was only the white flower on the pillow, its petals closed.

Outside, the redundant rain added its unwelcome measure to the swollen and angry stream. In the ghostly gray dawn the grotesque wreckage of flood-time floated and whirled and jiggled by, seeming to bob a mad obeisance as it passed the show boat which, in its turn, made stately bows from its moorings. There drifted past, in fantastic parade, great trees, uprooted and clutching at the water with stiff dead arms; logs, catapulted with terrific force; animal carcasses dreadful in their passivity; chicken coops; rafts; a piano, its ivory mouth fixed in a death grin; a two-room cabin, upright, and moving in a minuet of stately and ponderous swoops and advances and chassés; fence rails; an armchair whose white crocheted antimacassar stared in prim disapproval at the wild antics of its fellow voyagers; a live sheep, bleating as it came, but soon still; a bed with its covers, by some freak of suction, still snugly tucked in as when its erstwhile occupant had fled from it in fright—all these, and more, contributed to the weird terror of the morning. The Mississippi itself was a tawny tiger, roused, furious, bloodthirsty, lashing out with its great tail, tearing with its cruel claws, and burying its fangs deep in the shore to swallow at a gulp land, houses, trees, cattle—humans, even; and roaring, snarling, howling hideously as it did so.

Inside Magnolia Ravenal's cabin all was snug and warm and bright. A wood fire snapped and crackled cosily in the little pot-bellied iron stove. Over it bent a veritable Sairey Gamp stirring something hot and savoury in a saucepan. She stirred noisily, and talked as she stirred, and glanced from time to time at the mute white figure in the bed. Her own bulky figure was made more ponderous by layer on layer of ill- assorted garments of the kind donned from time to time as night wears on by one who, having been aroused hastily and in emergency, has arrived scantily clad. A gray flannel nightgown probably formed the basis of this costume, for its grizzled cuffs could just be seen emerging from the man's coat whose sleeves she wore turned back from the wrists for comfort and convenience. This coat was of box cut, double-breasted, blue with brass buttons and gold braid, of the sort that river captains wear. It gave her a racy and nautical look absurdly at variance with her bulk and occupation. Peeping beneath and above and around this, the baffled eye could just glimpse oddments and elegancies such as a red flannel dressing gown; a flower-besprigged challis sacque whose frill of doubtful lace made the captain's coat even more incongruous; a brown cashmere skirt, very bustled and bunchy; a pair of scuffed tan kid bedroom slippers (men's) of the sort known as romeos. This lady's back hair was twisted into a knob strictly utilitarian; her front hair bristled with the wired ends of kid curlers assumed, doubtless, the evening before the hasty summons. Her face and head were long and horse-like, at variance with her bulk. This, you sensed immediately, was a person possessed of enormous energy, determination, and the gift of making exquisitely uncomfortable any one who happened to be within hearing radius. She was the sort who rattles anything that can be rattled; slams anything that can be slammed; bumps anything that can be bumped. Her name, by some miracle of fitness, was Parthenia Ann Hawks; wife of Andy Hawks, captain and owner of the Cotton Blossom Floating Palace Theatre; and mother of this Magnolia Ravenal who, having just been delivered of a daughter, lay supine in her bed.

Now, as Mrs. Hawks stirred the mess over which she was bending, her spoon regularly scraped the bottom of the pan with a rasping sound that would have tortured any nerves but her own iron-encased set. She removed the spoon, freeing it of clinging drops by rapping it smartly and metallically against the rim of the basin. Magnolia Ravenal's eyelids fluttered ever so slightly.

"Now then!" spake Parthy Ann Hawks, briskly, in that commanding tone against which even the most spiritless instinctively rebelled, "Now then, young lady, want it or not, you'll eat some of this broth, good and hot and stren'th'ning, and maybe you won't look so much like a wet dish rag." Pan in one hand, spoon in the other, she advanced toward the bed with a tread that jarred the furniture and set the dainty dimity window curtains to fluttering. She brought up against the side of the bed with a bump. A shadow of pain flitted across the white face on the pillow. The eyes still were closed. As the smell of the hot liquid reached her nostrils, the lips of the girl on the bed curled in distaste. "Here, I'll just spoon it right up to you out of the pan, so's it'll be good and hot. Open your mouth! Open your eyes! I say open——— Well, for land's sakes, how do you expect a body to do anything for you if you———"

With a motion shocking in its swift unexpectedness Magnolia Ravenal's hand emerged from beneath the coverlet, dashed aside the spoon with its steaming contents, and sent it clattering to the floor. Then her hand stole beneath the coverlet again and with a little relaxed sigh of satisfaction she lay passive as before. She had not opened her eyes. She was smiling ever so slightly.

"That's right! Act like a wildcat just because I try to get you to sup up a little soup that Jo's been hours cooking, and two pounds of good mutton in it if there's an ounce, besides vegetables and barley, and your pa practically risked his life getting the meat down at Cairo and the water going up by the foot every hour. No, you're not satisfied to get us caught here in the flood, and how we'll ever get out alive or dead, God knows, and me and everybody on the boat up all night long with your goings on so you'd think nobody'd ever had a baby before. Time I had you there wasn't a whimper out of me. Not a whimper. I'd have died, first. I never saw anything as indelicate as the way you carried on, and your own husband in the room." Here Magnolia conveyed with a flutter of the lids that this had not been an immaculate conception. "Well, if you could see yourself now. A drowned rat isn't the word. Now you take this broth, my fine lady, or we'll see who's———" She paused in this dramatic threat to blow a cooling breath on a generous spoonful of the steaming liquid, to sup it up with audible appreciation, and to take another. She smacked her lips. "Now then, no more of your monkey-shines, Maggie Hawks!"

No one but her mother had ever called Magnolia Ravenal Maggie Hawks. It was unthinkable that a name so harsh and unlovely could be applied to this fragile person. Having picked up the rejected spoon and wiped it on the lace ruffle of the challis sacque, that terrible termagant grasped it firmly against surprise in her right hand and, saucepan in left, now advanced a second time toward the bed. You saw the flower on the pillow frosted by an icy mask of utter unyieldingness; you caught a word that sounded like shenanigans from the woman bending over the bed, when the cabin door opened and two twittering females entered attired in garments strangely akin to the haphazard costume worn by Mrs. Hawks. The foremost of these moved in a manner so bustling as to be unmistakably official. She was at once ponderous, playful, and menacing—this last attribute due, perhaps, to the rather splendid dark moustache which stamped her upper lip. In her arms she carried a swaddled bundle under one flannel flap of which the second female kept peering and uttering strange clucking sounds and words that resembled izzer and yesseris.

"Fine a gal's I ever see!" exclaimed the bustling one. She approached the bed with the bundle. "Mis' Means says the same and so"—she glanced contemptuously over her shoulder at a pale and haggard young man, bearded but boyish, who followed close behind them—"does the doctor."

She paused before the word doctor so that the title, when finally it was uttered, carried with it a poisonous derision. This mysterious sally earned a little snigger from Mis' Means and a baleful snort from Mrs. Hawks. Flushed with success, the lady with the swaddled bundle (unmistakably a midwife and, like all her craft, royally accustomed to homage and applause) waxed more malicious. "Fact is, he says only a minute ago, he never brought a finer baby that he can remember."

At this the sniggers and snorts became unmistakable guffaws. The wan young man became a flushed young man. He fumbled awkwardly with the professionally massive watch chain that so unnecessarily guarded his cheap nickel blob of a watch. He glanced at the flowerlike face on the pillow. Its aloofness, its remoteness from the three frowzy females that hovered about it, seemed to lend him a momentary dignity and courage. He thrust his hands behind the tails of his Prince Albert coat and strode toward the bed. A wave of the hand, a slight shove with the shoulder, dismissed the three as nuisances. "One moment, my good woman. . . . *If* you please, Mrs. Hawks. . . . Kindly don't jiggle . . ."

The midwife stepped aside with the bundle. Mrs. Hawks fell back a step, the ineffectual spoon and saucepan in her hands. Mis' Means ceased to cluck and to lean on the bed's footboard. From a capacious inner coat pocket he produced a stethoscope, applied it, listened, straightened. From the waistcoat pocket came the timepiece, telltale of his youth and impecuniosity. He extracted his patient's limp wrist from beneath the coverlet and held it in his own strong spatulate fingers—the fingers of the son of a farmer.

"H'm! Fine!" he exclaimed. "Splendid!"

An unmistakable sniff from the midwife. The boy's florid manner dropped from him. He cringed a little. The sensitive hand he still held in his great grasp seemed to feel this change in him, though Magnolia Ravenal had not opened her eyes even at the entrance of the three. Her wrist slid itself out of his hold and down until her fingers met his and pressed them lightly, reassuringly. The youth looked down, startled. Magnolia Ravenal, white-lipped, was smiling her wide gay gorgeous smile that melted the very vitals of you. It was a smile at once poignant and brilliant. It showed her gums a little, and softened the planes of her high cheek-bones, and subdued the angles of the too-prominent jaw. A comradely smile, an understanding and warming one. Strange that this woman on the bed, so lately torn and racked with the agonies of childbirth, should be the one to encourage the man whose clumsy ministrations had so nearly cost her her life. That she could smile at all was sheer triumph of the spirit over the flesh. And that she could smile in sympathy for and encouragement of this bungling inexpert young medico was incredible. But that was Magnolia Ravenal. Properly directed and managed, her smile, in later years, could have won her a fortune. But direction and management were as futile when applied to her as to the great untamed Mississippi that even now was flouting man-built barriers; laughing at levees that said so far and no farther; jeering at jetties that said do thus and so; for that matter, roaring this very moment in derision of Magnolia Ravenal herself, and her puny pangs and her mortal plans; and her father Captain Andy Hawks, and her mother Parthenia Ann Hawks, and her husband Gaylord Ravenal, and the whole troupe of the show boat, and the Cotton Blossom Floating Palace Theatre itself, now bobbing about like a cork on the yellow flood that tugged and sucked and tore at its moorings.

Two tantrums of nature had been responsible for the present precarious position of the show boat and its occupants. The Mississippi had furnished one; Magnolia Ravenal the other. Or perhaps it might be fairer to fix the blame, not on nature, but on human stupidity that had failed to take into account its vagaries.

Certainly Captain Andy Hawks should have known better, after thirty-five years of experience on keelboats, steamboats, packets, and show boats up and down the great Mississippi and her tributaries (the Indians might call this stream the Father of Waters but your riverman respectfully used the feminine pronoun). The brand-new show boat had done it. Built in the St. Louis shipyards, the new *Cotton Blossom* was to have been ready for him by February. But February had come and gone, and March as well. He had meant to be in New Orleans by this time, with his fine new show boat and his troupe and his band of musicians in their fresh glittering red-and-gold uniforms, and the marvellous steam calliope that could be heard for miles up and down the bayous and plantations. Starting at St. Louis, he had planned a swift trip downstream, playing just enough towns on the way to make expenses. Then, beginning with Bayou Teche and pushed by the sturdy steamer *Mollie Able,* they would proceed grandly upstream, calliope screaming, flags flying, band tooting to play every little town and landing and plantation from New Orleans to Baton Rouge, from Baton Rouge to Vicksburg; to Memphis, to Cairo, to St. Louis, up and up to Minnesota itself; then over to the coal towns on the Monongahela River and the Kanawha, and down again to New Orleans, following the crops as they ripened—the corn belt, the cotton belt, the sugar cane; north when the wheat yellowed, following with the sun the ripening of the peas, the tomatoes, the crabs, the peaches, the apples; and as the farmer garnered his golden crops so would shrewd Captain Andy Hawks gather his harvest of gold.

It was April before the new *Cotton Blossom* was finished and ready to take to the rivers. Late though it was, when Captain Andy Hawks beheld her, glittering from texas to keel in white paint with green trimmings, and with Cotton Blossom Floating Palace Theatre done in letters two feet high on her upper deck, he was vain enough, or foolhardy enough, or both, to resolve to stand by his original plan. A little nervous fussy man, Andy Hawks, with a horrible habit of clawing and scratching from side to side, when aroused or when deep in thought, at the little mutton-chop whiskers that sprang out like twin brushes just below his leather-visored white canvas cap, always a trifle too large for his head, so that it settled down over his ears. A capering figure, in light linen pants very wrinkled and baggy, and a blue coat, double-breasted; with a darting manner, bright brown eyes, and a trick of talking very fast as he clawed the mutton-chop whiskers first this side, then that, with one brown hairy little hand. There was about him something grotesque, something simian. He beheld the new *Cotton Blossom* as a bridegroom gazes upon a bride, and frenziedly clawing his whiskers he made his unwise decision.

"She won't high-water this year till June." He was speaking of that tawny tigress, the Mississippi; and certainly no one knew her moods better than he. "Not much snow last winter, north; and no rain to speak of, yet. Yessir, we'll just blow down to New Orleans ahead of French's *Sensation*"—his bitterest rival in the showboat business—"and start to work the bayous. Show him a clean pair of heels up and down the river."

So they had started. And because the tigress lay smooth and unruffled now, with only the currents playing gently below the surface like muscles beneath the golden yellow skin, they fancied she would remain complaisant until they had had their way. That was the first mistake.

The second was as unreasoning. Magnolia Ravenal's child was going to be a boy. Ma Hawks and the wise married women of the troupe knew the signs. She felt thus-and-so. She had such-and-such sensations. She was carrying the child high. Boys always were slower in being born than girls. Besides, this was a first child, and the first child always is late. They got together, in mysterious female conclave, and counted on the fingers of their two hands—August, September, October, November, December—why, the end of April, the soonest. They'd be safe in New Orleans by then, with the best of doctors for Magnolia, and she on land while one of the other women in the company played her parts until she was strong again—a matter of two or three weeks at most.

No sooner had they started than the rains began. No early April showers, these, but torrents that blotted out the river banks on either side and sent the clay tumbling in great cave-ins, down to the water, jaundicing it afresh where already it seethed an ochreous mass. Day after day, night after night, the rains came down, melting the Northern ice and snow, filtering through the land of the Mississippi basin and finding its way, whether trickle, rivulet, creek, stream, or river, to the great hungry mother, Mississippi. And she grew swollen, and tossed and flung her huge limbs about and shrieked in labour even as Magnolia Ravenal was so soon to do.

Eager for entertainment as the dwellers were along the little Illinois and Missouri towns, after a long winter of dull routine on farm and in store and schoolhouse, they came sparsely to the show boat. Posters had told them of her coming, and the news filtered to the backcountry. Town and village thrilled to the sound of the steam calliope as the Cotton Blossom Floating Palace Theatre, propelled by the square-cut clucking old steamer, *Mollie Able,* swept grandly down the river to the landing. But the back-country roads were impassable bogs by now, and growing worse with every hour of rain. Wagon wheels sank to the hubs in mud. There were crude signs, stuck on poles, reading, "No bottom here." The dodgers posted on walls and fences in the towns were rain-soaked and bleary. And as for the Cotton Blossom Floating Palace Theatre Ten Piece Band (which numbered six)— how could it risk ruin of its smart new red coats, gold-braided and gold-buttoned, by marching up the water-logged streets of these little towns whose occupants only stared wistfully out through storm-blurred windows? It was dreary even at night, when the show boat glowed invitingly with the blaze of a hundred oil lamps that lighted the auditorium seating six hundred (One Thousand Seats! A Luxurious Floating Theatre within an Unrivalled Floating Palace!). Usually the flaming oil-flares on their tall poles stuck in the steep clay banks that led down to the show boat at the water's edge made a path of fiery splendour. Now they hissed and spluttered dismally, almost extinguished by the deluge. Even when the bill was St. Elmo or East Lynne, those tried and trusty winners, the announcement of which always packed the show boat's auditorium to the very last seat in the balcony reserved for Negroes, there was now only a damp handful of shuffle-footed men and giggling girls and a few children in the cheaper rear seats. The Mississippi Valley dwellers, wise with the terrible wisdom born of much suffering under the dominance of this voracious and untamed monster, so ruthless when roused, were preparing against catastrophe should these days of rain continue.

Captain Andy Hawks clawed his mutton-chop whiskers, this side and that, and scanned the skies, and searched the yellowing swollen stream with his bright brown eyes. "We'll make for Cairo," he said. "Full steam ahead. I don't like the looks of her—the big yella snake."

But full steam ahead was impossible for long in a snag-infested river, as

Andy Hawks well knew; and in a river whose treacherous channel shifted almost daily in normal times, and hourly in flood-time. Cautiously they made for Cairo. Cape Girardeau, Gray's Point, Commerce—then, suddenly, near evening, the false sun shone for a brief hour. At once everyone took heart. The rains, they assured each other, were over. The spring freshet would subside twice as quickly as it had risen. Fittingly enough, the play billed for that evening was Tempest and Sunshine, always a favourite. Magnolia Ravenal cheerfully laced herself into the cruel steel-stiffened high-busted corset of the period, and donned the golden curls and the prim rufffles of the part. A goodish crowd scrambled and slipped and slid down the rain-soaked clay bank, torch-illumined, to the show boat, their boots leaving a trail of mud and water up and down the aisles of the theatre and between the seats. It was a restless audience, and hard to hold. There had been an angry sunset, and threatening clouds to the northwest. The crowd shuffled its feet, coughed, stirred constantly. There was in the air something electric, menacing, heavy. Suddenly, during the last act, the north wind sprang up with a whistling sound, and the little choppy hard waves could be heard slapping against the boat's flat sides. She began to rock, too, and pitch, flat though she was and securely moored to the river bank. Lightning, a fusillade of thunder, and then the rain again, heavy, like drops of molten lead, and driven by the north wind. The crowd scrambled up the perilous clay banks, slipping, falling, cursing, laughing, frightened. To this day it is told that the river rose seven feet in twenty-four hours. Captain Andy Hawks, still clawing his whiskers, still bent on making for Cairo, cast off and ordered the gang plank in as the last scurrying villager clawed his way up the slimy incline whose heights the river was scaling inch by inch.

"The Ohio's the place," he insisted, his voice high and squeaky with excitement. "High water at Cincinnati, St. Louis, Evansville, or even Paducah don't have to mean high water on the Ohio. It's the old yella serpent making all this kick-up. But the Ohio's the river gives Cairo the real trouble. Yessir! And she don't flood till June. We'll make for the Ohio and stay on her till this comes to a stand, anyway."

Then followed the bedlam of putting off. Yells, hoarse shouts, bells ringing, wheels churning the water to foam. Lively now! Cramp her down! Snatch her! SNATCH her!

Faintly, above the storm, you heard the cracked falsetto of little Captain Andy Hawks, a pilot for years, squeaking to himself in his nervousness the orders that river etiquette forbade his actually giving that ruler, that ultimate sovereign, the pilot, old Mark Hooper, whose real name was no more Mark than Twain's had been: relic of his leadsmen days, with the cry of, "Mark three! Mark three! Half twain! Quarter twain! M-A-R-K twain!" gruffly shouted along the hurricane deck.

It was told, on the rivers, that little Andy Hawks had been known, under excitement, to walk off the deck into the river and to bob afloat there until rescued, still spluttering and shrieking orders in a profane falsetto.

Down the river they went, floating easily over bars that in normal times stood six feet out of the water; clattering through chutes; shaving the shores. Thunder, lightning, rain, chaos outside. Within, the orderly routine of bedtime on the show boat. Mis' Means, the female half of the character team, heating over a tiny spirit flame a spoonful of goose grease which she would later rub on her husband's meagre cough-racked chest; Maudie Rainger, of the general business team, sipping her bedtime cup of coffee; Bert Forbush, utility man, in shirt sleeves, check pants, and carpet slippers, playing a sleep-inducing game of canfield—all this on the stage, bare now of scenery and turned into a haphazard and impromptu lounging room for the members of this floating theatrical company. Mrs. Hawks, in her fine new cabin on the second deck, off the gallery, was putting her sparse hair in crimpers as she would do if this were the night before Judgment Day. Flood, storm, danger—all part of river show-boat life. Ordinarily, it is true, they did not proceed down river until daybreak. After the performance, the show boat and its steamer would stay snug and still alongside the wharf of this little town or that. By midnight, company and crew would have fallen asleep to the sound of the water slap-slapping gently against the boat's sides.

To-night there probably would be little sleep for some of the company, what with the storm, the motion, the unwonted stir, and the noise that came from the sturdy *Mollie Able,* bracing her cautious bulk against the flood's swift urging; and certainly none for Captain Andy Hawks, for pilot Mark Hooper and the crew of the *Mollie Able.* But that, too, was all part of the life.

Midnight had found Gaylord Ravenal, in nightshirt and dressing gown, a handsome and distraught figure, pounding on the door of his mother-in-law's cabin. From the cabin he had just left came harrowing sounds—whimpers, and little groans, and great moans, like an animal in agony. Magnolia Ravenal was not one of your silent sufferers. She was too dramatic for that. Man-oeuvred magically by the expert Hooper, they managed to make a perilous landing just above Cairo. The region was scoured for a doctor, without success, for accident had followed on flood. Captain Andy had tracked down a stout and reluctant midwife who consented only after an enormous bribe to make the perilous trip to the levee, clambering ponderously down the slippery bank with many groanings and forebodings, and being sustained, both in bulk and spirit, by the agile and vivacious little captain much as a tiny fussy river tug guides a gigantic and unwieldy ocean liner. He was almost frantically distraught, for between Andy Hawks and his daughter Magnolia Ravenal was that strong bond of affection and mutual understanding that always exists between the henpecked husband and the harassed offspring of a shrew such as Parthy Ann Hawks.

When, an hour later, Gaylord Ravenal, rain-soaked and mud-spattered, arrived with a white-faced young doctor's assistant whose first obstetrical call this was, he found the fat midwife already in charge and inclined to elbow about any young medical upstart who might presume to dictate to a female of her experience.

It was a sordid and ravaging confinement which, at its climax, teetered for one dreadful moment between tragedy and broad comedy. For at the crisis, just before dawn, the fat midwife, busy with ministrations, had said to the perspiring young doctor, "D'you think it's time to snuff her?"

Bewildered, and not daring to show his ignorance, he had replied, judicially, "Uh—not just yet. No, not just yet."

Again the woman had said, ten minutes later, "Time to snuff her, I'd say."

"Well, perhaps it is." He watched her, fearfully, wondering what she might mean; cursing his own lack of knowledge. To his horror and amazement, before he could stop her, she had stuffed a great pinch of strong snuff up either nostril of Magnolia Ravenal's delicate nose. And thus Kim Ravenal was born into the world on the gust of a series of convulsive a-CHOOs!

"God almighty, woman!" cried the young medico, in a frenzy. "You've killed her."

"Run along, do!" retorted the fat midwife, testily, for she was tired by now, and hungry, and wanted her coffee badly. "H'm! It's a gal. And they had their minds all made up to a boy. Never knew it to fail." She turned to Magnolia's mother, a ponderous and unwieldy figure at the foot of the bed.

"Well, now, Mis'—Hawks, ain't it?—that's right—Hawks. Well, now, Mis' Hawks, we'll get this young lady washed up and then I'd thank you for a pot of coffee and some breakfast. I'm partial to a meat breakfast."

All this had been a full hour ago. Magnolia Ravenal still lay inert, unheeding. She had not even looked at her child. Her mother now uttered bitter complaint to the others in the room.

"Won't touch a drop of this good nourishing broth. Knocked the spoon right out of my hand, would you believe it! for all she lays there looking so gone. Well! I'm going to open her mouth and pour it down."

The young doctor raised a protesting palm. "No, no, I wouldn't do that." He bent over the white face on the pillow. "Just a spoonful," he coaxed, softly. "Just a swallow?"

She did not vouchsafe him another smile. He glanced at the irate woman with the saucepan; at the two attendant vestals. "Isn't there somebody———?"

The men of the company and the crew were out, he well knew, with pike poles in hand, working to keep the drifting objects clear of the boats. Gaylord Ravenal would be with them. He had been in and out a score of times through the night, his handsome young face (too handsome, the awkward young doctor had privately decided) twisted with horror and pity and self-reproach. He had noticed, too, that the girl's cries had abated not a whit when the husband was there. But when he took her writhing fingers, and put one hand on her wet forehead, and said, in a voice that broke with agony, "Oh, Nola! Nola! Don't. I didn't know it was like . . . Not like this. . . . Magnolia . . ."—she had said, through clenched teeth and white lips, surprisingly enough, with a knowledge handed down to her through centuries of women writhing in childbirth, "It's all right, Gay. . . . Always . . . like this . . . damn it. . . . Don't you worry. . . . It's . . . all . . ." And the harassed young doctor had then seen for the first time the wonder of Magnolia Ravenal's poignant smile.

So now when he said, shyly, "Isn't there somebody else———" he was thinking that if the young and handsome husband could be spared for but a moment from his pike pole it would be better to chance a drifting log sent crashing against the side of the boat by the flood than that this white still figure on the bed should be allowed to grow one whit whiter or more still.

"Somebody else's fiddlesticks!" exploded Mrs. Hawks, inelegantly. They were all terribly rude to him, poor lad, except the one who might have felt justified in being so. "If her own mother can't———" She had reheated the broth on the little iron stove, and now made a third advance, armed with spoon and saucepan. The midwife had put the swaddled bundle on the pillow so that it lay just beside Magnolia Ravenal's arm. It was she who now interrupted Mrs. Hawks, and abetted her.

"How in time d'you expect to nurse," she demanded, "if you don't eat!"

Magnolia Ravenal didn't know and, seemingly, didn't care.

A crisis was imminent. It was the moment for drama. And it was furnished, obligingly enough, by the opening of the door to admit the two whom Magnolia Ravenal loved in all the world. There came first the handsome, haggard Gaylord Ravenal, actually managing, in some incredible way, to appear elegant, well-dressed, dapper, at a time, under circumstances, and in a costume which would have rendered most men unsightly, if not repulsive. But his gifts were many, and not the least of them was the trick of appearing sartorially and tonsorially flawless when dishevelment and a stubble were inevitable in any other male. Close behind him trotted Andy Hawks, just as he had been twenty-four hours, before—wrinkled linen pants, double-breasted blue coat, oversize visored cap, mutton-chop whiskers and all.

Together he and Ma Hawks, in her blue brass-buttoned coat that was a twin of his, managed to give the gathering quite a military aspect. Certainly Mrs. Hawks' manner was martial enough at the moment. She raised her voice now in complaint.

"Won't touch her broth. Ain't half as sick as she lets on or she wouldn't be so stubborn. Wouldn't have the strength to be, 's what I say."

Gaylord Ravenal took from her the saucepan and the spoon. The saucepan he returned to the stove. He espied a cup on the washstand; with a glance at Captain Andy he pointed silently to this. Andy Hawks emptied its contents into the slop jar, rinsed it carefully, and half filled it with the steaming hot broth. The two men approached the bedside. There was about both a clumsy and touching but magically effective tenderness. Gay Ravenal slipped his left arm under the girl's head with its hair all spread so dank and wild on the pillow. Captain Andy Hawks leaned forward, cup in hand, holding it close to her mouth. With his right hand, delicately, Gay Ravenal brought the first hot revivifying spoonful to her mouth and let it trickle slowly, drop by drop, through her lips. He spoke to her as he did this, but softly, softly, so that the others could not hear the words. Only the cadence of his voice, and that was a caress. Another spoonful, and another, and another. He lowered her again to the pillow, his arm still under her head. A faint tinge of palest pink showed under the waxen skin. She opened her eyes; looked up at him. She adored him. Her pain-dulled eyes even then said so. Her lips moved. He bent closer. She was smiling almost mischievously.

"Fooled them."

"What's she say?" rasped Mrs. Hawks, fearfully, for she loved the girl. Over his shoulder he repeated the two words she had whispered.

"Oh," said Parthy Ann Hawks, and laughed. "She means fooled 'em because it's a girl instead of a boy."

But at that Magnolia Ravenal shook her head ever so slightly, and looked up at him again and held up one slim forefinger and turned her eyes toward the corners with a listening look. And in obedience he held up his hand then, a warning for silence, though he was as mystified as they. And in the stillness of the room you heard the roar and howl and crash of the great river whose flood had caught them and shaken them and brought Magnolia Ravenal to bed ahead of her time. And now he knew what she meant. She wasn't thinking of the child that lay against her arms. Her lips moved again. He bent closer. And what she said was:

"The River."

2

SURELY NO LITTLE girl had ever had a more fantastic little girlhood than this Magnolia Ravenal who had been Magnolia Hawks. By the time she was eight she had fallen into and been fished out of practically every river in the Mississippi Basin from the Gulf of Mexico to Minnesota. The ordinary routine of her life, in childhood, had been made up of doing those things that usually are strictly forbidden the average child. She swam muddy streams; stayed up until midnight; read the lurid yellow-backed novels found in the cabins of the women of the company; went to school but rarely; caught catfish; drank river water out of the river itself; roamed the streets of strange towns alone; learned to strut and shuffle and buck-and-wing from the Negroes whose black faces dotted the boards of the Southern wharves as thickly as grace notes sprinkle a bar of lively music. And all this despite constant watchfulness, nagging, and admonition from her spinster-like mother; for Parthy Ann Hawks, matron though she was, still was one of those women who, confined as favourite wife in the harem of a lascivious Turk, would have remained a spinster at heart and in manner. And though she lived on her husband's show boat season after season, and tried to rule it from pilot house to cook's galley, she was always an incongruous figure in the gay, careless vagabond life of this band of floating players. The very fact of her presence on the boat was a paradox. Life, for Parthy Ann Hawks, was meant to be made up of crisp white dimity curtains at kitchen windows; of biweekly bread bakings; of Sunday morning service and Wednesday night prayer meeting; of small gossip rolled evilly under the tongue. The male biped, to her, was a two-footed animal who tracked up a clean kitchen floor just after it was scoured and smoked a pipe in defiance of decency. Yet here she was— and had been for ten years—leading an existence which would have made that of the Stratford strollers seem orderly and prim by comparison.

She had been a Massachusetts school teacher, living with a henpecked fisherman father, and keeping house expertly for him with one hand while she taught school with the other. The villagers held her up as an example of all the feminine virtues, but the young males of the village were to be seen walking home from church with this or that plump twitterer who might be a notoriously bad cook but who had an undeniable way of tying a blue sash about a tempting waist. Parthenia Ann, prayer book clasped in mitted hands, walked sedately home with her father. The vivacious little Andy Hawks, drifting up into Massachusetts one summer, on a visit to fishermen kin, had encountered the father, and, through him, the daughter. He had eaten her light flaky biscuit, her golden-brown fries; her ruddy jell; her succulent pickles; her juicy pies. He had stood in her kitchen doorway, shyly yet boldly watching her as she moved briskly from table to stove, from stove to pantry. The sleeves of her crisp print dress were rolled to the elbow, and if those elbows were not dimpled they were undeniably expert in batter-beating, dough-kneading, pan-scouring. Her sallow cheeks were usually a little flushed with the heat of the kitchen and the energy of her movements, and, perhaps, with the consciousness of the unaccustomed masculine eye so warmly turned upon her. She looked her bustling best, and to little impulsive warm-hearted Andy she represented all he had ever known and dreamed, in his roving life, of order, womanliness, comfort. She was some years older than he. The intolerance with which women of Parthenia Ann's type regard all men was heightened by this fact to something resembling contempt. Even before their marriage, she bossed him about much as she did her old father, but while she nagged she also fed them toothsome viands, and the balm of bland, well-cooked food counteracted the acid of her words. Then, too, Nature, the old witchwanton, had set the yeast to working in the flabby dough of Parthy Ann's organism. Andy told her that his real name was André and that he was descended, through his mother, from a long line of Basque fisher folk who had lived in the vicinity of St. Jean-de-Luz, Basses-Pyrénées. It probably was true, and certainly accounted for his swarthy skin, his bright brown eyes, his impulsiveness, his vivacious manner. The first time he kissed this tall, raw-boned New England woman he was startled at the robustness with which she met and returned the caress. They were married and went to Illinois to live in the little town of Thebes, on the Mississippi. In the village from which she had married it was said that, after she left, her old father, naturally neat and trained through years of nagging to superneatness, indulged in an orgy of disorder that lasted days. As other men turn to strong drink in time of exuberance or relief from strain, so the tidy old septuagenarian strewed the kitchen with dirty dishes and scummy pots and pans; slept for a week in an unmade bed; padded in stocking feet; chewed tobacco and spat where he pleased; smoked the lace curtains brown; was even reported by a spying neighbour to have been seen seated at the reedy old cottage organ whose palsied pipes had always quavered to hymn tunes, picking out with one gnarled forefinger the chorus of a bawdy song. He lived one free, blissful year and died of his own cooking.

As pilot, river captain, and finally, as they thrived, owner and captain of a steamer accommodating both passengers and freight, Captain Andy was seldom in a position to be guilty of tracking the white-scoured kitchen floor or discolouring with pipe smoke the stiff folds of the window curtains. The prim little Illinois cottage saw him but rarely during the season when river navigation was at its height. For many months in the year Parthy Ann Hawks was free to lead the spinsterish existence for which nature had so evidently planned her. Her window panes glittered, her linen was immaculate, her floors unsullied. When Captain Andy came home there was constant friction between them. Sometimes her gay, capering little husband used to look at this woman as at a stranger. Perhaps his nervous habit of clawing at his mutton-chop whiskers had started as a gesture of puzzlement or despair.

The child Magnolia was not born until seven years after their marriage. That Parthy Ann Hawks could produce actual offspring was a miracle to give one renewed faith in certain disputed incidents recorded in the New Testament. The child was all Andy—manner, temperament, colouring. Between father and daughter there sprang up such a bond of love and understanding as to make their relation a perfect thing, and so sturdy as successfully to defy even the destructive forces bent upon it by Mrs. Hawks. Now the little captain came home whenever it was physically possible, sacrificing time, sleep, money—everything but the safety of his boat and its passengers—for a glimpse of the child's piquant face, her gay vivacious manner, her smile that wrung you even then.

It was years before Captain Andy could persuade his wife to take a river trip with him on his steamer down to New Orleans and back again, bringing the child. It was, of course, only a ruse for having the girl with him. River captains' wives were not popular on the steamers their husbands commanded. And Parthy Ann, from that first trip, proved a terror. It was due only to tireless threats, pleadings, blandishments, and actual bribes on the part of Andy that his crew did not mutiny daily. Half an hour after embarking on that first trip, Parthy Ann poked her head into the cook's galley and told him the place was a disgrace. The cook was a woollyheaded black with a rolling protuberant eye and the quick temper of his calling.

Furthermore, though a capable craftsman, and in good standing on the river boats, he had come aboard drunk, according to time-honoured custom; not drunk to the point of being quarrelsome or incompetent, but entertaining delusions of grandeur, varied by ominous spells of sullen silence. In another twelve hours, and for the remainder of the trip, he would be sober and himself. Captain Andy knew this, understood him, was satisfied with him.

Now one of his minions was seated on an upturned pail just outside the door, peeling a great boiler full of potatoes with almost magic celerity and very little economy.

Parthy Ann's gimlet eye noted the plump peelings as they fell in long spirals under the sharp blade. She lost no time.

"Well, I declare! Of all the shameful waste I ever clapped my eyes on, that's the worst."

The black at the stove turned to face her, startled and uncomprehending. Visitors were not welcome in the cook's galley. He surveyed without enthusiasm the lean figure with the long finger pointing accusingly at a quite innocent pan of potato parings.

"Wha' that you say, missy?"

"Don't you missy me!" snapped Parthy Ann Hawks. "And what I said was that I never saw such criminal waste as those potato parings. An inch thick if they're a speck, and no decent cook would allow it."

A simple, ignorant soul, the black man, and a somewhat savage; as mighty in his small domain as Captain Andy in his larger one. All about him now were his helpers, black men like himself, with rolling eyes and great lips all too ready to gash into grins if this hard-visaged female intruder were to worst him.

"Yo-all passenger on this boat, missy?"

Parthy Ann surveyed disdainfully the galley's interior, cluttered with the disorder attendant on the preparation of the noonday meal.

"Passenger! H'mph! No, I'm not. And passenger or no passenger, a filthier hole I never saw in my born days. I'll let you know that I shall make it my business to report this state of things to the Captain. Good food going to waste———"

A red light seemed to leap then from the big Negro's eyeballs. His lips parted in a kind of savage and mirthless grin, so that you saw his great square gleaming teeth and the blue gums above them. Quick as a panther he reached down with one great black paw into the pan of parings, straightened, and threw the mass, wet and slimy as it was, full at her. The spirals clung and curled about her—on her shoulders, around her neck, in the folds of her gown, on her head, Medusa-like.

"They's something for you take to the Captain to show him, missy."

He turned sombrely back to his stove. The other blacks were little less grave than he. They sensed something sinister in the fury with which this garbage-hung figure ran screaming to the upper deck. The scene above decks must have been a harrowing one.

They put him off at Memphis and shipped another cook there, and the big Negro, thoroughly sobered now, went quite meekly down the gangplank and up the levee, his carpet bag in hand. In fact, it was said that, when he had learned it was the Captain's wife whom he had treated thus, he had turned a sort of ashen gray and had tried to jump overboard and swim ashore. The gay little Captain Andy was a prime favourite with his crew. Shamefaced though the Negro was, there appeared something akin to pity in the look he turned on Captain Andy as he was put ashore. If that was true, then the look on the little captain's face as he regarded the miscreant was certainly born of an inward and badly concealed admiration. It was said, too, but never verified, that something round and gold and gleaming was seen to pass from the Captain's hairy little brown hand to the big black paw.

For the remainder of the trip Mrs. Hawks constituted herself a sort of nightmarish housekeeper, prowling from corridor to cabins, from dining saloon to pantry. She made life wretched for the pert yellow wenches who performed the cabin chamber-work. She pounced upon them when they gathered in little whispering groups, gossiping. Thin-lipped and baleful of eye, she withered the very words they were about to utter to a waiter or deck-hand, so that the flowers of coquetry became ashes on their tongues. She regarded the female passengers with suspicion and the males with contempt. This was the latter '70s, and gambling was as much a part of river-boat life as eating and drinking. Professional gamblers often infested the boats. It was no uncommon sight to see a poker game that had started in the saloon in the early evening still in progress when sunrise reddened the river. It was the day of the flowing moustache, the broad-brimmed hat, the open-faced collar, and the diamond stud. It constituted masculine America's last feeble flicker of the picturesque before he sank for ever into the drab ashes of uniformity. A Southern gentleman, particularly, clad thus, took on a dashing and dangerous aspect. The rakish angle of the hat with its curling brim, the flowing ends of the string tie, the movement of the slender virile fingers as they stroked the moustache, all were things to thrill the feminine beholder. Even that frigid female, Parthenia Ann Hawks, must have known a little flutter of the senses as she beheld these romantic and—according to her standards—dissolute passengers seated, silent, wary, pale, about the gaming table. But in her stern code, that which thrilled was wicked. She belonged to the tribe of the Knitting Women; of the Salem Witch Burners; of all fanatics who count nature as an enemy to be suppressed; and in whose veins the wine of life runs vinegar. If the deep seepage of Parthy Ann's mind could have been brought to the surface, it would have analyzed chemically thus: "I find these men beautiful, stirring, desirable. But that is an abomination. I must not admit to myself that I am affected thus. Therefore I think and I say that they are disgusting, ridiculous, contemptible."

Her attitude was somewhat complicated by the fact that, as wife of the steamer's captain, she was treated with a courtly deference on the part of these very gentlemen whom she affected to despise; and with a gracious cordiality by their ladies. The Southern men, especially, gave an actual effect of plumes on their wide-brimmed soft hats as they bowed and addressed her in their soft drawling vernacular.

"Well, ma'am, and how are you enjoying your trip on your good husband's magnificent boat?" It sounded much richer and more flattering as they actually said it. " . . . Yo' trip on yo' good husband's ma-a-a-ygnif'cent . . ." They gave one the feeling that they were really garbed in satin, sword, red heels, lace ruffles.

Parthenia Ann, whose stays always seemed, somehow, to support her form more stiffly than did those of any other female, would regard her inquirers with a cold and fishy eye.

"The boat's well enough, I suppose. But what with the carousing by night and the waste by day, a Christian soul can hardly look on at it without feeling that some dreadful punishment will overtake us all before we arrive at the end of our journey." From her tone you would almost have gathered that she hoped it.

He of the broad-brimmed hat, and his bustled, basqued alpaca lady, would perhaps exchange a glance not altogether amused. Collisions, explosions, snagfounderings were all too common in the river traffic of the day to risk this deliberate calling down of wrath.

Moving away, the soft-tongued Southern voices would be found to be as effective in vituperation as in flattery. "Pole cat!" he of the phantom plumes would say, aside, to his lady.

Fortunately, Parthy Ann's dour misgivings did not materialize. The trip downstream proved a delightful one, and as tranquil as might be with Mrs. Hawks on board. Captain Andy's steamer, though by no means as large as some of the so-called floating palaces that plied the Mississippi, was known for the excellence of its table, the comfort of its appointments, and the affability of its crew. So now the passengers endured the irritation of Mrs. Hawks' presence under the balm of appetizing food and good-natured service. The crew suffered her nagging for the sake of the little captain, whom they liked and respected; and for his wages, which were generous.

Though Parthenia Ann Hawks regarded the great river—if, indeed, she noticed it at all—merely as a moist highway down which one travelled with ease to New Orleans; untouched by its mystery, unmoved by its majesty, unsubdued by its sinister power, she must still, in spite of herself, have come, however faintly and remotely, under the spell of its enchantment. For this trip proved, for her, to be the first of many, and led, finally, to her spending seven months out of the twelve, not only on the Mississippi, but on the Ohio, the Missouri, the Kanawha, the Big Sandy. Indeed, her liking for the river life, together with her zeal for reforming it, became so marked that in time river travellers began to show a preference for steamers other than Captain Andy's, excellently though they fared thereon.

Perhaps the attitude of the lady passengers toward the little captain and the manner of the little captain as he addressed the lady passengers did much to feed the flame of Parthy Ann's belligerence. Until the coming of Andy Hawks she had found favour in no man's eyes. Cut in the very pattern of spinsterhood, she must actually have had moments of surprise and even incredulity at finding herself a wife and mother. The art of coquetry was unknown to her; because the soft blandishments of love had early been denied her she now repudiated them as sinful; did her hair in a knob; eschewed flounces; assumed a severe demeanour; and would have been the last to understand that any one of these repressions was a confession. All about her—and Captain Andy—on the steamship were captivating females, full of winning wiles; wives of Southern planters; cream-skinned Creoles from New Orleans, indolent, heavy-lidded, bewitching; or women folk of prosperous Illinois or Iowa merchants, lawyers, or manufacturers making a pleasure jaunt of the Southern business trip with husband or father.

And, "Oh, Captain Hawks!" they said; and, "Oh, Captain Andy! Do come here like a nice man and tell us what it means when that little bell rings so fast? . . . And why do they call it the hurricane deck? . . . Oh, Captain Hawks, is that a serpent tattooed on the back of your hand! I declare it is! Look, Emmaline! Emmaline, look! This naughty Captain Andy has a serpent . . ."

Captain Andy's social deportment toward women was made up of that most devastating of combinations, a deferential manner together with an audacious tongue. A tapering white finger, daringly tracing a rosy nail over the blue coils of the tattooed serpent, would find itself gently imprisoned beneath the hard little brown paw that was Andy's free hand.

"After this," the little captain would say, thoughtfully, "it won't be long before that particular tattoo will be entirely worn away. Yes, ma'am! No more serpent."

"But why?"

"Erosion, ma'am."

"E—but I don't understand. I'm so stupid. I———"

Meltingly, the wicked little monkey, "I'll be so often kissing the spot your lovely finger has traced, ma'am."

"Oh-h-h-h!" A smart tap of rebuke with her palmleaf fan. "You *are* a saucy thing. Emmaline, did you hear what this wicked captain said!"

Much of the freedom that Magnolia enjoyed on this first trip she owed to her mother's quivering preoccupation with these vivacious ladies.

If the enchantment of the river had been insidious enough to lure even Mrs. Hawks, certainly the child Magnolia fell completely under its magic spell. From that first trip on the Mississippi she was captive in its coils. Twenty times daily, during that leisurely journey from St. Louis to New Orleans, Mrs. Hawks dragged her child, squirming and protesting, from the pilot house perched atop the steamer or from the engine room in its bowels. Refurbished, the grime removed from face and hands, dressed in a clean pinafore, she was thumped on one of the red plush fauteuils of the gaudy saloon. Magnolia's hair was almost black and without a vestige of natural curl. This last was a great cross to Mrs. Hawks, who spent hours wetting and twining the long dank strands about her forefinger with a fine-toothed comb in an unconvincing attempt to make a swan out of her duckling. The rebellious little figure stood clamped between her mother's relentless knees. Captured thus, and made fresh, her restless feet in their clean white stockings and little strapped black slippers sticking straight out before her, her starched skirts stiffly spread, she was told to conduct herself as a young lady of her years and high position should.

"Listen to the conversation of the ladies and gentlemen about you," Mrs. Hawks counselled her, severely, "instead of to the low talk of those greasy engineers and pilots you're always running off to. I declare I don't know what your father is thinking of, to allow it. . . . Or read your book. . . . Then where is it? Where is the book I bought you especially to read on this trip? You haven't opened it, I'll be bound. . . . Go get it and come back directly."

A prissy tale about a female Rollo so prim that Magnolia was sure she turned her toes out even in her sleep. When she returned with a book (if she returned at all) it was likely to be of a quite different sort—a blood-curdling tale of the old days of river-banditry—a story, perhaps, of the rapacious and brutal Murrel and his following of ten hundred cut-throats sworn to do his evil will; and compared to whom Jesse James was a philanthropist. The book would have been loaned her by one of the crew. She adored these bloody tales and devoured them with the avidity that she always showed for any theme that smacked of the river. It was snatched away soon enough when it came under her mother's watchful eye.

Magnolia loathed the red plush and gilt saloon except at night, when its gilding and mirrors took on a false glitter and richness from the kerosene lamps that filled wall brackets and chandeliers. Then it was that the lady passengers, their daytime alpacas and serges replaced by silks, sat genteelly conversing, reading, or embroidering. Then, if ever, the gentlemen twirled their mustachios most fiercely so that the diamond on the third finger of the right hand sparkled entrancingly. Magnolia derived a sensory satisfaction from the scene. The rich red of the carpet fed her, and the yellow glow of the lamps. In her best cashmere dress of brown with the polonaise cut up the front and around the bottom in deep turrets she sat alertly watching the elaborate posturings of the silken ladies and the broadcloth gentlemen.

Sometimes one of the ladies sang to the hoarse accompaniment of the ship's piano, whose tones always sounded as though the Mississippi River mist had lodged permanently in its chords. The Southern ladies rendered tinkling and sentimental ballads. The Midwestern wives were wont to deliver themselves of songs of a somewhat sterner stuff. There was one song in particular, sung by a plain and falsetto lady hailing from Iowa, that aroused in Magnolia a savage (though quite reasoning) loathing. It was entitled Waste Not, Want Not; Or: You Never Miss The Water Till The Well Runs Dry. Not being a psychologist, Magnolia did not know why, during the rendition of the first verse and the chorus, she always longed to tear her best dress into ribbons and throw a barrel of flour and a dozen hams into the river. The song ran:

> When a child I lived at Lincoln
> With my parents at the farm,
> The lessons that my mother taught,
> To me were quite a charm.
> She would often take me on her knee,
> When tired of childish play,

And as she press'd me to her breast,
I've heard my mother say:

Chorus: Waste not, want not, is a maxim I would teach————

Escape to the decks or the pilot house was impossible of accomplishment by night. She extracted what savour she could from the situation. This, at least, was better than being sent off to bed. All her disorderly life Magnolia went to bed only when all else failed. Then, too, once in her tiny cabin she could pose and swoop before the inadequate mirror in pitiless imitation of the arch alpacas and silks of the red plush saloon; tapping an imaginary masculine shoulder with a phantom fan; laughing in an elegant falsetto; grimacing animatedly as she squeaked, "Deah, yes!" and "Deah, no!" moistening a forelock of her straight black hair with a generous dressing of saliva wherewith to paste flat to her forehead the modish spit-curl that graced the feminine adult coiffure.

But during the day she and her father often contrived to elude the maternal duenna. With her hand in that of the little captain, she roamed the boat from stem to stern, from bunkers to pilot house. Down in the engine room she delightedly heard the sweating engineer denounce the pilot, decks above him, as a goddam Pittsburgh brass pounder because that monarch, to achieve a difficult landing, had to ring more bells than the engineer below thought necessary to an expert. But best of all Magnolia loved the bright, gay, glass-enclosed pilot house high above the rest of the boat and reached by the ultimate flight of steep narrow stairs. From this vantage point you saw the turbulent flood of the Mississippi, a vast yellow expanse, spread before you and all around you; for ever rushing ahead of you, no matter how fast you travelled; sometimes whirling about in its own tracks to turn and taunt you with your unwieldy ponderosity; then leaping on again. Sometimes the waters widened like a sea so that one could not discern the dim shadow of the farther shore; again they narrowed, snake-like, crawling so craftily that the side-wheeler boomed through the chutes with the willows brushing the decks. You never knew what lay ahead of you—that is, Magnolia never knew. That was part of the fascination of it. The river curved and twisted and turned and doubled. Mystery always lay just around the corner of the next bend. But her father knew. And Mr. Pepper, the chief pilot, always knew. You couldn't believe that it was possible for any human brain to remember the things that Captain Andy and Mr. Pepper knew about that treacherous, shifting, baffling river. Magnolia delighted to test them. She played a game with Mr. Pepper and with her father, thus:

"What's next?"

"Kinney's woodpile."

"Now what?"

"Ealer's Bend."

"What'll be there, when we come round that corner?"

"Patrie's Plantation."

"What's around that bend?"

"An old cottonwood with one limb hanging down, struck by lightning."

"What's coming now?"

"A stump sticking out of the water at Higgin's Point."

They always were right. It was magic. It was incredible. They knew, too, the depth of the water. They could point out a spot and say, "That used to be an island—Buckle's Island."

"But it's water! It couldn't be an island. It's water. We're—why, we're riding on it now."

Mr. Pepper would persist, unmoved. "Used to be an island." Or, pointing again, "Two years ago I took her right down through there where that point lays."

"But it's dry land. You're just fooling, aren't you, Mr. Pepper? Because you couldn't take a boat on dry land. It's got things growing on it! Little trees, even. So how could you?"

"Water there two years ago—good eleven foot."

Small wonder Magnolia was early impressed with this writhing monster that, with a single lash of its tail, could wipe a solid island from the face of the earth, or with a convulsion of its huge tawny body spew up a tract of land where only water had been.

Mr. Pepper had respect for his river. "Yessir, the Mississippi and this here Nile, over in Egypt, they're a couple of old demons. I ain't seen the Nile River, myself. Don't expect to. This old river's enough for one man to meet up with in his life. Like marrying. Get to learn one woman's ways real good, you know about all there is to women and you got about all you can do one lifetime."

Not at all the salty old graybeard pilot of fiction, this Mr. Pepper. A youth of twenty-four, nerveless, taciturn, gentle, profane, charming. His clear brown eyes, gazing unblinkingly out upon the river, had tiny golden flecks in them, as though something of the river itself had taken possession of him, and become part of him. Born fifty years later, he would have been the steel stuff of which aviation aces are made.

Sometimes, in deep water, Mr. Pepper actually permitted Magnolia to turn the great pilot wheel that measured twice as high as she. He stood beside her, of course; or her father, if he chanced to be present, stood behind her. It was thrilling, too, when her father took the wheel in an exciting place—where the water was very shoal, perhaps; or where the steamer found a stiff current pushing behind her, and the tricky dusk coming on. At first it puzzled Magnolia that her father, omnipotent in all other parts of the *Creole Belle,* should defer to this stripling; should actually be obliged, on his own steamer, to ask permission of the pilot to take the wheel. They were both beautifully formal and polite about it.

"What say to my taking her a little spell, Mr. Pepper?"

"Not at all, Captain Hawks. Not at all, sir," Mr. Pepper would reply, cordially if ambiguously. His gesture as he stepped aside and relinquished the wheel was that of one craftsman who recognizes and respects the ability of another. Andy Hawks had been a crack Mississippi River pilot in his day. And then to watch Captain Andy skinning the wheel—climbing it round and round, hands and feet, and looking for all the world like a talented little monkey.

Magnolia even learned to distinguish the bells by tone. There was the Go Ahead, soprano-voiced. Mr. Pepper called it the Jingle. He explained to Magnolia:

"When I give the engineer the Jingle, why, he knows I mean for him to give her all she's got." Strangely enough, the child, accustomed to the sex of boats and with an uncannily quick comprehension of river jargon, understood him, nodded her head so briskly that the hand-made curls jerked up and down like bell-ropes. "Sometimes it's called the Soprano. Then the Centre Bell—the Stopping Bell—that's middle tone. About alto. This here, that's the Astern Bell—the backup bell. That's bass. The Boom-Boom, you call it. Here's how you can remember them: The Jingle, the Alto, and the Boom-Boom."

A charming medium through which to know the river, Mr. Pepper. An enchanting place from which to view the river, that pilot house. Magnolia

loved its shining orderliness, disorderly little creature that she was. The
wilderness of water and woodland outside made its glass-enclosed cosiness
seem the snugger. Oilcloth on the floor. You opened the drawer of the little
table and there lay Mr. Pepper's pistol, glittering and sinister; and Mr.
Pepper's Pilot Rules. Magnolia lingered over the title printed on the brick-
coloured paper binding:

PILOT RULES
FOR THE
RIVERS WHOSE WATERS FLOW INTO THE GULF OF
MEXICO AND THEIR TRIBUTARIES
AND FOR
THE RED RIVER OF THE NORTH

The Red River of the North! There was something in the words that thrilled
her; sent little delicious prickles up and down her spine.

There was a bright brass cuspidor. The expertness with which Mr. Pepper
and, for that matter, Captain Hawks himself, aimed for the centre of this
glittering receptacle and sustained a one-hundred-per-cent record was as
fascinating as any other feature of this delightful place. Visitors were rarely
allowed up there. Passengers might peer wistfully through the glass enclosure
from the steps below, but there they were confronted by a stern and forbidding sign which read: No Visitors Allowed. Magnolia felt very superior
and slightly contemptuous as she looked down from her vantage point upon
these unfortunates below. Sometimes, during mid-watch, a very black texas-
tender in a very white starched apron would appear with coffee and cakes
or ices for Mr. Pepper. Magnolia would have an ice, too, shaving it very
fine to make it last; licking the spoon luxuriously with little lightning flicks
of her tongue and letting the frozen sweet slide, a slow delicious trickle,
down her grateful throat.

"Have another cake, Miss Magnolia," Mr. Pepper would urge her. "A
pink one, I'd recommend, this time."

"I don't hardly think my mother———"

Mr. Pepper, himself, surprisingly enough, the father of twins, was sure
her mother would have no objection; would, if present, probably encourage
the suggestion. Magnolia bit quickly into the pink cake. A wild sense of
freedom flooded her. She felt like the river, rushing headlong on her way.

To be snatched from this ecstatic state was agony. The shadow of the
austere and disapproving maternal figure loomed always just around the
corner. At any moment it might become reality. The knowledge that this
was so made Magnolia's first taste of Mississippi River life all the more
delicious.

3

GRIM FORCE THOUGH she was, it would be absurd to fix upon Parthy Ann
Hawks as the sole engine whose relentless functioning cut down the profits
of Captain Andy's steamboat enterprise. That other metal monster, the railroad, with its swift-turning wheels and its growing network of lines, was
weaving the doom of river traffic. The Prince Albert coats and the alpaca
basques were choosing a speedier, if less romantic, way to travel from
Natchez to Memphis, or from Cairo to Vicksburg. Illinois, Minnesota, and
Iowa business men were favouring a less hazardous means of transporting

their merchandise. Farmers were freighting their crops by land instead of water. The river steamboat was fast becoming an anachronism. The jig, Captain Andy saw, was up. Yet the river was inextricably interwoven with his life—was his life, actually. He knew no other background, was happy in no other surroundings, had learned no other trade. These streams, large and small of the North, the Mid-west, the South, with their harsh yet musical Indian names—Kaskaskia, Cahokia, Yazoo, Monongahela, Kanawha—he knew in every season: their currents, depths, landings, banks, perils. The French strain in him on the distaff side did not save him from pronouncing the foreign names of Southern rivers as murderously as did the other rivermen. La Fourche was the Foosh. Bayou Teche was Bayo Tash. As for names such as Plaquemine, Paincourteville, and Thibodaux—they emerged mutilated beyond recognition, with entire syllables lopped off, and flat vowels protruding everywhere. Anything else would have been considered affected.

Captain Andy thought only in terms of waterways. Despite the prim little house in Thebes, home, to Andy, was a boat. Towns and cities were to him mere sources of supplies and passengers, set along the river banks for the convenience of steamboats. He knew every plank in every river-landing from St. Paul to Baton Rouge. As the sky is revealed, a printed page, to the astronomer, so Andy Hawks knew and interpreted every reef, sand bar, current, and eddy in the rivers that drained the great Mississippi Basin. And of these he knew best of all the Mississippi herself. He loved her, feared her, respected her. Now her courtiers and lovers were deserting her, one by one, for an iron-throated, great-footed, brazen-voiced hussy. Andy, among the few, remained true.

To leave the river—to engage, perforce, in some landlubberly pursuit was to him unthinkable. On the rivers he was a man of consequence. As a captain and pilot of knowledge and experience his opinion was deferred to. Once permanently ashore, penduluming prosaically between the precise little household and some dull town job, he would degenerate and wither until inevitably he who now was Captain Andy Hawks, owner and master of the steamboat *Creole Belle,* would be known merely as the husband of Parthy Ann Hawks, that Mistress of the Lace Curtains, Priestess of the Parlour Carpet, and Keeper of the Kitchen Floor. All this he did not definitely put into words; but he sensed it.

He cast about in his alert mind, and made his plans craftily, and put them warily, for he knew the force of Parthenia's opposition.

"I see here where old Ollie Pegram's fixing to sell his show boat." He was seated in the kitchen, smoking his pipe and reading the local newspaper. *"Cotton Blossom,* she's called."

Parthy Ann was not one to simulate interest where she felt none. Bustling between stove and pantry she only half heard him. "Well, what of it?"

Captain Andy rattled the sheet he was holding, turned a page leisurely, meanwhile idly swinging one leg, as he sat with knees crossed. Each movement was calculated to give the effect of casualness.

"Made a fortune in the show-boat business, Ollie has. Ain't a town on the river doesn't wait for the *Cotton Blossom.* Yessir. Anybody buys that outfit is walking into money."

"Scallywags." Thus, succinctly, Parthenia thought to dismiss the subject while voicing her opinion of water thespians.

"Scallywags nothing! Some of the finest men on the river in the show-boat business. Look at Pegram! Look at Finnegan! Look at Hosey Watts!"

It was Mrs. Hawks' habit to express contempt by reference to a ten-foot pole, this being an imaginary implement of disdain and a weapon of defence which was her Excalibur. She now announced that not only would she decline to look at the above-named gentlemen, but that she could not be induced to touch any of them with a ten-foot pole. She concluded with the repetitious "Scallywags!" and evidently considered the subject closed.

Two days later, the first pang of suspicion darted through her when Andy renewed the topic with an assumption of nonchalance that failed to deceive her this time. It was plain to this astute woman that he had been thinking concentratedly about show boats since their last brief conversation. It was at supper. Andy should have enjoyed his home-cooked meals more than he actually did. They always were hot, punctual, palatable. Parthenia had kept her cooking hand. Yet he often ate abstractedly and unappreciatively. Perhaps he missed the ceremony, the animation, the sociability that marked the meal hours in the dining saloon of the *Creole Belle*. The Latin in him, and the unconsciously theatrical in him, loved the mental picture of himself in his blue coat with brass buttons and gold braid, seated at the head of the long table while the alpacas twittered, "Do you think so, Captain Hawks?" and the Prince Alberts deferred to him with, "What's your opinion, sir?" and the soft-spoken black stewards in crackling white jackets bent over him with steaming platters and tureens.

Parthenia did not hold with conversation at meal time. Andy and Magnolia usually carried on such talk as occurred at table. Strangely enough, there was in his tone toward the child none of the usual patronizing attitude of the adult. No what-did-you-learn-at-school; no have-you-been-a-good-girl-to-day. They conversed like two somewhat rowdy grown-ups, constantly chafed by the reprovals of the prim Parthenia. It was a habit of Andy seldom to remain seated in his chair throughout a meal. Perhaps this was due to the fact that he frequently was called away from table while in command of his steamer. At home his jumpiness was a source of great irritation to Mrs. Hawks. Her contributions to the conversation varied little.

"Pity's sake, Hawks, sit still! That's the third time you've been up and down, and supper not five minutes on the table. . . . Eat your potato, Magnolia, or not a bite of cup cake do you get. . . . That's a fine story to be telling a child, I must say, Andy Hawks. . . . Can't you talk of anything but a lot of good-for-nothing drunken river roustabouts! . . . Drink your milk, Maggie. . . . Oh, stop fidgeting, Hawks! . . . Don't cut away all the fat like that, Magnolia. No wonder you're so skinny I'm ashamed of you and the neighbours think you don't get enough to eat."

Like a swarm of maddening mosquitoes, these admonitions buzzed through and above and around the conversation of the man and the child.

To-night Andy's talk dwelt on a dramatic incident that had been told him that day by the pilot of the show boat *New Sensation,* lately burned to the water's edge. He went on vivaciously, his bright brown eyes sparkling with interest and animation. Now and then, he jumped up from the table the better to illustrate a situation. Magnolia was following his every word and gesture with spellbound attention. She never had been permitted to see a show-boat performance. When one of these gay water travellers came prancing down the river, band playing, calliope tooting, flags flying, towboat puffing, bringing up with a final flare and flourish at the landing, there to tie up for two or three days, or even, sometimes, for a week, Magnolia was admonished not to go near it. Other children of the town might swarm over it by day, enchanted by its mystery, enthralled by its red-coated musicians when the band marched up the main street; might even, at night, witness the performance of a play and actually stay for the song-and-dance numbers which comprised the "concert" held after the play, and for which an additional charge of fifteen cents was made.

Magnolia hungered for a glimpse of these forbidden delights. The little white house at Thebes commanded a view up the river toward Cape Girardeau. At night from her bedroom window she could see the lights shining golden yellow through the boat's many windows, was fired with excitement at sight of the kerosene flares stuck in the river bank to light the way of the lucky, could actually hear the beat and blare of the band. Again and again, in her very early childhood, the spring nights when the show boats were headed downstream and the autumn nights when they were returning up river were stamped indelibly on her mind as she knelt in her nightgown at the little window of the dark room that faced the river with its dazzling and forbidden spectacle. Her bare feet would be as icy as her cheeks were hot. Her ears were straining to catch the jaunty strains of the music, and her eyes tried to discern the faces that passed under the weird glow of the torch flares. Usually she did not hear the approaching tread of discovery until the metallic, "Magnolia Hawks, get into your bed this very minute!" smote cruelly on her entranced ears. Sometimes she glimpsed men and women of the show-boat troupe on Front Street or Third Street, idling or shopping. Occasionally you saw them driving in a rig hired from Deffler's Livery Stable. They were known to the townspeople as Show Folks, and the term carried with it the sting of opprobrium. You could mark them by something different in their dress, in their faces, in the way they walked. The women were not always young. Magnolia noticed that often they were actually older than her mother (Parthy was then about thirty-nine). Yet they looked lively and somehow youthful, though their faces bore wrinkles. There was about them a certain care-free gaiety, a jauntiness. They looked, Magnolia decided, as if they had just come from some interesting place and were going to another even more interesting. This was rather shrewd of her. She had sensed that the dulness of village and farm life, the look that routine, drudgery, and boredom stamp indelibly on the countenance of the farm woman or the village housewife, were absent in these animated and often odd faces. Once she had encountered a little group of three—two women and a man—strolling along the narrow plank sidewalk near the Hawks house. They were eating fruit out of a bag, sociably, and spitting out the seeds, and laughing and chatting and dawdling. One of the women was young and very pretty, and her dress, Magnolia thought, was the loveliest she had ever seen. Its skirt of navy blue was kilted in the back, and there were puffs up each side edged with passementerie. On her head, at a saucy angle, was a chip bonnet of blue, trimmed with beaded lace, and ribbon, and adorable pink roses. The other woman was much older. There were queer deep lines in her face—not wrinkles, though Magnolia could not know this, but the scars left when the gashes of experience have healed. Her eyes were deep, and dark, and dead. She was carelessly dressed, and the boxpleated tail of her flounced black gown trailed in the street, so that it was filmed with a gray coating of dust. The veil wound round her bonnet hung down her back, imparting a Spanish and mysterious look. The man, too, though young and tall and not bad-looking, wore an unkempt look. His garments were ill assorted. His collar boasted no cravat. But all three had a charming air of insouciance as they strolled up the tree-shaded village street, laughing and chatting and munching and spitting out cherry stones with a little childish ballooning of the cheeks. Magnolia hung on the Hawks fence gate and stared. The older woman caught her eye and smiled, and immediately Magnolia decided that she liked her better than she did the pretty, young one, so after a moment's grave inspection she smiled in return her sudden, brilliant wide smile.

"Look at that child," said the older woman. "All of a sudden she's beautiful."

The other two surveyed her idly. Magnolia's smile had vanished now. They saw a scrawny sallow little girl, big-eyed, whose jaw conformation was too plainly marked, whose forehead was too high and broad, and whose black hair deceived no one into believing that its dank curls were other than tortured.

"You're crazy, Julie," remarked the pretty girl, without heat; and looked away, uninterested.

But between Magnolia and the older woman a filament of live liking had leaped. "Hello, little girl," said the older woman.

Magnolia continued to stare, gravely; said nothing.

"Won't you say hello to me?" the woman persisted; and smiled again. And again Magnolia returned her smile. "There!" the woman exclaimed, in triumph. "What did I tell you!"

"Cat's got her tongue," the sloppy young man remarked as his contribution to the conversation.

"Oh, come on," said the pretty girl; and popped another cherry into her mouth.

But the woman persisted. She addressed Magnolia gravely. "When you grow up, don't smile too often; but smile whenever you want anything very much, or like any one, or want them to like you. But I guess maybe you'll learn that without my telling you. . . . Listen, won't you say hello to me? H'm?"

Magnolia melted. "I'm not allowed," she explained.

"Not—? Why not? Pity's sake!"

"Because you're show-boat folks. My mama won't let me talk to show-boat folks."

"Damned little brat," said the pretty girl, and spat out a cherry stone. The man laughed.

With a lightning gesture the older woman took off her hat, stuffed it under the man's arm, twisted her abundant hair into a knob off her face, pulled down her mouth and made a narrow line of her lips, brought her elbows sharply to her side, her hands clasped, her shoulders suddenly pinched.

"Your mama looks like this," she said.

" Why, how did you know!" cried Magnolia, amazed. The three burst into sudden loud laughter. And at that Parthy Hawks appeared at the door, bristling, protective.

"Maggie Hawks, come into the house this minute!"

The laughter of the three then was redoubled. The quiet little village street rang with it as they continued their leisurely care-free ramble up the sun-dappled leafy path.

Now her father, at supper, had a tale to tell of these forbidden fascinators. The story had been told him that afternoon by Hard Harry Swager, river pilot, just in at the landing after a thrilling experience.

"Seems they were playing at China Grove, on the Chappelia. Yessir. Well, this girl—La Verne, her name was, or something—anyway, she was on the stage singing, he says. It was the concert, after the show. She comes off and the next thing you know there's a little blaze in the flies. Next minute she was afire and no saving her." To one less initiated it might have been difficult to differentiate in his use of the pronoun, third person, feminine. Sometimes he referred to the girl, sometimes to the boat. "Thirty years old if she's a day and burns like greased paper. Went up in ten minutes. Hard Harry goes running to the pilot house to get his clothes. Time he reaches the boiler deck, fire has cut off the gangway. He tries to lower himself twelve feet from the boiler deck to the main, and falls and breaks his leg. By that time they were cutting the towboat away from the *Sensation* to save her.

Did save her, too, finally. But the *Sensation* don't last long's it takes to tell it. Well, there he was, and what did they have to do but send four miles inland for a doctor, and when he comes, the skunk, guess what?''

"What!" cries Magnolia not merely to be obliging in this dramatic crisis, but because she is frantic to know. Captain Andy is on his feet by this time, fork in hand.

"When the doc comes he takes a look around, and there they all are in any kind of clothes they could grab or had on. So he says he won't set the leg unless he's paid in advance, twenty-five dollars. 'Oh, you won't, won't you!' says Hard Harry, laying there with his broken leg. And draws. 'You'll set it or I'll shoot yours off so you won't ever walk again, you son of a bitch!' ''

"Captain Andy Hawks!"

He has acted it out. The fork is his gun. Magnolia is breathless. Now both gaze, stricken, at Mrs. Hawks. Their horror is not occasioned by the word spoken but by the interruption.

"Go on!" shouts Magnolia; and bounces up and down in her chair. "Go *on!*"

But the first fine histrionic flavour has been poisoned by that interruption. Andy takes his seat at table. He resumes the eating of his pork steak and potatoes, but listlessly. Perhaps he is a little ashamed of the extent to which he has been carried away by his own recital. "Slipped out," he mumbled.

"Well, I should say as much!" Parthy retorted, ambiguously. "What kind of language can a body expect, you hanging around show-boat riff-raff."

Magnolia would not be cheated of her dénouement. "But did he? Did he shoot it off, or did he fix it, or what? What did he do?"

"He set it, all right. They gave him his twenty-five and told him to get the h——— to get out of there, and he got. But they had to get the boat out— the towboat they'd saved—and no pilot but Hard Harry. So next day they put him on the hurricane deck, under a tarpaulin because the rain was pouring the way it does down there worse than any place in the world, just about. And with two men steering, he brings the boat to Baton Rouge seventy-five miles through bayou and Mississippi. Yessir.''

Magnolia breathed again.

"And who's this," demanded Mrs. Hawks, was telling you all this fol-de-rol, did you say?"

"Swager himself. Harry. Hard Harry Swager, they call him." (You could see the ten-foot pole leap of itself into Mrs. Hawks' hand as her fingers drummed the tablecloth.) "I was talking to him to-day. Here of late he's been with the *New Sensation*. He piloted the *Cotton Blossom* for years till Pegram decided to quit. Well, sir! He says five hundred people a night on the show boat was nothing, and eight hundred on Saturday nights in towns with a good back-country. Let me tell you right here and now that runs into money. Say a quarter of 'em's fifty centers, a half thirty-five, and the rest twenty-five. The niggers all twenty-five up in the gallery, course. Naught . . . five times five's . . . five and carry the two . . . five times two's ten carry the one . . . five . . .''

Parthy was no fool. She sensed that here threatened a situation demanding measures even more than ordinarily firm.

"I may not know much"—another form of locution often favoured by her. The tone in which it was spoken utterly belied the words; the tone told you that not only did she know much, but all. "I may not know much, but this I do know. You've got something better to do with your time than loafing down at the landing like a river rat with that scamp Swager. Hard Harry! He comes honestly enough by that name, I'll be bound, if he never came

honestly by anything else in his life. And before the child, too. Show boats!
And language!''

"What's wrong with show boats?''

"Everything, and more, too. A lot of loose-living worthless scallywags,
men *and* women. Scum, that's what. Trollops!'' Parthy could use a good
old Anglo-Saxon word herself, on occasion.

Captain Andy made frantic foray among the whiskers. He clawed like a
furious little monkey—always the sign of mental disturbance in him. "No
more scum than your own husband, Mrs. Hawks, ma'am. I used to be with
a show-boat troupe myself.''

"Pilot, yes.''

"Pilot be damned.'' He was up now and capering like a Quilp. "Actor,
Mrs. Hawks, and pretty good I was, too, time I was seventeen or eighteen.
You ought to've seen me in the after-piece. Red Hot Coffee it was called.
I played the nigger. Doubled in brass, too. I pounded the bass drum in the
band, and it was bigger than me.''

Magnolia was enchanted. She sprang up, flew round to him. "Were you
really? An actor? You never told me. Mama, did you know? Did you know
Papa was an actor on a show boat?''

Parthy Ann rose in her wrath. Always taller than her husband, she seemed
now to tower above him. He defied her, a terrier facing a mastiff.

"What kind of talk is this, Andy Hawks! If you're making up tales to tease
me before the child I'm surprised at you, that thought nothing you could do
would ever surprise me again.''

"It's the truth. The *Sunny South,* she was called. Captain Jake Bofinger,
owner. Married ten times, old Jake was. A pretty rough lot we were in those
days, let me tell you. I remember time we————''

"Not another word, Captain Hawks. And let me tell you it's a good thing
for you that you kept it from me all these years. I'd never have married you
if I'd known. A show-boat actor!''

"Oh, yes, you would, Parthy. And glad of the chance.''

Words. Bickering. Recriminations. Finally, "I'll thank you not to mention
show boats again in front of the child. You with your La Vernes and your
Hard Harrys and your concerts and broken legs and fires and ten wives and
language and what not! I don't want to be dirtied by it, nor the child. . . .
Run out and play, Magnolia. . . . And let this be the last of show boat talk
in this house.''

Andy breathed deep, clung with both hands to his whiskers, and took the
plunge. "It's far from being the last of it, Parthy. I've bought the *Cotton
Blossom* from Pegram.''

4

MANY QUARRELS HAD marked their married life, but this one assumed serious proportions. It was a truly sinister note in the pageant of mismating
that passed constantly before Magnolia's uncomprehending eyes in childhood. Parthenia had opposed him often, and certainly always when a new
venture or plan held something of the element of unconventionality. But
now the Puritan in her ran rampant. He would disgrace her before the
community. He was ruining the life of his child. She would return to her
native New England. He would not see Magnolia again. He had explained
to her—rather, it had come out piecemeal—that his new project would ne-
cessitate his absence from home for months at a time. He would be away,

surely, from April until November. If Parthy and the child would live with him on the show boat part of that time—summers—easy life—lots to see— learn the country——

The storm broke, raged, beat about his head, battered his diminutive frame. He clutched his whiskers and hung on for dear life. In the end he won.

All that Parthy ever had in her life of colour, of romance, of change, he brought her. But for him she would still be ploughing through the drifts or mud of the New England road on her way to and from the frigid little schoolhouse. But for him she would still be living her barren spinster life with her salty old father in the grim coast town whence she had come. She was to trail through the vine-hung bayous of Louisiana; float down the generous rivers of the Carolinas, of Tennessee, of Mississippi, with the silver-green weeping willows misting the water's edge. She was to hear the mellow plaintive voices of Negroes singing on the levees and in cabin door-ways as the boat swept by. She would taste exotic fruits; see stirring sights; meet the fantastic figures that passed up and down the rivers like shadows drifting in and out of a weird dream. Yet always she was to resent loveliness; fight the influence of each new experience; combat the lure of each new face. Tight-lipped, belligerent, she met beauty and adventure and defied them to work a change in her.

For three days, then, following Andy's stupendous announcement, Par-thenia threatened to leave him, though certainly, in an age that looked upon the marriage tie as well-nigh indissoluble by any agent other than death, she could not have meant it, straight-laced as she was. For another three days she refused to speak to him, conveying her communications to him through a third person who was, perforce, Magnolia. "Tell your father thus-and-so." This in his very presence. "Ask your father this-and-that."

Experience had taught Magnolia not to be bewildered by these tactics; she was even amused, as at a game. But finally the game wearied her; or perhaps, child though she was, an instinctive sympathy between her and her father made her aware of the pain twisting the face of the man. Suddenly she stamped her foot, issued her edict. "I won't tell him another single word for you. It's silly. I thought it was kind of fun, but it isn't. It's silly for a great big grown-up person like you that's a million years old."

Andy was absent from home all day long, and often late into the night. The *Cotton Blossom* was being overhauled from keel to pilot house. She was lying just below the landing; painters and carpenters were making her ship-shape. Andy trotted up and down the town and the river bank, talking, gesticulating, capering excitedly. There were numberless supplies to be or-dered; a troupe to be assembled. He was never without a slip of paper on which he figured constantly. His pockets and the lining of his cap bristled with these paper scraps.

One week following their quarrel Parthy Ann began to evidence interest in these negotiations. She demanded details. How much had he paid for that old mass of kindling wood? (meaning, of course, the *Cotton Blossom*). How many would its theatre seat? What did the troupe number? What was their route? How many deckhands? One cook or two? Interspersed with these questions were grumblings and dire predictions anent money thrown away; poverty in old age; the advisability of a keeper being appointed for people whose minds had palpably given way. Still, her curiosity was obviously intense.

"Tell you what," suggested Andy with what he fancied to be infinite craft. "Get your hat on come on down and take a look at her."

"Never," said Parthenia; and untied her kitchen apron.

"Well, then, let Magnolia go down and see her. She likes boats, don't you, Nola? Same's her pa."

"H'm! Likely I'd let her go," sniffed Parthy.

Andy tried another tack. "Don't you want to come and see where your papa's going to live all the months and months he'll be away from you and ma?"

At which Magnolia, with splendid dramatic sense, began to cry wildly and inconsolably. Parthy remained grim. Yet she must have been immediately disturbed, for Magnolia wept so seldom as to be considered a queer child on this count, among many others.

"Hush your noise," commanded Parthy.

Great sobs racked Magnolia. Andy crudely followed up his advantage. "I guess you'll forget how your papa looks time he gets back."

Magnolia, perfectly aware of the implausibility of any such prediction, now hurled herself at her father, wrapped her arms about him, and howled, jerking back her head, beating a tattoo with her heels, interspersing the howls with piteous supplications not to be left behind. She wanted to see the show boat; and, with the delightful memory of the *Creole Belle* trip fresh in her mind, she wanted to travel on the *Cotton Blossom* as she had never wanted anything in her life. Her eyes were staring and distended; her fingers clutched; her body writhed; her moans were heart-breaking. She gave a magnificent performance.

Andy tried to comfort her. The howls increased. Parthy tried stern measures. Hysteria. The two united then, and alarm brought pleadings, and pleadings promises, and finally the three sat intertwined, Andy's arm about Magnolia and Parthenia; Parthenia's arm embracing Andy and Magnolia; Magnolia, clinging to both.

"Come get your hair combed. Mama'll change your dress. Now stop that crying." Magnolia had been shaken by a final series of racking sobs, real enough now that the mechanics had been started. Her lower lip quivered at intervals as the wet comb chased the strands of straight black hair around Mrs. Hawks' expert forefinger. When finally she appeared in starched muslin petticoats and second-best plaid serge, there followed behind her Parthy Ann herself bonneted and cloaked for the street. The thing was done. The wife of a showman. The Puritan in her shivered, but her curiosity was triumphant even over this. They marched down Oak Street to the river landing, the child skipping and capering in her excitement. There was, too, something of elation in Andy's walk. If it had not been for the grim figure at his side and the restraining hand on his arm, it is not unlikely that the two—father and child—would have skipped and capered together down to the water's edge. Mrs. Hawks' tread and mien were those of a matronly Christian martyr on her way to the lions. As they went the parents talked of unimportant things to which Magnolia properly paid no heed, having had her way. . . . Gone most of the time. . . . It wouldn't hurt her any, I tell you. . . . Learn more in a week than she would in a year out of books. . . . But they *ain't*, I tell you. Decent folks as you'd ever want to see. Married couples, most of 'em. . . . What do you think I'm running? A bawdy-boat? . . . Oh, language be damned! . . . Now, Parthy, you've got this far, don't start all over again. . . . There she is! Ain't she pretty! Look, Magnolia! That's where you're going to live. . . . Oh, all right, all right! I was just talking . . .

The *Cotton Blossom* lay moored to great stobs. Long, and wide and plump and comfortable she looked, like a rambling house that had taken perversely to the nautical life and now lay at ease on the river's broad breast. She had had two coats of white paint with green trimmings; and not the least of these green trimmings comprised letters, a foot high, that smote Parthy's anguished eye, causing her to groan, and Magnolia's delighted gaze, causing her to squeal. There it was in all the finality of painter's print:

CAPT. ANDY HAWKS COTTON BLOSSOM FLOATING PALACE THEATRE

Parthy gathered her dolman more tightly about her, as though smitten by a chill. The clay banks of the levee were strewn with cinders and ashes for a foothold. The steep sides of a river bank down which they would scramble and up which they would clamber were to be the home path for these three in the years to come.

An awninged upper deck, like a cosy veranda, gave the great flat boat a curiously homelike look. On the main deck, too, the gangplank ended in a forward deck which was like a comfortable front porch. Pillars, adorned with scroll-work, supported this. And there, its mouth open in a half-oval of welcome, was the ticket window through which could be seen the little box office with its desk and chair and its wall rack for tickets. There actually were tickets stuck in this, purple and red and blue. Parthy shut her eyes as at a leprous sight. A wide doorway led into the entrance hall. There again double doors opened to reveal a stairway.

"Balcony stairs," Andy explained, "and upper boxes. Seat hundred and fifty to two hundred, easy. Niggers mostly, upstairs, of course." Parthy shuddered. An aisle to the right, an aisle to the left of this stairway, and there was the auditorium of the theatre itself, with its rows of seats and its orchestra pit; its stage, its boxes, its painted curtain raised part way so that you saw only the lower half of the Venetian water scene it depicted; the legs of gondoliers in wooden attitudes; faded blue lagoon; palace steps. Magnolia knew a pang of disappointment. True, the boxes bore shiny brass railings and boasted red plush upholstered seats.

"But I thought it would be all light and glittery and like a fairy tale," she protested.

"At night," Andy assured her. He had her warm wriggling little fingers in his. "At night. That's when it's like a fairy tale. When the lamps are lighted; and all the people; and the band playing."

"Where's the kitchen?" demanded Mrs. Hawks.

Andy leaped nimbly down into the orchestra pit, stooped, opened a little door under the stage, and beckoned. Ponderously Parthy followed. Magnolia scampered after. Dining room and cook's galley were under the stage. Great cross-beams hung so low that even Andy was forced to stoop a little to avoid battering his head against them. Magnolia could touch them quite easily with her finger-tips. In time it came to seem quite natural to see the company and crew of the *Cotton Blossom* entering the dining room at meal time humbly bent as though in a preliminary attitude of grace before meat.

There were two long tables, each accommodating perhaps ten; and at the head of the room a smaller table for six.

"This is our table," Andy announced, boldly, as he indicated the third. Parthy snorted; but it seemed to the sensitive Andy that in this snort there was just a shade less resentment than there might have been. Between dining room and kitchen an opening, the size of a window frame, had been cut in the wall, and the base of this was a broad shelf for convenience in conveying hot dishes from stove to table. As the three passed from dining room to kitchen, Andy tossed over his shoulder further information for the possible approval of the bristling Parthy. "Jo and Queenie—she cooks and he waits and washes up and one thing another—they promised to be back April first, sure. Been with the *Cotton Blossom,* those two have, ten years and more. Painters been cluttering up here, and what not. And will you look at the way the kitchen looks, spite of 'em. Slick's a whistle. Look at that stove!" Crafty Andy.

Parthenia Ann Hawks looked at the stove. And what a stove it was! Broad-bosomed, ample, vast, like a huge fertile black mammal whose breast would suckle numberless eager sprawling bubbling pots and pans. It shone richly. Gazing upon this generous expanse you felt that from its source could emerge nothing that was not savoury, nourishing, satisfying. Above it, and around the walls, on hooks, hung rows of pans and kettles of every size and shape, all neatly suspended by their pigtails. Here was the wherewithal for bound-less cooking. You pictured whole hams, sizzling; fowls neatly trussed in rows; platoons of brown loaves; hampers of green vegetables; vast plateaus of pies. Crockery, thick, white, coarse, was piled, plate on plate, platter on platter, behind the neat doors of the pantry. A supplementary and redundant kerosene stove stood obligingly in the corner.

"Little hot snack at night, after the show," Andy explained. "Coffee or an egg, maybe, and no lighting the big wood burner."

There crept slowly, slowly over Parthy's face a look of speculation, and this in turn was replaced by an expression that was, paradoxically, at once eager and dreamy. As though aware of this she tried with words to belie her look. "All this cooking for a crowd. Take a mint of money, that's what it will."

"Make a mint," Andy retorted, blithely. A black cat, sleek, lithe, at ease, paced slowly across the floor, stood a moment surveying the two with wary yellow eyes, then sidled toward Parthy and rubbed his arched back against her skirts. "Mouser," said Andy.

"Scat!" cried Parthy; but her tone was half-hearted, and she did not move away. In her eyes gleamed the unholy light of the housewife who beholds for the first time the domain of her dreams. Jo and Queenie to boss. Wholesale marketing. Do this. Do that. Perhaps Andy, in his zeal, had even overdone the thing a little. Suddenly, "Where's that child! Where's—— Oh, my goodness, Hawks!" Visions of Magnolia having fallen into the river. She was, later, always to have visions of Magnolia having fallen into rivers so that Magnolia sometimes fell into them out of sheer perversity as other children, cautioned to remain in the yard, wilfully run away from home.

Andy darted out of the kitchen, through the little rabbit-hutch door. Mrs. Hawks gathered up her voluminous skirts and flew after; scrambled across the orchestra pit, turned at the sound of a voice, Magnolia's, and yet not Magnolia's, coming from that portion of the stage exposed below the half-raised curtain. In tones at once throaty, mincing, and falsely elegant—that arrogant voice which is childhood's unconscious imitation of pretence in its elders—Magnolia was reciting nothing in particular, and bringing great gusto to the rendition. The words were palpably made up as she went along— "Oh, do you rully think so! . . . My little girl is very naughty . . . we are rich, oh dear me yes, ice cream every day for breakfast, dinner, and sup-per. . . ." She wore her mother's dolman which that lady had unclasped and left hanging over one of the brass railings of a box. From somewhere she had rummaged a bonnet whose jet aigrette quivered with the earnestness of its wearer's artistic effort. The dolman trailed in the dust of the floor. Magnolia's right hand was held in a graceful position, the little finger ele-gantly crooked.

"Maggie Hawks, will you come down out of there this instant!" Parthy whirled on Andy. "There! That's what it comes to, minute she sets foot on this sink of iniquity. Play acting!"

Andy clawed his whiskers, chuckling. He stepped to the proscenium and held out his arms for the child and she stood looking down at him, flushed, smiling, radiant. "You're about as good as your pa was, Nola. And that's no compliment." He swung her to the floor, a whirl of dolman, short starched skirt and bonnet askew. Then, as Parthy snatched the dolman from her and glared at the bonnet, he saw that he must create again a favourable impression—contrive a new diversion—or his recent gain was lost. A born show-man, Andy.

"Where'd you get that bonnet, Magnolia?"

"In there." She pointed to one of a row of doors facing them at the rear of the stage. "In one of those little bedrooms—cabins—what are they, Papa?"

"Dressing rooms, Nola, and bedrooms, too. Want to see them, Parthy?" He opened a little door leading from the right-hand box to the stage, crossed the stage followed by the reluctant Parthenia, threw open one of the doors at the back. There was revealed a tiny cabin holding a single bed, a diminutive dresser, and washstand. Handy rows of shelves were fastened to the wall above the bed. Dimity curtains hung at the window. The window itself framed a view of river and shore. A crudely coloured calendar hung on the wall, and some photographs and newspaper clippings, time-yellowed. There was about the little chamber a cosiness, a snugness, and, paradoxically enough, a sense of space. That was the open window, doubtless, with its vista of water and sky giving the effect of freedom.

"Dressing rooms during the performance," Andy explained, "and bed-rooms the rest of the time. That's the way we work it."

Mrs. Hawks, with a single glance, encompassed the tiny room and rejected it. "Expect me to live in a cubby-hole like that!" It was, unconsciously, her first admission.

Magnolia, behind her mother's skirts, was peering, wide-eyed, into the room. "Why, I *love* it! Why, I'd love to live in it. Why, look, there's a little bed, and a dresser, and a———"

Andy interrupted hastily. "Course I don't expect you to live in a cubby-hole, Parthy. No, nor the child, neither. Just you step along with me. Now don't say anything; and stop your grumbling till you see. Put that bonnet back, Nola, where you got it. That's wardrobe. Which room'd you get it out of?"

Across the stage, then, up the aisle to the stairway that led to the balcony, Andy leading, Mrs. Hawks following funereally, Magnolia playing a zigzag game between the rows of seats yet managing mysteriously to arrive at the foot of the stairs just as they did. The balcony reached, Magnolia had to be rescued from the death that in Mrs. Hawks' opinion inevitably would result from her leaning over the railing to gaze enthralled on the auditorium and stage below. "Hawks, will you look at that child! I declare, if I ever get her off this boat alive I'll never set foot on it again."

But her tone somehow lacked conviction. And when she beheld those two upper bedrooms forward, leading off the balcony—those two square roomy bedrooms, as large, actually, as her bedroom in the cottage, she was lost. The kitchen had scored. But the bedrooms won. They were connected by a little washroom. Each had two windows. Each held bed, dresser, rocker, stove. Bedraggled dimity curtains hung at the windows. Matting covered the floors. Parthy did an astonishing—though characteristic—thing. She walked to the dresser, passed a practised forefinger over its surface, examined the finger critically, and uttered that universal tongue-and-tooth sound indicating disapproval. "An inch thick," she then said. "A sight of cleaning this boat will take, I can tell you. Not a curtain in the place but'll have to come down and washed and starched and ironed."

Instinct or a superhuman wisdom cautioned Andy to say nothing. From the next room came a shout of joy. "Is this my room? It's got a chair that rocks and a stove with a res'vore and I can see my whole self in the looking glass, it's so big. Is this my room? Is it? Mama!"

Parthy passed into the next room. "We'll see. We'll see. We'll see." Andy followed after, almost a-tiptoe; aaffraid to break the spell with a sudden sound.

"But is it? I want to know. Papa, make her tell me. Look! The window here is a little door. It's a door and I can go right out on the upstairs porch. And there's the whole river."

"I should say as much, and a fine way to fall and drown without anybody being the wiser."

But the child was beside herself with excitement and suspense. She could endure it no longer; flew to her stern parent and actually shook that adamantine figure in its dolman and bonnet. "Is it? Is it? Is it?"

"We'll see." A look, then, of almost comic despair flashed between father and child—a curiously adult look for one of Magnolia's years. It said: "What a woman this is! Can we stand it? I can only if you can."

Andy tried suggestion. "Could paint this furniture any colour Nola says————"

"Blue," put in Magnolia, promptly.

"—and new curtains, maybe, with ribbons to match————" He had, among other unexpected traits, a keen eye for colour and line; a love for fabrics.

Parthy said nothing. Her lips were compressed. The look that passed between Andy and Magnolia now was pure despair, with no humour to relieve it. So they went disconsolately out of the door; crossed the balcony, clumped down the stairs, like mutes at a funeral. At the foot of the stairs they heard voices from without—women's voices, high and clear—and laughter. The sounds came from the little porch-like deck forward. Parthy swooped through the door; had scarcely time to gaze upon two sprightly females in gay plumage before both fell upon her lawful husband Captain Andy Hawks and embraced him. And the young pretty one kissed him on his left-hand mutton-chop whisker. And the older plain one kissed him on the right-hand mutton-chop whisker. And, "Oh, dear Captain Hawks!" they cried. "Aren't you surprised to see us! And happy! Do say you're happy. We drove over from Cairo specially to see you and the *Cotton Blossom*. Doc's with us."

Andy flung an obliging arm about the waist of each and gave each armful a little squeeze. "Happy ain't the word." And indeed it scarcely seemed to cover the situation; for there stood Parthy viewing the three entwined, and as she stood she seemed to grow visibly taller, broader, more ominous, like a menacing cloud. Andy's expression was a protean thing in which bravado and apprehension battled.

Magnolia had recognized them at once as the pretty young woman in the rose-trimmed hat and the dark woman who had told her not to smile too often that day when, in company with the sloppy young man, they had passed the Hawks house, laughing and chatting and spitting cherry stones idly and comfortably into the dust of the village street. So she now took a step forward from behind her mother's voluminous skirts and made a little tentative gesture with one hand toward the older woman. And that lively female at once said, "Why, bless me! Look, Elly! It's the little girl!"

Elly looked. "What little girl?"

"The little girl with the smile." And at that, quite without premeditation, and to her own surprise, Magnolia ran to her and put her hand in hers and looked up into her strange ravaged face and smiled. "There!" exclaimed the woman, exactly as she had done that first time.

"Maggie Hawks!" came the voice.

And, "Oh, my God!" exclaimed the one called Elly, "it's the———" sensed something dangerous in the air, laughed, and stopped short.

Andy extricated himself from his physical entanglements and attempted to do likewise with the social snarl that now held them all.

"Meet my wife Mrs. Hawks. Parthy, this is Julie Dozier, female half of our general business team and one of the finest actresses on the river besides being as nice a little lady as you'd meet in a month of Sundays. . . . This here little beauty is Elly Chipley—Lenore La Verne on the bills. Our ingénue lead and a favourite from Duluth to New Orleans. . . . Where's Doc?"

At which, with true dramatic instinct, Doc appeared scrambling down the cinder path toward the boat; leaped across the gangplank, poised on one toe, spread his arms and carolled, "Tra-da!" A hard-visaged man of about fifty-five, yet with kindness, too, written there; the deep-furrowed, sad-eyed ageless face of the circus shillaber and showman.

"Girls say you drove over. Must be flush with your spondulicks, Doc. . . . Parthy, meet Doc. He's got another name, I guess, but nobody's ever used it. Doc's enough for anybody on the river. Doc goes ahead of the show and bills us and does the dirty work, don't you, Doc?"

"That's about the size of it," agreed Doc, and sped sadly and accurately a comet of brown juice from his lips over the boat's side into the river. "Pleased to make your acquaintance."

Andy indicated Magnolia. "Here's my girl Magnolia you've heard me talk about."

"Well, well! Lookit them eyes! They oughtn't to go bad in the show business, little later." A sound from Parthy who until now had stood a graven image, a portent. Doc turned to her, soft-spoken, courteous. "Fixin' to take a little ride with us for good luck I hope, ma'am, our first trip out with Cap here?"

Mrs. Hawks glanced then at the arresting face of Julie Dozier, female half of our general business team and one of the finest actresses on the river. Mrs. Hawks looked at Elly Chipley (Lenore La Verne on the bills) the little beauty, and favourite from Duluth to New Orleans. She breathed deep.

"Yes. I am." And with those three monosyllables Parthenia Ann Hawks renounced the ties of land, of conventionality; forsook the staid orderliness of the little white-painted cottage at Thebes; shut her ears to the scandalized gossip of her sedate neighbours; yielded grimly to the urge of the river and became at last its unwilling mistress.

5

WHEN APRIL CAME, and the dogwood flashed its spectral white in the woods, the show boat started. It was the most leisurely and dreamlike of journeys. In all the hurried harried country that still was intent on repairing the ravages of a Civil War, they alone seemed to be leading an enchanted existence, suspended on another plane. Miles—hundreds—thousands of miles of willow-fringed streams flowing aquamarine in the sunlight, olive-green in the shade. Wild honeysuckle clambering over black tree trunks. Mules. Negroes. Bare unpainted cabins the colour of the sandy soil itself. Sleepy little villages blinking drowsily down upon a river which was some almost forgotten offspring spawned years before by the Mississippi. The nearest railroad perhaps twenty-five miles distant.

They floated down the rivers. They floated down the rivers. Sometimes they were broad majestic streams rolling turbulently to the sea, and draining a continent. Sometimes they were shallow narrow streams little more than creeks, through which the *Cotton Blossom* picked her way as cautiously as a timid girl picking her way among stepping stones. Behind them, pushing them maternally along like a fat puffing duck with her silly little gosling, was the steamboat *Mollie Able*.

To the people dwelling in the towns, plantations, and hamlets along the many tributaries of the Mississippi and Ohio, the show boat was no longer a novelty. It had been a familiar and welcome sight since 1817 when the first crude barge of that type had drifted down the Cumberland River. But familiarity with these craft had failed to dispel their glamour. To the farmers and villagers of the Midwest; and to the small planters—black and white—of the South, the show boat meant music, romance, gaiety. It visited towns whose leafy crypts had never echoed the shrill hoot of an engine whistle. It penetrated settlements whose backwoods dwellers had never witnessed a theatrical performance in all their lives—simple child-like credulous people to whom the make-believe villainies, heroics, loves, adventures of the drama were so real as sometimes to cause the *Cotton Blossom* troupe actual embarrassment. Often quality folk came to the show boat. The perfume and silks and broadcloth of the Big House took frequent possession of the lower boxes and the front seats.

That first summer was, to Magnolia, a dream of pure delight. Nothing could mar it except that haunting spectre of autumn when she would have to return to Thebes and to the ordinary routine of a little girl in a second-best pinafore that was donned for school in the morning and thriftily replaced by a less important pinafore on her return from school in the late afternoon. But throughout those summer months Magnolia was a fairy princess. She was Cinderella at the ball. She shut her mind to the horrid certainty that the clock would inevitably strike twelve.

Year by year, as the spell of the river grew stronger and the easy indolence of the life took firmer hold, Mrs. Hawks and the child spent longer and longer periods on the show boat; less and less time in the humdrum security of the cottage ashore. Usually the boat started in April. But sometimes, when the season was mild, it was March. Mrs. Hawks would announce with a good deal of firmness that Magnolia must finish the school term, which ended in June. Later she and the child would join the boat wherever it happened to be showing at the time.

"Couple of months missed won't hurt her," Captain Andy would argue, loath as always to be separated from his daughter. "May's the grandest month on the rivers—and April. Everything coming out fresh. Outdoors all day. Do her good."

"I may not know much, but this I do know, Andy Hawks: No child of mine is going to grow up an ignoramus just because her father has nothing better to do than go galumphing around the country with a lot of riff-raff."

But in the end, when the show boat started its leisurely journey, there was Mrs. Hawks hanging fresh dimity curtains; bickering with Queenie; preventing, by her acid presence, the possibility of a too-saccharine existence for the members of the *Cotton Blossom* troupe. In her old capacity as school teacher, Parthy undertook the task of carrying on Magnolia's education during these truant spring months. It was an acrimonious and painful business ending, almost invariably, in temper, tears, disobedience, upbraidings. Unconsciously Andy Hawks had done much for the youth of New England when he ended Parthy's public teaching career.

"Nine times seven, I said. . . . No, it isn't! Just because fifty-six was the right answer last time it isn't right every time. That was seven times eight and I'll thank you to look at the book and not out of the window. I declare, Maggie Hawks, sometimes I think you're downright simple."

Magnolia's under lip would come out. Her brow was lowering. She somehow always looked her plainest and sallowest during these sessions with her mother. "I don't care what nine times seven is. Elly doesn't know, either. I asked her and she said she never had nine of anything, much less nine times seven of anything; and Elly's the most beautiful person in the world, except Julie sometimes—and me when I smile. And my name isn't Maggie Hawks, either."

"I'd like to know what it is if it isn't. And if you talk to me like that again, young lady, I'll smack you just as sure as I'm sitting here."

"It's Magnolia—Magnolia—uh—something beautiful—I don't know what. But not Hawks. Magnolia—uh———" a gesture with her right hand meant to convey some idea of the exquisiteness of her real name.

Mrs. Hawks clapped a maternal hand to her daughter's somewhat bulging brow, decided that she was feverish, needed a physic, and promptly administered one.

As for geography, if Magnolia did not learn it, she lived it. She came to know her country by travelling up and down its waterways. She learned its people by meeting them, of all sorts and conditions. She learned folkways; river lore; Negro songs; bird calls; pilot rules; profanity; the art of stage make-up; all the parts in the *Cotton Blossom* troupe's repertoire including East Lynne, Lady Audley's Secret, Tempest and Sunshine, Spanish Gipsy, Madcap Margery, and Uncle Tom's Cabin.

There probably was much that was sordid about the life. But to the imaginative and volatile little girl of ten or thereabouts it was a combination playhouse, make-believe theatre, and picnic jaunt. Hers were days of enchantment—or would have been were it not for the practical Parthy who, iron woman that she was, saw to it that the child was properly fed, well clothed, and sufficiently refreshed by sleep. But Parthy's interests now were too manifold and diverse to permit of her accustomed concentration on Magnolia. She had an entire boatload of people to boss—two boatloads, in fact, for she did not hesitate to investigate and criticize the manners and morals of the crew that manned the towboat *Mollie Able*. A man was never safe from her as he sat smoking his after-dinner pipe and spitting contemplatively into the river. It came about that Magnolia's life was infinitely more free afloat than it had ever been on land.

Up and down the rivers the story went that the *Cotton Blossom* was the sternest-disciplined, best-managed, and most generously provisioned boat in the business. And it was notorious that a sign back-stage and in each dressing room read: "No lady of the company allowed on deck in a wrapper." It also was known that drunkenness on the *Cotton Blossom* was punished by instant dismissal; that Mrs. Captain Andy Hawks was a holy terror; that the platters of fried chicken on Sunday were inexhaustible. All of this was true.

Magnolia's existence became a weird mixture of lawlessness and order; of humdrum and fantasy. She slipped into the life as though she had been born to it. Parthy alone kept her from being utterly spoiled by the members of the troupe.

Mrs. Hawks' stern tread never adjusted itself to the leisurely rhythm of the show boat's tempo. This was obvious even to Magnolia. The very first week of their initial trip she had heard her mother say briskly to Julie, "What time is it?" Mrs. Hawks was marching from one end of the boat to the other, intent on some fell domestic errand of her own. Julie, seated in a low chair on deck, sewing and gazing out upon the yellow turbulence of the Mississippi, had replied in her deep indolent voice, without glancing up, "What does it matter?"

The four words epitomized the divinely care-free existence of the *Cotton Blossom* show-boat troupe.

Sometimes they played a new town every night. Sometimes, in regions that were populous and that boasted a good back-country, they remained a week. In such towns, as the boat returned year after year until it became a recognized institution, there grew up between the show-boat troupe and the townspeople a sort of friendly intimacy. They were warmly greeted o.. their arrival; sped regretfully on their departure. They almost never travelled at night. Usually they went to bed with the sound of the water slap-slapping gently against the boat's flat sides, and proceeded down river at daybreak. This meant that constant warfare raged between the steamboat crew of the *Mollie Able* and the show-boat troupe of the *Cotton Blossom*. The steamer crew, its work done, retired early, for it must be up and about at daybreak. It breakfasted at four-thirty or five. The actors never were abed before midnight or one o'clock and rose for a nine o'clock breakfast. They complained that the steamer crew, with its bells, whistles, hoarse shouts, hammerings, puffings, and general to-do attendant upon casting off and getting under way, robbed them of their morning sleep. The crew grumbled and cursed as it tried to get a night's rest in spite of the noise of the band, the departing audience, the midnight sociability of the players who, still at high tension after their night's work, could not yet retire meekly to bed.

"Lot of damn scenery chewers," growled the crew, turning in sleep.

"Filthy roustabouts," retorted the troupers, disturbed at dawn. "Yell because they can't talk like human beings."

They rarely mingled, except such members of the crew as played in the band; and never exchanged civilities. This state of affairs lent spice to an existence that might otherwise have proved too placid for comfort. The bickering acted as a safety valve.

It all was, perhaps, the worst possible environment for a skinny, high-strung, and sensitive little girl who was one-quarter French. But Magnolia thrived on it. She had the solid and lumpy Puritanism of Parthy's presence to counteract the leaven of her volatile father. This saved her from being utterly consumed.

The life was at once indolent and busy. Captain Andy, scurrying hither and thither, into the town, up the river bank, rushing down the aisle at rehearsal to squeak a false direction to the hard-working company, driving off into the country to return in triumph laden with farm produce, was fond of saying, "We're just like one big happy family."

Captain Andy knew and liked good food (the Frenchman in him). They ate the best that the countryside afforded—not a great deal of meat in the height of summer when they were, perhaps, playing the hot humid Southern river towns, but plenty of vegetables and fruit—great melons bought from the patch with the sun still hot on their rounded bulging sides, and then chilled to dripping deliciousness before eating; luscious yams; country butter and cream. They all drank the water dipped out of the river on which they happened to be floating. They quaffed great dippersful of the Mississippi, the Ohio, and even the turbid Missouri, and seemed none the worse for it. At the stern was the settling barrel. Here the river water, dipped up in buckets, was left to settle before drinking. At the bottom of this receptacle, after it was three-quarters empty, one might find a rich layer of Mississippi silt intermingled with plummy odds and ends of every description including, sometimes, a sizable catfish.

In everything but actual rehearsing and playing, Magnolia lived the life of the company. The boat was their home. They ate, slept, worked, played on it. The company must be prompt at meal time, at rehearsals, and at the evening performances. There all responsibility ended for them.

Breakfast was at nine; and under Parthy's stern régime this meant nine. They were a motley lot as they assembled. In that bizarre setting the homely, everyday garb of the men and women took on a grotesque aspect. It was as though they were dressed for a part. As they appeared in the dining room, singly, in couples, or in groups, with a cheerful or a dour greeting, depending on the morning mood of each, an onlooker could think only of the home life of the Vincent Crummleses. Having seen Elly the night before as Miss Lenore La Verne in the golden curls, short skirts, and wide-eyed innocence of Bessie, the backwoodsman's daughter, who turned out, in the last act, to be none other than the Lady Clarice Trelawney, carelessly mislaid at birth, her appearance at breakfast was likely to have something of the shock of disillusionment. The baby stare of her great blue eyes was due to near-sightedness to correct which she wore silver-rimmed spectacles when not under the public gaze. Her breakfast jacket, though frilly, was not of the freshest, and her kid curlers were not entirely hidden by a silk-and-lace cap. Elly was, despite these grotesqueries, undeniably and triumphantly pretty, and thus arrayed gave the effect of a lttle girl mischievously tricked out in her grandmother's wardrobe. Her husband, known as Schultzy in private and Harold Westbrook on the bills, acted as director of the company. He was what is known in actor's parlance as a raver, and his method of acting was designated in the show-boat world as spitting scenery. A somewhat furtive young man in very tight pants and high collar always a trifle too large. He was a cuffshooter, and those cuffs were secured and embellished with great square shiny chunks of quartz-like stuff which he frequently breathed upon heavily and then rubbed with his handkerchief. Schultzy played juvenile leads opposite his wife's ingénue rôles; had a real flair for the theatre.

Sometimes they were in mid-river when the breakfast bell sounded; sometimes tied to a landing. The view might be plantation, woods, or small town—it was all one to the *Cotton Blossom* company, intent on coffee and bacon. Long before white-aproned Jo, breakfast bell in hand, emerged head first from the little doorway beneath the stage back of the orchestra pit, like an amiable black python from its lair, Mrs. Hawks was on the scene, squinting critically into cream jugs, attacking flies as though they were dragons, infuriating Queenie with the remark that the biscuits seemed soggy this morning. Five minutes after the bell was brandished, Jo had placed the breakfast on the table, hot: oatmeal, steaming pots of coffee, platters of fried eggs with ham or bacon, stacks of toast, biscuits fresh from the oven. If you were prompt you got a hot breakfast; tardy, you took it cold.

Parthy, whose breakfast cap, designed to hide her curl papers, always gave the effect, somehow, of a martial helmet, invariably was first at the small table that stood at the head of the room farthest from the little doorway. So she must have sat at her schoolhouse desk during those New England winters, awaiting the tardy morning arrival of reluctant and chilblained urchins. Magnolia was one of those children whom breakfast does not interest. Left to her own devices, she would have ignored the meal altogether. She usually entered late, her black hair still wet from the comb, her eyes wide with her eagerness to impart the day's first bit of nautical news.

"Doc says there's a family going down river on a bumboat, and they've got a teensy baby no bigger than a———"

"Drink your milk."

"—doll and he says it must have been born on the boat and he bets it's not more than a week old. Oh, I hope they'll tie up somewhere near———"

"Eat your toast with your egg."

"Do I have to eat my egg?"

"Yes."

If Magnolia was late, Andy was always later. He ate quickly and abstractedly. As he swallowed his coffee you could almost see his agile mind darting here and there, so that you wondered how his electric little body resisted following it as a lesser force follows a greater—up into the pilot house, down in the engine room, into the town, leaping ahead to the next landing; dickering with storekeepers for supplies. He was always the first to finish and was off at a quick trot, clawing the mutton-chop whiskers as he went.

Early or late, Julie and Steve came in together, Steve's great height ludicrously bent to avoid the low rafters of the dining room. Julie and Steve were the character team—Julie usually cast as adventuress, older sister, foil for Elly, the ingénue. Julie was a natural and intuitive actress, probably the best in the company. Sometimes she watched Elly's unintelligent work, heard her slovenly speech and her silly inflections, and a little contemptuous look would come into her face.

Steve played villains and could never have kept the job, even in that uncritical group, had it not been for Julie. He was very big and very fair, and almost entirely lacking in dramatic sense. A quiet gentle giant, he always seemed almost grotesquely miscast, his blondeur and his trusting faithful blue eyes belying the sable hirsuteness of villainy. Julie coached him patiently, tirelessly. The result was fairly satisfactory. But a nuance, an inflection, was beyond him.

"Who has a better right!" his line would be, perhaps. Schultzy, directing at rehearsal, would endeavour fruitlessly to convey to him its correct reading. After rehearsal, Julie could be heard going over the line again and again.

"Who has a better *right!* " Steve would thunder, dramatically.

"No, dear. The accent is on 'better.' Like this: 'Who has a *better* right!' "

Steve's blue eyes would be very earnest, his face red with effort. "Oh, I see. Come down hard on 'better,' huh? 'Who has a better *right!'* "

It was useless.

The two were very much in love. The others in the company sometimes teased them about this, but not often. Julie and Steve did not respond to this badinage gracefully. There existed between the two a relation that made the outsider almost uncomfortable. When they looked at each other, there vibrated between them a current that sent a little shiver through the beholder. Julie's eyes were deep-set and really black, and there was about them a curious indefinable quality. Magnolia liked to look into their soft and mournful depths. Her own eyes were dark, but not like Julie's. Perhaps it was the whites of Julie's eyes that were different.

Magnolia had once seen them kiss. She had come upon them quietly and unexpectedly, on deck, in the dusk. Certainly she had never witnessed a like passage of love between her parents; and even her recent familiarity with stage romance had not prepared her for it. It was long before the day of the motion picture fadeout. Olga Nethersole's famous osculation was yet to shock a Puritan America. Steve had held Julie a long long minute, wordlessly. Her slimness had seemed to melt into him. Julie's eyes were closed.

She was quite limp as he tipped her upright. She stood thus a moment, swaying, her eyes still shut. When she opened them they were clouded, misty, as were his. The two then beheld a staring and fascinated little girl quite palpably unable to move from the spot. Julie had laughed a little low laugh. She had not flushed, exactly. Her sallow colouring had taken on a tone at once deeper and clearer and brighter, like amber underlaid with gold. Her eyes had widened until they were enormous in her thin dark glowing face. It was as though a lamp had been lighted somewhere behind them.

"What makes you look like that?" Magnolia had demanded, being a forthright young person.

"Like what?" Julie had asked.

"Like you do. All—all shiny."

"Love," Julie had answered, quite simply. Magnolia had not in the least understood; but she remembered. And years later she did understand.

Besides Elly, the ingénue, Schultzy, juvenile lead, Julie and Steve, character team, there were Mr. and Mrs. Means, general business team, Frank, the heavy, and Ralph, general utility man. Elly and Schultzy sat at table with the Hawkses, the mark of favour customary to their lofty theatrical eminence. The others of the company, together with Doc, and three of the band members, sat at the long table in the centre of the room. Mrs. Means played haughty dowagers, old Kentucky crones, widows, mothers, and middle-aged females. Mr. Means did bankers, Scrooges, old hunters and trappers, comics, and the like.

At the table nearest the door and the kitchen sat the captain and crew of the *Mollie Able*. There were no morning newspapers to read between sips of coffee; no mail to open. They were all men and women of experience. They had knocked about the world. In their faces was a lived look, together with an expression that had in it a curiously child-like quality. Captain Andy was not far wrong in his boast that they were like one big family—a close and jealous family needing no outside stimulus for its amusement. They were extraordinarily able to amuse themselves. Their talk was racy, piquant, pungent. The women were, for the most part, made of sterner stuff than the men—that is, among the actors. That the men had chosen this drifting, carefree, protected life, and were satisfied with it, proved that. Certainly Julie was a force stronger than Steve; Elly made a slave of Schultzy; Mrs. Means was a sternly maternal wife to her weak-chested and drily humorous little husband.

Usually they lingered over their coffee. Jo, padding in from the kitchen, would bring on a hot potful.

Julie had a marmoset which she had come by in New Orleans, where it had been brought from equatorial waters by some swarthy earringed sailor. This she frequently carried to the table with her, tucked under her arm, its tiny dark head with the tragic mask of a face peering out from beneath her elbow. To Mrs. Hawks' intense disgust, Julie fed the tiny creature out of her own dish. In her cabin its bed was an old sealskin muff from whose depths its mournful dark eyes looked appealingly out from a face that was like nothing so much as that of an old old baby.

"I declare," Parthy would protest, almost daily, "it fairly turns a body's stomach to see her eating out of the same dish with that dirty little rat."

"Why, Mama! it isn't a rat any such thing! It's a monkey and you know it. Julie says maybe Schultzy can get one for me in New Orleans if I promise to be very very careful of it."

"I'd like to see her try," grimly putting an end to that dream.

The women took care of their own cabins. The detail of this occupied them until mid-morning. Often there was a rehearsal at ten that lasted an hour or more. Schultzy announced it at breakfast.

As they swept up a river, or floated down, their approach to the town was announced by the shrill iron-throated calliope, pride of Captain Andy's heart. Its blatant voice heralded the coming of the show boat long before the boat itself could be seen from the river bank. It had solid brass keys and could plainly be heard for five miles. George, who played the calliope, was also the pianist. He was known, like all calliope players, as the Whistler. Magnolia delighted in watching him at the instrument. He wore a slicker and a slicker hat and heavy gloves to protect his hands, for the steam of the whistles turned to hot raindrops and showered his hands and his head and shoulders as he played. As they neared the landing, the band, perched atop the show boat, forward, alternated with the calliope. From the town, hurrying down the streets, through the woods, dotting the levee and the landing, came eager figures, black and white. Almost invariably some magic-footed Negro, overcome by the music, could be seen on the wharf executing the complicated and rhythmic steps of a double shuffle, his rags flapping grotesquely about him, his mouth a gash of white. By nine o'clock in the morning every human being within a radius of five miles knew that the Cotton Blossom Floating Palace Theatre had docked at the waterfront.

By half-past eleven the band, augmented by two or three men of the company who doubled in brass, must be ready for the morning concert on the main street corner. Often, queerly enough, the town at which they made their landing was no longer there. The Mississippi, in prankish mood, had dumped millions of tons of silt in front of the street that faced the river. Year by year, perhaps, this had gone on, until now that which had been a river town was an inland town, with a mile of woodland and sandy road between its main street and the waterfront. The old serpent now stretched its sluggish yellow coils in another channel.

By eleven o'clock the band would have donned its scarlet coats with the magnificent gold braid and brass buttons. The nether part of these costumes always irritated Magnolia. Her colour-loving eye turned away from them, offended. For while the upper costume was splendidly martial, the lower part was composed merely of such everyday pants as the band members might be wearing at the time of the concert hour, and were a rude shock to the ravished eye as it travelled from the gay flame and gold of the jacket and the dashing impudence of the cap. Especially in the drum major did this offend her. He was called the baton spinner and wore, instead of the scarlet cap of the other band members, an imposing (though a slightly mangy) fur shako, very black and shaggy and fierce-looking, and with a strap under the chin. Pete, the bass drummer, worked in the engine room. Usually, at the last minute, he washed up hastily, grabbed his drum, buttoned on his coat, and was dazzlingly transformed from a sooty crow into a scarlet tanager.

Up the levee they scrambled—two cornets, a clarinet, a tuba, an alto (called a peck horn. Magnolia loved its ump-a ump-a ta-ta-ta-ta, ump-a ump-a ta-ta-ta-ta), a snare drummer who was always called a "sticks," and the bass drum, known as the bull.

When the landing was a waterfront town, the band concert was a pleasant enough interval in the day's light duties. But when a mile or more of dusty road lay between the show boat and the main street it became a real chore. Carrying their heavy instruments, their scarlet coats open, their caps in their hands, they would trudge, tired, hot, and sweating, the long dusty road that led through the woods. When the road became a clearing and they emerged abruptly into the town, they would button their coats, mop their hot faces, adjust cap or shako, stiffen their drooping shoulders. Their gait would change from one of plodding weariness to a sprightly strut. Their pepper-and-salt, or brown, or black trousered legs would move with rhythmic precision in time to the music. From tired, sticky, wilted plodders, they would be transformed into heroic and romantic figures. Up came the chest of the baton spinner. His left hand rested elegantly on his hip, his head and shoulders were held stiffly, arrogantly; his right hand twirled the glittering baton until it dazzled the eyes like a second noonday sun. Hotel waitresses, their hearts beating high, scurried to the windows: children rushed pell-mell from the school yard into the street; clerks in their black sateen aprons and straw sleevelets stood in the shop doorways; housewives left their pots a-boil as they lingered a wistful moment on the front porch, shading their eyes with a work-seamed hand; loafers spilled out of the saloons and stood agape and blinking. And as the music blared and soared, the lethargic little town was transformed for an hour into a gay and lively scene. Even the old white fly-bitten nags in the streets stepped with a jerky liveliness in their spring-halted gait, and a gleam came into their lacklustre eyes as they pricked up their ears to the sound. Seeking out the busiest corner of the dull little main street, the band would take their stand, bleating and blaring, the sun playing magnificently on the polished brass of their instruments.

Although he never started with them, at this point Captain Andy always turned up, having overtaken them in some mysterious way. Perhaps he swung from tree to tree through the woods. There he was in his blue coat, his wrinkled baggy linen pants, his white canvas cap with the leather visor; fussy, nervous, animated, bright-eyed, clawing the mutton-chop whiskers from side to side. Under his arm he carried a sheaf of playbills announcing the programmes and extolling the talents of the players. After the band had played two lively numbers, he would make his speech, couched in the absurd grandiloquence of the showman. He talked well. He made his audience laugh, bizarre yet strangely appealing little figure that he was. "Most magnificent company of players every assembled on the rivers . . . unrivalled scenery and costumes . . . Miss Lenore La Verne . . . dazzling array of talent . . . fresh from triumphs in the East . . . concert after the show . . . singing and dancing . . bring the children . . . come one, come all. . . . *Cotton Blossom* troupe just one big happy family. . . ."

The band would strike up again. Captain Andy would whisk through the crowd with uncanny swiftness distributing his playbills, greeting an acquaintance met on previous trips, chucking a child under the chin, extolling the brilliance and gaiety of the performance scheduled for that evening. At the end of a half hour the band would turn and march playing down the street. In the dispersing crowd could be discerned Andy's agile little figure darting, stooping, swooping as he thriftily collected again the playbills that, once perused, had been dropped in the dust by careless spectators.

Dinner was at four, a hearty meal. Before dinner, and after, the *Cotton Blossom* troupe was free to spend its time as it would. The women read or sewed. There were always new costumes to be contrived, or old ones to mend and refurbish. The black-hearted adventuress of that morning's rehearsal sat neatly darning a pair of her husband's socks. There was always the nearby town to visit; a spool of thread to be purchased, a stamp, a sack of peppermint drops, a bit of muslin, a toothbrush. The indolence of the life was such that they rarely took any premeditated exercise. Sometimes they strolled in the woods at springtime when the first tender yellow-green hazed the forest vistas. They fished, though the catch was usually catfish. On hot days the more adventuresome of them swam. The river was their front yard, grown as accustomed as a stretch of lawn. They were extraordinarily able to amuse themselves. Hardly one that did not play piano, violin, flute, banjo, mandolin.

By six o'clock a stir—a little electric unrest—an undercurrent of excitement could be sensed aboard the show boat. They came sauntering back from the woods, the town, the levee. They drifted down the aisles and in and out of their dressing rooms. Years of trouping failed to still in them the quickened pulse that always came with the approach of the evening's performance.

Down in the orchestra pit the band was tuning up. They would play atop the show boat on the forward deck before the show, alternating with the calliope, as in the morning. The daytime lethargy had vanished. On the stage the men of the company were setting the scene. Hoarse shouts. Lift 'er up there! No—down a little. H'ist her up. Back! Closer! Dressing room doors opened and shut. Calls from one room to another. Twilight came on. Doc began to light the auditorium kerosene lamps whose metal reflectors sent back their yellow glow. Outside the kerosene search light, cunningly rigged on top of the *Mollie Able's* pilot house, threw its broad beam up the river bank to the levee.

Of all the hours in the day this was the one most beloved of Magnolia's heart. She enjoyed the stir, the colour, the music, the people. Anything might happen on board the Cotton Blossom Floating Palace Theatre between the night hours of seven and eleven. And then it was that she was banished to bed. There was a nightly struggle in which, during the first months of their life on the rivers, Mrs. Hawks almost always won. Infrequently, by hook or crook, Magnolia managed to evade the stern parental eye.

"Let me just stay up for the first act—where Elly shoots him."

"Not a minute."

"Let me stay till the curtain goes up, then."

"You march yourself off to bed, young lady, or no trip to the pirate's cave tomorrow with Doc, and so I tell you."

Doc's knowledge of the gruesome history of river banditry and piracy provided Magnolia with many a goose-skinned hour of delicious terror. Together they went excursioning ashore in search of the blood-curdling all the way from Little Egypt to the bayous of Louisiana.

Lying there in her bed, then, wide-eyed, tense, Magnolia would strain her ears to catch the words of the play's dialogue as it came faintly up to her through the locked door that opened on the balcony; the almost incredibly naïve lines of a hackneyed play that still held its audience because of its full measure of fundamental human emotions. Hate, love, revenge, despair, hope, joy, terror.

"I will bring you to your knees yet, my proud beauty!"

"Never. I would rather die than accept help from your blood-stained hand."

Once Parthy, warned by some maternal instinct, stole softly to Magnolia's room to find the prisoner flown. She had managed to undo the special lock with which Mrs. Hawks had thought to make impossible her little daughter's access to the upper veranda deck just off her room. Magnolia had crept around the perilously narrow ledge enclosed by a low railing just below the upper deck and was there found, a shawl over her nightgown, knitted bedslippers on her feet, peering in at the upper windows together with adventuresome and indigent urchins of the town who had managed somehow to scramble to this uncertain foothold.

After fitting punishment, the ban was gradually removed; or perhaps Mrs. Hawks realized the futility of trying to bring up a show-boat child according to Massachusetts small-town standards. With natural human perversity, thereafter, Magnolia frequently betook herself quietly to bed of her own accord the while the band blared below, guns were fired, love lost, villains foiled, beauty endangered, and blood spilled. Curiously enough, she never tired of watching these simple blood-and-thunder dramas. Automatically she learned every part in every play in the Cotton Blossom's repertoire, so that by the time she was thirteen she could have leaped on the stage at a moment's notice to play anything from Simon Legree to Lena Rivers.

But best of all she liked to watch the audience assembling. Unconsciously the child's mind beheld the moving living drama of a nation's peasantry. It was such an audience as could be got together in no other kind of theatre in all the world. Farmers, labourers, Negroes; housewives, children, yokels, lovers; roustabouts, dock wallopers, backwoodsmen, rivermen, gamblers. The coal-mining regions furnished the roughest audiences. The actors rather dreaded the coal towns of West Virginia or Pennsylvania. They knew that when they played the Monongahela River or the Kanawha there were likely to be more brawls and bloodshed off the stage than on.

By half-past six the levee and landing were already dotted with the curious, the loafers, the impecunious, the barefoot urchins who had gathered to snatch such crumbs as could be gathered without pay. They fed richly on the colour, the crowds, the music, the glimpses they caught of another world through the show boat's glowing windows.

Up the river bank from the boat landing to the top of the bluff flared kerosene torches suspended on long spikes stuck in the ground. Magnolia knew they were only kerosene torches, but their orange and scarlet flames never failed to excite her. There was something barbaric and splendid about them against the dusk of the sky and woods beyond, the sinister mystery of the river below. Something savage and elemental stirred in her at sight of them; a momentary reversion to tribal days, though she could not know that. She did know that she liked the fantastic dancing shadows cast by their vivid tongues on the figures that now teetered and slid and scrambled down the steep clay bank to the boat landing. They made a weird spectacle of the commonplace. The whites of the Negroes' eyes gleamed whiter. The lights turned their cheeks to copper and bronze and polished ebony. The swarthy coal miners and their shawled and sallow wives, the farmers of the corn and wheat lands, the backwoods poor whites, the cotton pickers of Tennessee, Louisiana, Mississippi, the smalltown merchants, the shambling loafers, the lovers two by two were magically transformed into witches, giants, princesses, crones, gnomes, Nubians, genii.

At the little ticket window sat Doc, the astute, or Captain Andy. Later Mrs. Hawks was found to possess a grim genius for handling ticket-seeking crowds and the intricacies of ticket rack and small coins. Those dimes, quarters, and half dollars poured so willingly into the half-oval of the ticket window's open mouth found their way there, often enough, through a trail of pain and sweat and blood. It was all one to Parthy. Black faces. White faces. Hands gnarled. Hands calloused. Men in jeans. Women in calico. Babies. Children. Gimme a ticket. I only got fifteen. How much for her here? Many of them had never seen a theatre or a play. It was a strangely quiet crowd, usually. Little of laughter, of shouting. They came to the show boat timid, wide-eyed, wondering, like children. Two men of the steamboat crew or two of the musicians acted as ushers. After the first act was over they had often to assure these simple folk that the play was not yet ended. "This is just a recess. You come back to your seat in a couple of minutes. No, it isn't over. There's lots more to the show."

After the play there was the concert. Doc, Andy, and the ushers passed up and down between the acts selling tickets for this. They required an additional fifteen cents. Every member of the *Cotton Blossom* troupe must be able to sing, dance, play some musical instrument, or give a monologuge—in some way contribute to the half hour of entertainment following the regular performance.

Now the band struck up. The kerosene lamps on the walls were turned low. The scuffling, shuffling, coughing audience became quiet, quiet. There was in that stillness something of fright. Seamed faces. Furrowed faces. Drab. Bitter. Sodden. Childlike. Weary. Sometimes, startlingly clear-cut in that half light, could be glimpsed a profile of some gaunt Southern labourer, or backwoodsman; and it was the profile of a portrait seen in some gallery or in the illustration of a book of history. A nose high-bred, aquiline; a sensitive, haughty mouth; eyes deep-set, arrogant. Spanish, French, English? The blood of a Stuart, a Plantagenet? Some royal rogue or adventurer of many many years ago whose seed, perhaps, this was.

The curtain rose. The music ceased jerkily, in midbar. They became little children listening to a fairy tale. A glorious world of unreality opened before their eyes. Things happened. They knew that in life things did not happen thus. But here they saw, believed, and were happy. Innocence wore golden curls. Wickedness wore black. Love triumphed, right conquered, virtue was rewarded, evil punished.

They forgot the cotton fields, the wheatfields, the cornfields. They forgot the coal mines, the potato patch, the stable, the barn, the shed. They forgot the labour under the pitiless blaze of the noonday sun; the bitter marrow-numbing chill of winter; the blistered skin; the frozen road; wind, snow, rain, flood. The women forgot for an hour their washtubs, their kitchen stoves, childbirth pains, drudgery, worry, disappointment. Here were blood, lust, love, passion. Here were warmth, enchantment, laughter, music. It was Anodyne. It was Lethe. It was Escape. It was the Theatre.

6

IT WAS THE theatre, perhaps, as the theatre was meant to be. A place in which one saw one's dreams come true. A place in which one could live a vicarious life of splendour and achievement; winning in love, foiling the evildoer; a place in which one could weep unashamed, laugh aloud, give way to emotions long pent-up. When the show was over, and they had clambered up the steep bank, and the music of the band had ceased, and there was left only the dying glow of the kerosene flares, you saw them stumble a little and blink, dazedly, like one rudely awakened to reality from a lovely dream.

By eleven the torches had been gathered in. The show-boat lights were dimmed. Troupers as they were, no member of the *Cotton Blossom* company could go meekly off to sleep once the work day was over. They still were at high tension. So they discussed for the thousandth time the performance that they had given a thousand times. They dissected the audience.

"Well, they were sitting on their hands to-night, all right. Seemed they never would warm up. "

"I got a big laugh on that new business with the pillow. Did you notice? "

"Notice! Yeh, the next time you introduce any new business you got a right to leave me know beforehand. I went right up. If Schultzy hadn't thrown me my line where'd I been! "

"I never thought of it till that minute, so help me! I just noticed the pillow on the sofa and that minute it came to me it'd be a good piece of business to grab it up like it was a baby in my arms. I didn't expect any such laugh as I got on it. I didn't go to throw you off. "

From Schultzy, in the rôle of director: "Next time you get one of those inspirations you try it out at rehearsal first. "

"God, they was a million babies to-night. Cap, I guess you must of threw a little something extra into your spiel about come and bring the children. They sure took you seriously and brought 'em, all right. I'd just soon play for a orphan asylum and be done with it. "

Julie was cooking a pot of coffee over a little spirit lamp. They used the stage as a common gathering place. Bare of scenery now, in readiness for next night's set, it was their living room. Stark and shadowy as it was, there was about it an air of coziness, of domesticity. Mrs. Means, ponderous in dressing gown and slippers, was heating some oily mess for use in the nightly ministrations on her frail little husband's delicate chest. Usually Andy, Parthy, Elly, and Schultzy, as the *haute monde,* together with the occasional addition of the *Mollie Able's* captain and pilot, supped together at a table below-stage in the dining room, where Jo and Queenie had set out a cold collation—cheese, ham, bread, a pie left from dinner. Parthy cooked the coffee on the kerosene stove. On stage the women of the company hung their costumes carefully away in the tiny cubicles provided for such purpose just outside the dressing-room doors. The men smoked a sedative pipe. The lights of the little town on the river bank had long been extinguished. Even the saloons on the waterfront showed only an occasional glow. Sometimes George at the piano tried out a new song for Elly or Schultzy or Ralph, in preparation for to-morrow night's concert. The tinkle of the piano, the sound of the singer's voice drifted across the river. Up in the little town in a drab cottage near the waterfront a restless soul would turn in his sleep and start up at the sound and listen between waking and sleeping; wondering about these strange people singing on their boat at midnight; envying them their fantastic vagabond life.

A peaceful enough existence in its routine, yet a curiously crowded and colourful one for a child. She saw town after town whose waterfront street was a solid block of saloons, one next the other, open day and night. Her childhood impressions were formed of stories, happenings, accidents, events born of the rivers. Towns and cities and people came to be associated in her mind with this or that bizarre bit of river life. The junction of the Ohio and Big Sandy rivers always was remembered by Magnolia as the place where the Black Diamond Saloon was opened on the day the *Cotton Blossom* played Catlettsburg. Catlettsburg, typical waterfront town of the times, was like a knot that drew together the two rivers. Ohio, West Virginia, and Kentucky met just there. And at the junction of the rivers there was opened with high and appropriate ceremonies the Black Diamond Saloon, owned by those picturesque two, Big Wayne Damron and Little Wayne Damron. From the deck of the *Cotton Blossom* Magnolia saw the crowd waiting for the opening of the Black Diamond doors—free drinks, free lunch, river town hospitality. And then Big Wayne opened the doors, and the crowd surged back while their giant host, holding the key aloft in his hand, walked down to the river bank, held the key high for a moment, then hurled it far into the yellow waters of the Big Sandy. The Black Diamond Saloon was open for business.

The shifting colourful life of the rivers unfolded before her ambient eyes. She saw and learned and remembered. Rough sights, brutal sights; sights of beauty and colour; deeds of bravery; dirty deeds. Through the wheat lands, the corn country, the fruit belt, the cotton, the timber region. The river life flowed and changed like the river itself. Shanty boats. Bumboats.

Side-wheelers . Stern-wheelers. Fussy packets, self-important. Races ending often in death and disaster. Coal barges. A fleet of rafts, log-laden. The timber rafts, drifting down to Louisville, were steered with great sweeps. As they swept down the Ohio, the timbermen sang their chantey, their great shoulders and strong muscular torsos bending, straightening to the rhythm of the rowing song. Magnolia had learned the words from Doc, and when she espied the oarsmen from the deck of the *Cotton Blossom* she joined in the song and rocked with their motion out of sheer dramatic love of it:

> "The river is up,
> The channel is deep,
> The wind blows steady and strong.
> Oh, Dinah's got the hoe cake on,
> So row your boat along.
> Down the river,
> Down the river,
> Down the O-hi-o.
> Down the river,
> Down the river,
> Down the O-
>
> > hi-
> >
> > O!' "

Three tremendous pulls accompanied those last three long-drawn syllables. Magnolia found it most invigorating. Doc had told her, too, that the Ohio had got its name from the time when the Indians, standing on one shore and wishing to cross to the other, would cup their hands and send out the call to the opposite bank, loud and high and clear, "O-*HE*-O! "

"Do you think it's true? " Magnolia would say; for Mrs. Hawks had got into the way of calling Doc's stories stuff-and-nonsense. All those tales, it would seem, to which Magnolia most thrilled, turned out, according to Parthy, to be stuff-and-nonsense. So then, "Do you think it's true? " she would demand, fearfully.

"Think it! Why, pshaw! I know it's true. Sure as shootin'."

It was noteworthy and characteristic of Magnolia that she liked best the rampant rivers. The Illinois which had possessed such fascination for Tonti, for Joliet, for Marquette—for countless *coureurs du bois* who had frequented this trail to the southwest—left her cold. Its clear water, its gentle current, its fretless channel, its green hillsides, its tidy bordering grain fields, bored her. From Doc and from her father she learned a haphazard and picturesque chronicle of its history, and that of like rivers—a tale of voyageurs and trappers, of flatboat and keelboat men, of rafters in the great logging days, of shanty boaters, water gipsies, steamboats. She listened, and remembered, but was unmoved. When the *Cotton Blossom* floated down the tranquil bosom of the Illinois Magnolia read a book. She drank its limpid waters and missed the mud-tang to be found in a draught of the Mississippi.

"If I was going to be a river, " she announced, "I wouldn't want to be the Illinois, or like those. I'd want to be the Mississippi."

'How's that?" asked Captain Andy.

"Because the Illinois, it's always the same. But the Mississippi is always different. It's like a person, that you never know what they're going to do next, and that makes them interesting."

Doc was oftenest her cicerone and playmate ashore. His knowledge of the countryside, the rivers, the dwellers along the shore and in the back country, was almost godlike in its omniscience. At his tongue's end were tales of buccaneers, of pirates, of adventurers. He told her of the bloodthirsty and rapacious Murrel who, not content with robbing and killing his victims, ripped them open, disembowelled them, and threw them into the river.

"Oh my!" Magnolia would exclaim, inadequately; and peer with some distaste into the water rushing past the boat's flat sides. "How did he look? Like Steve when he plays Legree?"

"Not by a jugful, he didn't. Dressed up like a parson, and used to travel from town to town, giving sermons. He had a slick tongue, and while the congregation inside was all stirred up getting their souls saved, Murrel's gang outside would steal their horses."

Stories of slaves stolen, sold, restolen, resold, and murdered. Murrel's attempted capture of New Orleans by rousing the blacks to insurrection against the whites. Tales of Crenshaw, the vulture; of Mason, terror of the Natchez road. On excursions ashore, Doc showed her pirates' caves, abandoned graveyards, ancient robber retreats along the river banks or in the woods. They visited Sam Grity's soap kettle, a great iron pot half hidden in a rocky unused field, in which Grity used to cache his stolen plunder. She never again saw an old soap kettle sitting plumply in some Southern kitchen doorway, its sides covered with a handsome black velvet coat of soot, that she did not shiver deliciously. Strong fare for a child at an age when other little girls were reading the Dotty Dimple Series and Little Prudy books.

Doc enjoyed these sanguinary chronicles in the telling as much as Magnolia in the listening. His lined and leathery face would take on the changing expressions suitable to the tenor of the tale. Cunning, cruelty, greed, chased each other across his mobile countenance. Doc had been a show-boat actor himself at some time back in his kaleidoscopic career. So together he and Magnolia and his ancient barrel-bellied black-and-white terrier Catchem roamed the woods and towns and hills and fields and churchyards from Cairo to the Gulf.

Sometimes, in the spring, she went with Julie, the indolent. Elly almost never walked and often did not leave the *Cotton Blossom* for days together. Elly was extremely neat and fastidious about her person. She was for ever heating kettles and pans of water for bathing, for washing stockings and handkerchiefs. She had a knack with the needle and could devise a quite plausible third-act ball gown out of a length of satin, some limp tulle, and a yard or two of tinsel. She never read. Her industry irked Julie as Julie's indolence irritated her.

Elly was something of a shrew (Schultzy had learned to his sorrow that your blue-eyed blondes are not always doves). "Pity's sake, Julie, how you can sit there doing nothing, staring out at that everlasting river's more than I can see. I should think you'd go plumb crazy."

"What would you have me do?"

"Do! Mend the hole in your stocking, for one thing."

"I should say as much," Mrs. Hawks would agree, if she chanced to be present. She had no love for Elly; but her own passion for industry and order could not but cause her to approve a like trait in another.

Julie would glance down disinterestedly at her long slim foot in its shabby shoe. "Is there a hole in my stocking?"

"You know perfectly well there is, Julie Dozier. You must have seen it the size of a half dollar when you put it on this morning. It was there yesterday, same's to-day."

Julie smiled charmingly. "I know. I declare to goodness I hoped it wouldn't be. When I woke up this morning I thought maybe the good fairies would have darned it up neat's a pin while I slept." Julie's voice was as indolent as Julie herself. She spoke with a Southern drawl. Her I was Ah. Ah declah to goodness—or approximately that.

Magnolia would smile in appreciation of Julie's gentle raillery. She adored Julie. She thought Elly, with her fair skin and china-blue eyes, as beautiful as a princess in a fairy tale, as was natural in a child of her sallow colouring and straight black hair. But the two were antipathetic. Elly, in ill-tempered moments, had been known to speak of Magnolia as "that brat," though her vanity was fed by the child's admiration of her beauty. But she never allowed her to dress up in her discarded stage finery, as Julie often did. Elly openly considered herself a gifted actress whose talent and beauty were, thanks to her shiftless husband, pearls cast before the river-town swinery. Pretty though she was, she found small favour in the eyes of men of the company and crew. Strangely enough, it was Julie who drew them, quite without intent on her part. There was something about her life-scarred face, her mournful eyes, her languor, her effortlessness, her very carelessness of dress that seemed to fascinate and hold them. Steve's jealousy of her was notorious. It was common boat talk, too, that Pete, the engineer of the *Mollie Able,* who played the bull drum in the band, was openly enamoured of her and had tried to steal her from Steve. He followed Julie into town if she so much as stepped ashore. He was found lurking in corners of the *Cotton Blossom* decks; loitering about the stage where he had no business to be. He even sent her presents of imitation jewellery and gaudy handkerchiefs and work boxes, which she promptly presented to Queenie, first urging that mass of ebon royalty to bedeck herself with her new gifts when dishing up the dinner. In that close community the news of the disposal of these favours soon reached Pete's sooty ears. There had even been a brawl between Steve and Pete—one of those sudden tempestuous battles, animal-like in its fierceness and brutality. An oath in the darkness; voices low, ominous; the thud of feet; the impact of bone against flesh; deep sob-like breathing; a high weird cry of pain, terror, rage. Pete was overboard and floundering in the swift current of the Mississippi. Powerful swimmer though he was, they had some trouble in fishing him out. It was well that the *Cotton Blossom* and the *Mollie Able* were lying at anchor. Bruised and dripping, Pete had repaired to the engine room to dry, and to nurse his wounds, swearing in terms ridiculously like those frequently heard in the second act of a *Cotton Blossom* play that he would get his revenge on the two of them. He had never, since then, openly molested Julie, but his threats, mutterings, and innuendoes continued. Steve had forbidden his wife to leave the show boat unaccompanied. So it was that when spring came round, and the dogwood gleaming white among the black trunks of the pines and firs was like a bride and her shining attendants in a great cathedral, Julie would tie one of her floppy careless hats under her chin and, together with Magnolia, range the forests for wild flowers. They would wander inland until they found trees other than the willows, the live oaks, and the elms that lined the river banks. They would come upon wild honeysuckle, opalescent pink. In autumn they went nutting, returning with sackfuls of hickory and hazel nuts—anything but the black walnut which any show-boat dweller knows will cause a storm if brought aboard. Sometimes they experienced the shock of gay surprise that follows the sudden sight of gentian, a flash of that rarest of flower colours, blue; almost poignant in its beauty. It always made Magnolia catch her breath a little.

Julie's flounces trailing in the dust, the two would start out sedately enough, though to the accompaniment of a chorus of admonition and criticism.

From Mrs. Hawks: "Now keep your hat pulled down over your eyes so's

you won't get all sunburned, Magnolia. Black enough as 'tis. Don't run and
get all overheated. Don't eat any berries or anything you find in the woods,
now. . . . Back by four o'clock the latest . . . poison ivy . . . snakes . . .
lost . . . gipsies. . . .

From Elly, trimming her rosy nails in the cool shade of the front deck:
"Julie, your placket's gaping. And tuck your hair in. No, there, on the side."

So they made their way up the bank, across the little town, and into the
woods. Once out of sight of the boat the two turned and looked back. Then,
without a word, each would snatch her hat from her head; and they would
look at each other, and Julie would smile her wide slow smile, and Magnolia's
dark plain pointed little face would flash into sudden beauty. From some
part of her person where it doubtless was needed Julie would extract a pin
and with it fasten up the tail of her skirt. Having thus hoisted the red flag
of rebellion, they would plunge into the woods to emerge hot, sticky, bram-
ble-torn, stained, flower-laden, and late. They met Parthy's upbraidings and
Steve's reproaches with cheerful unconcern.

Often Magnolia went to town with her father, or drove with him or Doc
into the back country. Andy did much of the marketing for the boat's food,
frequently hampered, supplemented, or interfered with by Parthy's less
openhanded methods. He loved good food, considered it important to happiness, liked to order it and talk about it; was himself an excellent cook,
like most boatmen, and had been known to spend a pleasant half hour reading
the cook book. The butchers, grocers, and general store keepers of the river
towns knew Andy, understood his fussy ways, liked him. He bought
shrewdly but generously, without haggling; and often presented a store acquaintance of long standing with a pair of tickets for the night's performance.
When he and Magnolia had time to range the countryside in a livery rig,
Andy would select the smartest and most glittering buggy and the liveliest
nag to be had. Being a poor driver and jerky, with no knowledge of a horse's
nerves and mouth, the ride was likely to be exhilarating to the point of
danger. The animal always was returned to the stable in a lather, the vehicle
spattered with mud-flecks to the hood. Certainly, it was due to Andy more
than Parthy that the *Cotton Blossom* was reputed the best-fed show boat on
the rivers. He was always bringing home in triumph a great juicy ham, a
side of beef. He liked to forage the season's first and best: a bushel of downy
peaches, fresh-picked; watermelons; little honey-sweet seckel pears; a dozen
plump broilers; new corn; a great yellow cheese ripe for cutting.

He would plump his purchases down on the kitchen table while Queenie
surveyed his booty, hands on ample hips. She never resented his suggestions,
though Parthy's offended her. Capering, Andy would poke a forefinger into
a pullet's fat sides. "Rub 'em over with a little garlic, Queenie, to flavour
'em up. Plenty of butter and strips of bacon. Cover' em over till they're
tender and then give 'em a quick brown the last twenty minutes."

Queenie, knowing all this, still did not resent his direction. "That shif'less
no-'count Jo knew 'bout cookin' like you do, Cap'n Andy, Ah'd git to rest
mah feet now an' again, Ah sure would."

Magnolia liked to loiter in the big, low-raftered kitchen. It was a place of
pleasant smells and sights and sounds. It was here that she learned Negro
spirituals from Jo and cooking from Queenie, both of which accomplishments
stood her in good stead in later years. Queenie had, for example, a way of
stuffing a ham for baking. It was a fascinating process to behold, and one
that took hours. Spices—bay; thyme, onion, clove, mustard, allspice, pepper—chopped and mixed and stirred together. A sharp-pointed knife plunged
deep into the juicy ham. The incision stuffed with the spicy mixture. Another
plunge with the knife. Another filling. Again and again and again until the

great ham had grown to twice its size. Then a heavy clean white cloth, needle and coarse thread. Sewed up tight and plump in its jacket the ham was immersed in a pot of water and boiled. Out when tender, the jacket removed; into the oven with it. Basting and basting from Queenie's long-handled spoon. The long sharp knife again for cutting, and then the slices, juicy and scented, with the stuffing of spices making a mosaic pattern against the pink of the meat. Many years later Kim Ravenal, the actress, would serve at the famous little Sunday night suppers that she and her husband Kenneth Cameron were so fond of giving a dish that she called ham*à la* Queenie.

"How does your cook do it!" her friends would say—Ethel Barrymore or Kit Cornell or Frank Crowninshield or Charley Towne or Woollcott. "I'll bet it isn't real at all. It's painted on the platter."

"It is not! It's a practical ham, stuffed with all kinds of devilment. The recipe is my mother's. She got it from an old Southern cook named Queenie."

'Listen, Kim. You're among friends. Your dear public is not present. You don't have to pretend any old Southern aristocracy Virginia belle mammy stuff with *us.*"

"Pretend, you great oaf! I was born on a show boat on the Mississippi, and proud of it. Everybody knows that."

Mrs. Hawks, bustling into the show-boat kitchen with her unerring gift for scenting an atmosphere of mellow enjoyment, and dissipating it, would find Magnolia perched on a chair, both elbows on the table, her palms propping her chin as she regarded with roundeyed fascination Queenie's magic manipulations. Or perhaps Jo, the charming and shiftless, would be singing for her one of the Negro plantation songs, wistful with longing and pain; the folk songs of a wronged race, later to come into a blaze of popularity as spirituals.

For some nautical reason, a broad beam, about six inches high and correspondingly wide, stretched across the kitchen floor from side to side, dividing the room. Through long use Jo and Queenie had become accustomed to stepping over this obstruction, Queenie ponderously, Jo with an effortless swing of his lank legs. On this Magnolia used to sit, her arms hugging her knees, her great eyes in the little sallow pointed face fixed attentively on Jo. The kitchen was very clean and shining and stuffy. Jo's legs were crossed, one foot in its great low shapeless shoe hooked in the chair rung, his banjo cradled in his lap. The once white parchment face of the instrument was now almost as black as Jo's, what with much strumming by work-stained fingers.

"Which one, Miss Magnolia?"

"I Got Shoes," Magnolia would answer, promptly.

Jo would throw back his head, his sombre eyes half shut:

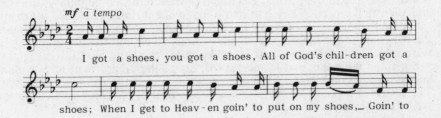

mf a tempo

I got a shoes, you got a shoes, All of God's chil-dren got a shoes; When I get to Heav-en goin' to put on my shoes,— Goin' to

walk all o-ver God's Heav'n.— Heav'n,— Heav'n,—

Ev-'ry bod-y talk-in' 'bout heav'n ain't go-in' there; Heav'n,

Heav-en,—— Goin' to shout all o-ver God's Heav'n.—

The longing of a footsore, ragged, driven race expressed in the tragically childlike terms of shoes, white robes, wings, and the wise and simple insight into hypocrisy: "Ev'rybody talkin 'bout Heav'n ain't goin' there. . . ."

"Now which one?" His fingers still picking the strings, ready at a word to slip into the opening chords of the next song.

"Go Down, Moses."

She liked this one—at once the most majestic and supplicating of all the Negro folk songs—because it always made her cry a little. Sometimes Queenie, busy at the stove or the kitchen table, joined in with her high rich camp-meeting voice. Jo's voice was a reedy tenor, but soft and husky with the indescribable Negro vocal quality. Magnolia soon knew the tune and the words of every song in Jo's repertoire. Unconsciously, being an excellent mimic, she sang as Jo and Queenie sang, her head thrown slightly back, her eyes rolling or half closed, one foot beating rhythmic time to the music's cadence. Her voice was true, though mediocre; but she got into this the hoarsely sweet Negro overtone—purple velvet muffling a flute.

Between Jo and Queenie flourished a fighting affection, deep, true, and lasting. There was some doubt as to the actual legal existence of their marriage, but the union was sound and normal enough. At each season's close they left the show boat the richer by three hundred dollars, clean new calico for Queenie, and proper jeans for Jo. Shoes on their feet. Hats on their heads. Bundles in their arms. Each spring they returned penniless, in rags, and slightly liquored. They had had a magnificent time. They did not drink again while the *Cotton Blossom* kitchen was their home. But the next winter the programme repeated itself. Captain Andy liked and trusted them. They were as faithful to him as their childlike vagaries would permit.

So, filled with the healthy ecstasy of song, the Negro man and woman and the white child would sit in deep contentment in the show-boat kitchen. The sound of a door slammed. Quick heavy footsteps. Three sets of nerves went taut. Parthy.

"Maggie Hawks, have you practised to-day?"

"Some."

"How much?"

"Oh, half an hour—more."

"When?"

"'Smorning."

"I didn't hear you."

The sulky lower lip out. The high forehead wrinkled by a frown. Song flown. Peace gone.

"I did so. Jo, didn't you hear me practising? "

"Ah suah did, Miss Magnolia."

"You march right out of here, young lady, and practise another half hour. Do you think your father's made of money, that I can throw fifty-cent pieces away on George for nothing? Now you do your exercises fifteen minutes and the Maiden's Prayer fifteen. . . . Idea!"

Magnolia marched. Out of earshot Parthy expressed her opinion of nigger songs. "I declare I don't know where you get your low ways from! White people aren't good enough for you, I suppose, that you've got to run with blacks in the kitchen. Now you sit yourself down on that stool."

Magnolia was actually having music lessons. George, the Whistler and piano player, was her teacher, receiving fifty cents an hour for weekly instruction. Driven by her stern parent, she practised an hour daily on the tinny old piano in the orchestra pit, a rebellious, skinny, pathetic little figure strumming painstakingly away in the great emptiness of the show-boat auditorium. She must needs choose her time for practice when a rehearsal of the night's play was not in progress on the stage or when the band was not struggling with the music of a new song and dance number. Incredibly enough, she actually learned something of the mechanics of music, if not of its technique. She had an excellent rhythm sense, and this was aided by none other than Jo, whose feeling for time and beat and measure and pitch was flawless. Queenie lumped his song gift in with his general shiftlessness. Born fifty years later he might have known brief fame in some midnight revue or Club Alabam' on Broadway. Certainly Magnolia unwittingly learned more of real music from black Jo and many another Negro wharf minstrel than she did from hours of the heavy-handed and unlyrical George.

That Mrs. Hawks could introduce into the indolent tenor of show-boat life, anything so methodical and humdrum as five-finger exercises done an hour daily was triumphant proof of her indomitable driving force. Life had miscast her in the rôle of wife and mother. She was born to be a Madam Chairman. Committees, Votes, Movements, Drives, Platforms, Gavels, Reports all showed in her stars. Cheated of these, she had to be content with such outlet of her enormous energies as the *Cotton Blossom* afforded. Parthy had never heard the word Feminist, and wouldn't have recognized it if she had. One spoke at that time not of Women's Rights but of Women's Wrongs. On these Parthenia often waxed tartly eloquent. Her housekeeping fervour was the natural result of her lack of a more impersonal safety valve. The *Cotton Blossom* shone like a Methodist Sunday household. Only Julie and Windy, the *Mollie Able* pilot, defied her. She actually indulged in those most domestic of rites, canning and preserving, on board the boat. Donning an all-enveloping gingham apron, she would set frenziedly to work on two bushels of peaches or seckel pears; baskets of tomatoes; pecks of apples. Pickled pears, peach marmalade, grape jell in jars and pots and glasses filled shelves and cupboards. Queenie found a great deal of satisfaction in the fact that occasionally, owing to some culinary accident or to the unusual motion of the flat-bottomed *Cotton Blossom* in the rough waters of an open bay, one of these jars was found smashed on the floor, its rich purple or amber contents mingling with splinters of glass. No one—not even Parthy—ever dared connect Queenie with these quite explicable mishaps.

Parthy was an expert needlewoman. She often assisted Julie or Elly or Mis' Means with their costumes. To see her stern implacable face bent over a heap of frivolous stuffs while her industrious fingers swiftly sent the needle flashing through unvarying seams was to receive the shock that comes of beholding the incongruous. The enormity of it penetrated even her blunt sensibilities.

"If anybody'd ever told me that I'd live to see the day when I'd be sewing on costumes for show folks!"

"Run along, Parthy. You like it," Andy would say.

But she never would admit that. 'Like it or lump it, what can I do! Married you for better or worse, didn't I!'' Her tone leaving no doubt as to the path down which that act had led her. Actually she was having a rich, care-free, and varied life such as she had never dreamed of and of which she secretly was enamoured.

Dwellers in this or that river town loitering down at the landing to see what manner of sin and loose living went on in and about this show boat with its painted women and play-acting men would be startled to hear sounds and sniff smells which were identical with those which might be issuing that very moment from their own smug and godly dwellings ashore. From out the open doors of the Cotton Blossom Floating Palace Theatre came the unmistakable and humdrum sounds of scales and five-finger exercises done painfully and unwillingly by rebellious childish hands. Ta-ta-ta—*TA*—ta-ta-ta. From below decks there floated up the mouth-watering savour of tomato ketchup, of boiling vinegar and spices, or the perfumed aroma of luscious fruits seething in sugary kettles.

"Smells for all the world like somebody was doing up sweet pickles." One village matron to another.

"Well, I suppose they got to eat like other folks. "

Ta-ta-ta—*TA*—ta-ta-ta.

It was inevitable, however, that the ease and indolence of the life, as well as the daily contact with odd and unconventional characters must leave some imprint on even so adamantine an exterior as Parthy's. Little by little her school-teacherly diction dropped from her. Slowly her vowels began to slur, her aren'ts became ain'ts, her crisp new England utterance took on something of the slovenly Southern drawl, her consonants were missing from the end of a word here and there. True, she still bustled and nagged, managed and scolded, drove and reproached. She still had the power to make Andy jump with nervousness. Whether consciously or unconsciously, the influence of this virago was more definitely felt than that of any other one of the *Cotton Blossom's* company and crew. Of these only Julie Dozier, and Windy, the pilot (so called because he almost never talked) actually triumphed over Mrs. Hawks. Julie's was a negative victory. She never voluntarily spoke to Parthy and had the power to aggravate that lady to the point of frenzy by remaining limp, supine, and idle when Parthy thought she should be most active; by raising her right eyebrow quizzically in response to a more than usually energetic tirade; by the habitual disorder of the tiny room which she shared with Steve; by the flagrant carelessness and untidiness of her own gaunt graceful person.

"I declare, Hawks, what you keep that slatternly yellow cat around this boat for beats me."

"Best actress in the whole caboodle, that's why." Something fine in little Captain Andy had seen and recognized the flame that might have glorified Julie had it not instead consumed her. "That girl had the right backing she'd make her mark, and not in any show boat, either. I've been to New York. I've seen 'em down at Wallack's and Daly's and around."

"A slut, that's what she is. If I had my way she'd leave this boat bag and baggage."

"Well, this is one time you won't have your way, Mrs. Hawks, ma'am." She had not yet killed the spirit in Andy.

"Mark my words, you'll live to regret it. The way she looks out of those black eyes of hers! Gives me the creeps."

"What would you have the girl look out of," retorted Andy, not very brilliantly. "Her ears?"

Julie could not but know of this antagonism toward her. Some perverse streak in her otherwise rich and gentle make-up caused her to find a sinister pleasure in arousing it.

Windy's victory was more definitely dramatic, though his defensive method against Parthy's attacks resembled in sardonic quiet and poise Julie's own. Windy was accounted one of the most expert pilots on the Mississippi. He knew every coil and sinew and stripe of the yellow serpent. River men used his name as a synonym for magic with the pilot's wheel. Starless night or misty day; shoal water or deep, it was all one to Windy. Though Andy's senior by more than fifteen years, the two had been friends for twenty. Captain Andy had enormous respect for his steersmanship; was impressed by his taciturnity (being himself so talkative and vivacious); enjoyed talking with him in the bright quiet security of the pilot house. He was absolute czar of the *Mollie Able* and the *Cotton Blossom,* as befitted his high accomplishments. No one ever dreamed of opposing him except Parthy. He was slovenly of person, careless of habit. These shortcomings Parthy undertook to correct early in her show-boat career. She met with defeat so prompt, so complete, so crushing as to cause her for ever after to leave him unmolested.

Windy had muddy boots. They were, it seemed, congenitally so. He would go ashore in mid-afternoon of a hot August day when farmers for miles around had been praying for rain these weeks past and return in a downpour with half the muck and clay of the countryside clinging to his number eleven black square-toed elastic-side boots. A tall, emaciated drooping old man, Windy; with long gnarled muscular hands whose enlarged knuckles and leathery palms were the result of almost half a century at the wheel. His pants were always grease-stained; his black string tie and gray shirt spattered with tobacco juice; his brown jersey frayed and ragged. Across his front he wore a fine anchor watch chain, or "log" chain, as it was called. And gleaming behind the long flowing tobacco-splotched gray beard that reached almost to his waist could be glimpsed a milkily pink pearl stud like a star behind a dirty cloud-bank. The jewel had been come by, doubtless, in payment of some waterfront saloon gambling debt. Surely its exquisite curves had once glowed upon fine and perfumed linen.

It was against this taciturn and omnipotent conquerer of the rivers that Parthy raised the flag of battle.

"Traipsin' up and down this boat and the *Mollie Able,* spitting his filthy tobacco and leaving mud tracks like an elephant that's been in a bog. If I've had those steps leading up to the pilot house scrubbed once, I've had 'em scrubbed ten times this week, and now look at them! I won't have it, and so I tell you. Why can't he go up the side of the boat the way a pilot is supposed to do! What's that side ladder for, I'd like to know! He's supposed to go up it; not the steps."

"Now, Parthy, you can't run a boat the way you would a kitchen back in Thebes. Windy's no hired man. He's the best pilot on the rivers, and I'm lucky to have him. A hundred jobs better than this ready to jump at him if he so much as crooks a finger. He's pulled this tub through good many tight places where any other pilot'd landed us high and dry on a sand bar. And don't you forget it.''

"He's a dirty old man. And I won't have it. Muddying up my clean . . .

Parthy was not one of your scolds who takes her grievances out in mere words. With her, to threaten was to act. That very morning, just before the *Cotton Blossom* was making a late departure from Greenville, where they had played the night before, to Sunnisie Side Landing, twelve miles below, this formidable woman, armed with hammer and nails, took advantage of Windy's temporary absence below decks to nail down the hatch above the steps leading to the pilot house. She was the kind of woman who can drive a nail straight. She drove ten of them, long and firm and deep. A pity that no one saw her. It was a sight worth seeing, this accomplished and indomitable virago in curl papers, driving nails with a sure and steady stroke.

Below stairs Windy, coming aboard from an early morning look around, knocked the ashes out of his pipe, sank his great yellow fangs into a generous wedge of Honest Scrap, and prepared to climb the stairs to the *Cotton Blossom* pilot house, there to manipulate wheel and cord that would convey his orders to Pete in the engine room.

Up the stairs, leaving a mud spoor behind. One hand raised to lift the hatch; wondering, meanwhile, to find it closed. A mighty heave; a pounding with the great fist; another heave, then, with the powerful old shoulder.

"Nailed,'' said Windy aloud to himself, mildly, Then, still mildly, "The old hell cat.'' He spat, then, on the hatchway steps and clumped leisurely down again. He leaned over the boat rail, looking benignly down at the crowd of idlers gathered at the wharf to watch the show boat cast off. Then he crossed the deck again to where a capacious and carpet-seated easy chair held out its inviting arms. Into this he sank with a grunt of relaxation. From his pocket he took the pipe so recently relinquished, filled it, tamped it, lighted it. From another pocket he took a month-old copy of the New Orleans *Times-Democrat,* turned to the column marked Shipping News, and settled down, apparently, for a long quiet day with literature.

Up came the anchor. In came the hawser. Chains clanked. The sound of the gangplank drawn up. The hoarse shouts from land and water that always attend the departure of a river boat. "Throw her over there! Lift 'er! Heh, Pete! Gimme hand here! Little to the left. Other side! Hold on! Easy!''

The faces of the crowd ashore turned expectantly toward the boat. Everything shipshape. Pete in the engine room. Captain Andy scampering for the texas. Silence. No bells. No steam. No hoarse shouts of command. God A'mighty, where's Windy? Windy! Windy!

Windy lowers his shielding newspaper and mildly regards the capering captain and bewildered crew and startled company. He is wearing his silver-rimmed reading spectacles slightly askew on his biblical-looking hooked nose. Andy rushes up to him, all the Basque in him bubbling. "God's sake, Windy, what's . . . why don't you take her! We're going.''

Windy chewed rhythmically for a moment, spat a long brown jet of juice, wiped his hairy mouth with the back of one gnarled hand. "We ain't going, Cap'n Hawks, because she can't go till I give her the go-ahead. And I ain't give her the go-ahead. I'm the pilot of this here boat.''

"But why? What the . . . Wh———''

"The hatch is nailed down above the steps leading to the pilot house, Cap'n Andy. Till that hatchway's open, I don't climb up to no pilot house. And till I climb up to the pilot house, she don't get no go-ahead. And till I give her the go-ahead, she don't go, not if we stay here alongside this landing till the *Cotton Blossom* rots.''

He looked around benignly and resumed his reading of the New Orleans *Times-Democrat*.

Profanity, frowned upon under Parthy's régime, now welled up in Andy and burst from him in spangled geysers. Words seethed to the surface and exploded like fireworks. Twenty-five years of river life had equipped him with a vocabulary rich, varied, purple. He neglected neither the heavens above nor the earth beneath. Revolt and rage shook his wiry little frame. Years of henpecking, years of natural gaiety suppressed, years of mincing when he wished to stride, years of silence when he wished to sing, now were wiped away by the stream of undiluted rage that burst from Captain Andy Hawks. It was a torrent, a flood, a Mississippi of profanity in which hells and damns were mere drops in the mighty roaring mass.

"Out with your crowbars there. Pry up that hatch! I'm captain of this boat, by God, and anybody, man or woman, who nails down that hatch again without my orders gets put off this boat wherever we are, and so I say."

Did Parthenia Ann Hawks shrink and cower and pale under the blinding glare of this pyrotechnic profanity? Not that indomitable woman. The picture of outraged virtue in curl papers, she stood her ground like a Roman matron. She had even, when the flood broke, sent Magnolia indoors with a gesture meant to convey protection from the pollution of this verbal stream.

"Well, Captain Hawks, a fine example you have set for your company and crew I must say."

"*You* must say! You————! Let me tell you, Mrs. Hawks, ma'am, the less you say the better. And I repeat, anybody touches that hatchway again————"

"Touch it!" echoed Parthy in icy disdain. "I wouldn't touch it, nor the pilot house, nor the pilot either, if you'll excuse my saying so, with a ten-foot pole."

And swept away with as much dignity as a *Cotton Blossom* early morning costume would permit. Her head bloody but unbowed.

7

JULIE WAS GONE. Steve was gone. Tragedy had stalked into Magnolia's life; had cast its sable mantle over the *Cotton Blossom*. Pete had kept his promise and revenge had been his. But the taste of triumph had not, after all, been sweet in his mouth. There was little of the peace of satisfaction in his sooty face stuck out of the engine-room door. The arm that beat the bull drum in the band was now a listless member, so that a hollow mournful thump issued from that which should have given forth a rousing boom.

The day the *Cotton Blossom* was due to play Lemoyne, Mississippi, Julie Dozier took sick. In show-boat troupes, as well as in every other theatrical company in the world, it is an unwritten law that an actor must never be too sick to play. He may be sick. Before the performance he may be too sick to stand; immediately after the performance he may collapse. He may, if necessary, die on the stage and the curtain will then be lowered. But no real trouper while conscious will ever confess himself too sick to go on when the overture ends and the lights go down.

Julie knew this. She had played show boats for years, up and down the rivers of the Middle West and the South. She had a large and loyal following. Lemoyne was a good town, situated on the river, prosperous, sizable.

Julie lay on her bed in her darkened room, refusing all offers of aid. She did not want food. She did not want cold compresses on her head. She did not want hot compresses on her head. She wanted to be left alone—with Steve. Together the two stayed in the darkened room, and when some member of the company came to the door with offers of aid or comfort, there came into their faces a look that was strangely like one of fear, followed immediately by a look of relief.

Queenie sent Jo to the door with soup, her panacea for all ailments, whether of the flesh or the spirit. Julie made a show of eating it, but when Jo had clumped across the stage and down to his kitchen Julie motioned to Steve. He threw the contents of the bowl out of the window into the yellow waters of the Mississippi.

Doc appeared at Julie's door for the tenth time though it was only mid-morning. "Think you can play all right, to-night, though, don't you, Julie?"

In the semi-darkness of her shaded room Julie's eyes glowed suddenly wide and luminous. She sat up in bed, pushing her hair back from her forehead with a gesture so wild as to startle the old trouper.

"No!" she cried, in a sort of terror. "No! I can't play to-night. Don't ask me."

Blank astonishment made Doc's face almost ludicrous. For an actress to announce ten hours before the time set for the curtain's rising that she would not be able to go on that evening—an actress who had not suffered decapitation or an amputation—was a thing unheard of in Doc's experience.

"God a'mighty, Julie! If you're sick as all that, you'd better see a doctor. Steve, what say?"

The great blond giant seated at the side of Julie's bed did not look round at his questioner. His eyes were on Julie's face. "Julie's funny that way. She's set against doctors. Won't have one, that's all. Don't coax her. It'll only make her worse."

Inured as he was to the vagaries of woman, this apparently was too much for Doc. Schultzy appeared in the doorway; peered into the dimness of the little room.

"Funny thing. I guess you must have an admirer in this town, Jule. Somebody's stole your picture, frame and all, out of the layout in the lobby there. First I thought it might be that crazy Pete, used to be so stuck on you. . . . Now, now, Steve! Keep your shirt on! Keep your shirt on! . . . I asked him, straight, but he was surprised all right. He ain't good enough actor to fool me. He didn't do it. Must be some town rube all right, Julie, got stuck on your shape or something. I put up another one." He stood a moment, thoughtfully. Elly came up behind him, hatted and gloved.

"I'm going up to town, Julie. Can I fetch you something? An orange, maybe? Or something from the drug store?"

Julie's head on the pillow moved a negative. "She says no, thanks," Steve answered for her, shortly. It was as though both laboured under a strain. The three in the doorway sensed it. Elly shrugged her shoulders, though whether from pique or indifference it was hard to say. Doc still stood puzzled, bewildered. Schultzy half turned away. "S'long's you're all right by to-night," he said cheerfully.

"Says she won't be," Doc put in, lowering his voice.

"Won't be!" repeated Schultzy, almost shrilly. "Why, she ain't *sick,* is she! I mean, sick!"

Schultzy sent his voice shrilling from Julie's little bedroom doorway across the bare stage, up the aisles of the empty auditorium, so that it penetrated the box office at the far end of the boat, where Andy, at the ticket window, was just about to be relieved by Parthy.

"Heh, Cap! Cap!. Come here. Julie's sick. Julie's too sick to go on. Says she's too sick to . . .

"Here," said Andy, summarily, to Parthy; and left her in charge of business. Down the aisle with the light quick step that was almost a scamper; up the stage at a bound. "Best advance sale we've had since we started out. We never played this town before. License was too high. But here it is, not eleven o'clock, and half the house gone already." He peered into the darkened room.

From its soft fur nest in the old sealskin muff the marmoset poked its tragic mask and whimpered like a sick baby. This morning there was a strange resemblance between the pinched and pathetic face on the pillow and that of the little sombre-eyed monkey.

By now there was quite a little crowd about Julie's door. Mis' Means had joined them and could be heard murmuring about mustard plasters and a good hot something or other. Andy entered the little room with the freedom of an old friend. He looked sharply down at the face on the pillow. The keen eyes plunged deep into the tortured eyes that stared piteously up at him. Something he saw there caused him to reach out with one brown paw, none too immaculate, and pat that other slim brown hand clutching the coverlet so tensely. "Why, Jule, what's———Say, s'pose you folks clear out and let me and Jule and Steve here talk things over quiet. Nobody ain't going to get well with this mob scene you're putting on. Scat!" Andy could distinguish between mental and physical anguish.

They shifted—Doc, Elly, Schultzy, Mis' Means, Catchem the torpid. Another moment and they would have moved reluctantly away. But Parthy, torn between her duty at the ticket window and her feminine curiosity as to the cause of the commotion at Julie's door became, suddenly, all woman. Besides—demon statistician that she was—she suddenly had remembered a curious coincidence in connection with this sudden illness of Julie's. She slammed down the ticket window, banged the box-office door, sailed down the aisle. As she approached Doc was saying for the dozenth time:

"Person's too sick to play, they're sick enough to have a doctor's what I say. Playing Xenia to-morrow. Good a stand's we got. Prolly won't be able to open there, neither, if you're sick's all that."

"I'll be able to play to-morrow!" cried Julie, in a high strained voice. "I'll be able to play to-morrow. To-morrow I'll be all right."

"How do you know?" demanded Doc.

Steve turned on him in sudden desperation. "She'll be all right, I tell you. She'll be all right as soon as she gets out of this town."

"That's a funny thing," exclaimed Parthy. She swept through the little crowd at the door, seeming to mow them down with the energy of her progress. "That's a funny thing."

"What?" demanded Steve, his tone belligerent. "What's funny?"

Captain Andy raised a placating palm. "Now, Parthy, now, Parthy. Sh-sh!"

"Don't shush *me,* Hawks. I know what I'm talking about. It came over me just this minute. Julie took sick at this very town of Lemoyne time we came down river last year. Soon as you and Doc decided we wouldn't open here because the license was too high she got well all of a sudden, just like that!" She snapped a thumb and forefinger.

Silence, thick, uncomfortable, heavy with foreboding, settled down upon the little group in the doorway.

"Nothing so funny about that," said Captain Andy, stoutly; and threw a sharp glance at the face on the pillow. "This hot sticky climate down here after the cold up north is liable to get anybody to feeling queer. None too chipper myself, far's that goes. Affects some people that way." He scratched frenziedly at the mutton-chop whiskers, this side and that.

"Well, I may not know *much*——" began Parthy.

Down the aisle skimmed Magnolia, shouting as she came, her child's voice high and sharp with excitement. "Mom! Mom! Look. What do you think! Julie's picture's been stolen again right out of the front of the lobby. Julie, they've taken your picture again. Somebody took one and Schultzy put another in and now it's been stolen too."

She was delighted with her news; radiant with it. Her face fell a little at the sight of the figure on the bed, the serious group about the doorway that received her news with much gravity. She flew to the bed then, all contrition. "Oh, Julie darling, I'm so sorry you're sick." Julie turned her face away from the child toward the wall.

Captain Andy, simulating fury, capered a threatening step toward the doorway crowd now increased by the deprecating figure of Mr. Means and Ralph's tall shambling bulk. "Will you folks clear out of here or will I have to use force! A body'd think a girl didn't have the right to feel sick. Doc, you get down and 'tend to that ticket window, or Parthy. If we can't show tonight we got to leave 'em know. Ralph, you write out a sign and get it pasted up at the post office. . . . Sure you won't be feeling better by night time, are you, Julie?" He looked doubtfully down at the girl on the bed.

With a sudden lithe movement Julie flung herself into Steve's arms, clung to him, weeping. "No!" she cried, her voice high, hysterical. "No! No! No! Leave me alone, can't you! Leave me alone!"

"Sure," Andy motioned, then, fiercely to the company. "Sure we'll leave you alone, Julie."

But Tragedy, having stalked her victim surely, relentlessly, all the morning, now was about to close in upon her. She had sent emissary after emissary down the show-boat aisle, and each had helped to deepen the look of terror in Julie's eyes. Now sounded the slow shambling heavy tread of Windy the pilot, bearded, sombre, ominous as the figure of fate itself. The little group turned toward him automatically, almost absurdly, like a badly directed mob scene in one of their own improbable plays.

He clumped up the little flight of steps that led from the lower left-hand box to the stage. Clump, clump, clump. Irresistibly Parthy's eyes peered sharply in pursuit of the muddy tracks that followed each step. She snorted indignantly. Across the stage, his beard waggling up and down as his jaws worked slowly, rhythmically on a wedge of Honest Scrap. As he approached Julie's doorway he took off his cap and rubbed his pate with his palm, sure sign of great mental perturbation in this monumental old leviathan. The yellow skin of his knobby bald dome-like head shone gold in the rays of the late morning sun that came in through the high windows at the side of the stage.

He stood a moment, chewing, and peering mildly into the dimness of the bedroom, Sphinx-like, it seemed that he never would speak. He stood, champing. The *Cotton Blossom* troupe waited. They had not played melodrama for years without being able to sense it when they saw it. He spoke. "Seems that skunk Pete's up to something." They waited. The long tobacco-stained beard moved up and down, up and down. "Skinned out half an hour back streaking toward town like possessed. He yanked that picture of Julie out of the hall there. Seen him. I see good deal goes on around here."

Steve sprang to his feet with a great ripping river oath. "I'll kill him this time, the——"

"Seen you take that first picture out, Steve." The deep red that had darkened Steve's face and swelled the veins on his great neck receded now, leaving his china-blue eyes staring out of a white and stricken face.

"I never did! I never did!"

Julie sat up, clutching her wrapper at the throat. She laughed shrilly. "What would he want to steal my picture for! His own wife's picture. Likely!"

"So nobody in this town'd see it, Julie," said Windy, mildly. "Listen. Fifty years piloting on the rivers you got to have pretty good eyesight. Mine's as good to-day as it was time I was twenty. I just stepped down from the texas to warn you I see Pete coming along the levee with Ike Keener. Ike's the sheriff. He'll be in here now any minute."

"Let him," Andy said, stoutly. "Our license is paid. Sheriff's as welcome around this boat as anybody. Let him."

But no one heard him; no one heeded him. A strange and terrible thing was happening. Julie had sprung from her bed. In her white nightgown and her wrapper, her long black hair all tumbled and wild about her face, a stricken and hunted thing, she clung to Steve, and he to her. There came a pounding at the door that led into the show-boat auditorium from the fore deck. Steve's eyes seemed suddenly to sink far back in his head. His cheek-bones showed gaunt and sharp as Julie's own. His jaw was set so that a livid ridge stood out on either side like bars of white-hot steel. He loosened Julie's hold almost roughly. From his pocket he whipped a great clasp-knife and opened its flashing blade. Julie did not scream, but the other women did, shriek on shriek. Captain Andy sprang for him, a mouse attacking a mastodon. Steve shook him off with a fling of his powerful shoulders.

"I'm not going to hurt her, you fool. Leave me be. I know what I'm doing." The pounding came again, louder and more insistent. "Somebody go down and let him in—but keep him there a minute."

No one stirred. The pounding ceased. The doors opened. The boots of Ike Keener, the sheriff, clattered down the aisle of the *Cotton Blossom*.

"Stop those women screeching," Steve shouted. Then, to Julie, "It won't hurt much, darling." With incredible swiftness he seized Julie's hand in his left one and ran the keen glittering blade of his knife firmly across the tip of her forefinger. A scarlet line followed it. He bent his blond head, pressed his lips to the wound, sucked it greedily. With a little moan Julie fell back on the bed. Steve snapped the blade into its socket, thrust the knife into his pocket. The boots of Sheriff Ike Keener were clattering across the stage now. The white faces clustered in the doorway—the stricken, bewildered, horrified faces—turned from the two within the room to the one approaching it. They made way for this one silently. Even Parthy was dumb. Magnolia clung to her, wide-eyed, uncomprehending, sensing tragedy though she had never before encountered it.

The lapel of his coat flung back, Ike Keener confronted the little cowed group on the stage. A star shone on his left breast. The scene was like a rehearsal of a *Cotton Blossom* thriller.

"Who's captain of this here boat?"

Andy, his fingers clutching his whiskers, stepped forward. "I am. What's wanted with him? Hawks is my name—Captain Andy Hawks, twenty years on the rivers."

He looked the sheriff of melodrama, did Ike Keener—boots, black moustaches, wide-brimmed black hat, flowing tie, high boots, and all. Steve himself, made up for the part, couldn't have done it better. "Well, Cap, kind of unpleasant, but I understand there's a miscegenation case on board."

"What?" whispered Magnolia. "What's that? What does he mean, Mom?"

"Hush!" hissed Parthy, and jerked the child's arm.

"How's tha?" asked Andy, but he knew.

"Miscegenation. Case of a Negro woman married to a white man. Criminal offense in this state, as you well know."

"No such thing," shouted Andy. "No such thing on board this boat."

Sheriff Ike Keener produced a piece of paper. "Name of the white man is Steve Baker. Name of the negress"— he squinted again at the slip of paper—"name of the negress is Julie Dozier." He looked around at the group. "Which one's them?"

"Oh, my God!" screamed Elly. "Oh, my God! Oh, my God!"

"Shut up," said Schultzy, roughly.

Steve stepped to the window and threw up the shade, letting the morning light into the crowded disorderly little cubicle. On the bed lay Julie, her eyes enormous in her sallow pinched face.

"I'm Steve Baker. This is my wife."

Sheriff Ike Keener tucked the paper in his pocket. "You two better dress and come along with me."

Julie stood up. She looked an old woman. The marmoset whimpered and whined in his fur nest. She put out a hand, automatically, and plucked it from the muff and held it in the warm hollow of her breast. Her great black eyes stared at the sheriff like the wide-open unseeing eyes of a sleep walker.

Steve Baker grinned—rather, his lips drew back from his teeth in a horrid semblance of mirth. He threw a jovial arm about Julie's shrinking shoulder. For once she had no need to coach him in his part. He looked Ike Keener in the eye. "You wouldn't call a man a white man that's got Negro blood in him, would you?"

"No, I wouldn't; not in Mississippi. One drop of nigger blood makes you a nigger in these parts."

"Well, I got more than a drop of—nigger blood in me, and that's a fact. You can't make miscegenation out of that."

"You ready to swear to that in a court of law?"

"I'll swear to it any place. I'll swear it now." Steve took a step forward, one hand outstretched. "I'll do more than that. Look at all these folks here. There ain't one of them but can swear I got Negro blood in me this minute. That's how white I am."

Sheriff Ike Keener swept the crowd with his eye. Perhaps what he saw in their faces failed to convince him. "Well, I seen fairer men than you was niggers. Still, you better tell that——

Mild, benevolent, patriarchal, the figure of old Windy stepped out from among the rest. "Guess you've known me, Ike, better part of twenty-five years. I was keelboatin' time you was runnin' around, a barefoot on the landin'. Now I'm tellin' you—me, Windy McKlain—that that white man there's got nigger blood in him. I'll take my oath to that."

Having thus delivered himself of what was, perhaps, the second longest speech in his career, he clumped off again, across the stage, down the stairs, up the aisle, looking, even in that bizarre environment, like something out of Genesis.

Sheriff Ike Keener was frankly puzzled. "If it was anybody else but Windy—but I got this straight from—from somebody ought to know."

"From who?" shouted Andy, all indignation. "From a sooty-faced scab of a bull-drumming engineer named Pete. And why? Because he's been stuck on Julie here I don't know how long, and she wouldn't have anything to do with him."

"Is that right?"

"Yes, it is," Steve put in, quickly. "He was after my wife. Anybody in the company'll bear me out. He wouldn't leave her alone, though she hated the sight of him, and Cap here give him a talking—didn't you, Cap? So finally, when he wouldn't quit, then there was nothing for it but lick him, and I licked him good, and soused him in the river to get his dirty face clean. He crawls out swearing he'll get me for it. Now you know.''

Keener now addressed himself to Julie for the first time. "He says—this Pete—that you was born here in Lemoyne, and that your pop was white and your mammy black. That right?''

Julie moistened her lips with the tip of her tongue. "Yes,'' she said. "That's—right.''

A sudden commotion in the group that had been so still. Elly's voice, shrill with hysteria. "I will! I'll tell right out. The wench! The lying black———''

Suddenly stifled, as though a hand had been clapped none too gently across her mouth. Incoherent blubberings; a scuffle. Schultzy had picked Elly up like a sack of meal, one hand still firmly held over her mouth; had carried her into her room and slammed the door.

"What's she say?'' inquired Keener.

Again Andy stepped into the breach. "That's our ingénue lead. She's kind of high strung. You see, she's been friends with this—with Julie Dozier, here—without knowing about her—about her blood, and like that. Kind of give her a shock, I guess. Natural.''

It was plain that Sheriff Ike Keener was on the point of departure, puzzled though convinced. He took off his broad-brimmed hat, scratched his head, replaced the hat at an angle that spelled bewilderment. His eye, as he turned away, fell on the majestic figure of Parthenia Ann Hawks, and on Magnolia cowering, wide-eyed, in the folds of her mother's ample skirts.

"You look like a respectable woman, ma'am.''

Imposing enough at all times, Parthy now grew visibly taller. Cold sparks flew from her eyes. "I am.''

"That your little girl?''

Andy did the honours. "My wife, Sheriff. My little girl, Magnolia. What do you say to the Sheriff, Magnolia?''

Thus urged, Magnolia spoke that which had been seething within her. "You're bad!'' she shouted, her face twisted with the effort to control her tears. "You're a bad mean man, that's what! You called Julie names and made her look all funny. You're a———''

The maternal hand stifled her.

"If I was you, ma'am, I wouldn't bring up no child on a boat like this. No, nor stay on it, neither. Fine place to rear a child!''

Whereupon, surprisingly enough, Parthy turned defensive. "My child's as well brought up as your own, and probably better, and so I tell you. And I'll thank you to keep your advice to yourself, Mr. Sheriff.''

"Parthy! Parthy!'' from the alarmed Andy.

But Sheriff Ike Keener was a man of parts. "Well, women folks are all alike. I'll be going. I kind of smell a nigger in the woodpile here in more ways than one. But I'll take your word for it.'' He looked Captain Andy sternly in the eye. "Only let me tell you this, Captain Hawks. You better not try to give your show in this town to-night. We got some public-spirited folks here in Lemoyne and this fix you're in has kind of leaked around. You go to work and try to give your show with this mixed blood you got here and first thing you know you'll be riding out of town on something don't sit so easy as a boat.''

His broad-brimmed hat at an angle of authority, his coat tails flirting as he strode, he marched up the aisle then and out.

The little huddling group seemed visibly to collapse. It was as though an unseen hand had removed a sustaining iron support from the spine of each. Magnolia would have flown to Julie, but Parthy jerked her back. Whispering then; glance of disdain.

"Well, Julie, m'girl," began Andy Hawks, kindly. Julie turned to him.

"We're going," she said, quietly.

The door of Elly's room burst open. Elly, a rumpled, distraught, unlovely figure, appeared in Julie's doorway, Schultzy trying in vain to placate her.

"You get out of here!" She turned in a frenzy to Andy. "She gets out of here with that white trash she calls her husband or I go, and so I warn you. She's black! She's black! God, I was a fool not to see it all the time. Look at her, the nasty yellow————" A stream of abuse, vile, obscene, born of the dregs of river talk heard through the years, now welled to Elly's lips, distorting them horribly.

"Come away from here," Parthy said, through set lips, to Magnolia. And bore the child, protesting, up the aisle and into the security of her own room forward.

"I want to stay with Julie! I want to stay with Julie!" wailed Magnolia, overwrought, as the inexorable hand dragged her up the stairs.

In her tiny disordered room Julie was binding up her wild hair with a swift twist. She barely glanced at Elly. "Shut that woman up," she said, quietly. "Tell her I'm going." She began to open boxes and drawers.

Steve approached Andy, low-voiced. "Cap, take us down as far as Xenia, will you, for God's sake! Don't make us get off here."

"Down as far as Xenia you go," shouted Captain Andy at the top of his voice, "and anybody in this company don't like it they're free to git, bag and baggage, now. We'll pull out of here now. Xenia by afternoon at four, latest. And you two want to stay the night on board you're welcome. I'm master of this boat, by God!"

They left, these two, when the *Cotton Blossom* docked at Xenia in the late afternoon. Andy shook hands with them, gravely; and Windy clumped down from the pilot house to perform the same solemn ceremony. You sensed unseen peering eyes at every door and window of the *Cotton Blossom* and the *Mollie Able*.

"How you fixed for money?" Andy demanded, bluntly.

"We're fixed all right," Julie replied, quietly. Of the two of them she was the more composed. "We've been saving. You took too good care of us on the *Cotton Blossom*. No call to spend our money." The glance from her dark shadow-encircled eyes was one of utter gratefulness. She took up the lighter pieces of luggage. Steve was weighed down with the others—bulging boxes and carpet bags and bundles—their clothing and their show-boat wardrobe and their pitifully few trinkets and personal belongings. A pin cushion, very lumpy, that Magnolia had made for her at Christmas a year ago. Photographs of the *Cotton Blossom*. A book of pressed wild flowers. Old newspaper clippings.

Julie lingered. Steve crossed the gangplank, turned, beckoned with his head. Julie lingered. An unspoken question in her eyes.

Andy flushed and scratched the mutton-chop whiskers this side and that. "Well, you know how she is Julie. She don't mean no harm. But she didn't let on to Magnolia just what time you were going. Told her to-morrow, likely. Women folks are funny, that way. She don't mean no harm."

"That's all right," said Julie; picked up the valises, was at Steve's side. Together the two toiled painfully up the steep river bank, Steve turning to aid her as best he could. They reached the top of the levee. They stood a moment, breathless; then turned and trudged down the dusty Southern country road, the setting sun in their faces. Julie's slight figure was bent under the weight of the burden she carried. You saw Steve's find blond head turned toward her, tender, concerned, encouraging.

Suddenly from the upper deck that fronted Magnolia's room and Parthy's came the sound of screams, a scuffle, a smart slap, feet clattering pell-mell down the narrow wooden balcony stairs. A wild little figure in a torn white frock, its face scratched and tear-stained, its great eyes ablaze in the white face, flew past Andy, across the gangplank, up the levee, down the road. Behind her, belated and panting, came Parthy. Her hand on her heart, her bosom heaving, she leaned against the inadequate support offered by Andy's right arm, threatening momentarily to topple him, by her own dead weight, into the river.

"To think that I should live to see the day when—my own child—she slapped me—her mother! I saw them out of the window, so I told her to straighten her bureau drawers—a sight! All of a sudden she heard that woman's voice, low as it was, and she to the window. When she saw her going she makes for the door. I caught her on the steps, but she was like a wildcat, and raised her hand against me—her own mother—and tore away, with me holding this in my hand." She held out a fragment of torn white stuff. "Raised her hand against her own————"

Andy grinned. "Good for her."

"What say, Andy Hawks!"

But Andy refused to answer. His gaze followed the flying little figure silhouetted against the evening sky at the top of the high river bank. The slim sagging figure of the woman and the broad-shouldered figure of the man trudged down the road ahead. The child's voice could be heard high and clear, with a note of hysteria in it. "Julie! Julie! Wait for me! I want to say goodbye! Julie!"

The slender woman in the black dress turned and made as though to start back and then, with a kind of crazy fear in her pace, began to run away from the pursuing little figure—away from something that she had not the courage to face. And when she saw this Magnolia ran on yet a little while, faltering, and then she stopped and buried her head in her hands and sobbed. The woman glanced over her shoulder, fearfully. And at what she saw she dropped her bags and bundles in the road and started back toward her, running fleetly in spite of her long ruffled awkward skirts; and she held out her arms long before they were able to reach her. And when finally they came together, the woman dropped on her knees in the dust of the road and gathered the weeping child to her and held her close, so that as you saw them sharply outlined against the sunset the black of the woman's dress and the white of the child's frock were as one.

8

MAGNOLIA, AT FIFTEEN, was a gangling gawky child whose eyes were too big for her face and whose legs were too long for her skirts. She looked, in fact, all legs, eyes, and elbows. It was a constant race between her knees and her skirt hems. Parthy was for ever lengthening frocks. Frequently Magnolia, looking down at herself, was surprised, like Alice in Wonderland after she had eaten the magic currant cake, to discover how far away from her head her feet were. Being possessed of a natural creamy pallor which her mother mistook for lack of red corpuscles, she was dosed into chronic biliousness on cod liver oil, cream, eggs, and butter, all of which she loathed.

Then suddenly, at sixteen, legs, elbows, and eyes assumed their natural proportions. Overnight, seemingly, she emerged from adolescence a rather amazing looking young creature with a high broad forehead, a wide mobile mouth, great dark liquid eyes, and a most lovely speaking voice which nobody noticed. Her dress was transformed, with Cinderella-like celerity, from the pinafore to the bustle variety. She was not a beauty. She was, in fact, considered rather plain by the unnoticing. Being hipless and almost boyishly flat of bust in a day when the female form was a thing not only of curves but of loops, she was driven by her mother into wearing all sorts of pads and ruffled corset covers and contrivances which somehow failed to conceal the slimness of the frame beneath. She was, even at sixteen, what might be termed distinguished-looking. Merely by standing tall, pale, dark-haired, next to Elly, that plump and pretty ingénue was transformed into a dumpy and rather dough-faced blonde in whose countenance selfishness and dissatisfaction were beginning to etch telltale lines.

She had been now almost seven years on the show boat. These seven years had spread a tapestry of life and colour before her eyes. Broad rivers flowing to the sea. Little towns perched high on the river banks or cowering flat and fearful, at the mercy of the waters that often crept like hungry and devouring monsters, stealthily over the levee and into the valley below. Singing Negroes. Fighting whites. Spawning Negroes. A life fantastic, bizarre, peaceful, rowdy, prim, eventful, calm. On the rivers anything might happen and everything did. She saw convict chain gangs working on the roads. Grisly nightmarish figures of striped horror, manacled leg to leg. At night you heard them singing plantation songs in the fitful glare of their camp fires in the woods; simple songs full of hope. Didn't My Lord Deliver Daniel? they sang. Swing Low Sweet Chariot, Comin' for to Carry Me Home. In the Louisiana bayou country she saw the Negroes perform that weird religious rite known as a ring shout, semi-savage, hysterical, mesmerizing.

Iowa, Illinois, and Missouri small-town housewives came to be Magnolia's friends, and even Parthy's. The coming of the show boat was the one flash of blazing colour in the drab routine of their existence. To them Schultzy was the John Drew of the rivers, Elly the Lillian Russell. You saw them scudding down the placid tree-shaded streets in their morning ginghams and calicoes, their bits of silver clasped in their workseamed hands, or knotted into the corner of a handkerchief. Fifty cents for two seats at to-night's show.

"How are you, Mis' Hawks? . . . And the little girl? . . . My! Look at the way she's shot up in a year's time! Well, you can't call her little girl any more. . . . I brought you a glass of my homemade damson preserve. I take cup of sugar to cup of juice. Real rich, but it is good if I do say so. . . . I told Will I was coming to the show every night you were here, and he could like it or lump it. I been saving out of the housekeeping money."

They brought vast chocolate cakes; batches of cookies; jugs of home-brewed grape wine; loaves of fresh bread; jars of strained honey; stiff tight bunches of garden flowers. Offerings on the shrine of Art.

Periodically Parthy threatened to give up this roving life and take Magnolia with her. She held this as a weapon over Andy's head when he crossed her will, or displeased her. Immediately boarding shcool,convents, and seminaries yawned for Magnolia.

Perhaps Parthy was right. "What kind of a life is this for a child!" she demanded. And later, "A fine kind of a way for a young lady to be living—slopping up and down these rivers, seeing nothing but loafers and gamblers and niggers and worse. What about her Future?" Future, as she pronounced it, was spelled with a capital F and was a thin disguise for the word husband.

"Future'll take care of itself," Andy assured her, blithely.

"If that isn't just like a man!"

It was inevitable that Magnolia should, sooner or later, find herself through force of circumstance treading the boards as an actress in the Cotton Blossom Floating Theatre company. Not only that, she found herself playing ingénue leads. She had been thrown in as a stop-gap following Elly's defection, and had become, quite without previous planning, a permanent member of the troupe. Strangely enough, she developed an enormous following, though she lacked that saccharine quality which river towns had come to expect in their show-boat ingénues. True, her long legs were a little lanky beneath the short skirts of the woodman's pure daughter, but what she lacked in one extremity she made up in another. They got full measure when they looked at her eyes, and her voice made the small-town housewives weep. Yet when their husbands nudged them, saying, "What you sniffling about?" they could only reply, "I don't know." And no more did they.

Elly was twenty-eight when she deserted Schultzy for a gambler from Mobile. For three years she had been restless, fault-finding, dissatisfied. Each autumn she would announce to Captain Andy her intention to forsake the rivers and bestow her talents ashore. During the winter she would try to get an engagement through the Chicago booking offices contrary to the custom of show-boat actors whose habit it was to hibernate in the winter on the savings of a long and economical summer. But the Chicago field was sparse and uncertain. She never had the courage or the imagination to go as far as New York. April would find her back on the *Cotton Blossom*. Between her and Schultzy the bickerings and the quarrels became more and more frequent. She openly defied Schultzy as he directed rehearsals. She refused to follow his suggestions though he had a real sense of direction. Everything she knew he had taught her. She invariably misread a line and had to be coached in it, word by word; inflection; business; everything.

Yet now, when Schultzy said, "No! Listen. You been kidnapped and smuggled on board this rich fella's yacht, see. And he thinks he's got you in his power. He goes to grab you. You're here, see. Then you point toward the door back of him, see, like you saw something there scared the life out of you. He turns around and you grab the gun off the table, see, and cover him, and there's your big speech. *So* and so and *so* and so and *so* and so and *so* and so————" the *ad lib.* directions that have held since the day of Shakespeare.

Elly would deliberately defy him. Others in the company—new members— began to take their cue from her.

She complained about her wardrobe; refused to interest herself in it, though she had been an indefatigable needlewoman. Now, instead of sewing, you saw her looking moodily out across the river, her hands idle, her brows black. An unintelligent and unresourceful woman turned moody and thoughtful must come to mischief, for within herself she finds no solace.

At Mobile, then, she was gone. It was, they all knew, the black-moustached gambler who had been following the show boat down the river since they played Paducah, Kentucky. Elly had had dozens of admirers in her show-boat career; had received much attention from Southern gallants, gamblers, loafers, adventurers—all the romantic beaux of the river towns of the '80s. Her attitude toward them had been puritanical to the point of sniffiness, though she had enjoyed their homage and always displayed any amorous missives or gifts that came her way.

True to the melodramatic tradition of her environment, she left a note for Schultzy, written in a flourishing Spencerian hand that made up, in part, for the spelling. She was gone. He need not try to follow her ot find her or bring her back. She was going to star at the head of her own company and play Camille and even Juliet. He had promised her. She was good and sick and tired of this everlasting flopping up and down the rivers. She wouldn't go back to it, no matter what. Her successor could have her wardrobe. They had bookings through Iowa, Illinois, Missouri, and Kansas. She might even get to New York. (Incredibly enough, she did actually play Juliet through the Mid-west, to audiences of the bewildered yokelry.) She was sorry to leave Cap in the lurch like this. And she would close, and begged to remain his loving Wife (this inked out but still decipherable)—begged to remain, his truly, Elly Chipley. Just below this signature the added one of Lenore La Verne, done in tremendous sable downstrokes and shaded curlecues, especially about the L's.

It was a crushing blow for Schultzy, who loved her. Stricken, he thought only of her happiness. "She can't get along without me," he groaned. Then, in a stunned way, "Juliet!" There was nothing of bitterness or rancour in his tone; only a dumb despairing wonder, "Juliet! And she couldn't play Little Eva without making her out a slut." He pondered this a moment. "She's got it into her head she's Bernhardt, or something. . . . Well, she'll come back."

"Do you mean to say you'd take her back!"

Parthy demanded. "Why, sure," Schultzy replied, simply. "She never packed a trunk in her life, or anything. I done all those things for her. Some ways she's a child. I guess that's how she kept me so tight. She needed me all the time. . . . Well, she'll come back."

Captain Andy sent to Chicago for an ingénue lead. It was then, pending her arrival, that Magnolia stepped into the breach—the step being made, incidentally, over what was practically Parthy's dead body. For at Magnolia's calm announcement that she knew every line of the part and all the business, her mother stormed, had hysterics, and finally took to her bed (until nearly time for the rise of the curtain). The bill that night was The Parson's Bride. Show-boat companies to this day still tell the story of what happened during that performance on the *Cotton Blossom*.

They had two rehearsals, one in the morning, another that lasted throughout the afternoon. Of the company, Magnolia was the calmest. Captain Andy seemed to swing, by invisible pulleys, from the orchestra pit below to Parthy's chamber above. One moment he would be sprawled in the kerosene footlights, his eyes deep in wrinkles of delight, his little brown paws scratching the mutton-chop whiskers in a frenzy of excitement.

"That's right. That's the stuff! Elly never give it half the—— 'Scuse me, Schultzy—I didn't go for to hurt your feelings, but by golly, Nollie! I wouldn't of believed you had it in you, not if your own mother told——" Then, self-reminded, he would cast a fearful glance over his shoulder, that shoulder would droop, he would extricate himself from the welter of footlights and music racks and prompt books in which he squatted, and scamper up the aisle. The dim outline of a female head in curl papers certainly could not have been seen peering over the top of the balcony rail as he fancied, for when he had clattered up the balcony stairs and had gently turned the knob of the bedroom door, there lay the curl-papered head on the pillow of the big bed, and from it issued hollow groans, and plastered over one cheek of it was a large moist white cloth soaked in some pungent and nostril-pricking stuff. The eyes were closed. The whole figure was shaken by shivers. Mortal agony, you would have said (had you not known Parthy), had this stricken and monumental creature in its horrid clutches.

In a whisper—"Parthy!"

A groan, hollow, heartrending, mortuary.

He entered, shut the door softly, tiptoed over to the bed, laid a comforting brown paw on the shivering shoulder. The shoulder became convulsive, the shivers swelled to heaves. "Now, now, Parthy! What you taking on so for? God A'mighty, person'd think she'd done something to shame you instead of make you mighty proud. If you'd see her! Why, say, she's a born actress."

The groans now became a wail. The eyes unclosed. The figure raised itself to a sitting posture. The sopping rag rolled limply off. Parthy rocked herself to and fro. "My own daughter! An actress! That I should have lived to see this day! . . . Rather have . . . in her grave . . . why I ever allowed her to set foot on this filthy scow. . . .

"Now, Parthy, you're just working yourself up. Matter of fact, that time Mis'Means turned her ankle and we thought she couldn't step on it, you was all for going on in her part, and I bet if Sophy Means hadn't tied up her foot and gone on like a soldier she is, we'd of had you acting that night. You was rarin' to. I watched you."

"Me! Acting on the stage! Not that I couldn't play better than any Sophy Means, and that's no compliment. A poor stick if I couldn't." But her defence lacked conviction. Andy had surprised a secret ambition in this iron-armoured bosom.

"Now, come on! Cheer up! Ought to be proud your own daughter stepping in and saving us money like this. We'd of closed. Had to. God knows when that new baggage'll get here, if she gets here at all. What do you think of that Chipley! Way I've treated that girl, if she'd been my own daughter—well! . . . How'd you like a nice little sip of whisky, Parthy? Then you come on down give Nollie a hand with her costumes. Chipley's stuff comes up on her like ballet skirts.—Now, now, now! I didn't say she——— Oh, my God!"

Parthy had gone off again into hysterics. "My own daughter! My little girl!"

The time for severe measures had come. Andy had not dealt with actresses for years without learning something of the weapons with which to fight hysteria.

"All right. I'll give you something to screech for. The boys paraded this noon with a banner six feet long and red letters a foot high announcing the Appearance Extraordinaire of Magnolia the Mysterious Comedy Trage-dienne in The Parson's Bride. I made a special spiel on the corner. We got the biggest advance sale we had this season. Yessir! Doc's downstairs raking it in with both hands and you had the least bit of gumption in you, instead of laying here whining and carrying on, you'd———"

"What's the advance?" spake up Parthy, the box-office expert.

"Three hundred; and not anywheres near four o'clock."

With one movement Parthy had flung aside the bedclothes and stepped out of bed revealing, rather inexplicably, a complete lower costume including shoes.

Andy was off, down the stairs, up the aisle, into the orchestra pit just in time to hear Magnolia say, "Schultzy, *please!* Don't throw me the line like that, I know it. I didn't stop because I was stuck."

"What'd you stop for, then, and look like you'd seen spooks!"

"I stopped a-purpose. She sees her husband that she hates and that she thought was dead for years come sneaking in, and she wouldn't start right in to talk. She'd just stand there, kind of frozen and stiff, staring at him."

"All right, if you know so much about directing go ahead and di———"

She ran to him, threw her arms about him, hugged him, all contrition. "Oh, Schultzy, don't be mad. I didn't go to boss. I just wanted to act it like I felt. And I'm awfully sorry about Elly and everything. I'll do as you say, only I just can't help thinking, Schultzy dear, that she'd stand there, staring kind of silly, almost.''

"You're right. I guess my mind ain't on my work. I ought to know how right you are. I got that letter Elly left for me, I just stood there gawping with my mouth open, and never said a word for I don't know how long———— Oh, my God!''

"There, there, Schultzy.''

By a tremendous effiort (the mechanics of which were not entirely concealed) Schultzy, the man, gave way to Harold Westbrook, the artist.

"You're right, Magnolia. That'll get 'em. You standing there like that, stunned and pale.''

"How'll I get pale, Schultzy?''

"You'll feel pale inside and the audience'll think you are.'' (The whole art of acting unconsciously expressed by Schultzy.) "Then Frank here has his sneery speech—*so* and so and *so* and so and *so* and so—and thought you'd marry the parson, huh? And then you open up with your big scene-so and so and *so* and so and *so* and so————''

Outwardly calm, Magnolia took only a cup of coffee at dinner, and Parthy, for once, did not press her to eat. That mournful matron, though still occasionally shaken by a convulsive shudder, managed her usual heartening repast and actually spent the time from four to seven lengthening Elly's frocks for Magnolia and taking them in to fit the girl's slight frame.

Schultzy made her up, and rather overdid it so that, as the deserted wife and school teacher and, later, as the Parson's prospective bride, she looked a pass between a healthy Camille and Cleopatra just before she applied the asp. In fact, in their effort to bridge the gap left by Elly's sudden flight, the entire company overdid everything and thus brought about the cataclysmic moment which is theatrical show-boat history.

Magnolia, so sure of her lines during rehearsal, forgot them a score of times during the performance and, had it not been for Schultzy, who threw them to her unerringly and swiftly, would have made a dismal failure of this, her first stage appearance. They were playing Vidallia, always a good showboat town. The house was filled from the balcony boxes to the last row downstairs near the door, from which point very little could be seen and practically nothing heard. Something of the undercurrent of excitement which pervaded the *Cotton Blossom* troupe seemed to seep through the audience; or perhaps even an audience so unsophisticated as this could not but sense the unusual in this performance. Every one of the troupe— Schultzy, Mis' Means, Mr. Means, Frank, Ralph, the Soapers (Character Team that had succeeded Julie and Steve)—all were trembling for Magnolia. And because they were fearful for her they threw themselves frantically into their parts. Magnolia, taking her cue (literally as well as figuratively) from them, did likewise. As ingénue lead, her part was that of a young school mistress earning her livelihood in a little town. Deserted some years before by her worthless husband, she learns now of his death. The town parson has long been in love with her, and she with him. Now they can marry. The wedding gown is finished. The guests are invited.

This is her last day as school teacher. She is alone in the empty schoolroom. Farewell, dear pupils. Farewell, dear schoolroom, blackboard, erasers, waterbucket, desk, etc. She picks up her key. But what is this evil face in the doorway! Who is this drunken, leering tramp, grisly in rags, repulsive———— My God! You! My husband!

(Never was villain so black and diabolical as Frank. Never was heroine so lovely and frail and trembling and helpless and white—as per Schultzy's directions. As for Schultzy himself, the heroic parson, very heavily made up and pure yet brave withal, it was a poor stick of a maiden who wouldn't have contrived to get into some sort of distressing circumstance just for the joy of being got out of it by this godly yet godlike young cleric.)

Frank, then: "I reckon you thought I was dead. Well, I'm about the livest corpse you ever saw.'''A diabolical laugh. "Too damn bad you won't be able to wear that new wedding dress."

Pleadings, agony, despair.

Now his true villainy comes out. A thousand dollars, then, and quick, or you don't walk down the aisle to the music of no wedding march.

"I haven't got it."

"No! Where's the money you been saving all these years?"

"I haven't a thousand dollars. I swear it."

'So!'' Seizes her. Drags her across the room. Screams. His hand stifles them.

Unfortunately, in their very desire to help Magnolia, they all exaggerated their villainy, their heroism, their business. Being a trifle uncertain of her lines, Magnolia, too, sought to cover her deficiencies by stressing her emotional scenes. When terror was required her face was distorted with it. Her screams of fright were real screams of mortal fear. Her writhings would have wrung pity from a fiend. Frank bared his teeth, chortled like a maniac. He wound his fingers in her long black hair and rather justified her outcry. In contrast, Schultzy's nobility and purity stood out as crudely and unmistakably as white against black. Nuances were not for show-boat audiences.

So then, screams, protestations, snarls, ha-ha's, pleadings, agony, cruelty, anguish.

Something—intuition—or perhaps a sound from the left upper box made Frank, the villain, glance up. There, leaning over the box rail, his face a mask of hatred, his eyes glinting, sat a huge hairy backwoodsman. And in his hand glittered the barrel of a businesslike gun. He was taking careful aim. Drama had come late into the life of this literal mind. He had, in the course of a quick-shooting rough-and-tumble career, often seen the brutal male mishandling beauty in distress. His code was simple. One second more and he would act on it.

Frank's hand released his struggling victim. Gentleness and love overspread his features, dispelling their villainy. To Magnolia's staring and openmouthed amazement he made a gesture of abnegation. "Well, Marge, I ain't got nothin' more to say if you and the parson want to get married." After which astounding utterance he slunk rapidly off, leaving the field to what was perhaps the most abject huddle of heroism that every graced a show-boat stage.

The curtain came down. The audience, intuitively glancing toward the upper box, ducked, screamed, or swore. The band struck up. The backwoodsman, a little bewildered but still truculent, subsided somewhat. A trifle mystified, but labouring under the impression that this was, perhaps, the ordinary routine of the theatre, the audience heard Schultzy, in front of the curtain, explaining that the villain was taken suddenly ill; that the concert would now be given free of charge; that each and every man, woman, and child was invited to retain his seat. The backwoodsman, rather sheepish now, took a huge bite of Honest Scrap and looked about him belligerently. Out came Mr. Means to do his comic Chinaman. Order reigned on one side of the footlights at least, though behind the heaving Venetian lagoon was a company saved from collapse only by a quite human uncertainty as to whether tears or laughter would best express their state of mind.

The new ingénue lead, scheduled to meet the *Cotton Blossom* at Natchez, failed to appear. Magnolia, following her trial by firearms, had played the absent Elly's parts for a week. There seemed to be no good reason why she should not continue to do so at least until Captain Andy could engage an ingénue who would join the troupe at New Orleans.

A year passed. Magnolia was a fixture in the company. Now, as she, in company with Parthy or Mis' Means or Mrs. Soaper, appeared on the front street of this or that little river town, she was stared at and commented on. Round-eyed little girls, swinging on the front gate, gazed at her much as she had gazed, not so many years before, at Elly and Julie as they had sauntered own the shady path of her own street in Thebes.

She loved the life. She worked hard. She cherished the admiration and applause. She took her work seriously. Certainly she did not consider herself an apostle of art. She had no illusions about herself as an actress. But she did thrive on the warm electric current that flowed from those river audiences made up of miners, farmers, Negroes, housewives, harvesters, backwoodsmen, villagers, over the footlights, to her. A naïve people, they accepted their theatre without question, like children. That which they saw they believed. They hissed the villain, applauded the heroine, wept over the plight of the wronged. The plays were as naïve as the audience. In them, onrushing engines were cheated of their victims; mill wheels were stopped in the nick of time; heroes, bound hand and foot and left to be crushed under iron wheels, were rescued by the switchman's ubiquitous daughter. Sheriffs popped up unexpectedly in hidden caves. The sound of horses' hoofs could always be heard when virtue was about to be ravished. They were the minstrels of the rivers, these players, telling in terms of blood, love, and adventure the crude saga of a new country.

Frank, the Heavy, promptly fell in love with Magnolia. Parthy, quick to mark the sheep's eyes he cast in the direction of the ingénue lead, watched him with a tigress glare, and though he lived on the *Cotton Blossom,* as did Magnolia; saw her all day, daily; probably was seldom more than a hundred feet removed from her, he never spoke to her alone and certainly never was able to touch her except in the very public glare of the footlights with some hundreds of pairs of eyes turned on the two by the *Cotton Blossom* audiences. He lounged disconsolately after her, a large and somewhat splay-footed fellow whose head was too small for his shoulders, giving him the look of an inverted exclamation point.

His unrequited and unexpressed passion for Magnolia would have bothered that young lady and her parents very little were it not for the fact that his emotions began to influence his art. In his scenes on the stage with her he became more and more uncertain of his lines. Not only that, his attitude and tone as villain of the piece took on a tender note most mystifying to the audience, accustomed to seeing villainy black, with no half tones. When he should have been hurling Magnolia into the mill stream or tying her brutally to the track, or lashing her with a horsewhip or snarling at her like a wolf, he became a cooing dove. His blows were caresses. His baleful glare became a simper of adoration.

"Do you intend to speak to that sheep, or shall I?" demanded Parthy of her husband.

"I'll do it," Andy assured her, hurriedly. "Leave him be till we get to New Orleans. Then, if anything busts, why, I can always get some kind of a fill-in there."

They had been playing the Louisiana parishes—little Catholic settlements between New Orleans and Baton Rouge, their inhabitants a mixture of French and Creole. Frank had wandered disconsolately through the miniature cathedral which each little parish boasted and, returning, had spoken darkly of abandoning the stage for the Church.

New Orleans meant mail for the *Cotton Blossom* troupe. With that mail came trouble. Schultzy, white but determined, approached Captain Andy, letter in hand.

"I got to go, Cap. She needs me."

"Go!" squeaked Andy. His squeak was equivalent to a bellow in a man of ordinary stature. "Go where? What d'you mean, she?" But he knew.

Out popped Parthy, scenting trouble.

Schultzy held out a letter written on cheap paper, lined, and smelling faintly of antiseptic. "She's in the hospital at Little Rock. Says she's had an operation. He's left her, the skunk. She ain't got a cent."

"I'll take my oath on that,"Parthy put in, pungently.

"You can't go and leave me flat now, Schultzy."

"I got to go, I tell you. Frank can play leads till you get somebody, or till I get back. Old Means can play utility at a pinch, and Doc can do general business."

"Frank," announced Parthy, with terrible distinctness, "will play no leads in this company, and so I tell you, Hawks."

"Who says he's going to! A fine-looking lead he'd make, with that pin-head of his, and those elephant's hoofs. . . . Now looka here, Schultzy. You been a trouper long enough to know you can't leave a show in the ditch like this. No real show-boat actor'd do it, and you know it."

"Sure I know it. I wouldn't do it for myself, no matter what. But it's her. I wrote her a letter, time she left. I got her bookings. I said if the time comes you need me, leave me know, and I'll come. And she needs me, and she left me know, and I'm coming."

"How about us!" demanded Parthy. "Leaving us in the lurch like that, first Elly and now you after all these years. A fine pair, the two of you."

"Now, Parthy!"

"Oh, I've no patience with you, Hawks. Always letting people get the best of you."

"But I told you," Schultzy began again, almost tearfully, "it's for her, not me. She's sick. You can pick up somebody here in New Orleans. I bet there's a dozen better actors than me laying around the docks this minute. I got to talking to a fellow while ago, down on the wharf. The place was all jammed up with freight, and I was waiting to get by so's I could come aboard. I said I was an actor on the *Cotton Blossom,* and he said he'd acted and that was a life he'd like."

"Yes," snapped Parthy. "I suppose he would. What does he think this is! A bumboat! Plenty of wharf rats in New Orleans'd like nothing better———"

Schultzy pointed to where a slim figure leaned indolently against a huge packing case—one of hundreds of idlers dotting the great New Orleans plank landing.

Andy adjusted the pair of ancient binoculars through which he recently had been scanning the wharf and the city beyond the levee. He surveyed the graceful lounging figure.

"I'd go ashore and talk to him, I was you," advised Schultzy.

Andy put down the glasses and stared at Schultzy in amazement. "Him! Why, I couldn't go up and talk to him about acting on no show boat. He's a gentleman."

"Here," said Parthy, abruptly, her curiosity piqued. She in turn trained the glasses on the object of the discussion. Her survey was brief but ample. "He may be a gentleman. But nobody feels a gentleman with a crack in his shoe, and he's got one. I can't say I like the looks of him, specially. But with Schultzy playing us this dirty trick—well, that's what it amounts to, and there's no sense trying to prettify it—we can't be choosers. I'd just step down talk to him if I was you, Hawks.''

9

THIS, THEN, TURNED out to be Magnolia's first glimpse of Gaylord Ravenal—an idle elegant figure in garments whose modish cut and fine material served, at a distance, to conceal their shabbiness. Leaning moodily against a tall packing case dumped on the wharf by some freighter, he gazed about him and tapped indolently the tip of his shining (and cracked) boot with an exquisite little ivory-topped malacca cane. There was about him an air of distinction, an atmosphere of richness. On closer proximity you saw that the broadcloth was shiny, the fine linen of the shirt front and cuffs the least bit frayed, the slim boots undeniably split, the hat (a delicate gray and set a little on one side) soiled as a pale gray hat must never be. From the *Cotton Blossom* deck you saw him as the son, perhaps, of some rich Louisiana planter, idling a moment at the water's edge. Waiting, doubtless, for one of the big river packets—the floating palaces of the Mississippi—to bear him luxuriously away up the river to his plantation landing.

The truth was that Gaylord Ravenal was what the river gamblers called broke. Stony, he would have told you. No one had a better right to use the term than he. Of his two possessions, save the sorry clothes he had on, one was the little malacca cane. And though he might part with cuff links, shirt studs and if necessary, shirt itself, he would always cling to that little malacca cane, emblem of good fortune, his mascot. It had turned on him temporarily. Yet his was the gambler's superstitious nature. To-morrow the cane would bring him luck.

Not only was Gaylord Ravenal broke; he had just politely notified the Chief of Police of New Orleans that he was in town. The call was not entirely one of social obligation. It had a certain statutory side as well.

In the first place, Chief of Police Vallon, in a sudden political spasm of virtue, endeavouring to clear New Orleans of professional gamblers, had given them all twenty-four hours' shrift. In the second place, this particular visitor would have come under the head of New Orleans undesirables on his own private account, even though his profession had been that of philanthropist. Gaylord Ravenal had one year-old notch to his gun.

It had not been murder in cold blood or in rage, but a shot fired in self-defence just the fraction of a second before the other man could turn the trick. The evidence proved this, and Ravenal's final vindication followed. But New Orleans gathered her civic skirts about her and pointed a finger of dismissal toward the door. Hereafter, should he enter, his first visit must be to the Chief of Police; and twenty-four hours—no more—must be the limit of his stay in the city whose pompano and crayfish and Creoles and roses and Ramos gin fizzes he loved.

The evening before, he had stepped off the river packet *Lady Lee,* now to be seen lying alongside the New Orleans landing together with a hundred other craft. His twenty-four hours would expire this evening.

Certainly he had not meant to find himself in New Orleans. He had come aboard the *Lady Lee* at St. Louis, his finances low, his hopes high, his erstwhile elegant garments in their present precarious state. He had planned, following the game of stud poker in which he immediately immersed himself, to come ashore at Memphis or, at the latest, Natchez, with his finances raised to the high level of his hopes. Unfortunately his was an honest and over-eager game. His sole possession, beside the little slim malacca cane (itself of small tangible value) was a singularly clear blue-white diamond ring which he never wore. It was a relic of luckier days before his broadcloth had become shiny, his linen frayed, his boots split. He had clung to it, as he had to the cane, through almost incredible hazards. His feeling about it was neither sentimental nor superstitious. The tenuous streak of canniness in him told him that, possessed of a clear white diamond, one can hold up one's head and one's hopes, no matter what the state of coat, linen, boots, and hat. It had never belonged, fiction-fashion, to his sainted (if any) mother, nor was it an old Ravenal heirloom. It was a relic of winnings in luckier days and represented, he knew, potential hundreds. In the trip that lasted, unexpectedly, from St. Louis to New Orleans, he had won and lost that ring six times. When the *Lady Lee* had nosed her way into the Memphis landing, and again at Natchez, it had been out of his possession. He had stayed on board, perforce. Half an hour before coming into New Orleans he had had it again, and had kept it. The game of stud poker had lasted days, and he rose from it the richer by exactly nothing at all.

He had glanced out of the *Lady Lee's* saloon window, his eyes bloodshot from sleeplessness, his nerves jangling, his hands twitching, his face drawn; but that face shaven, those hands immaculate. Gaylord Ravenal, in luck or out, had the habits and instincts of a gentleman.

"Good God!" he exclaimed now, "this looks like it is New Orleans!" It was N'Yawlins as he said it.

"What did you think it was?" growled one of the players, who had temporarily owned the diamond several times during the journey down river. "What did you think it was? Shanghai?"

"I wish it was," said Gaylord Ravenal. Somewhat dazedly he walked down the *Lady Lee's* gangplank and retorted testily to a beady-eyed giant-footed gentleman who immediately spoke to him in a low and not unfriendly tone, "Give me time, can't you! I haven't been twenty-four hours stepping from the gangplank to this wharf, have I? Well, then!"

"No offence, Gay," said the gentleman, his eyes still searching the other passengers as they filed across the narrow gangplank. "Just thought I'd remind you, case of trouble. You know how Vallon is."

Vallon had said, briefly, later, "That's all right, Gay. But by this time to-morrow evening———" He had eyed Ravenal's raiment with a comprehending eye. "Cigar?" The weed he proffered was slim, pale, and frayed as the man who stood before him. Gaylord Ravenal's jangling nerves ached for the solace of tobacco; but he viewed this palpably second-hand gift with a glance of disdain that was a triumph of the spirit over the flesh. Certainly no man handicapped by his present sartorial and social deficiencies was justified in raising a quizzical right eyebrow in the manner employed by Ravenal.

"What did you call it?" said he now.

Vallon looked at it. He was not a quick-witted gentleman. " Cigar."

"Optimist." And strolled out of the chief's office, swinging the little malacca cane.

So then, you now saw him leaning moodily against a wooden case on the New Orleans plank wharf, distinguished, shabby, dapper, handsome, broke, and twentyfour.

It was with some amusement that he had watched the crew of the *Mollie Able* bring the flat unwieldy bulk of the *Cotton Blossom* into the wharfside in the midst of the confusion of packets, barges, steamboats, tugs, flats, tramp boats, shanty boats. He had spoken briefly and casually to Schultzy while that bearer of evil tidings, letter in hand, waited impatiently on the dock as the *Cotton Blossom* was shifted to a landing position farther up-stream. He had seen these floating theatres of the Mississippi and the Ohio many times, but he had never before engaged one of their actors in con-versation.

"Juvenile lead!" he had exclaimed, unable to hide something of incredulity in his voice. Schultzy, an anxious eye on the *Mollie Able's* tedious man-oeuvres, had just made clear to Ravenal his own position in the *Cotton Blossom* troupe. Ravenal, surveying the furrowed brow, the unshaven cheeks, the careless dress, the lack-lustre eye, had involuntarily allowed to creep into his tone something of the astonishment he felt.

Schultzy made a little deprecating gesture with his hands, his shoulders. "I guess I don't look like no juvenile lead, and that's a fact. But I'm all shot to pieces. Took a drink the size of this"—indicating perhaps five fingers—"up yonder on Canal Street; straight whisky. No drinking allowed on the show boat. Well, sir, never felt it no more'n it had been water. just got news my wife's sick in the hospital."

Ravenal made a little perfunctory sound of sympathy. "In New Orleans?"

"Little Rock, Arkansas. I'm going. It's a dirty trick, but I'm going."

"How do you mean, dirty trick?" Ravenal was mildly interested in this confiding stranger.

"Leave the show flat like that. I don't know what they'll do. I————" He saw that the *Cotton Blossom* was now snugly at ease in her new position, and that her gangplank had again been lowered. He turned away abruptly, without a good-bye, went perhaps ten paces, came back five and called to Ravenal. "You ever acted?"

"Acted!"

"On the stage. Acted. Been an actor."

Ravenal threw back his handsome head and laughed as he would have thought, ten minutes ago, he never could laugh again. "Me! An actor! N—" then, suddenly sober, thoughtful even—"Why, yes. Yes." And eyeing Schultzy through half-shut lids he tapped the tip of his shiny shabby boot with the smart little malacca cane. Schultzy was off again toward the *Cotton Blossom*.

If Ravenal was aware of the scrutiny to which he was subjected through the binoculars, he gave no sign as he lounged elegantly on the wharf watching the busy waterside scene with an air of indulgent amusement that would have made the onlooker receive with incredulity the information that the law was even then snapping at his heels.

Captain Andy Hawks scampered off the *Cotton Blossom* and approached this figure, employing none of the finesse that the situation called for.

"I understand you've acted on the stage."

Gaylord Ravenal elevated the right eyebrow and looked down his aris-tocratic nose at the rapering little captain. "I am Gaylord Ravenal, of the Tennessee Ravenals. I failed to catch your name."

"Andy Hawks, captain and owner of the Cotton Blossom Floating Palace Theatre." He jerked a thumb over his shoulder at the show boat.

"Ah, yes," said Ravenal, with polite unenthusiasm. He allowed his pa-trician glance to rest idly a moment on the *Cotton Blossom,* lying squat and dumpy alongside the landing.

Captain Andy found himself suddenly regretting that he had not had her painted and overhauled. He clutched his whiskers in embarrassment, and, under stress of that same emotion, blurted the wrong thing. "I guess Parthy was mistaken." The Ravenal eyebrow became interrogatory. Andy floun-dered on. "She said that no man with a crack in the shoe————" he stopped, then, appalled.

Gaylord Ravenal looked down at the footgear under discussion. He looked up at the grim and ponderous female figure on the forward deck of the show boat. Parthy was wearing one of her most uncompromising bonnets and a gown noticeably bunchy even in that day of unsymmetrical feminine fashions. Black was not becoming to Mrs. Hawks' sallow colouring. Lumpy black was fatal. If anything could have made this figure less attractive than it actually was, Ravenal's glance would seem to have done so. "That—ah—lady ?"

"My wife," said Andy. Then, mindful of the maxim of the sheep and the lamb, he went the whole way. "We've lost our juvenile lead. Fifteen a week and found. Chance to see the world. No responsibility. Schultzy said you said . . . I said . . . Parthy said . . ." Hopelessly entangled, he stopped.

"Am I to understand that I am being offered the position of—ah—juvenile lead on the—" the devastating glance upward—"Cotton Blossom Floating Palace————"

"That's the size of it," interrupted Andy, briskly. After all, even this young man's tone and manner could not quite dispel that crack in the boot. Andy knew that no one wears a split shoe from choice.

"No responsibility," he repeated. "A chance to see life."

"I've seen it," in the tone of one who did not care for what he has beheld. His eyes were on a line with the *Cotton Blossom's* deck. His gaze suddenly became concentrated. A tall slim figure in white had just appeared on the upper deck, forward—the bit of deck that looked for all the world like a nautical veranda. It led off Magnolia's bedroom. The slim white figure was Magnolia. Prepatory to going ashore she was taking a look at this romantic city which she always had loved, and which she, in company with Andy or Doc, had roamed a dozen times since her first early childhood trip on the *Creole Belle*.

Her dress was bunchy, too, as the mode demanded. But where it was not bunchy it was very tight. And its bunchiness thus only served to emphasize the slimness of the snug areas. Her black hair was drawn smoothly away from the temples and into a waterfall at the back. Her long fine head and throat rose exquisitely above the little pleated frill that finished the neckline of her gown She carried her absurd beribboned and beflowered high—crowned hat in her hand. A graceful, pliant, slim young figure in white, surveying the pandemonium that was the New Orleans levee. Columns of black rose from a hundred steamer stacks. Freight barrels and boxes went hurtling through the air, or were shoved or carried across the plank wharf to the accompaniment of shouting and sweating and swearing. Negroes everywhere. Band boxes, carpet bags, babies, drays, carriages, wheelbarrows, carts. Beyond the levee rose the old salt warehouses. Beyond these lay Canal Street. Magnolia was going into town with her father and her mother. Andy had promised her supper at Antoine's and an evening at the old French theatre. She knew scarcely ten words of French. Andy, if he had known it in his childhood, had quite forgotten it now. Parthy looked upon it as the language of sin and the yellowback paper novels. But all three found enjoyment in the grace and colour and brilliance of the performance and the audience—both of a sort to be found nowhere else in the whole country. Andy's enjoyment was tinged and heightened by a vague nostalgia; Magnolia's was that of one artist for the work of another; Parthy's was the enjoyment of suspicion. She always hoped the play's high scenes were going to be more risqué than they actually were.

From her vantage point Magnolia stood glancing alertly about her, enjoying the babel that was the New Orleans plank wharves. She now espied and recognized the familiarly capering little figure below with its right hand scratching the mutton-chop whiskers this side and that. She was impatient to be starting for their jaunt ashore. She waved at him with the hand that held the hat. The upraised arm served to enhance the delicate curve of the pliant young figure in its sheath of white.

Andy, catching sight of her, waved in return.

"Is that," inquired Gaylord Ravenal, "a member of your company?"

Andy's ace softened and glowed. "That? That's my daughter Magnolia."

"Magnolia. Magnol—- Does she is she a————"

"I should smile she is! She's our ingénue lead, Magnolia is. Plays opposite the juvenile lead. But if you've been a trouper you know that, I guess." A sudden suspicion darted through him. "Say, young man —what's your name?—oh, yes, Ravenal. Well, Ravenal, you a quick study? That's what I got to know, first off. Because we leave New Orleans tonight to play the bayous. Bayou Teche to-morrow night in Tempest and Sunshine. . . . You a quick study?"

"Lightning," said Gaylord Ravenal.

Five minutes later, bowing over her hand, he did not know whether to curse the crack in his shoe for shaming him before her, or to bless it for having been the cause of his being where he was.

That he and Magnolia should become lovers was as inevitable as the cosmic course. Certainly some force greater than human must have been at work on it, for it overcame even Parthy's opposition. Everything conspired to bring the two together, including their being kept forcibly apart. Himself a picturesque, mysterious, and romantic figure, Gaylord Ravenal, immediately after joining the *Cotton Blossom* troupe, became the centre of a series of dramatic episodes any one of which would have made him glamorous in Magnolia's eyes, even though he had not already assumed for her the glory of a Galahad.

She had never before met a man of Ravenal's stamp. In this dingy motley company he moved aloof, remote, yet irresistibly attracting all of them—except Parthy. She, too, must have felt drawn to this charming and magnetic man, but she fought the attraction with all the strength of her powerful and vindictive nature. Sensing that here lay his bitterest opposition, Ravenal deliberately set about exercising his charm to win Parthy to friendliness. For the first time in his life he received rebuff so bristling, so unmistakable, as to cause him temporarily to doubt his own gifts.

Women had always adored Gaylord Ravenal. He was not a villain. He was, in fact, rather gentle, and more than a little weak. His method, coupled with strong personal attractiveness, was simple in the extreme. He made love to all women and demanded nothing of them. Swept off their feet, they waited, trembling deliciously, for the final attack. At its failure to materialize they looked up, wondering, to see his handsome face made more handsome by a certain wistful sadness. At that their hearts melted within them. That which they had meant to defend they now offered. For the rest, his was a paradoxical nature. A courtliness of manner, contradicted by a bluff boyishness. A certain shy boldness. He was not an especially intelligent man. He had no need to be. His upturned glance at a dining-room waitress bent over him was in no way different from that which he directed straight at Parthy now; or at the daughter of a prosperous Southern lawyer, or at that daughter's vaguely uneasy mama. It wasn't deliberate evil in him or lack of fastidiousness. He was helpless to do otherwise.

Certainly he had never meant to remain a member of this motley troupe, drifting up and down the rivers. He had not, for that matter, meant to fall in love with Magnolia, much less marry her. Propinquity and opposition, either of which usually is sufficient to fan the flame, together caused the final conflagration. For weeks after he came on board, he literally never spoke to Magnolia alone. Parthy attended to that. He saw her not only daily but almost hourly. He considered himself lucky to be deft enough to say, "Lovely day, isn't it, Miss Magn———" before Mrs. Hawks swept her offspring out of earshot. Parthy was wise enough to see that this handsome, graceful, insidious young stranger would appear desirable and romantic in the eyes or women a hundredfold more sophisticated than the child-like and unawakened Magnolia. She took refuge in the knowledge that this dangerous male was the most impermanent of additions to the *Cotton Blossom* His connection with them would end on Schultzy s return.

Gaylord Ravenal was, in the meantime, a vastly amused and prodigiously busy young man. To learn the juvenile leads in the plays that made up the *Cotton Blossom* troupe's repertoire was no light matter. Not only must he memorize lines, business, and cues of the regular bills—Uncle Tom's Cabin, East Lynne, Tempest and Sunshine, Lady Audley's Secret, The Parson's Bride, The Gambler, and others— but he must be ready to go on in the concert afterpiece, whatever it might be —sometimes A Dollar for a Kiss, sometimes Red Hot Coffee. The company rehearsed day and night; during the day they rehearsed that night's play; after the performance they rehearsed next night's bill. With some astonishment the Cotton Blossom troupe realized, at the end of two weeks, that Gaylord Ravenal was acting as director. It had come about naturally and inevitably. Ravenal had a definite theatre sense—a feeling for tempo, rhythm, line, grouping, inflection, characterization—any, or all, of these. The atmosphere had freshness for him; he was interested; he wished to impress Andy and Parthy and Magnolia; he considered the whole business a gay adventure; and an amusing interlude. For a month they played the bayous and plantations of Louisiana, leaving behind them a whole countryside whose planters, villagers, Negroes had been startled out of their Southern lethargy. These had known show boats and show-boat performances all their lives. They had been visited by this or that raffish, dingy, slap-dash, or decent and painstaking troupe. The *Cotton Blossom* company had the reputation for being the last-named variety, and always were patronized accordingly. The plays seldom varied. The performance was, usually, less than mediocre. They were, then, quite unprepared for the entertainment given them by the two handsome, passionate, and dramatic young people who now were cast as ingénue and juvenile lead of the Cotton Blossom Floating Palace Theatre company. Here was Gaylord Ravenal, fresh, young, personable, aristocratic, romantic of aspect. Here was Magnolia, slim, girlish, ardent, electric, lovely. Their make-believe adventures as they lived them on the stage became real; their dangers and misfortunes set the natives to trembling; their love-making was a fragrant and exquisite thing. News of this troupe seeped through from plantation to plantation, from bayou to bayou, from settlement to settlement, in some mysterious underground way. The *Cotton Blossom* did a record-breaking business in a region that had never been markedly profitable. Andy was jubilant, Parthy apprehensive, Magnolia starry-eyed, tremulous, glowing. Her lips seemed to take on a riper curve. Her skin was, somehow, softly radiant as though lighted by an inner glow, as Julie's amber colouring, in the years gone by, had seemed to deepen into golden brilliance. Her eyes were enormous, luminous. The gangling, hobbledehoy, sallow girl of seventeen was a woman of eighteen, lovely, and in love.

Back again in New Orleans there was a letter from Schultzy, a pathetic scrawl; illiterate; loyal. Elly was out of the hospital, but weak and helpless. He had a job, temporarily, whose nature he did not indicate. ("Porter in a Little Rock saloon, I'll be bound," ventured Parthy, shrewdly, "rubbing up the brass and the cuspidors.'') He had met a man who ran a rag-front carnival company. He could use them for one attraction called The Old Plantation; or, The South Before the War. They were booked through the Middle West. In a few weeks, if Elly was stronger . . .

He said nothing about money. He said nothing of their possible return to the Cotton Blossom. That, Andy knew, was because of Elly. Unknown to Parth, he sent Schultzy two hundred dollars. Schultzy never returned to the rivers. It was, after all, oddly enough. Elly who, many many years later, completed the circle which brought her again to the show boat.

Together, Andy, Parthy, and Doc went into consultation. They must keep Ravenal. But Ravenal obviously was not of the stuff of show-boat actors. He had made it plain, when first he came aboard, that he was the most impermanent of troupers; that his connection with the *Cotton Blossom* would continue, at the latest, only until Schultzy's return. He meant to leave them, not at New Orleans, as they had at first feared, but at Natchez, on the up trip.

"Don't tell him Schultzy ain't coming back," Doc offered, brilliantly.

"Have to know it some time," was Andy's obvious reply.

"Person'd think," said Parthy, "he was the only juvenile lead left in the world. Matter of fact, I can't see where he's such great shakes of an actor. Rolls those eyes of his a good deal, and talks deep-voiced, but he's got hands white's a woman's and fusses with his nails. I'll wager if you ask around in New Orleans you'll find something queer, for all he talks so high about being a Ravenal of Tennessee and his folks governors in the old days, and slabs about 'em in the church, and what not. Shifty, that's what he is. Mark my words."

"Best juvenile lead ever played the rivers. And I never heard that having clean finger nails hurt an actor any."

"Oh, it isn't just clean finger nails," snapped Parthy. "It's everything."

"Wouldn't hold that against him, either," roared Doc. The two men then infuriated the humourless Mrs. Hawks by indulging in a great deal of guffawing and knee-slapping.

"That's right, Hawks. Laugh at your own wife. And you, too, Doc."

"You ain't my wife," retorted Doc, with the privilege of sixty-odd. And roared again.

The gossamer thread that leashed Parthy's temper dissolved now. "I can't bear the sight of him. Palavering and soft-soaping. Thinks he can get round a woman my age. Well, I'm worth a dozen of him when it comes to smart." She leaned closer to Andy, her face actually drawn with fear and a sort of jealousy. "He looks at Magnolia, I tell you."

"A fool if he didn't."

"Andy Hawks, you mean to tell me you'd sit there and see your own daughter married to a worthless tramp of a wharf rat, or worse, that hadn't a shirt to his back when you picked him up!"

"Oh, God A'mighty, woman, can't a man look at a girl without having to marry her!"

"*Having* to marry her, Captain Hawks! *having*—— Well, what can a body expect when her own husband talks like that, and before strangers, too. Having——!"

Doc rubbed his leathery chin a trifle ruefully.

"Stretching a point, Mrs. Hawks, ma'am, calling me a stranger, ain't you?"

"All right. Keep him with the show, you two. Who warned you about that yellow-skinned Julie! And what happened! If sheriffs is what you want, I'll wager you could get them fast enough if you spoke his name in certain parts of this country. Wait till we get back to New Orleans. I intend to do some asking around, and so does Frank.''

"What's Frank got to do with it?''

But at this final exhibition of male obtuseness Parthy flounced out of the conference.

On their return from the bayous the *Cotton Blossom* lay idle a day at the New Orleans landing. Early on the morning of their arrival Gaylord Ravenal went ashore. On his stepping off the gangplank he spoke briefly to that same gimlet-eyed gentleman who was still loitering on the wharf. To the observer, the greeting between them seemed amiable enough.

"Back again, Gay!" he of the keen gaze had exclaimed. "Seems like you can't keep away from the scene of the————''

"Oh, go to hell,'' said Ravenal.

He returned to the *Cotton Blossom* at three o'clock. At his appearance the idler who had accosted him (and who was still mysteriously lolling at the waterside) shut his eyes and then opened them quickly as though to dispel a vision.

"Cripes, Ravenal! Robbed a bank?''

From the tip of his shining shoes to the top of his pale gray hat, Ravenal was sartorial perfection, nothing less. The boots were hand-made, slim, aristocratic. The cloth of his clothes was patently out of England, and tailored for no casual purchaser, but for Ravenal's figure alone. The trousers tapered elegantly to the instep. The collar was moulded expertly so that it hugged the neck. The linen was of the finest and whitest, and cunning needlecraft had gone into the embroidering of the austere monogram that almost escaped showing in one corner of the handkerchief that peeped above his left breast pocket. The malacca stick seemed to take on a new lustre and richness now that it found itself once more in fitting company. With the earnings of his first two weeks on the *Cotton Blossom* enclosed as evidence of good faith, and future payment assured, Gaylord Ravenal had sent by mail from the Louisiana bayous to Plumbridge, the only English tailor in New Orleans, the order which had resulted in his present splendour.

He now paused a moment to relieve himself of that which had long annoyed him in the beady-eyed one. "Listen to me, Flat Foot. The *Cotton Blossom* dropped anchor at seven o'clock this morning at the New Orleans dock. I came ashore at nine. It is now three. I am free to stay on shore or not, as I like, until nine to-morrow morning. Until then, if I hear any more of your offensive conversation, I shall have to punish you.''

Flat Foot, thus objurgated, stared at Ravenal with an expression in which amazement and admiration fought for supremacy. "By God, Ravenal, with any luck at all, that gall of yours ought to get you a million some day.''

"I wouldn't be bothered with any sum so vulgar.'' From an inside pocket he drew a perfecto, long, dark, sappy. "Have a smoke.'' He drew out another. "And give this to Vallon when you go back to report. Tell him I wanted him to know the flavour of a decent cigar for once in his life.''

As he crossed the gangplank he encountered Mrs. Hawks and Frank, the lumbering heavy, evidently shore-bound together. He stepped aside with a courtliness that the Ravenals of Tennessee could not have excelled in the days of swords, satins, and periwigs.

Mrs. Hawks was, after all, a woman; and no woman could look unmoved upon the figure of cool elegance that now stood before her. "Sakes alive!'' she said, inadequately. Frank, whose costumes, ashore or afloat, always were négligée to the point of causing the beholder some actual nervousness, attempted to sneer without the aid of makeup and made a failure of it.

Ravenal now addressed Mrs. Hawks. "You are not staying long ashore, I hope?"

"And why not?" inquired Mrs. Hawks, with her usual delicacy.

"I had hoped that perhaps you and Captain Hawks and Miss Magnolia might do me the honour of dining with me ashore and going to the theatre afterward. I know a little restaurant where—"

"Likely," retorted Parthy, by way of polite refusal; and moved majestically down the gangplank, followed by the gratified heavy.

Ravenal continued thoughtfully on his way. Captain Andy was in the box office just off the little forward deck that served as an entrance to the show boat. With him was Magnolia—Magnolia minus her mother's protecting wings. After all, even Parthy had not the power to be in more than one place at a time. At this moment she was deep in conversation with Flat Foot on the wharf.

Magnolia was evidently dressed for a festive occasion. The skirt of her light écru silk dress was a polonaise draped over a cream-white surah silk, and the front of the tight bodice-basque was of the same cream-white stuff. Her round hat of Milan straw, with its modishly high crown, had an artful brim that shaded her fine eyes, and this brim was faced with deep rose velvet, and a bow of deep rose flared high against the crown. The black of her hair was all the blacker for this vivid colour. An écru parasol and long suede gloves completed the costume. She might have stepped out of *Harper's Bazaar*—in fact, she had. The dress was a faithful copy of a costume which she had considered particularly fetching as she pored over the pages of that book of fashion.

Andy was busy at his desk. Ranged in rows on that desk were canvas sacks, plump, squat; canvas sacks limp, lop-sided; canvas sacks which, when lifted and set down again, gave forth a pleasant clinking sound. Piled high in front of these were neat packets of greenbacks, ones and ones and ones, in bundles of fifty, each bound with a tidy belt of white paper pinned about its middle. Forming a kind of Chinese wall around these were stacked half dollars, quarters, dimes, and nickels, with now and then a campanile of silver dollars. In the midst of this Andy resembled an amiable and highly solvent gnome stepped out of a Grimm's fairy tale. The bayou trip had been a record-breaking one in point of profit.

". . . And fifty's six hundred and fifty," Andy was crooning happily, as he jotted figures down on a sheet of yellow lined paper, ". . . and fifty's seven hundred, and twenty-five's seven hundred twenty-five and twenty-five's . . ."

"Oh, Papa!" Magnolia exclaimed impatiently, and turned toward the little window through which one saw New Orleans lying so invitingly in the protecting arms of the levee. "It's almost four, and you haven't even changed your clothes, and you keep counting that old money, and Mama's gone on some horrid business with that sneaky Frank. I know it's horrid because she looked so pleased. And you promised me. We won't see New Orleans again for a whole year. You said you'd get a carriage and two horses and we'd drive out to Lake Pontchartrain, and have dinner, and drive back, and go to the theatre, and now it's almost four and you haven't even changed your clothes and you keep counting that old money, and Mama's————"

After all, in certain ways, Magnolia the ingénue lead had not changed much from that child who had promptly had hysterics to gain her own ends that day in Thebes many years before.

"Minute," Andy muttered, absently. "Can't leave this money laying around like buttons, can I? Germania National's letting me in the side door as a special favour after hours, as 'tis, just so's I can deposit. . . . And fifty's eight-fifty, and fifty's nine . . ."

"I don't *care!*" cried Magnolia, and stamped her foot. "It's downright mean of you, Papa. You promised. And I'm all dressed. And you haven't even changed your————"

"Oh, God A'mighty, Nollie, you ain't going to turn out an unreasonable woman like your ma, are you! Here I sit, slaving away————"

"Oh! How beautiful you look!" exclaimed Magnolia now, to Andy's bewilderment. He looked up at her. Her gaze was directed over his head at someone standing in the doorway. Andy creaked hastily around in the ancient swivel chair. Ravenal, of course, in the doorway. Andy pursed his lips in the sky-rocket whistle, starting high and ending low, expressive of surprise and admiration.

"How beautiful you look!" said Magnolia again; and clasped her hands like a child.

"And you, Miss Magnolia," said Ravenal; and advanced into the cubby hole that was the office, and took one of Magnolia's surprised hands delicately in his, and bent over it, and kissed it. Magnolia was an excellent enough actress, and sufficiently the daughter of the gallant and Gallic Andy, to acknowledge this salute with a little gracious inclination of the head, and no apparent surprise whatever. Andy himself showed nothing of astonishment at the sight of this suave and elegant figure bent over his daughter's hand. He looked rather pleased than otherwise. But suddenly then the look on his face changed to one of alarm. He jumped to his feet. He scratched the mutton-chop whiskers, sure evidence of perturbation.

"Look here, Ravenal! That ain't a sign you're leaving, is it? Those clothes, and now kissing Nollie's hand. God A'mighty, Ravenal, you ain't leaving us!"

Ravenal flicked an imaginary bit of dust from the cuff of his flawless sleeve. "These are my ordinary clothes, Captain Hawks, sir. I mean to say, I usually am attired as you now see me. When first we met I was in temporary difficulties. The sort of thing that can happen to any gentleman."

"Certainly can," Andy agreed, heartily and hastily. "Sure can. Well, you gave me a turn. I thought you come in to give me notice. And while we're on it, you're foolish to quit at Natchez like you said, Ravenal. don't know what you been doing, but you're cut out for a show-boat actor, and that's the truth. Stick with us and I'll raise you to twenty—" as Ravenal shook his head—"twenty-five" again the shake of the head-"thirty! And, God A'mighty, they ain't a juvenile lead on the rivers ever got anywheres near that."

Ravenal held up one white shapely hand. "Let's not talk money now, Captain. Though if you would care to advance me a fifty, I . . . Thanks I was going to say I came in to ask if you and Mrs. Hawks and Miss Magnolia here would do me the honour to dine with me ashore this evening, and go to the theatre. I know a little French restaurant . . ."

"Papa!" She swooped down upon little Andy then, enveloping him in her ruffles, in her surah silk, her rose velvet, her perfume. Her arms were about his neck. Her fresh young cheek pressed the top of his grizzled head. Her eyes were enormous—and they looked into Ravenal's eyes. "Papa!"

But years of contact with the prim Parthy had taught him caution. "Your ma————" he began, feebly.

Magnolia deserted him, flew to Ravenal, clutched his am. Her lovely eyes held tears. Involuntarily his free hand covered her hand that clung so appealingly to his sleeve. "He promised me. And now because he's got all that money to count because Doc was delayed at Baton Rouge and didn't meet us here like he expected he would this afternoon and Mama's gone ashore and we were to drive to Lake Pontchartrain and have dinner and he hasn't even changed his clothes and it's almost four o'clock—probably is four by now—and he keeps counting that old money———''

"Magnolia!" shouted Andy in a French frenzy, clutching the whiskers as though to raise himself by them from the floor.

Magnolia must have been enjoying the situation. Here were two men, both of whom adored her, and she them. She therefore set about testing their love. Her expression became tragic—but not so tragic as to mar her delightful appearance. To the one who loved her most deeply and unselfishly she said:

"You don't care anything about me or my happiness. It's all this old boat, and business, and money. Haven't I worked, night after night, year in, year out! And now, when I have a chance to enjoy myself—it isn't as if you hadn't promised me—''

"We're going, I tell you, Nollie. But your ma isn't even here. And how did I know Doc was going to be stuck at Baton Rouge! We got plenty of time to have dinner ashore and go to the theatre, but we'll have to give up the drive to Pontchartrain———''

A heartbroken wail from Magnolia. Her great dark eyes turned in appeal to Ravenal. "It's the drive I like better than anything in the world. And horses. I'm crazy about horses, and I don't get a chance to drive—oh, well—'' at an objection from Andy— "sometimes but what kind of horses do they have in those little towns! And here you can get a splendid pair, all shiny, and their nostrils working, and a victoria and lovely long tails and a clanky harness and fawn cushions and the lake and soft-shell crabs———'' She was becoming incoherent, but remained as lovely as ever, and grew more appealing by the moment.

Ravenal resisted a mad urge to take her in his arms. He addressed himself earnestly to the agonized Andy. "If you will trust me, Captain Hawks, I have a plan which I have just thought of. I know New Orleans very well and I am—uh—very well known in New Orleans. Miss Magnolia has set her heart on this little holiday. I know where I can get a splendid turnout, Chestnuts—very high steppers, but quite safe.'' An unadult squeal of delight from Magnolia. "If we start immediately, we can enjoy quite a drive—Miss Magnolia and I. If you like, we can take Mrs. Means with us, or Mrs. Soaper———''

"No," from the brazen beauty.

"—and return in time to meet you and Mrs. Hawks at, say, Antoine's for dinner.''

"Oh, Papa!" cried Magnolia now. "Oh, Papa!"

"Your ma———'' began Andy again, feebly. The stacks and piles still lay uncounted on the desk. This thing must be settled somehow. He scuttled to the window, scanned the wharf, the streets that led up from it. "I don't know where she's got to.'' He turned from the window to survey the pair, helplessly. Something about them—the very fitness of their standing there together, so young, so beautiful, so eager, so alive, so vibrant—melted the romantic heart within him. Magnolia in her holiday garb; Ravenal in his tailored perfection. "Oh, well, I don't see how it'll hurt any. Your ma and I will meet you at Antoine's at, say, half-past six———''

They were off. It was as if they had been lifted bodily and blown together out of the little office, across the gangplank to the landing. Flat Foot stared after them almost benignly.

Andy returned to his desk. Resumed his contented crooning. Four o'clock struck. Half-past four. His pencil beat a rat-a-tat-tat as he jotted down the splendid figures. A gold mine, this Ravenal. A fine figger of a boy. Cheap at thirty. Rat-a-tat-tat. And fifty's one thousand. And twenty-five's one thousand twenty-five. And fifty's—and fifty's—twelve twenty-five— gosh a'mighty!——

A shriek. A bouncing across the gangplank and into the cubby hole just as Andy was rounding, happily, into thirteen hundred. A hand clutching his shoulder frantically, whirling him bodily out of the creaking swivel chair. Parthy, hat awry, bosom palpitating, eyes starting, mouth working.

"On Canal Street!" she wheezed. It was as though the shriek she had intended were choked in her throat by the very force of the feeling behind it, so that it emerged a strangled thing. "Canal Street! The two of them . . . with my own eyes . . . driving . . . in a . . . in a——"

She sank into a chair. There seemed to be no pretense about this. Andy, for once, was alarmed. The tall shambling figure of Frank the heavy assed the little ticket window, blocked the low doorway. He stared, open-mouthed, at the almost recumbent Parthy He was breathing heavily and looked aggrieved.

"She ran away from me," he said. "Sees 'em in the crowd, driving, and tries to run after the carriage on Canal, with everybody thinking she's gone loony. Then she runs down here to the landing, me after her. Woman her age. What d'yah take me for, anyway!"

But Parthy did not hear him. He did not exist. Her face was ashen. "He's a murderer!" she now gasped.

Andy's patience, never too long-suffering, snapped under the strain of the afternoon's happenings. "What's wrong with you, woman! Have you gone clean crazy! Who's a murderer! Frank? Who's he murdered? For two cents I'd murder the both of you, come howling in here when a man's trying to run his business *like* a business and not like a yowling insane asylum——"

Parthy stood up, shaking. Her voice was high and quavering. "Listen to me, you fool. I talked to the man on the docks—the one he was talking to— and he wouldn't tell me anything and he said I could ask the chief of police if I wanted to know about anybody, and I went to the chief of police, and a perfect gentleman if there ever was one, and he's killed a man."

"The chief of police! Killed a man! What man!" killed a man."

"God A'mighty, when!" He started as though to rescue Magnolia. A year ago. A year ago, in this very town." The shock of relief was too much for Andy He was furious. "They didn't hang him for it, did they?"

"Hang who?" asked Parthy, feebly.

"Who! Ravenal! They didn't hang him?"

"Why, no, they let him go. He said he shot him in self——"

"He killed a man and they let him go. What does that prove? He'd a right to. All right. What of it!"

"What of it! Your own daughter is out driving in an open carriage this minute with a murderer, that's what, Andy Hawks. I saw them with my own eyes. There I was, out trying to protect her from contamination by finding out . . . and I saw her the minute my back was turned . . . your doings your own daughter driving in the open streets in an open carriage with a murderer——"

"Oh, open murderer be damned!" squeaked Andy in his falsetto of utter rage. "I killed a man when I was nineteen, Mrs. Hawks, ma'am, and I've been twenty-five years and more as respected a man as there is on the rivers, and that's the truth if you want to talk about mur——"

But Parthenia Ann Hawks, for the first time in her vigorous life, had fainted.

10

GAYLORD RAVENAL HAD had not meant to fall in love. Certainly he had not dreamed of marrying. He was not, he would have told you, a marrying man. Yet Natchez had come and gone, and here he was, still playing juvenile leads on the *Cotton Blossom;* still planning, days ahead for an opportunity to outwit Mrs. Hawks and see Magnolia alone. He was thoroughly and devastatingly in love. Alternately he pranced and cringed. To-day he would leave this dingy scow. What was he, Gaylord Ravenal, doing aboard a show boat, play-acting for a miserable thirty dollars a week! He who had won (and lost) a thousand a night at poker or faro. Tomorrow he was resolved to give up gambling for ever; to make himself worthy of this lovely creature; to make himself indispensable to Andy; to find the weak chink in Parthy's armour.

He had met all sorts of women in his twenty-four years. He had loved some of them, and many of them had loved him. He had never met a woman like Magnolia. She was a paradoxical product of the life she had led. The contact with the curious and unconventional characters that made up the *Cotton Blossom* troupe; the sights and sounds of river life, sordid, romantic, homely, Rabelaisian, tragic, humorous; the tolerant and meaty wisdom imbibed from her sprightly little father; the spirit of *laissez faire* that pervaded the whole atmosphere about her, had given her a flavour, a mellowness, a camaraderie found usually only in women twice her age and a hundredfold more experienced. Weaving in and out of this was an engaging primness directly traceable to Parthy. She had, too, a certain dignity that was, perhaps, the result of years of being deferred to as the daughter of a river captain. Sometimes she looked at Ravenal with the wide-eyed gaze of a child. At such times he wished that he might leap into the Mississippi (though muddy) and wash himself clean of his sins as did the pilgrims in the River Jordan.

On that day following Parthy's excursion ashore at New Orleans there had been between her and Captain Andy a struggle, brief and bitter, from which Andy had emerged battered but victorious.

"That murdering gambler goes or I go," Parthy had announced, rashly. It was one of those pronunciamentos that can only bring embarrassment to one who utters it.

"He stays." Andy was iron for once.

He stayed. So did Parthy, of course.

You saw the two—Parthy and Ravenal—eyeing each other, backs to the wall, waiting for a chance to lunge and thrust.

Cotton Blossom business was booming. News of the show boat's ingénue and juvenile lead filtered up and down the rivers. During the more romantic scenes of this or that play Parthy invariably stationed herself in the wings and glowered and made muttering sounds to which the two on stage—Magnolia starry-eyed as the heroine, Ravenal ardent and passionate as the lover— were oblivious. It was their only opportunity to express to each other what they actually felt. It probably was, too, the most public and convincing lovemaking that ever graced the stage of this or any other theatre.

Ravenal made himself useful in many ways. He took in hand, for example, the *Cotton Blossom's* battered scenery. It was customary on all show boats to use both sides of a set. One canvas side would represent, perhaps, a drawing room. Its reverse would show the greens and browns of leaves and tree trunks in a forest scene. Both economy and lack of stage space were responsible for this. Painted by a clumsy and unimaginative hand, each leaf daubed as a leaf, each inch of wainscoting drawn to scale, the effect of any *Cotton Blossom* set, when viewed from the other side of the footlights, was unconvincing even to rural and inexperienced eyes. Ravenal set to work with paint and brush and evolved two sets of double scenery which brought forth shrieks of ridicule and protest from the company grouped about the stage.

"It isn't supposed to look like a forest," Ravenal explained, slapping on the green paint with a lavish hand. "It's supposed to give the effect of a forest. The audience isn't going to sit on the stage, is it? Well, then! Here— this is to be a gate. Well, there's no use trying to paint a flat thing with slats that nobody will ever believe looks like a gate. I'll just do this . . . and this . . ."

"It does!" cried Magnolia from the middle of the house where she had stationed herself, head held critically on one side. "It does make you think there's a gate there, without its actually being . . . Look, Papa! . . . And the trees. All those lumpy green spots we used to have somehow never looked like leaves."

All unconsciously Ravenal was using in that day, and in that crude milieu, a method which was to make a certain Bobby Jones famous in the New York theatre of a quarter of a century later.

"Where did you learn to———" some one of the troupe would marvel; Magnolia, perhaps, or Mis' Means, or Ralph.

"Paris," Ravenal would reply, briefly. Yet he had never spoken of Paris. He often referred thus casually to a mysterious past.

"Paris fiddlesticks!" rapped out Parthy, promptly. "No more Paris than he's a Ravenal of Tennessee, or whatever rascally highfalutin story he's made up for himself."

Whereupon, when they were playing Tennessee, weeks later, he strolled one day with Magnolia and Andy into the old vine-covered church of the village, its churchyard fragrant and mysterious with magnolia and ilex; its doorstep worn, its pillars sagging. And there, in a glass case, together with a tattered leather-bound Bible a century and a half old, you saw a time-yellowed document. The black of the ink strokes had, perhaps, taken on a tinge of gray, but the handwriting, clear and legible, met the eye.

WILL OF JEAN BAPTISTA RAVENAL.

I, Jean Baptista Ravenal, of this Province, being through the mercy of Almighty God of sound mind and memory do make, appoint, declare and ordain this and this only to be my last Will and Testament. It is my will that my sons have their estates delivered to them as they severally arrive at the age of twenty and one years, the eldest being Samuel, the second Jean, the third Gaylord.

I will that my slaves be kept to work on my lands that my estate be managed to the best advantage so as my sons may have as liberal an education as the profits thereof will afford. Let them be taught to read and write and be introduced into the practical part of Arithmetic not too hastily hurrying them to Latin and Grammar. To my sons, when they arrive at age I recommend the pursuit and study of some profession or business (I would wish one to ye Law, the other to Merchandise).

"The other?" cried Magnolia softly then, looking up very bright-eyed and flushed from the case over which she had been bending. "But the third? Gaylord? It doesn't say————"

"The black sheep. My great-grandfather. There always was a Gaylord. And he always was the black sheep. My grandfather, Gaylord Ravenal and my father Gaylord Ravenal, and————" he bowed.

"Black too, are you?" said Andy then, drily.

"As pitch."

Magnolia bent again to the book, her brow thoughtful, her lips forming the words and uttering them softly as she deciphered the quaint script.

> I give and bequeath unto my son Samuel the lands called Ashwood, which are situated, lying and being on the South Side of the Cumberland River, together with my other land on the North side of said River. . . .
>
> I give and bequeath unto my son Jean, to him and his heirs and assigns for ever a tract of land containing seven hundred and forty acres lying on Stumpy Sound . . . also another tract containing one thousand acres . . .
>
> I give and bequeath to my son Samuel four hunded and fifty acres lying above William Lowrie's plantation on the main branch of Old Town Creek . . .

Magnolia stood erect. Indignation blazed in her fine eyes. "But, Gaylord!" she said.

"Yes!" Certainly she had never before called him that.

"I mean this Gaylord. I mean the one who came after Samuel and Jean. Why isn't—why didn't————"

"Naughty boy," said Ravenal, with his charming smile.

She actually yearned toward him then. He could not have said anything more calculated to bind his enchantment for her. They swayed toward each other over the top of the little glass-encased relic. Andy coughed hastily. They swayed gently apart. They were as though mesmerized.

"Folks out here in the churchyard?" inquired Andy, briskly, to break the spell. "Ravenal kin?"

"Acres of 'em," Gaylord assured him, cheerfully. "Son of . . . and daughter of . . . and beloved father of. . . . For that matter, there's one just beside you."

Andy side-stepped hastily, with a little exclamation. He cast a somewhat fearful glance at the spot toward which Ravenal so carelessly pointed. A neat gray stone slab set in the wall. Andy peered at the lettering it bore; stooped a little. "Here—you read it, Nollie. You've got young eyes."

Her fresh young cheek so near the cold gray slab, she read in her lovely flexible voice:

> Here lies the body of M^{rs}. Suzanne Ravenal, wife of Jean Baptista Ravenal Esqr., one of his Majesty's Council and Surveyor General of the Lands of this Province, who departed this life Octr 19^t 1765. Aged 37 Years. After labouring ten of them under the severest Bodily afflictions brought on by Change of Climate, and tho' she went to her native land received no relief but returned and bore them with uncommon Resolution and Resignation to the last.

Magnolia rose, slowly, from the petals of her flounced skirt spread about her as she had stooped to read.

"Poor darling!" Her eyes were soft with pity. Again the two seemed to sway a little toward each other, as though blown by a gust of passion. And this time little Captain Andy turned his back and clattered down the aisle. When they emerged again into the sunshine they found him, a pixie figure, leaning pensively against the great black trunk of a live oak. He was smoking a pipe somewhat apologetically, as though he hoped the recumbent Ravenals would not find it objectionable.

"I guess," he remarked, as Magnolia and Ravenal came up to him, "I'll have to bring your ma over. She's partial to history, her having been a schoolma'am, and all."

Like the stage sets he so cleverly devised for the show boat, Gaylord Ravenal had a gift for painting about himself the scenery of romance. These settings, too, did not bear the test of too close scrutiny. But in a favourable light, and viewed from a distance, they were charmingly effective and convincing.

His sense of the dramatic did not confine itself to the stage. He was the juvenile lead, on or off. Audiences adored him. Mid-western village housewives, good mothers and helpmates for years, were, for days after seeing him as the heroic figure of some gore-and-glory drama, mysteriously silent and irritably waspish by turn. Disfavour was writ large on their faces as they viewed their good commonplace dull husbands across the midday table set with steaming vegetables and meat.

"Why'n't you shave once in a while middle of the week," they would snap, "'stead of coming to the table looking like a gorilla?"

Mild surprise on the part of the husband. "I shaved Sat'dy, like always."

"Lookit your hands!"

"Hands? . . . Say, Bella, what in time's got into you, anyway?"

"Nothing." A relapse into moody silence on the part of Bella.

Mrs. Hawks fought a good fight, but what chance had her maternal jealousy against youth and love and romance? For a week she would pour poison into Magnolia's unwilling ear. Only making a fool of you . . . probably walk off and leave the show any day . . . common gambler . . . look at his eyes . . . murderer and you know it . . . rather see you in your grave. . . .

Then, in one brief moment, Ravenal, by some act of courage or grace or sheer deviltry, would show Parthy that all her pains were for nothing.

That night, for example, when they were playing Kentucky Sue. Ravenal's part was what is known as a blue-shirt lead—the rough brave woodsman, with the uncouth speech and the heart of gold. Magnolia, naturally, was Sue. They were playing Gains Landing, always a tough town, often good for a fight. It was a capacity audience and a surprisingly well-behaved and attentive. Midway in the play's progress a drawling drunken voice from the middle of the house began a taunting and ridiculous chant whose burden was, "Is *'at* so!" After each thrilling speech; punctuating each flowery period, "Is *'at* so!" came the maddening and disrupting refrain. You had to step carefully at Gains Landing. The *Cotton Blossom* troupe knew that. One word at the wrong moment, and knives flashed, guns popped. Still, this could not go on.

"Don't mind him," Magnolia whispered fearfully to Ravenal. "He's drunk. He'll stop. Don't pay any attention."

The scene was theirs. They were approaching the big moment in the play when the brave Kentuckian renounces his love that Kentucky Sue may be happy with her villainous bridegroom-to-be (Frank, of course). Show-boat audiences up and down the rivers had known that play for years; had committed the speech word for word, through long familiarity. "Sue," it ran, "ef he loves yuh and you love him, go with him. Ef he h'ain't good to yuh, come back where there's honest hearts under homespun shirts. Back to Kaintucky and home!''

Thus the speech ran. But as they approached it the blurred and mocking voice from the middle of the house kept up its drawling skepticism. "Is *'at* so! Is *'at* so!''

"Damned drunken lout!'' said Ravenal under his breath, looking unutterable love meanwhile at the languishing Kentucky Sue.

"Oh, dear!'' said Magnolia, feeling Ravenal's muscles tightening under the blue shirt sleeves; seeing the telltale white ridge of mounting anger under the grease paint of his jaw line. "Do be careful.''

Ravenal stepped out of his part. He came down to the footlights. The house, restless and irritable, suddenly became quiet. He looked out over the faces of the audience. "See here, pardner, there's others here want to hear this, even if you don't.''

The voice subsided. There was a little desultory applause from the audience and some cries of, "That's right! Make him shut up.'' They refused to manhandle one of their own, but they ached to see someone else do it.

The play went on. The voice was silent. The time approached for the big speech of renunciation. It was here. "Sue, ef he loves yuh and you love him, go with him. Ef he———''

"Is *'at* so!'' drawled the amused voice, with an element of surprise in it now. "Is *'at* so!''

Ravenal cast Kentucky Sue from him. "Well, if you will have it,'' he threatened, grimly. He sprang over the footlights, down to the piano top, to the keyboard, to the piano stool, all in four swift strides, was up the aisle, had plucked the limp and sprawling figure out of his seat by the collar, clutched him then firmly by this collar hold and the seat of his pants, and was up the aisle again to the doorway, out of the door, across the gangplank, and into the darkness. He was down the aisle then in a moment, spatting his hands briskly as he came; was up on the piano stool, on to the piano keyboard, on the piano top, over the footlights, back in position. There he paused a moment, breathing fast. Nothing had been said. There had actually been no sound other than his footsteps and the discordant jangle of protest that the piano keyboard had emitted when he had stepped on its fingers. Now a little startled expression came into Ravenal's face.

"Let's see,'' he said, aloud. "Where was I———''

And as one man the audience chanted, happily, "Sue, ef he loves yuh and you love him———''

What weapon has a Parthenia against a man like that? And what chance a Frank?

Drama leaped to him. There was, less than a week later, the incident of the minister. He happened to be a rather dirty little minister in a forlorn little Kentucky river town. He ran a second-hand store on the side, was new to the region, and all unaware of the popularity and good-will enjoyed by the members of the *Cotton Blossom* troupe. To him an actor was a burning brand. Doc had placarded the little town with dodgers and handbills. There was one, especially effective even in that day of crude photography, showing Magnolia in the angelic part of the ingénue lead in Tempest and Sunshine. These might be seen displayed in the windows of such ramshackle stores as the town's river front street boasted. Gaylord Ravenal, strolling disdainfully up into the sordid village that was little more than a welter of mud and flies and mules and Negroes, stopped aghast as his eye chanced to fall upon the words scrawled beneath a picture of Magnolia amidst the dusty disorderly mélange of the ministerial second-hand window. There was the likeness of the woman he loved looking starry-eyed, out upon the passer-by. And beneath it, in the black, fanatic penmanship of the itinerant parson:

A Lost Soul

In his fine English clothes, swinging the slim malacca cane, Gaylord Ravenal, very narrow-eyed, entered the fusty shop and called to its owner to come forward. From the cobwebby gloom of the rear reaches emerged the merchant parson, a tall, shambling large-knuckled figure of the anaconda variety. You thought of Uriah Heep and of Ichabod Crane, experiencing meanwhile a sensation of distaste.

Ravenal, very elegant, very cool, very quiet, pointed with the tip of his cane. "Take that picture out of the window. Tear it up. Apologize."

"I won't do anything of the kind," retorted the holy man. "You're a this-and-that, and a such-and-such, and a so-and-so, and she's another, and the whole boatload of you ought to be sunk in the river you contaminate."

"Take off your coat," said Ravenal, divesting himself neatly of his own faultless garment as he spoke.

A yellow flame of fear leaped into the man's eyes. He edged toward the door. With a quick step Ravenal blocked his way. "Take it off before I rip it off. Or fight with your coat on."

"You touch a man of God and I'll put the law on you. The sheriff's office is just next door. I'll have you————"

Ravenal whirled him round, seized the collar of his grimy coat, peeled it dexterously off, revealing what was, perhaps, as maculate a shirt as ever defiled the human form. The Ravenal lip curled in disgust.

"If cleanliness is next to godliness," he remarked, swiftly turning back his own snowy cuffs meanwhile, "you'll be shovelling coal in hell." And swung. The minister was taller and heavier than this slight and dandified figure. But Ravenal had an adrenal advantage, being stimulated by the fury of his anger. The godly one lay, a soiled heap, among his soiled wares. The usual demands of the victor.

"Take that thing out of the window! . . . Apologize to me! . . . Apologize publicly for defaming a lady!"

The man crept groaning to the window, plucked the picture, with its offensive caption, from amongst the miscellany there, handed it to Ravenal in response to a gesture from him. "Now then, I think you're pretty badly bruised, but I doubt that anything's broken. I'm going next door to the sheriff. You will write a public apology in letters corresponding to these and place it in your filthy window. I'll be back." He resumed his coat, picked up the malacca cane, blithely sought out the sheriff, displayed the sign, heard that gallant Kentuckian's most Southern expression of regard for Captain Andy Hawks, his wife and gifted daughter, together with a promise to see to it that the written apology remained in the varmint's window throughout the day and until the departure of the *Cotton Blossom*. Ravenal then went his elegant and unruffled way up the sunny sleepy street.

By noon the story was known throughout the village, up and down the river for a distance of ten miles each way, and into the back country, all in some mysterious word-of-mouth way peculiar to isolated districts. Ravenal, returning to the boat, was met by news of his own exploit. Business, which had been booming for this month or more, grew to phenomenal proportions. Ravenal became a sort of legendary figure on the rivers. Magnolia went to her mother. "I am never allowed to talk to him. I won't stand it. You treat him like a criminal."

"What else is he?"

"He's the———" A long emotional speech, ringing with words such as hero, gentleman, wonderful, honourable, nobility, glorious—a speech such as Schultzy, in his show-boat days as director, would have designated as a so-and-so-and-so-and-so-and-so-and-so.

Ravenal went to Captain Andy. I am treated as an outcast. I'm a Ravenal. Nothing but the most honourable conduct. A leper. Never permitted to speak to your daughter. Humiliation. Prefer to discontinue connection which can only be distasteful to the Captain and Mrs. Hawks, in view of your conduct. Leaving the *Cotton Blossom* at Cairo.

In a panic Captain Andy scampered to his lady and declared for a more lenient chaperonage.

"Willing to sacrifice your own daughter, are you, for the sake of a picking up a few more dollars here and there with this miserable upstart!"

"Sacrificing her, is it, to tell her she can speak civilly to as handsome a young feller and good-mannered as I ever set eyes on, or you either!"

"Young squirt, that's what he is."

"I was a girl like Nollie I'd run off with him, by God, and that's the truth. She had any spirit left in her after you've devilled her these eighteen years past, she'd do it."

"That's right! Put ideas into her head! How do you know who he is?"

"He's a Rav———"

"He says he is."

"Didn't he show me the church———"

"Oh, Hawks, you're a zany. I could show you gravestones. I could say my name was Bonaparte and show you Napoleon's tomb, but that wouldn't make him my grandfather, would it!"

After all, there was wisdom in what she said. She may even have been right, as she so often was in her shrewish intuition. Certainly they never learned more of this scion of the Ravenal family than the meagre information gleaned from the chronicles of the village church and graveyard.

Grudgingly, protestingly, she allowed the two to converse genteelly between the hours of five and six, after dinner. But no oriental princess was ever more heavily chaperoned than was Magnolia during these prim meetings. For a month, then, they met on the port side of the upper deck, forward. Their chairs were spaced well apart. On the starboard side, twenty-five feet away, sat Parthy in her chair, grim, watchful; radiating opposition.

Magnolia, feeling the gimlet eye boring her spine, would sit bolt upright, her long nervous fingers tightly interwoven, her ankles neatly crossed, the pleats and flounces of her skirts spread sedately enough yet seeming to vibrate with an electric force that gave them the effect of standing upright, a-quiver, like a kitten's fur when she is agitated.

He sat, one arm negligently over the back of his chair, facing the girl. His knees were crossed. He seemed at ease, relaxed. Yet a slim foot in its well-made boot swung gently to and fro. And when Parthy made one of her sudden moves, as was her jerky habit, or when she coughed raspingly by way of emphasizing her presence, he could be felt, rather than seen, to tighten in all his nerves and muscles, and the idly swinging foot took a clonic leap.

The words they spoke with their lips and the words they spoke with their eyes were absurdly at variance.

"Have you really been in Paris, Mr. Ravenal! How I should love to see it!" (How handsome you are, sitting there like that. I really don't care anything about Paris. I only care about you.)

"No doubt you will, some day, Miss Magnolia" (You darling! How I should like to take you there. How I should like to take you in my arms.)

"Oh, I've never even seen Chicago. Only these river towns." (I love the way your hair grows away from your temples in that clean line. I want to put my finger on it, and stroke it. My dear.)

"A sordid kind of city. Crude. Though it has some pleasant aspects. New York————" (What do I care if that old tabby is sitting there! What's to prevent me from getting up and kissing you a long long while on your lovely pomegranate mouth.)

Lowering, inflexible, sat Parthy. "She'll soon enough tire of that sort of popinjay talk," she told herself. She saw the bland and almost vacuous expression on the countenance of the young man, and being ignorant of the fact that he was famous from St. Louis to Chicago for his perfect poker face, was equally ignorant of the tides that were seething and roaring within him now.

They were prisoners on this boat; together, yet miles apart. Guarded, watched. They had their scenes together on the stage. These were only aggravations. The rather high planes of Magnolia's cheek-bones began to show a trifle too flat. Ravenal, as he walked along the grass-grown dusty streets of this or that little river town, switched viciously at weed and flower stalks with the slim malacca cane.

They hit upon a pathetic little scheme whereby they might occasionally, if lucky, steal the ecstasy of a goodnight kiss. After the performance he would stroll carelessly out to the stern where stood the settling barrel. Ostensibly he was taking a bedtime drink of water. Magnolia was, if possible, to meet him there for a brief and perilous moment. It was rarely accomplished. The signal to him was the slamming of the screen door. But often the screen door slammed as he stood there, a tense quivering figure in the velvet dark of the Southern night, and it was Frank, or Mrs. Soaper, or Mis' Means, or puny Mr. Means, coughing his bronchial wheeze. Crack! went the screen door. Disappointment. Often he sloshed down whole gallons of river water before she came—if she came at all.

He had managed to save almost a hundred dollars. He was restless, irritable. Except for a mild pinochle game now and then with the men of the company, he had not touched a card in weeks. If he could get into a real game, somehow; manage a sweepstakes. Chicago. St. Louis, even. These little rotten river towns. No chance here. If he could with luck get together enough to take her away with him. Away from the old hell-cat, and this tub, and these damned eternal rivers. God, but he was sick of them!

They were playing the Ohio River—Paducah, Kentucky. He found himself seated at mid-afternoon round a table in the back room of a waterfront saloon. What time is it? Five. Plenty of time. Just for that raise you five. A few hundred dollars would do it. Six o'clock. Seven. Seven-thirty. Eight. Half-past—Who said half past! Ralph in the doorway. Can't be! Been looking everywhere for you. This's a fine way . . . Come on outa here you. . . . Christ! . . . Ten dollars in his pocket. The curtain up at eight. Out, the shouts of the men echoing in his ears. Down to the landing. A frantic company, Andy clawing at his whiskers. Magnolia in tears, Parthy grim but triumphant, Frank made up to go on in Ravenal's part.

He dashed before the curtain, raised his shaking hand to quiet the cat-calling angry audience.

"Ladies and gentlemen, I ask your patience. There has been an unfortunate but unavoidable delay. The curtain will rise in exactly five minutes. In the name of the management I wish to offer you all apologies. We hope, by our performance, to make up for the inconvenience you have suffered. I thank you." A wave of his hand.

The band.

Parthy in the wings. "Well, Captain Hawks, I guess this settles it. Maybe you'll listen to your wife after this. In a saloon—that's where he was—gambling. If Ralph hadn't found him—a pretty kettle of fish. Years building up a reputation on the rivers and then along comes a soft-soaping murdering gambler . . ."

Ravenal had got into his costume with the celerity of a fireman, and together he and Magnolia were giving a performance that was notable for its tempo and a certain vibratory quality. The drama that unrolled itself before the Paducah gaze was as nothing compared to the one that was being secretly enacted.

Between the lines of her part she whispered between immovable lips: "Oh, Gay, why did you do it?"

A wait, perhaps, of ten minutes before the business of the play brought him back within whispering distance of her.

"Money" (very difficult to whisper without moving the lips. It really emerged, "Uh-ney," but she understood). "For you. Marry you. Take you away."

All this while the lines of the play went on. When they stood close together it was fairly easy.

Magnolia (in the play) : What! Have all your friends deserted you! (Mama'll make Andy send you away.)

Ravenal: No, but friendship is too cold a passion to stir my heart now. (Will you come with me?)

Magnolia: Oh, give me a friend in preference to a sweetheart. (But how can I?)

Ravenal: My dear Miss Brown—Miss Lucy——— (Marry me).

Magnolia: Oh, please don't call me Miss Brown. (When?)

Ravenal: Lucy! (Where do we play to-morrow? Marry me there.)

Magnolia: Defender of the fatherless! (Metropolis. I'm frightened.)

Ravenal: Will you be a poor man's bride? (Darling!)

For fear of arousing suspicion, she did not dare put on her best dress in which to be married. One's best dress does not escape the eye of a Parthy at ten o'clock in the morning, when the landing is Metropolis. With a sigh Magnolia donned her second best—the reseda sateen, basqued, its overskirt caught up coquettishly at the side. She determined on her Milan hat trimmed with the grosgrain ribbon and pink roses. After all, Parthy or no Parthy, if one has a hat with pink roses, the time to wear it is at one's wedding, or never.

Ravenal vanished beyond the river bank immediately after breakfast next day; a meal which he had eaten in haste and in silence. He did not, the general opinion ran, look as crushed as his misdemeanour warranted. He had, after all, been guilty of the crime of crimes in the theatre, be it a Texas tent show or an all-star production on Broadway; he had held up the performance. For once the *Cotton Blossom* troupe felt that Mrs. Hawks' bristling attitude was justified. All through the breakfast hour the stern ribbon bow on her breakfast cap had quivered like a seismographic needle registering the degree of her inward upheaval.

"I think," said Magnolia, drinking her coffee in very small sips, and eating nothing, "I'll just go to town and match the ribbon on my grosgrain striped silk———"

"You'll do nothing of the kind, miss, and so I tell you."

"But, Mama, why? You'd think I was a child instead of a———"

"You are, and no more. I can't go with you. So you'll stop at home."

"But Mis' Means is going with me. I promised her I'd go. She wants to get some ointment for Mr. Means' chest. And a yard of elastic. And half a dozen oranges. . . . Papa, don't you think it's unreasonable to make me suffer just because everybody's in a bad temper this morning? I'm sure I haven't done anything. I'm sure I————"

Captain Andy clawed his whiskers in a frenzy. "Don't come to me with your yards of elastic and your oranges. God A'mighty!" He rushed off, a distraught little figure, as well he might be after a wretched night during which Mrs. Hawks had out-caudled Mrs. Caudle. When finally he had dropped off to sleep to the sound of the monotonously nagging voice, it was to dream of murderous gamblers abducting Magnolia who always turned out to be Parthy.

In her second best sateen and the Milan with the pink roses Magnolia went off to town at a pace that rather inconvenienced the short-breathed Mis' Means.

"What's your hurry!" wheezed that lady, puffing up the steep cinder path to the levee.

"We're late."

"Late! Late for what? Nothing to do all day till four, far's I know."

"Oh, I just meant—uh—I mean we started kind of late————" her voice trailed off, lamely.

Fifteen minutes later Mis' Means stood in indecision before a counter crawling with unwound bolts of elastic that twined all about her like garter snakes. The little general store smelled of old apples and broom straw and kerosene and bacon and potatoes and burlap and mice. Sixteen minutes later she turned to ask Magnolia's advice. White elastic half an inch wide? Black elastic three quarters of an inch wide? Magnolia had vanished from her side. Mis' Means peered through the dimness of the fusty little shop. Magnolia! White elastic in one hand, black in the other, Mis' Means scurried to the door. Magnolia had gone.

Magnolia had gone to be married in her second best dress and her hat with the pink roses. She flew down the street. Mis' Means certainly could have achieved no such gait; much less could she have bettered it to the extent of overtaking Magnolia. Magnolia made such speed that when her waiting bridegroom, leaning against the white picket fence in front of the minister's house next the church, espied her and came swiftly to meet her, she was so breathless a bride that he could make nothing out of her panted—"Elastic . . . Mis' Means . . . ran away . . .''

She leaned against the picket fence to catch her breath, a lovely flushed figure, and not a little frightened. And though it was early April with Easter just gone, there was a dogwood in bridal bloom in the minister's front yard, and a magnolia as well. And along the inside of the picket fence tulips and jonquils lifted their radiant heads. She looked at Gaylord Ravenal then and smiled her wide and gorgeous smile. "Let's go," she said, "and be married. I've caught my breath."

"All right," said Ravenal. Then he took from his pocket the diamond ring that was much too large for her. "Let's be engaged first, while we go up the path." And slipped it on her finger.

"Why, Gay! It's a diamond! Look what the sun does to it! Gay!"

"That's nothing compared to what the sun does to you," he said; and leaned toward her.

"Right at noon, in the minister's front yard!"

"I know. But I've had only those few moments in the dark by the settling barrel—it's been terrible."

The minister's wife opened the door. She looked at the two.

"I saw you from the parlour window. We were wondering—I thought maybe you'd like to be married in the church. The Easter decorations are

still up. It looks lovely, all palms and lilies and smilax, too, from down
South, sent up. The altar's banked with it. Mr. Seldon's gone there."

"Oh, I'd love to be married in church. Oh, Gay, I'd love to be married
in church."

The minister's wife smoothed the front of her dress with one hand, and
the back of her hair with the other, and, having made these preparations for
the rôle of bridal attendant, conducted them to the little flowerbanked church
next door.

Magnolia never did remember very clearly the brief ceremony that followed. There were Easter lilies—whole rows of them—and palms and smilax,
as the minister's wife had said. And the sun shone, picturebook fashion,
through the crude yellows and blues and scarlets of the windows. And there
was the Reverend Something-or-other Seldon, saying solemn words. But
these things, strangely enough, seemed unimportant. Two little pig-tailed
girls, passing by from school, had seen them enter the church and had tiptoed
in, scenting a wedding. Now they were up in the choir loft, tittering hysterically. Magnolia could hear them above the Reverend Seldon's intonings.
In sickness and in health—tee-hee-hee—for richer, for poorer—tee-hee-
hee—for better, for worse—tee-hee-hee.

They were kneeling. Ravenal was wearing his elegantly sharp-pointed
shoes. As he knelt his heels began to describe an arc—small at first, then
wider and wider as he trembled more and more, until, at the end, they were
all but striking the floor from side to side. Outwardly Magnolia was the bride
of tradition, calm and pale.

. . . pronounce you man and wife.

Ravenal had a ten-dollar bill—that last ten-dollar bill—all neatly folded in
his waistcoat pocket. This he now transferred to the Reverend Seldon's
somewhat surprised palm.

"And," the minister's wife was saying, "while it isn't much—we're church
mice, you see—you're welcome to it, and we'd be happy to have you
take your wedding dinner with us. Veal loaf, I'm afraid, and butter
beets————"

So Magnolia Ravenal was married in church, as proper as could be. And
had her wedding dinner with the minister vis-à-vis. And when she came out
of the church, the two little giggling girls, rather bold and rather frightened,
but romantically stirred, pelted her with flowers. Pelted may be rather an
exaggeration, because one threw a jonquil at her, and one a tulip, and both
missed her. But it helped, enormously. They went to the minister's house
and ate veal loaf and buttered beets and bread pudding, or ambrosia or
whatever it was. And so they lived h———— and so they lived . . . ever
after.

11

EVEN AFTER SHE had seen the Atlantic in a January hurricane, Kim Ravenal
always insisted that the one body of water capable of striking terror to her
was the Mississippi River. Surely she should have known. She had literally
been born on that turbid torrent. All through her childhood her mother,
Magnolia Ravenal, had told her tales of its vagaries, its cruelties, its moods;
of the towns along its banks; of the people in those towns; of the boats that
moved upon it and the fantastic figures that went up and down in those
boats. Her grandfather, Captain Andy Hawks, had lost his life in the treacherous swift current of its channel; her grandmother, Parthenia Ann Hawks

was, at eighty, a living legend of the Mississippi; the Flying Dutchman of the rivers, except that the boat touched many ports. One heard strange tales about Hawks' widow. She had gone on with the business after his tragic death. She was the richest show-boat owner on the rivers. She ran the boat like a female seminary. If an actor uttered so much as a damn, he was instantly dismissed from the troupe. Couples in the company had to show a marriage certificate. Every bill—even such innocuous old-timers as East Lynne and The Gambler's Daughter and Tempest and Sunshine—were subject to a purifying process before the stern-visaged female owner of the new *Cotton Blossom* would sanction their performance on her show boat.

Kim herself remembered many things about the Mississippi, though after her very early childhood she did not see it for many years; and her mother rarely spoke of it. She even shook her head when Kim would ask her for the hundredth time to tell her the story of how she escaped being named Mississippi.

"Tell about the time the river got so high, and all kinds of things floated on it—animals and furniture and houses, even—and you were so scared, and I was born, and you wanted to call me Mississippi, but you were too sleepy or something to say it. And the place was near Kentucky and Illinois and Missouri, all at once, so they made up a name from the letters K and I and M, just till you could think of a real name. And you never did. And it stayed Kim. . . . People laugh when I tell them my name's Kim. Other girls are named Ellen and Mary and Elizabeth. . . . Tell me about that time on the Mississippi. And the Cotton Blossom Floating Palace Theatre."

"But you know all about it. You've just told me."

"I like to hear you tell it."

"Your father doesn't like to have me talk so much about the rivers and the show boat."

"Why not?"

"He wasn't very happy on them. I wasn't, either, after Grandpa Hawks———"

Kim knew that, too. She had heard her father say, "God's sake, Nola, don't fill the kid's head full of that stuff about the rivers and the show boat. The way you tell it, it sounds romantic and idle and picturesque."

"Well, wasn't———?"

"No. It was rotten and sordid and dull. Flies on the food and filthy water to drink and yokels to play to. And that old harridan———"

"Gay!"

He would come over to her, kiss her tenderly, contritely. "Sorry, darling."

Kim knew that her mother had a strange deep feeling about the rivers. The ugly wide muddy ruthless rushing rivers of the Middle West.

Kim Ravenal's earliest river memories were bizarre and startling flashes. One of these was of her mother seated in a straight-backed chair on the upper deck of the *Cotton Blossom,* sewing spangles all over a highbusted corset. It was a white webbed corset with a pinched-in waist and high full bosom and flaring hips. This humdrum garment Magnolia Ravenal was covering with shining silver spangles, one overlapping the other so that the whole made a glittering basque. She took quick sure stitches that jerked the fantastic garment in her lap, and when she did this the sun caught the brilliant heap aslant and turned it into a blaze of gold and orange and ice-blue and silver.

Kim was enchanted. Her mother was a fairy princess. It was nothing to her that the spangle-covered basque, modestly eked out with tulle and worn with astonishingly long skirts for a bareback rider, was to serve as Magnolia's costume in The Circus Clown's Daughter.

Kim's grandmother had scolded a good deal about that costume. But then, she had scolded a good deal about everything. It was years before Kim realized that all grandmothers were not like that. At three she thought that scolding and grandmothers went together, like sulphur and molasses. The same was true of fun and grandfathers, only they went together like ice cream and cake. You called your grandmother grandma. You called your grandfather Andy, or, if you felt very roguish, Cap'n. When you called him that, he cackled and squealed, which was his way of laughing, and he clawed his delightful whiskers this side and that. Kim would laugh then, too, and look at him knowingly from under her long lashes. She had large eyes, deep-set like her mother's and her mother's wide mobile mouth. For the rest, she was much like her father—a Ravenal, he said. His fastidious ways (high-falutin, her grandmother called them); his slim hands and feet; his somewhat drawling speech, indirect though strangely melting glance, calculatedly impulsive and winning manner.

Another childhood memory was that of a confused and terrible morning. Asleep in her small bed in the room with her father and mother, she had been wakened by a bump, followed by a lurch, a scream, shouts, bells, clamour. Wrapped in her comforter, hastily snatched up from her bed by her mother, she was carried to the deck in her mother's arms. Gray dawn. A misty morning with fog hanging an impenetrable curtain over the river, the shore. The child was sleepy, bewildered. It was all one to her—the confusion, the shouting, the fog, the bells. Close in her mother's arms, she did not in the least understand what had happened when the confusion became pandemonium; the shouts rose to screams. Her grandfather's high squeaky voice that had been heard above the din—"La'berd lead there! Sta'berd lead! Snatch her! *SNATCH HER!*" was heard no more. Something more had happened. Someone was in the water, hidden by the fog, whirled in the swift treacherous current. Kim was thrown on her bed like a bundle of rags, all rolled in her blanket. She was left there, alone. She had cried a little, from fright and bewilderment, but had soon fallen asleep again. When she woke up her mother was bending over her, so wild-eyed, so frightening with her black hair streaming about her face and her face swollen and mottled with weeping, that Kim began to cry again in sheer terror. Her mother had snatched her to her. Curiously enough the words Magnolia Ravenal now whispered in a ghastly kind of agony were the very words she had whispered after the agony of Kim's birth—though the child could not know that.

"The river!" Magnolia said, over and over. Gaylord Ravenal came to her, flung an arm about her shoulder, but she shook him off wildly. "The river! The river!"

Kim never saw her grandfather again. Because of the look it brought to her mother's face, she soon learned not to say, "Where's Andy?" or—the roguish question that had always made him appear, squealing with delight: "Where's Cap'n?"

Baby though she was, the years—three or four—just preceding her grandfather's tragic death were indelibly stamped on the infant's mind. He had adored her; made much of her. Andy, dead, was actually a more vital figure than many another alive.

It had been a startling but nevertheless actual fact that Parthenia Ann Hawks had not wanted her daughter Magnolia to have a child. Parthy's strange psychology had entered into this, of course—a pathological twist. Of this she was quite unaware.

"How're you going to play ingénue lead, I'd like to know, if you—when you—while you———" She simply could not utter the word "pregnant" or say, " while you are carrying your child," or even the simpering evasion of her type and class—"in the family way."

Magnolia laughed a little at that. "I'll play as long as I can. Toward the end I'll play ruffly parts. Then some night, probably between the second and third acts—though they may have to hold the curtain for five minutes or so—I'll excuse myself———"

Mrs. Hawks declared that she had never heard anything so indelicate in her life. "Besides, a show boat's no place to bring up a child."

"You brought me up on one."

"Yes," said Mrs. Hawks, grimly. Her tone added, "And now look at you!"

Even before Kim's birth the antagonism between Parthy and her son-in-law deepened to actual hatred. She treated him like a criminal; regarded Magnolia's quite normal condition as a reproach to him.

"Look here, Magnolia, I can't stand this, you know. I'm so sick of this old mud-scow and everything that goes with it."

"Gay! Everything!"

"You know what I mean. Let's get out of it. I'm no actor. I don't belong here. If I hadn't happened to see you when you stepped out on deck that day at New Orleans———"

"Are you sorry?"

"Darling! It's the only luck I've ever had that lasted."

She looked thoughtfully down at the clear colourful brilliance of the diamond on her third finger. Always too large for her, it now hung so loosely on her thin hand that she had been obliged to wind it with a great pad of thread to keep it from dropping off, though hers were the large-knuckled fingers of the generous and resourceful nature. It was to see much of life, that ring.

She longed to say to him, "Where do you belong, Gay? Who are you? Don't tell me you're a Ravenal. That isn't a profession, is it? You can't live on that."

But she knew it was useless. There was a strange deep streak of the secretive in him; baffling, mystifying. Questioned, he would say nothing. It was not a moody silence, or a resentful one. He simply would not speak. She had learned not to ask.

"We can't go away now, Gay dear. I can't go. You don't want to go without me, do you? You wouldn't leave me! Maybe next winter, after the boat's put up, we can go to St. Louis, or even New Orleans—that would be nice, wouldn't it? The winter in New Orleans."

One of his silences.

He never had any money—that is, he never had it for long. It vanished. He would have one hundred dollars. He would go ashore at some sizable town and return with five hundred—a thousand. "Got into a little game with some of the boys," he would explain, cheerfully. And give her three hundred of it, four hundred, five. "Buy yourself a dress, Nola. Something rich, with a hat to match. You're too pretty to wear those home-made things you're always messing with."

Some woman wisdom in her told her to put by a portion of these sums. She got into the habit of tucking away ten dollars, twenty, fifty. At times she reproached herself for this; called it disloyal, sneaking, underhand. When she heard him say, as he frequently did, "I'm strapped. If I had fifty dollars I could turn a trick that would make five hundred out of it. You haven't got fifty, have you, Nola? No, of course not."

She wanted then to give him every cent of her tiny hoard. It was the tenuous strain of her mother in her, doubtless—the pale thread of the Parthy in her make up—that caused her to listen to an inner voice. "Don't do it," whispered the voice, nudging her, "keep it. You'll need it badly by and by."

It did not take many months for her to discover that her husband was a gambler by profession—one of those smooth and plausible gentry with whom years of river life had made her familiar. It was, after all, not so much a discovery as a forced admission. She knew, but refused to admit that she knew. Certainly no one could have been long in ignorance with Mrs. Hawks in possession of the facts.

Ten days after Magnolia's marriage to Ravenal (and what a ten days those had been! Parthy alone crowded into them a lifetime of reproach), Mrs. Hawks came to her husband, triumph in her mien, portent in her voice:

"Well, Hawks, I hope you're satisfied now." This was another of Parthy's favourite locutions. The implication was that the unfortunate whom she addressed had howled heaven-high his demands for hideous misfortune and would not be content until horror had piled upon horror. "I hope you're satisfied now, Hawks. Your son-in-law is a gambler, and no more. A common barroom gambler, without a cent to his trousers longer'n it takes to transfer his money from his pocket to the table. That's what your only daughter has married. Understand, I'm not saying he gambles, and that's all. I say he's a gambler by calling. That's the way he made his living before he came aboard this boat. I wish he had died before he ever set foot on the *Cotton Blossom* gangplank, and so I tell you, Hawks. A smooth-tongued, oily, good-for-nothing; no better than the scum Elly ran off with."

"Now, Parthy, what's done's done. Why'n't you try to make the best of things once in a while, instead of the worst? Magnolia's happy with him."

"She ain't lived her life out with him yet. Mark my words. He's got a roving eye for a petticoat."

"Funny thing, Parthy. Your father was a man, and so's your husband, and your son-in-law's another. Yet seems you never did get the hang of a man's ways."

Andy liked Ravenal. There was about the fellow a grace, an ease, a certain elegance that appealed to the aesthetic in the little Gallic captain. When the two men talked together sometimes, after dinner, it was amiably, in low tones, with an air of leisure and relaxation. Two gentlemen enjoying each other's company. There existed between the two a sound respect and liking.

Certainly Ravenal's vogue on the rivers was tremendous. Andy paid him as juvenile lead a salary that was unheard of in show-boat records. But he accounted him worth it. Shortly after Kim's birth, Andy spoke of giving Ravenal a share in the *Cotton Blossom*. But this Mrs. Hawks fought with such actual ferocity that Andy temporarily at least relinquished the idea.

Magnolia had learned to dread the idle winter months. During this annual period of the *Cotton Blossom's* hibernation the Hawks family had, before Magnolia's marriage, gone back to the house near the river at Thebes. Sometimes Andy had urged Parthy to spend these winter months in the South, evading the harsh Illinois climate for a part of the time at least in New Orleans, or one of the towns of southern Mississippi where one might have roses instead of holly for Christmas. He sometimes envied black Jo and Queenie their period of absence from the boat. In spite of the disreputable state in which they annually returned to the *Cotton Blossom* in the early spring, they always looked as if they had spent the intervening months seated in the dappled shade, under a vine, with the drone of insects in the air, and the heavy scent of white-petalled blossoms; eating fruit that dripped juice between their fingers; sleeping, slack-jawed and heavily content, through the heat of the Southern mid-afternoon; supping greasily and plentifully on fried catfish and corn bread; watching the moon come up to the accompaniment of Jo's coaxing banjo.

"We ought to lazy around more, winters" Andy said to his energetic wife. She was, perhaps, setting the Thebes house to rights after their long absence; thwacking pillows, pounding carpets, sloshing pails, scouring tables, hanging fresh curtains, flapping drapes, banging bureau drawers. A towel wrapped about her head, turban-wise, her skirts well pinned up, she would throw a frenzy of energy into her already exaggerated housewifeliness until Andy, stepping fearfully out of the way of mop and broom and pail, would seek waterfront cronies for solace.

"Lazy! I've enough of lazying on that boat of yours month in month out all summer long. No South for me, thank you. Eight months of flies and niggers and dirty mud-tracking loafers is enough for me, Captain Hawks. I'm thankful to get back for a few weeks where I can live like a decent white woman." Thwack! Thump! Bang!

After one trial lasting but a few days, the Thebes house was found by Magnolia to be impossible for Gaylord Ravenal. That first winter after their marriage they spent in various towns and cities. Memphis for a short time; a rather hurried departure; St. Louis; Chicago. That brief glimpse of Chicago terrified her, but she would not admit it. After all, she told herself, as the astounding roar and din and jangle and clatter of State Street and Wabash Avenue beat at her ears, this city was only an urban Mississippi. The cobblestones were the river bed. The high grim buildings the river banks. The men, women, horses, trucks, drays, carriages, street cars that surged through those streets; creating new channels where some obstacle blocked their progress; felling whole sections of stone and brick and wood and sweeping over that section, obliterating all trace of its former existence; lifting other huge blocks and sweeping them bodily downstream to deposit them in a new spot; making a boulevard out of what had been a mud swamp—all this, Magnolia thought, was only the Mississippi in another form and environment; ruthless, relentless, Gargantuan, terrible. One might think to know its currents and channels ever so well, but once caught unprepared in the maelstrom, one would be sucked down and devoured as Captain Andy Hawks had been in that other turbid hungry flood.

"You'll get used to it," Ravenal told his bride, a trifle patronizingly, as one who had this monster tamed and fawning. "Don't be frightened. It's mostly noise,"

"I'm not frightened, really. It's just the kind of noise that I'm not used to. The rivers, you know, all these years—so quiet. At night and in the morning."

That winter she lived the life of a gambler's wife. Streak o' lean, streak o' fat. Turtle soup and terrapin at the Palmer House to-day. Ham and eggs in some obscure eating house to-morrow. They rose at noon. They never retired until the morning hours. Gay seemed to know a great many people, but to his wife he presented few of these.

"Business acquaintance," he would say. "You wouldn't care for him."

Hers had been a fantastic enough life on the show boat. But always there had been about it an orderliness, a routine, due, perhaps, to the presence of the martinet, Parthenia Ann Hawks. Indolent as the days appeared on the rivers, they still bore a methodical aspect. Breakfast at nine. Rehearsal. Parade. Dinner at four. Make-up. Curtain. Wardrobe to mend or refurbish; parts to study; new songs to learn for the concert. But this new existence seemed to have no plot or plan. Ravenal was a being for the most part unlike the lover and husband of *Cotton Blossom* days. Expansive and secretive by turn; now high-spirited, now depressed; frequently absent-minded. His manner toward her was always tender, courteous, thoughtful. He loved her as deeply as he was capable of loving. She knew that. She had to tell herself all this one evening when she sat in their hotel room, dressed and waiting for him to take her to dinner and to the theatre. They were going to Mc-Vicker's Theatre, the handsome new auditorium that had risen out of the ashes of the old (to quote the owner's florid announcement). Ravenal was startled to learn how little Magnolia knew of the great names of the stage. He had told her something of the history of McVicker's, in an expansive burst of pride in Chicago. He seemed to have a definite feeling about this great uncouth giant of a city.

"When you go to McVicker's," Ravenal said, "you are in the theatre where Booth has played, and Sothern, and Lotta, and Kean, and Mrs. Siddons."

"Who," asked Magnolia, "are they?"

He was so much in love that he found this ignorance of her own calling actually delightful. He laughed, of course, but kissed her when she pouted a little, and explained to her what these names meant, investing them with all the glamour and romance that the theatre—the theatre of sophistication, that is—had for him; for he had the gambler's love of the play. It must have been something of that which had held him so long to the *Cotton Blossom*. Perhaps, after all, his infatuation for Magnolia alone could not have done it.

And now she was going to McVicker's. And she had on her dress with the open-throated basque, which she considered rather daring, though now that she was a married woman it was all right. She was dressed long before the time when she might expect him back. She had put out fresh linen for him. He was most fastidious about his dress. Accustomed to the sloppy deshabille of the show boat's male troupers, this sartorial niceness in Ravenal had impressed her from the first.

She regarded herself in the mirror now. She knew she was not beautiful. She affected, in fact, to despise her looks; bemoaned her high forehead and prominent cheek-bones, her large-knuckled fingers, her slenderness, her wide mouth. Yet she did not quite believe these things she said about herself; loved to hear Ravenal say she was beautiful. As she looked at her reflection now in the long gilt-framed mirror of the heavy sombre walnut bedroom, she found herself secretly agreeing with him. This was the first year of her marriage. She was pregnant. It was December. The child was expected in April. There was nothing distorted about her figure or her face. As is infrequently the case, her condition had given her an almost uncanny radiance of aspect. Her usually pallid skin showed a delicious glow of rosy colouring; her eyes were enormous and strangely luminous; tiny blue veins were faintly, exquisitely etched against the cream tint of her temples; her rather angular slimness was replaced by a delicate roundness; she bore herself well, her shoulders back, her head high. A happy woman, beloved, and in love.

Six o'clock. A little late, but he would be here at any moment now. Half-past six. She was opening the door every five minutes to peer up the red-carpeted corridor. Seven. Impatience had given way to fear, fear to terror, terror to certain agony. He was dead. He had been killed. She knew by now that he frequented the well-known resorts of the city, that he played cards in them. "Just for pastime," he told her. "Game of cards to while away the afternoon. What's the harm in that? Now, Nola! Don't look like your mother. Please!"

She knew about them. Red plush and gilt, mahogany and mirrors. Food and drink. River-front saloons and river-front life had long ago taught her not to be squeamish. She was not a foolish woman, nor an intolerant. She was, in fact, in many ways wise beyond her years. But this was 1888. The papers had been full of the shooting of Simeon Peake, the gambler, in Jeff Hankins' place over on Clark Street. The bullet had been meant for someone else—a well-known newspaper publisher, in fact. But a woman, hysterical, crazed, revengeful, had fired it. It had gone astray. Ravenal had known Simeon Peake. The shooting had been a shock to him. It had, indeed, thrown him so much off his guard that he had talked to Magnolia about it for relief. Peake had had a young daughter Selina. She was left practically penniless.

Now the memory of this affair came rushing back to her. She was frantic. Half-past seven. It was too late, now, for the dinner they had planned for the gala evening—dinner at the Wellington Hotel, down in the white marble café. The Wellington was just across the street from McVicker's. It would make everything simple and easy; no rush, no hurrying over that last delightful sweet sip of coffee.

Eight o'clock. He had been killed. She no longer merely opened the door to peer into the corridor. She left the room door open and paced from room to hall, from hall to room, wildly; down the corridor. Finally, in desperation, down to the hotel lobby into which she had never stepped in the evening without her husband. There were two clerks at the office desk. One was an ancient man, flabby and wattled, as much a part of the hotel as the stones that paved the lobby. He had soft wisps of sparse white hair that seemed to float just above his head instead of being attached to it; and little tufts of beard, like bits of cotton stuck on his cheeks. He looked like an old baby. The other was a glittering young man; his hair glittered, his eyes, his teeth, his nails, his shirt-front, his cuffs. Both these men knew Ravenal; had greeted him on their arrival; had bowed impressively to her. The young man had looked flattering things; the old man had pursed his soft withered lips.

Magnolia glanced from one to the other. There were people at the clerks' desk leaning against the marble slab. She waited nervous, uncertain. She would speak to the old man. She did not want, somehow, to appeal to the glittering one. But he saw her, smiled, left the man to whom he was talking, came toward her. Quickly she touched the sleeve of the old man—leaned forward over the marble to do it—jerked his sleeve, really, so that he glanced up at her testily.

"I—I want—may I speak to you?"

"A moment, madam. I shall be free in a moment."

The sparkler leaned toward her. "What can I do for you, Mrs. Ravenal?"

"I just wanted to speak to this gentleman————"

"But I can assist you, I'm sure, as well as————"

She glanced at him and he was a row of teeth, all white and even, ready to bite. She shook her head miserably; glanced appealingly at the old man. The sparkler's eyebrows came up. He gave the effect of stepping back, courteously, without actually doing so. Now that the old clerk faced her, questioningly, she almost regretted her choice.

She blushed, stammered; her voice was little more than a whisper. "I . . . my husband . . . have been . . . he hasn't returned . . . worried . . . killed or . . . theatre . . ."

The old baby cupped one hand behind his ear. "What say?"

Her beautiful eyes, in their agony, begged the sparkler now to forgive her for having been rude. She needed him. She could not shout this. He stepped forward, but the teeth were hidden. After all, a chief clerk is a chief clerk. Miraculously, he had heard the whisper.

"You say your husband————?"

She nodded. She was terribly afraid that she was going to cry. She opened her eyes very wide and tried not to blink. If she so much as moved her lids she knew the mist that was making everything swim in a rainbow haze would crystallize into tears.

"He is terribly late. I—I've been so worried. We were going to the—to McVicker's—and dinner—and now it's after seven————"

"After eight," wheezed cotton whiskers, peering at the clock on the wall.

"—after eight," she echoed, wretchedly. There! She had winked. Two great drops plumped themselves down on the silk bosom of her bodice with the openthroated neckline. It seemed to her that she heard them splash.

"H'm!" cackled the old man.

The glittering one leaned toward her. She was enveloped in a waft of perfume. "Now, now, Mrs. Ravenal! There's absolutely nothing to worry about. Your husband has been delayed. That's all. Unavoidably delayed."

She snatched at this. "Do you think—? Are you sure? But he always is back by six, at the latest. Always. And we were going to dinner—and Mc————"

"You brides!" smiled the young man. He actually patted her hand, then. Just a touch. "Now you just have a bite of dinner, like a sensible little woman."

"Oh, I couldn't eat a bite! I couldn't!"

"A cup of tea. Let me send up a cup of tea."

The old one made a sucking sound with tongue and teeth, rubbed his chin, and proffered his suggestion in a voice that seemed to Magnolia to echo and reëcho through the hotel lobby. "Why'n't you send a messenger around for him, madam?"

"Messenger? Around? Where?"

Sparkler made a little gesture—a tactful gesture. "Perhaps he's having a little game of—uh—cards; and you know how time flies. I've done the same thing myself. Look up at the clock and first thing you know it's eight. Now if I were you, Mrs. Ravenal————"

She knew, then. There was something so sure about this young man; and so pitying. And suddenly she, too, was sure. She recalled in a flash that time when they were playing Paducah, and he had not come. They had held the curtain until after eight. Ralph had searched for him. He had been playing poker in a waterfront saloon. Send around for him! Not she. The words of a popular sentimental song of the day went through her mind, absurdly.

> Father, dear father, come home with me now.
> The clock in the steeple strikes one.

She drew herself up, now. The actress. She even managed a smile, as even and sparkling and toothy as the sparkler's own. "Of course. I'm very silly. Thank you so . . . I'll just have a bit of supper in my room. . . ." She turned away with a little gracious bow. The eyes very wide again.

"H'm!" The old man. Translated it meant, "Little idiot!"

She took off the dress with the two dark spots on the silk of the basque. She put away his linen and his shiny shoes. She took up some sewing. But the mist interfered with that. She threw herself on the bed. An agony of tears. That was better. Ten o'clock. She fell asleep, the gas lights burning. At a little before midnight he came in. She awoke with a little cry. Queerly enough, the first thing she noticed was that he had not his cane—the richly mottled malacca stick that he always carried. She heard herself saying ridiculously, half awake, half asleep, "Where's your cane?"

His surprise at this matter-of-fact reception made his expression almost ludicrous. "Cane! Oh, that's so. Why I left it. Must have left it."

In the years that followed she learned what the absence of the malacca stick meant. It had come to be a symbol in every pawnshop on Clark Street. Its appearance was bond for a sum a hundred times its actual value. Gaylord Ravenal always paid his debts.

She finished undressing, in silence. Her face was red and swollen. She looked young and helpless and almost ugly. He was uncomfortable and self-reproachful. "I'm sorry, Nola. I was detained. We'll go to the theatre to-morrow night."

She almost hated him then. Being, after all, a normal woman, there followed a normal scene—tears, reproaches, accusations, threats, pleadings, forgiveness. Then:

"Uh—Nola, will you let me take your ring—just for a day or two?"

"Ring?" But she knew.

"You'll have it back. This is Wednesday. You'll have it by Saturday. I swear it."

The clear white diamond had begun its travels with the malacca stick.

He had spoken the truth when he said that he had been unavoidably detained.

She had meant not to sleep. She had felt sure that she would not sleep. But she was young and healthy and exhausted from emotion. She slept. As she lay there by his side she thought, before she slept, that life was very terrible—but fascinating. Even got from this a glow of discovery. She felt old and experienced and married and tragic. She thought of her mother. She was much, much older and more married, she decided, than her mother ever had been.

They returned to Thebes in February. Magnolia longed to be near her father. She even felt a pang of loneliness for her mother. The little white cottage near the river, at Thebes, looked like a toy house. Her bedroom was doll-size. The town was a miniature village, like a child's Christmas set. Her mother's bonnet was a bit of grotesquerie. Her father's face was etched with lines that she did not remember having seen there when she left. The home-cooked food, prepared by Parthy's expert hands, was delicious beyond belief. She was a traveller returned from a far place.

Captain Andy had ordered a new boat. He talked of nothing else. The old *Cotton Blossom,* bought from Pegram years before, was to be discarded. The new boat was to be lighted by some newfangled gas arrangement instead of the old kerosene lamps. Carbide or some such thing Andy said it was. There were to be special footlights, new scenery, improved dressing and sleeping rooms. She was being built at the St. Louis shipyards.

"She's a daisy!" squeaked Andy, capering. He had just returned from a trip to the place of the *Cotton Blossom's* imminent birth. Of the two impending accouchements—that which was to bring forth a grandchild and that which was to produce a new show boat—it was difficult to say which caused him keenest anticipation. Perhaps, secretly, it was the boat, much as he loved Magnolia. He was, first, the river man; second, the showman; third, the father.

"Like to know what you want a new boat for!" Parthy scolded. "Take all the money you've earned these years past with the old tub, and throw it away on a new one."

"Old one a'n't good enough."

"Good enough for the riff-raff we get on it."

"Now, Parthy, you know's well's I do you couldn't be shooed off the rivers now you've got used to 'em. Any other way of living'd seem stale to you."

"I'm a woman loves her home and asks for nothing better."

"Bet you wouldn't stay ashore, permanent, if you had the chance."

He won the wager, though he had to die to do it.

The new *Cotton Blossom* and the new grandchild had a trial by flood on their entrance into life. The Mississippi, savage mother that she was, gave them both a baptism that threatened for a time to make their entrance into and their exit from the world a simultaneous act. But both, after some perilous hours, were piloted to safety; the one by old Windy, who swore that this was his last year on the rivers; the other by a fat midwife and a frightened young doctor. Through storm and flood was heard the voice of Parthenia Ann Hawks, the scold, berating Captain Hawks her husband, and Magnolia Ravenal her daughter, as though they, and not the elements, were responsible for the predicament in which they now found themselves.

There followed four years of war and peace. The strife was internal. It raged between Parthy and her son-in-law. The conflict of the two was a chemical thing. Combustion followed inevitably upon their meeting. The biting acid of Mrs. Hawks' discernment cut relentlessly through the outer layers of the young man's charm and grace and melting manner and revealed the alloy. Ravenal's nature recoiled at sight of a woman who employed none of the arts of her sex and despised and penetrated those of the opposite sex. She had no vanity, no coquetry, no reticences, no respect for the reticence of others; treated compliment as insult, met flattery with contempt.

A hundred times during those four years he threatened to leave the *Cotton Blossom,* yet he was held to his wife Magnolia and to the child Kim by too many tender ties. His revolt usually took the form of a gambling spree ashore during which he often lost every dollar he had saved throughout weeks of enforced economy. There was no opportunity to spend money legitimately in the straggling hamlets to whose landings the *Cotton Blossom* was so often fastened. Then, too, the easy indolence of the life was, beginning to claim him—its effortlessness, its freedom from responsibility. Perhaps a new part to learn at the beginning of the season—that was all. River audiences liked the old plays. Came to see them again and again. It was Ravenal who always made the little speech in front of the curtain. Wish to thank you one and all . . . always glad to come back to the old . . . to-morrow night that thrilling comedy–drama entitled . . . each and every one . . . . concert after the show . . .

Never had the *Cotton Blossom* troupe so revelled in home-baked cakes, pies, cookies; home-brewed wine; fruits of tree and vine. The female population of the river towns from the Great Lakes to the Gulf beheld in him the lover of their secret dreams and laid at his feet burnt offerings and shewbread. Ravenal, it was said by the *Cotton Blossom* troupe, could charm the gold out of their teeth.

Perhaps, with the passing of the years, he might have grown quite content with this life. Sometimes the little captain, when the two men were conversing quietly apart, dropped a word about the future.

"When I'm gone—you and Magnolia—the boat'll be yours, of course."

Ravenal would laugh. Little Captain Andy looked so very much alive, his bright brown eyes glancing here and there, missing nothing on land or shore, his brown paw scratching the whiskers that showed so little of gray, his nimble legs scampering from texas to gangplank, never still for more than a minute.

" No need to worry about that for another fifty years," Ravenal assured him.

The end had in it, perhaps, a touch of the ludicrous, as had almost everything the little capering captain did. The *Cotton Blossom,* headed upstream on the Mississippi, bound for St. Louis, had struck a snag in Cakohia Bend, three miles from the city. It was barely dawn, and a dense fog swathed the

river. The old *Cotton Blossom* probably would have sunk midstream. The
new boat stood the shock bravely. In the midst of the pandemonium that
followed the high shrill falsetto of the little captain's voice could be heard
giving commands which he, most of all, knew he had no right to give. The
pilot only was to be obeyed under such conditions. The crew understood
this, as did the pilot. It was, in fact, a legend that more than once in a crisis
Captain Andy on the upper deck had screamed his orders in a kind of
dramatic frenzy of satisfaction, interspersing these with picturesque and
vivid oaths during which he had capered and bounced his way right off the
deck and into the river, from which damp station he had continued to screech
his orders and profanities in cheerful unconcern until fished aboard again.
Exactly this happened. High above the clamour rose the voice of Andy. His
little figure whirled like that of a dervish. Up, down, fore, aft—suddenly he
was overboard unseen in the dimness, in the fog, in the savage swift current
of the Miississippi, wrapped in the coils of the old yellow serpent, tighter,
tighter, deeper, deeper, until his struggles ceased. She had him at last.

"The river," Magnolia had said, over and over, "The river. The river."

12

THEBES?" ECHOED PARTHENIA Ann Hawks, widow. The stiff crêpe of her
weeds seemed to bristle. "I'll do nothing of the kind, miss! If you and that
fine husband of yours think to rid yourself of me *that* way————"

"But, Mama, we're not trying to rid ourselves of you. How can you think
of such things! You've always said you hated the boat. Always. And now
that Papa—now that you needn't stay with the show any longer, I thought
you'd want to go back to Thebes to live."

"Indeed! And what's to become of the *Cotton Blossom,* tell me that,
Maggie Hawks!"

"I don't know," confessed Magnolia, miserably. "I don't—know. That's
what I think we ought to talk about." The *Cotton Blossom,* after her tragic
encounter with the hidden snag in the Mississippi, was in for repairs. The
damage to the show boat had been greater than they had thought. The snag
had, after all, inflicted a jagged wound. So, too, had it torn and wounded
something deep and hidden in Magnolia's soul. Suddenly she had a horror
of the great river whose treacherous secret fangs had struck so poisonously.
The sight of the yellow turbid flood sickened her; yet held her hypnotized.
Now she thought that she must run from it, with her husband and her child,
to safety. Now she knew that she never could be content away from it. She
wanted to flee. She longed to stay. This, if ever, was her chance. But the
river had Captain Andy. Somewhere in its secret coils he lay. She could not
leave him. On the rivers the three great mysteries—Love and Birth and
Death—had been revealed to her. All that she had known of happiness and
tragedy and tranquillity and adventure and romance and fulfilment was bound
up in the rivers. Their willow-fringed banks framed her world. The motley
figures that went up and down upon them or that dwelt on their shores were
her people. She knew them; was of them. The Mississippi had her as surely
as it had little Andy Hawks.

"Well, we're talking about it, ain't we?" Mrs. Hawks now demanded.

"I mean—the repairs are going to be quite expensive. She'll be laid up
for a month or more, right in the season. Now's the time to decide whether
we're going to try to run her ourselves just as if Papa were still————"

"I can see you've been talking things over pretty hard and fast with

Ravenal. Well, I'll tell you what we're going to do, miss. We're going to run her ourselves—leastways, I am."

"But, Mama!"

"Your pa left no will. Hawks all over. I've as much say-so as you have. More. I'm his widow. You won't see me willing to throw away the good-will of a business that it's taken years to build up. The boat's insurance'll take care of the repairs. Your pa's life insurance is paid up, and quite a decent sum—for him. I saw to that. You'll get your share, I'll get mine. The boat goes on like it always has. No Thebes for me. You'll go on playing ingénue leads; Ravenal juvenile. Kim———"

"No!" cried Magnolia much as Parthy had, years before. "Not Kim."

"Why not?"

There was about the Widow Hawks a terrifying and invincible energy. Her black habiliments of woe billowed about her like the sable wings of a destroying angel. With Captain Andy gone, she would appoint herself commander of the Cotton Blossom Floating Palace Theatre. Magnolia knew that. Who, knowing Parthy, could imagine it otherwise? She would appoint herself commander of their lives. Magnolia was no weakling. She was a woman of mettle. But no mettle could withstand the sledge-hammer blows of Parthy Ann Hawks' iron.

It was impossible that such an arrangement could hold. From the first Ravenal rejected it. But Magnolia's pleadings for at least a trial won him over, but grudgingly.

"It won't work, Nola, I tell you. We'll be at each other's throats. She's got all kinds of plans. I can see them whirling around in her eye."

"But you will try to be patient, won't you, Gay? For my sake and Kim's?"

But they had not been out a week before mutiny struck the *Cotton Blossom*. The first to go was Windy. Once his great feet were set toward the gangplank there was no stopping him. He was over seventy now, but he looked not an hour older than when he had come aboard the *Cotton Blossom* almost fifteen years before. To the irate widow he spoke briefly but with finality.

"You're Hawks' widow. That's why I said I'd take her same's if Andy was alive. I thought Nollie's husband would boss this boat, but seems you're running it. Well, ma'am, I ain't no petticoat-pilot. I'm off the end of this trip down. Young Tanner'll come aboard there and pilot you."

"Tanner! Who's he? How d'you know I want him? I'm running this boat."

"You better take him, Mrs. Hawks, ma'am. He's young, and not set in his ways, and likely won't mind your nagging. I'm too old. Lost my taste for the rivers, anyway, since Cap went. Lost my nerve, too, seems like. . . . Well, ma'am, I'm going."

And he went.

Changes came then, tripping on each other's heels. Mis' Means stayed, and little weak-chested Mr. Means. Frank had gone after Magnolia's marriage. Ralph left.

Parthy met these difficulties and defeats with magnificent generalship. She seemed actually to thrive on them. Do this. Do that. Ravenal's right eyebrow was cocked in a perpetual circumflex of disdain. One could feel the impact of opposition whenever the two came together. Every fibre of Ravenal's silent secretive nature was taut in rejection of this managerial mother-in-law. Every nerve and muscle of that energetic female's frame tingled with enmity toward this suave soft-spoken contemptuous husband of her daughter.

Finally, "Choose," said Gaylord Ravenal "between your mother and me."

Magnolia chose. Her decision met with such terrific opposition from Parthy as would have shaken any woman less determined and less in love.

"Where you going with that fine husband of yours? Tell me that!"

"I don't know."

"I'll warrant you don't. No more does he. Why're you going? You've got a good home on the boat."

"Kim . . . school . . ."

"Fiddlesticks!"

Magnolia took the plunge. "We're not—I'm not—Gay's not happy any more on the rivers."

"You'll be a sight unhappier on land before you're through, make no mistake about that, young lady. Where'll you go? Chicago, h'm? What'll you do there? Starve, and worse. I know. Many's the time you'll wish yourself back here."

Magnolia, nervous, apprehensive, torn, now burst into sudden rebellion against the iron hand that had gripped her all these years.

"How do you know? How can you be so sure? And even if you are right, what of it? You're always trying to keep people from doing the things they want to do. You're always wanting people to live cautiously. You fought to keep Papa from buying the *Cotton Blosson* in the first place, and made his life a hell. And now you won't leave it. You didn't want me to act. You didn't want me to marry Gay. You didn't want me to have Kim. Maybe you were right. Maybe I shouldn't have done any of those things. But how do you know? You can't twist people's lives around like that, even if you twist them right. Because how do you know that even when you're right you mayn't be wrong? If Papa had listened to you, we'd be living in Thebes. He'd be alive, probably. I'd be married to the butcher, maybe. You can't do it. Even God lets people have their own way, though they have to fall down and break their necks to find out they were wrong. . . . You can't do it . . . and you're glad when it turns out badly . . ."

She was growing incoherent.

Back of Parthy's opposition to their going was a deep relief of which even she was unaware, and whose existence she would have denied had she been informed of it. Her business talent, so long dormant, was leaping into life. Her energy was cataclysmic. One would almost have said she was happy. She discharged actors, crew; engaged actors, crew. Ordered supplies. Spoke of shifting to an entirely new territory the following year—perhaps to the rivers of North Carolina and Maryland. She actually did this, though not until much later. Magnolia, years afterward reading her mother's terse and maddening letters, would be seized with a nostalgia not for the writer but for the lovely sounding places of which she wrote—though they probably were as barren and unpicturesque as the river towns of the Mississippi and Ohio and Big Sandy and Kanawha. "We're playing the town of Bath, on the Pamlico River," Parthy's letter would say. Or, "We had a good week at Queenstown, on the Sassafras."

Magnolia, looking out into the gray Chicago streets, slippery with black ice, thick with the Lake Michigan fog, would repeat the names over to herself. Bath on the Pamlico. Queenstown on the Sassafras.

Mrs. Hawks, at parting, was all for Magnolia's retaining her financial share in the *Cotton Blossom,* the money accruing therefrom to be paid at regular intervals. In this she was right. She knew Ravenal. In her hard and managing way she loved her daughter; wished to insure her best interests. But Magnolia and Ravenal preferred to sell their share outright if she would buy. Ravenal would probably invest it in some business, Magnolia said.

"Yes—monkey business," retorted Mrs. Hawks. Then added, earnestly,

"Now mind, don't you come snivelling to me when it's gone and you and your child haven't a penny to bless yourselves with. For that's what it'll come to in the end. Mark my words. I don't say I wouldn't be happy to see you and Kim back. But not him. When he's run through every penny of your money, he needn't look to me for more. You can come back to the boat; you and Kim. I'll look for you. But him! Never!"

The two women faced each other, and they were no longer mother and daughter but two forces opposing each other with all the strength that lay in the deep and powerful nature of both.

Magnolia made one of those fine speeches. "I wouldn't come to you for help—not if I were starving to death, and Kim too."

"Oh, there's worse things than starving to death."

"I wouldn't come to you no matter what."

"You will, just the same. I'd take my oath on that"

"I never will."

Secretly she was filled with terror at leaving the rivers; for the rivers, and the little inaccessible river towns, and the indolent and naïve people of those towns whose very presence in them confessed them failures, had with the years taken on in Magnolia's eyes the friendly aspect of the accustomed. Here was comfort assured; here were friends; here the ease that goes with familiarity. Even her mother's bristling generalship had in it a protective quality. The very show boat was a second mother, shielding her from the problems and cares that beset the land-dweller. The *Cotton Blossom* had been a little world in itself on which life was a thing detached dream-like, narcotic.

As Magnolia Ravenal, with her husband and her child, turned from this existence of ease to the outside world of which she already had had one bitter taste, she was beset by hordes of fears and doubts. Yet opposing these, and all but vanquishing them, was the strong love of adventure—the eager curiosity about the unknown—which had always characterized her and her dead father, the little captain, and caused them both to triumph, thus far, over the clutching cautious admonitions of Parthenia Ann Hawks.

Fright and anticipation; nostalgia and curiosity; a soaring sense of freedom at leaving her mother's too-protective wing; a pang of compunction that she should feel this unfilial surge of relief.

They were going. You saw the three of them scrambling up the steep river bank to the levee (perhaps for the last time, Magnolia thought with a great pang. And within herself a voice cried no! no!) Ravenal slim, cool, contained; Magnolia whiter than usual, and frankly tearful; the child Kim waving an insouciant farewell with both small fists. They carried no bundles, no parcels, no valises. Ravenal disdained to carry parcels; he did not permit those of his party to carry them. Two Negroes in tattered and faded blue overalls made much of the luggage, stowing it inefficiently under the seats and over the floor of the livery rig which had been hired to take the three to the nearest railway station, a good twelve miles distant.

The *Cotton Blossom* troupe was grouped on the forward deck to see them off. The *Cotton Blossom* lay, smug, safe, plump, at the water's edge. A passing side-wheeler, flopping ponderously downstream, sent little flirty waves across the calm waters to her, and set her to palpitating coyly. Good-bye! Good-bye! Write, now. Mis' Means' face distorted in a ridiculous pucker of woe. Ravenal in the front seat with the driver. Magnolia and Kim in the back seat with the luggage protruding at uncomfortable angles all about them. Parthenia Ann Hawks, the better to see them, had stationed herself on the little protruding upper deck, forward—the deck that resembled a balcony much like that on the old *Cotton Blossom*. The livery nags started with a lurch up the dusty village street. They clattered across the bridge toward the upper road. Magnolia turned for a last glimpse through her tears. There stood Parthenia Ann Hawks, silhouetted against sky and water, a massive and almost menacing figure in her robes of black—tall, erect, indomitable. Her face was set. The keen eyes gazed, unblinking, across the sunlit waters. One arm was raised in a gesture of farewell. Ruthless, unconquerable, headstrong, untamed, terrible.

"She's like the River," Magnolia thought, through her grief, in a sudden flash of vision. "She's the one, after all, who's like the Mississippi."

A bend in the upper road. A clump of sycamores. The river, the show boat, the silent black-robed figure were lost to view.

13

THE MOST CASUAL onlooker could gauge the fluctuations of the Ravenal fortunes by any one of three signs. There was Magnolia Ravenal's sealskin sacque; there was Magnolia Ravenal's diamond ring; there was Gaylord Ravenal's malacca cane. Any or all of these had a way of vanishing and reappearing in a manner that would have been baffling to one not an habitué of South Clark Street, Chicago. Of the three, the malacca stick, though of almost no tangible value, disappeared first and oftenest, for it came to be recognized as an I O U by every reputable Clark Street pawnbroker. Deep in a losing game of faro at Jeff Hankins' or Mike McDonald's, Ravenal would summon a Negro boy to him. He would hand him the little ivory-topped cane. "Here—take this down to Abe Lipman's, corner Clark and Monroe. Tell him I want two hundred dollars. Hurry." Or: "Run over to Goldsmith's with this. Tell him a hundred."

The black boy would understand. In ten minutes he would return minus the stick and bearing a wilted sheaf of ten-dollar bills. If Ravenal's luck turned, the cane was redeemed. If it still stayed stubborn, the diamond ring must go; that failing, then the sealskin sacque. Ravenal, contrary to the custom of his confrères, wore no jewellery; possessed none. There were certain sinister aspects of these outward signs, as when, for example, the reigning sealskin sacque was known to skip an entire winter.

Perhaps none of these three symbols was as significant a betrayal of the Ravenal finances as was Gay Ravenal's choice of a breakfasting place. He almost never breakfasted at home. This was a reversion to one of the habits of his bachelor days; was, doubtless, a tardy rebellion, too, against the years spent under Mrs. Hawks' harsh régime. He always had hated those *Cotton Blossom* nine o'clock family breakfasts ominously presided over by Parthy in cap and curl papers.

Since their coming to Chicago Gay liked to breakfast between eleven and twelve, and certainly never rose before ten. If the Ravenal luck was high, the meal was eaten in leisurely luxury at Billy Boyle's Chop House between Clark and Dearborn streets. This was most agreeable, for at Billy Boyle's, during the noon hour, you encountered Chicago's sporting blood—political overlords, gamblers, jockeys, actors, reporters—these last mere nobodies— lean and somewhat morose young fellows vaguely known as George Ade, Brand Whitlock, John McCutcheon, Pete Dunne. Here the news and gossip of the day went round. Here you saw the Prince Albert coat, the silk hat, the rattling cuffs, the glittering collar, the diamond stud of the professional gamester. Old Carter Harrison, Mayor of Chicago, would drop in daily, a good twenty-five-cent cigar waggling between his lips as he greeted this friend and that. In came the brokers from the Board of Trade across the way. Smoke-blue air. The rich heavy smell of thick steaks cut from prime Western beef. Massive glasses of beer through which shone the pale amber of light brew, or the seal-brown of dark. The scent of strong black coffee. Rye bread pungent with caraway. Little crisp round breakfast rolls sprinkled with poppy-seed.

Calories, high blood pressure, vegetable luncheons, golf, were words not yet included in the American everyday vocabulary. Fried potatoes were still considered a breakfast dish, and a meatless meal was a snack.

Here it was, then, that Gay Ravenal, slim, pale, quiet, elegant, liked best to begin his day; listening charmingly and attentively to the talk that swirled about him—talk of yesterday's lucky winners in Gamblers' Alley, at Prince Varnell's place, or Jeff Hankins' or Mike McDonald's; of the Washington Park racetrack entries; of the new blonde girl at Hetty Chilson's, of politics in their simplest terms. Occasionally he took part in this talk, but like most professional gamblers, his was not the conversational gift. He was given credit for the astuteness he did not possess merely on the strength of his cool evasive glance, his habit of listening and saying little, and his bland poker face.

"Ravenal doesn't say much but there's damned little he misses. Watch him an hour straight and you can't make out from his face whether he's cleaning up a thousand or losing his shirt." An enviable Clark Street reputation.

Still, this availed him nothing when funds were low. At such times he eschewed Billy Boyle's and breakfasted meagrely instead at the Cockeyed Bakery just east of Clark. That famous refuge for the temporarily insolvent was so named because of the optical peculiarity of the lady who owned it and who dispensed its coffee and sinkers. This refreshment cost ten cents. The coffee was hot, strong, reviving; the sinkers crisp and fresh. Every Clark Street gambler was, at one time or another, through the vagaries of Lady Luck, to be found moodily munching the plain fare that made up the limited menu to be had at the Cockeyed Bakery. For that matter lacking even the modest sum required for this sustenance, he knew that there he would be allowed to "throw up a tab" until luck should turn.

Many a morning Gaylord Ravenal, dapper, nonchalant, sartorially exquisite, fared forth at eleven with but fifty cents in the pocket of his excellently tailored pants. Usually, on these occasions, the malacca stick was significantly absent. Of the fifty cents, ten went for the glassy shoeshine; twenty-five for a boutonnière; ten for coffee and sinkers at the Cockeyed Bakery. The remaining five cents stayed in his pocket as a sop to the superstition that no coin breeds no more coins. Stopping first to look in a moment at Weeping Willy Mangler's, or at Reilly's pool room for a glance at the racing chart, or to hear a bit of the talk missed through his enforced absence from Boyle's, he would end at Hankins' or McDonald's, there to woo fortune with nothing at all to offer as oblation. But affairs did not reach this pass until after the first year.

It was incredible that Magnolia Ravenal could so soon have adapted herself to the life in which she now moved. Yet it was explicable, perhaps, when one took into consideration her inclusive nature. She was interested, alert, eager—and still in love with Gaylord Ravenal. Her life on the rivers had accustomed her to all that was bizarre in humanity. Queenie and Jo had been as much a part of her existence as Elly and Schultzy. The housewives in the little towns, the Negroes lounging on the wharves, the gamblers in the river-front saloons, the miners of the coal belt, the Northern fruit-pickers, the boatmen, the Southern poor whites, the Louisiana aristocracy, all had passed in fantastic parade before her ambient eyes. And she, too, had marched in a parade, a figure as gorgeous, as colourful as the rest.

Now, in this new life, she accepted everything, enjoyed everything with a naïveté that was, perhaps, her greatest charm. It was, doubtless, the thing that held the roving Ravenal to her. Nothing shocked her; this was her singularly pure and open mind. She brought to this new life an interest and a curiosity as fresh as that which had characterized the little girl who had so eagerly and companionably sat with Mr. Pepper, the pilot, in the bright cosy glass-enclosed pilot house atop the old *Creole Belle* on that first enchanting trip down the Mississippi to New Orleans.

To him she had said, "What's around that bend? . . . Now what's coming? . . . How deep is it here? . . . What used to be there? . . . What island is that?"

Mr. Pepper, the pilot, had answered her questions amply and with a feeling of satisfaction to himself as he beheld her childish hunger for knowledge being appeased.

Now she said to her husband with equal eagerness: "Who is that stout woman with the pretty yellowhaired girl? What queer eyes they have! . . . What does it mean when it says odds are two to one? . . . Why do they call him Bath House John? . . . Who is that large woman in the victoria, with the lovely sunshade? How rich her dress is, yet it's plain. Why don't you introduce me to——— Oh! That! Hetty Chilson! Oh! . . . Why do they call him Bad Jimmy Connerton? . . . But why do they call it the Levee? It's really Clark Street, and no water anywhere near, so why do they call it the Levee? . . . What's a percentage game? . . . Hieronymus! What a funny word! . . . Mike McDonald? That! Why, he looks like a farmer, doesn't he? A farmer in his Sunday-best black clothes that don't fit him. The Boss of the Gamblers. Why do they call his place 'The Store'? . . . Oh, Gay darling, I wish you wouldn't. . . . Now don't frown like that. I just mean I—when I think of Kim, I get scared because, how about Kim—I mean when she grows up? . . . Why are they called owl cars? . . . But I don't understand why Lipman lets you have money just for a cane that isn't worth more than ten or twenty . . . How do pawnbrokers . . . Mont Tennes— what a queer name! . . . Al Hankins? Oh, you're joking now. Really killed by having a folding bed close up on him! Oh, I'll never again sleep in a . . . Boiler Avenue? . . . Hooley's Theatre? . . . Cinquevalli? . . . Fanny Davenport? . . . Derby Day? . . . Weber and Fields? . . . Sauterne? . . . Rector's? . . ."

Quite another world about which to be curious—a world as sordid and colourful and crude and passionate and cruel and rich and varied as that other had been.

It had taken Ravenal little more than a year to dissipate the tidy fortune which had been Magnolia's share of Captain Andy's estate, including the *Cotton Blossom* interest. He had, of course, meant to double the sum—to multiply it many times so that the plump thousands should increase to tens— to hundreds of thousands. Once you had money—a really respectable amount of it—it was simple enough to manipulate that money so as to make it magically produce more and more money.

They had made straight for Chicago, at that period the gamblers' paradise. When Ravenal announced this step, a little look of panic had come into Magnolia's eyes. She was reluctant to demur at his plans. It was the thing her mother always had done when her father had proposed a new move. Always Captain Andy's enthusiasm had suffered the cold douche of Parthy's disapproval. At the prospect of Chicago, the old haunts, congenial companions, the restaurants, the theatres, the races, Ravenal had been more elated than she had ever seen him. He had become almost loquacious. He could even be charming to Mrs. Hawks, now that he was so nearly free of her. That iron woman had regarded him as her enemy to the last and, in making over to Magnolia the goodish sum of money which was due her, had uttered dire predictions, all of which promptly came true.

That first year in Chicago was a picture so kaleidoscopic, so extravagant, so ridiculous that even the child Kim retained in her memory's eye something of its colour and pageantry. This father and mother in their twenties seemed really little older than their child. Certainly there was something pathetically childish in their evident belief that they could at once spend their money and keep it intact. Just a fur coat—what was that! Bonnets. A smart high yellow trap. Horses. The races. Suppers. A nursemaid for Kim. Magnolia knew nothing of money. She never had had any. On the *Cotton Blossom* money was a commodity of which one had little need.

On coming to Chicago they had gone directly to the Sherman House. Compared with this, that first visit to Chicago before Kim's birth had been a mere picnic jaunt. Ravenal was proud of his young wife and of his quiet, grave big-eyed child; of the nursemaid in a smart uniform; of the pair of English hackneys which he sometimes allowed Magnolia to drive, to her exquisite delight. Magnolia had her first real evening dress, cut décolleté; tasted champagne; went to the races at the Washington Park race track; sat in a box at Hooley's; was horrified at witnessing the hootchiekootchie dance on the Midway Plaisance at the World's Fair.

The first fur coat was worthy of note. The wives of the well-to-do wore sealskin sacques as proof of their husband's prosperity. Magnolia descended to these later. But the pelts which warmed her during that first winter of Chicago lake blasts and numbing cold had been cunningly matched in Paris, and French fingers had fashioned them into a wrap.

Ravenal had selected it for her, of course. He always accompanied her on her shopping trips. He liked to loll elegantly at ease like a pasha while the keen-eyed saleswomen brought out this gown and that for his expert inspection. To these alert ladies it was plain to see that Magnolia knew little enough about chic attire. The gentleman, though—he knew what was what. Magnolia had been aghast at the cost of that first fur coat, but then, how should she know of such things? Between them, she and Parthy had made most of the costumes she had worn in her *Cotton Blossom* days, both for stage and private use. The new coat was a black astrakhan jacket; the fur lay in large smooth waves known as baby lamb. Magnolia said it made her feel like a cannibal to wear a thing like that. The salesladies did not smile at this, but that was all right because Magnolia had not intended that they should. The revers and cuffs were of Russian sable, dark and rich and deep; and it had large mutton-leg sleeves—large enough to contain her dress sleeves comfortably, with a little expert aid in the way of stuffing. "Stuff my sleeves in," was one of the directions always given a gentleman when he assisted a lady with her wrap.

This royal garment had cost————"Oh, Gay!" Magnolia had protested, in a low shocked voice (but not so low that the sharp-eared saleswomen failed to hear it)—"Oh, Gay! I honestly don't think we ought————"

"Mrs. Potter Palmer," spoke up the chief saleswoman in a voice at once sharp and suave, "has a coat identically similar. They are the only two of the kind in the whole country. To tell you the truth, I think the sable skins on this garment of madam's are just a little finer than Mrs. Palmer's. Though perhaps it's just that madam sets it off better, being so young and all."

He liked her to wear, nestling in the rich depths of the sable revers, a bunch of violets. For the theatre she had one of those new winged bonnets, representing a butterfly, cunningly contrived of mousseline de soie wired and brilliantly spangled so that it quivered and trembled with the movements of her head and sparkled enchantingly. Kim adored the smell of the violet-scented creature who Kissed her good-night and swept out, glittering. The impression must have gone deep, deep into the childish mind, for twenty years later she still retained a sort of story-book mental picture of this black-haired creamy mother who would come in late of a winter afternoon laughing and bright-eyed after a drive up Grand Boulevard in the sleigh behind the swift English hackneys. This vision would seem to fill the warm room with a delightful mixture of violets, and fur, and cold fresh air and velvet and spangles and love and laughter. Kim would plunge her face deep into the soft scented bosom.

"Oh, Gay, do see how she loves the violets! You won't mind if I take them off and put them here in this glass so she———— No, you mustn't buy me any fresh ones. Please! I wish she didn't look quite so much like me . . . her mouth . . . but it's going to be a great wide one, like mine. . . . Oh, Bernhardt! Who wants her little girl to look like Bernhardt! Besides, Kim isn't going to be an actress."

At the end of a year or so of this the money was gone—simply gone. Of course, it hadn't been only the hackneys, and the races, and the trap, and the furs, and the suppers and the theatres and dresses and Gay's fine garments and the nurse and the hotel. For, as Ravenal explained, the hackneys hadn't even been pure-blooded, which would have brought them up to one thousand each. He had never been really happy about them, because of a slight blot on their family escutcheon which had brought them down to a mere six hundred apiece. This flaw was apparent, surely, to no one who was not an accredited judge at a horse show. Yet when Ravenal and Magnolia on Derby Day joined the gay stream of tallyhos, wagonettes, coaches, phaetons, tandems, cocking carts, and dog-carts sweeping up Michigan Avenue and Grand Boulevard toward the Washington Park race track he was likely to fall into one of his moody silences and to flick the hackneys with little contemptuous cuts of the long lithe whip in a way that only they—and Magnolia—understood. On such occasions he called them nags.

"Ah! That off nag broke again. That's because they're not thorough-breds."

"But, Gay, you're hurting their mouths, sawing like that."

"Please, Nola. This isn't a Mississippi barge I'm driving."

She learned many things that first year, and saw so much that part of what she saw was mercifully soon forgotten. You said Darby Day, very English. You pretended not to mind when your husband went down to speak to Hetty Chilson and her girls in their box. For that matter, you pretended not to see Hetty Chilson and her girls at all, though they had driven out in a sort of private procession of victorias, landaus, broughams, and were by far the best-dressed women at the races. They actually set the styles, Gay had told her. Hetty Chilson's girls wore rich, quiet, almost sedate clothes; and no paint on their faces. They seemed an accepted part of the world in which Gaylord Ravenal moved. Even in the rough life of the rivers, Magnolia had always understood that women of Hetty Chilson's calling simply did not exist in the public sense. They were not of the substance of everyday life, but were shadows, sinister, menacing, evil. But with this new life of Magnolia's came the startling knowledge that these ladies played an important part in the social and political life of this huge sprawling Mid-western city. This stout, blonde, rather handsome woman who carried herself with an air of prosperous assurance; whose shrewd keen glance and hearty laugh rather attracted you—this one was Hetty Chilson. The horsewomen you saw riding in the Lincoln Park bridle path, handsomely habited in black close-fitting riding clothes, were, likely as not, Hetty Chilson's girls. She was actually a power in her way. When strangers were shown places of interest in Chicago—the Potter Palmer castle on Lake Shore Drive, the Art Museum, the Stockyards, the Auditorium Hotel, the great mansions of Phil Armour and his son on Michigan Avenue, with the garden embracing an entire city block—Hetty Chilson's place, too, was pointed out (with a lowering of the voice, of course, and a little leer, and perhaps an elbow dug into the ribs). A substantial brick house on Clark Street, near Polk, with two lions, carved in stone, absurdly guarding its profane portals.

"Hetty Chilson's place," Gay explained to his wide-eyed young wife, "is like a club. You're likely to find every prominent politician in Chicago there, smoking and having a sociable drink. And half the political plots that you read about in the newspapers later are hatched at Hetty's. She's as smart as they make 'em. Bought a farm, fifteen acres, out at Ninetieth and State, for her father and mother. And she's got a country place out on the Kankakee River, near Momence—about sixty miles south of here—that's known to have one of the finest libraries in the country. Cervantes—Balzac—rare editions. Stable full of horses—rose garden————"

" But, Gay dear!"

You saw Hetty driving down State Street during the shopping hour in her Kimball-made Victoria, an equipage such as royalty might have used, its ebony body fashioned by master craftsmen, its enamel as rich and deep and shining as a piano top. Her ample skirts would be spread upon the plum-coloured cushions. If it was summer the lace ruffles of her sunshade would plume gently in the breeze. In winter her mink coat swathed her full firm figure. One of her girls sat beside her, faultlessly dressed, pale, unvivacious. Two men in livery on the box. Harness that shone with polished metal and jingled splendidly. Two slim, quivering, high-stepping chestnuts. Queen of her world—Chicago's underworld.

"But, Gay dear!"

"Well, how about France!"

"France?"

"How about the women you used to read about—learned about them in your history books, for that matter, at school? Pompadour and Maintenon and Du Barry! Didn't they mix up in the politics of their day—and weren't they recognized? Courtesans, every one of them. You think just because they wore white wigs and flowered silk hoops and patches————"

A little unaccustomed flush surged over Magnolia's pallor—the deep, almost painful red of indignation. She was an inexperienced woman, but she was no fool. These last few months had taught her many things. Also the teachings of her school-teacher mother had not, after all, been quite forgotten, it appeared.

"She's a common woman of the town, Gaylord Ravenal. All the wigs and patches and silks in the world wouldn't make her anything else. She's no more a Du Barry than your Hinky Dink is a—uh—Mazarin."

It was as though he took a sort of perverse pleasure in thus startling her. It wasn't that she was shocked in the prim sense of the word. She was bewildered and a little frightened. At such times the austere form and the grim visage of Parthenia Ann Hawks would rise up before her puzzled eyes. What would Parthy have said of these unsavoury figures now passing in parade before Magnolia's confused vision—Hetty Chilson, Doc Haggerty, Mike McDonald, "Prince" Varnell, Effie Hankins? Uneasy though she was, Magnolia could manage to smile at the thought of her mother's verbal destruction of this raffish crew. There were no half tones in Parthy's vocabulary. A hussy was a hussy; a rake a rake. But her father, she thought, would have been interested in all this, and more than a little amused. His bright brown eyes would have missed nothing; the little nimble figure would have scampered inquisitively up and down the narrow and somewhat sinister lane that lay between Washington and Madison streets, known as Gamblers' Alley; he would have taken a turn at faro; appraised the Levee ladies at their worth; visited Sam T. Jack's Burlesque Show over on Madison, and Kohl & Middleton's Museum, probably, and Hooley's Theatre certainly. Nothing in Chicago's Levee life would have escaped little Captain Andy, and nothing would have changed him.

"See it all, Nollie," he had said to her in the old *Cotton Blossom* days, when Parthy would object to their taking this or that jaunt ashore between shows. "Don't you believe 'em when they say that what you don't know won't hurt you. Biggest lie ever was. See it all and go your own way and nothing'll hurt you. If what you see ain't pretty, what's the odds! See it anyway. Then next time you don't have to look."

Magnolia, gazing about her, decided that she was seeing it all.

The bulk of the money had gone at faro. The suckers played roulette, stud poker, hazard, the bird-cage, chuck-a-luck (the old army game). But your gambler played faro. Faro was Gaylord Ravenal's game, and he played at Hankins'—not at George Hankins' where they catered to the cheap trade who played percentage games—but at Jeff Hankins' or Mike McDonald's where were found the highest stakes in Chicago. Faro was not a game with Ravenal—it was for him at once his profession, his science, his drug, his drink, his mistress. He had, unhappily, as was so often the case with your confirmed gambler, no other vice. He rarely drank, and then abstemiously; smoked little and then a mild cigar, ate sparingly and fastidiously; eschewed even the diamond ring and shirt-stud of his kind.

The two did not, of course, watch the money go, or despair because it would soon be gone. There seemed to be plenty of it. There always would be enough. Next week they would invest it securely. Ravenal had inside tips on the market. He had heard of a Good Thing. This was not the right time, but They would let him know when the magic moment was at hand. In the meantime there was faro. And there were the luxurious hotel rooms with their soft thick carpets, and their big comfortable beds; ice water tinkling at the door in answer to your ring; special dishes to tempt the taste of Mr. Ravenal and his lady. The sharp-eyed gentleman in evening clothes who stood near the little ticket box as you entered the theatre said, "Good-evening, Mr. Ravenal," when they went to Hooley's or McVicker's or the Grand Opera House, or Kohl and Castle's. The heads of departments in Mandel's or Carson Pirie's or even Marshall Field's said, "I have something rather special to show you, Mrs. Ravenal. I thought of you the minute it came in."

Sometimes it seemed to Magnolia that the *Cotton Blossom* had been only a phantom ship—the rivers a dream—a legend.

It was all very pleasant and luxurious and strange. And Magnolia tried not to mind the clang of Clark Street by day and by night. The hideous cacophony of noise invaded their hotel apartment and filled its every corner. She wondered why the street-car motormen jangled their warning bells so persistently. Did they do it as an antidote to relieve their own jangled nerves? *Pay*-pes! MO'-nin' *pay*-pes! Crack! Crack! Crackcrackcrack! The shooting gallery across the street. Someone passing the bedroom door, walking heavily and clanking the metal disk of his room key. The sound of voices, laughter, from the street, and the unceasing shuffle of footsteps on stone. Whee-e-e-e! Whoop-a! Ye-e-eow! A drunkard. She knew about that, too. Part of her recently acquired knowledge. Ravenal had told her about Big Steve Rowan, the three-hundred-pound policeman, who, partly because of his goatee and moustache, and partly because of his expert manipulation of his official weapon, was called the Jack of Clubs.

"You'll never see Big Steve arrest a drunk at night," Gay had explained to her, laughing. "No, sir! Nor any other Clark Street cop if he can help it. If they arrest a man they have to appear against him the next morning at the nine o'clock police court. That means getting up early. So if he's able to navigate at all, they pass him on down the street from corner to corner until they get him headed west somewhere, or north across the bridge. Great system.

All this was amusing and colourful, perhaps, but scarcely conducive to tranquillity and repose. Often Magnolia, lying awake by the side of the sleeping man, or lying awake awaiting his late return, would close her stinging eyelids the better to visualize and sense the deep velvet silence of the rivers of her girlhood—the black velvet nights, quiet, quiet. The lisping clucksuck of the water against the hull.

Clang! MO'nin' *pay*-pes! Crack! E-e-eee-yow!

And then, suddenly, one day: "But, Gay dear, how do you mean you haven't one hundred dollars? It's for that bronze-green velvet that you like so much, though I always think it makes me look sallow. You did urge me to get it, you know, dear. And now this is the third time they've sent the bill. So if you'll give me the money—or write a check, if you'd rather."

"I tell you I haven't got it, Nola."

"Oh, well, to-morrow'll do. But please be sure tomorrow, because I hate———"

"I can't be any surer to-morrow than I am to-day. I haven't got a hundred dollars in the world. And that's a fact."

Even after he had finished explaining, she did not understand; could not believe it; continued to stare at him with those great dark startled eyes.

Bad luck. At what? Faro. But, Gay—thousands! Well, thousands don't last forever. Took a flyer. Flyer? Yes. A tip on the market. Market? The stock market. Stock? Oh, you wouldn't understand. But all of it, Gay? Well, some of it lost at faro. Where? Hankins'. How much? What does it matter?— it's gone. But, Gay, how much at faro? Oh, a few thousands. Five? Y-y- yes. Yes, five. More than that? Well, nearer ten, probably.

She noticed then that the malacca cane was gone. She slipped her diamond ring off her finger. Gave it to him. With the years, that became an automatic gesture.

Thus the change in their mode of living did not come about gradually. They were wafted, with Cinderella-like celerity, from the coach-and-four to the kitchen ashes. They left the plush and ice water and fresh linen and rich food and luxurious service of the Sherman House for a grubby little family hotel that was really a sort of actors' boarding house, on the north side, just across the Clark Street bridge, on Ontario Street. It was, Ravenal said, within convenient walking distance of places.

"What places?" Magnolia asked. But she knew. A ten minutes' saunter brought you to Gamblers' Alley. In the next fifteen years there was never a morning when Gaylord Ravenal failed to prove this interesting geographical fact.

14

THE RAVENAL REVERSES, if they were noticed at all in Gamblers' Alley, went politely unremarked. There was a curious and definite code of honour among the frequenters of Chicago's Levee. You paid your gambling debts. You never revealed your own financial status by way of conversation. You talked little. You maintained a certain physical, sartorial, and social standard in the face of all reverses. There were, of course, always unmistakable signs to be read even at the most passing glance. You drew your conclusions; made no comment. If you were seen to breakfast for days—a week—two weeks—at the Cockeyed Bakery, you were greeted by your confréres with the same suavity that would have been accorded you had you been standing treat at Billy Boyle's or the Palmer House. Your shoe might be cracked, but it must shine. Your linen might be frayed, but it must be clean. Your cheeks were perhaps a trifle hollow, but they must be shaven and smell pleasantly of bay rum. You might dine at Burkey and Milan's (Full Meal 15c.) with ravenous preliminary onslaughts upon the bread-and-butter and piccalilli. But you consumed, delicately and fastidiously, just so much and no more of the bountiful and rich repast spread out for your taking at Jeff Hankins' or at Mike McDonald's. Though your suit was shabby, it must bear the mark of that tailor to the well-dressed sporting man—Billy McLean. If you were too impecunious for Hetty Chilson's you disdained the window-tapping dives on Boiler Avenue and lower Clark Street and State; the sinister and foul shanties of Big Maud and her ilk. You bathed, shaved, dressed, ate, smoked with the same exotic care when you were broke as when luck was running your way. Your cigar was a mild one (also part of the code), and this mild one usually a dead one as you played. And no one is too broke for one cigar a day. Twelve o'clock—noon—found you awake. Twelve o'clock—midnight—found you awake. Somewhere between those hours you slept the deep sweet sleep of the abstemious. You were, in short, a gambler—and a gentleman.

Thus, when the Ravenals moved, perforce, from the comfort of the Sherman to the threadbare shabbiness of the Ontario Street boarding house, there was nothing in Gaylord Ravenal's appearance to tell the tale. If his cronies knew of his financial straits, they said nothing. Magnolia had no women friends. During the year or more of their residence in Chicago she had been richly content with Kim and Gay. The child had a prim and winning gravity that gave her a curiously grown-up air.

"Do you know, Gay," Magnolia frequently said, "Kim sometimes makes me feel so gawky and foolish and young. When she looks at me after I've been amused about something, or am enthusiastic or excited or—you know—anyway, she looks at me out of those big eyes of hers, very solemn, and I feel—— Oh, Gay, you don't think she resembles—that is—do you think she is much like Mama?"

"God forbid!" ejaculated Ravenal, piously.

Kim had been Magnolia's delight during the late morning hours and the early afternoon. In company with the stolid nurse, they had fared forth in search of such amusement as the city provided for a child brought up amidst the unnatural surroundings of this one. The child had grown accustomed to seeing her nurse stand finger on lips, eyes commanding silence, before the closed door of her parents ' room at ten in the morning—at eleven, even— and she got it into her baby head that this attitude, then, was the proper and normal one in which to approach the closed door of that hushed chamber.

Late one morning Magnolia, in nightgown and silken wrapper, had opened this door suddenly to find the child stationed there, silent, grave-eyed, admonitory, while in one corner, against the door case, reposed the favourite doll of her collection—a lymphatic blonde whose eyes had met with some unfortunate interior mishap which gave them a dying-calf look. This sprawling and inert lady was being shushed in a threatening and dramatic manner by the sternly maternal Kim. There was, at sight of this, that which brought the quick sting of tears to Magnolia's eyes. She gathered the child up in her arms, kissed her passionately, held her close, brought her to Ravenal as he lay yawning.

"Gay, look at her! She was standing by the door telling her doll not to make any noise. She's only a baby. We don't pay enough attention to her. Do you think I neglect her? Standing there by the door! And it's nearly noon. Oh, Gay, we oughtn't to be living here. We ought to be living in a house—a little house where it's quiet and peaceful and she can play."

"Lovely," said Gay. "Thebes, for example. Now don't get dramatic, Nola, for God's sake. I thought we'd finished with that."

With the change in their fortunes the English nurse had vanished with the rest. She had gone, together with the hackneys, the high smart yellow cart, the violets, the green velvets, the box seats at the theatre, the champagne. She, or her counterpart, never returned, but many of the lost luxuries did, from time to time. There were better days to come, and worse. Their real fortune gone, there now was something almost humdrum and methodical about the regularity of their ups and downs. There rarely was an intermediate state. It was feast or famine, always. They actually settled down to the life of a professional gambler and his family. Ravenal would have a run of luck at faro. Presto! Rooms at the Palmer House. A box at the races. The theatre. Supper at Rector's after the theatre. Hello, Gay! Evening, Mrs. Ravenal. Somebody's looking mighty lovely to-night. A new sealskin sacque. Her diamond ring on her finger. Two new suits of clothes for Ravenal, made by Billy McLean. A little dinner for Gay's friends at Cardinal Bemis's famous place on Michigan Avenue. You couldn't fool the Cardinal.

He would ask suavely, "What kind of a dinner, Mr. Ravenal?" If Gay replied, "Oh—uh—a cocktail and a little red wine," Cardinal Bemis knew that luck was only so-so, and that the dinner was to be good, but plainish. But if, in reply to the tactful question, Gay said, magnificently, " A cocktail, Cardinal; claret, sauterne, champagne, and liqueurs," Bemis knew that Ravenal had had a real run of luck and prepared the canvasbacks boiled in champagne; or there were squabs or plover, with all sorts of delicacies, and the famous frozen watermelon that had been plugged, filled with champagne, put on ice for a day, and served in such chunks of scarlet fragrance as made the nectar and ambrosia of the gods seem poor, flavourless fare indeed.

Magnolia, when luck was high, tried to put a little money by as she had instinctively been prompted to do during those first months of their marriage, when they still were on the *Cotton Blossom*. But she rarely had money of her own. Gay, when he had ready cash, was generous—but not with the handing over of the actual coin itself.

"Buy yourself some decent clothes, Nola; and the kid. Tell them to send me the bill. That thing you're wearing is a terrible sight. It seems to me you haven't worn anything else for months." Which was true enough. There was something fantastic about the magnificence with which he ignored the reason for her not having worn anything else for months. It had been, certainly, her one decent garment during the lean period just passed, and she had cleaned and darned and refurbished to keep it so. Her experience in sewing during the old *Cotton Blossom* days stood her in good stead now.

There were times when even the Ontario Street hotel took on the aspect of unattainable luxury. That meant rock bottom. Then it was that the Ravenals took a room at three dollars a week in a frowzy rooming house on Ohio or Indiana or Erie; the Bloomsbury of Chicago. There you saw unshaven men, their coat collars turned up in artless attempt to conceal the absence of linen, sallying forth, pail in hand, at ten or eleven in the morning in search of the matutinal milk and rolls to accompany the coffee that was even now cooking over the gas jet. Morning was a musty jade on these streets; nothing fresh and dewy and sparkling about her. The ladies of the neighbourhood lolled huge, unwieldy, flaccid, in wrappers. In the afternoon you saw them amazingly transformed into plump and pinkly powdered persons, snugly corseted, high-heeled, rustling in silk petticoats, giving out a heady scent. They were friendly voluble ladies who beamed on the pale slim Magnolia, and said, "Won't you smile for me just a little bit? H'm?" to the sedate and solemn-eyed Kim.

Magnolia, too, boiled coffee and eggs over the gas jet in these lean times. Gravely she counted out the two nickels that would bring her and Kim home from Lincoln Park on the street car. Lincoln Park was an oasis—a life-giving breathing spot to the mother and child. They sallied forth in the afternoon; left the gas jet, the three-dollar room, the musty halls, the stout females behind them. There was the zoo; there was the lake; there was the grass. If the lake was their choice it led inevitably to tales of the rivers. It was in this way that the background of her mother's life was first etched upon Kim's mind. The sight of the water always filled Magnolia with a nostalgia so acute as to amount to an actual physical pain.

The childish treble would repeat the words as the two sat on a park bench facing the great blue sea that was Lake Michigan.

" You remember the boat, don't you, Kim?"

"Do I?" Kim's diction was curiously adult, due, doubtless, to the fact that she had known almost no children.

"Of course you do, darling. Don't you remember the river, and Grandma and Grandpa————"

"Cap'n!"

"Yes! I knew you remembered. And all the little darkies on the landing. And the band. And the steam organ. You used to put your hands over your ears and run and hide, because it frightened you. And Jo and Queenie."

"Tell me about it."

And Magnolia would assuage her own longing by telling and retelling the things she liked to remember. The stories, with the years, became a saga. Figures appeared, vanished, reappeared. The rivers wound through the whole. Elly, Schultzy, Julie, Steve; the man in the box with the gun; the old *Creole Belle* and Magnolia's first trip on the Mississippi; Mr. Pepper and the pilot house; all these became familiar and yet legendary figures and incidents to the child. They were her Three Bears, her Bo-peep, her Red Riding Hood, her Cinderella. Magnolia must have painted these stories with the colour of life itself, for the child never wearied of them.

"Tell me the one about the time you were a little girl and Gra'ma locked you in the bedroom because she didn't want you to see the show and you climbed out of the window in your nightie . . .."

Kim Ravenal was probably the only white child north of the Mason and Dixon line who was sung to sleep to the tune of those plaintive, wistful Negro plantation songs which later were to come into such vogue a spirituals. They were the songs that Magnolia had learned from black Jo and from Queenie, the erstwhile rulers of the *Cotton Blossom* galley. Swing Low Sweet Chariot, she sang. O, Wasn't Dat a Wide River! And, of course, All

God's Chillun Got Wings. Kim loved them. When she happened to be ill
with some childhood ailment, they soothed her. Magnolia sang these songs,
always, as she had learned to sing them in unconscious imitation of the soft
husky Negro voice of her teacher. Through the years of Kim's early childhood, Magnolia's voice might have been heard thus wherever the shifting
Ravenal fortunes had tossed the three, whether the red-plush luxury of the
Sherman House, the respectable dulness of the family hotel, or the sordid
fustiness of the cheap rooming house. Once, when they were living at the
Sherman, Magnolia, seated in a rocking chair with Kim in her arms, had
stopped suddenly in her song at a curious sound in the corridor. She had
gone swiftly to the door, had opened it, and had been unable to stifle a little
shriek of surprise and terror mingled. There stood a knot of black faces,
teeth gleaming, eyes rolling. Attracted by the songs so rarely heard in the
North, the Sherman House bell boys and waiters had eagerly gathered outside the closed door in what was, perhaps, as flattering and sincere a compliment as ever a singer received.

Never did child know such ups and downs as did this daughter of the
Chicago gambler and the showboat actress. She came to take quite for
granted sudden and complete changes that would have disorganized any one
more conventionally bred. One week she would find herself living in grubby
quarters where the clammy fetid ghost of cabbage lurked always in the halls;
the next would be a gay panorama of whisking waiters, new lace petticoats,
drives along the lake front, ice cream for dessert, front seats at the matinée.
The theatre bulked large in the life of the Ravenals. Magnolia loved it without
being possessed of much discrimination with regard to it. Farce, comedy,
melodrama—the whole gamut as outlined by Polonius—all held her interested, enthralled. Ravenal was much more critical than she. You saw him
smoking in the lobby, bored, dégagé. It might be the opening of the rebuilt
Lincoln Theatre on Clark near Division, with Gustave Frohman's company
playing The Charity Ball.

"Oh, Gay, isn't it exciting!"

"I don't think much of it. Cheap-looking theatre, too, isn't it? They might
better have left it alone after it burned down."

Kim's introduction to the metropolitan theatre was when she was taken,
a mere baby, to see the spectacle America at the Auditorium. Before she
was ten she had seen everyone from Julia Marlowe to Anna Held; from
Bernhardt to Lillian Russell. Gravely she beheld the antics of the Rogers
Brothers. As gravely saw Klaw and Erlanger's company in Foxey Quiller.

"It isn't that she doesn't see the joke," Magnolia confided to Ravenal,
almost worriedly. "She actually doesn't seem to approve. Of course, I suppose I ought to be glad that she prefers the more serious things, but I wish
she wouldn't seem quite so grown-up at ten. By the time she's twenty she'll
probably be spanking me and putting me to bed."

Certainly Magnolia was young enough for two. She was the sort of theatre-
goer who clutches the hand of her neighbour when stirred. When Ravenal
was absent Kim learned to sustain her mother at such emotional moments.
They two frequently attended the theatre together. Their precarious mode
of living cut them off from sustained human friendships. But the theatre was
always there to stimulate them, to amuse them, to make them forget or
remember. There were long afternoons to be filled, and many evenings as
Ravenal became more and more deeply involved in the intricacies of Chicago's night world.

There was, curiously enough, a pendulum-like regularity about his irregular life. His comings and goings could be depended on almost as though
he were a clerk or a humdrum bookkeeper. Though his fortunes changed

with bewildering rapidity, his habits remained the same. Indeed, he felt these changes much less than did Magnolia and Kim. No matter what their habitation—cheap rooming house or expensive hotel—he left at about the same hour each morning, took the same leisurely course toward town, returned richer or poorer—but unruffled—well after midnight. On his off nights he and Magnolia went to the theatre. Curiously they seemed always to have enough money for that.

Usually they dwelt somewhere north, just the other side of the Chicago River, at that time a foul-smelling and viscid stream, with no drainage canal to deodorize it. Ravenal, in lean times, emerging from his dingy hotel or rooming house on Ontario or Ohio, was as dapper, as suave, as elegant as that younger Ravenal had been who, leaning against the packing case on the wharf at New Orleans, had managed to triumph over the handicap of a cracked boot. He would stand a moment, much as he had stood that southern spring morning, coolly surveying the world about him. That his viewpoint was the dingy front stoop of a run-down Chicago rooming house and his view the sordid street that held it, apparently disturbed his equanimity not at all. On rising he had observed exactly the same niceties that would have been his had he enjoyed the services of a hotel valet. He bathed, shaved, dressed meticulously. Magnolia had early learned that the slatternly morning habits which she had taken for granted in the *Cotton Blossom* wives—Julie, Mis' Means, Mrs. Soaper, even the rather fastidious Elly—would be found inexcusable in the wife of Ravenal. The sternly utilitarian undergarments of Parthy's choosing had soon enough been done away with, to be replaced with a froth of lace and tucks and embroidery and batiste. The laundering of these was a pretty problem when faro's frown decreed Ohio Street.

Ravenal was spared these worrisome details. Once out of the dingy boarding house, he could take his day in his two hands and turn it over, like a bright, freshminted coin. Each day was a new start. How could you know that you would not break the bank! It had been done on a dollar.

Down the street Ravenal would stroll past the ship chandlers' and commission houses south of Ontario, to the swinging bridge that spanned the slimy river. There he would slacken his already leisurely pace, or even pause a moment, perhaps, to glance at the steamers tied up at the docks. There was an occasional sailboat. A three-masted schooner, *The Finney,* a grain boat, was in from up North. Over to Clark and Lake. You could sniff in the air the pleasant scent of coffee. That was Reid & Murdock's big warehouse a little to the east. He sometimes went a block out of his way just to sniff this delicious odour. A glittering shoeshine at the Sherman House or the Tremont.

"Good-morning, George."

"Mawnin' Mist' Ravenal ! Mawnin'! Papah, suh?"

"Ah—n-n-no. No. H'm!" His fifty cents, budgeted, did not include the dispensing of those extra pennies for the *Times-Herald,* the *Inter-Ocean,* or the *Tribune.* They could be seen at McDonald's for nothing. A fine Chicago morning. The lake mist had lifted. That was one of the advantages of never rising early. Into the Cockeyed Bakery for breakfast. Tomorrow it would be Boyle's. Surely his bad luck would break to-day. He felt it. Had felt it the moment he opened his eyes.

"Terrapin and champagne to-morrow, Nola. Feel it in my bones. I woke up with my palm itching, and passed a hunchback at Clark and Randolph last night."

"Why don't you let me give you your coffee and toast here this morning, Gay dear? It'll only take a minute. And it's so much better than the coffee you get at the—uh—downtown."

Ravenal, after surveying his necktie critically in the mirror of the crazy little bureau, would shrug himself into his well-made coat. "You know I never eat in a room in which I have slept."

Past the Court House; corner of Washington reached. Cut flowers in the glass case outside the basement florist's. A tapping on the glass with a coin, or a rapping on the pavement with his stick—if the malacca stick was in evidence. "Heh, Joe!"

Joe clattering up the wooden steps.

"Here you are, sir. All ready for you. just came in fresh." A white carnation. Ravenal would sniff the spicy bloom, snap the brittle stem, thrust it through the buttonhole of his lapel.

A fine figure of a man from his boots to his hat. Young, handsome, well-dressed, leisurely. Joe, the Greek florist, pocketing his quarter, would reflect gloomily on luck—his own and that of others.

Ravenal might drop in a moment at Weeping Willy Mangler's, thence to Reilly's pool room near Madison, for a look at the racing odds. But no matter how low his finances, he scorned the cheaper gambling room that catered to the clerks and the working men. There was a great difference between Jeff Hankins' place and that of his brother, George. At George's place, and others of that class, barkers stood outside. "Game upstairs, gentlemen! Game upstairs! Come in and try your luck! Ten cents can make you a millionaire."

At George Hankins' the faro checks actually were ten cents. You saw there labouring men with their tin dinner pails, their boots lime-spattered, their garments reeking of cheap pipe tobacco. There, too, you found stud poker, roulette, hazard—percentage games. None of these for Ravenal. He played a gentleman's game, broke or flush.

This game he found at Mike McDonald's "The Store." Here he was at home. Here were excitement, luxury, companionship. Here he was Gaylord Ravenal. Fortune lurked just around the corner. At McDonald's his credit always was good for enough to start the play. On the first floor was the saloon, with its rich walnut panelling, its great mirrors, its tables of teakwood and ivory inlay, its paintings of lolling ladies. Chicago's saloons and gambling resorts vied with each other in rich and massive decoration. None of your soapscrawled mirrors and fancy bottle structures for these. "Prince" Varnell's place had, for years, been famous for its magnificent built-in mantel of Mexican onyx, its great marble statue of the death of Cleopatra, its enormous Sèvres vases.

The second floor was Ravenal's goal. He did not even glance at the whirling of the elaborately inlaid roulette wheels. He nodded to the dealers and his greeting was deferentially returned. It was said that most of these men had come of fine old Southern families. They dressed the part. But McDonald himself looked like a farmer. His black clothes, though well made, never seemed to fit him. His black string tie never varied. Thin, short, gray-haired, Mike McDonald the Boss of the gamblers would have passed anywhere for a kindly rustic.

"Playing to-day, Mr. Ravenal?"

"Why, yes. Yes, I thought I'd play a while."

"Anything we can do to make you comfortable?"

"Well—uh—yes- "

McDonald would raise a benevolent though authoritative hand. His finger would summon a menial. "Dave, take care of Mr. Ravenal."

Ravenal joined the others then, a gentleman gambler among gentleman gamblers. A group smartly dressed like himself, well groomed, quiet, almost elegant. Most of them wore jewellery—a diamond scarf pin, a diamond ring, sometimes even a diamond stud, though this was frowned on by players of Ravenal's class. A dead cigar in the mouth of each. Little fine lines etched about their eyes. They addressed each other as "sir." Thank you, sir. . . . Yours I believe, sir. . . . They were quiet, quiet. Yet there was an electric vibration in the air above and about the faro table. Only the dealer seemed remote, detached, unmoved. An hour passed; two, three, four, five. The Negro waiters in very white starched aprons moved deferentially from group to group. One would have said that no favouritism was being shown, but they knew the piker from the plunger. Soft-voiced, coaxing: "Something to drink, suh? A little whisky, suh? Cigar? Might be you'd relish a little chicken white meat and a bottle of wine?"

Ravenal would glance up abstractedly. "Time is it?"

"Pushin' six o'clock, suh."

Ravenal might interrupt his game to eat something, but this was not his rule. He ate usually after he had finished his play for the day. It was understood that he and others of his stamp were the guests of McDonald or of Hankins. Twenty-five-cent cigars were to be had for the taking. Drinks of every description. Hot food of the choicest sort and of almost any variety could be ordered and eaten as though this were one's own house, and the servants at one's command. Hot soups and broths. Steaks. Chops. Hot birds. You could eat this at a little white-spread table alone, or with your companions, or you could have it brought to you as you played. On long tables in the adjoining room were spread the cold viands—roast chickens, tongue, sausages, cheese, joints of roast beef, salads. Everything about the place gave to its habitués the illusion of plenty, of ease, of luxury. Soft red carpets; great prism-hung chandeliers; the clink of ice; the scent of sappy cigars and rich food; the soft slap-slap of the cards; the low voices of the dealers. It was all friendly, relaxed, soothing. Yet when the dealer opened the little drawer that was so cleverly concealed under his side of the table —the money drawer with its orderly stacks of yellow-backs, and green-backs and gold and silver—you saw, if your glance was quick and sharp enough, the gleam of still another metal: the glittering, sinister blue-gray of steel.

A hundred superstitions swayed their play. Luck was a creature to be wooed, flattered, coaxed, feared. No jungle voodoo worshipper ever lent himself to simpler or more childish practices and beliefs than did these hard-faced men.

Sometimes Ravenal left the faro table penniless or even deeper in Mike McDonald's debt. His face at such times was not more impassive than the bucolic host's own. " Better luck next time, Mr. Ravenal."

"She's due to turn to-morrow, Mike. Watch out for me to-morrow. I'll probably clean you."

And if not to-morrow, to-morrow. Luck must turn, sooner or later. There! Five hundred! A thousand! Five thousand! Did you hear about Ravenal? Yes, he had a wonderful run. It happened in an hour. He walked out with ten thousand. More, some say.

On these nights Ravenal would stroll coolly home as on losing nights. Up Clark Street, the money in neat rolls in his pocket. There were almost no street robberies in those simpler Chicago days. If you were, like Ravenal, a well-dressed sporting looking man, strolling up Clark Street at midnight or thereabouts, you were likely to be stopped for the price of a meal. You gave it as a matter of course, unwrapping a bill, perhaps, from the roll you carried in your pocket.

They might be living in modest comfort at the Revere House on Clark and Austin. They might be living in decent discomfort at the little theatrical boarding house on Ontario. They might be huddled in actual discomfort in the sordid room of the Ohio Street rooming house. Be that as it may, Ravenal would take highhanded possession, but in a way so blithe, so gay, so charming that no one could have withstood him, least of all his wife who, though she knew him and understood him as well as any one could understand this secretive and baffling nature, frequently despised him, often hated him, still was in love with him and always would be.

The child would be asleep in her corner, but Magnolia would be wide awake, reading or sewing or simply sitting there waiting. She never reproached him for the hours he kept. Though they quarrelled frequently it was never about this. Sometimes, as she sat there, half dozing, her mind would go back to the rivers and gently float there. An hour—two hours—would slip by. Now the curtain would be going down on the last act. Now the crowd staying for the after-piece and concert would be moving down to occupy the seats nearer the stage. A song number by the ingénue finishing with a clog or a soft-shoe dance. The comic tramp. The character team in a patter act, with a song. The afterpiece now; probably Red Hot Coffee, or some similar stand-by. Now the crowd was leaving. The band struck up its last number. Up the river bank scrambled the last straggler. You never threw me my line at all. There I was like a stuck pig. Well, how did I know you was going to leave out that business with the door. Why'n't you tell me? Say, Ed, will you go over my song with me a minute? You know, that place where it goes TUM-ty-ty TUM-ty-ty TUM-TUM-TUM and then I vamp. It kind of went sour to-night, seemed to me. A bit of supper. Coffee cooked over a spirit lamp. Lumps of yellow cheese, a bite of ham. Relaxation after strain. A daubing with cold cream. A sloshing of water. Quieter. More quiet. Quiet. Darkness. Security. No sound but that of the river flowing by. Sometimes if she dozed she was wakened by the familiar hoot of a steamer whistle—some big lake boat, perhaps, bound for Michigan or Minnesota; or a river barge or tug on the Chicago River near by. She would start up, bewildered, scarcely knowing whether she had heard this hoarse blast or whether it was only, after all, part of her dream about the river and the *Cotton Blossom*.

Ravenal coming swiftly up the stairs. Ravenal's quick light tead in the hall.

"Come on, Nola! We're leaving this rat's nest."

"Gay, dear! Not now. You don't mean to-night."

"Now! It'll only take a minute. I'll wake up the slavey. She'll help."

"No! No! I'd rather do it myself. Oh, Gay, Kim's asleep. Can't we wait until morning?"

But somehow the fantastic procedure appealed tremendously to her love of the unexpected. Packing up and moving on. The irresponsible gaiety of it. The gas turned high. Out tumbled the contents of bureau drawers and boxes and trunks. Finery saved from just such another lucky day. Froth and foam of lace and silk strewn incongruously about this murky little chamber with its frayed carpet and stained walls and crazy chairs. They spoke in half whispers so as not to wake the child. They were themselves like two children, eager, excited, laughing.

"Where are we going, Gay?"

"Sherman. Or how would you like to try the Auditorium for a change? Rooms looking out over the lake."

'Gay!'' Her hands clasped as she knelt in front of a trunk.

"Next week we'll run down to West Baden. Do us good. During the day we can walk and drive or ride. You ought to learn to ride, Nola. In the evening we can take a whirl at Sam Maddock's layout."

"Oh, don't play there—not much, I mean. Let's try to keep what we have for a little while."

"After all, we may as well give Sam a chance to pay our expenses. Remember the last time we were down I won a thousand at roulette alone—and roulette isn't my game."

He awoke the landlady and paid his bill in the middle of the night. She did not resent being thus disturbed. Women rarely resented Gaylord Ravenal's lack of consideration. They were off in a hack fetched by Ravenal from the near-by cab stand. It was no novelty for Kim to fall asleep in the dingy discomfort of a north side rooming house and to wake up amidst the bright luxuriousness of a hotel suite, without ever having been conscious of the events which had wrought this change. Instead of milk out of the bottle and an egg cooked over the gas jet, there was a shining breakfast tray bearing mysterious round-domed dishes whose covers you whipped off to disclose what not of savoury delights! Crisp curls of bacon, parsley-decked; eggs baked and actually bubbling in a brown crockery container; hot golden buttered toast. And her mother calling gaily in from the next room, "Drink your milk with your breakfast, Kim darling! Don't gulp it all down in one swallow at the end."

It was easy enough for Kim to believe in those fairy tales that had to do with kindly sprites who worked miracles overnight. A whole staff of such good creatures seemed pretty regularly occupied with the Ravenal affairs.

Once a month there came a letter from Mrs. Hawks. No more and no less. That indomitable woman was making a great success of her business. Her letters bristled with complaint, but between the lines Magnolia could read satisfaction and even a certain grim happiness. She was boss of her world, such as it was. Her word was final. The modern business woman had not yet begun her almost universal battle against the male in his own field. She was considered unique. Tales of her prowess became river lore. Parthy Ann Hawks, owner and manager of the Cotton Blossom Floating Palace Theatre, strong, erect, massive, her eyebrows black above her keen cold eyes, her abundant hair scarcely touched with gray, was now a well-known and important figure on the rivers. She ran her boat like a pirate captain. He who displeased her walked the plank. It was said that the more religious rivermen who hailed from the Louisiana parishes always crossed themselves fearfully at her approach and considered a meeting with the *Cotton Blossom* a bad omen. The towering blackgarbed form standing like a ship's figurehead, grim and portentous, as the boat swept downstream, had been known to give a really devout Catholic captain a severe and instantaneous case of chills and fever.

Her letters to Magnolia were. characteristic:

Well, Maggie, I hope you and the child are in good health. Often and often I think land knows what kind of a bringing up she is getting with the life you are leading. I can imagine. Well, you made your own bed and now you can lie in it. I have no doubt that he has run through ever penny of your money that your poor father worked so hard to get as I predicted he would. I suppose you heard all about French's *New Sensation*. French has the worst luck it does seem. She sank six weeks ago at Medley's just above New Madrid. The fault of the pilot it was. Carelessness if ever I heard it. He got caught in the down draft of a gravel bar and snagged her they say. I think of your poor pa and how he met his end. It took two weeks to raise her though she was only in

six feet of water. On top of that his other boat the *Golden
Rod* you remember went down about four weeks ago in the
Illinois near Hardin. A total loss. Did you ever hear of such
luck. Business is pretty good. I can't complain. But I have
to be right on hand every minute or they would steal me
blind and that's the truth. I have got a new heavy. No great
shakes as an actor but handy enough and a pretty good black
face in the concert and they seem to like him. We had a
pretty rough audience all through the coal country but whenever it looked like a fight starting I'd come out in front and
stand there a minute and say if anybody started anything I
would have the boat run out into the middle of the river and
sink her. That I'd never had a fight on my boat and wasn't
going to being any such low life shenanigans now.

(Magnolia got a swift mental picture of this menacing, black-garbed figure
standing before the gay crude curtain, the footlights throwing grim shadows
on her stern face. That implacable woman was capable of cowering even a
tough coal-belt audience bent on a fight.)

Crops are pretty good so business is according. I put up
grape jell last week. A terrible job but I can't abide this store
stuff made of gelatine or something and no real grape in it.
Well I suppose you are too stylish for the *Cotton Blossom*
by now and Kim never hears of it. I got the picture you
sent. I think she looks kind of peaked. Up all hours of the
night I suppose and no proper food. What kind of an education is she getting? You wrote about how you were going
to send her to a convent school. I never heard of such a
thing. Well I will close as goodness knows I have enough
to do besides writing letters where they are probably not
wanted. Still I like to know how you and the child are doing
and all.

Your mother,
PARTHENIA ANN HAWKS.

These epistles always filled Magnolia with an emotion that was a poisonous
mixture of rage and tenderness and nostalgia. She knew that her mother, in
her harsh way, loved her, loved her grandchild, often longed to see both of
them. Parthy's perverse and inhibited nature would not permit her to confess
this. She would help them with money, Magnolia knew, if they needed help.
But first she must know the grisly satisfaction of having them say so. This
Magnolia would not do, though there were many times when her need was
great. There was Kim, no longer a baby. This feverish and irregular life
could not go on for her. Magnolia's letters to her mother, especially in lean
times, were triumphs of lying pride. Sentimental Tommy's mother, writing
boastfully home about her black silks and her gold chain, was never more
stiff-necked than she.

Gay is more than good to me. . . . I have only to wish for a thing . . .
Everyone says Kim is unusually tall and bright for her age. . . . He speaks
of a trip to Europe next year . . . new furcoat . . . never an unkind word
. . . very happy . . .

Still, if Magnolia was clever at reading between the lines of her mother's
bald letters, so, too, was Parthenia at hers. In fact, Parthy took many a

random shot that struck home, as when once she wrote, tartly, "Fur coat one day and none the next I'll be bound."

15

THE PROBLEM OF Kim's education, of Kim's future, was more and more insistently borne in upon her. She wanted money—money of her own with which to provide security for the child. Ravenal's improvident method was that of Paddy and the leaky roof. When luck was high and he was showering her and Kim with luxuries, he would say, "But, good God, haven't you got everything you want? There's no satisfying you any more, Nola."

When he had nothing he would throw out his hands, palms upward, in a gesture of despair. "I haven't got it, I tell you. I give you everything I can think of when I am flush. And now, when I'm broke, you nag me."

"But, Gay, that's just it. Everything one day and nothing the next. Couldn't we live like other people, in between? Enough, and none of this horrible worrying about to-morrow. I can't bear it."

"You should have married a plumber."

She found herself casting about in her mind for ways in which she could earn money of her own. She took stock of her talents: a slim array. There was her experience on the show-boat stage. She could play the piano a little. She could strum the banjo (relic of Jo's and Queenie's days in the old *Cotton Blossom* low-raftered kitchen). She had an untrained, true, and rather moving voice of mediocre quality.

Timidly, with a little nervous spot of red showing in either cheek, she broached this to Ravenal one fine afternoon when they were driving out to the Sunnyside Hotel for dinner. Gaylord had had a run of luck the week before. Two sleek handsome chestnuts seemed barely to flick the road with their hoofs as they flew along. The smart high cart glittered with yellow varnish. None of your cheap livery rigs for Ravenal. Magnolia was exhilarated, happy. Above all else she loved to drive into the country or the suburbs behind a swift pair of horses. Ravenal was charming; pleased with himself; with his handsome, well-dressed young wife; with the cart, the horses, the weather, the prospect of one of Old Man Dowling's excellent dinners. They sped through Lincoln Park. Their destination was a two-hours' drive north, outside the city limits: a favourite rendezvous for Chicago's sporting world. At Dowling's one had supper at a dollar a head—and such a supper! The beefsteak could be cut with a fork. Old Man Dowling bred his own fine fat cattle. Old Lady Dowling raised the plump broilers that followed the beefsteak. There was green corn grown in the Dowling garden; fresh-plucked tomatoes, young onions. There was homemade ice cream. There was a huge chocolate cake, each slice a gigantic edifice alternating layers of black and white.

"Can't I drive a while, Gay dear?"

"They're pretty frisky. You'd better wait till we get out a ways, where there aren't so many rigs." The fine cool late summer day had brought out all manner of vehicles. "By that time the nags'll have some of the skittishness worked out of them, too."

"But I like to have them when they're skittish. Papa always used to let me take them."

"Yes—well, these aren't canal-boat mules, you know. Why can't you be content just to sit back and enjoy the drive? You're getting to be like one of those bloomer girls they joke about. You'll be waiting to wear the family pants next."

"I am enjoying it, only———"

"Only don't be like your mother, Nola."

She lapsed into silence. During one of their many sojourns at the Ontario Street hotel she had struck up a passing acquaintance with a large, over-friendly blonde actress with green-gold hair and the tightest of black bodices stretched over an imposing shelf of bosom. This one had surveyed the Ravenal ménage with a shrewd and kindly though slightly bleary eye, and had given Magnolia some sound advice.

"Why'n't you go out more, dearie?" she had asked one evening when she herself was arrayed for festivity in such a bewilderment of flounces, bugles, jets, plumes, bracelets, and chains as to give the effect of a lighted Christmas tree in the narrow dim hallway. She had encountered Magnolia in the corridor and Nola had returned the woman's gusty greeting with a shy and faintly wistful smile. "Out more, evenin's. Young thing like you. I notice you're home with the little girl most the time. I guess you think that run, run is about all I do."

Magnolia resented this somewhat. But she reflected instantly this was a friendly and well-meaning creature. She reminded her faintly of Elly, somehow; Elly as she might be now, perhaps; blowsy, over-blown, middle-aged. "Oh, I go out a great deal," she said, politely.

"Husband home?" demanded the woman, bluntly. She was engaged in the apparently hopeless task of pulling a black kid glove over her massive arm.

Magnolia's fine eyebrows came up in a look of hauteur that she unconsciously had borrowed from Ravenal. "Mr. Ravenal is out." And started on toward her room.

The woman caught her hand. "Now don't get huffy, dear. I'm a older woman than you and I've seen a good deal. You stay home with the kid and your husband goes out, and will he like you any better for it! Nit! Now leave me tell you when he asks you to go out somewheres with him you go, want to or not, because if you don't there's those that will, and pretty soon he'll quit asking you."

She had waddled stiffly down the hallway then, in her absurdly high-heeled slippers, leaving a miasma of perfume in the passage. Magnolia had been furious, then amused, then thoughtful, then grateful. In the last few years she had met or seen the wives of professional gamblers. It was strange: they were all quiet, rather sad-faced women, home-loving and usually accompanied by a well-dressed and serious child. Much like herself and Kim, she thought. Sometimes she met them on Ohio Street. She thought she could recognize the wife of a gambler by the look in her face.

Frequently she saw them coming hurriedly out of one of the many pawn-shops on North Clark, near the river. The windows of these shops fascinated her. They held, often, such intimate, revealing, and mutely appealing things—a doll, a wedding ring, a cornet, a meerschaum pipe, a Masonic emblem, a Bible, a piece of lace, a pair of gold-rimmed spectacles.

She thought of these things now as she sat so straight and smartly dressed beside Ravenal in the high yellow cart. She stole a glance at him. The colour was high in his cheeks. His box-cut covert coat with the big pearl buttons was a dashingly becoming garment. In the buttonhole bloomed a great pompon of a chrysanthemum. He looked very handsome. Magnolia's head came up spiritedly.

"I don't want to wear the pants. But I would like to have some say-so about things. There's Kim. She isn't getting the right kind of schooling. Half the time she goes to private schools and half the time to public and half the time to no school at all—oh, well, I know there aren't three halves, but anyway . . . and it isn't fair. It's because half the time we've got money and half the time we haven't any."

"Oh, God, here we are, driving out for pleasure————"

"But, Gay dear, you've got to think of those things. And so I thought— I wondered—Gay, I'd like to earn some money of my own."

Ravenal cut the chestnuts sharply with his whip.

"Pooh!" thought Magnolia. "He can't scare me that way. How like a man—to take it out on the horses just because he's angry." She slipped her hand through his arm.

"Don't! Don't jerk my arm like that. You'll have them running away in a minute."

"I should think they would, after the way you slashed them. Sometimes I think you don't care about horses—as horses—any more than you do about————" She stopped, aghast. She had almost said, "than you do about me as a wife." A long breath. Then, "Gay darling, I'd like to go back on the stage. I'd like to act again. Here, I mean. In Chicago."

She was braced for a storm and could have weathered it. But his shouts of laughter startled and bewildered her and the sensitive chestnuts as well. At this final affront they bolted, and for the next fifteen minutes Magnolia clutched the little iron rod at the end of the seat with one hand and clung to her hat with the other as the outraged horses stretched their length down the rutty country road, eyes flaming, nostrils distended, hoofs clattering, the light high cart rocking and leaping behind them. Ravenal's slender weight was braced against the footboard. The veins in his wrists shone blue against dead white. With a tearing sound his right sleeve ripped from his coat. Little beads of moisture stood out about his mouth and chin. Magnolia, white-lipped, tense, and terribly frightened, magnificently uttered no sound. If she had been one of your screamers there probably would have been a sad end. Slowly, gradually, the chestnuts slowed a trifle, slackened, resumed a normal pace, stood panting as Ravenal drew up at the side of the road. They actually essayed to nibble innocently at some sprigs of grass growing by the roadside while Ravenal wiped his face and neck and hands, slowly, with his fine perfumed linen handkerchief. He took off his black derby hat and mopped his forehead and the headband of his hat's splendid white satin lining. He fell to swearing, softly, this being the form in which the male, relieved after fright, tries to deny that he has been frightened.

He turned to look at her, his eyes narrow. She turned to look at him, her great eyes wide. She leaned toward him a little, her hand over her heart. And then, suddenly, they both began to laugh, so that the chestnuts pricked up their ears again and Ravenal grabbed the reins. They laughed because they were young, and had been terribly frightened, and were now a little hysterical following the strain. And because they loved each other, so that their fear of injury and possible death had been for each a double horror.

"That's what happens when you talk about going on the stage," said Ravenal. "Even the horses run at the thought. I hope this will be a lesson to you." He gathered up the reins.

"A person would think I'd never been an actress and knew nothing of the stage."

"You don't think that catch-as-catch-can performance was acting, do you? Or that hole in the wall a stage! Or that old tub a theatre! Or those plays- Good God! Do you remember . . . 'Sue, if he loves yuh, go with him. Ef he ain't good to yuh————'"

"But I do!" cried Magnolia. "I do think so. I loved it. Everybody in the company was acting because they liked it. They'd rather do it than anything in the wrld. Maybe we weren't very good but the audiences thought we were; and they cried in the places where they were supposed to cry, and laughed when they should have laughed, and believed it all, and were happy, and if that isn't the theatre then what is?''

"Chicago isn't a river dump; and Chicago audiences aren't rubes. You've seen Modjeska and Mansfield and Bernhardt and Jefferson and Ada Rehan since then. Surely you know the difference.''

"That's the funny part of it. I don't, much. Oh, I don't mean they haven't got genius. And they've been beautifully directed. And the scenery and costumes and all. But—I don't know—they do exactly the same things—do them better, but the same things that Schultzy told us to do—and the audiences laugh at the same things and cry at the same things—and they go trouping around the country, on land instead of water, but trouping just the same. They play heroes and heroines in plays all about love and adventure; and the audiences go out blinking with the same kind of look on their faces that the river-town audiences used to have, as though somebody had just waked them up.''

"Don't be silly, darling. . . . Ah, here we are!''

And here they were. They had arrived in ample time, so that Magnolia chatted shyly and Ravenal chatted charmingly with Pa and Ma Dowling; and Magnolia was reminded of Thebes as she examined the shells and paper roses and china figurines in the parlour. The dinner was excellent, abundant, appetizing. Scarcely were they seated at the long table near the window when there was heard a great fanfare and hullabaloo outside. Up the winding driveway swept a tallyho, and out of it spilled a party of Chicago bloods in fawn covert coats and derby hats and ascot ties and shiny pointed shoes; and they gallantly assisted the very fashionable ladies who descended the perilous steps with much shrill squealing and shrieking and maidenly clutching at skirts, which clutchings failed satisfactorily of their purpose. Some of the young men carried banjos and mandolins. The four horses jangled their metaltrimmed harness and curveted magnificently. Up the steps swarmed the gay young men and the shrill young women. On closer sight Magnolia noticed that some of these were not, after all, so young.

"Good God!'' Ravenal had exclaimed; and had frowned portentously.

"Do you know them, Gay?''

"It's Bliss Chapin's gang. He's giving a party. He's going to be married day after to-morrow. They're making a night of it.''

"Really! How lovely! Which one's the girl he's to marry? Point her out.''

And for the second time Ravenal said, "Don't be silly, darling.''

They entered the big dining room on a wave of sound and colour. They swarmed the table. They snatched up bits of bread and pickles and celery, and munched them before they were seated. They caught sight of Ravenal.

"Gay! Well, I'm damned! Gay, you old Foxey Quiller, so that's why you wouldn't come out! Heh, Blanche, look! Here's Gay, the bad boy. Look who's here!''

"I thought you were going out to Cramp's place,'' Gay said, sullenly, in a low voice, to one of the men.

He chose the wrong confidant, the gentleman being neither reticent nor ebriate. He raised his voice to a shout. "That's a good 'un! Listen! Foxey Gay thought we were going out to Cramp's place, so what does he do? He brings his lady here. Heh, Blanche, d'you hear that? Now you know why he couldn't come.'' He bent upon Magnolia a look of melting admiration. "And can you blame him? All together! NO!''

"You go to hell,'' said the lady named Blanche from the far end of the table, though without anger; rather in the manner of one who is ready with a choice bit of repartee. Indeed it must have been so considered, for at its utterance Mr. Bliss Chapin's pre-nuptial group uttered shouts of approbation.

"Shut up, you jackass," said Ravenal then, sotto voce.

And "Oho!" bellowed the teaser. "Little Gay's afraid he'll get in trouble with his lady friend."

Gay's lady friend now disproved for all time her gentleman friend's recent accusation that she knew nothing about the art of acting. She raised her head and gazed upon the roistering crew about the long table. Her face was very white, her dark eyes were enormous; she was smiling.

"Won't you introduce me to your friends, Gay?" she said, in her clear and lovely voice.

"Don't be a fool," whispered Ravenal at her side.

The host, Bliss Chapin, stood up rather red-faced and fumbling with his napkin. He was not sober, but his manner was formal—deferential, even. "Mrs.—uh—Rav'nal—I—uh—charmed. I rem'ber seeing you—someone pointed you out in a box at th—th—th—" he gave it up and decided to run the two words together—"ththeatre. Chapin's my name. Bliss Chapin. Call me Bliss. Ever'body calls me Bliss. Uh—" he decided to do the honours. He indicated each guest with a graceful though vague wave of the hand. " 'S Tantine . . . Fifi . . . Gerty . . . Vi'let . . . Blanche . . . Mignon. Lovely girls. Lovely. But—we'll let that pass. Uh . . . Georgie Skiff. . . . Tom Haggerty . . . Billy Little—Li'l' Billee we call him. Pretty cute, huh? . . . Know what I mean? . . . Dave Lansing . . . Jerry Darling— that's his actu-al name. Can you 'mazhine what the girls can do with name like that! Boys 'n girls, this's Mrs. Gaylord Ravenal, wife of the well-known faro expert. An' a lucky dog he is, too. No offense, I hope. Jus' my rough way. I'm going to be married to-morr'. An'thing goes'sevening."

Prolonged applause and shouting. A twanging of mandolins and banjos.

"Speech!" shouted the man who had first called attention to Magnolia. "Speech by Mrs. Ravenal!"

They took it up shrilly, hoarsely, the Fifis, the Violets, the Billys, the Gertys, the Jerrys. Speech! Speech!

Ravenal got to his feet. "We've got to go," he began. "Sorry————"

"Sit down! Throw him out! Foxey Gay! Shut up, Gay!"

Ravenal turned to Magnolia. "We'll have to get out of this," he said. He put a hand on her arm. His hand was trembling. She turned her head slowly and looked up at him, her eyes blank, the smile still on her face. "Oh, no," she said, and shook her head. "Oh, no. I like it here, Gay dear."

"Speech!" yelled the Tantines, the Mignons, the Daves, beating on their plates with their spoons.

Magnolia brought one hand up to her throat in a little involuntary gesture that betokened breathlessness. There was nothing else to indicate how her heart was hammering. "I—I can't make a speech," she began in her lovely voice.

"Speech! Speech!"

She looked at Ravenal. She felt a little sorry for him.

"But I'll sing you a song if you'll lend me a banjo, someone."

She took the first of a half-dozen instruments thrust toward her.

"Magnolia!"

"Do sit down, Gay dear, and stop fidgeting about so. It's all right. I'm glad to entertain your friends." She still wore the little set smile. "I'm going to sing a song I learned from the Negroes when I was a little girl and lived on a show boat on the Mississippi River." She bent her head above the

banjo and began to thumb it softly. Then she threw her head back slightly.
One foot tapped emphasis to the music's cadence. Her lids came down over
her eyes—closed down over them. She swayed a little, gently. It was an
unconscious imitation of old Jo's attitude. "It's called Deep River. It doesn't
mean—anything. It's just a song the niggers used to———" She began to
sing, softly. "Deep———river———"

When she had finished there was polite applause.

"I think it's real sweet," announced the one they called Violet. And began
to snivel, unbecomingly.

Mr. Tom Haggerty now voiced the puzzlement which had been clouding
his normally cheerful countenance.

"You call that a coon song and maybe it is. I don't dispute you, mind.
But I never heard any song like *that* called a coon song, and I heard a good
many coon songs in my day. I Wan Them Presents Back, and A Hot Time,
and Mistah Johnson, Turn Me Loose."

"Sing another," they said, still more politely. "Maybe something not quite
so sad. You'll have us thinking we're at prayer meeting next. First thing you
know Violet here will start to repent her sins."

So she sang All God's Chillun Got Wings. They wagged their heads and
tapped their feet to that. I got a wings. You got a wings. All o' God's chillun
got a wings. When I get to heab'n I'm goin' to put on my wings, I'm goin'
to fly all ovah God's heab'n . . . heab'n . . .

Well, that, they agreed, was better. That was more like it. The red-faced
cut-up rose on imaginary wings to show how he, too, was going to fly all
over God's heab'n. The forthright Blanche refused to be drawn into the
polite acclaim. "If you ask me," she announced, moodily, "I think they're
rotten." "I like somepin' a little more lively, myself," said the girl they
called Fifi. "Do you know What! Marry Dat Gal! I heard May Irwin sing
it. She was grand."

"No," said Magnolia. "That's the only kind of song I know, really." She
stood up. "I think we must be going now." She looked across the table, her
great dark eyes fixed on the red-faced bridegroom. "I hope you will be very
happy."

"A toast to the Ravenals! To Gaylord Ravenal and Mrs. Ravenal!" She
acknowledged that too, charmingly. Ravenal bowed stiffly and glowered and
for the second time that day wiped his forehead and chin and wrists with
his fine linen handkerchief.

The chestnuts were brought round. Bliss Chapin's crew crowded out to
the veranda off the dining room. Magnolia stepped lightly up to the seat
beside Ravenal in the high dog-cart. It was dusk. A sudden sharpness had
come into the evening air as always, toward autumn, in that Lake Michigan
region. Magnolia shivered a little and drew about her the little absurd
flounced shoulder cape so recently purchased. The crowd on the veranda
had caught the last tune and were strumming it now on their banjos and
mandolins. The kindly light behind them threw their foolish faces into
shadow. You heard their voices, plaintive, even sweet; the raucous note fled
for the moment. Fifi's voice and Jerry's; Gerty's voice and little Billee's.
I got a wings. You got a wings. All God's chillun got a wings. When I get
to heab'n I'm goin' to put on my wings, I'm goin' to fly . . .

Magnolia turned to wave to them as the chestnuts made the final curve
in the driveway and stretched eagerly toward home.

Silence between the two for a long half hour. Then Ravenal, almost humbly: "Well—I suppose I'm in for it, Nola. Shoot!"

But she had been thinking, "I must take things in hand now. I have been
like a foolish young girl when I'm really quite an old married woman. I

suppose being bossed by Mama so much did that. I must take Kim in hand now. What a fool I've been. 'Don't be silly, darling.' He was right. I have been———'' Aloud she said, only half conscious that he had spoken, "What did you say?"

"You know very well what I said. I suppose I'm in for one of your mother's curtain lectures. Go on. Shoot and get it over."

"Don't be silly, darling," said Magnolia, a trifle maliciously. "What a lovely starlight night it is! . . . " She laughed a little. "Do you know, those dough-faced Fifis and Tantines and Mignons were just like the Ohio and Illinois farm girls, dressed up. The ignorant girls who used to come to see the show. I'll bet that when they were on the farm, barefooted, poor things, they were Annie and Jenny and Tillie and Emma right enough."

16

"AND THIS," SAID Sister Cecilia, "is the chapel." She took still another key from the great bunch on her key chain and unlocked the big gloomy double doors. It was incredible that doors and floors and wainscotings so shining with varnish could still diffuse such an atmosphere of gloom. She entered ahead of them with the air of a cicerone. It seemed to Magnolia that the corridors were tunnels of murk. It was like a prison. Magnolia took advantage of this moment to draw closer still to Kim. She whispered hurriedly in her ear:

"Kim darling, you don't need to stay. If you don't like it we'll slip away and you needn't come back. It's so gloomy."

"But I do like it," said Kim in her clear, decisive voice. "It's so shiny and clean and quiet." In spite of her lovely Ravenal features, which still retained something of their infantile curves, she looked at that moment startlingly like her grandmother, Parthenia Ann Hawks. They followed Sister Cecilia into the chapel. Magnolia shivered a little.

In giving Kim a convent education it was not in Magnolia's mind to prepare her for those Sunday theatrical page interviews beginning, "I was brought up by the dear Sisters in the Convent." For that matter, the theatre as having any part in Kim's future never once entered Magnolia's mind. Why this should have been true it is difficult to say, considering the child's background, together with the fact that she was seeing Camille and Ben Hur, and the Rogers Brothers in Central Park at an age when other little girls were barely permitted to go to cocoa parties in white muslin and blue sashes where they might, if they were lucky, see the funny man take the rabbit out of the hat.

The non-sectarian girls' schools of good standing looked askance at would-be entrants whose parentage was as socially questionable, not to say bizarre, as that represented by Ravenal mère and père. The daughter of a professional gambler and an ex-show-boat actress would have received short shrift at the hands of the head mistress of Miss Dignam's School for Girls at Somethin-gorother-on-the-Hudson. The convent school, then, opened its gloomy portals to as motley a collection of *jeunes filles* as could be imagined under one roof. In the prim dim corridors and cubicles of St. Agatha's on Wabash Avenue, south, you might see a score of girlish pupils who, in spite of the demure face, the sleek braids, the severe uniform, the modest manner, the prunes-and-prism expression, still resembled in a startling degree this or that vivacious lady whose name was associated with the notorious Everleigh Club, or with the music halls and museums thriving along Clark Street or

Madison or Dearborn. Visiting day at St. Agatha's saw an impressive line
of smart broughams outside the great solemn brick building; and the ladies
who emerged therefrom, while invariably dressed in garments of sombre
colour and restrained cut, still produced the effect of being attired in what
is known as fast black. They gave forth a heady musky scent. And the mould
of their features, even when transformed by the expression that crept over
them as they gazed upon those girlish faces so markedly resembling their
own, had a look as though the potter had used a heavy thumb.

The convent had been Magnolia's idea. Ravenal had laughed when she
broached the subject to him. "She'll be well fed and housed and generally
cared for there," he agreed. "And she'll learn French and embroidery and
deportment and maybe some arithmetic, if she's lucky. But every t—uh—
every shady lady on Clark Street sends her daughter there."

"She's got to go somewhere, Gay. This pillar-to-post life we're leading
is terrible for a child."

"What about your own life when you were a child? I suppose you led a
prissy existence."

"It was routine compared to Kim's. When I went to bed in my little room
on the *Cotton Blossom* I at least woke up in it next morning. Kim goes to
sleep on north Clark and wakes up on Michigan Avenue. She never sees a
child her own age. She knows more bell boys and chambermaids and waiters
than a travelling man. She thinks a dollar bill is something to buy candy with
and that when a stocking has a hole in it you throw it away. She can't do
the simplest problem in arithmetic, and yesterday I found her leaning over
the second floor rotunda rail spitting on the heads of people in the———"

"Did she hit anybody?"

"It isn't funny, Gay."

"It is, too. I've always wanted to do it."

"Well, so have I—but, anyway, it won't be funny five years from now."

St. Agatha's occupied half of one of Chicago's huge square blocks. Its
great flight of front steps was flush with the street, but at the back was a
garden discreetly protected by a thick brick wall fully ten feet high and
belligerently spiked. St. Agatha herself and a whole host of attendant cher-
ubim looked critically down upon Magnolia and Kim as they ascended the
long broad flight of steps that led to the elaborately (and lumpily) carved
front door. Of the two Magnolia was the more terrified. The windows glittered so sharply. The stairs were so clean. The bell, as they rang it, seemed
to echo so hollowly through endless unseen halls and halls and halls. The
hand that opened the door had been preceded by no sound of human footsteps. The door had loomed before them seemingly as immovable as the
building itself. There was the effect of black magic in its sudden and noiseless
opening. The great entrance hall waited still and dim. The black-robed figure
before them was vaguely surmounted by a round white face that had the
look of being no face at all but a flat circular surface on which features had
been clumsily daubed.

"I came to see about placing my little girl in school."

The flat surface broke up surprisingly into a smile. She was no longer a
mysterious and sombre figure but a middle-aged person, kindly, but not
especially bright. "This way."

This way led to a small and shiny office presided over by another flat
circular surface. This, in turn, gave way to a large and almost startlingly
sunny room, one flight up, where sat at a desk a black-robed figure different
from the rest. A large pink face. Penetrating shrewd blue eyes behind gold-
rimmed spectacles. A voice that was deep without resonance. A woman

with the look of the ruler. Parthy, practically, in the garb of a Mother Superior.

"Oh, my goodness!" thought Magnolia, in a panic. She held Kim's cool little hand tight in her own agitated fingers. Of the two, she was incalculably the younger. The classrooms. The sewing room. Sister This. Sister That. The garden. Little hard-benches. Prim gravel paths. Holy figures in stone brooding down upon the well-kept flower beds. Saints and angels and apostles. When all those glittering windows were dark, and the black-robed figures within lay in slumber, their hands (surely) crossed on their barren breasts and the flat circular surfaces reposed exactly in the centre of the hard pillows, and the moonlight flooded this cloistered garden spot with the same wanton witchery that enveloped a Sicilian bower, did these pious stone images turn suddenly into fauns and nymphs and dryads, Magnolia wondered, wickedly.

Aloud: "I see . . . I see . . . Oh, the refectory . . . I see. . . . Prayers . . . seven o'clock . . . dark blue dresses . . . every Thursday from two to five . . . and sewing and music and painting as well. . . ."

And this was the chapel. I see. And this was her bedroom to be shared with another pupil. But she has always had her own. It is the rule. I see. I'll let you know. It's Kim. I know it is, but that's her name, really. It's—she was born—in Kentucky and Illinois and Missouri—that is—yes, it does sound—no, I don't think she'd like to have you call her anything else, she's so used—I'll let you know, may I? I'd like to talk it over with her to see if she thinks she'd be happy . . .

In the garden, in various classrooms, in the corridors, and on the stairs they had encountered girls from ten to sixteen or even eighteen years of age, and they were all dressed exactly alike, and they had all flashed a quick prim look at the visitors from beneath demure lids. Magnolia had sensed a curious undercurrent of plot, of mischief. Hidden secret thoughts scurried up the bare varnished halls, lurked grinning in the stairway niches.

They were back in the big sunny second-floor room after their tour of inspection. The pink-faced Parthy person was regarding them with level brows. Magnolia was clinging more tightly than ever to Kim's hand. It was as though the child were supporting her, not she the child.

"But I know now whether I like it or not," Kim had spoken up, astonishingly. "I like it."

Magnolia was horrified to find that she had almost cried, "Oh, no! No, Kim!" aloud. She said, instead, "Are you sure, darling? You needn't stay unless you want to. Mother just brought you to see if you might like it."

"I do," repeated Kim, patiently, as one speaks to an irritating child.

Magnolia was conscious of a sinking sense of disappointment. She had hoped, perversely enough, that Kim would stamp her feet, throw herself screaming on the floor, and demand to be carried out of the bare clean orderly place back to the delightful welter of Clark Street. She could not overcome the feeling that in thus bestowing upon Kim a ladylike education and background she was depriving her of something rich and precious and colourful. She thought of her own childhood. She shut her eyes so as to see more clearly the pictures passing in her mind. Deep rivers. Wide rivers. Willows by the water's edge trailing gray-green. Dogwood in fairy bloom. Darkies on the landing. Plinketty-plunk-plunk-plunk, plinketty-plunk-plunk-plunk. Cotton bales. Sweating black bodies. Sue, ef he loves yuh, go with him. To-morrow night, ladies and gentlemen, that magnificent comedy-drama, Honest Hearts and Willing Hands. The band, red-coated, its brass screaming defiance at the noonday sun.

The steely blue eyes in the pink face surrounded by the white wimple and the black coif seemed to be boring into her own eyes. "If you yourself would rather not have her here with us we would prefer not to take her."

"Oh, but I would! I do!" Magnolia cried hastily.

So it was arranged. Next week. Monday. Half a dozen woollen this. Half a dozen cotton that.

Descending the great broad flight of outside steps Magnolia said, like a child, "From now until Monday we'll do things, shall we? Fun. What would you like to do?"

"Oh, a matinée on Saturday————" began Kim eagerly. Magnolia was enormously relieved. She had been afraid that this brief glimpse into the more spiritual life might already have had a chastening effect upon the cosmopolitan Kim.

Thus the child was removed from the pernicious atmosphere of the Chicago Levee just when the Levee itself began to feel the chastening hand of reform. Suddenly, overnight, Chicago went civic. For a quarter of a century she had been a strident, ample-bosomed, loud-mouthed Rabelaisian giantess in red satin and diamonds, who kept open house day and night and welcomed all comers. There were food and drink and cheer. Her great muscular arms embraced ranchers from Montana and farmers from Indiana and bankers from New York. At Bath House John's Workingmen's Exchange you got a tub of beer for a nickel; the stubble-faced bums lined the curb outside his ceaselessly swinging door on Clark Street. The visiting ranchers and farmers and bankers were told to go over to the Palmer House and see the real silver dollars sunk in the tiled floor of that hostelry's barroom. The garrulous Coughlin, known as The Bath, and the silent little Hinky Dink Mike Kenna were Chicago's First Ward aldermen and her favourite naughty sons. The roulette wheels in Gamblers' Alley spun merrily by day and by night. The Mayor of the city called a genial, "Hope you're all winning, boys!" as he dropped in for a sociable drink and a look at the play; or even to take a hand. "What'll you have?" was Chicago's greeting, and "Don't care if I do," her catch phrase. Hetty Chilson was the recognized leader of her sinister world, and that this world happened to be prefaced by the qualifying word, "under" made little difference in Chicago's eyes. Pawnshops, saloons, dives, and gambling houses lined Clark Street from Twelfth to the river, and dotted the near-by streets for blocks around. The wind-burned ranchmen in bearskin coats and sombreros at Polk and Clark were as common a sight as the suave white fingered gentry in Prince Alberts and diamonds at Clark and Madison. It was all one to Chicago. "Game upstairs, gentlemen! Game upstairs!"

New York, eyeing her Western cousin through disapproving lorgnettes, said, "What a crude and vulgar person!"

"Me!" blustered Chicago, dabbing futilely at the food and wine spots on her broad satin bosom. "Me! I'll learn you I'm a lady."

The names of University of Chicago professors (Economics Department) began to appear on the lists of aldermanic candidates. Earnest young men and women with notebooks and fountain pens knocked at barred doors, stated that they were occupied in compiling a Survey, and asked intimate questions. Down came whole blocks of rats' nests on Clark and Dearborn, with the rats scuttling frantically to cover. Up went office buildings that actually sneered down upon the Masonic Temple's boasted height. Brisk gentlemen in eyeglasses and sack suits whisked in and out of these chaste edifices. The clicking sound to be heard on Clark Street was no longer that of the roulette wheel but of the stock market ticker and the Western Union transmitter.

It was rumoured that they were going to close Jeff Hankins'. They were going to close Mike McDonald's. They were going to banish the Washington Park race track.

"They can't do it," declared Gaylord Ravenal.

"Oh, can't we!" sneered the reformers. Snick-snack, went the bars on Hankins' doors and on Mike McDonald's. It actually began to be difficult to find an open game. It began to be well-nigh impossible. It came to such a pass that you had to know the signal knock. You had to submit to a silent scrutiny from unseen eyes peering through a slit somewhere behind a bland closed door. The Prince Alberts grew shiny. The fine linen showed frayed edges. The diamonds reposed unredeemed for longer and longer periods at Lipman's or Goldsmith's. The Ravenal ring and the succession of sealskin sacques seemed permanently to have passed out of the Ravenal possession. The malacca stick, on the other hand, was now a fixture. It had lost its magic. It was no longer a symbol of security. The day was past when its appearance at Lipman's or Goldsmith's meant an I O U for whatever sum Gay Ravenal's messenger might demand. There actually were mornings when even the Cockeyed Bakery represented luxury. As for breakfast at Billy Boyle's! An event.

The Ravenals' past experience in Chicago seemed, in comparison with their present precarious position, a secure and even humdrum existence. Ohio and Ontario streets knew them for longer and longer periods. Now when Magnolia looked into the motley assemblage of objects in the more obscure pawnshop windows, she was likely to avert her eyes quickly at recognition of some object not only intimate but familiar. Magnolia thought of Kim, safe, secure, comfortable, in the convent on Wabash Avenue.

"I must have felt this thing coming," she said to Ravenal. "Felt it in my bones. She's out of all this. It makes me happy just to think of it; to think of her there."

"How're you going to keep her there?" demanded Ravenal, gloomily. "I'm strapped. You might as well know it, if you don't already. I've had the damnedest run of luck."

Magnolia's eyes grew wide with horror. "Keep her there! Gay! We've got to. I wouldn't have her knocking around here with us. Gay, can't you do something? Something real, I mean. Some kind of work like other—I mean, you're so wonderful. Aren't there things—positions—you know—with banks or—uh—those offices where they buy stocks and sell them and make money in wheat and—wheat and things?" Lamely.

Ravenal kissed her. "What a darling you are, Nola. A darling simpleton."

It was a curious and rather terrible thing, this love bond between them. All that Parthy had grimly predicted had come to pass. Magnolia knew him for what he was. Often she hated him. Often he hated her. Often he hated her because she shamed him with her gaiety, her loyalty, her courage, her tenderness. He was not true to her. She knew this now. He knew she knew this. She was a one-man woman. Frequently they quarrelled hideously. Tied to you. . . . Tied! God knows I'd be happier without you. You've never brought me anything but misery. . . . Always finding fault. . . . Put on those fine lady airs with me. What'd I take you out of! . . . An honest living, anyway. Look people in the face. Accusations. Bitterness. Longing. Passion. The long periods of living in sordid surroundings made impossible most of the finer reticences. Garments washed out in the basin. Food cooked over the gas jet. One room. One bed. Badly balanced meals. Reproaches. Tears. Sneers. Laughter. Understanding. Reconciliation.

They loved each other. Over and above and through and beneath it all, thick and thin, warp and woof, they loved each other.

It was when their fortunes were at lowest ebb; when the convent tuition had now been two terms unpaid; when the rent on the Ontario Street lodgings was overdue; when even Ravenal, handsome and morose, was forced to content himself with the coffee and rolls of the bedroom breakfast; when a stroll up Clark Street meant meeting a dozen McLean suits as shabby as his own—it was at this unpropitious time that Parthenia Ann Hawks was seized with the idea of visiting her daughter, her son-in-law, and her grandchild in Chicago. Her letters always came to the Sherman House—had been called for there through these years though the fluctuations of fortune had carried the Ravenals away from the hotel and back again with a tide-like regularity. Twice Magnolia had taken Kim to see her grim grandmamma at Thebes when the *Cotton Blossom* was in for repairs during the winter season. These visits had always been timed when the Ravenal tide was high. Magnolia and Kim had come back to Thebes on the crest of a wave foaming with silks and laces and plumes and furs. The visits could not, however, be said to have been a success. Magnolia always came prepared to be the fond and dutiful daughter. Invariably she left seething between humorous rage and angry laughter.

"It wasn't anything she actually did," she would explain afterward, ruefully, to Ravenal. "It's just that she treats me with such disrespect." She pondered this a moment. "I honestly think Mama's the vainest woman I have ever met."

Strangely enough, Kim and her grandmother did not get on very satisfactorily, either. It dawned on Magnolia that the two were much alike. Their methods were different, but the result was the same. Each was possessed of an iron determination; boundless vitality; enormous resistance; canny foresight; definite ambition. Parthy was the blustering sort; Kim the quietly stubborn. When the two met in opposition they stood braced, horn to horn, like bulls.

On both occasions these visits had terminated abruptly in less than a week. The bare, wind-swept little town, winter-locked, had seemed unspeakably dreary to Magnolia. In the chill parlour of the cottage there was a wooden portrait of her father done in crayon. It was an enlargement which Parthy had had done from a small photograph of Andy in his blue coat and visored cap and baggy wrinkled pants. An atrocious thing, but the artist, clumsy though he was, had somehow happened to catch the alert and fun-loving brightness of the keen brown eyes. The mutton-chop whiskers looked like tufts of dirty cotton; the cheeks were pink as a chorus girl's. But the eyes were Andy's. Magnolia wandered into the parlour to stand before this picture, looking up at it with a smile. She wandered, too, down to the river to gaze at the sluggish yellow flood thick now with ice, but as enthralling as ever to her. She stood on the river bank in her rich furs, a lonely, wind-swept figure, gazing down the river, down the river, and her eyes that had grown so weary with looking always at great gray buildings and grim gray streets and swarming gray crowds now lost their look of strain, of unrepose, as they beheld in the far still distance the lazy Southern wharves, the sleepy Southern bayous—Cairo, Memphis, Vicksburg, Natchez, New Orleans—Queenie, Jo, Elly, Schultzy, Andy, Julie, Steve.

She took Kim eagerly to the water's edge—gave her the river with a sweep of her arm. Kim did not like it.

"Is that the river?" she asked.

"Why, yes, darling. Don't you remember! The river!"

"The river you told me about?"

"Of course!"

"It's all dirty and ugly. You said it was beautiful."

"Oh, Kim, isn't it?"

"No."

She showed her the picture of Captain Andy.

"Grampa?"

"Yes."

"Cap'n?"

"Yes, dear. He used to laugh so when you called him that when you were a little baby. Look at his eyes, Kim. Aren't they nice? He's laughing."

"He's funny-looking," said Kim.

Parthy asked blunt questions. "Sherman House? What do you go living in a hotel for all these years, with the way they charge for food and all! You and that husband of yours must have money to throw away. Why don't you live in a house, with your own things, like civilized people?"

"Gay likes hotels."

"Shiftless way to live. It must cost a mint of money."

"It does," agreed Magnolia, amiably.

"Like to know where you get it, that's what."

"Gay is very successful."

A snort as maddening as it was expressive from Parthy. The widow Hawks did not hesitate to catechize the child in the temporary absence of her mother. From these sessions Parthy must have gained some knowledge of the Ohio and Ontario street interludes, for she emerged from them with a look of grim satisfaction.

And now Parthenia Ann Hawks was coming to Chicago. She had never seen it. The letter announced her arrival as two weeks distant. The show-boat season was at an end. She would stay at the Sherman House where they were, if it wasn't too expensive. They were not to pay. She wouldn't be beholden to any one. She might stay a week, she might stay two weeks or longer, if she liked it. She wanted to see the Stockyards, the Grand Opera House, the Masonic Temple, Marshall Field's, Lincoln Park, and the Chicago River.

"My God!" said Gaylord Ravenal, almost piously. "My GOD!"

Stricken, they looked at each other. Stared. It was a thing beyond laughter. Every inch of space about them spelled failure. Just such failure as had been predicted for them by the woman who was now coming, and whose coming would prove to her the triumph of that prediction. They were living in a huddle of discomfort on Ontario Street. Magnolia, on her visits to Kim at the convent, was hard put to it to manage the little surprise gift planned to bring to the girl's face the flashing look of gay expectancy. A Henrici cake elaborately iced, to share with her intimates; a book; a pair of matinée tickets as a special treat; flowers for the Mother Superior; chocolates. Now the Christmas holidays were approaching. Kim would expect to spend them with her parents. But where? They would not bring her to this sordid lodging. And somehow, before the new term began, the unpaid tuition fee must be got together. Still, the Ravenals had faced such problems as these before now. They could have met them, they assured each other, as they always had. Luck always turned when things looked blackest. Life did that to tease you. But this was different. Gaylord Ravenal's world was crumbling. And Parthy! Parthy! Here was a situation fraught with what of horror! Here was humiliation. Here was acknowledged defeat.

" Borrow," suggested Magnolia.

"On what security?"

"I don't mean that kind of—I don't mean businesslike borrowing. I mean borrowing from friends. Friends. All these men————"

"Men! What men?"

"The men at the—at the places." She had always pretended that she did not actually know he came by his livelihood as he did. She never said, "Gamblers' Alley." She refused to admit that daily he had disappeared within the narrow slit of lane that was really a Clark Street alley; that he had spent the hours there watching bits of pasteboard for a living. "The men you have known so many years."

Grimly: "They've all been trying to borrow of me."

"But Mike McDonald. Hankins. Varnell." She cast pretense aside now. "Thousands. They've had thousands of dollars. All the money we brought with us to Chicago. Won't they give some of it back?"

This he found engaging rather than irritating, as well he might have. He shouted with laughter as he always did at a fresh proof of her almost incredible naïveté. At times such as these he invariably would be impelled to caress her much as one laughs at a child and then fondles it delightedly after it has surprised one with an unexpected and charming trick. He would kiss the back of her neck and then her wide, flexible mouth, and she would push him away, bewildered and annoyed that this should be his reaction to what she had meant so seriously.

"Nola, you're priceless! You're a darling. There's no one like you." He went off again into a shout of laughter. "Give it back! McDonald, h'm? There's an idea for you."

"How can you act like that when you know how serious it is!"

"Serious! Why, damn it, it's desperate. I tell you I'll never have her come here and see us living like this. We'll get out, first. . . . Say, Nola, what's to prevent us getting out, anyway? Chicago's no good any more. Why not get out of this! I'm sick of this town."

"We haven't any money to get out with, for one reason. And Kim's at school and she's going to stay there. She's going to stay there if I have to———"

"Have to what?"

"Ask Mama for the money." She said this mischievously, troubled though she was. Out he flew into a rage.

"I'll see her in——— I've been in deeper holes than this and managed to crawl out." He sat a moment in silence, staring with unseeing eyes at the shabby sticks of furniture that emphasized the room's dreariness. Magnolia, seated as quietly opposite him, sewing on a petticoat for Kim, suddenly let her hands sink in her lap. She realized, with a sort of fright, that he was as completely outside the room as though his body had been wafted magically through the window. And for him she, too, had vanished. He was deep in thought. The mask was off. She sat looking at him. She saw, clearly, the man her mother had so bitterly fought her marrying. The face of this man now in his late thirties was singularly unlined. Perhaps that was what you missed in it. The skin and hair and eyes, the set of the shoulders, the lead of the hand from the wrist, bespoke a virile man. But vigour—vigorous — no, he was not that. This was a fencer, not a fighter. But he had fought for her, years ago. The shambling preacher in the little river town whose name she had forgotten. That simple ignorant soul who preached hell fire and thought that play actors were damned. He had not expected to be knocked down in his own musty little shop. Not much of a victory, that. Gay had opposed that iron woman, her mother. But the soft life since then. Red plush, rich food, Clark Street. Weak. What was it? No lines about the mouth. Why was it weak? Why was it weak now if it had not been twelve years ago? A handsome man. Hard. But you couldn't be hard and weak at the same time, could you? What was he thinking of so intently? His face was so exposed, so defenceless, as sometimes when she awoke in the early morning and looked at him, asleep. Almost ashamed to look at his face, so naked was it of the customary daytime covering.

Now resolve suddenly tightened it. He stood up. He adjusted the smart and shabby hat at an angle that defied its shabbiness. He reached for the malacca stick. It was nine o'clock in the evening. They had had a frugal and unappetizing meal at a little near-by lunch room. Ravenal had eaten nothing. He had, for the most part, stared at the dishes with a detached and slightly amused air as though they had been served him by mistake and soon would be apologetically reclaimed by the slovenly waitress who had placed them before him.

She had never been one to say, "Where are you going?" Yet now her face was so moving in its appeal that he answered its unspoken question.

"Cheer up, old girl! I know somebody."

"Who? Who, Gay?"

"Somebody I've done favours for. She owes me a good turn." He was thinking aloud.

"She?"

"Never mind."

"She, Gay?"

"Did I say—now never mind, Nola. I'll do the worrying."

He was off.

She had become accustomed, through these years, to taking money without question when there was money; to doing without, uncomplainingly, when there was none. They had had to scheme before now, and scurry this way and that, seeking a way out of a tight corner. They had had to borrow as they had often lent. It had all been part of the Clark Street life—the gay, wasteful, lax, improvident sporting life of a crude new Mid-west city. But that life was vanishing now. That city was vanishing with it. In its place a newer, harder, more sophisticated metropolis was rearing its ambitious head.

Magnolia, inured to money crises, realized that the situation to-night was different. This was not a crisis. It was an impasse.

Let's get out of here," Gay had said. There was no way out. The men from whom he had borrowed in the past were themselves as harried as he. The sources from which he had gained his precarious livelihood were drying up; had almost ceased to exist, except furtively. I know somebody. Somebody who would like to do me a favour. Somebody—who—would—like—— horrid suspicion darted through her mind, released from the subconscious. Appalled at its ugliness, she tried to send it back to its hiding place. It would not go. It stayed there before her mind's eye, grinning, evil, unspeakably repulsive. She took up her sewing again. She endeavoured to fix her mind on Kim. Kim asleep in the cold calm quiet of the great walled convent on South Wabash. French and embroidery and deportment and china painting and wimples and black wings and long dark shining halls and round white faces and slim white tapers and statues of the saints that turned into fauns and why was that not surprising? A clatter. One of the saints had dropped her rosary on the bare shining floor. It wasn't a rosary. It was an anchor ringing against the metal stanchion of the *Cotton Blossom*.

Magnolia awoke. Her sewing scissors had fallen from her lap. Her face felt stiff and drawn. She hugged herself a little, and shivered, and looked about her. Her little gold watch on the dresser—no, of course not. That was gone. She folded her sewing. It was late, she knew. She was accustomed to being up until twelve, one, two. But this was later. Something told her that this was later. The black hush of the city outside. The feel of the room in which she sat. The sinister quiet of the very walls about her. The cheap clock on the shelf had stopped. The hands said twenty minutes after two. Twenty-one minutes after, she told herself in a foolish triumph of precision.

She took down her fine long black hair. Brushed it. Plaited it. One of the lacy nightgowns so absurd in the sordid shabbiness of the rooming-house bedroom; so alien to the coarse gray sheets. She had no other kind. She went to bed. She fell asleep.

It was just before dawn when he returned. The black of the window panes showed the promise of gray. His step had an unaccustomed sound. He fumbled for the gas jet. His very presence was strange in the dark. The light flared blue, but she knew; she knew even before it illumined his face that bore queer slack lines she had never before seen there. For the first time in their life together Gaylord Ravenal was drunk.

She sat up; reached for her wrapper at the foot of the bed and bunched it about her shivering shoulders. He was immensely serious and dignified. He swayed a little. The slack look on his face. That was all.

"I'll do the worrying," he said, as though continuing the conversation that had held them at nine o'clock. He placed the malacca stick carefully in its corner. He removed his coat, keeping his hat on. The effect was startlingly rowdy, perhaps because he had always so meticulously observed the niceties. Standing thus, weaving back and forth ever so slightly, he pulled from his left vest pocket, where it fitted much too snugly, a plump bill-folder. Custom probably cautioned him to retain this, merely widening its open side to reveal the sheaf of notes within. But his condition, and all that had gone to bring it about, caused him to forego his cunning. With a vague, but successful, gesture, and a little lurch as he stood, he tossed the leather folder to the counterpane. "Coun' it!" he commanded, very distinctly. "Ten one hun'er' dollar bills and ten one hun'er' dollar bills makes twen'y one hun'er' dollar bills an' anybody says it doesn' is a liar. Two thousan' dollars. Would you kin'ly count 'em, Mrs. Rav'nal? I believe"—with businesslike dignity—"I b'lieve you'll find that correc'."

Magnolia Ravenal in her nightgown with her wrapper hunched about her shoulders sat staring at the little leather booklet on the bed. Its gaping mouth mocked her. She did not touch it.

"Two thousand dollars?" she said.

"I b'lieve you'll fin' tha's correc'." He seemed to be growing less distinct.

"Where did you get this, Gay?"

"Never min'. I'll do th' worrying."

He unbuttoned his vest with some difficulty. Yawned prodigiously, like one who has earned his rest after a good day's work.

She looked at him. She was like a drawing in French ink—her face so white, her eyes so enormous, her hair so black.

"You got this from Hetty Chilson."

His collar came off with a crack-snap. He held it in the hand that pointed toward the money. He seemed offended at something. Not angry, but hurt. "How can you say that, M'nolia! I got one thousan' from good ol' Het and not cen' more. Wha' do I do then! Marsh up to Sheedy's and win a thousan' more at roulette. Ha! That's a great joke on Sheedy because, look, roulette isn' my game. Nev' has been. Faro's my game. Tha's a gen'leman's game, faro. One thousan' Hetty, and marsh ri' up . . . roulette . . . win . . . 'nother . . . Thous . . ." He lurched to the bed.

He was asleep at once, heavily, deeply, beside her on the bed, his fine long head lolling off the pillow. She knelt in her place and tried to lift the inert figure to a more comfortable position; succeeded, finally, after some tugging. She drew the lumpy coverlet over him. Then she sat as before, hunched in her nightgown and the wrapper, staring at the open wallet with its many leaves. It was dawn now. The room was gray with it. She ought to turn out the gas. She arose. She picked up the wallet. Before extinguishing the light she counted out ten one-hundred-dollar bills from the sheaf within the wallet. One thousand dollars. Her fingers touched the bills gingerly, fastidiously, and a little wrinkle of disgust curled her lip. She placed the bills on the dresser. She folded the leather holder and tucked it, with its remaining contents, under his pillow. He did not waken. She turned out the light then, and coming back to the bedside drew on the slippers that lay on the floor. She got her shirtwaist—a fresh white one with a Gibson tuck—from the drawer, and her skirt and jacket from the hooks covered over with a protecting length of calico against the wall. She heated a little water, and washed; combed and dressed her hair; put on her clothes, laid her hat on the dresser. Then she sat in the one comfortable chair that the room afforded—a crazy and decayed armchair done in dingy red plush, relic of some past grandeur—and waited. She even slept a little there in the sagging old chair, with the morning light glaring pitilessly in upon her face. When she awoke it must have been nearly noon. A dour day, but she had grown accustomed to the half lights of the Chicago fogs. She glanced sharply at him. He had not moved. He had not stirred. He looked, somehow, young, helpless, innocent, pathetic. She busied herself in making a cup of coffee as quietly as might be. This might rouse him, but it would make little difference. She knew what she had to do. She drank the hot revivifying liquid in great gulps. Then she put on her jacket, pinned on her hat, took up the bills and placed them neatly in her handbag. She glanced at herself in the mirror.

"My, you're plain!" she thought, meaninglessly. She went down the dim stairway. The fusty landlady was flapping a gray rag in the outer doorway as her contribution to the grime of the street.

"What's taking you out so bright and early, Mis' Ravenal? Business or pleasure?" She liked her little joke.

"Business," said Magnolia.

17

THE KNELL HAD sounded for the red brick house with the lions guarding its portals. The Chicago soot hung like a pall over it. The front steps sagged. Even the stone lions had a mangy look. The lemon-water sunshine of a Chicago winter day despoiled the dwelling of any sinister exterior aspect. That light, filtering through the lake mist, gave to the house-front the look of a pock-marked, wrinkled, and evil old hag who squats in the market place with her face to the sun and thinks of her purple past and does not regret it.

It was half-past one. Magnolia Ravenal had figured this out nicely. That part of Clark Street would be astir by now. As she approached the house on Clark, near Polk, her courage had momentarily failed her, and she had passed it, hurriedly. She had walked a block south, wretchedly. But the feel of the bills in her bag gave her new resolve. She opened the handbag to look at them, turned and walked swiftly back to the house. She rang the bell this time, firmly, demandingly; stood looking down at its clean-scrubbed doorstep and tried to ignore the prickling sensation that ran up and down her spine and the weak and trembling feeling in her legs. The people passing by could see her. She was knocking at Hetty Chilson's notorious door, and the people passing by could see her: Magnolia Ravenal. Well, what of it! Don't be silly. She rang again.

The door was opened by a Negro in a clean starched white house coat. Magnolia did not know why the sight of this rather sad-eyed looking black man should have reassured her; but it did. She knew exactly what she wanted to say.

"My name is Mrs. Ravenal. I want to speak to Hetty Chilson."

"Mis' Chilson is busy, ma'am," he said, as though repeating a lesson. Still, something about the pale, well-dressed, earnest woman evidently impressed him. Of late, when he opened the door there had been frequent surprises for him in the shape of similar earnest and well-dressed young women who, when you refused them admittance, flashed an official-looking badge, whipped out notebook and pencil and insisted pleasantly but firmly that he make quite sure Miss Chilson was not in. "You-all one them Suhveys?"

Uncomprehending, she shook her head. He made as though to shut the door, gently. Magnolia had not spent years in the South for nothing. "Don't you shut that door on me! I want to see Hetty Chilson."

The man recognized the tone of white authority.

"Wha' you want?"

Magnolia recovered herself. After all, this was not the front door of a home, but of a House. "Tell her Mrs. Gaylord Ravenal wants to speak to her. Tell her that I have one thousand dollars that belongs to her, and I want to give it to her." Foolishly she opened her bag and he saw the neat sheaf of bills. His eyes popped a little.

"Yes'm. Ah tell huh. Step in ma'am"

Magnolia entered Hetty Chilson's house. She was frightened. The trembling had taken hold of her knees again. But she clutched the handbag and looked about her, frankly curious. A dim hallway, richly carpeted, its walls covered with a red satin brocade. There were deep soft cushioned chairs, and others of carved wood, high-backed. A lighted lamp on the stairway newel post cast a rosy glow over the whole. Huge Sèvres vases stood in the stained-glass window niches. It was an entrance hall such as might have been seen in the Prairie Avenue or Michigan Avenue house of a new rich Chicago packer. The place was quiet. Now and then you heard a door shut. There was the scent of coffee in the air. No footfall on the soft carpet, even though the tread were heavy. Hetty Chilson descended the stairs, a massive, imposing figure in a black-and-white patterned foulard dress. She gave the effect of activity hampered by some physical impediment. Her descent was one of impatient deliberateness. One hand clung to the railing. She appeared a stout, middle-aged, well-to-do householder summoned from some domestic task abovestairs. She had aged much in the last ten years. Magnolia, startled, realized that the distortion of her stout figure was due to a tumour.

"How do you do?" said Hetty Chilson. Her keen eyes searched her visitor's face. The Negro hovered near by in the dim hallway. "Are you Mrs. Ravenal?"

"Yes."

"What is it, please?"

Magnolia felt like a schoolgirl interrogated by a stern but well-intentioned preceptress. Her cheeks were burning as she opened her handbag, took out the sheaf of hundred-dollar bills, tendered them to this woman. "The money," she stammered, "the money you gave my—you gave my husband. Here it is."

Hetty Chilson looked at the bills. "I didn't give it to him. I loaned it to him. He said he'd pay it back and I believe he will. Ravenal's got the name for being square."

Magnolia touched Hetty Chilson's hand with the folded bills; pressed them on her so that the hand opened automatically to take them. "We don't want it."

"Don't want it! Well, what'd he come asking me for it for, then? I'm no bank that you can take money out and put money in."

"I'm sorry. He didn't know. I can't—we don't—I can't take it."

Hetty Chilson looked down at the bills. Her eyeglasses hung on the bodice of her dress, near the right shoulder, attached to a patent gold chain. This she pulled out now with a businesslike gesture and adjusted the eyeglasses to her nose. "Oh, you're that kind, huh?" She counted the bills once and then again; folded them. "Does your husband know about this?" Magnolia did not answer. She looked dignified and felt foolish. The very matter-of-factness of this world-hardened woman made this thing Magnolia had done seem overdramatic and silly. Hetty Chilson glanced over her shoulder to where the white-coated Negro stood. "Mose, tell Jule I want her. Tell her to bring her receipt book and a pen." Mose ran up the soft-carpeted stairs. You heard a deferential rap at an upper door; voices. Hetty turned again to Magnolia. "You'll want a receipt for this. Anyway, you'll have that to show him when he kicks up a fuss." She moved ponderously to the foot of the stairway; waited a moment there, looking up. Magnolia's eyes followed her gaze. Mose had vanished, evidently, down some rear passage and stairway, for he again appeared mysteriously at the back of the lower hall though he had not descended the stairway up which he had gone a moment before. Down this stair came a straight slim gray-haired figure. Genteel, was the word that popped into Magnolia's mind. A genteel figure in decent black silk, plain and good. It rustled discreetly. A white fine turnover collar finished it at the throat. Narrow cuffs at the wrist. It was difficult to see her face in the dim light. She paused a moment in the glow of the hall lamp as Hetty Chilson instructed her. A white face—no, not white—ivory. Like something dead. White hair still faintly streaked with black. In this clearer light the woman seemed almost gaunt. The eyes were incredibly black in that ivory face; like dull coals, Magnolia thought, staring at her, fascinated. Something in her memory stirred at sight of this woman in the garb of a companion-secretary and with a face like burned-out ashes. Perhaps she had seen her with Hetty Chilson at the theatre or the races. She could not remember.

"Make out a receipt for one thousand dollars received from Mrs. Gaylord Ravenal. R-a-v-e-n-a-l. Yes, that's right. Here; I'll sign it." Hetty Chilson penned her name swiftly as the woman held the book for her. She turned to Magnolia. "Excuse me," she said. "I have to be at the bank at two. Jule, give this receipt to Mrs. Ravenal. Come up as soon as you're through."

With a kind of ponderous dignity this strange and terrible woman ascended her infamous stairway. Magnolia stood, watching her. Her plump, well-shaped hand clung to the railing. An old woman, her sins heavy upon her. She had somehow made Magnolia feel a fool.

The companion tore the slip of paper from the booklet, advanced to Magnolia and held it out to her. "One thousand dollars," she said. Her voice was deep and rich and strange. "Mrs. Gaylord Ravenal. Correct?" Magnolia put out her hand, blindly. Unaccountably she was trembling again. The slip of paper dropped from her hand. The woman uttered a little exclamation of apology. They both stooped to pick it up as the paper fluttered to the floor. They bumped awkwardly, actually laughed a little, ruefully, and straightening, looked at each other, smiling. And as Magnolia smiled, shyly, she saw the smile on the face of the woman freeze into a terrible contortion of horror. Horror stamped itself on her every feature. Her eyes were wild and enormous with it; her mouth gaped with it. So the two stood staring at each other for one hideous moment. Then the woman turned, blindly, and vanished up the stairs like a black ghost. Magnolia stood staring after her. Then, with a little cry, she made as though to follow her up the stairway. Strangely she cried, "Julie! Julie, wait for me!" Mose, the Negro, came swiftly forward. "This way out, miss," he said, deferentially. He held the street door open, Magnolia passed through it, down the steps of the brick house with the lions couchant, into the midday brightness of Clark Street. Suddenly she was crying, who so rarely wept. South Clark Street paid little attention to her, inured as it was to queer sights. And if a passer-by had stopped and said, "What is it? Can I help you?" she would have been at a loss to reply. Certainly she could not have said, "I think I have just seen the ghost of a woman I knew when I was a little girl—a woman I first saw when I was swinging on the gate of our house at Thebes, and she went by in a longtailed flounced black dress and a lace veil tied around her hat. And I last saw her— oh, I can't be sure. I can't be sure. It might not————"

Clark Street, even if it had understood (which is impossible), would not have been interested. And presently, as she walked along, she composed herself. She dabbed at her face with her handkerchief and pulled down her neat veil. She had still another task to perform. But the day seemed already so old. She was not sleepy, but her mind felt thick and slow. The events of the past night and of the morning did not stand out clearly. It was as if they had happened long ago. Perhaps she should eat something. She had had only that cup of coffee; had eaten almost nothing the night before.

She had a little silver in her purse. She counted it as it lay next to the carefully folded thousand-dollar receipt signed in Hetty Chilson's firm businesslike hand. Twenty-five—thirty-five—forty—fifty—seventy-three cents. Ample. She stopped at a lunch room on Harrison, near Wabash; ate a sandwich and drank two cups of coffee. She felt much better. On leaving she caught a glimpse of herself in a wall mirror—a haggard woman with a skin blotched from tears, and a shiny nose and with little untidy wisps of hair showing beneath her hat. Her shoes—she remembered having heard or read somewhere that neat shoes were the first requisite for an applicant seeking work. Furtively and childishly she rubbed the toe of either shoe on the back of each stocking. She decided to go to one of the department-store rest rooms for women and there repair her toilette. Field's was the nicest; the Boston store the nearest. She went up State Street to Field's. The white marble mirrored room was full of women. It was warm and bright and smelled pleasantly of powder and soap and perfume. Magnolia took off her hat, bathed her face, tidied her hair, powdered. Now she felt less alien to these others about her—these comfortable chattering shopping women; wives of husbands who worked in offices, who worked in shops, who worked in factories. She wondered about them. She was standing before a mirror adjusting her veil, and a woman was standing beside her, peering into the same glass, each seemingly oblivious of the other. "I wonder," Magnolia thought, fancifully, "what she would say if I were to turn to her and tell her that I used to be a show-boat actress, and that my father was drowned in the Mississippi, and my mother, at sixty, runs a show boat all alone, and that my husband is a gambler and we have no money, and that I have just come from the most notorious brothel in Chicago, where I returned a thousand dollars my husband had got there, and that I'm on my way to try to get work in a variety theatre." She was smiling a little at this absurd thought. The other woman saw the smile, met it with a frozen stare of utter respectability, and walked away.

There were few theatrical booking offices in Chicago and these were of
doubtful reputation. Magnolia knew nothing of their location, though she
thought, vaguely, that they probably would be somewhere in the vicinity of
Clark, Madison, Randolph. She was wise enough in the ways of the theatre
to realize that these shoddy agencies could do little for her. She had heard
Ravenal speak of the variety houses and museums on State Street and Clark
and Madison. The word "vaudeville" was just coming into use. In company
with her husband she had even visited Kohl & Middleton's Museum—that
smoke-filled comfortable shabby variety house on Clark, where the admission was ten cents. It had been during that first Chicago trip, before Kim's
birth. Women seldom were seen in the audience, but Ravenal, for some
reason, had wanted her to get a glimpse of this form of theatrical entertainment. Here Weber and Fields had played for fifteen dollars a week. Here
you saw the funny Irishman, Eddie Foy; and May Howard had sung and
danced.

"They'll probably build big expensive theatres some day for variety
shows," Ravenal had predicted.

The performance was, Magnolia thought, much like that given as the
concert after the evening's bill on the *Cotton Blossom*. "A whole evening
of that?" she said. Years later the Masonic Temple Roof was opened for
vaudeville.

"There!" Ravenal had triumphantly exclaimed. "What did I tell you!
Some of those people get three and four hundred a week, and even more."
Here the juggling Agoust family threw plates and lighted lamps and tables
and chairs and ended by keeping aloft a whole dinner service and parlour
suite, with lamps, soup tureens, and plush chairs passing each other affably
in midair without mishap. Jessie Bartlett Davis sang, sentimentally, Tuh-rue
LOVE, That's The Simple Charm That Opens Every Woman's Heart.

At the other end of the scale were the all-night restaurants with a stage
at the rear where the waiters did an occasional song and dance, or where
some amateur tried to prove his talent. Between these were two or three
variety shows of decent enough reputation though frequented by the sporting
world of Chicago. Chief of these was Jopper's Varieties, a basement theatre
on Wabash supposed to be copied after the Criterion in London. There was
a restaurant on the ground floor. A flight of marble steps led down to the
underground auditorium. Here new acts were sometimes tried out. Lillian
Russell, it was said, had got her first hearing at Jopper's. For some reason,
Magnolia had her mind fixed on this place. She made straight for it, probably
as unbusinesslike a performer as ever presented herself for a hearing. It was
now well on toward mid-afternoon. Already the early December dusk was
gathering, aided by the Chicago smoke and the lake fog. Her fright at Hetty
Chilson's door was as nothing compared to the sickening fear that filled her
now. She was physically and nervously exhausted. The false energy of the
morning had vanished. She tried to goad herself into fresh courage by
thoughts of Kim at the convent; of Parthy's impending visitation. As she
approached the place on Wabash she resolved not to pass it, weakly. If she
passed it but once she never would have the bravery to turn and go in. She
and Ravenal had driven by many times on their way to the South Side races.
It was in this block. It was four doors away. It was here. She wheeled stiffly,
like a soldier, and went in. The restaurant was dark and deserted. One dim
light showed at the far end. The tablecloths were white patches in the gray-
ness. But a yellow path of light flowed up the stairway that led to the
basement, and she heard the sound of a piano. She descended the swimming
marble steps, aware of the most alarming sensation in her legs—rather, of

no sensation in them. It was as though no solid structure of bone and flesh and muscle lay in the region between her faltering feet and her pounding heart.

There was a red-carpeted foyer; a little ticket window; the doors of the auditorium stood open. She put out a hand, blindly, to steady herself against the door jamb. She looked into the theatre; the badly lighted empty theatre, with its rows and rows of vacant seats; its stage at the far end, the curtain half raised, the set a crudely painted interior. As she looked there came over her—flowed over her like balm—a feeling of security, of peace, of home-coming. Here were accustomed surroundings. Here were the very sights and smells and sounds she knew best. Those men with their hats on the backs of their heads and their cigars waggling comfortably and their feet on the chair in front of them might have been Schultzy, Frank, Ralph, Pa Means. Evidently a song was being tried out in rehearsal. The man at the piano was hammering it and speaking the words in a voice as hoarse and unmusical as a boat whistle coming through the fog. It was a coon song full of mah babys and choo-choos and Alabam's.

Magnolia waited quietly until he had come to a full stop.

A thin pale young man in a striped shirt and a surprising gray derby who had been sitting with his wooden kitchen chair tipped up against the proscenium now brought his chair down on all fours.

"You was with Haverly's, you say?"

"I cer'nly was. Ask Jim. Ask Sam. Ask anybody."

"Well, go back to 'em is what I say. If you ever was more than a singin' waiter then I'm new to the show business." He took his coat from where it lay on top of the piano. "That's all for to-day, ain't it, Jo?" He addressed a large huddle whose thick shoulders and round head could just be seen above the back of a second-row centre seat. The fat huddle rose and stretched and yawned, and grunted an affirmative.

Magnolia came swiftly down the aisle. She looked up at the thin young man; he stared at her across the footlight gutter.

"Will you let me try some songs?" she said,

"Who're you?" demanded the young man.

"My name is Magnolia Ravenal."

"Never heard of it. What do you do?"

"I sing. I sing Negro songs with a banjo."

"All right," said the thin young man, resignedly. "Get out your banjo and sing us one."

"I haven't got one."

"Haven't got one what?"

"One—a banjo."

"Well, you said you—didn' you just say you sung nigger songs with a banjo!"

"I haven't got it with me. Isn't there one?" Actually, until this moment, she had not given the banjo a thought. She looked about her in the orchestra pit.

"Well, for God's sakes!" said the gray derby.

The hoarse-voiced singer who had just met with rebuff and who was shrugging himself into a shabby overcoat now showed himself a knight. He took an instrument case from the piano top. "Here," he said. "Take mine, sister."

Magnolia looked to left, to right. "There." The fat man in the second row jerked a thumb toward the right stage box back of which was the stage door. Magnolia passed swiftly up the aisle; was on the stage. She was quite at ease, relaxed, at home. She seated herself in one of the deal chairs; crossed her knees.

"Take your hat off," commanded the pasty young man.

She removed her veil and hat. A sallow big-eyed young woman, too thin, in a well-made suit and a modish rather crumpled shirtwaist and nothing of the look of the stage about her. She thumbed the instrument again. She remembered something dimly, dimly, far, far back; far back and yet very recent; this morning. "Don't smile too often. But if you ever want anything . . ."

She smiled. The thin young man did not appear overwhelmed. She threw back her head then as Jo had taught her, half closed her eyes, tapped time with the right foot, smartly. Imitative in this, she managed, too, to get into her voice that soft and husky Negro quality which for years she had heard on river boats, bayous, landings. I got a wings. You got a wings. All God's chillun got a wings.

"Sing another," said the old young man. She sang the one she had always liked best.

> "Go down,Moses,
> 'Way down in Egypt land,
> Tell ole Pharaoh,
> To let my people go."

Husky, mournful, melodious voice. Tapping foot. Rolling eye.
Silence.

"What kind of a coon song do you call that?" inquired the gray derby.

"Why, it's a Negro melody—they sing them in the South."

"Sounds like a church hymn to me." He paused. His pale shrewd eyes searched her face. " You a nigger?"

The unaccustomed red surged into Magnolia's cheeks, dyed her forehead, her throat, painfully. "No, I'm not a—nigger."

"Well, you cer'nly sing like one. Voice and—I don't know—way you sing. Ain't that right, Jo?"

"Cer'nly is," agreed Jo.

The young man appeared a trifle embarrassed, which made him look all the younger. Years later, in New York, Kim was to know him as one of the most powerful theatrical producers of his day. And he was to say to Kim, "Ravenal, h'm? Why, say, I knew your mother when she was better-looking than you'll ever be. And smart! Say, she tried to sell me a coon song turn down in Jopper's in the old days, long before your time. "I thought they were hymns and wouldn't touch them. Seems they're hot stuff now. Spirituals, they call them. You hear 'em in every show on Broadway. 'S fact! Got to go to church to get away from 'em. Well, live and learn's what I say."

It was through this shrewd, tough, stage-wise boy that Magnolia had her chance. He did not understand or like her Negro folk songs then, but he did recognize the quality she possessed. And it was due to this precociousness in him that Magnolia, a little more than a year later, was singing American coon songs in the Masonic Roof bill, her name on the programme with those of Cissie Loftus and Marshall Wilder and the Four Cohans.

But now she stood up, the scarlet receding from her face, leaving it paler than before. Silently she handed the husky singer his banjo; tried to murmur a word of thanks; choked. She put on her hat, adjusted her veil.

"Here, wait a minute, sister. No offense. I've seen 'em lighter'n you.

Your voice sounds like a—ain't that the truth, Jo?'' Actually distressed, he appealed again to his unloquacious ally in the third row.

"Sure does," agreed Jo.

The unfortunate hoarse-voiced man who had loaned her the banjo now departed. He seemed to bear no rancour. Magnolia, seeing this, tried again to smile on the theory that, if he could be game, then so, too, could she. And this time, it was the real Magnolia Ravenal smile of which the newspapers made much in the years to come. The ravishing Ravenal smile, they said (someone having considered that alliterative phrase rather neat).

Seeing it now the young showman exclaimed, without too much elegance, "Lookit that, Jo!" Then, to Magnolia: "Listen, sister. You won't get far with those. Your songs are too much like church tunes, see? They're for a funeral, not a theaytre. And that's a fact. But I like the way you got of singing them. How about singing me a real coon song? You know. Hello, Mah Baby! or something like that."

"I don't know any. These are the only songs I know."

"Well, for——! Listen. You learn some real coon songs and come back, see, in a week. Here. Try these over at home, see." He selected some song sheets from the accommodating piano top. She took them, numbly.

She was again in the cold moist winter street. Quite dark now. She walked over to State Street and took a northbound car. The door of their room on the third floor was locked, and when she had opened it she felt that the room was empty. Not empty merely; deserted. Before she had lighted the gas jet she had an icy feeling of desolation, of impending and piled-up tragedy at the close of a day that already toppled with it. Her gaze went straight to the dresser.

An envelope was there. Her name on it in Ravenal's neat delicate hand. Magnolia. Darling, I am going away for a few weeks . . . return when your mother is gone . . . or send for you . . . six hundred dollars for you on shelf under clock . . . Kim . . . convent . . . enough . . . weeks . . . darling . . . love . . . best . . . always. . . .

She never saw him again.

She must have been a little light-headed by this time, for certainly no deserted wife in her right senses would have followed the course that Magnolia Ravenal now took. She read the note again, her lips forming some of the words aloud. She walked to the little painted shelf over the wash stand. Six hundred. That was right. Six hundred. Perhaps this really belonged to that woman, too. She couldn't go there again. Even if it did, she couldn't go there again.

She left the room, the gas flaring. She hurried down Clark Street, going a few blocks south. Into one of the pawnshops. That was nothing new. The man actually greeted her by name. "Good-evening, Mrs. Ravenal. And what can I do for you?"

"A banjo."

"What?"

"I want to buy a banjo."

She bargained for it, shrewdly. When she tendered a hundred-dollar bill in payment the man's face fell. "Oh now Mrs. Ravenal I gave you that special price because you——"

"I'll go somewhere else."

She got it. Hurried back with it. Into her room again. She had not even locked the door. Five of the six one-hundred-dollar bills lay as she had tossed them on the dresser. A little crazy, certainly. Years, years afterward she actually could relate the fantastic demoniac events of this day that had begun at four in the morning and ended almost twenty hours later. It made a very good story, dramatic, humorous, tragic. Kim's crowd thought it was wonderful.

She took off her veil and hat and jacket. Her black hair lay in loose limp ugly loops about her face. She opened one of the sheets of music—Whose Black Baby Are You?—and propped it up against the centre section of the old-fashioned dresser. She crossed her knees. Cradled the banjo. One foot tapped the time rhythmically. An hour. Two hours.

A knock at the door. The landlady, twelve hours fustier than she had been that morning. "It ain't me, Mis' Ravenal, but Downstairs says she can't sleep for the noise. She's that sickly one. She says she pounded but you didn't———"

"I'll stop. I didn't hear her. I'm sorry."

"For me you could go on all night." The landlady leaned bulkily and sociably against the door. "I'm crazy about music. I never knew you was musical."

"Oh, yes," said Magnolia. "Very."

18

"I WAS EDUCATED," began Kim Ravenal, studying her reflection in the mirror, and deftly placing a dab of rouge on either ear lobe, "in Chicago, by the dear Sisters there in St. Agatha's Convent."

She then had the grace to snigger, knowing well what the young second assistant dramatic critic would say to that. She was being interviewed in her dressing room at the Booth between the second and third acts of Needles and Pins. She had opened in this English comedy in October. Now it was April. Her play before this had run a year. Her play before that had run two years. Her play—well, there was nothing new to be said in an interview with Kim Ravenal, no matter how young or how dramatic the interviewer. There was, therefore, a touch of mischievous malice in this trite statement of hers. She knew what the bright young man would say in protest.

He said it. He said: "Oh, now, Pete's sake, Miss Ravenal! Quit kidding."

"But I was. I can't help it. I was! Ask my mother. Ask my husband. Ask anybody. Educated by the dear Sisters in the con———"

"Oh, I know it! So does everybody else who reads the papers. And you know as well as I do that that educated-in-a-convent stuff is rubber-stamp. It ceased to be readable publicity when Mrs. Siddons was a gal. Now be reasonable. Kaufman wants a bright piece about you for the Sunday page."

"All right. You ask intelligent questions and I'll answer them." Kim then leaned forward to peer intently at her own reflection in the dressing-room mirror with its brilliant border of amber lights. She reached for the rabbit's foot and applied to her cheeks that nervous and redundant film of rouge which means that the next curtain is four minutes away.

He was a very cagey New York second assistant dramatic critic, who did not confine his talents to second-assistant dramatic criticism. The pages of *Vanity Fair* and *The New Yorker* (locally known as the Fly Papers) frequently accepted first (assistant dramatic) aid from his pen. And, naturally, he had written one of those expressionistic plays so daringly different that three intrepid managers had decided not to put it on after all. Embittered, the second assistant dramatic critic threatened sardonically to get a production through the ruse of taking up residence in Prague or Budapest, changing his name to Capek or Vajda, and sending his manuscript back to New York as a foreign play for them to fight over.

Though she had now known New York for many years, there were phases of its theatrical life that still puzzled Kim's mother, Magnolia Ravenal; and this was one of them. "The critics all seem to write plays," she complained. "It makes the life of a successful actress like Kim so complicated. And the actors and actresses all lecture on the Trend of the Modern Drama at League Luncheons given at the Astor. I went to one once, with Kim. Blue voile ladies from Englewood. In my day critics criticized and actors acted."

Her suave and gifted son-in-law, Kenneth Cameron, himself a producer of plays of the more precious pattern (The Road to Sunrise, 1921; Jock o' Dreams, 1924), teased her gently about this attitude of intolerance. "Why, Nola! And you a famous stage mama! You ought to know that even Kim occasionally has to do things for publicity."

"In my *Cotton Blossom* days we were more subtle. The band marched down Main Street and played on the corner and Papa gave out handbills. That was our publicity. I didn't have to turn handsprings up the levee."

There was little that the public did not know about Kim Ravenal. There was nothing that the cagey young assistant critic did not know. He now assumed a tone of deep bitterness.

"All right, my fine lady. I'll go back and write a pattern piece. Started in stock in Chicago. Went to New York National Theatre School. Star pupil and Teacher's Pet while there. Got a bit in—uh—Mufti, wasn't it?—and walked away with the play just like the aspiring young actress in a bum short story. Born on a show boat in Kentucky and Illinois and Missouri simultaneously—say, explain that to me some time, will you?—hence name of Kim. Also mother was a show boat actress and later famous singer of coon—— Say, where is your mother these days, anyway? Gosh, I think she's grand! I'm stuck on her. She's the burning passion of my youth. No kidding. I don't know. She's got that kind of haunted hungry et-up look, like Bernhardt or Duse or one of them. You've got a little of it, yourself."

"Oh, sir!" murmured Kim, gratefully.

"Cultivate it, is my advice. And when she smiles! . . . Boy! I work like a dawg to get her to smile whenever I see her. She thinks I'm one of those cut-ups. I'm really a professional suicide at heart, but I'd wiggle my ears if it would win one of those slow, dazzling——"

"Listen! Who—or whom—are you interviewing, young man? Me or my mama?"

"She around?"

"No. She's at the Shaw opening with Ken."

"Well, then, you'll do."

"Just for that I think I'll turn elegant on you and not grant any more interviews. Maude Adams never did. Look at Mrs. Fiske! And Duse. Anyway, interviews always sound so dumb when they appear in print. Dignified silence is the thing. Mystery. Everybody knows too much about the stage, nowadays."

"Believe me, *I* do!" said the young second assistant dramatic critic, in a tone of intense acerbity.

A neat little triple tap at the dressing-room door. "Curtain already!" exclaimed Kim in a kind of panic. You would have thought this was her first stage summons. Another hasty application with the rabbit's foot.

A mulatto girl in black silk so crisp, and white batiste cap and apron so correct that she might have doubled as stage and practical maid, now opened the door outside which she had been discreetly stationed. "Curtain, Blanche?"

"Half a minute more, Miss Ravenal. Telegram." She handed a yellow envelope to Kim.

As Kim read it there settled over her face the rigidity of shock, so plain that the second assistant dramatic critic almost was guilty of, "No bad news, I hope?" But as though he had said it Kim Ravenal handed him the slip of paper.

"They've misspelled it," she said, irrelevantly. "It ought to be Parthenia."

He read:

> Mrs. Parthna A. Hawks died suddenly eight o'clock before evening show Cotton Blossom playing Cold Spring Tennessee advise sympathy company.
>
> CHAS. K. BARNATO.

"Hawks?"

"My grandmother."

"I'm sorry." Lamely. "Is there anything————"

"I haven't seen her in years. She was very old—over eighty. I can't quite realize. She was famous on the rivers. A sort of legendary figure. She owned and managed the *Cotton Blossom*. There was a curious kind of feud between her and Mother and my father. She was really a pretty terrible—I wonder—Mother————"

"Curtain, Miss Ravenal!"

She went swiftly toward the door.

"Can I do anything? Fetch your mother from the theatre?"

"She'll be back here with Ken after the play. Half an hour. No use————"

He followed her as she went swiftly toward the door from which she made her third-act entrance. "I don't want to be offensive, Miss Ravenal. But if there's a story in this—your grandmother, I mean—eighty, you know————"

Over her shoulder, in a whisper, "There is. See Ken." She stood a moment; seemed to set her whole figure; relaxed it then; vanished. You heard her lovely bbut synthetic voice as the American wife of the English husband in the opening lines of the third act:

"I'm so sick of soggy British breakfast. Devilled kidneys! Ugh! Who but the English could face food so visceral at nine A. M.!"

She was thinking as she played the third act for the three hundredth time that she must tuck the telegram under a cold cream jar or back of her mirror as soon as she returned to her dressing room. What if Magnolia should take it into her head to leave the Shaw play early and find it there on her dressing table! She must tell her gently. Magnolia never had learned to take telegrams calmly. They always threw her into a panic. Ever since that one about Gaylord Ravenal's death in San Francisco. Gaylord Ravenal. A lovely name. What a tin-horn sport he must have been. Charming though, probably.

Curtain. Bows. Curtain. Bows. Curtain. Bows. Curtain.

She was back in her dressing room, had removed her make-up, was almost dressed when Ken returned with her mother. She had made desperate haste, aided expertly by her maid.

The two entered laughing, talking, bickering good-naturedly. Kim heard her husband's jejune plangent voice outside her dressing-room door.

"I'm going to tell your daughter on you, Nola! Yes, I am."

"I don't care. He started it."

Kim looked round at them. Why need they be so horribly high-spirited just to-night? It was like comedy relief in a clumsily written play, put in to make the tragedy seem deeper. Still, this news was hardly tragic. Yet her mother might————

For years, now, Kim Ravenal had shielded her mother; protected her; spoiled her, Magnolia said, almost resentfully.

She stood now with her son-in-law in the cruel glare of the dressing-room lights. Her face was animated, almost flushed. Her fine head rose splendidly from the furred frame of her luxurious coat collar. Her breast and throat were firm and creamy above the square-cut décolletage of her black gown. Her brows looked the blacker and more startling for the wing of white that crossed the black of her straight thick hair. There was about this woman past middle age a breath-taking vitality. Her distinguished young son-in-law appeared rather anaemic in contrast.

"How was the play?" Kim asked, possibly in the hope of changing their ebullient mood.

"Nice production," said Cameron. "Lunt was flawless. Fontanne's turned just a shade cute on us. She'd better stop that. Shaw, revived, tastes a little mouldy. Westley yelled. Simonson's sets were—uh—meticulous I think the word is. . . . And I want to inform you, my dear Mrs. C., that your mama has been a very naughty girl."

This would never do, thought Kim, her mind on the yellow envelope. She put an arm about her mother.

"Kiss me and I'll forgive you," she said.

"You don't know what she's done."

"Whatever it is————"

"Woollcott started it, anyway," protested Magnolia Ravenal, lighting her cigarette. "I should think a man who's dramatic critic of the New York *World* would have more consideration for the dignity of his————"

Cameron took up the story. "Our seats turned out to be next to his. Nola sat between us. You know how she always clutches somebody's hand during the emotional scenes."

"The last time I went to the theatre with Woollcott he said he'd slap my hands hard if I ever again————" put in Magnolia. But Cameron once more interrupted.

"Then in the second act she clutched him instead of me and he slapped her hand————"

"And pinched————"

"And Nola gave him a sharp dig in the stomach, I'm afraid, with her elbow, and there was quite a commotion. Mothers-in-law are a terrible responsibility."

"Mother *dear!* A first night of a Shaw revival at the National!"

"He started it. And anyway, you've brought me up wrong."

There was about her suddenly a curious effect of weariness. It was as though, until now, she had been acting, and had discarded her rôle. She stood up. "Ken, if you'll get me a taxi I'll run along home. I'm tired. You two are going to the Swopes', aren't you? That means three o'clock."

"I'm not going," said Kim. "Wait a minute, Ken." She came over to Magnolia. "Mother, I just got a telegram."

"Mama?" She uttered the word as though she were a little girl.

"Yes."

"Where is it?"

Kim indicated it. "There, Ken. Get it for me, will you? Under the make-up tray."

"Dead?" Magnolia had not unfolded the yellow slip.

"Yes."

She read it. She looked up. The last shadow had vanished of that mood in which she had entered ten minutes earlier. She looked, suddenly, sallow and sixty. "Let me see. Tennessee. Trains."

" But not to-night, Mother!"

"Yes. Ken, there's something to St. Louis—Memphis—I'm sure. And then from there to-morrow morning."

"Ken will go with you."

"No!" sharply. "No!"

She had her way in the end; left that night, and alone, over Kim's protests and Ken's. "If I need you, Ken dear, I'll telegraph. All those people in the troupe, you know. Some of them have been with her for ten years—fifteen."

All sorts of trains before you reached this remote little town. Little dusty red-plush trains with sociable brakemen and passengers whose clothes and bearing now seemed almost grotesque to the eyes that once had looked upon them without criticism. A long, hard, trying journey. Little towns at which you left this train and waited long hours for the next. Cinder-strewn junctions whose stations were little better than sheds.

Mile after mile the years had receded as New York was left behind. The sandy soil of the South. Little straggling villages. Unpainted weather-stained cabins, black as the faces that peered from their doorways. When Magnolia Ravenal caught the first gleam of April dogwood flashing white in the forest depths as the train bumbled by, her heart gave a great leap. In a curious and dreamlike way the years of her life with Ravenal in Chicago, the years following Ravenal's desertion of her there, the years of Magnolia's sudden success in New York seemed to fade into unreality; they became unimportant fragmentary interludes. This was her life. She had never left it. They would be there—Julie, and Steve, and Windy, and Doc, and Parthy, and Andy, and Schultzy—somehow, they would be there. They were real. The others were dream people: Mike McDonald, Hankins, Hetty Chilson, all that raffish Chicago crew; the New York group—Kim's gay, fly, brittle brilliant crowd with which Magnolia had always assumed an ease she did not feel.

She decided, sensibly, that she was tired, a little dazed, even. She had slept scarcely at all the night before. Perhaps this news of her mother's death had been, after all, more of a shock than she thought. She would not pretend to be grief-stricken. The breach between her and the indomitable old woman had been a thing of many years' standing, and it had grown wider and wider with the years following that day when, descending upon her daughter in Chicago, Mrs. Hawks had learned that the handsome dashing Gaylord Ravenal had flown. She had been unable to resist her triumphant, "What did I tell you!" It had been the last straw.

She had wondered, vaguely, what sort of conveyance she might hire to carry her to Cold Spring, for she knew no railroad passed through this little river town. But when she descended from the train at this, the last stage but one in her wearisome journey, there was a little group at the red brick station to meet her. A man came toward her (he turned out to be the Chas. K. Barnato of the telegram). He was the general manager and press agent. Doc's old job, modernized. "How did you know me?" she had asked, and was startled when he replied:

"You look like your ma." Then, before she could recover from this: "But Elly told me it was you."

A rather amazing old lady came toward her. She looked like the ancient ruins of a bisque doll. Her cheeks were pink, her eyes bright, her skin parchment, her hat incredible.

"Don't you remember me, Nollie?" she said. And pouted her withered old lips. Then, as Magnolia stared, bewildered, she had chirped like an annoyed cockatoo, "Elly Chipley—Lenore La Verne."

"But it isn't possible!" Magnolia had cried.

This had appeared to annoy Miss Chipley afresh. "Why not, I'd like to know! I've been back with the *Cotton Blossom* the last ten years. Your ma advertised in the *Billboard* for a general utility team. My husband answered the ad, giving his name————"

"Not————?"

"Schultzy? Oh, no, dearie. I buried poor Schultzy in Douglas, Wyoming, twenty-two years ago. Yes, indeed. Clyde!" She wheeled briskly. "Clyde!" The man came forward. He was, perhaps, fifty. Surely twenty years younger than the erstwhile ingénue lead. A sheepish, grizzled man whose mouth looked as if a drawstring had been pulled out of it, leaving it limp and sprawling. "Meet my husband, Mr. Clyde Mellhop. This is Nollie. Mrs. Ravenal, it is, ain't it? Seems funny, you being married and got a famous daughter and all. Last time I saw you you was just a skinny little girl, dark-complected——— Well, your ma was hoity-toity with me when she seen it was me was the other half of the Mellhop General Utility Team. Wasn't going to let me stay, would you believe it! Well, she was glad enough to have me, in the end."

This, Magnolia realized, must be stopped. She met the understanding look of the man Barnato. He nodded. "I guess you must be pretty tuckered out, Mrs. Ravenal. Now, if you'll just step over to the car there." He indicated an important-looking closed car that stood at the far end of the station platform.

Gratefully Magnolia moved toward it. She was a little impressed with its appearance. "Your car! That was thoughtful of you. I was wondering how I'd get————"

"No, ma'am. That ain't mine. I got a little car of my own, but this is your ma's—that is—well, it's yours, now, I reckon." He helped her into the back seat with Elly. He seated himself before the wheel, with Mellhop beside him. He turned to her, solemnly. "I suppose you'd like to go right over to see your—to view the remains. She's—they're at Breitweiler's Undertaking Parlours. I kind of tended to everything, like your son-in-law's telegram said. I hope everything will suit you. Of course, if you'd like to go over to the hotel first. I took a room for you—best they had. It's real comfortable. To-morrow morning we take her—we go to Thebes on the ten-fif-teen————"

"The hotel!" cried Magnolia. "But I want to sleep on the boat to-night. I want to go back to the boat."

"It's a good three-quarters of an hour run from here, even in this car."

"I know it. But I want to stay on the boat to-night."

"It's for you to say, ma'am."

The main business street of the little town was bustling and prosperous-looking. Where, in her childhood river-town days the farm wagons and buggies had stood hitched at the curb, she now saw rows of automobiles parked, side by side. Five-and-Ten-Cent Stores. Motion Pictures. Piggly-Wiggly. Popular magazines in the drug-store window. She had thought that everything would be the same.

Breitweiler's Undertaking Parlours. Quite a little throng outside; and within an actual crowd, close-packed. They made way respectfully for Barnato and his party. "What is it?" whispered Magnolia. "What are all these people here for? What has happened?"

"Your ma was quite a famous person in these parts, Mrs. Ravenal. Up and down the rivers and around she was quite a character. I've saved the pieces for you in the paper."

"You don't mean these people—all these people have come here to see————"

"Yes, ma'am. In state. I hope you don't object, ma'am. I wouldn't want to feel I'd done something you wouldn't like."

She felt a little faint. "I'd like them to go away now."

Parthenia Ann Hawks in her best black silk. Her strong black eyebrows punctuated the implacable old face with a kind of surprised resentment. She had not succumbed to the Conqueror without a battle. Magnolia, gazing down upon the stern waxen features, the competent hands crossed in unwilling submission upon her breast, could read the message of revolt that was stamped, even in death, upon that strong and terrible brow. Here! I'm mistress of this craft. You can't do this to me! I'm Parthenia Ann Hawks! Death? Fiddlesticks and nonsense! For others, perhaps. But not for me.

Presently they were driving swiftly out along the smooth asphalt road toward Cold Spring. Elly Chipley was telling her tale with relish, palpably for the hundredth time.

". . . seven o'clock in the evening or maybe a few minutes past and her standing in front of the looking-glass in her room doing her hair. Clyde and me, we had the room next to hers, for'ard, the last few years, on account I used to do for her, little ways. Not that she was feeble or like that. But she needed somebody younger to do for her, now and then"—with the bridling self-consciousness of a girlish seventy, as compared to Parthy's eighty and over. "Well, I was in the next room, and just thinking I'd better be making up for the evening show when I hear a funny sound, and then a voice I didn't hardly recognize sort of squeaks, 'Elly! A stroke!' And then a crash."

Magnolia was surprised to find herself weeping: not for grief; in almost unwilling admiration of this powerful mind and will that had recognized the Enemy even as he stole up on her and struck the blow from behind.

"There, there!" cooed Elly Chipley, pleased that her recital had at last moved this handsome silent woman to proper tears. "There, there!" She patted her hand. "Look, Nollie dear. There's the boat. Seems funny not to see her lighted up for the show this time of night."

Magnolia peered through the dusk, a kind of dread in her heart. Would this, too, be changed beyond recognition? A great white long craft docked at the water's edge. Larger, yes. But much the same. In the gloom she could just make out the enormous letters painted in black against the white upper deck.

COTTON BLOSSOM FLOATING PALACE THEATRE
Parthenia Ann Hawks, Prop.

And there was the River. It was high with the April rains and the snows that nourished it from all the hundreds of miles of its vast domain—the Mississippi Basin.

Vaguely she heard Barnato—"Just started out and promised to be the biggest paying season we had for years. Yessir! Crops what they were last fall, and the country so prosperous. . . . Course, we don't aim to bother you with such details now. . . . Troupe wondering—ain't no more'n natural—what's to become of 'em now. . . . Finest show boat on the rivers. . . . Our own electric power plant. . . . Ice machine. . . . Seats fifteen hundred, easy. . . ."

And there was the River. Broad, yellow, turbulent. Magnolia was trembling. Down the embankment, across the gangplank, to the lower forward deck that was like a comfortable front porch. The bright semicircle of the little ticket window. A little group of Negro loungers and dock-hands making way respectfully, gently for the white folks. The sound of a banjo tinkling somewhere ashore, or perhaps on an old sidewheeler docked a short distance downstream. A playbill in the lobby. She stared at it. Tempest and Sunshine. The letters began to go oddly askew. A voice, far away—"Look out! She's going to faint!"

A tremendous effort. "No, I'm not. I'm—all right. I don't think I've eaten anything since early morning."

She was up in the bedroom. Dimity curtains at the windows, fresh and crisp. Clean. Shining. Orderly. Quiet. "Now you just get into bed. A hot-water bag. We'll fix you a tray and a good cup of tea. To-morrow morning you'll be feeling fine again. We got to get an early start."

She ate, gratefully. Anything I can do for you now, Nollie? No, nothing, thanks. Well, I'm kind of beat, myself. It's been a day, I can tell you. Good-night. Good-night. Now I'll leave my door open, so's if you call me———

Nine o'clock. Ten. The hoarse hoot of a boat whistle. The clank of anchor chains. Swish. Swash. Fainter. Cluck-suck against the hull. Quieter. More quiet. Quiet. Black velvet. The River. Home.

19

KIM RAVENAL'S TENTH letter to her mother was the decisive one. It arrived late in May, when the Cotton Blossom Floating Palace Theatre was playing Lulu, Mississippi. From where the show boat lay just below the landing there was little enough to indicate that a town was situated near by. Lulu, Mississippi, in May, was humid and drowsy and dusty and fly-ridden. The Negroes lolled in the shade of their cabins and loafed at the water's edge. Thick-petalled white flowers amidst glossy dark green foliage filled the air with a drugging sweetness, and scarlet-petalled flowers stuck their wicked yellow tongues out at the passer-by.

Magnolia, on the *Cotton Blossom* upper deck that was like a cosy veranda, sat half in the shade and half in the sun and let the moist heat envelop her. The little nervous lines that New York had etched about her eyes and mouth seemed to vanish magically under the languorous touch of the saturant Southern air. She was again like the lovely creamy blossom for which she had been named; a little drooping, perhaps; a little faded: but Magnolia.

Elly Chipley, setting to rights her privileged bedroom on the boat's port side, came to the screen door in cotton morning frock and boudoir cap. The frock was a gay gingham of girlish cut, its colour a delicate pink. The cap was a trifle of lace and ribbon. From this frame her withered life-scarred old mask looked out, almost fascinating in its grotesquerie.

"Beats me how you can sit out there in the heat like a lizard or a cat or something and not get a stroke. Will, too, one these fine days."

Magnolia, glancing up from the perusal of her letter, stretched her arms above her head luxuriously. I love it."

Elly Chipley's sharp old eyes snapped at the typewritten sheets of the letter in Magnolia's hand. "Heard from your daughter again, did you?"

"Yes."

"I never seen anybody such a hand at writing letters. You got one about every stand since you started, with the boat, seems. I was saying to Clyde only yesterday, I says, what's she find to write about!''

This, Magnolia knew, was not a mere figure of speech. In some mysterious way the knowledge had seeped through the *Cotton Blossom* company that in these frequent letters between mother and daughter a battle was being waged. They sensed, too, that in the outcome of this battle lay their own future.

The erstwhile ingénue now assumed an elaborate carelessness of manner which, to the doubting onlooker, would forever have decided the question of her dramatic ability. "What's she got to say, h'm? What———'' here she giggled in shrill falsetto appreciation of her own wit—"what news on the Rialto?''

Magnolia glanced down again at the letter. "I think Kim may come down for a few days to visit us, in June. With her husband.''

The ribbons of Ely's cap trembled. The little withered well-kept hand in which she still took such pride went to her lips that were working nervously. "You don't say! Well, that'll be nice.'' After which triumph of simulated casualness you heard her incautious steps clattering down the stairs and up the aisle to the lesser dressing rooms and bedrooms at the rear of the stage.

Magnolia picked up the letter again. Kim hated to write letters. The number that she had written her mother in the past month testified her perturbation.

> Nola darling, you've gone gaga, that's all. What do mean
> by staying down there in that wretched malarial heat! Now
> listen to me. We close June first. They plan to open in Boston
> in September, then Philadelphia, Chicago. My contract, of
> course, doesn't call for the road. Cruger offered me an in-
> crease and a house percent if I'd go when the road season
> opens, but you know how I hate touring. You're the trouper
> of this family. Besides, I wouldn't leave Andy. He misses
> you as much as Ken and I do. If he could talk, he would
> demand his grandmother's immediate presence. If you
> aren't in New York by June third I shall come and get you.
> I mean this. Ken and I sail on the *Olympic* June tenth.
> There's a play in London that Cruger wants me to see for
> next season. You know. Casualty. We'll go to Paris, Vienna,
> Budapest, and back August first. Come along or stay in the
> country with Andy. Nate Fried says he'll settle up your
> business affairs if that's what's bothering you. What is there
> to do except sell the old tub or give it away or something,
> and take the next train for New York? You bookings say
> Lazare, Mississippi, June fourth, fifth and sixth. Nate looked
> it up and reports it's twenty miles from a railroad. Now,
> Nola, that's just too mad. Come on home.
>
> KIM.

The hand that held the letter dropped to her lap again. Magnolia lay relaxed in the low deck chair and surveyed through half-closed lids the turgid, swift-flowing stream that led on to Louisiana and the sea. Above the clay banks that rose from the river lay the scrubby little settlement shimmering in the noonday heat. A mule team toiled along the river road drawing a decrepit cart on whose sagging seat a Negro sat slumped, the rope lines slack in his listless hands, his body swaying with the motion of the vehicle. From the cook's galley, aft, came the yee-yah-yah-yah of Negro laughter. Then a sudden crash of piano, drum, horn, and cymbals. The band was rehearsing.

The porcine squeal and bleat and grunt of the saxophone. Mississippi Blues they were playing. Ort Hanley, of the Character Team, sang it in the concert after the show. I got the blues. I said the blues. I got the M-i-s-, I said the s-i-s, I said the s-i-pp-i, Mississippi, I got them Miss-is-*sippi blu*-hoo-hoos.

The heat and the music and the laughter and the squeak of the mule cart up the road blended and made a colourful background against which the woman in the chair viewed the procession of the last twenty-five years.

It had turned out well enough. She had gone on, blindly, and it had turned out well enough. Kim. Kim was different. Nothing blind about Kim. She had emerged from the cloistral calm of the Chicago convent with her competent mind quite made up. I am going to be a actress. Oh, no Kim! Not you! But Kim had gone about it as she went about everything. Clear-headed. Thoughtful. Deliberate. But actresses were not made in this way, Magnolia argued. Oh, yes, they were. Five years in stock on Chicago's North Side. A tiny part in musical comedy. Kim decided that she knew nothing. She would go to the National Theatre School of Acting in New York and start all over again. Magnolia's vaudeville days were drawing to an end. A middle-aged woman, still able to hold her audience, still possessing a haunting kind of melancholy beauty. But more than this was needed to hold one's head above the roaring tide of ragtime jazz-time youngsters surging now toward the footlights. She had known what it was to be a headliner, but she had never commanded the fantastic figures of the more spectacular acts. She had been thrifty, though, and canny. She easily saw Kim through the National Theatre School. The idea of Kim in a school of acting struck her as being absurd, though Kim gravely explained to her its uses. Finally she took a tiny apartment in New York so that she and Kim might have a home together. Kim worked slavishly, ferociously. The idea of the school did not amuse Magnolia as much as it had at first.

Fencing lessons. Gymnastic dancing. Interpretive dancing. Singing lessons. Voice placing. French lessons.

"Are you studying to be an acrobat or a singer or a dancer? I can't make it out."

"Now, Nola, don't be an old-fashioned frumpy darling. Spend a day at the school and you'll know what I'm getting at."

The dancing class. A big bright bare room. A phonograph. Ten girls bare-legged, bare-footed, dressed in wisps. A sturdy, bare-legged woman teacher in a hard-worked green chiffon wisp. They stood in a circle, perhaps five feet apart, and jumped on one foot and swung the other leg behind them, and kept this up, alternating right leg and left, for ten minutes. It looked ridiculously simple. Magnolia tried it when she got home and found she couldn't do it at all. Bar work. Make a straight line of that leg. Back! Back! Stretch! Stretch! Stretch! Some of it was too precious. The girls in line formation and the green chiffon person facing them, saying, idiotically, and suiting actions to words:

"Reach down into the valley! Gather handfuls of mist. Up, up, facing the sun! Oh, how lovely!"

The Voice class. The Instructor, wearing a hat with an imposing façade and clanking with plaques of arts-and-crafts jewellery, resembled, as she sat at her table fronting the seated semi-circle of young men and women, the chairman of a woman's club during the business session of a committee meeting.

Her voice was "placed." Magnolia, listening and beholding, would not have been surprised to see her remove her voice, an entity, from her throat and hold it up for inspection. It was a thing so artificial, so studied, so manufactured. She articulated carefully and with great elegance.

"I don't need to go into the wide-open throat to-day. We will start with the jaw exercises. Down! To the side! Side! Rotate!"

With immense gravity and earnestness twelve young men and women took hold of their respective jaws and pulled these down; from side to side; around. They showed no embarrassment.

"Now then! The sound of *b*. Bub-ub-ub-ub. *They bribed Bob with a bib.* Sound of *t*. *It isn't a bit hot.* Sound of *d*. *Dad did the deed.* Sound of *n*. *None of the nine nuns came at noon.*"

Singly and en masse they disposed of Bob and Dad and the nine nuns. Pharynx resonance. Say, "Clear and free, Miss Ravenal." Miss Ravenal said clear and free, distinctly. No, no, no! Not clear-and-free, but clear—and free. Do you see what I mean? Good. Now take it again. Miss Ravenal took it again. Clear—and free. *That's* better.

Now then. Words that differ in the *wh* sound. Mr. Karel, let us hear your list. Mr. Karel obliges. Whether-weather, when-wen, whinny-winnow, whither-wither; why do you spell it with a y?

Miss Rogers, *l* sounds. Miss Rogers, enormously solemn (fated for Lady Macbeth at the lightest)—level, loyal, lull, lily, lentil, love, lust, liberty, boil, coral———

Now then! The nerve vitalizing breath! We'll all stand. Hold the breath. Stretch out arms. Arms in—and IN—AND IN—out—in—head up—mouth open———

Shades of Modjeska, Duse, Rachel, Mrs. Siddons, Bernhardt! Was this the way an actress was made!

"You wait and see," said Kim, grimly. Dancing, singing, fencing, voice, French. One year. Two. Three. Magnolia had waited, and she had seen.

Kim had had none of those preliminary hardships and errors and temptations, then, that are supposed to beset the path of the attractive young woman who would travel the road to theatrical achievement. Her success actually had been instantaneous and sustained. She had been given the part of the daughter of a worldly mother in a new piece by Ford Salter and had taken the play away from the star who did the mother. Her performance had been clear-cut, modern, deft, convincing. She was fresh, but finished.

She was intelligent, successful, workmanlike, intuitive, vigorous, adaptable. She was almost the first of this new crop of intelligent, successful, deft, workmanlike, intuitive, vigorous, adaptable young women of the theatre. There was about her—or them—nothing of genius, of greatness, of the divine fire. But the dramatic critics of the younger school who were too late to have seen past genius in its heyday and for whom the theatrical genius of their day was yet to come, viewed her performance and waxed hysterical, mistaking talent and intelligence and hard work and ambition for something more rare. It became the thing to proclaim each smart young woman the Duse of her day if she had a decent feeling for stage tempo, could sustain a character throughout three acts, speak the English language intelligibly, cross a stage or sit in a chair naturally. By the time Kim had been five years out of the National Theatre School there were Duses by the dozen, and a Broadway Bernhardt was born at least once a season.

These gave, invariably, what is known as a fine performance. As you stood in the lobby between the acts, smoking your cigarette, you said, "She's giving a fine performance."

"A fine performance!" Magnolia echoed one evening, rather irritably, after she and Kim had returned from the opening of a play in which one of Kim's friends was featured. "But she doesn't act. Everything she did and everything she said was right. And I was as carried out of myself as though I were listening to a clock strike. When I go to the theatre I want to care."

In the old days maybe they didn't know so much about tempo and rhythm, but in the audience strong men wept and women fainted————''

"Now listen, Nola darling. One of your old-day gals would last about four seconds on Broadway. I've heard about Clara Morris and Mrs. Siddons, and Modjeska, and Bernhardt all my life. If the sentimental old dears were to come back in an all-star revival to-day the intelligent modern theatre-going audience would walk out on them.''

The new-school actresses went in for the smarter teas, eschewed cocktails, visited the art exhibits, had their portraits painted in the new manner, never were seen at night clubs, were glimpsed coming out of Scribner's with a thick volume of modern biography, used practically no make-up when in mufti, kept their names out of the New York telephone directory, wore flat-heeled shoes and woollen stockings while walking briskly in Central Park, went to Symphony Concerts; were, in short, figures as glamorous and ro-mantic as a pint of milk. Everything they did on the stage was right. Intel-ligent, well thought out, and right. Watching them, you knew it was right—tempo, tone, mood, character. Right. As right as an engineering blueprint. Your pulses, as you sat in the theatre, were normal.

Usually, their third season, you saw them unwisely lunching too often at the Algonquin Round Table and wise-cracking with the critics there. The fourth they took a bit in that new English comedy just until O'Neill should have finished the play he was doing for them. The fifth they married that little Whatshisname. The sixth they said, mysteriously, that they were Writ-ing.

Kim kept away from the Algonquin, did not attend first nights with Wooll-cott or Broun, had a full-page Steichen picture in *Vanity Fair,* and married Kenneth Cameron. She went out rarely. Sunday night dinners, sometimes; or she had people in (ham *à la* Queenie part of the cold buffet). Her list of Sunday night guests or engagements read like a roster of the New York Telephone Company's Exchanges. Stuyvesant, Beekman, Bleeker, Murray, Rhinelander, Vanderbilt, Jerome, Wadsworth, Tremont. She learned to say, "It's just one of those things————" She finished an unfinished sentence with, "I *mean*————" and a throwing up of the open palms.

Kenneth Cameron. Her marriage with Kenneth Cameron was successful and happy and very nice. Separate bedrooms and those lovely negligées—velvet with Venetian sleeves and square neck-line. Excellent friends. Noth-ing sordid. Personal liberty and privacy of thought and action—those were the things that made for happiness in marriage. Magnolia wondered, some-times, but certainly it was not for her to venture opinion. Her own marriage had been no such glittering example of perfection. Yet she wondered, seeing this well-ordered and respectful union, if Kim was not, after all, missing something. Wasn't marriage, like life, unstimulating and unprofitable and somewhat empty when too well ordered and protected and guarded? Wasn't it finer, more splendid, more nourishing, when it was, like life itself, a mixture of the sordid and the magnificent; of mud and stars; of earth and flowers; of love and hate and laughter and tears and ugliness and beauty and hurt? She was wrong, of course. Ken's manner toward Kim was polite, tender, thoughtful. Kim's manner toward Ken was polite, tender, thoughtful. Are you free next Thursday, dear? The Paynes are having those Russians. It might be rather interesting. . . . Sorry. Ken's voice. Soft, light. It was the—well, Magnolia never acknowledged this, even to herself, but it was what she called the male interior decorator's voice. You heard it a good deal at teas, and at the Algonquin, and in the lobby between the acts on first nights and in those fascinating shops on Madison Avenue where furniture and old glass and brasses and pictures were shown you by slim young men with delicate hands. I *mean*———! It's just one of those things. . . .

There was no Mississippi in Kim. Kim was like the Illinois River of Magnolia's childhood days. Kim's life flowed tranquilly between gentle green-clad shores, orderly, well regulated, dependable.

"For the land's sakes, Magnolia Hawks, you sitting out there yet! Here it's after three and nearly dinner time!" Elly Chipley at the screen door. "And in the blazing sun, too. You need somebody to look after you worse than your ma did."

Elly was justified, for Magnolia had a headache that night.

Kim and Ken arrived unexpectedly together on June second, clattering up to the boat landing in a scarecrow Ford driven by a stout Negro in khaki pants, puttees, and an army shirt.

Kim was breathless, but exhilarated. "He says he drove in France in '17, and I believe it. Good God! Every bolt, screw, bar, nut, curttain, and door in the thing rattled and flapped and opened and fell in and fell out. I've been working like a Swiss bell-ringer trying to keep things together there in the back seat. Nola darling, what do you mean by staying down in this miserable hole all these weeks! Ken, dear, take another aspirin and a pinch of bicarb and lie down a minute. . . . Ken's got a headache from the heat and the awful trip. . . . We're going back to-night, and we sail on the tenth, and, Nola darling, for heaven's sake . . .

They had a talk. The customary four o'clock dinner was delayed until nearly five because of it. They sat in Magnolia's green-shaded bedroom with its frilled white bedspread and dimity curtains—rather, Kim and Magnolia sat and Ken sprawled his lean length on the bed, looking a little yellow and haggard, what with the heat and the headache. And in the cook's galley, and on the stage, and in the little dressing rooms that looked out on the river, and on deck, and in the box office, the company and crew of the Cotton Blossom Floating Palace Theatre lounged and waited, played pinochle and waited, sewed and napped and read and wondered and waited.

"You can't mean it, Nola darling. Flopping up and down these muddy wretched rivers in this heat! You could be out at the Bay with Andy. Or in London with Ken and me—Ken, dear, isn't it any better?—or even in New York, in the lovely airy apartment, it's cooler than———"

Magnolia sat forward.

"Listen, Kim. I love it. The rivers. And the people. And the show boat. And the life. I don't know why. It's bred in me, I suppose. Yes, I do know why. Your grandpa died when you were too little to remember him, really. Or you'd know why. Now, if you two are set on going back on the night train, you'll have to listen to me for a minute. I went over things with the lawyer and the banker in Thebes when we took Mama back there. Your grandmother left a fortune. I don't mean a few thousand dollars. She left half a million, made out of this boat in the last twenty-five years. I'm giving it to you, Kim, and Ken."

Refusal, of course. Protest. Consideration. Acquiescence. Agreement. Acceptance. Ken was sitting up now, pallidly. Kim was lyric. "Half a million! Mother! Ken! It means the plays I want, and Ken to produce them. It means that I can establish a real American theatre in New York. I can do the plays I've been longing to do—Ibsen and Hauptmann, and Werfel, and Schnitzler, and Molnar, and Chekhov, and Shakespeare even. Ken! We'll call it the American Theatre!"

"The American Theatre," Magnolia repeated after her, thoughtfully. And smiled then. "The American Theatre." She looked a trifle uncomfortable, as one who has heard a good joke, and has no one with whom to share it.

A loud-tongued bell clanged and reverberated through the show boat's length. Dinner.

Kim and Ken pretended not to notice the heat and flies and the molten state of the butter. They met everyone from the captain to the cook; from the ingénue lead to the drum.

"Well, Miss Ravenal, this is an—or Mrs. Cameron, I suppose I should say—an honour. We know all about you, even if you don't know about us." Not one of them had ever seen her.

A little tour of the show boat after dinner. Ken, still pale, but refreshed by tea, was moved to exclamations of admiration. Look at that, Kim! Ingenious. Oh, say, we must stay over and see a performance. I'd no idea! And these combination dressing rooms and bedrooms, eh? Well, I'll be damned!

Elly Chipley was making up in her special dressing room, infinitesimal in size, just off the stage. Her part for to-night was that of a grande dame in black silk and lace cap and fichu. The play was The Planter's Daughter. She had been rather sniffy in her attitude toward the distinguished visitors. They couldn't patronize *her*. She applied the rouge to her withered cheeks in little pettish dabs, and leaned critically forward to scrutinize her old mask of a face. What did she see there? Kim wondered, watching her, fascinated.

"Mother tells me you played Juliet, years ago. How marvellous!"

Elly Chipley tossed her head skittishly. "Yes, indeed! Played Juliet, and was known as the Western Favourite. I wasn't always on a show boat, I promise you."

"What a thrill—to play Juliet when you were so young! Usually we have to wait until we're fifty. Tell me, dear Miss La Verne"—elaborately polite, and determined to mollify this old harridan—"tell me, who was your Romeo?"

And then Life laughed at Elly Chipley (Lenore La Verne on the bills) and at Kim Ravenal, and the institution known as the Stage. For Elly Chipley tapped her cheek thoughtfully with her powder puff, and blinked her old eyes, and screwed up her tremulous old mouth, and pondered, and finally shook her head. "My Romeo? Let me see. Let—me—see. Who *was* my Romeo?"

They must go now. Oh, Nola darling, half a million! It's too fantastic. Mother, I can't bear to leave you down in this God-forsaken hole. Flies and Negroes and mud and all this yellow terrible river that you love more than me. Stand up there—high up—where we can see you as long as possible.

The usual crowd was drifting down to the landing as the show-boat lights began to glow. Twilight was coming on. On the landing, up the river bank, sauntering down the road, came the Negroes, and the hangers-on, the farmhands, the river folk, the curious, the idle, the amusement-hungry. Snatches of song. Feet shuffling upon the wharf boards. A banjo twanging.

They were being taken back to the nearest railroad connection, but not in the Ford that had brought them. They sat luxuriously in the car that had been Parthy's and that was Magnolia's now.

"Mother, dearest, you'll be back in New York in October or November at the latest, won't you? Promise me. When the boat closes? You will!"

Kim was weeping. The car started smoothly. She turned for a last glimpse through her tears. "Oh, Ken, do you think I ought to leave her like this?"

"She'll be all right, dear. Look at her! Jove!"

There stood Magnolia Ravenal on the upper deck of the Cotton Blossom Floating Palace Theatre, silhouetted against sunset sky and water—tall, erect, indomitable. Her mouth was smiling but her great eyes were wide and sombre. They gazed, unwinking, across the sunlit waters. One arm was raised in a gesture of farewell.

"Isn't she splendid, Ken!" cried Kim, through her tears. "There's something about her that's eternal and unconquerable—like the River."

A bend in the upper road. A clump of sycamores. The river, the show boat, the straight silent figure were lost to view.

Cimarron

FOREWORD

ONLY THE MORE fantastic and improbable events contained in this book are true. There is no attempt to set down a literal history of Oklahoma. All the characters, the towns, and many of the happenings contained herein are imaginary. But through reading the scant available records, documents, and histories (including the Oklahoma State Historical Library collection) and through many talks with men and women who have lived in Oklahoma since the day of the Opening, something of the spirit, the color, the movement, the life of that incredible commonwealth has, I hope, been caught. Certainly the Run, the Sunday service in the gambling tent, the death of Isaiah and of Arita Red Feather, the catching of the can of nitroglycerin, many of the shooting affrays, most descriptive passages, all of the oil phase, and the Osage Indian material complete—these are based on actual happenings. In many cases material entirely true was discarded as unfit for use because it was so melodramatic, so absurd as to be too strange for the realm of fiction.

There is no city of Osage, Oklahoma. It is a composite of, perhaps, five existent Oklahoma cities. The Kid is not meant to be the notorious Billy the Kid of an earlier day. There was no Yancey Cravat—he is a blending of a number of dashing Oklahoma figures of a past and present day. There is no Sabra Cravat, but she exists in a score of bright-eyed, white-haired, intensely interesting women of sixty-five or thereabouts who told me many strange things as we talked and rocked on an Oklahoma front porch (tree-shaded now).

Anything can have happened in Oklahoma. Practically everything has.

EDNA FERBER

1

ALL THE VENABLES sat at Sunday dinner. All those handsome inbred Venable faces were turned, enthralled, toward Yancey Cravat, who was talking. The combined effect was almost blinding, as of incandescence; but Yancey Cravat was not bedazzled. A sun surrounded by lesser planets, he gave out a radiance so powerful as to dim the luminous circle about him.

Yancey had a disconcerting habit of abruptly concluding a meal—for himself, at least—by throwing down his napkin at the side of his plate, rising, and striding about the room, or even leaving it. It was not deliberate rudeness. He ate little. His appetite satisfied, he instinctively ceased to eat; ceased to wish to contemplate food. But the Venables sat hours at table, leisurely shelling almonds, sipping sherry; Cousin Dabney Venable peeling an orange for Cousin Bella French Vian with the absorbed concentration of a sculptor molding his clay.

The Venables, dining, strangely resembled one of those fertile and dramatic family groups portrayed lolling unconventionally at meat in the less spiritual of those Biblical canvases that glow richly down at one from the great gallery walls of Europe. Though their garb was sober enough, being characteristic of the time—1889—and the place—Kansas—it yet conveyed an impression as of purple and scarlet robes enveloping these gracile shoulders. You would not have been surprised to see, moving silently about this board, Nubian blacks in loincloths, bearing aloft golden vessels piled with exotic fruits or steaming with strange pasties in which nightingales' tongues figured prominently. Blacks, as a matter of fact, did move about the Venable table, but these, too, wore the conventional garb of the servitor.

This branch of the Venable family tree had been transplanted from Mississippi to Kansas more than two decades before, but the mid-west had failed to set her bourgeois stamp upon them. Straitened though it was, there still obtained in that household, by some genealogical miracle, many of those charming ways, remotely Oriental, that were of the South whence they had sprung. The midday meal was, more often than not, a sort of tribal feast at which sprawled hosts of impecunious kin, mysteriously sprung up at the sound of the dinner bell and the scent of baking meats. Unwilling émigrés, war ruined, Lewis Venable and his wife Felice had brought their dear customs with them into exile, as well as the superb mahogany oval at which they now sat, and the war-salvaged silver which gave elegance to the Wichita, Kansas, board. Certainly the mahogany had suffered in transit; and many of their Southern ways, transplanted to Kansas, seemed slightly silly—or would have, had they not been tinged with pathos. The hot breads of the South, heaped high at every meal, still wrought alimentary havoc. The frying pan and the deep-fat kettle (both, perhaps, as much as anything responsible for the tragedy of '64) still spattered their deadly fusillade in this household. Indeed, the creamy pallor of the Venable women, so like that of a magnolia petal in their girlhood, and tending so surely toward the ocherous in middle age, was less a matter of pigment than of liver. Impecunious though the family now was, three or four negro servants went about the house, soft-footed, slack, charming. "Rest yo' wrap?" they suggested, velvet voiced and hospitable, as you entered the wide hallway that was at once so bare and so cluttered. And, "Beat biscuit, Miss Adeline?" as they proffered a fragrant plate.

Even that Kansas garden was of another latitude. Lean hounds drowsed in the sun-drenched untidiness of the doorway, and that untidiness was hidden and transformed by a miracle of color and scent and bloom. Here were passion flower and wisteria and even Bougainvillea in season. Honeysuckle gave out its swooning sweetness. In the early spring lilies of the valley thrust the phantom green of their spears up through the dead brown banking the lilac bushes. That coarse vulgarian, the Kansas sunflower, was a thing despised of the Venables. If one so much as showed its broad face among the scented élégantes of that garden it suffered instant decapitation. On one occasion Felice Venable had been known to ruin a pair of very fine-tempered embroidery scissors while impetuously acting as headsman. She had even been heard to bewail the absence of Spanish moss in this northerly climate. A neighboring mid-west matron, miffed, resented this.

"But that's a parasite! And real creepy, almost. I was in South Carolina and saw it. Kind of floating, like ghosts. And no earthly good."

"Do even the flowers have to be useful in Kansas?" drawled Felice Venable. She was not very popular with the bustling wives of Wichita. They resented her ruffled and trailing white wrappers of cross-barred dimity; her pointed slippers, her arched instep, her indifference to all that went on outside the hedge that surrounded the Venable yard; they resented the hedge itself, symbol of exclusiveness in that open-faced Kansas town. Sheathed in the velvet of Felice Venable's languor was a sharp-edged poniard of wit inherited from her French forbears, the old Marcys of St. Louis; Missouri fur traders of almost a century earlier. You saw the Marcy mark in the black of her still bountiful hair, in the curve of the brows above the dark eyes—in the dark eyes themselves, so alive in the otherwise immobile face.

As the family now sat at its noonday meal it was plain that while two decades of living in the Middle West had done little to quicken the speech or hasten the movements of Lewis Venable and his wife Felice (they still "you-alled"; they declared to goodness; the eighteenth letter of the alphabet would forever be ah to them) it had made a noticeable difference in the younger generation. Up and down the long table they ranged, sons and daughters, sons-in-law and daughters-in-law; grandchildren; remoter kin such as visiting nieces and nephews and cousins, offshoots of this far-flung family. As the more northern-bred members of the company exclaimed at the tale they now were hearing you noted that their vowels were shorter, their diction more clipped, the turn of the head, the lift of the hand less leisurely. In all those faces there was a resemblance, one to the other. Perhaps the listening look which all of them now wore served to accentuate this.

It was late May, and unseasonably hot for the altitude. Then, too, there had been an early pest of moths and June flies this spring. High above the table, and directly over it, on a narrow board suspended by rods from the lofty ceiling sat perched Isaiah, the little black boy. With one hand he clung to the side rods of his precarious roost; with the other he wielded a shoofly of feathery asparagus ferns cut from the early garden. Its soft susurrus as he swished it back and forth was an obbligato to the music of Yancey Cravat's golden voice. Clinging thus aloft the black boy looked a simian version of one of Raphael's ceilinged angels. His round head, fuzzed with little tight tufts, as of woolly astrachan through which the black of his poll gleamed richly, was cocked at an impish angle the better to catch the words that flowed from the lips of the speaker. His eyes, popping with excitement, were fixed in an entrancement on the great lounging figure of Yancey Cravat. So bewitched was the boy that frequently his hand fell limp and he forgot altogether his task of bestirring with his verdant fan the hot moist air above the food-laden table. An impatient upward glance from Felice Venable's darting black eyes, together with a sharply admonitory "*Ah*-saiah!" would set him to swishing vigorously until the enchantment again stayed his arm.

The Venables saw nothing untoward in this remnant of Mississippi feudalism. Dozens of Isaiah's forbears had sat perched thus, bestirring the air so that generations of Mississippi Venables might the more agreeably sup and eat and talk. Wichita had first beheld this phenomenon aghast; and even now, after twenty years, it was a subject for local tongue waggings.

Yancey Cravat was talking. He had been talking for the better part of an hour. This very morning he had returned from the Oklahoma country—the newly opened Indian Territory where he had made the Run that marked the settling of this vast tract of virgin land known colloquially as the Nation. Now, as he talked, the faces of the others had the rapt look of those who listen to a saga. It was the look that Jason's listeners must have had, and Ulysses'; and the eager crowd that gathered about Francisco Vasquez de Coronado before they learned that his search for the Seven Cities of Cibolo had been in vain.

The men at table leaned forward, their hands clasped rather loosely between their knees or on the cloth before them, their plates pushed away, their chairs shoved back. Now and then the sudden white ridge of a hardset muscle showed along the line of a masculine jaw. Their eyes were those of men who follow a game in which they would fain take part. The women listened, a little frightened, their lips parted. They shushed their children when they moved or whimpered, or, that failing, sent them, with a half-tender, half-admonitory slap behind, to play in the sunny dooryard. Sometimes a woman's hand reached out possessively, remindingly, and was laid on the arm or the hand of the man seated beside her. "I am here," the hand's pressure said. "Your place is with me. Don't listen to him like that. Don't believe him. I am your wife. I am safety. I am security. I am comfort. I am habit. I am convention. Don't listen like that. Don't look like that."

But the man would shake off the hand, not roughly, but with absent-minded resentment.

Of all that circlet of faces, linked by the enchantment of the tale now being unfolded before them, there stood out lambent as a flame the face of Sabra Cravat as she sat there at table, her child Cim in her lap. Though she, like her mother Felice Venable, was definitely of the olive-skinned type, her face seemed luminously white as she listened to the amazing, incredible, and slightly ridiculous story now being unfolded by her husband. It was plain, too, that in her, as in her mother, the strain of the pioneering French Marcys was strong. Her abundant hair was as black, and her eyes; and the strong brows arched with a swooping curve like the twin scimitars that hung above the fireplace in the company room. Sabra was secretly ashamed of her heavy brows and given to surveying them disapprovingly in her mirror while running a forefinger (slightly moistened by her tongue) along their sable curves. For the rest, there was something more New England than Southern in the directness of her glance, the quick turn of her head, the briskness of her speech and manner. Twenty-one now, married at sixteen, mother of a four-year-old boy, and still in love with her picturesque giant of a husband, there was about Sabra Cravat a bloom, a glow, sometimes seen at that exquisite and transitory time in a woman's life when her chemical, emotional, and physical make-up attains its highest point and fuses.

It was easy to trace the resemblance, both in face and spirit, between this glowing girl and the sallow woman at the foot of the table. But to turn from her to old Lewis Venable was to find one's self baffled by the mysteries of paternity. Old Lewis Venable was not old, but aged; a futile, fumbling, gentle man, somewhat hag-ridden and rendered the more unvital by malaria. Face and hands had a yellow ivory quality born of generations subjected to hot breads, lowlands, bad liver, port wine. To say nothing of a resident unexplored bullet somewhere between the third and fifth ribs, got at Murfreesboro as a member of Stanford's Battery, Heavy Artillery, long long before Roentgen had conceived an eye like God's.

Lewis Venable, in his armchair at the head of the table, was as spellbound as black Isaiah in his high perch above it. Curiously enough, even the boy Cim had listened, or seemed to listen, as he sat in his mother's lap. Sabra had eaten her dinner over the child's head in absent-minded bites, her eyes always on her husband's face. She rarely had had to say, "Hush, Cim, hush!" or to wrest a knife or fork or forbidden tidbit from his clutching fingers. Perhaps it was the curiously musical quality of the story-teller's voice that lulled him. Sabra Venable's disgruntled suitors had said when she married Yancey Cravat, a stranger, mysterious, out of Texas and the Cimarron, that it was his voice that had bewitched her. They were in a measure right, for though Yancey Cravat was verbose, frequently even windy, and though much that he said was dry enough in actual content, he had those priceless gifts of the born orator, a vibrant and flexible voice, great sweetness and charm of manner, an hypnotic eye, and the power of making each listener feel that what was being said was intended for his ear alone. Something of the charlatan was in him, much of the actor, a dash of the fanatic.

Any tale told by Yancey Cravat was likely to contain enchantment, incredibility (though this last was not present while he was telling it), and a tinge of the absurd. Yancey himself, even at this early time, was a bizarre, glamorous, and slightly mythical figure. No room seemed big enough for his gigantic frame; no chair but dwindled beneath the breadth of his shoulders. He seemed actually to loom more than his six feet two. His black locks he wore overlong, so that they curled a little about his neck in the manner of Booth. His cheeks and forehead were, in places, deeply pitted, as with the pox. Women, perversely enough, found this attractive.

But first of all you noted his head, his huge head, like a buffalo's, so heavy that it seemed to loll of its own weight. It was with a shock of astonishment that you remarked about him certain things totally at variance with his bulk, his virility, his appearance of enormous power. His mouth, full and sensual, had still an expression of great sweetness. His eyelashes were long and curling, like a beautiful girl's, and when he raised his heavy head to look at you, beneath the long black locks and the dark lashes you saw with something of bewilderment that his eyes were a deep and unfathomable ocean gray.

Now, in the course of his story, and under the excitement of it, he left the table and sprang to his feet, striding about and talking as he strode. His step was amazingly light and graceful for a man of his powerful frame. Fascinated, you saw that his feet were small and arched like a woman's, and he wore, even in this year of 1889, Texas star boots of fine soft flexible calf, very high heeled, thin soled, and ornamented with cunningly wrought gold stars around the tops. His hands, too, were disproportionate to a man of his stature; slim, pliant, white. He used them as he talked, and the eye followed their movements, bewitched. For the rest, his costume was a Prince Albert of fine black broadcloth whose skirts swooped and spread with the vigor of his move-ments; a pleated white shirt, soft and of exquisite material; a black string tie; trousers tucked into the gay boot-tops; and, always, a white felt hat, broad-brimmed and rolling. On occasion he simply blubbered Shakespeare, the Old Testament, the Odyssey, the Iliad. His speech was spattered with bits of Latin, and with occasional Spanish phrases, relic of his Texas days. He flattered you with his fine eyes; he bewitched you with his voice; he mesmerized you with his hands. He drank a quart of whisky a day; was almost never drunk, but on rare occasions when the liquor fumes bested him he would invariably select a hapless victim and, whipping out the pair of mother-o'-pearl-handled six-shooters he always wore at his belt, would force him to dance by shooting at his feet—a pleasing fancy brought with him from Texas and the Cimarron. Afterward, sobered, he was always filled with shame. Wine, he quoted sadly, is a mocker, strong drink is raging. Yancey Cravat could have been (in fact was, though most of America never knew it) the greatest criminal lawyer of his day. It was said that he hypnotized a jury with his eyes and his hands and his voice. His law practice yielded him nothing, or less than that, for being sentimental and melodramatic he usually found himself out of pocket following his brilliant and successful defense of some Dodge City dancehall girl or roistering cowboy whose six-shooter had been pointed the wrong way.

His past, before his coming to Wichita, was clouded with myths and surmises. Gossip said this; slander whispered that. Rumor, romantic, un-savory, fantastic, shifting and changing like clouds on a mountain peak, floated about the head of Yancey Cravat. They say he has Indian blood in him. They say he has an Indian wife somewhere, and a lot of papooses. Cherokee. They say he used to be known as "Cimarron" Cravat, hence his son's name, corrupted to Cim. They say his real name is Cimarron Seven, of the Choctaw Indian family of Sevens; he was raised in a tepee; a wickiup had been his bedroom, a blanket his robe. It was known he had been one of the early Boomers who followed the banner of the picturesque and splen-didly mad David Payne in the first wild dash of that adventurer into Indian Territory. He had dwelt, others whispered, in that sinister strip, thirty-four miles wide and almost two hundred miles long, called No-Man's-Land as early as 1854, and, later, known as the Cimarron, a Spanish word meaning wild or unruly. Here, in this strange unowned empire without laws and without a government, a paradise for horse thieves, murderers, desperadoes it was rumored he had spent at least a year (and for good reason). They said the evidences of his Indian blood were plain; look at his skin, his hair, his manner of walking. And why did he protest in his newspaper against the government's treatment of those dirty, thieving, lazy, good-for-nothing wards of a beneficent country! As for his newspaper—its very name was a scandal: The Wichita *Wigwam*. And just below this: All the News. Any Scandal Not Libelous. Published Once a week if Convenient. For that matter, who ever heard of a practising lawyer who ran a newspaper at the same time? Its columns were echoes of his own thundering oratory in the court-room or on the platform. He had started his paper in opposition to the old established Wichita *Eagle*. Wichita, roaring, said he should have called his sheet the *Rooster*. The combination law and newspaper office itself was a jumble and welter of pied type, unopened exchanges, boiler plate, legal volumes, paste pots, loose tobacco, old coats, and racing posters, Wichita, professing scorn of the *Wigwam*, read it. Wichita perused his maiden editorial entitled Shall the Blue Blood of the Decayed South Poison the Red Blood of the Great Middle West? and saw him, two months later, carry off in triumph as his bride Sabra Venable, daughter of that same Decay; Sabra

Venable, whose cerulean stream might have mingled with the more vulgarly sanguine life fluid of any youth in Wichita. In spite of the garden hedge, the parental pride, the arched insteps, the colored servants, and the general air of what-would-you-varlet that pervaded the Venable household at the entrance of a local male awooing, Sabra Venable, at sixteen, might have had her pick of the red-blooded lads of Kansas, all the way from Salina to Winfield. Not to mention more legitimate suitors of blue-blooded stock up from the South, such as Dabney Venable himself, Sabra's cousin, who resembled at once Lafayette and old Lewis, even to the premature silver of his hair, the length of the fine, dolichocephalic, slightly decadent head, and the black stock at sight of which Wichita gasped. When, from among all these eligibles, Sabra had chosen the romantic but mysterious Cravat, Wichita mothers of marriageable daughters felt themselves revenged of the Venable airs. Strangely enough, the marriageable daughters seemed more resentful than ever, and there was a noticeable falling off in the number of young ladies who had been wont to drop round at the *Wigwam* office with notices of this or that meeting or social event to be inserted in the columns of the paper.

During the course of the bountiful meal with which the Venable table was spread Yancey Cravat had eaten almost nothing. Here was an audience to his liking. Here was a tale to his taste. His story, wild, unbelievable, yet true, was of the opening of the Oklahoma country; of a wilderness made populous in an hour; of cities numbering thousands literally sprung up overnight, where the day before had been only prairie, coyotes, rattlesnakes, red clay, scrub oak, and an occasional nester hidden in the security of a weedy draw.

He had been a month absent. Like thousands of others he had gone in search of free land, and a fortune. Here was an empire to be had for the taking. He talked, as always, in the highfalutin terms of the speaker who is ever conscious of his audience. Yet, fantastic as it was, all that he said was woven of the warp and woof of truth. Whole scenes, as he talked, seemed to be happening before his listeners' eyes.

2

COAT TAILS SWISHING, eyes flashing, arms waving, voice soaring.

"Folks, there's never been anything like it since Creation. Creation! Hell! That took six days. This was done in one. It was History made in an hour— and I helped make it. Thousands and thousands of people from all over this vast commonwealth of ours" (he talked like that) "traveled hundreds of miles to get a bare piece of land for nothing. But what land! Virgin, except when the Indians had roamed it. 'Lands of lost gods, and godlike men!' They came like a procession—a crazy procession—all the way to the Border, covering the ground as fast as they could, by any means at hand—scrambling over the ground, pushing and shoving each other into the ditches to get there first. God knows why—for they all knew that once arrived there they'd have to wait like penned cattle for the firing of the signal shot that opened the promised land. As I got nearer the line it was like ants swarming on sugar. Over the little hills they came, and out of the scrub-oak woods and across the prairie. They came from Texas, and Arkansas and Colorado and Missouri. They came on foot, by God, all the way from Iowa and Nebraska! They came in buggies and wagons and on horseback and muleback. In prairie schooners and ox carts and carriages. I saw a surrey, honey colored, with a fringe around the top, and two elegant bays drawing it, still stepping high along those rutted clay roads as if out for a drive in the Presidio. There was a black boy driving it, brass buttons and all, and in the back seat was a dude in a light tan coat and a cigar in his mouth and a diamond in his shirtfront; and a woman beside him in a big hat and a pink dress laughing and urging the horses along the red dust that was halfway up to the wheel spokes and fit to choke you. They had driven like that from Denver, damned if they hadn't. I met up with one old homesteader by the roadside—a face dried and wrinkled as a nutmeg—who told me he had started weeks and weeks before, and had made the long trip as best he could, on foot or by rail and boat and wagon, just as kind-hearted people along the way would pick him up. I wonder if he ever got his piece of land in that savage rush—poor old devil."

He paused a moment, perhaps in retrospect, perhaps cunningly to whet the appetites of his listeners. He wrung a breathless, "Oh, Yancey, go on! Go on!" from Sabra.

"Well, the Border at last, and it was like a Fourth of July celebration on Judgment Day. The militia was lined up at the boundary. No one was allowed to set foot on the new land until noon next day, at the firing of the guns. Two million acres of land were to be given away for the grabbing. Noon was the time. They all knew it by heart. April twenty-second, at noon. It takes generations of people hundreds of years to settle a new land. This was going to be made livable territory over night—was made—like a miracle out of the Old Testament. Compared to this, the Loaves and the Fishes and the parting of the Red Sea were nothing—mere tricks."

"Don't be blasphemous, Yancey!" spoke up Aunt Cassandra Venable.

Cousin Dabney Venable tittered into his stock.

"A wilderness one day—except for an occasional wandering band of Indians—an empire the next. If that isn't a modern miracle———"

"Indians, h'm?" sneered Cousin Dabney, meaningly.

"Oh, Dabney!" exclaimed Sabra, sharply. "Why do you interrupt? Why don't you just listen!"

Yancey Cravat raised a pacifying hand, but the great buffalo head was lowered toward Cousin Dabney, as though charging. The sweetest of smiles wreathed his lips. "It's all right, Sabra. Let Cousin Dabney speak. And why not? *Un cabello haze sombra.*"

Cousin Dabney's ivory face flushed a delicate pink. "What's that, Cravat? Cherokee talk?"

"Spanish, my lad. Spanish."

A little moment of silent expectation. Yancey did not explain. A plump and pretty daughter-in-law (not a Venable born) put the question.

"Spanish, Cousin Yancey! I declare! Whatever in the world does it mean? Something romantic, I do hope."

"Not exactly. A Spanish proverb. It means, literally, 'Even a hair casts a shadow.' "

Another second's silence. The pretty daughter-in-law's face became quite vacuous. "Oh. A hair—but I don't see what that's got to do with . . ."

The time had come for Felice Venable to take charge. Her drawling, querulous voice dripped its slow sweetness upon the bitter feud that lay, a poisonous pool, between the two men.

"Well, I must say I call it downright bad manners, I do indeed. Here we all are with our ears just a-flapping to hear the first sound of the militia guns at high noon on the Border, and here's Cousin Jouett Goforth all the way up from Louisiana the first time in fifteen years, and just a-quivering with curiosity, and what do we hear but chit-chat about Spanish proverbs and shadows.'' She broke off abruptly, cast a lightning glance aloft, and in a tone that would have been called a shout had it issued from the throat of any but a Venable, said, ''*Ah*-saiah!''

The black boy's shoo-fly, hanging limp from his inert hand, took up its frantic swishing. The air was cleared. The figures around the table relaxed. Their faces again turned toward Yancey Cravat. Yancey glanced at Sabra. Sabra's lips puckered into a phantom kiss. They formed two words, unseen, unheard by the rest of the company. ''Please, darling.''

''*Cede Deo*,'' said Yancey, with a little bow to her. Then, with a still slighter bow, he turned to Cousin Dabney. '' 'Let there be no strife, I pray thee, between thee and me.' You may not recognize that either, Dabney. It's from the Old Testament.''

Cousin Dabney Venable ran a finger along the top of his black silk stock, as though to ease his throat.

With a switch of his coat tails Yancey was off again, pausing only a moment at the sideboard to toss off three fingers of Spanish brandy, like burning liquid amber. He patted his lips with his fine linen handkerchief. ''I've tasted nothing like that in a month, I can tell you. Raw corn whisky fit to tear your throat out. And as for the water! Red mud. There wasn't a drink of water to be had in the town after the first twenty-four hours. There we were, thousands and thousands of us, milling around the Border like cattle, with the burning sun baking us all day, nowhere to go for shade, and the thick red dust clogging eyes and nose and mouth. No place to wash, no place to sleep, nothing to eat. Queer enough, they didn't seem to mind. Didn't seem to notice. They were feeding on a kind of crazy excitement, ₋nd there was a wild light in their eyes. They laughed and joked and just milled around, all day and all night and until near noon next day. If you had a bit of food you divided it with someone. I finally got a cup of water for a dollar, after standing in line for three hours, and then a woman just behind me————''

''A woman!'' Cousin Arminta Greenwood (of the Georgia Greenwoods). And Sabra Cravat echoed the words in a shocked whisper.

''You wouldn't believe, would you, that women would go it alone in a fracas like that. But they did. They were there with their husbands, some of them, but there were women who made the Run alone.''

''What kind of women?'' Felice Venable's tone was not one of inquiry but of condemnation.

''Women with iron in 'em. Women who wanted land and a home. Pioneer women.''

From Aunt Cassandra Venable's end of the table there came a word that sounded like, ''Hussies!''

Yancey Cravat caught the word beneath his teeth and spat it back. ''Hussies, heh! The one behind me in the line was a woman of forty—or looked it—in a calico dress and a sunbonnet. She had driven across the prairies all the way from the north of Arkansas in a springless wagon. She was like the women who crossed the continent to California in '49. A gaunt woman, with a weather-beaten face; the terribly neglected skin''—he glanced at Sabra with her creamy coloring—''that means alkali water and sun and dust and wind. Rough hair, and unlovely hands, and boots with the mud caked on them. It's women like her who've made this country what it is. You can't read the history of the United States, my friends'' (all this he later used in an Oklahoma Fourth of July speech when they tried to make him Governor) ''without learning the great story of those thousands of unnamed women— women like this one I've described—women in mud-caked boots and calico dresses and sunbonnets, crossing the prairie and the desert and the mountains enduring hardship and privation. Good women, with a terrible and rigid goodness that comes of work and self-denial. Nothing picturesque or romantic about them, I suppose—though occasionally one of them flashes—Belle Starr the outlaw—Rose of the Cimarron—Jeannette Daisy who jumped from a moving Santa Fé train to stake her claim—but the others—no, their story's never really been told. But it's there, just the same. And if it's ever told straight you'll know it's the sunbonnet and not the sombrero that has settled this country."

"Talking nonsense," drawled Felice Venable.

Yancey whirled on his high heels to face her, his fine eyes blazing. "You're one of them. You came up from the South with your husband to make a new home in this Kansas———"

"I am not!" retorted Felice Venable, with enormous dignity. "And I'll thank you not to say any such thing. Sunbonnet indeed! I've never worn a sunbonnet in my life. And as for my skin and hair and hands, they were the toast of the South, as I can prove by anyone here, all the way from Louisiana to Tennessee. And feet so small my slippers had to be made to order. Calico and muddy boots indeed!"

"Oh, Mamma, Yancey didn't mean—he meant courage to leave your home in the South and come up—he wasn't thinking of——— Yancey, do get on with your story of the Run. You got a drink of water for a dollar—dear me!—and shared it with the woman in the calico and the sunbonnet . . ."

He looked a little sheepish. "Well, matter of fact, it turned out she didn't have a dollar to spare, or anywhere near it, but even if she had it wouldn't have done her any good. The fellow selling it was a rat-faced hombre with one eye and Mexican pants. The trigger finger of his right hand had been shot away in some fracas or other, so he ladled out water with that hand and toted his gun in his left. Bunged up he was, plenty. A scar on his nose, healed up, but showing the marks of where human teeth had bit him in a fight, as neat and clear as a dentist's signboard. By the time I got to him there was one cup of water left in the bucket. He tipped it while I held the dipper, and it trickled out, just an even dipperful. The last cup of water on the Border. The crowd waiting in line behind me gave a kind of sound between a groan and a moan. The sound you hear a herd of cow animals give, out on the prairie, when their tongues are hanging out for water in the dry spell. I tipped up the dipper and had downed a big mouthful—filthy tasting stuff it was, too. Gyp water. You could feel the alkali cake on your tongue. Well, my head went back as I drank, and I got one look at that woman's face. Her eyes were on me—on my throat, where the Adam's apple had just given that one big gulp after the first swallow. All bloodshot the whites of her eyes, and a look in them like a dying man looks at a light. Her mouth was open, and her lips were all split with the heat and the dust and the sun, and dry and flaky as ashes. And then she shut her lips a little and tried to swallow nothing, and couldn't. There wasn't any spit in her mouth. I couldn't down another mouthful, parching as I was. I'd have seen her terrible face to the last day of my life. So I righted it, and held it out to her and said, 'Here, sister, take the rest of it. I'm through.' "

Cousin Jouett Goforth essayed his little joke. "Are you right sure she was forty, Yancey, and weather-beaten? And that about her hair and boots and hands?"

Cravat, standing behind his wife's chair, looked down at her; at the fine white line that marked the parting of her thick black hair. With one forefinger he touched her cheek, gently. He allowed the finger to slip down the creamy surface of her skin, from cheek bone to chin. "Dead sure, Jouett. I left out one thing, though." Cousin Jouett made a sound signifying, ah, I thought so. "Her teeth," Yancey Cravat went on thoughtfully. "Broken and discolored like those of a woman of seventy. And most of them gone at the side."

Here Yancey could not resist charging up and down, flirting his coat tails and generally ruining the fine flavor of his victory over the Venable mind. The Venable mind (or the prospect of escaping it) had been one of the reasons for his dash into the wild mêlée of the Run in the first place. Now he stood surveying these handsome futile faces, and a great impatience shook him, and a flame of rage shot through him, and a tongue of malice flicked him. With these to goad him, and the knowledge of how he had failed, he plunged again into his story to the end.

"I had planned to try and get a place on the Santa Fé train that was standing, steam up, ready to run into the Nation. But you couldn't get on. There wasn't room for a flea. They were hanging on the cow-catcher and swarming all over the engine, and sitting on top of the cars. It was keyed down to make no more speed than a horse. It turned out they didn't even do that. They went twenty miles in ninety minutes. I decided I'd use my Indian pony. I knew I'd get endurance, anyway, if not speed. And that's what counted in the end.

"There we stood, by the thousands, all night. Morning, and we began to line up at the Border, as near as they'd let us go. Militia all along to keep us back. They had burned the prairie ahead for miles into the Nation, so as to keep the grass down and make the way clearer. To smoke out the Sooners, too, who had sneaked in and were hiding in the scrub oaks, in the draws, wherever they could. Most of the killing was due to them. They had crawled in and staked the land and stood ready to shoot those of us who came in, fair and square, in the Run. I knew the piece I wanted. An old freighters' trail, out of use, but still marked with deep ruts, led almost straight to it, once you found the trail, all overgrown as it was. A little creek ran through the land, and the prairie rolled a little there, too. Nothing but blackjacks for miles around it, but on that section, because of the water, I suppose, there were elms and persimmons and cottonwoods and even a grove of pecans. I had noticed it many a time, riding the range."

(H'm! Riding the range! All the Venables made a quick mental note of that. It was thus, by stray bits and snatches, that they managed to piece together something of Yancey Cravat's past.)

"Ten o'clock, and the crowd was nervous and restless. Hundreds of us had been followers of Payne and had gone as Boomers in the old Payne colonies, and had been driven out, and had come back again. Thousands from all parts of the country had waited ten years for this day when the land-hungry would be fed. They were like people starving. I've seen the same look exactly on the faces of men who were ravenous for food.

"Well, eleven o'clock, and they were crowding and cursing and fighting for places near the Line. They shouted and sang and yelled and argued, and the sound they made wasn't human at all, but like thousands of wild animals penned up. The sun blazed down. It was cruel. The dust hung over everything in a thick cloud, blinding you and choking you. The black dust of the burned prairie was over everything. We were like a horde of fiends with our red eyes and our cracked lips and our blackened faces. Eleven-thirty. It was a picture straight out of hell. The roar grew louder. People fought for an inch of gain on the Border. Just next to me was a girl who looked about eighteen— she turned out to be twenty-five—and a beauty she was, too—on a coal-black thoroughbred."

"Aha!" said Cousin Jouett Goforth. He was the kind of man who says, "Aha."

"On the other side was an old fellow with a long gray beard—a plainsman, he was—a six-shooter in his belt, one wooden leg, and a flask of whisky. He took a pull out of that every minute or two. He was mounted on an Indian pony like mine. Every now and then he'd throw back his head and let out a yell that would curdle your blood, even in that chorus of fiends. As we waited we fell to talking, the three of us, though you couldn't hear much in that uproar. The girl said she had trained her thoroughbred for the race. He was from Kentucky, and so was she. She was bound to get her hundred and sixty acres, she said. She had to have it. She didn't say why, and I didn't ask her. We were all too keyed up, anyway, to make sense. Oh, I forgot. She had on a get-up that took the attention of anyone that saw her, even in that crazy mob. The better to cut the wind, she had shortened sail and wore a short skirt, black tights, and a skullcap.''

Here there was quite a bombardment of sound as silver spoons and knives and forks were dropped from shocked and nerveless feminine Venable fingers.

"It turned out that the three of us, there in the front line, were headed down the old freighters' trail toward the creek land. I said, 'I'll be the first in the Run to reach Little Bear.' That was the name of the creek on the section. The girl pulled her cap down tight over her ears. 'Follow me,' she laughed. 'I'll show you the way.' Then the old fellow with the wooden leg and the whiskers yelled out, 'Whoop-ee! I'll tell 'em along the Little Bear you're both a-comin.'

"There we were, the girl on my left, the old plainsman on my right. Eleven forty-five. Along the Border were the soldiers, their guns in one hand, their watches in the other. Those last five minutes seemed years long; and funny, they'd quieted till there wasn't a sound. Listening. The last minute was an eternity. Twelve o'clock. There went up a roar that drowned the crack of the soldiers' musketry as they fired in the air as the signal of noon and the start of the Run. You could see the puffs of smoke from their guns, but you couldn't hear a sound. The thousands surged over the Line. It was like water going over a broken dam. The rush had started, and it was devil take the hindmost. We swept across the prairie in a cloud of black and red dust that covered our faces and hands in a minute, so that we looked like black demons from hell. Off we went, down the old freight trail that was two wheel ruts, a foot wide each, worn into the prairie soil. The old man on his pony kept in one rut, the girl on her thoroughbred in the other, and I on my Whitefoot on the raised place in the middle. That first half mile was almost a neck-and-neck race. The old fellow was yelling and waving one arm and hanging on somehow. He was beating his pony with the flask on his flanks. Then he began to drop behind. Next thing I heard a terrible scream and a great shouting behind me. I threw a quick glance over my shoulder. The old plainsman's pony had stumbled and fallen. His bottle smashed into bits, his six-shooter flew in another direction, and he lay sprawling full length in the rut of the trail. The next instant he was hidden in a welter of pounding hoofs and flying dirt and cinders and wagon wheels.''

A dramatic pause. Black Isaiah was hanging from his perch like a monkey on a branch. His asparagus shoofly was limp. The faces around the table were balloons pulled by a single string. They swung this way and that with Yancey Cravat's pace as he strode the room, his Prince Albert coat tails billowing. This way—the faces turned toward the sideboard. That way— they turned toward the windows. Yancey held the little moment of silence like a jewel in the circlet of faces. Sabra Cravat's voice, high and sharp with suspense, cut the stillness.

"What happened? What happened to the old man?''

Yancey's pliant hands flew up in a gesture of inevitability. "Oh, he was trampled to death in the mad mob that charged over him. Crazy. They couldn't stop for a one-legged old whiskers with a quart flask."

Out of the well-bred murmur of horror that now arose about the Venable board there emerged the voice of Felice Venable, sharp-edged with disapproval. "And the girl. The girl with the black———". Unable to say it. Southern.

"The girl and I—funny, I never did learn her name—were in the lead because we had stuck to the old trail, rutted though it was, rather than strike out across the prairie that by this time was beyond the burned area and was covered with a heavy growth of blue stem grass almost six feet high in places. A horse could only be forced through that at a slow pace. That jungle of grass kept many a racer from winning his section that day.

"The girl followed close behind me. That thoroughbred she rode was built for speed, not distance. A race horse, blooded. I could hear him blowing. He was trained to short bursts. My Indian pony was just getting his second wind as her horse slackened into a trot. We had come nearly sixteen miles. I was well in the lead by that time, with the girl following. She was crouched low over his neck, like a jockey, and I could hear her talking to him, low and sweet and eager, as if he were a human being. We were far in the lead now. We had left the others behind, hundreds going this way, hundreds that, scattering for miles over the prairie. Then I saw that the prairie ahead was afire. The tall grass was blazing. Only the narrow trail down which we were galloping was open. On either side of it was a wall of flame. Some skunk of a Sooner, sneaking in ahead of the Run, had set the blaze to keep the Boomers off, saving the land for himself. The dry grass burned like oiled paper. I turned around. The girl was there, her racer stumbling, breaking and going on, his head lolling now. I saw her motion with her hand. She was coming. I whipped off my hat and clapped it over Whitefoot's eyes, gave him the spurs, crouched down low and tight, shut my own eyes, and down the trail we went into the furnace. Hot! It was hell! The crackling and snapping on either side was like a fusillade. I could smell the singed hair on the flanks of the mustang. My own hair was singeing. I could feel the flames licking my legs and back. Another hundred yards and neither the horse nor I could have come through it. But we broke out into the open choking and blinded and half suffocated. I looked down the lane of flame. The girl hung on her horse's neck. Her skullcap was pulled down over her eyes. She was coming through, game. I knew that my land—the piece that I had come through hell for—was not more than a mile ahead. I knew that hanging around here would probably get me a shot through the head, for the Sooner that started that fire must be lurking somewhere in the high grass ready to kill anybody that tried to lay claim to his land. I began to wonder, too, if that girl wasn't headed for the same section that I was bound for. I made up my mind that, woman or no woman, this was a race, and devil take the hindmost. My poor little pony was coughing and sneezing and trembling. Her racer must have been ready to drop. I wheeled and went on. I kept thinking how, when I came to Little Bear Creek, I'd bathe my little mustang's nose and face and his poor heaving flanks, and how I mustn't let him drink too much, once he got his muzzle in the water.

"Just before I reached the land I was riding for I had to leave the trail and cut across the prairie. I could see a clump of elms ahead. I knew the creek was near by. But just before I got to it I came to one of those deep gullies you find in the plains country. Drought does it—a crack in the dry earth to begin with, widening with every rain until it becomes a small cañon. Almost ten feet across this one was, and deep. No way around it that I could see, and no time to look for one. I put Whitefoot to the leap and, by God, he took it, landing on the other side with hardly an inch to spare. I heard a wild scream behind me. I turned. The girl on her spent racer had tried to make the gulch. He had actually taken it—a thoroughbred and a gentleman, that animal—but he came down on his knees just on the farther edge, rolled, and slid down the gully side into the ditch. The girl had flung herself free. My claim was fifty yards away. So was the girl, with her dying horse. She lay there on the prairie. As I raced toward her—my own poor little mount was nearly gone by this time—she scrambled to her knees. I can see her face now, black with cinders and soot and dirt, her hair all over her shoulders, her cheek bleeding where she had struck a stone in her fall, her black tights torn, her little short skirt sagging. She sort of sat up and looked around her. Then she staggered to her feet before I reached her and stood there swaying, and pushing her hair out of her eyes like someone who'd been asleep. She pointed down the gully. The black of her face was streaked with tears.

"Shoot him!' she said. 'I can't. His two forelegs are broken. I heard them crack. Shoot him! For God's sake!'

"So I off my horse and down to the gully's edge. There the animal lay, his eyes all whites, his poor legs doubled under him, his flanks black and sticky with sweat and dirt. He was done for, all right. I took out my six-shooter and aimed right between his eyes. He kicked once, sort of leaped— or tried to, and then lay still. I stood there a minute, to see if he had to have another. He was so game that, some way, I didn't want to give him more than he needed.

"Then something made me turn around. The girl had mounted my mustang. She was off toward the creek section. Before I had moved ten paces she had reached the very piece I had marked in my mind for my own. She leaped from the horse, ripped off her skirt, tied it to her riding whip that she still held tight in her hand, dug the whip butt into the soil of the prairie— planted her flag—and the land was hers by right of claim."

Yancey Cravat stopped talking. There was a moment of stricken silence. Sabra Cravat staring, staring at her husband with great round eyes. Lewis Venable, limp, yellow, tremulous. Felice Venable, upright and quivering. It was she who spoke first. And when she did she was every inch the thrifty descendant of French forbears; nothing of the Southern belle about her.

"Yancey Cravat, do you mean that you let her have your quarter section on the creek that you had gone to the Indian Territory for! That you had been gone a month for! That you had left your wife and child for! That———"

"Now, Mamma!" You saw that all the Venable in Sabra was summoned to keep the tears from her eyes, and that thus denied they had crowded themselves into her trembling voice. "Now, Mamma!"

"Don't you 'now Mamma' me! What of the land that you were to have had! It was bad enough to think of your going to that wilderness, but to—" She paused. Her voice took on a new and more sinister note. "I don't believe a word of it." She whirled on Yancey, her black eyes blazing. "Why did you let that trollop in the black tights have that land?"

Yancey regarded this question with considerable judicial calm, but Felice, knowing him, might have been warned by the way his great head was lowered like that of a charging bull buffalo.

"If it had been a man I could have shot him. A good many had to, to keep the land they'd run fairly for. But you can't shoot a woman."

"Why not?" demanded the erstwhile Southern belle, sharply.

The Venables, as one man, gave a little jump. A nervous sound, that was half gasp and half shocked titter, went round the Venable board. A startled "Felice!" was wrung from Lewis Venable. "Why, Mamma!" said Sabra.

Yancey Cravat, enormously vital, felt rising within him the tide of irritability which this vitiated family always stirred in him. Something now about their shocked and staring faces, their lolling and graceful forms, roused in him an unreasoning rebellion. He suddenly hated them. He wanted to be free of them. He wanted to be free of them—of Wichita—of convention—of smooth custom—of—no, not of her. He now smiled his brilliant sweet smile which alone should have warned Felice Venable. But that intrepid matriarch was not one to let a tale go unpointed.

"I'm mighty pleased, for one, that it turned out as it did. Do you suppose I'd have allowed a daughter of mine—a Venable—to go traipsing down into the wilderness to live among drunken one-legged plainsmen, and toothless scrags in calico, and trollops in tights! Never! It's over now, and a mighty good thing, too. Perhaps now, Yancey, you'll stop this ramping up and down and be content to run that newspaper of yours and conduct your law practice—such as it is—with no more talk of this Indian Territory. A daughter of mine in boots and calico and sunbonnet, if you please, a-pioneering among savages. Reared as she was! No, indeed."

Yancey was strangely silent. He was surveying his fine white hands critically, interestedly, as though seeing them in admiration for the first time—another sign that should have warned the brash Felice. When he spoke it was with utter gentleness.

"I'm no farmer. I'm no rancher. I didn't want a section of farm land, anyway. The town's where I belong, and I should have made for the town sites. There were towns of ten thousand and over sprung up in a night during the Run. Wagallala—Sperry—Wawhuska—Osage. It's the last frontier in America, that new country. There isn't a newspaper in one of those towns—or wasn't, when I left. I want to go back there and help build a state out of prairie and Indians and scrub oaks and red clay. For it'll be a state some day—mark my words."

"That wilderness a state!" sneered Cousin Dabney Venable. "With an Osage buck or a Cherokee chief for governor, I suppose."

"Why not? What a revenge on a government that has cheated them and driven them like cattle from place to place and broken its treaties with them and robbed them of their land. Look at Georgia! Look at Mississippi! Remember the Trail of Tears!"

"Ho hum," yawned Cousin Jouett Goforth, and rose, fumblingly. "This has all been very interesting—odd, but interesting. But if you will excuse me now I shall have my little siesta. I am accustomed after dinner . . . ."

Lewis Venable, so long silent, now too reached for his cane and prepared to rise. He was not quick enough. Felice Venable's hand, thin, febrile, darted out and clutched his coat sleeve—pressed him back so that he became at once prisoner and judge in his chair at the head of the table.

"Lewis Venable, you heard him! Are you going to sit there? He says he's going back. How about your daughter?" She turned blazing black eyes on her son-in-law. "Do you mean you're going back to that Indian country? Do you?"

"I'll be back there in two weeks. And remember, it's white man's country now."

Sabra stood up, the boy Cim grasped about his middle in her arms, so that he began to whimper, dangling there. Her eyes were startled, enormous. "Yancey! Yancey, you're not leaving me again!"

"Leaving you, my beauty!" He strode over to her. "Not by a long shot. This time you're going with me."

"And I say she's not!" Felice Venable rapped it out. "And neither are you, my fine fellow. You were tricked out of your land by a trollop in tights, and that ends it. You'll stay here with your wife and child."

He shook his great head gently. His voice was dulcet.

"I'm going back to the Oklahoma country; and Sabra and Cim with me."

Felice whirled on her husband. "Lewis! You can sit there and see your daughter dragged off to be scalped among savages!"

The sick man raised his fine white head. The faded blue eyes were turned on the girl. The child, sensing conflict, had buried his head in her shoulder. "You came with me, Felice, more than twenty years ago, and your mother thought you were going to the wilderness, too. You remember? She cried and made mourning for weeks."

"Sabra's different. Sabra's different.

The reedy voice of the sick man had the ghostly carrying quality of an echo. You heard it above the women's shrill clamor. "No, she isn't, Felice. She's more like you this minute than you are yourself. She favors those pioneer women Yancey was telling about in the old days. Look at her."

The Venable eye, from one end of the table to the other, turned like a single orb in its socket toward the young woman facing them with defiance in her bearing. Not defiance, perhaps, so much as resolve. Seeing her, head up, standing there beside her husband, one arm about the child, you saw that what her father said was indeed true. She was her mother, the Felice Venable of two decades ago; she was the woman in sunbonnet and calico to whom Yancey had given his cup of water; she was the women jolting endless miles in covered wagons, spinning in log cabins, cooking over crude fires; she was all women who have traveled American prairie and desert and mountain and plain. Here was that inner rectitude, that chastity of lip, that clearness of eye, that refinement of feature, that absence of allure that comes with cold white fire. The pioneer type, as Yancey had said. Potentially a more formidable woman than her mother.

Seeing something of this, Felice Venable said again, more loudly, as though to convince herself, "She's not to go."

Looking more than ever like her mother, Sabra met this stubbornly. "But I want to go, Mamma."

"I forbid it. You don't know what you want. You don't know what you're talking about. I say you'll stay here with your mother and father in decent civilization. I've heard enough. I hope this will serve a lesson to you, Yancey."

"I'm going back to the Nation," said Yancey, quite pleasantly.

Sabra stiffened. "I'm going with him." In her new resolve she must have squeezed the hand of the child Cim, for he gave a little yelp. The combined Venables, nerves on edge, leaped in their chairs and then looked at each other with some hostility.

"And I say you're not."

"But I want to go."

"You don't."

Perhaps Sabra had not realized until now how terribly she had counted on her husband's return as marking the time when she would be free to leave the Venable board, to break away from the Venable clan; no more to be handled, talked over, peered at by the Venable eye—and most of all by the maternal Venable eye. Twenty-one, and the yoke of her mother's dominance was beginning to gall her. Now, at her own inner rage and sickening disappointment, all the iron in her fused and hardened. It had gone less often to the fire than the older woman's had. For the first time this quality in her met that of her mother, and the metal of the older woman bent.

"I *will* go," said Sabra Cravat.

If anyone had been looking at Lewis Venable at that moment (which no one ever thought of doing) he could have seen a ghostly smile momentarily irradiating the transparent ivory face. But now it was Yancey Cravat who held their fascinated eye. With a cowboy yip he swung the defiant Sabra and the boy Cim high in the air in his great arms—tossed them up, so that Sabra screamed, and Cim squealed in mingled terror and delight. It was the kind of horseplay (her word) at which Felice Venable always shuddered. Altogether the three seemed suddenly an outrage in that seemly room with its mahogany and its decanters and its circle of staring high-bred faces.

"Week from to-morrow," announced Yancey, in something like a shout, so exulting it seemed. "We'll start on a Monday, fresh and fair. Two wagons. One with the printing outfit—you'll drive that, Sabra—and one with the household goods and bedding and camp stuff and the rest. We ought to make it in nine days. . . . Wichita!" His glance went round the room, and in that glance you saw not only Wichita! but Venables! "I've had enough of it. Sabra, my girl, we'll leave all the goddamned middle-class respectability of Wichita, Kansas, behind us. We're going out, by God, to a brand-new, two-fisted, rip-snorting country, full of Injuns and rattlesnakes and two-gun toters and gyp water and desper-*ah*-dos! Whoop-*ee!*"

It was too much for black Isaiah in his perilous perch high above the table. He had long ago ceased to wield his asparagus fan. He had been leaning farther and farther forward, the better to hear and see all of the scene that was spread beneath him. Now, at Yancey's cowboy whoop, he started violently, his slight hold was loosed, and he fell like a great black grape from the vine directly into the midst of one of Felice Venable's white and virgin frosted silver cakes.

Shouts, screams, upleapings. Isaiah plucked, white-bottomed, out of the center of the vast pastry. The sudden grayish pallor of his face matched the silver tone of his pants' seat. Felice Venable, nerves strained to breaking, lifted her hand to cuff him smartly. But the black boy was too quick for her. With the swiftness of a wild thing he scuttled across the table to where Yancey Cravat stood with his wife and child, leaped nimbly to the floor, crept between the man's legs like a whimpering little dog, and lay there, locked in the safety of Yancey's great knees.

3

INDIANS WERE NO novelty to the townspeople of Wichita. Sabra had seen them all her life. At the age of three Cim was held up in his father's arms to watch a great band of them go by on one of their annual pilgrimages. He played Indian, of course, patting his lips to simulate the Indian yodeling yell. He had a war bonnet made of chicken feathers sewed to the edge of a long strip of red calico.

Twice a year, chaperoned by old General "Bull" Plummer, the Indians swept through the streets of Wichita in their visiting regalia—feathers, beads, blankets, chains—a brilliant sight. Ahead of them and behind them was the reassuring blue of United States army uniforms worn by the Kansas regiment from Fort Riley. All Wichita, accustomed to them though it was, rushed out to gaze at them from store doorways and offices and kitchens. Bucks, braves, chiefs, squaws, papooses; tepees, poles, pots, dogs, ponies, the cavalcade swept through the quiet sunny streets of the midwestern town, a vivid frieze of color against the drab monotony of the prairies.

In late spring it was likely to be the Cheyennes going north from their reservation in the Indian Territory to visit their cousins the Sioux in Dakota. In the late autumn it was the Sioux riding south to return the visit of the Cheyennes. Both of these were horse Indians, and of the Plains tribes, great visitors among themselves, and as gossipy and highly gregarious as old women on a hotel veranda. Usually they called a halt in their journey to make camp for the night outside the town. Though watched over by martial eye, they usually managed to pilfer, in a friendly sort of way, anything they could lay hands on—chickens, wash unwisely left on the line, the very clothes off the scarecrows in the field.

Throughout the year there were always little groups of Indians to be seen on the streets of the town—Kaws, Osages, and Poncas. They came on ponies or in wagons from their reservations; bought bacon, calico, whisky if they could get it. You saw them squatting on their haunches in the dust of the sunny street, silent, sloe eyed, aloof. They seemed to be studying the townspeople passing to and fro. Only their eyes moved. Their dress was a mixture of savagery and civilization. The Osages, especially, clung to the blanket. Trousers, coat, and even hat might be in the conventional pattern of the whites. But over this the Osage wore his striped blanket of vivid orange and purple and red. It was as though he defied the whites to take from him that last insignia of race.

A cowed enough people they seemed by now; dirty, degraded. Since the Custer Massacre of '76 they had been pretty thoroughly beaten into submission. Only occasionally there seemed to emanate from a band of them a sullen, enduring hate. It had no definite expression. It was not in their bearing; it could not be said to look out from the dead black Indian eye, nor was it anywhere about the immobile parchment face. Yet somewhere black implacable resentment smoldered in the heart of this dying race.

In one way or another, at school, in books and newspapers of the time, in her father's talk with the men and women of his own generation, Sabra had picked up odds and ends of information about these silent, slothful, yet sinister figures. She had been surprised—even incredulous—at her husband's partisanship of the redskins. It was one of his absurdities. He seemed actually to consider them as human beings.

Tears came to his own eyes when he spoke of that blot on southern civilization, the Trail of Tears, in which the Cherokees, a peaceful and home-loving Indian tribe, were torn from the land which a government had given them by sworn treaty, to be sent far away on a march which, from cold, hunger, exposure, and heartbreak, was marked by bleaching bones from Georgia to Oklahoma. Yancey and old Lewis Venable had a longstanding feud on the subject of Mississippi's treatment of the Choctaws and Georgia's cruelty to the Cherokees.

"Oh, treaties!" sneered Yancey's father-in-law, outraged at some blistering editorial with which Yancey had enlivened the pages of the Wichita *Wigwam*. "One doesn't make treaties with savages—and expect to keep them."

"You call the Choctaws, the Creeks, the Chickasaws, the Cherokees and the Seminoles savages! They are the Five Civilized Tribes! They had their laws, they had their religion, they cultivated the land, they were peaceful, home-loving, wise. Would you call Chief Apushmataha a savage?"

"Certainly, sir! Most assuredly."

"How about Sequoyah? John Ross? Stand Waitie? Quanah Parker? They were wise men. Great men."

"Savages, with enough white blood in them to make them leaders of their dull-witted, full-blood brothers. The Creeks, sir" (he pronounced it "suh") "intermarried with niggers. And so did the Choctaws; and the Seminoles down in Florida."

Yancey smiled his winning smile. "I understand that while you Southerners didn't exactly marry————"

"Marriage, sir, is one thing. Nature, sir, is another. Far from signing treaties with these creatures and giving them valuable American land to call their own————"

"Which was their own before we took it away from them."

"——I would be in favor of extermination by some humane but effective process. They are a sore on the benign bosom of an otherwise healthy government."

"It is now being done as effectively as even you could wish, though perhaps lacking a little something on the humane side."

From her father and mother, too, Sabra had heard much of this sort of talk before Yancey had come into her life. She had heard of them at school, as well. Their savagery and trickiness had been emphasized; their tragedy had been glossed over or scarcely touched upon. Sabra, if she considered them at all, thought of them as dirty and useless two-footed animals. In her girlhood she had gone to a school conducted by the Sisters of Loretto, under the jurisdiction of the Jesuit Fathers. Early in the history of Kansas, long before Sabra's day, it had started as a Mission school, and the indefatigable Jesuit priests had traveled the country on horseback, riding the weary and dangerous miles over the prairies to convert the Indians. Mother Bridget, a powerful, heavy woman of past sixty now, shrewd, dominating, yet strangely childlike, had come to the Mission when a girl just past her novitiate, in the wild and woolly days of Kansas. She had seen the oxen haul the native yellow limestone of which the building was made; she had known the fear of the scalping knife; with her own big, capable, curiously masculine hands she had planted the first young fruit trees, the vegetable and flower garden that now flourished in the encircling Osage hedge; she had superintended the building of the great hedge itself, made of the tough yet supple wood that the exploring pioneer French had called *bois d'arc,* because in the early days the Indians had fashioned their bows of it. The Kansans had corrupted the word until now the wood was known as " bodark." The Mission had been an Indian school then, with a constantly fluctuating attendance. One day there would be forty pairs of curiously dead black Indian eyes intent on a primer of reading, writing, or arithmetic; the next there would be none. The tribe had gone on a visit to a neighboring friendly tribe. Bucks and squaws, ponies and dogs and children, they were off on society bent, the Osages visiting the Kaws, or the Kaws the Quapaws. At other times their absence might mean something more sinister—an uprising in the brewing, or an attack on an enemy tribe. Mother Bridget had terrible tales to tell. She could even make grim jokes about those early days. "Hair-raising times they were," she would tell you (it was her pet pun), "in more ways than one, as many a poor white settler could prove to you who'd had the scalp lifted off him by the knife." She had taught the Indian girls to sew, to exchange wigwams for cabins, and to wear sunbonnets and to speak about their souls and their earthly troubles as well to a Great Father named God who was much more powerful than the Sun and the Rain and the Wind to whom they attributed such potency. These things they did with gratifying docility for weeks at a time, or even months, after which it was discovered that they buried their dead under the cabins, removing enough of the puncheon floor to enable them to dig a grave, laying the timbers back neatly, and then deserting the cabins to live outdoors again, going back to the blanket at the same time and holding elaborate placating ceremonies to various gods of the elements. Mother Bridget (Sister Bridget then, red cheeked in her wimple, her beads clicking a stubborn race against the treachery of the savages) and the other Sisters of Loretto had it all to do over again from the start.

All this was past now. The Indians were herded on reservations in the Indian Territory. Mother Bridget and her helpers taught embroidery and music and kindred ladylike accomplishments to the bonneted and gloved young ladies of Wichita's gentry. The Osage hedge now shielded prim and docile misses where once it had tried to confine the wild things of the prairie. The wild things seemed tame enough now, herded together on their reservations, spirit broken, pride destroyed.

Sabra had her calico pony hitched to the phaëton (a matron now, it was no longer seemly to ride him as she used to, up and down the rutted prairie roads, her black hair in a long thick braid switching to the speed of the hard-bitten hoofs). Mother Bridget was in the Mission vegetable garden, superintending the cutting of great rosy stalks of late pie plant. The skirt of her habit was hitched up informally above her list shoes, muddied by the soft loam of the garden.

"Indian Territory! What does your ma say?"

"She's wild."

"Do you want to go?"

"Oh, yes, yes!" Then added hastily: "Of course, I hate to leave Mamma and Papa. But the Bible says, 'Whither thou———' "

"I know what the Bible says," interrupted the old nun shrewdly. "Why does he want to go—Cravat?"

Sabra glowed with pride. "Yancey says it's a chance to build an empire out of the last frontier in America. He says its lawmakers can profit by the mistakes of the other states, so that when the Indian Territory becomes a state some day it will know wherein the other states have failed, and knowing—uh—avoid the pitfalls———"

"Stuff!" interrupted Mother Bridget. "He's going for the adventure of it. They always have, no matter what excuse they've given, from the Holy Grail to the California gold fields. The difference in America is that the women have always gone along. When you read the history of France you're peeking through a bedroom keyhole. The history of England is a joust. The womenfolks were always Elaineish and anemic, seems. When Ladye Guinevere had pinned a bow of ribbon to her knight's sleeve, why, her job was done for the day. He could ride off to be killed while she stayed home and stitched at a tapestry. But here in this land, Sabra, my girl, the women, they've been the real hewers of wood and drawers of water. You'll want to remember that."

"But that's what Yancey said. Exactly."

"Did he now!" She stood up and released the full folds of her skirt from the waist cord that had served to loop it away from the moist earth. She lifted her voice in an order to the figure that stooped over the pie-plant bed. "Enough, Sister Norah, enough. Tell Sister Agnes plenty of sugar and not like the last pie, fit to pucker your mouth." She turned back to Sabra. "When do you start? How do you go?"

"Next Monday. Two wagons. One with the printing outfit, the other with the household goods and bedding. Yancey will have it that we've got to take along bedsprings for me, right out of our bed here and laid flat in the wagon."

Mother Bridget seemed not to hear. She looked out across the garden to where prairie met sky. Her eyes, behind the steel-rimmed spectacles, saw a pageant that Sabra had never known. "So. It's come to that. They've opened it to the whites after all—the land that was to belong to the Indians forever. 'As long as grass grows and the rivers flow.' That's what the treaty said. H'm. Well, what next!"

"Oh, Indians . . ." said Sabra. Her tone was that of one who speaks of prairie dogs, seven-year locusts, or any like Western nuisance.

"I know," said Mother Bridget. "You can't change them. Nobody knows better than I. I've had Indian girls here in the school for two years at a stretch. We'd teach them to wash themselves every day; they'd learn to sew, and embroider, and cook and read and write. They were taught worsted and coral work and drawing and even painting and vocal music. They learned the Gospel of the Son of God. They'd leave here as neat and pretty and well behaved as any girl you'd care to see. In two weeks I'd hear they'd gone back to the blanket. Say what you like, the full-blood Indian to-day is just about where he was before Joshua. Well————"

Sabra was a little bored by all this. She had not come out to the old Mission to hear about Indians. She had come to say farewell to Mother Bridget, and have a fuss made over her, and to be exclaimed over. Wasn't she going to be a pioneer woman such as you read about in the books?

"I must be going, dear Mother Bridget. I just came out—there's so much to do." She was vaguely disappointed in the dramatics of this visit.

"I've something for you. Come along." She led the way through the garden, across the sandstone flagging of the porch, into the dim cool mustiness of the Mission hall. She left Sabra there and went swiftly down the corridor. Sabra waited, grateful for this shady haven after the heat of the Kansas sun. She had known this hall, and the bare bright rooms that opened off it, all through her girlhood. The fragrance of pie crust, baking crisply, came to her nostrils: the shell, of course, that was to hold the succulent rhubarb. There was the sound of a heavy door opening, shutting, click, thud, somewhere down a turn in the corridor. She had never seen Mother Bridget's room. No one had. Sabra wondered about it. The Sisters of Loretto owned nothing. It was a rule of the Order. The possessive pronoun, first person, was never used by them. Sabra recalled how Sister Innocenta had come running in one morning in great distress. "Our rosary!" she had cried. "I have lost our rosary!" The string of devotional beads she always wore at her waist had somehow slipped or broken and was missing. They kept nothing for themselves. Strange and sometimes beautiful things came into their hands and were immediately disposed of. Sabra had seen Mother Bridget part with queer objects. Once it had been a scalping knife with brown stains on it that looked like rust and were not; another time an Osage papoose board with its gay and intricately beaded pocket in which some Indian woman had carried her babies strapped to her tireless back. There had been a crewelwork motto done in bright-colored wool threads by the fingers of some hopeful New England émigrée of years ago. Its curlycue letters announced: Music Hath Charms to Soothe the Savage Breast. It had been found hanging on the wall just above the prim little parlor organ in the cabin of a settler whose young wife and children had been killed during a sudden uprising of Indians in his absence.

Suddenly, as she waited there in the peace of the old building, there swept over Sabra a great wave of nostalgia for the very scenes she was leaving. It was as though she already had put behind her these familiar things of her girlhood: the calico pony and the little yellow phaëton; the oblong of Kansas sunshine and sky and garden seen through the Mission doorway; the scents and sounds and security of the solid stone building itself. She was shaken by terror. Indian Territory! Indian—why, she couldn't go there to live. To live forever, the rest of her life. Yancey Cravat, her husband, became suddenly remote, a stranger, terrible. She was Sabra Venable, Sabra Venable, here, safe from harm, in the Mission school. She wouldn't go. Her mother was right.

A door at the end of the corridor opened. The huge figure of Mother Bridget appeared, filling the oblong, blotting out the sunlight. In her arms was a thick roll of cloth. "Here," she said, and turned to let the light fall on it. It was a blanket or coverlet woven in a block pattern of white and a deep, brilliant blue. "It's to keep you and little Cim warm, in the wagon, on the way to the Indian Territory. I wove it myself, on a hand loom. There's no wear-out to it. The blue is Indian dye, and nothing can fade it. It's a wild country you'll be going to. But there's something in the blue of this makes any room fit to live in, no matter how bare and ugly. If they ask you out there what it is, tell 'em a Kansas tapestry."

She walked with Sabra to the phaëton and produced from a capacious pocket hidden in the folds of her habit a little scarlet June apple for the pony. Sabra kissed her on both plump cheeks quickly and stepped into the buggy, placing the blue and white blanket on the seat beside her. Her face was screwed up comically—the face of a little girl who is pretending not to be crying. "Good-bye," she said, and was surprised to find that her voice was no more than a whisper. And at that, feeling very sorry for herself, she began to cry, openly, even as she matter-of-factly gathered up the reins in her strong young fingers.

Mother Bridget stepped close to the wheel. "It'll be all right. There's no such thing as a new country for the people who come to it. They bring along their own ways and their own bits of things and make it like the old as fast as they can."

"I'm taking along my china dishes," breathed Sabra through her tears, "and my lovely linen and the mantel set that Cousin Dabney gave me for a wedding present, and my own rocker to sit in, and my wine-color silkwarp henrietta, and some slips from the garden, because Yancey says there isn't much growing."

Behind her spectacles the eyes of the wise old nun were soft with pity. "That'll be lovely." She watched the calico pony and the phaëton drive off up the dusty Kansas road. She turned toward the Mission house. The beads clicked. Hail, Mary, full of grace . . .

4

THE CHILD CIM had got it into his head that this was to be a picnic. He had smelled pies and cakes baking; had seen hampers packed. Certainly, except for the bizarre load that both wagons contained, this might have been one of those informal excursions into a nearby wood which Cim so loved, where they lunched in the open, camped near a stream, and he was allowed to run barefoot in the shadow of his aristocratic grandmother's cool disapproval. Felice Venable loathed all forms of bucolic diversion and could, with a glance, cause more discomfort at an al fresco luncheon than a whole battalion of red ants.

There was a lunatic week preceding their departure from Wichita. Felice fought their going to the last, and finally took to her bed with threats of impending dissolution which failed to achieve the desired effect owing to the preoccupation of the persons supposed to be stricken by her plight. From time to time, intrigued by the thumpings, scurryings, shouts, laughter, quarrels, and general upheaval attendant on the Cravats' departure, Felice rose from her bed and trailed wanly about the house, looking, in her white dimity wrapper, like a bilious and distracted ghost. She issued orders. Take this. Don't take that. It can't be that you're leaving those behind! Your own Aunt Sarah Moncrief du Tisne embroidered every inch of them with her own———

"But, Mamma, you don't understand. Yancey says there's very little society, and it's all quite rough and unsettled—wild, almost."

"That needn't prevent you from remembering you're a lady, I hope. Unless you are planning to be one of those hags in a sunbonnet and no teeth that Yancey seems to have taken such a fancy to."

So Sabra Cravat took along to the frontier wilderness such oddments and elegancies as her training, lack of experience, and Southern family tradition dictated. A dozen silver knives, forks, and spoons in the DeGrasse pattern; actually, too, a dozen silver after-dinner coffee spoons; a silver cake dish, very handsome, upheld by three solid silver cupids in care-free attitudes; linen that had been spun by hand and that bore vine-wreathed monograms; many ruffled and embroidered and starched white muslin petticoats to be sullied in the red clay of the Western muck; her heavy black grosgrain silk with the three box pleats on each side, and trimmed with black passementerie; her black hat with the five black plumes; her beautiful green nun's veiling; her tulle bonnet with the little pink flowers; forty jars of preserves; her own rocker, a lady's chair whose seat and back were upholstered fashionably with bright colored Brussels carpeting. There were two wagons, canvas covered and lumbering. Dishes, trunks, bedding, boxes were snugly stowed away in the capacious belly of one; the printing outfit, securely roped and lashed, went in the other. This wagon held the little hand press; two six-column forms; the case rack containing the type (cardboard was tacked snugly over this to keep the type from escaping); the rollers; a stock of paper; a can of printer's ink, tubes of job ink, a box of wooden quoins used in locking the forms.

There was, to the Wichita eye, nothing unusual in the sight of these huge covered freighters that would soon go lumbering off toward the horizon. Their like had worn many a track in the Kansas prairie. The wagon train had wound its perilous way westward since the day of the old Spanish trail, deeply rutted by the heavy wheels of Mexican carts. The very Indians who trafficked in pelts and furs and human beings had used the white man's trails for their trading. Yet in this small expedition faring forth there was something that held the poignancy of the tragic and the ridiculous. The man, huge, bizarre, impractical; the woman, tight lipped, terribly determined, her eyes staring with the fixed, unseeing gaze of one who knows that to blink but once is to be awash with tears; the child, out of hand with excitement and impatience to be gone. From the day of Yancey's recital of the Run, black Isaiah had begged to be taken along. Denied this, he had sulked for a week and now was nowhere to be found.

The wagons, packed, stood waiting before the Venable house. Perhaps never in the history of the settling of the West did a woman go a-pioneering in such a costume. Sabra had driven horses all her life; so now she stepped agilely from ground to hub, from hub to wheel top, perched herself on the high wagon seat and gathered up the reins with deftness and outward composure. Her eyes were enormous, her pale face paler. She wore last year's second best gray cheviot, lined, boned, basqued, and (though plain for its day) braided all the way down the front with an elaborate pattern of curlycues. Her gray straw bonnet was trimmed only with a puff of velvet and a bird. Her feet, in high buttoned shoes, were found to touch the wagon floor with difficulty, so at the last minute a footstool was snatched from the house and placed so that she might brace herself properly during the long and racking drive. This article of furniture was no more at variance with its surroundings than the driver herself. A plump round mahogany foot rest it was, covered with a gay tapestry that had been stitched by Sabra's grandmother on the distaff side. Its pattern of faded scarlet and yellow and blue represented what seemed to be a pair of cockatoos sparring in a rose bush. Yancey had swung Cim up to the calico-cushioned seat beside Sabra. His short legs, in their copper-toed boots, stuck straight out in front of him. His dark eyes were huge with excitement. "Why don't we go?" he demanded, over and over, in something like a scream. He shouted to the horses as he had heard teamsters do. "Giddap in 'ere! Gee-op! G'larng!" His grandmother and grandfather, gazing up with sudden agony in their faces at sight of this little expedition actually faring forth so absurdly into the unknown, had ceased to exist for Cim. As Sabra drove one wagon and Yancey the other, the boy pivoted between them through the long drive, spending the morning in the seat beside his mother, the afternoon beside his father, with intervals of napping curled up on the bedding at the back of the wagon. All through the first day they could do nothing with him. He yelled, "Giddap! Whoa! Gee-op!" until he was hoarse, pausing only to shoot imaginary bears, panthers, wildcats and Indians, and altogether working himself up into such a state of excitement and exhaustion that he became glittering eyed and feverish and subsequently had to be inconveniently dosed with castor oil.

Now, with a lurch and a rattle and a great clatter of hoofs the two wagons were off. Sabra had scarcely time for one final frantic look at her father and mother, at minor massed Venables, at the servants' black faces that seemed all rolling eyeballs. She was so busy with the horses, with Cim, so filled with a dizzy mixture of fright and exhilaration and a kind of terror-stricken happiness that she forgot to turn and look back, as she had meant to, like the heroine in a melodrama, at the big white house, at the hedge, at the lovely untidy garden, at the three great elms. Later she reproached herself for this. And she would say to the boy, in the bare treeless ugliness of the town that became their home, "Cim, do you remember the yellow and purple flags that used to come up first thing in the spring, in the yard?"

"What yard?"

"Granny's yard, back home."

"Nope."

"Oh, Cim!"

It was as though the boy's life had begun with this trip. The four previous years of his existence seemed to be sponged from his mind like yesterday's exercise from a slate. Perched beside his father on the high wagon seat his thirsty little mind drank in tales that became forever part of his consciousness and influenced his whole life.

They had made an early start. By ten the boy's eyes were heavy with sleep. He refused stubbornly to lie on the mattress inside the larger wagon; denied that he was sleepy. Sabra coaxed him to curl up on the wagon seat, his head in her lap. She held the reins in one hand; one arm was about the child. It was hot and still and drowsy. Noon came with surprising swiftness. They had brought along a precious keg of water and a food supply sufficient, they thought, to last through most of the trip—salt pork, mince and apple pies, bread, doughnuts—but their appetites were enormous. At midday they stopped and ate in the shade. Sabra prepared the meal while Yancey tended the horses. Cim, wide awake now and refreshed, ate largely with them of the fried salt pork and potatoes, the hard-boiled eggs, the mince pie. He was even given one of the precious oranges with which the journey had been provided by his grandparents. It was all very gay and comfortable and relaxed. Short as the morning had been, the afternoon stretched out, somehow, endless. Sabra began to be horribly tired, cramped. The boy whimpered. It was mid-afternoon and hot; it was late afternoon; then the brilliant Western sunset began to paint the sky. Yancey, in the wagon ahead, drew up, gazed about, got out, tied his team to one of a clump of cottonwoods.

"We'll camp here," he called to Sabra and came toward her wagon, prepared to lift her down, and the boy. She was stiff, utterly weary. She stared down at him, dully, then around the landscape.

"Camp?"

"Yes. For the night. Come, Cim." He lifted the boy down with a great swoop.

"You mean for the night? Sleep here?"

He was quite matter-of-fact. "Yes. It's a good place. Water and trees. I'll have a fire before you can say Jack Robinson. Where'd you think you were going to sleep? Back home?"

Somehow she had not thought. She had not believed it. To sleep out of doors like this, in the open, with only a wagon top as roof! All her neat conventional life she had slept in a four-poster bed with a dotted Swiss canopy and net curtains and linen sheets that smelled sweetly of the sun and the air.

Yancey began to make camp. Already the duties of this new manner of living had become familiar. There was wood to gather, a fire to start, water to be boiled. Cim, very wide awake now, trotted after his father, after his mother. Meat began to sizzle appetizingly in the pan. The exquisite scent of coffee revived them with its promise of stimulation.

"That roll of carpet," called Sabra, busy at the fire, to Yancey at the wagon. "Under the seat. I want Cim to sit on it . . . ground may be damp. . . ."

A sudden shout from Yancey. A squeal of terror from the bundle of carpeting in his arms—a bundle that suddenly was alive and wriggling. Yancey dropped it with an oath. The bundle lay on the ground a moment, heaving, then it began to unroll itself while the three regarded it with starting eyes. A black paw, a woolly head, a face all open mouth and whites of eyes. Black Isaiah. He had found a way to come with them to the Indian Territory.

5

BY NOON NEXT day they were wondering how they had got on at all without him. He gathered wood. He started fires. He tended Cim like a nurse, played with him, sang to him, helped put him to bed, slept anywhere, like a little dog. He even helped Sabra to drive her team, change and change about, for after all there was little to it but the holding of the reins slackly in one's fingers while the horses plodded across the prairie, mile on mile, mile on mile.

Yancey pointed out the definiteness with which the land changed when they left Kansas and came into the Oklahoma country. "Okla-homa," he explained to Cim. "That's Choctaw. Okla—people. Humma—red. Red People. That's what they called it when the Indians came here to live."

Suddenly the land, too, had become red: red clay as far as the eye could see. The rivers and little creeks were sanguine with it, and at sunset the sky seemed to reflect it, so that sometimes Sabra's eyes burned with all this scarlet. When the trail led through a cleft in a hill the blood red of the clay on either side was like a gaping wound. Sabra shrank from it. She longed for the green of Kansas. The Oklahoma sky was not blue but steel color, and all through the day it was a brazen sheet of glittering tin over their heads. Its glare seared the eyeballs.

It was a hard trip for the child. He was by turns unruly and listless. He could not run about, except when they stopped to make camp. Sabra, curiously enough, had not the gift of amusing him as Yancey had, or even Isaiah. Isaiah told him tales that were negro folklore, handed down by word of mouth through the years. Like the songs he sang, these were primitive accounts of the sorrows and the tribulations of a wronged people and their inevitable reward in after life.

"An' de angel say to him, he say, 'Mose, come on up on dis'ya throne an' eat 'case yo' hongry, an' drink 'case yo' parch, and res' yo' weary an' achin' feet . . .' "

But when he rode with his father he heard thrilling tales. If it was just before his bedtime, after their early supper had been eaten, Yancey invariably began his story with the magic words, "It was on just such a night as this . . ."

There would follow a legend of buried treasure. Spanish conquistadores wandered weary miles over plains and prairie and desert, led, perhaps, by the false golden promises of some captured Indian eager to get back to the home of his own tribe far away. Like all newly settled countries, there were here hundreds of such tales. The sparsely settled land was full of them. The poorer the class the more glittering the treasure. These people, wresting a meager living from the barren plains, consoled themselves with tales of buried Spanish gold; of jewels. No hairy squatter or nester in his log cabin with his bony parchment-skinned wife and litter of barelegged brats but had some tale of long-sought treasure. Cim heard dozens of these tales as they dragged their way across the red clay of Oklahoma, as they forded rivers, passed little patches of blackjack or cottonwood. He was full of them. They became as real to him as the rivers and trees themselves.

During the day Yancey told him stories of the Indians. He taught him the names of the Five Civilized Tribes, and Cim remembered the difficult Indian words and repeated them—Cherokee, Choctaw, Creek, Seminole, and Chickasaw. He heard the Indian story, not in terms of raids, scalpings, tomahawk, and tom-tom, but as the saga of a tricked and wronged people. Yancey Cravat needed only a listener. That that listener was four, and quite incapable of comprehending the significance of what he heard, made no difference to Cravat. He told the boy the terrific story of the Trail of Tears— of the Cherokee Nation, a simple and unnomadic people, driven from their homes in Georgia, like cattle across hundreds of miles of plain and prairie to die by the thousands before they reached the Oklahoma land that had been allotted to them, with two thousand troops under General Winfield Scott to urge on their flagging footsteps.

"Why did they make the Indians go away?"

"They wanted the land for themselves."

"Why?"

"It had marble, and gold and silver and iron and lead, and great forests. So they took all this away from them and drove them out. They promised them things and then broke their promise."

Sabra was horrified at Cim's second-hand recital of this saga. He told her all about it as he later sat on the seat beside her. "Uncle Sam is a mean bad man. He took all the farms and the gold and the silver and the buff'-loes away from the Indians and made them go away and they didn't want to go and so they went and they died."

He knew more about David Payne than about Columbus. He was more familiar with Quanah Parker, the Comanche, with Elias Boudinot and General Stand Waitie, his brother, both full-blooded Cherokees, than he was with the names of Lincoln and Washington.

Sabra, in her turn, undertook to wipe this impression from the boy's mind. "Indians are bad people. They take little boys from their mammas and never bring them back. They burn down people's houses, and hurt them. They're dirty and lazy, and they steal."

She was unprepared for the hysterical burst of protest that greeted this. The boy grew white with rage. "They're not. You're a liar. I hate you. I won't ride with you."

He actually prepared to climb down over the wagon wheel. She clutched at him with one hand, shook him smartly, cuffed him. He kicked her. She stopped the team, wound the reins, took him over her knee and spanked him soundly. He announced, through his tears, that he was going to run away and join the Indians and never come back. If she could have known that his later life was to be shaped by Yancey's tales and this incident, certainly her protests would have been even more forceful than they were.

"Why can't you talk to him about something besides those dirty thieving Indians? There's enough to teach him about the history of his country, I should think. George Washington and Jefferson Davis and Captain John Smith . . ."

"The one who married Pocahontas, you mean?"

"I declare, Yancey, sometimes I wonder if———"

"What?"

"Oh—nothing."

But often the days were gay enough. They fell into the routine, adjusted themselves to the discomfort. At first Sabra had been so racked with the jolting of the wagon that she was a cripple by night. Yancey taught her how to relax; not to brace herself against the wagon's jolting but to sway easily with it. By the second day her young body had accustomed itself to the motion. She actually began to enjoy it, and at the journey's end missed it as a traveler at sea misses the roll and dip of a ship. By this time she had the second-best gray cheviot open at the throat and her hair in a long black braid. She looked like a schoolgirl. She had got out the sunbonnet which one of the less formidable Venables had jokingly given her at parting, and this she wore to shield her eyes from the pitiless glare of sky and plain. The gray straw bonnet, with its puff of velvet and its bird, reposed in its box in the back of the wagon. The sight of her in that prairie wilderness engaged in the domestic task of beating up a bowl of biscuit dough struck no one as being incongruous. The bread supply was early exhausted. She baked in a little portable tin oven that Yancey had fitted out for her.

As for Yancey himself, Sabra had never known him so happy. He was tireless, charming, varied. She herself was fascinated by his tales of hidden mines, of Spanish doubloons, of iron chests plowed up by some gaunt homesteader's hand plow hitched to a stumbling mule. Yancey roared snatches of cowboy songs:

> When I was young I was a reckless lad,
> Lots of fun with the gals I had,
> I took one out each day fur a ride,
> An' I always had one by my side.
> I'd hug 'em an' kiss 'em just fur fun,
> An' I've proposed to more'n one,
> If there's a gal here got a kiss for me,
> She'll find me as young as I used to be.

Hi rickety whoop ti do,
How I love to sing to you.
Oh, I could sing an' dance with glee,
If I was as young as I used to be.

Once they saw him whip a rattlesnake to death with his wagon whip. They had unhitched the horses to water them. Yancey, whip in hand, had taken them down to the muddy stream, Cim leaping and shouting at his side. His two guns, in their holsters, lay on the ground with the belt which he had just now unstrapped from about his waist. Sabra saw the thick coil, the wicked head. Perhaps she sensed it. She screamed horribly, stood transfixed. The boy's face was a mask of fright. Yancey lashed out once with his whip, the thing struck out, he lashed again, again, again, in a kind of fury. She turned away, sickened. The whip kept up its whistle, its snap. The coiled thing lay in ribbons. Isaiah, though ashen with fright, still had to be forcibly restrained from prowling among the mass for the rattlers which, with some combination of sunset and human saliva, were supposed to be a charm against practically every misfortune known to man. Cim had nightmare all that night and awoke screaming.

Once they saw the figure of a solitary horseman against the sunset sky. Inexplicably the figure dismounted, stood a moment, mounted swiftly and vanished.

"What was that?"

"That was an Indian."

"How could you tell?"

"He dismounted on the opposite side from a white man."

That night it was Sabra who did not sleep. She held the boy tight in her arms. Every snap of a twig, every stamp of a horse's hoof caused her to start up in terror.

Yancey tried in vain to reassure her. "Indian? What of it? Indians aren't anything to be scared of. Not any more."

She remembered something that Mother Bridget had said. "They're no different. They haven't changed since Joshua."

"Since what?" He was very sleepy.

"Joshua."

He could make nothing of this. He was asleep again, heavily, worn out with the day's journey.

The wind, at certain periods of the year, blows almost without ceasing in Oklahoma. And when it rains the roads become slithering bogs of greased red dough, so that a wagon will sink and slide at the same time. They had two days of rain during which they plodded miserably, inch by inch. Cim squalled, Isaiah became just a shivering black lump of misery, and Sabra thought of her dimity-hung bed back home in Wichita; of the garden in the cool of the evening; of the family gathered in the dining room; of the pleasant food, the easy talk, the luxurious ease. "Lak yo' breakfus' in bed, Miss Sabra? Mizzly mo'nin'."

At Pawnee Yancey saw fresh deer tracks. He saddled a horse and was off. They had, before this, caught bass in the streams, and Yancey had shot prairie chicken and quail, and Sabra had fried them delicately. But this was their first promise of big game. Sabra felt no fear at being left alone with the two children. It was mid-afternoon. She was happy, peaceful. There was about this existence a delightful detachment. Her prim girlhood, which, because she had continued to live in her parents' household, had lasted into her marriage, was now behind her. Ahead of her lay all manner of unknown terrors and strangeness, but here in the wilderness she was secure. She ruled her little world. Her husband was hers, alone. Her child, too. The little black boy Isaiah was as much her slave as though the Emancipation Proclamation had never been. Here, in the wide freedom of the prairie, she was, temporarily at least, suspended out of the reach of human interference.

Now she welcomed this unexpected halt. She and Isaiah carried water from the creek and washed a few bits of clothes and hung them to dry. She bathed Cim. She heated water for herself and bathed gratefully. She set Isaiah to gathering fuel for the evening meal, while Cim played in the shade of the clump of scrub oak. She was quite serene. She listened for the sound of horse's hoofs that would announce Yancey's triumphant return. She could hear Cim as he played under the trees, crooning to himself some snatch of song that Yancey had taught him. Vaguely she began to wonder if Yancey should not have returned by now. She brushed her hair thoroughly, enjoying the motion, throwing it over her head and bending far forward in that contortionistic attitude required by her task. After she had braided it she decided to leave it in a long thick plait down her back. Audaciously she tied it with a bright red ribbon, smiling to think of what Yancey would say. She tidied the wagon. She was frankly worried now. Nothing could happen. Of course nothing could happen. And in another part of her mind she thought that any one of a dozen dreadful things could happen. Indians. Why not? Some wild thing in the woods. Broken bones. A fall from his horse. He might lose his way. Suppose she had to spend the night alone here on the prairie with the two children. Here was the little clump of scrub oaks. The land just beyond showed a series of tiny hillocks that rolled gently away toward the horizon— rolled just enough to conceal what not of horror! A head perhaps even now peering craftily over the slope's edge to see what it could see.

In a sudden panic she stepped out of the wagon with the feeling that she must have her own human things near her—Cim, Isaiah—to talk to. Cim was not there playing with his bits of stone and twigs. He had gone off with Isaiah to gather fuel, though she had forbidden it. Isaiah, his long arms full of dead twigs and small branches, was coming toward the wagon now. Cim was not with him.

"Where's Cim?"

He dropped his load, looked around. "I lef' him playin' by hisself right hyah when Ah go fetch de wood. Ain' he in de wagon?"

"No. No."

"Might be he crep' in de print wagon."

"Wagon?" She ran to the other wagon, peered inside, called. He was not there.

Together they looked under the wagons, behind the trees. Cim! Cim! Cimarron Cravat, if you are hiding I shall punish you if you don't come out this minute. A shrill note of terror crept into her voice. She began to run up and down, calling him. She began to scream his name, her voice cracking grotesquely. Cim! Cim! She prayed as she ran, mumblingly. O God, help me find him. O God, don't let anything happen to him. Dear God, help me find him—Cim! Cim! Cim!

She had heard among pioneer stories that of the McAlastair wagon train crossing the continent toward California in '49. The Benson party had got separated perhaps a half day's journey from the front section when scouts brought news of Indians on the trail. Immediately they must break camp and hurry on to join the section ahead for mutual protection. In the midst of the bustle and confusion it was discovered that a child—a boy of three—was missing. The whole party searched at first confidently, then frenziedly, then despairingly. The parents of the missing child had three other small children and another on the way. Every second's delay meant possible death to every other member of the party. They must push on. They appealed to the mother. "I'll go on," she said, and the wagon train wound its dusty way across the plains. The woman sat ashen faced, stony, her eyes fixed in a kind of perpetual horror. She never spoke of the child again.

O God! whimpered Sabra, running this way and that. O God! Oh, Cim! Cim!

She came to a little mound that dipped suddenly and unexpectedly to a draw. And there, in a hollow, she came upon him, seated before a cave in the side of the hill, the front and roof ingeniously timbered to make a log cabin. One might pass within five feet of it and never find it. Four men were seated about the doorstep outside the rude cabin. Cim was perched on the knee of one of them, who was cracking nuts for him. They were laughing and talking and munching nuts and having altogether a delightful time of it. Sabra's knees suddenly became weak. She was trembling. She stumbled as she ran toward him. Her face worked queerly. The men sprang up, their hands at their hips.

"The man is cracking nuts for me," remarked Cim, sociably, and not especially glad to see her.

The man on whose knee he sat was a slim young fellow with a sandy mustache and a red handkerchief knotted cowboy fashion around his throat. He put the boy down gently as Sabra came up, and rose with a kind of easy grace.

"You ran away—you—we hunted every—Cim———" she stammered, and burst into tears of mingled anger and relief.

The slim young man seemed the spokesman, though the other three were obviously older than he.

"Why, I'm real sorry you was distressed, ma'am. We was going to bring the boy back safe enough. He wandered down here lookin' for his pa, he said." He was standing with one hand resting lightly, tenderly, on Cim's head, and looking down at Sabra with a smile of utter sweetness. His was the soft-spoken, almost caressing voice of the Southwestern cowman and ranger. At this Sabra's anger, born of fright, vanished. Besides, he was so young—scarcely more than a boy.

"Well," she explained, a little sheepishly, "I was worried. . . . My husband went off on the track of a deer . . . hours ago . . . he hasn't come back . . . then when Cim . . . I came out and he was gone. . . . I was so—so terribly . . ."

She looked very wan and schoolgirlish in her prim gray dress and with her hair in a braid tied with a bright red ribbon, and her tear-stained cheeks.

One of the men who had strolled off a little way with the appearance of utmost casualness returned to the group in time to hear this. "He'll be back any minute now," he announced. "He didn't get no deer."

"But how do you know?"

The soft-spoken young man shot a malignant look at the other, and the older man looked suddenly abashed. Sabra's question went unanswered. "Won't you sit and rest yourself, ma'am?" suggested the spokesman. The words were hospitable enough, yet there was that in the boy's tone which conveyed to Sabra the suggestion that she and Cim had better be gone. She took Cim's hand. Now that her fright was past she thought she must have looked very silly running down the draw with her tears and her pigtail and her screaming. She thanked them, using a little Southern charm and Southern drawl, which she often legitimately borrowed from the ancestral Venables for special occasions such as this.

"I'm ve'y grateful to you-all," she now said. "You've been mighty kind.

If you would just drop around to our camp I'm sure my husband would be delighted to meet you."

The young man smiled more sweetly than ever, and the others looked at him, an inexplicable glint of humor in their weather-beaten faces.

"I sure thank you, ma'am. We're movin' on, my friends here and me. Pronto. Floyd, how about you getting a piece of deer meat for the lady, seeing she's been cheated of her supper. Now, if you and the little fella don't mind sittin' up behind and before, why, I'll take you back a ways. You probably run fu'ther than you expected, ma'am, scared as you was." She had, as a matter of fact, in her terror, run almost half a mile from camp.

He mounted first. His method of accomplishing this was something of a miracle. At one moment the horse was standing ready and he was at its side. The next there was a flash, and he was on its back. It was like an optical illusion in which he seemed to have been drawn to the saddle as a needle flies to the magnet. Cim he drew up to the pommel, holding him with one hand; Sabra, perched on the horse's rump, clung with both arms round the lad's slim waist. Something of a horsewoman, she noticed his fine Mexican saddle, studded with silver. From the sides of the saddle hung hair-covered pockets whose bulge was the outline of a gun. A slicker such as is carried by those who ride the trails made a compact ship-shape roll behind the saddle. The horse had a velvet gait, even with this triple load. Sabra found herself wishing that this exhilarating ride might go on for miles. Suddenly she noticed that the young rider wore gloves. The sight of them made her vaguely uneasy, as though some memory had been stirred. She had never seen a plainsman wearing gloves. It was absurd, somehow.

A hundred feet or so from the camp he reined in his horse abruptly, half turned in his saddle, and with his free hand swung Sabra gently to the ground, leaning far from his saddle and keeping a firm hold on Cim and reins as he did so. He placed the child in her upraised arms, wheeled, and was gone before she could open her lips to frame a word of thanks. The piece of deer meat, neatly wrapped, lay on the ground at her feet. She stood staring after the galloping figure, dumbly. She took Cim's hand. Together they ran toward the camp. Isaiah had a fire going, a pot of coffee bubbling. His greeting to Cim was sternly admonitory. Ten minutes later Yancey galloped in, empty handed.

"What a chase he led me! Twice I thought I had him. I'd have run him into Texas if I hadn't thought you'd be———"

Sabra, for the first time since her marriage, felt superior to him; was impatient of his tale of prowess. She had her own story to tell, spiced with indignation. She was not interested in his mythical deer. She had an actual piece of fresh deer meat to cook for their supper.

". . . and just when I was ready to die with fright, there he was, talking to those four men, and sitting on the knee of one of them as though he'd known him all his life eating nuts. . . . Anything might have happened to him and to me while you were off after your old deer."

Yancey seemed less interested in the part that she and Cim had played in the adventure than in the appearance and behavior of the four men in the draw, and especially the charming young man who had so gallantly brought them back.

"Thin faced, was he? And a youngster? About nineteen or twenty? What else?"

"Oh, a low voice, and kind of sweet, as though he sang tenor. And his teeth———"

Yancey interrupted. "Long, weren't they? The two at the side, I mean. Like a wolf's?"

"Yes. How did you———— Do you know him?"

"Sort of," Yancey answered, thoughtfully.

Sabra was piqued. "It was lucky for us it was someone who knows you, probably. Because you don't seem to care much about what happened to us—what might have happened."

"You said you wanted to go a-pioneering."

"Well?"

"This is it. Stir that fire, Isaiah. Sabra, get that deer meat a-frizzling that your friend gave you. Because we're moving on."

"Now? To-night? But it's late. I thought we were camping here for the night."

"We'll eat and get going. Moonlight to-night. I don't just like it here. There's been a lot of time lost this afternoon. We'll push on. In another day or so. with luck, we'll be in Osage, snug and safe."

They ate hurriedly. Yancey seemed restless, anxious to be off.

They jolted on. Cim slept, a little ball of weariness, in the back of the wagon. Isaiah drowsed beside Sabra, and she herself was half asleep, the reins slack in her hands. The scent of the sun-warmed prairie came up to her, and the pungent smell of the sagebrush. The Indians had swept over this plain in hordes; and buffalo by the millions. She wondered if the early Spaniards, in their lust for gold, had trod this ground—perhaps this very trail. Coronado, De Soto, Narvaez. She had seen pictures of them, these dark-skinned élégantes in their cumbersome trappings of leather and heavy metal, tramping the pitiless plains of this vast Southwest, searching like children for cities of gold. . . . The steady clop-clop of the horses' feet, the rattle of the wagon, the squeak of the wheels, the smell of sun-baked earth . . .

She must have dozed off, for suddenly the sun's rays were sharply slanted, and she shivered with the cool of the prairie night air. Voices had awakened her. Three horsemen had dashed out of a little copse and stood in the path of Yancey's lead wagon. They were heavily armed. Their hands rested on their guns. Their faces were grim. They wore the mournful mustaches of the Western plainsman, their eyes were the eyes of men accustomed to great distances; their gaze was searing. All three wore the badge of United States marshals, but there was about them something that announced this even before the eye was caught by their badge of office. The leader addressed Yancey, his voice mild, even gentle.

"Howdy."

"Howdy."

"Where you bound for, pardner?"

"Osage."

The questioner's hand rested lightly on the butt of the six-shooter at his waist. "What might your name be?"

"Cravat—Yancey Cravat."

The spokesman's face lighted up with the slow, incredulous smile of a delighted child. "I'll be doggoned!" He turned his slow grin on the man at his right, on the man at his left. "Yancey Cravat!" he said again, as though they had not heard. "I sure am pleased to make your acquaintance. Heard about you till I feel like I knew you."

"Why, thanks," replied Yancey, unusually modest and laconic. Sabra knew then that Yancey was playing one of his rôles. He would talk as they talked. Be one of them.

"Aimin' to make quite a stay in Osage?"

"Aim to live there."

"Go on! I've a notion to swear you in as Deputy Marshal right now, darned if I ain't. Citizens like you is what we need, and no mistake. Lawy'in'?''

"I'm planning to take up my law practice in Osage, yes," Yancey answered, "and start a newspaper as well."

The three looked a little perturbed at this. They glanced at each other, then at Yancey, then away, uncomfortably. "Oh, newspaper, huh?" There was little enthusiasm in the marshal's voice. "Well, we did have a newspaper there for a little while in Osage, 'bout a week."

"A daily?"

"A weekly."

There was something sinister in this. "What became of it?"

"Well, seems the editor—name of Pegler—died."

There was a little silence. Sabra gathered up her reins and brought her team alongside Yancey's, the better to hear. The three mustached ones acknowledged her more formal presence by briefly touching their hat brims with the forefinger of the hand that had rested on their guns.

"Who killed him?"

A little shadow of pained surprise passed over the features of the marshal. "He was just found dead one morning on the banks of the Canadian. Bullet wounds. But bullets is all pretty much alike, out here. He might 'a' killed himself, plumb discouraged."

The silence fell again. Yancey broke it. "The first edition of the *Oklahoma Wigwam* will be off the press two weeks from to-morrow."

He gathered up the reins as though to end this chance meeting, however agreeable. "Well, gentlemen, good-evening. Glad to have met you."

The three did not budge. "What we stopped to ask you," said the spokesman, in his gentle drawl, "was, did you happen to glimpse four men anywhere on the road? They're nesting somewheres in here, the Kid and his gang. Stole four horses, robbed the bank at Red Fork, shot the cashier, and lit out for the prairie. Light complected, all of 'em. The Kid is a slim young fella, light hair, red handkerchief, soft spoken, and rides with gloves on. But then you know what he's like, Cravat, well's I do."

Yancey nodded in agreement. "Everybody's heard of the Kid. No, sir, I haven't seen him. Haven't seen anybody the last three days but a Kaw on a pony and a bunch of dirty Cheyennes in a wagon. Funny thing, I never yet knew a bad man who wasn't light complected—or, anyway, blue or gray eyes."

"Oh, say, now!" protested the marshal, stroking his sandy mustache.

"Fact. You take the Kid, and the James boys, and Tom O'Phalliard, and the whole Mullins gang."

"How about yourself? You're pretty good with the gun, from all accounts. And black as a crow."

Yancey lifted his great head and the heavy lids that usually drooped over the gray eyes and looked at the marshal. "That's so," said the other, as though in agreement at the end of an argument. "I reckon it goes fur killers and fur killers of killers. . . . Well, boys, we'll be lopin'. Good luck to you."

"Good luck to *you!*" responded Yancey, politely.

The three whirled their steeds spectacularly, raised their right hands in salute; the horses pivoted on their hind legs prettily; Cim crowed with delight. They were off in a cloud of red dust made redder by the last rays of the setting sun.

Yancey gathered up his reins. Sabra stared at him in bewildered indignation. "But the person who shields a criminal is just as bad as the criminal himself, isn't he?"

Yancey looked back at her around the side of his wagon top. His smile was mischievous, sparkling, irresistible. "Don't be righteous, Sabra. It's middle class—and a terrible trait in a woman."

Late next day, just before sunset, after pushing on relentlessly through the blistering sun of midday, Yancey pointed with his wagon whip to something that looked like a wallow of mud dotted with crazy shanties and tents. Theatrically he picked Cim up in his arms so that the child, too, might see. But he spoke to Sabra.

"There it is," he said. "That's our future home."

Sabra looked. And her brain seemed to have no order or reason about it, for she could think only of the green nun's veiling trimmed with ruchings of pink which lay so carefully folded, with its modish sleeves all stuffed out with soft paper, in the trunk under the canvas of the wagon.

6

LONG BEFORE THE end of that first nightmarish day in Osage, Sabra had confronted her husband with blazing eyes. "I won't bring up my boy in a town like this!"

It had been a night and a day fantastic with untoward happenings. Their wagons had rumbled wearily down the broad main street of the settlement— a raw gash in the prairie. All about, on either side, were wooden shacks, and Indians and dried mud and hitching posts and dogs and crude wagons like their own. It looked like pictures Sabra had seen of California in '49. They had supped on ham and eggs, fried potatoes, and muddy coffee in a place labeled Ice Cream and Oyster Parlor. They spent that first night in a rooming house above one of the score of saloons that enlivened the main street—Pawhuska Avenue, it was called. It was a longish street, for the Osage town settlers seemed to have felt the need of huddling together for company in this wilderness. The street stopped abruptly at either end and became suddenly prairie.

"Pawhuska Avenue," said a tipsy sign tacked on the front of a false-front pine shack. Yancey chose this unfortunate time to impart a little Indian lore to Cim, wide eyed on the wagon seat beside his mother.

"That's Osage," he shouted to the boy. "Pawhu—that means hair. And scah, that means white. White Hair. Pawhuska—White Hair—was an old Osage Chief———"

"Yancey Cravat!" Sabra called in a shout that almost equaled his own, and in a tone startlingly like one of Felice Venable's best (she was, in fact, slightly hysterical, what with weariness and disappointment and fear), "Yancey Cravat, will you stop talking Indian history and find us a place to eat and sleep! Where's your sense? Can't you see he's ready to drop, and so am I?"

The greasy food set before them in the eating house sickened her. She shrank from the slatternly bold-faced girl who slammed the dishes down in front of them on the oilcloth-covered table. At this same table with them— there was only one, a long board accommodating perhaps twenty—sat red-faced men talking in great rough voices, eating with a mechanical and absent-minded thoroughness, shoveling potatoes, canned vegetables, pie into their mouths with knives. Cim was terribly wide awake and noisily unruly, excited by the sounds and strangeness about him.

"I'm an Indian!" he would yell, making a great clatter with his spoon on the table. "Ol' White Hair! Wa-wa-wa-wa-wa-wa-wa!" Being reprimanded, and having the spoon forcibly removed from his clutching fingers, he burst into tears and howls.

Sabra had taken him up to the bare and clean enough little room which was to be their shelter for the night. From wide-eyed wakefulness Cim had become suddenly limp with sleep. Yancey had gone out to see to the horses, to get what information he could about renting a house, and a shack for the newspaper. A score of plans were teeming in his mind.

"You'll be all right," he had said. "A good night's sleep and everything'll look rosy in the morning. Don't look so down in the mouth, honey. You're going to like it."

"It's horrible! It's—and those men! Those dreadful men."

" 'For my part, I had rather be the first man among these fellows than the second man in Rome.' " Yancey struck an attitude.

Sabra looked at him dully. "Rome?"

"Plutarch, my sweet." He kissed her; was gone with a great flirt of his coat tails. She heard his light step clattering down the flimsy wooden stairs. She could distinguish his beautiful vibrant voice among the raucous speech of the other men below.

The boy was asleep in a rude box bed drawn up beside theirs. Black Isaiah was bedded down somewhere in a little kennel outside. Sabra sank suspiciously down on the doubtful mattress. The walls of the room were wafer thin; mere pine slats with cracks between. From the street below came women's shrill laughter, the sound of a piano hammered horribly. Horses clattered by. Voices came up in jocose greeting; there were conversations and arguments excruciatingly prolonged beneath her window.

"I was sellin' a thousand beef steers one time—holdin' a herd of about three thousand—and me and my foreman, we was countin' the cattle as they come between us. Well, the steers was wild long-legged coasters—and run! Say, they come through between us like scairt wolves, and I lost the count . . ."

"Heard where the Mullins gang rode in there this morning and cleaned up the town—both banks—eleven thousand in one and nineteen thousand in the other, and when they come out it looked like the whole county'd rallied against 'em. . . ."

"Say, he's a bad hombre, that fella. Got a poisoned tongue, like a rattlesnake. . . . Spades trump?"

"No, hearts. Say, I would of known how to handle him. One time we was campin' on Amarillo Creek . . ."

A loud knock at the door opposite Sabra's room. The knock repeated. Then a woman's voice, metallic, high. *"Quien es? Quien es?"* The impatient rattle of a door knob, and a man's gruff voice.

A long-drawn wail in the street below, "Oh, Joe! He-e-e-ere's your mule!" followed by a burst of laughter.

Yet somehow she had fallen asleep in utter exhaustion, only to be awakened by pistol shots, a series of blood-curdling yells, the crash and tinkle of broken glass. Then came screams of women, the sound of horses galloping. She lay there, cowering. Cim stirred in his bed, sighed deeply, slept again. She was too terrified to go to the window. Her shivering seemed to shake the bed. She wanted to waken the child for comfort, for company. She summoned courage to go to the window; peered fearfully out into the dim street below. Nothing. No one in the street. Yancey's bleeding body was not lying in the road; no masked men. Nothing again but the clink of glasses and plates; the tinny piano, the slap of cards.

She longed with unutterable longing, not for the sweet security of her bed back in Wichita—that seemed unreal now—but for those nights in the wagon on the prairie with no sound but the rustle of the scrub oaks, the occasional stamp of horses' hoofs on dry clay, the rippling of a near-by stream. She looked at her little gold watch, all engraved with a bird and a branch and a waterfall and a church spire. It was only nine.

It was midnight when Yancey came in. She sat up in bed in her high-necked, long-sleeved nightgown. Her eyes, in her white face, were two black holes burned in a piece of paper.

"What was it? What was it?"

"What was what? Why aren't you asleep, sugar?"

"Those shots. And the screaming. And the men hollering."

"Shots?" He was unstrapping his broad leather belt with its twin six-shooters whose menacing heads peered just above their holsters. He wore it always now. It came, in time, to represent for her a sinister symbol of all the terrors, all the perils that lay waiting for them in this new existence. "Why, sugar, I don't recollect hearing any—— Oh—that?" He threw back his great head and laughed. "That was just a cowboy, feeling high, shooting out the lights over in Strap Turket's saloon. On his way home and having a little fun with the boys. Scare you, did it?"

He came over to her, put a hand on her shoulder. She shrugged away from him, furious. She pressed her hand frantically to her forehead. It was cold and wet. She was panting a little. "I won't bring my boy up in a town like this. I won't. I'm going back. I'm going back home, I tell you."

"Wait till morning, anyhow, won't you, honey?" he said, and took her in his arms.

Next morning was, somehow, magically, next morning, with the terrors of the night vanished quite. The sun was shining. For a moment Sabra had the illusion that she was again at home in her own bed at Wichita. Then she realized that this was because she had been awakened by a familiar sound. It was the sound of Isaiah's voice somewhere below in the dusty yard. He was polishing Yancey's boots, spitting on them industriously and singing as he rubbed. His husky sweet voice came up to her as she lay there.

> Lis'en to de lambs, all a-cryin'
> Lis'en to de lambs, all a-cryin'
> Lis'en to de lambs, all a-cryin',
> Ah wanta go to heab'n when ah die.
> Come on, sister, wid yo' ups an' downs,
> Wanta go to heab'n when ah die,
> De angels waitin' fo' to gib yo' a crown,
> Wanta go to heab'n when ah die.

Lugubrious though the words were, Sabra knew he was utterly happy.

There was much to be done—a dwelling to be got somehow—a place in which to house the newspaper plant. If necessary, Yancey said, they could live in the rear and set up the printing and law office in the front. Almost everyone who conducted a business in the town did this. "Houses are mighty scarce," Yancey said, making a great masculine snorting and snuffling at the wash bowl as they dressed. "It's take what you can get or live in a tent. I heard last night that Doc Nisbett's got a good house. Five rooms, and he'll furnish us with water. There're a dozen families after it, and Doc's as independent as a hog on ice."

Sabra rather welcomed this idea of combining office and home. She would be near him all day. As soon as breakfast was over she and Yancey fared forth, leaving Cim in Isaiah's care (under many and detailed instructions from Sabra). She had put on her black grosgrain silk with the three box pleats on each side, trimmed with the passementerie and jet buttons—somewhat wrinkled from its long stay in the trunk—and her modish hat with the five ostrich plumes and the pink roses that had cost twelve dollars and fifty cents in Wichita, and her best black buttoned kid shoes and her black kid gloves. In the tightly basqued black silk she was nineteen inches round the waist and very proud of it. Her dark eyes, slightly shadowed now, what with weariness, excitement, and loss of sleep, were enormous beneath the brim of the romantic black plumed hat.

Yancey, seeing her thus attired in splendor after almost a fortnight of the gray cheviot, struck an attitude of dazzlement. Blank verse leaped to his ready lips. " 'But who is this, what thing of land or sea,—female of sex it seems—that so bedeck'd, ornate, and gay, comes this way sailing, like a stately ship of Tarsus, bound for th' isles of Javan or Gadire, with all her bravery on. . . .' "

"Oh, now, Yancey, don't talk nonsense. It's only my second-best black grosgrain."

"You're right, my darling. Even Milton has no words for such beauty."

"Do hurry, dear. We've so much to do."

With his curling locks, his broad-brimmed white sombrero, his high-heeled boots, his fine white shirt, the ample skirts of his Prince Albert spreading and swooping with the vigor of his movements, Yancey was an equally striking figure, though perhaps not so unusual as she, in this day and place.

The little haphazard town lay broiling in the summer sun. The sky that Sabra was to know so well hung flat and glaring, a gray-blue metal disk, over the prairie.

"Well, Sabra honey, this isn't so bad!" exclaimed Yancey, and looked about him largely. " 'Now Morning saffron-robed arose from the streams of Ocean to bring light to gods and men.' "

"Ocean!" echoed Sabra, the literal. "Mighty little water I've seen around here—unless you call that desert prairie the ocean."

"And so it is, my pet. That's very poetic of you. The prairie's an ocean of land." He seemed enormously elated—jubilant, almost. His coat tails switched; he stepped high in his fine Texas star boots. She tucked her hand in her handsome husband's arm. The air was sweet, and they were young, and it was morning. Perhaps it was not going to be so dreadful, after all.

Somehow, she had yet no feeling that she, Sabra Cravat, was part of this thing. She was an onlooker. The first thing she noticed, as she stepped into the dust of the street in her modish dress and hat, caused her heart to sink. The few women to be seen scuttling about wore sunbonnets and calico—the kind of garments in which Sabra had seen the women back home in Wichita hanging up the Monday wash to dry on the line in the back yard. Here they came out of butcher's shop or grocery store with the day's provisions in their arms; a packet of meat, tins of tomatoes or peaches, unwrapped. After sharp furtive glances at Sabra, they vanished into this little pine shack or that. Immediately afterward there was great agitation among the prim coarse window curtains in those dwellings boasting such elegance.

"But the others—the other kind of women———" Sabra faltered.

Yancey misunderstood. "Plenty of the other kind in a town like this, but they aren't stirring this time of day."

"Don't be coarse, Yancey. I mean ladies like myself—that I can talk to—who'll come calling—that is———"

He waved a hand this way and that. "Why, you just saw some women folks, didn't you?"

"Those!"

"Well, now, honey, you can't expect those ladies to be wearing their best bib and tucker mornings to do the housework in. Besides, most of the men came without their women folks. They'll send for them, and then you'll have plenty of company. It isn't every woman who'd have the courage you showed, roughing it out here. You're the stuff that Rachel was made of, and the mother of the Gracchi."

Rachel was, she knew, out of the Bible; she was a little hazy about the Gracchi, but basked serene in the knowledge that a compliment was intended.

There was the absurdly wide street—surely fifty feet wide—in this little one-street town. Here and there a straggling house or so branched off it. But the life of Osage seemed to be concentrated just here. There were tents still to be seen serving as dwellings. Houses and stores were built of unpainted wood. They looked as if they had been run up overnight, as indeed they had. They stared starkly out into the wide-rutted red clay road, and the muddy road glared back at them, and the brazen sky burned with fierce intensity down on both, with never a tree or bit of green to cheer the spirit or rest the eye. Tied to the crude hitching posts driven well into the ground were all sorts of vehicles: buckboards, crazy carts, dilapidated wagons, mule drawn; here and there a top buggy covered with the dust of the prairie; and everywhere, lording it, those four-footed kings without which life in this remote place could not have been sustained—horses of every size and type and color and degree. Indian ponies, pintos, pack horses, lean long-legged range horses, and occasionally a flashing-eyed creature who spurned the red clay with the disdainful hoof of one whose ancestors have known the mesas of Spain. Direct descendants, these, of the equine patricians who, almost four hundred years before, had been brought across the ocean by Coronado or Moscoso to the land of the Seven Cities of Gold.

There were the sounds of the hammer and the saw, the rattle of chains, the thud of hoofs, all very sharp and distinct, as though this mushroom town were pulling itself out of the red clay of the prairie by its own boot straps before one's very eyes. Crude and ugly though the scene was that now spread itself before Sabra and Yancey, it still was not squalid. It had vitality. You sensed that behind those bare boards people were planning and stirring mightily. There was life in the feel of it. The very names tacked up over the store fronts had bite and sting. Sam Pack. Mott Bixler. Strap Buckner. Ike Hawes. Clint Hopper. Jim Click.

Though they had come to town but the night before, it seemed to her that a surprising number of people knew Yancey and greeted him as they passed down the street. "H'are you, Yancey! Howdy, ma'am." Loungers in doorways stared at them curiously. Cowboys loping by gave her a long hard look that still had in it something of shyness—a boyish look, much like that with which the outlaws had greeted her down in the draw on the prairie when they learned that she was Cim's mother.

It struck Sabra suddenly with a little shock of discovery that the men really were doing nothing. They lounged in doorways and against hitching posts and talked; you heard their voices in animated conversation within saloon and store and office; they cantered by gracefully, and wheeled and whirled and cantered back again. She was to learn that many of these men were not builders but scavengers. The indomitable old '49ers were no kin of these. They were, frequently, soft, cruel, furtive, and avaricious. They had gathered here to pick up what they could and move on. Some were cowmen, full of resentment against a government that had taken the free range away from them and given it over to the homesteaders. Deprived of their only occupation, many of these became outlaws. Equipped with six-shooters, a deadly aim, and horsemanship that amounted to the miraculous, they took to the Gyp Hills or the Osage, swooping down from their hidden haunts to terrorize a town, shoot up a bank, hold up a train, and dash out again, leaving blood behind them. They risked their lives for a few hundred dollars. Here was a vast domain without written laws, without precedent, without the customs of civilization; part of a great country, yet no part of its government. Here a horse was more valuable than a human life. A horse thief, caught, was summarily hanged to the nearest tree; the killer of a man often went free.

Down the street these two stepped in their finery, the man swaggering a little as a man should in a white sombrero and with a pretty woman on his arm; the woman looking about her interestedly, terrified at what she saw and determined not to show it. If two can be said to make a procession, then Yancey and Sabra Cravat formed quite a parade as they walked down Pawhuska Avenue in the blaze of the morning sun. Certainly they seemed to be causing a stir. Lean rangers in buckboards turned to stare. Loungers in doorways nudged each other, yawping. Cowboys clattering by whooped a greeting. It was unreal, absurd, grotesque.

"Hi, Yancey! Howdy, ma'am."

Past the Red Dog Saloon. A group in chairs tilted up against the wall or standing about in high-heeled boots and sombreros greeted Yancey now with a familiarity that astonished Sabra. "Howdy, Cim! Hello, Yancey!"

"He called you Cim!"

He ignored her surprised remark. Narrowly he was watching them as he passed. "Boys are up to something. If they try to get funny while you're here with me . . ."

Sabra, glancing at the group from beneath her shielding hat brim, did see that they were behaving much like a lot of snickering schoolboys who are preparing to let fly a bombardment of snowballs. There was nudging, there was whispering, an air of secret mischief afoot.

"Why are they—what do you think makes them———" Sabra began, a trifle nervously.

"Oh, they're probably fixing up a little initiation for me," Yancey explained, his tone light but his eye wary. "Don't get nervous. They won't dare try any monkeyshines while you're with me."

"But who are they?" He evaded her question. She persisted. "Who are they?"

"I can't say for sure. But I suspect they're the boys that did Pegler dirt."

"Pegler? Who is—oh, isn't that the man—the editor—the one who was found dead—shot dead on the banks of the——— Yancey? Do you mean they did it!"

"I don't say they did it—exactly. They know more than is comfortable, even for these parts. I was inquiring around last night, and everybody shut up like a clam. I'm going to find out who killed Pegler and print it in the first number of the *Oklahoma Wigwam*."

"Oh, Yancey! Yancey, I'm frightened!" She clung tighter to his arm. The grinning mirthless faces of the men on the saloon porch seemed to her like the fanged and snarling muzzles of wolves in a pack.

"Nothing to be frightened of, honey. They know me. I'm no Pegler they can scare. They don't like my white hat, that's the truth of it. Dared me last night down at the Sunny Southwest Saloon to wear it this morning. Just to try me out. They won't have the guts to come out in the open———"

The sentence never was finished. Sabra heard a curious buzzing sound past her ear. Something sang—zing! Yancey's white sombrero went spinning into the dust of the road.

Sabra's mouth opened as though she were screaming, but the sounds she would have made emerged, feebly, as a croak.

"Stay where you are," Yancey ordered, his voice low and even. "The dirty dogs." She stood transfixed. She could not have run if she had wanted to. Her legs seemed suddenly no part of her—remote, melting beneath her, and yet pricked with a thousand pins and needles. Yancey strolled leisurely over to where the white hat lay in the dust. He stooped carelessly, his back to the crowd on the saloon porch, picked up the hat, surveyed it, and reached toward his pocket for his handkerchief. At that movement there was a rush and a scramble on the porch. Tilted chairs leaped forward, heels clattered, a door slammed. The white-aproned proprietor who, tray in hand, had been standing idly in the doorway, vanished as though he had been blotted out by blackness. Of the group only three men remained. One of these leaned insolently against a porch post, a second stood warily behind him, and a third was edging prudently toward the closed door. There was nothing to indicate who had fired the shot that had sent Yancey's hat spinning.

Yancey, now half turned toward them, had taken his fine white handkerchief from his pocket, had shaken out its ample folds with a gesture of elegant leisure, and, hat in hand, was flicking the dust from his headgear. This done he surveyed the hat critically, seemed to find it little the worse for its experience unless, perhaps, one excepts the two neat round holes that were drilled, back and front, through the peak of its crown. He now placed it on his head again with a gesture almost languid, tossed the fine handkerchief into the road, and with almost the same gesture, or with another so lightning quick that Sabra's eye never followed it, his hand went to his hip. There was the crack of a shot. The man who was edging toward the door clapped his hand to his ear and brought his hand away and looked at it, and it was darkly smeared. Yancey still stood in the road, his hand at his thigh, one slim foot, in its fine high-heeled Texas star boot, advanced carelessly. His great head was lowered menacingly. His eyes, steel gray beneath the brim of the white sombrero, looked as Sabra had never before seen them look. They were terrible eyes, merciless, cold, hypnotic. She could only think of the eyes of the rattler that Yancey had whipped to death with the wagon whip on the trip across the prairie.

"A three-cornered piece, you'll find it, Lon. The Cravat sheep brand."

"Can't you take a joke, Yancey?" whined one of the three, his eyes on Yancey's gun hand.

"Joke—hell!" snarled the man who had been nicked. His hand was clapped over his ear. "God help you, Cravat."

"He always has," replied Yancey, piously.

"If your missus wasn't with you——" began the man whom Yancey had called Lon. Perhaps the rough joke would have ended grimly enough. But here, suddenly, Sabra herself took a hand in the proceedings. Her fright had vanished. These were no longer men, evil, sinister, to be feared, but mean little boys to be put in their place. She now advanced on them in the majesty of her plumes and her silk, her fine eyes flashing, her gloved forefinger admonishing them as if they were indeed naughty children. She was every inch the descendant of the Marcys of France and the very essence of that iron woman, Felice Venable.

"Don't you 'missus' me! You're a lot of miserable, good-for-nothing loafers, that's what you are! Shooting at people in the streets. You leave my husband alone. I declare, I've a notion to——"

For one ridiculous dreadful moment it looked as though she meant to slap the leathery bearded cheek of the bad man known as Lon Yountis. Certainly she raised her little hand in its neat black kid. The eyes of the three were popping. Lon Yountis ducked his head exactly like an urchin who is about to be smacked by the schoolmarm. Then, with a yelp of pure terror he fled into the saloon, followed by the other two.

Sabra stood a moment. It really looked as though she might make after them. But she thought better of it and sailed down the steps in triumph to behold a crushed, a despairing Yancey.

"Oh, my God, Sabra! What have you done to me!"

"What's the matter?"

"This time to-morrow it'll be all over the whole Southwest, from Mexico to Arkansas, that Yancey Cravat hid behind a woman's petticoats."

"But you didn't. They can't say so. You shot him very nicely in the ear, darling." Thus had a scant eighteen hours in the Oklahoma country twisted her normal viewpoint so askew that she did not even notice the grotesquerie of what she had just said.

"They're telling it now, in there. My God, a woman's got no call to interfere when men are having a little dispute."

"Dispute! Why, Yancey Cravat! He shot your hat right off your head!"

"What of it! Little friendly shooting."

The enormity of this example of masculine clannishness left her temporarily speechless with indignation. "Let's be getting on," Yancey continued, calmly. "If we're going to look at Doc Nisbett's house we'd better look at it. There are only two or three to be had in the whole town, and his is the pick of them. It's central" (Central! she thought, looking about her) "and according to what he said last night there's a room in the front big enough for getting out the paper. It'll have to be newspaper and law office in one. Then there are four rooms in the back to live in. Plenty."

"Oh, plenty," echoed Sabra, thinking of the nine or ten visiting Venables always comfortably tucked away in the various high-ceilinged bedrooms in the Wichita house.

They resumed their walk. Sabra wondered if she had imagined the shooting outside the Red Dog Saloon.

Doc Nisbett (veterinarian) shirt sleeved, shrewd, with generations of New England ancestry behind him, was seated in a chair tipped up against the front of his coveted property. Nothing of the brilliant Southwest sun had mellowed the vinegar of his chemical make-up. In the rush for Territory town sites at the time of the Opening he had managed to lay his gnarled hands on five choice pieces. On these he erected dwellings, tilted his chair up against each in turn, and took his pick of late-comers frantic for some sort of shelter they could call a home. That perjury, thieving, trickery, gun play, and murder had gone into the acquiring of these—as well as many other—sites was not considered important or, for that matter, especially interesting.

The dwelling itself looked like one of Cim's childish drawings of a house. The roof was an inverted V; there was a front door, a side door, and a spindling little porch. It was a box, a shelter merely, as angular and unlovely as the man who owned it. The walls were no more than partitions, the floors boards laid on dirt.

Taking her cue from Yancey—"Lovely," murmured Sabra, agonized. The mantel ornaments that had been Cousin Dabney's wedding present! The hand-woven monogrammed linen! The silver cake dish with the carefree cupids. The dozen solid silver coffee spoons! "Do very nicely. Perfectly comfortable. I see. I see. I see."

"There you are!" They stood again on the porch, the tour completed. Yancey clapped his hands together gayly, as though by so doing he had summoned a genie who had tossed up the house before their very eyes. In the discussion of monthly rental he had been a child in the hands of this lean and grasping New Englander. "There you are! That's all settled." He struck an attitude. " 'Survey our empire, and behold our home!' "

"Heh, hold on a minute," rasped Doc Nisbett. "How about water?"

"Sabra, honey, you settle these little matters between you—you and the Doc—will you? I've got to run down the street and see Jesse Rickey about putting up the press and setting up the type racks and helping me haul the form tables, and then we've got the furniture to buy for the house. Meet you down the street at Hefner's Furniture Store. Ten minutes."

He was off, with a flirt of his coat tails. She would have called, "Yancey! Don't leave me!" but for a prideful reluctance to show fear before this dour-visaged man with the tight lips and the gimlet eyes. From the first he had seemed to regard her with disfavor. She could not imagine why. It was, of course, his Puritan New England revulsion against her plumes, her silks, her faintly Latin beauty.

"Well, now," repeated Doc Nisbett, nasally, "about water."

"Water?"

"How much you going to need? Renting this house depends on how much water you think you going to need. How many barrels."

Sabra had always taken water for granted, like air and sunshine. It was one of the elements. It was simply there. But since leaving Wichita there was always talk of water. Yancey, on the prairie journey, made it the basis of their camping site.

"Oh, barrels," she now repeated, trying to appear intensely practical. "Well, let—me—see. There's cooking, of course, and all the cleaning around the house, and drinking, and bathing. I always give Cim his bath in the evening if I can. You wouldn't believe how dirty that child gets by the end of the day. His knees—oh, yes—well, I should think ten barrels a day would be enough."

"Ten barrels," said Doc Nisbett, in a flat voice utterly devoid of expression, "a day."

"I should think that would be ample," Sabra repeated, judiciously.

Doc Nisbett now regarded Sabra with a look of active dislike. Then he did a strange thing. He walked across the little porch, shut the front door, locked it, put the key in his pocket, seated himself in the chair and tilted it up against the wall at exactly the angle at which they had come upon him.

Sabra stood there. Seeing her, it would have been almost impossible to believe that anyone so bravely decked out in silk and plumes and pink roses could present a figure so bewildered, so disconsolate, so defeated. Literally, she did not know what to do. She had met and surmounted many strange experiences in these last ten days. But she had been born of generations of women to whom men had paid homage. Perhaps in all her life she had never encountered the slightest discourtesy in a man, much less this abysmal boorishness.

She looked at him, her face white, shocked. She looked up, in embarrassment, at the glaring steel sky; she looked down at the blinding red dust, she looked helplessly in the direction that Yancey had so blithely taken. She glanced again at Doc Nisbett, propped so woodenly against the wall of his hateful house. His eye was as cold, as glassy, as unseeing as the eye of a dead fish.

She should, of course, have gone straight up to him and said, "Do you mean that ten barrels are too much? I didn't know. I am new to all this. Whatever you say."

But she was young, and inexperienced, and full of pride, and terribly offended. So without another word she turned and marched down the dusty street. Her head in its plumed hat was high. On either cheek burned a scarlet patch. Her eyes, in her effort to keep back the hot tears, were blazing, liquid, enormous. She saw nothing. From the saloons that lined the street there came, even at this hour of the morning, yelps and the sound of music.

And then a fearful thing happened to Sabra Cravat.

Down the street toward her came a galloping cowboy in sombrero and chaps and six-shooters. Sabra was used to such as he. Full of her troubles, she was scarcely aware that she had glanced at him. How could she know that he was just up from the plains of Texas, that this raw town represented for him the height of effete civilization, that he was, in celebration of his arrival, already howling drunk as befits a cowboy just off the range, and that never before in his life (he was barely twenty-three) had he seen a creature so gorgeous as this which now came toward him, all silk, plumes, roses, jet, scarlet cheeks, and great liquid eyes. Up he galloped; stared, wheeled, flung himself off his horse, ran toward her in his high-heeled cowboy boots (strangely enough all that Sabra could recall about him afterward were those boots as he came toward her. The gay tops were of shiny leather, and alternating around them was the figure of a dancing girl with flaring skirts, and a poker hand of cards which later she learned was a royal flush, all handsomely embossed on the patent leather cuffs of the boots). She realized, in a flash of pure terror, that he was making straight for her. She stood, petrified. He came nearer, he stood before her, he threw his arms like steel bands about her, he kissed her full on the lips, released her, leaped on his horse, and was off with a bloodcurdling yelp and a clatter and a whirl of dust.

She thought that she was going to be sick, there, in the road. Then she began to run, fleetly but awkwardly, in her flounced and bustled silken skirts. Hefner's Furniture Store. Hefner's Furniture Store. Hefner's Furniture Store. She saw it at last. Hefner's Furniture and Undertaking Parlors. A crude wooden shack, like the rest. She ran in. Yancey. Yancey! Everything looked dim to her bewildered and sun-blinded eyes. Someone came toward her. A large moist man, in shirt sleeves. Hefner, probably. My husband. My husband, Yancey Cravat. No. Sorry, ma'am. Ain't been in, I know of. Anything I can do for you, ma'am?

She blurted it, hysterically. "A man—a cowboy—I was walking along—he jumped off his horse—he—I never saw him b——— he kissed me—there on the street in broad daylight—a cowboy—he kissed———"

"Why, ma'am, don't take on so. Young fella off the range, prob'ly. Up from Texas, more'n likely, and never did see a gorgeous critter like yourself, if you'll pardon my mentioning it."

Her voice rose in her hysteria. "You don't understand! He kissed me. He k-k-k-k———" racking sobs.

"Now, now, lady. He was drunk, and you kind of went to his head. He'll ride back to Texas, and you'll be none the worse for it."

At this calloused viewpoint of a tragedy she broke down completely and buried her head on her folded arms atop the object nearest at hand. Her slim body shook with her sobs. Her tears flowed. She cried aloud like a child.

But at that a plaintive but firm note of protest entered Mr. Hefner's voice.

"Excuse me, ma'am, but that's velvet you're crying on, and water spots velvet something terrible. If you'd just lean on something else . . . "

She raised herself from the object on which she had collapsed, weeping, and looked at it with brimming eyes that widened in horror as she realized that she had showered her tears on that pride of Hefner's Furniture and Undertaking establishment, the newly arrived white velvet coffin (child's size) intended for show window purposes alone.

7

FROM DOC NISBETT, Yancey received laconic information to the effect that the house had been rented by a family whose aquatic demands were more modest than Sabra's. Sabra was inconsolable, but Yancey did not once reproach her for her mistake. It was characteristic of him that he was most charming and considerate in crises which might have been expected to infuriate him. "Never mind, sugar. Don't take on like that. We'll find a house. And, anyway, we're here. That's the main thing. God, when I think of those years in Wichita!"

"Why, Yancey! I thought you were happy there."

" 'A prison'd soul, lapped in Elysium.' Almost five years in one place—that's the longest stretch I've ever done, honey. Five years, back and forth like a trail horse; walking down to the *Wigwam* office in the morning, setting up personal and local items and writing editorials for a smug citizenry interested in nothing but the new waterworks. Walking back to dinner at noon, sitting on the veranda evenings, looking at the vegetables in the garden or the Venables in the house until I couldn't tell vegetables from Venables and began to think, by God, that I was turning into one or the other myself."

He groaned with relief, stretched his mighty arms, shook himself like a great shaggy lion. In all this welter of red clay and Indians and shirt sleeves and tobacco juice and drought he seemed to find a beauty and an exhilaration that eluded Sabra quite. But then Sabra, after those first two days, had ceased to search for a reason for anything. She met and accepted the most grotesque, the most fantastic happenings. When she looked back on the things she had done and the things she had said in the first few hours of her Oklahoma experience it was as though she were tolerantly regarding the naïvetés of a child. Ten barrels of water a day! She knew now that water, in this burning land, was a precious thing to be measured out like wine. Life here was an anachronism, a great crude joke. It was hard to realize that while the rest of the United States, in this year of 1889, was living a conventionally civilized and primly Victorian existence, in which plumbing, gaslight, trees, gardens, books, laws, millinery, Sunday churchgoing, were taken for granted, here in this Oklahoma country life had been set back according to the frontier standards of half a century earlier. Literally she was pioneering in a wilderness surrounded but untouched by civilization.

Yancey had reverted. Always—even in his staidest Wichita incarnation—a somewhat incredibly romantic figure, he now was remarkable even in this town of fantastic humans gathered from every corner of the brilliantly picturesque Southwest. His towering form, his curling locks, his massive head, his vibrant voice, his dashing dress, his florid speech, his magnetic personality drew attention wherever he went. On the day following their arrival Yancey had taken from his trunk a pair of silver-mounted ivory-handled six-shooters and a belt and holster studded with silver. She had never before seen them. She had not known that he possessed these grim and gaudy trappings. His white sombrero he had banded with a rattlesnake skin of gold and silver, with glass eyes, a treasure also produced from the secret trunk, as well as a pair of gold-mounted spurs which further enhanced the Texas star boots. Thus bedecked for his legal and editorial pursuits he was by far the best dressed and most spectacular male in all the cycloramic Oklahoma country. He had always patronized a good tailor, and because the local talent was still so limited in this new community he later sent as far as San Antonio, Texas, when his wardrobe needed replenishing.

Sabra learned many astounding things in these first few days, and among the most terrifying were the things she learned about the husband to whom she had been happily married for more than five years. She learned, for example, that this Yancey Cravat was famed as the deadliest shot in all the deadly shooting Southwest. He had the gift of being able to point his six-shooters without sighting, as one would point with a finger. It was a direction-born gift in him and an enviable one in this community. He was one of the few who could draw and fire two six-shooters at once with equal speed and accuracy. His hands would go to his hips with a lightning gesture that yet was so smooth, so economical that the onlooker's eye scarcely followed it. He could hit his mark as he walked, as he ran, as he rode his horse. He practised a great deal. From the back door of their cabin Sabra and Cim and rolling-eyed Isaiah used to stand watching him. He sometimes talked of wind and trajectory. You had to make allowance mathematically, he said, for this ever-blowing Oklahoma wind. Sabra was vaguely uneasy. Wichita had not been exactly effete, and Dodge City, Kansas, was notoriously a gunplay town. But here no man walked without his six-shooters strapped to his body. On the very day of her harrowing encounter with Doc Nisbett and the cowboy, Sabra, her composure regained, had gone with Yancey to see still another house owner about the possible renting of his treasure. The man was found in his crude one-room shack which he used as a combination dwelling and land office. He and Yancey seemed to know each other. Sabra was no longer astonished to find that Yancey, twenty-four hours after his arrival, appeared to be acquainted with everyone in the town. The man glanced up at them from the rough pine table at which he was writing.

"Howdy, Yancey!"

"Howdy, Cass!"

Yancey, all grace, performed an introduction. The lean, leather-skinned house owner wiped his palm on his pants' seat in courtly fashion and, thus purified, extended a hospitable hand to Sabra. Yancey revealed to him their plight.

"Well, now, say, that's plumb terr'ble, that is. Might be I can help you out—you and your good lady here. But say, Yancey, just let me step out, will you, to the corner, and mail this here letter. The bag's goin' any minute now."

He licked and stamped the envelope, rose, and took from the table beside him his broad leather belt with its pair of holstered six-shooters, evidently temporarily laid aside for comfort while writing. This he now strapped quickly about his waist with the same unconcern that another man would use in slipping into his coat. He merely was donning conventional street attire for the well-dressed man of the locality. He picked up his sheaf of envelopes and stepped out. In three minutes he was back, and affably ready to talk terms with them.

It was, perhaps, this simple and sinister act, more than anything she had hitherto witnessed, that impressed Sabra with the utter lawlessness of this new land to which her husband had brought her.

This house, so dearly held by the man called Cass, turned out to be a four-room dwelling inadequate to their needs, and they were in despair at the thought of being obliged to wait until a house could be built. Then Yancey had a brilliant idea. He found a two-room cabin made of rough boards. This was hauled to the site of the main house, plastered, and—added to it— provided them with a six-room combination dwelling, newspaper plant, and law office. There was all the splendor of sitting room, dining room, bedroom, and kitchen to live in. One room of the small attached cabin was a combination law and newspaper office. The other served as composing room and print shop. The Hefner Furniture and Undertaking Parlors provided them with furniture—a large wooden bedstead to fit Sabra's mattress and spring; a small bed for Cim; tables, chairs—the plainest of everything. The few bits of furnishing and ornament that Sabra had brought with her from Wichita were fortunately—or unfortunately—possessed of the enduring beauty of objects which have been carefully made by hands exquisitely aware of line, texture, color, and further enhanced by the rich mellow patina that comes with the years. Her pieces of silver, of china, of fine linen were as out of place in this roughly furnished cabin of unpainted lumber as a court lady in a peasant's hovel. In two days Sabra was a housewife established in her routine as though she had been at it for years. A pan of biscuits in the oven of the wood-burning kitchen stove; a dress pattern of calico, cut out and ready for basting, on the table in the sitting room.

Setting up the newspaper plant and law office was not so simple. Yancey, for example, was inclined to write his first editorial entitled Whither Oklahoma? before the hand press had been put together. He was more absorbed in the effect of the sign tacked up over the front of the shop than he was in the proper mechanical arrangement of the necessary appliances inside. THE OKLAHOMA WIGWAM, read the sign in block letters two feet high, so that the little cabin itself was almost obscured. Then, beneath, in letters scarcely less impressive: YANCEY CRAVAT, PROP. AND EDITOR. AT-TORNEY AT LAW. NOTARY.

The placing of this sign took the better part of a day, during which time all other work was suspended. While the operation was in progress Yancey crossed the road fifty times, ostensibly to direct matters from a proper vantage point of criticism, but really to bask in the dazzling effect of the bold fat black letters. As always in the course of such proceedings on the part of the laboring male there was much hoarse shouting, gesticulation, and general rumpus. To Sabra, coming to the door from time to time, dish towel or ladle in hand, the clamor seemed out of all proportion to the results achieved. She thought (privately) that two women could have finished the job in half the time with one tenth the fuss. She still was far too feminine, tactful, and in love with her husband to say so. Cim enjoyed the whole thing enormously, as did his black satellite, bodyguard, and playmate, Isaiah. They capered, shouted, whooped, and added much to the din.

Yancey, from across the road—"Lift her up a little higher that end!"

"What say?" from the perspiring Jesse Rickey, his assistant.

"That end—up! NO! UP! I said, UP!"

"Well, which end, f'r Chris' sakes, right or left?"

"Right! RIGHT! God Almighty, man, don't you know your right from your left?"

"Easy now. E-e-e-esy! Over now. Over! There! That's—no—yeh—now head her a little this way. . . ."

"How's that?"

"Oh, my land's sakes alive!" thought Sabra, going back to her orderly kitchen. "Men make such a lot of work of nothing."

It was her first admission that the male of the species might be fallible. A product of Southern training, even though a daily witness, during her girlhood, to the dominance of her matriarchal mother over her weak and war-shattered father, she had been bred to the tradition that the male was always right, always to be deferred to. Yancey, still her passionate lover, had always treated her, tenderly, as a charming little fool, and this rôle she had meekly—even gratefully—accepted. But now suspicion began to rear its ugly head. These last three weeks had shown her that the male was often mistaken, as a sex, and that Yancey was almost always wrong as an individual. But these frightening discoveries she would not yet admit even to herself. Also that he was enthralled by the dramatics of any plan he might conceive, but that he often was too impatient of its mechanics to carry it through to completion.

"Yancey, this case of type's badly pied." Jesse Rickey, journeyman printer and periodic drunkard, was responsible for this misfortune, having dropped a case, face down, in the dust of the road while assisting Yancey in the moving. "It'll have to be sorted before you can get out a paper."

"Oh, Rickey'll tend to that. I've got a lot of important work to do. Editorials to write, news to get, lot of real estate transfers—and I'm going to find out who killed Pegler and print it in the first issue if it takes the last drop of blood in me."

"Oh, please don't. What does it matter! He's dead. Maybe he did shoot himself. And besides, you've got Cim and me to think of. You can't let anything happen to you."

"Let that Yountis gang get away with a thing like that and anything *is* likely to happen to me; the same thing that happened to him. No, sir! I'll show them, first crack, that the *Oklahoma Wigwam* prints all the news, all the time, knowing no law but the Law of God and the government of these United States! Say, that's a pretty good slogan. Top of the page, just above the editorial column."

In the end it was she who sorted the case of pied type. The five years of Yancey's newspaper ownership in Wichita had familiarized her, almost unconsciously, with many of the mechanical aspects of a newspaper printing shop. She even liked the smell of printer's ink, of the metal type, of the paper wet from the hand press. She found that the brass and copper thin spaces, used for setting up ads, had no proper container, and at a loss to find one she hit upon the idea of using a muffin tin until a proper receptacle could be found. It never was found, and the muffin tin still served after a quarter of a century had gone by. She was, by that time, sentimental about it, and superstitious.

The hand press was finally set up, and the little job press, and the case rack containing the type. The rollers were in place, and their little stock of paper. Curiously enough, though neither Yancey nor Sabra was conscious of it, it was she who had directed most of this manual work and who had indeed actually performed much of it, with Isaiah and Jesse Rickey to help her. Yancey was off and up the street every ten minutes. Returning, he would lose himself in the placing of his law library, his books of reference, and his favorite volumes, for which he contended there was not enough shelf room in the house proper. He had brought along boxes of books stowed away in the covered wagons. If the combined book wealth contained in all the houses, offices, and shops of the entire Oklahoma country so newly settled could have been gathered in one spot it probably would have been found to number less than this preposterous library of the paradoxical Yancey Cravat. Glib and showy though he was with his book knowledge Yancey still had in these volumes of his the absorption of the true book lover. He gave more attention to the carpenter who put up these crude bookshelves than he had bestowed upon the actual coupling of the two cabins when first they had moved in. The books he insisted on placing himself, picking them up, one by one, and losing himself now in this page, now in that, so that at the end of the long hot afternoon he had accomplished nothing. Blackstone and Kent (ineffectual enough in this lawless land) were shocked to find themselves hobnobbing side by side with Childe Harold and the Decameron. Culpepper's Torts nestled cosily between the shameless tale of the sprightly

Wife of Bath and Yancey's new and joyously discovered copy of Fitzgerald's Omar Khayyám.

Lost to all else he would call happily in to Sabra as she bent over the case rack, her cheek streaked with ink, her fingers stained, her head close to Jesse Rickey's bleary-eyed one as she sorted type or filled the muffin tin with the metal thin spaces: "Sabe! Oh, Sabe—listen to this." He would clear his throat. " 'Son of Nestor, delight of my heart, mark the flashing of bronze through the echoing halls, and the flashing of gold and of amber and of silver and of ivory. Such like, methinks, is the court of Olympian Zeus within, for the world of things that are here; wonder comes over me as I look thereon.' . . . God, Sabra, it's as fine as the Old Testament. Finer!"

" 'The world of things that are here,' " echoed Sabra, not bitterly, but with grave common sense. "Perhaps if you'd pay more attention to those, and less to your nonsense in books about gold and silver and ivory, we might get settled."

But he was ready with a honeyed reply culled from the same book so dear to his heart and his grandiloquent tongue. " 'Be not wroth with me hereat, goddess and queen.' "

The goddess and queen pushed her hair back from her forehead with a sooty hand, leaving still another smudge of printer's ink upon that worried surface.

Jesse Rickey, the printer (known, naturally, to his familiars as "Gin" Rickey, owing to his periods of intemperance) and black Isaiah were, next to Sabra, most responsible for the astounding fact that the Cravat family finally was settled in house and office. The front door, which was the office entrance, faced the wide wallow of the main street. The back and the side doors of the dwelling looked out on a stretch of Oklahoma red clay, littered with the empty tin cans that mark any new American settlement, and especially one whose drought is relieved by the thirst-quenching coolness of tinned tomatoes and peaches. Perhaps the canned tomato, as much as anything, made possible the settling of the vast West and Southwest. In the midst of this clay and refuse, in a sort of shed-kennel, lived little Isaiah; rather, he slept there, like a faithful dog, for all day long he was about the house and the printing office, tireless, willing, invaluable. He belonged to Sabra, body and soul, as completely as though the Civil War had never been. A little servant of twelve, born to labor, he became as dear to Sabra, as accustomed, as one of her own children, despite her Southern training and his black skin. He dried the dishes, a towel tied round his neck; he laid the table; he was playmate and nursemaid for Cim; he ran errands, a swift and splay-footed Mercury; he was a born reporter, and in the course of his day's scurrying about the town on this errand or that brought into Sabra's kitchen more items of news and gossip (which were later transferred to the newspaper office) than a whole staff of trained newspaper men could have done. He was so little, so black, so lithe, so harmless looking, that his presence was, more often than not, completely overlooked. The saloon loungers, cowboys, rangers, and homesteaders in and about the town alternately spoiled and plagued him. One minute they were throwing him dimes in the dust for his rendition of his favorite song:

> King Jesus come a-ridin' on a milk-white steed,
> Wid a rainbow on his shoulder.

The next moment they were making his splay-feet dance frenziedly as the bullets from their six-shooters plopped playfully all about him and his kinky hair seemed to grow straight and dank with terror.

Sabra, in time, taught him to read, write, and figure. He was quick to
learn, industrious, lovable. He thought he actually belonged to her. Cim was
beginning to learn the alphabet, and as Sabra bent over the child, Isaiah,
too, would bring his little stool out of its corner. Perched on it like an
intelligent monkey he mastered the curlycues in their proper sequence. He
cleared the unsightly back yard of its litter of tin cans and refuse. Together
he and Sabra even tried to plant a little garden in this barren sanguine clay.
More than anything else, Sabra missed the trees and flowers. In the whole
town of almost ten thousand inhabitants there were two trees: stunted jack
oaks. Sometimes she dreamed of lilies of the valley—the translucent, almost
liquid green of their stems and leaves, the perfumed purity of their white
bells.

All this, however, came later. These first few days were filled to overflowing with the labor of making the house habitable and the office and plant
fit for Yancey's professional pursuits. Already his talents as a silver-tongue
were being sought in defense of murderers, horse thieves, land grabbers,
and more civil offenders in all the surrounding towns and counties. It was
known that the average jury was wax in his hands. Once started on his plea
it was as though he were painting the emotions that succeeded each other
across the faces of the twelve (or less, depending on the number available
in the community) good men (or good enough) and true. A tremolo tone—
their eyes began to moisten, their mouth muscles to sag with sympathy; a
wave of the hand, a lilt of the golden voice—they guffawed with mirth. Even
a horse thief, that blackest of criminals in this country, was said to have a
bare chance for his life if Yancey Cravat could be induced to plead for him—
and provided always, of course, that the posse had not dealt with the offender
first.

Yancey, from the time he rose in the morning until he went to bed late
at night, was always a little overstimulated by the whisky he drank. This,
together with a natural fearlessness, an enormous vitality, and a devouring
interest in everybody and everything in this fantastic Oklahoma country,
gained him friends and enemies in almost equal proportion.

In the ten days following their arrival in Osage, his one interest seemed
to be the tracing of the Pegler murder—for he scoffed at the idea that his
predecessor's death was due to any other cause.

He asked his question everywhere, even in the most foolhardy circumstances, and watched the effect of his question. Pegler had been a Denver
newspaper man; known, respected, decent. Yancey had sworn to bring his
murderers to justice.

Sabra argued with him, almost hysterically, but in vain. "You didn't do
anything about helping them catch the Kid, out there on the prairie, when
they were looking for him, and you knew where he was—or just about—
and he had killed a man, too, and robbed a bank, and I don't know what
all."

"That was different. The Kid's different," Yancey answered, unreasonably and infuriatingly.

"Different! How different? What's this Pegler to you! They'll kill you,
too—they'll shoot you down—and then what shall I do?—Cim—Cim—and
I here, alone—Yancey, darling—I love you so—if anything should happen
to you———" She waxed incoherent.

"Listen, honey. Hush your crying and listen. Try to understand. The
Kid's a terror. He's a bad one. But it isn't his fault. The government at
Washington made him an outlaw."

"Why, Yancey Cravat, what are you talking about? Don't you ever say
a thing like that before Cim."

"The Kid's father rode the range before there were fences or railroads in Kansas, and when this part of the country was running wild with longhorn cattle that had descended straight from the animals that the Spaniards had brought over four centuries ago. The railroads began coming in. The settlers came with it, from the Gulf Coast, up across Texas, through the Indian Territory to the end of steel at Abilene, Kansas. The Kid was brought up to all that. Freighters, bull whackers, mule skinners, hunters, and cowboys—that's all he knew. Into Dodge City, with perhaps nine months' pay jingling in his pocket. I'll bet neither the Kid nor his father before him ever saw a nickel or a dime. They wouldn't have bothered with such chicken feed. Silver dollars were the smallest coin they knew. They worked for it, too. I've seen seventy-five thousand cattle at a time waiting shipment to the East, with lads like the Kid in charge. The Kid's grandfather was a buffalo hunter. The range was the only life they wanted. Along comes the government. What happens?"

"What?" breathed Sabra, as always enthralled by one of Yancey's arguments, forgetting quite that she must oppose this very plea.

"They take the range away from the cattle men and cowboys—the free range that never belonged to them really, but that they had come to think of as theirs through right of use. Squatters come in, Sooners, too, and Nesters, and then the whole rush of the Opening. The range is cut up into town sites, and the town into lots, before their very eyes. Why, it must have sickened them—killed them almost—to see it."

"But that's progress, Yancey. The country's got to be settled."

"This was different. There's never been anything like this. Settling a great section of a country always has been a matter of years—decades—centuries, even. But here they swept over it in a day. You know that as well as I do. Wilderness one day; town sites the next. And the cowboys and rangers having no more chance than chips in a flood. Can't you see it? Shanties where the horizon used to be; grocery stores on the old buffalo trails. They went plumb locoed, I tell you. They couldn't fight progress, but they could get revenge on the people who had taken their world away from them and cut it into little strips and dirtied it."

"You're taking the part of criminals, of murderers, of bad men! I'm ashamed of you! I'm afraid of you! You're as bad as they are."

"Now, now, Sabra. No dramatics. Leave that for me. I'm better at it. The Kid's bad, yes. They don't come worse than he. And they'll get him, eventually. But he never kills unless he has to. When he robs a bank or holds up a train it's in broad daylight, by God, with a hundred guns against him. He runs a risk. He doesn't shoot in the dark. The other fellow always has a chance. It's three or four, usually, against fifty. He was brought up a reckless, lawless, unschooled youngster. He's a killer now, and he'll die by the gun, with his boots on. But the man who fathered him needn't be ashamed of him. There's no yellow in the Kid."

For one dreadful sickening second something closed with iron fingers around Sabra Cravat's heart and squeezed it, and it ceased to beat. White faced, her dark eyes searched her husband's face. Wichita whispers. Kansas slander. But that face was all exaltation, like the face of an evangelist, and as pure. His eyes were glowing. The iron fingers relaxed.

"But Pegler. The men who killed Pegler. Why are they so much worse————"

"Skunks. Dirty jackals hired by white-livered politicians."

"But why? Why?"

"Because Pegler had the same idea I have—that here's a chance to start clean, right from scratch. Live and let live. Clean politics instead of the skulduggery all around; a new way of living and of thinking, because we've had a chance to see how rotten and narrow and bigoted the other way has been. Here everything's fresh. It's all to do, and we can do it. There's never been a chance like it in the world. We can make a model empire out of this Oklahoma country, with all the mistakes of the other pioneers to profit by. New England, and California, and the settlers of the Middle West—it got away from them, and they fell into the rut. Ugly politics, ugly towns, ugly buildings, ugly minds.'' He was off again. Sabra, all impatience, stopped him.

"But Pegler. What's that got to do with Pegler?" She hated the name. She hated the dead man who was stalking their new life and threatening to destroy it.

"I saw that one copy of his paper. He called it the *New Day*—poor devil. And in it he named names, and he outlined a policy and a belief something like—well—along the lines I've tried to explain to you. He accused the government of robbing the Indians. He accused the settlers of cheating them. He told just how they got their whisky, in spite of its being forbidden, and how their monthly allotment was pinched out of their foolish fingers————''

"Oh, my heavens, Yancey! Indians! You and your miserable dirty Indians! You're always going on about them as if they mattered! The sooner they're all dead the better. What good are they? Filthy, thieving, lazy things. They won't work. You've said so yourself. They just squat there, rotting.''

"I've tried to explain to you," Yancey began, gently. "White men can't do those things to a helpless————''

"And so they killed him!" Sabra cried, irrelevantly. "And they'll kill you, too. Oh, Yancey—please—please—I don't want to be a pioneer woman. I thought I did, but I don't. I can't make things different. I liked them as they were. Comfortable and safe. Let them alone. I don't want to live in a model empire. Darling! Darling! Let's just make it a town like Wichita . . . with trees . . . and people being sociable . . . not killing each other all the time . . . church on Sunday . . . a school for Cim. . . .''

The face she adored was a mask. The ocean-gray eyes were slate-gray now, with the look she had seen and dreaded—cold, determined, relentless.

"All right. Go back there. Go back to your trees and your churches and your sidewalks and your Sunday roast beef and your whole goddamned, smug, dead-alive family. But not me! Me, I'm staying here. And when I find the man who killed Pegler I'll face him with it, and I'll publish his name, and if he's alive by then I'll bring him to justice and I'll see him strung up on a tree. If I don't it'll be because I'm not alive myself.''

"Oh, God!" whimpered Sabra, and sank, a limp bundle of misery, into his arms. But those arms were, suddenly, no haven, no shelter. He put her from him, gently, but with iron firmness, and walked out of the house, through the newspaper office, down the broad and sinister red road.

8

YANCEY PUT HIS question wherever he came upon a little group of three or four lounging on saloon or store porch or street corner. "How did Pegler come to die?" The effect of the question always was the same. One minute they were standing sociably, gossiping, rolling cigarettes; citizenry at ease in their shirt sleeves. Yancey would stroll up with his light, graceful step, his white sombrero with the two bullet holes in its crown, his Prince Albert, his fine high-heeled boots. He would ask his question. As though by magic the group dispersed, faded, vanished.

He visited Coroner Hefner, of Hefner's Furniture Store and Undertaking Parlor. That gentleman was seated, idle for the moment, in his combination office and laboratory. "Listen, Louie. How did Pegler come to die?"

Hefner's sun-kissed and whisky-rouged countenance became noticeably less roseate. His pale blue pop-eyes stared at Yancey in dismay. "Are you going around town askin' that there question, or just me?"

"Oh—around."

Hefner leaned forward. He looked about him furtively. He lowered his voice. "Yancey, you and your missus, you bought your furniture and so on here in my place, and what's more, you paid cash for it. I want you as a customer, see, but not in the other branch of my business. Don't go round askin' that there question."

"Think I'd better not, h'm?"

"I know you better not."

"Why not?"

The versatile Hefner made a little gesture of despair, rose, vanished by way of his own back door, and did not return.

Yancey strolled out into the glaring sunshine of Pawhuska Avenue. Indians, Mexicans, cowboys, solid citizens lounged in whatever of shade could be found in the hot, dry, dusty street. On the corner stood Pete Pitchlyn talking to the Spaniard, Estevan Miro. They were the gossips of the town, these two. This Yancey knew. News not only of the town, but of the Territory—not alone of the Territory but of the whole brilliant burning Southwest, from Texas through New Mexico into Arizona, sieved through this pair. Miro not only knew; he sold his knowledge. The Spaniard made a gay splash of color in the drab prairie street. He wore a sash of purple wound round his middle in place of a belt and his neckerchief was of scarlet. His face was tiny, like the face of a child, and pointed; his hair was thick, blueblack, and lay in definite strands, coarse and glossy, like fine wire. His two upper incisor teeth were separated by, perhaps, the width of an eighth of an inch. He was very quiet, and his movements appeared slow because of their feline grace. Eternally he rolled cigarettes in the cowboy fashion, with exquisite deftness, manipulating the tobacco and brown paper magically between the thumb and two fingers of his right hand. The smoke of these he inhaled, consuming a cigarette in three voracious pulls. The street corner on which he lounged was ringed with limp butts.

Pete Pitchlyn, famous Indian scout of a bygone day, has grown pot-bellied and flabby, now that the Indians were rotting on their reservations and there was no more work for him to do. He was a vast fellow, his height of six feet three now balanced by his bulk. His wife, a full-blood Cherokee squaw, squatted on the ground in the shade of a near-by frame shack about ten feet away, as befits a wife whose husband is conversing with another male. On the ground all around her, like a litter of puppies tumbling about a bitch, were their half-breed children. Late in his hazardous career as a scout on the plains Pitchlyn had been shot in the left heel by a poisoned Indian arrow. It was thought he would surely die. This failing, it was then thought he would lose that leg. But a combination of unlimited whisky, a constitution made up of chilled steel, and a determination that those varmints should never kill him, somehow caused him not only to live but to keep the poison-ravaged leg clinging to his carcase. Stubbornly he had refused to have it amputated, and by a miracle it had failed to send its poison through the rest of that iron frame. But the leg had withered and shrunk until now it was fully twelve inches shorter than the sound limb. He refused to use crutches or the clumsy mechanical devices of the day, and got about with astonishing speed and agility. When he stood on the sound leg he was, with his magnificent breadth of shoulders, a giant of six feet three. But occasionally the sound leg tired, and he would rest it by slumping for a moment on the other. He then became a runt five feet high.

The story was told of him that when he first came to Osage in the rush of the Run he, with hundreds of others, sought the refreshment of the Montezuma Saloon, which hospice—a mere tent—had opened its bar and stood ready for business as the earliest homesteader drew his red-eyed sweating horse up before the first town site to which claim was laid in the settlement of Osage (at that time—fully a month before—a piece of prairie as bare and flat as the palm of your hand). The crowd around the rough pine slab of the hastily improvised bar was parched, wild eyed, clamorous. The bartenders, hardened importations though they were, were soon ready to drop with fatigue. Even in this milling mob the towering figure of Pete Pitchlyn was one to command attention. Above the clamor he ordered his drink—three fingers of whisky. It was a long time coming. He had had a hard day. He leaned one elbow on the bar, while shouts emerged as croaks from parched throats, and glasses and bottles whirled all about him. Dead tired, he shifted his weight from the sound right leg to the withered left, and conversed half-heartedly with the thirsty ones on this side and that. The harried bartender poured Pitchlyn's whisky, shoved it toward him, saw in his place only a wearily pensive little man whose head barely showed above the bar, and, outraged, his patience tried beyond endurance, yelled:

"Hey, you runt! Get out of there! Where's the son of a bitch who ordered this whisky?"

Like a python Pete Pitchlyn uncoiled to his full height and glared down on the bewildered bartender.

Crowded though it was, the drinks were on the house.

These two specimens of the Southwest it was that Yancey now approached, his step a saunter, his manner carefree, even bland. Almost imperceptibly the two seemed to stiffen, as though bracing themselves for action. In the old scout it evidenced itself in his sudden emergence from lounging cripple to statuesque giant. In the Spaniard you sensed, rather than saw, only a curiously rippling motion of the muscles beneath the smooth tawny skin, like a snake that glides before it really moves to go.

"Howdy, Pete!"

"Howdy, Yancey!"

He looked at the Spaniard. Miro eyed him innocently. *"Que tal?"*

"Bien. Y tu?"

They stood, the three, wary, silent. Yancey balanced gayly from shining boot toe to high heel and back again. The Cherokee woman kept her sloe eyes on her man, as though, having received one signal, she were holding herself in readiness for another.

Yancey put the eternal question of the inquiring reporter. "Well, boys, what do you know?"

The two were braced for a query less airy. Their faces relaxed in an expression resembling disappointment. It was as when gunfire fails to explode. The Spaniard shrugged his shoulders, a protean gesture intended on this occasion to convey to the beholder the utter innocence and uneventfulness of the daily existence led by Estevan Miro. Pete Pitchlyn's eyes, in that ravaged face, were coals in an ash heap. It was not for him to be seen talking on the street corner with the man who was asking a fatal question— fatal not only to the asker but to the one who should be foolhardy enough to answer it. He knew Yancey, admired him, wished him well. Yet there was little he dared say now before the reptilian Miro. Yancey continued, conversationally:

"I understand there's an element rarin' around town bragging that they're going to make Osage the terror of the Southwest, like Abilene and Dodge City in the old days; and the Cimarron." The jaws of Pete Pitchlyn worked rhythmically on the form of nicotine to which he was addicted. Estevan Miro inhaled a deep draught of his brand of poison and sent forth its wraith, a pale gray jet, through his nostrils. Thus each maintained an air of nonchalance to hide his nervousness. "I'm interviewing citizens of note," continued Yancey, blandly, "on whether they think this town ought to be run on that principle or on a Socratic one that the more modern element has in mind." He lifted his great head and turned his rare gaze full on the little Spaniard. His gray eyes, quizzical, mocking, met the black eyes, and the darker ones shifted. "Are you at all familiar with the works of Socrates— 'Socrates . . . whom well inspir'd the oracle pronounced wisest of men'?"

Again Estevan Miro shrugged. This time the gesture was exquisitely complicated in its meaning, even for a low-class Spaniard. Slight embarrassment was in it, some bewilderment, and a grain—the merest fleck—of something as nearly approaching contempt as was possible in him for a man whom he feared.

"Yancey," said Pete Pitchlyn, deliberately, "stick to your lawy'in'."

"Why?"

"Anybody's got the gift of gab like you have is wastin' their time doin' anything else."

"Oh, I wouldn't say that," Yancey replied, all modesty. "Running a newspaper keeps me in touch with folks. I like it. Besides, the law isn't very remunerative in these parts. Running a newspaper's my way of earning a living. Of course," he continued brightly, as an afterthought, "there have been times when running a newspaper has saved the editor the trouble of ever again having to earn a living." The faces of the two were blank as a sponged slate. Suddenly—"Come on, boys. Who killed Pegler?"

Pete Pitchlyn, his Cherokee squaw, and the litter of babies dispersed. It was magic. They faded, vanished. It was as though the woman had tossed her young into a pouch, like a kangaroo. As for the cripple, he might have been a centipede. Yancey and the Spaniard were left alone on the sunny street corner. The face of Miro now became strangely pinched. The eyes were inky slits. He was summoning all his little bravado, pulling it out of his inmost depths.

"I know something. I have that to tell you," he said in Spanish, his lips barely moving.

Yancey replied in the same tongue, "Out with it."

The Spaniard did not speak. The slits looked at Yancey. Yancey knew that already he must have been well paid by someone to show such temerity when his very vitals were gripped with fear. "You know something, h'm? Well, Miro, *mas vale saber que haber.*" With which bit of philosophy he showed Miro what a Westerner can do in the way of a shrug; and sauntered off.

Miro leaped after him in one noiseless bound, like a cat. He seemed now to be more afraid of not revealing that which he had been paid to say than of saying it. He spoke rapidly, in Spanish. His hard *r* sounds drummed like hail on a tin roof. "I say only that which was told to me. The words are not mine. They say, 'Are you a friend of Yancey Cravat?' I say, 'Yes.' They say then, 'Tell your friend Yancey Cravat that wisdom is better than wealth. If he does not keep his damn mouth shut he will die.' The words are not mine."

"Thanks," replied Yancey, thoughtfully, speaking in English now. Then with one fine white hand he reached out swiftly and gave Miro's scarlet neckerchief a quick strong jerk and twist. The gesture was at once an insult and a threat. "Tell them———" Suddenly Yancey stopped. He opened his mouth, and there issued from it a sound so dreadful, so unearthly as to freeze the blood of any within hearing. It was a sound between the gobble of an angry turkey cock and the howl of a coyote. Throughout the Southwest it was known that this terrible sound, famed as the gobble, was Cherokee in origin and a death cry among the Territory Indians. It was known, too, that when an Indian gobbled it meant sudden destruction to any or all in his path.

The Spaniard's face went a curious dough gray. With a whimper he ran, a streak of purple and scarlet and brown, round the corner of the nearest shack, and vanished.

Unfortunately, Yancey could not resist the temptation of dilating to Sabra on this dramatic triumph. The story was, furthermore, told in the presence of Cim and Isaiah, and illustrated—before Sabra could prevent it—with a magnificent rendering of the blood-curdling gobble. They were seated at noonday dinner, with Isaiah slapping briskly back and forth between stove and table. Sabra's fork, halfway to her mouth, fell clattering on her plate. Her face blanched. Her appetite was gone. Cim, tutored by that natural Thespian and mimic, black Isaiah, spent the afternoon attempting faithfully to reproduce the hideous sound, to the disastrous end that Sabra, nerves torn to shreds, spanked him soundly and administered a smart cuff to Isaiah for good measure. Luckily, the full import of the sinister Indian gobble was lost on her, else she might have taken even stronger measures.

It was all like a nightmarish game, she thought. The shooting, the carousing, the brawls and high altercations; the sounds of laughter and ribaldry and drinking and song that issued from the flimsy cardboard false-front shacks that lined the preposterous street. Steadfastly she refused to believe that this was to be the accepted order of their existence. Yancey was always talking of a new code, a new day; live and let live. He was full of wisdom culled from the Old Testament, with which he pointed his remarks. " 'The fathers have eaten sour grapes, and the children's teeth are set on edge,' " when Sabra reminded him of this or that pleasant Wichita custom. But Sabra prepared herself with a retort, and was able, after some quiet research, to refute this with:

" 'Stand ye in the ways, and see, and ask for the old paths, where is the good way, and walk therein.' There! Now perhaps you'll stop quoting the Bible at me every time you want an excuse for something you do."

"The devil," retorted Yancey, "can cite Scripture for his purpose." But later she wondered whether by this he had intended a rather ungallant fling at her own quotation or a sheepish excuse for his own.

She refused to believe, too, that this business of the Pegler shooting was as serious as Yancey made it out to be. It was just one of his whims. He would, she told herself, publish something or other about it in the first edition of the *Oklahoma Wigwam*. Yancey stoutly maintained it was due off the press on Thursday. Privately, Sabra thought that this would have to be accomplished by a miracle. This was Friday. A fortnight had gone by. Nothing had been done. Perhaps he was exaggerating the danger as well as the importance of all this Pegler business. Something else would come up to attract his interest, arouse his indignation, or outrage his sense of justice.

She was overjoyed when, that same day, a solemn deputation of citizens, three in number, *de rigueur* in sombreros and six-shooters, called on Yancey in his office (where, by some chance, he happened momentarily to be) with the amazing request that he conduct divine service the following Sunday morning. Osage was over a month old. The women folks, they said, in effect, thought it high time that some contact be established between the little town sprawled on the prairie and the Power supposedly gazing down upon it from beyond the brilliant steel-blue dome suspended over it. Beneath the calico and sunbonnets despised of Sabra on that first day of her coming to Osage there apparently glowed the same urge for convention, discipline and the old order that so fired her to revolt. She warmed toward them. She made up her mind that, once the paper had gone to press, she would don the black silk and the hat with the plumes and go calling on such of the wooden shacks as she knew had fostered this meeting. Then she recollected her mother's training and the stern commands of fashion. The sunbonnets had been residents of Osage before she had arrived. They would have to call first. She pictured, mentally, a group of Mother Hubbards balanced stylishly on the edge of her parlor chairs, making small talk in this welter of Southwestern barbarism.

She got out a plaid silk tie for Cim. "Church meeting!" she exclaimed, joyously. Here, at last, was something familiar; something on which she could get a firm foothold in this quagmire. Yancey temporarily abandoned his journalistic mission in order to make proper arrangements for Sunday's meeting. There was, certainly, no building large enough to hold the thousands who, surprisingly enough, made up this settlement spawned overnight on the prairie. Yancey, born entrepreneur, took hold with the enthusiasm that he always displayed in the first spurt of a new enterprise. Already news of the prospective meeting had spread by the mysterious means common to isolated settlements. Nesters, homesteaders, rangers, cowboys for miles around somehow got wind of it. Saddles were polished, harnesses shined, calicoes washed and ironed, faces scrubbed. Church meeting.

Yancey turned quite naturally to the one shelter in the town adequate to the size of the crowd expected. It was the gambling tent that stood at the far north end of Pawhuska Avenue, flags waving gayly from its top in the brisk Oklahoma wind. For the men it was the social center of Osage. Faro, stud poker, chuckaluck diverted their minds from the stern business of citizenship and saved them the trouble of counting their ready cash on Saturday night. Sunday was, of course, the great day in the gambling tent. Rangers, cowboys, a generous sprinkling of professional bad men from the near-by hills and plains, and all the town women who were not respectable flocked to the tent on Sunday for recreation, society, and excitement. Shouts, the tinkle of glass, the sound of a tubercular piano playing Champagne Charley assailed the ears of the passers-by. The great canvas dome, measuring ninety by one hundred and fifty feet, was decorated with flags and bunting; cheerful, bright, gay.

It was a question whether the owner and dealer would be willing to sacrifice any portion of Sunday's brisk trade for the furtherance of the Lord's business, even though the goodwill of the townspeople were to be gained thereby. After all, he might argue, it was not this element that kept a faro game going.

Yancey, because of his professional position and his well-known power to charm, was delegated to confer with that citizen *du monde*, Mr. Grat Gotch, better known as Arkansas Grat, proprietor and dealer of the gambling tent. Mr. Gotch was in. Not only that, it being mid-afternoon and a slack hour for business, he was superintending the placing of a work of art recently purchased by him and just arrived via the Missouri, Kansas & Texas Railroad, familiarly known throughout the Territory, by a natural process of elision, as the Katy. The newly acquired treasure was a picture, done in oils of a robust and very pink lady of full habit who, apparently having expended all her energy upon the arrangement of her elaborate and highly modern coiffure, was temporarily unable to proceed further with her toilette until fortified by refreshment and repose. To this end she had flung herself in a complete state of nature (barring the hairpins) down on a convenient couch where she lolled at ease, her lips parted to receive a pair of ripe red cherries which she held dangling between thumb and forefinger of a hand whose little finger was elegantly crooked. Her eyes were not on the cherries but on the beholder, of whom she was, plainly, all unaware.

As a tent naturally boasts no walls, it was impossible properly to hang this *objet d'art,* and it was being suspended by guy ropes from the tent top so that it dangled just in front of the bar, as it properly should, flanked by mirrors. Arkansas Grat had pursued his profession in the bonanza days of Denver, San Francisco, White Oaks, and Dodge City. In these precocious cities his artistic tastes had been developed. He knew that the eye, as well as the gullet, must have refreshment in hours of ease. A little plump man, Grat, with a round and smiling countenance, strangely unlined. He looked like an old baby.

He now, at Yancey's entrance, called his attention to the newly acquired treasure, expressing at the same time his admiration for it.

"Ain't she," he demanded, "a lalapaloosa!"

Yancey surveyed the bright pink lady. He had come to ask a favor of Grat, but he would not sell his artistic soul for this mess of pottage.

"It's a calumny," he announced, with some vehemence, "on nature's fairest achievement."

The word was not contained in Mr. Gotch's vocabulary. He mistook Yancey's warmth of tone for enthusiasm. "That's right," he agreed, in triumphant satisfaction. "I was sayin' to the boys only this morning when she come."

Yancey ordered his drink and invited Gotch to have one with him. Arkansas Grat was not one of those abstemious characters frequently found in fiction who, being dispensers of alcoholic refreshment, never sample their own wares. Over the whisky Yancey put his case.

"Listen, Grat. The women folks have got it into their heads that there ought to be a church service Sunday, now that Osage is over a month old, with ten thousand inhabitants, and probably the metropolis of the great Southwest in another ten years. They want the thing done right. I'm chosen to conduct the meeting. There's no building in town big enough to hold the crowd. What I want to know is, can we have the loan of your tent here for about an hour Sunday morning for the purpose of divine worship?"

Arkansas Grat set down his glass, made a sweeping gesture with his right hand that included faro tables, lolling cherry eater, bar, piano, and all else that the tent contained.

"Divine worship! Why, hell, yes, Yancey," he replied, graciously.

They went to work early Sunday. So as not to mar the numbers they covered the faro and roulette tables with twenty-two-foot boards. Such of the prospective congregation as came early would use these for seats. There were, too, a few rude benches on which the players usually sat. The remainder must stand. The meeting was to be from eleven to twelve. As early as nine o'clock they began to arrive. They seemed to spring out of the earth. The horizon spewed up little hurrying figures, black against the brilliant Oklahoma sky. They came from lonely cabins, dugouts, tents. Ox carts, wagons, buggies, horsemen, mule teams. They were starving for company. It wasn't religion they sought; it was the stimulation that comes of meeting their kind in the mass. They brought picnic baskets and boxes, prepared for a holiday. The cowboys were gorgeous. They wore their pink and purple shirts, their five-gallon hats, their gayest neckerchiefs, their most ornate high-heeled boots. They rode up and down before the big tent, their horses curveting and stepping high. "Whoa there! Don't crowd the cattle! . . . You figgerin' on gettin' saved, Quince? . . . Yessir, I'm here for the circus and I'm stayin' for the concert and grand olio besides. . . . Say, you're too late, son. Good whisky and bad women has ruined you."

The town seemed alive with blanketed Indians.

They squatted in the shade of the wooden shacks. They walked in from their near-by reservations, or rode their mangy horses, or brought in their entire families—squaw, papoose, two or three children of assorted sizes, dogs. The family rarely was a large one. Sabra had once remarked this.

"They don't have big families, do they? Two or three children. You'd think savages like that—I mean————"

Yancey explained. "The Indian is a cold race—passionless, or almost. I don't know whether it's the food they eat—their diet—or the vigorous outdoor life they've lived for centuries, or whether they're a naturally sterile race. Funny. No hair on their faces—no beards. Did you ever see an Indian festival dance?"

"Oh, no! I've heard they————"

"They work themselves up, you know, at those dances. Insidious music, mutilations, hysteria—all kinds of orgies to get themselves up to pitch."

Sabra had shuddered with disgust.

This Sunday morning they flocked in by the dozens, with their sorry nags and their scabrous dogs. The men were decked in all their beads and chains with metal plaques. They camped outside the town, at the end of the street.

Sabra, seeing them, told herself sternly that she must remember to have a Christian spirit, and they were all God's children; that these red men had been converted. She didn't believe a word of it. "They're just where they were before Joshua," Mother Bridget had said.

Rangers, storekeepers, settlers. Lean squatters with their bony wives and their bare-legged, rickety children, as untamed as little wolves.

Sabra superintended the toilettes of her men folk from Yancey to Isaiah. She herself had stayed up the night before to iron his finest shirt. Isaiah had polished his boots until they glittered. Sabra sprinkled a drop of her own cherished cologne on his handkerchief. It was as though they were making ready a bridegroom.

He chided her, laughing, "My good woman, do you realize that this is no way to titivate for the work of delivering the Word of God? Sackcloth and ashes is, I believe, the prescribed costume." He poured and drank down three fingers of whisky, the third since breakfast.

Cim cavorted excitedly in his best suit, with the bright plaid silk tie and the buttoned shoes, tasseled at the top. The boy, Sabra thought as she dressed him, grew more and more like Yancey, except that he seemed to lack his father's driving force, his ebullience. But he was high spirited enough now, so that she had difficulty in dressing him.

"I'm going to church!" he shouted, his voice shrill. "Hi, Isaiah! Blessed be the name of the Lawd Amen hall'ujah glory be oh my fren's come and be save hell fire and brimstone————"

"Cimarron Cravat, stop that this minute or you'll have to stay home." Evidently he and Isaiah, full of the Sunday meeting, had been playing church on Saturday afternoon. This was the result of their rehearsal.

Yancey's sure dramatic instinct bade him delay until he could make an effective entrance. A dozen times Sabra called to him, as he sat in the front office busy with paper and pencil. This was, she decided, his sole preparation for the sermon he would be bound to deliver within the next hour. Later she found in the pocket of his sweeping Prince Albert the piece of paper on which he had made these notes. The paper was filled with those cabalistic whorls, crisscrosses, parallel lines and skulls with which the hand unconsciously gives relief to the troubled or restless mind. One word he had written on it, and then disguised it with meaningless marks—but not quite. Sabra, studying the paper after the events of the morning, made out the word "Yountis."

At last he was ready. As they stepped into the road they saw that stragglers were still hurrying toward the tent. Sabra had put on, not her second-best black grosgrain, but her best, and the hat with the plumes, none of which splendor she had worn since that eventful first day. She and Yancey stepped sedately down the street, with Cim's warm wriggling fingers in her own clasp. Sabra was a slimly elegant little figure in her modish black; Yancey, as always, a dashing one; Cim's clothes were identical with those being worn, perhaps, by a million little boys all over the United States, now on their unwilling way to church. Isaiah, on being summoned from his little kennel in the back yard, had announced that his churchgoing toilette was not quite completed, urged them to proceed without him, and promised to catch up with them before they should have gone a hundred feet.

They went on their way. It occurred neither to Sabra nor to Yancey that there was anything bizarre or even unusual in their thus proceeding, three well-dressed and reasonably conventional figures, toward a gambling tent and saloon which, packed to suffocation with the worst and the best that a frontier town has to offer, was for one short hour to become a House of God.

"Are you nervous, Yancey dear?"

"No, sugar. Though I will say I'd fifty times rather plead with a jury of Texas Panhandle cattlemen for the life of a professional horse thief than stand up to preach before this gang of———" He broke off abruptly. "What's everybody laughing at and pointing to?" Certainly passers-by were acting strangely. Instinctively Sabra and Yancey turned to look behind them. Down the street, perhaps fifty paces behind them, came Isaiah. He was strutting in an absurd and yet unmistakably recognizable imitation of Yancey's stride and swing. Around his waist was wound a red calico sash, and over that hung a holstered leather belt so large for his small waist that it hung to his knees and bumped against them at every step. Protruding from the holsters one saw the ugly heads of what seemed at first glance to be two six-shooters, but which turned out, on investigation by the infuriated Mrs. Cravat, to be the household monkey wrench and a bar of ink-soaked iron which went to make up one of the printing shop metal forms. On his head was a battered—an unspeakable—sombrero which he must have salvaged from the back-yard débris. But this was not, after all, the high point of his sartorial triumph. He had found somewhere a pair of Yancey's discarded boots. They were high heeled, slim, star trimmed. Even in their final degradation they still had something of the elegance of cut and material that Yancey's footgear always bore. Into these wrecks of splendor Isaiah had thrust, as far as possible, his own great bare splay feet. The high heels toppled. The arched insteps split under the pressure. Isaiah teetered, wobbled, walked now on his ankles as the treacherous heel betrayed him; now on his toes. Yet he managed, by the very power of his dramatic gift, to give to the appreciative onlooker a complete picture of Yancey Cravat in ludicrous—in grotesque miniature.

He advanced toward them, in spite of his pedestrian handicaps, with an appalling imitation of Yancey's stride. Sabra's face went curiously sallow, so that she was, suddenly, Felice Venable, enraged. Yancey gave a great roar of laughter, and at that Sabra's blazing eyes turned from the ludicrous figure of the black boy to her husband. She was literally panting with fury. Her idol, her god, was being mocked.

"You—laugh! . . . Stop. . . ."

She went in a kind of swoop of rage toward the now halting figure of Isaiah. Though Cim's hand was still tightly clutched by her own she had quite forgotten that he was there so that, as she flew toward the small mimic, Cim was yanked along as a cyclone carries small objects in its trail by the very force of its own velocity. She reached him. The black face, all eyes now (and those all whites), looked up at her, startled, terrorized. She raised her hand in its neat black kid glove to cuff him smartly. But Yancey was too quick for her. Swiftly as she had swooped upon Isaiah, Yancey's leap had been quicker. He caught her hand halfway in its descent. His fingers closed round her wrist in an iron grip.

"Let me go!" For that instant she hated him.

"If you touch him I swear before God I'll not set foot inside the tent. Look at him!"

The black face gazed up at him. In it was worship, utter devotion. Yancey, himself a born actor, knew that in Isaiah's grotesque costume, in his struttings and swaggerings, there had been only that sincerest of flattery, imitation of that which was adored. The eyes were those of a dog, faithful, hurt, bewildered.

Yancey released Sabra's wrist. He turned his brilliant winning smile on Isaiah. He put out his hand, removed the mangy sombrero from the child's head, and let his fine white hand rest a moment on the woolly poll.

Isaiah began to blubber, his fright giving way to injury. "Ah didn't go fo' to fret nobody. You-all was dress up fine fo' ch'ch meetin' so I crave to dress myself up Sunday style———"

"That's right, Isaiah. You look finer than any of us. Now listen to me. Do you want a real suit of Sunday clothes?"

The white teeth now vied with the rolling eyes. "Sunday suit fo' me to wear! Fo' true!"

"Listen close, Isaiah. I want you to do something for me. Something big. I don't want you to go to the church meeting." Then, as the black boy's expressive face, all smiles the instant before, became suddenly doleful: "Isaiah, listen hard. This is something important. Everybody in town's at the church meeting. Jesse Rickey's drunk. The house and the newspaper office are left alone. There are people in town who'd sooner set fire to the newspaper plant and the house than see the paper come out on Thursday. I want you to go back to the house and into the kitchen, where you can see the back yard and the side entrance, too. Patrol duty, that's what I'm putting you on."

"Yes, *suh,* Mr. Yancey!" agreed Isaiah. "Patrol." His dejected frame now underwent a transformation as it stiffened to fit the new martial rôle.

"Now listen close. If anybody comes up to the house—they won't come the front way, but at the back, probably, or the side—you take this—and shoot." He took from beneath the Prince Albert a gun which, well on the left, under the coat, was not visible as were the two six-shooters that he always carried at his belt. It was a six-shooter of the kind known as the single-action. The trigger was dead. It had been put out of commission. The dog—that part of the mechanism by which the hammer was held cocked and which was released at the pulling of the trigger—had been filed off. It was the deadliest of Southwestern weapons, a six-shooter whose hammer, when pulled back by the thumb, would fall again as soon as released. No need for Isaiah's small forefinger to wrestle with the trigger.

"Oh, Yancey!" breathed Sabra, in horror. She made as though to put Cim behind her—to shield him with her best black grosgrain silk from sight of this latest horror of pioneer existence. "Yancey! He's a child!" Now it was she who was protecting the black boy from Yancey. Yancey ignored her.

"You remember what I told you last week," he went on, equably. "When we were shooting at the tin can on the fence post in the yard. Do it just as you did it then —draw, aim, and shoot with the one motion."

"Yes, *suh,* Mr. Yancey! I kill 'em daid."

"You'll have a brand-new suit of Sunday clothes next week, remember, and boots to go with it. Now, scoot!"

Isaiah turned on the crazy high-heeled boots. "Take them off!" screamed Sabra. "You'll kill yourself. The gun. You'll stumble!"

But he flashed a brilliant, a glorified smile at her over his shoulder and was off, a ludicrous black Don Quixote miraculously keeping his balance; the boots slapping the deep dust of the road now this way, now that.

All Sabra's pleasurable anticipation in the church meeting had fled. "How could you give a gun to a child like that? You'll be giving one to Cim, here, next. Alone in the house, with a gun."

"It isn't loaded. Come on, honey. We're late."

For the first time in their married life she doubted his word absolutely. He strode along toward the tent. She hurried at his side. Cim trotted to keep up with her, his hand in hers.

"What did you mean when you said there were people who would set fire to the house? I never heard of such . . . Did you really mean that someone . . . or was it an excuse to send Isaiah back because of the way he looked?"

"That was it."

For the second time she doubted him. "I don't believe you. There's something going on—something you haven't told me. Yancey, tell me."

"I haven't time now. Don't be foolish. I just don't like the complexion of—I just thought that maybe this meeting was the idea of somebody who isn't altogether inspired by a desire for a closer communion with God. Just occurred to me. I don't know why. Good joke on me, if it's true."

"I'm not going to the meeting. I'm going back to the house." She was desperate. Her house was burning up, Isaiah was being murdered. Her linen, the silver in the DeGrasse pattern, the cake dish, the green nun's veiling.

"You're coming with me." He rarely used this tone toward her.

"Yancey! Yancey, I'm afraid to have you stand up there, before all those people. I'm afraid. Let's go back. Tell them you're sick. Tell them I'm sick. Tell them———"

They had reached the tent. The flap was open. A roar of talk came to them from within. The entrance was packed with lean figures smoking and spitting. "Hi, Yancey! How's the preacher? Where's your Bible, Yancey?"

"Right here, boys." And Yancey reached into the capacious skirt of his Prince Albert to produce in triumph the Word of God. "Come in or stay out, boys. No loafing in the doorway." With Sabra on his arm he marched through the close-packed tent. "They've saved two seats for you and Cim down front—or should have. Yes, there they are."

Sabra felt faint. She had seen the foxlike face of Lon Yountis in the doorway. "That man," she whispered to Yancey. "He was there. He looked at you as you passed by—he looked at you so———"

"That's fine, honey. Better than I hoped for. Nothing I like better than to have members of my flock right under my eye."

9

RANGED ALONG THE rear of the tent were the Indians. Osages, Poncas, Cherokees, Creeks. They had come from miles around. The Osages wore their blankets, striped orange, purple, green, scarlet, blue. The bucks wore hats—battered and dirty sombreros set high up on their heads. The thin snaky braids of their long black hair hung like wire ropes over their shoulders and down their breasts. Though they wore, for the most part, the checked gingham shirt of the white man there was always about them the gleam of metal, the flash of some brightly dyed fabric, the pattern of colored beads. The older women were shapeless bundles, with the exception of those of the Osage tribe. The Osage alone had never intermarried with the negro. Except for intermingled white blood, the tribe was pure. The Indian children tumbled all about. The savages viewed the proceedings impassively, their faces bronze masks in which only the eyes moved. Later, on their reservations, with no white man to see and hear, they would gossip like fishwives; they would shake with laughter; they would retail this or that absurdity which, with their own eyes, they had seen the white man perform. They would slap their knees and rock with mirth.

"Great jokers, the Indians," Yancey had once said, offhand, to Sabra. She had felt sure that he was mistaken. They were sullen, taciturn, grave. They did not speak; they grunted. They never laughed.

Holding Cim's hand tightly in her own, Sabra, escorted by Yancey, found that two chairs had been placed for them. Other fortunate ones sat perched on the saloon bar, on the gambling tables, on the benches, on upturned barrels. The rest of the congregation stood. Sabra glanced shyly about her. Men—hundreds of men. They were strangely alike, all those faces; young-old, weather-beaten, deeply seamed, and, for the most part, beardless. The Plains had taken them early, had scorched them with her sun, parched them with her drought, buffeted them with her wind, stung them with her dust. Sabra had grown accustomed to these faces during the past two weeks. But the women—she was not prepared for the women. Calico and sunbonnets there were in plenty; but the wives of Osage's citizenry had taken this first opportunity to show what they had in the way of finery; dresses that they had brought with them from Kansas, from Texas, from Arkansas, from Colorado, carefully laid away in layers of papers which in turn were smoothed into pasteboard boxes or into trunks. Headgear trembled with wired roses. Cheviot and lady's-cloth and henrietta graced shoulders that had known only cotton this month past. Near her, and occupying one of the seats evidently reserved for persons of distinction, was a woman who must be, Sabra thought, about her own age; perhaps twenty or twenty-one, fair, blue eyed, almost childlike in her girlish slimness and purity of contour. She was very well dressed in a wine-color silk-warp henrietta, bustled, very tightly basqued, and elaborate with fluting on sleeves and collar. Dress and bonnet were city made and very modish. From Denver, Sabra thought, or Kansas City, or even Chicago. Sabra further decided, with feminine unreason, that her nose was the most exquisite feature of the kind she had ever seen; that her fair skin could not long endure this burning, wind-deviled climate and that the man beside her, who looked old enough to be her father, must be, after all, her husband. It was in the way he spoke to her, gazed at her, touched her. Yancey had pointed him out one day. She remembered his name because it had amused her at the time: Waltz, Evergreen Waltz. He was a notorious Southwest gambler, earned his living by the cards, and was supposed to be the errant son of the former governor of some state or other—she thought it was Texas. The girl looked unhappy; and beneath that, rebellious.

Still, the sight of this lovely face, and of the other feminine faces looking out from at least fairly modish and decent straw bonnets and toques, gave Sabra a glow of reassurance. Immediately this was quenched at the late, showy, and dramatic entrance, just before Yancey took his place, of a group of women of whom Sabra had actually been unaware. As a matter of fact, the leader of this spectacular group, whose appearance caused a buzz and stir throughout the tent, had arrived in Osage only the day before, accompanied by a bevy of six young ladies. The group had stepped off the passenger coach of the Katy at the town of Wahoo arrayed in such cinder-strewn splendor as to cause the depot loafers to reel. The Katy had not yet been brought as far as Osage. It terminated at Wahoo, twenty-two miles away. The vision, in her purple grosgrain silk, with a parasol to match, and two purple plumes in her hat, with her six gayly bedecked companions had mounted a buckboard amid much shrill clamor and many giggles and a striking display of ankle. In this crude vehicle, their silks outspread, their astounding parasols unfurled, they had bumped their way over the prairie to the town. Osage, since that first mad day of its beginning, had had its quota of shady ladies, but these had been raddled creatures, driftwood from this or that deserted mining camp or abandoned town site, middle aged, unsavory, and doubtless slightly subnormal mentally.

These were different. The leader, a handsome black-haired woman of not more than twenty-two or -three, had taken for herself and her companions such rooms as they could get in the town. Osage gazed on the parasols, bedazzled. Within an hour it was known that the woman claimed the name of Dixie Lee. That she was a descendant of decayed Southern aristocracy. That her blooming companions boasted such fancy nomenclature as Cherry de St. Maurice, Carmen Brown, Belle Mansero, and the like. That the woman, shrewd as a man and sharp as a knife, had driven a bargain whereby she was to come into possession, at a stiff price, of the building known as the Elite Rooming House and Café, situated at the far end of Pawhuska Avenue, near the gambling tent; and that she contemplated building a house of her own, planned for her own peculiar needs, if business warranted. Finally, she brought the news, gained God knows how or where, that the Katy was to be extended to Osage and perhaps beyond it. Thus harlotry, heretofore a sordid enough slut in a wrapper and curling pins, came to Osage in silks and plumes, with a brain behind it and a promise of prosperity in its gaudy train.

Dixie Lee, shrewd saleswoman, had been quick to learn of Sunday's meeting, and quicker still to see the advantage of this opportunity for a public advertisement of her business. So now, at Osage's first church meeting, in marched the six, with Dixie Lee at their head making a seventh. They rustled in silks. The air of the close-packed tent became as suffocating with scent as a Persian garden at sunset. Necks were craned; whispers became a buzz; seats were miraculously found for these representatives of a recognized social order, as for visiting royalty. The dazzling tent top, seeming to focus rather than disseminate the glare of the Oklahoma sun, cast its revealing spotlight upon painted cheeks and beaded lashes. The nude and lolling lady of the cherries in Grat Gotch's newly acquired art treasure stared down at them, open-mouthed, with the look of one who is surprised and vanquished by an enemy from her own camp. The hard-working worthy wives of Osage, in their cheviots and their faded bonnets and cotton gloves, suddenly seemed sallow, scrawny, and almost spectacularly unalluring.

All this Sabra beheld in a single glance, as did the entire congregation. Only the Indians, standing or squatting in a row at the back, like an Egyptian frieze against the white of the tent, remained unagitated, remote. Yancey, having lifted Cim into the chair next his mother, looked up at the entrance of this splendid procession.

"God Almighty!" he said. His tone was as irreverent as the words were sacred. A dull flush suffused his face, a thing so rare in him as to startle Sabra more than the words he had uttered or the tone in which he had said them.

"What is it? Yancey! What's wrong?"

"That's the girl."

"What girl?"

"That one—Dixie Lee—she's the girl in the black tights and the skull-cap . . . in the Run . . . on the thoroughbred . . ." he was whispering.

"Oh, no!" cried Sabra, aloud. It was wrung from her. Those near by stared.

So this was the church meeting toward which she had looked with such hope, such happy assurance. Harlots, pictures of nude women, Indians, heat, glare, her house probably blazing at this moment, Isaiah weltering in his own gore, Lon Yountis's sinister face sneering in the tent entrance. And now this woman, unscrupulous, evil, who had stolen Yancey's quarter section from him by a trick.

Yancey made his way through the close-packed crowd, leaped to the top of the roulette table which was to be his platform, flung his broad-brimmed white sombrero dexterously to the outjutting base of a suspended oil lamp, where it spun and then clung, cocked rakishly; and, lifting the great lolling head, swept the expectant congregation with his mysterious, his magnetic eyes.

Probably never in the history of the Christian religion had the Word of God been preached by so romantic and dashing a figure. His long black locks curled on his shoulders; the fine eyes glowed; the Prince Albert swayed with his graceful movements; his six-shooters, one on each side, bulged reassuringly in their holsters.

His thrilling voice sounded through the tent, stilling its buzz and movement.

"Friends and fellow citizens, I have been called on to conduct this opening meeting of the Osage First Methodist, Episcopal, Lutheran, Presbyterian, Congregational, Baptist, Catholic, Unitarian Church. In the course of my career as a lawyer and an editor I have been required to speak on varied occasions and on many subjects. I have spoken in defense of my country and in criticism of it; I have been called on to defend and to convict horse thieves, harlots, murderers, samples of which professions could doubtless be found in any large gathering in the Indian Territory to-day. I name no names. I point no finger. Whether for good or for evil, the fact remains that any man or woman, for whatever purpose, found in this great Oklahoma country to-day is here because in his or her veins, actuated by motives lofty or base, there is the spirit of adventure. I ask with Shakespeare, 'Why should a man, whose blood is warm within, sit like his grandsire cut in alabaster?' Though I know the Bible from cover to cover, and while many of its passages and precepts are graven on my heart and in my memory, this, fellow citizens of Osage, is the first time that I have been required to speak the Word of God in His Temple." He glanced around the gaudy, glaring tent. "For any shelter, however sordid, however humble—no offense, Grat—becomes, while His Word is spoken within it, His Temple. Suppose, then, that we unite in spirit by uniting in song. We have, you will notice, no hymn books.

We will therefore open this auspicious occasion in the brief but inevitably glorious history of the city of Osage by singing—uh—what do you all know boys, anyway?"

There was a moment's slightly embarrassing pause. The hard-bitten faces of the motley congregation stared blankly up at Yancey. Yancey, self-possessed, vibrant, looked warmly down on them. He raised an arm in encouragement. "Come on, boys! Name it! Any suggestions, ladies and gentlemen?"

"How about Who Were You At Home? just for a starter," called out a voice belonging to a man with a shining dome-shaped bald head and a flowing silky beard, reddish in color. He was standing near the rear of the tent. It was Shanghai Wiley, up from Texas; owner of more than one hundred thousand long-horn cattle and of the Rancho Palacios, on Tres Palacios Creek. He was the most famous cattle singer in the whole Southwest, besides being one of its richest cattle and land owners. Possessed of a remarkably high sweet tenor voice that just escaped being a clear soprano, he had been known to quiet a whole herd of restless cattle on the verge of a mad stampede. It was an art he had learned when a cowboy on the range. Many cowboys had it, but none possessed the magic soothing quality of Shanghai's voice. It was reputed to have in it the sorcery of the superhuman. It was told of him that in a milling herd, their nostrils distended, their flanks heaving, he had been seen to leap from the back of one maddened steer to another, traveling the moving mass that was like a shifting sea, singing to them in his magic tenor, stopping them just as they were about to plunge into the Rio Grande.

Yancey acknowledged this suggestion with a grateful wave of the hand. "That's right, Shanghai. Thanks for speaking up. A good song, though a little secular for the occasion, perhaps. But anyway, you all know it, and that's the main thing. Kindly favor us with the pitch, will you, Shanghai? Will the ladies kindly join in with their sweet soprano voices? Now, then, all together!"

It was a well-known song in the Territory where, on coming to this new and wild country, so many settlers with a checkered—not to say plaid—past had found it convenient to change their names.

The congregation took it up feelingly, almost solemnly:

> Who were you at home?
> Who were you at home?
> God alone remembers
> Ere you first began to roam.
> Jack or Jo or Bill or Pete,
> Anyone you chance to meet,
> Sure to hit it just as neat,
> Oh, who were you at home?
> "Now, all together! Again!"

"Now, all together! Again!"

Somebody in the rear suddenly produced an accordion, and from the crowd perched on the saloon bar came the sound of a jew's harp. The chorus now swelled with all the fervor of song's ecstasy. They might have been singing Onward, Christian Soldiers. Through it all, high and clear, sounded Shanghai Wiley's piercing tenor, like brasses in a band, and sustaining it from the roulette table platform the 'cello of Yancey Cravat's powerful, rich barytone.

Oh, WHO were you at home?
WHO were you at HOME?

They had not risen to sing for the reason that most of the congregation was already standing, and the few who were seated were afraid to rise for fear that their seats would be snatched from under them.

Sabra had joined in the singing, not at first, but later, timidly. It had seemed, somehow, to relieve her. This, she thought, was better. Perhaps, after all, this new community was about to make a proper beginning. Yancey, she thought, looked terribly handsome, towering there on the roulette table, his eyes alight, his slim foot, in its shining boot, keeping time to the music. She began to feel prim and good and settled at last.

"Now, then," said Yancey, all aglow, "the next thing in order is to take up the collection before the sermon."

"What for?" yelled Pete De Vargas.

Yancey fixed him with a pitying gray eye. "Because, you Spanish infidel, part of a church service is taking up a collection. Southwest Davis, I appoint you to work this side of the house. Ike Bixler, you take that side. The collection, fellow citizens, ladies and gentlemen—and you, too, Pete—is for the new church organ."

"Why, hell, Yancey, we ain't even got a church!" bawled Pete again, aggrieved.

"That's all right, Pete. Once we buy an organ we'll have to build a church to put it in. Stands to reason. Members of the congregation, anybody putting in less than two bits will be thrown out of the tent by me. Indians not included."

The collection was taken up, in two five-gallon sombreros, the contents of which, as they passed from one hairy sunburned paw to the next, were watched with eagle eyes by Southwest Davis and Ike Bixler, and, in fact, by the entire gathering. The sombreros were then solemnly and with some hesitation brought to the roulette table pulpit for Yancey's inspection.

"Mr. Grat Gotch, being used to lightning calculations in the matter of coins, will kindly count the proceeds of the collection."

Arkansas Grat, red-faced and perspiring, elbowed his way to the pulpit and made his swift and accurate count. He muttered the result to Yancey. Yancey announced it publicly. "Fellow citizens, the sum of the first collection for the new church organ for the Osage church, whose denomination shall be nameless, is the gratifying total of one hundred and thirty-three dollars and fifty-five cents.—Heh, wait a minute, Grat! Fifty-five—did you say fifty-five cents?"

"That's right, Yancey."

Yancey's eye swept his flock. "Some miserable tight-fisted skinflint of a—— But maybe it was a Ponca or an Osage, by mistake."

"How about a Cherokee, Yancey?" came a taunting voice from somewhere in the rear.

"No, not a Cherokee, Sid. Recognized your voice by the squeak. A Cherokee—as you'd know if you knew anything at all—you and Yountis and the rest of your outfit—is too smart to put anything in the contribution box of a race that has robbed him of his birthright." He did not pause for the titter that went round. He now took from the rear pocket of the flowing Prince Albert the small and worn little Bible. "Friends! We've come to the sermon. What I have to say is going to take fifteen minutes. The first five minutes are going to be devoted to a confession by me to you, and I didn't expect to make it when I accepted the job of conducting this church meeting. Walt Whitman—say, boys, there's a poet with red blood in him, and the feel of the land, and a love of his fellow beings!—Walt Whitman has a line that has stuck in my memory. It is: 'I say the real and permanent grandeur of these states must be their religion.' That's what Walt says. And that's the text I intended to use for the subject of my sermon, though I know that the Bible should furnish it. And now, at the eleventh hour, I've changed my mind. It's from the Good Book, after all. I'll announce my text, and then I'll make my confession, and following that, any time left will be devoted to the sermon. Any lady or gent wishing to leave the tent will kindly do so now, before the confession, and with my full consent, or remain in his or her seat until the conclusion of the service, on pain of being publicly held up to scorn by me in the first issue of my newspaper, the *Oklahoma Wigwam,* due off the press next Thursday. Anyone wishing to leave the tent kindly rise now and pass as quietly as may be to the rear. Please make way for all departing—uh—worshipers.''

An earthquake might have moved a worshiper from his place in that hushed and expectant gathering: certainly no lesser cataclysm of nature. Yancey waited, Bible in hand, a sweet and brilliant smile on his face. He waited quietly, holding the eyes of the throng in that stifling tent. A kind of power seemed to flow from him to them, drawing them, fixing them, enthralling them. Yet in his eyes, and in the great head raised now as it so rarely was, there was that which sent a warning pang of fear through Sabra. She, too, felt his magnetic draw, but mingled with it was a dreadful terror—a stab of premonition. The little pitted places in the skin of forehead and cheeks were somehow more noticeable. Twice she had seen his eyes look like that.

Yancey waited yet another moment. Then he drew a long breath. "My text is from Proverbs. 'There is a lion in the way; a lion is in the streets.' Friends, there is a lion in the streets of Osage, our fair city, soon to be Queen of the Great Southwest. A lion is in the streets. And I have been a liar and a coward and an avaricious knave. For I pretended not to have knowledge which I have; and I went about asking for information of this lion—though I would change the word lion to jackal or dirty skunk if I did not feel it to be sacrilege to take liberties with Holy Writ—when already I had proof positive of his guilt—proof in writing, for which I paid, and about which I said nothing. And the reason for this deceit of mine I am ashamed to confess to you, but I shall confess it. I intended to announce to you all today that I had this knowledge, and I meant to announce to you from this pulpit—" he glanced down at the roulette table—"from this platform—that I would publish this knowledge in the columns of the *Oklahoma Wigwam* on Thursday, hoping thereby to gain profit and fame because of the circulation which this would gain for my paper, starting it off with a bang!'' At the word "bang," uttered with much vehemence, the congregation of Osage's First Methodist, Episcopal, Lutheran, etc., church jumped noticeably and nervously. "Friends and fellow citizens, I repent of my greed and of my desire for self-advancement at the expense of this community. I no longer intend to withhold, for my own profit, the name of the jackal in a lion's skin who, by threats of sudden death, has held this town abjectly terrorized. I stand here to announce to you that the name of that skunk, that skulking fiend and soulless murderer who shot down Jack Pegler when his back was turned—that coward and poltroon—'' he was gesturing with his Bible in his hand, brandishing it aloft—"was none other than———''

He dropped the Bible to the floor as if by accident, in his rage. As he stooped for it, on that instant, there was the crack of a revolver, a bullet from a six-shooter in the rear of the tent sang past the spot where his head had been, and there appeared in the white surface of the tent a tiny circlet of blue that was the Oklahoma sky. But before that dot of blue appeared

Yancey Cravat had raised himself halfway from the hips, had fired from the waist without, seemingly, pausing to take aim. His thumb flicked the hammer. That was all. The crack of his six-shooter was, in fact, so close on the heels of that first report that the two seemed almost simultaneous. The congregation was now on its feet, en masse, its back to the roulette table pulpit. Its eyes were on one figure; its breath was suspended. That figure—a man—was seen to perform some curious antics. He looked, first of all, surprised. With his left hand he had gripped one of the taut tent ropes, and now, with his hand still grasping the hempen line, his fingers slipping gently along it, as though loath to let go, he sank to the floor, sat there a moment, as if in meditation, loosed his hand's hold of the rope, turned slightly, rolled over on one side and lay there, quite still.

"—Lon Yountis," finished Yancey, neatly concluding his sentence and now holding an ivory-mounted six-shooter in right and left hand.

Screams. Shouts. A stampede for the door. Then the voice of Yancey Cravat, powerful, compelling, above the roar. He sent one shot through the dome of the tent to command attention. "Stop! Stand where you are! The first person who stampedes this crowd gets a bullet. Shut that tent flap, Jesse, like I told you to this morning. Louie Hefner, remove the body and do your duty."

"Okeh, Yancey. It's self-defense and justifiable homicide."

"I know it. Louie, . . . Fellow citizens! We will forego the sermon this morning, but next Sabbath, if requested, I shall be glad to take the pulpit again, unless a suitable and ordained minister of God can be procured. The subject of my sermon for next Sabbath will be from Proverbs XXVI, 27: 'Whoso diggeth a pit shall fall therein' . . . This church meeting, brethren and sisters, will now be concluded with prayer." There was a little thudding, scuffling sound as a heavy, inert burden was carried out through the tent flap into the noonday sunshine. His six-shooters still in his hands, Yancey Cravat bowed his magnificent buffalo head—but not too far—and sent the thrilling tones of his beautiful voice out into the agitated crowd before him.

". . . bless this community, O Lord. . . ."

10

MOURNFULLY, AND IN accordance with the custom of the community, Yancey carved a notch in the handsome ivory and silver-mounted butt of his six-shooter. It was then for the first time that Sabra, her eyes widening with horror, noticed that there were five earlier notches cut in the butts of Yancey's two guns—two on one, three on the other. This latest addition brought the number up to six.

Aghast, she gingerly investigated further. She saw that the two terrifying weapons were not worn completely encased in the holster but each was held within it by an ingenious steel clip, elastic and sensitive as a watch spring. This spring gripped the barrel securely and yet so lightly that the least effort would set it free. Yancey could pull his gun and thumb the hammer with but one motion, instead of two. The infinitesimal saving of time had saved his life that day.

"Oh, Yancey, you haven't killed six men!"

"I've never killed a man unless I knew he'd kill me if I didn't."

"But that's murder!"

"Would you have liked to see Yountis get me?"

"Oh, darling, no! I died a thousand deaths while you were standing there.

That terrible prayer, when I thought surely someone else would shoot you. But wasn't there some other way? Did you have to kill him? Like that?"

"Why, no, honey. I could have let him kill me."

"Cim has seen his own father shoot a man and kill him."

"Better than seeing a man shoot and kill his own father."

There was nothing more that she could say on this subject. But still another question was consuming her.

"That woman. That woman. I saw you talking to her, right on the street, in broad daylight to-day, after the meeting. All that horrible shooting—all those people around you—Cim screaming—and then to find that woman smirking and talking. Bad enough if you'd never seen her before. But she stole your land from you in the Run. You stood there, actually talking to her. Chatting."

"I know. She said she had made up her mind that day of the Run to get a piece of land, and farm it, and raise cattle. She wanted to give up her way of living. She's been at it since she was eighteen. Now she's twenty-six. Older than she looks. She comes of good stock. She was desperate."

"What she doing here, then?"

"Before the month was up she saw she couldn't make it go. One hundred and sixty acres. Then the other women homesteaders found out about her. It was no use. She sold out for five hundred dollars, added to it whatever money she had saved, and went to Denver."

"Why didn't she stay there?"

"Her business was overcrowded there. She got a tip that the railroad was coming through here. She's a smart girl. She got together her outfit, and down she came."

"You talk as though you admired her! That—that—" Felice Venable's word came to her lips—"that hussy!"

"Sne's a smart girl. She's a—" he hesitated, as though embarrassed— "in a way she's a—well, in a way, she's a good girl."

Sabra's voice rose to the pitch of hysteria.

"Don't you quote your Bible at me, Yancey Cravat! You with your Lukes and your Johns and your Magdalenes! I'm sick of them."

The first issue of the *Oklahoma Wigwam* actually appeared on Thursday, as scheduled. It was a masterly mixture of reticence and indiscretion. A half column, first page, was devoted to the church meeting. The incident of the shooting was not referred to in this account. An outsider, reading it, would have gathered that all had been sweetness and light. On an inside column of the four-page sheet was a brief notice:

> It is to be regretted that an unimportant but annoying shooting affray somewhat marred the otherwise splendid and truly impressive religious services held in the recreation tent last Sunday, kindness of the genial and popular proprietor, Mr. Grat Gotch. A ruffian, who too long had been infesting the streets of our fair city of Osage, terrorizing innocent citizens, and who was of the contemptible ilk that has done so much toward besmirching the dazzling fame of the magnificent Southwest, took this occasion to create a disturbance, during which he shot, with intent to kill, at the person presiding. It was necessary to reply in kind. The body, unclaimed, was interred in Boot Hill, with only the prowling jackals to mourn him, their own kin. It is hoped that his nameless grave will serve as a warning to others of his class.

Having thus modestly contained himself in the matter of the actual shooting, Yancey let himself go a little on the editorial page. His editorials, in fact, for a time threatened the paper's news items. Sabra and Jesse Rickey had to convince him that the coming of the Katy was of more interest to prospective subscribers than was the editorial entitled, Lower than the Rattlesnake. He was prevailed upon to cut it slightly, though under protest.

> The rattlesnake has a bad reputation. People accuse him
> of a great many mean things, and it cannot be denied that
> the world would be better off if his species were extermi-
> nated. Nine times out of ten his bite is fatal, and many homes
> have been saddened because of his venomous attacks. But
> the rattlesnake is a gentleman and a scholar beside some
> snakes. He always gives warning. It is the snake that takes
> you unawares that hurts the worst. . . .

Thus for a good half column.

Sabra, reading the damp galley proof, was murmurous with admiration. "It's just wonderful! But, Yancey, don't you think we ought to have more news items? Gossip, sort of. I don't mean gossip, really, but about people, and what they're doing, and so on. Those are the things I like to read in a newspaper. Of course men like editorials and important things like that. But women——"

"That's right, too," agreed Jesse Rickey, looking up, ink smeared, from his case. "Get the women folks to reading the paper."

Sabra was emerging slowly from her rôle of charming little fool. By degrees she was to take more and more of a hand in the assembling of the paper's intimate weekly items, while Yancey was concerned with cosmic affairs. Indeed, had it not been for Sabra and Jesse Rickey that first issue of the *Oklahoma Wigwam* might never have appeared, for the front office of the little wooden shack that served as newspaper plant was crowded, following that eventful Sunday, with congratulatory committees, so that it seemed stuffed to suffocation with sombreros, six-shooters, boots, tobacco, and repetitious talk.

"Yessir, Yancey, that was one of the quickest draws I ever see. . . . And you was on to him all the time, huh? Sa-a-ay, you're a slick one, all right. They don't come no slicker. . . . The rest of the gang has took to the Hills, I understand. That shows they're scairt, because they got a feud with the Kid and his outfit, and the Kid sees 'em he'll drop 'em like a row of gobblers at a turkey shootin'. Yessir, Yancey, you're the kind of stuff this country needs out here. First thing you know you'll be Governor of the Territory. How's that, boys! Come on out and have a drink to the future new Governor, the Honorable Yancey Cravat!"

The group moved in a body across the dusty street into the Sunny Southwest Saloon, from whence came further and more emphatic sounds of approbation.

Sabra, in her checked gingham kitchen apron, was selecting fascinating facts from the stock of ready-print brought with them from Wichita, fresh supplies of which they would receive spasmodically by mail or express via the Katy or the Santa Fé.

SWIMMING BRIDES

> Girls inhabiting the Island of Himla near Rhodes, are not
> allowed to marry until they have brought up a specified
> number of sponges, each taken from a certain depth. The
> people of the Island earn their living by the sponge fishery.

STRENGTH OF THE THUMB

The thumb is stronger than all the other fingers together.

COMPRESSED AIR FOR MINE HAULAGE

During the last ten years a great many mines have replaced
animal haulage with compressed air motors.

As the printing plant boasted only a little hand press, the two six-column
forms had to be inked with a hand roller. Over this was placed the damp
piece of white print paper. Each sheet was done by hand. The first issue of
the *Oklahoma Wigwam* numbered four hundred and fifty copies, and before
it was run off, Yancey, Jesse Rickey, Sabra, Isaiah—every member of the
household except little Cim—had taken a turn at the roller. Sabra's back
and arm muscles ached for a week.

Yancey made vigorous protest. "What! Ink on the white wonder of dear
Juliet's hand! Out, damned spot! See here, honey. This will never do. My
sweet Southern jasmine working over a miserable roller! I'd rather never
get out a paper, I tell you."

"It looks as if you never would, anyway." The sweet Southern jasmine
did not mean to be acid; but the events of the past two or three weeks were
beginning to tell on her nerves. The ready-print contained the opening chap-
ters of a novel by Bertha M. Clay in which beauty and virtue triumphed over
evil. An instalment of this would appear weekly. The second half of it was
missing. But Sabra sagely decided that this fragment, for a time at least,
would compensate the feminine readers of the *Oklahoma Wigwam* for the
preponderance of civic and political matter and the scarcity of social and
personal items. She made up her mind that she would conquer her shyness
and become better acquainted with some of those cheviots and straw bonnets
seen at the Sunday church meeting.

Yancey and Jesse Rickey seemed to have some joke between them. Sabra,
in her kitchen, could hear them snickering like a couple of schoolgirls. They
were up to some mischief. Yancey was possessed of the rough and childlike
notion of humor that was of the day and place.

"What are you boys up to?" she asked him at dinner.

He was all innocence. "Nothing. Not a thing! What a suspicious little
puss you're getting to be."

The paper came out on Thursday afternoon, as scheduled. Sabra was
astonished and a little terrified to see the occasion treated as an event, with
a crowd of cowboys and local citizens in front of the house, pistols fired,
whoops and yells; and Yancey himself, aided by Jesse Rickey, handing out
copies as if they had cost nothing to print. Perhaps twenty-five of these were
distributed, opened eagerly, perused by citizens leaning against the porch
posts, and by cowboys on horseback, before Sabra, peeking out of the office
window, saw an unmistakable look of surprise—even of shock—on their
faces and heard Cass Bixby drawl, "Say, Yancey, that's a hell of a name
for a newspaper."

She sent Isaiah out to get hold of a copy. He came back with it, grinning.
It was a single sheet. The *Oklahoma Galoot*. Motto: Take It or Leave It.
Beneath this a hastily assembled and somewhat pied collection of very personal items, calculated to reveal the weaknesses and foibles of certain prominent citizens now engaged in perusing the false sheet.

The practical joke being revealed and the *bona fide* paper issued, this was
considered a superb triumph for Yancey, and he was again borne away to
receive the congratulatory toasts of his somewhat sheepish associates.

It was a man's town. The men enjoyed it. They rode, gambled, swore, fought, fished, hunted, drank. The antics of many of them seemed like those of little boys playing robber's cave under the porch. The saloon was their club, the brothel their social rendezvous, the town women their sweethearts. Literally there were no other young girls of marriageable age; for the men and women who had come out here were, like Sabra and Yancey, married couples whose ages ranged between twenty and forty. It was no place for the very young, the very old, or even the middle-aged. Through it all wove the Indians, making a sad yet colorful pattern. The Osage reservation was that nearest the town of Osage. There now was some talk of changing the name of the town because of this, but it never was done. It had been named in the rush of the Run. The Osages, unlike many of the other Territory Plains tribes, were a handsome people—tall, broad shouldered, proud. The women carried themselves well, head up, shoulders firm, their step leisurely and light. Their garments were mean enough, but over them they wore the striped blanket of the tribe, orange and purple and scarlet and blue, dyed with the same brilliant lasting dyes that Mother Bridget had used in Sabra's coverlet. They came in from the Reservation on foot; sometimes a family rattled along the red clay road that led into town, huddled in a wagon, rickety, mud spattered. Sometimes a buck rode a scrofulous horse, his lean legs hugging its sorry flanks. The town treated them with less consideration than the mongrel curs that sunned themselves in the road. They bought their meager supplies with the stipend that the government allowed them; the men bought, stole, or begged whisky when they could, though fire water was strictly forbidden them, and to sell or give it to an Indian was a criminal offense. They lolled or squatted in the sun. They would not work. They raised a little corn which, mixed with lye, they called soffica. This mess, hot or cold, was eaten with a spoon made from the horn of a cow. Sabra hated them, even feared them, though Yancey laughed at her for this. Cim was forbidden by her to talk to them. This after she discovered that Yancey had taken him out to visit the Reservation one afternoon. Here, then, was the monstrous society in which Sabra Cravat now found herself. For her, and the other respectable women of the town, there was nothing but their housework, their children, their memories of the homes they had left.

And so the woman who was, after all, the most intelligent among them, set about creating some sort of social order for the good wives of the community. All her life Sabra had been accustomed to the open-handed hospitality of the South. The Venable household in Wichita had been as nearly as possible a duplicate of the Mississippi mansion which had housed generations of Sabra's luxury-loving and open-handed ancestors. Hordes of relatives came and went. Food and drink were constantly being passed in abundance. White muslin dresses and blue sashes whirled at the least provocative tinkle of the handsome old square piano with its great blobs of grapevine carving. Friends drove up for midday dinner and stayed a week. Felice Venable's musical drawl was always tempting the sated guest to further excesses. "I declare, Cousin Flora May, you haven't eaten enough to keep a bird alive. Angie'll think you don't fancy her cooking. . . . Lacy, just another quail. They're only a mouthful. . . . Mittie, pass the currant jell."

Grimly Sabra (and, in time, the other virtuous women of the community) set about making this new frontier town like the old as speedily as possible. Yancey, almost single handed, tried to make the new as unlike the old as possible. He fought a losing fight from the first. He was muddled; frequently insincere; a brilliant swaggerer. He himself was not very clear as to what he wanted, or how to go about getting it. He only knew that he was impatient of things as they were; that greed, injustice, and dishonesty in office were everywhere; that here, in this wild and virgin land, was a chance for a Utopian plan. But he had no plan. He was sentimental about the under dog; overgallant to women; emotional, quick-tempered, impulsive, dramatic, idealistic. And idealism does not flourish in a frontier settlement. Yancey Cravat, with his unformed dreams—much less the roistering play boys of saloon and plain and gambling house—never had a chance against the indomitable materialism of the women.

Like Sabra, most of the women had brought with them from their homes in Nebraska, in Arkansas, in Missouri, in Kansas, some household treasure that in their eyes represented elegance or which was meant to mark them as possessed of taste and background. A chair, a bed, a piece of silver, a vase, a set of linen. It was the period of the horrible gimcrack. Women all over the country were covering wire bread toasters with red plush, embroidering sulphurous yellow chenille roses on this, tying the whole with satin ribbons and hanging it on the wall to represent a paper rack (to be used on pain of death). They painted the backsides of frying pans with gold leaf and daisies, enhanced the handles of these, too, with bows of gay ribbon and, the utilitarian duckling thus turned into a swan, hung it on the wall opposite the toaster. Rolling pins were gilded or sheathed in velvet. Coal scuttles and tin shovels were surprised to find themselves elevated from the kitchen to the parlor, having first been subjected to the new beautifying process. Sabra's house became a sort of social center following the discovery that she received copies of *Harper's Bazar* with fair regularity. Felice Venable sometimes sent it to her, prompted, no doubt, by Sabra's rather guarded account of the lack of style hints for the person or for the home in this new community. Sabra's social triumph was complete when she displayed her new draped jars, done by her after minute instructions found in the latest copy of *Harper's*. She then graciously printed these instructions in the *Oklahoma Wigwam,* causing a flurry of excitement in a hundred homes and mystifying the local storekeepers by the sudden demand for jars.

> As everything [the fashion note announced, haughtily] is now draped, we give an illustration [Sabra did not—at least in the limited columns of the *Wigwam*] of a china or glass jar draped with India silk and trimmed with lace and ribbon, the decoration entirely concealing any native hideousness in the shape or ornamentation of the jar. Perfectly plain jars can also be draped with a pretty piece of silk and tied with ribbon bows or ornamented with an odd fragment of lace and thereby makes a pretty ornament at little or no cost.

Certainly the last four words of the hint were true.

With elegancies such as these the womenfolk of Osage tried to disguise the crudeness and bareness of their glaring wooden shacks. Usually, there was as well a plush chair which had survived the wagon journey; a tortured whatnot on which reposed painted seashells and the *objets d'art* above described; or, on the wall, a crayon portrait or even an oil painting of some stern and bewhiskered or black-silk and fichued parent looking down in surprised disapproval upon the ructions that comprised the daily activities of this town. From stark ugliness the house interiors were thus transformed into grotesque ugliness, but the Victorian sense of beauty was satisfied. The fact was that these women were hungry for the feel of soft silken things; their eyes, smarting with the glare, the wind, the dust, ached to rest on that which was rich and soothing; their hands, roughened by alkali water, and red dust, and burning sun and wind, dwelt lovingly on these absurd scraps of silk and velvet, snipped from an old wedding dress, from a bonnet, from finery that had found its way to the scrap bag.

Aside from the wedding silver and linen that she had brought with her, the loveliest thing that Sabra possessed was the hand-woven blue coverlet that Mother Bridget had given her. It made a true and brilliant spot of color in the sitting room, where it lay neatly folded at the foot of the sofa, partly masking the ugliness of that utilitarian piece of furniture. This Sabra did not know. As silk patchwork quilts, made in wheel and fan patterns, and embroidered in spider webs of bright-colored threads were quite the fashion, the blue coverlet was looked on with considerable disrespect. Thirty years later, its color undimmed, Sabra contributed it temporarily to an exhibition of early American handiwork held in the Venetian room of the Savoy-Bixby Hotel, and it was cooed and ah'd over by all the members of Osage's smart set. They said it was quaint and authentic and very native and a fine example of pioneer handicraft and Sabra said yes indeed, and told them of Mother Bridget. They said she must have been quaint, too. Sabra said she was.

Slowly, in Sabra's eyes, the other women of the town began to emerge from a mist of drabness into distinct personalities. There was one who had been a school teacher in Cairo, Illinois. Her husband, Tracy Wyatt, ran the spasmodic bus and dray line between Wahoo and Osage. They had no children. She was a sparse and simpering woman of thirty-nine, who talked a good deal of former trips to Chicago during which she had reveled in the culture of that effete city. Yancey was heard learnedly discoursing to her on the subject of Etruscan pottery, of which he knew nothing. The ex-school teacher rolled her eyes and tossed her head a good deal.

"You don't know what a privilege it is, Mr. Cravat, to find myself talking to someone whose mind can soar above the sordid life of this horrible town."

Yancey's ardent eyes took on their most melting look. "Madam, it is you who have carried me with you to your heights. 'In youth and beauty wisdom is but rare!' " It was simply his way. He could not help it.

"Ah, Shakespeare!" breathed Mrs. Wyatt, bridling.

"Shakespeare—hell!" said Yancey to Sabra, later. "She doesn't know Pope when she hears him. No woman ought to pretend to be intelligent. And if she is she ought to have the intelligence to pretend she isn't. And this one looks like Cornelia Blimber, to boot."

"Cornelia? . . ."

"A schoolmarm in Dickens's *Dombey and Son*. A magnificent book, honey. I want you to read it. I want Cim to read it by the time he's twelve. I've got it somewhere here on the shelves." He was searching among the jumble of books. Five minutes later he was deep in a copy of Plutarch which he had bewailed as lost.

Sabra persisted. "But why did you make her think she was so smart and attractive when you were talking to her?"

"Because she is so plain, darling."

"It's just that you can't bear not to have everybody think you're fascinating."

She never read *Dombey and Son*, after all. She decided that she preferred exchanging recipes and discussing the rearing of children with the other women to the more intellectual conversation of Mrs. Wyatt.

It was Sabra who started the Philomathean Club. The other women clutched at the idea. It was part of their defense against these wilds. After all, a town that boasted a culture club could not be altogether lost. Sabra had had no experience with this phase of social activity. The languorous yet acid Felice Venable had always scorned to take part in any civic social life that Wichita knew. Kansas, even then, had had its women's clubs, though they were not known by this title. The Ladies' Sewing Circle, one was called; the Twentieth Century Culture Society; the Hypatias.

Felice Venable, approached as a prospective member, had refused languidly.

"I just naturally hate sewing," she had drawled, looking up from the novel she was reading. "And as for culture! Why, the Venables and the Marcys have had it in this country for three hundred years, not to speak of England and France, where they practically started it going. Besides, I don't believe in women running around to club meetings. They'll be going into politics next."

Sabra timidly approached Mrs. Wyatt with her plan to form a woman's club, and Mrs. Wyatt snatched at it with such ferocity as almost to make it appear her own idea. Each was to invite four women of the town's élite. Ten, they decided, would be enough as charter members.

"I," began Mrs. Wyatt promptly, "am going to ask Mrs. Louie Hefner, Mrs. Doc Nisbett————"

"Her husband's horrid! I hate him. I don't want her in my club." The ten barrels of water still rankled.

"We're not asking husbands, my dear Mrs. Cravat. This is a ladies' club."

"Well, I don't think the wife of any such man could be a lady."

"Mrs. Nisbett," retorted Mrs. Wyatt, introducing snobbery into that welter of mud, Indians, pine shacks, drought, and semi-barbarism known as Osage, Indian Territory, "was a Krumpf, of Ouachita, Arkansas."

Sabra, descendant of the Marcys and the Venables, lifted her handsome black eyebrows. Privately, she decided to select her four from among the less vertebrate and more ebullient of Osage's matrons. Culture was all very well, but the thought of mingling once every fortnight with nine versions of the bony Mrs. Wyatt or the pedigreed Mrs. Nisbett (née Krumpf) was depressing. She made up her mind that next day, after the housework was done, she would call on her candidates, beginning with that pretty and stylish Mrs. Evergreen Waltz. Sabra had inherited a strain of frivolity from Felice Venable. At supper that evening she told Yancey of her plans.

"We're going to take up literature, you know. And maybe early American history."

"Why, honey, don't you know you're making it?"

This she did not take seriously. "And then current events, too."

"Well, the events in this town are current enough. I'll say that for them. The trick is to catch them as they go by. You girls'll have to be quick." She told him of her four prospective members.

"Waltz's wife!" Surprise and amusement, too, were in his voice, but she was too full of her plans to notice. Besides, Yancey often was mystifyingly amused at things that seemed to Sabra quite serious. "Why, that's fine, Sabra. That's fine! That's the spirit!"

"I noticed her at church meeting last Sunday. She's so pretty, it rests me to look at her, after all these—not that they're—I don't mean they're not very nice ladies. But after all, even if it's a culture club, someone nearer my own age would be much more fun."

"Oh, much," Yancey agreed, still smiling. "That's what a town like this should be. No class distinctions, no snobbery, no highfalutin notions."

"I saw her washing hanging on the line. Just by accident. You can tell she's a lady. Such pretty underthings, all trimmed with embroidery, and there were two embroidery petticoats all flounced and every bit as nice as the ones Cousin Belle French Vian made for me by hand, for my trousseau."

"I'm not surprised." Yancey was less loquacious than usual. But then, men were not interested in women's clothes.

"She looks kind of babyish and lonely, sitting there by the window sewing all day. And her husband's so much older, and a cripple, too, or almost. I noticed he limps quite badly. What's his trouble?"

"Shot in the leg."

"Oh." She had already learned to accept this form of injury as a matter of course. "I thought I'd ask her to prepare a paper for the third meeting on Mrs. Browning's 'Aurora Leigh.' I could lend her yours to read up on, if you don't mind, just in case she hasn't got it."

Yancey thought it unlikely.

Mrs. Wyatt's house was one of the few in Osage which were used for dwelling purposes alone. No store or office occupied the front of it. Tracy Wyatt's bus and dray line certainly could not be contained in a pine shack intended for family use. Mrs. Wyatt had five rooms. She was annoyingly proud of this, and referred to it on all possible occasions.

"The first meeting," she said, "will be held at my house, of course. It will be so much nicer."

She did not say nicer than what, but Sabra's face set itself in a sort of mask of icy stubbornness. "The first meeting of the Philomathean Society will be held at the home of the Founder." After all, Mrs. Wyatt's house could not boast a screen door, as Sabra's could. It was the only house in Osage that had one. Yancey had had Hefner order it from Kansas City. The wind and the flies seemed to torture Sabra. It was so unusual a luxury that frequently strangers came to the door by mistake, thinking that here was the butcher shop, which boasted the only other screen door in the town.

"I'll serve coffee and doughnuts," Sabra added, graciously. "And I'll move to elect you president. I"—this not without a flick of malice—"am too busy with my household and my child and the newspaper—I often assist my husband editorially—to take up with any more work."

The paper on Mrs. Browning's "Aurora Leigh" never was written by the pretty Mrs. Evergreen Waltz. Three days later Sabra, chancing to glance out of her sitting-room window, saw the crippled and middle-aged gambler passing her house, and in spite of his infirmity he was walking with great speed—running, almost. In his hand was a piece of white paper—a letter, Sabra thought. She hoped it was not bad news. He had looked, she thought, sort of odd and wild.

Evergreen Waltz, after weeks of tireless waiting and watching, had at last intercepted a letter from his young wife's lover. As he now came panting up the street the girl sat at the window, sewing. The single shot went just through the center of the wide white space between her great babyish blue eyes. They found her with the gold initialed thimble on her finger, and the bit of work on which she had been sewing, now brightly spotted with crimson, in her lap.

"Why didn't you tell me that when she married him she was a girl out of a—out of a—house!" Sabra demanded, between horror and wrath.

"I thought you knew. Women are supposed to have intuition, or whatever they call it, aren't they? All those embroidered underthings on the line in a town where water's scarce as champagne—scarcer. And then 'Aurora Leigh.' "

She was thoroughly enraged by now. "What, for pity's sake, has 'Aurora Leigh' got to do with her!"

He got down the volume. "I thought you'd been reading it yourself, perhaps." He opened it. " 'Dreams of doing good for good-for-nothing people.' "

11

SABRA'S SECOND CHILD, a girl, was born in June, a little more than a year after their coming to Osage. It was not as dreadful an ordeal there in those crude surroundings as one might have thought. She refused to send for her mother; indeed, Sabra insisted that Felice Venable be told nothing of the event until after her granddaughter had wailed her way into the Red Man's country. Yancey had been relieved at Sabra's decision. The thought of his luxury-loving and formidable mother-in-law with her flounced dimities and her high-heeled slippers in the midst of this Western wallow to which he had brought her daughter was a thing from which even the redoubtable Yancey shrank. Curiously enough, it was not the pain, the heat, nor the inexpert attention she received that most distressed Sabra. It was the wind. The Oklahoma wind tortured her. It rattled the doors and windows; it whirled the red dust through the house; its hot breath was on her agonized face as she lay there; if allowed its own way it leaped through the rooms, snatching the cloth off the table, the sheets off the bed, the dishes off the shelves.

"The wind!" Sabra moaned. "The wind! The wind! Make it stop." She was a little delirious. "Yancey! With your gun. Shoot it. Seven notches. I don't care. Only stop it."

She was tended, during her accouchement, by the best doctor in the county and certainly the most picturesque man of medicine in the whole Southwest, Dr. Don Valliant. Like thousands of others living in this new country, his past was his own secret. He rode to his calls on horseback, in a black velveteen coat and velveteen trousers tucked into fancy leather boots. His soft black hat, rivaling Yancey's white one, intensified the black of his eyes and hair. It was known that he often vanished for days, leaving the sick to get on as best they could. He would reappear as inexplicably as he had vanished; and it was noticed then that he was worn looking and his horse was jaded. It was no secret that he was often called to attend the bandits when one of their number, wounded in some outlaw raid, had taken to their hiding place in the Hills. He was tender and deft with Sabra, though between them he and Yancey consumed an incredible quantity of whisky during the racking hours of her confinement. At the end he held up a caterwauling morsel of flesh torn from Sabra's flesh—a thing perfect of its kind, with an astonishing mop of black hair.

"This is a Spanish beauty you have for a daughter, Yancey. I present to you Señorita Doña Cravat."

And Donna Cravat she remained. The town, somewhat scandalized, thought she had been named after Dr. Don himself. Besides, they did not consider Donna a name at all. The other women of the community fed their hunger for romance by endowing their girl children with such florid names as they could conjure up out of their imagination or from the novels they read between dish washings. The result was likely to range from the pathetic to the ridiculous. Czarina McKee; Emmeretta Folsom; Gazelle Slaughter; Maurine Turket; Cassandra Sipes; Jewel Riggs.

The neighborhood wives showered the Cravat household with the customary cakes, pies, meat loaves, and bowls of broth. Black Isaiah was touching, was wonderful. He washed dishes, he mopped floors, he actually cooked as though he had inherited the art from Angie, his vast black mother, left behind in Wichita. One of Sabra's gingham kitchen aprons, checked blue and white, was always hitched up under his arms, and beneath this utilitarian yet coquettish garment his great bare feet slapped in and out as he did the work of the household. He was utterly fascinated by the new baby. "Looka dat! She know me! Hi, who yo' rollin' yo' eyes at, makin' faces!" He danced for her, he sang negro songs to her, he rocked her to sleep. He was, as Donna grew older, her nursemaid, pushing her baby buggy up and down the dusty street, and later still her playmate as well as Cim's.

When Sabra Cravat arose from that bed something in her had crystallized. Perhaps it was that, for the first time in a year, she had had hours in which to rest her tired limbs; perhaps the ordeal itself worked a psychic as well as a physical change in her; it might have been that she realized she must cut a new pattern in this Oklahoma life of theirs. The boy Cim might surmount it; the girl Donna never. During the hours through which she had lain in her bed in the stifling wooden shack, mists seemed to have rolled away from before her eyes. She saw clearly. She felt light and terribly capable—so much so that she made the mistake of getting up, dizzily donning slippers and wrapper, and tottering into the newspaper office where Yancey was writing an editorial and shouting choice passages of it into the inattentive ear of Jesse Rickey, who was setting type in the printing shop.

". . . the most stupendous farce ever conceived by the mind of man in a civilized country. . . ."

He looked up to see in the doorway a wraith, all eyes and long black braids. "Why, sugar! What's this? You can't get up!"

She smiled rather feebly. "I'm up. I felt so light, so———"

"I should think you would. All that physic."

"I feel so strong. I'm going to do so many things. You'll see. I'm going to paper the whole house. Rosebuds in the bedroom. I'm going to plant two trees in the front. I'm going to start another club—not like the Philomathean—I think that's silly now—but one to make this town . . . no saloons . . . women like that Dixie Lee . . . going to have a real hired girl as soon as the newspaper begins to . . . feel so queer . . . Yancey . . ."

As she began to topple, Yancey caught the Osage Joan of Arc in his arms.

Incredibly enough, she actually did paper the entire house, aided by Isaiah and Jesse Rickey. Isaiah's ebony countenance splashed with the white paste mixture made a bizarre effect, a trifle startling to anyone coming upon the scene unawares. Also Jesse Rickey's inebriate eye, which so often resulted in many grotesque pied print lines appearing in unexpected and inconvenient places in the *Oklahoma Wigwam* columns, was none too dependable in the matching of rosebud patterns. The result, in spots, was Burbankian, with roses grafted on leaves and tendrils emerging from petals. Still, the effect was gay, even luxurious. The Philomathean Club, as one woman, fell upon wall paper and paste pot, as they had upon the covered jars in Sabra's earlier effort at decoration. Within a month Louie Hefner was compelled to install a full line of wall paper to satisfy the local demand.

Slowly, slowly, the life of the community, in the beginning so wild, so unrelated in its parts, began to weave in and out, warp and woof, to make a pattern. It was at first faint, almost undiscernible. But presently the eye could trace here a motif, there a figure, here a motif, there a figure. The shuttle swept back, forward, back, forward.

"It's almost time for the Jew," Sabra would say, looking up from her sewing. "I need some number forty sewing-machine needles."

And then perhaps next day, or the day after, Cim, playing in the yard, would see a familiar figure, bent almost double, gnomelike and grotesque, against the western sky. It was Sol Levy, the peddler, the Alsatian Jew. Cim would come running into the house, Donna, perhaps, trotting at his heels. "Mom, here comes the Jew!"

Sabra would fold up her work, brush the threads from her apron; or if her hands were in the dough she would hastily mold and crimp her pie crust so as to be ready for his visit.

Sol Levy had come over an immigrant in the noisome bowels of some dreadful ship. His hair was blue-black and very thick, and his face was white in spite of the burning Southwest sun. A black stubble of beard intensified this pallor. He had delicate blue-veined hands and narrow arched feet. His face was delicate, too, and narrow, and his eyes slanted ever so little at the outer corners, so that he had the faintly Oriental look sometimes seen in the student type of his race. He belonged in crowded places, in populous places, in the color and glow and swift drama of the bazaars. God knows how he had found his way to this vast wilderness. Perhaps in Chicago, or in Kansas City, or Omaha he had heard of this new country and the rush of thousands for its land. And he had bummed his way on foot. He had started to peddle with an oilcloth-covered pack on his back. Through the little hot Western towns in summer. Through the bitter cold Western towns in winter. They turned the dogs on him. The children cried, "Jew! Jew!" He was only a boy, disguised with that stubble of beard. He would enter the yard of a farmhouse or a dwelling in a town such as Osage. A wary eye on the dog. Nice Fido. Nice doggie. Down, down! Pins, sewing-machine needles, rolls of gingham and calico, and last, craftily, his Hamburg lace. Hamburg lace for the little girls' petticoats, for the aprons of the lady of the house; the white muslin apron edged with Hamburg lace, to be donned after the midday dinner dishes were done, the house set to rights, her hair tidied with a wet comb, the basket of mending got out, or the roll of strips for the rag rug, to be plaited in the precious hours between three and five. He brought news, too.

"The bridge is out below Gray Horse. . . . The Osages are having a powwow at Hominy. All night they kept me awake with their drums, those savages. . . . The Kid and his gang held up the Santa Fé near Wetoka and got thirty-five thousand dollars; but one of them will never hold up a train again. A shot in the head. Verdigris Bob, they call him. A name! They say the posse almost caught the Kid himself because this Verdigris Bob when he finds he is dying he begs the others to leave him and go on, but first they must stop to take his boots off. His boots he wants to have off, that murderer, to die a respectable man! The Kid stops to oblige him, and the posse in ten more minutes would have caught him, too. A feather in that sheriff's cap, to catch the Kid! . . . A country! My forefathers should have lived to see me here!"

His beautiful, civilized face, mobile as an actor's, was at once expressive of despair and bitter amusement. His long slender hands were spread in a gesture of wondering resignation.

Later he bought a horse—a quadruped possessed unbelievably of the power of locomotion—a thing rheumy-eyed, cadaverous, high rumped, like a cloth horse in a pantomime. Sol Levy was always a little afraid of it; timorous of those great square white teeth, like gravestones. He came of a race of scholars and traders. Horses had been no part of their experience. He had to nerve himself to wait on it, to give it the feed bag, an occasional apple or lump of sugar. With the horse and rickety wagon he now added kitchenware to his stock, coarse china, too; bolts of woollen cloth; and, slyly, bright colored silks and muslin flowers and ribbons. Dixie Lee and her girls fell upon these with feverish fingers and shrill cries, like children. He spread his wares for them silently. Sometimes they teased him, these pretty morons; they hung on his meager shoulders, stroked his beard. He regarded them remotely, almost sadly.

"Come on, Solly!" they said. "Why don't you smile? Don't you never have no fun? I bet you're rich. Jews is all rich. Ain't that the truth, Maude?"

His deep-sunk eyes looked at them. *Schicksas*. They grew uncomfortable under his gaze, then sullen, then angry. "Go on, get the hell out of here! You got your money, ain't you? Get, sheeny!"

He sometimes talked to Dixie Lee. There existed between these two a strange relation of understanding and something resembling respect. Outcasts, both of them, he because of his race, she because of her calling. "A smart girl like you, what do you want in such a business?"

"I've got to live, Solly. God knows why!"

"You come from a good family. You are young yet, you are smart. There are other ways."

"Ye-e-e-s? I guess I'll take up school teaching. Tell a lot of snotty-nosed brats that two and two make four and get handed eleven dollars at the end of the month for it. I tried a couple of things. Nix, nix!"

In a year or two he opened a little store in Osage. It was, at first, only a wooden shack containing two or three rough pine tables on which his wares were spread. He was the town Jew. He was a person apart. Sometimes the cowboys deviled him; or the saloon loungers and professional bad men. They looked upon him as fair game. He thought of them as savages. Yancey came to his rescue one day in the spectacular fashion he enjoyed. Seated at his desk in the *Wigwam* office Yancey heard hoots, howls, catcalls, and then the crack and rat-a-tat-tat of a fusillade. The porch of the Sunny Southwest Saloon was filled with grinning faces beneath sombreros. In the middle of the dusty road, his back against a Howe scale, stood Sol Levy. They had tried to force him to drink a great glass of whisky straight. He had struggled, coughed, sputtered; had succeeded in spitting out the burning stuff. They had got another. They were holding it up from their vantage point on the porch. Their six-shooters were in their hands. And they were shooting at him—at his feet, at his head, at his hands, expertly, devilishly, miraculously, never hitting him, but always careful to come within a fraction of an inch. He had no weapon. He would not have known how to use it if he had possessed one. He was not of a race of fighters.

"Drink it!" the yells were high and less than human. "You're a dead Jew if you don't. Dance, gol darn you! Dance for your drink!"

The bullets spat all about him, sang past his ears, whipped up the dust about his feet. He did not run. He stood there, facing them, frozen with fear. His arms hung at his sides. His face was deathly white. They had shot off his hat. He was bareheaded. His eyes were sunken, suffering, stricken. His head lolled a little on one side. His thick black locks hung dank on his forehead. At that first instant of seeing him as he rushed out of his office, Yancey thought, subconsciously, "He looks like—like———" But the resemblance eluded him then. It was only later, after the sickening incident had ended, that he realized of Whom it was that the Jew had reminded him as he stood there, crucified against the scale.

Yancey ran into the road. It is impossible to say how he escaped being killed by one of the bullets. He seemed to leap into the thick of them like a charmed thing. As he ran he whipped out his own ivory-handled guns, and at that half the crowd on the saloon porch made a dash for the door and were caught in it and fell sprawling, and picked themselves up, and crawled or ran again until they were inside. Yancey stood beside Sol Levy, the terrible look in his eyes, the great head thrust forward and down, like a buffalo charging. Here was a scene to his liking.

"I'll drill the first son of a bitch that fires another shot. I will, so help me

God! Go on, fire now, you dirty dogs. You filthy loafers. You stinking spawn of a rattlesnake!''

He was, by now, a person in the community—he was, in fact, the person in the town. The porch loafers looked sheepish. They sheathed their weapons, or twirled them, sulkily.

"Aw, Yancey, we was foolin'!"

"We was only kiddin' the Jew. . . . Lookit him, the white-livered son of a gun. Lookit—Holy Doggie, look at him! He's floppin'.''

With a little sigh Sol Levy slid to the dust of the road and lay in a crumpled heap at the foot of the Howe scale. It was at that moment, so curiously does the human mind work, that Yancey caught that elusive resemblance. Now he picked the man up and flung him over his great shoulder as he would a sack of meal.

"Yah!" hooted the jokesters, perhaps a little shamefaced now.

Yancey, on his way to his own house so near by, made first a small detour that brought him to the foot of the tobacco-stained saloon porch steps. His eyes were like two sword blades flashing in the sun.

"Greasers! Scum of the Run! Monkey skulls!''

His limp burden dangling over his shoulder, he now strode through the *Wigwam* office, into the house, and laid him gently down on the sitting-room couch. Revived, Sol Levy stopped to midday dinner with the Cravats. He sat, very white, very still, in his chair and made delicate pretense of eating. Sabra, because Yancey asked her to, though she was mystified, had got out her DeGrasse silver and a set of her linen. His long meager fingers dwelt lingeringly on the fine hand-wrought stuff. His deep-sunk haunting eyes went from Sabra's clear-cut features, with the bold determined brows, to Yancey's massive head, then to the dazzling freshness of the children's artless countenances.

"This is the first time that I have sat at such a table in two years. My mother's table was like this, in the old country. My father—peace to his soul!—lighted the candles. My mother—sainted—spread the table with her linen and her precious thin silver. Here in this country I eat as we would not have allowed a beggar to eat that came to the door for charity.''

"This Oklahoma country's no place for you, Sol. It's so rough, too hard. You come of a race of dreamers.''

The melancholy eyes took on a remote—a prophetic look. There was, suddenly, a slight cast in them, as though he were turning his vision toward something the others could not see. "It will not always be like this. Wait. Those savages to-day will be myths, like the pictures of monsters you see in books of prehistoric days.''

"Don't worry about those dirty skunks, Sol. I'll see that they leave you alone from now on.''

Sol Levy smiled a little bitter smile. His thin shoulders lifted in a weary shrug. "Those barbarians! My ancestors were studying the Talmud and writing the laws the civilized world now lives by when theirs were swinging from tree to tree.''

12

IN THE THREE and a half years of her residence in Osage Sabra had yielded hardly an inch. It was amazing. It was heroic. She had set herself certain standards, and those she had maintained in spite of almost overwhelming opposition. She had been bred on tradition. If she had yielded at all it was in minor matters and because to do so was expedient. True, she could be seen of a morning on her way to the butcher's or the grocer's shielded from the sun by one of the gingham sunbonnets which in the beginning she had despised. Certainly one could not don a straw bonnet, velvet or flower trimmed, to dart out in a calico house dress for the purchase of a pound and a half of round steak, ten cents worth of onions, and a yeast cake.

Once only in those three years had she gone back to Wichita. At the prospect of the journey she had been in a fever of anticipation for days. She had taken with her Cim and Donna. She was so proud of them, so intent on outfitting them with a wardrobe sufficiently splendid to set off their charms, that she neglected the matter of her own costuming and found herself arriving in Wichita with a trunk containing the very clothes with which she had departed from it almost four years earlier. Prominent among these was the green nun's veiling with the pink ruchings. She had had little enough use for it in these past years or for the wine-colored silk-warp henrietta.

"Your skin!" Felice Venable had exclaimed at sight of her daughter. "Your hands! Your hair! As dry as a bone! You look a million. What have you done to yourself?"

Sabra remembered something that Yancey once had said about Texas. Mischievously she paraphrased it in order to shock her tactless mother. "Oklahoma is fine for men and horses, but it's hell on women and oxen."

The visit was not a success. The very things she had expected to enjoy fell, somehow, flat. She missed the pace, the exhilarating uncertainty of the Oklahoma life. The teacup conversation of her girlhood friends seemed to lack tang and meaning. Their existence was orderly, calm, accepted. For herself and the other women of Osage there was everything still to do. There lay a city, a county, a whole vast Territory to be swept and garnished by an army of sunbonnets. Paradoxically enough, she was trying to implant in the red clay of Osage the very forms and institutions that now bored her in Wichita. Yet it was, perhaps, a very human trait. It was illustrated literally by the fact that she was, on her return, more thrilled to find that the scrawny elm, no larger than a baby's arm, which she had planted outside the doorway in Osage, actually had found some moisture for its thirsty roots, and was now feebly vernal, than she had been at sight of the cool glossy canopy of cedar, arbor vitae, sweet locust, and crêpe myrtle that shaded the Kansas garden. She took a perverse delight in bringing the shocked look to the faces of her Wichita friends, and to all the horde of Venables and Marcys and Vians that swarmed up from the South to greet the pioneer. Curiously enough, it was not the shooting affrays and Indian yarns that ruffled them so much as her stories of the town's social life.

". . . rubber boots to parties, often, because when it rains we wade up to our ankles in mud. We carry lanterns when we go to the church sociables. . . . Mrs. Buckner's sister came to visit her from St. Joseph, Missouri, and she remarked that she had noticed that the one pattern of table silver seemed to be such a favorite. She had seen it at all the little tea parties that had been given for her during her visit. Of course it was my set that had been the rounds. Everybody borrowed it. We borrow each other's lamps, too, and china, and even linen."

At this the Venables and Marcys and Vians and Goforths looked not only shocked but stricken. Chests of lavender-scented linen, sideboards flashing with stately silver, had always been part of the Venable and Marcy tradition.

Then the children. The visiting Venables insisted on calling Cim by his full name—Cimarron. Sabra had heard it so rarely since the day of his birth that she now realized, for the first time, how foolish she had been to yield to Yancey's whim in the naming of the boy. Cimarron. Spanish; wild, or unruly. The boy had made such an obstreperous entrance into the world, and Yancey had shouted, in delight, "Look at him! See him kick with his feet and strike out with his fists! He's a wild one. Heh, Cimarron! *Peceno Gitano.*"

Cousin Jouett Goforth or Cousin Dabney Venable said, pompously, "And now, Cimarron, my little man, tell us about the big red Indians. Did you ever fight Indians, eh, Cimarron?" The boy surveyed them from beneath his long lashes, his head lowered, looking for all the world like his father.

Cimarron was almost eight now. If it is possible for a boy of eight to be romantic in aspect, Cimarron Cravat was that. His head was not large, like Yancey's, but long and fine, like Sabra's—a Venable head. His eyes were Sabra's, too, dark and large, but they had the ardent look of Yancey's gray ones, and he had Yancey's absurdly long and curling lashes, like a beautiful girl's. His mannerisms—the head held down, the rare upward glance that cut you like a sword thrust when he turned it full on you—the swing of his walk, the way he gestured with his delicate hands—all these were Yancey in startling miniature.

His speech was strangely adult. This, perhaps, because of his close association with his elders in those first formative years in Osage. Yancey had delighted in talking to the boy; in taking him on rides and drives about the broad burning countryside. His skin was bronzed the color of his father's. He looked like a little patrician Spaniard or perhaps (the Venables thought privately) part Indian. Then, too, there had been few children of his age in the town's beginning. Sabra had been, at first, too suspicious of such as there were. He would, probably, have seemed a rather unpleasant and priggish little boy if his voice and manner had not been endowed miraculously with all the charm and magnetism that his father possessed in such disarming degree.

He now surveyed his middle-aged cousins with the concentrated and disconcerting gaze of the precocious child.

"Indians," he answered, with great distinctness, "don't fight white men any more. They can't. Their—uh—spirit is broken." Cousin Dabney Venable, who still affected black stocks (modified), now looked slightly apoplectic. "They only fought in the first place because the white men took their buff'loes away from them, that they lived on and ate and traded the skins and that was all they had; and their land away from them."

"Well," exclaimed Cousin Jouett Goforth, of the Louisiana Goforths, "this is quite a little Redskin you have here, Cousin Sabra."

"And," continued Cimarron, warming to his subject, "look at the Osage Indians where my father took me to visit the reservation near where we live. The white people made them move out of Missouri to Kansas because they wanted their land, and from there to another place—I forget—and then they wanted that, too, and they said, 'Look, you go and live in the Indian Territory where we tell you,' and it's all bare there, and nothing grows in that place—it's called the Bad Lands—unless you work and slave and the Osages they were used to hunting and fishing not farming, so they are just starving to death and my father says some day they will get their revenge on the white——"

Felice Venable turned her flashing dark gaze on her daughter.

"Aha!" said Cousin Jouett Goforth.

Cousin Dabney Venable, still the disgruntled suitor, brought malicious eyes to bear on Sabra. "Well, well, Cousin Sabra! Look out that you don't have a Pocahontas for a daughter-in-law some fine day."

Sabra was furious, though she tried in her pride to conceal it. "Oh, Cim has just heard the talk of the men around the newspaper office—the Indian agent, Mr. Heeney, sometimes drops in on his trips to Osage—they're talking now of having the Indian Agent's office transferred to Osage, though Oklahoma City is fighting for it—Yancey has always been very much stirred by the wretched Indians—Cim has heard him talking.''

Cim sensed that he had not made the desired effect on his listeners. "My father says,'' he announced, suddenly, striding up and down the room in absurd and unconscious imitation of his idol—one could almost see the Prince Albert coat tails switching—"my father says that some day an Indian will be President of the United States, and then you bet you'll all be sorry you were such dirty skunks to 'em.''

The eyes of the visiting Venables swung, as one orb, from the truculent figure of the boy to the agitated face of the mother.

"My poor child!'' came from Felice Venable in accents of rage rather than pity. She was addressing Sabra.

Sabra took refuge in hauteur. "You wouldn't understand. Our life there is so different from yours here. Yancey's Indian editorials in the *Wigwam* have made a sensation. They were spoken of in the Senate at Washington.'' Felice dismissed all Yancey's written works with a wave of her hand. "In fact,'' Sabra went on—she who hated Indians and all their ways—"in fact, his editorials on the subject have been so fearless and free that he has been in danger of his life from the people who have been cheating the Indians. It has been even more dangerous than when he tracked down the murderer of Pegler.''

"Pegler,'' repeated the Venables, disdainfully, and without the slightest curiosity in their voices.

Sabra gave it up. "You don't understand. The only thing you care about is whether the duck runs red or not.''

Even little Donna was not much of a success. The baby was an eerie little elf, as plain as the boy was handsome. She resembled her grandmother, Felice Venable, without a trace of that redoubtable matron's former beauty. But she had that almost indefinable thing known as style. At the age of two she wore with undeniable chic the rather clumsy little garments that Sabra had so painstakingly made for her; and when she was dressed, for the first time, in one of the exquisitely hemstitched, tucked and embroidered white frocks that her grandmother had wrought for her, that gifted though reluctant needlewomen said, tartly, "Thank God, she's got style, at least. She'll have to make out with that.''

All in all, Sabra found herself joyously returning to the barren burning country to which, four years earlier, she had gone in such dread and terror. She resented her mother's do-this, do-that. She saw Felice Venable now, no longer as a power, an authority in all matters of importance, but as a sallow old lady who tottered on heels that were too high and who, as she sat talking, pleated and unpleated with tremulous fingers the many ruffles of her white dimity wrapper. The matriarch had lost her crown. Sabra was matriarch now of her own little kingdom; and already she was planning to extend that realm beyond and beyond its present confines into who knows what vastness of demesne.

She decided that she must take the children more than ever in hand. No more of this talk of Indians, of freedom, or equality of man. She did not realize (it being long before the day of psychology as applied so glibly to the training of children) that she was, so far as Cim was concerned, years too late. At eight his character was formed. She had taught him the things that Felice Venable had taught her—stand up straight; eat your bread and butter; wash your hands; say how do you do to the lady; one and one are two; somebody has been eating *my* porridge, said the little wee bear. But Yancey had taught him poetry far beyond his years, and accustomed his ears to the superb cadences of the Bible; Yancey had told him, bit by bit, and all unconsciously, the saga of the settling of the great Southwest.

"Cowboys wear big sombreros to shield their faces from the rain and the sun when they're riding the range, and the snow from dripping down their backs. He wears a handkerchief knotted at the back of the neck and hanging down in front so that he can wipe the sweat and dust from his face with it, and then there it is, open, drying in the wind; and in a dust storm he pulls it over his mouth and nose, and in a blizzard it keeps his nose and chin from freezing. He wears chaps, with the hairy side out, to keep his legs warm in winter and to protect them from being torn by chaparral and cactus thorns in summer. His boots are high heeled to keep his feet from slipping in the stirrups when he has to work standing in the saddle, and because he can sink them in the sod when he's off his horse and roping a plunging bronc. He totes a six-shooter to keep the other fellow from shooting."

The child's eyes were enormous, glowing, enthralled. Yancey told him the story of the buffalo; he talked endlessly of the Indians. He even taught him some words of Comanche, which is the court language of the Indian. He put him on a horse at the age of six. A sentimentalist and a romantic, he talked to the boy of the sunset; of Spanish gold; of the wild days of the Cimarron and the empire so nearly founded there. The boy loved his mother dutifully, and as a matter of course, as a child loves the fount of food, of tender care, of shelter. But his father he worshiped, he adored.

Sabra's leave-taking held one regret, one pain. Mother Bridget had died two weeks before Sabra arrived in Wichita. It was not until she learned this sad news that Sabra realized how tremendously she had counted on telling her tale of Osage to the nun. She would have understood. She would have laughed at the story of the ten barrels of water; of the wild cowboy's kiss in the road; she would have sympathized with Sabra's terror during that Sunday church meeting. She had known that very life a half century ago, there in Kansas. Sabra, during her visit, did not go to the Mission School. She could not.

She had meant, at the last, to find occasion to inform her mother and the minor Venables that it was she who ironed Yancey's fine white linen shirts. But she was not a spiteful woman. And she reflected that this might be construed as a criticism of her husband.

So, gladly, eagerly, Sabra went back to the wilds she once had despised.

13

BEFORE THE KATY pulled in at the Osage station (the railroad actually had been extended, true to Dixie Lee's prediction, from Wahoo to Osage and beyond) Sabra's eyes were searching the glaring wooden platform. Len Orsen, the chatty and accommodating conductor, took Donna in his arms and stood with her at the foot of the car steps. His heavy gold plated watch chain, as broad as a cable, with its concomitant Masonic charm, elk's tooth, gold pencil and peach pit carved in the likeness of an ape, still held Donna enthralled, though she had snatched at it whenever he passed their seat or stood to relate the gossip of the Territory to Sabra. She was hungry for news, and Len was a notorious fishwife. Now, as she stepped off the train, Sabra's face wore that look of radiant expectancy characteristic of the returned traveler, confident of a welcome.

"Well, I guess I know somebody'll be pretty sorry to see you," Len said, archly. He looked about for powerful waiting arms in which to deposit Donna. The engine bell clanged, the whistle tooted. His kindly and inquisitive blue eyes swept the station platform. He plumped Donna, perforce, into Sabra's strangely slack arms, and planted one foot, in its square-toed easy black shoe, onto the car step in the nick of time, the other leg swinging out behind him as the train moved on.

Yancey was not there. The stark red-painted wooden station sat blistering in the sun. Yancey simply was not there. Not only that, the station platform, usually graced by a score of vacuous faces and limp figures gathered to witness the exciting event of the Katy's daily arrival and departure, was bare. Even the familiar figure of Pat Leary, the station agent, who always ran out in his shirt sleeves to wrestle such freight or express as was left on the Osage platform, could not be seen. From within the ticket office came the sound of his telegraph instrument. Its click was busy; was frantic. It chattered unceasingly in the hot afternoon stillness.

Sabra felt sick and weak. Something was wrong. She left her boxes and bags and parcels on the platform where Len Orsen had obligingly dumped them. Half an hour before their arrival in Osage she had entrusted the children to the care of a fellow passenger while she had gone to the washroom to put on one of the new dresses made in Wichita and bearing the style cachet of Kansas City: green, with cream colored ruchings at the throat and wrists, and a leghorn hat with pink roses. She had anticipated the look in Yancey's gray eyes at sight of it. She had made the children spotless and threatened them with dire things if they sullied their splendor before their father should see them.

And now he was not there.

With Donna in her arms and Cim at her heels she hurried toward the sound of the clicking. And as she went her eyes still scanned the dusty red road that led to the station, for sight of a great figure in a white sombrero, its coat tails swooping as it came.

She peered in at the station window. Pat Leary was bent over his telegraph key. A smart tight little Irishman who had come to the Territory with the railroad section crew when the Katy was being built. Station agent now, and studying law at night.

"Mr. Leary! Mr. Leary! Have you seen Yancey?" He looked up at her absently, his hand still on the key. Click . . . click . . . clickclickclickety—clicketyclickclick,

"Wha' say?"

"I'm Mrs. Cravat. I just got off the Katy. Where's my husband? Where's Yancey?"

He clicked on a moment longer; then wiped his wet forehead with his forearm protected by the black sateen sleevelet. "Ain't you heard?"

"No," whispered Sabra, with stiff lips that seemed no part of her. Then, in a voice rising to a scream, "No! No! No! What? Is he dead?"

The Irishman came over to her then, as she crouched at the window. "Oh, no, ma'am. Yancey's all right. He ain't hurt to speak of. Just a nick in the arm—and left arm at that."

"Oh, my God!"

"Don't take on. You goin' to faint or———?"

"No. Tell me."

"I been so busy. . . . Yancey got the Kid, you know. Killed him. The whole town's gone crazy. Pitched battle right there on Pawhuska Avenue in front of the bank, and bodies layin' around like a battlefield. I'm sending it out. I ain't got much time, but I'll give you an idea. Biggest thing that's happened in the history of the Territory—or the whole Southwest, for that matter. Shouldn't wonder if they'd make Yancey President. Governor, anyway. Seems Yancey was out hunting up in the Hills last Thursday——''

"Thursday! But that's the day the paper comes out."

"Well, the *Wigwam* ain't been so regular since you been away." She allowed that to pass without comment. "Up in the Hills he stumbles on Doc Valliant, drunk, but not so drunk he don't recognize Yancey. Funny thing about Doc Valliant. He can be drunker'n a fool, but one part of his brain stays clear as a diamond. I seen him take a bullet out of Luke Slaughter once and sew him up when he was so drunk he didn't know his right hand from his left, or where he was at, but he done it. What? Oh, yeh—well, he tells Yancey, drunk as he is, that he's right in the camp where the Kid and his gang is hiding out. One of them was hurt bad in that last Santa Fé holdup at Cimarron. Like to died, only they sent for Doc, and he come and saved him. They got close to thirty thousand that trick, and it kind of went to their head. Valliant overheard them planning to ride in here to Osage, like to-day, and hold up the Citizens' National in broad daylight like the Kid always does. They was already started. Well, Yancey off on his horse to warn the town, and knows he's got to detour or he'll come on the gang and they'll smell a rat. Well, say, he actually did meet 'em. Came on 'em, accidental. The Kid sees him and grins that wolf grin of his and sings out, 'Yancey, you still runnin' that paper of yourn down at Osage!' Yancey says, 'Yes.' 'Well, say,' he says, 'how much is it?' Yancey says a dollar a year. The Kid reaches down and throws Yancey a shot sack with ten silver dollars in it. 'Send me the paper for ten years,' he says. 'Where to?' Yancey asks him. Well, say, the Kid laughs that wolf laugh of his again and he says, 'I never thought of that. I'll have to leave you know later.' Well, Yancey, looking as meek and mealy-mouthed as a baby, he rides his way, he's got a little book of poems in his hand and he's reading as he rides, or pretending to, but first chance he sees he cuts across the Hills, puts his horse through the gullies and into the draws and across the scrub oaks like he was a circus horse or a centipede or something. He gets into Osage, dead tired and his horse in a lather, ten minutes before the Kid and his gang sweeps down Pawhuska Avenue, their six-shooters barking like a regiment was coming, and makes a rush for the bank. But the town is expecting them. Say! Blood!"

Sabra waited for no more. She turned. And as she turned she saw coming down the road in a cloud of dust a grotesque scarecrow, all shanks and teeth and rolling eyes. Black Isaiah.

"No'm, Miss Sabra, he ain't hurt—not what yo' rightly call hurt. No, ma'am. Jes'a nip in de arm, and he got it slung in a black silk hank'chief and looks right sma't handsome. They wouldn't let him alone noways. Ev'ybody in town they shakin' his hand caze he shoot the shot dat kill de Kid. An' you know what he do then, Miss Sabra? He kneel down an' he cry like a baby. . . . Le' me tote dis yere valise. Ah kin tote Miss Donna, too. My, she sho' growed!"

The newspaper office, the print shop, her parlor, her kitchen, her bedroom, were packed with men in boots, spurs, sombreros; men in overalls; with women; with children. Mrs. Wyatt was there—the Philomatheans as one woman were there; Dixie Lee, actually; everyone but—sinisterly—Louie Hefner.

"Well, Mis' Cravat, I guess you must be pretty proud of him! . . . This is a big day for Osage. I guess Oklahoma City knows this town's on the map now, all right. . . . You missed the shootin', Mis' Cravat, but you're in time to help Yancey celebrate. . . . Say, the Santa Fé alone offered five thousand dollars for the capture of the Kid, dead or alive. Yancey gets it, all right. And the Katy done the same. And they's a government price on his head, and the Citizens' National is making up a purse. You'll be ridin' in your own carriage, settin' in silks, from now.''

Yancey was standing at his desk in the *Wigwam* office. His back was against the desk, as though he were holding this crowd at bay instead of welcoming them as congratulatory guests. His long locks hung limp on his shoulders. His face was white beneath the tan, like silver under lacquer. His great head lolled on his chest. His left arm lay in a black and scarlet silk sling made of one of his more piratical handkerchiefs.

He looked up as she came in, and at the look in his face she forgave him his neglect of her; forgave him the house full of what Felice Venable would term riffraff and worse; his faithlessness to the *Wigwam*. Donna, tired and frightened, had set up a wail. Cim, bewildered, had gone on a rampage. But as Yancey took a stumbling step toward her she had only one child, and that one needed her. She thrust Donna again into Isaiah's arms; left Cim whirling among the throng; ran toward him. She was in his great arms, but it was her arms that seemed to sustain him.

"Sabra. Sugar. Send them away. I'm so tired. Oh, God, I'm so tired.''

Next day they exhibited the body of the Kid in the new plate glass show window of Hefner's Furniture Store and Undertaking Parlors. All Osage came to view him, all the county came to view him; they rode in on trains, on horses, in wagons, in ox carts for miles and miles around. The Kid. The boy who, in his early twenties, had sent no one knew how many men to their death—whose name was the symbol for terror and daring and merciless marauding throughout the Southwest. Even in the East—in New York—the name of the Kid was known. Stories had been written about him. He was, long before his death, a mythical figure. And now he, together with Clay McNulty, his lieutenant, lay side by side, quite still, quite passive. The crowd was so dense that it threatened Louie Hefner's window. He had to put up rope barriers to protect it, and when the mob surged through these he stationed guards with six-shooters, and there was talk of calling out the militia from Fort Tipton. Sabra said it was disgusting, uncivilized. She forbade Cim to go within five hundred yards of the place kept him, in fact, virtually a prisoner in the yard. Isaiah she could not hold. His lean black body could be seen squirming in and out of the crowds; his ebony face, its eyes popping, was always in the front row of the throng gloating before Hefner's window. He became, in fact, a sort of guide and unofficial lecturer, holding forth upon the Kid, his life, his desperate record, the battle in which he met his death in front of the bank he had meant to despoil.

"Well, you got to hand it to him," the men said, gazing their fill. "He wasn't no piker. When he held up a train or robbed a bank or shot up a posse it was always in broad daylight, by God. Middle of the day he'd come riding into town. No nitro-glycerin for him, or shootin' behind fence posts and trees in the dark. Nosiree! Out in the open, and takin' a bigger chance than them that was robbed. Ride! Say, you couldn't tell which was him and which was horse. They was one piece. And shoot! It wa'n't shootin'. It was magic. They say he's got half a million in gold cached away up in the Hills.''

For weeks, for months, the hills were honeycombed with prowlers in search of this buried treasure.

Sabra did a strange, a terrible thing. Yancey would not go near the grisly window. Sabra upheld him; denounced the gaping crowd as scavengers and ghouls. Then, suddenly, at the last minute, as the sun was setting blood red across the prairie, she walked out of the house, down the road, as if impelled, as if in a trance, like a sleep walker, and stood before Hefner's window. The crowd made way for her respectfully. They knew her. This was the wife of Yancey Cravat, the man whose name appeared in headlines in every newspaper throughout the United States, and even beyond the ocean.

They had dressed the two bandits in new cheap black suits of store clothes, square in cut, clumsy, so that they stood woodenly away from the lean hard bodies. Clay McNulty's face had a faintly surprised look. His long sandy mustaches drooped over a mouth singularly sweet and resigned. But the face of the boy was fixed in a smile that brought the lips in a sardonic snarl away from the wolf-like teeth. He looked older in death than he had in life, for his years had been too few for lines such as death's fingers usually erase; and the eyes, whose lightning glance had pierced you through and through like one of the bullets from his own dreaded six-shooters, now were extinguished forever behind the waxen shades of his eyelids.

It was at the boy that Sabra looked; and having looked she turned and walked back to the house.

They gave them a decent funeral and a burial with everything in proper order, and when the minister refused to read the service over these two sinners Yancey consented to do it and did, standing there with the fresh-turned mounds of red Oklahoma clay sullying his fine high-heeled boots, and the sun blazing down upon the curling locks of his uncovered head.

" 'Whoso sheddeth man's blood, by man shall his blood be shed. . . . His hand will be against every man, and every man's hand against him. . . . The words of his mouth were smoother than butter, but war was in his heart. . . . Fools make mock at sin. . . .' "

They put up two rough wooden slabs, marking the graves. But souvenir hunters with little bright knives soon made short work of those. The two mounds sank lower, lower. Soon nothing marked this spot on the prairie to differentiate it from the red clay that stretched for miles all about it.

They sent to Yancey, by mail, in checks, and through solemn committees in store clothes and white collars, the substantial money rewards that, for almost five years, had been offered by the Santa Fé road, the M.K. & T., the government itself, and various banks, for the capture of the Kid, dead or alive.

Yancey refused every penny of it. The committees, the townspeople, the county, were shocked and even offended. Sabra, tight lipped, at last broke out in protest.

"We could have a decent house—a new printing press—Cim's education—Donna———"

"I don't take money for killing a man," Yancey repeated, to each offer of money. The committees and the checks went back as they had come.

14

SABRA NOTICED THAT Yancey's hand shook with a perceptible palsy before breakfast, and that this was more than ever noticeable as that hand approached the first drink of whisky which he always swallowed before he ate a morsel. He tossed it down as one who, seeking relief from pain, takes medicine. When he returned the glass to the table he drew a deep breath. His hand was, miraculously, quite steady.

More and more he neglected the news and business details of the *Wigwam*. He was restless, moody, distrait. Sabra remembered with a pang of dismay something that he had said on first coming to Osage. "God, when I think of those years in Wichita! Almost five years in one place—that's the longest stretch I've ever done."

The newspaper was prospering, for Sabra gave more and more time to it. But Yancey seemed to have lost interest, as he did in any venture once it got under way. It was now a matter of getting advertisements, taking personal and local items, recording the events in legal, real estate, commercial, and social circles. Mr. and Mrs. Abel Dagley spent Sunday in Chuckmubbee. The Rev. McAlestar Couch is riding the Doakville circuit.

Even in the courtroom or while addressing a meeting of townspeople Yancey sometimes would behave strangely. He would stop in the midst of a florid period. At once a creature savage and overcivilized, the flaring lamps, the hot, breathless atmosphere, the vacuous white faces looming up at him like balloons would repel him. He had been known to stalk out, leaving them staring. In the courtroom he was an alarming figure. When he was defending a local county or Territorial case they flocked from miles around to hear him, and the crude pine shack that was the courtroom would be packed to suffocation. He towered over any jury of frontiersmen—a behemoth in a Prince Albert coat and fine linen, his great shaggy buffalo's head charging menacingly at his opponent. His was the florid hifalutin oratory of the day, full of sentiment, hyperbole, and wind. But he could be trenchant enough when needs be; and his charm, his magnetic power, were undeniable, and almost invariably he emerged from the courtroom victorious. He was not above employing tricks to win his case. On one occasion, when his client was being tried for an affair of gunplay which had ended disastrously, the jury, in spite of all that Yancey could do, turned out to be one which would be, he was certain, heavily for conviction. He deliberately worked himself up into an appearance of Brobdingnagian rage. He thundered, he roared, he stamped, he wept, he acted out the events leading up to the killing and then, while the jury's eyes rolled and the weaker among them wiped the sweat from their brows, he suddenly whipped his two well known and deadly ivory-handled and silver six-shooters from their holsters in his belt. "And this, gentlemen, is what my client did." He pointed them. But at that, with a concerted yelp of pure terror the jury rose as one man and leaped for the windows, the doors, and fled.

Yancey looked around, all surprise and injured innocence. The jury had disbanded. According to the law, a new jury had to be impaneled. The case was retried. Yancey won it.

Sabra saw more and more to the editing and to the actual printing of the *Oklahoma Wigwam*. She got in as general houseworker and helper an Osage Indian girl of fifteen who had been to the Indian school and who had learned some of the rudiments of household duties: cleaning, dishwashing, laundering, even some of the simpler forms of cookery. She tended Donna, as well. Her name was Arita Red Feather, a quiet gentle girl who went about the house in her calico dress and moccasins and had to be told everything over again, daily. Isaiah was beginning to be too big for these duties. He was something of a problem in the household. At the suggestion that he be sent back to Wichita he set up a howling and wailing and would not be consoled until both Sabra and Yancey assured him that he might remain with them forever. So he now helped Arita Red Feather with the heavier housework; did odd jobs about the printing shop; ran errands; saw that Donna kept from under horses' hoofs; he could even beat up a pan of good light biscuits in a pinch. When Jesse Rickey was too drunk to stand at the type case and Yancey was off on some legal matter, he slowly and painstakingly helped Sabra to make possible the weekly issue of the *Oklahoma Wigwam*. Arita Red 'Feather's dialect became a bewildering thing in which her native Osage, Sabra's refined diction, and Isaiah's Southern negro accent were rolled into an almost unintelligible jargon. "I'm gwine wash um clothes big rain water extremely nice um make um clothes white fo' true."

"That's fine!" Sabra would say. Then, an hour later, "Oh, Arita, don't you remember I've told you a hundred times you put the bluing in *after* they're rubbed, not before?"

Arita's dead black Indian eyes, utterly devoid of expression, would stare back at her.

Names of families of mixed Indian and white blood appeared from time to time in the columns of the *Wigwam,* for Sabra knew by now that there were in the Territory French-Indian families who looked upon themselves as aristocrats. This was the old French St. Louis, Missouri, background cropping up in the newly opened land. The early French who had come to St. Louis, there to trade furs and hides with the Osages, had taken Indian girls as squaws. You saw, sprinkled among the commonplace nomenclature of the frontier, such proud old names as Bellieu, Revard, Revelette, Tayrien, Perrier, Chouteau; and their owners had the unmistakable coloring and the bearing of the Indian. These dark-skinned people bore, often enough, and ridiculously enough, Irish names as well, for the Irish laborers who had come out with pickax and shovel and crowbar to build the Territory railroads had wooed and married the girls of the Indian tribes. You saw little Indian Kellys and Flahertys and Riordans and Caseys.

All this was bewildering to Sabra. But she did a man's job with the paper, often against frightening odds, for Yancey was frequently absent now, and she had no one but the wavering Jesse Rickey to consult. There were times when he, too, failed her. Still the weekly appeared regularly, somehow.

Grandma Rosey, living eleven miles northwest of town, is very ill with the la grippe. Mrs. Rosey is quite aged and fears are entertained for her recovery.

Preaching next Sunday morning and evening at the Presbyterian church by Rev. J. H. Canby. Come and hear the new bell.

Mrs. Wicksley is visiting with the Judge this week.

A movement is on foot to fill up the sink holes on Pawhuska Avenue. The street in its present state is a disgrace to the community.

C. H. Snack and family expect to leave next week for an extended visit with Mrs. Snack's relatives in southeastern Kansas. Mr. Snack disposed of his personal property at public sale last Monday. Our loss is Kansas's gain.

(A sinister paragraph this. You saw C. H. Snack, the failure, the defeated, led back to Kansas there to live the life of the nagged and unsuccessful husband tolerated by his wife's kin.)

Sabra, in a pinch, even tried her unaccustomed hand at an occasional editorial, though Yancey seldom failed her utterly in this department. A rival newspaper set up quarters across the street and, for two or three months, kept up a feeble pretense of existence. Yancey's editorials, during this period, were extremely personal.

The so-called publishers of the organ across the street

have again been looking through glasses that reflect their own images. A tree is known by its fruit. The course pursued by the *Dispatch* does not substantiate its claim that it is a Republican paper.

The men readers liked this sort of thing. It was Yancey who brought in such items as:

> Charles Flasher, wanted for murder, forgery, selling liquor without a license and breaking jail at Skiatook, was captured in Oklahoma City as he was trying to board a train in the Choctaw yards.

But it was Sabra who held the women readers with her accounts of the veal loaf, cole slaw, baked beans, and angel-food cake served at the church supper, and the somewhat touching decorations and costumes worn at the wedding of a local or county belle.

If, in the quarter of a century that followed, every trace of the settling of the Oklahoma country had been lost, excepting only the numbers of the *Oklahoma Wigwam,* there still would have been left a clear and inclusive record of the lives, morals, political and social and economic workings of this bizarre community. Week by week, month by month, the reader could have noticed in its columns whatever of progress was being made in this fantastic slice of the Republic of the United States.

It was the day of the practical joke, and Yancey was always neglecting his newspaper and his law practice to concoct, with a choice group of conspirators, some elaborate and gaudy scheme for the comic downfall of a fellow citizen or a newcomer to the region. These jokes often took weeks for their successful consummation. Frequently they were founded on the newcomer's misapprehension concerning the Indians. If this was the Indian Territory, he argued, not unreasonably, it was full of Indians. He had statistics. There were 200,000 Indians in the Territory. Indians meant tomahawks, scalping, burnings, raidings, and worse. When the local citizens assured him that all this was part of the dead past the tenderfoot quoted, sagely, that there was no good Indian but a dead Indian. Many of the jokes, then, hinged on the mythical bad Indian. The newcomer was told that there was a threatened uprising; the Cheyennes had been sold calico—bolts and bolts of it—with the stripes running the wrong way. This, it was explained, was a mistake most calculated to madden them. The jokesters armed themselves to the teeth. Six-shooters were put in the clammy, trembling hand of the tenderfoot. He was told that the nights were freezing cold. He was led to a near-by field that was man-high with sunflowers and cautioned not to fire unless he heard the yells of the maddened savages. There, shaking and sweating in overcoat, overshoes, mufflers, ear muffs, and leggings, he cowered for hours while all about him (at a safe distance) he heard the horrid, blood-curdling yells of the supposed Indians. His scalp, when finally he was rescued, usually was found to be almost lifted of its own accord.

Next day, Yancey would spend hours writing a humorous account of this Indian uprising for the Thursday issue of the *Wigwam.* The drinks were on the newcomer. That ceremony also took hours.

> O jest unseen, inscrutable, invisible,
> As a nose on a man's face, or a weathercock on a steeple.

Thus Yancey's article would begin with a quotation from his favorite poet.

"Oh, Yancey darling, sometimes I think you're younger than Cim."

"What would you like me to be, honey? A venerable Venable 'A man whose blood is very snow-broth; one who never feels the wanton stings and motions of the sense'?"

Sabra, except for Yancey's growing restlessness, was content enough. The children were well; the paper was prospering; she had her friends; the house had taken on an aspect of comfort; they had added another bedroom; Arita Red Feather and Isaiah together relieved her of the rougher work of the household. She was, in a way, a leader in the crude social life of the community. Church suppers; sewing societies; family picnics.

One thing rankled deep. Yancey had been urged to accept the office of Territorial delegate to Congress (without vote) and had refused. All sorts of Territorial political positions were held out to him. The city of Guthrie, Capital of the Territory, wooed him in vain. He laughed at political position, rejected all offers of public nature. Now he was being offered the position of Governor of the Territory. His oratory, his dramatic quality, his record in many affairs, including the Pegler murder and the shooting of the Kid, had spread his fame even beyond the Southwest.

"Oh, Yancey!" Sabra thought of the Venables, the Marcys, the Vians, the Goforths. At last her choice of a mate was to be vindicated. Governor!

But Yancey shook his great head. There was no moving him. He would go on the stump to make others Congressmen and Governors, but he himself would not take office. "Palavering to a lot of greasy office seekers and panhandlers! Dancing to the tune of that gang in Washington! I know the whole dirty lot of them."

Restless. Moody. Irritable. Riding out into the prairies to be gone for days. Coming back to regale Cim with stories of evenings spent on this or that far-off Reservation, smoking and talking with Chief Big Horse of the Cherokees, with Chief Buffalo Hide of the Chickasaws, with old Black Kettle of the Osages.

But he was not always like this. There were times when his old fiery spirit took possession. He entered the fight for the statehood of Oklahoma Territory, and here he encountered opposition enough even for him. He was for the consolidation of the Oklahoma Territory and the Indian Territory under single statehood. The thousands who were opposed to the Indians—who looked upon them as savages totally unfit for citizenship—fought him. A year after their coming to Oklahoma the land had been divided into two territories—one owned and occupied by the Indian Tribes, the other owned by the whites. Here the Cravats lived, on the border line. And here was Yancey, fighting week after week, in the editorial and news columns of the *Oklahoma Wigwam,* for the rights of the Indians; for the consolidation of the two halves as one state. Yet, unreasonably enough, he sympathized with the Five Civilized Tribes in their efforts to retain their tribal laws in place of the United States Court laws which were being forced upon them. He made a thousand bitter enemies. Many of the Indians themselves were opposed to him. These were for separate statehood for the Indian Territory, the state to be known as Sequoyah, after the great Cherokee leader of that name.

Sabra, who at first had paid little enough heed to these political problems, discovered that she must know something of them as protection against those times (increasingly frequent) when Yancey was absent and she must get out the paper with only the uncertain aid of Jesse Rickey.

She dared not, during these absences of Yancey, oppose outright his political and Territorial stand. But she edged as near the line as she could, for her hatred of the Indians was still deep and (she insisted) unconquerable.

She even published—slyly—the speeches and arguments of the Double State-hood party leaders, stating simply that these were the beliefs of the opposition. They sounded very reasonable and convincing as the *Wigwam* readers perused them.

Sabra came home one afternoon from a successful and stirring meeting of the Twentieth Century Philomathean Culture Club (the two had now formed a pleasing whole) at which she had read a paper entitled, Whither Oklahoma? It had been received with much applause on the part of Osage's twenty most exclusive ladies, who had heard scarcely a word of it, their minds being intent on Sabra's new dress. She had worn it for the first time at the club meeting, and it was a bombshell far exceeding any tumult that her paper might create.

Her wealthy Cousin Bella French Vian, visiting the World's Fair in Chicago, had sent it from Marshall Field's store. It consisted of a blue serge skirt, cut wide and flaring at the hem but snug at the hips; a waistlength blue serge Eton jacket trimmed with black soutache braid; and a garment called a shirtwaist to be worn beneath the jacket. But astounding—revolutionary—as all this was, it was not the thing that caused the eyes of feminine Osage to bulge with envy and despair. The sleeves! The sleeves riveted the attention of those present, to the utter neglect of Whither Oklahoma! The balloon sleeve now appeared for the first time in the Oklahoma Territory, sponsored by Mrs. Yancey Cravat. They were bouffant, enormous; a yard of material at least had gone into each of them. Every woman present was, in her mind, tearing to rag strips, bit by bit, every gown in her own scanty wardrobe.

Sabra returned home, flushed, elated. She entered by way of the newspaper office, seeking Yancey's approval. Curtseying and dimpling she stood before him. She wanted him to see the new costume before she must thriftily take it off for the preparation of supper. Yancey's comment, as she pirouetted for his approval, infuriated her.

"Good God! Sleeves! Let the squaws see those and they'll be throwing away their papoose boards and using the new fashion for carrying their babies, one in each sleeve."

"They're the very latest thing in Chicago. Cousin Bella French Vian wrote that they'll be even fuller than this, by autumn."

"By autumn," echoed Yancey. He held in his hand a slip of paper. Later she knew that it was a telegram—one of the few telegraphic messages which the *Wigwam's* somewhat sketchy service received. He was again completely oblivious of the new costume, the balloon sleeves. "Listen, sugar. President Cleveland's just issued a proclamation setting September sixteenth for the opening of the Cherokee Strip."

"Cherokee Strip?"

"Six million, three hundred thousand acres of Oklahoma land to be opened for white settlement. The government has bought it from the Cherokees. It was all to be theirs—all Oklahoma. Now they're pushing them farther and farther out."

"Good thing," snapped Sabra, still cross about the matter of Yancey's indifference to her costume. Indians. Who cared! She raised her arms to unpin her hat.

Yancey rose from his desk. He turned his rare full gaze on her, his handsome eyes aglow. "Honey, let's get out of this. Clubs, sleeves, church suppers—God! Let's get our hundred and sixty acre allotment of Cherokee Strip land and start a ranch—raise cattle— live in the open—ride—this town life is no good—it's hideous."

Her arms fell, leaden, to her side. "Ranch? Where?"

"You're not listening. There's to be a new Run. The Cherokee Strip

Opening. You know. You wrote news stories about it only last week, before the opening date had been announced. Let's go, Sabra. It's the biggest thing yet. The 1889 Run was nothing compared to it. Sell the *Wigwam,* take the children, make the Run, get our hundred and sixty, start a ranch, stock up with cattle and horses, build a ranch house and patio; in the saddle all day————"

"Never!" screamed Sabra. Her face was distorted. Her hands were clutching the air, as though she would tear to bits this plan of his for the future. "I won't, I won't go. I'd rather die first. You can't make me."

He came to her, tried to take her in his arms, to pacify her. "Sugar, you won't understand. It's the chance of a lifetime. It's the biggest thing in the history of Oklahoma. When the Territory's a state we'll own forever one hundred and sixty acres of the finest land anywhere. I know the section I want."

"Yes. You know. You know. You knew the last time, too. You let that slut—that hussy—take it away from you—or you gave it to her. Go and take her with you. You'll never make me go. I'll stay here with my children and run the paper. Mother! Cim! Donna!"

She had a rare and violent fit of hysterics, after which Yancey, aided clumsily by Arita Red Feather, divested her of the new finery, quieted the now screaming children, and finally restored to a semblance of supper time order the household into which he had hurled such a bomb. Felice Venable herself, in her heyday, could not have given a finer exhibition of Marcy temperament. It was intended, as are all hysterics (no one ever has hysterics in private), to intimidate the beholder and fill him with remorse. Yancey was properly solicitous, tender, charming as only he could be. From the shelter of her husband's arms Sabra looked about the cosy room, smiled wanly upon her children, bade Arita Red Feather bring on the belated supper. "That," thought Sabra to herself, bathing her eyes, smoothing her hair, and coming pale and wistful to the table, her lip quivering with a final effective sigh, "settles that."

But it did not. September actually saw Yancey making ready to go. Nothing that Sabra could say, nothing that she could do, served to stop him. She even negotiated for a little strip of farm land outside the town of Osage and managed to get Yancey to make a payment on it, in the hope that this would keep him from the Run. "If it's land you want you can stay here and farm the piece at Tuskamingo. You can raise cattle on it. You can breed horses on it."

Yancey shook his head. He took no interest in the farm. It was Sabra who saw to the erection of a crude little farmhouse, arranged for the planting of such crops as it was thought that land would yield. It was very near the Osage Reservation land and turned out, surprisingly enough, doubtless owing to some mineral or geological reason (they knew why, later), to be fertile, though the Osage land so near by was barren and flinty.

"Farm? That's no farm. It's a garden patch. D'you think I'm settling down to be a potato digger and chicken feeder, in a hayseed hat and manure on my boots!"

September, the month of the opening of the vast Cherokee Strip, saw him well on his way. Cim howled to be taken along, and would not be consoled for days.

Sabra's farewell was intended to be cold. Her heart, she told herself, was breaking. The change that these last four years had made in her never was more apparent than now.

"You felt the same way when I went off to the first Run," Yancey reminded her. " Remember? You carried on just one degree less than your mother. And if I hadn't gone you'd still be living in the house in Wichita, with your family smothering you in Southern fried chicken and advice."

There was much truth in this, she had to admit. She melted; clung to him.

"Yancey! Yancey!"

"Smile, sugar. Wait till you see Cim and Donna, five years from now, riding the Cravat acres."

After all, a hundred other men in Osage were going to make the Cherokee Strip Run. The town—the whole Territory—had talked of nothing else for months.

She dried her eyes. She even managed a watery smile. He was making the Run on a brilliant, wild-eyed mare named Cimarron, with a strain of Spanish in her for speed and grace, and a strain of American mustang for endurance. He had decided to make the trip from Osage to the Cherokee Outlet on horseback by easy stages so as to keep the animal in condition, though the Santa Fé and the Rock Island roads were to run trains into the Strip. He made a dashing, a magnificent figure as he sat the strong, graceful animal that now was pawing and pirouetting to be off. Though a score of others were starting with him, it was Yancey that the town turned out to see. He rode in his white sombrero, his fine white shirt, his suit with the Prince Albert coat, his glittering high-heeled Texas star boots with the gold-plated spurs. The start was made shortly after sunrise so as to make progress before the heat of the day. But a cavalcade awoke them before dawn with a rat-a-tat-tat of six-shooters and a blood-curdling series of cowboy yips. The escort rode with Yancey and the others for a distance out on the Plains. Sabra, at the last minute, had the family horse hitched to the buggy, bundled Cim and Donna in with her, and—Isaiah hanging on behind, somehow—the prim little vehicle bumped and reeled its way over the prairie road in the wake of the departing adventurers.

At the last Sabra threw the reins to Isaiah, sprang from the buggy, ran to Yancey as he pulled up his horse. He bent far over in his saddle, picked her up in one great arm, held her close while he kissed her long and hard.

"Sabra, come with me. Let's get clear away from this."

"You've gone crazy! The children!"

"The children, too. All of us. Come on. Now." His eyes were blazing. She saw that he actually meant it. A sudden premonition shook her.

"Where are you going? Where are you going?"

He set her down gently and was off, turned halfway in his saddle to face her, his white sombrero held aloft in his hand, his curling black locks tossing in the Oklahoma breeze.

Five years passed before she saw him again.

15

DIXIE LEE'S GIRLS were riding by on their daily afternoon parade. Sabra recognized their laughter and the easy measured clatter of their horses' hoofs before they came into view. She knew it was Dixie Lee's girls. Somehow, the virtuous women of Osage did not laugh much, though Sabra did not put this thought into words, even in her mind. She glanced up now as they drove by. She was seated at her desk by the window in the front office of the *Oklahoma Wigwam*. Their plumes, their parasols, their brilliant-hued dresses made a gay garden of color in the monotony of Pawhuska Avenue. They rode in open phaëtons, but without the usual top, so that they had only their parasols to shade their brightly painted faces from the ardent Southwest sun.

The color of the parasols and plumes and dresses was changed from day to day, but they always were done in ensemble effect. One day the eyes of Osage's male population were dazzled (and its female population's eyes affronted) by a burst of rosy splendor shading from pale pink to scarlet. The next day they would shade from palest lavender to deepest purple. The next, from delicate lemon to orange; the day following they ran the gamut of green. They came four by four, and usually one in each carriage handled the reins, though occasionally a negro driver occupied the front seat alone. They were not boisterous. Indeed, they conducted themselves in seemly enough fashion except perhaps for the little bursts of laughter and for the fact that they were generous with the ankles beneath the ruffled skirts. Often they carried dolls in their arms. Sometimes—rarely—they called to each other. Their voices were high and curiously unformed, like the voices of little children, and yet with a metallic note in them.

"Madge, looka! When we get to the end of Pawhuska we'll race you to Coley's Gulch and back." These afternoon races became almost daily sporting events, and the young bloods of Osage got into the habit of stationing themselves along the road to bet on the pale pink plumes or the deep rose plumes.

"Heh, go it, Clemmie! Whip him up, Carmen. Give him the whip! Come on! Whoop-ee! Yi!" Plumes whirling, parasols bobbing, skirts flying, shrill shouts and screams of laughter from the edge of town. But on the return drive their behavior was again seemly enough, their cheeks flushed with a natural color beneath the obvious red.

Sabra's face darkened now as she saw them driving slowly by. Dixie Lee never drove with them. Sabra knew where she was this afternoon. She was down in the back room of the Osage First National Bank talking business to the President, Murch Rankin. The business men of the town were negotiating for the bringing of the packing house and a plough works and a watch factory to Osage. Any one of these industries required a substantial bonus. The spirit of the day was the boom spirit. Boom the town of Osage. Dixie Lee was essentially a commercial woman—shrewd, clear headed. She had made a great success of her business. It was one of the crude town's industries, and now she, as well as the banker, the hardware man, the proprietor of the furniture store, the meat market, the clothing store, contributed her share toward coaxing new industries to favor Osage. That way lay prosperity.

Dixie Lee was a personage in the town. Visitors came to her house now from the cities and counties round about. She had built for herself and her thriving business the first brick structure in the wooden town; a square, solid, and imposing two-story house, its bricks formed from the native Oklahoma red clay. Cal Bixby had followed close on it with the Bixby Block on Pawhuska Avenue, but Dixie Lee had led the way. She had commissioned Louie Hefner to buy her red velvet and gold furniture and her long giltframed mirrors, her scarlet deep-pile carpet—that famous velvet-pile carpet in which Shanghai Wiley, that bearded, cultured, and magnetic barbarian, said he sank so deep that for a terrified moment he fell into a panic, being unable to tell which was red carpet and which his own flowing red beard. Dixie herself had gone East for her statues and pictures. The new house had been opened with a celebration the like of which had never been seen in the Southwest. Sabra Cravat, mentioning no names, had had an editorial about it in which the phrases "insult to the fair womanhood of America" and "orgy rivaling the Bacchanalian revels of history" (Yancey's library stood her in good stead these days) figured prominently. Both the Philomathean Society and the Twentieth Century Culture Club had, for the duration of one meeting at least, deserted literature and culture for the discussion of the more vital topic of Dixie Lee's new mansion.

It was—this red brick brothel—less sinister than these good and innocent women suspected. Dixie Lee, now a woman of thirty or more, ruled it with an iron hand. Within it obtained certain laws and rules of conduct so rigid as to be almost prim. In a crude, wild, and nearly lawless country the brick mansion occupied a strange place, filled a want foreign to its original purpose. It was, in a way, a club, a rendezvous, a salon. For hundreds of men who came there it was all they had ever known of richness, of color, of luxury. The red and gold, the plush and silk, the perfume, the draperies, the white arms, the gleaming shoulders sank deep into their hard-bitten senses, long starved from years on wind-swept ranches, plains dust bedeviled, prairies baked barren by the fierce Southwest sun. Here they lolled, sunk deep in rosy comfort, while they talked Territory politics, swapped yarns of the old cattle days, played cards, drank wines which tasted like sweet prickling water to their whisky-scarred palates. They kissed these women, embraced them fiercely, thought tenderly of many of them, and frequently married them; and these women, once married, settled down contentedly to an almost slavish domesticity.

A hard woman, Dixie Lee; a bad woman. Sabra was morally right in her attitude toward her. Yet this woman, as well as Sabra, filled her place in the early life of the Territory.

Now, as the laughter sounded nearer and the equipages came within her view, Sabra, seated at her desk in the newspaper office, put down the soft pencil with which she had been filling sheet after sheet of copy paper. She wrote easily now, with no pretense to style, but concisely and with an excellent sense of news values. The *Oklahoma Wigwam* had flourished in these last five years of her proprietorship. She was thinking seriously of making it a daily instead of a weekly; of using the entire building on Pawhuska Avenue for the newspaper plant and building a proper house for herself and the two children on one of the residence streets newly sprung up—streets that boasted neatly painted houses and elm and cottonwood trees in the front yards.

Someone came up the steps of the little porch and into the office. It was Mrs. Wyatt. She often brought club notices and social items to the *Wigwam:* rather fancied herself as a writer; a born woman's club corresponding secretary.

"Well!" she exclaimed now, simply, but managing to put enormous bite and significance into the monosyllable. Her glance followed Sabra's. Together the two women, tight lipped, condemnatory, watched the gay parade of Dixie Lee's girls go by.

The flashing company disappeared. A whiff of patchouli floated back to the two women standing by the open window. Their nostrils lifted in disdain. The sound of the horses' hoofs grew fainter,

"It's a disgrace to the community"—Mrs. Wyatt's voice took on its platform note—"and an insult to every wife and mother in the Territory. There ought to be a law."

Sabra turned away from the window. Her eyes sought the orderly rows of books, bound neatly in tan and red—Yancey's law books, so long unused now, except, perhaps, for occasional newspaper reference. Her face set itself in lines of resolve. "Perhaps there is."

It had taken almost three of those five years to bring those lines into Sabra Cravat's face. They were not, after all, lines. Her face was smooth, her skin still fresh in spite of dust and alkali water and sun and wind. It was, rather, that a certain hardening process had taken place—a crystallization. Yancey

had told her, tenderly, that she was a charming little fool, and she had
believed it—though perhaps with subconscious reservations. It was not until
he left her, and the years rolled round without him, that she developed her
powers. The sombrero had ridden gayly away. The head under the sunbonnet
had held itself high in spite of hints, innuendoes, gossip.

A man like Yancey Cravat—spectacular, dramatic, impulsive—has a thousand critics, scores of bitter enemies. As the weeks had gone by and Yancey
failed to return—had failed to write—rumor, clouded by scandal, leaped like
prairie fire from house to house in Osage, from town to town in the Oklahoma
Country, over the Southwest, indeed. All the old stories were revived, and
their ugly red tongues licked a sordid path through the newly opened land.

They say he is living with the Cherokee squaw who is really his wife.

They say he was seen making the Run in the Kickapoo Land Opening in
1895.

They say he killed a man in the Cherokee Strip Run and was caught by
a posse and hung.

They say he got a section of land, sold it at a high figure, and was seen
lording it around the bar of the Brown Palace Hotel in Denver, in his white
sombrero and his Prince Albert coat.

They say Dixie Lee is his real wife, and he left her when she was seventeen,
came to Wichita, and married Sabra Venable; and he is the one who has set
Dixie up in the brick house.

They say he drank five quarts of whisky one night and died and is buried
in an unmarked grave in Horseshoe Ranch, where the Doolin gang held
forth.

They say he is really the leader of the Doolin gang.

They say. They say. They say.

It is impossible to know how Sabra survived those first terrible weeks that
lengthened into months that lengthened into years. There was in her the
wiry endurance of the French Marcys; the pride of the Southern Venables.
Curiously enough, in spite of all that had happened to her she still had that
virginal look—that chastity of lip, that clearness of the eye, that purity of
brow. Men come back to the women who look as Sabra Cravat looked, but
the tempests of men's love pass them by.

She told herself that he was dead. She told the world that he was dead.
She knew, by some deep and unerring instinct, that he was alive. Donna
had been so young when he left that he now was all but wiped from her
memory. But Cim, strangely enough, spoke of Yancey Cravat as though he
were in the next room. "My father says . . . " Sometimes, when Sabra saw
the boy coming toward her with that familiar swinging stride, his head held
down and a little thrust forward, she was wrenched by a physical pang of
agony that was almost nausea.

She ran the paper competently; wrung from it a decent livelihood for
herself and the two children. When it had no longer been possible to keep
secret from her parents the fact of Yancey's prolonged absence, Felice
Venable had descended upon her prepared to gather to the family bosom
her deserted child and to bring her, together with her offspring, back to the
parental home. Lewis Venable had been too frail and ill to accompany his
wife, so Felice had brought with her the more imposing among the Venables,
Goforths, and Vians who chanced to be visiting the Wichita house at the
time of her departure. Osage had looked upon these stately figures with
much awe, but Sabra's reception of them had been as coolly cordial as her
rejection of their plans for her future was firm.

"I intend to stay right here in Osage," she announced, quietly, but in a
tone that even Felice Venable recognized as inflexible, "and run the paper,

and bring up my children as their father would have expected them to be brought up.''

"Their father!'' Felice Venable repeated, in withering accents.

The boy Cimarron, curiously sensitive to sounds and moods, stood before his grandmother, his head thrust forward, his handsome eyes glowing. "My father is the most famous man in Oklahoma. The Indians call him Buffalo Head."

Felice Venable pounced on this. "If that's what you mean by bringing them up as their father . . .''

The meeting degenerated into one of those family bickerings. "I do wish, Mamma, that you wouldn't repeat everything I say and twist it by your tone into something poisonous."

"*I* say! I can't help it if the things you say sound ridiculous when they are repeated. I simply mean————"

"I don't care what you mean. I mean to stay here in Osage until Yancey— until————" She never finished that sentence.

The Osage society notes became less simple. From bare accounts of quilt-ings, sewing bees, and church sociables they blossomed into flowery imi-tations of the metropolitan dailies' descriptions of social events. Refresh-ments were termed elegant. Osage matrons turned from the sturdy baked beans, cole slaw, and veal loaf of an earlier day to express themselves in food terms culled from the pictures in the household magazines. They heard about fruit salads. They built angel-food cakes whose basis was the whites of thirteen eggs, and their husbands, at breakfast, said, "What makes these scrambled eggs so yellow?" Countrified costumes were described in terms of fashion. The wilted prairie flowers that graced weddings and parties were transformed into rare hothouse blooms by the magic touch of the *Oklahoma Wigwam* hand press. Sabra cannily published all the brilliant social news items that somewhat belatedly came her way via the ready-print and the paper's scant outside news service.

> *Newport. Oct. 4*—One of the most brilliant weddings which Newport has seen for many years was solemnized in old Trinity Church to-day. The principals were Miss Geor-gina Harwood and Mr. Harold Blake, both members of fam-ilies within the charmed circle of the 400. The bride wore a gown of ivory satin with draperies and rufflings of rarest point lace, the lace veil being caught with a tiara of pearls and diamonds. After the ceremony a magnificent colla-tion . . .

The feminine population of Osage—of the county—felt that it had seen the ivory satin, the point lace, the tiara of pearls and diamonds, as these splendors moved down the aisle of old Trinity on the person of Miss Georgina Harwood of Newport. They derived from it the vicarious satisfaction that a dieting dyspeptic gets from reading the cook book.

Sabra was, without being fully aware of it, a power that shaped the social aspect of this crude Southwestern town. The Ladies of the new Happy Hour Club, on her declining to become a member, pleading lack of time and press of work (as well she might) made her an honorary member, resolved to have her influential name on their club roster, somehow. They were paying un-conscious tribute to Oklahoma's first feminist. She still ran the paper single handed, with the aid of Jesse Rickey, the most expert printer in the Southwest (when sober), and as good as the average when drunk.

Sabra, serene in the knowledge that the attacked could do little to wreak vengeance on a woman, printed stories and statements which for boldness and downright effrontery would have earned a male editor a horsewhipping. She publicly scolded the street loafers who, in useless sombreros and six-shooters and boots and spurs, relics of a bygone day, lolled limply on Pawhuska Avenue corners, spitting tobacco juice into the gutter. Sometimes she borrowed Yancey's vigorous and picturesque phraseology. She denounced a local politician as being too crooked to sleep in a roundhouse, and the phrase stuck, and in the end defeated him. Law, order, the sanctity of the home, prunes, prisms. Though the Gyp Hills and the Osage Hills still were as venomous with outlaws as the Plains were with rattlesnakes; though the six-shooter still was as ordinary a part of the Oklahoma male costume as boots or trousers; though outlawry still meant stealing a horse rather than killing a man; though the Territory itself had been settled and peopled, in thousands of cases, by men who had come to it, not in a spirit of adventure, but from cowardice, rapacity, or worse, Sabra Cravat and the other basically conventional women of the community were working unconsciously, yet with a quiet ferocity, toward that day when one of them would be able to say, standing in a doorway with a stiff little smile:

"Awfully nice of you to come."

"Awfully nice of you to ask me," the other would reply.

When that day came, Osage would no longer need to feel itself looked down upon by Kansas City, Denver, Chicago, St. Louis, and San Francisco.

Slowly, slowly, certain figures began to take on the proportions of personalities. No one had arisen in the Territory to fill Yancey Cravat's romantic boots. Pat Leary was coming on as a Territory lawyer, with an office in the Bixby Block and the railroads on which he had worked as section hand now consulting him on points of Territorial law. In his early railroad days he had married an Osage girl named Crook Nose. People shook their heads over this and said that he regretted it now, and that a lawyer could never hope to get on with this marital millstone round his neck.

There still was very little actual money in the Territory. People traded this for that. Sabra often translated subscriptions to the *Oklahoma Wigwam*—and even advertising space—into terms of fresh vegetables, berries, wild turkey, quail, prairie chickens, dress lengths and shoes and stockings for the children.

Sol Levy's store, grown to respectable proportions now, provided Sabra with countless necessities in return for the advertisement which, sent through the country via the *Oklahoma Wigwam,* urged its readers to Trade at Sol Levy's. Visit the Only Zoo in the Territory. This invitation, a trifle bewildering to the uninitiated, was meant to be taken literally. In the back of his store Sol Levy kept a sizable menagerie. It had started through one of those chance encounters. A gaunt and bearded plainsman had come into the store one day with the suggestion that the proprietor trade a pair of pants for a bear cub. The idea had amused Sol Levy; then he had glanced out into the glare of Pawhuska Avenue and had seen the man's ocherous wife, his litter of spindling children, huddled together in a crazy wagon attached by what appeared to be ropes, strings, and bits of nail and wire, to horses so cadaverous that his amusement was changed to pity. He gave the man the pants, stockings for the children, and—the sentimentalist in him—a piece of bright-colored cotton stuff for the woman.

The bear cub, little larger than a puppy, had been led gingerly into the welter of packing cases, straw, excelsior, and broken china which was the Levy Mercantile Company's back yard, and there tied with a piece of rope which he immediately bit in two. Five minutes later a local housewife, deep in the purchase of a dress length of gingham, and feeling something rubbing against her stout calves, looked down to see the bear cub sociably gnawing his way through her basket of provisions, carelessly placed on the floor by her side.

One week later the grateful ranger brought in a pair of catamounts. A crude wire cage was built. There were added coyotes, prairie dogs, an eagle. The zoo became famous, and all the town came to see it. It brought trade to the Mercantile Company, and free advertising. It was the nucleus for the zoo which, fifteen years later, Sol Levy shyly presented to the Osage City Park, and which contained every wild thing that the Southwest had known, from the buffalo to the rattlesnake.

In a quiet, dreamy way Sol Levy had managed to buy a surprising amount of Osage real estate by now. He owned the lot on which his store stood, the one just south of it, and, among other pieces, the building and lot which comprised the site of the *Wigwam* and the Cravat house. In the year following Yancey's departure Sabra's economic survival was made possible only through the almost shamefaced generosity of this quiet, sad-eyed man.

"I've got it all down in my books," Sabra would say, proudly. "You know that it will all be paid back some day."

He began in the *Oklahoma Wigwam* a campaign of advertising out of all proportions to his needs, and Sabra's debt to him began to shrink to the vanishing point. She got into the habit of talking to him about her business problems, and he advised her shrewdly. When she was utterly discouraged he would say, not triumphantly, but as one who states an irrefutable and not particularly happy fact:

"Some day, Mrs. Cravat, you and I will look back on this and we will laugh—but not very loud."

"How do you mean—laugh?"

The little curious cast came into his eyes. "Oh—I will be very rich, and you will be very famous. And Yancey————"

"Yancey!" The word was wrenched from her like a cry.

"They will tell stories about Yancey until he will grow into a legend. He will be part of the history of the Southwest. They will remember him and write about him when all these mealy-faced governors are dead and gone and forgotten. They will tell the little children about him, and they will dispute about him—he did this, he did that; he was like this, he was like that. You will see."

Sabra thought of her own children, who knew so little of their father. Donna, a thin secretive child of almost seven now, with dark, straight black hair and a sallow skin like Yancey's; Cim, almost thirteen, moody, charming, imaginative. Donna was more like her grandmother Felice Venable than her own mother; Cim resembled Yancey so strongly in mood, manner, and emotions as to have almost no trace of Sabra. She wondered, with a pang, if she had failed to impress herself on them because of her absorption in the town, in the newspaper, in the resolve to succeed. She got out a photograph of Yancey that she had hidden away because to see it was to feel a stab of pain, and had it framed, and hung it on the wall where the children could see it daily. He was shown in the familiar costume—the Prince Albert, the white sombrero, the six-shooters, the boots, the spurs, the long black locks curling beneath the hat brim, the hypnotic eyes startling you with their arresting gaze, so that it was as if he were examining you rather than that you were seeing his likeness in a photograph. One slim foot, in its high-heeled boot, was slightly advanced, the coat tails flared, the whole picture was somehow endowed with a sense of life and motion.

"Your father————" Sabra would begin, courageously, resolved to make him live again in the minds of the children. Donna was not especially interested. Cim said, "I know it," and capped her story with a tale of his own in which Yancey's feat of derring-do outrivaled any swashbuckling escapade of D'Artagnan.

"Oh, but Cim, that's not true! You mustn't believe stories like that about your father."

"It is true. Isaiah told me. I guess he ought to know." And then the question she dreaded. "When are Isaiah and Father coming back?"

She could answer, somehow, evasively, about Yancey, for her instinct concerning him was sure and strong. But at the fate that had overtaken the negro boy she cowered, afraid even to face the thought of it. For the thing that had happened to the black boy was so dreadful, so remorseless that when the truth of it came to Sabra she felt all this little world of propriety, of middle-class Middle West convention that she had built up about her turning to ashes under the sudden flaring fire of hidden savagery. She tried never to think of it, but sometimes, at night, the hideous thing took possession of her, and she was swept by such horror that she crouched there under the bedclothes, clammy and shivering with the sweat of utter fear. Her hatred of the Indians now amounted to an obsession.

It was in the fourth year of Yancey's absence that, coming suddenly and silently into the kitchen from the newspaper office, where she had been busy as usual, she saw Arita Red Feather twisted in a contortion in front of the table where she had been at work. Her face was grotesque, was wet, with agony. It was the agony which only one kind of pain can bring to a woman's face. The Indian girl was in the pangs of childbirth. Even as she saw her Sabra realized that something about her had vaguely disturbed her in the past few weeks. Yet she had not known, had not dreamed of this. The loose garment which the girl always wore—her strong natural slenderness—the erect dignity of her Indian carriage—the stoicism of her race—had served to keep secret her condition. She had had, too, Sabra now realized in a flash, a way of being out of the room when her mistress was in it; busy in the pantry when Sabra was in the kitchen; busy in the kitchen when Sabra was in the dining room; in and out like a dark, swift shadow.

"Arita! Here. Come. Lie down. I'll send for your father—your mother." Her father was Big Knee, well known and something of a power in the Osage tribe. Of the tribal officers he was one of the eight members of the Council and as such was part of the tribe's governing body.

Dreadful as the look on Arita Red Feather's face had been, it was now contorted almost beyond recognition. "No! No!" She broke into a storm of pleading in her own tongue. Her eyes were black pools of agony. Sabra had never thought that one of pure Indian blood would thus give way to any emotion before a white person.

She put the girl to bed. She sent Isaiah for Dr. Valliant, who luckily was in town and sober. He went to work quietly, efficiently, aided by Sabra, making the best of such crude and hasty necessities as came to hand. The girl made no outcry. Her eyes were a dull, dead black; her face was rigid. Sabra, passing from the kitchen to the girl's bedroom with hot water, cloths, blankets, saw Isaiah crouched in a corner by the wood box. He looked up at her mutely. His face was a curious ash gray. As Sabra looked at him she knew.

The child was a boy. His hair was coarse and kinky. His nose was wide. His lips were thick. He was a negro child. Doc Valliant looked at him as Sabra held the writhing red-purple bundle in her arms.

"This is a bad business."

"I'll send for her parents. I'll speak to Isaiah. They can marry."

"Marry! Don't you know?"

Something in his voice startled her. "What?"

"The Osages don't marry negroes. It's forbidden."

"Why, lots of them have. You see negroes who are Indians every day. On the street."

"Not Osages. Seminoles, yes. And Creeks, and Choctaws, and even Chickasaws. But the Osages, except for intermarriage with whites, have kept the tribe pure."

This information seemed to Sabra to be unimportant and slightly silly. Purity of the tribe, indeed! Osages! She resolved to be matter of fact and sensible now that the shocking event was at hand, waiting to be dealt with. She herself felt guilty, for this thing had happened in her own house. She should have foreseen danger and avoided it. Isaiah had been a faithful black child in her mind, whereas he was, in reality, a man grown.

Dr. Valliant had finished his work. The girl lay on the bed, her dull black eyes fixed on them; silent, watchful, hopeless. Isaiah crouched in the kitchen. The child lay now in Sabra's arms. Donna and Cim were, fortunately, asleep, for it was now long past midnight. The tense excitement past, the whole affair seemed to Sabra sordid, dreadful. What would the town say? What would the members of the Philomathean Club and the Twentieth Century Culture Club think?

Doc Valliant came over to her and looked down at the queer shriveled morsel in her arms. "We must let his father see him."

Sabra shrank. "Oh, no!"

He took the baby from her and turned toward the kitchen. "I'll do it. Let me have a drink of whisky, will you, Sabra! I'm dead tired."

She went past him into the dining room, without a glance at the negro boy cowering in the kitchen. Doc Valliant followed her. As she poured a drink of Yancey's store of whisky, almost untouched since he had left, she heard Valliant's voice, very gentle, and then the sound of Isaiah's blubbering. All the primness in her was outraged. Her firm mouth took on a still straighter line. Valliant took the child back to the Indian girl's bed and placed it by her side. He stumbled with weariness as he entered the dining room where Sabra stood at the table. As he reached for the drink Sabra saw that his hand shook a little as Yancey's used to do in that same gesture. She must not think of that. She must not think of that.

"There's no use talking now, Doctor, about what the Osages do or don't do that you say is so pure. The baby's born. I shall send for the old man—what's his name?—Big Knee. As soon as Arita can be moved he must take her home. As for Isaiah, I've a notion to send him back to Kansas, as I wanted to do years ago, only he begged so to stay, and Yancey let him. And now this."

Doc Valliant had swallowed the whisky at a gulp—had thrown it down his throat as one takes medicine to relieve pain. He poured another glass. His face was tired and drawn. It was late. His nerves were not what they had been, what with drink, overwork, and countless nights without sleep as he rode the country on his black horse, his handsome figure grown a little soft and sagging now. But he still was a dashing sight when he sat the saddle in his black corduroys and his soft-brimmed black hat.

He swallowed his second drink. His face seemed less drawn, his hand steadier, his whole bearing more alert. "Now listen, Sabra. You don't understand. You don't understand the Osages. This is serious."

Sabra interrupted quickly. "Don't think I'm hard. I'm not condemning her altogether, or Isaiah, either. I'm partly to blame. I should have seen. But I am so busy. Anyway, I can't have her here now, can I? With Isaiah. Even you . . ."

He filled his glass. She wished he would stop drinking; go home. She would sit up the night with the Indian girl. And in the morning—well, she must get someone in to help. They would know, sooner or later.

He was repeating rather listlessly what he had said. "The Osages have kept the tribe absolutely free of negro blood. This is a bad business."

Her patience was at an end. "What of it? And how do you know? How do you know?"

"Because they remove any member of the tribe that has had to do with a negro."

"Remove!"

"Kill. By torture."

She stared at him. He was drunk, of course. "You're talking nonsense," she said crisply. She was very angry.

"Don't let this get around. They might blame you. The Osages. They might——— I'll just go and take another look at her."

The girl was sleeping. Sabra felt a pang of pity as she gazed down at her. "Go to bed—off with you," said Doc Valliant to Isaiah. The boy's face was wet, pulpy with tears and sweat and fright. He walked slackly, as though exhausted.

"Wait." Sabra cut him some bread from the loaf, sliced a piece of meat left from supper. "Here. Eat this. Everything will be all right in the morning."

The news got round. Perhaps Doc Valliant talked in drink. Doubtless the girl who came in to help her. Perhaps Isaiah, who after a night's exhausted sleep had suddenly become proudly paternal and boasted loudly about the house (and no doubt out of it) of the size, beauty, and intelligence of the little lump of dusky flesh that lay beside Arita Red Feather's bed in the very cradle that had held Donna when an infant. Arita Red Feather was frantic to get up. They had to keep her in bed by main force. She had not spoken a dozen words since the birth of the child.

On the fourth day following the child's birth Sabra came into Arita Red Feather's room early in the morning and she was not there. The infant was not there. Their beds had been slept in and now were empty. She ran straight into the yard where Isaiah's little hut stood. He was not there. She questioned the girl who now helped with the housework and who slept on a couch in the dining room. She had heard nothing, seen nothing. The three had vanished in the night.

Well, Sabra thought, philosophically, they have gone off. Isaiah can make out, somehow. Perhaps he can even get a job as a printer somewhere. He was handy, quick, bright. He had some money, for she had given him, in these later years, a little weekly wage, and he had earned a quarter here, a half dollar there. Enough, perhaps, to take them by train back to Kansas. Certainly they had not gone to Arita's people, for Big Knee, questioned, denied all knowledge of his daughter, of her child, of the black boy. He behaved like an Indian in a Cooper novel. He grunted, looked blank, folded his arms, stared with dead black, expressionless eyes. They could make nothing of him. His squaw, stout, silent, only shook her head; pretended that she neither spoke nor understood English.

Then the rumor rose, spread, received credence. It was started by Pete Pitchlyn, the old Indian guide and plainsman who sometimes lived with the Indians for months at a time on their reservations, who went with them on their visiting jaunts, hunted, fished, ate with them, who was married to a Cherokee. and who had even been adopted into the Cherokee tribe. He had got the story from a Cherokee who in turn had had it from an Osage. The

Osage, having managed to lay hands on some whisky, and becoming very drunk, now told the grisly tale for the first time.

There had been an Osage meeting of the Principal Chief, old Howling Wolf; the Assistant Chief; the eight members of the Council, which included Big Knee, Arita's father. There the news of the girl's dereliction had been discussed, her punishment gravely decided upon, and that of Isaiah.

They had come in the night and got them—the black boy, the Indian girl, the infant—by what means no one knew. Arita Red Feather and her child had been bound together, placed in an untanned and uncured steer hide, the hide was securely fastened, they were carried then to the open, sun-baked, and deserted prairie and left there, with a guard. The hide shrank and shrank and shrank in the burning sun, closer and closer, day by day, until soon there was no movement within it.

Isaiah, already half dead with fright, was at noonday securely bound and fastened to a stake. Near by, but not near enough quite to touch him, was a rattlesnake so caught by a leather thong that, strike and coil and strike as it might, it could not quite reach, with its venomous head, the writhing, gibbering thing that lay staring with eyes that protruded out of all semblance to human features. But as dusk came on the dew fell, and the leather thong stretched a little with the wet. And as twilight deepened and the dew grew heavier the leather thong holding the horrible reptile stretched more and more. Presently it was long enough.

16

"REMEMBER THE *MAINE!* To hell with Spain!" You read this inflaming sentiment on posters and banners and on little white buttons pinned to coat lapels or dress fronts. There were other buttons and pennants bearing the likeness of an elderly gentleman with a mild face disguised behind a martial white mustache; and thousands of male children born within the United States in 1898 grew up under the slight handicap of the christened name of Dewey. The *Oklahoma Wigwam* bristled with new words: Manila Bay— Hobson—Philippines. Throughout the Southwest sombreros suddenly became dust-colored army hats with broad, flat brims and peaked crowns. People who, if they had thought of Spain at all, saw it in the romantic terms of the early Southwest explorers—Coronado, De Soto, Moscosco—and, with admiration for these intrepid and mistaken seekers after gold, now were told that they must hate Spain and the Spanish and kill as many little brown men living in the place called the Philippines as possible. This was done as dutifully as could be, but with less than complete enthusiasm.

Rough Riders! That was another matter. Here was something that the Oklahoma country knew and understood—tall, lean, hard young men who had practically been born with a horse under them and a gun in hand; riders, hunters, dead shots; sunburned, keen eyed, daredevil. Their uniforms, worn with a swagger, had about them a dashing something that the other regiments lacked. Their hat crowns were dented, not peaked, and the brims were turned romantically up at one side and caught with the insignia of the Regiment—the crossed sabers. And their lieutenant-colonel and leader was that energetic, toothy young fellow who was making something of a stir in New York State—Roosevelt, his name was. Theodore Roosevelt.

Osage was shaken by chills and fever; the hot spasms of patriotism, the cold rigors of virtue. One day the good wives of the community would have a meeting at which they arranged for a home-cooked supper, with coffee, to be served to this or that regiment. Their features would soften with sentiment, their bosoms heave with patriotic pride. Next day, eyes narrowed, lips forming a straight line, they met to condemn Dixie Lee and her ilk, and to discuss ways and means for ridding the town of their contaminating presence.

The existence of this woman in the town had always been a festering sore to Sabra. Dixie Lee, the saloons that still lined Pawhuska Avenue, the gambling houses, all the paraphernalia of vice, were anathema lumped together in the minds of the redoubtable sunbonnets. A new political group had sprung up, ostensibly on the platform of civic virtue. In reality they were tired of seeing all the plums dropping into the laps of the earlyday crew, made up of such strong-arm politicians as had been the first to shake the Territorial tree. In the righteous ladies of the Wyatt type they saw their chance for a strong ally. The saloons and the gamblers were too firmly intrenched to be moved by the reform element: they had tried it. Sabra had been urged to help. In the columns of the *Oklahoma Wigwam* she had unwisely essayed to conduct a campaign against Wick Mongold's saloon, in whose particularly lawless back room it was known that the young boys of the community were in the habit of meeting. With Cim's future in mind (and as an excuse) she wrote a stirring editorial in which she said bold things about shielding criminals and protecting the Flower of our Southwest's Manhood. Two days later a passer-by at seven in the morning saw brisk flames licking the foundations of the *Oklahoma Wigwam* office and the Cravat dwelling behind it. The whole had been nicely soaked in coal oil. But for the chance passer-by, Sabra, Cim, Donna, newspaper plant, and house would have been charred beyond recognition. As the town fire protection was still of the scantiest, the alarmed neighbors beat out the fire with blankets wet in the near-by horse trough. It was learned that a Mexican had been hired to do the job for twenty dollars. Mongold skipped out.

After an interval reform turned its attention to that always vulnerable objective known then as the Scarlet Woman. Here it met with less opposition. Almost five years after Yancey's departure it looked very much as though Dixie Lee and her fine brick house and her plumed and parasoled girls would soon be routed by the spiritual broomsticks and sunbonnets of the purity squad.

It was characteristic that at this moment in Osage's history, when the town was torn, now by martial music, now by the call of civic virtue, Yancey Cravat should have chosen to come riding home; and not that alone, but to come riding home in full panoply of war, more dashing, more romantic, more mysterious than on the day he had ridden away.

It was eight o'clock in the morning. The case of Dixie Lee (on the charge of disorderly conduct) was due to come up at ten in the local court. Sabra had been at her desk in the *Wigwam* office since seven. One ear was cocked for the sounds that came from the house; the other was intent on Jesse Rickey's erratic comings and goings in the printing shop just next the office.

"Cim! Cim Cravat! Will you stop teasing Donna and eat your breakfast. Miss Swisher's report said you were late three times last month, and all because you dawdle while you dress, you dawdle over breakfast, you dawdle——— Jesse! Oh, Jesse! The Dixie Lee case will be our news lead. Hold two columns open. . . ."

Horse's hoofs at a gallop, stopping spectacularly in front of the *Wigwam* office in a whirl of dust. A quick, light step. That step! But it couldn't be. Sabra sprang to her feet, one hand at her breast, one hand on the desk, to steady herself. He strode into the office. For five years she had pictured him returning to her in dramatic fashion; in his white sombrero, his Prince Albert, his high-heeled boots. For five years she had known what she would say, how she would look at him, in what manner she would conduct herself toward him—toward this man who had deserted her without a word, cruelly. In an instant, at sight of him, all this left her mind, her consciousness. She was in his arms with an inarticulate cry, she was weeping, her arms were about him, the buttons of his uniform crushed her breasts. His uniform. She realized then, without surprise, that he was in the uniform of the Oklahoma Rough Riders.

It is no use saying to a man who has been gone for five years, "Where have you been?" Besides, there was not time. Next morning he was on his way to the Philippines. It was not until he had gone that she realized her failure actually to put this question that had been haunting her for half a decade.

Cim and Donna took him for granted, as children do. So did Jesse Rickey, with his mind of a child. For that matter, Yancey took his own return for granted. His manner was nonchalant, his spirits high, his exuberance infectious. He set the pitch. There was about him nothing of the delinquent husband.

He now strode magnificently into the room where the children were at breakfast, snatched them up, kissed them. You would have thought he had been gone a week.

Donna was shy of him. "Your daughter's a Venable, Mrs. Cravat," he said, and turned to the boy. Cim, slender, graceful, taller than he seemed because of that trick of lowering his fine head and gazing at you from beneath his too-long lashes, reached almost to Yancey's broad shoulders. But he had not Yancey's heroic bulk, his vitality. The Cravat skull structure was contradicted by the narrow Venable face. The mouth was oversensitive, the hands and feet too exquisite, the smile almost girlish in its wistful sweetness.

" 'Gods! How the son degenerates from the sire!' "

"Yancey!" cried Sabra in shocked protest. It was as though the five years had never been.

"Do you want to see my dog?" Cim asked.

"Have you got a pony?"

"Oh, no."

"I'll buy you one this afternoon. A pinto. Here. Look."

He took from his pocket a little soft leathern pouch soiled and worn from much handling. It was laced through at the top with a bit of stout string. He loosed this, poured the bag's contents onto the breakfast table; a little heap of shining yellow. The three stood looking at it. Cim touched it with one finger.

"What is it?"

Yancey scooped up a handful of it and let it trickle through his fingers. "That's gold." He turned to Sabra. "It's all I've got to show, honey, for two years and more in Alaska."

"Alaska!" she could only repeat, feebly. So that was it.

"I'm famished. What's this? Bacon and eggs?" He reached for a slice of bread from the plate on the table, buttered it lavishly, clapped a strip of coldish bacon on top of that, and devoured it in eager bites. Sabra saw then, for the first time, that he was thinner; there were hollow shadows in the pock-marked cheeks; there was a scarcely perceptible sag to the massive shoulders. There was something about his hand. The forefinger of the right hand was gone. She felt suddenly faint, ill. She reeled a little and stumbled. As always, he sprang toward her. His lips were against her hair.

"Oh, God! How I've missed you, Sabra, sugar!"

"Yancey! The children!" It was the prim exclamation of a woman who had forgotten the pleasant ways of dalliance. Those five years had served to accentuate her spinsterish qualities; had made her more and more powerful; less human; had slowed the machinery of her emotional equipment. A man in the house. A possessive male, enfolding her in his arms; touching her hair, her throat with urgent fingers. She was embarrassed almost. Besides, this man had neglected her, deserted her, had left his children to get on as best they could. She shrugged herself free. Anger leaped within her. He was a stranger.

"Don't touch me. You can't come home like this—after years—after years———"

"Ah, Penelope!"

She stared. "Who!"

" 'Strange lady, surely to thee above all womankind the Olympians have given a heart that cannot be softened. No other woman in the world would harden her heart to stand thus aloof from her husband, who after travail and sore had come to her . . . to his own country.' "

"You and your miserable Milton!"

He looked only slightly surprised and did not correct her.

One by one, and then in groups and then in crowds, the neighbors and townspeople began to come in—the Wyatts, Louie Hefner, Cass Peery, Mott Bixler, Ike Hawes, Grat Gotch, Doc Nisbett—the local politicians, the storekeepers, their wives. They came out of curiosity, though they felt proper resentment toward this strange—this baffling creature who had ridden carelessly away, leaving his wife and children to fend for themselves, and now had ridden as casually back again. They would have stayed away if they could, but his enchantment was too strong. Perhaps he represented, for them, the thing they fain would be or have. When Yancey, flouting responsibility and convention, rode away to be gone for mysterious years, a hundred men, bound by ties of work and wife and child, escaped in spirit with him; a hundred women, faithful wives and dutiful mothers, thought of Yancey as the elusive, the romantic, the desirable male.

Well, they would see how she had met it, and take their cue from her. A smart woman, Sabra Cravat. Throw him out, likely as not, and serve him right. But at sight of Yancey Cravat in his Rough Rider uniform of khaki, U.S.V. on the collar, the hat brim dashingly caught up on the left side with the insignia of crossed sabers, they were snared again in the mesh of his enchantment. The Rough Riders. Remember the *Maine,* to hell with Spain! There'll Be a Hot Time in the Old Town To-night. He became a figure symbolic of the war, of the Oklahoma country, of the Territory, of the Southwest—impetuous, romantic, adventuring.

"Hi, Yancey! Well, say, where you been, you old son of a stampedin' steer!"

"Howdy, Cimarron! Where at's your white hat?"

"You and this Roosevelt get goin' in this war, I guess the Spaniards'll wish Columbus never been born."

And Yancey, in return, "Hello, Clint! Howdy, Sam! Well, damn' if it isn't you, Grat! H'are you, Ike, you old hoss thief!"

The great figure towered even above these tall plainsmen; the fine eyes glowed; the mellifluous voice worked its magic. The renegade was a hero; the outcast had returned a conqueror.

Alaska. Oklahoma had not been so busy with its own growing pains that it had failed to hear of Alaska and the Gold Rush. "Alaska! Go on, you wasn't never in Alaska! Heard you'd turned Injun. Heard you was buried up in Boot Hill along of the Doolins."

He got out the little leather sack. While they gathered round him he poured out before their glistening eyes the shining yellow heap of that treasure with which the whole history of the Southwest was intertwined. Gold. The hills and the plains had been honeycombed for it; men had hungered and fought and parched for it; had died for it; had been killed for it; had sacrificed honor, home, happiness in the hope of finding it. And here was the precious yellow stuff from far-off Alaska trickling through Yancey Cravat's slim white fingers.

"Damn it all, Yancey, some folks has all the luck."

And so he stood, this Odysseus, and wove for them this new chapter in his saga. And they listened, and wondered, and believed and were stirred with envy and admiration and the longing for like adventure. He talked, he laughed, he gesticulated, he strode up and down, and they never missed the flirt of the Prince Albert coat tails, for there were brass buttons and patch pockets and gold embroidery and the glitter of crossed sabers to take their place.

"Luck! Call it luck, do you, Mott, to be frozen, starved, lost, snow-blinded! One whole winter shut up alone in a one-room cabin with the snow piled to the roof-top and no living soul to talk to for months. Luck to have your pardner that you trusted cheat you out of your claim and rob you of your gold in the bargain! All but this handful. I was going to see Sabra covered in gold like an Aztec princess."

The eyes of listening Osage swung to the prim blue serge figure of the cheated Aztec princess, encountered the level gaze, the unsmiling lips; swung back again hastily to the dashing, the martial figure of the lately despised wanderer.

A tale of another world; a story of a land so remote from the brilliant scarlet and orange of the burning Southwest country that the very sound of the words he used in describing it fell with a strange cadence on the ears of the eager listeners. And as always when Yancey was telling the tale, he filled his hearers with a longing for the place he described; a longing that was like a nostalgia for something they had never known. Well, folks, winters at fifty below zero. Two hours of bitter winter sunshine, and then blackness. Long splendid summer days in May and June, with twenty hours of sunshine and four hours of twilight. Sabra, listening with the others, found this new vocabulary as strange, as terrifying, as the jargon of the Oklahoma country had been to her when first she had encountered it years ago.

Yukon. Chilkoot Pass. Skagway. Kuskokwim. Klondike. Moose. Caribou. Huskies. Sledges. Nome. Sitka. Blizzards. Snow blindness. Frozen fingers. Pemmican. Cold. Cold. Cold. Gold. Gold. Gold. To the fascinated figures crowded into the stuffy rooms of this little frame house squatting on the sun-baked Oklahoma prairie he brought, by the magic of his voice and his eloquence, the relentless movement of the glaciers, the black menace of icy rivers, the waste plains of blinding, treacherous snow. Two years of this, he said; and looked ruefully down at the stump that had been his famous trigger finger.

They, too, looked. Two years. Two years, and he had been gone five. That left three unaccounted for, right enough. The old stories seeped up in their minds. Their eyes, grown accustomed to the uniform, were less dazzled now. They saw the indefinable break that had come to the magnificent figure—not a break, really, but a loosening, a lowering of the resistance such as comes to steel that has been too often in the flaming furnace. You looked at the massive shoulders—they did not droop. The rare glance still pierced you like a sword thrust. The buffalo head, lowered, menaced you; lifted, thrilled you. Yet something had vanished.

"Where'd you join up, Yancey?"

"San Antonio. Leonard Wood's down there—Colonel Wood now—and young Roosevelt, Lieutenant Colonel. He's been drilling the boys. Most of them born on a horse and weaned on a Winchester. We're better equipped than the regulars that have been at it for years. Young Roosevelt's to thank for that. They were all for issuing us winter clothing, by God, to wear through a summer campaign in the tropics—those nincompoops in Washington—and they'd have done it if it hadn't been for him."

Southwest Davis spoke up from the crowd. "That case, you'll be leaving right soon, won't you? Week or so."

"Week!" echoed Yancey, and looked at Sabra. "I go back to San Antonio to-morrow. The regiment leaves for Tampa next day."

He had not told her before. Yet she said nothing, gave no sign. She had outfaced them with her pride and her spirit for five years; she would give them no satisfaction now. Five years. One day. San Antonio—Tampa—Cuba—the Philippines—War. She gave no sign. Curiously, the picture that was passing in her mind was this: she saw herself, as though it were someone she had known in the dim, far past, standing in the cool, shady corridor of the Mission School in Wichita. She saw, through the open door, the oblong of Kansas sunshine and sky and garden; there swept over her again that wave of nostalgia she had felt for the scene she was leaving; she was shaken by terror of this strange Indian country to which she was going with her husband.

". . . but here in this land, Sabra, my girl, the women, they've been the real hewers of wood and drawers of water. You'll want to remember that."

Sabra remembered it now, well enough.

Slowly the crowd began to disperse. The men had their business; the women their housework. Wives linked their arms through those of husbands, and the gesture was one of perhaps not entirely unconscious cruelty, accompanied as it was by a darting glance at Sabra.

"Rough Rider uniform, sack of gold, golden voice, and melting eye," that glance seemed to say. "You're welcome to all the happiness you can get from those. Security, permanence, home, husband—I wouldn't change places with you."

"Come on, Yancey!" shouted Strap Buckner. "Over to the Sunny Southwest and have a drink. We got a terrible lot of drinking to do, ain't we, boys! Come on, you old longhorn. We got to drink to you because you're back and because you're going away."

"And to the war!" yelled Bixler.

"And the Rough Riders!"

"And Alaska!"

Their boots clattered across the board floor of the newspaper office. They swept the towering figure in its khaki uniform with them. He turned, waved his hat at her. "Back in a minute, honey." They were gone.

Sabra turned to the children, Cim and Donna, flushed, both, with the unwonted excitement; out of hand. Her face set itself with that look of quiet resolve. "Half the morning's gone. But I want you to go along to school, anyway. Now, none of that! It's no use your staying around here. The paper must be got out. Jesse'll be no good to me the rest of the day. It's easy to see that. I'll write a note to your teachers. . . . Run along now. I must go to court."

She actually had made up her mind that she would see the day through as she had started it. The Dixie Lee case, seething for weeks, was coming to a crisis this morning—this very minute. She would be late if she did not hasten. She would not let the work of months go for nothing because this man—this stranger had seen fit to stride into her life for a day.

She pinned on her hat, saw that her handbag contained pencil and paper, hurried into the back room that was printing shop, composing room, press room combined. She had been right about Jesse Rickey. That consistently irresponsible one was even now leaning a familiar elbow on the polished surface of the Sunny Southwest bar as he helped toast the returned wanderer or the departing hero or the war in the semi-tropics, or the snows of Alaska "—or God knows what!" concluded Sabra, in her mind.

Cliff Means, the ink-smeared printer's devil who, at fifteen, served as Jesse Rickey's sole assistant in the mechanical end of the *Wigwam* office, looked up from his case rack as Sabra entered.

"It's all right, Mis' Cravat. I got the head all set up like you said. 'Vice Gets Death Blow. Reign of Scarlet Woman Ends. Judge Issues Ban.' Even if Jesse don't—even if he ain't—why, you and me can set up the story this afternoon so we can start the press goin' for Thursday. We ain't been late with the paper yet, have we?"

"Out on time every Thursday for five years," Sabra said, almost defiantly.

Suddenly, sharp and clear, Yancey's voice calling her from the office porch, from the front office, from the print-shop doorway; urgent, perturbed. "Sabra! Sabra! Sabra!"

He strode into the back shop. She faced him. Instinctively she knew. "What's this about Dixie Lee?" His news-trained eye leaped to the form. He read the setup head, upside down, expertly. "When's this case come up?"

"Now."

"Who's defending her?"

"Nobody in town would touch the case. They say she got a lawyer from Denver. He didn't show up. He knew better than to take her money."

"Prosecuting?"

"Pat Leary."

Without a word he turned. She caught him at the door, gripped his arm. "Where are you going?"

"Court."

"What for? What for?" But she knew. She actually interposed her body between him and the street door then, as though physically to prevent him from going. Her face was white. Her eyes stared enormous.

"You can't take the case of that woman."

"Why not?"

"Because you can't. Because I've been fighting her. Because the *Wigwam* has come out against all that she stands for."

"Why, Sabra, honey, where are you thinking of sending her?"

"Away. Away from Osage."

"But where?"

"I don't know. I don't care. Things have changed since you went away. Went away and left me."

"Nothing's changed. It's all the same. Dixie's been stoned in the market place for two thousand years and more. Driving her out is not going to do it. You've got to drive the devil out of———"

"Yancey Cravat, are you preaching to me? You who left your wife and children to starve, for all you cared! And now you come back and you take this creature's part against every respectable woman in Osage—against me!"

"I know it. I can't help it, Sabra."

"I'll tell you what I think," cried Sabra—the Sabra Cravat who had been evolved in the past five years. "I think you're crazy! They've all said so. And now I know they are right."

"Maybe so."

"If you dare to think of disgracing me by defending her. And your children. I've fought her for months in the paper. A miserable creature like that! Your own wife—a laughing stock—for a—a———"

"The Territory's rotten. But, by God, every citizen's still got the legal right to fight for existence!" He put her gently aside.

She went mad. She became a wildcat. She tried to hold him. She beat herself against him. It was like an infuriated sparrow hurling itself upon a mastodon. "If you dare! Why did you come back? I hate you. What's she to you? I say you won't. I'd rather see you dead. I'd kill you first. That scum! That filth! That harlot!"

Her dignity was gone. He lifted her, scratching, kicking, clawing, set her gently down in the chair in front of her desk. The screen slammed. His quick, light step across the porch, down the stair. Crumpled, tearstained, wild as she was, and with her hat on one side she reached automatically for her pencil, a pad of copy paper, and wrote a new head. Vice Again Triumphs Over Justice. Then, with what composure she could summon, she sped down the dusty road to where the combination jail and courthouse—a crude wooden building—sat broiling in the sun.

Because of the notoriety of the defendant the inadequate little courtroom would have been crowded enough in any case. But the news of Yancey's abrupt departure from the Sunny Southwest Saloon—and the reason for it— had spread from house to house through the little town with the rapidity of a forest fire leaping from tree to tree. Mad Yancey Cravat's latest freak. Men left their offices, their stores; women their cooking, their cleaning. The courtroom, stifling, fly infested, baked by the morning sun, was packed beyond endurance. The crowd perched on the window sills, stood on boxes outside the windows, suffocated in the doorway, squatted on the floor. The jury so hastily assembled, Pat Leary in a solemn suit of black, Dixie Lee with her girls, even Judge Sipes himself seemed in momentary danger of being trampled by the milling mob. It was a travesty of a courtroom. The Judge nervously champing his cud of tobacco, the corners of his mouth stained brown; Pat Leary neat, tight, representing law and order in his glittering celluloid collar; Dixie Lee, with a sense of the dramatic, all in black, her white cheeks unrouged, her dark abundant hair in neat smooth bands under the prim brim of her toque. But her girls were in full panoply of plumes. It was rather exhilarating to see them in that assemblage of drab respectability.

The jury was a hard-faced lot for the most part. Plucked from the plains or the hills; halting of speech, slow of mind, quick on the trigger. Two or three in overalls; one or two in the unaccustomed discomfort of store clothes. The rest in the conventional boots, corduroys or jeans, and rough shirt. A slow, rhythmic motion of the jaw was evidence that a generous preliminary bite of plug served as a precaution to soothe the nerves and steady the judgment.

This legal farce had already begun before Yancey made his spectacular entrance.

17

"CASE OF THE Territory of Oklahoma versus Dixie Lee!" (So they had made it a Territorial case. . . .) "Counsel for the Territory of Oklahoma!" Pat Leary stood up. ". . . for the defense." No one. The closepacked courtroom was a nightmare of staring eyes and fishlike mouths greedily devouring

Dixie Lee's white, ravaged face. Oddly enough, compared to these, she seemed pure, aloof, exquisite. "The defendant having failed to provide herself with counsel, it is my duty, according to the laws of the gover'ment of the United States and the Territory of Oklahoma to appoint counsel for the defendant." He shifted his quid, the while his cunning, red-rimmed eyes roved solemnly through the crowd seeking the shyster, Gwin Larkin. A stir in the close-packed crowd; a murmur. "I hereby appoint———" The murmur swelled. "Order in the court!"

"Your Honor!"

Towering above the crowd, forging his way through like some relentless force of nature, came the great buffalo head, the romantic Rough Rider hat with its turned-up brim caught by the crossed sabers; the massive khaki-clad figure. It was dramatic, it was melodramatic, it was ridiculous. It was superb. The fish faces turned their staring eyes and their gasping mouths away from the white-faced woman and upon him. Here was the kind of situation that the Southwest loved and craved; here was action, here was blood-and-thunder, here was adventure. Here, in a word, was Cimarron.

He stood before the shoddy judge. He swept off his hat with a gesture that invested it with plumes. "If it please Your Honor, I represent the defendant, Dixie Lee."

No Territorial judge, denying Yancey Cravat, would have dared to face that crowd. He cast another glance round—a helpless, baffled one, this time—waved the approaching Gwin Larkin back with a feeble gesture, and prepared to proceed with the case according to the laws of the Territory. Certainly the look that he turned on Sabra Cravat as she entered a scant ten minutes later, white faced, resolute, and took her place as representative of the press, was one of such mingled bewilderment and reproach as would have embarrassed anyone less utterly preoccupied than the editor and publisher of the *Oklahoma Wigwam*.

Objection on the part of the slick Pat Leary. Overruled, perforce, by the Judge. A shout from the crowd. Order! Bang! Another shout. Law in a lawless community not yet ten years old; a community made up, for the most part, of people whose very presence there meant impatience of the old order, defiance of the conventions. Ten minutes earlier they had been all for the cocky little Leary, erstwhile station agent; eager to cast the first stone at the woman in the temple. Now, with the inexplicable fickleness of the mob, the electric current of sympathy flowed out from them to the woman to be tried, to the man who would defend her. Hot and swift and plenty of action—that was the way the Southwest liked its justice.

Pat Leary. Irish, ambitious, fiery. His temper, none too even at best, had been lost before he ever rose. The thought of Yancey ahead of him, the purity brigade behind him, spurred him to his frantic, his disorderly charge.

His years as section hand on the railroad had equipped him with a vocabulary well suited to scourge this woman in black who sat so quietly, so white faced, before him, for all the crowd to see. Adjective on adjective; vituperation; words which are considered obscenity outside the Bible and the courtroom.

". . . all the vicious influences, your Honor, with which our glorious Territory is infested, can be laid at this woman's leprous door. . . . A refuge for the evil, for the diseased, for the criminal . . . waxed fat and sleek in her foul trade, on the money that should have been spent to help build up, to ennoble this fair Southwest land of ours . . . scavenger . . . vilest of humans . . . disgrace to the fair name of woman. . . ." Names, then, that writhed from his tongue like snakes.

A curious embarrassment seized the crowd. There were many in the packed room who had known the easy hospitality of Dixie's ménage; who had eaten at her board, who had been broken in Grat Gotch's gambling place and had borrowed money from Dixie to save themselves from rough frontier revenge. She had plied her trade and taken the town's money and given it out again with the other merchants of the town. The banker could testify to that; the mayor; this committee; that committee. Put Dixie Lee's name down for a thousand. Part of the order of that disorderly, haphazard town.

Names. Names. Names. The dull red of resentment deepened the natural red of their sunburned faces. The jurors shifted in their places. A low mutter, ominous, like a growl, sounded its distant thunder. Blunt. Sharp. Ruthless. Younger than Yancey, less experienced, he still should have known better. These men of the inadequate jury, these men in the courtroom crowd, had come of a frontier background, had lived in the frontier atmosphere. In their rough youth, and now, women were scarce, with the scarcity that the hard life predicated. And because they were scarce they were precious. No woman so plain, so hard, so undesirable that she did not take on, by the very fact of her sex, a value far beyond her deserts. The attitude of a whole nation had been touched by this sentimental fact which was, after all, largely geographic. For a full century the countries of Europe, bewildered by it, unable to account for it, had laughed at this adolescent reverence of the American man for the American woman.

Here was Pat Leary, jumping excitedly about, mouthing execrations, when he himself, working on the railroads ten years before, had married an Indian girl out of the scarcity of girls in the Oklahoma country. Out of the corner of his eye, as he harangued, he saw the great lolling figure of Yancey Cravat. The huge head was sunk on the breast; the eyelids were lowered. Beaten, Pat Leary thought. Defeated, and he knows it. Cravat, the wind bag, the wife deserter. He finished in a burst of oratory so ruthless, so brutal that he had the satisfaction of seeing the painful, unaccustomed red surge thickly over Dixie Lee's pale face from her brow down to where the ladylike white turnover of her high collar met the line of her throat.

The pompous little Irishman seated himself, chest out, head high, eye roving the crowd and the bench, lips open with self-satisfaction. A few more cases like this and maybe they'd see there was material for a Territory governor right here in Osage.

The crowd shifted, murmured, gabbled. Yancey still sat sunk in his chair as though lost in thought. The gabble rose, soared. "He's given it up," thought Sabra, exulting. "He sees how it is."

The eyes of the crowd so close packed in that suffocating little courtroom were concentrated on the inert figure lolling so limply in its chair. Perhaps they were going to be cheated of their show after all.

Slowly the big head lifted, the powerful shoulders straightened, he rose, he seemed to rise endlessly, he walked to Judge Sipes's crude desk with his light, graceful stride. The lids were still cast down over the lightning eyes. He stood a moment, that singularly sweet and winning smile wreathing his lips. He began to speak. The vibrant voice, after Leary's shouts, was so low pitched that the crowd held its breath in order to hear.

"Your Honor. Gentlemen of the Jury. I am the first to bow to achievement. Recognition where recognition is due—this, gentlemen, has ever been my way. May I, then, before I begin my poor plea in defense of this lady, my client, most respectfully call your attention to that which, in my humble opinion, has never before been achieved, much less duplicated, in the whole of the Southwest. Turn your eye to the figure which has so recently and so deservedly held your attention. Gaze once more upon him. Regard him well. You will not look upon his like again. For, gentlemen, in my opinion this

gifted person, Mr. Patrick Leary, is the only man in the Oklahoma Territory—in the Indian Territory—in the whole of the brilliant and glorious
Southwest—nay, I may even go so far as to say the only man in this
magnificent country, the United States of America!—of whom it actually
can be said that he is able to strut sitting down.''

The puffed little figure in the chair collapsed, then bounded to its feet, red
faced, gesticulating. ''Your Honor! I object!''

But the rest was lost in the gigantic roar of the delighted crowd.

''Go it, Yancey!''

''That's the stuff, Cimarron!''

Here was what they had come for. Doggone, there was nobody like him,
damn if they was!

Even to-day, though more than a quarter of a century has gone by, there
still are people in Oklahoma who have kept a copy, typed neatly now from
records made by hand, of the speech made that day by Yancey Cravat in
defense of the town woman, Dixie Lee. Yancey Cravat's Plea for a Fallen
Woman, it is called; and never was speech more sentimental, windy, false,
and utterly moving. The slang words hokum and bunk were not then in use,
but even had they been they never would have been applied, by that appreciative crowd, at least, to the flowery and impassioned oratory of the
Southwest Silver Tongue, Yancey Cravat.

Cheap, melodramatic, gorgeous, impassioned. A quart of whisky in him;
an enthralled audience behind him; a white-faced woman with hopeless eyes
to spur him on; the cry of his wronged and righteous wife still sounding in
his ears—Booth himself, in his heydey, never gave a more brilliant, a more
false performance.

''Your Honor! Gentlemen of the Jury! You have heard with what cruelty
the prosecution has referred to the sins of this woman, as if her condition
was of her own preference. A dreadful—a vicious—a revolting picture has
been painted for you of her life and surroundings. Tell me—tell me—do you
really think that she willingly embraced a life so repellent, so horrible? No,
gentlemen! A thousand times, no! This girl was bred in such luxury, such
refinement, as few of us have known. And just as the young girl was budding
into womanhood, cruel fate snatched all this from her, bereft her of her dear
ones, took from her, one by one, with a terrible and fierce rapidity, those
upon whom she had come to look for love and support. And then, in that
moment of darkest terror and loneliness, came one of our sex, gentlemen.
A wolf in sheep's clothing. A fiend in the guise of a human. False promises.
Lies. Deceit so palpable that it would have deceived no one but a young girl
as innocent, as pure, as starry eyed as was this woman you now see white
and trembling before you. One of our sex was the author of her ruin, more
to blame than she. What could be more pathetic than the spectacle she
presents? An immortal soul in ruin. The star of purity, once glittering on her
girlish brow, has set its seal, and forever. A moment ago you heard her
reviled, in the lowest terms a man can employ toward a woman, for the
depths to which she has sunk, for the company she keeps, for the life she
leads. Yet where can she go that her sin does not pursue her? You would
drive her out. But where? Gentlemen, the very promises of God are denied
her. Who was it said, ''Come unto me all ye that are heavy laden, and I will
give you rest'? She is indeed heavy laden, this trampled flower of the South,
but if at this instant she were to kneel down before us all and confess her
Redeemer, where is the Church that would receive her, where the community
that would take her in? Scorn and mockery would greet her; those she met
of her own sex would gather their skirts the more closely to avoid the
pollution of her touch. Our sex wrecked her once pure life. Her own sex

shrinks from her as from a pestilence. Society has reared its relentless walls
against her. Only in the friendly shelter of the grave can her betrayed and
broken heart ever find the Redeemer's promised rest. The gentleman who
so eloquently spoke before me told you of her assumed names, of her sins,
of her habits. He never, for all his eloquence, told you of her sorrows, her
agonies, her hopes, her despairs. But I could tell you. I could tell you of the
desperate day—the redletter day in the banner of the great Oklahoma country—when she tried to win a home for herself where she could live in decency
and quiet. . . . When the remembered voices of father and mother and
sisters and brothers fall like music on her erring ears . . . who shall tell what
this heavy heart, sinful though it may seem to you and to me . . . understanding, pity, help, like music on her erring soul . . . oh, gentlemen
. . . gentlemen . . .''

But by this time the gentlemen, between emotion and tobacco juice, were
having such difficulty with their Adam's apples as to make a wholesale
strangling seem inevitable. The beautiful flexible voice went on, the hands
wove their enchantment, the eyes held you in their spell. The pompous figure
of little Pat Leary shrank, dwindled, disappeared before their mind's eye.
The harlot Dixie Lee, in her black, became a woman romantic, piteous,
appealing. Sabra Cravat, her pencil flying over her paper, thought grimly:

"It isn't true. Don't believe him. He is wrong. He has always been wrong.
For fifteen years he has always been wrong. Don't believe him. I shall have
to print this. How lovely his voice is. It's like a knife in my heart. I mustn't
look at his eyes. His hands—what was that he said?—I must keep my mind
on . . . music on her erring soul . . . oh, my love . . . I ought to hate
him . . . I do hate him. . . .''

Dixie Lee's head drooped on her ravaged breast. Even her plumed satellites had the wit to languish like crushed lilies and to wipe their eyes with
filmy handkerchiefs the while they sniffled audibly.

It was finished. Yancey walked to his seat, sat as before, the great buffalo
head lowered, the lids closed over the compelling eyes, the beautiful hands
folded, relaxed.

The good men and true of the jury filed solemnly out through the crowd
that made way for them. As solemnly they crossed the dusty road and
repaired to a draw at the roadside, where they squatted on such bits of rock
or board as came to hand. Solemnly, briefly, and with utter disregard of its
legal aspect, they discussed the case—if their inarticulate monosyllables
could be termed discussion. The courtroom throng, scattering for refreshment, had barely time to down its drink before the jury stamped heavily
across the road and into the noisome courtroom.

". . . find the defendant, Dixie Lee, not guilty.''

18

IT WAS AS though Osage and the whole Oklahoma country now stopped and
took a deep breath. Well it might. Just ahead of it, all unknown, waited
years of such clangor and strife as would make the past years seem uneventful
in comparison. Ever since the day of the Run, more than fifteen years ago,
it had been racing helter-skelter, devil take the hindmost; shooting into the
air, prancing and yelping out of sheer vitality and cussedness. A rough roof
over its head; coarse food on its table; a horse to ride; a burning drink to
toss down its throat; border justice; gyp water; a girl to hug; mud roads to
the edge of the sun-baked prairie, and thereafter no road; grab what you

need; fight for what you want—the men who had come to the wilderness of the Oklahoma country had expected no more than this; and this they had got. A man's country it seemed to be, ruled by men for men. The women allowed them to think so. The word feminism was unknown to the Sabra Cravats, the Mrs. Wyatts, the Mrs. Hefners, the Mesdames Turket and Folsom and Sipes. Prim, good women and courageous, banded together by their goodness and by their common resolve to tame the wilderness. Their power was the more tremendous because they did not know they had it. They never once said, during those fifteen years, "We women will do this. We women will change that." Quietly, indomitably, relentlessly, without even a furtive glance of understanding exchanged between them, but secure in their common knowledge of the sentimental American male, they went ahead with their plans.

The Philomathean Club. The Twentieth Century Culture Club. The Eastern Star. The Daughters of Rebekah. The Venus Lodge.

"Ha-ha!" and "Ho-ho!" roared their menfolk. "What do you girls do at these meetings of yours? Swap cooking receipts and dress patterns?"

"Oh, yes. And we talk."

"I bet you do. Say, you don't have to tell any man that. Talk! Time about ten of you women folks start babblin' together I bet you get the whole Territory settled—politics, Injuns, land fights, and all."

"Just about."

Yancey had come home from the Spanish-American War a hero. Other men from Osage had been in the Philippines. One had even died there (dysentery and ptomaine from bad tinned beef). But Yancey was the town's Rough Rider. He had charged up San Juan Hill with Roosevelt. Osage, knowing Yancey and never having seen Roosevelt, assumed that Yancey Cravat—the Southwest Cimarron—had led the way, an ivory-and-silver-mounted six-shooter in either hand, the great buffalo head lowered with such menace that the little brown men had fled to their jungles in terror.

His return had been the occasion for such a celebration as the town had never known and never would know again, they assured each other, between drinks, until the day when statehood should come to the Territory. He returned a captain, unwounded, but thin and yellow, with the livery look that confirmed the stories one had heard of putrid food, typhoid, dysentery, and mosquitoes more deadly, in this semi-tropical country, than bullets or cannon.

Poisoned and enfeebled though he was, his return seemed to energize the crude little town. Wherever he might be he lived in a swirl of events that drew into its eddy all that came within its radius. Hi, Yancey! Hi, Clint! He shed the khaki and the cocked hat and actually appeared again in the familiar white sombrero, Prince Albert, and high-heeled boots. Osage breathed a sigh of satisfaction. His dereliction was forgiven, the rumors about him forgotten—or allowed to subside, at least. Again the editorial columns of the *Oklahoma Wigwam* blazed with hyperbole.

It was hard for Sabra to take second place (or to appear to take second place) in the office of the *Wigwam*. She had so long ruled there alone. Her word had been law to the wavering Jesse Rickey and to the worshiping Cliff Means. And now to say, "You'd better ask Mr. Cravat."

"He says leave it to you. He's went out."

Yancey did a good deal of going out. Sabra, after all, still did most of the work of the paper without having the satisfaction of dictating its policy. A linotype machine, that talented iron monster, now chattered and chittered and clanked in the composing room of the *Wigwam*. It was the first of its kind in the Oklahoma country. Very costly and uncannily human, Sabra never quite got over her fear of it. The long arm reached down with such leisurely assurance, snatched its handful of metal, carried it over, descended, dropped it. It opened its capacious maw to be fed bars of silvery lead which it spat forth again in the shape of neat cakes of type. Its keys were like grinning teeth. It grunted, shivered, clumped, spoke—or nearly.

"I never come near it," Sabra once admitted, "that I don't expect the thing to reach down with its iron arm and clap me on the shoulder and clatter, 'Hello, Sabra!' "

She was proud of the linotype machine, for it had been her five years at the head of the *Wigwam* that had made it possible. It was she who had gone out after job printing contracts; who had educated the local merchants to the value of advertising. Certainly Yancey, prancing and prating, had never given a thought to these substantial foundations on which the entire business success of the paper rested. They now got out with ease the daily *Wigwam* for the Osage townspeople and the weekly for county subscribers. Passing the windows of the *Wigwam* office on Pawhuska Avenue you could hear the thump and rattle of the iron monster. Between them Jesse Rickey and Cliff Means ran the linotype. Often they labored far into the night on job work, and the late passer-by would see the little light burning in the printing shop and hear the rattle and thump of the machine. In a pinch Sabra herself could run it. Yancey never went near it, and, strangely enough, young Cim had a horror of it, as he had of most things mechanical. After one attempt at the keyboard, during which he had hopelessly jammed the machine's delicate insides, he was forbidden ever to go near it again. For that matter, Cim had little enough taste for the newspaper business. He pied type at the case rack. He had no news sense. He had neither his father's gift for mingling with people and winning their confidence nor his mother's more orderly materialistic mind. He had much of Yancey Cravat's charm, and something of the vagueness of his grandfather, old Lewis Venable (dead these two years), but combining the worst features of both.

"Stop dreaming!" Sabra said to him, often and often. "What are you dreaming about?"

She had grown to love the atmosphere of the newspaper office and resented the boy's indifference to it. She loved the very smell of it—the mixed odor of hot metal, printer's ink, dust, white paper, acid, corncob pipe, and cats.

"Stop dreaming?" Yancey, hearing her thus admonishing Cim, whirled on her in one of his rare moments of utter rage. "God a'mighty, Sabra! That's what Ann Hathaway said to Shakespeare. Don't you women know that 'Dreams grow holy put in action; work grows fair through starry dreaming?' Leave the boy alone! Let him dream! Let him dream!"

"One starry dreamer in a family is enough," Sabra retorted, tartly.

Five years had gone by—six years since Yancey's return. Yet, strangely enough, Sabra never had a feeling of security. She never forgot what he had said about Wichita. "Almost five years in one place. That's the longest stretch I've ever done, honey." Five years. And this was well into the sixth. He had plunged head first into the statehood fight, into the Indian Territory situation. The anti-Indian faction was bitterly opposed to the plan for combining the Oklahoma Territory and the Indian Territory under the single state of Oklahoma. Their slogan was The White Man's State for the White Man.

"Who brought the Indian here to the Oklahoma country in the first place?" shouted Yancey in the editorial columns of the *Wigwam*. "White men. They hounded them from Missouri to Arkansas, from Arkansas to southern Kansas, then to northern Kansas, to northern Oklahoma, to southern Oklahoma. You white men sold them the piece of arid and barren land on which they now live in squalor and misery. It isn't fit for a white man to live on, or the Indians wouldn't be living on it now. Deprived of their tribal laws, deprived of their tribal rites, herded together in stockades like wild animals, robbed, cheated, kicked, hounded from place to place, give them the protection of the country that has taken their country away from them. Give them at least the right to become citizens of the state of Oklahoma.''

He was obsessed by it. He traveled to Washington in the hope of lobbying for it, and made quite a stir in that formal capital with his white sombrero, his Prince Albert, his Texas star boots, his great buffalo head, his charm, his grace, his manner. Roosevelt was characteristically cordial to his old campaign comrade. Washington ladies were captivated by the flowery speeches of this romantic, this story-book swaggerer out of the Southwest.

It was rumored on good authority that he was to be appointed the next Governor of the Oklahoma Territory.

"Oh, Yancey," Sabra said, "do be careful. Governor of the Territory! It would mean so much. It would help Cim in the future. Donna, too. Their father a governor." She thought, "Perhaps everything will be all right now. Perhaps all that I've gone through in the last ten years will be worth it, now. Perhaps it was for this. He'll settle down. . . . Mamma can't say now . . . and all the Venables and the Vians and the Goforths and the Greenwoods. . '. ." She had had to endure their pity, even from a distance, all these years.

The rumor took on substance. My husband, Yancey Cravat, Governor of the Territory of Oklahoma. And then, when statehood came, as it must in the next few years, perhaps Governor of the state of Oklahoma. Why not!

At which point Yancey blasted any possibility of his appointment to the governorship by hurling a red-hot editorial into the columns of the *Wigwam*. The gist of it was that the hundreds of thousands of Indians now living on reservations throughout the United States should be allowed to live where they pleased, at liberty. The whites of the Oklahoma Territory and the Indian Territory, with an Indian population of about one hundred and twenty thousand of various tribes—Poncas, Cherokees, Chickasaws, Creeks, Osages, Kiowas, Comanches, Kaws, Choctaws, Seminoles, and a score of others— read, emitted a roar of rage, and brandishing the paper ran screaming into the streets, cursing the name of Yancey Cravat.

Sabra had caught the editorial in the wet proof sheet. Her eye leaped down its lines.

> Herded like sheep in a corral—no, like wild animals in a cage—they are left to rot on their reservations by a government that has taken first their land, then their self-respect, then their liberty from them. The land of the free! When the very people who first dwelt on it are prisoners! Slaves, but slaves deprived of the solace of work. What hope have they, what ambition, what object in living? Their spirit is broken. Their pride is gone. Slothful, yes. Why not? Each month he receives his dole, his pittance. Look at the Osage Nation, now dwindled to a wretched two thousand souls. The men are still handsome, strong, vital; the women beautiful, dignified, often intelligent. Yet there they huddle in their miserable shanties like beaten animals eating the food that is thrown them by a great—a munificent—government. The government of these United States! Let them be free. Let the Red Man live a free man as the White Man lives. . . .

Much that he wrote was true, perhaps. Yet the plight of the Indian was not as pitiable as Yancey painted it. He cast over them the glamour of his own romantic nature. The truth was that they themselves cared little—except a few of their tribal leaders, more intelligent than the rest. They hunted a little, fished, slept, visited from tribe to tribe, the Poncas visiting the Osages, the Osages the Poncas, gossiping, eating, holding powwows. The men were great poker players, having learned the game from the white man, and spent hours at it.

They passed through the town of Osage in their brilliant striped blankets, sometimes walking, sometimes on sorry nags, sometimes in rickety wagons laden with pots, poles, rags, papooses, hounds. The towns people hastily removed such articles as might please the pilfering fancy.

Sabra picked up the proof sheet, still damp from the press, and walked into Yancey's office. Her face was white, set.

"You're going to run this, Yancey?"

"Yes."

"You'll never be Governor of the Territory."

"Never."

She stood a moment, her face working. She crushed the galley proof in her hand so that her knuckles stood out, white.

"I've forgiven you many, many things, God knows, in the last ten years. I'll never forgive you for this. Never."

"Yes, you will, honey. Never is a long time. Not while I'm alive, maybe. But some day, a long time from now—though not so very long, maybe—you'll be able to turn back to the old files of the *Oklahoma Wigwam* and lift this editorial of mine right out of it, word for word, and run it as your own."

"Never. . . . Donna . . . Cim . . ."

"I can't live my children's lives for them, Sabra, honey. They've got to live their own. I believe what I believe. This town is rotten—the Territory—the whole country. Rotten."

"You're a fine one to say what is or isn't rotten. You with your whisky and your Indians and your women. I despise you. So does everyone in the town—in the Territory."

" 'A prophet is not without honor, save in his own country and in his own home.' " A trifle sonorously.

She never really knew whether he had done this thing with the very purpose of making his governorship impossible. It was like him.

Curiously enough, the editorial, while it maddened the white population of the Territory, gained the paper many readers. The *Wigwam* prospered. Osage blossomed. The town was still rough, crude, wide open, even dangerous. But it began to take on an aspect of permanence. It was no longer a camp; it was a town. It began to build schools, churches, halls. Arkansas Grat's gambling tent had long ago been replaced by a solid wooden structure, just as gambling terms of the West and the Southwest had slowly been incorporated into the language of daily use. I'm keeping cases on him . . . standing pat . . . bluffing . . . bucking the tiger. Terms filched from the gaming table; poker and faro and keno.

Sol Levy's store—the Levy Mercantile Company—had two waxen ladies in the window, their features only slightly affected by the burning Southwest sun. Yancey boomed Sol Levy for mayor of Osage, but he never had a chance. It was remarkable how the *Oklahoma Wigwam* persisted, though its position in most public questions was violently unpopular. Perhaps it, like Yancey, had a vitality and a charm that no one could withstand.

Although Sol Levy was still the town Jew, respected, prosperous, the town had never quite absorbed this Oriental. A citizen of years' standing, he still was a stranger. He mingled little with his fellow townsmen outside business hours. He lived lonesomely at the Bixby House and ate the notoriously bad meals served by Mrs. Bixby. He was shy of the town women though the Women of the Town found him kindly, passionate, and generous. The business men liked him. They put him on committees. Occasionally Sabra or some other woman who knew him well enough would say, half playfully, half seriously, "Why don't you get married, Sol? A nice fellow like you. You'd make some girl happy."

Sometimes he thought vaguely of going to Wichita or Kansas City or even Chicago to meet some nice Jewish girl there, but he never did. It never entered his head to marry a Gentile. The social life of the town was almost unknown to him. Sometimes if a big local organization—the Elks, the Odd Fellows, the Sons of the Southwest—gave a benefit dance, you would glimpse him briefly, in the early part of the evening, standing shyly against the wall or leaning half hidden in the doorway, a darkling, remote, curiously Oriental figure in the midst of these robust red-faced plainsmen and ex-cowmen.

"Come on, Sol, mix in! Grab off one of the girls and get to dancin', why don't you? What you scairt of?" But Sol remained aloof. He regarded the hot, sweaty, shouting dancers with a kind of interested bewilderment and wonder, much as the dancers themselves sometimes watched the Indians during one of the Festival Dances on the outlying reservations. On occasion he made himself politely agreeable to a stout matron well past middle age. They looked up at his tragic dark eyes; they noticed his slim ivory hand as it passed them a plate of cake or a cup of coffee. "He's real nice when you get to know him," they said. "For a Jew, that is."

Between him and Yancey there existed a deep sympathy and understanding. Yancey campaigned for Sol Levy in the mayoralty race—if a thing so one-sided could be called a race. The *Wigwam* extolled him.

> Sol Levy, the genial proprietor of the Levy Mercantile Company, is the *Wigwam's* candidate for mayor. It behooves the people of Osage to do honor to one of its pioneer citizens whose career, since its early days, has been marked by industry, prosperity, generosity. He comes of a race of dreamers and doers. . . .

"Why, the very idea!" snorted the redoubtable virago, Mrs. Tracy Wyatt, whose husband was the opposing candidate. "A Jew for mayor of Osage! They'll be having an Indian mayor next. Mr. Wyatt's folks are real Americans. They helped settle Arkansas. And as for me, why, I can trace my ancestry right back to William Whipple, who was one of the signers of the Declaration of Independence."

Sol Levy never had a chance for public honor. He, in fact, did practically nothing to further his own possible election. He seemed to regard the whole matter with a remoteness slightly tinged with ironic humor. Yancey dropped into Sol's store to bring him this latest pronouncement of the bristling Mrs. Wyatt. Sol was busy in the back of the store, where he was helping the boy unpack a new invoice of china and lamps just received, for the Levy Mercantile Company had blossomed into a general store of parts. His head was in a barrel, and when he straightened and looked up at the towering Yancey there were bits of straw and excelsior clinging to his shirt sleeves and necktie and his black hair.

"Declaration of Independence!" he exclaimed, thoughtfully. "Tell her one of my ancestors wrote the Ten Commandments. Fella name of Moses."

Yancey, roaring with laughter, used this in the *Wigwam,* and it naturally helped as much as anything to defeat the already defeated candidate.

Sometimes the slim, white-faced proprietor, with his friend Yancey Cravat, stood in the doorway of the store, watching the town go by. They said little. It was as though they were outsiders, looking on at a strange pageant.

"What the hell are you doing here in this town, anyway, Sol?" Yancey would say, as though musing aloud.

"And you?" Sol would retort. "A civilized barbarian."

The town went by—Indians, cowboys up from Texas, plainsmen, ranchers. They still squatted at the curb, as in the early days. They chewed tobacco and spat. The big sombrero persisted, and even the boots and spurs.

"Howdy, Yancey! Howdy, Sol! H'are you, Cim!"

There was talk of paving Pawhuska Avenue, but this did not come for years. The town actually boasted a waterworks. The *Wigwam* office still stood on Pawhuska, but it now occupied the entire house. Two years after Yancey's return they had decided to build a home on Kihekah Street, where there actually were trees now almost ten years old.

Sabra had built the house as she wanted it, though at first there had been a spirited argument about this. Yancey's idea had been, of course, ridiculous, fantastic. He said he wanted the house built in native style.

"Native! What in the world! A wickiup?"

"Well, a house in the old Southwest Indian style—almost pueblo, I mean. Or Spanish, sort of, made of Oklahoma red clay—plaster, maybe. Not brick. And low, with a patio where you can be out of doors and yet away from the sun. And where you can have privacy."

Sabra made short work of that idea. Or perhaps Yancey did not persist. He withdrew his plan as suddenly as he had presented it; shrugged his great shoulders as though the house no longer interested him.

Osage built its new houses with an attached front porch gaping socially out into the street. It sat on the front porch in its shirt sleeves and kitchen apron. It called from porch to porch, "How's your tomato plants doing? I see the Packses got out-of-town company visiting." It didn't in the least want privacy.

Sabra built a white frame house in the style of the day, with turrets, towers, minarets, cupolas, and scroll work. There was a stained glass window in the hall, in purple and red and green and yellow, which, confronting the entering caller, gave him the look of being suddenly stricken with bubonic plague. There were parlor, sitting room, dining room, kitchen on the first floor; four bedrooms on the second floor, and a bathroom, actually, with a full-size bathtub, a toilet, and a marble washstand with varicose veins. In the cellar there was a hot air furnace. In the parlor were brown brocade-and-velvet settee and stuffed chairs. In the sitting room was a lamp with a leaded glass shade in the shape of a strange and bloated flower—a Burbankian monstrosity, half water lily, half petunia.

"As long as we're building and furnishing," Sabra said, "it might as well be the best." She had gone about planning the house, and furnishing it, with her customary energy and capability. With it all she found time to do her work on the *Wigwam*—for without her the paper would have been run to the ground in six months. Osage had long since ceased to consider it queer that she, a woman, and the wife of one of its most prominent citizens, should go to work every morning like a man.

By ten every morning she had attended to her household, seen it started for the day, had planned the meals, ordered them on her way downtown, and was at her desk in the *Wigwam* office, sorting mail, reading exchanges, taking ads, covering news, writing heads, pasting up. Yancey's contributions were brilliant but spasmodic. The necessary departmental items—real estate transfers, routine court news, out-of-town district and county gleanings—bored him, though he knew well that they were necessary to the success of the paper. He left these to Sabra, among many other things.

Sabra, in common with the other well-to-do housewives of the community, employed an Indian girl as a house servant. There was no other kind of help available. After her hideous experience with Arita Red Feather she had been careful to get Indian girls older, more settled, though this was difficult. She preferred Osage girls. These married young, often before they had finished their studies at the Indian school.

Ruby Big Elk had been with Sabra now for three years. A curious, big, silent girl of about twenty-two—almost handsome—one of six children—a large family for an Osage. Sabra was somewhat taken aback, after the girl had been with her for some months, to learn that she already had been twice married.

"What became of your husbands, Ruby?"

"Died."

She had a manner that bordered on the insolent. Sabra put it down to Indian dignity. When she walked she scuffed her feet ever so little, and this, for some inexplicable reason, seemed to add insolence to her bearing. "Oh, do lift your feet, Ruby! Don't scuffle when you walk." The girl made no reply. Went on scuffling. Sabra discovered that she was lame; the left leg was slightly shorter than the right. She did not limp—or, rather, hid the tendency to limp by the irritating sliding sound. Her walk was straight, leisurely, measured. Sabra was terribly embarrassed; apologized to the Indian girl. The girl only looked at her and said nothing. Sabra repressed a little shiver. She had never got accustomed to the Indians.

Sabra was a bustler and a driver. As she went about the house in the morning, performing a dozen household duties before leaving for the *Wigwam* office, her quick tapping step drummed like hail on a tin roof. It annoyed her intensely, always, to see Ruby Big Elk making up the beds with that regal manner, or moving about the kitchen with the pace and air of a Lady Macbeth. The girl's broad, immobile face, her unspeaking eyes, her secret manner all worked a slow constant poison in Sabra. She spoke seldom; never smiled. When Sabra spoke to her about some household task she would regard her mistress with an unblinking gaze that was highly disconcerting.

"Did you understand about the grape jell, Ruby? To let it get thoroughly cool before you pour on the wax?"

Ruby would majestically incline her fine head, large, like a man's head. The word sinister came into Sabra's mind. Still, Sabra argued, she was good to the children, fed them well, never complained about the work. Sometimes—on rare occasions—she would dig a little pit in the back yard and build a slow hot smothered fire by some secret Indian process, and there, to the intense delight of young Cim, she would roast meats deliciously in the Indian fashion, crisp and sweet, skewered with little shafts of wood that she herself whittled down. Donna refused to touch the meat, as did Sabra. Donna shared her mother's dislike of the Indians—or perhaps she had early been impressed with her mother's feeling about them. Sometimes Donna, the spoiled, the pampered, the imperious (every inch her grandmother Felice Venable) would feel Ruby Big Elk's eye on her—that expressionless, dead black Indian eye. Yet back of its deadness, its utter lack of expression, there still seemed to lurk a cold contempt.

"What are you staring at, Ruby?" Donna would cry, pettishly. Ruby would walk out of the room with her slow scuffling step, her body erect, her head regal, her eyes looking straight ahead. She said nothing. "Miserable squaw!'' Donna would hiss under her breath. ''Gives herself the airs of a princess because her greasy old father runs the tribe or something.''

Ruby's father, Big Elk, had in fact been Chief of the Osage tribe by election for ten years, and though he no longer held this highest office, was a man much looked up to in the Osage Nation. He had sent his six children and actually his fat wife to the Indian school, but he himself steadfastly refused to speak a word of English, though he knew enough of the language. He conversed in Osage, and when necessary used an interpreter. It was a kind of stubborn Indian pride in him. It was his enduring challenge to the white man. ''You have not defeated me.''

His pride did not, however, extend to more material things, and Sabra was frequently annoyed by the sight of the entire Big Elk family, the old ex-Chief, his squaw, and the five brothers and sisters, squatting in her kitchen doorway enjoying such juicy bits as Ruby saw fit to bestow upon them from the Cravat larder. When Sabra would have put a stop to this, Yancey intervened.

''He's a wise old man. If he had a little white blood in him he'd be as great as Quanah Parker was, or Sequoyah. Everything he says is wisdom. I like to talk with him. Leave him alone.''

This did not serve to lessen Sabra's irritation. Often she returned home to find Yancey squatting on the ground with old Big Elk, smoking and conversing in a mixture of Osage and English, for Big Elk did not refuse to understand the English language, even though he would not speak it. Yancey had some knowledge of Osage. Sabra, coming upon the two grunting and muttering and smoking and staring ahead into nothingness or (worse still) cracking some Indian joke and shaking with silent laughter, Indian fashion, was filled with fury. Nothing so maddened her.

It slowly dawned on Sabra that young Cim was always to be found lolling in the kitchen, talking to Ruby. Ruby, she discovered to her horror, was teaching Cim to speak Osage. A difficult language to the white, he seemed to have a natural aptitude for it. She came upon them, their heads close together over the kitchen table laughing and talking and singing. Rather, Ruby Big Elk was singing a song with a curious rhythm, and (to Sabra's ear, at least) no melody. There was a pulsation of the girl's voice on sustained notes such as is sometimes produced on a violin when the same note is sounded several times during a single bow stroke. Cim was trying to follow the strange gutturals, slurs, and accents, his eyes fixed on Ruby's face, his own expression utterly absorbed, rapt.

''What are you doing? What is this?''

The Indian girl's face took on its customary expression of proud disdain. She rose. ''Teach um song,'' she said; which was queer, for she spoke English perfectly.

''Well, I must say, Cimarron Cravat! When you know your father is expecting you down at the office———'' She stopped. Her quick eye had leaped to the table where lay the little round peyote disk or mescal button which is the hashish of the Indian.

She had heard about it; knew how prevalent among the Indian tribes from Nebraska down to Mexico had become the habit of eating this little buttonlike top of a Mexican cactus plant. In shape a disk about an inch and a half in diameter and a quarter of an inch thick, the mescal or peyote gave the eater a strange feeling of lightness, dispelled pain and fatigue, caused visions of marvelous beauty and grandeur. The use of it had become an Indian religious rite.

Like a fury Sabra advanced to the table, snatched up the little round button of soft green.

"Peyote!" She whirled on Cim. "What are you doing with this thing?"

Cim's eyes were cast down sullenly. His hands in his pockets, he leaned against the wall, very limp, very bored, very infuriating and insolent.

"Ruby was just teaching me one of the Mescal Ceremony songs. Darned interesting. It's the last song. They sing it at sunrise when they're just about all in. Goes like this."

To Sabra's horror he began an eerie song as he stood there leaning against the kitchen wall, his eyes half closed.

Ya   na   hi   yo   hi   ya   na

Ya   na   hi____   ya   na   hi____   yo

"Stop it!" screamed Sabra. With the gesture of a tragedy queen she motioned him out of the kitchen. He obeyed with very bad grace, his going more annoying in its manner, than his staying. Sabra followed him, silently. Suddenly she realized she hated his walk, and knew why. He walked with a queer little springing gait, on the very soles of his feet. It came over her that it always had annoyed her. She remembered that someone had laughingly told her what Pete Pitchlyn, the old Indian scout, lounging on his street corner, had said about young Cim:

"Every time I see that young Cimarron Cravat acomin' down the street I expect to hear a twig snap. Walks like a story-book Injun."

In the privacy of the sitting room Sabra confronted her son, the bit of peyote still crushed in her hand.

"So you've come to this! I'm ashamed of you!"

"Come to what?"

She opened her hand to show the button of pulpy green crushed in her palm. "Peyote. A son of mine. I'd rather see you dead————"

"Oh, for heaven's sake, Mom, don't get Biblical, like Dad. To hear you a person would think you'd found me drugged in a Chinese opium den."

"I think I'd almost rather."

"It's nothing but a miserable little piece of cactus. And what was I doing but sitting in the kitchen listening to Ruby tell how her father————"

"I should think a man of almost eighteen could find something better to do than sit in a kitchen in the middle of the day talking to an Indian hired girl. Where's your pride!"

Cim's eyes were still cast down. He still lounged insolently, his hands in his pockets. "How about these stories you've told me all your life about the love you Southerners had for your servants and how old Angie was like a second mother to you?"

"Niggers are different. They know their place."

He raised the heavy eyelids then and lifted his fine head with the menacing look that she knew so well in his father. "You're right. They are different. In the first place, Ruby isn't an Indian hired girl. She is the daughter of an Osage chief."

"Osage fiddlesticks! What of it!"

"Ruby Big Elk is just as important a person in the Osage Nation as Alice Roosevelt is in Washington."

"Now, listen here, Cimarron Cravat! I've heard about enough. A lot of dirty Indians! Just you march yourself down to the *Wigwam* office, young man, and don't you ever again let me catch you talking in that disrespectful manner about the daughter of the President of the United States. And if I ever hear that you've eaten a bite of this miserable stuff"—she held out her hand, shaking a little, the mescal button crushed in her palm—"I'll have your father thrash you within an inch of your life, big as you are. As it is, he shall hear of this."

But Yancey, on being told, only looked thoughtful and a little sad. "It's your own fault, Sabra. You're bound that the boy shall live the life you've planned for him instead of the one he wants. So he's trying to escape into a dream life. Like the Indians. It's all the same thing."

"I don't know what you're talking about. I don't think you know, either."

"The Indians started to eat peyote after the whites had taken their religious and spiritual and decent physical life away from them. They had owned the plains and the prairies for centuries. The whites took those. The whites killed off the buffalo, whose flesh had been the Indians' food, and whose skins had been their shelter, and gave them bacon and tumbledown wooden houses in their place. The whites told them that the gods they had worshiped were commonplace things. The Sun was a dying planet—the Stars lumps of hot metal—the Rain a thing that could be regulated by tree planting—the Wind just a current of air that a man in Washington knew all about and whose travels he could prophesy by looking at a piece of machinery."

"And they ought to be grateful for it. The government's given them food and clothes and homes and land. They're a shiftless good-for-nothing lot and won't work. They won't even plant crops."

" 'Man cannot live by bread alone.' He has got to have dreams, or life is unendurable. So the Indian turned to the peyote. He finds peace and comfort and beauty in his dreams."

A horrible suspicion darted through Sabra. "Yancey Cravat, have you ever——"

He nodded his magnificent head slowly, sadly. "Many times. Many times."

19

CIM WAS NINETEEN, Donna fifteen. And now Sabra lived quite alone in the new house on Kihekeh Street, except for a colored woman servant sent from Kansas. She ran the paper alone, as she wished it run. She ordered the house as she wished it. She very nearly ran the town of Osage. She was a power in the Territory. And Yancey was gone, Cim was gone, Donna was gone. Sabra had refused to compromise with life, and life had taken matters out of her hands.

Donna was away at an Eastern finishing school—Miss Dignum's on the Hudson. Yancey had opposed that, of course. It had been Sabra's idea to send Donna east to school.

"East?" Yancey had said. "Kansas City?"

"Certainly not."

"Oh—Chicago."

"I mean New York."

"You're crazy."

"I didn't expect you to approve. I suppose you'd like her to go to an Indian school. Donna's an unusual girl. She's not a beauty and never will be, but she's brilliant, that's what she is. Brilliant. I don't mean intellectual.

You needn't smile. I mean that she's got the ambition and the insight and the foresight, too, of a woman of twice her age."

"I'm sorry to hear that."

"I'm not. She's like Mamma in many ways, only she's got intelligence and drive. She doesn't get along with the girls here—Maurine Turket and Gazelle Slaughter and Jewel Riggs and Czarina McKee, and those. She's different. They go switching up and down Pawhuska Avenue. They'll marry one of these tobacco-chewing loafers and settle down like vegetables. Well, she won't. I'll see to that."

"Going to marry her off to an Eastern potentate—at fifteen?"

"You wait. You'll see. She knows what she wants. She'll get it, too."

"Sure it isn't you who know what you want her to want?"

But Sabra had sent her off to Miss Dignum's on a diet of prunes and prisms that even her high-and-mighty old grandmother Felice Venable approved.

Cim, walking the prairies beyond Osage with that peculiar light step of his, his eyes cast down; prowling the draws and sprawling upon the clay banks of the rivers that ran so red through the Red Man's Territory, said that he wanted to be a geologist. He spoke of the Colorado School of Mines. He worked in the *Wigwam* office and hated it. He could pi a case of type more quickly and completely than a drunken tramp printer. The familiar "shrdlu etaoin" was likely to appear in any column in which he had a hand. Even Jesse Rickey, his mournful mustaches more drooping than ever, protested to Yancey.

"She can't make a newspaper man out of that kid," he said. "Not in a million years. Newspaper men are born, not made. Cim, he just naturally hates news, let alone a newspaper office. He was born without a nose for news, like a fellow that's born without an arm, or something. You can't grow it if you haven't got it."

"I know it," said Yancey, wearily. "He'll find a way out."

For the first time a rival newspaper flourished in the town of Osage. The town was scarcely large enough to support two daily papers, but Yancey's political attitude so often was at variance with the feeling of the Territory politicians that the new daily, slipshod and dishonest though it was, and owned body and soul by Territorial interests, achieved a degree of popularity.

Sabra, unable to dictate the policy of the *Wigwam* with Yancey at its head, had to content herself with the management of its mechanical workings and with its increasingly important social and club columns. Osage swarmed with meetings, committees, lodges, Knights of This and Sisters of That. The Philomathean and the Twentieth Century clubs began to go in for Civic Betterment, and no Osage merchant or professional man was safe from cajoling and unattractive females in shirtwaists and skirts and eyeglasses demanding his name signed to this or that petition (with a contribution. Whatever you feel that you can give, Mr. Hefner. Of course, as a leading business man . . .).

They planted shrubs about the cinder-strewn environs of the Santa Fé and the Katy depots. They agitated for the immediate paving of Pawhuska Avenue (it wasn't done). The Ladies of the Eastern Star. The Venus Lodge. Sisters of Rebekah. Daughters of the Southwest. They came into the *Wigwam* office with notices to be printed about lodge suppers and church sociables. Strangely enough, they were likely to stay longer and to chat more freely if Yancey and not Sabra were there to receive them. Sabra was polite but businesslike to her own sex encountered in office hours. But Yancey made himself utterly charming. He could no more help it than he could help breathing. It was almost functional with him. He made the stout, common-

place, middle-aged women feel that they were royal—and seductive. He
flattered them with his fine eyes; he bowed them to the door; their eyeglasses
quivered. He was likely, on their departure, to crumple their carefully
worded notice and throw it on the floor. Sabra, though she made short work
of the visiting Venuses and Rebekahs, ran their notice and, if necessary,
carefully rewrote it.

"God A'mighty!" he would groan at noonday dinner. "The office was full
of Wenuses this morning. Like a swarm of overstuffed locusts."

Sabra was at the head of many of these Betterment movements. Also if
there could be said to be anything so formal as society in Osage, Sabra
Cravat was the leader of it. She was the first to electrify the ladies of the
Twentieth Century Culture Club by serving them Waldorf salad—that abom-
inable mixture of apple cubes, chopped nuts, whipped cream, and mayonnaise. The club fell upon it with little cries and murmurs. Thereafter it was
served at club meetings until Osage husbands, returning home to supper
after a day's work, and being offered this salvage from the feast, would push
it aside with masculine contempt for its contents and roar, "I can't eat this
stuff. Fix me some bacon and eggs."

From this culinary and social triumph Sabra proceeded to pineapple and
marshmallow salad, the recipe for which had been sent her by Donna in the
East. Its indirect effects were fatal.

When it again became her turn to act as hostess to the members of the
club she made her preparations for the afternoon meeting, held at the grisly
hour of half-past two. Refreshments were invariably served at four. With
all arrangements made, she was confronted by Ruby Big Elk with the astounding statement that this was a great Indian Festival day (September,
and the corn dances were on) and that she must go to the Reservation in
time for the Mescal Ceremony.

"You can't go," said Sabra, flatly. Midday dinner was over. Yancey had
returned to the office. Cim was lounging in the hammock on the porch. For
answer Ruby turned and walked with her stately, irritating step into her own
room just off the kitchen and closed the door.

"Well," shouted Sabra in the tones of Felice Venable herself, "if you do
go you needn't come back." She marched out to the front porch, where the
sight of the lounging Cim only aggravated her annoyance.

"This ends it. That girl has got to leave."

"What girl?"

"Ruby. Twenty women this afternoon, and she says she's going to the
Reservation. They'll be here at half-past two." It was rather incoherent, but
Cim, surprisingly enough, seemed to understand.

"But she told you a month ago."

"Told me what? How do you know?"

"Because she told me she told you, ever so long ago."

"Maybe she did. She never mentioned it again. I can't be expected to
remember every time the Indians have one of their powwows. I told her she
couldn't go. She's in there getting ready. Well, this ends it. She needn't
come back."

She flounced into the kitchen. There stood a mild-mannered young Indian
girl unknown to her.

"What do you want?"

"I am here," the girl answered, composedly, "to take Ruby Big Elk's
place this afternoon. I am Cherokee. She told me to come." She plucked
Ruby's blue and white checked gingham kitchen apron off the book behind
the door and tied it around her waist.

"Well!" gasped Sabra, relieved, but still angry. Through the kitchen window she saw Cim hitching up the two pintos to the racy little yellow phaëton that Yancey had bought. She must run out and tell him before he left. He had seemed disturbed. She was glad he was clearing out. She liked having the men folks out of the way when afternoon company was due.

Ruby's door opened. The girl came out. Her appearance was amazing. She wore a dress of white doeskin hanging straight from shoulders to ankles, and as soft and pliable as velvet. The hem was fringed. Front, sleeves, collar were finely beaded in an intricate pattern that was more like embroidery than beading. On her feet were moccasins in ivory white and as exquisitely beaded as the dress. It was the robe of a princess. Her dark Indian eyes were alive. Her skin seemed to glow in contrast with the garment. The girl was, for the moment, almost beautiful.

"Hello, Theresa Jump. . . . This is Theresa Jump. She will do my work this day. I have told her. She knows about the pineapple and marshmallow salad." For a moment it seemed to Sabra that just the faintest shadow of amusement flitted over Ruby's face as she said this. But then, Sabra never had pretended to understand these Indians. "I will be back to-morrow morning."

She walked slowly out of the house by way of the kitchen door, across the yard with her slow insolent dragging step. A stab of suspicion cut Sabra. She flew to the back porch, stood there a moment. Ruby Big Elk walked slowly toward the barn. Cim drove out with the phaëton and pintos. He saw the Indian woman in her white doeskin dress. His eyes shone enormous. He lifted his head as though to breathe deeply. At that look in his face Sabra ran across the yard. One hand was at her breast, as though an Indian arrow had pierced her. Ruby had set one foot in its cream white moccasin on the buggy step. Cim held out his free hand.

Sabra reached them, panting. "Where are you going?"

"I'm driving Ruby out to the Reservation."

"No, you're not. No, you're not." She put one hand in a futile gesture on the buggy wheel, as though to stop them by main force. She knew she must not lose her dignity before this Indian woman—before her son. Yet this thing was, to her way of thinking, monstrous.

Cim gathered up the reins, his eyes on the restive ponies. "I may stay to see some of the dancing and the Mescal Ceremony. Father says it's very interesting. Big Elk has invited me."

"Your father knows you're going? Like this?"

"Oh, yes." He cast a slight, an oblique glance at her hand on the wheel. Her hand dropped heavily to her side. He spoke to the horses. They were off. Ruby Big Elk looked straight ahead. She had uttered no word. Sabra turned and walked back to the house. The hot tears blinded her. She was choking. But her pride spoke, even then. You must not go the kitchen way. That Indian girl will see you. They are all alike. You must go around by the front way. Pretend it is nothing. Oh, God, what shall I do! All those women this afternoon. Perhaps I am making a fuss over nothing. Why shouldn't he take the Indian girl out to the Reservation and stop an hour or two to see the dances and the rites? . . . His face! His face when he saw her in that dress.

She bathed her eyes, powdered her nose, changed her dress, came into the kitchen, smiling. ". . . the pineapple cut into chunks about like this. Then you snip the marshmallow into it with the scissors. Mix whipped cream into your mayonnaise . . . a cherry on top . . . little thin sandwiches . . . damp napkin . . ." She went into the sitting room, adjusted a shade, plumped a pillow. The door bell rang. "Howdy-do, Mrs. Nisbett. . . . No, you're not. You're just on time. It's everybody else who's late." She thought, "Women are wonderful. No man could do what I am doing. Smiling and chatting when I am almost crazy." Her fine dark eyes were luminous. Her clear ivory skin was tinged now with a spot of red on either cheek. She looked very handsome.

Theresa Jump proved clumsy and unteachable. Sabra herself mixed and served the pineapple and marshmallow salad, and though this novelty proved a great success, the triumph of serving it was spoiled for Sabra. She bundled the girl off at six, after the dishes were done. Wearily she began to set the house to rights, but Yancey came home to a confusion of chairs and squashed pillows, a mingled odor of perfumery and coffee; a litter of cake crumbs, bits of embroidery silk, and crumpled tea napkins. His huge frame moving about the cluttered sitting room made these feminine remnants seem ridiculous. The disorder of the household irked him. Worst of all, Sabra, relieved now of her guests, was free to pour out upon him all the pent-up wrath, anxiety, and shock of the past few hours. Ruby. Cim. Theresa Jump. Peyote. Osages. If his own father allows such things—what will people say—no use trying to make something of yourself.

Yancey, usually so glib with quotations from this or that sonorous passage of poetry, said little. He did not even try to cajole her into a better humor with his flattery, his charm, his tenderness. His eyes were bloodshot, his hand more unsteady than usual. He had been drinking even more than was his wont, she knew that at once. By no means drunk (she had never seen him really drunk—no one had—he was seemingly incapable of reaching a visible state of drunkenness), he was in one of his fits of moody depression. The great shoulders sagged. The splendid head lolled on his breast. He seemed sunk in gloomy thought. She felt that he hardly heard what she was saying. She herself could eat nothing. She set a place for him at the dining-room table and plumped down before him a dish of the absurd salad, a cup of coffee, some cake, a plate of the left-over sandwiches, their edges curled dismally.

"What's this?" he said.

"Pineapple and marshmallow salad. With Ruby gone and all, I didn't get anything for your supper—I was so upset—all those women . . ."

He sat looking down at the slippery mass on his plate. His great arms were spread out on the table before him. The beautiful hands were opening and closing convulsively. So a mastodon might have looked at a worm. "Pineapple and marshmallow salad," he repeated, thoughtfully, almost wonderingly. Suddenly he threw back the magnificent head and began to laugh. Peal after peal of Herculean laughter. "Pineapple and marsh———" choking, the tears running down his cheeks. Sabra was angry, then frightened. For as suddenly as he had begun to laugh he became serious. He stood up, one hand on the table. Then he seemed to pull his whole body together like a tiger who is about to spring. He stood thus a moment, swaying a little. " 'Actum est de republica.' "

"What?" said Sabra, sharply.

"Latin, Latin, my love. Pineapple and marshmallow salad! "It is all over with the Republic.' " She shrugged her shoulders impatiently. Yancey turned, stiffly, like a soldier, walked out of the room, flicked his white sombrero off the hall rack and put it on at the usual jaunty angle, went down the porch stair with his light, graceful step, to the sidewalk and up the street, the great head lowered, the arms swinging despondently at his sides.

Sabra went on with her work of tidying up the house. Her eyes burned, her throat was constricted. Men! Men! Cim off with that squaw. Yancey angry because she had given him this very feminine dish of left-overs. What was the use of working, what was the use of pride, what was the use of ambition for your children, your home, your town if this was all it amounted to? Her work done, she allowed herself the luxury of a deliberate and cleansing storm of tears.

Eight o'clock. She heated some of the afternoon coffee and drank it sitting at the kitchen table. She went out on the front porch. Darkness had come on. A hot September evening. The crickets squeaked and ground away in the weeds. She was conscious of an aching weariness in all her body, but she could not sleep. Her eyes felt as though they were being pulled apart by invisible fingers. She put her palms over them, to shut them, to cool them. Nine. Ten. Eleven. Twelve. She undressed, unpinned the braids of her thick hair, brushed it, plaited it for the night. All the time she was listening. Listening. One.

Suddenly she began to dress again with icy fumbling fingers. She did up her hair, put on her hat and a jacket. She closed the door behind her, locked it, slipped the key into the mail box. The *Wigwam* office. Yancey was not there. The office was dark. She shook the door, rattled the knob, peered in, unlocked it with the key in her handbag. Her heart was pounding, but she was not afraid of the darkness. A cat's eyes gleamed at her from the printing shop. She struck a light. No one. No one. The linotype machine grinned at her with its white teeth. Its iron arm and hand shook tauntingly at her in the wavering light. With a sudden premonition she ran to Yancey's desk, opened the drawer in which he kept his holster and six-shooters, now that Osage had become so effete as to make them an unessential article of dress. They were not there. She knew then that Yancey had gone.

Doc Valliant. She closed and locked the door after her, stepped out into the quiet blackness of Pawhuska Avenue. Doc Valliant. He would go with her. He would drive her out there. But his office and the room at the rear, which was his dwelling, gave forth no response. Gone out somewhere—a case. Down the rickety wooden steps of the two-story brick building. She stood a moment in the street, looking this way and that. She struck her palms together in a kind of agony of futility. She would go alone if she had a horse and buggy. She could rent one at the livery stable. But what would they think —those men at the livery stable? They were the gossips of the town. It would be all over Osage, all over the county. Sabra Cravat driving out into the prairie alone in the middle of the night. Something up. Well, she couldn't help that. She had to go. She had to get him.

Toward the livery stable, past the Bixby House. A quiet little figure rose from the blackness of the porch where all through the day the traveling men and loafers sat with their chairs tilted back against the wall. The red coal of his cigar was an eye in the darkness.

"Sabra! What is this! What are you doing running around at this hour of the night?"

Sol Levy, sitting there in the Oklahoma night, a lonely little figure, sleepless, brooding. He had never before called her Sabra.

"Sol! Sol! Cim's out at the Reservation. Something's happened. I know. I feel it."

He did not scoff at this, as most men would. He seemed to understand her fear, her premonition, and to accept it with Oriental fatalism.

"What do you want to do?"

"Take me out there. Hitch up and drive me out there. Cim's got the buggy. He went out with her."

He did not ask where Yancey was. He asked nothing. "Go home," he said. "Wait on your porch. I will get my rig and come for you. They shouldn't see you. Do you want me to go home with you first?"

"No, no. I'm not afraid. I'm not afraid of anything."

Sol Levy had two very fine horses; really good animals. They won the races regularly at the local fairs. The little light rig with its smart rubber tires whirled behind them over the red dusty Oklahoma prairie roads. His slim hands were not expert with horses. He was a nervous, jerky driver. They left the town behind them, were swallowed up by the prairie. The Reservation was a full two hours distant. Sabra took off her hat. The night air rushed against her face, cooling it. A half hour.

"Let me drive, will you, Sol?"

Without a word he entrusted the reins to her strong, accustomed hands; the hands of one who had come of generations of horse lovers. The animals sensed the change. They leaped ahead in the darkness. The light buggy rocked and bounced over the rutted roads. Sol asked her nothing. They drove in silence. Presently she began to talk, disjointedly. Yet, surprisingly enough, he seemed intuitively to understand, to fill in the gaps with his own instinct and imagination. What she said sounded absurd; he knew it for tragedy.

". . . pineapple and marshamallow salad . . . hates that kind of thing . . . queer for a long time . . . moody . . . drinking . . . Ruby Big Elk . . . Cim . . . his face . . . peyote . . . Mescal Ceremony . . . Osage . . . white doeskin dress . . . Theresa Jump . . ."

"I see," said Sol Levy, soothingly. "Sure. Well, sure. The boy will be all right. The boy will be all right. Well, Yancey—you know how he is—Yancey. Do you think he has gone away again? I mean—gone?"

"I don't know." Then, "Yes."

Three o'clock and after. They came in sight of the Osage Reservation, a scattered settlement of sterile farms and wooden shanties sprawled on the bare unlovely prairie.

Darkness. The utter darkness that precedes the dawn. Stillness, except for the thud of their horses' flying hoofs and the whir and bump of the buggy wheels. Then, as Sabra slowed them down, uncertainly, undecided as to what they might best do, they heard it—the weird wavering cadences of the Mescal song, the haillike clatter of the gourd rattle shaken vigorously and monotonously; and beneath and above and around it all, reverberating, haunting, ominous, the beat of the buckskin drum. Through the still, cool night air of the prairie it came to them—to the overwrought woman, and to the little peaceful Jew. Barbaric sounds, wild, sinister. She pulled up the horses. They sat a moment, listening. Listening. The drum. The savage sound of the drum.

Fear was gnawing at her vitals, wringing her very heart with clammy fingers, yet Sabra spoke matter-of-factly, her voice holding a hard little note because she was trying to keep it from quavering.

"He'll be in the Mescal tepee next to Big Elk's House. They built it there when he was Chief, and they still use it regularly for the ceremony. Yancey showed it to me once, when he drove me out here." She stopped and cleared her throat, for her voice was suddenly husky. She wondered, confusedly, if that sound was the drum or her own heart beating. She gave a little cracked laugh that bordered on hysteria. "A drum in the night. It sounds so terrible. So savage."

Sol Levy took the reins from her shaking fingers. "Nothing to be frightened about. A lot of poor ignorant Indians trying to forget their misery. Come." Perhaps no man ever made a more courageous gesture, for the little sensitive Jew was terribly frightened.

Uncertainly, in the blackness, they made their way toward the drum beat. Nearer and nearer, louder and louder. And yet all about, darkness, silence.

Only that pulsing cry and rattle and beat pounding through the night like the tide. What if he is not there? thought Sabra.

Sol Levy pulled up in the roadway before the trampled yard that held the Mescal tepee, round, to typify the sun, built of wood, larger than any other building on the Reservation. The horses were frightened, restive. All about in the blackness you heard the stamp of other horses' hoofs, heard them crunching the dried herbage of the autumn prairie. With difficulty he groped his way to a stump that served as hitching post, tied the horses. As he helped Sabra down her knees suddenly bent, and he caught her as she sank. "Oh! It's all right. Stiff, I guess—from the ride." She leaned against him a moment, then straightened determinedly. He took her arm firmly. Together they made their way toward the tent-shaped wooden tepee.

Two great, silent blanketed figures at the door through which the fitful flame of the sacred fire flared. The figures did not speak. They stood there, barring the way. The little Jew felt Sabra's arm trembling in his hand. He peered up into the faces of the silent, immobile figures.

Suddenly, "Hello, Joe!" He turned to Sabra. "It's Joe Yellow Eyes. He was in the store only yesterday. Say, Joe, the lady here—Mrs. Cravat—she wants her son should come out and go home."

The blanketed figures stood silent.

Suddenly Sabra thought, "This is ridiculous."

She loosed her arm. She took a step forward, her profile sharp and clear in the firelight. "I am the woman of Yancey Cravat, the one you call Buffalo Head. If my son is in there I want to take him home now. It is time."

"Sure take um home," replied the blanket that Sol had addressed as Joe Yellow Eyes. He stood aside. Blinking, stumbling a little, Sol and Sabra entered the crowded Mescal tepee.

The ceremony was almost at an end. With daybreak it would be finished. Blinded by the light, Sabra at first could discern nothing except the central fire and the figure crouched before it. Yet her eyes went this way and that, searching for him. Gradually her vision cleared. The figures within the tepee paid no attention to those two white intruders. They stood there in the doorway, bewildered, terrified, brave.

In the center a crescent of earth about six inches high curved around a fire built of sticks so arranged that as the ashes fell they formed a second crescent within the other. A man squatted, tending this fire, watchfully, absorbedly. In the center of the crescent, upon a little star of sage twigs, lay the mescal, symbol of the rite. Facing them was the Chief, old Stump Horn, in the place of honor, the emblems of office in his hands—the rattle, the wand, the fan of eagle plumes. All about the tepee crouched or lay blanketed motionless figures. Some sat with heads bowed, others gazed fixedly upon the central mescal button. All had been eating the mescal or drinking a brew in which it had steeped. Now and then a figure would slowly draw the blanket over his head and sink back to receive the vision. And the song went on, the shaking of the gourd rattle, the beat-beat of the buckskin drum. The air of the room was stifling, the room itself scrupulously clean.

At intervals around the wall, and almost level with the dirt floor, were apertures perhaps sixteen inches square. A little wooden door was shut upon most of these. Near each lay figures limper, more spent even than the other inert bodies. As Sabra and Sol stood, blinking, they learned the use of these openings. For suddenly nausea overcame one of the Indians crouched in the semicircle near the flame. The man crawled swiftly to one of the little doors, opened it, thrust head and shoulders out into the night air, relieved his body of the drug's overdose.

Sabra only turned her eyes away, searching, searching. Then she saw where the boy lay under his gay striped blanket. His face was covered, but she knew. She knew well how the slim body curled in its blankets, how it lay at night, asleep. This was a different sleep, but she knew. They went to him, picking their way over the crouching figures with the fixed trancelike gaze; the recumbent forms that lay so still. She turned back the blanket. His face was smiling, peaceful, lovely.

She thought, "This is the way I should look at him if he were dead." Then, "He is dead." The boy lay breathing quietly. All about the room was an atmosphere of reverie, of swooning bliss. If the Indians looked at all at Sabra, at the Jew, at their efforts to rouse the boy, it was with the eyes of sleep-walkers. Their lips were gently smiling. Sometimes they swayed a little. The sacred fire leaped orange and scarlet and gold. Old Stump Horn wielded his eagle feather fan, back and forth, back and forth. The quavering cadences of the Mescal song rose and fell to the accompaniment of the gourd rattle and the unceasing drum. The white man and woman, frail both, tugged and strained at the inert figure of the boy.

"Oh, God!" whimpered Sabra. "He's so heavy. What shall we do?" They bent again, tugged with all their strength, lifted but could not carry him.

"We must drag him," Sol said, at last.

They took an arm each. So, dragging, tugging, past those rapt still forms, past those mazed smiling faces, they struggled with him to the door. The little beads of sweat stood out on her forehead, on her lip. She breathed in choking gasps. Her eyes were wide and staring and dreadful in their determination. The rattle. The drum beat. The high eerie song notes, wordless.

The blackness of the outer air; past the two towering motionless blanketed figures at the door. Dragging him along the earth, through the trampled weeds.

"We can't lift him into the buggy. We can't———" She ran back to the two at the door. She clasped her hands before the one called Joe Yellow Eyes. She lifted her white, agonized face to him. "Help me. Help me." She made a futile gesture of lifting.

The Indian looked at her a moment with a dead, unseeing gaze. Flecks of gold and red and yellow danced, reflected in the black pools of his eyes, and died there. Leisurely, wordless, he walked over to where the boy lay, picked him up lightly in his great arms as though he were a sack of meal, swung him into the buggy seat. He turned, then, and went back to his place at the door.

They drove back to the town of Osage. Cim's body leaned heavily, slackly against hers; his head lay in her lap, like a little boy's. One aching arm she held firmly about him to keep him from slipping to the floor of the buggy, so that finally it ceased to ache and became numb. The dawn came, and then the sunrise over the prairie, its red meeting the red of the Oklahoma earth, so that they drove through a fiery furnace.

She had been quiet enough until now, with a kind of stony quiet. She began to sob; a curious dry racking sound, like a hiccough.

"Now, now," said Sol Levy, and made a little comforting noise between tongue and teeth. "So bad it isn't. What did the boy do, he went out to see the sights on the Reservation and try what it was like to eat this dope stuff— this peyote. Say, when I was a boy I did lots worse."

She did not seem to pay much heed to this, but it must have penetrated her numbed brain at last, for presently she stopped the painful sobbing and looked down at his lovely smiling face in her lap, the long lashes, like a girl's, resting so fragilely on the olive cheek.

"He wanted to go. I wouldn't let him. Is it too late, Sol?"

"Go? Go where?"

"The Colorado School of Mines. Geology."

"Too late! That kid there! Don't talk foolish. September. This is the time to go. It just starts. Sure he'll go."

They drove through the yard, over Sabra's carefully tended grass, of which she was so proud, right to the edge of the porch steps, and so, dragging again and pulling, they got him in, undressed him; she washed his dust-smeared face.

"Well," said Sol Levy. "I guess I go and open the store and then have a good cup of coffee."

She put out her hand. Her lower lip was caught between her teeth, sharp and tight. Her face was distorted absurdly with her effort not to cry. But when he would have patted her grimed and trembling hand with his own, in a gesture of comforting, she caught his hand to her lips and kissed it.

The sound of the horses' hoofs died away on the still morning air. She looked down at Cim. She thought, I will take a bath, and then I will have some coffee, too. Yancey has gone again. Has left me. I know that. How do I know it? Well, nothing more can happen to me now. I have had it all, and I have borne it. Nothing more can happen to me now.

20

FOR YEARS OKLAHOMA had longed for statehood as a bride awaits the dawn of her wedding day. At last, "Behold the bridegroom!" said a paternal government, handing her over to the Union. "Here is a star for your forehead. Meet the family."

Then, at the very altar, the final words spoken, the pact sealed, the bride had turned to encounter a stranger—an unexpected guest, dazzling, breathtaking, embodying all her wildest girlish dreams.

"Bridegroom—hell!" yelled Oklahoma, hurling herself into the stranger's arms. "What's family to me! Go away! Don't bother me. I'm busy."

The name of the gorgeous stranger was Oil.

Oil. Nothing else mattered. Oklahoma, the dry, the wind-swept, the burning, was a sea of hidden oil. The red prairies, pricked, ran black and slimy with it. The work of years was undone in a day. The sunbonnets shrank back, aghast. Compared to that which now took place the early days following the Run in '89 were idyllic. They swarmed on Oklahoma from every state in the Union. The plains became black with little eager delving figures. The sanguine roads were choked with every sort of vehicle. Once more tent and shanty towns sprang up where the day before had been only open prairie staring up at a blazing sky. Again the gambling tent, the six-shooter, the roaring saloon, the dance hall, the harlot. Men fought, stole, killed, died for a piece of ground beneath whose arid surface lay who knew what wealth of fluid richness. Every barren sun-baked farm was a potential fortune; every ditch and draw and dried-up creek bed might conceal liquid treasure. The Wildcat Field—Panhandle—Cimarron—Crook Nose—Cartwright—Wahoo—Bear Creek—these became magic names; these were the Seven Cities of Cibola, rich beyond Coronado's wildest dream. Millions of barrels of oil burst through the sand and shale and clay and drenched the parched earth. Drill, pump, blast. Nitro-glycerin. Here she comes. A roar. Oklahoma went stark raving mad.

Sabra Cravat went oil mad with the rest of them. Just outside the town of Osage, for miles around, they were drilling. There was that piece of farm land she had bought years ago, when Yancey first showed signs of restlessness. She had thought herself shrewd to have picked up this fertile little oasis in the midst of the bare unlovely plain. She was proud of her bit of farm land with its plump yield of alfalfa, corn, potatoes, and garden truck. She knew now why it had been so prolific. By a whim of nature rich black oil lay under all that surrounding land, rendering it barren through its hidden riches. No taint of corroding oil ran beneath that tract of Cravat farm land, and because of this it lay there now, so green, so lush, with its beans, its squash, its ridiculous onions, taunting her, deriding her, like a mirage in the desert. Queerly enough, she had no better luck with her share in an oil lease for which she had paid a substantial sum—much more than she could afford to lose. Machinery, crew, days of drilling, weeks of drilling, sand, shale, salt. The well had come up dry—a duster.

That which happened to Sabra happened to thousands. The stuff was elusive, tantalizing. Here might be a gusher vomiting millions. Fifty feet away not so much as a spot of grease could be forced to the surface. Fortune seemed to take a delight in choosing strange victims for her pranks. Erv Wissler, the gawk who delivered the milk to Sabra's door each morning, found himself owner of a gusher whose outpourings yielded him seven thousand dollars a day. He could not grasp it. Seven dollars a day his mind might have encompassed. Seven thousand had no meaning.

"Why, Erv!" Sabra exclaimed, when he arrived at her kitchen door as usual, smelling of the barnyard. "Seven thousand dollars a day! What in the world are you going to do with it!"

Erv's putty features and all his loose-hung frame seemed to stiffen with the effort of his new and momentous resolve. "Well, I tell you, Mis' Cravat, I made up my mind I ain't going to make no more Sunday delivery myself. I'm a-going to hire Pete Lynch's boy to take the milk route Sundays."

Everyone in Osage knew the story of Ferd Sloat's wife when the news was brought to her that weeks of drilling on the sterile little Sloat farm had brought up a gusher. They had come running to her across the trampled fields with the news. She had stood there on the back porch of the shabby farmhouse, a bony drudge, as weather-beaten and unlovely as the house itself.

"Millions!" they shouted at her. "Millions and millions! What are you going to do?"

Ferd Sloat's wife had looked down at her hands, shriveled and gnarled from alkali water and rough work. She wiped them now on a corner of her gingham apron with a gesture of utter finality. Her meager shoulders straightened. The querulous voice took on a note of defiance.

"From now on I'm goin' to have the washin' done out."

In those first few frenzied weeks there was no time for scientific methods. That came later. Now, in the rush of it, they all but burrowed in the red clay with their finger nails. Men prowled the plains with divining rods, with absurd things called witch sticks, hoping thus to detect the precious stuff beneath the earth's surface.

For years the meandering red clay roads that were little more than trails had seen only occasional buggies, farm wagons, horsemen, an Indian family creeping along in a miserable cart or—rarely—an automobile making perilous progress through the thick dust in the dry season or the slippery dough in the wet. Now those same roads were choked, impassable. The frail wooden one-way bridges over creeks and draws sagged and splintered with the stream of traffic, but no one took the time to repair them. A torrent of vehicles of every description flowed without ceasing, night and day. Frequently the torrent choked itself with its own volume, and then the thousands were piled there, locked, cursing, writhing, battling, on their way to the oil fields. From the Crook Nose field to Wahoo was a scant four miles; it sometimes took half a day to cover it in a motor car. Trucks, drays, wagons, rigs, Fords, buckboards. Every day was like the day of the Opening back in '89. Millionaire promoters from the East, engineers, prospectors, drillers, tool dressers, shooters, pumpers, roustabouts, Indians. Men in oil-soaked overalls that hadn't been changed for days. Men in London tailored suits and shirts from Charvet's. Only the ruthless and desperate survived. In the days of the covered wagon scarcely twenty years earlier those roads had been trails over the hot, dry plains marked by the bleaching skull of a steer or the carcass of a horse, picked clean by the desert scavengers and turned white and desolate to the blazing sky. A wagon wheel, a rusted rim, a split wagon tongue lay at the side of the trail, mute evidence of a traveler laboriously crawling his way across the prairie. Now the ditches by the side of these same roads were strewn with the bodies of wrecked and abandoned automobiles, their skeletons stripped and rotting, their lamps staring up at the sky like sightless eyes, testimony to the passing of the modern ravisher of that tortured region. Up and down the dust-choked roads, fenders ripped off like flies' wings, wheels interlocking, trucks overturned, loads sunk in the mud, plank bridges splitting beneath the strain. Devil take the hindmost. It was like an army push, but without an army's morale or discipline. Bear Creek boasted a killing a day and not a jail nor a courthouse for miles around. Men and women, manacled to a common chain, were marched like slave convicts down the road to the nearest temple of justice, a rough pine shack in a town that had sprung overnight on the prairie. There were no railroads where there had been no towns.

Boilers loaded on two wagons were hauled by twenty-mule-team outfits. Stuck in the mud as they inevitably were, only mules could have pulled the load out. Long lines of them choked the already impassable road. Wagons were heaped with the pipes through which the oil must be led; with lumber, hardware, rigs, tools, portable houses—all the vast paraphernalia of sudden wealth and growth in a frontier community.

Tough careless young boys drove the nitro-glycerin cars, a deadly job on those rough and crowded roads. It was this precious and dreadful stuff that shot the oil up out of the earth. Hard lads in corduroys took their chances and pocketed their high pay, driving the death-dealing wagons, singing as they drove, a red shirt tail tied to a pole flaunting its warning at the back of the load. Often an expected wagon would fail to appear. The workers on the field never took the trouble to trace it or the time to wait for it. They knew that somewhere along the road was a great gaping hole, with never a sizable fragment of wood or steel or bone or flesh anywhere for yards around to tell the tale they already knew.

Acres that had been carefully tended so that they might yield their scanty crop of cabbages, onions, potatoes were abandoned to oil, the garden truck rotting in the ground. Rawboned farmers and their scrawny wives and pindling brats, grown spectacularly rich overnight, walked out of their houses without taking the trouble to move the furniture or lock the door. It was not worth while. They left the sleazy curtains on the windows, the pots on the stove. The oil crew, clanking in, did not bother to wreck the house unless they found it necessary. In the midst of an inferno of oil rigs, drills, smoke, steam, and seeping oil itself the passer-by would often see a weather-beaten farmhouse, its windows broken, its front askew, like a beldame gone mad, gray hair streaming about her crazed face as she stared out at the pandemonium of oil hell about her.

The farmers moved into Osage, or Oklahoma City, or Wahoo. They bought automobiles and silk shirts and gew-gaws, like children. The men sat on the front porch in shirt sleeves and stocking feet and spat tobacco juice into the fresh young grass.

Mile on mile, as far as the eye could see, were the skeleton frames of oil rigs outlined against the sky like giant Martian figures stalking across the landscape. Horrible new towns—Bret Harte wooden-front towns—sprang up overnight on the heels of an oil strike; towns inhabited by people who never meant to stay in them; stark and hideous houses thrown up by dwellers who never intended to remain in them; rude frontier crossroad stores stuffed with the necessities of frontier life and the luxuries of sudden wealth all jumbled together in a sort of mercantile miscegenation. The thump and clank of the pump and drill; curses, shouts; the clatter of thick dishes, the clink of glasses, the shrill laughter of women; fly-infested shanties. Oil, smearing itself over the prairies like a plague, killing the grass, blighting the trees, spreading over the surface of the creeks and rivers. Signs tacked to tree stumps or posts; For Ambulance Call 487. Sim Neeley Undertaker. Call 549. Call Dr. Keogh 735.

Oklahoma—the Red People's Country—lay heaving under the hot summer sun, a scarred and dreadful thing with the oil drooling down its face a viscid stream.

Tracy Wyatt, who used to drive the bus and dray line between Wahoo and Osage, standing up to the reins like a good-natured red-faced charioteer as the wagon bumped over the rough roads, was one of the richest men in Oklahoma—in the whole of the United States, for that matter. Wyatt. The Wyatt Oil Company. In another five years the Wyatt Oil Companies. You were to see their signs all over the world. The Big Boys from the East were to come to him, hat in hand, to ask his advice about this; to seek his favor for that. The sum of his daily income was fantastic. The mind simply did not grasp it. Tracy himself was, by now, a portly and not undignified looking man of a little more than fifty. His good-natured, rubicund face wore the grave slightly astonished look of a commonplace man who suddenly finds himself a personage.

Mrs. Wyatt, plainer, more horse-faced than ever in her expensive New York clothes, tried to patronize Sabra Cravat, but the Whipple blood was no match for the Marcy. The new money affected her queerly. She became nervous, full of spleen, and the Eastern doctors spoke to her of high blood pressure.

Sabra frankly envied these lucky ones. A letter from the adder-tongued Felice Venable to her daughter was characteristic of that awesome old matriarch. Sabra still dreaded to open her mother's letters. They always contained a sting.

> All this talk of oil and millions and everyone in Oklahoma rolling in it. I'll be bound that you and that husband of yours haven't so much as enough to fill a lamp. Trust Yancey Cravat to get hold of the wrong piece of land. Well, at least you can't be disappointed. It has been like that from the day you married him, though you can't say your mother didn't warn you. I hope Donna will show more sense.

Donna, home after two years at Miss Dignum's on the Hudson, seemed indeed to be a granddaughter after Felice Venable's own heart. She was, in coloring, contour, manner, and outlook, so unlike the other Oklahoma girls— Czarina McKee, Gazelle Slaughter, Jewel Riggs, Maurine Turket—as to make that tortured, wind-deviled day of her birth on the Oklahoma prairie almost nineteen years ago seem impossible. Even during her homecomings in the summer vacations she had about her an air of cool disdain together with a kind of disillusioned calculation very disconcerting to her former intimates, not to speak of her own family.

The other girls living in Osage and Oklahoma City and Guthrie and Wahoo were true products of the new raw Southwest country. They liked to dress in crude high colors—glaring pinks, cerise, yellow, red, vivid orange, magenta. They made up naïvely with white powder and big daubs of carmine paint on either cheek. The daughters of more wealthy parents drove their own cars in a day when this was considered rather daring for a woman. Donna came home tall, thin to the point of scrawniness in their opinion; sallow, unrouged, drawling, mysterious. She talked with an Eastern accent, ignored the letter *r*, said eyether and nyether and rih'ally and altogether made herself poisonously unpopular with the girls and undeniably stirring to the boys. She paid very little heed to the clumsy attentions of the Oklahoma home-town lads, adopting toward them a serpent-of-the-Nile attitude very baffling to these frank and open-faced prairie products.

Her school days finished, and she a finished product of those days, she now looked about her coolly, calculatingly. Her mother she regarded with a kind of affectionate amusement.

"What a rotten deal you've had, Sabra dear," she would drawl. "Really, I don't see how you've stood it all these years."

Sabra would come to her own defense, goaded by something strangely hostile in herself toward this remote, disdainful offspring. "Stood what?"

"Oh—you know. This being a pioneer woman and a professional Marcy and head-held-high in spite of a bum of a husband."

"Donna Cravat, if you ever again dare to speak like that of your father I shall punish you, big as you are."

"Sabra darling, how can you punish a grown woman? You might slap me, and I wouldn't slap you back, of course. But I'd be terribly embarrassed for you. As for Father—he is a museum piece. You know it."

"Your father is one of the greatest figures the Southwest has ever produced."

"Mm. Well, he's picturesque enough, I suppose. But I wish he hadn't worked so hard at it. And Cim? There's a brother! A great help to me in my career, the men folks of this quaint family."

"I wasn't aware that you were planning a career," Sabra retorted, very much in the manner of Felice Venable. "Unless getting up at noon, slopping around in a kimono most of the day, and lying in the hammock reading is called a career by Dignum graduates. If it is, you're the outstanding success of your class."

"Darling, I adore you when you get viperish and Venable like that. Perhaps you influenced me in my early youth. That's the new psychology, you know. You used to tell me about Grandma trailing around in her white ruffled dimity wrappers and her high heels, never lifting a lily hand."

"At least your grandmother didn't consider it a career."

"Neither do I. This lovely flower-like head isn't so empty as you think, lolling in the front porch hammock. I know it's no use counting on Father, even when he's not off on one of his mysterious jaunts. What is he doing, anyway? Living with some squaw? . . . Forgive me, Mother darling. I didn't mean to hurt you . . . Cim's just as bad, and worse, because he's weak and hasn't even Dad's phony ideals. You're busy with the paper. That's all right. I'm not blaming you. If it weren't for you we'd all be on the town— or back in Wichita living on Grandma in genteel poverty. I think you're wonderful, and I ought to try to be like you. But I don't want to be a girl reporter. Describing the sumptuous decorations of dandelions and sunflowers at one of Cassandra Sipes' parties."

Goaded by curiosity and a kind of wonder at this unnatural creature, Sabra must put her question: "What do you want to do, then?"

"I want to marry the richest man in Oklahoma, and build a palace that I'll hardly ever live in, and travel like royalty, and clank with emeralds. With my skin and hair they're my stone."

"Oh, emeralds, by all means," Sabra agreed, cuttingly. "Diamonds are so ordinary. And the gentleman that you consider honoring—let me see. From your requirements that would have to be Tracy Wyatt, wouldn't it?"

"Yes," replied Donna, calmly.

"You've probably overlooked Mrs. Wyatt. Of course, Tracey's only fifty-one, and you being nineteen, there's plenty of time if you'll just be patient." She was too amused to be really disturbed.

"I don't intend to be patient, Mamma darling."

Something in her hard, ruthless tone startled Sabra. "Donna Cravat, don't you start any of your monkey business. I saw you cooing and ah-ing at him the other day when we went over the Wyatts' new house. And I heard you saying some drivel about his being a man that craved beauty in his life, and that he should have it; and sneering politely at the new house until I could see him beginning to doubt everything in it, poor fellow. He had been so proud to show it. But I thought you were just talking that New York talk of yours."

"I wasn't. I was talking business."

Sabra was revolted, alarmed, and distressed, all at once. She gained reassurance by telling herself that this was just one of Donna's queer jokes—part of the streak in her that Sabra had never understood and that corresponded to the practical joker in Yancey. That, too, had always bewildered her. Absorbed in the workings of the growing, thriving newspaper the conversation faded to a dim and almost unimportant memory.

Sabra was sufficiently shrewd and level headed to take Sol Levy's sound advice. "You settle down to running your paper, Sabra, and you won't need any oil wells. You can have the best-paying paper and the most powerful in the Southwest. Bigger than Houston or Dallas or San Antonio. Because Osage is going to be bigger and richer than any of them. You mark what I say. Hardly any oil in the town of Osage, but billions of barrels of oil all around it. This town won't be torn to pieces, then. It'll grow and grow. Five years from now it'll look like Chicago."

"Oh, Sol, how can that be?"

"You'll see. There where the gambling tent stood with a mud hole in front of it a few years ago you'll see in another five years a skyscraper like those in New York."

She laughed at that.

Just as she had known that Yancey had again left her on that night of the Mescal ceremony, so now she sensed that he would come back in the midst of this new insanity that had seized all Oklahoma. And come back he did, from God knows where, on the very crest of the oil wave, and bringing with him news that overshadowed his return. He entered as he had left, with no word of explanation, and, as always, his entrance was so dramatic, so bizarre as to cause everything else to fade into the background.

He came riding, as always, but it was a sorry enough nag that he bestrode this time; and his white sombrero was grimed and battered, the Prince Albert coat was spotted, the linen frayed, the whole figure covered with the heavy red dust of the trampled road. He must have ridden like an avenging angel, for his long black locks were damp, his eyes red rimmed. And when she saw this Don Quixote, so sullied, so shabby, her blood turned to water within her veins for pity.

She thought, it will always be like this as long as he lives, and each time he will be a little more broken, older, less and less the figure of splendor I married, until at last . . .

She only said, "Yancey," quietly.

He was roaring, he was reeling with Jovian laughter as he strode into the *Wigwam* office where she sat at her neat orderly desk just as she had sat on that day years before. For a dreadful moment she thought that he was drunk or mad. He flung his soiled white sombrero to the desk top, he swept her into his arms, he set her down.

"Sabra! Here's news for you. Jesse! Heh, Jesse! Where's that rum-soaked son of a printer's devil? Jesse! Come in here! God, I've been laughing so that I almost rolled off my horse." He was striding up and down as of old, his shabby coat tails spreading with the vigor of his movements, the beautiful hands gesticulating, the fine eyes—bloodshot now—still flashing with the fire that would burn until it consumed him.

"Oil, my children! More oil than anybody ever thought there was in any one spot in the world. And where! Where? On the Osage Indian Reservation. It came in an hour ago, like the ocean. It makes every other field look like the Sahara. There never was such a joke! It's cosmic—it's terrible. How the gods must be roaring. 'Laughter unquenchable among the blessed gods!' "

"Yancey dear, we're used to oil out here. It's an old story. Come now. Come home and have a hot bath and clean clothes." In her mind's eye she saw those fine white linen shirts of his all neatly stacked in the drawer as he had left them.

For answer he reached out with one great arm and swept a pile of exchanges, copy paper, galley proofs, and clippings off the desk, while with the other hand he seized the typewriter by its steel bar and plumped it to the floor with a force that wrung a protesting whine and zing from its startled insides. He had always scorned to use a typewriter. The black swathes of his herculean pencil bit deeper into the paper's surface than any typewriter's metal teeth.

"Hot bath! Hot hell, honey! Do you realize what this means? Do you understand that two thousand Osage Indians, squatting in their rags in front of their miserable shanties, are now the richest nation in the world! In the world, I tell you. They were given that land—the barest, meanest desert land in the whole of the Oklahoma country. And the government of these United States said, 'There, you red dogs, take that and live on it. And if you can't live on it, then die on it.' God A'mighty, I could die myself with laughing. Millions and millions of dollars. They're spattering, I tell you, all over the Osage Reservation. There's no stopping that flow. Every buck and squaw on the Osage Reservation is a millionaire. They own that land, and, by God, I'm going to see that no one takes it away from them!"

"Oh, Yancey, be careful."

He was driving his pencil across the paper. "Send this out A.P. They tried to keep it dark when the flow came, but I'll show them. Sabra, kill your editorial lead, whatever it was. I'll write it. Make this your news lead, too. Listen. 'The gaudiest star-spangled cosmic joke that ever was played on a double-dealing government burst into fireworks to-day when, with a roar that could be heard for miles around, thousands of barrels of oil shot into the air on the miserable desert land known as the Osage Indian Reservation and occupied by those duped and wretched———!' "

"We can't use that, I tell you."

"Why not?"

"This isn't the Cimarron. It's the state of Oklahoma. That's treason—that's anarchy——"

"It's the truth. It's history. I can prove it. They'll be down on those Osages like a pack of wolves. At least I'll let them know they're expected. I'll run the story, by God, as I want it run, and they can shoot me for it."

"And I say you won't. You can't come in here like that. I'm the editor of this paper."

He turned quietly and looked at her, the great head jutting out, the eyes like cold steel. "Who is?"

"I am."

Without a word he grasped her wrist and led her out, across the old porch, down the steps and into the street. There, on Pawhuska Avenue, in the full glare of noonday, he pointed to the weather-worn sign that he himself, aided by Jesse Rickey, had hung there almost twenty years before. She had had it painted and repainted. She had had it repaired. She had never replaced it with another.

THE OKLAHOMA WIGWAM
YANCEY CRAVAT PROPR. AND EDITOR.

"When you take that down, Sabra honey, and paint your own name up in my place, you'll be the editor of this newspaper. Until you do that, I am."

As they stood there, she in her neat blue serge, he in his crumpled and shabby attire, she knew that she never would do it.

21

YOUNG CIM CAME home from Colorado for the summer vacation, was caught up in the oil flood, and never went back. With his geological knowledge, slight as it was, and his familiarity with the region, he was shuttled back and forth from one end of the state to the other. Curiously enough Cim, like his father, was more an onlooker than a participant in this fantastic spectacle. The quality of business acumen seemed to be lacking in both these men; or perhaps a certain mad fastidiousness in them kept them from taking part in the feverish fight. A hint of oil in this corner, a trace of oil in that, and the thousands were upon it, pushing, scrambling, nose to the ground, down on all-fours like pigs in a trough. A hundred times Yancey could have bought an oil lease share for a song. Head lolling on his breast, lids lowered over the lightning eyes, he shrugged indifferent shoulders.

"I don't want the filthy muck," he said. "It stinks. Let the Indians have it. It's theirs. And the Big Boys from the East—let them sweat and scheme for it. They know where Oklahoma is now, all right."

His comings and goings had ceased to cause Sabra the keen agony of earlier days. She knew now that their existence, so long as Yancey lived, would always be made up of just such unexplained absences and melodramatic homecomings. She had made up her mind to accept the inevitable.

She did not mind that Yancey spent much time on the oil fields. He knew the men he called the Big Boys from the East, and they often sought him out for his company, which they found amusing, and for a certain regional wisdom that they considered valuable. He despised them and spent most of his time with the pumpers and roustabouts, drillers and tool dressers and shooters—a hard-drinking, hard-talking, hard-fighting crew. In his white sombrero and his outdated Prince Albert and his high-heeled boots he was known as a picturesque character. Years of heavy drinking were taking their toll of the magnificent body and mind. The long locks showed streaks of gray.

Local townsmen who once had feared and admired him began to patronize him or to laugh at him, tolerantly. Many of them were rich now, counting their riches not in thousands but in millions. They had owned a piece of Oklahoma dirt, or a piece of a piece of dirt—and suddenly, through no act of theirs, it was worth its weight in diamonds. Pat Leary, the pugnacious little Irish lawyer who had once been a section hand in the early days of the building of the Santa Fé road, was now so rich through his vast oil holdings that his Indian wife, Crook Nose, was considered a quaint and picturesque note by the wives of Eastern operators who came down on oil business.

After the first shrill excitement of it Sabra Cravat relinquished the hope of making sudden millions as other luckier ones had done. Her land had yielded no oil; she owned no oil leases. It was a curious fact that Sabra still queened it in Osage and had actually become a power in the state. The paper was read, respected, and feared throughout the Southwest. It was said with pride by Osage's civic minded that no oil was rich enough to stain the pages of the *Oklahoma Wigwam*. Though few realized it, and though Sabra herself never admitted it, it was Yancey who had made this true. He neglected it for years together, but he always turned up in a crisis, whether political, economic, or social, to hurl his barbed editorials at the heads of the offenders, to sting with the poison of his ridicule. He championed the Indians, he denounced the oil kings, he laughed at the money grabbers, he exposed the land thieves. He was afraid of nothing. He would absent himself for six months. The *Wigwam* would run along smoothly, placidly. He would return, torch in hand, and again set fire to the paper until the town, the county, the state were ablaze. The Osages came to him with their legal problems, and he advised them soundly and took a minimum fee. He seemed always to sense an important happening from afar and to emerge, growling like an old lion, from his hidden jungle lair, broken, mangy, but fighting, the fine eyes still alight, the magnificent head still as menacing as that of a buffalo charging. He had, on one occasion, come back just in time to learn of Dixie Lee's death.

Dixie had struck oil and had retired, a rich woman. She had closed her house and gone to Oklahoma City, and there she bought a house in a decent neighborhood and adopted a baby girl. She had gone to Kansas City for it, and though she had engaged a capable and somewhat bewildered nurse on that trip, Dixie herself carried the child home in her arms, its head close against the expensive satin bosom.

No one knew what means she had used to pull the wool over the eyes of the Kansas City authorities. She never could have done it in Oklahoma. She had had the child almost a year when the women of Osage got wind of it. They say she took it out herself in its perambulator daily, and perhaps someone recognized her on the street, though she looked like any plump and respectable matron now, in her rich, quiet dress and her pince nez, a little gray showing in the black, abundant hair.

Sabra Cravat heard of it. Mrs. Wyatt. Mrs. Doc Nisbett. Mrs. Pack.

They took the child away from her by law. Six months later Dixie Lee died; the sentimental said of a broken heart. It was Yancey Cravat who wrote her obituary:

Dixie Lee, for years one of the most prominent citizens
of Osage and a pioneer in the early days of Oklahoma, having

made the Run in '89, one of the few women who had the
courage to enter that historic and terrible race, is dead.
She was murdered by the good women of Osage. . . .

The story was a nine-days' wonder, even in that melodramatic state. Sabra
read it, white faced. The circulation of the *Wigwam* took another bound
upward.

"Some day," said Osage, over its afternoon paper, "somebody is going
to come along and shoot old Cimarron."

"I should think his wife would save them the trouble," someone suggested.

If Yancey's sporadic contributions increased the paper's circulation it was
Sabra's steady drive that maintained it. It was a gigantic task to keep up
with the changes that were sweeping over Osage and all of Oklahoma. Yet
the columns of the *Wigwam* recorded these changes in its news columns,
in its editorial pages, in its personal and local items and its advertisements,
as faithfully as on that day of its first issue when Yancey had told them who
killed Pegler. Perhaps it was because Sabra, even during Yancey's many
absences, felt that the paper must be prepared any day to meet his scathing
eye.

Strange items began to appear daily in the paper's columns—strange to
the eye not interested in oil; but there was no such eye in Oklahoma, nor,
for that matter, in the whole Southwest. Cryptic though these items might
be to dwellers in other parts of the United States, they were of more absorbing interest to Oklahomans than front-page stories of war, romance,
intrigue, royalty, crime.

Indian Territory Illuminating Oil Company swabbed 42
barrels in its No. 3 Lizzie in the northwest corner of the
southwest of the northwest of 11–8–6 after having plugged
back to 4,268 feet, and shooting with 52 quarts.

The wildcat test of McComb two miles north of Kewoka
which is No. 1 Sutton in the southwest corner of the south-
east of the northeast of 35–2–9 was given a shot of 105 quarts
in the sand from 1,867 feet and hole bridged. As it stands
it is estimated good for 450 barrels daily.

The paper's ads reflected the change. The old livery stable, with its buggies
and phaëtons, its plugs to be hired, its tobacco-chewing loungers, its odor
of straw, manure, and axle grease, was swept away, and in its place was
Fink's Garage and Auto Livery. Repairs of All Kinds. Buy a Stimson Salient
Six. The smell of gasoline, the hiss of the hose, lean young lads with grease-
grimed fingers, engine wise.

Come to the Chamber of Commerce Dinner. The Oklahoma City College
Glee Club will sing.

Osage began to travel, to see the world. Their wanderings were no longer
local. Where, two years ago, you read that Dr. and Mrs. Horace McGill are
up from Concho to do their Christmas buying, you now saw that Mr. and
Mrs. W. Fletcher Busby have left for a trip to Europe, Egypt, and the Holy
Land. You knew that old Wick Busby had made his pile in oil and that Nettie
Busby was out to see the world.

Most astounding of all were the Indian items, for now the *Oklahoma
Wigwam* and every other paper in the county regularly ran news about those
incredible people who in one short year had leaped from the Neolithic Age
to Broadway.

The Osage Indians, a little more than two thousand in number, who but yesterday were a ragged, half-fed, and listless band, squatting wretchedly on the Reservation allotted them, waiting until time, sickness, and misery should blot them forever from the land, were now, by a miracle of nature, the richest nation in the world. The barren ground on which they had lived now yielded the most lavish oil flow in the state. Yancey Cravat's news story and editorial had been copied and read all over the country. A stunned government tried to bring order out of a chaos of riches. The two thousand Osages were swept off the Reservation to make way for the flood of oil that was transmuted into a flood of gold. They were transported to a new section called Wazhazhe, which is the ancient Indian word for Osage.

Agents appointed. Offices established. Millions of barrels of oil. Millions of dollars. Millions of dollars yearly to be divided somehow among two thousand Osage Indians, to whom a blanket, a bowl of soffica, a mangy pony, a bit of tobacco, a disk of peyote had meant riches. And now every full blood, half blood, or quarter blood Osage was put on the Indian Roll, and every name on the Indian Roll was entitled to a Head Right. Every head right meant a definite share in the millions. Five in a family—five head rights. Ten in a family—ten head rights. The Indian Agent's office was full of typewriters, files, pads, ledgers, neat young clerks all occupied with papers and documents that read like some fantastic nightmare. The white man's eye, traveling down the tidy list, with its story-book Indian names and its hard, cold, matter-of-fact figures, rejected what it read as being too absurd for the mind to grasp.

Clint Tall Meat	$523,000
Benny Warrior	$192,000
Ho ki ah se	$265,887
Long Foot Magpie	$387,942

The government bought them farms with their own oil money, and built big red brick houses near the roadside and furnished them in plush and pianos and linoleum and gas ranges and phonographs. You saw their powerful motor cars, dust covered, whirling up and down the red clay Oklahoma roads—those roads still rutted, unpaved, hazardous, for Oklahoma had had no time to attend to such matters. Fifty years before, whole bands of Osages on their wiry little ponies had traveled south in the winter and north in the summer to visit their Indian cousins. Later, huddled miserably on their Reservation, they had issued forth on foot or in wretched wagons to pay their seasonal visits and to try to recapture, by talk and song and dance and ritual, some pale ghost of their departed happiness. A shabby enough procession, guarded, furtive, smoldering.

But now you saw each Osage buck in his high-powered car, his inexpert hands grasping the wheel, his enormous sombrero—larger even than the white man's hat—flapping in the breeze that he made by his speed. In the back you saw the brilliance of feathers and blankets worn by the beady-eyed children and the great placid squaw crouched in the bottom of the car. The white man driving the same road gave these Indian cars a wide berth, for he knew they stopped for no one, kept the middle of the road, flew over bridges, draws, and ditches like mad things.

Grudgingly, for she still despised them, Sabra Cravat devoted a page of the *Wigwam* to news of the Osages, those moneyed, petted wards of a bewildered government. The page appeared under the title of Indian News, and its contents were more than tinged with the grotesque.

Long Foot Magpie and wife were week-end visitors of Plenty Horses at Watonga recently.

Grandma Standing Woman of near Hominy was a visitor at the home of Red Paint Woman.

Mr. and Mrs. Sampson Lame Bull have returned from Osage after accompanying Mrs. Twin Woman, who is now a patient in the Osage Hospital.

Albert Short Tooth and Robert White Eyes are batching it at the home of Mrs. Ghost Woman during her absence.

Laura Bird Woman and Thelma Eagle Nest of near here motored to Grey Horse to visit Sore Head but he was not at home.

Woodson Short Man and wife were shopping in Osage one day last week.

Red Bird Scabby has left the Reservation for a visit to Colorado Springs and Manitou.

Squaw Iki has returned recently after being a patient at the Concho Hospital for some time.

Joe Stump Horn and his wife Mrs. Long Dead are visiting Red Nose Scabby for a few days.

Sun Maker has given up the effort to find a first-class cook in Wazhazhe and is looking around in Osage.

The Osages were *Wigwam* subscribers. They read the paper, or had it read to them if they were of the older and less literate generation. Sabra was accustomed to seeing the doorway suddenly darkened by a huge blanketed form or to look up, startled, to behold the brilliant striped figure standing beside her desk in the business office. If Yancey chanced to be in the occasion became very social.

"How!"

"How!"

'Want um paper."

"All right, Short Tooth. Five dollars."

The blanketed figure would produce a wallet whose cheeks were plump to bursting with round silver dollars, for the Osage loved the sound and feel of the bright metal disks. Down on the desk they clinked.

The huge Osage stood then, waiting. Yancey knew what was wanted, as did Sabra.

"Me want see iron man. Make um name."

Whereupon Yancey or Sabra would conduct the visitor into the composing room. There were three linotype machines now, clanking and chattering away. Once Yancey had taken old Big Elk, Ruby's father, back there to see how the linotype turned liquid lead into printed words. He had had Jesse Rickey, at the linotype's keyboard, turn out old Big Elk's name in the form of a neat metal bar, together with the paper slip of its imprint.

There was no stopping it. The story of the iron monster that could talk and write and move spread like a prairie fire through Wazhazhe. Whole families subscribed separately for the *Oklahoma Wigwam*—bucks, squaws, girls, boys, papooses in arms. The iron monster had for them a fascination that was a mingling of admiration, awe, and fear. It was useless to explain that they need not take out a subscription in order to own one of these coveted metal bars. It had been done once. They always would do it that way. Sabra, if she happened to be in charge, always gave the five dollars to her pet charity, after trying in vain to refuse it when proffered. Yancey took it cheerfully and treated the boys at the new Sunny South Saloon, now a thing of splendor with its mahogany bar, its brass rail, its mirror, chandeliers, and flesh-tinted oil paintings.

Up and down the dusty Oklahoma roads at terrific speed, up and down Pawhuska Avenue, went the blanketed figures in their Packard and Pierce Arrow cars. The merchants of Osage liked to see them in town. It meant money freely spent on luxuries. The Osage Indian men were broad shouldered, magnificent, the women tall, stately. Now they grew huge with sloth and overfeeding. They ate enormously and richly. They paced Pawhuska Avenue with slow measured tread; calm, complete, grandly content. The women walked bareheaded, their brilliant blankets, striped purple and orange and green and red, wrapped about their shoulders and enveloping them from neck to heels. But beneath this you saw dresses of silk, American in make and style. On their feet were slippers of pale fine kid, high-heeled, or of patent-leather, ornamented with buckles of cut steel, shining and costly. The men wore the blanket, too, but beneath it they liked a shirt of silk brocade in gorgeous colors—bright green or purple or cerise—its tail worn outside the trousers, and the trousers often as not trimmed with a pattern of beadwork at the side. On their heads they wore huge sombreros trimmed with bands of snakeskin ornamented with silver. They hired white chauffeurs to drive their big sedan cars and sat back grandly after ordering them to drive round and round and round the main business block. Jewelry shops began to display their glistening wares in Osage, not so much in the hope of winning the favor of the white oil millionaire as the red. Bracelets, watches, gaudy rings and pins and bangles and beads and combs and buckles. Diamonds. These the Indians seemed instinctively to know about, and they bought them clear and blue-white and costly.

The Levy Mercantile Company had added a fancy grocery and market department to its three-story brick store. It was situated on the street floor and enhanced with a great plate-glass window. In this window Sol displayed a mouth-watering assortment of foods. Juicy white stalks of asparagus in glass, as large around as a man's two thumbs; great ripe olives, their purple-black cheeks glistening with oil; lobster, mushrooms, French peas, sardines, mountainous golden cheeses, tender broilers, peaches in syrup, pork roasts dressed in frills. Dozens of chickens, pounds of pork, baskets of delicacies were piled in the cars of homeward bound Osages. Often, when the food bills mounted too high, the Indian Agent at Wazhazhe threatened to let the bill go unpaid. He alone had the power to check the outpouring of Indian gold, and even he frequently was unable to cope with their mad extravagances.

"It's disgusting," Sabra Cravat said, again and again. "What are they good for? What earthly good are they? Ignorant savages who do nothing but eat and sleep and drive around in their ridiculous huge automobiles."

"Keep money in circulation," Sol Levy replied, for she often took him to task after seeing a line of Indian cars parked outside the Osage Mercantile Company's store.

"You ought to be ashamed of yourself."

"Now, now, Sabra. Not so grand, please, I don't do like dozens of other merchants here in town. Make out bills for goods they haven't bought and give them the money. Or charge them double on the bill that the Indian Agent sees, and return them the overcharge. They come in my store, they buy, they pay what the article is marked, and they get what they pay for. Inez Bull comes in and gets a silk step-in, or Sun Maker he buys twelve pounds of chicken and ten pounds of pork. I should tell them they can't have it! Let the President of the United States do it. The Big White Father."

Not only did Yancey agree with Sol, he seemed to find enormous satisfaction in the lavishness with which they spent their oil money; in the very absurdity of the things they bought.

"The joke gets better and better. We took their land away from them and exterminated the buffalo, then expected them to squat on the Reservations weaving baskets and molding pottery that nobody wanted to buy. Well, at least the Osages never did that. They're spending their money just as the white people do when they get a handful of it—chicken and plush and automobiles and phonographs and silk shirts and jewelry."

"Why don't they do some good with it?" Sabra demanded.

"What good's Wyatt doing? Or Nisbett, or old Buckner, or Ike Hawes, or their wives! Blowing it on houses and travel and diamonds and high-priced cars."

"The Osages could help the other tribes—poor Indian tribes that haven't struck oil."

"Maybe they will—when Bixby gives away his millions to down-and-out hotel keepers who are as poor as he was when he ran the Bixby House, back in the old days."

"Filthy savages!"

"No, honey. Just blanket Indians—horse Indians—Plains Indians, with about twenty-five millions of dollars a year gushing up out of the earth and splattering all around them. The wonder to me is that they don't die laughing and spoil their own good time."

Sometimes Sabra encountered old Big Elk and his vast squaw and Ruby Big Elk, together with others of the family—a large one for an Osage—driving through Pawhuska Avenue. With their assembled head rights the family was enormously rich—one of the wealthiest on the Wazhazhe Reservation. When the Big Elks drove through the town it was a parade. No one car could have contained the family, though they would have scorned such economy even if it had been possible.

They made a brilliant Indian frieze in the modern manner. Old Big Elk and his wife, somewhat conservatively, lolled in a glittering Lincoln driven by a white chauffeur. Through the generous glass windows you saw the two fat bronze faces, the massive bodies, the brilliant colors of their blankets and chains and beads. One of the Big Elk boys drove a snow-white Pierce Arrow roadster that tore and shrieked like an avenging demon up and down the dusty road between Osage and Wazhazhe. Ruby herself, and a sister-in-law or so, and a brother, might follow in one of the Packards, while still another brother or sister preferred a Cadillac. If they walked at all it was to ascend with stately step the entrance to the Indian Agent's Office. The boys wore American dress, with perhaps an occasional Indian incongruity—beaded pants, a five-gallon hat with an eagle feather in it, sometimes moccasins. Ruby and her sisters and her sister-in-law wore the fine and gaudy blanket over their American dresses, they were hatless, and their long bountiful hair was done Indian fashion. The dress of old Big Elk and his wife was a gorgeous mixture of Indian and American, with the Indian triumphantly predominating. About the whole party, as in the case of any of the Osage oil families, there was an air of quiet insolence, of deep rich triumph.

Sabra always greeted them politely enough. "How do you do, Ruby," she would say. "What a beautiful dress." Ruby would say nothing. She would look at Sabra's neat business dress of dark blue or gray, at Sabra's plain little hat and sensible oxford ties. "Give my regards to your father and mother," Sabra would continue, blandly, but inwardly furious to find herself feeling uncomfortable and awkward beneath this expressionless Indian gaze. She fancied that in it there was something menacing, something triumphant. She wondered if Ruby, the oft-married, had married yet again. Once she asked young Cim about her, making her tone casual. "Do you ever see that girl who used to work here—Ruby, wasn't that it? Ruby Big Elk?"

Cim's tone was even more casual than hers. "Oh, yes. We were working out Wazhazhe way, you know, on the Choteau field. That's near by."

"They're terribly rich, aren't they?"

"Oh, rotten. A fleet of cars and a regular flock of houses."

"It's a wonder that some miserable white squaw man hasn't married that big greasy Ruby for her head right. Mrs. Conn Sanders told me that one of the Big Elk boys was actually playing golf out at the Westchester Apawamis Club last Saturday. It's disgusting. He must know there's a rule against Indians. Mrs. Sanders reported him to the house committee."

"There's a rule, all right. But you ought to see the gallery when Standing Bear whams it out so straight and so far that he makes the pro look like a ping-pong player."

"How is he in a tomahawk contest?"

"Oh, Mother, you talk like Grandma when she used to visit here."

"The Marcys and the Venables didn't hobnob with dirty savages in blankets."

"Standing Bear doesn't wear his blanket when he plays golf," retorted Cim, coolly. "And he took a shower after he'd made the course in seven below par."

Donna came home from a bridge party one afternoon a week later, the creamy Venable pallor showing the Marcy tinge of ocherous rage. She burst in upon Sabra, home from the office.

"Do you know that Cim spends his time at the Big Elks' when we think he's out in the oil fields?"

Sabra met this as calmly as might be. "He's working near there. He told me he had seen them."

"Seen them! That miserable Gazelle Slaughter said that he's out there all the time. All the time, I tell you, and that he and Ruby drive around in her car, and he eats with them, he stays there, he————"

"I'll speak to your father. Cim's coming home Saturday. Gazelle is angry at Cim, you know that, because he won't notice her and she likes him."

She turned her clear appraising gaze upon this strange daughter of hers. She thought, suddenly, that Donna was like a cobra, with that sleek black head, that cold and slanting eye, that long creamy throat in which a pulse sometimes could be seen to beat and swell a little—the only sign of emotion in this baffling creature.

"I'll tell you what, Donna. If you'd pay a little less attention to your brother's social lapses and a little more to your own vulgar conduct, perhaps it would be better."

Donna bestowed her rare and brilliant smile upon her forthright mother. "Now, now, darling! I suppose I say, 'What do you mean?' And you say, 'You know very well what I mean.'"

"You certainly do know what I mean. If you weren't my own daughter I'd say your conduct with Tracy Wyatt was that of a—a————"

"Harlot," put in Donna, sweetly.

"Donna! How can you talk like that? You are breaking my heart. Haven't I had enough? I've never complained, have I? But now—you————"

Donna came over to her and put her arms about her, as though she were the older woman protecting the younger. "It's all right, Mamma darling. You just don't understand. Life isn't as simple as it was when you were a frontier gal. I know what I want and I'm going to get it."

Sabra shrugged away from her; faced her with scorn. "I've seen you. I'm ashamed for you. You press against him like a—like a————" Again she could not say it. Another generation. "And that horse you ride. You say he loans it to you. He gave it to you. It's yours. What for?"

She was weeping.

"I tell you it's all right, Mamma. He did give it to me.

He wants to give me lots of things, but I won't take them, yet. Tracy's in love with me. He thinks I'm young and beautiful and stimulating and wonderful. He's married to a dried-up, vinegary, bitter old hag who was just that when he married her, years ago. He's never known what love is. She has never given him children. He's insanely rich, and not too old, and rather sweet. We're going to be married. Tracy will get his divorce. Money does anything. It has taken me a year and a half to do it. I've never worked so hard in all my life. But it's going to be worth it. Don't worry, darling. Tracy's making an honest woman of your wayward daughter."

Sabra drew herself up, every inch the daughter of her mother, Felice Venable, née Marcy. "You are disgusting."

"Not really, if you just look at it without a lot of sentiment. I shall be happy, and Tracy, too. His wife will be unhappy, I suppose, for a while. But she isn't happy anyway, as it is. Better one than three. It'll work out. You'll see. Don't bother about me. It's Cim that needs looking after. He's got a streak of—of——" She looked at her mother. Did not finish the sentence. "When he comes home Saturday I wish you'd speak to him."

22

BUT CIM DID not come home on Saturday. On Saturday, at noon, when Sabra and Yancey drove from the office in their little utility car to the house on Kihekah Street for their noonday dinner they saw a great limousine drawn up at the curb. A chauffeur, vaguely familiar, lounged in front. The car was thick with the red dust of the country road.

A vague pang of premonition stabbed at Sabra's vitals. She clutched Yancey's arm. "Whose car is that?"

Yancey glanced at it indifferently. "Somebody drove Cim home, I suppose. Got enough dinner for company?"

Donna had gone to Oklahoma City to spend the week-end. It must be Cim.

"Cim!" Sabra called, as she entered the front door. "Cim!" But there was no answer. She went straight to the sitting room. Empty. But in the stiff little parlor, so seldom used, sat two massive, silent figures. With the Indian sense of ceremony and formality old Big Elk and his squaw had known the proper room to use for an occasion such as this.

"Why—Big Elk!"

"How!" replied Big Elk, and held up his palm in the gesture of greeting.

"Yancey!" cried Sabra suddenly, in a terrible voice. The two pairs of black Indian eyes stared at her. Sabra saw that their dress was elaborate; the formal dress reserved for great occasions. The woman wore a dark skirt and a bright cerise satin blouse, ample and shaped like a dressing sacque. Over her shoulders was the fine bright-hued blanket. Her hair was neatly braided and wound about her hatless head. She wore no ornaments. That was the prerogative of the male. Old Big Elk was a structure of splendor. His enormous bulk filled the chair. His great knees were wide apart. His blue trousers were slashed and beaded elaborately at the sides and on his feet were moccasins heavy with intricate beadwork. His huge upper body was covered with a shirt of brilliant green brocade worn outside the trousers, and his striped blanket hung regally from his shoulders. About his neck and on his broad breast hung chains, beads, necklaces. In the bright silk neckerchief knotted about his throat you saw the silver emblem of his former glory as chief of the tribe. There were other insignia of distinction made of beaten silver—the star, the crescent, the sun. On his head was a round high cap of brown beaver like a Cossack's. Up the back of this was stuck an eagle feather. His long locks, hanging about his shoulders, straight and stiff, were dyed a brilliant orange, like an old burlesque queen's, a startling, a fantastic background for the parchment face, lined and creased and crisscrossed with a thousand wrinkles. One hand rested on his knee. The other wielded languidly, back and forth, back and forth, an enormous semicircular fan made of eagle feathers. Side by side the two massive figures sat like things of bronze. Only their eyes moved, and that nightmarish eagle feather fan, back and forth, back and forth, regally.

Those dull black unsmiling eyes, that weaving fan, moved Sabra to nameless terror. "Yancey!" she cried again, through stiff lips. "Yancey!"

At the note of terror in her voice he was down the stairs and in the room with his quick light step. But at sight of old Big Elk and his wife his look of concern changed to one of relief. He smiled his utterly charming smile.

"How!"

"How!" croaked Big Elk.

Mrs. Big Elk nodded her greeting. She was a woman younger, perhaps, by thirty years than her aged husband; his third wife. She spoke English; had even attended an Indian Mission school in her girlhood. But through carelessness or indifference she used the broken, slovenly English of the unlettered Indian.

Now the two relapsed into impassive silence.

"What do they want? Ask them what they want."

Yancey spoke a few words in Osage. Big Elk replied with a monosyllable.

"What did he say? What is it?"

"I asked them to eat dinner with us. He says he cannot."

"I should hope not. Tell her to speak English. She speaks English."

Big Elk turned his great head, slowly, as though it moved on a mechanical pivot. He stared at his fat, round-faced wife. He uttered a brief command in his own tongue. The squaw smiled a little strange, embarrassed smile, like a schoolgirl—it was less a smile than a contortion of the face, so rare in her race as to be more frightening than a scowl.

"Big Elk and me come take you back to Wazhazhe."

"What for?" cried Sabra, sharply.

"Four o'clock big dinner, big dance. Your son want um come tell you. Want um know he marry Ruby this morning."

She was silent again, smiling her foolish fixed smile. Big Elk's fan went back and forth, back and forth.

"God A'mighty!" said Yancey Cravat. He looked at Sabra, came over to her quickly, but she waved him away.

"Don't. I'm not going to—it's all right." It was as though she shrank from his touch. She stood there, staring at the two barbaric figures staring so stonily back at her with their dead black Indian eyes. It was at times like this that the Marcy in her stood her in good stead. She came of iron stock, fit to stand the fire. Only beneath her fine dark eyes you now suddenly saw a smudge of purplish brown, as though a dirty thumb had rubbed there; and a sagging of all the muscles of her face, so that she looked wattled, lined, old.

"Don't look like that, honey. Come. Sit down."

Again the groping wave of her hand. "I'm all right, I tell you. Come. We must go there."

Yancey came forward. He shook hands formally with Big Elk, with the

Indian woman. Sabra, seeing him, suddenly realized that he was not displeased. She knew that no formal politeness would have prevented him from voicing his anger if this monstrous announcement had shattered him as it had her, so that her very vitals seemed to be withering within her.

"Sugar, shake hands with them, won't you?"

"No. No." She wet her dry lips a little with her tongue, like one in a fever. She turned, woodenly, and walked to the door, ignoring the Indians. Across the hall, slowly, like an old woman, down the porch steps, toward the shabby little car next to the big rich one. As she went she heard Yancey's voice (was there an exultant note in it?) at the telephone.

"Jesse! Take this. Get it in. Ready! . . . Ex-Chief Big Elk, of the Osage Nation, and Mrs. Big Elk, living at Wazhazhe, announce the marriage of their daughter Ruby Big Elk to Cimarron Cravat, son of—don't interrupt me—I'm in a hurry—son of Mr. and Mrs. Yancey Cravat, of this city. The wedding was solemnized at the home of the bride's parents and was followed by an elaborate dinner made up of many Indian and American dishes, partaken of by the parents of the bride and the groom, many relatives and numerous friends of the young . . ."

Sabra climbed heavily into the car and sat staring at the broad back of the car ahead of her. Chief Big Elk and his wife came out presently, unreal, bizarre in the brilliant noonday Oklahoma sunshine, ushered by Yancey. He was being charming. They heaved their ponderous bulk into the big car. Yancey got in beside Sabra. She spoke to him once only.

"I think you are glad."

"This is Oklahoma. In a way it's what I wanted it to be when I came here twenty years ago. Cim's like your father, Lewis Venable. Weak stuff, but good stock. Ruby's pure Indian blood and a magnificent animal. It's hard on you now, my darling. But their children and their grandchildren are going to be such stuff as Americans are made of. You'll see."

"I hope I shall die before that day."

The shabby little middle-class car followed the one whirling ahead of them over the red clay Oklahoma roads. Eating the dust of the big car just ahead.

She went through it and stood it, miraculously, until one grotesquerie proved too much for her strained nerves and broke them. But she went into the Indian house, and saw Cim sitting beside the Indian woman, and as she looked at his beautiful weak face she thought, I wish that I had never found him that day when he was lost on the prairie long ago. He came toward her, his head lowered with that familiar look, his fine eyes hidden by the lids.

"Look at me!" Sabra commanded, in the voice of Felice Venable. The boy raised his eyes. She looked at him, her face stony. Ruby Big Elk came toward her with that leisurely, insolent, scuffling step. The two women gazed at each other; rather, their looks clashed, like swords held high. They did not shake hands.

There were races, there were prizes, there was dancing. In the old Indian days the bucks had raced on foot for a prize that was a pony tethered at a distance and won by the fleetest to reach him, mount, and ride him back to the starting point. To-day the prize was a magnificent motor car that stood glittering in the open field half a mile distant. Sabra thought, I am dying, I am dying. And Donna. This squaw is her sister-in-law. Miss Dignum's on the Hudson.

Ruby's handsome head right had bought the young couple the house just across the road from Big Elk's—a one-story red brick bungalow, substantial, ugly. They showed Sabra and Yancey through it. It was furnished complete. Mongrel Spanish furniture in the living room—red plush, fringe, brass nail heads as big as twenty-dollar gold pieces. An upright piano. An oak dining-room set. A fine bathroom with heavy rich bath towels neatly hung on the racks. A shining stained oak bedroom set with a rose-colored taffeta spread. Sabra felt a wave of nausea. Cim's face was smiling, radiant. Yancey was joking and laughing with the Indians. In the kitchen sat a white girl in a gingham dress and a kitchen apron. The girl's hair was so light a yellow as to appear almost white. Her unintelligent eyes were palest blue. Her skin was so fair as to be quite colorless. In the midst of the roomful of dark Indian faces the white face of the new Cravat hired girl seemed to swim in a hazy blob before Sabra's eyes. But she held on. She felt Ruby's scornful dark eyes on her. Sabra had a feeling as though she had been disemboweled and now was a hollow thing, an empty shell that moved and walked and talked.

Dinner. White servants and negro servants to wait on them. A long table seating a score or more, and many such tables. Bowls and plates piled with food all down the length of it. Piles of crisp pork, roasted in the Indian fashion over hot embers sunk in a pit in the yard, and skewered with a sharp pointed stick. Bowls of dried corn. Great fat, black ripe olives. Tinned lobster. Chicken. Piles of dead ripe strawberries. Vast plateaus of angel-food cake covered with snow fields of icing.

Sabra went through the motions of eating. Sometimes she put a morsel into her mouth and actually swallowed it. There was a great clatter of knives and forks and dishes. Everything was eaten out of one plate. Platters and bowls were replenished. Sabra found herself seated beside Mrs. Big Elk. On her other side was Yancey. He was eating and laughing and talking. Mrs. Big Elk was being almost comically polite, solicitous. She pressed this tidbit, that dainty, on her stony guest.

Down the center of the table, at intervals, were huge bowls piled with a sort of pastry stuffed with forcemeat. It was like a great ravioli, and piles of it vanished beneath the onslaught of appreciative guests.

"For God's sake, pretend to eat something, Sabra," Yancey murmured, under his breath. "It's done now. They consider it an insult. Try to eat something."

She stirred the pastry and chopped meat that had been put on her plate.

"Good," said Mrs. Big Elk, beside her, and pointed at the mass with one dusky maculate finger.

Sabra lifted her fork to her lips and swallowed a bit of it. It was delicious—spicy, rich, appetizing. "Yes," she said, and thought, I am being wonderful. This is killing me. "Yes, it is very good. This meat—this stuffing—is it chopped or ground through a grinder?"

The huge Indian woman beside her turned her expressionless gaze on Sabra. Ponderously she shook her head from side to side in negation.

"Naw," she answered, politely. "Chawed."

The clatter of a fork dropped to the plate, a clash among the cups and saucers. Sabra Cravat had fainted.

23

OSAGE WAS SO sophisticated that it had again become simple. The society editor of the *Oklahoma Wigwam* used almost no adjectives. In the old days, you had read that "the house was beautifully decorated with an artistic arrangement of smilax, sent from Kansas City, pink and purple asters in profusion making a bower before which the young couple stood, while in the dining room the brilliance of golden glow, scarlet salvia, and autumn leaves gave a seasonal touch." But now the society column said, austerely, "The decorations were orchids and Pernet roses."

Osage, Oklahoma, was a city.

Where, scarcely two decades ago, prairie and sky had met the eye with here a buffalo wallow, there an Indian encampment, you now saw a twenty-story hotel: the Savoy-Bixby. The Italian head waiter bent from the waist and murmured in your ear his secret about the veal sauté with mushrooms or the spaghetti Caruso du jour. Sabra Cravat, Congresswoman from Oklahoma, lunching in the Louis XIV room with the members of the Women's State Republican Committee, would say, looking up at him with those intelligent dark eyes, "I'll leave it to you, Nick. Only quickly. We haven't much time." Niccolo Mazzarini would say yes, he understood. No one had much time in Osage, Oklahoma. A black jackanapes in a tight scarlet jacket with brass buttons and even tighter bright blue pants, an impudent round red cap cocked over one ear, strolled through the dining room bawling, "Mistah Thisandthat! Mistah Whoandwhat!" He carried messages on a silver salver. There were separate ice-water taps in every bedroom. Servidors. Ring once for the waiter. Twice for the chambermaid. A valet is at your service.

Twenty-five years earlier anybody who was anybody in Oklahoma had dilated on his or her Eastern connections. Iowa, if necessary, was East.

They had been a little ashamed of the Run. Bragged about the splendors of the homes from which they had come.

Now it was considered the height of chic to be able to say that your parents had come through in a covered wagon. Grandparents were still rather rare in Oklahoma. As for the Run of '89—it was Osage's *Mayflower*. At the huge dinner given in Sabra Cravat's honor when she was elected Congresswoman, and from which they tried to exclude Sol Levy over Sabra's vigorous (and triumphant) protest, the chairman of the Committee on Arrangements explained it all to Sol, patronizingly.

"You see, we're inviting only people who came to Oklahoma in the Run."

"Well, sure," said the former peddler, genially. "That's all right. I walked."

The Levy Mercantile Company's building now occupied an entire square block and was fifteen stories high. In the huge plate-glass windows on Pawhuska postured ladies waxen and coquettish, as on Fifth Avenue. You went to the Salon Moderne to buy Little French Dresses, and the saleswomen of this department wore black satin and a very nice little strand of imitation pearls, and their eyes were hard and shrewd and their phrases the latest. The Osage Indian women had learned about these Little French Dresses, and they often came in with their stately measured stride: soft and flaccid from easy living, rolls of fat about their hips and thighs. They tried on sequined dresses, satin dresses, chiffon. Sometimes even the younger Osage Indian girls still wore the brilliant striped blanket, in a kind of contemptuous defiance of the whites. And to these, as well as to the other women customers, the saleswomen said, "That's awfully good this year. . . . That's dreadfully smart on you, Mrs. Buffalo Hide. . . . I think that line isn't the thing for your figure, Mrs. Plenty Vest. . . . My dear, I want you to have that. It's perfect with your coloring."

The daughter of Mrs. Pat Leary (née Crook Nose) always caused quite a flutter when she came in, for accustomed though Osage was to money and the spending of it, the Learys' lavishness was something spectacular. Handmade silk underwear, the sheerest of cobweb French stockings, model hats, dresses—well, in the matter of gowns it was no good trying to influence Maude Leary or her mother. They frankly wanted beads, spangles, and paillettes on a foundation of crude color. The saleswomen were polite and acquiescent, but they cocked an eyebrow at one another. Squaw stuff. Now that little Cravat girl—Felice Cravat, Cimarron Cravat's daughter—was different. She insisted on plain, smart tailored things. Young though she was, she was Oklahoma State Woman Tennis Champion. She always said she looked a freak in fluffy things—like a boy dressed up in girl's clothes. She had long, lean, muscular arms and a surprising breadth of shoulder, was slim flanked and practically stomachless. She had a curious trick of holding her head down and looking up at you under her lashes and when she did that you forgot her boyishness, for her lashes were like fern fronds, and her eyes, in her dark face, an astounding ocean gray. She was a good sport, too. She didn't seem to mind the fact that her mother, when she accompanied her, wore the blanket and was hatless, just like any poor Kaw, instead of being one of the richest of the Osages. She was rather handsome for a squaw, in a big, insolent, slow-moving way. Felice Cravat, everyone agreed, was a chip of the old block, and by that they did not mean her father. They were thinking of Yancey Cravat—old Cimarron, her grandfather, who was now something of a legend in Osage and throughout Oklahoma. Young Cim and his Osage wife had had a second child—a boy—and they had called him Yancey, after the old boy. Young Yancey was a bewilderingly handsome mixture of a dozen types and forbears—Indian, Spanish, French, Southern, Southwest. With that long narrow face, the dolichocephalic head, people said he looked like the King of Spain—without that dreadful Hapsburg jaw. Others said he was the image of his grandmother, Sabra Cravat. Still others contended that he was his Indian mother over again—insolence and all. A third would come along and say, "You're crazy. He's old Yancey, born again. I guess you don't remember him. There, look, that's what I mean! The way he closes his eyes as if he were sleepy, and then when he does look at you straight you feel as if you'd been struck by lightning. They say he's so smart that the Osages believe he's one of their old gods come back to earth."

Mrs. Tracy Wyatt (she who had been Donna Cravat) had tried to adopt one of her brother's children, being herself childless, but Cim and his wife Ruby Big Elk had never consented to this. She was a case, that Donna Cravat, Oklahoma was agreed about that. She could get away with things that any other woman would be shot for. When old Tracy Wyatt had divorced his wife to marry this girl local feeling had been very much against her. Everyone had turned to the abandoned middle-aged wife with attentions and sympathy, but she had met their warmth and friendliness with such vitriol that they fell back in terror and finally came to believe the stories of how she had deviled and nagged old Tracy all through their marriage. They actually came to feel that he had been justified in deserting her and taking to wife this young and fascinating girl. Certainly he seemed to take a new lease on life, lost five inches around the waist line, played polo, regained something of the high color and good spirits of his old dray-driving days, and made a great hit in London during the season when Donna was presented at court. Besides, there was no withstanding the Wyatt money. Even in a country blasé of millionaires Tracy Wyatt's fortune was something to marvel about. The name of Wyatt seemed to be everywhere. As you rode in trains you saw the shining round black flanks of oil cars, thousands of them, and painted on them in letters of white, "Wyatt Oils." Motoring through Oklahoma and the whole of the Southwest you passed miles of Wyatt oil tanks, whole silent cities of monoliths, like something grimly Egyptian, squatting eunuch-like on the prairies.

As for the Wyatt house—it wasn't a house at all, but a combination of the palace of Versailles and the Grand Central Station in New York. It occupied grounds about the size of the duchy of Luxembourg, and on the grounds, once barren plain, had been set great trees brought from England.

A mile of avenue, planted in elms, led up to the mansion, and each elm, bought, transported, and stuck in the ground, had cost fifteen hundred dollars. There were rare plants, farms, forests, lakes, tennis courts, golf links, polo fields, race tracks, airdromes, swimming pools. Whole paneled rooms had been brought from France. In the bathrooms were electric cabinets, and sunken tubs of rare marble, and shower baths glass enclosed. These bathrooms were the size of bedrooms, and the bedrooms the size of ballrooms, and the ballroom as big as an auditorium. There was an ice plant and cooling system that could chill the air of every room in the house, even on the hottest Oklahoma windy day. The kitchen range looked like a house in itself, and the kitchen looked like that of the Biltmore, only larger. When you entered the dining room you felt that here should be seated solemn diplomats in gold braid signing world treaties and having their portraits painted doing it. Sixty gardeners manned the grounds. The house servants would have peopled a village.

Sabra Cravat rarely came to visit her daughter's house, and when she did the very simplicity of her slim straight little figure in its dark blue georgette or black crêpe was startling in the midst of these marble columns and vast corridors and royal hangings. She did come occasionally, and on those occasions you found her in the great central apartment that was like a throne room, standing there before the portraits of her son's two children, Felice and Yancey Cravat. Failing to possess either of the children for her own, Donna had had them painted and hung there, one either side of the enormous fireplace. She had meant them to be a gift to her mother, but Sabra Cravat had refused to take them.

"Don't you like them, Sabra darling! They're the best things Segovia has ever done. Is it because they're modern? I think they look like the kids—don't you?"

"They're just wonderful."

"Well, then!"

"I'd have to build a house for them. How would they look in the sitting room of the house on Kihekah! No, let me come here and look at them now and then. That way they're always a fresh surprise to me."

Certainly they were rather surprising, those portraits. Rather, one of them was. Segovia had got little Felice well enough, but he had made the mistake of painting her in Spanish costume, and somehow her angular contours and boyish frame had not lent themselves to these gorgeous lace and satin trappings. The boy, Yancey, had refused to dress up for the occasion—had, indeed, been impatient of posing at all. Segovia had caught him quickly and brilliantly, with startling results. He wore a pair of loose, rather grimy white tennis pants, a white woolly sweater with a hole in the elbow, and was hatless. In his right hand—that slim, beautiful, speaking hand—he held a limp, half-smoked cigarette, its blue-gray smoke spiraling faintly, its dull red eye the only note of color in the picture. Yet the whole portrait was colorful, moving, alive. The boy's pose was so insolent, so lithe, so careless. The eyes followed you. He was a person.

"Looks like Ruby, don't you think?" Donna had said, when first she had shown it to her mother.

"No!" Sabra had replied, with enormous vigor. "Not at all. Your father."

"Well—maybe—a little."

"A little! You're crazy! Look at his eyes. His hands. Of course they're not as beautiful as your father's hands were—are . . ."

It had been five years since Sabra had heard news of her husband, Yancey Cravat. And now, for the first time, she felt that he was dead, though she had never admitted this. In spite of his years she had heard that Yancey had gone to France during the war. The American and the English armies had rejected him, so he had dyed his graying hair, lied about his age, thrown back his still magnificent shoulders, and somehow, by his eyes, his voice, his hands, or a combination of all these, had hypnotized them into taking him. An unofficial report had listed him among the missing after the carnage had ceased in the shambles that had been a wooded plateau called the Argonne.

"He isn't dead," Sabra had said, almost calmly. "When Yancey Cravat dies he'll be on the front page, and the world will know it."

Donna, in talking it over with her brother Cim, had been inclined to agree with this, though she did not put it thus to her mother. "Dad wouldn't let himself die in a list. He's too good an actor to be lost in a mob scene."

But a year had gone by.

The *Oklahoma Wigwam* now issued a morning as well as an afternoon edition and was known as the most powerful newspaper in the Southwest. Its presses thundered out tens of thousands of copies an hour, and hour on hour—five editions. Its linotype room was now a regiment of iron men, its staff boasted executive editor, editor in chief, managing editor, city editor, editor, and on down into the dozens of minor minions. When Sabra was in town she made a practice of driving down to the office at eleven every night, remaining there for an hour looking over the layout, reading the wet galley proof of the night's news lead, scanning the A. P. wires. Her entrance was in the nature of the passage of royalty, and when she came into the city room the staff all but saluted. True, she wasn't there very much, except in the summer, when Congress was not in session.

The sight of a woman on the floor of the Congressional House was still something of a novelty. Sentimental America had shrunk from the thought of women in active politics. Woman's place was in the Home, and American Womanhood was too exquisite a flower to be subjected to the harsh atmosphere of the Assembly floor and the committee room.

Sabra stumped the state and developed a surprising gift of oratory.

"If American politics are too dirty for women to take part in, there's something wrong with American politics. . . . We weren't too delicate and flowerlike to cross the plains and prairies and deserts in a covered wagon and to stand the hardships and heartbreaks of frontier life . . . history of France peeking through a bedroom keyhole . . . history of England a joust . . . but here in this land the women have been the hewers of wood and drawers of water . . . thousands of unnamed heroines with weather-beaten faces and mud-caked boots . . . alkali water . . . sun . . . dust . . . wind. . . . I am not belittling the brave pioneer men but the sunbonnet as well as the sombrero has helped to settle this glorious land of ours. . . ."

It had been so many years since she had heard this ————it had sunk so deep into her consciousness—that perhaps she actually thought she had originated this speech. Certainly it was received with tremendous emotional response, copied throughout the Southwest, the Far West, the Mid-West states, and it won her the election and gained her fame that was nation wide.

Perhaps it was not altogether what Sabra Cravat said that counted in her favor. Her appearance must have had something to do with it. A slim, straight, dignified woman, yet touchingly feminine. Her voice not loud, but clear. Her white hair was shingled and beautifully waved and beneath this her soft dark eyes took on an added depth and brilliance. Her eyebrows had remained black and thick, still further enhancing her finest feature. Her dress was always dark, becoming, smart, and her silken ankles above the slim slippers with their cut-steel buckles were those of a young girl. The aristocratic Marcy feet and ankles.

Her speeches were not altogether romantic, by any means. She knew her state. Its politics were notoriously rotten. Governor after governor was impeached with musical comedy swiftness and regularity, and the impeachment proceedings stank to Washington. This governor was practically an outlaw and desperado; that governor, who resembled a traveling evangelist with his long locks and his sanctimonious face, flaunted his mistress, and all the office plums fell to her rapscallion kin. Sabra had statistics at her tongue's end. Millions of barrels of oil. Millions of tons of zinc. Third in mineral products. First in oil. Coal. Gypsum. Granite. Live stock.

In Washington she was quite a belle among the old boys in Congress and even the Senate. The opposition party tried to blackmail her with publicity about certain unproved items in the life of her dead (or missing) husband Yancey Cravat: a two-gun man, a desperado, a killer, a drunkard, a squaw man. Then they started on young Cim and his Osage Indian wife, but Sabra and Donna were too quick for them.

Donna Wyatt leased a handsome Washington house in Dupont Circle, staffed it, brought Tracy Wyatt's vast wealth and influence to bear, and planned a coup so brilliant that it routed the enemy forever. She brought her handsome, sleepy-eyed brother Cim and his wife Ruby Big Elk, and the youngsters Felice and Yancey to the house in Dupont Circle, and together she and Sabra gave a reception for them to which they invited a group so precious that it actually came.

Sabra and Donna, exquisitely dressed, stood in line at the head of the magnificent room, and between them stood Ruby Big Elk in her Indian dress of creamy white doeskin all embroidered in beads from shoulder to hem. She was an imposing figure, massive but not offensively fat as were many of the older Osage women, and her black abundant hair had taken on a mist of gray.

"My daughter-in-law, Mrs. Cimarron Cravat, of the Osage Indian tribe."

"My son's wife, Ruby Big Elk—Mrs. Cimarron Cravat."

"My sister-in-law, Mrs. Cimarron Cravat. A full-blood Osage Indian. . . . Yes, indeed. We think so, too."

And, "How do you do?" said Ruby, in her calm, insolent way.

For the benefit of those who had not quite been able to encompass the Indian woman in her native dress Ruby's next public appearance was made in a Paris gown of white. She became the rage, was considered picturesque, and left Washington in disgust, her work done. No one but her husband, whom she loved with a doglike devotion, could have induced her to go through this ceremony.

The opposition retired, vanquished.

Donna and Tracy Wyatt then hired a special train in which they took fifty Eastern potentates on a tour of Oklahoma. One vague and not very bright Washington matron, of great social prestige, impressed with what she saw, voiced her opinion to young Yancey Cravat, quite confused as to his identity and seeing only an attractive and very handsome young male seated beside her at a country club luncheon.

"I had no idea Oklahoma was like this. I thought it was all oil and dirty Indians."

"There is quite a lot of oil, but we're not all dirty."

"We?"

"I'm an Indian."

Osage, Oklahoma, was now just as much like New York as Osage could manage to make it. They built twenty-story office buildings in a city that had hundreds of miles of prairie to spread in. Tracy Wyatt built the first skyscraper—the Wyatt building. It was pointed out and advertised all over the flat prairie state. Then Pat Leary, dancing an Irish jig of jealousy, built the Leary building, twenty-three stories high. But the sweet fruits of triumph soon turned to ashes in his mouth. The Wyatt building's foundations were not built to stand the added strain of five full stories. So he had built a five-story tower, slim and tapering, a taunting finger pointing to the sky. Again Tracy Wyatt owned the tallest building in Oklahoma.

On the roof of the Levy Mercantile Company's Building Sol had had built a penthouse after his own plans. It was the only one of its kind in all Oklahoma, That small part of Osage which did not make an annual pilgrimage to New York was slightly bewildered by Sol Levy's roof life. They fed one another with scraps of gossip got from servants, clerks, stenographers who claimed to have seen the place at one time or another. It was, these said, filled with the rarest of carpets, rugs, books, hangings. Super radio, super phonograph, super player piano. Music hungry. There he lived, alone, in luxury, of the town, yet no part of it. At sunset, in the early morning, late of a star-spangled night he might have been seen leaning over the parapet of his sky house, a lonely little figure, lean, ivory, aloof, like a gargoyle brooding over the ridiculous city sprawled below; over the oil rigs that encircled it like giant Martian guards holding it in their power; beyond, to where the sky, in a veil of gray chiffon that commerce had wrought, stooped to meet the debauched red prairie.

Money was now the only standard. If Pat Leary had sixty-two million dollars on Tuesday he was Oklahoma's leading citizen. If Tracy Wyatt had seventy-eight million dollars on Wednesday then Tracy Wyatt was Oklahoma's leading citizen.

Osage had those fascinating little specialty shops and interior decorating shops on Pawhuska just like those you see on Madison Avenue, whose owners are the daughters of decayed Eastern aristocracy on the make. The head of the shop appeared only to special clients and then with a hat on. She wore the hat from morning until night, her badge of revolt against this position of service. "I am a lady," the hat said. "Make no mistake about that. Just because I am a shopkeeper don't think you can patronize me. I am not working. I am playing at work. This is my fad. At any moment I can walk out of here, just like any of you."

Feminine Osage's hat, by the way, was cut and fitted right on its head, just like Paris.

Sabra probably was the only woman of her own generation and social position in Osage who still wore on the third finger of her left hand the plain broad gold band of a long-past day. Synchronous with the permanent wave and the reducing diet the oil-rich Osage matrons of Sabra's age cast sentiment aside for fashion, quietly placed the clumsy gold band in a bureau drawer and appeared with a slim platinum circlet bearing, perhaps, the engraved anachronism, "M. G.-K. L. 1884." Certainly it was much more at ease among its square-cut emerald and oblong-diamond neighbors. These ladies explained (if at all) that the gold band had grown too tight for the finger, or too loose. Sabra looked down at the broad old-fashioned wedding ring on her own gemless finger. She had not once taken it off in over forty years. It was as much a part of her as the finger itself.

Osage began to rechristen streets, changing the fine native Indian names to commonplace American ones. Hetoappe Street became the Boston Road; very fashionable it was, too. Still, the very nicest people were building out a ways in the new section (formerly Okemah Hill) now River View. The river was the ruddy Canadian, the view the forest of oil rigs bristling on the opposite shore. The grounds sloped down to the river except on those occasions when the river rose in red anger and sloped down to the houses. The houses themselves were Italian palazzi or French châteaux or English manors; none, perhaps, quite so vast or inclusive as Tracy Wyatt's, but all provided with such necessities as pipe organs, sunken baths, Greek temples, ancient tapestries, Venetian glass, billiard rooms, and butlers. Pat Leary, the smart little erstwhile section hand, had a melodramatic idea. Not content with peacocks, golf links, and swimming pools on his estate he now had placed an old and weathered covered wagon, a rusted and splintered wagon tongue, the bleached skull of a buffalo, an Indian tepee, and a battered lantern on a little island at the foot of the artificial lake below the heights on which his house stood. At night a searchlight, red, green, or orange, played from the tower of the house upon the mute relics of frontier days.

"The covered wagon my folks crossed the prairies in," Pat Leary explained, with shy pride. Eastern visitors were much impressed. It was considered a great joke in Osage, intimately familiar with Pat's Oklahoma beginnings.

"Forgot something, ain't you Pat, in that outfit you got rigged up in the yard?" old Bixby asked.

"What's that?"

"Pickax and shovel," Bixby replied, laconically. "Keg of spikes and a hand car."

Old Sam Pack, who had made the Run on a mule, said that if Pat Leary's folks had come to Oklahoma in a covered wagon then his had made the trip in an airplane.

All the Oklahoma millionaire houses had libraries. Yards and yards of fine leather libraries, with gold tooling. Ike Hawkes's library had five sets of Dickens alone, handsomely bound in red, green, blue, brown, and black, and Ike all unaware of any of them.

Moving picture palaces, with white-gloved ushers, had all the big Broadway super-films. Gas filling stations on every corner. Hot dog, chili con carne, and hamburger stands on the most remote country road. The Arverne Grand Opera Company at the McKee Theater for a whole week every year, and the best of everything— *Traviata, Bohême, Carmen, Louise, The Barber of Seville*. The display of jewels during that week made the Diamond Horseshoe at the Metropolitan look like the Black Hole of Calcutta.

SMART DANCING PARTY

Social events of the week just closed were worthily concluded with the smart dancing party at which Mr. and Mrs. Clint Hopper entertained a small company at the Osage Club. The roof garden of the club . . .

SMALL DINNER

Mr. and Mrs. James Click honored two distinguished Eastern visitors on Wednesday at the small dinner at which they entertained in courtesy to Mr. and Mrs. C. Swearingen Church, of St. Paul, Minnesota. There were covers for eighty. . . .

Mr. and Mrs. Buchanan Ketcham and Miss Patricia Ketcham left for New York last night, from which city they will

sail for Europe, there to meet the J. C. McConnells on their
yacht at Monaco. . . .

Le Cercle Français will meet Tuesday evening at the home
of Mr. and Mrs. Everard Pack. . . .

The sunbonnets had triumphed.

24

STILL, OIL WAS oil, and Indians were Indians. There was no way in which
either of those native forces could quite be molded to fit the New York
pattern.

The Osages still whirled up and down the Oklahoma roads, and those
roads, for hundreds of miles, were still unpaved red prairie dust. They
crashed into ditches and draws and culverts as of old, walked back to town
and, entering the automobile salesroom in which they had bought the original
car, pointed with one dusky finger at a new and glittering model.

" 'Nother," they said, succinctly. And drove out with it.

It was common news that Charley Vest had smashed eight Cadillac cars
in a year, but then Charley had a mysterious source through which he
procured fire water. They bought airplanes now, but they were forbidden
the use of local and neighboring flying fields after a series of fatal smashes.
They seemed, for the most part (the full bloods, at least), to be totally lacking
in engine sense.

They had electric refrigerators—sometimes in the parlor, very proud. They
ate enormously and waxed fatter and fatter. The young Osages now wore
made-to-order shirts with monograms embroidered on them the size of a
saucer. The Osages had taken to spending their summers in Colorado Springs
or Manitou. At first the white residents of those cities had refused to rent
their fine houses, furnished, to the Indians for the season. But the vast sums
offered them soon overcame their reluctance. The Indian problem was still
a problem, for he was considered legitimate prey, and thousands of prairie
buzzards fed on his richness.

Sabra Cravat had introduced a bill for the further protection of the Osages,
and rather took away the breath of the House assembled by advocating
abolition of the Indian Reservation system. Her speech, radical though it
was, and sensational, was greeted with favor by some of the more liberal
of the Congressmen. They even conceded that this idea of hers, to the effect
that the Indian would never develop or express himself until he was as free
as the negro, might some day become a reality. These were the reformers—
the longhairs—fanatics.

Oklahoma was very proud of Sabra Cravat, editor, Congresswoman, pioneer. Osage said she embodied the finest spirit of the state and of the
Southwest. When ten of Osage's most unctuous millionaires contributed fifty
thousand dollars each for a five-hundred-thousand-dollar statue that should
embody the Oklahoma Pioneer no one was surprised to hear that the sculptor,
Masja Krbecek, wanted to interview Sabra Cravat.

Osage was not familiar with the sculpture of Krbecek, but it was impressed
with the price of it. Half a million dollars for a statue!

"Certainly," said the committee, calmly. "He's the best there is. Half a
million is nothing for his stuff. He wouldn't kick a pebble for less than a
quarter of a million."

"Do you suppose he'll do her as a pioneer woman in a sunbonnet? Holding little Cim by the hand, huh? Or maybe in a covered wagon."

Sabra received Krbecek in a simple (draped) dress. He turned out to be a quiet, rather snuffy little Pole in eyeglasses, who looked more like a tailor—a "little" tailor—than a sculptor. His eye roamed about the living room of the house on Kihekah. The old wooden house had been covered with plaster in a deep warm shade much the color of the native clay; the gimcrack porch and the cupolas had been torn away and a great square veranda and a terrace built at the side, away from the street and screened by a thick hedge and an iron grille. It was now, in fact, much the house that Yancey had planned when Sabra first built it years ago. The old pieces of mahogany and glass and silver were back, triumphant again over the plush and brocade with which Sabra had furnished the house when new. The old, despised since pioneer days, was again the fashion in Osage. There was the DeGrasse silver; the cake dish with the carefree cupids, the mantelpiece figures of china, even the hand-woven coverlet that Mother Bridget had given her that day in Wichita so long ago. Its rich deep blue was unfaded.

"You are very comfortable here in Oklahoma," said Masja Krbecek. He pronounced it syllable by syllable, painfully. O-kla-ho-ma.

"It is a very simple home," Sabra replied, "compared to the other places you have seen hereabouts."

"It is the home of a good woman," said Krbecek, dryly.

Sabra was a trifle startled, but she said thank you, primly.

"You are a Congress member, you are editor of a great newspaper, you are well known through the country. You American women, you are really amazing."

Again Sabra thanked him.

"Tell me, will you, my dear lady," he went on, "some of the many interesting things about your life and that of your husband, this Yancey Cravat who so far preceded his time."

So Sabra told him. Somehow, as she talked, the years rolled back, curtain after curtain, into the past. The Run. Then they were crossing the prairie, there was the first glimpse of the mud wallow that was Osage, the church meeting in the tent, the Pegler murder, the outlaws, the early years of the paper, the Indians, oil. She talked very well in her clear, decisive voice. At his request she showed him the time-yellowed photographs of Yancey, of herself. Krbecek listened. At the end, "It is touching," he said. "It makes me weep." Then he kissed her hand and went away, taking one or two of the old photographs with him.

The statue of the Spirit of the Oklahoma Pioneer was unveiled a year later, with terrific ceremonies. It was an heroic figure of Yancey Cravat stepping forward with that light graceful stride in the high-heeled Texas star. boots, the skirts of the Prince Albert billowing behind with the vigor of his movements, the sombrero atop the great menacing buffalo head, one beautiful hand resting lightly on the weapon in his two-gun holster. Behind him, one hand just touching his shoulder for support, stumbled the weary, blanketed figure of an Indian.

25

SABRA CRAVAT, CONGRESSWOMAN from Oklahoma, had started a campaign against the disgraceful condition of the new oil towns. With an imposing party of twenty made up of front-page oil men, Senators, Congressmen, and editors, she led the way to Bowlegs, newest and crudest of the new oil strikes.

Cities like Osage were suave enough in a surface way. But what could a state do when oil was forever surging up in unexpected places, bringing the days of the Run back again? At each newly discovered pool there followed the rush and scramble. Another Bret Harte town sprang up on the prairie; fields oozed slimy black; oil rigs clanked; false-front wooden shacks lined a one-street village. Dance halls. Brothels. Gunmen. Brawls. Heat. Flies. Dirt. Crime. The clank of machinery. The roar of traffic boiling over a road never meant for more than a plodding wagon. Nitro-glycerin cars bearing their deadly freight. Overalls, corduroys, blue prints, engines. The human scum of each new oil town was like the scum of the Run, but harder, crueler, more wolfish and degraded.

The imposing party, in high-powered motor cars, bumped over the terrible roads, creating a red dust barrage.

"It is all due to our rotten Oklahoma state politics," Sabra explained to the great Senator from Pennsylvania who sat at her right and the great editor from New York who sat at her left in the big luxurious car. "Our laws are laughed at. The Capitol is rotten with graft. Anything goes. Oklahoma is still a Territory in everything but title. This town of Bowlegs. It's a throw-back to the frontier days of forty years ago—and worse. It's like the old Cimarron. People who have lived in Osage all their lives don't know what goes on out here. They don't care. It's more oil, more millions. That's all. Any one of you men, well known as you are, could come out here, put on overalls, and be as lost as though you had vanished in the wilderness."

The Pennsylvania Senator laughed a plump laugh and with the elbow nearest Sabra made a little movement that would have amounted to a nudge— in anyone but a Senator from Pennsylvania. "What they need out here is a woman Governor—eh, Lippmann!" to the great editor.

Sabra said nothing.

On the drive out from Osage they stopped for lunch in an older oil town hotel dining room—a surprisingly good lunch, the Senators and editors were glad to find, with a tender steak, and little green onions, and near beer, and cheese, and coffee served in great thick cups, hot and strong and refreshing. The waitress was deft and friendly: a tall angular woman with something frank and engaging about the two circles of vermilion on the parchment of her withered cheeks.

"How are you, Nettie?" Sabra said to her.

"I'm grand, Mis' Cravat. How's all your folks?"

The Senator from Ohio winked at Sabra. "You're a politician, all right."

Arrived at Bowlegs, Sabra showed them everything, pitilessly. The dreadful town lay in the hot June sun, a scarred thing, flies buzzing over it, the oil drooling down its face, a slimy stream. A one-street wooden shanty town, like the towns of the old Territory days, but more sordid. A red-cheeked young Harvard engineer was their official guide: an engaging boy in bone-rimmed glasses and a very blue shirt that made his pink cheeks pinker. That is what I wanted my Cim to be, Sabra thought with a great wrench at her heart. I mustn't think of that now.

The drilling of the oil. The workmen's shanties. The trial of a dance-hall girl in the one-room pine shack that served as courtroom. The charge, non-payment of rent. The little room, stifling, stinking, was already crowded. Men and women filled the doorway, lounged in the windows. The judge was a yellow-faced fellow with a cud of tobacco in his cheek, and a Sears-Roebuck catalogue and a single law book on a shelf as his library. It was a trial by jury. The jurors were nine in number, their faces a rogues' gallery.

There had happened to be nine men loafing near by. It might have been less or more. Bowlegs did not consider these fine legal points. They wore overalls and shirts. The defendant was a a tiny rat-faced girl in a soiled green dress that parodied the fashions, a pathetic green poke bonnet, down-at-heel shoes, and a great run in her stocking. Her friends were there—a dozen or more dance-hall girls in striped overalls and jockey caps or knee-length gingham dresses with sashes. Their ages ranged from sixteen to nineteen, perhaps. It was incredible that life, in those few years, could have etched that look on their faces.

The girls were charming, hospitable. They made way for the imposing visitors. "Come on in," they said. "How-do! "—like friendly children. The mid-afternoon sun was pitiless on their sick eyes, their bad skin, their unhealthy hair. Clustered behind the rude bench on which the jury sat, the girls, from time to time, leaned a sociable elbow on a juryman's shoulder, occasionally enlivening the judicial proceedings by a spirited comment uttered in defense of their sister, and spoken in the near-by ear or aloud, for the benefit of the close-packed crowd.

"She never done no such thing!"

"He's a damn liar, an' I can prove it."

No one, least of all the tobacco-chewing judge, appeared to find these girlish informalities at all unusual in the legal conduct of the case.

In the corner of the little room was a kind of pen made of wooden slats, like a sizable chicken coop, and in it, on the floor, lay a man.

"What's he there for?" Sabra asked one of the girls. "What is that?"

"That's Bill. He's in jail. He shot a man last night, and he's up for carrying concealed weapons. It ain't allowed."

"I'm going to talk to him," said Sabra. And crossed the room, through the crowd. The jurors had just filed out. They repaired to a draw at the side of the road to make their finding. Two or three of the dance-hall girls, squatted on the floor, were talking to Bill through the bars. They asked Sabra her name, and she told them, and they gave her their own. Toots. Peewee. Bee.

The face of the boy on the floor was battered and blood-caked. There was a festering sore on his left hand, and the hand and arm were swollen and angry looking.

"You were carrying a concealed weapon?" Sabra asked, squatting there with the girls. A Senator or two and an editor were just behind her.

An injured look softened Bill's battered features. He pouted like a child. "No, ma'am. I run the dance hall, see? And I was standing in the middle of the floor, working, and I had the gun right in my hand. Anybody could see. I wasn't carrying no concealed weapon."

The jury filed back. Not guilty. The rat-faced girl's shyster lawyer said something in her ear. She spoke in a dreadful raucous voice, simpering.

"I sure thank you, gents."

The dance-hall girls cheered feebly.

Out of that fetid air into the late afternoon blaze. "The dance halls open about nine," Sabra said. "We'll wait for that. In the meantime I'll show you their rooms. Their rooms———" she looked about for the fresh-cheeked Harvard boy. "Why, where———"

"There's some kind of excitement," said the New York editor. "People have been running and shouting. Over there in that field we visited awhile ago. Here comes our young friend now. Perhaps he'll tell us."

The Harvard boy's color was higher still. He was breathing fast. He had been running. His eyes shone behind the bone-rimmed spectacles.

"Well, folks, we'll never have a narrower squeak than that."

"What?"

"They put fifty quarts in the Gypsy pool but before she got down the oil came up————"

"Quarts of what?" interrupted an editorial voice.

"Oh—excuse me—quarts of nitro-glycerin."

"My God?"

"It's in a can, you know. A thing like a can. It never had a chance to explode down there. It just shot up with the gas and oil. If it had hit the ground everything for miles around would have been shot to hell and all of us killed. But he caught it. They say he just ran back like an outfielder and gauged it with his eye while it was up in the air, and ran to where it would fall, and caught it in his two arms, like a baby, right on his chest. It didn't explode. But he's dying. Chest all caved in. They've sent for the ambulance."

"Who? Who's he?"

"I don't know his real name. He's an old bum that's been around the field, doing odd jobs and drinking. They say he used to be quite a fellow in Oklahoma in his day. Picturesque pioneer or something. Some call him old Yance and I've heard others call him Sim or Simeon or————"

Sabra began to run across the road.

"Mrs. Cravat! You mustn't—where are you going?"

She ran on, across the oil-soaked field and the dirt, in her little buckled high-heeled slippers. She did not even know that she was running. The crowd was dense around some central object. They formed a wall—roustabouts, drillers, tool dressers, shooters, pumpers. They were gazing down at something on the ground.

"Let me by! Let me by!" They fell back before this white-faced woman with the white hair.

He lay on the ground, a queer, crumpled, broken figure. She flung herself on the oil-soaked earth beside him and lifted the magnificent head gently, so that it lay cushioned by her arm. A little purplish bubble rose to his lips, and she wiped it away with her fine white handkerchief, and another rose to take its place.

"Yancey! Yancey!"

He opened his eyes—those ocean-gray eyes with the long curling lashes like a beautiful girl's. She had thought of them often and often, in an agony of pain. Glazed now, unseeing.

Then, dying, they cleared. His lips moved. He knew her. Even then, dying, he must speak in measured verse.

" 'Wife and mother—you stainless woman—hide me—hide me in your love!' "

She had never heard a line of it. She did not know that this was Peer Gynt, humbled before Solveig. The once magnetic eyes glazed, stared; were eyes no longer.

She closed them, gently. She forgave him everything. Quite simply, all unknowing, she murmured through her tears the very words of Solveig.

"Sleep, my boy, my dearest boy."

Saratoga Trunk

1

THEY WERE INTERVIEWING Clint Maroon. They were always interviewing old Colonel Maroon. Though he shunned publicity, never had held public office and wasn't really a Colonel at all, he possessed that magnetic flamboyant quality which makes readable news. It wasn't his wealth. America had fifty men as rich as he. Certainly it wasn't social position. He and the spectacularly beautiful Clio Maroon never had figured in formal New York society. It could not have been his great age merely which had brought the reporters into his hotel suite at Saratoga on this, his eighty-ninth birthday, for the newspapers had seized upon him with yelps of joy when first he had dawned dramatically upon their horizon at thirty. They had swarmed on him throughout the threescore years that had elapsed since then; when he turned forty; at his dashing half-century mark; at sixty, when there was scarcely a glint of gray in the reddish-brown hair that was exactly the color of a ripe pecan shell; at seventy, eighty, eighty-five. If Clint Maroon bought an old master or a new yacht, sold short or emerged from a chat with the President of the United States, streamlined one of his railroads or donated a million to charity or science, won the Grand National or took up ice-skating (ever so slightly bow-legged, proof of his Texas past) there the reporters were, clamoring for him.

"I'm from the *Times*, Mr. Maroon . . . *Herald Tribune*, Colonel . . . *News* . . . *American* . . . *Sun* . . . *Post* . . . *World-Telegram* . . . My paper would like to know if it's true that you . . ."

They liked him. He never said, "Hiyah, boys!" with that false jocularity they so quickly detected. He never whipped a brown oily cylinder out of his vest pocket with a patronizing, "Have a good cigar." His manner was courteous without being hearty. Quietly he answered their questions when he was able, always taking his time about it. Just as deliberately he had said, on occasion, "Sorry, young man, but I can't answer that question at this time." Curiously soft-voiced and rather drawling for so big and full-blooded a man, he sometimes gave the effect of being actually shy. Easterners for the most part, the New York newspapermen did not realize that in the Far West of the bad old days the man who was slowest in his speech was likely to be quickest on the draw. They had, in fact, forgotten that Texas was Clint Maroon's early background. He never had reminded them.

Certain wise ones among the fraternity said it was Mrs. Maroon who really ran the show. "She's always there," these wily craftsmen observed, "if you'll notice, standing beside him with her hand on his arm, like royalty, looking so damned beautiful and queenly you think, Boy! She must have wowed them when she was young. She doesn't talk much, but watch those eyes of hers. Big and black and soft, and what they miss you could put in your own eye. But when she does speak up, very soft and sort of Southern, she says something. Nice, too, both of them, but I don't know, cagey, in a way. I've seen her pinch him when he was headed for a boner, with that lovely kind of heartbreaking smile on her face all the time he took to cover up and start fresh. Some day I'd like to dig way back on those two. I'll bet there's gold in them thar hills."

Mr. and Mrs. Clinton Maroon, Fifth Avenue and Seventy-third Street. Clint and Clio back in the old Texas, New Orleans and Saratoga days. But curiously enough, for all their interviewing, none of the newspapermen or women really knew about that. These two had been rich, respectable and powerful for sixty years. Newspaper reporters die young, or quit their jobs.

Possessed of a dramatic quality, together with vitality and bounce, a zest for life and an exquisite sense of timing, the Maroons had brightened many a dull Monday morning news page. They were almost incredibly handsome, this pair, with a splendor of face and figure that had crumbled little under the onslaught of the years. Hospitable, friendly, interested in life—particularly in your life, your plans, your conversation—hundreds liked and respected them, but amazingly few really knew them. Seeming frank and accessible, the truth was that they went their way in a kind of splendid isolation. They consistently shied away from the photographers. It was the one point on which they met the news fraternity reluctantly.

"Oh, come on now, Colonel! Please, Mrs. Maroon! Just one shot. You haven't murdered anybody."

"That's what you think," Clint Maroon retorted.

Much as they liked him, the general opinion among the newsmen lately had been that the old boy was cracking up. When they came to interview him on business or political or philanthropic or international affairs he now tried to tell them outrageous yarns palpably culled from Western thrillers and lurid detective stories. It was difficult to lead him back to the hard modern facts about which they had come to see him. Among themselves they confided, "Old Maroon's getting a little balmy, if you ask me. At that, he's good for his age. Crowding ninety. Gosh, ninety! You should live so long, not me."

And now on this, his eighty-ninth birthday, old Clint Maroon, in spite of wars, panics, and world chaos, still was triumphantly news. Cameras, candid and flashlight; reporters, male and female, special and news, all had traveled up to Saratoga on this broiling August day. They were there not only because the ancient's natal day found him at the quaint little spa at the beginning of the racing season when the thermometer kissed the ninety-degree mark, but because he had just made a gesture so lavish, so dramatic that it promised to land him on the front page of every newspaper in the country along with other world phenomena.

Reporters had swarmed by plane, motorcar and train. It was four o'clock on a brilliant summer afternoon. "What the hell's the good of living to be eighty-nine and piling up eighty-nine millions and more if you can't take yourself a nap or go to the races at four in the afternoon on a day like this!" demanded Matt Quinlan.

"You're above all that at eighty-nine, with eighty-nine millions," said the astringent Trixie Nye of the *Post.*

Short, squat little Balmer of the *Sun,* oldest of the lot and most canny, shook his head while he lighted his pipe, in itself no mean feat. "Not that old bird. Clint's up to something, or Gaffer Balmer has missed his calling all these years."

They roamed the room or sat mopping their flushed faces or stared down at the street below which, for one brief month in the year, wakened from its Victorian serenity to receive the sporting blood, the moneyed, the horse-lovers, the gay, the social, the gambling fraternity of the whole country. The great ancient elms in front of the United States Hotel cast an ineffectual shade upon the burning asphalt and cement.

In the high-ceilinged dim old sitting room of the Maroon suite at the United States Hotel there was something incongruous about those modern hard young faces, that slick mechanical equipment. The carved walnut tables with their liver-colored marble tops, the prancing rockers, the Victorian drapes and steel engravings, the faded ingrain carpets and lumpy upholstery were anachronistic as a background for this dynamic group. The women writers stared with amused eyes at the gas globes of the ponderous chandelier, the men took a sporting shot at the vast cuspidor. Quinlan's lean, worldly face broke into a grin as he noticed the coil of stout rope dangling from a hook near the window. "It's a rope fire escape, by God! I heard they still had 'em but I never believed it."

Ellen Ford of the *Tribune* said, wistfully, "I wish they'd let me see the bathroom. They say the tub and the loo and the washstand are all boxed in black walnut, like coffins."

Tubby Krause wagged a fat and chiding forefinger. "Papa told you to go when you were downstairs."

There was a discreet tap at the outer door, they turned swiftly to face it, but it was a waiter, it was a little flock of waiters in the best Saratoga manner, white-clad, black-skinned, gold-toothed, aware of the dignity of their calling and the tradition of the house. Trays and trays and trays. Scotch, rye, bourbon. Iced coffee, iced tea. Mint and gin pleasantly mingled. Lemon, cream, sandwiches. Tinkle of ice, clink of silver.

"Hepp you ladies and geppmen or you prefer to hepp youseff?"

"Hepp ourseff," said Larry Conover, and lost no time. "One you boys got a tip on a horse?"

"Honey Chile, straight," the procession answered as one man; bowed and withdrew with a rustle of starched white uniforms.

"Is it always like this?" inquired one of the newer men. Before anyone could answer, the door to the adjoining room opened, the newspaper reporters turned their alert faces like a battery of searchlights on the pair who entered.

"Good afternoon, ladies! Glad to see you, gentlemen! Keep your seats. Go on with your drinks."

"Hiyah, Mr. Maroon!"

They looked like royalty—rowdy royalty, and handsome. Almost a century of life rested as rakishly on his head as the sombrero he so often wore. A columnist once said that Clint Maroon, even in top hat and tails, gave the effect of wearing spurs, chaps and sombrero.

"Clio, these are the ladies and gentlemen of the press. Some of them you have met before. . . . Mrs. Maroon." He pronounced her name with such effect that you felt you had almost heard a brass horn Ta-TA-ah-ah-ah!

Both wore white; there was almost an other-world look about them. The reporters reproached themselves inwardly for being so hot, so sweaty and unkempt. As though sensing this, Mrs. Maroon now said in her lovely leisurely voice, "How young you all are! It refreshes me just to look at you. Don't you feel that, Clint?"

"Swap you ten years for ten millions, Mr. Maroon," said the brash Quinlan.

"Wish I could do it, Matt. Or there was a time when I'd have wished it. Not so sure, now. Take your coats off, take your coats off! Be comfortable."

Clio Maroon at seventy-nine stood straight and slim as a girl. Her unwithered lips were soft and full, her skin was gently wrinkled like old silk crepe, its lines almost unnoticeable at a distance. Even the least perceptive among those present must have felt something exotic and quickening about her. Ten years younger than he, she still was beautiful with a timeless beauty like that of ivory or marble or a painting that takes on added magnificence with age. Her white hair was still so strongly mixed with black that the effect was steel-gray. In certain lights it had a bluish tinge. Springing strongly away from brow and temples, it was amazingly thick and vigorous for a woman of her age. But all this you remarked at a second or third glance. It was the eyes you first saw, liquid, clear, softly bright; merry, too, as though she enjoyed outer life with the added fillip of an inner secret. She stood beside her towering handsome husband, but a little behind him, too, as women of Victorian days had walked in deference to the male. Certain seasoned newspapermen knew there was more than mere symbolism in her standing thus. They had watched the workings of her quiet generalship; they knew she sustained and directed him. Her delicate brown hand resting so trustingly on his arm was not above giving him a furtive little pinch in warning or reproof. They had even seen him wince on occasion, and once or twice he had been known to emit an ouch of surprised remonstrance at a particularly sharp and sudden tweak.

"Oh, Clint, *chéri!*" Mrs. Maroon would say, her tone one of fond sympathy. "Is it your arthritis again?"

Though she appeared fragile there yet was about her a hair-wire resilience that bespoke more vitality than he possessed in spite of his bulk, his high color and the auburn still glowing in his hair that even now was only sprinkled with white. Though marked for the woodsman's ax, the juices still coursed through the old tree.

Now the photographers sprang into action. Almost automatically he and she raised protesting hands; then she smiled as though remembering something. Clint Maroon waved one great arm. "All right. Shoot! I'm through with skulking. My grandpappy fought in the Alamo. I reckon I can face a battery of cameras without flinching." Suddenly he winced. Then he reached across his own girth and patted his wife's hand that lay so innocently in the crook of his other arm. "No more pinching to shut me up, Clio. Time's past for that, too. From now on I'm making a clean breast of it. This is going to be a different America. We won't live to see it, but we said we were going to try to make up for what we'd done to it."

She smiled again, wistfully, and shook her head a little, and the reporters thought, she must have a time of it managing the old boy now that his mind is slipping a bit. The candid camera men stood on chairs and surveyed their victims from strange angles; the little boxes clicked. The two white-clad figures posed smiling and serene.

Len Brisk of the *Telegram* dismissed the camera men with a gesture of clearing the decks for action. "All right, boys! You've got yours. Beat it."

You heard the well-bred authoritative voice of Keppel of the New York *Times*. "Mr. Maroon, there are certain questions my paper would like me to ask you. Is it true . . ."

The barrage was on. Is it true you are giving your Fifth Avenue house to the city, outright, to be used for a Service Clubhouse? Is it true you've turned your collection of paintings over to the Metropolitan Museum? Is it true your yacht is to be a government training ship? Is it true your Adirondacks estate is to be a free summer camp for boys? Is it true you're giving away every penny of your fortune to the government after you've pensioned your old employes? And that you're keeping just enough for you and Mrs. Maroon to live on in comfort? Is it true . . . is it true . . . is it true . . .

He replied in the soft-spoken Texas drawl that had taken on the clipped overtones of authority. "All true. But unimportant. That stuff's not what

I want to tell you about. This time I can give you a real story. It isn't only
something to write about. It's something for Americans to read and realize,
and remember. They'll hate me for it. But anyway, they'll know."

"Yeah, that'll be fine. Uh—look, Colonel, we want————"

"All right, Colonel, but first————"

"First hell! This is first I tell you. In another year, if I live, I'll be ninety.
The way the world is headed I don't know's I want to. Ninety, nearly, and
I'm sick of being a railroad magnate and a collector of art and a Metropolitan
Opera stockholder and director of a lot of fool corporations. It's damned
dull, and always has been. If I was thirty I'd learn to run an airplane. Might
anyway. Next to breaking a bucking bronco that must be more fun than
anything."

"May we say that, Mr. Maroon?"

"God, yes. Say anything you like. I've got nothing to lose now. I'm coming
clean. Listen. Millions, and I had to be respectable. Me, a terror from Texas.
Here you are, smart as they make 'em, you and your kind have been interviewing me for sixty years, ever since I found that fool railroad hanging
around my neck—and you don't know a thing about the real Clint Maroon.
Not a damned thing. Or if you have got it filed away in the morgue somewhere
you're scared to print it while I'm alive. Well, go on. Use it! I'm a Texas
gambler and a killer. I've killed as many men as Jesse James, or almost.
I've robbed my country for sixty years. My father, he ran the town of San
Antonio back in 1840 before the damn Yankees came along and stole his
land for a railroad. That's one reason why I didn't hesitate to steal it back
from them. My grandpappy, old Dacey Maroon, fought the Santa Anna
Mexicans along with Jim Bowie and Bill Travis and Sam Houston. That's
the stock I come from. And what did I do for my country! Stole millions
from millionaires who were stealing each other blind. Another year and
I'll be ninety—the meanest old coot that ever lived to be nearly a hundred————"

"Oh, come on now, Colonel. You know you're a wonderful guy and
everybody's crazy about you and Mrs. Maroon. So stop kidding us and give
us our story in time for the first edition."

"God A'mighty, I'm giving it to you, I tell you! They called us financiers.
Financiers hell! We were a gang of racketeers that would make these apes
today look like kids stealing turnips out of the garden patch. We stole a
whole country—land, woods, rivers, metal. They've got our pictures in the
museums. We ought to be in the rogues' gallery. My day you could get away
with wholesale robbery, bribery in high places and murder—and brag about
it. I was brought up on the stories my father told about 'em—Huntington
and Stanford and Crocker. Two hundred thousand dollars is all they had
amongst them in 1861. And they wanted to build a railroad across a continent.
So they paid a visit to Washington, and they left that two hundred thousand
there. Made no secret of it. They came away with a charter and land grants
and the government's promise to pay in bonds for work in progress. What
did the Central Pacific crowd do! I heard my pa tell how in '63 Phil Stanford—
he was brother of the Governor—drove up to the polls in a buggy when they
were holding elections in San Francisco over a bond issue. Reached into a
bag and began throwing gold pieces to the crowd at the polls, yelling to 'em
to vote the bond issue. They voted it, all right. Do that today and where'd
you land? In jail! Lives and principles, they didn't matter. Same thing in
1880 when I got started. Say, I was as bad as the worst of 'em————"

"Sure, Colonel, we know, we know. You were a bad *hombre* all right."

"You tell us all about that some time. Some other time. And about the day you rode your horse right up to the bar of the Perfessor Saloon in San Antone."

They were being good-natured about it, but they did wish Mrs. Maroon would stop the old coot's nonsense. Pretty soon it would be too late, the races would be over and they'd have to hop back to New York without a chance to use that tip on Honey Chile.

"Sixty years ago, young fella, I'd have wiped that grin off your face with a six-shooter. Fights and feuds and fiestas and fandangoes, that was the program back in Texas where I came from in 1880. People call it romantic now. Well, maybe it was. Anyway we had the use of our legs and arms instead of being just limbless trunks riding around in automobiles the way you softies are today. It's got so you have to jump into a car to go down to the corner to get a pack of cigarettes. Two years ago I went down to Texas, went in an airplane from New York in less time than it used to take us to gallop into town on a Saturday night in the old days. Houston's a stinking oil town now, Dallas sets up to be a style center, San Antonio's full of art and they're starting a movement to run gondolas on the San Antonio River for tourists. My God, I almost had a stroke."

"That's very interesting, Mr. Maroon, but look————"

"I can tell you things if you think that's interesting. Ninety, or nearly. Let 'em put me in jail. If I was to eat two pieces of chocolate cake this minute and drink a quart of champagne I'd be dead in an hour. What can death do to you at ninety that life hasn't done to you already!"

"You're right, Colonel. Uh, look, we've got our edition to make, see. And if you'll just give us what we came for, first, and then————"

"You're deaf and dumb and blind, the lot of you!" His face was dangerously red considering his age and the weather. He snatched his arm free of his wife's restraining hand, his voice rang out with a resonance incredible in an organ that had known almost a century of use. "I tell you I'm giving you the real story if you'd have the sense to see it. I'm giving up my money now because I robbed widows and orphans to get it. That was considered smart in those days. But I'll say this for myself—I didn't want money or position or power for myself. I wanted Clio Dulaine and I had to have those to get her. So I outwitted them and I've outlived them, too, the whole sniveling lot of them—Gould and Vanderbilt and Rockefeller and Morgan and Fisk and Drew. We skimmed a whole nation—took the cream right off the top."

Tubby Krause spoke up soothingly, but even his unctuous voice had the gritty sound of patience nearing exhaustion. "Yep, that's right, Mr. Maroon. You ought to write a book about it. I bet it'd make 'em sit up. Ever read *The Robber Barons?* Great book. Yeh, those were the bad old boys all right. Now, Mr. Maroon, if you'll just answer a couple of questions."

Mrs. Maroon took his great freckled hand in her own two delicate ones; she looked up into his face, earnestly. "You see, Clint, they don't want to hear it. I told you they wouldn't. They don't believe it. Let it go. What does it matter now?"

"Thanks, Mrs. Maroon." It was Quinlan with an edge to his voice. "You understand how it is. We're here to get our story. We've always been on the square with you and the Colonel. And you've been more than square with us. This is our job, see."

"Yah, your jobs!" snarled Maroon to their astonishment, for he had always been as charming as he was considerate. "You young fools! You deserve to lose 'em. I suppose if I told you that Mrs. Maroon is the daughter of a Creole aristocrat and the most famous *placée* in New Orleans back in the '60's, you wouldn't be interested!"

"What's a *placée?*"

"I suppose you never heard of José Llulla, either? Pepe Llulla, they called him, isn't that right, Clio? Long before your day. He fought and won so many duels that he had to start his own cemetery to take care of them. Cemetery of St. Vincent de Paul on Louisa Street. Anybody'll show it to you. Well, now, Mrs. Maroon's grandmother was killed by Pepe Llulla. Jealousy."

The newspaper people were smiling rather uncertainly now. After all, a joke's a joke, they thought, but the old boy was going too far. Mrs. Maroon's musical indolent laugh reassured them. Mischievously she shook her husband's arm as one would remind a dear forgetful child.

"Don't leave out the important things, Clint, *chéri.*" She shut one handsome eye in an amazing and confidential wink. "Surely you won't forget to tell them that Mama was accused of murder. And the scandal was hushed up," Clio Maroon went on, equably. "They said he had died of a heart attack. So then Mama was smuggled out of New Orleans, they sent her to France, and of course that's how I———"

"—came to be educated in a convent," chimed in two of three rather weary voices.

Someone said, "Oh, listen, Mrs. Maroon! You going to start kidding us too? After we've given you the best years of our lives!"

Clio Maroon smiled up at her husband. "You see, dear? Next time. Next time."

"That's right," Len Brisk assured her. "Next time we'll run all that movie stuff, Mr. Maroon, just to show you our hearts are in the right place, even if our heads aren't. Then what'll you do to us?"

"Sue you for a million dollars," Mrs. Maroon put in, swiftly.

"But it's all true!" Clint Maroon shouted. "Damn it, it's all true I tell you! I just want you boys and girls to write it —to write it so that Americans will know that this country today is finer and more honest and more free and democratic than it has been since way back in Revolutionary days. For a century we big fellows could grab and run. They can't do it today. It's going to be the day of the little man. Tell them to have faith and believe that they're the best Americans in the decentest government the world has ever seen. It's true, I tell you. We're just coming out of the darkness. Don't let anyone tell you that America today isn't the———"

"Sure. Sure. We know."

She turned to go then, with a glance at them over her shoulder—a whimsical and appealing glance from those fine eyes that seemed to convey a little secret understanding between her and them. I am leaving an old and sick man in your care, the glance said. Be lenient. Be kind. Aloud, "Don't keep Mr. Maroon too long, will you? And please help yourselves to drinks and sandwiches there on the table. If I come back at the end of—oh—fifteen minutes don't be too cross with me. Mr. Maroon finds this heat rather trying."

"Thanks, Mrs. Maroon. You've been swell. . . . Think it's safe to leave a bunch of newspapermen with all this scotch and rye?"

She went then, carrying herself with such grace and dignity that if it had not been for her steel-gray hair you might have thought her a woman of thirty, her soft draperies flowing after her, her head held high. As she closed the door and vanished she heard Keppel's voice, not quite so suave now, for time was pressing. "Now then, Mr. Maroon, is it true that you . . ." And then the hard incisive tone of Larry Conover's voice keyed to the tempo of the tabloid he represented. "Hi, wait a minute, fellas. Something tells me

Mr. Maroon isn't kidding. Are you, Mr. Maroon? Say, listen, maybe we're missing the real story. What was that again about————"

She made as though to turn back and re-enter the room. But she only hesitated a moment there before the door, and shrugged her shoulders with a little Gallic gesture and smiled and did not listen for more.

She and Clint Maroon had met and fallen instantly in love at breakfast in Madame Begué's restaurant that April Sunday morning in New Orleans, almost sixty years ago. Though perhaps their encounter in the French Market earlier in the day should be called their first meeting. Certainly there he had persisted in staring at her and following her, and he had even attempted to speak to her. She had had to administer punishment, brisk though second-hand—for his boldness.

Clio Dulaine was back in New Orleans after an absence of fifteen years. Though she had left it as a child and had not seen it again until now, when she had just turned twenty, she was as much at home in it, as deeply in love with it as if she were a Creole aristocrat with a century's background of dwelling in the *Vieux Carré*. Throughout the years of her life in France she had heard of New Orleans and learned of it through the memories and longings of two exiled and homesick women—her mother, the lovely Rita Dulaine, and her aunt Belle Piquery. These two, filled with nostalgia for their native and beloved Louisiana city, had lived unwillingly and died resentfully in the Paris to which they had been banished—the Paris of the 1870's. In those years the mind of the girl Clio had become a brimming reservoir for their dreams, their bizarre recollections, their heartsick yearnings. Though they dwelt perforce in France, they really lived in their New Orleans past. The Franco-Prussian War, the occupation of Paris had been to them a minor and faintly annoying incident. Their chief concern with it was that in those confused years their copy of the New Orleans French newspaper *L'Abeille* sometimes failed to arrive on time. Its arrival was an event. They fell upon its meager pages with the eager little cries of women famished for news from home. They devoured every crumb of information— births, deaths, marriages, society, advertisements. Though these two women belonged to that strange and exotic stratum which was the New Orleans underworld, Rita's life had been for many years entwined with that of one of the city's oldest and most aristocratic of families. In that fantastic society she had been the mistress of Nicolas Dulaine, only son of that proud and wealthy family; not only that, she had been known by his name, she was Rita Dulaine, she had lived in the charming little house he had purchased for her in Rampart Street, she had borne him a daughter, she was queen of that half-world peopled by women of doubtful blood. She was a *placée*, she had taken the name of Dulaine, she was the acknowledged beauty in an almost macabre society of strangely lovely women. Her gowns came from Paris, her jewels from the Rue de la Paix, she had traveled abroad with Nicolas Dulaine as his wife. Love, luxury, adulation, even position of a sort, Rita Dulaine had had everything that a beautiful and beloved woman can have except the security of a legal name and a legal right as the consort of Nicolas Dulaine.

The tragedy of Dulaine's death had changed her from a high-spirited and imperious woman to a dazed and broken creature, suddenly sallow and almost plain at times. Even Aunt Belle Piquery, her older sister, Belle the practical, the realistic, had been unable to urge her out of her valley of *douleur*. Usually after a ship's mail had brought them a little bundle made up of back numbers of *L'Abeille*, Rita was plunged deeper than ever in gloom. Whenever the words appeared in the newspaper's columns—Madame

Nicolas Dulaine—they seemed to leap out at her as though printed in red letters a foot high. This was his widow. This woman lived and he was dead. It was she who had really killed him with her possessiveness and her arrogance and her spite. Rita was long past weeping, but she would begin to weep again, dry tears. Her face, lovely still, would become distorted, her eyes would stare out hot and bright, her hand would clutch her throat as if she were choking, the sobs would come, hard and dry, racking her.

Then Angélique Pluton, whom they called Kakaracou—Kaka, her maid and Clio's nurse—would hold her in her arms like a baby, and soothe her and murmur to her. She spoke in a curious jargon, a mixture of French, Spanish, New Orleans colloquialisms, African Negro. "Hush, my baby, my baby. Spare your pretty eyes. There are dukes over here and kings and princes waiting to marry you. You will go back to New Orleans in your own golden carriage and they'll crawl at your feet, those stony-faced ones."

"I'll never go back, Kaka. I'll die here. They won't let me come back. They said they'll put me in prison. They said I killed him. I was only trying to kill myself because I couldn't live without him."

Brisk Belle Piquery would say, "You're only making yourself sick, Rita. I think you enjoy it. After all, they threw me out, too, and said they'd put me in prison if I ever showed my face again in New Orleans. And I was only your sister."

"There you go reproaching me. I wish I were dead too. Why didn't I kill myself! I wanted to."

"You didn't really," the practical Belle would say. "People hardly ever do. You wanted to keep him, of course, and you thought if he saw you pressing a pistol against your heart—well, there, there, let's not talk about it. He should have known better than to snatch it away, poor boy. Anyway, he's dead. Nothing can bring him back now. We'll be dead, too, first thing you know. So let's enjoy life while we can."

"You've never really loved, Bella. You don't know."

"I've loved lots of them," Aunt Belle retorted blithely. "I spent my life at it, didn't I! Only with me it was a career and with you it was your whole existence."

This elicited a little scream of pained remonstrance from the New Orleans Camille. "Belle! How can you speak like that of my love for Nicolas!"

"Now don't flare up, Rita. I just meant I know he was your life, but you expected too much. You even thought he would marry you after Clio was born. Imagine! Such a *bêtise!*"

"He would have, if it hadn't been for Them and Her."

"If it makes you feel better to believe that, then go on believing it. All I ever expected in life was a little fun and a chance to die respectable and to be buried in the cemetery of St. Louis with my name in gold letters—Belle Piquery—and chrysanthemums on All Saints' Day—though who'd bring them I don't know But when I die, that's where I want to be. They'll let me come back to New Orleans then. You'll do that for your Aunt Bella, won't you, Clio?"

It was a strange life the two women lived in the charming little Paris flat overlooking the Bois—the flat paid for by Them with threat money and hush money. But it was stranger still for the child Clio when, at sixteen, she emerged from the convent school. And strangest of all was the sight they presented as they drove in the Bois or walked in the Champs Elysées. Rita Dulaine, tragic in black, her great dark eyes demanding sympathy, her sable garments chic as only the Paris couturiers could make them. By her side the bouncing Belle in such a welter of flounce and furbelow that it was almost impossible to tell where bosom began and bouffant draperies left off. Their carriage was a landaulet with a little cushioned seat opposite the large tufted one, and on this, her back to the driver's box, perched Clio, her legs, far too long for this cramped little bench, doubled under her voluminous skirts, primly. Beside her, bolt upright, her spare, straight back disdaining the upholstery, sat Kakaracou with dignity enough for all. Her skin was neither black nor coffee-colored but the shade of a ripe fig, purplish dusted with gray. Above this, and accentuating the tone, reared the tignon with which her head always was bound, a gaudy turbanlike arrangement of flaming orange or purple or pink or scarlet, characteristic of the New Orleans Negro.

Certainly the occupants of the landaulet were bizarre enough to attract attention even in the worldly Paris. But the figure perched on the driver's seat held the added fillip of surprise. Seated there, his legs braced against the high footboard, his knees covered with a driver's rug, his powerful arms and hands managing the two neat chestnuts with a true horseman's deftness of touch, there seemed nothing remarkable about the coachman, Cupidon. It was only when he threw aside the rug, clambered down over the wheel as agilely as a monkey and stood at the curb that you saw with staring unbelief the man's real dimensions. The large head, the powerful arms and chest belonged to a dwarf, a little man not more than three feet high. His bandy legs were like tiny stumps to which the wee feet were attached. This gave him a curiously rolling gait like that of a diminutive drunken sailor on shore leave. The eyes in the young-old face were tender, almost wistful; the mouth sardonic, the expression pugnacious or mischievous by turn. This was Cupidon, whom they fondly called Cupide; bodyguard, coachman, major-domo. When he spoke, which was rarely, it was in a surprisingly sweet clear tenor like that of a choirboy whose voice has just changed. He might have been any age—fifteen, twenty, thirty, forty. There were those who said that, though white, he was Kakaracou's son. Certainly she bullied and pampered him by turns. Sometimes you saw her withered hand resting tenderly on the tiny man's head; sometimes she cuffed him smartly as though he were a naughty child. She managed to save the choicest tidbits for his plate after the others had finished, she filled his glass with good red wine of the country as they sat at the servants' table, he in his specially built high chair on which he clambered so nimbly up and down.

"Drink your red wine, Little One. It will make you strong."

Instead of thumping his chest or flexing his arm he would rap his great head briskly. "I don't need red wine to make me strong. I'm strong enough. Here's my weapon." But he would toss down the glassful, nevertheless, giving the effect as he did so of a wickedly precocious little boy in his cups. Everyone in the household knew that his boast was no idle one. That head, hard and thick as a cannonball, was almost as effective when directed against an enemy. Thigh-high to a normally built man, he would run off a few steps, then charge like a missile, his head thrust forward and down, goat fashion. On a frontal attack, men twice his size had been known to go down with one grunt, like felled oxen.

Except for her years at the convent in Tours this, then, was the weird household in which Clio Dulaine had spent her girlhood exile. But then, it did not seem strange to her. Kakaracou and Cupidon both had been part of the Dulaine ménage in Clio's infancy when they had lived so luxiously, so gaily in the house on Rampart Street in New Orleans. They were as much a part of her life as her mother or Aunt Belle Piquery. And all four of them dinned New Orleans into her ears, all four spoke of it with the nostalgia of the exiled, each in his or her own wistful way.

Rita Dulaine from her couch before the fire would stare into the flames like one hypnotized. It was as though she saw the past there, flickering and dying. "There's no society here in Paris to compare with the salon that your papa and I had in Rampart Street. The élite came to us. Oh, not those Creole sticks with their dowdy black clothes and their cold, hard faces."

"But Papa was a Creole. The Dulaines, you always told me, were the oldest and most————"

"Yes, yes. But he was my—he was your papa. His family, though, they were cruel and hard, they made me leave New Orleans after the—the—accident—after your papa was hurt—after he had a heart attack————" She would fall to weeping again, after all these years, if the dry gasping sounds she made could be called weeping.

Clio would rush to her, she would put her strong young arms about the woman's racked body, she would press her fresh young cheek against the other's ravaged one. "Don't, *chérie*, don't. Let's not talk about that any more. Let's talk about Great-Grand'mère Clio Bonnevie, how she came to New Orleans with the troupe of Monsieur Louis Tabary, and how they had to play in tents or vacant shops, and how the audiences behaved—go on, tell me again, from the beginning."

The girl herself had the face of an actress, inherited from that other Clio who had come to New Orleans in 1791, one of a homeless refugee band of players who had fled the murderous Negro uprising in the French West Indies. The features hadn't quite crystallized yet, but the face was one of potential beauty—mobile, alight with intelligence, the eyes large and lustrous like her mother's, the mouth wide and sensual like that of her father, the dead Nicolas Dulaine.

"Well," Rita would begin, suddenly gay again. "I heard it only from Grand'mère Vaudreuil who was, of course, as you know, the daughter of Great-Grand'mère Bonnevie." Hearing her reminiscing thus, one would have thought her a descendant of a long line of Louisiana aristocrats rather than the woman she really was. The formality of marriage had not been part of her lineage. Grand'mère Vaudreuil and Great-Grand'mère Bonnevie had lived much as she lived. Men had loved them, they had begotten children, Rita Dulaine had emerged from this murky background as a water lily lifts its creamy petals out of the depths of a muddy pond. "Of course you know Grand'mère Vaudreuil was the talk of New Orleans in her day because she was so beautiful and because José Llulla—Pepe Llulla, they called him—fought a duel with her protector. The duel was fought in St. Anthony's Garden just behind the Cathedral of St. Louis. They say he had his own cemetery, José Llulla, he was such a hothead and so formidable a duellist. . . . Oh, yes, Great-Grand'mère Bonnevie, they say she was a superb actress, you know she came over from the French West Indies with Monsieur Tabary's troupe, they played in the very first theater in New Orleans. You should have heard Mama tell of how Great-Grand'mère told her about the way the audiences used to fight to get in, the roughs and the élite all mixed up together. We've always loved the theater, our family, it dates from then, no doubt. . . . Your papa and I used to go to the French Opera, and sometimes after the play we entertained friends at home. . . . The house in Rampart Street had a lovely garden at the back paved with red brick, cool and fresh, and a fountain in the center. There were camellias and azaleas and mimosa and crepe myrtle. In the evening, the perfume was so heavy it made you swoon . . ."

She would forget all about Grand'mère Vaudreuil and Great-Grand'mère Bonnevie, she would live again her own past, drinking deep though she knew it would not slake her thirst, as a wanderer in the desert drinks of the alkaline water because there is no other.

"Before you were born your papa had built a little *garçonnière* at the far end of the garden facing the house. You were to live there with Kaka as nurse; all the little New Orleans boys of good family lived in their own houses—*garçonnières,* they are called—near the big house. He was so sure you were going to be a boy. He was disappointed at first, but then he said the next would be a boy. I said we should call him Nicolas Dulaine, I am sure he would have consented if he . . . Your little dresses were the finest embroidery and handmade lace, they were brought from France; he always said there was nothing in New Orleans fine enough. My dresses, too, came from . . .''

Clio began to find this a trifle dull. Aunt Belle Piquery's memories were of lustier stuff.

"You needn't talk to me about the food of Paris. I never tasted here such bouillabaisse and such shrimps and crab as we have in New Orleans. Marseilles bouillabaisse isn't to be compared with it. And the pompano, the lovely pompano, where else in the world is there a fish so delicate and at the same time so rich . . . ? *Bisque écrevisse Louisiane* . . . the *bouilli* . . . the hard-shell crab stew . . . soft-shell turtle ragout . . . the six-course Sunday morning breakfasts at Begué's . . . I used to love to go to the French Market myself in the morning, it made you hungry just to see the vegetables and fruits and fish spread out so crisp and appetizing almost with the dew still on them. On Sunday morning the French Market is like a court levee''—— unconsciously Aunt Belle lapsed into the present tense, so vivid were her longings and memories—"it's the meeting place for society on Sunday mornings after early Mass at St. Louis Cathedral. Or we sometimes go to late Mass and then to Begué's for breakfast. But first usually we like to spoil our appetite by eating hot *jambalaya* in the French Market, and delicious hot coffee————''

"Jambalaya! What's that, Aunt Belle? It sounds heavenly.''

"It's a Creole dish, hot and savory. Garlic and chorices and ham and rice and tomatoes and onion and shrimp or oysters all stewed up together————''

By this time Clio's mouth would be watering. Aunt Belle Piquery was off on another excursion into the past. "During Mardi Gras we'd have a tallyho or a great victoria and there we'd sit, viewing the parades, or we'd see them from a balcony in North Rampart or Royal Street. We never went near Canal, it wasn't chic. Your mama never went with us. She and Nicolas were very grand and stayed by themselves; you'd have thought Rita was *chacalata.* But then, I never held it against her. If Rita did go out people stared at her more than at any Carnival Queen, she was so much more beautiful.''

The girl, listening avidly, would press a quick clutching hand on her aunt's plump knee. "Am I beautiful, Aunt Belle? Like Mama?''

"You, *minette!* A little scrawny thing like you!''

"I will be, though.''

"Maybe, when you fill out. Your eyes, they're not bad, but your mouth's too big.''

"You wait. You wait and see. I'll be beautiful, but I shan't be the way you and Mama were. I shall marry and be very rich and most respectable. But quite, quite respectable. Not like you.''

A smart little slap from Aunt Belle's open palm. "You nasty little *griffe,* you! How dare you talk to me like that!''

The girl did not even deign to put her hand to her smarting cheek. Her eyes blazed. It was the epithet she resented, not the slap. "Don't you dare call me that! I'm a Dulaine. The royal blood of France flows in my veins.''

"*Quelle blague!* Your Grandmama Vaudreuil was a free woman of color. Your mother's a————''

"I'm a Dulaine! My father was Nicolas Dulaine. You wait. You'll see! My life will be different."

Aunt Belle Piquery laughed comfortably and took another chocolate from the little silver bonbon dish that always somehow managed to be on a tabouret beside her chair. "You'll be a fool about men just the way we all were—your mama and me and your Grandmother Vaudreuil and Great-Grandmama Bonnevie."

"I won't I tell you!"

"Though I honestly can't say I regret a thing I've done. I've had a fine time and would have yet if Rita hadn't gone waving pistols around. Don't take 'em seriously, I always told Rita."

The girl Clio looked at the overplump aging woman; her eyes were pitying but not contemptuous. "You and Mama aren't Dulaines. I am. My life's going to be different. I shan't be a fool about men. They'll be fools about me."

At this Aunt Belle laughed until she choked on a bit of chocolate, gasped, coughed, and waddled off to regale Rita and Kakaracou with this chit's presumption.

"Wiser than her elders," Kakaracou commented sagely when she heard it.

And now Rita Dulaine lay in the little cemetery outside St. Cloud; and Aunt Belle Piquery too knew at last the belated respectability of a solitary—though earthy—resting place in the cemetery of St. Louis in New Orleans, with her name in gold letters on the tomb and Clio and Kakaracou and Cupidon to place upon it the chrysanthemums that marked All Saints' Day. Years before she had slyly bought the space under another name, for the cemetery of St. Louis was not for the Belle Piquerys. The stately white-washed tombs bore the names of the socially elect of New Orleans. There was sardonic humor in the fact that even in death respectability was not to be granted Aunt Belle. For by the time Clio, an orphan of twenty, had brought Belle Piquery's earthly remains back to the New Orleans she loved and had seen her safely entombed among the city's élite, certain changes had taken place in these hallowed precincts. The railroad had edged its way along the outskirts of the cemetery, and at night the red light of the semaphore glowed down upon the tomb as though the sign of Belle Piquery's earthly profession haunted her even in this, her last resting place.

2

FROM FRANCE they had sailed back together in the early spring—this strange trio, distributed as befitted their state of being and their station in life. A quartette they might really have been called, for Aunt Belle, the erstwhile voluble and bouncing, now went as a silent passenger in the freight hold; Kakaracou and Cupidon, in the servants' quarters, baffled the ship's officers, what with the color of Kakaracou and the impish proportions of the little man; while the girl Clio, silent, lovely, black-clad, was a piquant source of mystery to the other passengers. New Orleans was their destination, and they seemed to melt into the teeming picturesque city as though they never had left it. Daily, for fifteen years, they had talked of it, had heard its praises sung, had longed for it through the nostalgia of the languishing Rita and the lusty Belle.

But even Kakaracou, who treated her like a child, was a little awed by the imperious and strategic generalship with which Clio Dulaine took possession of her New Orleans patrimony. Shabby and neglected though it was, Clio went immediately to the old house on Rampart Street. Mice scuttled and squeaked in it, windows were cracked or broken, the jalousies rattled eerily, rank weeds choked the garden once heavy with the fragrance of camellias and mimosa. The little brick *garçonnière* that faced the house at the rear was overgrown with a tangle of wistaria and bougainvillaea so that the iron lacework of the lovely gallery was completely hidden. The very street itself had taken on a look of decay.

Clio Dulaine stood surveying this scene of ruin, the half-smile on her face curiously cynical for one so young. Then to the shocked dismay of Kakaracou and Cupidon she began to laugh. She looked at the dust and the torn brocades and the broken glass and the weather-stained draperies and she laughed and laughed until she held her sides and then she held her head, and the tears of laughter streamed down her cheeks.

At first Kakaracou had laughed with her, companionably, though not knowing why. But then she looked sober, then serious, finally alarmed.

"Hysterical," said Cupidon, in French. "Slap her. Hard, on the cheek. I'll go into the next room."

Kakaracou had gone to her, had taken her gently in her arms as she stood there, but Clio had shaken her off and gone on laughing. "Don't *bébé*, don't *chérie*," Kaka had murmured. Then, seeing that this was unavailing, she took Cupide's advice. She slapped the girl's cheek a stinging blow. Clio's laughter ceased as though turned off by a piece of mechanism, her eyes blazed at the Negress, she raised her hand to strike her, the woman cowered, and Clio's hand came down on her thin shoulder, gently, gently.

"Thank you, Kaka. I'm all right now. It was that sofa with one leg off. It looked so crazy and frowsy and dirty, like that old woman who used to limp along the quay in Paris, selling fish."

Kakaracou stared at it. Then she began to laugh with something of Clio's hysterical note in her voice. "So it does! Oh, that's very funny! So it———"

"Stop it! Don't you begin. That wasn't why I was laughing, really. Anyway, it's better than crying. That sofa was the one Mama always talked about. It was made and carved by Prudent Mallard, she said, and the crimson brocade came from France. Solid mahogany. Not so solid now, is it?"

Kaka leaped to the defense of her dead darling. "You should have seen her as she sat on it in her silks and jewels———"

"I know, I know. She told me a thousand times. This house—I remembered it as the most exquisite and luxurious———" She began to laugh again, then pulled herself together with an actual physical effort. She stood there, surveying the mildewed walls, the decrepit furniture. Her young face was stern, her eyes resolute and almost hard. "I suppose nothing in life is what we dreamed it would be. She spoke of this house as if it had been a palace. It's a shanty, tumbledown and filthy."

"Is it?" Kaka asked, dully, staring about her as though seeing the room for the first time. "Is it? Why, so it is!"

"It is not!" Clio then retorted with fine inconsistence. "It's beautiful! You wait. You'll see. We're *cagou* because we are sad and tired and everything's so neglected. But we'll make *ménage,* you and I and Cupide. We'll sweep and scrub and polish. The jalousies will be mended and the *garde-de-frise* out there, and the walls and the windows."

Kaka, the imitative, looked a shade less doleful, but she hugged her thin shoulders and edged closer to the doorway. "In the street they say this house is haunted. That's why it looks as it does. No one has come near it since he died here."

"It's very chic to be haunted by a Dulaine. Buy yourself a *gris-gris* from the *mamaloi*. That will keep off the spirits, you've always said. You used to complain because there was no voodoo woman in Paris to furnish you with one."

"You may laugh, but I know————"

"Yes, I can laugh. I'm going to be happy. Not like Mama. She had no pleasure in living those years in France. She talked of nothing but this house and its wonders. Look at it! She might much better have been enjoying a gay time—she and poor funny Aunt Belle. Well, I'm going to have a gay time! Glorious! This house will be lovely again."

"How? We've nothing."

"Mama's jewelry."

"You wouldn't part with that!"

"How else? Not the best of it, of course."

"The best! You haven't got the best of it. That went long ago. The magnificent pieces. She was extravagant, my poor *bébé* Rita, no doubt of that."

"*Stupide!* I'll keep the best for myself, of course, until someone gives me better. The unimportant pieces will pay for what I shall do to make this place right again. It won't be much. We shan't be here long."

Kakaracou was accustomed to dolorous middle-aged mistresses who wept on her bosom, required to be dressed and undressed like children, asked her advice as though she were a sibyl and berated her by turn. She now rolled her eyes at this strange new note of authority so that they seemed all whites. "Where we go!"

"Oh, wherever there's money and fun."

"Not here! Not New Orleans!"

"Pooh! It's dead here—finished. I saw that the moment I set foot in this town. I only came here to show them they can't frighten me and bully me the way they did Mama. Clio Dulaine! That's me. If they threaten me I'll tell the whole business. They can't do anything to me. I would, anyway, if it weren't for Mama. . . . Come on, I want to see the bedroom. She always said the dressing table—she called it a *duchesse*—was carved of palissandre, and the four-poster bed that Papa gave her was made long ago by Francois Seignouret, of rosewood, too, and signed by him, like a painting, it's so valuable. Will they be like that sofa, I wonder . . . well . . ."

At that moment Cupide waddled in from the dim bedroom across the wide central hall that divided the drawing room and dining room from the two bedrooms. His gait was a rollicking thing to see, quick, light, rolling, like the gay little Basque fishing boats that used to come bouncing into port from the Bay of Biscay with the sardine and herring catch. They had watched them on many a holiday along the Côte d'Argent. As he trotted, Cupide was whistling through his teeth, a talent in the perfection of which he was aided by nature, his two large square yellow incisors being separated by a generous eighth of an inch. He jerked a thumb over his shoulder.

"Blood in there on the carpet by the bed," he announced blithely.

Kakaracou shrieked, but Clio Dulaine stared at him a moment, silent. "Let me see," she said, then. She crossed the hall swiftly, her silken skirts flirting the dust. "Open the jalousies."

It had been the bedroom of a lovely and beloved woman. This was apparent in its furnishings, in its delicate coloring, in its arrangement. The exquisitely carved armoire of rosewood was meant to hold only the most fragile of silks and laces; the great arms of the vast palissandre bed were built to cradle love. The light that shone dimly through the broken blinds gave to the room a pale green translucence as it filtered through the rank growth of vines and trees that had spread a verdant coverlet protectingly about the house. The pastel grays and rose and fluid greens of the charming Aubusson carpet formed a pattern of wreaths and roses, faded and dusty now, but still lovely except for that great blotch there by the side of the bed. It must have been a pool, once, a pool that had grown viscid before it had been scoured in vain by hands that had striven to erase its marks. A great rusty brown irregular circle defacing the wistful flowers that strewed the floor.

Cupidon pointed with one tiny blunt forefinger. Kakaracou shrieked again and covered her staring eyes with her two hands, but she peeped through her latticed fingers, too, at once fascinated and terrified. The girl only stared in silence.

"I saw him as plain as if he was there now, the blood spurting out of his shirt like the fountains at Versailles," began the dwarf with gusto, "and she kneeling there screaming, her hair was dipping in it———"

Kakaracou leaped to him; she cuffed him a thwack across his hard head. He did not even blink. He merely brushed her hand away lightly as though it had been a mosquito.

"Let him be," the girl commanded. "I want to hear it." She dropped to her knees beside the sinister stain, she peeled off her fine French glove and, stooping, she passed her hand slowly, caressingly, over the rusty brown spot on the carpet. "His blood. My blood. They are the same. I love it, this spot. I will sleep here tonight, in this bed."

"No, no, no!" screamed Kakaracou. For a moment it looked as though she would run from the room, from the house, from the street itself.

"Yes, I say. Why not?"

"You can't. It isn't—it isn't decent." Then, as the girl's eyes blazed again, "It needs airing—the whole house—it's like a tomb."

"Cupide, open up here. Run down to Canal Street and fetch a pail, a mop, a broom. Tomorrow we'll find women to scrub and clean but we'll make it do for tonight. Kaka, open the bags and find me an old *blouse-volante*. This afternoon I'll engage workmen. A little paint, a few nails. A glazier. The garden made neat. Today is Monday. By the end of the week everything will be shining and in order."

Cupide rubbed his tiny hands together, he kicked up his heels like a colt. "This is fine!" he cried. "I like this. Are we going to eat here? Shall I bring things from the market?"

"Get on there!" shouted Kaka, entering into the spirit of the thing. "The marketing is my affair, you whelp. The stove probably doesn't march, and the chimney's sure to be stopped up. Well, we'll see."

"Shrimps!" ordered Clio. "And a *poulet chanteclair* and *omelette soufflée*. How Aunt Belle would love it, poor darling."

"You're crazy," Kaka muttered. "What do you think I am? A magician! If I can give you the plainest of omelettes and a cup of black coffee it will be a miracle. . . . Here is the *blouse-volante*. What do you want it for?"

"To put on, of course. I'm going to scrub too."

"Your hands!"

"Oh, the creams will put them right. I can't wait to see everything neat and gay, the chandelier glittering in the drawing room, and pots in the kitchen and flowers everywhere and the fountain singing in the garden. And Sunday!"

"Sunday?" Kaka was plainly afraid to hear what Sunday might bring out of this new strange mad mind, but she listened nevertheless.

"Sunday we'll go down to the French Market, just as Aunt Belle used to tell it. We'll buy everything. Everything delicious. I'll wear my gray half-mourning. We'll go to Mass at St. Louis Cathedral. We'll go to Madame

Begué's for breakfast. Perhaps They will come in for breakfast. Mama said They sometimes did. Then—well, I don't know. I may stare at Them—like this. Or I may go up to Them and say, 'How are you, Grandmama, how do you do, Grandpapa.' ''

"You wouldn't do that!"

"Ha, wouldn't I! What are they? Rich. Rich and dull and clannish, drooping around in black like those Paris snobs who think they're so grand that they have to dress down to keep from dazzling the *canaille*. I'll be richer than they. I'll be grander than they. I'll dress in the most exquisite———''

"Yes, well, that's very fine. Meantime, that dress you're wearing was your poor mama's but it was made by Worth. I can copy it, but where would I find such material? So take it off and put on the *blouse-volante* or stop pulling furniture about, one or the other. You won't get another dress like it in a hurry."

Clio Dulaine had never done a day's manual labor. It was a lesson in the adaptability of youth to see her now as she scrubbed, polished, scoured with Kakaracou and Cupidon. She produced carpenters, plumbers, glaziers, cabinetmakers and charmed them into doing their work at once, and swiftly. All that week there was a cacophony of sound throughout the house and garden, a domestic orchestra made up of the swish of the broom, the rub-a-dub of the washboard, the clink-clank of the plumber's tools, the sharp report of the carpenter's hammer, the slap-slap of the paint brush, the snip of the gardener's shears, the scrape of trowel on brick. Above this homely symphony soared the solo of Clio's song. As she worked she sang in a rich, true contralto a strange mixture of music—music she had heard at the Paris Opera; songs that Rita Dulaine had hummed in a sweet and melancholy tremolo; plantation songs, Negro spirituals, folk songs with which Kaka had sung her to sleep in her childhood; songs that Aunt Belle Piquery had sung in a shrill off-key soprano, risqué songs whose origins had been the brothels and gambling houses of the New Orleans of her heyday. *Po' Pitie Mamze Zizi*, she caroled. Then, *Robert, toi que j'aime*. Three minutes later her fresh young voice would fling gaily upward the broken beat of a Negro melody:

> Tell yuh 'bout a man wot live befo Chris'—
> He name was Adam, Eve was his wife,
> Tell yuh how dat man he lead a rugged life,
> All be-cause he tak-en de woman's ad-vice. . . .
> She made his trouble so hard—she made his trou-ble so hard———
> Lawd, Lawd, she made his trou-ble so hard. . . .

It had been Kakaracou who had taught her *Grenadie, ça-ça-yie*, a Creole song with its light and fatalistic treatment of death and love. Kaka, too, had taught her those mixtures of French and Negro dialects such as rose so naturally now to her lips in the Creole lullaby:

> Pov piti Lolotte a mouin
> Pov piti Lolotte a mouin
> Li gagnin bobo, bobo,
> Li gagnin doule, doule,
> Li gagnin doule dans ker a li.

The dialect was Gombo, soft and slurred; she hardly knew the meaning of the words, but her slim white throat pulsed and her voice swelled in song. She was happy who had been bred in such *douleur,* she was definite and sure who had been so bewildered by her life, shuttled as she was from convent to Paris flat, hearing of her real background always in terms of nostalgia and resentment, never hoping to see it. She worked singing or she worked silent, the tip of her little pink tongue just showing between her teeth as she rubbed and polished, an unusual glow tinting the creamy pallor of her cheeks. She had the happy energy of one who at last belongs; of the vital female who has been dominated all her life and who now, at last, is free. As she sang and polished and flitted from room to room, from garden to kitchen, from *garçonnière* to street, the house magically took on life, color, charm. She was like a butterfly emerging from a grub; the house was a *bijou* once dingy with long neglect, now glowing rich and lustrous. The fine chandelier, always too magnificent for the little drawing room, was now a huge jewel whose every hand-cut crystal gave back its own flashing ruby and topaz and sapphire and emerald.

Every few minutes she ran to the door or window at the call of a street vendor. Here was another opera, high, low, melodious, raucous. The chimney sweep came by. "R-r-ra-monay! R-r-ramonez la cheminée du haut en bas!" The French words fell sweetly on her ear, but the voice same from a black giant in a rusty frock coat, a battered and enormous top hat, over his shoulder a stout rope, a sheaf of broom straw, bunches of palmetto. She beckoned him in, he shook his kinky head over the state of the fireplaces and chimneys. Like a magician he pulled all sorts of creatures out of their nests of brick and plaster—bats, mice, birds. Clio would not have been surprised to learn that the cow that jumped over the moon had come to rest in one of the chimneys of the Rampart Street house.

The coal peddler, a perfect match for his wares, had his song, too.

> *Mah mule is white*
> *Mah face is black;*
> *Ah sells mah coal*
> *Two bits a sack.*

The brush man called, *"Latanier! Latanier!* Palmetto root!" Clothes poles and palmetto roots dangled from his cart. Fruit women, calling. Berry women. Clio bought every sort of thing, her lovely laughing face popping out at this door or that window. Vast black women stepped down the street carrying great bundles of wash on their heads; they walked superbly, their arms swinging free at their sides. Generations had carried their burdens thus; their neck, waist and shoulder muscles were made of steel. Clio Dulaine threw *lagniappe* to every passing beggar or minstrel. Street bands, ragged and rolling-eyed, made weird music done in a curious broken rhythm that later was to be called ragtime or jazz.

Now the doorstep, scoured with powdered brick, shone white. Kaka, down on her knees with pail and brush, gave short shrift to inquisitive neighborhood servants who loitered by in assumed innocence, but who obviously had been sent out on reconnaissance by their mistresses.

"Where you come from? France, like they say?"

"I come from New Orleans. Not like you, Congo."

"You make *ménage?*"

Kaka had easily dropped into her native New Orleans patois. "What you think! We carpetbaggers like you!"

"Your lady and you, you going stay here?"

The time had come to close the conversation. *"Zaffaire Cabritt ça pas zaffaire Mouton."* The goat's business is none of the sheep's concern. The inquirer moved on, little wiser for her pains. Cupide gave them even less information, but a better show. Among his talents was that of being able to twist his face into the most appalling shapes and expressions. His popeyes, his wide lips, his outstanding ears, his buttonlike nose were natural contributors to this grisly gift. Perched on a ladder, busy with his window-washing or occupied with brush and pail on the doorstep, or even shopping in one of the neighborhood stores he would ponder a question a moment as though giving it grave consideration. Then in a lightning and dreadful transformation he would peer up at his questioner, his face screwed into such a mask of distortion and horror as to send his questioner gibbering in fright. At first the neighborhood children and the loiterers in the near-by barrooms and groceries had mistaken him for fair game. But his cannonball head, his prehensile arms and his monkeylike agility had soon taught them caution and even respect. *Bébé Babouin,* they called him. Baby baboon.

At the end of the first week the house seemed to be in a state of chaos from which order never could emerge. Dust, plaster, paint, soapsuds, shavings, glue mingled in dreadful confusion. But by Friday of the second week order had miraculously been wrought. Kaka's waspishness waned, she began to talk of toothsome Creole dishes; Cupide, who had seemed to swing like a monkey from chandelier to mantel, from mantel to window, came down to earth, donned his Paris uniform of broadcloth and buttons and announced that the time had come to search New Orleans for a suitable carriage and pair.

Clio, disheveled and somewhat wan, looked down at him with affectionate amusement. "Our carriage and pair will be ourselves and our own two legs, Cupide. At any rate, until someone buys us others. So you may as well lay away your maroon coat and gold buttons."

"My livery goes where I go. And I go where Mad'moiselle goes," he announced dramatically. This was not so much loyalty as fury at the thought of being parted from the uniform he loved, the trappings which, in his own eyes, made him a figure of importance in spite of his deformity. Young as she was, Clio Dulaine sensed this. She laid her hand gently on his head, she tipped the froglike face up and smiled down at him her lovely poignant smile. "You are my bodyguard, Cupide. My escort. And we'll have carriages and the finest of horses. You wait. You'll see."

He brightened at that, he capered like a frolicsome goat, he rushed off to the kitchen to tell Kaka that he was once more Cupidon of the maroon livery, the gold buttons, the shiny boots. Kaka, the realist, did not share his happiness. "On the street! You'll look like a monkey without a string."

"Carencro!" Cupide spat out at her, for by now he had renewed acquaintance with old half-forgotten New Orleans epithets. This Acadian corruption of carrion crow or black vulture he found particularly suitable in his verbal battles with the sharp-tongued Kakaracou.

Now it was Saturday, and the house was not only habitable, it was charming and even luxurious. From the street one saw only a neat one-story dwelling of the simple plantation type, built well off the ground to avoid dampness. Its low-hanging roof came down like a hat shading its upper windows. It gave the house a misleadingly compressed look, for inside the rooms were high-ceilinged and spacious, with a wide central hall running straight through the house from front to back. Drawing room, dining room, bedroom, boudoir; beautifully proportioned rooms in this cottagelike structure. But the real life of the house was at the back. There was the courtyard with its paving of faded old orange brick; kitchen and servants' rooms were separated from the main house, forming an ell at one side of the courtyard. At right angles to this, and facing the house, was the *garçonnière.* Its two rooms, with a lacework balcony thrown across the front, were protected from dampness by the little basement that formed the ground floor. Here and there, where the plaster had fallen off, the old brick of the foundation showed through, yellow-pink like the courtyard pavement.

Inside the house the white woodwork had been freshly painted, the carpets scoured, the windows mended. The rosewood and mahogany of the fine furniture had been rubbed until it shone like satin. The gilt mirrors gave back the jewel colors of the chandeliers. Clio had brought to America bits and pieces from the Paris flat—plump little French chairs, Sèvres vases, inlaid tables of rosewood and tulipwood. These had stood the journey bravely and now fitted into the Rampart Street house as though they dated from the lavish New Orleans day of Rita Dulaine.

And now the three stood surveying their handiwork: the big-eyed girl with that look in her face of one whose life will hold surprising things, but who, even now, is planning not to be taken by surprise; the Negress, wiry, protective, indomitable; the dwarf, rollicking, pugnacious, always slightly improbable, like a creature out of drawing. Each wore the expression of one who, having done his work, finds that work well done. An ill-assorted trio, held together by a background of common experience and real affection and a kind of rowdy camaraderie.

"It looks well," said Kakaracou even as she breathed on a bit of crystal and rubbed it with her apron, needlessly.

The little man cocked an impish eye up at her. "It's well enough—until we can manage something better."

Clio's grin was as impish as his. "Now I know what Mama meant. Do you remember she used to say there was an old Louisiana proverb: 'Give a Creole a crystal chandelier and two mirrors to reflect it and he is satisfied.' Well, I've got the chandelier and the two mirrors. But I'm not satisfied."

"Who's Creole here?" demanded Kaka, sourly. Always, when speaking to outsiders, she boasted that the Creole blood flowing in Clio Dulaine's veins actually was tinged with the cerulean hue of royalty. In private she never missed an opportunity to remind the girl that her origin was one-half aristocratic Creole and one-half New Orleans underworld. Perhaps this was her instinctive desire to protect the girl from bruising herself against her own ambitions as her mother before her had done.

Yet, "I am!" Clio shouted now. "I'm Creole!"

"Take shame on yourself, denying your own mama."

"That's a lie! Don't you dare!" She stopped in the midst of her protest as though suddenly remembering something. She stood looking at these two human oddments as though seeing them clearly for the first time. It was a deliberate and measuring look. In that moment she seemed to shed her girlhood before their very eyes and become a woman. The daughter of a *placée,* the niece of the hearty shrewd strumpet Belle Piquery, most of her life had been spent in the company of two women whose every thought was devoted to pleasing men. Convent-schooled though the girl was, she had absorbed the very atmosphere of courtesanship. Because she had loved them, her voice, her glance, her movements were an unconscious imitation of theirs. Yet there was a difference even now. Where they had been fluid and easy-going she was firm; where they had wavered she was direct. The square little chin balanced the sensual mouth; the melting eyes were likely to cause you to overlook the free plane of the brow. Wan and disheveled with her two weeks of concentrated work, she now seemed to gather herself together in all her mental and physical and emotional being.

"Now then, listen to me, you two. You, Angélique Pluton. You, Cupidon." They stared at her with uncomprehending gaze as though she had spoken in a strange language. Never in her life had she called the woman anything but Kaka, or—crowing mischievously—Kakaracou. The dwarf had always been Cupide. "Do you want to stay with me?"

The little man's mouth fell open. It was the wrinkled woman who said, with an edge of fear in her voice, "Where else!"

"Then remember that no matter what I say I am—that I am. I shall be what it suits me to be. Life is something you must take by the tail or it runs away from you. . . . Now where did I hear that! That's clever. I must have made it up. Well, anyway, I don't want to hear any more of this telling me who I am and what I am to do. Do as I say, and we'll be rich. Which do you choose—stay or go?"

"Stay!" shouted Cupide, cutting a caper with those absurd bandy legs. The Negress voiced no choice. The fear was gone from her eyes. She stood with her lean arms crossed on her breast, assured and even a trifle arrogant.

"Play-acting," she sniffed, "like your great-grandmother. That's the Bonnevie in you. You and your cleverness! What will Your Highness choose to be tomorrow? Queen of England, I suppose!"

Clio dropped her role of adventuress. She pouted a moment as she had in her childhood when her nurse Kaka would not bend to her will. Then she threw her arms around the woman and hugged her. "Tomorrow, Kaka, we'll dress in our best and we'll have a wonderful time, you and Cupide and I. We'll go first to the Cathedral and then to the French Market and then to Begué's for breakfast—or we may go to the French Market first and then to Mass—well, anyway, now I'll have my hair washed, Kaka, and such a brushing, and my hands in oil, and then you'll rub me all over with that lovely sweet stuff that you used when Mama had one of her sad times and couldn't sleep. And tomorrow morning I'll wake up all fresh and gay in my own home in New Orleans. Oh, Kaka!" Here she gave an unadult squeal and clapped her hands. There was something touching, something moving about this, probably because it made plain that her stern and implacable role of the past fortnight had been only an acting part. At sight of this the faces of the two changed as a summer sky grows brilliant again when the sun drives off the clouds. For two weeks she had been a stranger to them, a managing mistress, hard, almost harsh, driving them and herself in a fury of energy. Now she was young again and gay; the house was fresh, cool, orderly; in the kitchen just off the courtyard Kaka's copper pans shone golden as the sauces they soon would contain, and on the kitchen table was a Basque cloth of coarse linen striped with bright green and red and yellow. The window panes glittered. The steps were scoured white. The courtyard bricks were newly swept and the fountain actually tinkled its lazy little tune; inside the high-ceilinged rooms you were met by the clean odor of fresh paint; silver, crystal, satin and glass reflected each other, surface for surface; the scent of perfume in Clio's bedroom, her peignoir softly slithering over a chair back.

"*En avant, mes enfants!*" cried Clio, satisfied.

"*A la bonne heure!*" shouted Cupide.

But, "*Tout doux,*" the acidulous old woman cautioned them. "Not so fast, you two."

3

BUT NEXT MORNING even Kakaracou's grim mask was brightened by a gleam of anticipation. Sunday morning, April, and steaming hot. New Orleans citizens did not remark the heat, or if they did they relished it. They were habituated to that moist and breathless atmosphere, they thrived on it, they paced their lives in accordance with it. Clio and Kaka and Cupide slipped easily into the new-old environment as one allows an accustomed garment, temporarily discarded, once more to rest gratefully upon one's shoulders.

Kaka's broad nostrils dilated with her noisy inhalations as the three emerged into the brilliant April morning sunshine of Rampart Street. Over all New Orleans there hung the pungent redolence that was the very flavor of the bewitching city.

First, as always, the heavy air bore the scent of coffee pervading everything like an incense wafted from the great wharves and roasting ovens. Over and under and around this dominant odor were other smells, salty, astringent or exotic. There were the smells of the Mississippi, of river shrimps and crayfish and silt and rotting wood and all manner of floating and sunken things that go to feed the monster stream; of sugar, spices, bananas, rum, sawdust; of flower-choked gardens; of black men sweating on the levees; of rich food bubbling in butter and cream and wine and condiments; the sweet, dank, moldy smell of old churches whose doors, closed throughout the week, were opened now for the stream of Sabbath worshipers. The smell of an old and carnal city, of a worldly and fascinating city.

"M-m-m!" said Clio. And "M-m-m!" chorused Kaka and Cupide.

Any one of the three, as they set out this Sunday morning, would have been enough to attract attention on the streets of New Orleans, sophisticated though the city was. Certainly Clio Dulaine alone was a figure to catch the eye and hold it, to say nothing of the bizarre attendants who walked in her wake.

She was wearing a dress of stiff rich gray silk faille, and it was amazing that so prim a color could take on, from its wearer, so dashing and even brilliant a look. Perhaps it was that the gray of the gown was the shade of a fine pearl with a hint of pink behind it. It made her black hair seem blacker, her skin whiter. It had, in fact, an effect almost of gaiety. For contrast, and doubtless because this gown was supposed to represent mourning in its second stage, the overskirt and basque were trimmed with little black velvet bows as was the pancake hat with its black curled ostrich tips, tilted well down over her eyes. Beneath this protection her eyes swam shaded and mysterious like twin pools beneath an overhanging ledge. In her ears were pearl screws, very foreign and French, and a pearl and black onyx brooch made effective contrast just beneath the creamy hollow of her throat. If one could have seen her brows below the down-tipped pancake hat it might have been remarked how thick and dark and winged they were—the brows of a forceful and vigorous woman. She was a figure of French elegance as depicted in the fashion papers. No well-bred French woman would have ventured out of doors in a costume so rich, so picturesque.

Beside her and perhaps just a half step behind her paced Kakaracou, looking at once vaguely Egyptian, New Orleans Negro duenna, and a figure out of the Arabian Nights. Her handsome black grosgrain silk gown was as rich and heavy as that of any grand lady, though severe in style. Over it her ample white apron and fichu were cobweb fine and exquisitely hemstitched. In the withered ears dangled heavy gold earrings of Byzantine pattern, and where the fichu folded at her breast was a gold brooch of Arabesque design. Surmounting all this was a brilliantly gay tignon wound about her head. The gray-brown face, like an old dried fig, had the look of a rather sardonic Egyptian mummy, yet it had a vaguely simian quality due partly to the broad upper lip but more definitely to the eyes, which had the sad yet compassionate quality found in an old race whose heritage is tragedies remembered.

As she walked she had a way of turning her head quickly, almost dartingly like a bird, and this set her earrings to swinging and glinting in the sun. The eyes beneath their heavy wrinkled lids noted everything.

Behind these two, a figure out of Elizabethan court days, except that he wore no brilliant turban, no puffed satin pantaloons, walked the dwarf Cupidon. He walked without self-consciousness other than that of pride; the tiny bandy legs, the powerful trunk and shoulders, the large head, the young-old face were made all the more bizarre by his coachman's plum broadcloth uniform ornamented with gilt buttons and topped by a glazed hat with a gay cockade on one side. The wistful yet merry eyes watched the slim, graceful figure that walked ahead of him as a dog watches his mistress even while he seems busy with his own affairs. A mischievous and pugnacious little figure yet touching and, somehow, formidable. Hooked over one tiny arm was a large woven basket, for they were on their way to the French Market, these three on a fine hot, humid New Orleans Sunday morning, just as Clio Dulaine had planned.

Now and then the girl would turn her head to toss a word over her shoulder to the stern, stalking figure just behind her.

"It smells exactly the way Aunt Belle said it did." A long deep inhalation. "But precisely!"

"How else!"

The little procession moved on up the street. Passers-by and loungers stared. In their faces you saw reflected a succession of emotions like the expressions of rather clumsy pantomimists. First there was the shock of beholding the three in all their splendor; then the eye was lit with admiration for the lovely girl; startled by the mingled magnificence and gaudiness of the Negress; shocked or amused by the little liveried escort strutting so pompously behind them. The three figures made a gay colorful frieze against the smooth plaster walls of the *Vieux Carré*. Past the old houses whose exquisitely wrought ironwork decoration was like a black lace shawl thrown across the white bosom of a Spanish *señora;* past the Cabildo with its massive arches and its delicate cornices, pilasters and pediment. The sound of music came to them as they passed the Cathedral, but Clio did not enter.

"America is lovely," said Clio graciously, gazing across the Place d'Armes to the stately double row of the Pontalba buildings facing the square. The remark was addressed to the world, over her shoulder, and was caught deftly by Kakaracou who in turn tossed it back to Cupide, like an echo.

"America is lovely."

Cupide looked about him, spaciously. "It's well enough."

With one little gray-gloved hand Clio pointed across the Place d'Armes to the stately brick front of the Pontalba buildings with their lacy festoons of ironwork. "As you probably know, Kaka, my Aunt Micaela, the Baroness Pontalba, built those apartments." She turned her head slightly to catch Kaka's eye. For a moment it seemed that Kaka must reject this statement, but Clio Dulaine's look did not waver, her eye held the other in command. The turbaned head turned again to enlighten the little man.

"Mad'moiselle's Aunt Micaela, the Baroness Pontalba, built those fine apartments, Little One."

Pattering along behind them the dwarf rolled his goggle eyes in mock admiration of this palpable fantasy. *"Ma foi!* My uncle, the Emperor Napoleon, built the Arc de Triomphe."

Clio laughed her slow, rich laugh that was so paced and deep-throated. This morning she was gay, eager, this morning nothing could offend her. She was finding it to her liking, this colorful, unconventional city. She sniffed the smells of river water and good cooking and tropical gardens; her young eyes did not flinch from the glare of the sun on the white buildings; as they approached the busy French Market she felt at home with these people walking and chatting and laughing. Some of them had come there solely for sociability, some had market baskets on their arms or servants walking behind them carrying the laden hamper. She liked the look of these people, they were dark and juicy like the lusty people of Marseilles; indeed she thought the city itself had the look of Marseilles down here by the French Market so near the water front. These people thronging the streets on a spring Sunday morning had French and Spanish and American blood running strong in their veins, a heady mixture. And the Negroes were here, there, everywhere accenting the scene, enriching it with their expressive tragi-comic faces, their fluid movements. You heard French spoken, Spanish too, English; the Negro dialect called Gombo; the patois called Cajun, which had been brought to the Bayou country by the Acadian settlers from Nova Scotia.

And now they were in the midst of the Market's clamor, the cackling of geese, the squawk of chickens, vendors' cries, the clatter of horses' hoofs. Footsteps rang on the flagstoned floor, the arcaded brick and plaster structure was a sounding board, the arched columns formed a setting for the leisurely promenading figures or the scurrying busy ones. Creole ladies severe in their plain street dress of black were buying food for the day fresh from the river or lake or near-by plantations, while the basket on the arm of the servant grew heavier by the minute.

Greeks, Italians, French, Negroes, Indians. Oysters, fish, vegetables, oranges, figs, nuts. Delicate lake shrimp like tiny pink petals; pompano, trout, soft-shell crabs, crayfish. Quail, partridge, snipe, rabbits.

"Oh, Kaka, look, some of that! And that! Look, Cupide, herbs and green for *gombo-zhebes* that Aunt Belle longed for in Paris and couldn't get. I can't wait to taste it. Kaka! Kakaracou! Where are you! Look! Crayfish for bisque. Or shall we have redfish with *court-bouillon?* Cupide, come here with that basket."

Fat Negro women, their heads bound in snowy white turbans, baskets of sandwiches on their arms, lifted the corner of a napkin to tempt the passer-by with the wares beneath. A hundred appetizing odors came from charcoal braziers glowing here, there, behind stalls or at the pavement's edge. The fragrant coffee stands with their cups of *café noir or café au lait* were situated at opposite ends of the market, but in the very heart of the food stalls they were selling hot Creole dishes to be served up on the spot and eaten standing. There was the favorite hot jambalaya steaming and enriching the already heavy air; the mouth watered as one passed it.

The trailing skirts of Clio's exquisite French dress had swished from stall to stall, the basket on Cupide's arm had grown heavier and heavier. The market men and stall vendors, their Latin temperament quick to respond to her beauty and her strong electric attraction, gave her overweight measure. Cupide was almost hidden behind the foliage of greens in his basket; now and then a crayfish claw reached feebly out to nip the maroon sleeve of his uniform only to be slapped smartly back in place by the little man. They were followed now by quite a little procession of the curious and the admiring and the amused. They paid no heed. Even in Paris they had become accustomed to this.

Clio stopped now and pointed to the pot of bubbling jambalaya. "Some of that!" she said. "A plateful of that. Mm, what a heavenly smell!"

"No. It will ruin your breakfast at Begué's."

"Nothing will ruin my breakfast. I have the appetite of a dock laborer. You know that. Here, Cupide. Set down that basket and fetch me a plateful of that lovely stuff. What's that it's called, Kaka?"

"Jambalaya. Heavy stuff. You'll be————"

"Quick, Cupide. Tell the man a heaping plateful for me—for Madame la Comtesse."

Cupide, in the act of setting down his basket, straightened again with a jerk. "For who!"

"You heard!" barked Kakaracou. "A plateful of jambalaya for Madame la Comtesse. Who else, *stupide!*"

The dwarf shook his bullet head as though to rid it of cobwebs, grinned impishly and trotted off. "Heh, you! A dish of that stuff for Madame la Comtesse."

"Who?"

"Madame la Comtesse there. And be quick about it."

The man looked up from stirring the pot, his eyes fell on the girl's eager face, he became all smiles, his eyes, his teeth flashed, he spooned up a great bowlful and placed it on a tray and himself would have carried it to her but Cupide reached up and took it from him and brought it to her miraculously without spilling a drop, brimming though it was. Then, because he was just table-high with arms strong as steel rods, he stood before her holding up the tray with its savory dish and she stood and ate it thus, daintily and eagerly, with quite a little circle of admiring but anxious New Orleans faces, black, olive, cream, *café au lait,* white, awaiting her verdict.

"Oh," Clio cried between hot heaping spoonfuls, "it's delicious, it's better than anything I've ever eaten in France."

Cupide, the living table, could just be seen from the eyes up, staring over the rim of the tray. He now turned his head to right to left while his stocky little body remained immovable. "Madame la Comtesse," he announced in his shrill boyish voice, "says that the dish is delicious, it is more delicious than anything she has eaten in France." He then lowered the tray an inch or two to peer into the half-empty dish. *"Relevé,"* he said under his breath. "Hash! Pfui!"

Clio took a final spoonful, her strong white teeth crunching the spicy mess; she broke a crust of fresh French bread, neatly mopped up the sauce in the bowl and popped this last rich morsel into her mouth. The onlookers breathed a satisfied sigh, and at that moment Clio encountered the bold and enveloping stare of one onlooker whose admiration quite evidently was not for her gustatory feats but for her face and figure. It was more than that. The look in the eyes of this man who stood regarding her was amused, was tender, was possessive. He was leaning indolently against one of the pillars forming the arcade, his hands thrust into the front pockets of his tight fawn trousers, one booted foot crossed over the other. Under the broad, rolling brim of his white felt hat his stare of open and flashing admiration was as personal as an embrace. Clio Dulaine was accustomed to stares, she even liked them. In France, especially at the races, the Parisians had followed the fantastic little group made up of the lovely Rita Dulaine, the full-blown Belle, the great-eyed girl, the attendant dwarf and Negress. They had stared and commented with the Gallic love of the bizarre. But this man's gaze was an actual intrusion. He was speaking to her, wordlessly. In another moment she thought he actually would approach her, address her. She felt the blood tingling in her cheeks that normally were so pale. Abruptly she set down her plate and spoon, she shoved the tray a little away from her.

"Bravo Madame la Comtesse!" cried the jambalaya man behind his brazier of charcoal. "Eaten like a true Creole!" The onlookers laughed a little, but it was an indulgent laugh; they liked to see a pretty woman who could polish off her plate with gusto. It flattered them. They, too, knew good food when they saw it. They knew a good-looking woman, as well, though she did have a fast look about her—or maybe it was merely foreign.

Kakaracou nudged her with one sharp elbow. "Come, I don't like the look of this. It's common. You, Cupide, take that miserable stuff away." Her shar eyes had not missed the tall stranger lolling there against the pillar with his bold intent gaze. She was still muttering as they moved on, and the words were not pretty, made up as they were of various epithets and obscenities culled from the French, from the Congo, from the Cajun, from the Negro French.

"Stop nudging me, you wicked old woman! I'm not a child. I'll go when I please." But Clio moved on, nevertheless, with a flick of her eye to see if the tall figure lounging against the pillar took note of their going. Here and there they stopped at this stall or that, though the basket by now squeaked its protest and Cupide was almost ambushed behind its foliage. Clio was like a greedy child, she wanted everything that went to make up the dishes of which she had heard in her Paris exile. Kaka, too, was throwing caution to the winds. All through the Paris years she had complained because she could not obtain this or that ingredient for a proper Creole dish. And now here it all was, spread lavishly before her. Native dainties, local tidbits. Her eyes glittered, the artist in her was aroused.

"Quail!" she could cry like a desert wanderer who stumbles upon water. "Pompano! Red beans! Soft-shell crabs! Creole lettuce! Oh, the wonderful things that I could never find in that place over there."

A turbaned Negress came by calling the wares from her napkin-covered basket. *"Calas tout chaud! Calas tout chaud!"* Undone, Kaka bought a hot rice cake and gulped it down greedily, poked another into Cupide's great mouth. Down it went with a single snap of his jaws.

So it happened that when they reached the end of the arcade there leaning against a pillar exactly as before was the sombreroed stranger of the burning gaze. He was refreshing himself with a cup of coffee bought at the near-by stall, and as he stirred this lazily and sipped its creamy contents he did not once take his eyes off Clio over the cup's rim.

New Orleans knew a Texan when it saw one. New Orleans regarded its Texas neighbors as little better than savages. Certainly this great handsome product of the plains made the New Orleans male, by contrast, seem a rather anemic not to say effeminate fellow. He was, perhaps, an inch or so over six feet but so well proportioned that he did not seem noticeably tall. His eyes were not so blue as his bronzed face made them appear. His ears stood out a little too far, he walked with the gait of the horseman whose feet are more at home in the stirrup than on the ground. Any of these points would have marked him for an outlander in the eyes of New Orleans. But even if these had failed, his clothes were unmistakable. The great white sombrero was ornamented with a beautifully marked snakeskin band, his belt was heavy with silver nailheads, his fawn trousers were tucked into high-heeled boots that came halfway up his shin. But as final contrast to the quietly dandified or somber garments of the sophisticated Louisiana gentry he wore a blue broadcloth coat of brightish hue strained across his broad shoulders and reaching almost to the knees; and his necktie was a great stiff four-in-hand of white satin on which blue forget-me-nots had been lavishly embroidered by some fair though misguided hand. He was magnificent, he was vast, he was beautiful, he was crude, he was rough, he was untamed, he was Texas.

"There he is!" hissed Kaka, rearing her lean black head like a snake ready to strike. "There he is, that great *badaud,* leaning there."

Clio was intently examining a head of cauliflower. She hated cauliflower and never ate it. "Who, Kaka dear?" she now asked absentmindedly. "H'm?" with an air of dreamy preoccupation which would have deceived no one, least of all the astute Kakaracou. "What a lovely *choufleur!*"

"Who, Kaka dear, who, Kaka dear!" Wickedly the Negress mimicked her in a kind of poisonous baby-talk. "You and your cauliflower head there, you're two of a kind."

Clio decided that the time had now come for dignity. In her role of Madame la Comtesse she now drew herself up and looked down her nose at Kaka. The effect of this was somewhat spoiled by the fact that Kaka glared balefully back, completely uncowed. "We will now go to the Cathedral. Kaka, you will accompany me. Cupide, you will go home with your basket, quickly, then return and wait outside the church. *Vite!*"

At the Market curb stood an open victoria for hire, its shabby cushions a faded green, its two sorry nags hanging listless heads. The black charioteer was as decrepit as his equipage. "We'll ride," Clio announced, grandly. "I'm tired. It's hot. I'm hungry."

The black man bowed, his smile a brilliant gash that made sunshine in the sable face. His gesture of invitation toward the sagging carriage made of it a state coach, of its occupants royalty. "Yas'm, yas'm. Jes' the evening for ride out to the lake, yas'm."

"Evening! Why, it's hardly noon!"

"Yas'm, yas'm. Puffic evening for ride out to the lake."

She set one foot in its gray kid shoe on the carriage step.

"Ma'am," said a soft, rather drawling voice behind her, "Ma'am, I hate to see anybody as plumb beautiful as you ride in a moth-eaten old basket like this, let alone those two nags to pull it. If you'll honor me, Ma'am, by using my carriage, I'm driving a pair of long-tailed bays to a clarence, I brought them all the way from Texas, and they're beauties and thorough-breds, just like—well, that sounds terrible, I didn't mean to compare you, Ma'am, with—I meant if you'd just allow me————"

Standing there on the carriage step she had turned in amazement to find her face almost on a level with his as he stood at the curb. The blue eyes were blazing down upon her. He had taken off the great white sombrero. The Texas wind and sun that had bronzed the cheeks so startlingly near her own had burned the chestnut hair to a lively red-gold. For one terrible moment the two swayed together as though drawn by some magnetic force; then she drew back, and as she did so she realized with great definiteness that she wanted to feel his ruddy sun-warmed cheek against hers. She said, "Sir!" like any milk-and-water miss, turned away from him in majestic disapproval and seated herself in the carriage, whose cushion springs, playing her false, let her down in a rather undignified heap. His left hand still held the coffee cup. Unrebuffed, he strode toward the stall to set this down, and at that moment the outraged Kakaracou gave the signal to Cupide. That imp set down his laden basket. The Texan's back was toward him, a broad target. With the force and precision of a goat Cupide ran straight at him, head lowered, and butted him from behind. The coffee cup went flying, spattering the *café au lait* trousers with a deeper tone. Another man would have fallen, but the Texan's muscles were steel, his balance perfect. He pitched forward, stumbled, bent almost double, but he did not fall, he miraculously recovered himself. The white hat had fallen from his hand, it rolled like a hoop into a little pile of decayed vegetables at the curb. Across the open square, skipping along toward the *Vieux Carré*, you saw the figure of the dwarf almost obscured by the heavy basket.

A gasp had gone up from the market, and a snicker—but a small and smothered snicker. The flying blue coattails had revealed the silver-studded belt as being not purely ornamental. A businesslike holster hung suspended on either hip.

Kaka had whisked into the carriage, the coachman had whipped up the listless nags, they were off to the accompaniment of squeaking springs and clattering hoofs and the high shrill cackle of Kaka's rare laughter.

Clio Dulaine's eyes were blazing; her fists were clenched; she craned to stare back at the tall blue-coated figure that had recovered the hat and now, standing at the Market curb, was brushing its sullied whiteness with one coat sleeve even while he gazed at the swaying vehicle bouncing over the cobblestones toward the Cathedral.

"I'll whip him! I'll take his uniform away from him. I'll send him up North among the savages in New York State. I'll never allow him to walk out with me again. I'll lock him in the *garçonnière* on bread and water. I'll————"

"Oh, so Madame la Comtesse enjoys to have loutish cowboys from Texas speak to her on the street. What next! Even your aunt Belle————"

"Shut up! Do you want to be slapped here in front of the Cathedral!"

Kaka took another tack. She began to whimper, her monkeyish face screwed into a wrinkled knot of woe. "I wish I had died when my Rita *bébé* died. I wish I could die now. I promised her I'd take care of you. It's no use. Common. Common as dirt." The carriage came to a halt before the church, Clio stepped out, her head held much too high for a Sunday penitent. "Wait here," Kaka instructed the driver, her air of injured innocence exchanged for a brisk and businesslike manner, "and if that lout in the market asks you if we are inside say no, we left on foot. There'll be *pourboire* for you if you do as I say."

Within the cool dim cathedral Clio's head was meekly bowed, her lips moved silently, she wiped away a tear as she prayed for the souls of the dead, for her lovely unfortunate mother, for her father, for her lusty aunt, but her eyes swam this way and that to see if, in the twilight gray of the aisles and pillars, she could discern a tall waiting figure. Out again into the blinding white sunshine of the Place d'Armes, the carriage was there, awaiting her; Cupide was there perched on the coachman's box, the reins in his own tiny hands; the Sunday throngs were there, but no graceful lounging Texan, no clarence drawn by long-tailed bays.

"Oh!" The girl's exclamation of disappointment was as involuntary as the sound of protest under pain. Kaka was jubilant. They had thrown him off. He had overheard the driver speaking of the lake. Plainly Clio was pouting.

"It's too late for Begué's, don't you think, Kaka? And too hot. Let's drive out to the lake, h'm? I'm not hungry. All that jambalaya."

Cupide had wrought a startling change in the brokendown chariot. Evidently he had brought back with him from the house sundry oddments and elegancies with which to refurbish his lady's carriage. A whisk broom had been vigorously plied, for the ancient cushions were dustless now and the floor cloth as well. Over the carriage seat he had thrown a wine-red silk shawl so that the gray faille should not be sullied further. He had rubbed the metal buckles of the rusty harness, he had foraged in the basement of the *garçonnière* for his cherished equipment of Paris days and had brought out the check reins, which now held the nags' heads high in a position of astonished protest. He himself, in his maroon livery, was perched on the driver's seat, his little feet barely reaching the dashboard against which he braced himself. It was the Negro, dispossessed but admiring, who clambered down to assist the two into the transformed coach.

"Never see such a funny little *maringouin!* He climb up there he make them nags look like steppers. Look him now! Hi-yah!"

Sulkily Clio took her place on the wine-silk shawl against which her gray gown glowed the pinker. Kaka triumphantly took the little seat facing her, her back to the coachman's seat. "Begué's!" she commanded over her shoulder to Cupide.

"Fold your arms!" Cupide commanded of the chuckling Negro beside him on the box. "Sit up straight, you Congo! Eyes ahead!"

The man wagged his head in delighted wonder. "Just like you say, *Quartee*. Look them horses step! My, my!"

Kaka, victorious, decided to follow up her advantage. "Madame la Comtesse looked very chic talking to that dock laborer. Is it for that we crossed the ocean and returned to New Orleans to live!"

"I didn't talk to him. He talked to me. He isn't a dockhand. He's a Texan, probably. Can I help it if————"

"Texan! Savages!"

"A clarence, he said. Thoroughbred bays. And serve you right if he has Cupide brought into court."

"That one! Not for him, courtrooms. I know the look of them. He's probably wanted in Texas himself, and skipped out with somebody's carriage and pair."

"Oh, Kaka, let's not quarrel. I was going to have such a lovely day. I looked forward to it." The morning was sunny; she was young; a clarence drawn by long-tailed bays and driven by a huge Texan in a white sombrero could not long remain hidden on the streets of New Orleans; instinct warned her that danger lay ahead, common sense told her that Kakaracou was right.

They turned into Decatur Street and drew up at Madame Begué's with quite a flourish.

"Let him wait," Clio commanded, loftily.

"No such thing. Sitting here, doing nothing, while we pay him for it. I'll pay him off now. If he wants to wait until we come out that's his business. You, Cupide!"

Cupide had heard. He tossed the shabby reins into the hands of their owner, and, agile as a monkey, scrambled out on the heaving back of one of the astonished horses, retrieved his check reins (at which the horses' heads, released, immediately slumped forward as though weighted with lead), leaped down and handed Clio out in his best Paris manner. The check reins he tucked away under his coat; he sprang to open the restaurant door, and the strange little procession of three climbed the narrow stair and entered as Rita Dulaine had entered so often twenty years before, with the woman to attend her like a duenna, the dwarf to stand behind her chair as though she were Elizabethan royalty.

4

NEW ORLEANS OF the late '50's had itself been sufficiently bizarre to have found nothing fantastic in the sight of the beautiful *placée* followed by her strange retinue. But the New Orleans of Clio's day, breakfasting solidly in its favorite restaurant, looked up from its plate to remain staring, its fork halfway to its mouth.

The three stood a moment in the doorway, their eyes blinking a little in the sudden change from the white glare of the midday streets to the cool half-light of the restaurant. In that instant Monsieur Begué himself stood before them in his towering stiffly starched chef's cap, his solid round belly burgeoning ahead of him. He bowed, he clasped his plump hands.

"Madame! But no. For a moment I thought you were—but of course it isn't possible————"

"I have heard my mother speak of you so often, Monsieur Begué. They say I resemble her. I am Comtesse de—uh—Trenaunay de Chanfret. But this is America, and my home now. Just Madame de Chanfret, please."

She was having a splendid time. She relished the little stir that her entrance had made; it was pleasant to be ushered by Hippolyte Begué himself to a choice table and to have him hovering over her chair as he presented for her inspection the menu handwritten in lively blue ink. Having entered with enormously dramatic effect, she now pretended to be a mixture of royalty incognito and modest young miss wide-eyed with wonder. She had seated herself with eyes cast down, she had handed her parasol to Cupide, her gloves to Kaka, she had pressed her hands to her hot cheeks in pretty confusion, she had thrown an appealing glance up at the attendant Begué.

"I want everything that you are famous for, Monsieur. You and Madame Begué." She cast an admiring glance at the plump black-garbed figure reigning behind the vast cashier's desk at the rear. "All the delicious things Mama used to describe to me in Paris."

"She spoke of my food! In Paris!" He was immensely flattered. He snapped his fingers for Léon, the headwaiter, he himself flicked open her napkin and presented it to her with a flourish. Then the three heads came close—the restaurateur, the waiter, the audacious girl—intent on the serious business of selecting a Sunday morning breakfast from among the famous list of viands at Begué's. Madame Begué's renowned crayfish bisque? Not a dish for even Sunday New Orleans breakfast. Pompano? Begué's celebrated calf's liver *à la bourgeoise, Filet de truite, Poulet chanteclair?* With an *omelette soufflée* to follow? *Grillades? Pain perdu?*

Clio, speaking her flawless Parisian French to the two attendant men, ordered delicately and fastidiously. Hippolyte Begué himself waddled off to the kitchen to prepare the dishes with his own magic hands.

Clio Dulaine now leaned back in her chair and breathed a gusty sigh of relief and satisfaction. She looked about her with the lively curiosity of a small girl and the air of leisurely contemplation befitting her recently assumed title and station. She was attempting to produce the effect of being a woman of the world, a connoisseur of food, a *femme fatale* of mystery and experience. Curiously enough, with her lovely face made up as Aunt Belle had taught her, her rich attire, her bizarre attendants, her high, clear voice speaking the colloquial French of the Paris she had just left, she actually achieved the Protean role.

That choice section of New Orleans which was engaged in the rite of Sunday breakfast at Madame Begué's stared, whispered, engaged in facial gymnastics that ranged all the way from looking down their noses to raising their eyebrows.

Well they might. Behind the newcomer's chair stood Cupide, a figure cut from a pantomime. He brushed away a fly. He summoned a waiter with the Gallic "P-s-s-s-t!" He handed his mistress a little black silk fan. He glared pugnaciously about him. He stood with his tiny arms folded across his chest, a bodyguard out of a nightmare. His face was on a level with the table top as he stood. Each new dish, on presentation, he viewed with a look of critical contempt, standing slightly on tiptoe the better to see it as he did so.

From time to time Clio handed him a bit of crisp buttered crust with a tidbit on it—a bit of rich meat or a corner of French toast crowned with a ruby of jelly, as one would toss a bite to a pampered dog.

Breakfasting New Orleans snorted or snickered, outraged.

"Not bad," Clio commented graciously from time to time, addressing Kaka or the world at large. "The food here is really good—but really good."

Kakaracou sat at table an attendant, aloof from food and being offered none. Certainly Begué's clients would have departed in a body had she eaten one bite. Her lean straight back was erect, disdaining to relax against Begué's comfortable chair. The eyes beneath the heavy hoodlike lids noted everything about the table, about the room; she marked each person who entered at the doorway that led up the stair from the hot noonday glare of Decatur Street. For the most part her hands remained folded quietly in her neat lap, the while her eyes slid this way and that and the darting movement of her head set her earrings to swinging and glinting. Occasionally the purple-black hand, skinny and agile, darted forth like a benevolent spider to place nearer for her mistress's convenience a sugar bowl, a spoon, a dish. She viewed the food with the hard clear gaze of the expert.

"Red wine enough in that sauce, you think? . . . The *pain perdu* could be a shade browner."

The delicate and lovely girl slowly demolished her substantial breakfast with proper appreciation. She might have been a lifelong *habituée* dawdling thus over her Sunday morning meal. The room watched her boldly or covertly. Monsieur Begué hovered paternally. The waiters approved her and her entourage. Here was someone dramatic and to their fancy; someone who, young though she was, knew food. Titled, too. From France. There was about these serving men nothing of the appearance of the gaunt and flat-footed of their tribe. They were fruity old boys with mustaches and side whiskers. In moments of leisure they sat in a corner near Madame Begué's high desk reading *L'Abeille* and engaging in the argumentative talk of their fraternity. Nothing meager about these servitors. They, like Madame and Monsieur Begué, were solid with red wine and gumbo soup and the rich food for which the city was famous. Their customers were clients; each meal was a problem to be weighed, discussed. They advised, gravely. They were quick to see that the lovely stranger knew the importance of good eating.

From time to time Léon reported in a sibilant whisper, "A Comtesse, that little one . . . The little monkey is old, his face is marked with wrinkles when you see him close . . . She orders like a true Creole. Grits, she said, one must always have with breakfast at Begué's."

The talk between mistress and maid was not at all the sort of conversation ordinarily found in this relation. It resembled the confidences exchanged between friends of long standing or even conspirators who have nothing to conceal from one another. And conspirators they were. As guest after guest entered the dim coolness of the restaurant Kaka commented on them succinctly and wittily. The girl munched and nodded. Now and then she laid down her knife and fork to laugh her indolent deep-throated laugh.

The women who entered now, decorously escorted by the men of their family, were, for the most part, dressed in quiet, rich black, like Parisian women; the men wore Sunday attire of Prince Albert coat or sack suits with dark ties. Sallow, reserved, rather forbidding, they conducted themselves like royalty incognito, aware of their own exalted state but pretending unconsciousness of it.

"*Chacalata,*" Kakaracou said, witheringly. It was a local New Orleans term, culled from heaven knows where, to describe the inner circle of New Orleans aristocracy, clannish, self-satisfied, resenting change or innovation.

"The same dresses they wore when we left for France fifteen or more years ago. They're so puffed with their own pride they think they don't have to dress fashionably. They'd come out in their *gabrielles,* those *chacalata* women, if they thought it decent."

Clio giggled at the thought of beholding these stately New Orleans Creole women in the informality of the loose wrapper locally known as a *gabrielle*. She preened herself in the consciousness of her own rich finery. "Dowdy old things, in their snuffy black. I could show them black. I wish I'd worn my black ottoman silk with the Spanish lace flounces."

"Too grand for the street," Kaka observed. "Ladies don't dress up on the street. But then, you're not a lady." She said this, not spitefully or insolently, but as one stating a fair fact to another.

"Not I!" Clio agreed, happily. "I'm going to enjoy myself, and laugh, and wear pretty clothes and do as I like."

"Like your mama."

"No, not like poor dear Mama. She didn't have any fun—at least not since I can remember. Always moping and reading old letters and trailing around in her *gabrielle*, ill and sad."

"She wasn't always like that, my poor *bébé* Rita."

"Look!" Clio interrupted, in French. "There! Coming in. Is it They?"

The head in its brilliant tignon jerked sharply in the direction of the doorway. The spare figure stiffened, then relaxed. "No. No, silly."

"Are you sure? You're sure you'd know them, after all these years?"

"I would know them, those faces of stone, after a hundred years. . . . Stop staring at the door. Drink your good red wine and eat another slice of that delicious liver. It will bring you strength and make your eyes bright and your cheeks pink."

Clio pushed her plate away like a willful child. "I don't want to be pink. Pink women bore me, just to look at them, like dolls."

Indeed the naturally creamy skin was dead white with the French liquid powder she used, so that her eyes seemed darker and more enormous; sadder too, and the wide mouth wider. Almost a clown's mask, except for its beauty. It was a make-up that Aunt Belle Piquery had taught her—Aunt Belle of the round blue eyes and the plump pink cheeks and the pert little nose. "I'm the type men take a fancy to, but you're the type they stay with and die for," the hearty old baggage used to say to Clio. "Like your ma."

"All right, pink or not, eat it anyway," Kaka now persisted.

"I won't. I'm not hungry. I just ordered everything because I wanted to taste everything."

Like an angry monkey Kakaracou chattered her disapproval. "I told you! It's that jambalaya you stuffed yourself with in the French Market."

"Oh, what's it matter! I eat what I like when I like. . . . It's getting late, isn't it? They're not coming. You said yourself They stopped coming after Mama and Papa—after They—when Mama moved into the Rampart Street house. It isn't likely They started coming after Papa died. Anyway They're millions of years old by now."

The eyes of the Negress narrowed, they were knifelike slits in her gray-black face. "They stopped. But They came again, after. Creoles are like that. Customs. Habits. Everything *de rigueur*."

The girl leaned forward, eagerly. "Do I look enough like her? When They come in will it be a shock to Them to see me sitting here? Do I look like the picture Mama and Papa had taken together? Will They think I am Mama—just for that first moment?"

The woman's eyes regarded her sadly across the table; she shook her turbaned head. "You are like her, yes, perhaps even enough to startle anyone who knew her when she was your age. But she was beautiful. She was the most beautiful woman in New Orleans."

"I'm beautiful too."

"You're well enough. But she! At the balls they used to stand on chairs just to see her come in. Pale pink satin—shell pink—with black lace, sent from Paris, and all her jewels.''

"I'll have jewels too. You wait. You'll see."

"But you have hers."

"Second best."

"Her second best were finer than the best of other women."

The girl's eyes were always on the door, though she pretended to be busy with her food. Each time it opened she glanced swiftly to see who it was that stood outlined against the bar of blinding white sunshine that leaped into the carefully shaded room. She smiled now a little secret smile. "Mama was more beautiful perhaps, but I have more chic and more spirit. You've said so yourself, when you weren't cross with me. I'll find a rich man—but colossally rich—and I'll marry him. Not like mama. No Rampart Street for me."

Her eyes always sliding round to the door. Kakaracou saw this. Kakaracou saw everything. "Yes, that will be fine. That's why you are watching the door like a spaniel. Don't think you're fooling me. It isn't that you expect to see Them come in. You are watching to see if he has followed you here, that tramp, that roustabout, that *cagnard* in the French Market. That's why you wanted the carriage to wait outside. He might see it there, and know."

"That's a lie!" Clio snapped, too hotly. "I'd forgotten all about him until you mentioned him, that *picaioun.*" To prove this she busied herself with the dish before her, her eyes on her plate, so that though the door swung open she did not glance up to see who entered.

Cupide behind her chair leaned forward suddenly and stood on tiptoe so that the great head was close to her ear. "There he is! That *Gros-Jean!* Shall I butt him again?"

The girl's face and throat flushed pink—the pink she despised—beneath the sallow white of her skin and the white powder overlaying it.

"It is he!" breathed Clio, drawing herself up very fine and straight and looking tremendously happy.

Kaka knew an emergency. "Come. We will go. Cupide, run, ask Madame Begué the bill. *Vite! Vite!*"

"No!" Clio commanded sharply as the dwarf started off with his waddling bandy-legged gait. "Back, Cupide! I'm not leaving."

The man had not blinked or peered as he entered the room. Those eyes were accustomed to the white-hot sun of the Texas plains. He loomed immense in the doorway, then he smiled, he took off the great white sombrero and gave it a little twirl of satisfaction on one forefinger before he crossed the room with his long, loping stride, the high heels of his boots tap-tapping smartly on the flagstoned floor. He ignored Léon, who was about to approach him, he deftly side-stepped waiters with laden trays, he made straight for the table just next to the one on which his gaze was concentrated. Pulling out a chair he sank into it with a sigh of relief that almost drowned out the protesting creak of the chair as it received his great frame. His long legs sprawled under the table and into the aisle, he flung the sombrero to the floor beside his chair, he smiled broadly and triumphantly even as he summoned Hippolyte Begué with one beckoning finger and a "Heh, cookee!" Monsieur Begué did not pause; he did not even look in the direction of the man; he walked on with the leisurely pushing strut of the potbellied and vanished into the kitchen.

Kakaracou leaned forward. Her undertone was a hiss. "You see! He's sitting at the next table. Come. We are leaving."

"And I say we're staying. I'm not nearly finished. I'm going to have an *omelette soufflée* and after that some strawberries with thick cream."

Kaka glared, her wrinkled face working. "Yes! Burst your corsets! Stuff yourself! With a figure like a cow you'll get a fine husband, oh, yes! Or maybe you've already picked that Texas *vacher* for a bridegroom. He's used to bulging sides."

"Texas, Texas! How do you know he's from Texas? Besides, what does it matter! I'm not even looking at him. What do I care where he's from!"

Kaka smothered a little cackle of contempt. "Well, look at him then. He's mumbling over the menu. He can't read a word of it; he never saw a French menu before. Beef and beans, that's what he's used to, that *imbécile!* Look, Léon is laughing at him; he doesn't even care to put his hand before his mouth to hide his laugh. Now he points—the *stupide*—with his great thick sausage finger."

"I think he's beautiful," Clio said, deliberately. She put one hand to her throat. "I think he's beautiful."

As Kaka said, the man was pointing with one forefinger; he looked up at the contemptuous waiter and smiled boyishly; there was something engaging, something infinitely appealing about this great creature's perplexed smile.

"What's that, sonny? I'm no Frenchy. In Texas where I came from we print our bill of fare in American."

"I make no doubt," sneered Léon.

The Texan mopped his forehead with a vast red handkerchief. "It sure is steamy in New Or-leens," he said.

You would have said that Clio had not even looked at him. Industriously she had cleared her plate in the good French manner, pursuing the last evasive drop of sauce with a relentless crust. Her gaze was on her empty dish; she had not seemed to flick an eyelid. Yet now she said to Kaka's horror, "If he were mine I would have for him four dozen of the finest white handkerchiefs of handwoven linen and you would embroider the initials in the most delicate scrolls."

"I!" Kaka's remonstrance was pure outrage. "Embroider for that cowboy! He's never seen a white linen handkerchief."

"Linen, too, for his shirts," Clio went on equably. "Fine pleated linen and his initials on that too."

"Initials, initials!" barked the infuriated Kaka. "What initials!"

"What does it matter?" Clio murmured with maddening dreaminess.

The man at the next table had made his reluctant decision. "I don't know what the hell runions are, but I'll take a chance on it. They say anything here is licking good."

Clio tapped smartly three times with her knife against her water glass. At the sound Léon, smirking at the adjoining table, turned sharply toward her. "Léon!" She beckoned him, he sped toward her, he leaned deferentially over her table, forsaking his later client without so much as a word of apology.

"Léon, please tell Monsieur Begué I will have one of his marvelous *omelettes soufflées.*"

Léon was all admiration. "It is *prodigieux,* the fine appetite that Madame la Comtesse has! Monsieur Begué will be enchanted, he———!"

"P-s-s-s-st!" The sibilant sound came so venomously from Kaka that even the chunky Cupidon gave a jerk of alarm, stationed though he was so stolidly behind Clio's chair. "They're here! They're entering. I told you so! See, Madame Begué herself comes down from her desk to greet them. Now will you try to act the lady!"

"Good," said Clio calmly, not even deigning to turn her head. "And Léon, tell Monsieur seated there at the next table—that one with the big hat and the boots—tell him that if he is having difficulty in choosing his breakfast I shall be happy to assist him.''

Léon stared, his mouth agape. "What! That one, you mean!"

"Oh, yes, we're old friends. Only this morning we happened to meet him in the French Market. That's why he is breakfasting here. Ask him if he wouldn't, perhaps, prefer to be served here at my table. Then we can chat.'' Stunned, he turned away. "A moment! Léon! That old couple there—Madame Begué is speaking to them—now Monsieur Begué is showing them to a table. Is that—are they the old Monsieur and Madame Dulaine?''

The man stared, startled, then burst into discreet laughter. "Madame will have her little joke. For a moment you fooled me. Of course Madame knows that old Monsieur and Madame Dulaine are"—he coughed apologetically—"are, in a word, dead.''

Léon approached the near-by table with a new deference. Clio turned a dazzling smile upon Kakaracou. The natural prune color of Kaka's skin had turned a sort of dirty gray. Her lips were drawn away from the strong yellow teeth.

"Wait out in the hallway, Kaka. Or go home if you like. Cupide will stay.''

"You're crazy. You're as crazy as your mother was. Worse! I've a mind to slap you right here.''

"Oh, have you! You're not my nurse any more, you know. You're my maid. You'll do as I say, or I'll send you away to starve. You'll never see me again. Look! He's coming. Now I'll have a man at my table to protect me, like those other women. The handsomest man in the room. The handsomest man I ever———''

He was standing by her chair looking down at her. He flushed, he stammered. In his haste and astonishment he had left his great white sombrero on the floor by his chair. "Did you—that fellow said you said—pardon me, Ma'am, do you want me to sit here—did you mean———''

"Please sit down. Kaka, a menu. Cupide, fetch the gentleman's hat at the other table beside the chair.''

"Well, say, thanks. Back where I come from we carry our hats with us on account of not knowing just when we might want to pull out of a place quick.'' He jerked out a chair and bumped the table so that the water and the red wine slopped over the glasses' rims. His face would have grown redder if that had been possible; he sat down in embarrassed bewilderment yet with the kind of grace that comes of superb muscular coordination.

Kaka had risen; she stood at the side of the table as though rooted to the spot; she clung to the chair back with one skinny hand so that the knuckles showed almost white. But the two were not looking at her, they were looking at each other. He sat forward in his chair, one great arm thrown across the white cloth; she sat back in her chair, cool, silent, her eyes enormous in the white face, the pearl and onyx brooch at her throat rising and falling quickly, giving the lie to her cool silence. So they faced one another, measuring quietly as combatants eye each other with wary curiosity before the beginning of a struggle. Then in a kind of exultant hysteria she began to laugh her deep-throated deliberate laugh. After a moment he joined in, ruefully at first, like a giant boy, then delightedly, like a man who senses victory. The restaurant rang with their laughter. Begué breakfasters looked up from their plates, frowning at first. Monsieur Begué in his towering white cap stood in the doorway that led to the kitchen; Madame Begué of the shrewd black eyes held her busy pen suspended in momentary disapproval; the waiters glanced over their shoulders at the unwonted sound. Then the infection of hysterical laughter made itself felt. As the fresh high sounds of young laughter pealed through the sedate room you saw Monsieur Hippolyte Begué's great white-aproned belly begin to shake with sympathetic mirth; Madame Begué's vast black silk bosom heaved; the waiters giggled behind their napkins; the guests smiled, chuckled, laughed foolishly and helplessly. A plague of laughter fell upon the place. Only Kakaracou showed no taint of senseless mirth. And Cupidon behind his mistress's chair, though he smiled broadly, was too bewildered by the sudden favors accorded the lately despised Texan to relax into the mood of the room.

"Forgive me," Clio gasped, rather wildly. "You looked, sitting there, so—so big!"

"Far's that goes, you look kind of funny yourself, Ma'am, with all that white stuff on your face."

As suddenly as it had begun, the laughter of the two stopped. The Texan wiped his eyes. Clio Dulaine pressed one hand to her heart and leaned back in her chair, spent. The breakfasters, looking a little foolish and resentful, applied themselves again to their food.

He said, companionably, as though they had known each other for years, "I don't know what we're laughing at, but I haven't had so much fun in a coon's age. And down in Texas they told me people were stand-offish in New Or-leens."

"New Orleans," she said, gently correcting him.

"You fixing to learn me the English language? They told me you were French."

"I'm not French. I'm American. And it's teach, not learn."

"All right. Play schoolma'am if you want to. I'll learn anything you say. When I first saw you there in the Market I thought you were a town woman parading around with those two, all dressed up———"

"How dare you!"

"Well, I'm just coming out and telling you like that because I want to explain how come I spoke to you there. I had you wrong. I want to start fair with you because something tells me you and me———"

"Pardon." The waiter placed before him the dish at which he had pointed just as Clio had summoned him to her table. It turned out to be Begué's famous kidney stew with red wine, at which the Texan looked rather doubtfully. Hours had gone into the preparation of the dish before it had reached the stage of being ready to serve at a Begué breakfast. Hippolyte Begué allowed no one but himself to take part in the rite of its cooking.

"Rognon. Ragoût de rognon."

The Texan stirred it doubtfully with his fork. He looked up. "Got any ketchup."

The waiter recoiled. "Ketchup! But this *ragoût* is cooked with Monsieur Begué's own sauce, it is prepared by the hands of Monsieur Begué him———"

"Ketchup!" commanded Clio, crisply. Then, in French, "In Paris now everything is eaten with ketchup. It is the chic thing for dinner in Paris. Ketchup for Monsieur."

Stunned, the man went in search of the condiment. "What's that you're talking—French? I thought you said you were American."

"I am! I am American. But I was brought up in France. I am Comtesse de Chanfret."

"Shucks! You don't say! Well, honey, I don't believe it. But just to prove to you I'm playing square with you I'll tell you my real name though I'd just as soon they didn't know where I am, back in Texas. My name's Maroon. Clint Maroon. Now come on—tell me yours."

"Clint Maroon," she repeated after him, softly. She looked up at the grim-visaged Kaka still stationed behind the chair in which she lately had been seated. "Do you hear that, Kaka? The initials to be embroidered are C. M. You may go now and wait in the hall."

5

HE HAD DRIVEN her home behind the highstepping bays that Sunday afternoon—home to the Rampart Street house. Cool and straight and fragrant she sat beside him in the clarence. Now and then he turned his head to look at her almost shyly. His was not a swiftworking mind. His growing bewilderment aroused an inner amusement in her mingled with a kind of tenderness; a mixture of emotions whose consequences she did not yet recognize. She looked at the muscles of his wrists and at his strong bronzed hands as, gloveless, he held the reins. The two had been voluble enough in the restaurant. Now they were silent. Once, as though obeying an overmastering impulse, he shifted the reins to one hand and reached over as though to touch her knee. She drew away. He flushed, boyishly; flicked the bays smartly with the whip.

"I can't figure out about you."

"Is that why you whip your horses?"

In the back seat sat Kakaracou, an unwilling chaperon whose glare of disapproval would have seared their necks if their own emotional warmth had not served as counteraction. Cupidon had walked home—rather, after one wistful look at the fiery horses and the dashing equipage he had whisked off at an incredible pace on his own stumpy legs. Taking short cuts, dodging through alleys, there he stood, purple-faced and puffing what with haste and the heat, waiting at the carriage block when the turnout drew up before the house. He took the horses' heads, one tiny hand stroking their necks and withers with the practiced touch of the horse-lover.

Clint Maroon handed Clio out. Agilely Kaka stepped down, but she stood waiting like a demon duenna. Maroon stared at the neat secret house, he looked around him at this neighborhood that had about it something flavorous, something faintly sinister, something shoddy, something of past dignity. He looked the girl full in the face.

She hesitated, she glanced at the waiting Kaka; like a young girl still a pupil at the school in France she said, primly, "Won't you come in?"

He said, crudely, "Say, what kind of a game is this, anyway? "

Without a word she turned and walked swiftly toward the house. Cupide dropped the bridle-hold, Kakaracou seemed to flow like a lithe snake into the house, the front door closed with a thud, leaving him staring after them. As if by magic the three had vanished. The house-front was blank as a vault. From the sidewalk there was no hint of the garden at the back with its vines and shrubs, its magnolia tree, its courtyard green with moss, the tiny fountain's tinkle giving the illusion of coolness.

For a week he haunted Rampart Street. At first he came with his horses and carriage and the neighborhood marked him and watched and waited, but the house door did not open to his knocking, and small boys, white and black, gathered to stare and the horses fidgeted. Clint Maroon felt a baleful eye upon him from somewhere within the house—an eye with yellowish whites in a prune-colored face. But there was no sound. He took to loitering in the neighborhood, he sauntered into the near-by provision shops and asked questions meant to be discreet. But the shopkeepers were sneeringly polite and completely noncommunicative; they looked at him, at his white sombrero, at his high-heeled boots with the lone star stitching in the top, at

his wide-skirted coat and the diamond in his shirt front and at his skin that
had been ruddied by sun and whipped by wind and stung by desert sand.
They said, "Ah, a visitor from Texas, I see." The inflection was not flattering. He had a room at the St. Charles Hotel, that favorite rendezvous of
Louisiana planters and Texas cattle men. Its columned façade, its magnificent shining dome, its famous Sazaracs made from the potent Sazarac
brandy, all contributed to its fame and flavor. From here he laboriously
composed a letter to her, written in his round, schoolboyish hand and delivered in style by a dapper Negro in hotel uniform. He had spent an entire
morning over it.

> DEAR LADY,
>   You might be a countess like you said but you are a queen
> to me. I did not go for to hurt your feelings when I said that
> about how I did not understand about you. I guess back in
> Texas we are kind of raw. Anyway I sure never met anybody
> like you before and you had me locoed. I think about you
> all day and all night and am fit to be tied. You were mighty
> kind to me there in Begué's eating house and I acted like
> a fool and impolite as though I never had any bringing up
> and a disgrace to my Mother. If you will let me talk to you
> I can explain. I have got to see you or I will bust the house
> in. Please. You are the most beautiful little lady I ever met.
>   Ever your friend and servant,
>   CLINT MAROON.

This moving epistle was wasted effort. Clio never saw it. Delivered into
the hands of the ubiquitous Kakaracou, it was thrust into her capacious skirt
pocket and brought out that evening under the kitchen lamplight. But reading
was not one of Kaka's talents. Discretion told her to throw the letter into
the fire. Curiosity as to its contents proved too strong. Over the kitchen
supper table with Cupide she drew out the sheet of paper and turned it over
in her skinny fingers. She had deciphered the signature, and this she had
torn off in the touching belief that without it the letter's source would be a
mystery to its reader.

It was characteristic of Kaka's adaptability that, after an absence of more
than fifteen years, the old New Orleans Negro patois and accent were creeping back into her speech. Gombo French, Negro English, Cajun, indefinably
mixed; the dropped consonants, the softly slurred vowels, the fine disregard
for tenses. Naturally imitative and a born mimic, she was likely to fit her
speech to the occasion. Weary, she unconsciously slipped back into the
patois of her childhood. To impress shopkeepers and people whom she
considered riffraff, such as Clint Maroon, she chattered a voluble and colloquial French of the Paris boulevards and the Paris gutters. Her accent
when speaking pure English was more British than American, having been
copied from Clio's own. Clio's English had been learned primarily from the
careful speech of Sister Félice at the convent. And Sister Félice had come
by her English in London itself, during her novitiate. Not alone Kaka, but
Clio and Cupide were adept in these lingual gymnastics. They were given
to talking among themselves in a spicy *ragoût* of French, English and Gombo
that was almost unintelligible to an outsider.

Kaka now fished the crumpled letter out of her capacious pocket,
smoothed it, and turned upon Cupide an eye meant to be guileless and which
would not for a moment have deceived a beholder much less astute than the
cynical Cupidon.

"I find letter today in big *armoire* in hall I guess must be there many years hiding heself."

"What's it say?"

Kaka rather reluctantly pushed it across the table to him. St. Charles Hotel. New paper, palpably fresh ink. Cupide, his fork poised, read it aloud in a brisk murmur. Intently the old woman leaned forward to hear. Finished, Cupide said, *"Tu mentis comme un arracheur de dents."* You lie like a dentist. And went on with his supper.

"What does it say, you monkey, you!"

He shrugged. "Wants to see her. He'll break into the house if she doesn't see him. Crazy about her. A *la folie."*

A flame of fear and hate flared in Kaka's eyes. She pushed back her plate. She remembered the days when strange people had come into Rita Dulaine's house, forcing their way into the room where she lay weeping after Nicolas was dead.

"We must leave here. It is no good for us here in New Orleans. It was good in Paris—*triste* but good."

Cupide wiped his plate clean with a crust of crisp French bread and popped the morsel into his mouth. "Old *prune sèche!* What do you know! It's fine here in America. Don't you bother your addled head about little Clio. She knows her way about. Anyway, I like that big *vacher* from Texas. He knows about horses. Yesterday I heard he won a thousand dollars at the races. At night he gambles down on Royal Street and wins. At Number 18 they say he never loses."

"Number 18, Number 18! What are you talking about!"

"That big marble building on the Rue Royal—the one that used to be the Merchants' Exchange. Everybody knows it's a gambling house now. You ought to see it! Mirrors and velvet, and supper spread out on tables———"

"So that's where you've been at night! Leaving us here two women unprotected alone in the house." A sudden thought struck her. "Has he seen you there? Have you been talking———"

"No, but I might if you don't feed me better. You with your everlasting pineapple and strawberries with kirsch, you're too lazy to prepare a real sweet—*baba au rhum* or a lovely *crème brûlè."*

"Little One, I make you sweets—*omelette soufflèe—crepe suzette*—baba cake—pie Saint-Honorè—effen you not speak to her about letter."

He strutted superior in his knowledge as a male. His answer fell into Gombo French. "Make no difference about letter, Old One. This going to be something. You see. You better go to voodoo woman get black devil's powder. But if you do I tell. Anyway, I am sick of nothing but women in the house, here and in Paris. A man around suit me fine."

Now Clio was definitely bored with her week of dignified seclusion. It was not for this that she had come to New Orleans—to sit alone in the dusk in a garden swooning sweet with jessamine and roses and magnolia. She dressed herself all in white and, with Kaka and Cupide keeping pace behind her, she walked to the Cathedral of St. Louis in the cool of the evening, prayer book in hand, eyes cast down, but not so far down that she failed to see him when he entered. For at last he was rewarded for his daily vigil at the corner of Rampart Street. He did not remain in the shadow of the dim cathedral columns but came swiftly to her and knelt beside her, wordlessly, his shoulder touching hers, and suddenly the candlelights swam before her eyes and there came a pounding in her ears. She did not glance up at him. She closed her eyes, she bowed her head, she thought, irreligiously, I must tell him not to use that sweetish hair pomade, it isn't chic. When, finally, she rose, he rose. Together they moved up the aisle and, dreamlike, walked out into the tropical dusk. Kakaracou and Cupide fell in behind them.

"Send them away," he said. It was the first word that had been uttered between them.

She turned and spoke to them in French. "Go home, you two, quickly. There will be two of us for supper. The cold *daube glacé,* soft-shell crabs— Cupide, fetch a block of ice from the *épicier* and get out a bottle of the Grand Montrachet."

They ate by candlelight with the French doors wide open into the garden. They ate the delicate food, they drank the cool dry wine, they talked a great deal at first and laughed and did not look at one another for longer than a flick of the eyelash; but then they talked less and less, their gaze dwelt the one on the other longer and more intently until finally, wordlessly, they rose and moved in a pulsating silence toward the French doors, down the cool stone steps into the velvet dark of the garden, and the white of her gown merged with the dark cloth of his coat and there was only the soft tinkle of the little fountain. In the bedroom the gaunt figure of Kaka was silhouetted against the light as she made her mistress's room ready for the night.

6

JUST AS SHE had inherited all that remained of her mother's magnificent Rue de la Paix jewelry, just as her mother's exquisite Paris gowns fitted her as well as her own frocks, so Clio Dulaine had been bequeathed other valuables of courtesanship less tangible but equally important. Now, in the Rampart Street house, she slipped fluidly into the way of life that had been Rita Dulaine's many years before. But with a difference. There was an iron quality in this girl that the other woman never had possessed.

From her lovely languorous mother and from her hearty jovial aunt Clio had early learned the art of being charming to everyone. A trick of the socially insecure, there yet was nothing servile about it. Clio had seen Rita Dulaine's poignant smile and wistful charm turned upon the musty old concierge as he opened the courtyard door of the Paris flat. The same smile and equal charm had been bestowed upon any man numbered among her few Paris acquaintances whom she might encounter on her rare visits to the opera or while driving in the Bois. Her graciousness was partly due, doubtless, to the inherent good nature of a woman who has been beautiful and beloved for years; partly to the fact that gracious charm was a necessary equipment of the born courtesan.

So, then, the manner of the girl Clio Dulaine stemmed from a combination of causes: unconscious imitation of the two women she most loved and admired; observation, training, habit, innate shrewdness. She had, too, something of her buxom aunt's lusty good humor; much of her mother's sultry enchantment.

Without effort, without a conscious thought to motivate it, Clio had turned the same warm, personal smile on the waiter Lègon and on Monsieur Hippolyte Begué; on the painters and glaziers who had smartened the Rampart Street house; on Clint Maroon.

The relation between these two, begun as a flirtation, had, in two weeks, taken on a serious depth and complexity. Though so strongly drawn together there was, too, a definite sex antagonism between them. Each had a plan of life selfishly devised, though vague. Each felt the fear of the other's power to change that plan. Each, curiously enough, nourished a deep resentment against the world that had hurt someone dear to them. Hers was a sophisticated viewpoint, for all her youth and inexperience; his a naïve one, for all his masculinity and daredevil past. Cautiously at first, then in a flood that burst the dam of caution and reticence, the two had confided to each other the details of their lives. Through long lazy afternoons, through hot sultry nights each knew the relief that comes of confidences exchanged, of sympathies expressed, of festering grievances long hidden brought now to light and cleansed by exposure. Adventurers, both, bent on cracking the shell of the world that was to be their oyster.

Though they did not know it, they were like two people who, searching for buried treasure, are caught in a quicksand. Every struggle to extricate themselves only made them sink deeper.

She had never met anyone like this dashing and slightly improbable figure who seemed to have stepped out of the pages of fiction.

"Tell me, the men in Texas, are they all like you?"

"Only the bad ones."

"You're not bad. You're only mad at the world. You are like someone in a story book. When we lived in Paris I read the stories of Bret Harte. Do you know him? He is wonderful."

"No. Who's he?"

"Oh, what a great stupid boy! He is a famous American writer. His story-book men carry a pistol, too, like you, at the hip. I don't like pistols. They make me nervous. You know why."

By now he knew the story of Rita Dulaine. The Comtesse de Trenaunay de Chanfret had vanished early in their acquaintance. "This is different, honey. You don't have to worry about a gun on me."

"But why! Why do you wear it? It is fantastic, a gun on the hip, like the Wild West."

"The West is wild, and don't you forget it. Anyway, I wouldn't feel I was dressed respectable without it, I'm so used to it. I'd as soon go out without my shirt or my hat."

"Tell me, *chèri,* have you killed men?" He was silent. She persisted. "Tell me. Have you?"

"Oh, two, three, maybe. It was them or me." "They," she said automatically and absurdly.

"Aim to make a gentleman out of me, don't you, honey?"

"I don't want to change you. You are perfect. But perfect!"

"Ye-e-es, you do. You're like all the rest of 'em. They all try to make their men over."

"Their men! You are not my man. You belong to that little lady who you say is the finest little lady in the world—she who made you the amazing white satin tie embroidered with the blue forget-me-nots. Oh, that tie!" She laughed her slow, indolent laugh.

"What's the matter with it! You're jealous, that's all."

"It is terrible. But terrible! Tell me about her—the finest little lady in the world who made you that work of art. Blue eyes, you said, and golden hair, and so little she only comes up to here. How nize! How nize!" When she mocked him she became increasingly French, but rather in the music-hall manner, very maddening. "Tell me, when are you going to marry, you two?"

She could not be sure whether the finest little woman in the world really existed back there in his Texas past or whether he had devised her as protection. Grown cautious, he would say, "I don't aim to marry anybody. Me, I'm a lone ranger, out for big game."

She in turn had no intention of allowing this man to shape her life. She, too, had her armor against infatuation. "I shall marry. I shall marry a husband very, very rich and very respectable."

"Yes, and I'll be best man at the wedding."

"Why not? But no, you would be too handsome. All the guests would wonder why I had not married you. Very, very rich and very respectable men are so rarely handsome. But then one can't have everything."

"Say, what kind of a woman are you, anyway!" he would shout, baffled. Back home in Texas the codes were simpler. There were two kinds of women; good women, bad women. But here was a paradoxical woman, gay, gentle, fiery, prim; brazenly unconventional, absurdly correct; tender, hard, generous, ruthless. Sometimes she seemed an innocent girl; sometimes an accomplished courtesan.

Even after their first week together they were watching one another warily, distrustful of the world and of each other, stepping carefully to avoid a possible trap.

The very morning after their reunion in the church of St. Louis she had sat brushing her hair that hung a curtain of black against the sheer white dotted swiss of her *gabrielle* with its ruffled lace edging of Valenciennes. She wielded the silver-backed brush and sniffed the air delicately and half closed her eyes. "A house isn't really a house," she murmured, "unless it has about it the scent of a good cigar after breakfast."

He stared at her, he strode over to her seated there before the rosewood *duchesse*. With one great hand he grasped her shoulder so that she winced. "Where did you learn that?"

"Mama used to say that, poor darling. Or maybe it was Aunt Belle."

"Did, heh? Look here, all that stuff you were telling me last night in the garden—it's the truth, isn't it? I don't mean that first stuff about being a countess, and all that. Sometimes you talk like a schoolgirl—and sometimes I think you've been————"

She looked up at him from the low bench before the dressing table. He put his hand on her long throat, tipping her head still farther back so that his eyes plumbed hers.

"Ask Kaka. Ask Cupide."

"Those two! They'd lie for you no matter what."

"Well," she said gently, with his hand still on her throat so that he could feel the muscles moving under his palm as she spoke. "Well, if you think that I am lying and Kaka is lying and Cupide is lying why don't you finish your business here in New Orleans and go back to the finest little lady in Texas?" His great fist doubled against her jaw, he pushed her delicate head back gently, ruefully, in tender imitation of a blow.

He was a bewildered, love-smitten Texan who had met a woman the like of whom he never had seen or dreamed of.

For a week—two—three—they spent lazy hours talking, listening. The girl always until now had taken third place. Her mother had come first, then Aunt Belle; Kakaracou had waited on them, cooked New Orleans dishes for them, sewed for them. Cupide had run about for them tirelessly; he had been coachman, footman, butler, boots, page. Clio had worn second-best, had fetched and carried for the two women, had played bezique with Belle Piquery, bathed her mother's forehead with eau-de-cologne when she was suffering from headache, pressed her fresh young cheek against Rita's tear-furrowed one when she was sad, fed the two with her youth and high spirits. Now she found it wonderful to be the center of interest. Now she and Clint Maroon, suspicious of the world and resentful of it, could pour out to each other their hopes, their schemes, their longings, their emotions. It was almost as fascinating to listen as to speak. Not quite, but almost. He had told her his story disjointedly, in bits and pieces, for he was not an articulate man, and he had been taught to think that emotion was weakness.

"I haven't got any money, honey. I mean, money. I make my living gambling. I wouldn't fool you. I raise horses some—or did, back home in Texas. Sometimes I race 'em. That's how come I left. I shot the man we caught trying to lame my three-year-old, Alamo. He's almost pure Spanish, that chestnut. He steps so he hardly touches the ground; it's like the way you see a dancer that never seems to have a foot on the floor he's so light. It was a plain case; no jury in the Southwest could convict me, but I reckoned I'd better leave for now, anyway. And besides, I was ready to go. I always told Pa I'd come up North and get the land and money back they'd stole off him. Why, say, they came in and they took his land away from him as slick as if he'd been a hick playing a shell game at a country circus. Everybody in Texas knew Dacey Maroon, the town we lived in was named after him, Daceyville. Grampaw Maroon fought the siege of the Alamo; I was brought up on the story; it was sacred history like the stories in the Bible, only more real. He had fought over the very land he owned. Pa used to say that Daceyville and San Antonio were watered with the blood of their defenders. In Texas schools they teach the young ones about Bunker Hill and Valley Forge and battles of the Civil War like it was history, but mighty few up North know the story of the Alamo and San Jacinto. They're as much a part of American history as the Revolution or Gettysburg, and more. Pa had come in and settled his land and married Ma and brought her to Texas from Virginia. Brought up gentle as she was you'd think, she never could have stood what she had to. She was little————"

"Like the one embroidered the forget-me-not tie?"

"Why—maybe." "Men often marry their mothers," Clio observed, dreamily. Then, hastily, she added, "I heard Aunt Belle say that, too."

But his was too literal a mind for Belle Piquery's unconsciously sound psychology.

"There'll never be anybody like her. Everything around the house just so, and yet she'd never chase the menfolks out of the house to smoke, the way some women would. I reckon that was the way she was brought up in Virginia. She could gentle the orneriest horse in Texas, and her two little hands weren't any bigger than magnolia petals. Time she was married they drove into Texas from Virginia, through hell and high water. Pa worked that land there in Texas, staked it and claimed it and laid out the town of Daceyville, but Grampaw, he came in with Austin when Texas belonged to Mexico. That was real pioneering. They cleared, and they built cabins and planted grain. Funny thing about Texas. Do you know about Texas, honey?"

"No. I have read that it is big. Enormous. And wild."

"It's big, all right. Bigger than France, bigger than Germany, bigger than most of Europe rolled into one. Lots has been written about Texas, but it's unknown territory. Maybe it's because it's so all-fired big. Grampaw Dacey Maroon, and Sam Houston and Martin and Jones and Pettus—the Old Three Hundred—and Bowie and Travis and Davy Crockett, why, they were my heroes the way other youngsters think of Washington or Napoleon or Daniel Boone. Bowie, sick and dying of pneumonia there in the Alamo, and hacking away at the Mexicans from his cot because he was too weak to stand up or even sit up, and twenty dead Mexicans heaped up on the floor around him when finally they got him—that's what I mean when I say Texas. And then along through the West came a fellow named Huntington that used to be a watch peddler, and Mark Hopkins, and a storekeeper named Leland Stanford and a peddler named Charley Crocker. Smart as all get-out. Well, say, they pulled deals in Washington that no cattle or horse thief would have stooped

to. They began to survey in Daceyville and they sent a low-down sneaking
polecat to Pa and said, 'You'll give us your land and right of way through
here and so many thousand dollars that you'll raise among the folks here in
Daceyville and we'll run our railroad line through here and make a real town
of it. If you don't we'll go ten miles the other side and you might as well be
living in a graveyard.'

" 'I'm damned if I will,' " Pa said, and he got his gun and he chased them
off the place. They turned Daceyville into Poverty Flat; they built the depot
ten miles away and we found we were living in a deserted village, everything
closed up; you had to drive ten miles to get a sack of salt. Daceyville was
nothing but a wide place in the road. Everybody moved out except us. Pa
said we'd stay, and we did. The railroad they built yonder wasn't even a
decent road, but they'd been granted all that land by a rotten Congress that
they'd bought up—land on both sides of the tracks for miles and miles, east
and west. That's what they were after, you see. They got all that land along
the right of way—hundreds of thousands of acres—and it never cost them
a cent of their own money. A handful of men owned the West. They were
like kings. Pa said it wasn't like America, it wasn't taking a piece of land
from the government and settling it and making it fit for civilized folks to
live on. It was taking the land by force and by tricks—land that others had
worked on and settled. Ma said it was like the days of the feudal lords in
Europe, only this was supposed to be free America. It was free for them,
all right. All the silver and iron and copper in the land they'd stolen, and the
forests that stood on it and the rivers that ran through.''

"But couldn't your father fight them? Couldn't he go to Washington and
couldn't he see those Congressmen? If it was his own land!"

"He tried. That's all he did for years till he was old and broke. I saw my
mother and my father die in poverty on the land they'd cleared and built up.
Pa couldn't even take her back to Virginia to be buried with her kin the way
she'd always asked to be. Texas was Grampaw Maroon's lifeblood, and
Pa's—and mine, for a while. Not now. Reckon it's turned to gall, my blood.''

"It is bad to be bitter, Clint."

"Cleent," he grinned, mocking her. "Can't you talk American! Short,
like this—Clint." He clipped it smartly so that the sound fell on the ear like
the clink of a coin. "Clint."

"Clint," in brisk imitation.

"That's it, *muchachita!*"

"What? What is that word?"

"Oh, that. I learned that off the Mexicans down home. Spanish, I reckon.
Muchachita. Means—uh—pretty little girl, kind of. Sweetheart.''

"Very nice—that *muchachita*. But rather long for a dear name. And to
be called *muchachita* one must be little."

He passed his hand slowly over his eyes as though to wipe away an inner
vision. "That's so. It doesn't suit you, somehow. It just slipped out. It
belongs to Texas."

"But I like you to be Texas. It is right for you. You must never be different.
I want to know more about Texas and these men. Tell me more."

"Nothing more to tell, honey. They're the men I hate—them and their
kind. Ever since I grew up I made up my mind they'd never get me like
they'd got Pa. I was going to live off the rich and the suckers—and I have.
Let 'em look out for themselves. I live by gambling and racing once in a
while and turning a trick when I can—decent most of the time. Not always.
When I can get it honestly, I do it. When I can't, I get it the best way I can.
I've lived a rough life. The way I talk, I know better. But I want to talk the
way the cowhands talk, and the folks back in Texas. I've come a far piece

and I aim to go further, but Texas is where I belong. I'm going to make my pile off of them. I hate 'em all. I'd as soon shoot them as I would a gray mule-deer or a cottonmouth out on the Black Prairie. I might as well tell you I've killed men, but never for money. I've known a lot of women; I've never married one of them and don't aim to. I could be crazy about you but I ain't going to be.''

She looked at him as though seeing him clearly for the first time. "In a way, *chèri,* we're two of a kind. You heard your mother and father talking of the wrong that had been done to them and it cut deeply into you. I heard my mother and Aunt Belle talking the same way when I was very young and they thought I didn't hear or didn't understand. I wonder why grownup people think that children are idiots. I made up my mind early that some day I would pay them back, those people. I'm going to be rich and I'll make them pay for what they did to Mama and Aunt Belle. Mama never hurt anybody————''

"Well, excuse me, honey, but even back in Texas if shooting a man and killing him ain't hurting him none why————''

"She didn't kill him, I tell you. She————''

"I know, I know. Anyway, she had the gun, no matter which way she was pointing it, and he grabbed it and the bullet went into him and he died. And they got an awful ugly name for that in the courts of law.''

"If they thought she had killed him then why did they send her money all those years in France, to the day of her death?''

"Not aiming to hurt your feelings, honey, but that's called hush money where I come from.''

"Then New Orleans is going to learn that a Dulaine has returned from France. I'm going to see New Orleans and New Orleans is going to see me.''

"They'll come down on you.''

"They'll wish they hadn't.''

"I've seen a lot of women but I never saw any woman like you, Clio.''

"There isn't anyone like me,'' she replied quite simply. Then, "They'll come to me. You'll see.''

"Better not rile 'em. They'll find a way to make it hot for you. Anyway, you don't want to stay down here steaming like a clam. We can clear out, go up to Saratoga for the races. That's where I'm heading for. I wouldn't be here this long if it wasn't for you. You got me roped and tied, seems like.''

"Saratoga? Is that a nice place?''

"July and August there's nothing like it in the whole country. Races every day, gambling, millionaires and pickpockets and sporting people and respectable family folks and politicians and famous theater actors and actresses, you'll find them all at Saratoga.''

"I'd like that. But I haven't enough money, unless I sell something.''

"Shucks, you'll be with me. I can make enough for two.''

She shook her head. "No, I am going to be free. You want to be free, too. Perhaps we can have a plan together though. Tell me, is it cool there in Saratoga—cool and fresh and gay?''

"Well, not to say real cool. I've never been there before, but I've heard it's up in the hills beyond Albany, and there's pine woods all around, real spicy. And lakes. July, I was fixing to go up North. Come on.''

She sat a moment very still, her eyes fixed, unblinking, deep in thought. When finally she spoke it was in a curious monotone, as though she were thinking aloud. "Two more months here. That will be enough for me. I have a plan. There are things I must find out, first. These past few weeks—lovely— but no more drifting, drifting.'' She sighed, straightened, looked at him with a keen directness. "Clint, will you stay here in New Orleans for a month or perhaps a little more?"

He laughed rather shortly. "Wasn't for you I'd been on my way before now. It's too soft and pretty down here for me, and wet-hot. A week or two here and I was heading for St. Louis or maybe Kansas City and up north to Chicago. Clark Street, Chicago."

"Go then."

He looked down at his own big clasped hands, he glanced at the letter C so beautifully embroidered on the lower sleeve of his fine cambric shirt as he sat, coatless. In his hip pocket was a fine linen handkerchief hemstitched and marked in a design even more exquisite by the same hand—that of Kakaracou, expert though unwilling.

"You got me roped, tied—and branded. It's all over me, burned into my hide. C. Stands for Clio."

"It is for Clint, the letter C. You know that!"

"I'd have a tough time making 'em see that down in the cattle country back home in Texas. Me, Clint Maroon, embroidered and hemstitched. God! I'll be wearing ruffles on my pants, next thing."

"Is it kind to talk like that?"

"No, honey. Only I was just thinking how you can start something just fooling around and not meaning anything but a little fun, like that day I up and spoke to you at the Market."

Another woman would have said the obvious thing. But Clio Dulaine did not say, "Are you sorry?" She sat very still, waiting.

He stood up. "I'm staying," he said, and came over to her and put a hand on her head and then rocked it a little so that it lolled on her slender neck; a gesture of helpless resentment on his part. Then he strolled toward the garden doorway, where the hot sun lay like a metal sheet. She watched him go, high-heeled boots, tight pants, slim hips, vast shoulders, the head a little too small, perhaps, for the width and height of the structure of bone and muscle; the ears a little outstanding giving him a boyish look. She rose swiftly and came up behind him and put her two arms about him so that her hands just met across his chest. She pressed her cheek against the hard muscles of his shoulder blade. "I am so happy."

"Say that again."

"I am so happy, Clint."

"Say it again."

She gave him a little push toward the garden doorway. He had told her he loved to listen to her voice, sometimes he caught himself listening to it without actually hearing what she said. Hers was an alive voice, it had a vital note that buoyed you like fresh air or fresh water, it had a life-giving quality as though it came from the deep well of her inner being, as indeed it did. He had once said to her, "Back home in Texas the womenfolks are mighty fine, they don't come any finer, but they've got kind of screechy voices; I don't know, maybe it's the dust or the alky water or maybe having to yell at the ornery menfolks to make 'em listen. Your voice, it puts me in mind of the Texas sky at night, kind of soft and purple."

Clint Maroon stood a moment on the steps facing the courtyard and looked about him and listened and let the sun beat down upon his bare head and on his shoulders covered by the unaccustomed fineness of the cambric shirt. From the house, from the kitchen ell, from the *garçonnière* with the stable beneath came the homely soothing sounds and smells of life lived comfortably, easily, safely. In the kitchen Kaka was preparing the early midday meal that followed the morning black coffee. Clio, vigorous, healthy, was an early riser, a habit formed, doubtless, in her schooldays in France. She had, too, the habit of the light continental breakfast and the hearty lunch. Clint Maroon sniffed the air. The scent of baking breads delicately rolled, richly shortened; coffee; butter sputtering. He thought of the chuck wagon. Beans. Pork. Leaden biscuits. Come and get it! Under Clio's tutelage he had learned about food in these past three weeks. He had learned to drink wine. Whisky, Clio said, was not a drink, it was a medicine. Wine, too, was something you cooked with, oddly enough. As for frying—that, it seemed, was for savages. Back in Texas everything went into the frying pan. You even fried bread. Clio was shocked or amused. Kaka was contemptuous. Things *à la*. Things *au*. He had learned about these, too.

From the stable came a swish and a clatter and the sound of Cupide's clear choirboy tenor. Cupide was in high spirits these past weeks. The little man worshiped the Texan. He scampered round him as a terrier frisks about a mastiff, he fetched and carried for him, he tried to imitate his gait, his drawling speech, his colloquialisms. Sprinkled through his own *pot-au-feu* of French, English, Gombo, this added a startling spice to his already piquant speech. *"Bon Jour!"* he would say in morning greeting. "Howdy! *Certainement!* I sure aim to. It is a pleasure to see you as you drive the bays, Monsieur Maroon. Uh–you sure do handle a horse pretty. Yessiree!"

Triumph irradiated the froglike face; the great square teeth gleamed in a grin. "I speak like a true *vacher,* yes?" Maroon delighted in teaching him bits of cowboy idiom. The peak of Cupide's new knowledge was reached when one evening, standing in the drawing-room doorway to announce dinner, he had shouted, gleefully, "Come and get it or I'll throw it away!" Ever since the death of Nicolas Dulaine the little man had been ruled by women in a manless household—Rita Dulaine, Belle Piquery, Clio, Kaka. Now he and Clint Maroon were two males together; it was fine; he smoked Clint's cigars, he tended his horses; together they went to the horse sales, to the races. He loved to polish the Texan's high-heeled boots, to brush his clothes; he neglected the work in the house where, in his little green baize apron, he used to rub and polish floors, furniture, crystal.

Now, as he sluiced down the horses in the stable, he sang and whistled softly a song he had picked up with a strange rhythm. Queer music with a curious off-beat that you caught just before it dropped. He had heard it played by a tatterdemalion crowd of Negro boys who wandered the streets, minstrels who played and danced and sang and turned handsprings for pennies. The Razzy Dazzy Spasm Band they called themselves. Their instruments were a fiddle made of an old cigar box, a kettle, a cowbell, a gourd filled with pebbles, a bull fiddle whose body was half an old barrel; horns, whistles, a harmonica. Out of these *dégagé* instruments issued a weird music that set your body twitching and your feet shuffling and your head wagging. A quarter of a century later this broken rhythm was to be known as ragtime, still later as jazz. Cupidon, whose ear was true and quick, had caught the broken rhythm perfectly. He had learned, too, not to strike the high note fairly but to lead up to it—"crying" up to it they called it later. His whistle sounded jubilantly above the swish and thump as he worked.

The man standing on the steps in the sun's hot glare was thinking, Clint, you better be drifting. Say *adios*. You're fixing to get into a sight of trouble. You're locoed. Suddenly, from within the house, Clio began to sing. A natural mimic, she was imitating the song of the blackberry woman who passed the house on her rounds, having walked miles from the woods and bayous, her skirts tucked high above her dusty legs, her soft, melancholy voice calling her wares. Now Clio imitated her perfectly and with complete unconsciousness of what she was doing. Artless and lovely the song rose above the fountain's faint tinkle, above Cupide's whistle, above the clatter of pans in the kitchen.

> *Black-ber-ries—fresh an' fine,*
> *Got black-berries, lady, fresh f'om de vine,*
> *Got black-berries, lady, three glass fo' dime,*
> *I got black-berries, I got black-berries,*
>   *black-BER-ees!*

The man looked back over his shoulder into the cool dim room he had just left. He looked about him. In the sight and the sounds of the mossy courtyard there was something blood-stirring, exhilarating. The pulse in his powerful throat throbbed. He knew he could not go. He went down the steps, quick and light. The bedroom, the stable, the kitchen. The kitchen. Discord there, he knew. Kakaracou was a powerful ally or an implacable foe. She knew no middle course.

He had spoken to Clio about her. "That mammy of yours, she hates me like poison. Every time I look at her she turns away from me like a horse. I'm just naturally peaceable, but I'm fixing to have a little talk with Kaka."

"It isn't you. It's men. You see, she lived with Mama and Aunt Belle all those years. Men, to her, mean trouble and tears."

Now he strolled across the courtyard to the kitchen doorway and stood there a moment while the delicious aroma of Kakaracou's cookery was wafted to him from stove and table. Kaka did not glance up as his broad shoulders shadowed the room. At the French Market she had got hold of some tiny trout, cool and glittering in their bed of green leaves, and these she was broiling delicately. Her workday tignon of plain brilliant blue was wound around her head; she was concentrating on her work or perhaps away from him. Her wattled neck stretched forward, her lower lip protruded, she looked like a particularly haughty cobra.

"You ain't got one kind thought for me, have you now, Mammy? "

Her swift upward glance at him, jagged and ominous, was like a lightning stroke. He went on, evenly,

"Funny thing. When I meet up with somebody I don't like, or they don't like me, why, either I get out or they do, depending on which is doing the hating. I'm staying."

She eyed him balefully; she began to speak in French, knowing that he comprehended no word of it; taking great satisfaction in spitting out the venomous phrases. "Lout! Common cowboy! Scum of the gutters! Spawn of the devil! I hate you! *Je l'dèteste!*"

"My, my!" drawled Maroon. "I don't parley Frongsay myself, but I sure do admire to hear other people go it. I kind of caught the drift of what you were saying, though, on account of that last word; it's the same in American as it is in French. So I caught on you weren't exactly paying me compliments, Mammy."

Suddenly, swiftly, like a panther, he stood beside her; he caught her meager body up in his two hands. Her own hands he pinned behind her neck, one of his powerful hands held them there, the other grasped her skinny legs at the ankles and thus he held her as if she had been a sack of feathers. A little series of tooting screams issued from her throat like the whistle of a calliope coming down the river on a showboat. But they could not be heard outside, what with Clio's singing, Cupide's whistling and swishing and the cries of the hucksters in the street. Kaka's eyes protruded with hate and fear. Her face had turned a dirty gray.

Clint Maroon looked down at her. Suddenly his eyes were not blue at all, but steel color. When he spoke he was smiling a little and his voice was gentle and drawling, as always.

"Holding you the way I am, Mammy, I could give you a little twist, two ways, would crack your backbone like you split those fish. You'd never talk or walk again and nobody'd know I'd done it."

Like a snake she twisted her head and tried to sink her teeth into his arms. "Uh-uh. Shucks, I won't hurt you. I just thought you ought to know. We're going to be friends, you and me." The glare she now cast up at him made this statement seem doubtful. "Oh, yes, we are. Miss Clio, she never had any fun—not to say, fun. Two sick old women a-whining and a-bellyaching all the time. Now you and me and maybe Cupide there, all together, maybe we can fix it so's she'll be rich and happy. She wants fun and love and somebody to look after her. I don't aim to do her any harm. I want to help her."

Suddenly he set her on her feet and gave her a gentle spank on her bony posterior cushioned with layers of stifly starched petticoats. She swayed and put out one hand, gropingly, as though about to fall. Then he curved his arm about her meager shoulders and pressed her to his side a moment and hugged her like a boy. "I love you because you love her," he said.

Kakaracou looked up at him . "You mean she will be rich? And everything *comme il faut*. Respectable."

"Sure respectable. But we got to play careful."

She looked up at him with the eyes of an old seeress, bright and wicked and wise and compassionate. She ignored his threatened brutality, his mad display of strength as though they never had been used against her.

"How you like pie Saint Honorè for dinner tonight, effen you and Miss Clio going to be home for one time?"

He replied in the wooing dovelike tones he reserved for all females of whatever age, color or class.

"What's in it, Mammy? Is it something lickin' good?"

"Uh, puff paste, first thing, and filling of striped vanilla and chocolate cream with liddy dabs of puff paste on top."

"Yes ma'am! "

She rolled a bawdy old eye at him. "It is good to have a man in the house to cook for. To cook only for women all these years, it make *un feu triste*."

"Whatever that is, Mammy."

"*Un feu triste*—oh, it mean a dull fire. To cook for women, *cela in'ennuie à la mort*. Though she eat well, my little Clio." She clutched his arm with one clawlike hand. "Only one thing I ask you. Do not call me that."

"What? "

"This—mammy." She drew herself up very tall. "It is a thing I hate. Out of the slave days."

"Why, sure. Name your own name. She calls you————"

"Me, I am Angélique Pluton. If you like you call me Kaka."

He eyed her with a measuring look that was a blend of amusement and resentment. "They sure ruined you in Paris, nigger."

Curiously enough, she laughed at this, her high cackling laugh. "Sure nuff, Mr. Clint. But don't you pay me no never mind. Half time I'm play-acting jess like Miss Clio."

7

"Faire du scandale," said Clio, as though thinking aloud.

"How's that? "

"I shall make a scandal. Not a great scandal. Just a little one, enough to cause them some worry."

"Now just what are you figuring on doing? You fixing up some sorry mischief in that little head of yours?"

The jalousies were three-quarters drawn, they were sitting in the cool dimness of the dining room facing the garden. It was too hot now that May was well on its way to sit at midday in the courtyard. Not even a vagrant breeze stirred the listless leaves, the air was heavy with moist heat. They had finished their delicate breakfast-lunch of trout and asparagus and pale golden pineapple dashed with kirsch. Clio's face had a luminous pearl-like quality in the gray-green shadow of the sheltered room. She wore one of her lace-filled white *gabrielles;* her eyes, her hair seemed blacker, more vital in contrast.

"You put me in mind of a spring I used to come on out on the Great Plains near the Brazos. You'd come on it, unexpected, and there it was, cool-looking and fresh, you'd kneel to touch it and you'd find it was a hot spring, so hot it like to burn your fingers."

She laughed her slow indolent laugh that was so at variance with her real character. "Some day we will go to Texas, Cleent. Before I am settled for life with my rich and respectable husband."

"Trying to tease me?"

"No. Haven't I told you from the beginning?"

"Honey, sometimes you talk Frenchified and now and again you talk just as American as I do. Are you putting on, or what? "

She shrugged her shoulders, her smile was mischievous. "Great-Grand'mère Bonnevie was an actress, you know. And if I am the Comtesse de Trenaunay de Chanfret, why then————"

"Shucks! I keep forgetting you're nothing but a little girl dressed up in her ma's long skirts."

She sat up briskly. "I am not! I am very grown up. I have planned everything. I am an adventuress like my grandmother and my mother, only I shall be more shrewd. I am going to have a fine time and I am going to fool the world."

"You don't say!" he drawled as one would talk to an amusing child.

"Ecoute! There is nothing for us here in New Orleans, for you or for me. To stay, I mean. But I have a plan. Will you listen very carefully?"

"I sure would admire for to hear it. You look downright wicked."

' Not wicked, Clint. Worldly. They were worldly women—my dear Mama, and Aunt Belle. And Kaka is a witch. And Cupide is a dear little monster. And I have been with these all my life. And so————"

"I love you the way you are. I wouldn't change a hair of your head."

"Listen, then. I have sent Cupide out through the town, and Kaka, too, and they have listened and learned. They can find out anything, those two. All the gossip, all the scandal. Well, there is a daughter. Charlotte Thérèse."

"Daughter? " he repeated, bewildered. "Now, wait a minute. Who? What daughter?"

She explained with the virtuous patience of the unreasonable. "The daughter of my father, Nicolas Dulaine, and his wife. Charlotte Thérèse she is called. My half-sister she is. Isn't she?"

"We-e-ell————"

"But of course. Now then. She is fifteen, she is Creole-*chacalata*—very stiff they are and clannish and everything *de rigueur*. She is to be introduced into society next winter, at sixteen. All very formal and proper, you see. But not so proper if there pops up an old scandal in the family."

He had been lolling in his chair, interested but relaxed. Now he sat up, tense. "Hold on! You're not fixing to try blackmail! "

"Clint! How can you think of such a thing!"

"There's a look in your eyes, I've seen the same look on a wild Spanish mare just before she rares up on her hind legs and throws you."

"How I should like to see that! The Wild West! Well, perhaps some day. But now we have work to do."

"What kind of work? What's going on in that head of yours? Sometimes I'm plumb scairt of you, especially when you look the way you do now, smooth as a pan of cream, but poison underneath if you was to skim it off."

"But it is nothing wicked! I am only arranging a gay little time for you and for me. Nows45will you listen—but carefully."

"Sure, honey. I like to hear your voice, it just goes over me like oil on a blister. I'm a-listening."

She held herself very quiet; her eyes were not looking straight ahead but were turned a bit toward their corners in the way of a plotter whose scheme is being made orderly.

"When I came back to New Orleans—before I met you, *chèri*— I was much much younger than I am now. Don't laugh! It is so. Only a few weeks ago, but it is so. I didn't know what I was going to do. Like a child I came back to my childhood home. I cleaned this house, repaired it, made it as you see, quite lovely again. I was going to live here and be happy like someone in a storybook. How childish! How silly! "

"What's silly about it?"

"Because I do not want to stay in this house. I do not even want the house to exist after I have finished with it. But now it is the house in which Nicolas Dulaine was k——— died. I am now going to bring that sad accident to life again."

"Hi, wait a minute!" He sat up with a jerk.

"No. You wait. It is very simple. I shall make New Orleans notice me. I shall go everywhere—to the restaurants, to the races, to the theater if it is not too late now, to the French Market; I shall ride in the Park, I shall wear my most extravagant frocks—and you will go everywhere with me in your great white hat, and your diamond shirt stud and your beautiful boots———"

"But what———"

"No. Wait. All these weeks I have been living quietly, quietly here in this house—I here, you at the St. Charles Hotel, all very proper and prim and decorous."

A glint in his eye, an edge to his drawling voice. "Well, hold on, now. I wouldn't say it was all so proper, exactly."

"Proper on the surface. And in my eyes because I am so fond of you, Clint. But now we must be different."

"How d'you mean, different? What you fixing to do?"

"Only what I have said. We will go everywhere, and everywhere we must attract attention. Everything orderly, but bold—dashing—much *èclat*—everything conspicuous. People will say, 'Who is that beautiful creature who goes always everywhere with the handsome Texan? Look at her clothes! They must come from Paris. Look at her jewels! See how she rides, so superbly. Who is she?' Then another will answer, 'Oh, don't you know? . . .

She is the daughter of Nicolas Dulaine who died. You remember? There was a great scandal————' ''

"Why, say, Clio, you wouldn't be as coldblooded as that, now, would you? What do you want to go and do that for? What's the idea?"

"Because it will revive the old scandal. That would be very inconvenient for a family whose daughter will be of marriageable age next season—a family that is very conventional—in a word—*chacalata*. And the daughter— this Charlotte Thérèse—she is, I hear, quite plain. And thin. *Maigre comme un clou.*" Clio smiled a dreamily sweet smile. "She was not made with love."

"They'll run you out of town."

"I'll go—for a price."

He stared at her while the meaning of this fully resolved itself in his mind. "You mean to say you came here to New Orleans knowing you could make these people pay————"

"No, Clint! I came because—well, where else could I go? All my life I had heard of nothing but New Orleans, New Orleans. It was home to them. That was because they were exiles. It isn't home to me. It is nothing to me but a dim blurred copy of the city Mama and Aunt Belle loved."

"That's a fine speech, honey. But I've got so I'm not more than one jump behind that steel-trap mind of yours. Sometimes I'm even ahead of it. Come on, come on, Clio. I'm not just a big dumb cowboy from Texas. What's in that head of yours, for all you're looking so droopy about the dear old days in New Orleans—you little hell-cat, you!"

She looked at him with utter directness. She was no longer a woman and he a man; it was the cold, clear, purposeful look of the indomitable.

"One must be practical. Will you help me?"

"Likely they'll have us both corraled. I'll do it—just for the hell of it, and if it's going to make you happier feeling. But don't say I didn't warn you."

"The idea was mine. The risk is mine, really. We can share the expenses— restaurants, races, theaters—it will not be cheap. Perhaps you should have more than one-third————"

He stood up then, his eyes were steel slots in the blank face, he pushed her roughly away from him so that she staggered backward and would have tripped over the flounced train of her *gabrielle* if she had not grasped a table for support.

"Why, you no-'count French rat, you! You offering to pay me—like a fast man, like I was a pander."

"Clint! You a *paillard!* No! I did not mean—I only meant—we are partners, you and I————"

His slow venomous drawl cut under her passionate denial. "Yes, you're right. The idea is yours, the risk is yours, the whole rotten outfit is yours, your murdering mother and those two freaks out there————"

"Clint! Don't! Don't talk like this to me. I only meant—I was only trying to be fair—businesslike and practical—not like Mama and Aunt Belle! Don't you see?" She went to him, she clung to him, so that the thin white robe, the flowing sleeves, the perfumed lace ruffles hung from his shoulders, covered his face, swirled about his legs.

"Get away from me!"

"No! No! I will give it up. I only thought then we would be free. It was just a little plan—not bad, not wicked. Then we can go together to Saratoga, where it is gay and fresh with pine woods and the little lakes."

He was listening now, he was holding her against him instead of pushing her away, his anger was less than halfhearted. "I don't want any part of it."

"But when you said you would help me I thought we would be partners."

"Not in this. Maybe up North, if we hit on a scheme. But this here—this is different. This goes way back to—to something else. It ain't a clean grudge. Maybe they owe you something—you and your ma. I'll tote you around, like you said. You know I'm crazy about you. But I ain't that crazy. Any money you get from throwing dirt at them, why, it's yours to keep. I'll have no part of it."

"Clint, you are marvelous, *Je t'adore!*"

"Listen, honey," he said, plaintively. "You take things too hard. Why'n't you just gentle down and quit snorting and rarin' and take it in your stride?"

"Now it is you who are trying to make me different."

"No, not different. Only let's be more ourselves if we're going to run together. All this play acting. You being so French and me playing Texas cowboy."

"But I am! I mean, I lived so long in France. And you—well, you are from Texas, you were a cowboy—at least you said————"

"I sure am. But we both been working too hard at it. Let's just take the world the way you would a ripe coconut down in the French Market. Crack the shell, drink the milk, eat what you want of the white meat and throw the rest away."

New Orleans had a small-town quality in spite of its cosmopolitanism. No couple so handsome, so vital and so flamboyant could long escape notice in any city. Her beauty, her Paris gowns, his white Texas sombrero, his diamond stud, the high-stepping bays and the glittering carriage—any of these would have served to attract attention. But added to these were the fantastic figures of Cupide and Kakaracou. The spectacular couple were seen everywhere, sometimes unattended, sometimes followed by the arrogant, richly dressed black woman and the dwarf in his uniform of maroon and gold.

It was late May, hot and humid, but the city had not yet taken on the indolent pace of summer. Summer or winter, New Orleans moved at a leisurely gait. It still closed its places of business at noon for a two-hour siesta, one of many old Spanish customs still obtaining here in this Spanish-French city. New Orleans deserted commerce for the races; it flocked to any one of a score of excellent restaurants there to lunch or dine lavishly; it gambled prodigally in Royal Street or in Southport or out at Jefferson Parish. New Orleans adored the theater, it was stagestruck en masse. As for the opera, that was almost a religion. Summer was close at hand. Now New Orleans, between the excesses of the Mardi Gras recently passed and the simmering inertia of the summer approaching, was having a final mid-season fling.

Into this revelry Clio Dulaine and Clint Maroon pranced gaily. The long, lazy mornings in the cool shaded house, the tropical dreamlike evenings in the scented garden were abandoned. The bays and the clarence were seen daily on Canal Street or in the Park. Purposely Clio overdressed—lace parasols, silks, plumes, jewels. In France she had learned to ride, and frequently in Paris she had ridden in the Bois while Rita Dulaine and Belle Piquery had followed demurely in the carriage. Now she got out the dark blue riding habit with the very tight bodice, the long looped skirt, the high-heeled boots, the little hat with the flowing veil. Clint rode à la Texas: sombrero, boots, handkerchief knotted at the throat, tight pants, the high-horned Western saddle silver-trimmed. They tore along the bridle paths, her veil streaming behind her, he holding his reins with one hand while the other waved in the air, cowboy fashion. "Yip-eee Eeeee-yo!" New Orleans, sedately taking the air in carriages or on horseback, stared, turned, gasped. Sometimes she rode without Maroon, Cupide as groom following, perched gnomelike on the big horse and handling his mount superbly. If possible, this bizarre escort attracted more attention than when she rode with the Texan.

She had inherited plenty of the acting instinct from her lively and gifted ancestor. When they went to the theater they entered just before the curtain's rise. Between the acts she stood up and surveyed the house through her jeweled opera glasses, leisurely, insolent.

"That looks like real bad manners to me," Clint observed when first she did this. "Who you looking for?"

"It is the continental custom."

Then one night on their way to the French Opera she said rather defiantly, "Cupide has found out that they are going to the play tonight. She and this Charlotte Thérèse and two others—an uncle and a young man. These Creoles marry very young, you know."

"Look, Clio, you're not figuring on anything wild, are you? Tonight?"

"Don't be absurd, darling. Cupide discovered that they are to sit in a box, the first stage box at the right. Very indiscreet of them. The mother must be a stupid woman."

She wore her pink faille with the black lace flounces and Rita's jewels, and when, after the first act, she stood up to survey the house through her glasses, the audience sat staring as though at a play within a play. Their seats were well front. She turned her head slowly toward the right box, she adjusted her opera glasses on their tiny jeweled stick, her back to the stage, so that there was unmistakable intention in her long, steady stare at the sallow midde-aged woman in black and the sallow young girl in prim white. She stared and stared and stared. All the audience, as though slowly moved by a giant magnet, turned its head to stare with her, hypnotized. Through her glasses Clio saw the dull red rise and spread over the woman's face and throat and bosom; she saw the girl twiddle her fan and look down and look up and then speak to her mother. And the woman made a gesture for silence and the two men bent forward to shield them and quickly made conversation. And finally Clio turned her head indolently away from them and toward Maroon, who by now was looking as uncomfortable as the four in the box.

"Very *chacalata*. Very plain. Very dowdy."

When the lights went up after the second act the four in the box were gone.

They went everywhere, Clio and Clint; she made sure that wherever they went all eyes should follow them. They went to the French Market on Sunday morning, they breakfasted at Hippolyte Beguè's. The white sombrero, the Lone Star boots, the coat-tails; the Paris dresses, the plumed hats, the exotic attendants were restaurant talk now and coffee-table gossip. They say his collar button is a diamond . . . that woman down in Rampart Street, remember? Very beautiful. . . mistress . . . shot him . . . hushed up . . . Charlotte Thérèse . . . Rita, she called herself Dulaine . . . Clio . . . this is the daughter . . . demi-mondaine . . . Paris . . . must be twenty years ago . . .

She actually went with him to the gambling houses where respectable women did not go and in many of which women were not allowed. She accompanied him to the old marble building in Royal Street that once had been the Merchants' Exchange where traders, gamblers, auctioneers and merchants had met in the old days for the transaction of every sort of business. The second-floor rooms, topped by the beautifully proportioned dome, were used as a gambling house now. Number 18 Royal Street. She stood at the gaming table with Clint, she placed her money quietly and decisively.

"Why do they stare so! After all, I'm only playing quietly."

"They don't see many women here, I reckon. Not like you, leastways."

"I always went with Mama and Aunt Belle when we were in Nice or Cannes or Monte Carlo."

"It's different here. Out West, the girls in the gambling saloons, why—if that's where they were, that's what they were. New Orleans is no cow-town, but I can't help seeing they kind of look at you funny. Let's go home, Clio."

"But that's what I'm here for, foolish boy!"

He rubbed his hand over his eyes in that bewildered way. "I should think sometimes you'd get mixed up yourself not knowing which kind of a woman you are."

"I do! Get mixed up, I mean. Sometimes I am all Mama's family and sometimes I am all Papa's family."

"But there's times when you're both at once."

"Then look out!"

New Orleans, in spite of its Creole aristocracy with their almost royal taboos, looked with a tolerant and sophisticated eye on manners and customs that would have shocked many larger American cities. Its ways had the tang of the old world; it liked its food, its fun, its women, its morals spiced with something racier than the bland and innocuous American cream sauce. So the Texan and the girl with their flamboyant ways and their *outrè* clothes, their bizarre attendants and their lavish spending became a sort of feature of the town. One day you saw them at the races, the next they were shopping at the French Market, or driving the length of Canal Street down to the banana wharves where, to the mystification of the townspeople, they watched the giant black men unloading or loading the sugar, bananas, or coffee that made up the fragrant cargo.

"I love to watch it," Clio had said. "It is so beautiful and rhythmic and mysterious, too, like the jungle. See the muscles of their arms and backs. They move like panthers, these black men."

Clio Dulaine was enjoying herself, no doubt of that. Interspersed with her flauntings and posturings as a florid woman of the world she managed to see the best and the worst of New Orleans. She was saying hail and farewell to the city whose praises and whose shortcomings, whose fascination and whose-sordidness had been drummed into her ears all her life. "Oh, I remember that!" she would say of a beautiful building or a shop or a restaurant. She never before had seen it except through the eyes and the memory of the two nostalgic women. "They've remodeled the front of that building. . . . They should have used a ham bone instead of bacon strips in this Gombo Zhebes, and I don't think they've browned the flour enough in the *roux*. . . . This used to be the shop of Prudent Mallard the cabinetmaker, he was a great artist. Oh, dear, it's a meat market now! He made the great palissandre bed in my bedroom."

Though her childhood and girlhood in France had been a fantastic mèlange of conventional school life and haphazard household she had an eye for architecture, an ear for music, a taste in food, a flair for clothes, a love of horses, and even some knowledge of literature.

So she and Clint Maroon, walking or driving about the streets of the heady old city, were frequently drunk with its charm, its potent perfume, its mellow flavor.

"Funny thing," Clint Maroon said. "Going up and down the town like this, you and me together, it's like being with a man sometimes."

"I don't know that I like that, quite."

"aybe that does sound funny. I didn't mean it that way. Only you make things come alive, the way you see them and talk about them."

"I love to see new sights and visit strange cities. I want to see all of America. And I shall, too."

"You and me."

"No, we mustn't get used to each other—too much. Here, yes. And perhaps Saratoga."

"If I didn't know different I'd say you were a coldblooded piece."

"That isn't coldblooded. It is just sensible. I want respectability and security and comfort. Most people don't give as much thought to planning their lives as Kaka does to a dinner menu. Then when it turns out wrong they think the world is to blame."

"But suppose you plan it and know just where you're heading and even then it turns out wrong?"

"That is fate. You can do nothing about that."

Now the newspapers were beginning to mention the two. The French newspaper *L'Abeille,* usually too conservative to make mention of so spectacular a pair, published a sneering reference to the beautiful and mysterious visitor who calls herself the Comtesse de Trenaunay de Chanfret and her devoted escort, the Texan, Monsieur Clint Maroon.

"La Comtesse," the story went on, "chooses to reside in a section of our beautiful city not ordinarily favored by members of the foreign nobility visiting our shores. It is said that the house at least is closely connected with a certain notorious New Orleans *femme fatale* now dead."

"It isn't enough," Clio said. "It must be something more. Something touched with *bizarrerie.*"

"I won three thousand dollars at Number 18 last night," Clint drawled, plaintively. "And there was a piece about it in the *Picayune.* Seems they got a woman there runs that paper, name of Mrs. Holbrook. I never heard of such a thing. Women'll be going into politics, next. This Mrs. Holbrook, she writes poetry, too, signs her name Pearl Rivers. Piece in the paper called me that romantic Texan. The boys back home ever get wind of that I'll never get shut of it. They'll ride me ragged."

Clio surveyed him thoughtfully, speculatively, the light of invention slowly dawning in her eyes. "A duel," she said, meditatively, as though thinking aloud. "Of course it really should be over me, but—what of Mr. Holbrook? Why doesn't he—you're a marvelous shot—you could challenge———"

"No ma'am! You won't make any Josè Llulla out of me. Besides, she's a widow woman."

Regretfully she abandoned the idea. "If only your racehorse Alamo were here. Cupide could ride him. That would make *réclame.*"

"It's getting too late for the races here. Besides, they're shipping him up to Saratoga. And I'm going to have my horse up there for you to ride, Blue Blazes, she's so black she's blue, the way your hair looks sometimes, and her little hoofs they never touch the ground. They'll sit up in Saratoga when they see you on her."

"It's going to be wonderful to feel the air clear and cool with pine trees. You know, Clint, I am a little tired of shrimp and pompano and maguolias and all things soft and sweet.

"Then come on!"

"No, first I must finish here. I must have money. I will not sell my jewels because I shall need them. Besides, I have a sentimental feeling about them. I have made up my mind that I shall not be sentimental about anything. But Mama's jewels—that's different."

"There you go! Taking things hard again. You put me in mind of the way I used to be; I never would just open a door and walk through, I had to bust it down for the hell of it. I just naturally liked doing things the hard way. Always shooting my way through a crowd instead of shouldering.''

"But people make way for you now, don't they?''

"Oh, it's all right—long's somebody doesn't think of shooting me first.''

"Now it's you who are taking things hard. After all, what can they do to me! I have done nothing but enjoy myself in New Orleans, and I've harmed no one. But I should think their pride would have sent them to me before this.'' She stared out at the hot little courtyard with its unavailing fountain, its brick paving oven-hot in the sun. "I suppose,'' musingly, "it's too late and too hot for a concert.''

"Concert! Who?''

"I sing quite nicely. You've said so yourself. A concert—a public concert—that would be very annoying, I should think. But it's too hot, isn't it?''

"Hell, yes. Anyway, honey, that's the first really bad idea you've had. Stand on a platform, open to insult!''

"M-m, perhaps you're right. Let me see. I could say that this place is to be opened as a gambling house. Cupide and Kaka could spread the rumor in no time at all.''

"Now you're talking wild, Clio.''

"Am, I, *chèri?* Well, perhaps you're right.''

But she must have mentioned it. Or perhaps the implike Cupidon was eavesdropping as they talked. Within two days there arrived at the Rampart Street house a messenger with a letter in a long legal envelope and written in a dry legal hand. Though the envelope was addressed to the Comtesse de Trenaunay de Chanfret the letter itself dismissed her briefly, thus:

MADAM:
 Will all you call at my office at the address given above so that I may communicate to you a matter of importance.
 I trust that you will find it convenient to come within the next two days, and that the hour of eleven will suit you.
 May I add that the matter which I wish to discuss will prove to be to your advantage.
 With the hope that I may be favored with your immediate reply I beg to remain,
Your obedient servant,
AUGUSTIN MATHIEU HAUSSY.

This curt epistle was greeted by Clio as though it had been lyric with love. "There! That's what I've been waiting for.''

"How do you know it's because of them?''

"Who else!'

"Want me to go along with you?''

"I'm not going. This Monsieur Augustin Mathieu Haussy—he will come to me.''

"Suppose he won't? ''

"He will.''

And two days later Kakaracou in her best black silk and her finest white fichu and most brilliant tignon opened the door of the Rampart Street house to a dapper little man carrying a portfolio. Clio received him alone in the dim drawing room, as she had arranged. "It is better that I see him alone, Clint. I am really a very good, shrewd woman of business. I learned to be because Mama and Aunt Belle were so bad.''

She wore a childishly simple little dress of white china silk like a girl at her first Communion: puffed sleeves like a baby's, and a single strand of pearls. Curiously enough, this was the one piece of jewelry which always had been hers. Nicolas Dulaine had given it to this, his child, on her first birthday.

She had been seated on the crimson brocade and mahogany sofa. As the visitor entered rather hesitantly, for the dimness was intensified in his sun-dazzled eyes, she rose, slowly, a slight, almost childish figure.

Cupide, in livery, bawled from the doorway, "Monsieur Augustin Mathieu Haussy!"

She inclined her head, wordlessly. She put out her hand. He bowed over it. When he straightened to look at her he had to raise his eyes a little, for she was tall, and he was of less than medium height. They looked at one another—a long measuring look.

A little man, with a good brow, a quizzical eye; not more than thirty; a keen face, a long clever nose. "This is no dusty fool," Clio thought.

As his eyes grew accustomed to the dimness of the room he saw that the demure white figure resolved itself into a purposeful and lovely woman.

"You are younger than I thought—from your letter," said Clio.

"And you, Mademoiselle, are so young that I am certain you do not yet consider it a compliment to be told that you seem younger."

"Madame," she corrected him, smiling; motioned him to a chair.

He perched on the edge of his chair like a sharp little bird, his toes pointing precisely ahead. "I had hoped that we were going to be honest and straight-forward."

She thought, this is not going to be so easy. He has a brain, this little man. Charm, too. Aloud she said, "But of course. I hope you noticed that I did not say to you, 'To what do I owe the honor of this visit?' "

"Good. I think I should tell you that I do not belong to the old-school New Orleans tradition. I belong to the postwar New Orleans. I have seen the Carpetbaggers come and go; I have seen New Orleans under Negro rule; I have lived through the yellow-fever scourge of two years ago; I am one of those who wish to rid New Orleans of its old-time unsavoriness. New Orleans of the Mississippi steamboat must pass. By the end of this year five railroad trunk lines will enter———"

"You did not come here to discuss railroads with me, Monsieur Haussy."

He laughed a little laugh, like a chirp, and sat back in his chair as though he had been given a cue to relax. "I was only going to add that in another two years Canal Street will be lighted by electricity. I was talking, Made-moiselle, in order to give myself a chance to study you."

"And now your lesson is learned, Monsieur."

"By heart," he replied, gallantly, with a little bob forward that gave an absurd effect of bowing while seated. "I am here———"

"I know," she interrupted, almost rudely. "One of my unpleasant habits is to be impatient of long discussions. I know why you are here."

He began to untie the portfolio that rested on his knees. "I have here—"

"Please, no papers. I am bored by papers. May I offer you some refreshment? A glass of sherry? A *coquetier?*" She raised her voice. "Cupide!"

"Nothing. You are brusque, Mademoiselle, for so young and so lovely a woman."

"It was you who asked for this interview, and you who proposed honesty and straightforwardness. . . . Cupide, go to the kitchen and stay there until I ring."

"You are right. Well, then I shall come straight to the point. You are causing a great deal of pain to my client, Madame Nicolas Dulaine, and her daughter, Charlotte Thérèse."

"I should be interested to meet my half-sister, Charlotte Thérèse Dulaine."

"I should scarcely call her that."

"I should. And do. Her father was Nicolas Dulaine. My father was Nicolas Dulaine."

"But there was a difference."

"Yes. My father loved my mother dearly. He did not love the mother of this little Charlotte Thérèse. It is curious, isn't it—the child of real love is usually beautiful, like me, and the child of a marriage *de convenance* is dull and sallow, like this Charlotte Thérèse. Poor child!"

Now he knew this was an adversary to be respected. He said again, "Your conduct is causing a great deal of pain to my client."

"Your client," Clio retorted, evenly, "for many years caused my mother and me much greater pain."

"The conditions are different."

"How?"

He waived this as being too obvious to require an answer. "We object to your calling yourself Dulaine."

"My mother and my father traveled everywhere, in this country and in Europe, as Mr. and Mrs. Nicolas Dulaine."

The little man smiled at her confidingly. "Mrs. Dulaine is very far from wealthy, you know."

"Not so far as I, Monsieur."

"Is this blackmail?"

Clio's dramatic instinct told her that this was the time to rise. She rose. Augustin Mathieu Haussy jumped to his feet, dropped the portfolio, picked it up. By this time her effect was somewhat spoiled. "I did not come to you. I was living here quietly, in New Orleans, in my mother's house————"

"Quietly!"

"Quietly. Disturbing no one. After all, I am young; I like to go about to the shops and the theaters and the races and the restaurants. I am not a nun. Still, if, as you suggest, your actions can be construed as blackmail————"

"Me!" squeaked Haussy. "It is you who are attempting something very like that ugly word."

She made a gesture toward the bell. "I shall live my life as I please. You cannot frighten me as you did my mother. Good day, Monsieur Haussy."

But he seated himself and opened his portfolio. "I have here five thousand dollars. It is that or nothing. It is all that my client can afford, I assure you. New Orleans is a pauper today. Well, Mademoiselle?"

"Five thousand dollars for—what?"

He extracted a paper from the portfolio, adjusted his glasses, looked at her over them as though to make sure that he had her attention, and read in his quiet, rather pleasing voice.

"I, who call myself Clio Dulaine, sometimes known as the Comtesse de Trenaunay de Chanfret, daughter of the woman Rita who called herself Dulaine, hereby agree and promise that I shall leave New Orleans within the period of the next thirty days, never to return . . .

"I shall cease to call myself Dulaine . . .

"While remaining in New Orleans I shall conduct myself quietly, taking care to attract no undue notice or attention . . .

"After leaving New Orleans never to return I shall do and say nothing that could in any way associate me with the family of Dulaine or the history or background of the family of Dulaine . . .

"I hereby promise . . ."

She listened quietly, her hands resting easily in her lap, her fine eyes thoughtful and untroubled, as though considering an impersonal legal problem.

When he had finished she sat silent a moment. The tinkle of the fountain in the courtyard came faintly to them, and the sound of Cupide's high boyish voice chattering in eager French to Kaka in the kitchen.

"And if I do not sign this very inhospitable paper?"

"I have political influence. I can make things very uncomfortable for you indeed."

"Not as uncomfortable as I can make them for you and your client. I have the hope of security and even respectability in my life. It is just as important to me as to the little Charlotte Thérèse. But if you try to make it impossible, I have little to lose, you know. I shall make the most frightful noise, I shall do something to make such a scandal that the old affair will seem nothing in comparison."

"Yes," the little man agreed, soothingly. "I am sure you could. But you won't. You are too intelligent."

"Ten thousand."

Now the bargaining began in earnest. Five! Ten! Six! Ten! Seven! Ten! She actually achieved the ten.

"Now then, I, too, have certain demands."

"Impossible! " said Augustin Haussy, exhausted.

"Oh, don't be alarmed. They are mostly sentimental. Nothing, really. The money is to be paid me as if for the sale of this house, and I should like the house to be torn down. Now, now, wait a moment. Don't you see that your client probably would like that too? I am sure of it. Then, in my absence, there is to be placed a bunch of chrysanthemums on the grave of my Aunt Belle Piquery once each year, on All Saints' Day. And her tomb is to be kept whitewashed. The furniture in this house will be destroyed————"

"But my dear child!"

"Burned. I myself shall see to it. Except for such bits and bibelots as I shall see fit to save. I want no dirty eyes gloating over these chairs and tables—the armoire—the dressing table—the bed————"

Augustin Haussy looked around the charming room. "But this—all this—is in the best tradition of the furniture of the period. That couch you are sitting on—it must be the work of Prudent Mallard."

"It is."

"This chandelier—the Aubusson carpet—"

Clio Dulaine rose as though to close the interview. "My mother and father both possessed great good taste, Monsieur Haussy. . . . I signed so many, many papers in France after Mama's death, and then Aunt Belle's. I know this one must be properly witnessed and notarized. Will you come again tomorrow, so that no time may be lost? And do you think you could bring Charlotte Thérèse to see me?"

He stared at her in horror. "But that is impossible!"

"I suppose it is. But I think she might have liked to learn something of her father's real life. She never knew him, you see. Oh, well, she must always live a very conventional and dull existence, the poor little one. Always *chacalata*. How I pity the child!"

"A strange thing for you to say."

"No. My father would have felt the same, I am sure."

She rang for Cupide. You heard his little feet pattering across the courtyard. The lawyer tucked his portfolio under his arm, he paused to regard the girl with an eye no less keen but now definitely unprofessional.

"I am interested to know what you are going to do. As a—a—man—an acquaintance, not a lawyer, I mean. Ten thousand dollars—that can't last long—at least, with you. Those pearls you are wearing are easily worth more than that.''

Clio stared a moment, rigid. Then she melted into her slow, indulgent laugh. ''You were right to say that you were not of old New Orleans, Monsieur Haussy. I was little more than a baby when we left here. But I am sure your manners are of a more recent and unfortunate day.''

''I thought you were too worldly to take offense. I meant none.''

''Dear Monsieur Haussy, I am not offended. I am amused. I don't in the least mind telling you. I am going to marry a very rich and powerful man.''

He stared, his face almost ludicrous in its astonishment. ''You mean this fellow—this—pardon me—this Texan is———''

''Oh, no. Not a penny except what he wins, gambling. A charming boy. No, I am going to Saratoga, where I shall become the fashion. Mrs. De Chanfret. It may be that I shall have to call upon you for verification. I shall do nothing objectionable. Daring, perhaps, but not too indiscreet.''

''But marry—who?'' so mystified as to be ungrammatical.

''How should I know? What does it matter?''

He turned toward the door. Cupide of the big ears stood in the hallway. The man came back a step or two. ''I shall see you tomorrow, then.''

''Yes.''

He stammered, ''You are—very—beautiful—that is—beautiful.''

''Yes,'' Clio Dulaine agreed, placidly. ''Isn't it lucky!''

The legal mind must reach its conclusion. ''Even so, you seem very sure of achieving this—this rich and—uh—powerful, wasn't it? —uh—husband.''

She shrugged her shoulders; her tone was more wistful than blithe. ''I have been in America such a short time. And I have seen nothing of it, really. But even here in New Orleans I can see that this country is a little ridiculous, it is so simple and so good. Its people. Clint—the one you call the Texan—he has told me such stories! Some day those Europeans they will find out how simple and how good and how rich this country is and they will come and try to take it, I'm afraid.''

''You know a great deal—for one so young.''

''Oh, I know things without learning them, like a witch. And I am adventurous, like my great-grandmother, who traveled here to New Orleans so long ago from the French West Indies. I am going to have a fine time. And I am going to fool the world.''

He bowed in farewell. ''I hope the ten thousand dollars will be of help.''

''A little, Monsieur Haussy. A little.''

8

SHE WAS GIVING the Texan last-minute counsel, for it was June, moist and sweltering, and he was off for the North.

''Go to the best hotel in Saratoga. As soon as you've had a good look around, write me—write me everything.''

''I feel like a skunk leaving you here in this heat, and everything to do. Why'n't you get shut of it all and come on along with me? We'll light out tomorrow, a couple of days in St. Louis, then up to Saratoga.''

''I've told you, Clint, we must not come to Saratoga together. We do not even know one another. Remember that. Don't seem eager to make friends. Swagger with the coattails. But do nothing until I come. Always be Texas. The white hat, the boots, the new blue satin tie, the diamond collar button and the diamond stud—everything is perfect. You have only to be yourself as you are. Only—*écoute, chéri*—you are very rich but you do not want this known—and you are a Western railroad and mining man—but you do not want this known, either. I should tell no one if I were you except, perhaps, the hotel manager and a *croupier* in the largest casino. There is a casino, you are sure? For gambling?''

"What's that? Croup—uh—what——?''

"A—a dealer, I suppose you'd call him .''

"Oh. Faro dealer. He sure is a good one to tell your secrets to. Look, Clio, you'll be there in two weeks? Sure? ''

"But sure. Where else! But write me—names—everything. It's going to be wonderful! I feel it. In my witch's bones. New places! New faces! A whole new life!''

"Don't talk that way.'' He was genuinely horrified.

"Why, what have I said?''

"You can't trifle like that with luck! Bragging about what's going to be wonderful. Luck's just naturally ornery and goes the other way if you try to drive her like that. You got to just ease her along.''

"Luck—fate—you've got to make your own. Bad luck—bad judgment. Good luck—good judgment. Well, my judgment is good, so my luck will be the same. You wait. You'll see.''

The bays and the clarence had been shipped to Saratoga. "Sure you'll be all right, honey? '' Clint Maroon said over and over again. "What're you studying to do that keeps you here two weeks and more?'' A sudden fear smote him. "Look here! You're not playing any tricks with me, are you? Fixing to light out somewheres?'' Actually his hand crept to the gun that always hung beneath the flowing skirt of his coat. He carried it as other men wear a wallet, quite naturally.

Clio Dulaine watched this byplay with almost childlike delight. "You are perfect, Clint! But perfect! All my life in France I read about you, and here you are, melodrama come to life.'' She grew serious. "Not another shooting in this house, Clint. Think how uncomfortable you would be in prison in New Orleans during August.''

He passed his hand over his eyes with that rueful and bewildered gesture made so touching because of his size and the swashbuckling clothes and the gun which was his symbol of defiance against the world.

"Play-acting again, the both of us. I thought we'd be shut of that when we got to Saratoga.''

"No, foolish boy! We're really only beginning there.''

"Shucks, all I aim to do is play me a little faro and clean up on those suckers they say are hanging around Saratoga with the money choking their wallets. Maybe enter Alamo in a race if she looks likely. And buy you something pretty in New York.''

"New York! Oh, Clint! Really! ''

"Why not? Maybe, by September, if we're lucky.''

So they parted, and their panic at parting was real enough. They had come together so casually, the ruthless powerful girl, the swaggering resentful man. A month or two had served to bind them, the one to the other. Each had been alone against a hostile world; now each sustained the other.

"I've a good mind to stay and wait for you, no matter what you say.''

"No. No! that would spoil everything.''

"I sure would like to. I get to thinking somebody might do you harm here in New Orleans. That's what's eating on me.''

"Kaka would scratch their eyes out, and enjoy it. Cupide is better than a gun—you ought to know that. I have a thousand things to do. I shall never see New Orleans again. We are Southerners, you and I. Those Northerners are sharp."

"Any sharper than you, they're walking razors."

"We'll see."

"Anything goes wrong you'll send me a telegram, won't you, honey? I'll mosey back here in two shakes."

"Remember to talk like that in Saratoga. . . . Send me a telegram just as soon as you are sure of your hotel."

Suddenly she began to cry with her eyes wide open—great pearly drops that made her eyes seem larger and more liquid, her face dew-drenched.

"How in tarnation can I go when you do that! Crying!"

"Pay no attention. I often do that when I'm excited. You know that. It doesn't mean anything. Just tears."

"Well, you sure cry pretty."

The tears were running down her cheeks and she was smiling as he left. It was he whose face was distorted with pain at parting. Cupide had begged to go with him. The big Texan had shown one of his rare flashes of anger. "Why, you little varmint, you! Go along with me and leave her alone with only Kaka! You'll stay. And remember, if I find you haven't done just like she wants, everything she says, when you get to Saratoga I'll kill you, sure. No regular killing. I'll tromp you to death like a crazy horse."

"Sure," Cupide agreed, blithely. *"Mais certainement."*

In the little musty shops whose shelves were laden with the oddments and elegancies of a decayed French aristocracy of a past century Clio and Kaka had little trouble in finding the things they sought. Leather goods, jewel cases, handkerchiefs, bonbon boxes, lacy pillows, purses, jeweled *bibelots,* all monogrammed with the letter C. On these forays she dressed in the plainest black and oftener than not did not take Kaka with her. Cupide, instead, trailed far behind and lolled innocently outside the shop door until she emerged.

Kaka's needle flew. But Clio's wardrobe needed little replenishing. Her silks, satins, muslins, jewels were of the finest. Some of them were of a fashion that had not yet even penetrated to America.

Having made a gesture of melodramatic magnificence in speaking to Augustin Haussy about the furnishings of the Rampart Street house, she now thriftily changed her mind and her tactics, in part at least. The fine Aubusson carpets, the massive crystal chandelier, the unmarked silver and glass and such other impersonal pieces as had an intrinsic market value almost as permanent as that of precious stones she sold deliberately and shrewdly, driving as hard a bargain as she could. Certain exquisite pieces of porcelain and glass she had packed in stout packing cases, and these she sent to be stored at a warehouse. Luxury-loving, and possessed of a sure dramatic sense, she set aside for her own use such odds and ends as would lend authority and richness to a hotel suite—heavy wrought-silver photograph frames, antique brocade pillows, vases; the bonbon boxes from which the plump Belle Piquery had nibbled until her plumpness grew to obesity; a Corot landscape, misty and cool, that Nicolas Dulaine had long ago purchased for his Rita because she had said that just to look at it revived her on the hottest day; a paper-knife with a jeweled handle; a cloisonné desk set from the Rue de la Paix; a fabulous little gold clock.

A kind of frenzy of exhilaration filled the three—Clio, Kakaracou and Cupidon. They had an unconscious sense of release, of impending adventure. None of them had felt really secure or at peace in the New Orleans to which they had been so eager to return.

"Now then, my children," Clio announced to Kaka and Cupide, "we are

going to have a bonfire and to the tune of music. Not one thing will be left
that people can finger and gloat over and point at and say, 'See! That belonged
to Rita Dulaine. There is the mark.' Cupide, you will take the hammer and
you will pull apart the big bed and the couch and the dressing table and the
armoire, and you will roll up the carpet in the bedroom. You will burn all
these, a little at a time, in the courtyard."

"No," screamed Kaka, in real pain. "No!"

"I say yes. The marked glass you will throw against the brick wall of the
garçonnière so that it breaks into bits, and then you will gather it into the
dust bin to be thrown away. The center of the courtyard, Cupide. Smash
up the fountain first."

There was something dreadful in the sight of the glee with which the little
man went about his task of destruction. Ghoulish, powerful, grinning, he
rent and pounded, hammered and smashed. Now the massive hand-carved
posts and headboard, the superb mirror frames, the delicate chair legs went
to feed the fire that rose, a pillar of orange and scarlet destruction, at the
rear of the Rampart Street house. The heat was dreadful, though the fire
had to be fed slowly, for safety's sake. The mahogany burned reluctantly.
Cupide's face became soot-streaked; he pranced between house and courtyard, between fire and wall. Crash, tinkle. Crash, tinkle, as the glass was
hurled against the brick wall by his strong simian arm. Then another load
of wood on the flames. Begrimed, sweating, filled with the lust for destruction, he was like an imp from hell as he worked, trotted, smashed, poked,
hammered. The day was New Orleans at its worst—saturated with heat and
moisture, windless, dead. Fortunate, this, or the Rampart Street house itself
might have taken part in the holocaust. Perhaps Clio had hoped it would.

"More," she urged Cupide. "More. Everything. I will sleep on the mattress on the floor these next few days. Nothing must be left."

The telegram came from the Texan, and then, as speedily as might be, his
letter, written in his schoolboy hand, round and simple and somehow touching.

> DEAR CLIO (it began, formally enough)
> Honey I miss you something terrible. I thought I was used
> to being alone but it seems right queer now and lonesome
> as the range. This place beats anything I ever saw. Hotels
> pack jammed and you talk about style and some ways rough
> too all mixed up the old days in Texas couldn't hold a candle
> to it. The United States Hotel is the place to stay which is
> where I am as you see. The biggest gambling place is called
> the Club House it was built by Morrissey he is dead. You
> ought to see it, the carpet alone cost $25,000 they say, there
> is a colored woman housekeeper runs the kitchen and so on
> her name is Mrs. Lewis I found this out and thought that
> Kaka could get friendly there. Honey you ought to see who
> all is here. This is a bigger lay-out than we figured on. Wil-
> liam Vanderbilt, Jay Gould, Whitney, Crocker, Keene, Bart
> Van Steed, why they are all millionaires fifty times over
> besides a thousand who are just plain rich with only a million
> or so in their pants pocket. Jay Gould sits on the front porch
> he is here at the United States and rocks a soft-spoken quiet-
> stepping fellow I wouldn't trust him with a plugged dime.
> I notice he's got a bodyguard since they tried to shoot him
> a while back. They call it the Milllionaires' Piazza. The
> turnouts would take your breath away. A four-in-hand is

nothing out of the ordinary. Vanderbilt drives a pair I would give anything just to get my hands on they are Maude S. and Adelina, the horses I mean, the prettiest team I ever saw and the fastest pair in the world. Bart Van Steed drives a pair of big sorrels to a dogcart with a footman sitting up behind like a monkey. We got acquainted through my bays racing him on Broadway. They are as fine a pair as there is in town except of course Vanderbilt's if I do say so.

Well, honey they call me White Hat Maroon, I am playing up Texas like you said. Peabody of Philadelphia has a pretty team of dapple grays he drives to a landau. The races are just beginning. Better get you one of those new trunks they call Saratoga trunks big as a house and it will hold those fancy dresses of yours I haven't seen anybody can come within a mile of you for looks and style though they dress up day and night like a fancy dress ball. It beats anything I bet even Paris France. The girls are all out after Bart Van Steed and even yours truly they say their mamas bring them here to catch a husband. And a lot of the other kind here too, bold as brass. The race when it comes to looks and clothes and bows is between a Mrs. Porcelain from the East somewhere and Miss Giulia Forosini her pa is the banker from California she drives three white mares down Broadway with snow-white reins, it's as good as a circus. Well honey sweetheart that gives you some idea. Van Steed is a mama boy they say afraid of his ma, she isn't here yet but coming and he is trying to make hay while the sun shines they say if he looks at a girl his ma snatches him away pronto. Bring all your pretty dresses. My room number is 239 at the front of the house there are rooms at the back on the balconies facing the garden very expensive they call them cottages which they are not but too quiet for my taste. Try to get 237 and 238 bedroom and sitting room they are vacant I paid for them for a week I said I wanted plenty of room and talked big. You make up a good reason for wanting them specially and I'll be a little gentleman and give them up when the manager asks me to. There is something big here if we play our cards right. Hurry up and come on but let me know everything about it as soon as you can. You drive to the lake for fish dinners and catch the fish yourself if you want to as good as New Orleans and better—black bass, canvasbacks, brook trout, woodcock, reed birds, soft shell crabs, red raspberries. You won't even remember Begue's with their kidney stew they make such a fuss about. They give you something called Saratoga chips it is potatoes as thin as tissue paper and crackly like popcorn. Everything free and easy, plenty of money, not too hot and big shady trees and you can smell the pines. This is bigger than I thought. I wish there was some way I could get at the big money boys I am studying how I can do it. I hate them worse than a cow man hates a sheep man. Well, if the cards run right and the horses run right and the little ball falls right we ought to clean up here. And if I do honey I'm going to buy you the biggest whitest diamond on Fifth Avenue New

York. Only hurry away from that stew-kettle down there and come up here to,

Your friend,
WHITE HAT MAROON.

P.S. Crazier than ever about you I don't like you being down there alone old Kaka and Cupide don't count.

Clio Dulaine's reply to this rambling letter was characteristically direct and astute.

CLINT CHÉRI:—

It has been very queer here. All things. But I am well and I am safe and I shall arrive in Saratoga on July 14th at half-past two. Do not meet me. Be at the hotel desk when I enter. The hotel will expect me on the 15th. Find out immediately, as soon as you have read this letter, if Van Steed's mother is arriving in Saratoga before that time. Telegraph me at once. This is important. If she is not there he will receive a telegram sent by me en route at the last minute to say that she is on the train and that he is to meet her. It may not work but I shall try. Remember, you do not know me. I think this will not be a little holiday with perhaps some luck at cards and horses. This is the chance of a lifetime. I am bringing Kaka and Cupide of course and eight trunks besides boxes. *A bientôt chèri,* Big Texas. Remember we are business partners. I have written the hotel.

CLIO DE CHANFRET.

Her letter to the United States Hotel was as brief and more to the point.

MY DEAR SIR:—

My physician Dr. Fossat has advised me to go to Saratoga for the waters following my recent illness due to my bereavement of which you doubtless have heard. I shall require a bedroom and sitting room for myself and accommodations elsewhere in the hotel for my maid and my groom. Many years ago my dear husband occupied apartment 237 and 238 in the United States Hotel. It will make me very happy if you can arrange to give me this same apartment. If it is difficult I shall be happy to recompense the hotel for its trouble.

One thing more I must ask of you. Though I am the Comtesse de Trenaunay de Chanfret I wish to be known only as plain Mrs. De Chanfret. I want to remain quiet while at Saratoga. I wish no formal ceremonies. I must rely completely on you to comply with my request to remain incognito.

I shall arrive on July 15th at half-past two o'clock.

I remain,

Sincerely yours,
COMTESSE DE TRENAUNAY DE CHANFRET
(MRS. DE CHANFRET *Please!*)

Twenty-four hours after the arrival of this letter everyone in Saratoga knew that nobility was coming incognito. Saratoga made much of its train arrivals in this, the height of the season. The natives themselves flocked down to see the notables and fashionables as they stepped off the train. The bell in the old station cupola added its clamor to the pandemonium of train bell, whistle, screech; the cries of greeting or farewell; the shouts of hotel porters and omnibus and hack drivers; the thud of heavy trunks; the stamp of nervous horses' hoofs. Landaus and dogcarts and phaetons and even a barouche or two were drawn up at the platform's edge. There was a swishing of silks and bouncing of bustles and trailing of draperies. Bewhiskered and mustached beaux in midsummer suits of striped seersucker or checked linen, horsey men in driving coats of fawn color or buckskin made a great show of gallantry as they bowed and postured and twirled their mustaches and took charge of the light hand-luggage and gave authoritative masculine orders regarding the disposal of trunks and boxes.

Clio Dulaine had lingered and dawdled in the train so that she was almost the last passenger to step onto the depot platform. The confusion was at its height. Bells clanged, whistles tooted, horses plunged and reared, the hotel runners shouted, "Grand Union bus here! Take your bus for the United States Hotel! Clarendon! Congress Hall this way!"

As she stepped off the train at Saratoga Spa it was characteristic of Clio Dulaine that she was not dressed in the utilitarian black or snuffy brown ordinarily worn for traveling by the more practical feminine world. She was wearing gray, sedate yet frivolous, the costume of a luxurious woman who need not concern herself with travel stains and dust. The little gray shoulder cape of ottoman silk was edged with narrow black French lace and its postilion back made her small waist look still tinier. Even her traveling hat (known as a Langtry turban) was relieved by its curl of gray and mauve ostrich tips nestling against the black of her hair. A traveling costume de luxe; a hint of half-mourning whose wearer has long since dried her tears.

As she stepped off the train she looked about her in pretty bewilderment, her expression touched with the half-smile of expectancy. The noise and confusion were at their height as passengers were swept off into waiting carriages or buses; then the whistle, the clangor and the slow acceleration of the engine's choo-choo-choo-choo-choochoo-choochoochoo as the train drew out. The noise reached a crescendo, died down, became a murmur. Sheriff O'Brien's sorrels whirled him off in his dogcart, the Bissells' long-tailed bays were twin streaks of red-brown against the landscape, the Forosini landau rolled richly off, the coats of the blooded blacks glinting like satin in the sunlight. Cupide had trotted off to wrestle with the pyramid of trunks and boxes. And still the slim gray-clad figure, drooping a little now, stood on the station platform. Behind her, a sable pillar of support, was Kakaracou. But Clio's speech, incisive though whispered, belied her attitude of forlorn uncertainty.

"Yes, I was right, Kaka. He's the one who has been running up and down like a chick without its hen-mother. That must be his carriage with the sorrels and the groom. Look! Now he's rushing into the waiting room. Quick, fetch Cupide, never mind about the trunks, when he comes out we must be standing near his cart, the three of us, put on your gloves, fool! Hold the jewel box well forward. Cupide! Quick! Here!"

She maneuvered the little group so that they stood between the waiting-room door and the team at the platform's edge. When he came out he must pass them. And now Bartholomew Van Steed emerged, a somewhat frantic figure. A final searching look up and down the station platform—a look that included and rejected the group of three as being no part of his problem—

and he sped, dejected, toward the waiting groom and horses. As swiftly Clio intercepted him.

"Pardon, Monsieur!" He stopped, stared. "Can you tell me where I may find a carriage to take me to the United States Hotel? Please."

"Uh—why————?" He waved a vague arm in the direction of the public hack stand, for he was full of his own troubles. He now saw that the space was deserted. Frowning, he looked back at her, into the lovely pleading face, seeing it now for the first time. His gaze traveled to the black woman behind her, to the strange little man in livery, then returned to her, and now her lip was quivering just a little, and she caught it between her teeth and clasped her graygloved hands.

"I was to have been met. Naturally. I cannot understand." She turned and spoke rapidly to Kakaracou in French, "This is terrible. I don't want to embarrass this gentleman. Can we send Cupide somewhere, perhaps————?" Her appealing look came back to Van Steed. And now for the first time he seemed to see the striking group as a whole —the richly dressed young woman, the dignified Negress, the dwarf attendant, all surrounded by a barricade of hatboxes, monogrammed leather cases, fine leather bags, all the appurtenances of luxurious travel.

The brusqueness of perplexity now gave way to his natural shyness. He blushed, stammered, bowed. A tall man who appeared short perhaps because of his own inner uncertainty, perhaps because he stooped a little. Side whiskers and a rather ferocious mustache that did not hide the timidity of the lower face; a fine brow; brown eyes with a hurt look in them; a strong, arrogant hooked nose—the Van Steed nose. Clio Dulaine saw and weighed all this swiftly as she looked at him, her lips slightly parted now like a child's. Something of a dandy, poor darling, she thought, with that fawn-colored coat and the *sans souci* hat like that of a little boy playing in the Luxembourg Garden.

"Madame," he began, "that is—Miss—uh————"

"I am the Comtesse—I mean I am Mrs. De Chanfret. I am sorry to have troubled you. It has been such a long and tiring trip. I had expected to be met. I am not fully recovered from————"

Two great pearly tears welled up, clung a moment to her lashes; she blinked bravely but they eluded her and sped down her cheeks. She dabbed at them with a tiny lace-bordered handkerchief.

"But Mrs. De Chanfret! Please! Uh—allow me to drive you to the United States Hotel. I am stopping there myself. I am Bart Van Steed, if I may————"

"Not—not Bartholomew Van Steed!" He admitted this with a bow and with that air of embarrassment which, oddly enough, seizes one when confronted with one's own name. "But how enchanting! Like being met unexpectedly by a friend in a strange land. It is a strange land for me. But perhaps you are meeting someone else————"

At this his worried look returned, he glanced right and left as though the possibility still remained that he might have overlooked a passenger on the little depot platform. "I was expecting my mother. She telegraphed me that she would be on this train."

Clio was all concern. "And she didn't come?"

"I can't imagine what happened. Maybe she's on another train. But she never misses a train. And she never changes her mind."

"Perhaps someone was playing a joke."

"People do not play jokes on me," said Bart Van Steed. "I shall send a telegram as soon as we reach the hotel." He waved her toward the waiting carriage. "Lucky I drove the phaeton. Mother won't ride in the dogcart. But I'm afraid there isn't room for all———"

"You are so kind. This will do beautifully—for all of us." The groom had jumped down, had handed the reins to Van Steed, and now was barely in time to hand Clio up, for her foot was on the step and she was seated beside Van Steed before he had well adjusted the ribbons. "My woman can sit back there with your groom—she's very thin. And Cupidon can stand on the step, if necessary. . . . The bags just there . . . So . . . Kaka, have you my jewel-case? . . .That large bag here at my feet. I don't mind. . . . The hotel porter will see to the trunks. . . . Cupide! There, on the step . . . You see he's so very little you will never notice he's . . . It's not far, I suppose . . . This is wonderful! So kind! So very kind! I don't know what I should have done if you hadn't appeared like a shining knight. . . ."

She leaned a little toward him, she smiled her lovely poignant smile. She sighed. She thought, well, lucky I know how to manage, we'd never have been able to pile in. Not with this weak-chinned one.

Away they whirled. White-painted houses. Greek revival columns. Gingerbread fretwork. Ancient wine-glass elms. Smooth green lawns. "Oh, I like this! This is very American!" Clio clapped her hands like a child, and for once she was not acting. "Charming" She turned slightly to call over her shoulder to Kakaracou, speaking in French. "Look, Kaka, look! This is America—but the real America!"

"Tiens!" said Kaka, putting incredible sarcasm into the monosyllable.

"I gather that you have not visited Saratoga before," said Bart Van Steed, weightily. "I—uh—I speak some French." Then, as she turned to him, eager to express her delight in the language with which she was most at ease, he added, hastily, "But only a little. A very little. I—uh—read it better than I speak it. You haven't been here before, I gather."

"I haven't been anywhere. I am discovering America. It is amazing! So big! So new! All my life I have lived in France." She was having a fine time being very French; little Gallic gestures; her hands, her inflection, the cooing note in her voice. He had noted the crest on her luggage, the initials on the filmy handkerchief, the tiny jeweled monogram on her reticule. The letter C was entwined with vines and fragile leaves and spirals.

"Are you here for the racing season?"

"I am a lover of horses. But I am here in the hope that the waters and the air will help me. Not," she hastily added, "that I am ill. I never have been ill in my life. But I have heard that the waters are tonic and I hoped that the fresh bracing pine air and the tonic waters would restore my appetite."

His little blond mustache quivered, his pale blue eyes turned to her sympathetically. "I've got a delicate digestion too."

She thought, grimly, I'll be bound you have! Aloud she said, "All sensitive people—especially those whose lives are lived in the midst of great responsibilities—are likely to have delicate digestions. Because of his diplomatic duties my husband the Count de—I mean for years my late husband had to have everything *purée,* almost like an infant's food, really. Yet he was a man of the most brilliant mentality and marvelous achievement, like yourself."

"My mother," he announced, plaintively, "can digest anything. Anything. Sixty-seven."

"How marvelous! But then, she probably isn't your temperament. Not so delicately organized."

"She's as strong," he announced with surprising and unconscious bitterness, "as an ox—that is—she's got great strength and—uh—strength."

"How—wond-er-ful!" she cooed in that paced leisurely voice. "And yet, do you know, sometimes these very, very strong wonderful people become sort of annoying to more highly sensitive ones like you and me—I don't mean your dear mother, of course."

He had barely time to say, "No, certainly not!" with guilty emphasis when they drew up before the fantastically columned entrance of the United States Hotel. The three passengers in Bartholomew Van Steed's equipage stared in stunned unbelief at a sight which could be duplicated nowhere else in America—or in the world, for that matter. Slim columns rose three stories high from a piazza whose width and length were of the dimensions of a vast assembly room. A gay frieze of petunias and scarlet geraniums in huge boxes blazed like footlights to illumine the bizarre company that now crowded the space on the other side of the porch rail.

"*Grand Dieu!*" was wrung from Clio Dulaine as she stared in shocked unbelief.

"*Nom d'une pipe!*" squeaked Cupide.

"*Mais, bizarre! Fantastique!*" muttered Kakaracou.

Up and down, up and down the length of the enormous piazza moved a mass of people, slowly, solemnly, almost treading on each other's heels. The guests of the United States Hotel were digesting their gargantuan midday meal. Carriages and buses had already disgorged the passengers who had arrived on the half-past-two train, and these had been duly viewed, criticized and docketed by the promenaders. It was part of the daily program.

And now here was an unexpected morsel—a delicious bit to roll under the tongue. The vast company goggled, slowed its pace, came almost to a standstill like a regiment under command. En masse they stared with unabashed American curiosity at Bart Van Steed's carriage and its occupants. Bartholomew Van Steed, the unattainable bachelor, the despair of matchmaking mamas, the quarry of all marriageable daughters, dashing up to the hotel entrance in broad daylight with a woman—with a young, beautiful and strange woman. One could discern that before she emerged.

Down jumped a midget in livery, gold buttons and all. Out stepped a majestic turbaned black woman looking for all the world like an exiled Nubian queen. Out jumped Bart Van Steed's groom, then Van Steed threw him the reins and himself handed out the modish figure in gray and mauve.

A simple day, a crude society. Like figures in a gigantic marionette show the piazza faces turned toward the little procession as Clio, her skirts lifted ever so slightly, swept up the broad steps of the piazza into the vast white lobby. Beside her strode Bart Van Steed, and behind her a stream of satellites. Out rushed a covey of black bellboys and joined the parade, each snatching a hatbox, a case, a bag. The women noted the cut of the stranger's ottoman silk gown, the fineness of the black French lace so wantonly edging a traveling cape; they saw the sly line of the Lily Langtry hat, the way the gray kid boots matched the richly rustling skirt. The men saw the slender ankle beneath the demurely lifted skirt, the curve of the figure in the postilion cape, the lovely cream-white coloring and the great dark eyes beneath the low-tipped hat.

"Why, the sly dog! I wouldn't have believed it of him He said it was his mother he was going to meet."

Out pranced Roscoe Bean, the oily head usher, from his corner under the great winding stairway—Roscoe Bean, who winnowed the hotel wheat from the piazza chaff, who boasted he could tell the beau monde from the demimonde at first glance. A snob of colossal proportions, unctuous, flattering, malicious, he now skimmed toward the party so that the tails of his Prince

Albert coat spread fanlike behind him. His arms were outspread, he swayed
from the hips, it was a form of locomotion more like swimming han walking.

"Your ladyship!" he began, breathlessly, for his pervasive eye had
glimpsed the omnipresent monograms and crests. "Your ladyship! We didn't
expect you until tomorrow."

"Please!" She raised a protesting hand. "I am Mrs. De Chanfret."

"Yes, of course. Beg your pardon. Your letter said————"

She approached the desk. She did not even glance at the tall figure lounging
against a pillar just next to the clerk's desk—a figure whose long legs were
booted Western style, whose broad-brimmed white sombrero was pushed
back slightly from his forehead, whose gaze lazily followed the spiraled
smoke of the large fragrant cigar in his hand.

Even as she signed her name in the bold almost masculine hand—Mrs.
De Chanfret—maid—groom—the room clerk, the subclerk, the hastily summoned manager and assistant manager wrung their hands and wailed in
unison like a frock-coated Greek chorus.

"But Mrs. De Chanfret! Your letter said the fifteenth. Here it is. In your
own hand. The fifteenth! Two thirty-seven and two thirty-eight were to be
vacated early tomorrow morning. We were sending a staff of cleaners in to
prepare them for you first thing in the morning. We wouldn't have had this
happen for the world!"

"Perhaps I should have gone to one of the other hotels."

"Mrs. De Chanfret! No! We can give you a temporary suite in one of the
cottages————"

"Cottages!"

"Magnificent suites at the rear————"

"I! At the rear!"

"But the cottages aren't cottages—that is—they're suites on the balconies
overlooking the gardens. Our most élite guests refuse to occupy any other
rooms . . . Mr. William Vanderbilt . . . Lispenards . . . Chisholms . . .
Mr. Jay Gould himself . . . even President Arthur has . . ."

She shook her head gently; she turned away. To his own astonishment
Van Steed heard himself saying, "This is preposterous! You must accommodate Mrs. De Chanfret. I myself will give up————"

The turmoil had now reached a dramatic height exactly to Clio Dulaine's
liking. Behind her stood Kakaracou, an ebony statue, the jewel case clutched
prominently in front of her. Cupide, his tiny legs crossed, was lolling negligently against a stack of luggage while his froglike eyes made lively survey
of the immense lobby. A group of Negro bellboys, their clustered heads like
black grapes on a stem, stared down at him, enthralled. Inured though the
little man was to the cruel gaze of gaping strangers, he now was irked by
the attention he was receiving. Suddenly he contorted his face into the most
gruesome and inhuman aspect, accompanying this with an evil and obscene
voodoo gesture unmistakable even to these Northern boys. They scattered,
only to peer at him again, eyes popping, from behind a near-by pillar or
desk.

And outside, the piazza-walkers were savoring this unexpected after-dinner delicacy, or dropping into the lobby on any pretext. . . . It's that countess or whatever she is . . . but I thought she wasn't coming until tomorrow
. . . did you see the midget I thought it was a little boy until I saw his face
he looks . . . this morning I happened to meet Bart he said he was expecting
his mother on the two . . . well all I can say is that when old Madam Van
Steed hears of this she'll have a . . . rules him with a rod of iron . . . Mrs.
De Chanfret . . . they say she doesn't want to be called . . .

For this hotel was like a little self-contained town; the piazza like a daily meeting of a rural sewing society made up of gossips of both sexes. Every one of the promenaders longed to be in the lobby now. Yet even they realized that a concerted move in this direction would inevitably result in a stampede. Still, the hardier souls among them would not be denied. Singly or in pairs you heard them muttering a trumped-up excuse as they drifted out of the throng and made for the door that framed the enormous lobby.

"Well—uh—guess I'll get me forty winks after all that dinner . . . if I'm going to the races I'd better be starting . . . I'll go up to the room and see how Mama is. She had one of her headaches and wouldn't come down to dinner . . . Mr. Gillis said he'd have the information for me at the desk this afternoon so I'll just drop by and ask . . ."

Within the hotel the apologies and explanations behind the desk now rose to a babble through which could be heard a single word emerging like a leitmotif. Maroon. Maroon. Maroon. Colonel Maroon's occupying those rooms, but by tomorrow he——

Now the tall figure that had been so indolently viewing this scene from the vantage point of the near-by pillar uncrossed its legs, came forward with a slow easy grace and, removing the white sombrero with a sweeping gesture that invested it with imaginary plumes, bowed before the elegant and somewhat agitated figure of Mrs. De Chanfret.

"Excuse me, Ma'am, but I couldn't help hearing what you-all were saying. My name is Maroon, Ma'am—Clint Maroon. Texas."

Clio Dulaine looked up at him, she turned a bewildered face toward Bart Van Steed, then quickly to the men at the desk, "Well, really, gentlemen! This is too——"

"No offense, Ma'am," drawled Maroon.

Bart Van Steed now found himself not only aiding beauty in distress, but playing the defender of injured innocence. "Look here, Maroon, you can't address a lady you've never met."

"Listen at him! Introduce us, then, and make it legal. I'm aiming to help the little lady. She can have the rooms she wants right now. How's that, Ma'am!"

Grudgingly Van Steed went through the form of introduction. Again the Texan bowed with astonishing courtliness. Clio Dulaine held out her little gloved hand. He took it in his great clasp, he clung to it like an embarrassed boy. "But I couldn't think of turning you out of your rooms, Mr. Maroon."

"Make nothing of it, Ma'am. It's thisaway. I'm just occupying two thirty-seven, thirty-eight and thirty-nine for the hell of it. Shucks, Ma'am, excuse me. I didn't go for to use language." He came closer. He still held her hand in his. She did not retreat. "No sense in my having it. I just like to spread out and be comfortable. I'll go get me my stuff and you can move in right now. I never really used those two extra rooms, anyway."

"How good of you, Mr.——"

"Maroon," he prompted her. "Clint Maroon."

"What a delightful name! So American."

"Texas, Ma'am."

"Texas! I should love to see Texas."

"Play your cards right and you will, Ma'am. No offense, Mrs.—uh——"

"De Chanfret."

"De—uh—yes. Well, I meant that was just an expression we use. I sure would like to be the one to show you Texas." He raised a hand toward the clerks behind the desk. "I'll mosey along and be out of there in two shakes. You-all can come on along right now, if you've got a mind to."

This surprising suggestion was seized upon by Mrs. De Chanfret with alacrity. "Kaka! Cupide!"

The room clerk, the manager, the assistant manager, the head usher, relaxed beaming. "Madame is wonderful," cooed Roscoe Bean, "to accommodate herself like this."

Clio graciously murmured something about being a woman of the world. Cupide, a gargoyle come alive, bestirred himself among the bags. Kaka moved to her mistress's side. The little procession formed again, now taking on the proportions of a safari. Bells were tapped smartly. Orders given. A squad of chambermaids and scrub-women summoned. Clint Maroon did not precede the party. He waited. Clio turned to Bartholomew Van Steed.

"How can I thank you! You have been so kind, so friendly. I feel, really, that we actually are friends."

Caution settled like a glaze over Van Steed's face. The quarry scented the pursuer. "I am happy to have been of service." He bowed rather stiffly. "I trust that you will be comfortable."

"And I hope," Clio said, all sweetness and light, "that your dear mother's telegram will soon be followed by her coming. But I can't help being selfish enough to realize that her failure to arrive was my gain. Good-by, Mr. Van Steed." She half turned away.

Caution fled. He took a step toward her. "I shall see you soon, I—that is—we shall meet again soon, I trust—guests under the same roof, naturally——"

She bowed, she smiled, she moved off with her entourage; she had given him a swimming glance intended to convey fatigue, gratitude, aloofness. Incredibly enough, she actually managed all three. But even as she turned away she paused a moment. "Who is this gentleman,"—she indicated the tall figure of the Texan strolling toward the elevator—"your friend in the white hat? He is the real figure of an American. Who is he?" Her words were quite clear to the attendants at the desk.

Van Steed eyed him obliquely. "Maroon? Why—uh—Texas cattle man, I'm told. Some such matter. He's no friend of mine."

"A pity. In Paris he would be the rage." Bart Van Steed's pale golden eyes widened in surprise. How annoying those white eyelashes are, Clio thought, even as she smiled sweetly in farewell. Then the slender gray-clad figure moved off with a soft susurrus of silks, followed by the discreeter rustle of the majestic black woman's skirts. He was still looking after her as the elevator with its grillwork, its groaning ropes and clanking cables, lumbered heavily upward and bore her from his sight.

A little pink-and-white figure, pretty as a Dresden china shepherdess, approached the desk, paused a moment in passing and gave an extremely bad imitation of surprise at the encounter. "Your mother didn't come, Mr. Van Steed? What a disappointment for you!"

"Oh, howdy-do, Mrs. Porcelain! No—uh—that is—no."

"I do hope nothing's wrong," she cooed. "Saratoga isn't Saratoga without her."

A momentary gleam lighted his eye, then faded. "Nothing's wrong," he replied, as though thinking aloud. "The telegraph company must have made the mistake. Mother never does. I'm sending her a telegram now. The funny part of it is that I thought she was up in Newport at my sister's house. Mrs. Schermerhorn. She's expecting a—uh—she isn't well, that's why Mother—but her telegram was sent from New York."

Mrs. Porcelain wagged a coy forefinger at him. "Now, now! You're not playing a little joke on us, are you, Mr. Van Steed? You didn't drive down to the depot to meet a Certain Somebody Else? I just happened to be on the piazza taking a little constitutional when you drove up.''

For years Madam Van Steed, that iron matriarch, had checked relentlessly on his every coming and going. His solicitude when she was present only testified to his guilty inner hatred—a hatred which occasionally brimmed over into a fury of resentment. So now he was seized with the seemingly unreasonable rage of the hag-ridden male.

"My dear Mrs. Porcelain, am I to understand that I am obliged to cloak my actions or explain my behavior to a lot of harpies on a hotel piazza!"

"Harpies!" The round blue eyes, the round pink mouth showed her shocked surprise, but the social training of years triumphed. "You're quite right, Mr. Van Steed. We do become like small-town gossips here in dear little old Saratoga, don't we?" She managed an arch smile. "She is really lovely."

"But I tell you I don't know the lady!" he almost shouted.

But Mrs. Porcelain was not to be diverted from her purpose by mere insult.

"You must introduce me some time soon. I should so love to meet her."

9

CLIO DULAINE STOOD in the middle of the sitting room, surveying the suite with its grim and rigid furnishings. Black walnut chairs, mustard walls, a vast cuspidor. Through the open door of the bedroom she glimpsed the carved black walnut bed, the livery marble-topped table, the boxed-in wash-stand. Beyond that was the dim cavern of the bathroom with its zinc-lined tub. Bellboys were raising windows, lowering shades, muttering about ice water. Clint Maroon was standing discreetly in the outer hall doorway under the chaperonage of Roscoe Bean's eye.

"Looks like we're neighbors, Ma'am," he said, genially. "Seeing how I'm right next door." He waved his hand toward the closed double door.

"So kind of you to give up your rooms to me, Mr.—uh—Maroon. I really feel quite guilty."

"No call to. I never used 'em. Well, I'll be moseying along. Good day, Mrs. De Chanfret, Ma'am."

With considerable ostentation Roscoe Bean glided to the large double door between the sitting room and the bedroom just now designated by Maroon. "I'll lock the door on this side, Your Lady—that is, Mrs. De Chanfret—if you'll kindly turn the lock on your side, Mr. Maroon. It's a double lock, you see, both sides. Mmmm." His murmur conveyed a nice sense of the proprieties. He proceeded to turn the lock with precision and snap.

"Good day, Ma'am," Clint Maroon vanished from the doorway. Clio Dulaine waited. Roscoe Bean waited. Kakaracou waited. Cupide, grinning, cocked his impish head. A bolt shot into place, a key grated. "Ah!" sighed Roscoe Bean. Then, briskly, "The chambermaid and the scrubwoman and the housekeeper will be up at once. Have you had your dinner? Is there anything? Would you———"

Already Kaka was going about her duties with the utmost efficiency. She had immediately vanished into the bedroom to poke the mattress with an investigating forefinger. Now she was opening boxes, hanging clothes in the wardrobe, laying out toilet things, shooing the loitering bellboys. *"Allez, allez!* Go! *Carencro! Congo! Dépêche toi!"*

With a protesting palm and a voice of quiet authority Clio interrupted the usher's chatter. "Nothing now. Thank you. No maids. My maid will do all that is necessary for the present. Cupide, go with this gentleman. See that my trunks are brought up at once from the station. The hotel maids later, later. I must rest now."

She closed the outer hall door after them sharply, she turned the key, she stood a moment, listening, her head resting against the door. She turned, her body leaning against the door now, and surveyed the ugly room with a little secret smile of satisfaction and triumph. Her physical weariness was forgotten in a surge of elation. She listened again, her head thrown back. From the depths of her being she sighed with exquisite relief. The flurry of arrival was over, the fatigue of the trip was forgotten. From the bedroom came the reassuring sounds of Kaka's expert ministrations. Through the open windows facing the street she saw the green lace of giant elms, heard the clatter of horses' hoofs, snatches of talk, laughter, the cry of a vendor. Exultingly she thought, well, Clio Dulaine, here you are in Saratoga! You have left New Orleans and its sorrows behind you. You have already met the most eligible man in the East. You have money enough to last you the summer. You are a wonderful woman, Clio. But marvelous!

Swiftly she went to the forbidding slab of the somber double door, drew back the bolt, turned the massive key. But even as she did this she heard, in perfect unison, the bolt shot back, the key turned on the other door. Her hand never touched the knob, for as she instinctively stepped back the door was thrown open from the other side. As on their first real meeting the two burst into laughter spontaneous and a little hysterical before he gathered her up into his arms, caught her up and held her to him so that she lay in her gray and mauve like a scarf flung across his breast. There was no sound but the discreet rustling that betokened Kaka's hands busy in the adjoining room with tissue paper and silks. When, finally, he tipped her gently to her feet, one great arm spanned her shoulders, one hand tilted her face up toward his and silently, leisurely, he bent over her and his lips touched her hair, her brow, were pressed against her closed eyelids, her lips, her throat, her breast as he held her yielding as a reed.

"Send her away. Shut the door."

"Tonight, *chéri*. That endless journey. Tired."

He sighed, he released her, he passed a hand across his eyes with the old gesture of one dispelling a mist. "How are you, Ma'am?" Then they both giggled as though he had said something exquisitely witty.

"If you had called me Ma'am once more down there I'd have screamed."

"I sure would have admired to hear you, Ma'am. Only I'd hated to have you scared Bart thataway. Say, how in Sam Hill did you get him eating out of your hand? When I saw you come in with him easing along beside you I thought for a minute, well, hell's bells, how in tarnation can I stand here pretending I don't know her when that little mama's boy is bowing and scraping and running the whole shebang!"

"Jealous already!"

"You're damn whistlin' I am!"

"There is much more to come. You must remember what we're here for."

"Look, honey. I've been thinking. I can make out for both of us. There's money to burn around here at the Club House and over at the track. I'm used to stud and red dog but I've been making out pretty good at roulette and faro. And I've been sitting in on poker games upstairs at the Club House in the private rooms. Say! Look!" He brought forth a wallet, his dexterous hands ruffled a sheaf of yellow-backed bills. "We can clean up pretty and then light out for somewhere else."

Anger, cold and hard, stiffened her whole body. Her eyes narrowed, her jaw set so that the muscles suddenly showed rigid. Maroon had tossed the fat wallet onto the marble-topped center table. Now her hand seized on it, she drew in her breath with a little hiss, then she hurled the leather-enclosed packet across the room where it lay in a corner of the floor, its golden leaves fluttering a moment before it subsided. He stared at her, uncertainly. He had never before seen her in such anger.

"Poker games!" Her tone was venomous. "Poker games, when there are fools here worth millions and millions! Do you think I came here to pick up dollar bills like those girls you told me of in your cheap dance halls in the West! Do you! Do you!" Then quietly, venomously, "Get out! Get out of my room."

Kaka appeared in the bedroom doorway, a silken garment in her hand. The bewildered Texan stared at her. Kaka tossed the garment onto a chair and glided swiftly to the distraught woman. Clio thrust her away, but the Negress heeded this no more than if she had been dealing with a tired child. She began to unfasten the snug bodice of Clio's dress, swiftly and deftly she peeled it from her as she stood, and the heavy silken garment slid to the floor with a soft slithering sound and lay in a crumpled circle at the girl's feet while she still glared at the Texan and he stared dazedly at her. "My poor little tired baby!" Kakaracou murmured to the figure standing there in the embroidered and beribboned corset-cover and petticoats. Then, over her shoulder to Maroon, "Come, lift her out, lak lil *bébé,* I put her in bed."

"Too hot," murmured Clio, her eyes half closed, her anger fled as suddenly as it had come. "I'll lie on that funny couch there in the bedroom. And you'll sit and talk to me, Clint, and Kaka will go on unpacking. I love it like that, cozy, and everyone near me, and things stirring."

As though she had been a doll he picked her up in his arms while Kaka scooped up the dress, and together they deposited her on the couch with its unyielding expanse of brocatel, its lumpy head-rest, in the room littered with the silks and ribbons and bottles and jars and gowns and bonnets only now unpacked by Kakaracou.

"Hep shoes," ordered Kaka. Maroon knelt with the Negress while each removed one of the little gray kid boots. She slipped a sheer white wrapper over Clio's head, thrust the girl's limp arms into the long beribboned sleeves, briskly buttoned it at the throat and tucked a tiny French hand-wrought pillow under the weary head.

"Ah-h-h-h!" breathed Clio, luxuriously. Suddenly she was wide awake, alert. *Chéri,* I am so sorry. No, don't go away. Presently I will sleep. Not now. Come, sit here, talk to me. I didn't sleep, not one hour on that dreadful train, all the way from New Orleans I have not slept. Kaka can sleep standing upright like a cow. Really. And Cupide curled anywhere in a corner, like a monkey. Now, let us talk. This is wonderful. So cozy and gay but peaceful, too. I am happy! I am happy!"

"Hold on, look here," Maroon remonstrated, though only half-heartedly, for she looked so young and small there on the sofa amongst the cushions. "Now you say you're happy. But I've got a temper too, strong as horse-radish. You ever let go at me like that again, why, I'm sure liable to punish you, pronto. Screeching at me like a crazy mare. You try that again, girl, you'll be here alone."

She pretended to cower in fright among the pillows; it was impossible to maintain a role of offended dignity in the face of her outrageous simperings. But he refused to smile, he took on a gruffly paternal tone. "Likely you're lightheaded on account of having no sleep and no decent food, probably."

He strolled into the sitting room, retrieved the scorned wallet, came back, still talking, and stuffed the billfold into his breast pocket. "Easy come, easy go, that's my motto, but just the same I've got more respect for money than to take and throw it thataway. Better let Kaka fetch you some dinner, maybe that'll settle you."

"No. When the train stopped at that town—Poughkeepsie—what a name! When the train stopped there everyone got out and there were women with baskets covered over with clean white napkins, and underneath the most delicious chicken and biscuits and cake. We bought everything. Even Kaka had to say it was not bad. Didn't you, Kaka?" Kaka made an unladylike sound. "Well, at least we could eat it."

The Texan was not yet quite mollified. "I never did see a woman grown treated like a baby before. Getting undressed and put to sleep in the middle of the day. Ma, she stayed on her feet and not a yip out of her when she was just about dying."

"I know. She must have been wonderful, like the pioneer American women in the books. I am not at all like that." She dismissed the whole matter with the air of one who finds it unimportant. "When I am ill I complain and when I am angry I shout and when I am happy I laugh. It is simpler." She stirred luxuriously among the pillows, she smiled engagingly up at him. "Stop scowling like a cross little boy! Let's talk, all cozy and comfortable. Kaka, move that chair nearer. Now. Tell me. Tell me everything. From the beginning." She clasped her hands like a child waiting to be told a fairy tale.

Rather sulkily he lounged in the armchair by the sofa, his long booted legs stretched out. "Nothing much to tell, comes to that."

"Clint, *chéri,* don't be like that. Here we are in Saratoga where we shall make our fortunes. Now then, those rich old men, those wicked old men who sit and rock on that huge fantastic piazza, tell me about them. Have you talked with them? Do they think you are big and important and Western, as we planned?"

In spite of himself he began to kindle to his story. "Well, it ain't as easy as all that, sugar. They're a special breed of varmints. I thought I knew something about what was behind men's faces from watching poker players. I've sat in twenty-four-hour games where I got to know that a muscle that kind of twitched in a player's jaw meant four aces, and once I spotted a royal flush from just happening to notice that Steve Fargo's face was dead pan but the pupils of his eyes had widened till you couldn't rightly see the real color of his eyes. But these fellas, they ain't human . . . Don't raise your left eyebrow when I say ain't. I know better but I'm talking Texas every day now, like you said, practicing . . . Well, there's a kind of cold-blooded quiet about them you can't get at. It ain't money they're after. It's each other's skins. They've already got so much money they can't keep track of it, no way. I got it straight. Look at Willie Vanderbilt, his pa, the old Commodore—and say, he was no more a Commodore than I'm a Colonel—did I tell you they took to calling me Colonel around here, down at the track and over to the Club House—Colonel Maroon—well, as I was saying, the old Commodore left Willie ninety-four million dollars and damned if he hasn't run it up to two hundred million. Two hundred million, honey! We don't sit in that game, Clio."

"Why not! Why not, I'd like to know! Are you afraid?"

"No. I just ain't interested enough in money to go out and knife these sharks for it. It ain't money with them. It ain't even power. It's like they were playing a game, and the cards are people and the stakes are railroads or mines or water power. They ain't human. They don't care for human beings or for their own country or honesty or any decent living thing. These men, they're not like anybody you ever met up with. They don't run with the herd, they don't hunt in packs. They go it alone, dog eat dog. And yet you wouldn't rightly call what they've got by a name like—say—courage or independence. They put me in mind of jackals more than anything—they ain't dogs and they ain't wolves—they've just got the worst habits and make-up of both. You want me to be like them, Clio?''

"You don't have to be like them. You only have to be cleverer than they are.''

"Yep. That's all. I could scheme to grab ahead of 'em. But you see, my folks, they were the giving kind, not the taking. They liked to build up, not tear down. When you think how people came over here from the old country and worked like slaves and went through hardships would kill us today. Pa clearing the land and planting it up and Grandpaw at the Alamo—why, say, my fingers they just itch to take out my gun when I see that pack of varmints sitting there, rocking, so soft-spoken and mild-looking. They're so poison mean their lives are threatened all the time. And that's why you never see them without two or three big kind of dumb-looking fellows standing around near by, faces like big biscuits with a couple of raisins for eyes. They're bodyguards. I bet I could pick one or two off right here from this window.''

"Don't talk like a foolish boy, Clint. They must be quite simple, really, these American millionaires. Simple and cruel, like children. Taking each other's toys away by force and running off with them. This Van Steed—he seemed rather silly, I thought. Actually frightened of his mother. And a weak digestion. Pink cheeks and white eyelashes and stammers a little. Wouldn't you think he would have suspected my clumsy little trick! But he swallowed it. Well, now—really!''

He got up and began to pace the floor; then he perched on the footboard of the bed, slouching a little as though he were sitting on the top rail of a Texas corral fence. "Funny thing, they're all like that, one way or another. Sick men. It's like they knew death was on 'em, and they had to work fast. Vanderbilt looks like he'd burst a blood vessel any minute, his face is red but it isn't a red you get from health. Now Gould, he's got a bad heart and they say consumption. It's common talk he hardly ever sleeps, and times he spits up blood. Nights when everybody's asleep, two, three o'clock in the morning, he's sitting there on the piazza, rocking, and gets spasms of coughing you'd think he'd split in two. Spends all day sending telegrams to New York or talking to the men he sends for, so quiet you couldn't catch a word if you were passing by slow. Asks the band to play his favorite tune, 'Lead, Kindly Light.' . . . You think you can come here and lasso a critter like this Bart Van Steed! He's one-third bronco, one-third mule and one-third Mama's boy.''

"I thought he seemed quite charming.''

"Quite charming,'' he mimicked in a maddening falsetto.

But she only smiled at him as at a rather naughty but engaging child. "Oh, I wish I weren't so sleepy. There is so much I want to know. Just to hear your voice. But this cool delicious air after all that heat. It is as if I were drugged.''

He forsook his perch on the footboard to stand over Kaka busy with her bags and boxes. "Kaka, pull down the shades, she'll go to sleep, and we'll have a drive at five o'clock, or maybe a horseback ride if you feel like it, Clio.''

Kaka glanced over her shoulder at her mistress, feverish and heavy-eyed. She spoke as if Clio were not in the room, her English very precise. "When she looks like that she will do things her own way. She has been like that for a month now, until she is ready to drop with fatigue, and me I ache in every bone and Cupide's legs are an inch shorter from running.''

"Well, do something, can't you! She'll make herself sick.''

"She was like that in Paris before we came to America. She was like that before she met you in the Market." She dropped her voice, she became suddenly the black woman, superstitious, witchlike. "She under a *wanga.*"

"A what? What's that?"

"*Wanga.* A spell. I give her witch powder but"—her voice dropped so that her mobile lips mouthed the words almost soundlessly—"no good because Miss Clio she a witch woman herself."

He laughed a little uncomfortably. "Listen at you!"

"What are you two whispering about? Kaka, don't unpack everything. We may not stay in these rooms."

He strode over to her then and stood over her menacingly. "What do you mean—not stay here! You're plumb crazy. You've been talking crazy ever since you got here. Where're you aiming to go!"

"He said the cottages—that man downstairs. Is it more chic, there in the cottages?"

"God, I don't know! Nothing you've said since you drove in here makes a mite of sense. I've a mind to get out of here myself, and leave you."

"No, you won't, Clint *chéri.*"

"Why won't I!" In a miserable imitation of truculence.

"You won't," she repeated, equably. Then, persisting, "The cottages. Tell me."

"Hell's bells! I don't know, I tell you! I don't even know why they call them cottages. It's crazy. They're the rooms at the back where the hotel's kind of U-shaped and verandas running all around. I don't want to talk about hotels!"

"He said a garden."

"Well, there's a garden back there, right pretty, with big trees and flower-beds. Mornings and evenings the hotel band plays there, and when there's a hotel hop, why, they string up colored lanterns. Some folks they like to sit there in the garden. Oh, God, I don't know! This is the looniest talk I ever heard! Look, you're what they call punch-drunk, you need sleep, you'd better let Kaka put you————"

She got up then, trailing her long white draperies over the oddments and elegancies with which the floor was strewn. "I tell you I must know a thousand things before I can sleep. Then I shall sleep and sleep and sleep, hours and hours, a thousand miles deep, and when I wake up everything will be clear and right in my mind. Isn't it so, Kaka! Tell him."

A certain affirmation was in Kaka's eyes, but she cackled derisively. "Heh-heh, yes, she think she a *mamaloi,* she go off in a spell and when she wake up everything come right like she want it."

"That's just dumb talk. All this milling around. What's eatin' on you, anyway! You don't rightly know what you're saying."

"But I do. Or I will. This little fellow—this little Van Steed—do you imagine he is cleverer than you and I?"

"Clever! It's money. They've got millions."

"They didn't always have millions."

"Listen, honey, you just don't understand. Why, the women around here, they'll tear you to pieces if you step in their way. You pretending to be here alone—that's bad medicine. A woman without a man here in Saratoga— they'll make cold hash out of you in a week."

"But I have a man. You. And in a week there will be two men—you and little Bartholomew."

"He's going to be too busy to bother about you, honey. I heard yesterday they're out to get him."

She whirled at this. "Who? How? Why?"

Restlessly he began to pace the littered room, stepping over piles of neatly stacked lingerie, trampling stray bits of tissue paper.

"I don't rightly know yet. I pieced it together from what I picked up. Van Steed owns a hundred miles of road between Albany and Binghamton. Right up near Saratoga here. It's what they call a trunk line. Only a hundred miles or thereabouts. Years ago his mama gave it to him to play with, his first little railroad. Now it's turned up worth millions."

"But why? Why? . . . Kaka, stop that rattling of paper! . . . Why is this—this Saratoga trunk worth millions? These—these are the things I want to know. How can I sleep when there are things like these I must know! Tell me—why millions?"

"Seems it's the link between the new Pennsylvania hard-coal lands and New England. That little stretch of one hundred miles is what they want to get their claws into. It's the coal has made all the difference. It's a coal haul, direct, for all of New England. Sure thing it's worth millions."

"Does he know this—Van Steed?"

"Why wouldn't he know it! He isn't as dumb as he looks. Van Steed, he's president of the Albany & Tuscarora, and this trunk line was just a kind of link—it didn't mean anything until these new coal fields were opened up. They've been fighting it out for months now. Gould's crowd have been buying up town councilors all along the line. The way they work it's so simple it sounds kind of crazy—or I'd think it was crazy if I hadn't heard the same kind of story all my life from the way Pa was treated. Honey, you wouldn't believe it. I can't even explain it to you. I won't try. It's everybody for himself and catch as catch can. Now Van Steed, he's got a smart fella on his side, a friend named Morgan, a banker lives in New York—J. P. Morgan his name is. He's a scrapper; they say he's smarter than Gould or Fisk was or any of them. But he hasn't started to fight the way the other crowd does, where anything goes. He's being legal, everything open and aboveboard. And Van Steed, he's the kind has got to have everything down on paper. Meantime, the Gould crowd, they're hitting below the belt. Gouge and bite and kick—that's their way. Talk about the East being civilized, why, say, it makes the West look like a church meeting. I have to laugh when I see these people here, dressed up in their silks and their swallowtails, driving up and down, smirking and bowing."

"But these men with their railroads, what are they doing, then? What are they doing? Tell me."

"What they're doing they'd be strung up for as outlaws, West. You wouldn't believe. The Gould crowd, they hire gangs to go out and tear up tracks and chop down trestles. Folks won't ride the railroad any more. It ain't safe. That's just what the old crowd is figuring on. Run it down to nothing."

"But the government. Where is the government to stop these *apaches?*"

"Sa-a-ay, they took care of that right early. They've got the government bought up, hair and hide, horns and tallow."

Weary though she was her mind persisted in its clear reasoning. "We will make ourselves valuable to this little Van Steed. He must be told that you are clever with railroads. I will tell him."

"Look here, Clio, honey, we don't aim to be any part of that crowd."

She ignored this. "If it's only a hundred miles—this road into the coal fields—why don't they—the Gould crowd—build their own hundred miles of railroad?"

"Because they can't get the land. Twenty years ago—even ten, maybe— they could have bought the land or stolen it from the government by going

down to Washington and buying up Congress and so on. It's not so easy
now. These railroad men———"

Suddenly she yawned prodigiously. "Railroads, railroads! Railroads bore
me. I have no mind for railroads."

"But you said———"

"I know, I know. But you and I must do things very simply and directly,
with our little minds. We have only a month, really."

"Do? Do what? What things?"

"Oh—I don't know, *chéri*. I think I shall marry this little Van Steed.
Maybe———"

"Ha! Likely. I sure would like to know how you're fixing to do that."

"Oh, he is a simple fellow, really———"

"Don't fool yourself."

"Well———" She stretched luxuriously, then stopped abruptly, listening,
in the midst offf another yawn. "Cupide with my trunks. Kaka, quick, have
them put in the hall and left there. My great new Saratoga trunk would
hardly squeeze through the door, anyway. Quick, Kaka!"

Here Kaka rebelled. "How you going dress for dinner effen I don't take
out and press!"

"Because I'm not going down, stupid! Do as I say."

"Not going down!" repeated Maroon. "Tonight!"

"Of course not. And probably not tomorrow. Where's your dramatic
sense, Clint? I made a superb entrance. You will admit that was a great
stroke of luck—of course I'd planned it, but who would have thought it
would work so magically!"

But he was by now thoroughly exasperated. "Look here, you stop this
play-acting or I'll light out. Hell's bells, you can't do this———"

"Wouldn't it be won-der-ful to have some champagne now—immediately—very very cold—so cold that a little mist stands outside the glass.
Clint dearest, call Kaka—no, don't let them see you, of course—Kaka!
Kaka! Tell Cupide to order me a bottle of champagne in ice—they will bring
it up. Sit down, Clint, sit down." She picked up the pamphlet on the table
by the sofa and flicked its leaves. "The waters, of course. Tell me, which
one do you take?"

"Me! I wouldn't touch the stuff, I can't stomach it. Tastes worse than
desert alky water."

"But doesn't everybody? Drink it, I mean. When I used to go to Aix with
Mama and Aunt Belle everyone took the waters—there was a *régime* for
the day—you took the waters, you walked, there were baths, you went to
the Casino. Mama and Aunt Belle loved it—especially Aunt Belle. It made
her thinner for a little while."

"That's the way they pass the time of day here. Out before breakfast,
some of them over to the Springs. But mostly they don't take it the way you
say—not to say seriously."

She was reading from the booklet, her pretty nose wrinkling a little with
distaste. "M-m-m, let me see—uh—Empire waters. Rheumatism, gout, irritated condition of the stomach, pimples, blotches, ulcers"—hastily she
turned the page—"Columbia water. Possesses valuable di-diur—what is the
meaning of that word, Clint? Well, anyway, I shall not drink Columbia water.
Liver complaints—dyspepsia—erysipelas—gravel and vitiated condition of
the—mmmmmmmm——— A pint mornings. Ugh! Excelsior Springs—kidney, bladder, gravel— Congress Spring———*Mon Dieu!*"

"Congress is the one you want, honey. It's the stylish one. That's the
place to go, mornings, before breakfast or after. Band plays. Everybody
bowing and prancing."

"I can't imagine you———" She laughed deliciously at the picture of the Texan, booted, mincing, glass in hand, at Congress Spring.

"Me! No Ma'am! Mostly I'm over at the track, mornings, having my breakfast at the stables."

"Oh, Clint, I'd love that! Could I———" She stopped abruptly. From the street below came the call of a fruit vendor.

"Peaches! Fresh ripe peaches! Raspberries! Red raspberries!"

She was off the couch and across the floor, her head at the window. "Heh! You! Peaches! Peaches here!"

He leaped to the window just ahead of the vigilant Kakaracou. "God A'mighty, Clio! You can't do that."

Unwillingly she turned away. "Well, send down, then. Cupide. Or you go. Fresh peaches bobbing in a glass of champagne. That is the way Mama used to eat them in Paris, and Aunt Belle. Delicious, and cool, cool. I am so hot and tired, *chéri.*"

"*Stupide!*" Kaka scolded, thrusting her back from the window. "A fine lady you are, screaming into the street. You think this is New Orleans!"

"Well, where's Cupide? Kaka, see if he's outside the door. I told him to stay there. Send him down before the peach man is gone. Tell him big ripe yellow ones, with pink cheeks, and the pits like great pigeon-blood rubies in a nest of yellow velvet."

Cupide, stationed outside the door, was having a fine time. Already he had discovered that the exhilarating and speedy way to reach the ground floor was to slide down the banisters which curved from floor to floor around the stairwell. In Paris and in New Orleans he had had no fine slippery banisters. Now, cautioned by Kaka to make all haste in order to catch the fruit vendor, he nevertheless followed his usual procedure, which was to run up the stairs to the floor above in order to enjoy to the full his new and thrilling form of travel. Starting from these heights it was possible to attain sufficient momentum to swing round the polished curves and slide the entire distance down to the lobby itself, which was the end of the line. As he skimmed down from the third to the second floor a colored chambermaid, ascending the stairs with broom and pail, put out a horrified arm to stop him.

"You, little boy! Don't you know you ain't allowed slide down no banisters you kill youseff! I going tell you mammy on you you do that again." His powerful arm jerked her hand that attempted to hold him, he leaped off the banister, the impish face confronted the girl, he scurried around and nipped her smartly behind and, amidst her shriek of surprise, leaped again to the rail, his gargoyle face grinning impishly up at her until he vanished round the curve.

Half an hour later Clio Dulaine was sipping from a tall dewy glass in whose bubbling contents a fat peach bobbed, fragrant and tempting.

"But won't you just try it, Clint? A sip. It's heavenly!"

"That's no drink for a man," Clint Maroon had said. "Champagne and peaches in the middle of the day. No Ma'am!" Then, as Clio sipped and purred contentedly, "Look, sugar. You put on one of your prettiest dresses and come down for supper tonight, won't you? There's a hop tonight. We were introduced downstairs, weren't we, all regular and proper, by Bart Van Steed. I can talk to you, same as anybody else. No secret in that."

"Oh, no. I must have my dinner up here."

"You feel sick, Clio!"

"No, no! I feel so well and happy—happier than I've ever been."

"Then why in tarnation do you want to mope up here?"

"Because they expect me to come down. Because they all saw me arrive and stood there gaping like a lot of peasants. Because they'll be waiting for

me to come down this evening and tomorrow morning and tomorrow noon
and tomorrow night. And I shan't. I shan't come down until day after to-
morrow, in the morning, on my way to the spring. And by that time they
will be dying with eagerness to see me. Especially little Van Steed.''

"It sure sounds silly to me."

She looked at him over the rim of her glass, round-eyed. "Sometimes,
Clint, I wonder if it was a good thing or a bad thing, for both of us—that day
we met in the French Market.''

"One thing's sure. If we hadn't, you wouldn't be here in Saratoga, drinking
champagne out of a big water tumbler with a peach floating around in it.''

She tapped the glass's rim thoughtfully against her teeth. "You are right.''
Suddenly she sat bolt upright, her eyes strained, her lips quivering. "What
am I doing here!" she cried, wildly. "Mama is dead! Aunt Belle is dead!
What am I doing here! Who are you! How do I know who you are! Kaka!
Cupide!''

Swiftly, as before, the Negress ran to her, she took the hysterical girl in
her arms. "Hush! Hush your mouth!" She turned to speak to Maroon over
her shoulder, as she rocked the girl back and forth. "Champagne make her
sad. My lil Rita was the same way, her mama.''

Even as Clint Maroon stared at this new manifestation of his unpredictable
lady, the sitting-room door opened to admit a Cupide almost completely
hidden by an ambush of very pink roses. The years with Rita Dulaine and
Belle Piquery and Kakaracou had accustomed him to more dramatic bedroom scenes than this, with its welter of gowns, shoes, hats, hysteria; and
a discomfited male standing by in the background. He now advanced behind
the thicket of roses. Unceremoniously he dumped them in the lap of the
distraught Clio, who stopped in the midst of a disconsolate wail, her mouth
open.

"I could hear you way out in the hall," Cupide announced, scrutinizing
a thorn-pricked thumb and nursing it with his tongue. "There's quite a crowd
out there—chambermaids, waiting, and a woman to scrub and a boy with
ice water, and a woman who says she's the housekeeper. I told 'em if
anybody tried to come in they'd probably be killed. The roses are from that
man who drove us from the station.''

"Dutch pink roses!" Clio exclaimed. "I loathe the color. No taste, that
little man.'' And threw them to the floor. "Kaka, tell them to go away, those
people outside. I shall be changing anyway, tomorrow, to the cottage side.
Maybe even this afternoon if I'm not too tired————''

Maroon flung his arms out in a gesture that encircled the littered room.
"Look at this place! It's enough to make anybody tired. You don't even
know what you're saying. That champagne wine's gone to your head, middle
of the day. There you've been, cooped up in trains this long trip. No real
air. A drive would do you good. A little later, maybe, cool of the day.''

Drowsily she shook her head. "No. I don't want to be wide awake. I
don't want to drive. I want to be still, still. Talk to me. Tell me more. Little
things that are important to know, and then I will dream about them and
when I wake they will be settled in my mind. Who is the important woman,
par exemple. Who is it among them that they all follow? This Mrs. Porcelain?
Or the Forosini? Who?''

"Nope!" piped up Cupide in his clear boyish voice. "There's a fat old
woman, I heard her talking to that man—the one who stays in the corner
under the stairs. They call him the head usher. I heard her say De Chanfret,
so I listened way back under the stairs. She said, 'I knew the De Chanfrets.
Never heard of this one.' He said something about look it up in somebody's
peerage; she said, 'That's no good, it's English.' '' The midget's manner

was somewhat absent-minded, for his attention was fixed on his thorn-pricked thumb.

"Get out!" scolded Kakaracou. "What do you know, imp!"

"No, stay. Kaka, make yourself neat, go downstairs, say I do not find it quiet here, I shall move into the cottage wing tomorrow. Go, look at the rooms. Don't take the first apartment they offer. It must have a servant's room for you . . .Cupide, who is this fat woman?"

"Bellop," blurted Cupide.

"Don't make ugly noises."

"That's her name. I asked the bellboys. They call her Bellhop behind her back, but they say everybody in Saratoga is afraid of her. She looks like a washwoman. Big!" He stuck out his chest, he puffed his cheeks, he waddled, his voice suddenly became a booming bass. "Like that. And talks like a man. She called me to her when I was coming up the stairs just now and tried to question me. Where did you come from and how long had we been in this country and what was your name before you married. She gave me a silver dollar. I took it and pretended I spoke only French. I spoke very fast in French and I called her a fat old *truie* and what do you think! She speaks French like anything!" He went off into peals of laughter. "So I ran away."

"Oh, dear. I wish I weren't so terribly sleepy. You sound, all of you, as if you were speaking to me far away. Clint, who is this woman with the ridiculous name?"

Maroon, striding the room impatiently, tousled the dwarf's head not unkindly, and sent him into the next room with a little push. "That's what I've been telling you. That's the kind of thing you get yourself into here. The town is full of bunko steerers. This crowd here in the hotel, millionaires and sharpers, they're onto each other, no matter which. Our best bet is to be ourselves, get what money we can, have some fun, and light out. I hate'em like I hate rattlesnakes, but we'll never be able to sit in on the big game, honey."

"This woman," she persisted. "Who is this woman?"

"Well, far as I know, I'd say she looks about the way Cupide says. Mrs. Coventry Bellop. That's her name. Lives in New York but they say she hails from out West somewhere, years back. Got a tongue like an adder. Some say she gets her income from blackmail in a kind of quiet way. They say she lives here at the hotel free of charge, gets up parties, keeps 'em going, says who is who. Just a fat woman, about fifty-five, in black, plain-featured. I don't understand it. Maybe you do, Clio, but smart as you are I bet you'll make nothing out of her."

"I like the sound of her," Clio murmured, sleepily. "When a fat and frumpy old woman with no money can rule a place like this Saratoga then she is something uncommon—something original. I think we should know each other."

In a fury of masculine exasperation and bewilderment he stamped away from her. "Oh, to hell with all your planning and contriving, it's like something out of a storybook you've read somewhere." He came back to the couch. "Now look here, we're going to drive out to the lake at six, say, when it's cool, and have a fish dinner at Moon's, you can catch'em yourself right out of the lake. I'm bossing this outfit."

She had fished the dripping peach out of the glass and had taken a bite out of its luscious wine-drenched cheek. Now, as he looked at her, the plump fruit fell with a thud from her inert hand and rolled a little way, tipsily. Clio didn't reply, she did not hear him. He saw that suddenly, like a child, she was asleep, the long lashes very black against the tear-stained white cheeks.

At the sudden silence Kakaracou looked up.

"Looks like she's clean beat out," Maroon whispered. "A nap'll do her good."

Quietly Kaka began to make ready the bed. "She will sleep," she said, and her tone was like that of a watcher who has at last seen a fever break. "She will sleep perhaps until tomorrow, perhaps until next day. Carry her there to the bed. That is well."

A sudden suspicion smote him. He strode over to Kaka, he took her bony arms in his great grasp. "Look here, if you've given her anything—if this is some of your monkeyshines I'll break every————"

The black woman looked into his face calmly. "It is bad to be long without sleep." She went about pulling down the shades. "I will rest here on this couch. Cupide will keep watch there in the next room. But here, until she wakes, it must be quiet. Quiet." She stood there, in silence, waiting. He paused, irresolutely. The room and the two women in it seemed suddenly of another world, eerie, apart. He turned and walked toward his own door. He felt a stranger to them. He heard the door close after him, the key was turned, the bolt shot. Then he heard the closing of the bedroom door. He stood in the center of his own room, an outsider. To himself he said, "Now's your chance, Clint. Vamoose. Drag it outa here and drag it quick. You stay in these parts you're going to get into a heap of trouble. If you're smart you'll git—pronto."

But he knew he would never go.

10

IN THE FORTNIGHT following Clio's arrival old Madam Van Steed was made to realize that her male offspring in Saratoga was even more in need of her maternal protection than was her ailing daughter in Newport. News of Bartholomew's preoccupation with a mysterious and dazzling widow traveled to her on the lightning wings of hotel gossip. Bag and baggage, the beldame arrived, took one look at what she termed the shenanigans of the dramatic Mrs. De Chanfret, and boomed in her deepest chest tones, "De Trenaunay de Chanfret de Fiddlesticks! The woman's an adventuress! It's written all over her!"

But before her antagonist's arrival Clio Dulaine had had a fortnight's advantage. And in less than two days after Madam Van Steed's pronouncement the Widow De Chanfret had managed to bring about a cleavage in the none too solid structure of that bizarre edifice called Saratoga society.

On one side were ranged the embattled dowagers holding the piazza front lines, their substantial backs to the wall at the Friday night hops. Behind their General, Madam Van Steed, rallied the conservatives, the bootlickers, the socially insecure and ambitious, mothers with marriageable daughters, daughters for whom Bartholomew Van Steed was a target. Defying these pranced Clio Dulaine and her motley crew made up of such variegated members as Clint Maroon, a frightened but quaveringly defiant Bart Van Steed, Kakaracou and Cupidon, all the Negro waiters, bellboys and chambermaids, a number of piazza rockers who for years had been regularly snubbed by Madam Van Steed, and, astonishingly enough, that walking arsenal of insult, bonhomie, and social ammunition large and small, Mrs. Coventry Bellop of the Western Hemisphere.

The battle had started with a bang the very morning on which Clio, refreshed to the point òf feeling actually reborn, awoke from a thirty-six-hour sleep. The hotel management had been politely concerned, then mystified, then alarmed by the tomblike silence which pervaded 237 and 238. Messages went unanswered, chambermaids were shooed away, food was almost entirely ignored, a discreet knock at the door brought no response, a hammering, if persisted in, might cause the door to be opened a crack through which could be discerned the tousled head and goggle-eye of a haggard Cupidon or the heavy-lidded countenance of Kakaracou looking like nothing so much as a python aroused from a winter's hibernation.

"What you want? . . . Madame is resting. . . . We have all that is needed. Come back tomorrow. . . . Go away. Go away. Go away."

Once a tray was demanded. The Negro waiter saw that the bedroom door remained shut, and it was evident that it had been the Negress and the dwarf who had partaken of the food.

Then, suddenly, on the morning of the second day following the arrival of Mrs. De Chanfret and her attendants all was changed. The chambermaid slouching along the hall in her easy slippers at seven in the morning heard a gay snatch of song whose tune was familiar but whose words differed from those she knew. A fresh young voice, a white voice, for all its fidelity to the dialect:

> *Buckwheat cakes and good strong butter*
> *Makes mah mouf go flit-ter flut-ter.*
> *Look a-way a-way a-way in Dix-ay.*

"Them funny folks is up an' stirrin'," she confided to her colleague down the hall. "I thought they was sure 'nuff daid."

Except for three brief intervals Clio Dulaine actually had slept through that first night, through the following day and the second night. Once Kaka had brought her a *tisane* of soothing herbs brewed over the spirit-lamp, once she had fed her half an orange, slipping the slim golden moonlets between the girl's parted lips as you would feed a child. Clio's eyes were half shut during those ministrations, she murmured drowsily, almost incoherently, ". . . sleepy . . . what time . . . Mama . . . no more . . . Cleent . . . *chéri* . . . Cleent . . ." And she had giggled at this last coquettishly and then had sighed and snuggled her face into the pillow and slept again. During the heat of the noon hour Cupide had stood in his shirt sleeves, a tireless little sentinel fanning her gently with a great palmleaf fan as she lay asleep. Time after time Clint Maroon had knocked at the inner door. Sometimes he was admitted, often not. He had tiptoed away mystified and resentful but satisfied that nothing was seriously wrong.

"When she wake up," Kaka droned each time, "zoomba! Look out!"

Clio had opened her eyes at six in the morning. It was fresh and cool thus early. Wide awake at once, alert, renewed, she stood in the middle of the room in her bare feet and nightgown and surveyed the world about her. Kaka, fully dressed, lay on the sofa, her tignon askew so that you saw her grizzled skull, so rarely visible that now it gave the effect of nakedness. She, too, was at once awake at this first sign of fresh life in her mistress. She got to her feet, her tignon still tipped rakishly.

"My *gabrielle*," Clio commanded, crisply. "Go down to your own quarters. Make yourself fresh from head to foot, everything. Roll up those shades. Where is Cupide? In there?" She passed into the sitting room where Cupide lay curled like a little dog in one of the upholstered armchairs. Awake, he was either merry or pugnacious. Now, asleep, he looked defenseless and submissive as a child. "Poor little man," murmured Clio, looking down at him. She picked up a shawl from a near-by chair and placed it gently over him. But at that he, too, awoke, he cocked one ribald eye up at her, then he leaped to the floor in his tiny stockinged feet, shook himself like a puppy, and, running to a corner, slipped into his boots, shrugged himself into his coat.

"Why didn't you sleep downstairs in the room provided for you?" demanded Clio, not unkindly.

"I wanted to be near you and Kaka," he answered, simply.

"Get down there now, both of you. I want you to wash and make yourselves neat and smart. You, Cupide, look to your shoes and your buttons. Be quiet. And above all, polite to the hotel servants." She eyed Cupide severely. "No tricks. And you, Kaka. No voodoo, no witchwork. Your best black silk. I am going to bathe in that funny box. Like a coffin, isn't it! But to have one's own bath in a hotel—how wonderful! America is really marvelous. When you are fresh and clean come back. Then you will make me a cup of your coffee, Kaka, hot and strong. How good that will be! Then I'll dress and we'll go to the Congress Spring, early. It will be the fashion to walk to the Congress Spring, early. I'll make it so. You'll see. Get along now! Quick. *Vite!*"

When the door had closed behind them she stood at the window a moment looking down at Broadway, watching the little green-shaded town come to life.

The long trancelike sleep had left her mind clear and sharp as mountain air. She felt detached from her surroundings, as though she were seeing them from some godlike height. Curious and haphazard as her life was, there always had been about it some slight sense of security at least. In her babyhood there had been her mother, the luxurious little house in Rampart Street; later there had been the orderly routine of school in France and the rather frowsy comfort of the Paris flat with Rita Dulaine and Belle Piquery and Kakaracou and Cupidon to give it substance. Even on her return to New Orleans, brief as the interlude had been, the Rampart Street house had again given her the illusion of security that accompanies the accustomed, the familiar or the remembered. Now, she thought, as she stared down at the main street of the little spa, what have I? In the whole world. Well, an old woman and a dwarf. In the next room a man I have known a few weeks. A *blagueur,* for all I know. Trunks full of clothes. Some good jewelry. Money enough to last me a year if I am careful. No home, no name, no background, nothing. I want comfort, security, money, respectability. Love? Mama had that and it ruined her life.

"Food. That is what I need," she said, aloud. She looked around the disheveled room. Hot, hot coffee, very strong. It was then that she began to sing as she turned on the water for her bath. By the time Kaka and Cupide returned and she had her second cup of Kaka's coffee she was buoyant, decisive, gay.

"Cupide, go downstairs, tell the man in the office that I have decided to move into the cottages. Kaka, you yourself look at the rooms. Make a great *bruit,* but everything dignified and proper. Tell them I will not pay more than I pay here in this location. Here it is noisy and hot, and anyway, for my plan it is better to seem to be alone. This is not discreet, here. The rooms must be ready when I return from the Spring."

Kaka, rustling importantly in her best silk and her embroidered petticoats, stood sociably drinking her own cup of coffee.

"How you going drink spring water after all that coffee?"

"I'm not going to drink the water, silly. Vile stuff!"

"*Faire parade,* h'm?" She rather liked this faring forth to stare and be stared at. "It's time. Two days lost."

"Not lost at all, idiot! I could go for days now without rest or sleep. I've stored up sleep as a camel stores water . . . Let me see. I think I shall wear the mauve flowered cretonne and the shoes with the little red heels."

"Red heels are not for widows," grumbled Kaka. She began deftly to dress Clio's hair in a Marquise Catogan coiffure, bangs on the forehead, very smooth at the back and tied in a club with a black ribbon á la George Washington. It was a youthful, a girlish arrangement.

Clio grinned. "But my dear husband, the Count de Trenaunay de Chanfret died—oh—at least two years ago. So I'm out of mourning. Even second mourning. I only keep on wearing it because my heart is broken. . . . The large leghorn hat, Kaka, with the black velvet facing."

It was scarcely half-past eight when they appeared in the hotel lobby. Clio, followed by Kaka and Cupide, looked spaciously about her, seeing everything, enjoying everything—the vast brass spittoons, the ponderous brass gas-chandeliers, the glimpse of garden at the back, the dapper and alert Northern black boys in uniform, so different from the slow-moving, soft-spoken Southern Negro.

As she approached the great open doorway Roscoe Bean, looking more than ever like Uriah Heep, slithered out of his cubbyhole under the stairs. "Why Your Ladyship—Why Mrs. De Chanfret! You are an early riser indeed! Is your carriage at the door? May I assist you?"

"I am walking to Congress Spring."

"Walking!" His surprise and horror could not have been greater if she had said crawling.

"Certainly. I am in Saratoga for my health. I shall do here as I and everyone else did in Aix-le-Bains, in Vichy, in Evian, in Wiesbaden. No one in Europe would dream of driving to the springs. It is part of the *régime* to walk."

Bean, murmuring at her side, was all deference. "Of course. Naturally. So sensible."

She stood a moment in the doorway, surveying the vast spaces of the piazza. A scattering of portly and rather puffy-eyed men smoking large cigars. A few very settled matrons in the iron embrace of practical morning costumes—sturdy sateens, bison serge, relentless brown canvas, snuffy cashmere, high-necked, long-sleeved. Clio thought, I'd as soon wear a hair shirt for my sins, and done with it.

Well back near the wall in a rocking chair that almost engulfed him sat a little man, thin-chested, meager, with brilliant feverish eyes. With sudden conviction, "That is Mr. Gould, isn't it?" Clio demanded.

"Yes." Bean managed magically to inject awe, admiration and wonder into the monosyllable.

Audaciously she moved toward him, Kaka and Cupide in her wake, a reluctant Bean deferentially at her side. "I must speak to him. Though perhaps he may not remember me. Perhaps you'd better introduce us."

"Oh, Mrs. De Chanfret! I really——"

But it was too late. Deftly she covered his remonstrance by taking the office from him. "Oh, Mr. Gould, I was just saying to him—uh—to this— I used to hear my dear husband speak of you. I am Mrs. De Chanfret."

He rose, his eyes hostile, his face impassive. "I do not know the name."

Nasty little man, thought Clio. She smiled sweetly. "You will recall him as the Count de Trenaunay de Chanfret, no doubt. Please don't stand. After all, we're all here for our health, aren't we? So charming. So American!" Rather abruptly she moved away toward the street steps. No knowing what a man like that might do, she thought.

But I've been seen in conversation with Mr. Jay Gould. All these frumps on the piazza saw it. That should soon be spread about. She dismissed Bean with a soulful smile and a honeyed good day and moved down the street, her attendants in her wake. She looked about her with the liveliest interest. A neat New England town with a veneer of temporary sophistication, like a spinster schoolteacher gone gay. Wall Street tickers in the brokerage branch occupying a little street-floor shop in the United States Hotel; millinery and fancy goods, stationery and groceries in the windows of the two-story brick buildings to catch the fancy of the summer visitor. A spruced-up little town with an air of striving to put its best foot forward, innocently ignorant of the fact that its white-painted houses, its scroll-work Victorian porches, the greenery of lawn and shrub and ancient trees furuished its real charm. Past the Club House, Morrissey's realized dream of splendor, its substantial red-brick front so demure amidst the greenery of Congress Spring Park.

Clio Dulaine was ecstatically aware of a lightness and gayety of spirit and body and mind such as she had never before experienced. She had eaten almost nothing in the past three days. The hot, strong coffee had been a powerful stimulant. Every nerve, artery, muscle and vein had been refreshed by her trancelike sleep. After the clammy and stifling heat of New Orleans the pine-pricked air of Saratoga seemed clear, dry and exhilarating as a bottle of Grand Montrachet. Added to these were youth, ambition and a deadly seriousness of purpose.

Here, in July, were gathered the worst and the best of America. Even if Maroon had not told her she would have sensed this. Here, for three months in the year, was a raffish, provincial and swaggering society; a snobbish, conservative, Victorian society; religious sects meeting in tents; gamblers and race-track habitués swarming in hotels and paddocks and game rooms. Millionaires glutted with grabbing, still reaching out for more; black-satin madams, peroxided and portly, driving the length of Broadway at four in the afternoon, their girls, befeathered and bedizened, clustered about them like overblown flowers. Invalids in search of health; girls in search of husbands. Politicians, speculators, jockeys; dowagers, sporting men, sporting women; middle-class merchants with their plump wives and hopeful daughters; trollops, railroad tycoons, croupiers, thugs; judges, actresses, Western ranchers and cattle men. Prim, bawdy, vulgar, sedate, flashy, substantial. Saratoga.

I knew America would be like this, Clio Dulaine thought, exultantly. Everything into the kettle, like a French *pot-au-feu*. Everything simmering together in a beautiful rich stew. I'm going to have a glorious time. How Aunt Belle Piquery would have loved it, poor darling. She'd have had one of these dried-up millionaires in no time. Well, so shall I, but not in her way. Though I'm more like Aunt Belle, I do believe, than like Mama.

She turned her head to catch Kaka's jaundiced eye and the strutting Cupide's merry look. "It is well," she said, speaking to them in French. "This is going to be very good. I can feel it."

Kaka shrugged, skeptically. *"Peut-être que oui.* Not so fast, my pigeon." But the volatile Cupide whistled between his teeth, slyly, and the tune was Kaka's old Gombo song of "Compair Bouki Et Macaques"; Compair Bouki who thought to cook the monkeys in the boiling pot and was himself cooked instead.

> *Sam-bombel! Sam-bombel tam!*
> *Sam-bombel! Sam-bombel dam!*

Now there was the sound of music. The band was playing in Congress

Spring Park. They turned up the neat walk with its bordering flower-beds of geraniums and petunias and sweet alyssum. There at the spring were the dipper boys, ragamuffins who poked into the spring with their tin cups at the end of a long stick and brought up a dripping dipperful. Kaka had brought her mistress's own fine silver monogrammed cup, holding it primly in front of her as she walked. The little crowd of early-morning walkers and drinkers gaped, nudged, tittered, depending on their station in life. Saratoga's residents, both permanent and transient, were well accustomed to all that was dramatic and bizarre in humanity. But this beautiful and extravagantly dressed young woman with her two fantastic attendants were more than even the sophisticated eye could assimilate. One tended to reject the whole pattern as an optical illusion.

Dipper boys stared, promenaders stared, the band trombone struck a sour note. Clio, enjoying herself, walked serenely on toward the little ornate pavilion with its scrolled woodwork and colored glass windows and its tables and chairs invitingly set forth. Kaka, very stiff and haughty, held out her cup to be filled. Then she turned and marched off to tender the brimming potion, while Cupide, in turn, flipped a penny at the spring boy and strutted on. Strolling thus while Clio seemed to sip and contemplate the scene about her, they circled the little green square three times, and three times the cup was filled. If Clio poured its contents deftly into the shrubbery, no one saw. And now fashion began to arrive. They came in carriages, in dogcarts, on horseback; a few nobodies came afoot, the women's flounced skirts flirting the dusty street.

The crowds began to arrive in swarms. Clio had been waiting for this. She would leave as they came, moving against the incoming tide of morning visitors to the Congress Spring. She did not know these people but she marked them with a shrewd eye. Later she was to learn that it had been the Jefferson Deckers who had dashed up in the magnificent Brewster coach, black, with the yellow running gear, drawn by four handsome bays. The black-haired, black-eyed beauty, partridge-plump, guiding two snow-white horses tandem with white reins, for all the world, Clio thought, like a rider in a circus, could be only Guilia Forosini. The handsome old fellow beside her, with a mane of white hair and the neat white goatee was her father, of course, Forosini, the California banker-millionaire. There came Van Steed. Now he had seen her. The doll-like blonde stopping him now must be the Mrs. Porcelain that Clint wrote about. Where is he? Where is he? Some left their carriages and walked into the park to the spring; others were served at the carriage steps, the grooms or spring boys scampering back and forth with brimming cups.

There he was at last! There was Clint Maroon in the glittering dear familiar clarence with the fleet bays. Now Clio made her leisurely way up the path, her head high, Cupide following, Kaka, stately and rather forbidding, walking, duennalike, almost beside her.

And now she was passing Van Steed. She did not pause, she nodded, her smile was remote, almost impersonal. She felt the china-blue Porcelain eye appraising her—figure, gown, hat, face. Van Steed was not accustomed to being passed thus by any woman. These past two days he had watched for her.

"Mrs. De Chanfret! I heard you were—have you been ill? You haven't been down. I hope———" Van Steed at his shyest.

"Not ill. Weary."

"I can understand that. But you look—uh—you seem quite recovered if appearances are any—uh—that is, Mrs. Porcelain would like to meet you. . . . Mrs. Porcelain . . . Mrs. De Chanfret."

M7s. Porcelain's was a little soft chirrupy voice with a gurgle in it. "Oh—Mrs. De Chanfret, you must have driven down very early."

"I didn't drive. I walked."

"Walked!"

Van Steed waxed suddenly daring, emboldened as he was by temporary freedom from maternal restraint. "Then you must allow me to drive you back."

"No. No, I'm walking back. There is that fascinating Mr. Maroon. Isn't it? You presented him—remember? And he will ask to drive me back, too. You are all so kind. But I really never heard of driving to a spring when one is taking the waters. I intend to walk down and back every morning, early, as everyone does at the European cures. . . . I must say *au revoir*, now. *Au revoir*, Mrs. Porcelain." She was moving on, then seemed suddenly to recall something, came back a step, held up a chiding foreffiger. *"Méchant homme!* It was naughty of you to pretend you didn't know that this Mr. Maroon is a great famous American railroad king, dear Mr. Van Steed. You were having your little joke with me because I have been so long in France. Was that it?"

"Who?"

"That Mr. Maroon. Do you know, that is why I have been so weary until now. All that first night I was unable to sleep. Talk, talk, talk in the next room. Railroads, railroads! I thought I should go mad. I am moving to a cottage apartment this morning. For quiet."

Bart Van Steed's pink cheeks grew pinker, and the amber eyes suddenly widened and then narrowed like a jungle thing scenting prey. Ah, there it is, thought Clio. Those eyes. He isn't such a booby after all.

"Oh, talking railroads, were they? Now what could they say about railroads to keep a charming woman awake?"

"Dear me, I don't know. Such things are too much for me. But they argued and shouted until really I thought I must send one of my servants to protest. Albany and Something or Other—a railroad they were shouting about—and trunk lines—tell me, what is a trunk line?—and—oh, yes, they were talking about you, too, Mr. Van Steed. I even heard Mr. Maroon's voice say that you were smarter than any of them. By that time they really were shouting. I couldn't help hearing it. But maddening it was. No repose. You have such vitality here in America."

"Who? Who was there?"

"Why, how should I know! I know no one in Saratoga. When I was talking with Mr. Gould early this morning on the piazza I thought his voice sounded like the one that was disputing Mr. Maroon. Of course, I don't know. Perhaps I shouldn't have mentioned it. I don't understand such things. I just thought I would twit you with it because you had said he wasn't a friend of yours, teasing me I suppose, and I couldn't help overhearing him say that he was with you, or something like that . . . *Mon Dieu*, have I said anything? You look so troubled. I am so strange here, perhaps I shouldn't have . . . Please don't repeat what I have said. It is so different here in America after . . . Good-by. *Au revoir*." She was thinking, even as she talked, it can't be as simple as this. Now really!

They saw her move on. The eyes over the cups of water followed her as she went, dipping and swooping so gracefully in the flowered cretonne and the great leghorn turned up saucily at one side to reveal the black velvet facing. They saw White Hat Maroon jump down and bow low with a sweep of the sombrero, they saw him motion toward the clarence in invitation; there was no mistaking the negative shake of her head, the appreciative though fleeting smile as she moved on down the street, the Texan staring after her.

"Dear me!" tittered the pink Mrs. Porcelain. "You don't think she's strong-minded, do you? Walking!"

"I admire strong-minded women," declared Bartholomew Van Steed somewhat to his own surprise. "Excuse me. I must speak to Maroon." But Maroon had turned the clarence on one wheel and was even now driving away from Congress Spring toward the United States Hotel. But the spirited bays had been slowed down to a walk. They stepped high and daintily so as not to overpace the woman walking. It was as though the equipage and its occupant were guarding her.

11

THOUGH FOR TWO weeks they ran as fast they could, feminine Saratoga could never quite catch up with Mrs. De Chanfret. Clio Dulaine's instinct as a showman was sound; and if it had not been for the arrival of old Madam Van Steed, Clio's success might actually have been assured at the end of a fortnight. Certain sly letters of warning must have been dispatched to the matriarch watching over her female progeny in Newport. Torn between fear and duty, she must have convinced herself that while nature, even lacking her supervision, must inevitably pursue its course with her daughter, the enceinte Mrs. Schermerhorn of Newport, it could be thwarted if it threatened her son Bartholomew, weakest of her offspring and the most cherished. "Your dear son," the letters had said, "seems to be really interested in a charming widow, a Mrs. De Chanfret. . . . Bart has at last . . . they say she is the Countess de Trenaunay de Chanfret . . . no one seems to know exactly . . ." Like a lioness scenting danger to her young, Madam Van Steed descended upon Saratoga, claws unsheathed, fangs bared.

But those two weeks before the arrival of the iron woman had been sufficiently dramatic to last Saratoga the season.

You never knew. You never knew what that Mrs. De Chanfret was going to do or wear or say next. By the time they had copied her Marquise Catogan coiffure, she had discarded it for a madonna arrangement, her black hair parted in the middle and drawn down to frame the white face with the great liquid dark eyes. She had attended the first Saturday night hop escorted by that rich Texan Clint Maroon and wearing a breath-taking black satin *merveilleux* trimmed with flounce after flounce of cobweb fine black Chantilly lace as a background for a fabulous *parure* of diamond necklace, bracelets, rings, brooch, earrings. The Mrs. Porcelains, the Guilia Forosinis, the Peabody sisters of Philadelphia, the feminine Lispenards and Rhinelanders and Keenes, the Denards, the Willoughbys appeared at the following Wednesday hop in such panoply of satins, passementerie, galloons and garnitures as to call for a hysterical outburst of verbiage from Miss Sophie Sparkle, the local society correspondent for the New York newspapers. Into this blaze of splendor there entered on the somewhat unsteady arm of Bartholomew Van Steed a slim figure in girlish white china silk, the front of the skirt veiled by two deep flounces of Valenciennes lace, the modest square-cut corsage edged with lace, the sleeves mere puffs like a baby's. A single strand of pearls. Every woman in the room felt overdressed and, somehow, brazen.

Everything she did seemed unconventional because it was unexpected. The women found it most exasperating. The men thought it piquant.

On that first morning at Congress Spring she had returned to the hotel at a serene and leisurely gait and had waved demurely once to the dashing Texan, Clint Maroon, as he kept pace with her in his turnout. Arrived at the hotel, she had again encountered the full battery of the piazza barrage and had crossed the vast lobby to the dining room.

"Oh, no!" she cried at the door of that stupendous cavern. "I couldn't! I could never breakfast here!"

The headwaiter, black, majestic, with the assurance of one who has been patronized by presidents and millionaires and visiting nobility, surveyed the vast acreage of his domain and bestowed a reassuring smile upon his new client.

"No call for you to feel scairt, Madam. Ah'll escort you personally to your table."

Startled, she recovered herself and bestowed upon him her most poignant smile. "I so love to breakfast out of doors. It is a European custom. I would so like to have my breakfast out there under the trees in the garden. Or perhaps on the gallery just outside."

"We are not in the habit of serving meals out of doors, Madam. Our dining room is———" But his eye had caught the verdant promise of a crisp bill as her fingers dipped into her purse. "It might be arranged, though, Madam. It might be arranged."

Clio turned her head ever so slightly. "Kaka." Kaka advanced to take charge, fixing the man with her terrible eye. "Kaka, an American breakfast, just this once. Enormous. Everything. *Je meurs de faim.*"

As she turned away she heard Kaka's most scathing tones. "*Canaille!* You know who that was you talking to! La Comtesse de Trenaunay de———"

I could almost believe it myself, Clio thought, strolling toward the garden, Cupide strutting in her wake. "Cupide, run, find Mr. Maroon, tell him I am breakfasting in the garden."

Cupide looked up into her face, all eagerness. "When we go to the stables he promised to teach me roping as they do it in the Wild West. The lariat. He can lasso anything that runs. Like this. Z-z-zing!" He swung an imaginary rope round his head and let it fly.

"M-m-m," said Clio, absently. Then, "In the garden, while I am having my breakfast. I should like to see that. Tell Colonel Maroon that I should love to see an exhibition of this Wild West roping with the lariat. In the garden."

So the guests of the United States Hotel, breakfasting sedately in the dining room or returning from the springs or emerging from their bedrooms, saw the beautiful Mrs. De Chanfret seated at breakfast on the garden piazza, polishing off what appeared to be a farm-hand meal of ham and eggs and waffles and marmalade and coffee, pausing now and then to applaud the performance evidently in progress for her benefit. On the neat lawn of the garden just below the piazza rail the dashing Texan, Colonel Clint Maroon, was throwing a lariat in the most intricate and expert way, now causing it to whirl round his booted feet, now around his sombreroed head, now unexpectedly snaking it out with a zing and a whining whistle so that it spun round the head of the entranced dwarf who was watching him and bound the little figure's arms to its sides.

"Bravo!" Mrs. De Chanfret would cry from time to time, between bites of hot biscuit topped with strawberry jam. Maroon had supplied the little man with a shorter and lighter rope of his own, and with this he was valiantly striving to follow the wrist twists of his teacher. The front piazza was deserted now. Out of the tail of her eye Clio saw Van Steed's astonished face; the nervous smile of Roscoe Bean as he peered over the shoulder of Hiram

Tompkins, the hotel manager. Here was a situation outside the experience of the urbane Bean. He writhed with doubt. Was this good for the United States Hotel? Would the conservative guests object? Breakfast on the veranda! But now they'd all be demanding breakfast on the veranda. Black waiters, white-clad, skimming across the garden, were carrying breakfast trays to the cottage apartments, balancing them miraculously upon their heads in the famous Saratoga manner but threatening now at every step to send their burdens crashing as they gazed, pop-eyed, at the unprecedented goings-on in the sedate and cloistral confines of the elm-shaded garden. Now the hotel band was assembling in the stand for the ten o'clock morning concert under the trees. Instinct told Clio that the moment was over. Abruptly she motioned Cupide to her, she rose and leaned a little over the veranda rail, smiling down upon the gallant Maroon who now stood, hat in hand, idly twirling his lariat as he received her praises. "Oh, Colonel Maroon. Brilliant! As good as a circus."

Very low, without moving her lips, she was saying, swiftly, *Moving into the cottages, chéri. I think it is better. I must talk to you. Van Steed.*

"Will you honor me by driving to the races with me, Ma'am, at eleven?"

"I shall be delighted." *Go quickly. Before he can talk to you. I'll tell you then.*

She turned to encounter a stout, plain woman in dowdy black standing directly in her path. Fiftyish. Formidable. "Mrs. De Chanfret!" she boomed. "I am Mrs. Coventry Bellop." Remarkably beautiful eyes in that plain dumpling of a face. Gray eyes, purposeful, lively, penetrating. *En garde!* Clio thought.

"Ah, yes?" With the rising inflection indicating just the proper degree of well-bred surprise at being thus accosted by a stranger.

"I want to welcome you to Saratoga."

"So kind." Coolly.

"And to tell you that I had the great pleasure of knowing your late departed husband. Dear, dear Bimbi!"

The polite smile stiffened a little on Clio's face, but she was equal to the occasion. "Is it possible!"

Clio was aghast to see Mrs. Coventry Bellop close one lively eye in a portentous wink. "Well, isn't it?"

"Hardly. He was almost a recluse. Perhaps you are thinking of his younger brother the—the black sheep, I'm afraid. I believe he was known as—uh—Bimbi among his friends."

To her relief Mrs. Coventry Bellop now patted her smartly on the shoulder. "I shouldn't wonder. If you say so. Well, let me know if I can be of any—assistance. I really run Saratoga, you know," she boomed. "Though old lady Van Steed thinks she does."

"Indeed!" Vaguely.

"You'll soon be in a position to judge, I should say." With which astonishing prediction Mrs. Coventry Bellop again patted her arm and waddled off with surprising lightness and agility for one of her proportions.

Escorted by the ubiquitous Bean to her new quarters in the cottage section, Clio graciously expressed herself as pleased as she looked about the cool veranda-shaded apartment. It boasted its own outer entrance and hallway, its row of bells meant to summon chambermaid, waiter, valet (none of which functioned and none of which she needed, luckily, what with Kakaracou and Cupidon), its own cryptlike bathroom, a grim little sitting room, a black walnut bedroom. The garden greenery could be glimpsed just beyond the veranda.

"Now then," Clio announced, briskly, as she looked about her after

Bean's departure. "This is more like it. Privacy. Here, Cupide! Take this note to Mr. Maroon quickly. Kaka, I can't go to the races in flowered cretonne. I think the almond-shell *poult-de-soie*. The straw bonnet with the velvet ruche and the flower melange. My scarlet embroidered parasol for color. Brown silk stockings, brown shoes."

"M'm. *Chic,* that," Kaka murmured in approval. "I am happy to see the widow now vanishes."

"While I am at the races unpack the scarves and shawls and ornaments. The clock put there on the mantel. The photographs on the table and the desk. The ornaments—the *bibelots*—those I'll place about when I return. There will be fresh flowers sent by Mr. Van Steed and Mr. Maroon from the hotel florist. At least there should be. What horrible furniture! But it won't be so bad and it won't be so long—I hope. Though I like it, on the whole. Here I can receive—guests. With no maids poking about in the halls."

Kaka sniffed maddeningly. "High-heeled Texas boots make a great deal of noise on a wooden veranda floor."

"Oh, you old crow! Always croaking, croaking. A bundle of dried sticks! I tell you I like it here in Saratoga. I feel gay and young and light for the first time in my life."

Panic distorted Kaka's face. "Don't say it! The *Zambi* will hear and be displeased. Here, quick! Touch the *gris-gris.*" She groped in her bosom and pulled out an amulet on a bit of string that hung around her scrawny neck. She snatched up Clio's hand and forcibly rubbed her fingers over the dingy charm, muttering as she did so.

Clio slapped the woman's hand smartly. "Stop it, you witch! I'll send you back to New Orleans; you'll live there in a wretched hovel the rest of your life."

"*Laissez-donc!* You know I speak the truth." She thrust the gris-gris back into her bosom and went equally on fastening her mistress's smart little brown shoes.

Cupide poked his head in at the door. "He's at the curb with the carriage. What do you think! It's a new one to surprise you!" His voice rose to a squeal. "It's a four-in-hand! Everyone's out to see it. Two bays and two blacks, and a regular coach to match, black with red wheels. And the harness trimmed with silver!" Unable to contain himself, he flung open the door that led to the veranda, and the next instant the two women saw the impish figure in its maroon livery turning an exultant series of handsprings past the veranda window.

Escorted by Cupidon, Clio was horrified to see, as she reached the street doorway, that the situation she had schemed to avoid had taken place. There at the curb was the splendid coach and four, like something out of a fairy tale. There in the driver's seat in a white driving coat, fawn vest, fawn trousers and the now-famous white sombrero, was Clint Maroon, his expert hands holding the ribbons over the backs of the four horses whose satin-smooth coats glistened in the sun. Looking up at him, deep in earnest conversation, one foot on the step, was Bart Van Steed.

"*Dieu!*" exclaimed Clio, aloud; skimmed across the piazza and down the steps at such speed that Cupide, having opened the scarlet parasol, was a frantic little figure pattering after her, his tiny arm stretched full length to hold the parasol high.

Her quick ear caught the Texan's words as she came toward them. From his vantage, perched on the driver's seat, he had seen her approach. Van Steed's back was toward her.

". . . Texas is a young state run by young men. You Easterners take no account of Texas. That's where you make a mistake."

"Oh, Mr. Maroon! I do hope I haven't kept you waiting!" Van Steed spun on his heel. His pink cheeks flushed pinker. "What a glorious coach! And four——— Oh, Mr. Van Steed. Oh, dear! You haven't repeated my indiscreet conversation!" She put her palm prettily to her cheek as though she, too, were blushing, which she wasn't.

His girlish skin now took on a definite rose tint as he handed her up to the seat beside Maroon and Cupide proffered her the crimson parasol. There was something anguished in the amber eyes of young Van Steed as from his position at the curb he looked up at these two resplendent figures, young, seemingly carefree, certainly beautiful. Clio's crimson sunshade cast a roseate glow over them both. It was as if these two dwelt aloft in a glowing world of their own.

She leaned a little toward him over the wheel, her lovely ardent eyes meeting his. "I didn't thank you for the roses. That Mrs. Crockery was with you . . . no, that's not right . . . Porcelain . . . Porcelain, that's it . . . so stupid of me . . . she's really charming . . . may I, an utter stranger, offer you my congratulations . . . I hear you are to be married . . . Mrs. Porcelain . . . really enchanting . . ."

"Married! " His voice was a shout. Then he remembered the piazza and repeated, "Married!" in a voice that rose to a squeak vibrant with outrage. "Mrs. De Chanfret, whoever told you that is a liar!"

Clint Maroon's drawl cast its cooling shadow upon the heated words. "Why, Mrs. De Chanfret, Ma'am, you-all certainly are putting your pretty little foot in it today. First you tell this gentleman here that I'm out to get his railroad off him———"

"Oh, then he did tell you that! How naughty of you, Mr. Van Steed. Especially as I said that Colonel Maroon admired———"

"Shucks, he didn't rightly say that, no. It was this way. I told this little runt of yours to go fetch you my message I was waiting. He says you've moved to the cottages. It's natural I'd be surprised, being as I'd given up my rooms—not that that matters, Ma'am, I'm glad to be of service—but when I remarked how come you went and did that, why, friend Van Steed here speaks up and says it's because I and my friends raised such a holler up there last night talking railroads. Seems he got the idea I was fixing to skin him out of his millions, or some such sorry trick."

Her lips quivered. There were tears in her eyes. She looked at Maroon, she turned her stricken glance down upon Van Steed's upturned face.

"How dreadful! How really frightful. How could I be so clumsy. Dear Mr. Maroon! Dear Mr. Van Steed! After you've both been so kind, so helpful to a weary stranger. To have made trouble between you! How can I make amends!"

"Married!" Van Steed was still quivering. "I must ask you, Mrs. De Chanfret, to tell me who gave you that piece of complete misinformation." So that's stabbed him deepest, Clio thought. Poor little man.

"I don't know. Really! I've talked to so many people. I'm all confused and oh, so unhappy. It may have been Mr. Gould, it may have been the chambermaid—or Mrs. Coventry Bellop—or the hotel manager—or perhaps Cupide picked it up from the bellboys—yes, now that I recall it, I seem to remember it was you, wasn't it, Cupide?"

The dwarf poured out his protest in a flood of colloquial French that was, fortunately, completely unintelligible to all but Clio. Much of it was highly uncomplimentary to Mr. Van Steed, to Saratoga, and to the human race in general.

"*En voilà assez!*" She was all concern as she bent toward the injured Van

Steed. "He swears it wasn't he. But I'm quite certain now. Please forgive me." She turned to Maroon. "And you, too. How could I be so tiresome!"

Maroon laughed an easy laugh, his warm gaze upon her. "Why, Ma'am, just to know you've had my name on your lips gives me pleasure. And I'm not denying I'm interested in railroads. And if I didn't feel the way I do about Mr. Van Steed here, and his road we were talking about, why I'd say leave him roar. But I'm for you, Mr. Van Steed. Not against you. There ain't any call for you to be wrathy. I happen to know something of the fix you're in. Down in Texas we'd know what to do, but maybe we're too rough for you Eastern folks. Leastways, for folks like you." He gathered up the reins. The horses were stamping restlessly, the silver harness jingled, the piazza by now resembled a group of statuary frozen into vain attitudes of strained attention. "But I know what I'd do in your place."

Bart Van Steed did not take his foot off the carriage step.

"Just what would you do, Colonel Maroon? I'd be interested to know."

"I'll bet you would. Well, sir, that's something to talk about sometime, friendly, over a cigar. It might be worth nothing to you; it might be worth a million." He leaned over so that his shoulder pressed against Clio, he lowered his voice confidentially. "I might as well tell you I'd go the whole hog to put my brand on a certain crowd—and a certain man in that crowd. If I ever aim to get tangled with that bunch, look out! I been studying railroads a good many years now——" He broke off suddenly. "Shucks! This here's no place to talk business. With this little lady looking like a thoroughbred, rarin' for the races. Well, we'll be easin' along."

It was plain the conversation was ended. Curious that Van Steed had been the suppliant, there at the curb, and Clint Maroon a splendid figure with his lady beside him high up on the glittering coach. Van Steed's face, upturned, was almost wistful. Reluctantly he took his foot from the step. The reins became taut in Maroon's gloved hands.

"Ma'm'selle!" came Cupide's voice from the curb. "Ma'm'selle Clio! You're not going without me! Ma'm'selle!" His voice rose to a squeal of anguish. He held up his two little arms like a child.

"Let him come, Clint," she said, very low.

Maroon beckoned with a jerk of his head. Like a fly blown by the wind the dwarf soared up the side of the coach, perched on the edge of the rear seat.

"Ne bougez pas de là," Clio commanded. But she could have saved her breath. His arms folded across his chest, his head held high, he was the footman in livery, a statue in little. Only the fine eyes danced as he watched the movements of the splendid horses and heard the music of their fleet hoofs accompanied by the clink of the silver-mounted harness. The coach and four dashed down Broadway on its way to the races.

Clio gave a little childish bounce of delight. "Clint, I am so happy. Forgive me for behaving so badly the day I came." He did not reply. She turned to look into his face. It was stern and unsmiling. "Clint! *Chéri!*"

Still he said nothing. They whirled among the sundappled streets. His eyes were on the horses. She put a hand on his arm. She shook it a little, pettishly. The off lead horse broke a trifle in his stride, regained it immediately.

"Take your hand off my arm," Maroon said between his teeth. "What d'you reckon I'm driving—cattle!"

"How can you talk to me like that? No one has ever talked to me like that!"

"Time they did, then. You've been high-tailing it about long enough."

"What is that?"

"Back in Texas the menfolks run things. You've been living with a bunch of women so long it's like a herd of mares think they can run a stallion right off the range. I've got every reverence for womenkind. There'll never be anybody like Ma. And there's others back home———''

"Like the finest little woman in the world," she put in, mischievously.

"That's so. My way of thinking, women should have minds of their own and plenty of spirit. But back in Texas it's the men who wear the pants. Looks like you listened to so much poison talk back there in Paris on account of your ma and your aunty, they figured they'd been done wrong by, why, you've taken on a kind of sneery feeling about menfolks. You got 'em all scaled down to about the size of that poor little fellow perched up back there. Well, you're dead wrong."

"What have I done! What have I said?"

"I'm aimin' to tell you. I'm crazy about you, honey, but I reckon you'd best know that if you try to run me I'll leave you, pronto. I don't mean your pretty little ways, and thinking of things that are smart as all get-out, and trying 'em to see if they work. That's all fair enough."

"But Clint, we said this was to be a partnership."

"That's right. But that don't say you can put words in my mouth I never said. I'm just naturally ornery enough not to want to be stampeded into doing something I didn't aim to do. I can be nagged by women and I can be fooled by women and I can be coaxed by women, but no woman's going to run me, by God! Now you pin back those pretty little ears of yours and take heed of what I'm saying. I'm boss of this outfit or I'll drag it out of here and drag it quick. You heard me."

If he had anticipated tears and protestations he was happily disappointed. Like all domineering women she wanted, more than anything in the world, to be dominated by someone stronger than she. Now, at her silence, he turned his gaze from the road ahead to steal a glance at her. She was regarding him with such shining adoration as to cause him to forget road, coach, four-in-hand. *"Chéri,"* she said in her most melting tones; and then, in English, as though the French word could not convey her emotion, "Darling! Darling! Darling!"

"Attention!" screamed Cupide from the back seat. *"Nom d'un———"*

Almost automatically Maroon swerved the animals to the right, missing by a fraction of an inch a smart dogcart whose occupants' faces were two white discs of fright as the coach swept by.

"Hell's bells!" yelled Maroon. But the danger seemed to restore his customary good humor. "See what you do to me, honey? Good thing you coaxed me to let Cupide come along. Don't look at me like that when I've got a parcel of horses on my hands or we're liable to end in the ditch."

"With you I'm never afraid."

"Uh-huh."

"Tell me, Clint, have you really a plan, as you said to Van Steed? I mean, really?"

"Well, not to say rightly a plan. Anyway, nothing he'd hear to. I don't want to get mixed in with that crowd. Look, Clio. I came up here to Saratoga to get myself a little honest money—cards, roulette, horses and so forth. I figured we'd have a high old time, clean up and get out. New York, maybe, September, though it's not my meat. But here you are, starting trouble, cutting up didoes, acting downright locoed."

"What have I done! I arrived only a day—two days———"

"And then what! Screeching out of hotel windows, champagne and peaches in the middle of the day, sleeping like drugged straight through for better than thirty hours, sashaying over to the cottages after all that hocus-pocus about the rooms, and now telling the doggonedest mess of lies—excuse me, honey, I didn't go for to sound mean-tempered, but you going to keep this up?''

"Oh, yes. I've thought of the most wonderful things. It's going to be better and better all the time.''

He regarded with great concentration the glistening haunches of the four fine horses speeding so fleetly under his expert guidance. But it was plain that his horse-loving mind was not really on them. "Well—uh—now—countesses, they don't carry on thataway, do they? I mean, for a girl that's up to the tricks you are, why, you sure are getting yourself noticed.''

"That's my Paris background, I suppose. It's the Aunt Belle in me. We never went out in Paris that people didn't stare and even follow us. I'm used to it.''

"It don't make good sense to me.''

Out of her murky past she waxed sententious beyond her years. "The only people who can afford to go unnoticed and quiet are the very very rich and secure and the really wicked. No one would know I was here if I didn't make a great furor. *Faire le diable à quatre*. It was a success in New Orleans, wasn't it? My little technique?''

He laughed tolerantly at the memory of her recent triumph. "Yes, those sure were cute didoes you cut down there. But this is different. I didn't mind—much. But you don't figure on catching a husband any such way, do you? Leastways, not Van Steed. He was brought up prim and proper.''

Into her voice there came a hard determination. "He was brought up by a woman who was stronger and harder and more possessive than he. His mother. Well, I'll be stronger and harder and more possessive than she. And cleverer. You wait. You'll see.''

"Uh-huh,'' he said again.

Pleased with herself she smoothed the shining folds of her silken gown, she looked down at the glittering coach, at the four superb horses, at the silver harness. She just touched his knee with one gloved forefinger. "This is rather wonderful. I feel like Cinderella. You haven't told me how you came by this splendid coach and four. How Aunt Belle and Mama would have adored it!''

"Right nice little poker game at the Club House night before last,'' he explained, laconically. "I was kind of put out when you went off into the Sleeping Beauty act of yours, so I figured I might as well get me a little extra change. Nothing better to do with my time. Ever since then I've been real worried about your friend Bart Van Steed.''

"You have! Why? ''

"You know that old saying. And he sure is unlucky at cards.''

Now she looked at the coach and four with fresh appreciation and with a kind of proprietary approval, as though she had earned it. They were passing the stables now. With his whip he pointed to one. "Alamo's in there. We'll go down to the stables tomorrow morning and see him.''

"And breakfast at the stables?''

"I don't know about that. Women don't do that. Men go down there and eat, early mornings, six seven o'clock. But no women.''

"I'm going. I don't care what other women do. I'm different.''

"You are. You sure are. That's what———'' He stopped.

"What what?'' she asked, mischievously. But he did not go on, and they swept dramatically into the race-track enclosure, the most spectacular coach among all the glittering vehicles gathered there. Down jumped Cupide and scurried round and stood at the near lead horse's head, his hand on the bridle rein; and at sight of this diminutive figure pitted against the huge equipage and the four fiery horses, the staring crowd burst into laughter; a voice shouted, "Hold 'em, Goliath! " Another yelled, "Look out they don't eat you for a fly." But Cupidon spat between his teeth, taking careful aim, and his deriders were seen to wipe their faces hastily.

"We can watch the races from up here," Maroon said. "Only I reckoned maybe you'd like to stroll around some. Cupide can't hold these critters, though."

"He's got the strength of an orang-utan in his arms. All his life he has been around horses."

Maroon looked dubious as he stepped down. "I don't know about that. Up on that box." He walked over to Cupide and stared down on him. "You sitting up there I'm afraid if they took a notion to pull a little, why, you'd be over the dashboard and landed on one of their ears."

The impish face peered up at him wickedly. "If I wanted to I could lift you off your feet where you stand, and carry you."

Maroon backed away, hastily. "God A'mighty, don't do that! All right, get up there on the seat. Anybody starts monkeying with the horses, scaring 'em, give him a cut with the whip. We'll be back, anyway, in two shakes."

There they all were—the Rhinelanders, the Forosinis, the Vanderbilts, the Lorillards, the Chisholms, Mrs. Porcelain. Mrs. Coventry Bellop, looking more than ever like a cook, was squired by three young dandies who seemed to find her conversation vastly edifying, judging by their bursts of laughter. No sign anywhere of that meager figure, those burning eyes.

"They're all here except Mr. Gould. Doesn't he care for the races?"

"Gould, he doesn't care for anything that's fixed as easy as a horse race. He's been playing with millions and whole railroads and telegraph companies and hundreds of thousands of human beings and foreign empires so long he wouldn't get any feeling about whether a horse came in first or not. Do you know what he does for a pastime? Grows orchids out at his place in the country. Nope, you can't figure him out the way you can other people. Or get the best of him."

"There is a way," Clio persisted; "a very simple way. We will find it. No big thing. Something childish."

"I just like to hear you talk, honey. I don't care what you say."

"You will listen, though, won't you? And if we have a plan you will help? You promised."

"Why, sure thing. Fact is, I have got an idea, like I said to Van Steed. Don't know's it's any good, though. It came to me while I was talking to him. I was so riled at the way you'd gone and mixed me up with him that it came into my head, just like that."

"Listen, *chéri,* we won't stay here long at the races. There are other things to talk about much more exciting than this. Are you going to enter Alamo sometime soon?"

"He hasn't got much of a chance in this field. He's a little too young, anyway. And I haven't got a jockey I just like."

"Cupide will ride him."

"You're crazy."

"I say he can. He can ride anything. In France he used to be always around the stables; they called him their mascot at Longchamp and Auteuil; they let him exercise the horses at the tracks. He used to run off and be gone for days. Mama was always threatening to send him back to America. It would be chic to enter your horse; it would look successful and solid. Cupide knows a hundred ways, if Alamo is good and has a chance. Cupide would get something from Kaka; he would give the other horse something; no one would suspect it."

"Holy snakes!" Maroon glanced quickly around in horrorrr. "If anybody hears you say a thing like that! We'd be run out of town on a rail."

"Pooh! These piazza millionaires they cheat and rob and kill people, even. You've said so yourself."

"That's different. If you steal five millions and a railroad, that's high finance. But if you cheat on a horse race, that's worse than murder."

"I just thought you'd like to win. And you said Alamo wasn't very good yet. Why did you have him sent up here then?"

"Because. A hundred reasons. God A'mighty, women are the most immoral people there is. Don't seem to know right from wrong."

"Such a fuss about a horse race."

"Look, Clio, be like you were in New Orleans that first month, will you?"

"But how is that possible, Clint? I am at least ten years older since then."

"Let's be young again, just for now. Let's quit figuring and contriving. Here it is, midday, middle of the summer. Look at that pretty little race track! Even if you had you your million right now what could you get with it you haven't got this minute?"

Half-past eleven in the morning. Saratoga managed somehow to assemble its sporting blood at this matutinal hour. Even rakish New Yorkers whose lives were adjusted to a schedule in which night ended at noon were certain to appear at the Saratoga track by eleven, haggard perhaps, and not quite free of last night's fumes, but bravely armed with field-glasses, pencil, and strong black cigars. Even those imported flowers of the frailer species arrived in wilted clusters, buttressed by their stout black-satin madams and looking slightly ocherous in spite of the layers of rouge and rice powder.

Against the background of elms and pungent pines, richly green, the little track lay like a prim nosegay with its pinks and blues and heliotropes and scarlet of parasols and millinery.

Descended from their gaudy coach, Clint and Clio prepared to take their places, but not before a stroll in the paddock so that Clint could inspect the horses and the feminine world could inspect Clio's Paris *poult-de-soie* glowing under the rosy shade of the scarlet embroidered parasol.

Smiling, exquisite, seeming to glance neither to right nor left, Clio saw everything, everyone. "Who's that?" she said again and again, low-voiced, and she pinched Clint's arm a sharp little tweak to take his attention from the horses. "Who's that? Who's that? Why are they standing around that stout, homely little peasant? There, with the red face."

"Because that's Willie Vanderbilt, that's why."

"That! *Dieu!* That clod is a millionaire!"

"Only about a hundred and fifty million, that's all."

"But he looks wretched!"

"Sure does. They call him Public-Be-Damned Vanderbilt on account of what he said. They hate him. He's scared of his life. I bet he wishes he could have stayed there on Staten Island, farming, and hauling scows full of manure across the bay from the old Commodore's stables. He and Gould, they're dead enemies. In Texas they'd be shooting it out. Here they just try to steal each other's railroads."

"I'm almost sorry that I must marry a millionaire. They are so unattractive."

"You can't have everything, honey. Little Van Steed isn't so bad looking," he observed, with irritating tolerance. "Get him to grow a beard, now, hide that place where his chin ought to be, why————"

She pinched his arm now, in sheer spitefulness. Leisurely, they strolled toward the grandstand. Suddenly there was a tug at Clio's skirt. She turned quickly, but she knew even before she turned that she would see the goggle-eyed Cupide looking up at her. His voice was a whisper.

"Ma'm'selle, bet on Mavourneen in the third. Everything. Fixed. *Mais soyez sur de là*. Tell to Monsieur Clint."

"Heh! What the hell you doing away from those horses! Who———"

But the little man had darted off, was lost in the crowd.

"It's all right," Clio assured him placidly. "He would not neglect them. He has someone watching them, be sure of that. He has found valuable information, little Cupide. How much money have you? Here is my purse. In the third—Mavourneen—everything. He has ways of knowing, that *diablotin*. He has just now found out."

Together they walked to their places, a thousand eyes followed them. Curiously enough, aside from Clio the most distinguished feminine figure to be peered at by the crowd was not that of the beflowered Mrs. Porcelain or the over-dramatic Guilia Forosini but the stout black-clad Mrs. Coventry Bellop, whose rollicking laugh boomed out as she chatted and joked with her three attendant swains.

"She is good company, that one," Clio observed to Clint, very low. She was shutting her rosy parasol and adjusting her draperies as she looked about her languidly. "I've seen her sort in France, she is like one of those fat, mustached old women who sell fruit in the Paris market—tough and gay and impudent and full of good bread and soup. I like her, that one."

The first race was about to start. Suddenly, above the buzz of voices in the grandstand there could be heard the booming chest tones of Mrs. Bellop calling, "Countess! Countess!"

"She means you, Clio," said Clint out of the corner of his mouth. "The old trollop!"

"Countess!"

Clio turned her head ever so slightly. Sophie Bellop's ugly, broad face was grinning cheerily down at her. "Are you betting, Countess? You look to me like somebody who'd be lucky at picking winners."

"I am," said Clio, very quietly, just forming the words with her lips. Smiled her slow, sad smile for the benefit of the crowd and turned back to Maroon. "I think she means me well, that cow. I feel her friendly."

"I wouldn't give you a plugged nickel for any of 'em," Clint observed, morosely.

"Oh, come now, *chéri*. How could she harm me, that one?"

"She runs this place, I tell you."

"All the more reason, then. She took care to call me Countess though she surely knows———"

"She's after something. When an old coyote comes prowling around the chicken roost it ain't because she's friendly to the hens."

"Clint, Clint! You are suspicious of everyone. You probably are suspicious of me, even."

"No, sugar, I'm not suspicious of you. I'm dead sure of you. I know you're crooked, so I don't have to worry none."

Her lovely leisurely laugh rang out.

It was just after the second race that she said, "Your pencil," as Clint was leaving to place his bet and hers. "I want to write a note."

"Don't be foolish," he said.

"Wait a moment. I will go with you. Look, there is Van Steed arriving. How hot and cross he looks. There, the little Porcelain is happy; see how she grows all pink, like a milkmaid; and the one you tell me is the Forosini she shows all her teeth with happy hunger. Let us place our bet and go."

"Now!"

"After this race. Let us watch it from the carriage, standing. This grows a little tiresome, don't you think? After all, I know that one horse can run faster than another."

She scrawled one word in her childish hand on a scrap of paper, she folded it tight and cocked one corner. As they rose to leave she tossed it swiftly and accurately into Sophie Bellop's capacious lap. As that surprised face looked up at her, Clio put a finger to her lips, the ageless gesture of caution and secrecy. They had scarcely regained the carriage when they saw the stout black-clad figure rushing toward the window.

"Did you tell her Mavourneen?"

"Yes."

"Kind of foolish, weren't you? It's all right us throwing away a few hundred dollars on a chance. But what does that little imp know!"

"He doesn't always know. Only sometimes. But when he says he knows, like today, then you can be sure. He has ways, that little one."

"What kind of ways?"

"Never mind. You will see Mavourneen come in. And we shall leave here, and the Bellop will tell everyone she has won. There will be great *réclame*. And we will have—how much will we have in our pockets?"

"Thousand, maybe. I don't know's I like it, myself. I—there they are. Wait a minute. Here, take the glasses. That one. Seven. Green and white."

"M'm. Seven is lucky for me. And I adore green. But I think I must be like this Mr. Gould and even that little stubborn Van Steed. I would find it more exciting to gamble with railroads and millions and people and the law than with horses running. You see, I am by nature mercenary. How lucky for you that we are not serious, you and I."

"Yeh," said Maroon. "I'd just as soon take up steady with a rattlesnake." But his tone was hollow.

12

BY THE END of that first week the women had their knives out. A prick here, a prick there, the ladies of Saratoga's summer society were intent on drawing blood from their thrusts at the spectacular, the unpredictable Mrs. De Chanfret. But as yet they had been no match for her. She parried every thrust, she disarmed them by her sheer audacity. She was having a superb time, she was squired by the two most dashing bachelors in Saratoga. If she went to the races with Clint Maroon in the morning, then she drove to the lake with Van Steed in the afternoon. Occasionally she vanished for twenty-four hours. Resting. Madame is resting, Kakaracou said, barring the cottage suite doorway with her neat black silk, her stony white-fichued bosom, her basilisk eye. Bart Van Steed stood at the door; he actually found himself arguing with the woman.

"But Mrs. De Chanfret was going to have dinner with me at Moon's Lake House. I've ordered the dinner, exactly as she wanted it. Lobster shipped down specially from Maine." As though the very mention of this dish could somehow bring her out of her retirement.

"Madame is very sorry." Kaka was being very grand. "Madame La Com—Madame De Chanfret is fatigued. She asked me to tell you she is *désolée* she cannot go. Madame De Chanfret is resting today."

No one had ever before done a thing like this to the most eligible bachelor in New York—in the Western Hemisphere. He was piqued, bewildered, angered, bewitched.

When later he reproached her she said, "You are angry. *Vous avez raison.* You will never again ask me to dine with you."

"You know that isn't true."

"After all, why should you bother about a poor weary widow about whom you know nothing? I may be an adventuress for all you know. And there are such lovely creatures just longing for a word with you—that pretty little Porcelain, and that big handsome Forosini with the rolling dark eyes, and those really sweet little McAllister sisters. And Mr. Maroon tells me that there has come to town a new little beauty, Nellie Leonard. He says she is escorted by a person called Diamond Jim Brady. What a freshness of language you have here in America! But surely a man like that would have no chance if you happened to fancy this pretty little Leonard."

"Thank you." He was stammering with rage. The amber eyes were like a cat's, the pink cheeks were curiously white. "I am quite capable of selecting my own company. You needn't dictate to me the company I may or may not keep. It's bad enough that my mother————" He stopped, horrified at what he had almost said.

Instinct told her the right thing to do. As though to hide her hurt, she lowered her eyelids a moment in silence; the long lashes were dewy when she raised them.

"Why will you misunderstand me! You are so strong and powerful. I have known such unhappiness in my marriage—I mean, you have been from the first so kind when you rescued me at the station—I only want you to be happy. Forgive me if I seemed presumptuous and managing. Women are like that, you know, with men they—they admire and respect. Especially women who have known misfortune, perhaps, in—in love."

Mollified, bewildered, but still sulky, he floundered deeper in confusion. "But suppose I don't like the kind of women you keep throwing at my head! You and my mother."

"Do you think of me as of your mother, dear Mr. Van Steed! Oh, that is sweet of you. But though I have seen so much of the world I am, after all, young and sympathetic and at least I hope————" She faltered, stopped.

In desperation he almost shouted, "I always seem to say the wrong thing to you."

"But no, no. It is I who am clumsy—*sans savoir faire.* You must help me to do and say the right thing. Will you?"

He sent flowers, remorsefully. Mounds of them.

Kaka, divesting these chaste offerings of their tissue-paper wrappings, surveyed them with a jaundiced eye. "Flowers! Posies!" Her tone should have withered them on their stems. "That's a Northerner for you! Your mama, gentlemen just see her riding out in her carriage would send her jewelry. You say he got money—this little pink man?"

"Millions. Millions and millions and millions!"

"Why'n't he send you jewelry gifts, then? Diamonds and big stone necklace and ruby rings like your mama got."

"Because I'm a respectable widow, that's why. To take jewelry from a man who isn't your husband, that is not *convenable.*"

"Your aunt Belle was a widow. She never had a husband no more than you. But she got jewelry. She never had to put up with no flowers."

Clio regaled Clint with this bit of conversation; she gave a superb imitation of the black woman's disdain for mere roses; she enjoyed her performance as much as he. The two conspirators, at ease with one another, went into gales of laughter.

He said, ruefully, "You haven't had any jewelry off of me, either. I sure would like to load you with it, honey. You can have my diamond stud, and welcome, if you'll take it.''

"Clint! I'm ashamed of you. Where is your loyalty! You know that diamond is for the ring when you marry the little blonde Texas beauty—the finest little woman in the world.''

Morosely he retorted, "Some day you'll be play-acting yourself right out of Saratoga if you don't watch out.''

"No,'' she said, "I was quite wonderful with Van Steed. Real tears. I must make him think he is strong and masterful. He must feel he is deciding everything. You know, it's a great strain, this pretending. Mama never had to pretend. She was actually like that. Languid and lovely and sort of looking up at one with those eyes. I try to be like that—when I think of it.''

"You're really a strong-minded female, honey. No use your soft-soaping and fluttering around. You wouldn't fool any man.''

She flared at that. "I never bothered to try to fool you.''

"Yessir, Countess,'' he drawled, "that's right. I reckon I just wasn't worth fretting about, that day in the French Market.''

"Touché," she laughed, good-naturedly.

Sometimes even she found it difficult to tell when she was herself and when she was the mysterious Mrs. De Chanfret. Perhaps no one enjoyed her performance more than she. Frequently she actually convinced herself of her own assumed role. In a way she enjoyed everything—even the things she disliked.

She regarded the vast dining room with a mingling of amusement and horror; rarely entered it. The crowd, the clatter, the rush, the heavy smells of too-profuse food repelled her. When she did choose to dine there it always was late, when the hordes were almost finished. She kept her table, she selected special dishes ordered ahead by Kakaracou, she tipped well but not so lavishly as to cause the waiters to disrespect her judgment. She refused to countenance the heavy midday dinner.

"Barbaric! All that rich food in the middle of the day. I dine at night.''

Her cottage apartment was situated on the other side of the U-shaped wing. She frequently dined or lunched in her own sitting room. You saw the black waiters in stiffly starched white skimming across the garden, mounting the wooden steps, racing along the veranda toward her apartment, their laden trays miraculously balanced atop their heads. The dining-room meals were stupendous; the United States Hotel guests stuffed themselves with a dozen courses to the meal, for everything was included in the American plan. Clio fancied the specially prepared delicacies for which the outlying inns and restaurants were famous. There she grew ecstatic over savory American dishes, new to a palate trained to the French cuisine.

"I never saw a woman enjoy her vittles more than you do,'' Clint Maroon said admiringly, as she started on her third ear of hot corn on the cob, cooked in the husk and now dripping with butter.

"Mama said always that the only decent food in America was to be found in New Orleans. Of course the food at the hotel is—you know—no imagination. And cooked in such quantities, as for an army. How can food be properly cooked that way! Naturally not. But here it's delicious—all these American dishes, what a pity they don't know of them in France. In France, they think Americans live on buffalo meat and flapjacks.''

Woodcock, reed birds, brook trout, black bass, red raspberries at Riley's. Steak, corn on the cob, at Crum's.

Maroon said, "I get to where I can't look at all that fancy fodder at the hotel. I just want to wrassle with a good thick T-bone steak.'' The two enjoyed food and understood it. They would taste a dish in silence, let the flavor send its message to the palate, then they would solemnly look at one another across the table and nod.

"Ma, coming from Virginia, she fancied her food. I reckon that's how I came to be a kind of finicky feeder. Ma, she used to say she didn't trust people who said they didn't care about what they ate. Said there was something wrong with them. Texas, though, it isn't a good-feeding state. Everything into the frying skillet."

It was at Moon's that Clio first tasted the famous Saratoga chips, said to have originated there, and it was she who first scandalized spa society by strolling along Broadway and about the paddock at the race track crunching the crisp circlets out of a paper sack as though they were candy or peanuts. She made it the fashion, and soon you saw all Saratoga dipping into cornucopias filled with golden-brown paper-thin potatoes; a gathered crowd was likely to create a sound like a scuffling through dried autumn leaves.

Concluding a dinner with Maroon, she was conscious of her tight stays. In contrast, dining with the dyspeptic Van Steed was definitely lacking in gusto. The De Chanfret veneer frequently cracked here and there so that Belle Piquery, Rita Dulaine and the hotblooded Nicolas showed through to the most casual observer. But in Saratoga it was, for the most part, put down to the forgivable idiosyncrasies of the titled and the foreign.

The first time she lighted a cigarette in public the piazza shook to the topmost capital of its columns. A woman who smoked! But even fast women didn't smoke in public. She had lighted a tiny white cylinder one evening strolling in the hotel garden under the rosy light of the gay Japanese lanterns. It was just before the nine o'clock hop. She was accompanied by the timorous Van Steed and she was looking her most bewitching in a short Spanish jacket over a tight basque, a full skirt of flowered silk with a sash draped to the side and caught with a tremendous bow.

Van Steed had watched her with dazed unbelief that grew to consternation as she extracted the cigarette from a tiny diamond-studded case which she took from her flowered silk bag, tapped it daintily and expertly, placed it between her lips and motioned him wordlessly for a light. He struck a match, his hand trembling so that the flame flickered and died. He struck another; she smiled at him across the little pool of light that illumined their two intent faces.

"You smoke cigarettes, Mrs. De Chanfret!" This obviously was a rhetorical question, since she was now blowing a smoke spiral through her pursed lips into the evening dusk. "I—I've never seen a lady smoke cigarettes before." His shocked tone had in it a hint of almost husbandly proprietorship. Even the stout professional madams who marshaled their bevy of girls in the afternoon Broadway carriage parade knew better than to allow them to smoke in public.

Clio shrugged carelessly. "It's a continental custom, I suppose. I've smoked since I was thirteen. There's nothing so delicious as that single cigarette after dinner."

Nervously he glanced about, sensing a hundred peering eyes in the dusk. "People will—people will misunderstand. In a hotel, people talk."

"Oh, how sweet—how kind of you to protect me like that! Perhaps you are right. I am not used to American ways. But a cigarette"—she held it away from her delicately, she looked at it, she laughed a little poignant laugh—"a cigarette is sometimes cozy when one is lonely. Don't you find this so, dear Mr. Van Steed?"

"Cigar smoker myself," he said gruffly.

She murmured her admiration. "But of course. So masculine."

He cleared his throat. "I shouldn't think you'd be lonely, Mrs. De Chanfret. You never—that is, you're so popular—a woman of the world." She was silent. The silence lengthened, became unbearable. In a kind of panic he looked at her. Her face was almost hidden from him; she had turned her head aside, the lashes lay on the white cheeks. "Mrs. De Chanfret! Have I said something! I didn't mean————"

Still she was silent. They walked beneath the rosy glow of the Japanese lanterns. Inside the hotel the orchestra struck up the popular strains of "Champagne Charlie." Now she turned to him, she just touched her lashes with her lace handkerchief. "A woman of the world," she repeated, very low. Her tone was not reproachful; merely sad. "Imagine for yourself that your dear sister should suddenly find herself a widow, and her dear mother dead, too, suddenly—forgive me that I even speak of such a thing—but *par exemple* only—and she finds herself alone in—shall we say—France. Alone, with only a servant or two, and knowing no one. No one. She follows the ways to which she is accustomed in her own loved America. Is that a woman of the world!" She pressed the handkerchief to her lips.

"Mrs. De Chanfret! Clio! "

Her face was suddenly radiant; she just touched his arm with the tips of her fingers, and pressed it gently and gave the effect of gazing up at him, starry-eyed, by leaning just a little. "You called me Clio. How dear, how good, how friendly! Bart!"

"Shall we go in? The—uh—the music has started."

"She's smoking a cigarette!" It was as though the scarlet tip of the little white cylinder had lighted a conflagration in the United States Hotel. "He lighted it for her right there in the garden as bold as you please, and now she's smoking it, walking up and down with a lace thing over her head, and a short velvet jacket like a gypsy. . . . She's thrown away the cigarette. . . . She's taking his arm!"

These were the oddments which were dispatched by letter to old Madam Van Steed maintaining her grudging vigil over her expectant daughter in Newport. With the breath of the harpies hot on her neck, Clio Dulaine went her unconventional way.

It became known that she frequently rose at six and ate breakfast with the stable-boys and jockeys and grooms and trainers and horsemen at the race-track stables. Later, this became the last word in chic. Now the very idea was considered brazen beyond belief. The early-morning air was exquisitely cool and pungent with pine; the mist across the meadows pearled every tree and roof and fence and paddock. Clio made friends with everything and everyone from waterboys to track favorites. She was fascinated by the tough, engaging faces of the stable hangers-on. Theirs was a kind of terse astringent wit. Their faces were, for the most part, curiously hard-bitten and twisted as to features; a wry mouth like a crooked slit in a box; a nose that swerved oddly; an eye that seemed higher than its mate, or that drooped in one corner, with sinister effect. Their hands were slim, flexible, almost fragile looking; their feet, too, slim and high-arched. They wore jerseys, shapeless pants or baggy riding breeches that hugged their incredibly meager knees. There was about them an indefinable style.

"*Chic, ça,*" Clio would say. "*Un véritable type.*"

"What's a teep? " Maroon asked.

"Uh—I must think————" She was being very French for the benefit of Van Steed. The three were breakfasting together.

Van Steed now said, yes, indeed, you're right, he is, and nodded to show that he too was familiar with the French language. This did little to soothe Maroon's irritation.

"Spell it," demanded Maroon.

"Why, t-y-p-e. *Type.*" She gave it again the French pronunciation.

"T-y—well, hell's bells! Teep! Type, you mean. Well, it's too bad you can't speak American. Are you fixing to stay over in this country long, Mrs. De Chanfret? You ought to learn the language."

"That depends, dear Colonel Maroon, on so many, many things."

"What, for instance?" Van Steed asked with pronounced eagerness.

"Oh, things you would consider quite sordid, I'm afraid, Mr. Van Steed. Everything is so expensive over here. It takes so many francs to make one American dollar."

He spoke with a rush, as though the words had tumbled out before he could check them. "You should never have to worry about money. You're so—so—you ought to have everything that's beautiful and—uh—beautiful." He stammered, floundered, blushed furiously.

"Perhaps," wistfully, "if—ah—Edouard had lived."

"Edouard? "

"My husband."

"Oh. Oh, I thought you said—that is—I understood his name was Etienne."

"It was. I—I always called him Edouard. A little pet name, you understand."

Phew, Maroon thought. That'll learn her not to be so cute.

Unruffled, she went placidly on eating the hearty stable breakfast of scalding coffee and ham and eggs and steak and fried potatoes and hot biscuits. Everything seemed to her serene and friendly at this hour of the morning. Even the race horses, so fiery and untouchable as they pranced out to the track a few hours later, haughtily spurning the ground with their delicate hoofs, seeming scarcely to touch it, like the toes of a ballet dancer, now put their friendly heads outside their stalls looking almost benign as they lipped a bit of sugar.

Cupide usually accompanied her on these excursions to the stable. It was his heaven. The stables were quick to recognize his magic with horses. They permitted him to exercise their horses, grudgingly at first but freely after they had seen what he did with the fiery Alamo, who was as yet not entirely broken to the race track.

Darting in and out of the stables and paddocks, under horses' hoofs, into back rooms, he picked up the most astonishing and valuable bits of information, which he imparted to Clint and Clio.

"That Nellie Leonard is an actress, they say she is going to be famous because that James Buchanan Brady has lots of money to put into plays for her. She is taking singing lessons every day. . . . Bet on Champagne Charlie in the third race, don't let them talk you out of it. I know what I know. . . . That girl in the cottages with Sam Lamar isn't his daughter at all, she's his mistress. . . . President of the United States Arthur is coming to the United States Hotel next week. . . . They are going to have a great ball. . . . The Forosini has a new riding horse, pure white. He is trained to bow his head and swing toward her when she mounts the block. . . . Gould is going to buy the Manhattan Elevated Company. He is trying to ruin them so he can get it cheap. I listened at the keyhole when he was talking. . . . Kaka is teaching Creole cooking to Mrs. Lewis at the Club House, and Kaka is playing the roulette wheel from the kitchen. The waiters place her money for her. She won seventy-five dollars last night. They're afraid to keep any out for themselves because they know she is a witch. . . . The old lady who is the mother of that Van Steed is coming to Saratoga. She doesn't like you. . . . Tonight Mrs. Porcelain is going to wear a pink dress, tulle, with rosebuds. . . ."

He knew everything. His sources of news were devious but infallible.
Bellboys, chambermaids, waiters, grooms, bartenders, faro dealers, stable
hands, jockeys, trainers, prostitutes all brought him tidbits and spices with
which to flavor the *pot-au-feu* which was forever stewing in his great domed
skull. When he slipped into the hotel front lobby (where he was not permitted), the Negro boys swarmed around him, their faces gashed with anticipatory grins. He postured for them, he danced, he told droll dirty stories,
he fabricated tremendous gargantuan lies. For the chambermaids he seemed
to have a kind of fascination that was at once unwholesome and maternal.
At the track the stablemen and even the jockeys admitted that his knowledge
of horseflesh was uncanny.

Now he began his campaign. He wanted Maroon to enter Alamo. He
begged to be allowed to ride him. Dawn daily found him at the track. He
cajoled, begged, bribed, pleaded until Maroon, trainer, stable-boys, all were
worn down. He took the horse into his charge, bit by bit. Soon he was riding
him daily in the early-morning track work. Crouched over the neck of the
beautiful two-year-old he looked like a tiny bedizened monkey.

"Let me ride him, Mr. Clint. Let me race him; I promise you he will win.
I swear it. Perhaps not first, but we will not shame you, Alamo and I. Think
how chic it will be, your own horse to race at Saratoga . . . Miss Clio, speak
for me. Speak for me!"

He was like a thwarted lover pleading that they intercede with a mistress.
It was difficult to tell whether he was motivated by his slavish admiration
for Maroon, his doglike devotion to Clio, or his worship of the spirited
animal.

In the beginning Maroon had laughed indulgently at the dwarf's pleadings
as one treats a child who cries for the moon.

"Listen at him! You'd be a sorry figure and so would Alamo, trailing along
at the end of the field like a yearling strayed from the herd."

Cupide turned to Clio. "Mad'moiselle, tell him how in France I rode in
all the most famous races. Tell him————"

"What a lie!" Clio retorted.

Maroon roared good-naturedly. "Get going, Cupide, before I take a boot
to you. Why, Alamo's a big critter; he'd likely turn his head if you were up
there on his back, racing, and eat you for a fly."

"I've mounted him every day. You know this!" The little man was near
to tears. His barrel-like chest was heaving. "I have the strength of a giant."
He clenched his fists, he made the muscles bulge in the tight sleeves of his
uniform.

"Git! Scat! Drag it out of here!"

Suddenly the little man began to shake all over as with a chill. His popeyes
searched the room wildly. With a bound he stood before the dreary little
fireplace, he seized the iron poker, took it in his two tiny hands and bent
it into a circle as though it were a willow twig. As suddenly, then, he threw
it, rattling, to the floor, burst into tears and ran from the room.

Maroon, staring after him, shook his handsome head in bewilderment.
"How come I ever got mixed up with a hystericky outfit like you folks I'm
damned if I know! Why, say, that midget's downright dangerous. If he was
mine I'd sure enough tan him good. Did you see what he just did there!
Why—say!"

Unreasonably, then, Clio turned about-face and sided with Cupide. "He's
wonderful with horses. You yourself have seen that. He can ride anything.
You are jealous because Alamo loves him more than you."

"God A'mighty!" shouted Maroon. "Let the sorry scoundrel ride him

then. Serve him right if he gets throwed and killed. Only don't blame me."
He stamped from the room as irate as a humdrum husband.

Cupide was not yet finished. He knew power when he saw it; he had not
listened at keyholes in vain. Straight as his little bandy legs would take him
he ran to the room where power resided. It was napping time for the feminine
guests of the United States Hotel—that hour which stretched, a desert waste,
when the heavy midday meal was in the process of digestion and the three
o'clock Broadway carriage parade had not yet begun.

Smartly, peremptorily, he rapped at the door of a third-floor suite. There
was no answer. He rapped again.

"Go away!" bellowed the voice of Mrs. Coventry Bellop. "I'm sleeping."

Rat-a-tat-tat, went the knuckles. Then again. Silence within the room.
Rat-a-tat-tat. To a mind keyed to plots and petty conspiracies the peremptory
knocking spelled exigency. A key turned, the door was opened, Mrs. Bellop,
a huge shapeless mass in a rumpled muslin wrapper, peered out into the hall,
saw nothing, then, feeling a tweak at her skirts, looked down in amazement
over the shelf of her own tremendous bust to see the tiny figure hovering
in the neighborhood of her be-ruffled knees.

"Good God!" she boomed. "You gave me a start. What are you doing
down there?"

"I must talk to you." He laid one finger alongside his nose like a midget
in a pantomime. Perhaps he had, in fact, seen this gesture of secrecy in some
puppet show and with his gift of mimicry was unconsciously using it now.

She stood a moment, staring down at him. Then, without a word, she
stood aside to let him enter. Accustomed to the fastidious neatness of Clio
Dulaine's apartment, he looked about Mrs. Bellop's chamber with considerable distaste. A cluttered place in which chairs, tables, shelf were littered
with a burden of odds and ends of every description. The froglike eyes of
the little man saw everything, made a mental note of all they saw. Garments,
letters, papers, half-smoked stubs of very small black cigars; food, gloves,
wilted flowers, a hairbrush full of combings; stockings, a cockatoo in a cage,
a fat wheezing pug dog whose resemblance to Cupide was striking.

"What do you want?" demanded the forthright Mrs. Bellop. "Who sent
you?"

He held his hat in his hand, the polite and well-trained groom, but his tone
was that of a plotter who knows an accomplice when he sees one.

"No one sent me. I came."

"What for? Nothing good, I'll be bound."

He looked pained at this. "Would you like to make a thousand dollars?"

"Get out of here!" said Mrs. Bellop.

He put up his little hand, palm out, almost peremptorily. "You need only
say one word to Mad'moiselle—to Mrs. De Chanfret, I mean. And spend
fifty dollars. You have fifty dollars? "

"Get out of here!" Mrs. Bellop said again. But halfheartedly. It was plain
that her interest was at least piqued.

"Madam Bellop," he began, earnestly, "I am a great and famous jockey."

"Likely story."

"It is true. Look at me. Imagine my featherweight on a good horse, with
my hands of iron. Listen. I am serious. I want to ride Alamo. You know—
Monsieur Clint's horse. If I ride him I shall win."

"Ride him then. What d'you mean, rousing me out of my sleep! What's
behind all this twaddle? Quick, or I'll have you thrown out of the hotel!"

Yet storm as she would, the sad eyes, the sardonic mouth, the stunted
body commanded her interest, held her attention. He spoke simply, briefly,

like one who is himself so convinced that he feels he will have no trouble convincing another.

"I will ride Alamo. I will win. That I can assure you."

"Bosh! How?"

"I will win. Will you tell Mad'moiselle that it would be a good thing for Monsieur Clint and for her? To have a winning horse is very *chic*. All my life I have wanted to ride a winning horse. But all my life. It is my dream."

"Look here," interrupted Mrs. Bellop, testily. "Sometimes you talk like a nigger bootblack and sometimes you talk like a character in a book. I can't make it out. For that matter, I don't know why I'm wasting time on you. Get along, now, before I call the front office." But her tone lacked conviction.

The midget could not be serious long. He shook himself like a little dog, he grinned engagingly, the big front teeth, spaced wide apart, were friendly as a white picket fence. Suddenly he was all Negro. "Please tell her like I say, Miz Bellop. She do what you say. Looky, effen you ain't got fifty, why, I put it in for you, you win a thousand dollars. Only"—his face now was a mask of cunning—"only you mustn't speak a breathin' word to any folks about it. Just you and Mr. Clint and Miss Clio."

"Dirty work if I ever saw it," said the forthright Mrs. Bellop. "She send you?"

"No *ma'am!*"

"He send you?"

"No *ma'am!*"

It was impossible to doubt his sincerity. Mrs. Bellop possessed the spirit of adventure; and she was not a lady to forego a chance at gain. Still she hesitated, pondering. Her fine eyes, shrewd, intelligent, searched the froglike face upturned to her. Honor among thieves. Desperate, he played his last card. "No call to feel backward about the fifty, Miz Bellop. No call at all. I can spare it and you can pay me back when you win. I stole it."

At this engaging example of candor she burst into rollicking laughter, her bosom heaved, her sides shook. "Run along, you imp! I've a mind to do it, just out of curiosity. If you're lying———"

Always dramatic, he finished the sentence for her. "You can kill me."

"I know worse ways than that to punish you. Get, now! Shoo!"

But he must have final assurance. "You the boss of this here whole Saratoga. You going to do it, Miz Bellop? H'm?"

"I might." But he saw that he had won.

It was almost too simple. Sophie Bellop, bidding her usual train of attendants to remain where they were, waddled into the paddock at next day's race, alone. Her sharp eye had caught sight of Clint and Clio, but even if she had not seen them she need only have followed the turning of heads, like the waving of grain in the wind, as they passed through any crowd. Accustomed though Saratoga was to the dramatic, there always was a stir when these two handsome and compelling creatures appeared together.

Mrs. Coventry Bellop wasted no time on finesse. Hers was an almost brutal directness of method, always. "Good morning, Countess! How are you, Colonel Maroon!" She scarcely paused to hear their courteous return of greeting. "What's become of that horse of yours, Colonel?"

"He's here, Ma'am. In the stables. Eating his pretty head off."

"Race him, why don't you? Isn't that what a race horse is for?"

A light leaped in Clio's eye. So! she thought. Cupide. She said, aloud, "I've been urging Colonel Maroon to enter him, Mrs. Bellop."

"Certainly," said the blunt Sophie, brisk and businesslike as any bookie. "Get that little dwarf imp of yours to ride him, he's just made for a jockey.

I've watched him with horses; he's born to ride. Saratoga needs a new sensation. Come on. Surprise them.''

The man's mind sensed intrigue; he looked from the girl's sparkling face to the purposeful countenance of the powerful woman. "What're you two girls cooking up!'' His caressing laugh was sheer flattery, as always, but his eyes were unsmiling. He had a feeling of helplessness, of being propelled into something by wills stronger than his. This very morning Kaka had fixed him with her hypnotic eye and had murmured, "I had a dream last night, Mr. Clint. I saw a horse and it seemed like the horse belonged to you and yet it didn't. And the jockey, he was Cupide and yet it wasn't, riding him. And it was like a race, and at the same time it wasn't exactly a race, neither.''

"M'm,'' Clint cut in, laconically. "You'd better change your voodoo powders, Kaka.''

Gently, persistently, they wore down his resistance.

"It would give you great *réclame*,'' Clio said. "The New York papers.''

An unknown horse. An unknown jockey. They ordered—rather, Clio ordered—for the diminutive figure a suit of silks in the historic colors of the stormy Texas flag. Kakaracou, when the shining suit arrived, embroidered the Lone Star on his sleeve.

"All right, all right,'' Maroon had said. "You'll make a laughing stock of me, but maybe it'll teach you a lesson.''

But he knew Cupide; he had watched Kaka's secret impassive face. He had taken his own precautions the night before the race.

In the sitting room of Clio's apartment the big Texan had called Cupide to him. The little man had trotted over to him and the Texan, lolling in an armchair, had locked the midget firmly between his steel-muscled horseman's knees.

"Now listen at what I'm fixing to say, Cupide. I'm not just passin' the time of day. You're riding Alamo tomorrow. You haven't a Chinaman's chance to win, but you might bring him in fourth or even third, if you're smart. But if I hear you've been too smart, you might as well light out somewheres right from the stables and never come back. I reckon you know what I mean. Don't you touch another horse, hear me! Don't you even show your ugly little face in another stall, only Alamo's. If I hear of any monkeyshines I'll tie you to the bedpost here and I'll pay Kaka to do such voodoo over you that———''

"No!'' Cupide screamed. "I promise. I promise.''

"All right. Now fork over, pronto, before I shake it out of you. Everything you got on you, because I'm going to search you, later, down to your toenails. Don't figure to throw off on me, because I'm watching you.''

For a moment the midget was still, still. His lips drew back from his teeth like those of an animal about to sink his fangs into an enemy. Then he looked up pitifully into Maroon's stern face. "You going to make me?''

"Surest thing you know.''

"You'll be sorry.''

Maroon made a threatening gesture.

"Here!'' squealed Cupide. From the inside hidden pocket of his tight little jacket he took a tiny folded packet like a powder paper; from the lining of his hat he took another; he took a stubby pencil from some inner recess of his clothing, unscrewed its top and brought forth a vial hardly thicker than a darning needle. "Here. Take them. This is only a powder, it makes a horse sneeze and his eyes water, it does no harm—after the race. This makes him chill. And cough. This, under the hoof, you can't even find it once it's in, but———''

Maroon turned him inside out. He threatened to scratch Alamo in next day's race. He himself put Cupide to bed, took away his clothes.

"I'm driving you to the track myself," he said, next morning, "and staying with you till you're mounted."

"Mais certainement," Cupide said, amiably, "why not? Have I not been good, Monsieur Clint! I have not smoked a single cigar now for two weeks, so well I have trained."

"You're up to something," Clint mused, regarding the midget thoughtfully. "When you get to putting on French like that it means mischief."

"I must say good-by to Kaka, she will make magic to help me win."

"M'm. I'll go with you."

But though Kaka did a good deal of eye-rolling with facial contortions and mumbling and passing of hands over the little man's head and down the length of his body, her hands were flat, her fingers spread. In spite of himself Maroon watched her, fascinated. He drove Cupide to the track, stayed with him until he actually was mounted, a grotesque little bundle of satin in the brilliant colors of the state of Texas.

"Phew!" he exploded, mopping his face as he joined Clio just before the start of the race. "Why in tarnation I ever said I'd leave him ride Alamo! He shouldn't ought to be allowed to enter any kind of sporting event except maybe to see who can spit the farthest. He's got no moral sense, no more than a goat."

"Such a fuss, *chéri"* Clio laughed. "You've upset him, poor little man! Taking his silly powders away and watching him as if he were a criminal. What harm to give another horse a bit of something, not to hurt him?"

"God A'mighty, the both of you'll end in jail yet, doggone if I don't think so!"

Maroon sat moodily as the race began, staring as Alamo cantered to the head of the stretch. But when the field broke away suddenly he stood up, wildly waving his white sombrero, shouting, "Eeeeee-yipeeee! Stay with him, Cupide! EEEEE-YOW!" Something very odd seemed to be happening. Alamo had started at a curiously mincing gait, more like the spirited step of a high-bred horse showing his paces in the Broadway carriage parade than the swift steady pace of a racer. The field swept past him, left him behind with two straggling nags. The tiny mounted figure crouched almost astride the animal's neck, and now Cupide's stumpy arm, whip in hand, came up, came down, came up, down. "Leave him be!" howled Maroon. The grandstand and paddock roared. Who had ever heard of whipping a horse at the beginning of a two-mile race! And the whip came down on Alamo's neck, not his rump. Alamo lurched, recovered, abandoned his high-school gait for a curious bunching of the four feet followed by flinging them wide. It gave him a ridiculous plunging gait like that of a nursery rocking-horse. "Oh, my God!" groaned Maroon; and covered his eyes. But Clio remained smiling, smiling. Mrs. Coventry Bellop was staring at them. Clio smiled. Bart Van Steed, very pink-cheeked, shook a sympathetic head. Clio's smile grew sweeter. "I'd give a million dollars to be out of here," groaned Maroon. "Twenty to one shot. Well, anyway, nobody bet on him, that's sure. Only our couple of hundred between us."

"He seems to be running quite well," Clio now observed, mildly. There was something unnatural in her serene composure. Women take things different from men, Maroon thought, somewhat to his own surprise. She's a wonder and no mistake. His hand rested on her knee, he looked again at the track.

"Take your hand away. They're watching us," Clio said, between her teeth. But she need not have bothered. He had leaped again to his feet, the white sombrero was describing circles in the air. Alamo's gait still was grotesque but it was covering magnificent distances in the beginning of the second mile. He was running, not like a horse, but as a greyhound runs, or a jack rabbit. All four feet bunched under him, then all four spread to unbelievable length. He seemed to go through the air in a series of leaps. From a roar of amusement the crowd now grew hysterical.

"Kangaroo!" they were yelling. "Go it, Kangaroo! Tom Thumb! Let him out, Tom Thumb! He wants to fly!"

The tiny arm had ceased to rise and fall. Cupide, against the dark sweating neck, was like a bluebottle that will not be shaken off.

"He—why he's—he's—Clio, it looks like he's got a chance to win!"

"He will win," Clio said, calmly.

The curious bounding gait passed the last half-mile, passed the last five in the field of seven, passed the favorite Oh Susanna, reached the post and kept steadily on, bunch and spread, bunch and spread until a score of track-hands and stable-boys swarmed out to stop him. He stopped, too, in a bunch. "Four feet on a dime," Maroon said later, ruefully. With difficulty they brought him to a standstill, his eyes were rolling, he jerked, pranced, reared.

It was Maroon who lifted Cupide off the horse, hugged him, lighted for him the huge black cigar that he had denied himself like any jockey in training. And Maroon, smiling now, smiling a curious smile with Clio at his side, said, over and over, "Yes, it sure surprised me as much as anybody. I just entered him to please the little fellow, but he like to sawed Alamo's head off; it was a wonder the poor critter didn't roll him off his back. . . . Well, thanks . . . Well, that's mighty kind of you. . . . Why, no, I just had a few dollars up, not anything to speak of . . . I'd no *i*-dea he'd come in, his first race like that."

But once Clio's sitting room sheltered them, Maroon confronted her. He was white with rage.

"What did he give him? I'm going to wring his neck, and Kaka's too. But first tell me—what did he give him?"

"Give him? But who? What is this you are talking?"

"Don't start that Frenchified stuff with me. You and that witch bitch in there. Disgracing me for life! Kaka!" He strode toward the inner door. "Kaka! Come on out of there or I'll drag———"

As though on signal there came a knocking at the outer door even as Kaka flung open the bedroom door. She was an imposing figure in her best black silk, stiff and rich, a filmy fichu crossed on her flat breast, her gold earrings dangling, her brooch flashing, her turbaned head held high. In her hand was a silver tray holding small amber-filled glasses.

"Come in! Come in!" Clio called gaily in answer to the knocking at the outer door.

"*Coquetier?*" said Kaka, gently, proffering her tray to Maroon. "*Coquetier?*"

A Negro bellboy stood in the hall doorway. "Gepmun from the newspapers like to speak to Colonel Maroon. New York papers and everywhere."

"I won't see 'em. Tell them to go to hell!"

"Oh, I'd see them if I were you, dear Colonel Maroon," cooed Clio. "They'll think it so very queer, if you don't. Isn't that true?"

Sulkily he followed the boy across the balcony, down the stairs.

"How much you win?" Kaka asked her, smoothly.

"Ten thousand."

"M'm-m'm! The Colonel's wrathy. But he wouldn't let Cupide give the other horses the stop powders, like he wanted to, so he had to give Mr. Clint's horse the go-ahead medicine."

"True. In some ways—a few only—Colonel Maroon *il n'a point de raison.*"

"*Mais un homme comme il faut, toutefois,*" Kaka tittered. "Only we must keep away from him for a few days that other one—that monkey—that *homme des bois.*"

"Quick, stop that giggling, put down that glass, run after that bellboy, tell him to tell the newspaper reporters that the beautiful Mrs. De Chanfret won ten thousand dollars. Make it fifteen. And let it be known that Mrs. Coventry Bellop, too, was a winner. The well-known society leader . . . That stuff Cupide stuck into him with the butt of his whip—it won't hurt Alamo, will it? After?"

"No." Kaka scurried toward the door with a swish of her silks. "Only hurry-up powders. Wouldn't hurt a fly."

13

IT IS AN interesting thing," Clio reflected, her eyes narrowed in her thoughtful expression. "He's as shy as a bird, Van Steed, but he likes to be seen with women who are *dramatique*—spectacular—is that the word?"

"No spika de Angleesh," retorted Maroon, sulkily. He had not yet quite come round, though three days had elapsed since the race—the Kangaroo race it was called in Saratoga. There had been some ugly talk, but this had quickly died down when it became known beyond a shadow of a doubt that Maroon himself had had a mere hundred dollars on his own horse.

"Clint, I don't understand you now. You are so different."

"So are you."

"No. I am exactly what I said I would be when we planned it all in New Orleans. I did not pretend. I did not try to make you believe that I was one of those good women like your dear mama, and that other you so admire. Everything *convenable*. I am here to make somehow a great deal of money—by marriage, if possible. But safely. You know that."

"You make me sick," he said, brutally.

But her tone was equable. "Yes, it makes me a little sick, too. But Mama—and Aunt Belle—and all that in New Orleans—that I saw for years, and there if you like was something to make one really sick. I won't be like them. I won't be. I won't be!" The tears streaming from her wide-open eyes, her lips quivering.

"You sure cry pretty." But he came over to her and ran his hand almost roughly over her sleek black hair, and then the hand gripped her shoulder, her arms were about him, they clung together, he drank the tears from her eyes.

"You will help me, won't you, *chéri*? Darling. Darling." Always she accented the last syllable—dar-*ling*. Dar-*ling*. It seemed to make the word a thousand times more caressing.

"Now what?"

She sat up, flushed but composed again and almost businesslike. "That Forosini. He rides with her sometimes in the afternoon."

"I reckon he's still got the right."

"But it's because she behaves like a circus rider. I want to do something that will make her seem dull."

"Well, get yourself pink tights and spangles and ride down Broadway bareback." But even as she pouted he said, thoughtfully, "S-a-a-ay! Maybe we can teach Blue Blazes to do her licking trick with you. She likes you."

Like a child she hugged him. "Clint, you are a good, good man!"

"Oh, my God!" he groaned in protest.

She ran into the next room. "Quick, Kaka! My riding habit."

Guilia Forosini in her trim black habit was the center of an admiring crowd when she mounted her white horse every afternoon at five. It was quite a ceremony. Her father, white-haired, military of bearing, known to all by his shock of curly white hair, his iron-gray imperial and mustache, led her by the hand down the piazza steps. Always, as she approached her horse, the animal bowed his beautiful head and swung toward her as though inviting her to mount. Usually two grooms accompanied the dark-eyed beauty, often one of the young bloods among the summer visitors; occasionally even Bart Van Steed had been seen to canter with her through the pine-scented paths.

After that first afternoon at five when Mrs. De Chanfret had descended the piazza steps to mount Colonel Maroon's horse, Blue Blazes, the fickle crowd had deserted the Forosini en masse. The reason was simple enough. Mrs. De Chanfret gave them a better show.

Blue Blazes was blue black. His coat was the color of Clio's hair. Her gloves were white, her stock was white, she sported a fresh white flower in her buttonhole, her boots shone like Blue Blazes' back. There was about her the indefinable neatness of the Parisienne. She made the Forosini in contrast seem somehow blowzy. But it was not this alone the crowd had come to see; it was not for this that they had deserted the Forosini just in the act of mounting there at the other horse block. For as she reached Blue Blazes' side, Clio lifted her veil and Blue Blazes turned his magnificent head and kissed her cheek. The crowd was rapturous.

"Just a little sugar water on your cheek, honey," Maroon had said when he taught her the trick down at the stables. "Blue Blazes he'll do anything for a lick of sugar water. I taught him that little knack when he was just a foal."

Mrs. De Chanfret. That Countess de Traysomething de Chanfret. She uses mascara on her eyelashes you can't tell me they can be as long and black as that and kind of thick looking. (She used mascara quite artlessly, having seen Aunt Belle Piquery do it for years.) They say she walked right into the gambling room at the Club House where ladies simply aren't allowed and when they told her that it was against the rules she just smiled and stayed on as brazen as you please. Al Spencer, the manager, came up and spoke to her. She was with that Colonel Maroon. And she stayed, mind you. She says it's the fashion in Europe, well, all I can say is she'd better go back there—bringing ideas like that into the minds of American womanhood! Even Mrs. Coventry Bellop never went that far, and she certainly does as she likes.

Though Clio Dulaine was busily throwing dust in the eyes of Saratoga so that her real business could be accomplished, she now and then found herself the center of a sensation out of sheer innocence or worldliness; it was difficult to say which.

Though she enjoyed the al fresco dining at the outlying inns and restaurants, there was something very gala about dining at the ornate Club House with its mirrors and gilt, its frescoes and chandeliers. The full-length portrait of John Morrissey, its founder, hung in the hallway, black mustache, gold watch-chain, the famous $5,000 diamond stud, the diamond sleeve links, Prince Albert coat and all. Though death had ended his reign, the lavish standard of the Morrissey ménage persisted.

As for the blatant bronzes and flowered carpets and the writhing figures carved in every defenseless inch of wood, Clio, after one look, said, "Isn't it frightful! I adore it! And that portrait! His coat of arms should be over the door. A cuspidor couchant, with two cigars and a plug of tobacco rampant.''

This got about and caused mingled resentment and hilarity.

But even Clio's fastidious palate, accustomed to the most artful French and Creole cookery, could not deny the flavor and variety of the gaudy Club House restaurant. On cool evenings it was pleasant to dine where wines actually were known by name and age and where caviar and *crêpes suzette* were recognized as the alpha and omega of a good meal. It was pleasant, too, to be squired by the flamboyant Colonel Maroon or the shy but equally sensational Bart Van Steed.

She had been accompanied by Maroon on that first night when she entered the gaming rooms in defiance of the house rules. There were women in the parlors, in the lounge, but certainly they were not the cream of Saratoga summer society. They were adventurous nobodies who derived a vicarious sense of sin from being so near its portals; all the more titillating because it was forbidden them.

Clio had by now had quite enough of the hotel parlors with their shrill feminine chatter; she had had enough and to spare of the restaurants, of the drives, of the gargantuan hotel dining room. At the Club House she had eaten her dinner with enormous gusto, had mopped up the last drop of fragrant cointreau and orange sauce with a little pillow of pancake.

"That was heavenly! Now I am going to play a little roulette. I'm always lucky at roulette.''

"Womenfolks not allowed in the gaming room. You know that, honey.''

"*Ridicule!* Provincial nonsense. Tell me about the owner of this Club House. Who is he?''

"There's two of them. They bought it after Morrissey died. Charley Reed, he killed a man back in New Orleans in 1862 and they sentenced him to death but there was a lot of hocus-pocus and they got him pardoned. The Federal troops were in there by that time and the head of the gambling outfit was a fellow named Butler, brother of Major General Benjamin Butler. So Reed he got off and went right on with his gambling place. Well, say, now he's all for society here in Saratoga; built himself a fifty-thousand-dollar house on Union Avenue, goes to the Episcopal church every Sunday. At the races every day, but you don't see him around the Club House much.''

"And the other?''

"Al Spencer, he's the quietest spoken fellow you'd ever meet, stingy as all get-out. He's got a hobby of collecting paintings but it isn't just for fun. He buys 'em cheap and sells at a profit.''

"What a country! A convicted murderer and an art dealer conduct a gambling house in the most famous watering-place in America.''

"That's so. But look at us!''

"Look at all of them," Clio interrupted. "I only marvel more and more that any country could be so rich and so vital as to survive the plundering of these past years. We are all thieves together, the lot of us.''

She actually entered the gaming room, a thing unheard of in the history of Saratoga. Followed by the protesting and rather sheepish Maroon, she had swept past the doorman before he could recover from his surprise and was strolling past the faro and roulette tables with a professionally interested eye.

"Madam," an attendant protested. "Ladies are not allowed in the gaming rooms.''

"Nonsense. Send for Mr. Reed. Send for Mr. Spencer." The pious ex-murderer was not to be found, but Spencer, resembling a shabby clerk in a lawyer's office rather than the owner of the most notorious and gaudy gambling house in America, glided in and surveyed Mrs. De Chanfret with a fishy eye before he turned his reproachful gaze on Clint Maroon.

"Now, Colonel Maroon, after all the money you've taken out of this place————"

"It isn't his fault, Mr. Spencer," Clio interrupted quickly. "I am Mrs. De Chanfret. I have begged Mr. Van Steed and Mr. Maroon to escort me into your beautiful gaming rooms but they said it was forbidden. I couldn't believe it. I have been everywhere in Europe—Monte Carlo, Aix, Nice, Cannes—and never have I heard of such a thing."

"Hear of it now," replied the laconic Spencer.

"Think of all the money you're losing. Women are bad gamblers they say."

"Yes, ma'am. That's just it. Hystericky. Get to screechin'."

Every eye in the room was on them. She was wearing her dress of crème Beaupré veiling in the shade of Kioto porcelain and a blue surah vest bordered with red velvet. It was a costume in which she would have attracted attention under the most conventional circumstances. Now, in the midst of the men's dark coats and snuffy midsummer seersuckers, she stood out like a flag in a breeze. Only the fish-eyed Spencer surveyed her unmoved.

"Thanks, Al," Maroon said, uncomfortably. "Come on, Cl—uh—Mrs. De Chanfret. We'd better mosey along now."

But as always, opposition made her the more determined. "Mr. Spencer, I'll make a confession to you. Colonel Maroon wagered me five hundred dollars that you wouldn't let me play. I bet five hundred you would. If you'll let me play just once I'll put the five hundred on Number Five and, win or lose, I'll go. Will you? Just this once?"

The chance to recoup something, if only five hundred dollars, from the lucky Texan proved too much for the avaricious Spencer.

"Win or lose. Promise?"

"Win or lose. Promise."

Without a word Maroon peeled five one-hundred-dollar bills from the sheaf in his wallet and handed them to Spencer. Spencer in turn gave them to Clio. Wordlessly, without waiting to buy chips, she flung them down on the five.

Five won. She pointed to the winnings. "Thank you so much, dear Mr. Spencer. The original five please give to Mr. Maroon. The rest you will please give to your favorite charity in Saratoga"—in a definitely clear tone. The cream-and-blue Beaupré veiling floated out of the room followed by a fuming Maroon and leaving in its wake a buzz of talk that sounded like a badly directed mob scene in a pageant.

"Now what in tarnation did you do that for, Clio!"

"You're not angry, are you, Clint *chéri?* I had to play, once. It's very bad for me to be forbidden things I want to do. Harmless things, I mean."

"Suppose you'd lost the five?"

"I'd have paid you back. You know that."

"God help any man who takes up with you for life. I wouldn't be in his shoes, not for a million."

"Oh, I'm hoping he'll have more than a mere million."

"Pretty sure of yourself, aren't you?"

"No. No, I'm not. Not sure of myself or of you or anything or of any-one————" Her voice trailed off into wistful nothingness.

"There you go! Hard as nails to begin with, and then you get to feeling sorry for yourself and next thing you've got me and Kaka and Cupide and everybody else babying you like you were two years old. Well, that's about what you act like—two years old."

They were walking toward the hotel in the soft midsummer darkness.

"Do I? Yes, I suppose I do." There was something disarming about her unexpected acquiescence. "But what chance had we here in a place like this unless we made a great fuss? My little plan with Van Steed—it has thrown you two together, hasn't it? Everyone here knows you and me, they think we are rich and important. They suspect nothing."

He put his hand over hers that lay on his arm as they walked. "Honey, this kind of game, you've got to work quick and get out before they find the pea under the walnut shell."

"Then what have you done with Van Steed? I have done what I could. I've told him that he is wonderful. I've told him that you are wonderful. If I can have ten more days I think he would have the courage to be serious. You say you have a plan. Why don't you tell me! I can see no chance for big money unless this plan of yours is one that he——What is it, this plan, anyway? I've no head for railroads. Railroads bore me. But tell me simply."

"Same old plan we used to use when the sheep men tried to crowd the cattle men off the range. The quickest draw and the hardest fist and the smartest one to outguess the other, he won."

"Yes, but tell me. Tell me what is being done with this railroad. I'll try to understand."

"Anybody could understand. That's the trouble. Did you ever hear of a fellow named Morgan—J. P. Morgan?"

"You once spoke of him."

Strolling along in the soft darkness, his hand on hers, he told his story of ruthlessness, and his gentle drawling voice that she so loved to hear made it seem stirring and almost romantic.

"Well sir, he's a scrapper for you. New fellow. Banker. Smart as Gould and just as hard, but he ain't rough. Not poor white trash with no bringing up, like Rockefeller and Huntington and Gould and Jim Hill, Carnegie and Vanderbilt and Astor. Morgan, his pa was a banker before him. I don't mean he's any sissy, even if his name is Pierpont. But he sits quiet; he's as close-mouthed as an Indian. Matter of that, they're all in the same kettle. Yellow-livered, wouldn't fight in the Civil War, Pa said. Paid substitutes to fight for 'em; they were too busy robbing the country, themselves. But this Morgan, he's been to Europe, worked in a bank there; he's had a college education."

"Is he rich?"

"Rich! Hell, yes!"

"Married?"

His laugh rang out. "No, honey, no. I mean, no for you. Seems he married young, and she died. But no, sugar."

"*Eh bien!* One never knows. Do go on, *chéri*. I am fascinated."

"Folks have a lot of respect for him. Scared of him, too, I reckon; because he keeps his mouth shut, they don't know what he's thinking. I told him what I wanted to do——"

"When? Where?"

"Oh, last week, you were busy as a bird-dog hatching one of your plots with Kaka and Cupide, I guess, and off making little Bart think butter wouldn't melt in your mouth. I went to New York."

"New York! Without me!"

"Honey, you can't go traveling around with Colonel Maroon—a respectable widow like you. You got your work cut out, according to your own pattern."

She jerked his arm, irritably for her. "Go on, then. Go on! Never mind about my plan. Yours."

"You couldn't call it a plan. It's so dumb and simple nobody's willing to believe it'll work. That's Easterners for you! Course, it is rough, maybe, a mite. But not any rougher than they were with Pa. Now, that hundred miles of road between Albany and Binghamton, it keeps on breaking down all the time. The other crowd sees to that. The trains go off the tracks. The trestles break down. There's fights in the trains and people get hurt. It's got so nobody'll use the road for freight or passengers. Scairt to. It's all done by Gould and his gang. They're trying to make the trunk line worthless so little Bart will sell it to them cheap and good riddance. He's tried law and order by calling on the citizens of the towns the road runs through. Well, the Gould gang gets them beaten up, and now he's got agents going through the towns with bundles of cash buying up stock that's held by the townships. They even tried to take over the books and the headquarters by force. That's always been the system of men like Fisk and Gould and Drew—you don't know about 'em, but I've heard of 'em all my life. Their scheme is, run it into the ground, make it worthless and you'll get it for nothing. The Delaware, Lackawanna & Western crowd would help little Bart Van Steed—that's a coal company—and back of it all that J. P. Morgan—if Van Steed would only fight. I mean, fight. I'd be willing to lead a gang down there. I'd get together a certain crowd I know. I'd put men in every office and railroad yard and station, and on every train and in every engine. I'd battle 'em bloody. I'd run 'em off the range.''

They had reached the hotel. She took her hand from his arm, she stopped dead in the light that streamed from the open windows facing the piazza. "But this is a civilized day. These are like stories of Indian fighters. It is savage. I can't believe that business in America is conducted like this! You are laughing at me!''

"Nope. That's the straight of it.''

She shook her head, she looked up at him. "Poor little Bartholomew Van Steed!''

"Honey, come on away from here with me.''

But now she shook her head again, and this time it was for him. "When I leave Saratoga I intend to be settled for life—settled and safe and sure. But sure.''

"I can always make enough for the two of us.''

"But you just said God help any man who takes up with me for life.''

"Who's talking about a lifetime!''

"I am.''

Up the broad piazza steps and into the lobby. The cream-and-blue veiling, the white sombrero immediately were aware of an overtone of shrillness, an added quiver of excitement in the babble that issued from the hotel parlor.

Roscoe Bean skimmed by, his coat-tails vibrant. "What's up?'' drawled Maroon. "The cats seem to be miaouing louder than ordinary tonight.''

"Sh-sh!'' Bean's unctuous smile had in it a touch of apprehension. "Oh, Colonel Maroon, you kill me the way you put things.'' He dropped his voice as though speaking of the sacred. "It's Madam Van Steed. Madam Van Steed has arrived.''

14

MADAM VAN STEED sat on the piazza next morning, and her subjects paid her court. Frelinghuysens and Belmonts, Burnsides and Stewarts were reduced to their proper stations in the presence of royalty. Even Miss P. Vanderbilt, aunt of the fabulous William, whose first name no one seemed to know and wouldn't have dared use if they had, paid her respects to the monolithic figure whose iron-gray hair and iron-gray eyes and iron-gray gown seemed hewn from the very material of which she was made. Miss P. Vanderbilt ruled her own Vanderbilt clan with a terrible and devastating sweetness, a wistful blue eye, a tremulous smile, a tiny childlike voice. She wore little white *lisse* caps beneath which her faded curls bobbed jauntily. In the hotel dining room the Vanderbilt table was fourth from the door but the Van Steed table was second from the door and on the garden side. Madam Van Steed conducted herself like a comedy duchess in a bad American play about a duchess. Yet, once explained, her foibles were legitimate enough. Her companion, Miss Diggs, was there to drape shawls, read aloud, fetch and carry, pat pillows, write letters. Her crook-handled walking stick was a necessary adjunct to one who was ridden by rheumatism. The temper was induced by pain, for the arthritic right hand was curled into a claw. Her possessiveness toward her son was the frustrated love which had been rejected by the philandering Van Steed *pére*. Her arrogance, her spitefulness and her domineering habit were probably glandular, but added up to pure meanness, and could have existed only in one to whom the grace of humor had been completely denied. `

This bulky and aged Borgia now sat enthroned in her corner of the United States Hotel piazza. Each subject received his meed of poison as he approached the presence. The strident, overbearing voice carried up and down half the length of the enormous promenade.

"Oh, it's Miss Vanderbilt! Still wearing your little caps, I see." Then, in a piercing aside to Miss Diggs: "Bald as a billiard ball. Those curls are stitched to the cap."

Bart Van Steed hung over her chair, captive. "Well, I'll just drive down to Congress Spring, Mother. Shall I bring you a fresh bottle of water?"

"Diggs fetched it early this morning. Stay here with me, Bartholomew. After all, I arrived only last night, I haven't had a chance to talk to you. . . . Who's this? Oh, Mrs. Porcelain. You are still Mrs. Porcelain, I suppose? What's the matter with the men these days! They want nothing but young chits of sixteen. The sillies! As soon as a woman gets along toward her thirties and has some sense they count her as shopworn. . . . Is there a circus in town? But then who's that driving tandem with the white reins? Oh, the Forosini! No wonder. The old man himself looks like a ringmaster and now all the daughter needs is spangles and a hoop to make it perfect."

Only Mrs. Coventry Bellop gave her dart for dart. For well over a decade these two had been coming to Saratoga to partake of the waters and to enjoy their ancient feud. Madam Van Steed had the money, Mrs. Coventry Bellop the blood. She regarded Madam Van Steed as a parvenu and the Goulds, the Vanderbilts, the Astors, the Belmonts as upstarts. She loathed stupidity and dullness, played poker with the men; it was said she had been seen to smoke a pipe. Madam Van Steed, the conventional, regarded her with horror mingled with a wholesome fear. Bellop made no secret of her poverty. She knew the characters and the scandals of the Club House since the day of Morrissey; every hotel register was an open book to her. She knew how much the faro dealers were paid; which actually were secretaries and which were not in the cottages of the lonely millionaires whose wives were in Europe; had the most terrific inside political information about the doings, past, present and future of the late Boss Tweed, and of Samuel Tilden, James G. Blaine, Sanford Church. The lives of the Lorillards, the Kips, the Lelands were not only an open book to her but one from whose pages she gave free and delightful readings. She boasted that she was helping General Ulysses S. Grant with his memoirs; she gossiped with Mark Twain when he came to near-by Mount McGregor to visit General Grant. She was the confidante of chambermaids, race-track touts, millionaires, cooks, dowagers, bookies, debutantes, brokers, jockeys and, amazingly enough, she rarely betrayed a genuine confidence. Hers was the expansive, sympathetic and outgoing nature which attracts emotional confession. She was at once generous and grasping. She never had a penny long.

Clio had been conscious that this woman marked her comings and goings; suspected her plans; coolly appraised her jewelry and her exhibitionistic outbursts. The plump good-natured face, like the Cheshire cat, seemed to materialize out of thin air. The humorous intelligent eyes seemed to be weighing her, evaluating her.

This morning, as Clio ascended the steps of the United States Hotel with Clint Maroon at her side, her quick eye noted the staring group in the center of the piazza, her dramatic instinct sensed a tense moment impending. A bevy of sycophantic mamas and daughters clustered round the chair of an imperious old woman; the captive Bart leaned over her, offering filial attentions.

Clio had walked to Congress Spring, she had taken a glass of the water, she was conscious of a feeling of unusual alertness and excitement. Maroon, having breakfasted at the stables, had driven swiftly to Congress Park and had picked her up and driven her to the hotel in spite of her halfhearted protests. Kaka and Cupide, who had accompanied her as always, had been tucked into the back seat of the high cart. It was this picturesque company upon which Madam Van Steed's eye now fell—fell, flickered and widened in astonishment. Cupide leaped down to hold the horses, Maroon in white hat, white full-skirted coat, Texas boots and fawn trousers, handed down a Clio all cream and black in cool India silk and a lush leghorn hat trimmed with lace and yellow roses. Cream lace and leghorn enhanced the black of her smooth hair, her creamy skin, accented the dark eyes; the cream-colored India silk was set off by black velvet bows. A lace-ruffled parasol made perfect the whole.

Up the piazza steps, Maroon's eyes warm upon her. The statuesque Kakaracou walked behind. Cupide scrambled up to the driver's seat to await Maroon's return.

"Bless my soul!" came the trumpet tones of Madam Van Steed. "What's this? We've not only a circus but a sideshow!"

There was a murmur of remonstrance from the wretched Bart and a snicker of amusement from the piazza collection.

Clio heard a murmur of French from Kaka in the rear. "The old devil has arrived, then, to protect her imp."

Clio nodded coolly in the direction of Van Steed, Maroon swept off the white sombrero in salute, the little group entered the hotel, but not before they heard the beldame's next words shrilled from her nook and evidently addressed to her son. "Who? De Chanfret? What's the world coming to! Well, run along, run after them, fetch her over to me, and the cowboy too. I want to see them."

Another murmur of remonstrance from the wretched Bart; another titter from the group. Hurried footsteps behind them; Bartholomew Van Steed caught up with them. He stood before them, his cheeks were very pink, his amber eyes held a look of pleading.

"Mrs. De Chanfret, my mother arrived unexpectedly last evening—she wants so much to meet you—uh—you, too, Maroon—if you'd—do you mind—she's out on the piazza—not very well, you know—heard so much about you———"

"But I'd be enchanted to meet your dear mother," Clio said; and tossing her parasol to Kaka she gaily tucked one hand in Bart's limp and unresponsive arm, the other in Maroon's, and so through the screened doorway and down the piazza's length, a radiant smiling figure squired by two devoted swains. Now Clio saw that the stout black-clad Bellop was among the group and yet apart from it. She was leaning against one of the piazza pillars, her hands on her broad hips, her mocking eyes regarding the scene before her with anticipatory relish.

She called out to Clio in her deep hearty voice, "Good morning, Countess! *Comment ça va!*" A look of friendly warning in her eye, a something in her tone.

Clio grinned. *"C'est ce que nous verrons."* That remains to be seen.

Stumblingly Van Steed began the introduction. "Mother, this is Mrs. De Chanfret—Colonel Maroon—my————"

"Howdy do! I hear you call yourself a countess."

"I call myself Mrs. De Chanfret."

"Touché!" boomed Mrs. Coventry Bellop.

"Colonel Maroon, eh?" the rasping voice went on. "What war was that? You look a bit young to have been a colonel in the Civil War, young man."

The Texan looked down at her, the sunburned face crinkled in laughter, the drawling voice had in it a note of amused admiration.

"Shucks, Ma'am, I'm no Colonel, any more than old Vanderbilt was a Commodore. You know how it is, Ma'am. Vanderbilt, he ran a Staten Island ferry and some scows loaded with cow manure, and that's all the Commodore he ever was."

In the little ripple of laughter that followed this the cold gray eyes shifted to Clio's lovely face. "That ninny, Bean, the head usher, couldn't find your husband's signature in the old hotel register. Isn't that odd!"

This is going to be bad, after all, Clio thought. Aloud she said, "Signature?"

"I've been coming to the United States Hotel for years. Before it was burned down and after it was rebuilt. I've met every well-known person that ever stopped here—in my day, that is. They saved the old registers from the big fire, you know. You'd be interested to see the signatures. There's the Marquis de Lafayette and General Burnside and General Grant and Washington Irving and even Joseph Bonaparte, the late King of Spain. But no Count of Trenaunay de Chanfret. You say he stayed here?"

"Incognito." Serenely. "When a French diplomat is in America on affairs of state connected with his country, it is sometimes wise to discard titles."

"Mother doesn't mean————" stammered Bart Van Steed, miserably.

Mrs. Coventry Bellop's hearty voice cut in. "She doesn't mean a thing—do you, Clarissa? It doesn't pay to inquire too closely into the background of us Saratoga summer folks. Now you, Clarissa, you call yourself a lady. But that doesn't necessarily mean you are one, does it! Come on, Mrs. De Chanfret. Let's take a turn in the garden along with this handsome Texan. It's too hot out here in the sun for a woman of my girth."

"Good day to you, Ma'am," said Maroon to Madam Van Steed; and bowed, the white sombrero held over his heart.

Clio looked into Sophie Bellop's steady eyes, and her own were warm with gratitude for this new ally. "The garden? That will be charming, dear Mrs. Bellop. . . . Enchanted to have met you, Madam Van Steed. You are all that your dear son had led me to expect."

Into the grateful coolness of the hotel lobby. "Phew!" exclaimed Mrs. Coventry Bellop inelegantly and wiped her flushed face. "The old hell-cat!" Then, as Clint Maroon stared at her with new eyes, she proceeded to take charge. "Look, Colonel, I want to talk to this young lady. You're probably off, anyway, to the track. By the way, that little jockey of yours—where did he ever race before?"

"Why—uh———" floundered Clint.

"He rode *Sans Nom* at Longchamp two years ago," Clio snapped, for she was by now cross, tired, hot. "What a curious custom you Americans have of asking questions!"

Mrs. Bellop's round white cheeks crinkled in a grin. "You're a wonderful girl," she boomed. "Run along, Colonel. Mrs. De Chanfret and I, we're going to have a little chat, just us girls."

He looked at Clio. "Would you care to go to the races at eleven?"

"I am weary of the races."

"We'll drive at three."

"I am bored with the parade of carriages, like a funeral procession, up and down this Broadway."

"What do you say to dinner out at the Lake?"

"I am sick to death of black bass—corn on the cob—red raspberries— ugh!"

"Why—honey———!"

Sophie Bellop's comfortable laugh cut the little silence. "That's Saratoga sickness. Everybody feels that way after two weeks. If you can stand it after two weeks of it you can stand it for two months, and like it." She waved him away with a flirt of her strangely small, lean hand. "She'll be all right by this evening. You run along, Colonel Maroon."

He looked at Clio. She nodded. He was off, his Texas boots tapping smartly on the flagstones, the broad shoulders straightening in relief at being out of this feminine pother.

Clio thought, I must be rid of this woman. There is a reason for this sudden friendliness. She held out her hand. "I hope you weren't too sharp, after all, with that very provincial old lady. But thank you. Good-by."

"Nonsense. I want to talk to you. It's important. Don't be silly, child."

"The garden?"

"No. Your room. We can talk there."

With a shrug Clio turned toward the cottages. Kakaracou was accustomed to surprises. Her face, as she opened the door, remained impassive. Only the eyes narrowed a little in suspicion.

"Make me some coffee, Kaka. Will you have some, Mrs. Bellop? I've had no breakfast. But these huge trays of heavy food—I can't face them any more. How I should love a crisp *croissant* with sweet butter! Ah, well." She took off the broad-brimmed leghorn with its heavy trimming of blond lace and roses and ribbons, she flung it on the table among a litter of books and trinkets and *bibelots*. The grim little hotel sitting room had, with her occupancy, taken on a luxurious and feminine air. Sophie Bellop's eyes, intelligent, materialistic, encompassed the room and its contents, stared openly, without obliqueness, into the bedroom beyond with its lacy pink pillows, its scent bottles, its flowers and yellow-backed French books and its froth of furbelows.

"If you'd ask me," boomed Sophie Bellop, "who I'd rather be than anyone in the world this minute, I'd say—you."

Clio had gone straight to the bedroom and, Southern fashion, she was unconcernedly getting out of her elaborate street clothes and into an airy ruffled wrapper. Thus she had seen Rita Dulaine and Belle Piquery do, thus she always would do. Kaka, on her knees, was unlacing her. Now, as Clio, in petticoats and corset cover, moved toward the door the better to gaze upon the astonishing Mrs. Bellop, Kaka too moved forward, still on her knees.

"Me!" Bare-armed, her hands on her hips, Clio stared in unbelief. "But why?"

Mrs. Bellop had discovered a dish of large meaty black cherries on the sitting-room table and was munching them and blowing the pits into her palm. "No reason. No reason, my girl, except that you're young and beautiful and smart and brassy and have two dashing young men in love with you—at least, poor Bart would be dashing if that old harridan didn't catch on to his coat-tails every time he tries to dash—and are going to be rich if you use some sense. That's all." She popped another cherry into her mouth.

Clio said nothing. She moved back into her bedroom. Her corsets came off; you heard a little sigh of relief as lungs and muscles expanded. The cool flimsy gabrielle enveloped her. "The coffee, Kaka. Quickly. In there. A napkin and bowl for Mrs. Bellop's hands."

She crossed the little sitting room then with her easy indolent stride and sank back against the lumpy couch whose bleakness was enlivened by the Spanish silk shawl of lemon yellow thrown over its back.

Mrs. Bellop, relieved of the cherry pits, relaxed in her chair, belched a little and began to drum dreamily on the marble table top with her slim sensitive fingers. A silence fell between the two women—a silence of deliberate waiting, weighing, measuring.

At last Clio spoke, deliberately. "Just what is it you want of me?"

"Money."

"I have no money."

"You will have."

"How?"

"By listening to me."

"You have no money. Why have you not listened to yourself?"

"Because I'm not you. I explained that to you a minute ago. And I've been a fool most of my life."

Kaka brought the coffee, fragrant, steaming. Clio sugared it generously, drank it, creamless, in great grateful gulps. "Ah! That's wonderful! Another cup, Kaka." Kaka, in the bedroom, busied herself with the India silk, the froth of garments lately discarded.

"Tell your woman to shut that door."

"It doesn't matter. Kaka knows everything. She never talks. If you mean me harm she would be likely to kill you. She would make a little figure like you, out of soap or dough, and she would stick pins in it through the place where the heart and the brain and the bowels would be if it were alive. And you'd sicken and die."

"Not I," retorted Mrs. Coventry Bellop, briskly. "I've had pins stuck in me all my life, and knives, too. Clarissa Van Steed alone would have been the death of me if I hadn't the hide of a rhinoceros."

Clio, sipping her second cup of coffee, set the cup down on the saucer now with a little decisive clack. "All my life, Mrs. Bellop, I have been very direct. If I wanted to do a thing, and it was possible to do it, I did it. I say what I want to say. That old woman on the piazza, she is a terrible old woman, she dislikes me, she makes no pretense. I rather admire her for it. I shall be grateful if you will be as honest." She placed the cup and saucer on the tabouret at her side; she leaned back and regarded the woman before her with a level look.

"You're a babe," Mrs. Bellop began, briskly, "if you think that old adder is honest. She isn't. But that's neither here nor there. You're right, she hates you and she wants to run you out of Saratoga and she'll do it unless————"

"Unless?"

Sophie Bellop spread her feet wide apart, leaned forward, rested her hands on her plump knees and looked Clio straight in the eye. "Look, my girl. I know you're no more the Comtesse de Trumpery and Choo-Choo than I am Queen Victoria. But if I say you are, if I take you in hand, if I stand up for you against this old buzzard and her crew, the world will believe you are. I've watched you now for two weeks. And I'll say this: you've been wonderful. Bold and dramatic and believable. But from now on you'll need a strong arm behind you, and that handsome Texan's arm won't be enough. It's got to be a woman who's smarter than old lady Van Steed and who they're scared of."

As the woman talked, Clio was thinking, well, here it is. I wonder if she knows everything. I suppose I was foolish to think that America was so simple. It's no good being grand and denying things and telling her to go.

"What is it you want?"

"I'm coming to that. Let me just rattle on a little, will you? I'm gabby, but what I've got to say to you is important to both of us. And I like you more than ever for not trying to pretend you don't know what I'm talking about. Now listen. I know my way around this world. I've known what it was to be very rich. I know what it is to be very poor; I've lived on nothing for years. In luxury."

"Blackmail?" inquired Clio, pleasantly, as one would say, for example—farming?

"Give me credit for being smarter than that. Listen, my child. You've been shrewd, but you can't beat this combination without inside help any more than you can beat the roulette and faro games at the Club House simply because you happen to win once or twice. You lose in the end unless you know how the wheel is fixed or can fix it yourself. Same with Saratoga; same way with everything. I know everybody. I've been everywhere. I know Europe. I know America. If I give a party that somebody else pays for, everybody comes because I'm giving it. Don't ask me why. I don't know. I'm nearly sixty. I dress and look like a washwoman, so the women are never envious of me and the men never fall in love with me and I have a fine time. I'm afraid of nobody. If you know anything about America, which you probably don't, you know that Coventry Bellop was one of the wealthiest of the really rich men of the 1860's. He was in on Erie—maybe you don't know what that meant and I won't go into it now—but the New York Central crowd took it away from him, and then Astor and Drew and old Van Steed and Fisk and Gould came in on Erie—well, when Covey died of a stroke in '69, I was left as bare as the day I was born and people began to call me not Sophie Bellop or Mrs. Coventry Bellop, but Poorsophiebellop, just like that, all in one word. Poorsophiebellop. The wives of the very men who'd ruined him. Not that I blame them. Covey'd have done the same to them if he'd been smart enough to beat them. Well, they thought Poorsophiebellop would take their old clothes and live in that fourth-floor back bedroom in a rich relation's house and be glad to be asked in for tea. Right then I made it my motto to insult them before they could insult me. I was earning my living—and fairly honestly, too—in a day when it wasn't just downright common and vulgar for a woman to work for her living the way it is now—it was considered criminal. Not that I really worked. I schemed. I planned. I tricked and contrived. I made certain hotels fashionable by touting for them. I put Saratoga on the map. I made Newport, though I must say I can't bear the place. Remember, I've known the cream of two continents in my day—Daniel Webster, Washington Irving, Henry Clay, William Makepeace Thackeray, Henry James, for brains—not to speak of rich riffraff like the Astors, Drew, Jim Hill, the Vanderbilts, the Goulds, and plenty of dressed-up circus mountebanks like Jim Fisk and his brawling crew. As for the gloating friends like Clarissa Van Steed and the rich relations—I threw their cast-off clothes back in their faces and I snapped my fingers at the hall bedrooms. If I'd been a beauty, like you, I could have had the world. I don't know, though. There's always been a soft streak in me that crops out when I least want it. Now Bellop. I knew he was weak when I married him. But his eyes were so blue and he cried when I refused him. I thought I could make him strong and self-reliant. But you can't make iron out of lead. . . . So then, there I was, a widow and a pauper; I had two black dresses, one for daytime, one for evening, and that's been my uniform ever since. I don't bother about clothes and it's wonderful. Nobody cares how I look, anyway. I'm the life of the party. Most people don't know how to have a good time, any more than spoiled children. I show them. I spend their money for them, and they're grateful for it. I've got nothing to lose because I live by my wits. They can't take that away from me. So I say and I do as I please. It's a grand feeling."

Clio laughed suddenly, spontaneously, in sheer delight. "You're like Aunt Belle. It's wonderful!"

"Who's she?"

"Mama's sister. My Aunt Belle Piquery. Only she was more—well—légére. But she used a word—a Northern word. Spunky. She used to say she liked people with spunk."

"M'm. I know about your mama. I made it my business to find out. I've got connections in New Orleans."

"Then it is blackmail, after all?"

"No, child. I tell you I like you. And I hate Clarissa Van Steed and everything she stands for. She and women like her have kept America back fifty years. Hard and rigid and provincial. And mean. She's got the ugliest house in New York; the curtains at her front windows amount to a drawbridge moat and bastion. What's a bastion, anyway?"

Clio laughed again. "You came here just to talk. But I think you are really wonderful. The one amusing person I have met in America."

"That's right. Keep up that French accent. Your natural theater sense is one of your most valuable assets—though sometimes you overdo it. . . . So you're set on marrying little Bart Van Steed, eh?"

"I do not think that concerns you."

"You can't do it without me. He hasn't asked you yet, and he never will, now that the old devil's here, unless he's properly managed."

Suddenly, "I do not think I care to go on with this conversation."

But Sophie Bellop blithely waved aside this blunt statement which Clio had followed by rising as though to end the visit. Brightly, chattily, she went on, her attitude more relaxed now, her big body leaning comfortably against the chair back.

"Sit down, child, and stop fussing. Now then. Bart's really rich. I don't mean just rich—he's got seventy, eighty millions if he's got a cent and even if the Gould crowd trick him out of the trunk line————"

Clio sat down then. "You know about that, too?"

"Of course. I'm coming to that later. Maroon. Let's see—what was I saying? Oh, yes. Well, I've watched you like a hawk, you're a smart girl, you've got the jaw of success, and if you manage that big handsome brute right, even if he isn't as smart as you are—oh, I forgot, you're set on marrying Van Steed instead. Well, perhaps you're right, but I suppose if I had it to do I'd be a fool and marry the Texan though he hasn't a penny. I never could resist a magnificent specimen like that. Those shoulders, and small through the hips, and the way he looks at you. Ah, me! Well, lucky I haven't turned

silly in my old age. I play the piano like an angel, I never forget a face, I'm
healthy, I don't nip away at a bottle the way some women do, my age, poor
things."

She had not yet put her cards on the table. Her handsome shrewd eyes
were on Clio; she was talking now in order to give the girl time in which to
digest what she had heard. "They'll be after you now; they've only been
waiting for a leader; they'll tear you to pieces if you try to go it alone from
now on. But they're afraid of me. It was I who fixed on the number Four
Hundred for the Centennial Ball in '76. You probably don't know about that.
Most of the world thinks that Ward McAllister and Mrs. William Astor
picked the Four Hundred. But the inner circle knows I did it. More heads
fell that winter than at the time of the Bastille. Those daughters and granddaughters of peddlers and butchers and fur dealers and land grabbers are
afraid of me because I'm not scared of them. And I give them a good time,
poor dears, and show them how to have fun with their money."

Now that Clio Dulaine understood thoroughly, she put her question
bluntly. "How much do you want?"

"Understand," parried Mrs. Coventry Bellop, "you don't need anyone
to manage you; you've been clever as can be from the very first. That
spectacular entrance and then disappearing for two days. They nearly died.
I see you've got a crest on almost everything. Can't make it out, though."

"Kaka embroiders so beautifully. My name is Clio. She combined that
with the crest of the Duc de Chaulnes and part of the coat-of-arms of the
Dulaines. Sometimes I use just the plain letter C, with a vine or a wreath."

Sophie Bellop burst into laughter. "That's what I mean. You're a natural
success. You have the right instinct. Nothing can stop you—with me behind
you."

"How much do you want?"

"Of course," Mrs. Bellop rattled on, "you've got the right to help yourself
to a couple of crests and titles. Look at the people who've come over this
land like vultures. Not only Americans. Lord Dunmore's got a hundred
thousand acres of good American land if he's got a grain. Dunraven's got
sixty thousand up in Colorado. We're fools. We're fools. We think it can
go on forever. Too much of everything. I'll bet in another hundred years or
even less we'll find out. We'll be a ruined country unless they stop this
grabbing. We'll be so soft that anybody can come and take us like picking
a ripe plum. It's something to scare you, this country, I always say. There's
never been anything like it. Floods, grasshoppers, snowstorms—never
anything in moderation. Too hot or too cold or too high or too big. The
whole West from North Dakota on buried in snow last winter. You can't
begin to———"

"How much do you want?"

"I think you can get him if you want him. Mrs. Porcelain's too Dolly
Vardenish and pink for him. And the Forosini's too common. I'm nearly
sixty. I won't live more than another ten or twelve years. I'll take twenty-
five thousand down on the day of your settlement and ten thousand a year
for ten years. I don't want to be grasping."

"How do you know—how do I know—that I can't do this alone?"

"Very well. Try it."

"Or suppose, together, we don't succeed. Then what?"

"Nothing. You'll have learned from me and I from you. You can give me
a present—something negotiable, I hope. Now then, I like everything in
writing, black on white. It saves a lot of rumpus in the end."

The sound of swift, light footsteps on the cottage veranda, the hall door opened and shut, a tap at the door of the little sitting room. Clio stood up, an unaccustomed scarlet suddenly showing beneath the cream-white skin.

"Come in!"

Maroon's height and breadth seemed to fill the little room. He brought with him the smell of the stables and of barber's ointment and cigars and leather.

The lusty Sophie sniffed the air. "You smell nice and masculine. It's grand."

His blue plainsman's eyes looked from Clio to Sophie and back again. "You two plotting something? You look guilty as all hell."

Clio trailed her laces over to him, she picked up his great hand, she looked at it intently as though examining it for the first time. An intimate gesture, childlike. "Mrs. Bellop is going to be my—my chaperon."

He grinned. "Little late, I'd say."

Mrs. Bellop stood up and shook herself like an amiable poodle. "Not too late. We hope."

He eyed Clio straight. "Not too late for—what?"

Clio dropped his hand then and walked to the window that looked out on the sun-dappled garden. She shrugged her shoulders evasively.

Mrs. Bellop furnished a brisk answer. "For social success and a brilliant marriage—with someone who is really mad about her. You know who." She came over to Maroon, the plump poodle looked saucily up at the mastiff. "Though I'll say this: how any girl can look at any other man when you're around is more than I can see. If I was twenty years younger—well—twenty-five, say—I'd snatch you off if I had to drug you to do it. Speaking of drugs, that horse of yours—well, we won't go into that. Thanks for the tip, though. Comes in handy when a girl's got her own way to make. . . . What was I saying—oh, yes. If she wants to marry money, why, that's her business. I did. And now look at me. But don't think I'm going to neglect you, dear boy. I've got a scheme I want you to present to Bart Van Steed—you can say you thought of it—and I'll swear it will save that trunk line of the Albany and Tuscarora from falling into the clutches of———"

"Hold on there! Hold on! Just because Clio there has got me saddle broke don't get the idea that you can gentle me. If Clio is hankering for social success and a brilliant marriage, and you're the one to rope and tie the bridegroom, why here's wishing you luck. But you got me wrong, sister. When it comes to riding my own range, why, I'm the one that wears the pants. That matter, Clio, I'd say—only I don't want to get mixed up in any woman business—I'd say you've gone this far alone, I'd go the rest of the way and play the game out."

Slowly, as though emerging from a spell, Clio turned from the window. "You would?" she said, uncertainly. "You would?"

"Sure would. You're smarter than any woman in this town. Go it alone. . . . Sa-a-ay, that coffee sure smells good. Kaka! How about rustling me a cup!"

Clio Dulaine walked over to Mrs. Bellop. She held out her hand. "Thank you so much, Mrs. Bellop. You have been so kind. Don't think me ungrateful. I like you. But he is right."

Mrs. Bellop looked from one to the other, she laughed a little discomfited laugh. "Well, you can't say I didn't warn you."

"You are wonderful. So honest. And really good. Here. Please take this." To her own surprise Clio took a ring from her finger, pressed it into Mrs. Bellop's hand. "You are the only woman who has shown me kindness."

"Women," murmured Mrs. Bellop as she turned the ring this way and that to catch the light, "are a hundred years behind the times. They don't know their own strength. Some day they'll catch up with themselves and then this will be a different world. Look here, Clio, I'm going to stay behind you anyway, not being bossy but just in case. And just to prove to you I like you I'm going to keep your ring. Giving it to me is the first foolish thing you've done. Hang onto your jewelry, I always say. It's a woman's best friend.''

15

SUDDENLY CLIO DULAINE felt herself curiously alone in Saratoga; not alone merely, but neglected. She had arrived at an impasse. She knew she must break through this or devise another way. Her flouncings, her paradings, her dramatic entrances, her outrageous flouting of the conventions had begun to pall on her audience. Her sure dramatic sense warned her of this. At this crucial moment her two swains had grown distrait and even neglectful.

"Business," Clint would say, when she reproached him. "I'd like to go along with you, honey, but I've got a little matter of business to tend to. Now, Bart, he'd come a-running if he knew you wanted to drive out. Why'n't you send Cupide over with a note?"

"How dare you!" she would say, melodramatically.

Innocently, almost absently, he would stare at her. "What's up? Have I said something? I didn't go to."

"How dare you say to me that you're busy! And suggest that I go about begging other men to take me here and there! Perhaps the kind of women you have——"

"Hold on! I didn't say anything about other men. I said Bart. He's the man you're fixing to marry."

"Oh, so that's it. You're jealous."

"Oh. Yes. Uh-huh. Leastways, I would be if I had time. But I am busier than a sheep dog. Look, I'm seeing Van Steed right soon. Shall I tell him?"

"Get out! Get out of my sight!"

There was about him nothing of the chagrined suitor. On the contrary, he seemed elated and thoroughly the male pleased with himself. This in itself was sufficiently annoying to the high-handed Clio. But now, to her bewilderment, the timorous Van Steed was sometimes guilty of similiar conduct. Even in her company he actually seemed unconscious of her presence. It wasn't a lessening of his devotion, she felt, nor of Clint's. It was an intangible barrier that had come up between her and them. Her small personal plans seemed insignificant. From first place she sensed herself relegated to second position. Awaiting a reply to a question, she would find Van Steed's face blank. A silence. Then, "Oh, I beg your pardon! What was that you said? I was thinking——" he would stammer.

Baffled, Clio turned waspishly on Kakaracou and Cupidon. But in Cupide she encountered the same maddening preoccupation with something beyond her ken. Do this, do that, she would snap at him. But his goggle gaze would be fixed dreamily on some inner vision. "Do you hear me, you *suppôt!*"

"Did you say something, Ma'm'selle?"

Kaka, brushing the girl's hair and seeing the wrathful face in the mirror, attempted to offer her soothing solution.

"They cooking up something. Don't you fuss your head. They doing business."

"I don't care what they're doing. I'm bored with it here, anyway. Silly place, third-rate, provincial. Mama would have loathed it. I think I shall leave next week.''

At this Cupide set up a howl of protest. "No! I won't go! I won't go!''

Clio surveyed the dwarf through narrowed lids. "Oh, you won't go, is that what I hear!'' Then, in a surprising shout that topped his own, "Why not? Why not, *petit drôle?* Quick! Answer me!''

"Business,'' said Cupide. "I have business.''

With practiced ease he dodged as she reached swiftly for the hairbrush and let fly at him.

The truth of it was that he had. Van Steed had business. Maroon had business. Cupidon, blessed by nature with keyhole height, had made their business his.

Even when they had no engagement, Clint had always rushed to her side at sight of her, whether in the garden, at the springs, in the lobby, on the piazza. Van Steed's method had been less forthright, yet he too had seemed always somehow to be standing near, even if his mother's hand clutched his arm as she leaned on him not only for support but to stay him. Yet now she could pass the two men as they stood in the lobby talking together earnestly, seriously, and her bewilderment mounted to fury as they bowed and held their hats aloft with the kind of exaggeration which comes of absentminded courtesy. They were thinking of something other than herself; they were so deeply interested in what they were saying that she, Clio Dulaine, was actually only another woman passing. She listened sharply as she undulated by. The Texan's drawling voice:

"The government ought to get back of the railroads. Now, take Texas. It's a young state run by young men. Neither I nor my father before me cared a hoot for public office but railroads———''

"In arriving at the cost of production less depreciation, why, the local conditions such as service required and maintenance———''

Then for three days he was gone. He had announced his going, casually, the night before his departure. A shade too casually.

"Almost forgot to tell you, honey, I'm taking a little trip on business.'' This was the new Clint Maroon, in the saddle, and, as he phrased it, rarin' to go.

"Where? Where are you going?''

"Oh, Albany. Albany and New York.''

"What for? You used to tell me everything. What are you keeping from me?''

"I'm showing your little friend Van Steed that he can't go on trying to make agreements with these pirates. Next thing he knows they're going to get more than that little trunk-line railroad away from him. Maybe his pa left him millions, but hanging on to'em is something different.''

"Oh, really! If you know so much about making millions why don't you tell him this?''

"I did. I said, look, Van Steed, the way you're going I reckon you'll lose your piece of railroad and what goes with it. What's it mean to you, losing that hundred miles of coal haul? In figures, I mean. You know how he is, him and his kind. Afraid to give you a straight answer to a straight question. Well, what do I know about railroads and so on? Nothing! I said, will you give me a share in the road if I save it for you? Save it how? he said. Fighting it out, I told him, the way we used to fight the sheep men to save the cattle range.''

Clio stared, aghast. "But Clint, you can't do that! This isn't the Wild West.''

"Worse. It's the wild East. They've got the shareholdings deadlocked down there now. The board of directors are divided, half the Erie crowd, half the Morgan-Van Steed crowd. They actually wrestle for the stock books. I mean wrestle. Van Steed, he's about ready to give up; he's not much of a scrapper. But this J. P. Morgan, he's the boy for my money. I never thought I'd be in a railroad fight, but say, honey, this last week I've had more fun than any time since I came up North from Texas. And they're paying me for it. A fistful of shares if we————''

She grasped his arm, she shook him as though to bring him to his senses. "This is a dangerous business. What do they care for you! What are you doing down there! What is it you have been doing this week away from me? Tell me!''

"Well, I got a gang together from here and around. Went away to New York for some of 'em—there's quite a bunch of Texas boys around, you'd be surprised. Hard times. Hard times. Look at the wealth in the country, and hundreds and thousands begging in the streets. Look at Frick, a millionaire at thirty! Look at Carnegie down at the Thompson Steel Works, getting a hundred and thirty percent for his money. Pirates. You can't deal with 'em. You have to fight 'em, barehanded. That's how I put it to Morgan, and I'll say this for him, he was with me. There's been scraps in every railroad station along the line, but last week—time I was away there—we got wind of the plan they had to take over the office headquarters at Albany by force. Sent up a bunch of brass-knuckle boys and mavericks, said they were deputies, with fake badges pinned on'em. Well, say, honey, force is what they got. I had the boys rounded up, so when Jim Briscoe and his gang of thugs stepped through the door expecting to find nobody but old Gid Fish with his eyeshade on and sleeve-protectors, why, Briscoe he yelled, 'Rush in, boys, and take possession! Throw him out! Grab the books!' That's where we came in, yelling like Comanches and threw the whole crowd, Briscoe first of all, right down the stairs of the Tuscarora office. You never saw such a boiling of arms and legs there at the foot of the stairs. Nobody hurt serious— couple arms and legs and so on—but we were laughing so, seeing their faces, we like to fell down the stairs ourselves, on top of 'em.''

Clio clasped her hands to her head, as nearly distraught as he had ever seen her. "I won't listen. I won't listen!''

"Why, Clio, honey, you asked me what I'd been up to, didn't you?''

"But it's savage! It's disgusting!''

"Y-e-e-es,'' he drawled. "Perfectly disgusting.'' His tone, so quiet, so even, was venomous. "Almost as disgusting as what they did to my folks. A real delicate little flower like you, brought up in Paris and so on, you wouldn't understand. No! Van Steed, he's more your kind. Ladylike, he wouldn't hurt a fly. Pay somebody, though, to swat the fly for him.''

"*Chéri,* we didn't come here to this Saratoga to fight railroads.''

"Oh, yes we did.''

"To fight them with tricks, yes, and to get some of their millions if we could. But not to fight with fists and boots, like savages. I am frightened. I am frightened—for you.''

But the surly mood was still on him. There had been a time when he would have melted at this evidence of her solicitude, but now he said sneeringly, "Say, that's fine! I've got you to look after me, and little Bart, he's got his mama, why, no boogy man can get us thataway.''

Clio had battles of her own in plenty by now, but these brutal tales of Clint Maroon's adventures in railroading filled her with apprehension. Bewildered, she brought up the subject as casually as possible when next she saw Van Steed. It was interesting to see his struggles, buffeted as he now was between the filial habit of years and the powerful new emotion which this beautiful and unconventional woman had aroused in him. Inexperienced in love and wary of its unexplored dangers, he tried rather clumsily to be in her company when the maternal eye was not upon him.

"Uh—Mrs. De Chanfret—I—I hear you have a charming apartment in the cottages with your own beautiful—uh—bric-a-brac and ornaments and—uh—so forth. I never have had the privilege of seeing you surrounded by your—uh—own personal—that is————"

"Who told you this?"

"Why, Mrs. Bellop, I believe. That is, Mrs. Bellop."

"What an amazing woman! What energy! She has been most friendly to me."

"Would you—could I come to call some—some afternoon, perhaps, and have—that is—tea? You never have invited me, you know." He felt very audacious.

"Tea! I never could understand tea—except as medicine, of course. At night, when I am weary, Kaka brews me a tisane to soothe me. But tea as tea!"

"Oh, well, I just meant—you know—tea as a—a—symbol—I mean————"

"Dear Mr. Van Steed, that is almost as if you meant to sound improper!"

"Oh, no, Mrs. De Chanfret. I assure you!" It was too easy to bring the deeper pink into the already roseate cheeks.

"I was only teasing. Do come—tomorrow afternoon? And perhaps your mama would like to come, too." With innocent cordiality.

"I'm afraid not. She rarely goes anywhere; she isn't well, you know. Rheumatism—her age—difficult."

"So I have heard. It is diffiicult to believe. She is so very—alert." Then the direct attack. "Your mama does not like me."

"Oh, I wouldn't say that, Mrs. De Chanfret."

"Oh, it's quite natural. There are reasons, natural and unnatural. She wants to keep you by her—wait! I don't mean to offend you. She herself probably would be the first to deny it. She fears—and hates—any young and attractive woman who may snatch you from her. Particularly one like myself who is not of her little world—who is not *chacalata*."

"Not what? What's that mean?"

"Oh, that's a word, a foreign sort of word, it means conventional—*comme il faut*. It's a word out of my childhood. Well, she has nothing to fear from me, dear Mr. Van Steed. My heart lies buried in my beloved France." She saw the stubborn look come into his face. I've almost got him, she thought, exultantly. And even as this conviction came to her she perversely put it away from her. How silly he looks simpering at me like that! "Tomorrow afternoon, then. And do bring your dear mama if she cares to come."

He came alone, as she had known he would. She had set her stage. The heritage of Great-Grand'mére Bonnevie, the actress, always welled strong in her at times such as this. She wore simple white with the little girlish strand of pearls as ornament; she looked young, cool, virginal. Bart Van Steed, staring at her in the dim seclusion of the sitting room, blurted his thoughts as always.

"You look—different."

"Different?" She put one hand to her breast, posed fingers up like that portrait of the Empress Louise.

"Younger. That is, younger."

"Oh dear Mr. Van Steed! Have I seemed so old!"

It was too easy to make him blush, stammer, fidget. "No! No! Only about the hotel and in the evening and at the races you always seemed so much more—that is—your clothes usually so sophisticated and now you look"—fatuously—"you are like a little girl."

"Oh, Mr. Van Steed! How sweet! How sweet of you! After all, I was widowed at nineteen———"

Kaka and two black waiters crackling in stiffly starched linens now appeared with the tea-things. "Tea!" Van Steed cried in considerable dismay.

"You said tea," Clio reminded him, gently.

They sipped, stirred, munched. Years of this, Clio thought, grimly. Millions and security—but years of this.

Kaka in her best silk and best manner served them, shooing away the hotel waiters who had brought the tray.

"Wouldn't you rather have something cold to drink, perhaps?" Clio suggested, for he had placed the cup, almost untouched, on the table beside his chair. "Lemonade, or one of Kaka's delicious rum———"

"No. No, really. My digestion. Uh———"

"I have asked dear Mrs. Bellop to drop in, since your mama couldn't chaperon us. Not that we need a chaperon. A poor old widow like myself."

His pink face clouded with displeasure. "Mrs. Bellop!" Then hastily, "I wanted to ask you—could I fetch you for the ball tonight? I'd be delighted to call for you."

"I should have loved it. But I've promised to go with Colonel Maroon."

"Maroon's away." Bluntly.

"Yes. Yes, I know. But he'll be back. He assured me he would be back." She leaned forward. Something in his face alarmed her. "He went only to Albany, he said. Tell me, isn't this Albany very near Saratoga?"

"Why, yes. You passed it on your way traveling here in the train. Must have."

"Colonel Maroon has told me it is the capital of the state of New York."

"Yes. That's right."

"But Mr. Van Steed! I am bewildered. I cannot understand! What manner of country is this! There in Albany, the capital of the state, I hear that hordes of—of roughs they fight like savages for a railroad. Where are the laws! Where are the police! The military!"

The tale of banditry had seemed fantastic enough coming from the lips of the big Texan; but now to hear it retold and augmented by the shy and pink-cheeked Van Steed had the effect of wild absurdity.

"Oh. Well. You see, they've bought up the town councilors and so on." Very matter-of-factly. "We've met trick with trick and bribe with bribe. It's a matter of—uh—force now, you know." He patted her hand timidly. "You shouldn't worry your pretty head about such matters, dear Mrs. De Chanfret. In fact, Colonel Maroon shouldn't have told you. It's—uh—man's business."

She looked at him scornfully. "Really! What are you doing about it? You yourself, I mean."

He smiled tolerantly. "I'm afraid you wouldn't understand. But I may tell you—in confidence—that we now have possession of the Albany end of the road. Briscoe and his crowd have retreated to the Binghamton end." He looked about him, cautiously. He lowered his voice. "Traffic has stopped entirely. The people living along the line are terrified. We are planning to send down fully five hundred men by train and take the stations along the Binghamton route by force."

"Whose plan is this?"

"Well, Colonel Maroon proposed it, really———"

Suddenly, like a madness, little darts of rage and hate shot through her body; she wanted to hurt this shy and nervous little man, she hated him, she hated Saratoga, she hated the hotel, Madam Van Steed, Congress Spring, the race track, the lake, the food, the piazza, the world. She felt her fingers tingling with the desire to strike him—to slap him across his delicate pink face.

In a fury of cruelty she said, "You are afraid. You are afraid to fight for your own railroad, you are afraid of your mother, you are afraid of me, you are afraid of life, you are afraid of everything! Go away! Go away! I want to be alone."

She saw the look in his amber eyes; she saw the color drain out of his face. Abruptly she left him, flew to her room, fell to berating Kaka, and ended in a burst of tears, a thing in itself so rare in her that even Kakaracou was alarmed. The man in the front room stood a moment, his palms pressed to his eyes. Then he went, closing the front door gently.

In Kaka's arms, her head against the bony breast, she sniffled, "I detest this place! I wish I had never come. I wish we had stayed in Paris. I wish we had stayed in New Orleans. At least we belonged there. After a fashion. Even he doesn't care any more; he leaves me alone. Alone!"

Kaka rocked her to and fro. *"Pauvre bébé!* My pretty one, like my beautiful Rita! Alone."

But at that Clio Dulaine sat up, dried her eyes. *"Idiote!* I am not Rita! I am Clio! And I shall make my life as I said. No whining and weeping for me. There! I'm strong again. I'll show them, those devils who sit all day on the piazza brewing their witches' brew! And what do you think, he goes to fight like a common *Apache* in railroads!"

Kaka sniffed her disdain. "That *vacher!* That *gascon* with his swagger!"

Hearing him attacked by another, Clio now sprang to his defense. "He is no *gascon.* He doesn't swagger. He is too brave, that's the trouble. He fights the battles of little men who are too weak and cowardly to fight their own."

"You know what I think?" Kakaracou went on, maddeningly. "I think we have seen the last of him, that one. I hear he is to have a big lump of money for this work he is doing like a roustabout on the docks in New Orleans."

Fortunately it was a powder puff that Clio was holding in her right hand. If it had been a paperweight, a knife, a lump of iron, it would have been the same. She threw it into Kaka's face, she began to scream in French, English and Gombo, somewhat to her own surprise, epithets she had not known she knew. *"Cochonne!* Black devil! *Carencro!* Congo! Witch from hell! How dare you say he will not come back! He'll be back for the ball tonight. He promised me. He is going in real cowboy costume—chaps and spurs and lariat—and Cupide is———"

"Cupide is—where?" Kaka interrupted, her voice ominous.

"Cupide? Why—I haven't seen him today. I suppose he's over at the stables again; he fancies himself since he stole that race. I'll have a talk with him, that *suppôt!"*

"Cupide is with him."

"He can't be! Howdo you know?"

"For days now he has been pleading to go with him."

"Yes, but he refused to take him. I heard him."

"They have some big dangerous plan. I know that. Cupide knew it too. He listened. He must have hidden himself somewhere when the Maroon went off, and now he is with him. I know. I am sure."

"I'll whip him myself. I'll take my riding crop and I'll———What's that plan? What dangerous plan? Tell me!"

"Something crazy. He is driving to this Albany, then a train, the lot of them, toward a town———"

"Binghamton?"

"Yes, that's it. There are a lot of them, they are going to take each station along the way, Cupide said, as if they were fighting in a war—it is crazy I tell you—bizarre, like this place—this Saratoga—I tell you if anything happens to Cupide because of him, I'll kill him, I'll———"

Now it was Clio who was comforting the black woman, her arms about Kaka's meager shoulders, her lovely cheek pressed against the withered one.

"What stupid talk Kaka. Nothing will happen to them. We are simply not used to the way things are done here. We've been gone so long. It is like that in America. It is quite the thing. If you want a thing—land—a railroad—you simply take it. *Drôle, ça.*"

The Negress shook her head. "I tell you it's not good, I don't like it. Railroads. And fights with engines. What has Cupide to do with railroads! I tell you———" Her high thin voice rose in a wail.

Brisk knuckles rapped at the door. A hearty voice boomed, "What's going on here!"

Kaka jerked herself erect. "That great cow!" Miraculously she assumed her usual dignity like a garment as she opened the door. Sophie Bellop bounced in, a bombazine ball.

"What a to-do! I could hear you across the garden, screeching like a couple of fishwives. And Bart Van Steed looking up at your window as if he had seen a ghost. You can't afford to do this, Clio."

"I can afford to do what I please. What do I care for these old gossips? I spit on them. . . . Kaka, mix me a *coquetier*. I have been very upset. Will you have a *coquetier*, Mrs. Bellop?"

"What's that?"

"That is a little drink to hearten and steady one. A *coquetier* it is called. Aunt Belle used to take one when she felt upset. She used to let me taste hers, and Mama would scold her, but I loved it."

"Oh, no! Not for me. It's a drink, is it? I take nothing. You know that."

"No, no, it's a medicine, really. Aunt Belle said it was brought to New Orleans from Santo Domingo by Peychaud, the apothecary. Bitters, and a dash of cognac, and a twist of lemon peel. He mixed it in an egg-shaped cup. That's why it's called a *coquetier*. Lovely. Do just sip it, to try."

"Well, I'll just taste it, that's all, to please you."

Kaka glimpsed a black waiter, white-coated, crossing the garden. "Ice!" she bawled, thrusting her head out of the window. "Ice! For *coquetier!*"

Sophie Bellop shook her head reproachfully. "You folks have outlandish manners. It's all very well to be original, I think that's very clever, but with everyone against you as they are now———"

"Pooh! What do I care!" Clio curled herself up on the hard little sofa, she kicked off her slippers, she rolled up the voluminous sleeves of her gown. "Phew! It is hot here in this miserable Saratoga. I shall be glad to go. I think I shall go to the mountains. Where are there mountains here? Like the Alps."

Sophie Bellop's usually placid face was serious. "In this country we'd consider the Alps as foothills. Anyway, you're not going. Now look here. You've done wonderfully until now. All of a sudden you're behaving like a ninny. What's come over you?"

"*Ennui.* I am bored with Saratoga. With these railroad *parvenus*. I thought it would be wonderful to be very rich and secure and respectable for the rest of my life. Well, look at them. They're afraid of one another, they're afraid of me! Bart Van Steed is a *lâche*. The old one is a shrew and a devil. That Forosini and the Porcelain have the taste of vulgar provincials.''

"Yes, well, let's stop all this fancy talk and be sensible.''

"Sensible! Sensible! Sensible about what?''

"About the way you're behaving. It's really kind of crazy.''

"Oh *zut!* You have found out. You learn everything. Very well. I have done something wrong. I told little Van Steed he is a coward. What do I care! I managed before I came to this Saratoga. I can manage again.''

"But it's turned out right—or it may. Listen to me, child————''

But an imp of contrariness dominated the girl. "Ah, Kaka! There you are! Drink that, Mrs. Bellop, and then we shall be as sensible as sensible can be.'' She took the little glass from Kaka, she sniffed, she tasted, she nodded in approval, she quaffed it down. Potent, slightly bitter, the *coquetier* seemed to leap like a tiny tongue of liquid flame from her throat down to her vitals. Mrs. Bellop sipped, said, "Ugh! Bitter as gall,'' made a wry face, drank it down. "What's that you called it?''

"*Coquetier.*''

"Oh, now I get it. *Coquetier.* Cocktail! Of course. What's that in it? Brandy? Well, if that's medicine, everybody in Saratoga is going to have the complaint it's good for. I'll tell the barman at the Club about it. No, I won't have another, and neither will you. Give me the recipe, there's a good girl. I'll make old Spencer pay me for it.''

Clio's lip curled a little, contemptuously. "Kaka, Mrs. Bellop would like the recipe for the *coquetier*. Tell Cupide to write it out————'' Suddenly she remembered, she sat up, she pushed her hair away from her brow with a fevered frantic gesture. "Cupide went with him. He ran away and went with him to that mad—that insane—place where they battle like savages for a piece of railroad track! I don't understand this country! I don't understand. And now Clint is gone and Cupide is gone and you''—she turned blazing eyes on Kakaracou—"you will go next, I suppose. Why don't you go! Why don't you————''

Calmly and majestically, Kaka gathered up the little glasses and the great tumbler in which she had mixed the drink. A portion of the red-brown concoction still remained. "Is too hot for *coquetier*,'' she observed, and nonchalantly emptied the contents of the tumbler into the hotel cuspidor. "Why'n't you catch yourself a little nap, Miss Clio?'' She shot a malignant glance at Sophie Bellop, patted a couch pillow invitingly, then pressed her strong withered hand on the girl's shoulder. "Kaka is not going leave her Clio *bébé*.''

"Everybody can leave me! I don't need anyone! I'm not like Mama and Aunt Belle. I'm strong, I'm clever, I'm free!'' The tears were rolling down her cheeks.

"Well, good God!'' exclaimed Mrs. Bellop. "What was in that cocktail thing, Kaka?''

Kaka shook her head. She was all deep-south Negress, the veneer of Paris, of Northern travel was gone. "He like this when he tired.''

"He! He who? Oh, my God, I never heard such talk. What's wrong with you two! You've reverted right back to—to whatever it was you came from. Now you listen to me, Clio.''

"Go away,'' Clio said, sleepily. "Go away.''

"I'll do nothing of the kind. You're right on the doorstep—or threshold or whatever they call it—of success, and I'm not going to let you stop now. So quit rolling your eyes and listen to me. You can make the match of the year. I know a man head over heels in love when I see one. And he is, even if you did screech at him like a fishwife. He's used to being screeched at by a woman. He'd never marry anyone who wasn't stronger than his ma. And you're that. Besides, I need the money—and I like you. Are you listening?''

"You have said nothing."

"All right then. You're going to hear something. Bart and his ma have had a terrible quarrel. Oh, I thought that would make you open those eyes. The old devil is wild. Bart told her that he wasn't afraid of her any more— that he hated her—that he was in love with you. The chambermaid on their floor is paid to—that is, she does some laundry work for me, you understand. She said it was awful; she thought the old lady would have a stroke. Miss Diggs was dousing her with eau de cologne and spirits of ammonia and she slapped Diggs' face—not that that matters, but I just thought you'd like— well, she said she was going to run you out of town—out of the country— out of———''

"There is no other place," Clio murmured, her lids half closed, "except out of the world, and I don't think the poor old lady will have the courage to murder me. Do you?'' She cocked an amused eye at Sophie Bellop. One eye. The other was closed.

"Stop that! This is no laughing matter, I tell you."

"Oh, but let us laugh, anyway. The world—life—is no laughing matter. But one must laugh."

"If I hadn't seen with my own eyes that you'd had only one of those cocktail things, I'd say you were just plain drunk. Even though you're not, I ought to march right out of here and leave you. But I'm not going to be beaten by that old buzzard, Van Steed. It's a matter of pride."

"Pride," echoed Clio in a maddening murmur. "That is what the Dulaines have. I am a Dulaine, but not *chacalata*. I have very little pride, really."

"You're talking nonsense. Listen. Do you know what the old woman said to her son? And what she's saying to everyone in the hotel? That you're not a countess at all; that you're not even Mrs. De Chanfret; that you're an adventuress; that you've got a touch of the tarbrush!"

Clio now settled herself rather cozily as for a nap. "There is much in what she says. She is no fool, that old *mégère*."

The patience of the good-natured Bellop snapped. She bounced out of her chair, she shook Clio's shoulder, she stood over her in elephantine anger. "No, but you are. If I weren't sure that creepy woman of yours would put a knife into me, I'd slap you here and now. I'm only talking to you out of kindness of my heart."

"And out of your hatred for Mama Van Steed."

"You're an ungrateful brat!"

Clio sprang up, she took Sophie Bellop's hand, she looked beseechingly into her face. "I am! I am! But I am so troubled. I don't know what is the matter with me. Suddenly I don't care. I don't care about the very thing for which I've worked and planned and schemed."

"Maybe that's because you've almost got it."

"You think so?"

"Of course. Where's your spirit! He's never looked at a woman before, except just by way of politeness. When he came here today it was on the tip of his tongue to ask you to marry him. I'm sure of it. That's why I stayed away until I saw him come out, wobbling like a man who'd been hit. I don't say you'd make a suitable wife for him—but then, you wouldn't make a suitable wife for anyone—unless it was a Bengal tiger. You like him, don't you? Of course you're not in love with him. He doesn't expect it. Look here, are you listening to what I'm saying?"

"What? Who?"

"Good God! She says who! A fortune of millions in her very hand, and she says who!"

"Oh. Yes. You mean little Van Steed. Do you know, Mrs. Bellop, the women in America are very powerful. The men seem to spend their whole time and their energies on business matters while the women manage their lives for them. Here in the North, especially. I myself seem to be like that now. In France I remember it was quite different, it————"

"We haven't time to talk about France now, or whether American women are strong-minded. You know perfectly well that I got up this fancy-dress ball just for you. It won't be like the regular hops. We're having a supper at eleven—not just fruit-punch and cakes. Every millionaire in Saratoga will be there. The New York newspapers will call it the Millionaires' Ball. And that old harpy, Van Steed, is arranging to have everybody cut you."

"How nice!" cooed Clio at her most French.

"But I'll be there. It's my ball—at least, I got the hotel to give it. The Grand Union is wild with jealousy. I've found out that Guilia Forosini is coming as a Spanish gypsy—orange satin skirt, red velvet jacket, gold braid, epaulets, gold-ball fringe. Mrs. Porcelain's wearing a rose trellis costume. Ankle-length skirt of ciel blue tulle and satin, garlands of roses on her shoulders, and a headdress made to represent a gilt trellis covered with roses. Now you—what's the matter!"

Clio was laughing. She was laughing as she hadn't laughed since she came to Saratoga; she was staggering with laughter; the tears of laughter were filling her eyes.

Kakaracou, grimly disapproving, was in the bedroom doorway. "I told you leave Miss Clio alone when she like this."

"It's all right," Clio gasped. "Go away, Kaka. Dear Mrs. Bellop, forgive me. But the Spanish gypsy—and the gilt trellis on the head—it is so—so————" She was off again into the peals of hysterical laughter.

But even the good nature of the ebullient Sophie Bellop was cooled by now. "I'm going. You're right, Kaka. For that matter, I'm beginning to think that old viper Clarissa Van Steed is right, too, for the first time in her life. I came here to tell you that I think you ought to outdo them by coming as a French marquise—satin hoops, powdered wig, all your jewelry. I would help you, and your woman here is a seamstress, I'm sure."

Clio was suddenly very sober, deeply interested. "Pink satin, do you think? Over great hoops. With flounces of fine black Spanish lace? It was my mother's. I have it here in my unopened trunks."

"That's it! Wonderful!"

"Satin slippers with great diamond buckles?"

"Really! Can you manage?"

"It is nothing. And powdered hair and a little black patch here—and here—and all my jewels. All, you think?"

"Certainly. All. You'll look dazzling. Simply dazzling."

"How nize! How nize!" Clio's eyes were very narrow. There was something in her face and in the face of the Negress that made Sophie Bellop vaguely uncomfortable.

"You'll have to send him a note telling him you were ill or hysterical or something. He'll understand—I hope. Look, I'll tell him myself. You've got to make an entrance with him—not too early."

"I am coming to the dance with—with him. With Clint."

"But you can't. It'll spoil everything. Besides, he isn't here."

"He will be." Her face set in iron stubbornness. "No matter afterward. But I am going with him."

16

THIRTY MILES TO Albany. Clint Maroon was tooling along in the cool of the August day. Day, in fact, had not yet come. At four in the morning the road between Saratoga and Albany was still a dark mystery ahead, but the twin bays, fresh, glossy, restive after forty-eight hours of idleness, swung along as sure-footed as though the bright sun shone for them. For this trip Maroon had abandoned the clarence for a light, springy cart. Its four wheels seemed simultaneously off the ground, the cart and driver suspended in mid-air, so little did the bays make of the weight they were pulling along the road to Albany.

Clint Maroon was happy. He was happier than he had been in months. The reins in his hands, the cool moist air against his face, no sound except the hoofbeats and the skim of the wheels over the hard-baked road. No sun, no moon, no stars, no women, no fuss, no crowds; and the exhilarating prospect of a tough fight ahead. As blackness melted to a ghostly gray the good burghers sleeping lightly in the gray dawn stirred restlessly between rumpled sheets and started up in nightmarish fright, recalling the legend of the Headless Horseman of Sleepy Hollow, or old Indian stories of the region in earlier days—tales of sudden massacres and Iroquois uprisings. But it was only Clint Maroon, though they did not know, whirling along behind the light-stepping bays, high, wide and handsome, and singing the cowboy songs of old Texas as he went his nostalgic way.

> *I jumped in my saddle*
> *An' I give a li'l' yell*
> *An' the swing cattle broke*
> *An' the leaders went to hell.*
> *Tum-a-ti-yi, yippi, yippi, yea, yea, yea.*
> *Tum-a-ti-yi, yippi, yippi, yea, yea, yea.*

Aside from Van Steed he had taken no one into his confidence. To Clio he had said, "I'm fixing to go away, Clio, on business. Couple of days."

"Business. What business?"

He evaded this. "Cupide'll look after you. And Bart." He grinned.

Her hand on his arm, her tone wistfully reproachful. "But I thought we were here as partners, Clint. When we talked in New Orleans of this Saratoga we made the adventure together."

"Shucks, honey, you don't need me any more. You set out to catch you a millionaire and you've got him, roped and tied. All you've got to do now is cinch the saddle on him. He's already been gentled by his ma."

They glared at each other, the two partners. "Yes, I know I have been successful," she said, evenly. "I shan't forget you. When the time comes."

"Poor little Bart! If I didn't hate him and all his kind like poison I'd have a mind to warn him he was making a misjudgment. In his place I sure would feel cheap to think I was being married for my money."

"You need never fear. When you win five hundred at cards you feel yourself rich. The sweet little woman in Texas has just such ambitions, I am sure—she who makes the ravishing white satin neckties with the blue forget-me-nots."

"Yep, sure is comical the way a woman likes to put her mark on a man with a needle. You couldn't sit nor sleep till you had me crawling with those fancy initials all over my handkerchiefs and shirts. I looked to wake up any morning and find a big C, with a pretty vine, branded on my rump."

With the most disarming candor she said, "He hasn't asked me to marry him."

"Bart, he isn't the asking kind. You have to tell him."

They fell silent there in the dim coolness of her cottage sitting room. It was a warm pulsating silence such as they often had known in the dusk of the fragrant little garden in Rampart Street. As though sensing this he said, "It was different in New Orleans. Why can't it be like that here? You were mighty sweet, those days. Ornery—but mighty sweet."

In sudden fright, "Clint! *Chéri!* You're not leaving me!" She flung herself against him, she clung to him.

"Times I wish I could."

"Where are you going? Don't go! Don't go! Stay, stay!" Her arms about him, her scented laces smothering him.

He took her head in his two hands and looked down into her face. "Do you want to come away from here now, honey? Say the word."

But at that she hesitated a moment. In that moment he put her gently from him. "I have to go get me some sleep," he said, soberly. "Up before daybreak tomorrow." He strode toward the door.

"But you will be back for the hop—no, it is a ball that the Bellop is giving. A ball, no less, for these *canailles*. If you like you may escort me."

"I reckoned you were fixing to go with Bart."

"I was, but———"

"Better go with him. *Adios,* honey. Pleasant dreams." Suddenly he strode over to her, caught her up and kissed her roughly, punishingly, set her down so that she swayed dizzily. The next instant she heard the tap of his high-heeled boots on the veranda stairs.

Now, as Clint Maroon drove along toward Albany in the dawn, he thought, why don't you light out of here, cowboy? High-tail it out of there, and stay out. What call have you got to get yourself mixed up with railroads and foreign women and voodoo witches and dwarfs? You're Clint Maroon, of the Texas Maroons. Why don't you just keep on traveling away from here? They'll ship Alamo after you. That's about all you got to leave.

Clint! *Chéri!* You're not leaving me!

He knew he could not do it. Not yet.

The sun was higher now. The world was beginning drowsily to awake. From roadside farmhouses, as the turnout whirled by, there came the scent of coffee and of frizzling ham.

I'd like mighty well, Clint thought, to stop by and sit down to a good farm breakfast of biscuits and fried potatoes and ham like I used to back home. None of this la-de-da New Orleans and Saratoga stuff. Another month of that, I'm likely to be a sissy worse than Van Steed. Van Steed. No real harm in him. Not to say, harm. Not pure cussedness like the others. I wonder what the Gould crowd will do if they're licked. What was that Pappy said old Neely Vanderbilt said—it never pays to kick a skunk. Well, stink or not, I'm enjoying this. I don't recollect when I've felt more like tackling a job. Getting soft as mud sitting around eating quail, drinking wine, parading good horseflesh up and down that sinkhole Broadway in Saratoga like a dammed Easterner.

He had not pressed the bays, for he knew he was in ample time. Nevertheless they had, in three hours, easily covered the distance between Saratoga and Albany. He made straight for the Albany station. He knew he could get breakfast there. And there his drive would end and the business of the day begin. Few people were astir in the early-morning streets of Albany, yet these few stared, smiled, and a few even waved and broke into laughter as the handsome bays and their dashing driver and the dusty light cart flashed past. What the tarnation is eating on folks in this town! Clint thought, puzzled. You'd think they'd never seen a horse before, or a man driving. He whirled up to the Albany station, drew up at a hitching post and saw the faces of the loungers and Negro porters break into broad grins. Instinctively now he turned to glance over his shoulder. There behind him, snug as a jack-in-the-box and markedly resembling one, sat Cupide. Grinning, goggle-eyed, he was wedged neatly into the back of the cart. His glossy hat sat at a debonair angle, his maroon uniform was neatly buttoned, his arms were folded across his chest, his smile was an ivory gash, but his gaze was apprehensive as it met Maroon's stupefied stare.

In what seemed like a single fluid motion Clint Maroon had leaped to the ground, had thrown the reins to a waiting boy and advanced on Cupide, whip in hand.

"Get down out of there, you varmint! Get down or I'll haul you down."

Cupide stood up while the onlookers guffawed as for the first time they realized the stature of this strangely attired passenger. Nimbly he leaped to the ground, his tiny feet in their glittering top boots landing neatly as a cat's. As Maroon reached for him, the sad eyes looked up at him, the clear boyish voice broke a little with a note of pathos beneath its engaging humor.

"It was like riding on a donkey's tail, Monsieur Clint. Bumpitty-bump, bumpitty-bump. I'm hollow as a drum."

Maroon laid a heavy hand on the dwarf's shoulder. "What do you want here?"

"Breakfast. I am hungry for my breakfast."

Maroon's voice dropped. "Did she send you?"

"No. I ran away. I hid in the back of the cart. It was fine—but bumpy."

"You get out of here."

"No, Monsieur Clint. No! I want to fight, too, with you and the rest. I'm strong. You know how I am strong."

"Doggone if I haven't got a mind to tan you good, here and now, you little rat. Skin you and pin your hide to a fence, that's what I ought to do. How'd you know where I was going?"

The old face on the childlike body was turned up to him, its look all candor and simplicity. "I listened at the keyhole. I heard everything. It's going to be a fine fight."

He rubbed his tiny hands together. "I can't wait until I begin butting them in the stomach, the *canailles*."

Maroon's reply was a venomous mutter, out of which son-of-a-bitch emerged as the least offensive term. "You're going to get the hell out of here. . . . Hi, boy! What's the next train to Saratoga? . . . . D'you want to earn five dollars? You go rustle some breakfast—coffee and so on—for this little runt. You've got a good half an hour before train time. You buy a ticket and set him on that train headed for Saratoga, and don't you let him out of your sight till the train's started. Go on, get going, act like you're alive!"

"Monsieur Clint! You're not going to send me back!"

"You're damn whistlin' I am!" An aggrieved note crept into his voice. "Tagging me around. I bet she put you up to it."

"No, no! No one. Not Mad'moiselle, not Kaka. No one knows. Please let me stay. I will help, I will work, I will fight——"

"Shut up!" He dropped his voice, his very quietness was venomous. "And if you let out a word of what you know, here or in Saratoga, I'll kill you when I get back, sure as shooting." He turned to the fellow who now had emerged from the depot, railway ticket in hand. "Now, you. Hang on to that ticket till he's on the train. Give him his breakfast. If he gets balky leave him go without. One thing. Look out he don't butt you."

A bewildered look came into the face of the newly appointed guardian. "Don't what?"

"Butt you. He's got a head like a cannon ball. . . . I'll learn you to tag around after me. And remember! One word out of you about you know what and————" He snapped his fingers and flung the sound away, dead. Suddenly, to his horror, the little man dropped to his knees, he clasped his arms about Maroon's legs.

"Don't do this to me! Don't! Don't! I am strong. You know how strong. I am stronger than three regular men, I will fight————"

With terrible ruthlessness Maroon plucked the dwarf from him as you would fling off an insect. "Get away from me, you varmint you! I'll learn you to flap those big ears of yours at keyholes!"

The childlike figure was on its feet at once, like a thing made of steel springs. Even as the onlookers guffawed Clint Maroon felt his first pang of contrition, felt his face redden with shame at what he had done.

Cupidon brushed himself off, methodically. Quietly he looked at Maroon. His eyes gazed straight into those of his idol. "Monsieur, I am a man," he said. For that instant he was somehow tall.

A moment the two stared at one another. Then Maroon turned and walked quickly away.

He knew where he must go. He was late, and cursed his lateness and the cause of it, but his heart was not in it. You'll be hitting children next, he said to himself, and women too, likely. What's come over you! He strode along in his high-heeled boots, his great white sombrero, his fine cloth suit with its full-skirted coat, but he felt a diminished man.

The light cart and the bays would be cared for. That had been carefully arranged days ago. Everything had been arranged. All that money could insure had been carefully planned and carried out by men of millions. Only physical courage and devil-may-care love of adventure had been lacking. And these he, Clint Maroon, had provided.

Into the hot, dusty office of the stationmaster. Sparse, taciturn, Gid Fish looked up under his green eyeshade at the dashing figure in the doorway. His voice was as dry, his gaze as detached as though sombreroed figures in high-heeled Texas boots were daily visitors in the Albany depot office. The physical contrast between the two men was ludicrous—the one so full-blooded, so virile, so dramatic, the other so dry, dusty and sallow. Yet the two seemed to like and respect one another; their speech had the terseness of mutual understanding.

"Howdy, Gid!"

"Howdy, Clint!"

"Came in my rig like I said."

"Seen you."

"Boys in?"

"Yep."

"Steam up?"

"Yep."

"Road clear?"

"Yep."

"Well, *adios!*"

Maroon turned to go, his coat-tails flirting about his legs with the vigor of his movements. Gid Fish's rasping voice suddenly stopped him, held him with its note of urgency. "Somebody must of blabbed."

Maroon whirled. "Who says so?"

"Just come over the wire. They got wind."

Maroon's right hand went to his hip. "Who blabbed?"

"Gould's a smart fella."

Even as he said this there came the clack-clack-clack of the telegraph instrument on Gid Fish's desk. A moment of silence broken only by the clacking sound. "Says there's hell to pay in Binghamton," said Fish, laconically. "Git."

Clint Maroon's high heels clattered on the bare boards as he dashed from the room. Across the tracks, down the yards to where an engine waited, steam up.

The head that now thrust itself out of the engine-cab window was surmounted by the customary long-visored striped linen cap, the body was garbed in engineer's overalls, but the face that looked down at the hurrying figure of Clint Maroon was not an engineer's face as one usually sees it—the keen-eyed, quizzical and curiously benevolent countenance of the born mechanic. It was a hard-bitten ruthless face, but the eyes redeemed it. Devil-may-care, they were merry now with amusement and anticipation.

"You're going to get them nice clothes mussed up, Clint."

Maroon ignored this. His eye traveled the engine, end to end. "Sure enough big."

Pride irradiated the face framed in the engine cab. "She's the heaviest engine in the East."

"Better had be. Gid Fish says they got wind of us down in Binghamton. No telling what they'll do. Of course they don't know about the boys. Can't. They all back in there?" He nodded in the direction of the two coaches attached to the puffing engine.

"Yep. Rarin'."

"Get going, Les. I'll go talk to the boys. After the first stop I'll come up there in the engine with you. I want to see what's ahead. Where at's Tracy?"

Like a figure in a Punch and Judy show a smoke-grimed face bobbed up in the window beside that of Les, the engineer. His teeth gleamed white against their sooty background. "Feeding the critter," he said. "She eats like a hungry maverick." Les, the engineer; Tracy, the fireman; Clint Maroon, the leader. All three had the Western flavor in their speech—laconic, gentle, almost drawling. Les surveyed Clint with a kind of amused admiration.

"You come up here you're liable to ruin them pretty pants, Clint."

Maroon grinned back at him good-naturedly. "Got any coffee up there, left over?"

"Sure have. Wait a minute."

"Can't stop for it now. When I climb up in there I'll take it, and welcome. Get her going. We got to lick the whey out of the Binghamton outfit before noon and clean up all along the line to boot."

The two heads stuck out of the cab window turned to gaze after him a moment; they saw him leap into the doorway of the first car with a flirting whisk of his coat-tails.

"Son-of-a-gun!" said Tracy, affectionately. In another moment the big engine moved.

Passing swiftly from car to car, Clint Maroon faced three hundred men; he stood swaying at the head of each car; he repeated his brief speech, they made laconic answer.

"Howdy, boys!"

"Howdy, Clint!"

They strangely resembled one another, these silent men. Lean, tall, wiry; their faces weather-beaten, their eyes had the look of those accustomed to far horizons. Yet they were ruined faces, the faces of men who, though fearless, had known defeat and succumbed to it. Hard times had searched them out with her bony fingers and sent them wandering, drink-scarred and jobless, into the inhospitable East. Danger meant nothing to them. Risk was their daily ration. Violence flavored their food. Life they held lightly. Guns were merely part of their wardrobe.

"Like I said, no guns—only maybe the butts in a pinch, You got your clubs and spades and axes and your fists, and you'll likely need 'em. No shooting. Every station between here and Binghamton we're out quick before they can telegraph word ahead. We throw 'em out, take the books, and leave a bunch behind to hold the fort. Where we're in we stay in, and we've got to be in every station between here and there before nightfall, sure. Whenever you hear three screeches from the engine ahead—no matter where we're at or what you're doing—that means out, pronto. We're going. Hold on to your hats."

It was child's play to these men. They treated it as though it were a roundup; they felt that they lacked only the horses under them to make their day perfect. Town followed town, station followed station. The procedure never varied; it even took on a sort of monotony after the first hour. The train would come to a grinding, jolting halt that shook the marrow of even these hard-boned Westerners. Three shrill screeches from the engine. Out the men swarmed armed with bludgeons, spades, shovels; their guns handy in their holsters in spite of Clint's warning. Quick as they were, Maroon was quicker. The crew was, for the most part, sombreroed as he, but it was the figure in the great white sombrero and the flying coat-tails that led the charge into the station. A rush into the ticket office, bursting into the stationmaster's room; a scuffle, oaths, yells.

"Come on you son-a-kabitchee!"

"Stay with him, cowboy!"

"Heel that booger, Red. Heel him!"

"Hot iron! Hot iron!"

The old language of the range and the branding pen and the corral returned joyously to their lips. The West they had known was vanishing—had vanished, indeed, for them. Resentful, fearless, they were blurred copies of Clint Maroon. The thing they had been hired to do was absurd—was almost touching in its childlike simplicity and crudeness. But then, so, too, were they.

In each town they left behind them the bewildered buzz and chatter of the townspeople. Long-suffering as these were, and accustomed to the violence and destruction with which the now-notorious railroad fight had been carried on in the past year, the lightning sortie of these Westerners was a new and melodramatic experience. There was, in the first place, a kind of grim enjoyment in their faces, a sardonic humor in their speech, as they poured out of their modern Trojan horse. Booted, sombreroed like the dashing figure that led them, they seemed, in the eyes of the staid York State burghers, to be creatures from another world. Binghamton was their goal, Binghamton was to be the final test, for there the enemy was fortified in numbers probably equal to theirs, if not greater. Meanwhile their zest was tremendous, their purpose grim, their spirits rollicking. Strange wild yells, bred of the plains, the range, the Indian country, issued from their leather throats. Yip-ee! Eee-yow! And always, bringing up the rear, though the white-hatted leader never knew it, was a grotesque little figure rolling on stumpy legs. In wine-colored livery and top hat and glittering diminutive boots he was, the staring onlookers assumed, a creature strayed from a circus. The whole effect was, in fact, that of a circus minus its tent and tigers and elephants. This little figure followed an erratic pattern of its own, dodging, hiding, mingling whenever possible where the melee was thickest, darting back to the refuge of the train coaches before the white-hatted leader strode back to his eyrie in the engine cab. Evidently there was some sort of understanding between him and the tall rangey fellows who made up the company. Almost absent-mindedly they seemed to protect him; they shielded him in little clusters when it appeared that Maroon's eye might fall upon him. Here was a mascot. Here was a good-luck piece. Look at the little runt, they said. Says he's Maroon's bodyguard. Reckon he's lying.

In the engine cab Clint Maroon, incredibly neat in spite of the heat, the dust, the soot that belched from the smokestack, leaned far out of the window to peer up the track. Each time he withdrew his head from this watch-tower he heaved a sigh of relief.

"No sign of them, hide nor hair," he remarked to Les, the engineer. "D'you reckon Gid Fish was just throwin' off on me, saying he'd heard somebody'd blabbed up in Binghamton?"

"Nope," said Les, cheerfully, above the roar and jolt of the massive engine.

"We've only got a matter of fifteen miles to go," Clint argued.

Tracy, the fireman, his red-rimmed eyes rolling grotesquely in his sooty face, turned his head away from the fire to throw a terse reminder over his shoulder.

"Long tunnel between here and Binghamton. Keep your head stuck out going through there. You're liable to get kind of specked, but you sure might see something at the end of it."

Maroon's hand went to his hip. "You keeping back something you know!"

A grin gashed the black face. "My, my, ain't you touchy, Clint, since you come East and got to going with New York mmillionaires!"

With an oath Maroon lunged forward, but the drawling voice of Les with a sharp overtone in it now served to stop him short.

"Something down the line," he yelled. "I can feel it. On our track. God A'Mighty, they wouldn't mix it in the tunnel!"

For an instant the three men stared, each seeing in the other's eyes confirmation of his own worst dread. "Open her up!" yelled Clint. "Wide! We've got to get out of here." For they had slowed down going through the tunnel. From his window Clint could now see the blue sky through the tunnel mouth a hundred yards ahead.

"They can't jump if I speed her up."

"They've jumped off wild bucking horses, they can clear a greasy train, you got to get us the hell out of here. We'll be caught like rats in a———" His head was far out of the window, he was peering through the curtain of smoke and soot and cinders that belched from the smokestack. The heat in the tunnel was insufferable, the blazing temperature in the engine cab was indescribable, Maroon's face was ludicrously streaked now with sweat and grime, his white hat was polka-dotted with black, his diamond scarfpin sparkled bravely in the sullied nest of the satin necktie. He leaned perilously out, he turned his head now to peer back at the laden cars and he could dimly discern the heads and shoulders of the men thrust far out of the train windows and hanging from the car steps. Theirs had been perilous paths; instinctively they sensed danger; they were ready to jump. Now by straddling the car window Clint could see ahead. There it was, down the track, down their own track and headed straight for them. He could see the locomotive, it was sending out a column of smoke like a fiery monster breathing defiance.

"Give 'em the whistle!" yelled Maroon. "They're on the track!"

Three shrill blasts seemed to rend the roof of the tunnel. Three more. The figures in the cars behind now leaped, tumbled from the train, shouting, cursing, running.

"Jump!" howled Les above the turmoil. "Jump, you crazy sons-of-bitches, I'm letting her out."

Poised for the leap, with Tracy behind him, Maroon clung by one hand. "Come on! God damn it, come on, Les."

They had cleared the tunnel. "Coming. Jump! I'm letting her out. They didn't get us in the tunnel, the stinkin' yellowbellies."

Neatly and without fluster, as though he were sliding out of a saddle onto the ground, Clint Maroon stepped to the ground, swung round like a dancer, caught his balance magically and started to run as Tracy landed just behind him. He had had, as he leaped, a last glimpse of Les's face as he bent forward to give the powerful engine its last notch of speed before he, too, leaped for his life.

Bells were ringing, whistles tooting, sparks pouring from the two engines, men were leaping from doors and windows, they ran wide of the track, they yelled like Comanches as the two engines, like something out of a crazy dream, met in the terrible impact of a head-on collision. The heavy engine crumpled the lighter, pushed it aside like a toy. Above the crash and the splintering of wood and the smashing of glass sounded the wild shouts of the men in the blood-curdling yells of the Western plains. Yip-eeee! Eeeeeee-yow! Clubs in their hands, axes, guns, shovels. Swarming along the tracks they came toward each other, the two bands of men. It was plain that Maroon's crew outnumbered the Binghamton crowd, but on these you saw the flash of deputies' badges glinting in the sun. But the faces above these were the flabby drinksodden faces of such Bowery toughs and slum riffraff as the opposition had been able hastily to press into service when news of the Albany foray reached their ears.

"Heel them! Catch them! Brand them! Go get'em! Go get'em! Hot iron! Hot iron!"

At the head of the throng ran Clint Maroon. He was smiling, happily. His men were at his heels, and in another moment the two sides had met with an impact of blows, oaths, shouts. It was a glorious free-for-all, a primitive battle of fists and clubs and feet. The thud of knuckles on flesh; grunts; the scuffle of leather on cinders; the screams of men in pain; howls of rage.

"No guns!" Clint shouted. "Ear'em down, slug'em, kick them in the guts! Hammer'em! No guns."

Here was a strange new rule of the game to these men accustomed to fair gun play in a fight, but they cheerfully made the best of it. Fists, boots, axes, clubs. The early training of their cowboy days stood them in good stead now. Five hundred men writhed and pushed, stamped and cursed, punched and hammered and wrestled in a gargantuan bloody welter.

Suddenly, out of a corner of his eye, Clint Maroon glimpsed a familiar figure, diminutive, implike, in a wine-red coat and a shiny top hat, a grin of dreadful joy on his face. Busily, methodically, he was running between men's legs, he was butting them behind, tipping them over neatly and jumping on them, a look of immense happiness and satisfaction irradiating him as he did so.

Beset though he was, Clint stopped to stare, open-mouthed, then he burst into laughter, and even as he roared with mirth he waved the dwarf back and shouted at him above the din. "Get out of here, you son-of-a-gun! . . . Get out of here, run away from here! Drag it, or I'll bust every——"

The little man came running toward him, dodging this way and that. He was making frantic motions, he pointed with one tiny hand at something behind Maroon and mouthed as he ran. Instinctively Maroon whirled to look behind him. There stood a stubble-bearded ruffian, arms upraised to bring down a shovel on his head. He had only time to duck, an instinctive gesture, and to raise one arm to shield his head. The flat of the shovel crashed down on his elbow and came to a rest against his ribs. Maroon stumbled, sank to one knee, and saw with horror that the fellow again held the shovel high, poised for a finishing blow. Into Clint's mind flashed the thought, here's a Maroon being killed with a shovel and disgracing the family. Then Cupide leaped, not like a human being but like a monkey; he used his head as a projectile and landed squarely in the man's stomach as he stood arms upraised. There was a grunt, the shovel flew from his hands, and, falling, nicked Maroon smartly just above the eye. Then shovel-wielder, Cupide, Maroon, and the shovel itself mingled in a welter of legs, arms, curses, pain. But Maroon's shattered arm was doubled under his shattered rib and both felt the weight of his own body and that of the fantastic combatants. He was conscious of a wave of unbearable nausea before the kindly curtain of unconsciousness blacked out the daylight.

17

IN A SOCIETY which dined in the middle of the day and had supper at half-past six, the hour set for the grand ball of the United States Hotel season did not seem at all unsophisticated. But then, Saratoga, which considered itself very worldly and delightfully wicked, still had a Cinderella attitude toward the midnight hour. Eight-thirty to midnight the announcement had said.

Supper had been rushed through in the dining room or ignored completely by the belles of the evening. From behind bedroom doors and up and down the hotel corridors could be heard the sounds of gala preparation— excited squeals, the splashing of water, the tinkle of supper trays, the ringing of bells, the hurried steps of waiters and bellboys and chambermaids, the tuning of fiddle and horn. Every gas jet in the great brass chandeliers was flaring; even the crystal chandelier in the parlor, which was lighted only on special occasions. In the garden the daytime geraniums and petunias and alyssum and pansies had vanished in the dusk. In their place bloomed the gaudy orange and scarlet and rose color of the paper lanterns glowing between the trees.

Grudgingly, yet with a certain elation, the United States Hotel had permitted a very few choice guests of their rival, the Grand Union Hotel, to attend this crowning event of the hotel's summer season: the Jefferson De Forests, the Deckers of Rittenhouse Square, Mrs. Blood of Boston, the Rhinelanders, the Willoughby Kilps, General Roscoe E. Flower.

At the head of the ballroom, directly opposite the musicians' platform, enthroned among the dowagers, sat Madam Van Steed. About her clustered her ladies-in-waiting—the insecure, the jealous, the malicious, the grudging, the envious. They made elegant conversation and they watched the door; they commented on the success or the dismal failure of the costumes which had been devised under the generous rules of fancy dress; and they watched the door.

"How sweet!" they had cooed at sight of the rose-trellised Mrs. Porcelain. "How dashing and romantic!" on the entrance of the Spanish gypsy. They made stilted talk, generously larded with hints concerning their own lofty place in society.

"I had a letter today from my cousin, Mrs. Fortesque, of London. She says the Queen is suffering from low spirits. She will take no exercise. Letitia—that's Mrs. Fortesque— says the dear Queen will go to Italy in the autumn."

"I see that Mrs. De Chanfret isn't here yet. Do you think she's not coming! Dear me, I hope . . ."

"Letitia says that the Prince of Wales—they call him Jumbo, isn't that shocking!—no longer wears a buttonhole flower. . . ."

"A draft, Clarissa! Dear me, it's really very warm in here. I don't believe they'll want to shut the garden doors, so early . . ."

"They say it is a diet for corpulency devised by a Mr. Banting. I don't think it can be good for one's health, starving oneself. The Banting Regimen For Corpulency it is called. My dear, for breakfast you're allowed whitefish and bacon, or cold beef or broiled kidney, toast, and tea with milk and no cream, the way the English take it. For dinner some fish and a bit of poultry or game, a green vegetable, fruit. For supper only meat or fish, a vegetable . . . for tea . . ."

"My maid who has a friend who is a friend of a maid who knows Sophie Bellop's maid happened to mention to me—I didn't ask her—she just spoke of it the way they do—she happened to mention that she had heard that the De Chanfret woman, or whatever she calls herself, is coming as a French marquise in a powdered wig. Well, really! Couldn't you die! After all we know . . ."

"I always thought Creoles were colored people . . ."

". . . New Orleans aristocracy—French and Spanish blood . . ."

"But where is she? Your son seems worried, Clarissa dear . . ."

"I see your son isn't dancing, dear Mrs. Van Steed."

"He is worried. It's about business. I almost had to use force to keep him from going to Binghamton tonight. Something about a railroad. Some railroad trouble. Nothing to speak of. Bart is so clever. He'll make it come right."

Eight-thirty. Nine. Half-past nine. Ten. At half-past nine Mrs. Bellop had sent a bellboy with a message to Clio's rooms. He had returned with the news that the cottage apartment was in darkness, the door locked, the windows closed. No sound from within.

"But I felt," he said, solemnly, "like eyes was watching me."

Decidedly the ball was not going well. There was about it a thin quality, as though a prime ingredient were lacking. People danced, but listlessly. Mrs. Porcelain, the ciel tulle somewhat wilted, the rose trellis headdress askew, smiled and cooed unconvincingly, her eyes on the doorway. The rolling-eyed Forosini found that a velvet gypsy jacket for dancing in August was a mistake. The dowagers grouped against the wall were tigresses robbed of their prey.

"It doesn't seem to be going, Mrs. Bellop," complained Tompkins, the hotel manager. "It's too early for supper. They've just stuffed themselves with dinner. What's wrong?"

"It's that Mrs. De Chanfret."

"Why, what's the matter with her? I don't see her. Has she done something?"

"No. That's the trouble. She isn't here. And they've got so used to seeing her and expecting her to do something dramatic that when she isn't around everything goes stale, like flat champagne."

"Well, fetch her then. Fetch her."

"I can't find her."

"Nonsense! She must be somewhere. I can't have the Grand Union saying this ball was a failure. If they do, it's your fault, Mrs. Bellop."

"Oh, run along, Tompkins. Who do you think you're talking to! A chambermaid! I could make the United States Hotel look like a haunted house in two weeks if I chose. So mind your manners. Where's Van Steed? Now he's disappeared, too. Drat the man!"

She left the listless ballroom, her eyes searching the corridors, the lobby; she sent bellboys scurrying into the garden, the men's washroom, up to Van Steed's apartment, out to the piazza; she even tried Clio's apartment again, in vain. "The bar. He wouldn't be there. He doesn't drink anything. Can't. Well, try it, anyway." She herself followed the boy; she poked her head in at the swinging door to survey the territory forbidden to females. There sat Van Steed at a far corner table. "Fetch him! Fetch him at once. Tell him it's important."

As the boy bent over him he raised his head, his eyes followed the boy's pointing finger to where Mrs. Bellop stood in the doorway. Knowing her, perhaps he feared that she was not above coming in and buttonholing him in the bar itself. He rose and came toward her, and she saw that his cheeks had lost their wonted pink and were a curious clay-gray. He had had a drink too potent for the hot night, for little beads of moisture stood out on his forehead, yet his hand, when she grasped it, was cold. A grin that was a grimace sat awry on his lips. My, he's taking it hard, she thought.

"What's wrong? Are you sick? Has something happened to her?"

He opened his clenched left hand. In it was a moist wad of yellow paper. Mrs. Bellop had met enough bad news in her day to recognize it at sight. Yet the staring grin baffled her.

"Not bad news I hope, Bart. No, of course—you're smiling—that is—not bad news I hope."

He looked up from the slip of paper. He stared at her. He wet his lips with his tongue.

"Where is she?" he said, without preliminaries.

"I don't know. I sent over. The place is dark."

"Maybe she's heard."

"Heard what?"

"It's stifling in here. Come out on the piazza a minute, will you? I'm—"

She followed him. The piazza was almost deserted. A few solid couples sat there taking the evening air before their bedtime. A little low-voiced knot of sporting men talking of the day's races and tomorrow's possibilities. Van Steed glanced around quickly, seeking a secluded spot. Far off, in a dim corner at the end of the long piazza, there glowed the red eye of a cigar. They could not discern the lonely, meager, hollow-chested figure behind it, but they knew. And the grin came again, fleetingly, into Van Steed's drawn face.

"Well, we've licked him, anyway."

"So that's it!"

"He knows it. He's been sitting there like that; they've been sending him messages ever since this afternoon. I guess that will show him there are some people smarter than the Gould gang." Then, "Oh, my God!" The exclamation was wrung from him like a groan.

"For heaven's sake, what is it! Tell me quickly. I've got to go back in there. There's a musical concert at ten-thirty. Not that I care a damn about those ninnies. Stop staring like that and tell me!"

But shrewd and quick as her mind was in its workings, she could make little of his whispered babble. "They took every station between Albany and Binghamton———"

"Who? Who did?"

He ignored her question. "I didn't think he could do it —I thought he was all blow and bluster. Pierpont Morgan knew better; he took to him right away . . . Maroon had almost five hundred men . . . Gould's gang had more . . . but that Texas crowd six feet all of them and made of iron like him . . . engine too . . . the Binghamton locomotive rolled right off the track but they backed their own way down to . . . jumped first . . . if he's alive but he's disappeared and the dwarf . . . Morgan sent the telegram a thousand words . . . Morgan says he's a wonder Morgan thinks he's the biggest . . . of course maybe it's not so bad . . . but they can't find the little chap . . . only his hat that top hat of his mashed in . . . she'll never forgive me . . .''

Mrs. Bellop actually shook him. "For God's sake stop standing there mumbling! I can't make out what you're saying; it sounds crazy.''

Here she jumped and uttered a little scream as an oily voice sounded close to her ear. "Oop, sorry!" It was Bean, the head usher, unctuous, deferential. "They're waiting for you in the ballroom, Mrs. Bellop. Mr. Tompkins. The concert, you know.''

Mrs. Bellop clapped a frantic hand to her head. "No need to scare me to death with your pussycat ways. Look here, Bean, have you seen Mrs. De Chanfret? D'you know where she is? You make it your business to know everything.''

Bean's fatuous smile gleamed in the light from the parlor windows. He giggled a little. "I regret to say that I have not set eyes on that fairest of her sex since an early hour this m———''

"Oh, shut up!" barked Sophie Bellop. "Bart, pull yourself together.''

"—orning," the usher went on, urbanely. "And Mr. Van Steed, sir, your lady mother asked me to request you to come to her side, she seemed much perturbed, if I may venture to say so.''

"Go away, Bean. Run along! Scat!" She eyed the man sharply. "I suppose you were listening to everything we said. Read telegrams, too, before they're delivered. I'm sure of that. Oh, well.''

Sophie Bellop took Van Steed's arm; briskly she began to propel him toward the door. "Now pull yourself together, Bart. You're the color of dough.''

"He can't be hurt badly, can he?"

"My land, I don't know. I suppose he's made of flesh and blood like the———''

"Blood!" echoed Van Steed, and went a pale green.

"Come, come, he's probably all right, celebrating somewhere with his Texas friends. And the dwarf too.''

"But where is she? Do you think she's heard and has gone off to find him? Perhaps he sent for her. Perhaps———''

Mrs. Bellop looked serious. "I never thought of that. It's like her to do that. But this very evening she was planning to come in pink satin. I had planned it as a kind of triumph for her against all those harpies like that precious mother of yours.''

A changed man, he made no protest at this. He had transferred his every emotion to another strong woman. And of her, as had been true before, he stood in fear. "Do you think she'll blame me? It wasn't my plan, you know. It was his idea. I didn't approve, really. I thought it was crazy. I said so to Morgan. He'll have to admit that himself.''

Sophie glared at him with considerable distaste. "He grabbed your railroad for you, didn't he? Took it with his bare hands, like—like a hero—or a bandit—I'm not sure which. Anyway, you've got it.''

"I know," miserably. "I know.''

"If she comes down—maybe she's just overdoing her entrance—if she comes down don't say anything to her about Maroon being hurt or—well, hurt. Or the dwarf. Not tonight. Tonight is your chance. Now come along. Perk up! Be a man!''

Even this he did not resent.

As they entered the ballroom doorway, five hundred reproachful faces turned toward them like balloons pulled by a single string. The United States Hotel grand ball had bogged down in a morass of apathy. Leaderless, it flopped feebly, lifting first one foot then another, but without progress.

"Really, Mrs. Bellop!" hissed Tompkins, the manager, reproachfully. "Really, Mrs. Bellop! I haven't deserved this at your hands."

"Oh, hush your fuss!" snapped Sophie. Nimbly she clambered to the musicians' platform, she motioned the drum to beat a ruffle for silence. "Ladies and gentlemen! Before partaking of the magnificent collation which our genial host, Manager Tompkins, has ordered prepared for us, there has been planned a surprise concert in which the most talented of Saratoga's visiting guests will favor us. The first number is a bass solo entitled 'Rocked in the Cradle of the Deep,' rendered by Mr. Archibald McElroy of Cincinnati. Following this, Miss Charlotte Chisholm will lend her lovely soprano to the musical number entitled 'Her Bright Smile Haunts Me Still.' . . . Comedy number rendered by Mr. Len Porter, entitled 'I've Only Been Down to the Club.' . . . Duet by the justly popular Pettingill twins: 'Wait Till the Clouds Roll By, Jennie.' . . . Seats will be placed by the ushers, following which supper will be . . . and a prize will be given by the management for the most original fancy dress costume in this evening's . . .''

There followed a spatter of appreciative applause, the buzz of conversation; a fiddle squeaked, a flute emitted a tentative giggle. But their hearts were not in it. "A circus without the elephant," said Mrs. Bellop to Van Steed. "They're so disappointed they could cry. Your lady mother looks as if she'd have a stroke.''

"Praw-leens! Praw-leens!" A clear powerful voice sounded from the outer corridor. In the doorway appeared a black mammy in voluminous calico and a vast white apron, a kerchief crossed on her bosom, her head swathed in a brilliant orange tignon. Gold and diamond hoop earrings dangled from beneath the turban's folds (Aunt Belle Piquery's jewelry). The teeth gleamed white in the blackened face, the dark eyes flashed, on her arm was a great woven basket neatly covered with a white napkin. The slim figure was stuffed fore and aft into ponderous curves. "Praw-leens! Praw-leens!"

The basket actually was laden with the toothsome New Orleans confections; she was handing out pralines here and there as she made her way through the crowd; they were gathering round her laughing; the adventurous were biting into the sugary nut-laden circlets.

Sophie Bellop stood up, shaking. "They'll never forgive her for this," she muttered aloud to no one in particular, "they'll never———" With amazing agility for a woman of her weight, Sophie scurried through the crowd; she reached Mrs. De Chanfret's side just as the buxom calicoed figure stood before the anguished Bart Van Steed, just as his voice pleaded in an agonized whisper, "Mrs. De Chanfret. Go home. Please. Please. Don't!"

She tossed her head so that the earrings bobbed and glittered. "Go 'long, honey chile, you quality folks, you don't want no truck with a no-count black wench like me! You jes' shut you mouth with one o' these prawleens, Mammy made um herself, yassuh!" She laughed a great throaty Negro guffaw; she actually thrust a praline into his wretched hand and went on; she traveled the leisurely circle toward Madam Van Steed; her rolling eye encompassed the group; her grin was a scarlet and white gash in the blackened face. Recovering from their first surprise, the orchestra now entered

into the spirit of the thing. They struck up the strains of "Whoa, Emma!"
Clio Dulaine hoisted the basket a trifle higher on her arm, she raised the
voluminous calico skirts a little, the feet in the white cotton stockings and
the strapped flat slippers broke into the shuffle of a Negro dance as in her
childhood she had been taught it by Cupide and Kaka in the kitchen of the
Paris flat. Madam Van Steed's face, the faces of the satellite dowagers were
masks of horror as they beheld the shuffling slapping feet, the heaving rump,
the rolling eye, the insolent grin.

"Whoa, Emma!" boomed the band.

"Whoa, Emma!" yelled the crowd, delighted. The party had come alive
at last.

Clio's hand, in its white cotton glove, plunged into her basket; she began
to throw handfuls of pralines, like giant confetti, into the gray satin lap of
Madam Van Steed, into the brocade and satin laps of the ladies grouped
about her. "Praw-leen for sweeten dem sour faces! Praw-leens!" She rolled
her eyes, she raised her hands high, palms out, she threw back her head,
she was imitating every wandering New Orleans minstrel and cavorting street
band she had ever seen, every caroling berry vendor from the bayous; she
was Belle Piquery, she was Kakaracou and Cupide in the old carefree Southern days of her early childhood; she was defiance against every convention
she so hated. And so shuffling, shouting, clapping her hands, the empty
basket now hooked round her neck by its handle and hanging at her back,
Clio Dulaine made her fantastic way to the veranda door that led onto the
garden and disappeared from the sight of a somewhat hysterical company
made up of the flower of Saratoga.

The length of the curved veranda, down the steps to the floor below,
running along the veranda tier and into her own apartment, the heavy basket
bobbing at her back. A wild figure, her eyes rolling in the blackened face,
she stood in the center of the little sitting room, laughing, crying, while Kaka
divested her of the ridiculous garments—the full-skirted calico, the padding
that had stuffed bosom and hips, the brilliant tignon, the dangling hoop
earrings.

"Their faces, Kaka! Their silly faces with their mouths open and their
eyes staring, and those stiff old women in their satin dresses. And Mrs.
Porcelain with her trellis! Kaka! Kaka!" Tears streaked the blackened
cheeks.

With cream and a soft cloth Kaka was cleansing the girl's face and throat,
and as she worked she kept up a grumbling and a mumbling, as though to
herself.

"Somepin fret me . . . maybe now we come away from here but where
at is Cupide where at is Cupide I got a feeling deep down somepin fret me
. . . I knew you turn out like your mama . . . no luck with menfolks
. . . plan and contrive but no luck with menfolks . . . you fixing to marry
a millionaire but all the time you crazy in you head for that *vacher* he leave
you . . . just like Mister Nicolas he leave . . ."

With the flat of her hand Clio slapped the woman full in the face. But
Kakaracou caught her hand and kissed it and said, "Now! That is better.
Now will you put on the pink satin and your mama's diamonds and Kaka
fix your hair *à la marquise!*"

"Yes," said Clio, laughing. "Yes. Why not! Quick! Quick! I could marry
him yet, if I wanted to."

The black woman's fingers were lightning. Powder on the piled black hair;
the pink satin and black lace springing stiff and glistening from her slender
waist, the necklaces, bracelets, the pendants, the parure, the flashing earrings; the rings with which Nicolas Dulaine had loaded his mistress. "There!

Now, Kaka, you'll come with me, my attendant, all very proper, since I have no man now. I really do look beautiful, don't I! Am I as beautiful as my mother was? I am! I am!"

But Kakaracou shook her head. The two fantastic figures, the girl in her powdered hair and her pink satin hoops and her blazing jewels, the stately black woman in her turban and stiff silk, swept down the cottage balcony stairs and were halfway across the garden when a distracted figure stumbled toward them. His face was in shadow, but the light from the ballroom windows was full on the two women.

"Clio! Clio!"

"Oh, Mr. Van Steed, how you frightened me! I was just coming to have a little peek at the ball. The music sounded so enticing."

"Clio!"

She slipped her hand in his arm, she pulled him round with quite a hearty jerk. "Will you be my escort, since Colonel Maroon could not return in time?"

"Clio, I must talk to you. How could you————"

"Not now. Later. Who is that, singing? How sweet! How very sweet!"

They stood together in the ballroom doorway. On the platform Miss Charlotte Chisholm's soprano warbling wavered, faltered, went bravely on. Clio did not enter; she did not take advantage of a chair indicated by a dazzled usher; she stood there with the wretched Van Steed; she shook her lovely powdered head; she put a finger to her lips for quiet and glanced toward the platform; and if Miss Chisholm had been turning cartwheels, uttering the notes of a Patti meanwhile, no one in that crowded room would have seen her or heard.

The singer finished, lamely. Clio applauded delicately and said, "Charming, charming!" She smiled across the room at the glaring Madam Van Steed, she waved to Sophie Bellop, who was waddling toward her, making her way through the crowd with astonishing swiftness.

"Clio, will you come into the garden for a stroll? I must talk to you. Now."

"Wouldn't it look strange?"

"No. No."

But Mrs. Bellop was upon them. "Well, young lady, you must have taken leave of your senses!"

"Why, dear Mrs. Bellop!"

"A pretty how-d'you-do! It's sure to be in the New York papers. They'll never forgive you, those————"

Clio laid a hand affectionately on the arm of Saratoga's social arbiter. "Dear, dear Mrs. Bellop, don't scold me! And you, too, Bart. The party seemed so dull and stuffy I thought I would liven it up a little. It was in fun. I am so sorry. Tell me, have you heard news of Colonel Maroon? He was to have been my escort, the naughty man." A lightning look leaped between Sophie Bellop and Bart Van Steed. But swift as it was, Clio caught it. The day's vague unrest, the fear that had held her all evening, now became a terrible certainty. "What is it? You two. What's happened?"

"Nothing. Run along into the garden. You've made trouble enough for one evening."

Clio's face hardened into a dreadful mask of resolved fury. "Tell me. Tell me what you know or I shall do something dreadful. But really frightful. I shall tear off my clothes and scream. I shall beat you with my fists. I care for nothing. Tell me! Tell me!"

"Sh-sh-sh! All right. All right. Later."

"Now! Now!" Her voice was rising.

Mrs. Bellop spoke soothingly while Bart's mouth opened and closed like that of a gasping fish. "The railroad—they—Bart got word that everything was—was—successful— isn't that lovely!"

Clio spat the word through her teeth. "Successful! Successful! Clint! Where is he?" She actually shook Van Steed's arm as one would try to shake an answer out of a stubborn little boy.

He had not the gift of dissembling. Her fingers were biting into his arm. Ruthless in business, he was water-weak against the browbeating of a determined woman. "It's nothing. We heard that little—uh—the dwarf was hurt somewhat. Somewhat. Quite a fight," he went on, with a rickety attempt at jocularity. "Quite a little fracas the boys had. But you'll be glad to know that they won."

"Do you want me to strike you here before all these people! Maroon! Tell me what has happened to him! Maroon!"

"Well, I understand he was hurt a little—nothing serious—no direct word from him, but you know how he is—he can take care of himself————"

Her face was livid, her eyes narrowed to black slits, her lips drew back from her teeth. It was a face venomous, murderous, terrible.

"He's dead. He's dead. I can see it in your face. Your cowardly face. He fought for you and your miserable crawling railroad that brings you your dirty coal. I tell you I despise you. I would sooner marry a snake that crawls on its belly. I would————"

But they were not looking at her, they were looking at something beyond her, down the long hallway. She turned, then, to see Clint Maroon almost in the doorway. A stained and soiled bandage wrapped his head, his right arm rested in a sling, he leaned a little sideways as though to ease some inward strain. And behind him strutted a grotesque little figure on whose head rose a bump the size of an egg—a figure in a stained and ragged uniform of wine red and muddied boots whose left member lacked a heel, so that he limped and hopped as he came.

"Howdy, folks," drawled Maroon. "My, my, Mrs. De Chanfret, you look right pretty. I reckon I'm a sight————"

She seemed not to run to him merely but to spring like an arrow shot from the bow. "Clint! Clint *chéri!*"

But at the impact of her body flung against his Clint Maroon said, "Ouch'" like a little boy. And then his long body crumpled to the floor, dragging Clio to her knees as he went.

18

PROPPED UP AMONG the pillows of his bed, Clint Maroon looked out almost sheepishly from beneath his head bandage at the faces turned so solicitously toward him. The bandage was a proper one now; the arm in its splint rested comfortably against his side; the room smelled of drugs and eau de cologne and coffee. He looked very clean and boyish. The doctor had come and gone.

"Shucks! I feel fine. That's the first time a Maroon ever did a sissy thing like that. I sure hope you-all will excuse me being so womanish. Fainting away. I'm plumb ashamed."

"Don't talk now, *chéri*. Rest. Here. Another sip of this."

"Why, say, many a time back in Texas I've been hurt worse than this throwed by a bucking horse. Never made such a to-do about it. Nothing to eat all day—that was it, only a swallow of whisky one of the boys—say, that cup of Kaka's good coffee, the way she makes it, is better than any medicine. Where's Cupide?''

Two hands grasped the bed's footboard, the dwarf's powerful arms pulled him up so that the great head, decorated now with a plaster where the lump had risen, rose like a nightmarish sun over the horizon.

"You would have been killed—but smashed dead—if it had not been for me, Monsieur Clint.''

"I know, I know. I reckon it might have been better, at that, than having you around my neck the rest of my life.''

"Then why you take him along?'' Kaka demanded.

"Take him!'' Maroon yelled. "I tried the worst way to get shut of him.'' He glared wrathfully at the gnomelike figure perched now on the footboard. "How come you got on that train, anyway, after I turned you off at the Albany station?''

"Oh, that was easy,'' Cupide explained. His tiny hands made an airy nothing of it. "I butted him in the stomach, he grunted like a stuck pig, then I took the five dollars you had given him and I ran just as the train was moving—it was dangerous, I can tell you it was—and I hid in the water closet or under the seats when you came near. The boys were very nice to me—*mais gentil*—very.''

"Insecte!" said Kaka, fondly. *"Fou furieux!"*

Clio pushed the hair back from her forehead with a frantic gesture. "I tell you, I don't understand, I don't understand such people. You are hurt and broken and this monkey here might be dead—you, too—and all that a fool who has already millions may have another million. What nonsense is this!''

"You didn't think he was such a fool a week ago.''

"I did. I did. But when I heard you were hurt I hated him, I called him every name, I said terrible things.''

"Sorry?''

"Only if I have hurt the little man. Clint, let us go away from here. Take me with you. I have decided I do not care so much to marry a man with millions.''

"Looks like you'll have to now, care or not.''

She stared, uncomprehending, startled. "What is this! Clint! What are you saying!''

"Well, sugar, it's like this———''

But she knelt at the side of his bed, she put her head on the pillow beside him, she cradled his head in her arms. "I won't leave you. I tell you I will follow you, I will make such a *bruit* that you will be ashamed.''

"Now, now, wait a minute. Hold your horses. I got a taste of this railroad and money thing, and say, it's easier than riding fence. Even a dumb cowboy like me can get the hang of it. These fellows, they don't only skin the country and the people—they're out to skin each other. I've got a piece of that little Saratoga trunk railroad; Mr. Morgan gave it to me if I licked the Gould crowd, and I did. So now I'm figuring to get the whole of that railroad away from little Bart, and I will, too. I'm going to be hog rich. Just for the hell of it. And it's all your doings, Clio. Only now things have got to be different between us.''

"Different?'' she repeated with stiff lips.

"Sure thing. There's no way out, honey. I aim to be worth millions and millions. That's the way you wanted it. But our fun's over. Folks as rich as we're going to be, why, we just naturally have got to get married. Yes ma'am. Married and respectable, that's us.''

19

THERE WAS A light knock—light but firm—on the sitting-room door of the Maroon suite, and Mrs. Maroon entered, cool, smiling, lovely. The newspapermen scrambled to their feet.

"I'm sorry, but the time is up. I said fifteen minutes, and it has been nearly half an hour." She looked up at him, anxiety in her eyes. "Tired, *chéri?*" Her hand on his arm.

"No. You'd think I was ten years old—instead of nearly ten times ten."

She still smiled, her eyes were questioning them—what had he said, how much did they know? "You know, Mr. Maroon was hurt some years ago in a—in an accident. And sometimes now, when he overexerts himself, he feels it."

"What accident was that?" the *Post* reporter asked.

"Uh—railroad accident, you might say," Colonel Maroon replied.

"Recent?"

"Well, no, you couldn't exactly call it recent. Matter of, say, sixty years ago."

The reporters relaxed. "Now you're kidding us again, Mrs. Maroon. Honestly, how a woman who looks the way you do can have a stony heart like that!"

She glanced up at her handsome ruddy husband; her eyes were searching to know more than the question implied. "Did you tell the young people what they wanted to know?"

There were lines of weariness in his face; he was polite, but it was plain that he longed now to be rid of them.

"Yes, honey. They wouldn't listen to what I wanted to tell 'em. So I told them what they wanted to know. It's their job to get what they were sent for." He raised a hand in farewell. "Good day to you, boys and girls. I wish some time before the last roundup you'd listen to the story I want to tell you. I could show you this country's gone a long ways in the last fifty, sixty years. I don't mean machinery and education and that. I mean folks' rights. They've clamped down on fellows like me who damn near ruined this country."

"Oh, now, Colonel! You've been reading books. You're one of America's famous citizens. No kidding."

"Famous for what! Another quarter century of grabbers like us and there wouldn't have been a decent stretch of forest or soil or waterway that hadn't been divided among us. Museums and paintings and libraries—that was our way of trying to make peace with our conscience. I'm the last of the crowd that had all four feet in the trough and nothing to stop 'em. We're getting along toward a real democracy now and don't let anybody tell you different. These will be known as the good new days and those were the bad old days. The time's coming when there'll be no such thing as a multi-millionaire in America, and no such thing as a pauper. You'll live to see it but I won't. That'll be a real democracy."

"Sure, Colonel. That'll make a great story."

"That'll be swell. Don't forget to tell us all about it next time."

"Thanks, Mrs. Maroon. Thanks, Colonel. Look, we've got to beat it."

Standing there, handsome and straight, his wife's delicate hand resting on his arm, he waved to them a Western salute with his free hand as though he were whirling a sombrero round his fine head. They were gone.

"They didn't want to hear it, Clint?"

"No." Gruff with disappointment.

"Ah, well, it doesn't matter now."

"But honey, I sure would have liked to have them hear it. We were a couple of bad characters, I suppose, the way you'd look at it now."

She looked down at the simple flowing folds of her white gown. She smiled her lovely smile. "Streamlined. Saratoga trunks are streamlined now, and so are railroads and houses and people. Everything except this hotel. It's kind of wonderful to come back and find it the same."

He wiped his forehead with his fine linen handkerchief. "The storybooks made the old days seem right pretty. But it's better this way. I'll be glad to get rid of the money. . . . Want to go to the races, honey? Like we did in the old days!"

"But do you think you could stand it, *chéri?* The noise, the heat, the cameras, the crowds staring."

"Shucks, I've stood it for sixty years. I guess I can stand it a while longer. Anyway, if it's going to kill me I don't know anywhere I'd rather die than sitting out there at the Saratoga track watching the horses coming round the curve. Remember the time that little devil Cupide————?"

Giant

1

THIS MARCH DAY the vast and brassy sky, always spangled with the silver glint of airplanes, roared and glittered with celestial traffic. Gigantic though they loomed against the white-hot heavens there was nothing martial about these winged mammoths. They were merely private vehicles bearing nice little alligator jewel cases and fabulous gowns and overbred furs. No sordid freight sullied these four-engined family jobs whose occupants were Dallas or Houston or Vientecito or Waco women in Paris gowns from Neiman-Marcus; and men from Amarillo or Corpus Christi or San Angelo or Benedict in boots and Stetsons and shirt sleeves.

All Texas was flying to Jett Rink's party. All Texas, that is, possessed of more than ten millions in cash or cattle or cotton or wheat or oil. Thus was created an aerial stampede. Monsters in a Jovian quadrille, the planes converged from the Timber Belt and the Rio Grande Valley, from the Llano Estacado and the Trans-Pecos; the Blacklands the Balcones Escarpment the Granite Mountains the Central Plains the Edwards Plateau the boundless Panhandle. High, high they soared above the skyscraper office buildings that rose idiotically out of the endless plain; above the sluggish rivers and the arroyos, above the lush new hotels and the anachronistic white-pillared mansions; the race horses in rich pasture, the swimming pools the drives of transplanted palms the huge motion picture palaces the cattle herds and the sheep and mountains and wild antelope and cotton fields and Martian chemical plants whose aluminum stacks gave back the airplanes glitter for glitter. And above the grey dust-bitten shanties of the Mexican barrios and the roadside barbecue shacks and the windmills and the water holes and the miles of mesquite and cactus.

There were, of course, a few party-goers so conservative or so sure of their position in society, or even so impecunious, as to make the journey by automobile, choosing to cover the distance at a leisurely ninety miles an hour along the flat concrete ribbon that spanned the thousand miles of Texas from north horizon to the Gulf.

Though the pitiless southwest sun glared down on the airborne and the groundling it met defeat in the vine-veiled veranda of Reata Ranch Main House. Even the ever present Gulf wind arriving dry and dust-laden after its journey from the coast here took on a pretense of cool moisture as it filtered through the green and spacious shade. Cushions of palest pastel sailcoth on couches and chairs refreshed the eye even before the heat-tortured body found comfort, and through the day there was always the tinkle of ice against glass to soothe the senses. Through the verdant screen one caught glimpses of a heaven-blue swimming pool and actually, too, a lake in this arid land. Radios yelped and brayed from automobiles and ranch houses, towns and cities throughout the length and breadth of this huge and lonely commonwealth from the Gulf of Mexico to the Oklahoma border, from the Rio Grande to Louisiana, but here at Reata Ranch no such raucous sounds intensified the heat waves. Jett Rink's name splintered the air everywhere else, but not here. It stalked in black three-inch headlines across the front page of every newspaper from El Paso to Bowie. It stared out from billboards and newsreels. It was emblazoned on the very heavens in skywriting. Omnipresent, like Jett Rink's oil derricks straddling the land. At every turn the ears and eyes were assaulted by the stale and contrived news of Jett Rink's munificence.

The JETT RINK AIRPORT . . . gift of JETT RINK to the city of Hermoso . . . biggest airport in the Southwest . . . private preopening celebration . . . two thousand invited guests . . . magnificent banquet in the Grand Concourse . . . most important citizens . . . champagne . . . motion picture stars . . . Name Bands . . . millions . . . first Texas billionaire . . . orchids . . . caviar flown from New York . . . zillions . . . lobster flown from Maine . . . millions . . . oil . . . strictly private . . . millions . . . biggest-millionsbiggestbillionsbiggesttrillionsbiggestzillions . . .

Mrs. Jordan Benedict, dressed for the air journey—blue shantung and no hat—sat in her bedroom at Reata Ranch, quiet, quiet. She sat very relaxed in the cool chintz slipper chair, her long slim hands loosely clasped in her lap. The quiet and the cool laved her. She sat storing coolness and quiet against the time when her senses would be hammered and racked by noise and heat; big men and bourbon, the high shrill voices of Texas women, blare of brass, crash of china, odors of profuse food, roar of plane motors.

Now, as she sat, little sounds came faintly to her ears, little accustomed soothing sounds. A light laugh from the far-off kitchen wing—one of the Mexican girls, Delfina probably, the gay careless one, the others were more serious about their work. The clip-snip of Dimodeo's garden shears—Dimodeo and his swarming crew who seemed to spend their days on their knees clip-snipping, coaxing fine grass to grow green, and hedges to flower and water to spurt in this desert country. The muffled thud of a horse's hoofs on sun-baked clay; one of the vaqueros who still despised the jeep or Ford as a means of locomotion. The clang of a bell, deep-throated, resonant, an ancient bell that announced the nooning at Reata Ranch schoolhouse. The soft plaint of the mourning doves. The town of Benedict, bustling and thriving, lay four miles distant but here at Reata Main House set back a mile from the highway there was no sound of traffic or commerce. So Leslie Benedict sat very still within this bubble of quiet suspended for the moment before it must burst at the onslaught of high-pitched voices and high-powered motors. For all the family was going, and all the guests up at the huge Guest House there at the other end of the drive. The big plane was in readiness at Reata Ranch airfield and the Cadillacs were waiting to take them all to the plane.

The giant kingdom that was the Reata Ranch lay dozing in the sun, its feet laved by the waters of the Gulf of Mexico many miles distant, its head in the cloud-wreathed mountains far far to the north, its gargantuan arms flung east and west in careless might.

2

THOUGH THEY HAD been only an hour on the road the thought of this verdant haven tormented Mrs. Mott Snyth as she and her husband tore with cycloramic speed past miles and miles of Reata fence and field and range. The highway poured into the maw of the big car, the torrid wind seared the purpling face of Vashti Snyth and—now that he had removed his big cream Stetson—tossed the little white curls that so incongruously crowned the unlined and seemingly guileless face of Pinky, her husband. Vashti Snyth's vast bosom heaved, her hands fluttered with the vague almost infantile gestures of the hypothyroid.

"My!" she whimpered in helpless repetition. "My! It's a hot of a day!"

"March, what do you expect? The tiny high-heeled boot on the accelerator, the small strong hands on the wheel, the bland blue eyes seeming focused on nothing in particular, he appeared relaxed, almost lethargic; those eyes saw everything to the right to left and ahead, he was as relaxed as a steel spring. "Reata looks good. Salubrious. Bick must have had the stinger over this section again, not a mesquite far's you can see."

"Mott, let's stop by the house a minute, can't we?" This massive woman alone called him by his given name though to the rest of his world he was Pinky; she actually gave the effect of looking up at him though her elephantine bulk towered above his miniature frame; and in spite of the fact (or perhaps because of it) that she as Vashti Hake, inheritor of the third biggest ranch in all Texas, had years ago committed the unpardonable social crime of marrying one of her father's cow hands.

"Not if you're going to do a lot of shopping in Hermoso before we check in at the hotel we can't. Mathematically speaking."

"I'm only going to buy a little white mink cape throw."

"How long will that take?"

"Fifteen minutes."

"You said you didn't want to take the plane. You said you wanted to drive because the bluebonnets would be so pretty. It'll take us another five hours anyway to get to Hermoso. The dinner is seven. How do you figure———"

"I'm sick of bluebonnets. They're right pretty, but I'm sick of 'em miles back. We can leave the car at Reata, hitch a ride in the big plane with Les and Bick."

"How do you know?"

"They're taking their big plane. I know. That's why I didn't want to fly down. You wouldn't take the big plane. I won't come down in that little bitty old two-engine job, front of everybody in Texas."

"We'd look good, wouldn't we, just the two of us sitting in the four-engine job holds fifty! Crew of four, gas and all, cost us about five thousand dollars to go four hundred miles."

"What of it!"

"How do you know how many they got going! Maybe they're full up."

"Company of course, up at the Guest House. But not more then ten or twenty, usually. Then there's Bick and Leslie and young Doctor Jordy and his wife probably and Luz———"

"Luz! Thought she was at school there in Switzerland somewheres."

"She quit it. Didn't like it."

"Like it! I should think if anybody didn't like it it'd be Bick. Heard her schooling there was costing him a heifer a day."

"Well, anyway, she's home and tearing up the place as usual, driving the jeeps like they were quarter horses they say, jumping mesquites with 'em, practically. You know Luz. But that's neither here nor there. Mott, I want to see what Leslie's wearing."

The cool blue eye turned from its task of pouring the road into the car to glance briefly at the beige mound palpitating beside him. "Whatever Leslie's wearing I want to tell you it's away yonder better than that sorry outfit you're carrying."

"Why Mott Snyth! This! What's wrong with it?"

"Plain. Plain as a fence post."

"Plain is the smart thing this year," Vashti boomed with the hauteur of one who knows her ground. "Shows what you men know. Neat and plain and expensive as all hell, like those pictures in *Harper's Bazaar* of the Duchess. That's the thing. Ask anybody. Ask Leslie. Nobody in Texas or anywhere knows better than Leslie what's being worn, she doesn't have to be told, she knows by instinct, the way you can pick a horse. Simple and girlish—" she flicked an imaginary speck off her big beige bosom—"is the keynote of this year's styles."

A flash of amusement wrinkled Pinky's guileless face. "Simple and girlish is all right for Leslie, maybe, granted the way she is. But you're packing plenty tallow, Vash."

Mischievously he pronounced the abbreviation of her name so that it became a French noun unflattering to her figure. She heard, she understood, she chose momentarily to ignore it. Blandly she resumed her description of the mode of the day.

"Everything but jewelry, that is. You're supposed to wear a hunk of a bracelet like this one I got on, no matter what, even with a sweater or a cotton wash dress. And a big clip with a lot of good stones or a flock of diamond or ruby or sapphire scatter pins is smart worn just stuck somewhere offhand like you'd jab safety pins into the front of your dress diapering a baby. But not even your engagement ring."

"How about wedding rings, Vash? Wedding rings still okay?"

"Oh sure. But no other jewelry daytimes. Only evenings."

He threw intense anxiety into his tone. "You got stuff with you, I hope?"

"Mott Snyth, I got enough rocks in that little bitty old handbag back there I'll bet if they take us on board Bick and the crew'll have to jettison some before they can lift the plane up in the air. Yes sir! Tonight I'm really going to rise and shine!."

Again Pinky Snyth turned a brief instant to survey the tentlike mound beside him. His glance was affectionate and possesive.

"Ruffles," he said. "I like ruffles on a female. But no matter what you wear you're sassy. You're as sassy as pink shoes."

Vashti, taking advantage of this rare approval, pressed her point. "Well then, we'll stop by like I said, see who's going and all and maybe catch a ride. And let me tell you, Mott Snyth, don't you go calling me Vash, like that, front of company. You and I ain't the only two in Texas know the French for cow. And one compliment don't cover an insult, either." But she was smiling upon him indulgently. "Look! There's the tower of the Big House. I bet it's crammed with company. We're not a mile away from the ranch."

"No place in all of Texas," Pinky announced without bitterness, "is more than a mile away from Reata Ranch somewheres."

Vashti bridled. "We are so! House to house we're more than ninety miles."

"House to house maybe. But fence lines, that's what counts. Fence lines you adjoin as you know well and good. Like I said, nothing's a far piece from Reata, including Oklahoma one side and Mexico another and the Gulf and Louisiana throwed in. Here we are. My, those palms have took hold. Never know they'd been set in."

Any Texan overhearing this artless chitchat would have known that these two were talking Texas. Both had had a decent education, yet their conversation sounded like the dialogue in a third-rate parody of Texans. This was due partly to habit and partly to affectation born of a mixture of su-

periority and inferiority, as a certain type of Englishman becomes exces-
sively Oxford or a Southern politician intensifies his drawl. Each was playing
a role, deliberately. It was part of the Texas ritual. We're rich as son-of-a-
bitch stew but look how homely we are, just as plain-folksy as Grandpappy
back in 1836. We know about champagne and caviar but we talk hog and
hominy.

They turned in at the open gateway with the Reata Ranch brand, the
lariat—la reata as the Mexican vaquero wove it himself out of rawhide—
copied in artful iron as an ornament for the gateposts. You saw its twists
and coils over the gatehouse too, as it could be seen a thousand thousand
times throughout this ranch empire with its millions of acres. Over the door
of the Main House, the Big House, countless bunkhouses, line houses;
burned into the hide of hundreds of thousands of bulls, steers, cows, calves;
embroidered on the silks of the jockeys who rode the Reata race horses;
monogramming the household linen, the table silver; wrought into andirons
for the fireplaces; adorning the ranch business stationery and Leslie's own
delicate blue-grey; stamped on the jeeps, the pickups, the station wagons,
the Cadillacs, the saddles. A simple brand but difficult to distort. No cattle
rustler of the old Texas days could successfully burn this braided loop into
another pattern or symbol. It was for this reason that shrewd old Jordan
Benedict had chosen it in 1855 with his first thousand acres of Texas land.

The nose of the Snyth car had not passed the gateway before Ezequiel
was out of the gatehouse and into the road, barring the way with his outstretched left arm, his right hand close to his body. The black eyes pierced
the windshield. Then the tense dark face relaxed, the arm dropped, the right
hand came up in a gesture that was less a salute than an obeisance.

Pinky Snyth lifted his hand from the wheel, open-palmed. "Cómo estás,
Ezequiel?"

The white teeth flashed. "Bienvenido! Señor Snyth! Señora!" He waved
them on.

Vashti tossed her head. "About time Bick Benedict got over guarding his
country like he was royalty."

"Now Vashti, you know he tried it and the place was stampeded like a
fat stock show, the okies were fixing barbecue under every mesquite."

Up the long drive beneath the date palms so incredibly rich under the
white-hot blaze. They stood row on orderly row, green-topped, mammoth,
like pillars in a monumental cathedral. Only a brush-country Texan could
even dimly realize what had gone into the planting and sustaining of these
trees in this land. Between the rows were the clean straight lines of irrigation
ditches. The fertilized soil lay in tidy ridges at the base of the tree trunks.

"Bick sets out to do something can't be done, why, he's possessed till he
does it better than anybody," Pinky observed. "Be putting in a ski jump
next, shouldn't wonder, middle of August middle of the range, bringing snow
by air lift from Alaska."

Past the old whitewashed adobe schoolhouse, the Big House with its
towers and intricate grillwork, past the old carriage house and the vast
garage. But no cars stood waiting there, only the vine leaves stirred in the
hot wind as the visitors drew up before the Main House and peered toward
the shaded enclosure.

Vashti essayed a "Yoo—hoo!" It emerged a croak from her parched
throat. "Either they're gone or they're all dead. Can't be gone, this hour."
With amazing agility she climbed out of the car, smoothing her crumpled
skirts, adjusting her belt, wiping her flushed face as she went toward the
porch, her feet and ankles slim and small and neat beneath the ponderous
superstructure.

"Leslie! Bick! Where've you all got to, anyway?"

Instantly it was as though the enchantment under which Reata Ranch had lain now was broken. The volley of shouts as the Mexican children were freed from the schoolroom; the crunch of gravel under heavy tires; a telephone ringing and a man's voice answering it; Dimodeo rising from where he had knelt near the pool and calling in Spanish to his men. "El mediodía! Noon!" A distant hum of noonday sounds from the houses of the Mexican section on the outskirts of the headquarters building.

Leslie Benedict emerged from the house, cool, slim; about her a sort of careless elegance. The Paris buyer at Neiman's in Dallas had said of Leslie Benedict that she wore indistinct clothes with utter distinction. The buyer was rather proud of this mot. Sometimes she elaborated on it. "What she wears never hits you in the eye. It sneaks up on you. No tough colors, ever. And no faddy stuff. You know. Never too long or too short or too full or too tight or bustles or busy doodads. My opinion, Mrs. Jordan Benedict's the best-dressed woman in Texas and doesn't even know it. Or care."

Now at sight of her guest Leslie's rather set smile of greeting became one of warmth and affection.

"Vashti! What a nice surprise!"

"Thought you'd all gone off and died."

"Where's Pinky?"

"In the car there. We're so hot we're spittin' cotton."

The contrast between the two voices was startling; the one low, vibrant; the other high, strident.

"I thought it was the others from the Big House. Come in, come in! Something cold to drink?"

"Hot coffee I'd druther if it's handy."

"Of course. After twenty years and more in Texas wouldn't you think I'd know it's always hot coffee?" She called in Spanish to someone unseen within the house. She went to the veranda entrance. "Pinky! Come in!"

"Where at's Bick?"

"He'll be here any minute. Come in out of the sun."

Vashti, sunk in the depths of a cool chartreuse chair, fanned her flushed face with an unavailing handkerchief. Her inward eye on her own expanse of beige silk, her outward eye on Leslie's slim grey-blue shantung, she voiced the self-doubt that tormented her.

"Look, Les, does this look too fussy? Traveling, I mean. Light beige?"

"Well—beige is—is good in Texas. The dust." The soft dark eyes kind, friendly.

"I don't know," Vashti panted unhappily. She narrowed her baby-blue eyes to contemplate the entire effect of Leslie's costume. "Now, take you, piece by piece—shoes and stockings and dress and everything, why they're just right, every single thing. But to look at you quick you don't look like anything."

At the startled glance and then the quick flashing smile of the other woman Vashti's customary high color took on the scarlet of embarrassment. "Oh, Leslie, I didn't mean it mean! I just meant no matter what you've got on it doesn't hit you in the eye the first thing, but take you apart, why, everything is perfect. Just perfect."

On her way to greet Mott Snyth Leslie Benedict's hand rested a moment on the shoulder of her guest's moist and crumpled bulk. "Dear Vashti, that's the nicest thing any woman ever said to another woman."

"Coffee, Pinky?" she called to him. "Don't sit there under glass."

The little man, a Watteau figure in Western masquerade, emerged from the big car. Legs actually slightly bowed like those of a cowboy in a Grade

B movie; the unvenerable white head was a dot beneath the great brimmed Stetson. "Me and Vashti got to mosey along, all that way to drive." This was a cunning opening wedge. "Where's Bick?"

"Out since five this morning. You know Jordan. He's probably down at the hangar now. He's always fussy about the big plane, I don't know why. You can fall just as far from a little one as a big one, but he's alway's casual about the little ones."

"Mott's the same way." Vashti had taken off one tiny beige slipper and was wriggling her toes ecstatically. "Climbs into the little Piper Cub, kind of flips his foot and shoves off like he was in a kiddiekar. Years back, when we first got a flock of planes and Mott used to fly the kids to school mornings———, coffee!"

Delfina, soft-stepping, concealing her shyness with a childish insolence of bearing. As she placed the coffee tray on the glass-topped table she stared at the two women with the steady disconcerting gaze of a four-year-old, the bright dark eyes making leisurely appraisal from foot to throat encompassing their clothes. Their faces did not interest her. Masses of vital black hair hung about her shoulders, her blouse was low-cut, her stockingless feet shuffled in huaraches.

"Thank you, Delfina," Mrs. Benedict said—a shade too nicely—in English. Her eyes met Vashti's as the girl disappeared.

"New?" inquired Vashti over the scalding rim of her coffee cup.

"Alvaro's granddaughter. I can't do a thing about her hair! She copies the girls in the movies and the dime store in town. She's been working as elevator operator at the Hake. You must have seen her. Her cousin is a bellboy there. Raul Salazar. Alvaro asked Jordan to bring her back here to work in the house, she'd got into trouble———"

"Oh well, if you and Bick are going to look after all of old Alvaro's sons and daughters and grandchildren and great-grandchildren, all that patriarchal Texas stuff."

Pinky choked over his coffee. "Listen at who's talking! Vashti's always up to her hocks in a Mexican wedding or a borning or a family ruckus. Takes enormous cantle off her life. How's old Alvaro, anyway? Must be pushing a hundred."

"Oh, who cares about who's pushing a hundred!" Vashti, now miraculously refreshed by the strong hot coffee, led up to the purpose of her visit. She peered through the vine leaves, her gaze squinting skyward. "Nice flying weather."

Quite as though she cared about the weather, about flying, about anything that had to do with this hideous day Leslie Benedict took her cue as hostess, she said smoothly, "Do you think so? What do you think, Pinky? Some of those fat black clouds look like rain."

"Rain!" Pinky scoffed. "Can easy tell you've only been twenty-five years in Texas. No rain in those clouds. They're just empties coming back from California. Come on now, Vashti. We got to get going. Vashti says she's got to pick up a new fur piece in Hermoso. White mink cape or some such doodad."

"How does it happen you're not flying?"

Hastily Pinky raised a protesting hand. "We better not go into that. Well, I didn't want to haul out the big plane, Vashti wouldn't hear to the little one." The rosy face crinkled in a grin. "They used to be a saying, in Texas a man is no better than his horse, and a man on foot is no man atall. Nowadays a fella without an airplane has got no rating, might as well be a Mexican."

At last. "Don't you want to leave the car here and fly down with us?"

"Oh, Leslie!" Vashti's tone of astonishment would not have deceived an amoeba.

"Well, say, if you're sure it wouldn't crowd you none————"

Quickly Vashti cinched it. "Love it! Just purely love it, and thank you kindly. Who all's going? Who's over at the Big House, h'm?"

As Leslie Benedict answered there was a half-smile on her lips, a rueful little smile. She thought, This is ludicrous I suppose. Twenty-five years ago I'd have said it was too fantastic to be true. When I introduce Pinky and Vashti, these good and kind people, there are no terms in which I can define them. They are of a world unknown outside Texas. Even as she answered Vashti she was seeing these two with the eye of one who would always be an outsider in this land. Pinky. As unlike the cowboy of the motion picture and the Western novel as one could be in the likeness of a man. Small, his bone structure as delicate as a woman's. His feet in their high-heeled ornately tooled cowboy boots were arched and slim as a girl's. Pink cheeks, pansy-blue eyes, white hair that waved in thick clusters of curls. In the dust-clouded past he had come to Texas from nowhere. They had deviled him and ridiculed him with their rough jokes and rougher horseplay. He must compensate for his miniature frame and his innocent blue eyes and pink cheeks. So he had been tougher, more daring than the biggest and most daredevil cow hand in the brush country. He used big words whose meaning they did not always understand, he spoke softly but at times his tongue was a whiplash. The small hands were steel-strong, there was no horse he could not gentle. He had come to the Hake ranch—the vast Double B—possessed of nothing but the saddle he carried under his arm—his ridin' riggin' in the ranch idiom. And Vashti Hake actually had married him on the rebound—this big booming woman who had been a big awkward girl—this daughter of old Cliff Hake, now long dead. Two million acres of ranch land, oil wells, cattle, millions.

"Who all's going, Les? Who's over at the Big House, h'm?"

Leslie walked to the veranda screen door, she listened a moment. "The cars went out to call for them."

"Yeh, but who, Les?"

"Well—uh—there's Cal Otter the cowboy movie star. You know—with the white hat and white buckskin chaps and white horse and all those white teeth. And the King and Queen of Sargovia and Joe Glotch the ex-heavyweight champion and Lona Lane that new movie girl and her husband and my sister Lady Karfrey————"

"She here! When'd she come?" Vashti interrupted.

"Leigh flew over from London on Tuesday and flew on here next day. And Jordan's brother Bowie and his sister from Buffalo————"

"Uh-uh! Trouble. And who else?"

"Well—the Moreys are here from Dallas, and Congressman Bale Clinch, and Gabe Target stopped on his way down and Judge Whiteside and a South American ex-Presidente who's Ambassador now—I've forgotten which country—and Tara Tarova and some others—and Cal Otter's taking his white horse." The absurd list gave her a mischievous pleasure.

"On the plane?" Vashti asked somewhat nervously.

"It's all right. In the forward compartment. He's used to flying. We'll be up only an hour or two, Jordan wants to show the King and Queen something of the ranch from the air, they're thinking of buying a few thousand acres up north in the Panhandle. They spent a day or two at the King ranch. Jordan says they bought some of Bob Kleberg's prize Brahman bulls."

"Kind of nice selling foreign royalty a bill of goods for a change. They been taking us for a couple hundred years. They better watch out or Jett Rink'll be unloading one of his dusters on'em."

"That's a funny thing for them to do, go to ranching," Vashti commented. "A real king and queen like that."

"Nothing so funny about it," Pinky said. "The Prince of Wales —Duke of Windsor he is now—he owns a big country up in Canada, don't he!" He ruminated a moment. "Don't know's I ever met a king and queen. Socially, I mean. Course, they're out of business now, those two, you might say. But what do you call them, talking to them I mean?"

But before Pinky could benefit by an elementary lesson in the etiquette of royalty a battered jeep crunched to a jolting stop in the driveway as though it had been lassoed and a gaunt girl in boots, jeans and a fifty-dollar shirt swung long legs around the side. "Hi!" she said. She was hatless, her sun-bleached hair was tied back into a sort of horse's tail. She entered the veranda, she went through a routine that was the perfection of pretty manners. So-and-so Mrs. Snyth . . . this-and-that Pinky . . . see you at the party it sounds horrible doesn't it . . . where's Dad . . . I'm off . . .

"Luz, they'll all be here in a minute. Why don't you go with us in the big plane?"

"Oh, Ma! That hearse!"

"Amador's packing the lunch. We're eating on the plane. Don't you want something before you go?"

"How you going?" Pinky asked, though he knew well enough.

"I'm flying the little Snazzy. I'll stop on my way to the field and grab a hamburger at Jerky's place."

Pinky wagged his head knowingly. "You taking any passengers in that footbath?"

"Don't be roguish, Pinky."

"He ain't going to the rumpus, for God's sake!"

"He wouldn't be seen dead at it."

"He sure would if he went," Pinky asserted, quite solemnly.

She was off with a neat little clatter of scuffed boots. Pinky called after her. "I am informed that Jerky's hamburgers are made of horse meat. Old beat-up quarter horses shot for their hides."

She stuck her head out of the jeep. "Plenty of onions and barbecue sauce, it'll be better than tough Texas beef." To the shouts of remonstrance at this heresy the jeep scuttled off like a frightened bug.

The eyes of the three followed her out of sight. They looked at each other. Silence hung momentarily between them. Vashti was not given to silences.

"Honey, she ain't serious about that dirt farmer, is she?"

But before Leslie could answer Pinky cut in, deftly.

"Now, Vashti, look who's talking. You married a low-down cow hand, didn't you?"

"Cow hand is different. This fella works afoot. Telling everybody, going around lecturing at Grange halls about this grass and that, blue grama—yella bluestem—side-oats grama—telling Texans been ranching all their life and their fathers and grandfathers how to run things. He don't even act like a Texan. Cornell University! Texas U. ain't good enough."

"What you think of Bob Dietz, Leslie?" Pinky asked baldly. "Might as well ask out, now Vashti's been and choused things up. Me, I got the opinion that boy is an unexception."

Very quietly Leslie Benedict said, "I think Bob Dietz may change the whole face of Texas—its system and its politics and its future."

Vashti Snyth gave a little yelp of shock. "Why Leslie Benedict, he ain't got five hundred dollars cash to his name!"

"I'd have said a hundred," Leslie replied quietly.

Now there came an acceleration of sound and movement from within the house and without. It was like the quickening of the tempo in a discordant modern symphony. From the dim interior of one of the rooms along the veranda emerged young Jordy Benedict with the Mexican girl who was his wife. They were hand in hand, like children afraid. There was between them a resemblance so marked that they might have been brother and sister. His hair was black but hers was blacker. He had inherited his from Leslie, his mother; she from centuries of Spanish forebears. Her skin was camellia-white, the Texas sun had hurled its red rays in vain. In their bearing, too, this young pair had a strange diffidence in common. Withdrawn, these two, as though alien to this familiar group. So young, so beautiful, they bore themselves with a shy uncertainty. Nothing about them of the confidence with which Luz had come and gone. The girl was dressed in black, very simple in cut, a strand of small pearls at her throat; and that throat and the face above it seemed almost translucent, as though a light were glowing behind them.

They knew their manners. Hers were quaintly old-world in their formality. She had been born in Texas, as he had been. Her father and mother, her grandfather and grandmother, her great-grandfather and great-grandmother and their forebears had been native to this land centuries before the word Texas had ever been heard. In a vortex of airplanes and bourbon and Brahman cattle and millions and little white mink capes and Cadillac cars and oil rigs and skyscrapers this girl moved and spoke in the manner of an ancient people in an ancient land.

"Hiyah, honey!" yelled Vashti as though addressing a deaf foreigner. "My, you sure look pretty."

To this the girl said nothing. With grave dignity she gave her hand to Vashti Snyth, to Pinky. "Sure do," echoed Pinky, and took her hand in his bone-crushing grip. She gave a little yelp, then she laughed like a child at sight of Jordan's startled look. For the moment the tension that had followed their entrance was broken.

"What do you think you're doing!" Jordy Benedict said, laughing, and pretending to shy away from Pinky's extended hand. "Bulldogging a steer?" He spoke with a slight stammer—not always marked when he was at ease, but now noticeable as he negotiated the word bulldogging.

"Hiyah, Jordan!" Pinky pronounced it Jurden, Texas fashion. "You and Juana flying down to the big blow, Doc?"

"No," Jordy said and turned away. He sat then on the arm of his wife's chair and flung one arm across the back. There was something defiant, something protective about the gesture. "We're driving—if we go."

Leslie put her hand lightly on the girl's knee. "Juana doesn't like flying. But then," she added quickly, "neither do I, really. I never have learned to take it for granted. I guess I belong to the generation that still thinks the automobile is a wonderful invention."

"What you wearing black for all the time, anyway?" Vashti shrilled at the girl. "Like a Mex——" She stopped, appalled. "I mean a little bitty thing like you, whyn't you wearing bright stuff, look at me, I got age on me but I go busting out like a rainbow."

Pinky shook his head in a mood of ruminant wonder. "Funny thing about women folks like Vashti here. Her young'uns growed up and married away, she's got to be riding herd on everybody else's."

"Mott Snyth!" The vast bosom heaved, the plump pink face crinkled like a baby's who is about to cry. "You go to saying things like that, mean, I've a good mind to——"

But at the sound of the quick drum of horse's hoofs the infantile face cleared magically. As Bick Benedict leaped off his horse a Mexican boy sprang from nowhere to mount the brisk little animal and, wheeling, clatter off to the stables.

There was nothing regal, certainly, in the outer aspect of this broad-shouldered figure in the everyday clothes of a Texas cowman. Yet here was the ruler of an empire. His high-heeled boots of black leather were stitched in colored thread, scuffed by hard wear, handmade, had cost perhaps sixty dollars; tight brown canvas pants tucked into the boot tops; brown shirt open at the throat; a canvas brush jacket; a Stetson, dust-stained, and rolled at the brim to make an exaggerated tricorne. Every garment he wore was suited to the work and the climate of his world; and everything from his lariat to his saddle, from his boots to his hat, had been copied from the Mexican horsemen whose land this Texas had been little more than a century ago.

Just below the leather belt with its hand-tooled design of the reata the hard lean body was beginning to show a suspicion of a bulge. Sun wind dust had etched Bick Benedict's face, tanned the skin to warm russet. A strangely contradictory face, benign and arrogant. Benevolent and ruthless. The smile was nervous rather than mirthful. His was a deceptive gentleness; soft-spoken, almost mild. The eyes were completely baffling; guileless, visionary; calculating, shrewd.

Up since five, he was late, he was weary, he was beset, he had nicked his right forefinger in a magic new weighing machine they were installing down at the main corral. He threw a lot of Texas into his greeting now.

"Vashti! And Pinky! Well! This is mighty nice!" He clasped Pinky's little hand of steel, he took Vashti's plump fingers in his hand that was tough as rawhide. Vashti's color, normally pink, now became enriched by a maroon overlay. She had blushed in this way, painfully, at sight or touch of him ever since the day, over twenty years ago, when he had surprised Nueces County and the whole of Texas by bringing this Leslie, this Virginia girl unknown to them all, to Reata Ranch as his wife. Jilted they said. At least the same as jilted Vashti Hake. Even his sister Luz had as much as admitted they'd be married someday and you know how she glared if any woman so much as looked at him.

"Nearly winded Pronto getting here. Anything wrong, Leslie?" He poured a cup of coffee, drank it black and hot with the eagerness of need. People frequently were annoyed by the fact that as they talked to him he appeared not to be listening. He listened to nothing that did not vitally interest him; and nothing held his interest that was not vitally connected with this vast this fantastic kingdom over which he and his father and his grandfather had reigned for a hundred years. His was the detachment, the aloofness, the politely absent-minded isolation of royalty.

"They're late too," Leslie now said. "The cars went to the Big House half an hour ago."

He tensed to a distant sound. "There they are now. I'll change and be back before they're out of the cars."

"Pinky and Vashti are going with us. I thought we could drive down now, and all these people needn't get out of the cars————"

Over his shoulder as he strode indoors. "Better not do that. But I'll only be five minutes. Shave on the plane." He vanished into the shaded recesses of the house whose dim rooms seen from the veranda seemed to have a pale green quality like a scene glimpsed under water.

The gaze of the two older women followed him. In Vashti's eyes were bafflement and adoration and poignant hurt; in Leslie's wisdom and tenderness and the steady glowing warmth of a wife who, after many years of marriage and disillusionment, is still deeply in love with her husband.

A covey of long sleek grey cars; talk, over-hearty laughter. Two people only occupied the passenger space of the roomy first car though each following car held six or seven.

Leslie stood up. It was not merely the act of rising to her feet; there was about the simple act something that communicated itself to Vashti, relaxed and bountifully disposed in the depths of her chair, and to Pinky, squatting on his haunches as he tousled and played with the frisking dog, and to the two young people so silent and politely aloof.

A tall thin man in a black Homburg scrambled hastily down from the front seat which he had occupied with the Mexican driver and opened the door of the lead car. The urban incongruity of the black Homburg in that scene and climate gave the wearer the comic aspect of a masquerader. The King and Queen of Sargovia stepped out of the car. A thin somewhat horse-faced sad girl in a not very new French dress and a long double string of large genuine pearls which dangled drearily and looked dated because all the women were wearing two-strand chokers of cultured pearls that looked smarter and more genuine. The man was shorter than she with a long neck as though he had stretched it in an attempt to appear taller; and his Habsburg blood showed in his prognathous jaw which should have looked strong but didn't. He wore one of those suits carefully made by a Central European tailor who long ago had served an apprenticeship in London's Savile Row. But he had apparently lost the knack of line for the suit was tight where it should have been easy.

Leslie went forward to meet them as Vashti scrambled for the slipper at the side of her chair.

"I hope you slept, Sir. And you, Ma'am. Everyone was warned to be very quiet on pain of death, but you know . . . ranch noises are so . . . Sir, may I present Mrs. Mott Snyth. Mr. Mott Snyth . . . Ma'am, may I present . . . ."

3

"IT ISN'T FAR," Bick Benedict assured them. "Four hundred miles. We're early. We can cruise around. I'd like to show you something of the Pecos section of Reata—from the air, of course. And you could have a look at historic old Beaumont later. That's the site of old Spindletop, you know."

"Spindletop?" said Miss Lona Lane, the movie girl. "Is that a mountain or something? I don't like flying over mountains very much."

The Texans present looked very serious which meant that they were bursting inside with laughter. The Dallas Moreys and Congressman Bale Clinch and Gabe Target of Houston and Judge Whiteside did not glance at each other. It was as though a tourist in Paris had asked if Notre Dame was a football team.

"Uh—no," Bick Benedict said, turning on all his charm which was considerable. Miss Lona Lane was extremely photogenic.

"Spindletop was the first big oil gusher in Texas. It dates back to 1901." The Texans relaxed.

"What's this San Antone?" inquired Joe Glotch, the former heavyweight champion turned sportsman and New Jersey restaurateur. "I heard that's quite a spot."

"Nothing there but Randolph Field," the Congressman assured him.

Bick Benedict addressed himself to the King.

"Perhaps tomorrow we can fly up to Deaf Smith County in the Panhandle. There are some Herefords up there I'd like to show you————"

"That would be interesting. What is the distance?"

"About eight hundred miles."

The young man smiled nervously, he fingered his neat dark necktie. "To tell you the truth, I am not as accustomed to this flying as you Texans. You see, my little country could be hidden in one corner of your Texas. At home I rarely flew. It was considered too great a risk. Of course, that was when kings were . . . Our pilots were always falling into the Aegean Sea. Or somewhere. Perhaps it is because we are not the natural mechanics that you here in the great industrial United States————"

His English was precise and correct as was his wife's, clearly the triumph of the Oxford tutor and English governess system over the mid-European consonant.

"That's right," said Congressman Bale Clinch. "Here every kid's got a car or anyway a motorbike. And a tractor or a jeep is child's play. Flying comes natural, like walking, to these kids."

The group had been whisked to the ranch airfield where the vast winged ship stood awaiting them. A miniature airport, complete, set down like an extravagant toy in the midst of the endless plain. The airport station itself in the Spanish style, brilliantly white in the sunlight with its control tower and its sky deck and its neat pocket-handkerchief square of coarse grass and specimen cactus and the wind-sock bellying in the tireless Texas wind. A flock of small planes, two medium large Company planes, and the mammoth private plane of Jordan Benedict. Down the runway Luz was warming up for her flight, you could see the trembling of the little bright yellow bug, its wings glinting in the sun, gay as a clip in a Fifth Avenue jeweler's window.

They all climbed the metal steps, jauntily, into the hot shade of the plane's interior.

"It'll be cooler as soon as we get up," Bick Benedict called out. "We're pressurized." Seats upholstered in brilliant blue and yellow and rose and green, very modern and capacious. It was startling to see that they did not stand in orderly rows like the seats in a commercial plane, but were firmly fixed near the windows as casually as you would place chairs in a living room. The safety belts were in bright colors to match and the metal clasps bore the Reata brand. In the tail was a cozy section with banquettes upholstered in crimson leather and a circular table in the center for cards or for dining.

And there at the door as they entered was a slim dark-haired young steward in a smart French-blue uniform and beside him stood the blonde young stewardess in her slick skirted version of the same, and in the inner distance an assistant steward busy with wraps and little jewel cases and magazines.

A vibration, a humming, a buzzing a roaring; they lifted they soared, the strained expression left the faces of the King, the Queen, the Motion Picture Star, the Congressman, the South American—all the passengers who did not feet secure in life, whether up in the air or down on the ground.

"Bourbon!" boomed a big male voice. It was Judge Whiteside in reply to a question from the steward standing before him with tray and glasses.

The royal pair jumped perceptibly. The steward turned to them. "Bourbon? Scotch? Old-fashioned? Martini?"

"Oh, it's a—its something to drink!" It was the first time the Queen had spoken since leaving the house.

"Well, sure," said Bale Clinch, "bourbon whiskey, what else would it be?"

"I have some relatives whose family name this is, in a way of speaking.

May I know how the name of Bourbon came to be used for a whiskey?'' the girl asked shyly.

"Well, ma'am," the Congressman began to explain, quite unconsciously addressing her correctly as he used the Texas colloquialism, "it's the best old whiskey there is, and it's made of mash that's better than fifty percent corn. It's named because they say it was first made in Bourbon County, Kentucky. My opinion, it was originally made in Texas."

Vashti Snyth's shrill voice came through with the piercing quality of a calliope whistle. "He'll tell you everything was originally made in Texas. Texas brag. Worse than the Russians."

Leslie made herself heard above the roar of the motors. "Here in the United States the word has still another meaning. Anyone who is extremely conservative—well, reactionary you know. We say he is a Bourbon. I hope you don't mind."

"Not at all," said the girl with an effort at gaiety. "But to have a good whiskey named after one is more flattering."

Fascinated, the two watched the male Texans tossing down straight bourbon. Bent on pleasing though they were, they refused it themselves knowing that this was no refreshment for a royal stomach, sedentary by habit and weak by inheritance. On the wagon, said the heavyweight ex-champion. Not before six P.M., said the cowboy movie star.

For Leslie Benedict there was about this vast and improbable vehicle and its motley company a dreamlike quality. Her sister Lady Karfrey was being studiedly rude to royalty, she had no time for the deposed or unsuccessful. They're behaving like refugees, Leslie thought. Worried and uncertain and insecure and over-anxious to please. Kings and queens deposed once were called exiles—splendid romantic exiles. Now they're only refugees, I suppose.

They alone stared out of the plane windows, in their eyes fright and unbelief mingled. Seen from the sky the arid landscape lay, a lovely thing. The plains were gold and purple, the clouds cast great blue-black shadows, there were toy boxes in a dark green patch that marked the oasis of an occasional ranch house, and near by the jade-green circlets that meant water holes. So, in the almost unbearably brilliant blue sky, they soared and roared aloft in a giant iridescent bubble. The ship was steady as a bathtub, the stewards were preparing lunch, there was a tantalizing scent of coffee. Everybody said everything was wonderful.

The casual arrangement of the seats and the roar of the engines made conversation difficult. So the company sat for the most part in a splendor of aerial isolation, earthly mortals helplessly caught up in a godlike environment.

The canny and taciturn Gabe Target, who was said to hold the mortgage on every skyscraper in Texas and to own at least half of all the oil leases, now turned conversationally to the royal pair. His face was benign and mild, his abundant white hair parted very precisely in the middle, he resembled a good old baby until he lifted the hooded eyelids and you saw the twin cold grey phlegms through which his ophidian soul regarded the world. His voice was low and somewhat drawling. "Understand you're fixing to buy a ranch, you and the—uh—your good lady here. Takes a powerful sight of work, ranching. What you aiming to stock? Herefords?"

Frantically the King snatched at the one familiar word which had emerged audibly from the rest.

"Ah yes, work! Everyone in your country works that is one of the wonderful things." In a panic lest Gabe Target should make further inaudible offerings he turned to encounter the fascinated stare of Lona Lane's husband seated just across the way. His royal training, drilled into him from the age of six, had taught him to file diplomatically in his memory names faces careers. At a loss now he regarded the tall moonfaced man smelling faintly of antiseptic. The eyes were myopically enlarged behind thick octagonal lenses, his maroon necktie matched his socks, his socks matched the faint stripe of his shirt. His beautifully manicured fingernails bore little white flecks under their glistening surface.

The King's voice was high and plangent, it had the effect of a hoot in a cave. "I know of your charming wife's career of course who does not but tell me what is your work your profession. Everyone works in this marvelous country of yours. And your name—I did not quite————"

The man, caught off guard, took a too hasty sip from the glass in his hand, coughed, managed to bow apologetically though seated. Recovering, "Lamax!" he roared. "G. Irwin Lamax. Oral specialist."

An expression of absolute incomprehension glazed his listener's face. Noting this, G. Irwin Lamax smiled and nodded understandingly. "Say, pardon *me*. I clean forgot you were a foreigner. I didn't go for to get you buffaloed with American talk." Smiling still more broadly he tapped his large even front teeth with a polished fingernail. "Oral specialist. Extractions. Teeth. Dentist."

The King stared, stiffened, remembered, smiled a frosty smile, he was trying hard to say democracy democracy in his mind. He glanced at the lovely Lona Lane, he looked out of the window at the seemingly endless reaches of Bick Benedict's empire, he closed his world-weary eyes a moment and wished himself quietly dead.

Bick Benedict, in response to a summoning glance from Leslie, came swiftly up the broad aisle between the seats. "Feeling all right, Sir? Well, I just thought . . . We're flying over the south section now, we always buzz them a little when we go over." He turned to face the assembled company, he stood an easy handsome figure in his very good tropical suit and his high-heeled polished tan boots; that boyish rather shy smile. He raised his voice. "Hold your hats, boys and girls! Hang on to your drinks. We're going to give the south section a little buzz. Here we go!"

For perhaps thirty seconds then the huge ship did a series of banks, swoops and dives. It was an utterly idiotic and wantonly frightening performance, Leslie thought. Unadult and cruel. Some of the women visitors from outside Texas screamed. The Texas men grinned, they said, "Now nothing to be scared of, honey. This ship's just feeling frisky as a cutting horse." The Texas-bred women looked unruffled and resigned like mothers who are accustomed to the antics of high-spirited children.

From her aloof place near the tail of the big room the aquiline Lady Karfrey barked, "Why don't you Texans grow up!"

Bick Benedict's brother Bowie and Bick's sister Maudie Placer from Buffalo turned upon her the gaze which native Texans usually reserve for rattlesnakes.

The ship righted itself, Leslie's lovely voice projected itself miraculously above the roar and the chatter. She pointed toward the windows and the plains below. "They're using the stinger on the mesquite. You might like to see it—those of you who aren't Texans."

"Stinger? What is a stinger?" the South American asked. Obedient faces were pressed against the windows, they surveyed a toy world.

"It's that yellow speck. Now we're a bit lower, you can see. The black patch is brush. The little thing moving along is the stinger, it's a kind of tank with great knives and arms and head like a steel monster. It's called a tree dozer too. It's rather fascinating to watch."

Up there, high in the sky, they could see the green patch of brushland that was a wilderness of mesquite. The trees were large and the thickness was dense and the yellow monster snorted and clanked and backed and attacked but they could not hear the snorts or sense the power. There was the green patch and then a path no longer green as the trees fell right and left like ninepins.

The King turned a shocked face away from the window. "But why do you cut down a forest like that!"

"That's no forest," Bick Benedict said. "That's mesquite."

"But these are trees. Trees."

Leslie turned from the window, she began to explain, brightly. "You see, the whole country's overrun with mesquite."

"Really! The whole of the United States!"

Oh dear! Leslie thought. Now I'm talking that way too. "No, I meant only Texas. All this once was open prairie. Grazing country. Then the mesquite came in a little, it wasn't bad because there are no trees to speak of, you know. Then they brought cattle in from Mexico where the mesquite was growing. Some say that the cattle droppings carried the seed. Others say that when they built all these thousands of miles of automobile roads they stopped the prairie fires that used to sweep the earth clean of everything but grass————"

The voice of Maudie Placer, Bick's perpetually angry sister, broke in with a sneering quality of almost comic dimensions. "Really, Leslie, you're getting to be quite a rancher, aren't you! You must have been reading books again." But no one heeded this or even heard it except the three women who knew—Leslie herself, and her good friend Adarene Morey and the outspoken amiable Vashti Snyth.

"But your serfs," said the King. "The peons I see everywhere here. Could they not have removed this mesquite with hand labor before it grew to such————"

"Serfs!" roared Bale Clinch. "Why, we got no serfs here in this country! Everybody here is a free American."

"Yes, of course," agreed the King hastily. "Certainly. I see. I see."

He does see, Leslie thought. He's only a frightened little king without a kingdom but he sees.

"Lunch!" cried Vashti happily as the steward and the stewardess and the assistant steward appeared, quite a little procession, with trays. "Mm! Leslie, you do have the loveliest food! Nobody in Texas has food like Leslie's. Avocados stuffed with crab meat to begin with! My!"

It was midafternoon as they came down at the Hermoso airport, the shabby old municipal airport. As they buckled their seat belts for the landing their faces were pressed against the windows, they beheld glittering beside the scrofulous old airport the splendid white and silver palace which Jett Rink had flung down on the prairie. Spanning the roof of the building was a gigantic silver sign that, treated with some magic chemical, shone day and night so that the words JETT RINK AIRPORT could be seen from the air and from the ground for miles across the flat plains from noon to midnight to noon.

"Oh, look!" cried Adarene Morey. A trail of heaven-blue as if a streamer of sky had been tossed like a scarf to the earth spelled out the omnipresent name of Jett Rink.

"It's bluebonnets!" Leslie said, and her voice vibrated with resentment. "He has had bluebonnets planted and clipped and they spell his name. In bluebonnets!"

"How cute!" said Lona Lane. "It's simply fabulous! I'm dying to meet him."

It was the pallid Queen who put forward the query this time. "We ask a great many questions, I am afraid. But bluebonnets—what is it that this is?" In a literal translation from the French.

"Why girlie!" bawled Bale Clinch—he had had three bourbons—"girlie, you been neglected in your Texas education down there at the Benedicts'. Bick, you old sonofagun, what's a matter with that old schoolhouse you got on your country you're always bragging on!" He beamed now on the Queen. "Bluebonnets! Everybody knows they're the national state flower of Texas. The most beautiful flower in the most wonderful state in the world. That's all bluebonnets is." He pondered a moment. "Are."

The huge craft touched the runway as delicately, as sensitively as a moth on a windowpane. The clank of metal as straps were unbuckled. The Texans strolled to the door as casually as one would proceed from the house to the street. The visitors breathed a sigh of relief. They stood ready to disembark, huddled at the door, king and cowboy and rancher and politician and actress and statesman and shrewd operator and housewife. Royalty in the lead.

At the door, smiling but military in bearing, stood the slim young steward and the pretty stewardess. "Come back quick now!" the girl chirped.

"I beg your pardon!" said the King, startled.

"It's a—a phrase," Leslie explained. "It's the Texas way of saying goodbye."

Just before they descended the aluminum stairway that had been trundled quickly across the field for their landing Bick Benedict made a little speech, as host.

"Look, I'm going to brief you, kind of. Those of you who aren't Texians. This is the old airport, you know. The new one isn't open for traffic until after tonight. That's where the party's to be. I'm afraid there'll be photographers and so forth waiting out there; and reporters."

"You don't think Jett Rink's going to lose a chance like this for publicity, do you, Bick?" Lucius Morey called out, and a little laugh went up among the Texans.

"This is going to be a stampede," Gabe Target predicted.

"No, now, Gabe. Everything'll be fine if you'll just trail me, you know I'm a good top hand, Gabe. There's a flock of cars waiting, we'll pile right in and head for the hotel. And remember, everything's pilone. No one touches a pocket—except to pull a gun of course."

Even the outsiders knew this was a standard laugh. But, "Pilone?" inquired Joe Glotch.

"Means everything free," yelled Congressman Bale Clinch, "from Jett Rink's hotel and back again."

"Yes," drawled Pinky Snyth. "And I'll give anybody odds that Gabe Target here will own the hotel and the airport and the whole outfit away from Jett Rink inside of three years."

There were the photographers kneeling for close shots, standing on trucks for far shots. There were planes and planes and planes overhead and underfoot. A Texas big town commercial airfield. Squalling kids, cattlemen in big hats and high-heeled boots—the old-timers. The modern young business and professional men, hatless, their faces set and serious behind bone-rimmed spectacles, their brief cases under their arms as they descended the planes from Dallas and Lubbock and Austin and El Paso. Local air lines with cosmic names tacked to and fro between cotton towns and oil towns, wheat towns and vegetable valleys. Hatless housewives in jeans or ginghams with an infant on one arm and a child by the hand flew a few hundred miles to do a bit of shopping and see the home folks. Everywhere you saw the pilots in uniform—slightly balding young men who had been godlike young aviators with war records of incredible courage. Years ago they had come down out of the wild blue yonder; and now they found themselves staring out at the Southwest sky in two-engined jobs that ferried from Nacogdoches to Midland, from Brownsville on the Mexican border to Corpus Christi on the Gulf. In the duller intervals of the trip they would emerge from the cockpit to chat with a sympathetic passenger and to display the photograph of the thin and anxious-looking young wife and the three kids, the oldest of these invariably a boy and always of an age to make the beholder certain that he had been born of their frantic love and their agonized parting in '42 and '43.

The Wonder Bird, the dazzling invention of the twentieth century, had become a common carrier, as unremarkable here in Texas as the bus line of another day.

"This way!" Bick Benedict called. "Just follow me through this gate, it's supposed to be closed but I know the . . . right through here . . . those are our cars lined up out there. . . ."

There were signs printed in large black letters on the walls. One sign read DAMAS. Another, CABALLEROS. "What's that?" inquired Lona Lane scurrying by. "What's that sign mean?"

"Sh-sh.!" Vashti Snyth hissed as she puffed along. "That's Spanish. Means toilets for the Mexicans. Men and women, it means."

Through the motor entrance another sign read RECLAME SU EQUIPAJE AFUERA A SU DERECHA. Miss Lane glanced at this, decided against inquiring.

"H'm," said the ex-Presidente. "I find this interesting, these signs in Spanish. It is like another country, a foreign country in the midst of the United States."

"Texas!" protested old Judge Whiteside puffing along, red-faced and pot-bellied. "Why, sir, Texas is the most American country in the whole United States."

"I should have thought New England, or perhaps the Middle West. Kansas or even Illinois."

"East!" scoffed Judge Whiteside. "The East stinks."

Through the withering blast of the white-hot sun again and then into the inferno of the waiting motorcars that had been standing so long in the glare. The newspaper men and women crowded around the windows, they said lean forward a little will you king, as they tried for another picture.

Bick Benedict's eyes blazed blue-black. "Look here, you fellas!" But Leslie put a hand on his arm, she was the diplomatic buffer between Bick and his rages against the intruding world forever trying to peer into the windows of his life.

"We'll see you all later," she called in that soft clear voice of hers. "Tonight." She pressed her husband's arm.

"See you later, boys," Bick muttered grumpily, not looking at them. He climbed into the huge car in which the King and Queen were seated in solitary grandeur except for the driver and their aide in the front.

"You all going to be at the Conky?" one of the reporters yelled after them as they moved off. Leslie, with the others about to step into one of the line of waiting cars, smiled over her shoulder at the cluster of reporters and cameramen. "Conky," she repeated after them with distaste. She caught a glimpse of the royal pair, an artificial smile still pasted, slightly askew, on their faces. Then their car picked up speed and was away like the lead car in a funeral cortege. The grimace of forced amiability faded from their weary features. With a gesture Leslie seemed to wipe the smile from her own countenance, she thought, I'm one of a family of rulers, too, by marriage. The Benedicts of Texas. I wonder how soon we're going to be deposed.

Somehow the first formality of the earlier hours was gone. Helter-skelter they had piled into the capacious cars and now there mingled affably in one big interior the prize fighter and Vashti and Pinky, Leslie, the South American and the Congressman. The car doors were slammed with the rich unctuous sound of heavy costly mechanism.

"Do you object," inquired the ex-Presidente as the cortege drove off, "that I ask so many questions? After all, I am here to learn. We are Good Neighbors, are we not?"

"Oh, please!" Leslie said quickly. "Please do."

"Uh—Conqui? However it is spelled. Is that the name of a man like this Jettrink?"

"That's two names, you know. His first name is Jett. His last name is Rink. Conky. Well, they just call it that, it's a sort of nickname for the big new hotel. The Conquistador. Jett Rink built that too."

"Mm! The Spanish is very popular here, I can see. And this Jett Rink whose name I hear so often. He is a great figure in the United States of America?"

"Say, that's a good one," said Mott Snyth. Then, at a nudge from his wife, "Pardon me." A little cloud of ominous quiet settled down upon the occupants of the car.

Through this Leslie Benedict spoke coolly. "This Jett Rink about whom you hear so much—he's a spectacular figure here in Texas."

"They say he was weaned on loco weed when he was a baby," Vashti babbled. "He's always trying to do something bigger or costs more money than anybody else. They say this Hermoso airport's bigger than any in the whole United States. La Guardia, even. And this hotel we're going to, why, ever since he saw the Shamrock in Houston he said he was going to put up a hotel bigger and fancier and costing more than even it did. And that's the way he always does. Ants," she concluded, smiling her cherubic smile at the gravely attentive South American diplomat, "in his pants."

Congressman Bale Clinch spoke cautiously. "You'd be put to it, trying to explain Jett Rink outside of Texas."

Whirling along the broad roads, past the huddled clusters of barbecue shacks and sun-baked little dwellings like boxes strewn on the prairie. Oleanders grew weed-wild by the roadside, the green leaves and pink blossoms uniformly grey with dust.

Little Pinky Snyth, grinning impishly, addressed himself to the visitors. He spoke in the Texas patois, perhaps perversely perhaps because instinct told him that this was the proper sauce with which to serve up a story about Jett Rink.

"Well, say, maybe this'll give you some notion of Jett."

Congressman Bale Clinch cleared his throat, obviously in warning.

"Pinky, you ain't aiming to tell about that little trouble with the veteran, are you, I wouldn't if I was you, it's liable to give a wrong notion of Texas."

"No. No this is nothing serious, this is about that fellow up to Dalhart," he addressed himself to the Ambassador, and to Joe Glotch, impartially. "That's way up in Dallam County in the Panhandle. This fella, name of Mody—yes, Mody, that was it—he had a little barbecue shack by the road up on Route 87. He got a knack of fixing barbecued ribs they say it had a different taste from anybody else's and nobody can get the hang of the flavor even tasting it and nobody's wangled the receipt off of him, he won't give. So Jett Rink he hears about these ribs and one night when he's good and stinking he gets in his plane with a couple of other umbrys, he always travels with a bunch of bodyguards, they fly up to Dalhart it's as good as a thousand miles or nearly and the place is closed the fella's gone to bed. Jett and the

others they rout him out they make him fix them a mess of barbecued ribs
and they eat it and Jett says it's larrupin' and what has he got in the barbecue
sauce makes it taste different. This Mody says it's his receipt it's his own
original mix and he don't give it out to nobody. Well, Jett gets hot the way
he does, he started out just rawhiding but now he gets wild the way he does
when he's by-passed, he gets serious he starts fighting like he does when
he's been drinking they had beer and whiskey too with the barbecue. He
hits the fella over the head with a beer bottle, the fella dies, Jett has to pay
his widow ten fifteen thousand dollars besides all the other expenses and
lawyers and fixers and the plane trip and all, why it must of cost Jett Rink
better than twenty-five thousand dollars to eat that plate of barbecue. It'd
been cheaper for Jett to buy that fella and his barbecue shack and all that
part of town including the grain elevator. Funny thing about Jett. If he can
get a thing he don't want it. But if he wants it and can't get it, watch out."

"That's right," ruminated Congressman Bale Clinch. "Yes sir. You got
to say this for Jett Rink. He goes after what he wants."

A heavy silence fell upon the occupants of the great rich car as it swept
along the sun-drenched streets of Hermoso's outskirts.

Leslie Benedict had been sitting with her eyes shut. Vashti Snyth reached
over and patted her hand almost protectively as a mother might touch a
child. She ignored the presence of the others.

"Mott got one fault, it's talking. Talktalktalk. What he missed out in
growing he makes up in gab."

Congressman Bale Clinch smiled chidingly upon her. "Now now, Vashti.
You hadn't ought to talk about your lord and master thataway." He then
roared as at an exquisitely original witticism.

"We will soon be there," Leslie said to the Ambassador. "Just another
minute or two. The Conquistador isn't in the heart of the city, you know.
Like the other hotels. It's almost like a big resort hotel. Very lavish."

"Air-conditioned," shrilled Vashti, "from cellar to roof, every inch of
it—except the help's quarters, a course. They say there's guests there never
had their faces outdoors since Jett flang it open—or sealed it shut, you might
put it."

"And the recipe for the barbecue," the South American persisted gently.
"Did he get it then?"

Pinky looked doubtful. "Well sir, I never rightly heard. The place was
closed down or sold out. Jett he felt terrible about the whole thing when he
sobered up. There was a daughter, girl about eighteen, she got a job in Jett's
outfit somewheres. In the office in Hermoso or Houston or Dallas or somewheres. Did real well."

"She sure did!" said Vashti with more bite than her speech usually carried.

Silence again. The streets were broad boulevards now, the houses were
larger, they became pretentious. Hermoso oil and cattle society had gone
in for azaleas, the motorcars flashed past masses of brilliant salmon-pink
and white and orchid and now you could see the towers of the Conqueror,
the Conquistador, rising so incongruously there in suburban Hermoso thirty
stories up from the flat Texas plain. Towers, balconies, penthouses, palm
trees, swimming pool. Flags and pennants swirled and flirted in the hot Gulf
breeze—the single-starred flag of the Lone Star State, the Stars and Stripes
above this, but grudgingly; and fluttering from every corner and entrance
and tower the personal flag of Jett Rink, the emblem of his success and his
arrogance and his power, with his ranch brand centered gold on royal blue
as he had sketched it years ago in his own hand—years and years before he
had owned so much as a maverick cow or a gallon of oil: the J and the R
combined to make the brand JR. Houses had been razed, families dispos-

sessed, businesses uprooted, streets demolished to make way for this giant edifice. All about it, clustered near—but not too near—like poor relations and servitors around a reigning despot, were the little structures that served the giant one.

4

ROYAL BLUE AND gold smote the eye, the air swam with it. The doorman's uniform, the porter, the swarm of bellboys that sprang up like locusts. Royal-blue carpet in the vast lobby. Gold pillars. Masses of hothouse blue hydrangeas and yellow lilies. The distinguished guests were engulfed in a maelstrom of boots, spurs, ten-gallon hats, six-foot men; high shrill voices of women, soft drawling voices of sunburned men; deep-cushioned couches and chairs hidden under their burden of lolling figures staring slack-jawed at the milling throng, their aching feet wide-flung on the thick-piled carpet. An unavailing vacuum cleaner whined in a corner, an orchestra (in blue and gold) sawed discordantly against a cacophony of canned music which someone had senselessly turned on and which now streamed from outlets throughout the gigantic room and the corridors and shops that bounded it. The Conquistador was a city in itself, self-contained, self-complacent, almost majestically vulgar. Downstairs and upstairs, inside and out, on awnings carpets couches chairs desks rugs; towels linen; metal cloth wood china glass, the brand JR was stamped etched embroidered embossed woven painted inlaid.

Later, over a soothing bourbon consumed in the privacy of the Snyth suite together with ten or twelve neighboring guests who had drifted in from this floor or that, Pinky incautiously observed, "Jett's sure got his brand on everything. Prolly got his initials cut in the palm trees out there. Puts me in mind of a little feist dog gets excited and leaves his mark on everything he can lift his leg against."

What with Bick Benedict's familiarity with fiestas such as this, and Leslie Benedict's clear orderly sense of situation, the members of their group had, for the most part, been safely disposed in their Conquistador quarters, each according to his importance as seen through the eyes of the Manager, the Assistant Manager and the Room Clerk, guided perhaps for this very special occasion by the bloodshot orb of Jett Rink himself. Protean couches could magically transform single sitting rooms into bedrooms. Good enough for an ex-Presidente, the hard-pressed Management instantly decided. Sitting room and bedroom in a nice spot for the heavyweight ex-champion. Nice little suite for Cal Otter the Cowboy Movie Star, where the crowd could get at him for autographs and so on. Snappy little balcony job for Lona Lane where the photographers could catch her for outside shots if the swimming pool section got too rough. Never could tell with a gang like this, liquored up and out with the bridle off. The Coronado penthouse suite for the Bick Benedicts and the Hernando de Soto apartment for the King and Queen, ex or not, the Management said in solemn discussion, they were a bona fide king and queen even if they had been cut out, you couldn't laugh that off and it would look good in publicity. This festive opening of Hermoso's airport, gift of the fabulous Jett Rink, had turned Jett Rink's hotel (mortgaged or not, as gossip said, for something like thirty millions) into a vast and horrendous house party. There wasn't a room or a closet or a cupboard to be had by an outsider. From lobby to roof the structure was crammed with guests each of whom had a precious pasteboard, named and numbered, which would identify and place him at Jett Rink's gigantic airport banquet tonight.

The contrast between the blazing white-hot atmosphere of Hermoso's streets and the air-conditioned chill of every Conquistador room, restaurant, hall, was breath-taking, like encountering a glacier in the tropics. From every corridor, hurtling out through every room whether open-doored or closed, you heard the shrieks of high shrill laughter, booming guffaws, the tinkle of glass, a babble of voices; and through and above it all the unceasing chatter of radios, the twang and throb of cheap music, the rumble of rolling tables laden with food or drink trundled along the halls by stiffly starched blue-and-gold waiters or tightly tailored blue-and-gold bellboys bearing themselves like the militia, discreet as secret service men; wise, tough, avaricious, baby-faced.

Tee-hee ho-ho yak-yak. Wham. Whoopee!

"I wish we had friends as amusing as that," Leslie Benedict said to her husband across the vast spaces of the Coronado suite.

"No you don't," said Bick Benedict. "And don't be like that."

"Like what?" Leslie said. She was standing at the window which was tightly closed because of the air conditioning, and looking out at the view which consisted of nothing—unless one found refreshing an endless expanse of flat prairie pushing the horizon into obscurity.

"Like the kind of person you aren't. Like dear Lady Karfrey your bitter bitchy sister. Bitternesss doesn't become you."

"What's the opposite of lebensraum, Bick? That's what's the matter with them. They've got too much space. It gives them delusions of grandeur. In the plane they kept on yelling about it being the most wonderful place in the world—the most wonderful people in the world, the biggest cattle, fruit, flowers, vegetables, climate, horses. It isn't. They aren't. And what's so important about bigness, anyway? Bigness doesn't make a thing better."

"All right. I'll bite. What is?" He was at the telephone. "Room Clerk. . . . Well, I'll hold on. . . . Don't say that damned Riviera. Or California."

"No. No, I think the temperate climate of the United States. New York, or Pennsylvania, or Virginia or even Ohio. Cold in the winter with lemon-yellow sunshine and enough snow to make you long for spring. Hot in summer, cool in the spring, tangy in the autumn. You know where you are and you don't have to explain about it all the time and try to sell it as they do here in Texas."

". . . Hello! Room Clerk? . . . This is Bick Benedict. . . . Oh, fine fine! . . . No, I don't want to speak to the Manager, I just want to know if . . . Oh, God, he's connecting me with the . . . Hello there, Liggett! . . . Yes, everything's wonderful . . . yes, she's here looking at the view . . . yes, she thinks the furnishings are wonderful . . . no, don't bother to send anything up thanks just the same we brought a lot of stuff with us . . . sure sure if we need anything we'll . . . Look, I called the Room Clerk to find out if my daughter Luz—uh—Miss Luz Benedict you know—had come in yet, I . . . oh, for . . . he's putting me back on the Room Clerk. . . . Hello! Look, can you tell me if Miss Luz Benedict . . ."

They were in the enormous bedroom. Blond wood, bleached like a Broadway chorus girl. Their feet seemed to flounder ankle-deep in chenille. "They ought to give you snowshoes for these carpets," Bick said. "Or skis. Liable to get in up to your neck and never get out."

A half acre of dressing table laden with perfumes, china, glass. A dining room of bleached mahogany but vaguely oriental in defiance of Coronado. The dining table could seat thirty. There was a metal kitchen complete and

as virgin as the culinary unit in a utilities company window. Vast consoles
in the entrance hall and living room. Overpowering lamps with tent-size
shades. Three bedrooms. Terraces. A bathroom in pink tile, a bathroom in
yellow tile, a bathroom in aquamarine, and here deference was done to
Coronado in terms of brilliant varnished wallpaper depicting conquistadores
in armor dallying with maidens of obscure origin amongst flora not now
indigenous to Texas.

Leslie had taken off the blue shantung and was making a tour of the vast
and absurd living room, so cold in its metal and satin and brocade and glass
and pale wood and air conditioning. She surveyed this splendor with an
accustomed eye. It had been theirs on the occasion of the hotel's opening
a year earlier. With one hand Leslie hugged her peignoir more tightly about
her for warmth while with the other hand she patted cold cream on her face,
walking slowly the length of the room and pausing now and then before
some monstrous structure of porcelain or carved wood or painting.

"There's no JR on the Meissen or the pictures," she called back to Bick.
"What must Coronado think! Except for a few liquor spots on the carpet
and cigarette burns on the wood everything has stood up wonderfully this
past year. I hope Hernando de Soto has done as well for the King and
Queen."

"You were all right on the plane. You promised me you would be and
you were." He stood in the great doorway in shirt and shorts and bedroom
slippers, a costume becoming only to males of twenty and those in the men's
underwear advertisements. "I know you didn't want to come but we had
to and you damn well know why. Even if millions are dross to you. I don't
bother you with business affairs but you had to know that and now I'm
telling you again. . . . And where's Luz I'd like to know! And Jordy and
Juana. Why couldn't they come with us the way other people's kids would!
No, Luz had to fly her own, and Jordan and Juana had to drive. And now
where are they! And you stand there and talk about the climate of Pennsylvania and Meissen and Coronado and what's the opposite of lebensraum.
And spots on the carpet."

She went to him, she had to stand on tiptoe, tall though she was.

"If you don't mind the cold cream I can stand the shaving soap." She
kissed him not at all gingerly. "No soap there, at least."

"You hate the whole thing, don't you? As much as ever. That's why you
talk like a—like a————"

"Like one of those women in the Marquand novels you don't read. Very
quippy. Don't worry about the children. They'll make the dinner. Their
behavior is odd but their manners are beautiful."

"Like their mother, wouldn't you say?"

"That's right, amigo. We'd better dress. Entacucharse, eh?"

"Now listen, Leslie. It's bad enough having Luz talking pachuco. Where
do you hear it? The boys on our place don't talk like that."

"Oh, yes they do. The young ones. The kids in the garage. And on the
street corners in Benedict. Just today in the kitchen that young Domingo
Quiroz, Ezequiel's grandson, was looking at a leaky pipe that needed weld-
ing. He said, 'La paipa está likeando hay que hueldearla.' That's the sort
of Spanish the kids are speaking."

"Entacucharse, eh? Dress to kill. Well, I haven't a zoot suit, have I?"

"I had Eusebio pack your white dinner clothes and black cummerbund
and I've even ordered a deep red carnation for your buttonhole—probably
the only red carnation in Texas. You'll be smart as paint."

He glanced down at himself, he contracted his stomach muscles sharply.

"Riding does it. Everybody else lolling around in cars all the time. Even the vaqueros ride herd in jeeps half the time."

"Just remember to tuck in like that when you wrap your lithe frame into your cummerbund or you'll never make the first button. Look. We'll have to dress."

Here in southern Texas as in the tropics, there was little lingering twilight. It was glaring daylight, it was dark.

"Where're those damned kids!"

"Luz is probably out at the airfield chumming with the mechanics. Perhaps Jordy and Juana decided not to come. And even if they did, you know they're driving. That takes————"

"Thanks. I know how long it takes. I'm kind of from Texas too, remember?"

He was like that now. On the defensive, moody.

"Yes, dear. Get into our clothes and then we'd better give our Noah's Ark a roll call. Shall we go as we came out—you with the King and Queen and I with—doesn't it sound silly!"

Hermoso's old airport, so soon to be discarded, seemed a dim and dated thing huddling shabbily, wistfully, outside the glow and sparkle of the Jett Rink palace. Planes were coming and going on the old strip. Against the solid fences that separated the two fields were massed thousands of townspeople staring, staring, their white faces almost luminous in the reflected light. They talked and milled and shoved and drank Coca-Cola and the small children chased each other round and about their elders' legs, and the men shifted the sleeping babies hanging limp on their shoulders. "Lookit," they said. "Lookit the big lights up yonder. . . . I bet that's the Governor coming in there. . . . Stop that stompin' around, Alvin. Come here, I say, afore I whup you."

"Biggest airport in the whole state of Texas. Texas hell! In the whole United States Hermoso's the biggest. They say it makes anything they got in the East—New York or anywheres—look like a prairie-dog hole."

And in the deeper shadows stood the Hermosans of Mexican heritage, their darker faces almost indistinguishable in the gloom. These were quiet, the children did not run about with squawking catcalls; the boys and girls of sixteen, seventeen, sometimes stood with their arms about each other's waists, but demurely, almost primly, with their parents' eyes approvingly upon them. The roads beyond were choked with every kind of motorcar and in these, too, the people stood up and stared and wondered and applauded in their curious psychological consciousness, which was a mixture of childlike hope and provincial self-satisfaction.

"They lease that piece I got up in Tom Green County and it don't come in a duster I can be in there next year along with any of 'em, Jett Rink or any of 'em. All you need is one good break. What was he but a ranch hand, and not even a riding hand. Afoot. And now lookit!"

Lookit indeed. The guests came in cars the size of hearses and these were not stuck in the common traffic. Each carried a magic card and whole streets and outlying roads were open only to them. The women had got their dresses in New York or at Neiman's in Dallas or Opper-Schlink's in Houston. Given three plumes, they could have been presented just as they stood at the Court of St. James's. Their jewels were the blazing plaques and chains you see in a Fifth Avenue window outside of which a special policeman with a bulge on his hip is stationed on eight-hour duty. Slim, even chic, there still was lacking in these women an almost indefinable quality that was inherent in the women of the Eastern and Midwestern United States. Leslie Benedict thought she could define it. In the early days of her marriage she had tried to discuss it with her husband as she had been accustomed to talk with her father during her girlhood and young womanhood—freely and gaily and intelligently, lunge and riposte, very exhilarating, adult to adult.

"They lack confidence," she had said in the tones of one who has made a discovery after long search. "That's it. Unsure and sort of deferential. Like oriental women."

"What do you think they should be? Masculine?"

"I was just speaking impersonally, darling. You know. Even their voices go up at the end of a declarative sentence, instead of down. It's sort of touching, as though they weren't sure you'd like what they've said and were willing to withdraw it. Like this. I asked that Mrs. Skaggs where she lived and she said, 'Uvalde?' with the rising inflection. It's appealing but sort of maddening, too."

"Well, you know the old Texas saying. In Texas the cattle come first, then the men, then the horses and last the women."

Now, as they drove into the vast airfield and stopped at the floodlighted entrance, Leslie was thinking of these things without emotion, but almost clinically as she had learned she must if she would survive. Mindful of their two most distinguished guests in the crush and glare and clamor of the entrance they had somehow lost the South American. "It's all right," Bick said. "We'll pick him up inside. And we're all at the same table."

"Oh, Bick!" Leslie called through the roar and din. "Did you give him his card, I think it would have been better to give everyone a card just in case they were lost—oh, there he is in the doorway. Why—what———!"

The olive-skinned aquiline face, the slim and elegant figure in full evening dress, was easily distinguishable in the midst of the gigantic Texans in cream-colored suits, in dun-colored tropicals, in Texas boots and great cream Stetsons, worn in arrogance and in defiance of the negligible universe outside their private world. Even in the welter of waving arms, the shrill greetings, the booming laughter, the shoving and milling, the handshaking the back-slapping, "Well, if it ain't Lutch, you old sonofagun! You telling me you left that wind-blown sand-stung Muleshoe town of yours and all those cow critters to come to this———" even in the midst of this hullabaloo it was plain that something was wrong.

"Hurry, Bick. What is it?"

The men behind the door ropes were none of your oily headwaiters full of false deference and distaste for the human race in evening clothes. Giants in khaki guarded the entrance, and on their slim hips their guns, black and evil, gleamed above the holster flaps. And now, as Bick Benedict elbowed his way through the throng near the doorway, he heard one of the most gigantic of these guardians say, as he snapped with a contemptuous thumb and middle finger the stiff card in his other hand: "Well, you sure look like a cholo to me, and no Mexicans allowed at this party, that's orders and besides none's invited that's sure."

"Oh God, no!" cried Bick Benedict, and battered his way past resistant flesh and muscle to reach the giant cerberus. He called to him as he came. "Hi, Tod! Tod! Hold that, will you! Hold on there!" And the other man's head turning toward him, a curious greyish tone like a film over the olive skin, his dark eyes stony with outrage. Bick reached them, he put a hand on the faultlessly tailored sleeve, the other on Tod's steely wrist. "Look, Tod, this gentleman is one of the honored guests this evening, he's going to be the new Ambassador from Nuevo Bandera, down in South America. He's come all the way from Washington to———" His voice was low, insistent.

Tod's sunburned face broke into a grin that rippled from the lips to the eyes, he spoke in the soft winning drawl of his native region. "Well, I'm a hollow horn! I sure didn't go for to hurt your feelings. I made a lot of mistakes in my day but this does take the rag off the bush." He held out his great hand. "Glad to make your acquaintance. Sure sorry, Bick. Pass right along, gentlemen. Hi there, Miz Benedict, you're looking mighty purty."

There isn't anything to do, Leslie said to herself as she slipped her hand through her guest's arm, there isn't anything to do but ignore the whole thing unless he speaks of it.

She chatted gaily. "It's going to be a shambles, so crowded. We don't have to stay late after the dinner if you want to leave—you and the others. It's just one of those things—everybody's supposed to show up—you know—like a Washington reception when you can't get near the buffet. You've probably never before in your life seen Stetsons worn with black dinner coats or women in Mainbocher evening gowns escorted by men in shirt sleeves and boots." She looked about her. "Perhaps escorted isn't exactly the word."

Dinner, presaged by a jungle of tables and tables and tables, was to be served in the great domed main concourse. A bedlam, designated on the engraved invitations as a reception, was in progress in great sections and halls and rooms that next week would be restaurants, lunch rooms, baggage rooms, shops, offices. Every ticket and travel counter tonight was a bar. Travel signs were up, neat placards bearing the names of a half dozen air lines. And off the main hall were arrowed signs that said LADIES and others that said COLORED WOMEN. Orchids and great palms and tubs of blossoming trees. Banners, pennants, blinding lights. The reception now was spilling over into the concourse, into the patio and out to the runways. Kin Kollomore's Band over there. Oddie Boogen's Band over here. The loudspeakers were on, the blare was frightening, it beat on the brain like a pile driver.

Perhaps escorted isn't the word, Leslie had said somewhat maliciously. The men—the great mahogany-faced men bred on beef—who somehow had taken on Physical dimensions in proportion to the vast empire they had conquered—stood close together, shoulder to shoulder, as male as bulls; massive of shoulder, slim of flank, powerful, quiet and purposeful as diesel engines. On the opposite side of the room, huddled too, but restless, electric, yearning, stood the women in their satins and chiffons and jewels. The men talked together quietly, their voices low and almost musical in tone. The women were shrill as peacocks, they spread their handmade flounces and ruffles; white arms waved and beckoned.

"Ay-yud!" a wife called to a recalcitrant husband. "Mary Lou Ellen says at Jett's big bowil last year at the Conky opening they was ten thousand——"

"Sure nuff," Ed calls back, nodding and smiling agreeably, though no sound is heard above the din. He remains with the men.

"Ay-yud's had the one over the eight he's feelin' no pain," his wife says philosophically, turning back to her women friends.

The Ambassador regarded this with an impassive face. "It is interesting," he said, "that the people of this country of Texas——"

"Country!"

"It is like a country apart. It is different from any other North American state I have seen and I have traveled very widely here in the United States. It is curious that the citizens of Texas have adopted so many of the ways and customs of the people they despise."

"How do you mean?" Leslie asked as though politely conversational. She knew.

"In Latin countries—in Mexico and in Spain and Brazil and other South American countries including my own Nuevo Bandera—you often will find the men gathered separately from the women, they are talking politics and business and war and national affairs in which the women are assumed not to be interested."

"Or informed?"

Leslie, the outspoken, looked at him, she felt admiration and almost affection for this man who had met insult with such dignity. "Here in Texas we are very modern in matters of machinery and agriculture and certain ways of living. Very high buildings on very broad prairies. But very little high thinking or broad viewpoint. But they're the most hospitable people, they love entertaining visitors————"

He inclined toward her in a little formal diplomatic bow. "I am happily aware of that, madame."

"Oh, I didn't mean—I just—sometimes I forget I'm a Texan by marriage. But thank you. I—you see they're really wonderful in a crisis. In the last war—and the First World War too—the Texans were the most patriotic and courageous————"

"Yes. I know. But war is, as you say, a crisis—an excrescence, a cancer on the body of civilization. It is what a people do and think in the time of health and peace that is most important." He was very quiet and collected and somehow aloof in the midst of the turmoil all about them. Like Jordy's wife Juana, she thought suddenly. Remote, like Juana. He was speaking again, through the uproar. "But you are not a Texan?"

"No. But my husband is, of course, and all his people since the beginning of———— Oh, it must be dinner. They're moving toward the other room. Our party is all at the same table, it's Number One on the dais with our host, Jett Rink."

"Ah yes, the host who spends twenty-five thousand dollars for a dish of barbecue." He glanced about at the incredible scene. "I can well believe it now."

"There's Jordan—there's my husband—with the others. Now if only we can stay together." She raised her voice to reach her husband struggling toward them. "Luz? Jordy?"

His shoulders were making a path for the royal pair behind him "Haven't seen them" he shouted. "Catch on like a conga line and we'll make it."

Breathless, disheveled, they found themselves half an hour later seated on a platform at an orchid-covered table like a huge catafalque. From the hundreds of tables below a foam of faces stared up at them. Flashlights seared the air. Bands blared. The loudspeakers created pandemonium.

"And when," said the King seated beside Leslie, "does our host appear?"

With awful suddenness the loudspeaker system went off. It had exaggerated every sound. Conversation had necessarily been carried on at a shout. Now the abrupt quiet was as shocking as the noise had been. The comparative silence stunned one. From the dais where he sat with the guests of honor boomed the unctuous voice of Congressman Bale Clinch in tones which, under stress of the megaphones, had been meant for the confidential ear of his dinner neighbor alone. In the sudden silence they now rang out with all the strength and authority with which, in Washington Congress assembled, he frequently addressed his compatriots on the subject of Texas oil rights in general and Jett Rink's claims in particular.

"That wildcattin' son-of-a-bitch Jett Rink is drunk again or I'll eat a live rattlesnake. They're soberin' him up in there————" He stopped, aghast, as a thousand faces turned toward him like balloons in a breeze.

Big though his voice was it had carried only through a fraction of the great concourse. But the repetition from mouth to mouth had taken only a few seconds. A roar, a Niagara of laughter, shook the room.

In the midst of this Luz Benedict appeared suddenly at the main table, she had not made her way through the main room, she seemed to have materialized out of the air. She was wearing a white chiffon gown, not quite fresh; no jewelry, her fair hair still tied back in the absurd horse's tail coiffure, though now a little spray of tiny fresh white orchids replaced the black ribbon that had held it.

She leaned over her father's chair as casually as though she were in the dining room at the ranch. "Who told the joke?" she inquired casually. "I could use a laugh."

Bick Benedict turned his head slightly, he bit the words out of the corner of his mouth. "Where've you been? And Jordan?"

"Parn me, lady," said a waiter, and placed a huge slab of rare roast beef before Bick Benedict. It almost covered the large plate, it was an inch thick, astonishingly like the map of Texas in shape, and it had been cut from the prime carcasses flown by refrigerated plane from Kansas City. Luz viewed it with distaste as she leaned over her father's shoulder.

"Listen. Jordy's looking for Jett, he says he's going to beat him up he———"

A girl in a strapless scarlet evening dress appeared on the platform at the far end of the great hall, she began to sing to the accompaniment of the orchestra, her lips formed words but no note was heard in the absence of the sound mechanism, there was an absurd quality in her mute coquetry as she mouthed the words of the familiar Texas song that now opened the evening's program.

Bick Benedict jerked around in his chair to face his daughter. "You're crazy! Where is he?"

"Louder!" yelled a man in the audience. "Louder!" someone echoed from a far corner. "What's the matter with the loudspeaker! Jett! Jett, get busy in there!" With knives and forks they began to tap the sides of their water glasses or wineglasses or bourbon tumblers, the clinking rose to an anvil chorus. The girl in the red dress faltered, stopped, smiled uncertainly, went on with her soundless song.

From the far far end of the room young Jordan Benedict strode down through the jungle of tables close-packed as mesquite on the plains. He was alone. A neat grey suit, a neat blue bow tie, his blue-black hair that was so like his mother's seemed a heavy black cap above his white face. Straight toward the table marked Number One—the table on the dais.

Bick Benedict muttered an apology to the right to the left, quickly he pushed back his chair and stood facing Luz. He grasped her wrist. "What's the matter with him! What happened!" He shook her arm a little as though to hurry her into speech.

"He smashed up the Beauty Parlor at the hotel, he threw chairs into the mirrors and shot out the lights like 'an old Western movie———"

"Beauty Parlor! What the hell do you m———"

"Oh, you know—where we have our hair done and everything. Don't be—anyway, he wrecked it and now he's looking for Jett he says he's going to smash his face he says it's Jett's hotel and his orders———"

"Why! Why! Why! Quick!"

"Juana went down to keep an appointment to have her nails done. She'd telephoned, and given her name of course. When she got down there the girl at the desk looked at her and said they didn't take Mexicans, she came upstairs and Jordy went———" She stopped abruptly. "There comes Jett. Look. He's been drinking."

With a sudden blare that jolted the eardrums the loudspeaker went on. From the two bands there was a ruffle of the drums. Jett Rink came through the door marked Office. Private. White dinner clothes, a tight little boutonniere of bluebonnets on his lapel. The curiously square face, thin-lipped, ruthless, the head set too low on the neck that in turn was too massive for the small-boned body. He walked, not as a man who has authority and power but as a man does who boasts of these. On his right walked a man, on his left walked a man, the two looked oddly alike in an indefinable way, as though the resemblance came from some quality within them rather than from any facial kinship. Their clothes seemed too tight as though they covered muscles permanently flexed, and their shaves were fresh, close and unavailing. Their faces impassive, the cold hard eyes regnant as searchlights.

"Hi, Jett!" bawled the cowboy movie star.

"Which is he?" the King inquired, not very astutely.

Congressman Bale Clinch answered somewhat impatiently. "The middle one of course. The other two are strong-arms."

Now that the sound system had been restored the girl in red and the accompanying band were in full swing with a childish song which the state had adopted as its own. The tune was that of the old ballad, "I've Been Working on the Railroad" to words which someone had written.

> The eyes of Texas are upon you,
> All the live-long day.
> The eyes of Texas are upon you,
> You cannot get away. . . .

Jordy Benedict reached the dais, he leaped upon it nimbly, crept beneath the table opposite his father's empty chair like a boy playing hide-and-seek, he bobbed up to face Jett Rink. At the tables below the dais the diners had got to their feet leaving the slabs of red roast to congeal on their plates.

Jordy Benedict called no names. He looked absurdly young and slim as he faced the three burly figures.

"Stand away," he said quietly, "and fight." His arm came back and up like a piston. A spurt of crimson from Jett Rink's nose made a bizarre red white and blue of his costume. A dozen hands pinned Jordy's arms, the flint-faced men held Jett Rink, the two glaring antagonists, pinioned thus, strained toward each other like caged and maddened animals.

Jett Rink jumped then, swinging hammock-like between the two guards whose arms held his. His feet, with all his powerful bulk behind them, struck Jordy low with practiced vicious aim so that the grunt as the boy fell could be heard by the guests of honor on the dais even above the blare of the band.

Quick though Bick was, Leslie was there before him, kneeling on the floor beside her son. For the moment he was mercifully unconscious. The first exquisite agony of this blow had distorted the boy's face, his body was twisted with it. His eyes were closed.

Bick, kneeling, made as though to rise now. His eyes were terrible as he looked at the panting Jett Rink. But Leslie reached across the boy's crumpled form, she gripped Bick's arm so that her fingers bit into his muscles. Quietly, as though continuing a conversation, she said, "You see. It's caught up with you, it's caught up with us. It always does."

But now the boy stirred and groaned and his eyes opened and his face was a mask of hideous pain as he looked up into the two stricken faces bent over him. The physician in him rose valiantly to meet the moment, the distorted lips spoke the truth to reassure them.

"Morphine . . . pain . . . horrible . . . not serious . . . morphine . . ."

5

THOUGH THE THREE Lynnton girls always were spoken of as the Beautiful Lynnton Sisters of Virginia they weren't really beautiful. For that matter, they weren't Virginians, having been born in Ohio. But undeniably there was about these three young women an aura, a glow, a dash of what used to be called diablerie that served as handily as beauty and sometimes handier. These exhilarating qualities wore well, too, for they lasted the girls their lifetime, which beauty frequently fails to do.

The three Lynntons were always doing things first or better or more outrageously than other girls of their age and station in Virginia and Washington society. Leigh, the eldest—the one who married Sir Alfred Karfrey and went to England to live—scandalized Washington when, as a young woman in that capital's society circles, she had smoked a cigarette in public long before her friend Alice Roosevelt Longworth shocked the whole United States with a puff or two. Leigh certainly was the least lovely of the three Lynnton Lovelies as they sometimes were fatuously called. She had the long aquiline face of her mother—horse-faced, her feminine detractors said—and she was further handicapped for dalliance by a mordant tongue that should have scared the wits out of the young male Virginians who came courting with Southern sweet talk. People said that with her scarifying wit she actually had whiplashed the timorous Karfrey into marrying her.

Leslie the second sister was, as the term went, a bluestocking. She was forever reading books, but not the sort of books which other Southern young women consumed like bonbons as they lay, indolent and slightly liverish from too many hot breads, in the well-worn hammock under the trees. Leslie Lynnton had opinions of her own, she conversed and even argued with her distinguished father and his friends on matters political, sociological, medical and literary just as if she were a man. Though her eyes were large, dark, and warmly lustrous there undeniably was a slight cast in the left one which gave her, at times, a sort of stricken look. Oddly enough, men found this attractive, perhaps because it imparted a momentarily helpless and appealing aspect.

The third girl, Lacey, was seven years younger than her second sister and represented Mrs. Lynnton's last try for a son. Lacey turned out a tomboy and small wonder. As each of the three had been intended by their parents to be males only masculine names had been provided for them before birth. With the advent of the third girl Mrs. Lynnton, admitting final defeat, had hastily attempted to change the name from Lacey to Laura. But Lacey it remained.

You were always seeing photographs of the three in airy organdies and sashes posed with arms about one another's waists in front of white-columned porticoes with a well-bred hunting dog or two crouched in the foreground. But Race Lynnton—Doctor Horace Lynnton in all the encyclopedias and Who's Whos and medical journals—had really brought them up with a free hand and an open mind. Though the girls moved with grace and distinction they were generally considered too thin. Theirs were long cleverlooking hands rather than little dimpled ones; theirs a spirited manner; little money and small prospect of more, being daughters of a very dedicated surgeon-physician-scientist.

In spite of these handicaps the Lynnton ladies somehow emerged feminine and alluring. The life juices were strong in them, they possessed the gifts of warmth and sympathetic understanding which tempered their wit. Some-

times, talking before the fire with a gay and friendly group, Leslie had a way
of sitting on the hearth rug, her shoulder and arm pillowed against her father's
knee, her face turned up to him as he talked, her fine intelligent eyes seeming
to absorb the light in his face. At such times the younger men present were
likely to take their handkerchiefs furtively from their pockets and wipe their
brows. Electra, even in that fairly recent day, was merely a Greek legend,
together with the equally bemused Oedipus.

"I declare," Mrs. Lynnton would say—she frequently prefaced her statements with a warning salvo such as I declare or I must say or if you want
my opinion—"I declare, Leslie, I sometimes think your father and I will
have you on our hands as an old maid. Leigh was late enough, twenty-three
when she married, but look at her now, Lady Karfrey! So it turned out well
enough in spite of her sarcastic ways when she was a girl."

"But Mama, you didn't marry Papa until you were past twenty. And you
did pretty well for yourself, you will admit. Married to the most wonderful
man in the world, that's all."

"I married your father because he asked me, and that's the truth. I was
no beauty and neither are you. You treat men as if they were girl friends,
though you've had a hundred chances I must say."

"Not quite a hundred, Mama. Perhaps ten."

"Most girls have one, and snatch at it, and don't let them tell you anything
different. If you're not married next year I'm going to dress up Lacey and
put her in the parlor. She'll be seventeen soon and there she is out at the
stables day and night. It's time she learned that all males aren't quadrupeds."
She had a somewhat tangy tongue of her own, Nancy Lynnton.

Equipped thus rather meagerly for matrimony, one would justifiably have
thought the three Lynnton sisters fated for spinsterhood. On the contrary
the big shabby Virginia house was clogged with yearning swains. Young
Washington career men; slightly balding European sub-diplomats and em-
bassy secretaries in striped trousers and cutaways; Virginia and Maryland
squires of the huntin' ridin' and slightly run-down set; with a sprinkling of
New York lawyers and Wall Street men and even an occasional Midwestern
businessman. Doctors who came ostensibly to confer with Horace Lynnton
ended up in the vast hospitable kitchen (for the Lynntons were famous cooks
in defiance of a day and place in which cooking was considered menial).
Beaux haunted the verandas the parlors the stables. They swarmed all over
the place—to the dismay of neighboring beauties—much as bees will sometimes desert the stately cool rose for a field of heady wild red clover.

As for the boasted Virginia background, this lay so far in the past as to
be misted by the centuries and discernible only to Mrs. Lynnton's somewhat
bemused eye. A great-great-great-grandfather had sailed overseas to Virginia
in the 1600s, one of those indentured servants or jail bait whose descendants
later became First Families of Virginia perhaps as legitimately as their more
aristocratic contemporaries. But this traveler's son too had possessed the
spirit of roving adventure. He had moved with the tide of travel from Virginia
to Kentucky to Indiana to Ohio. Mrs. Lynnton always skipped lightly over
these geographical intervals when she spoke of herself as having descended
from one of the F.F.V.s. Leslie and Lacey made nothing of this, or at best
regarded it as a family joke. Leigh—now Lady Karfrey—having inherited
something of her mother's snobbishness, took the doubtful distinction more
seriously. As for Doctor Horace Lynnton, late of Ohio, here was a great
human being and a dedicated spirit disguised as a tall somewhat shambling
man in a crumpled suit and a bow tie slightly askew so that his wife or one
of three daughters seemed always to be busy under his chin. When finally
he had moved with his family to the once stately but now rather ramshackle

house in Virginia it was because he could give his brilliant brain his surgical genius and his magic hands to the rehabilitation of the thousands of broken boys who, veterans of the gruesome 1917-18 war years, filled the nearby hospitals of Washington Virginia and Maryland. Offered the cushiony post of White House Physician, he had refused it as casually as though he had been handed an over-sweet dessert.

Though there was only a physician's income behind it, profusion was characteristic of the Lynnton ménage. Horses in the weathered stables; the most delicate and savory of American cooking in the kitchen with no Southern grease-fried indigestibles to mar it. There were succulent soft-shell crabs from Maryland, smoked Virginia hams, Ohio maple sugar and pancakes, little plump white chickens, button-size hot biscuits with golden pools of butter between their brown cheeks. Terrapin. Oysters. Succotash. Devil's food cake. Profusion not only of food but of gaiety and laughter; of good talk at dinner and after; of guests, of servants, of books, of courtesy, of horses and dogs and crystal and silver. Sweet-scented flowers in the rambling garden, deep-cushioned shabby handsome chairs, vast beds and capacious fireplaces, sherry on the sideboard, leisure in the air, and wit to spice the whole of this.

Bick Benedict was no fool, and he hadn't been twenty minutes on the place before he realized that this was a run-down old Southern shebang in need of about fifty thousand dollars in repairs. Not that he was there in the role of anything but guest, and that of the most transitory nature. In Washington on business he had come down to the Lynnton place in Virginia to look at a horse and to buy it if possible.

By the purest of accidents Doctor Horace Lynnton had found himself owner of a long-legged rangy filly who had turned out to be a gold mine. As horses, to him, were four-legged animals meant for riding or for driving he was more bewildered than pleased. He was forever evading gifts from money-eyed patients who sent them in gratitude, or from insolvent patients who proffered them in lieu of cash. The filly had come from a long-standing friend who fell just between these two classifications. Doctor Lynnton had good-naturedly accepted the unwanted animal offered in part payment of a bill already absurdly small.

"She's an accident," the owner had confessed. "And I won't say she's any good except for one of your girls to ride. She's one of Wind Wings'."

"But I can't accept her," Doctor Lynnton had in the beginning protested. "You say her sire was Wind Wings!"

"Yes, but the dam was a stray plug that we kept for my little Betsy to jog around on. She got into the paddock by mistake, and the damage was done. Not that it matters, except that I want you to know that on her mother's side she hasn't a drop of good blood in her that I know of. She'll never run."

"Prince and peasant girl," said Horace Lynnton. "A combination that has been known to produce amazing results. Sire for speed, they say. Dam for stamina."

They named her My Mistake but in spite of this by the time she was three years old it began to appear that she would soon romp away with everything from New York to Mexico.

Bick Benedict of Texas had sought out Horace Lynnton in Washington not as the famous man of science but as the owner of My Mistake.

"Is she for sale?" he had asked.

"I suppose so. I don't go in for racing. She was meant for my youngest daughter—to ride around the country roads. Turned out to be a lightning bolt."

"Could I see her?"

"Drive out with me this afternoon, if you care to, stay for dinner and overnight."

"Thanks, I'll be glad to drive out but I can't stay. I've got business engagements here in Washington————"

But he never left—or practically never—until he and Leslie were off for their honeymoon and Texas.

In the first twenty-four hours of his stay at the Lynntons' Jordan Benedict experienced a series of shocks which left him dazed but strangely exhilarated too. The first shock to his Southwest sensibilities came when Doctor Lynnton introduced the young Negro who drove them down to Virginia. The little ceremony was as casual (but also as formal) as though he were introducing any two friends or acquaintances.

"Benedict, this is Jefferson Swazey who'll drive us down. Jeff, this is Mr. Jordan Benedict from Texas."

Well I'll be damned, thought Jordan Benedict. On the way down the two men talked of this and that—of the freakish little filly; of the dead Harding, that pitiful and scandal-ridden figure with his imposing façade concealing the termite-riddled interior; of Coolidge, the new President of the United States; the rigid and vinegary Vermonter.

Arrived, "Jeff will show us the filly," Horace Lynnton said, "or perhaps one of the girls will, though they don't ride her nowadays. She's in training, very hoity-toity and has ideas about who's in the saddle."

Jordan Benedict's eye, trained to estimate millions of acres and dozens of dwellings as a single unit, made brief work of the wistaria and honeysuckle. They did not hide from his expert gaze the sagging columns or disguise the fact that the outbuildings were in urgent need of repair. But then the family, as he met them one by one, made no effort at disguise, either.

It was almost dusk as they arrived. The two men entered the house. A wide and beautifully proportioned hall ran from front to back with great arched doorways opening off it. Shabby rugs on a caramel floor. Riding crops, tennis racquets; books and papers and magazines on the overflowing hall table; a friendly lean and lazy dog; a delicious scent of something baking or broiling or both. They peered into the big living room. Here was a feminine world, all crystal and flowers and faded yellow satin curtains. Bits of jade. The ruby glow of Bohemian glass. The flicker of flame in the fireplace.

Doctor Lynnton shook his head. "The girls are somewhere around, but they're probably busy. Perhaps you'd like to wash up."

"I'd like to have a look at the filly while it's still light."

"Yes—the horse," Doctor Lynnton agreed somewhat vaguely. From a nearby room there came the sound of voices. He raised his voice to a shout. "Leslie!" Then, still more loudly, "Leslie!"

Bick Benedict turned expecting to see a son, perhaps, or a manservant answering to this name. There emerged from the room that later he was to know as the library two figures, a man and a woman. The woman was wearing riding clothes, he was startled to see that it was a sidesaddle habit complete with glistening black boots, crop, white-starched stock. He had seen nothing like this in years—certainly not in Texas. A tall slim girl, not pretty.

"Leslie, this is Jordan Benedict, here from Texas. My daughter Leslie."

The young man with her was in riding clothes and not only riding clothes but actually a pink coat of the hunting variety. Well I'm damned, Jordan Benedict said to himself for the second time in an hour. Then his ear was caught by the girl's voice, which was lovely, warm and vibrant.

"Texas! How interesting! Father, you know Nicky Rorik. Mr. Benedict, this is Count Nicholas Rorik, Mr. Jordan Benedict."

Doctor Lynnton moved toward the rear doorway. "We're on our way to the paddock. Mr. Benedict's come to look at My Mistake."

"I'm coming along," said Leslie, "to tell you all her bad points. I don't want anyone to buy her."

"Dear daughter, kindly remember that Mr. Benedict is a Texan and your father is a country doctor. You two go on down to the stable. I'll join you directly, Jordan."

Rorik, Benedict was saying in his mind. Rorik. Now let's see. He comes from one of those kicked-around kingdoms, or a midget principality or something, it's one of those musical-comedy places.

Then the slim dark young man said something about seeing everyone at dinner. And vanished with a bow that gave the impresssion of heel-clicking, though nothing of the sort took place. Weeks later Jordan Benedict dredged the young man up from the depths of his memory and put to his wife Leslie the questions which even now were stirring in his thoughts.

"That first day I met you, Leslie, when I came into the house with your father. You were tucked away in the library with that Rorik guy. What kind of hanky-panky was going on, anyway? Quiet as mice until your father called you."

"Oh, that. Well, I never quite knew myself. It was a serious proposal of a sort, but it had a morganatic tinge. When his uncle dies he'll become ruler or Grand Duke or whatever it's called—if any. I've lost track."

Now, on their way to the paddock he waited for her to speak. In Texas the women talked a lot, they chattered on and on about little inconsequential things calculated to please but not strain the masculine mind. Leslie Lynnton did not start the conversation. She strolled composedly and quietly beside him in her absurdly chic riding clothes. All about them were the ancient trees, the scent of flowers whose perfume yielded itself to the cool evening air. The orchard was cloudy with blossoms.

"How green it is!" he said inadequately.

"Isn't it green in Texas?"

The girl must be a fool. "Don't you know about Texas?"

"No. Except that it's big. And the men wear hats like yours."

"Yes, I suppose this does look funny to you. But then that rigging you're wearing looks funny to me." For some reason he wanted to jar her composure. "And your friend's red coat."

She laughed and paused a moment in her walk and looked directly at him for the first time. And he thought, She might be kind of pretty if she filled out a little. Lovely eyes but there's a little kind of thing about one of them. A cast in it. She was saying, "They're called pink, not red. Don't ask me why. And you're right about these riding clothes of mine. They're ridiculous. I never wear them, really."

"But you're wearing———"

"I mean I never wear them for riding. Just today. It's a special day down here. Once a year they do a lot of rather silly stuff that was Virginia a century or two ago. You know—scarlet coats and floating veils and yoicks. The men dig their pink coats out of moth balls and the women wear this sort of thing out of the attic if they still can stick on a sidesaddle. Tonight's the Hunt Ball—not at our house, thank heaven!—and you're invited."

"How veddy veddy British!"

"I was born in Ohio so don't be sneery."

"I'd look good at a Hunt Ball in these clothes."

"Oh well. We're having dinner here—just the family and two or three others. Do stay for that."

He muttered something about an engagement in Washington, to which she said politely, well, another time perhaps. And there they were at the stables and My Mistake was being paced in the paddock by a young Negro boy. Bick saw instantly that the satin-coated sorrel had the proper conformation; long of leg, neat of hoof, long muscular neck, deep chest. Her hoofs seemed scarcely to touch the ground, they flicked the earth as delicately as a ballet dancer's toes.

"Well, there she is," said Doctor Lynnton, coming up behind them.

Horses had been a vital part of Jordan Benedict's life since birth. "And way before," he sometimes said. "They tell me that when I was born my mother slid off her horse and into bed at practically the same moment. She had been taking part in an equestrian quadrille at the rodeo in Benedict. All the young women for miles around tried for the quadrille, but only the top riders made it. The women rode in divided skirts those days."

It could not be said that he prided himself on his horsemanship any more than he could be said to be proud of his breathing or walking. Certainly walking was more foreign to this Texan than riding.

"I'd like to try her out if you've no objection," he said to Doctor Lynnton.

"Of course. How would you like to try her on the track? We've rigged up a little half-mile track there just beyond."

"How about your clothes?" Leslie called to him as he mounted in his Texas tans, his great wide-brimmed Texas Stetson, his brown oxfords.

He flung up his arm. "My grandmother could rope a steer in hoop skirts."

Perhaps it was the upflung arm that startled My Mistake. Jordan had ridden a thousand quarter horses, bucking ponies, racing horses. This filly was a live electric wire carrying a thousand volts. She was out of the gate and on the track like a lightning flash. Accustomed all his life to the high-pommeled Western saddle, he sat the Eastern saddle well enough but his style was a revelation to Eastern eyes. The stable boys stared, their eyes their mouths making three wide circles in each amazed face. Jordan's arms were akimbo, he held the reins high, his loose-jointed seat in the saddle irked the little filly, she jerked her head around to glare at him with rolling resentful eyeballs, she skittered sidewise. She gave him a nasty five minutes. Damned girl, watching. He knew he must master her, he did master her, he took her twice around, drew up before his startled audience and dismounted before the animal had come to a stop.

Leslie Lynnton was laughing like a child, peal on peal of helpless spontaneous laughter.

"Now Leslie," her father said chidingly, "don't you tease Mr. Benedict. That's the way they ride in Texas. Informal, their riding."

Leslie drew a deep breath and choked a little. "That wasn't riding. That was scuffling with a horse."

He was deeply offended, it was almost as if a man had impugned his honor—a phrase still used in Texas editorials. Instantly she sensed this, she went to him she spoke so that the grinning boys could hear. "I'm sorry. Forgive me. I'm ignorant about your part of the country. Our way of riding seems queer to you too. You'd laugh at me if you saw me in this habit all bunched up on the side of a horse."

He was furious. He said nothing. There was a little frown between his eyes and his eyes were steel.

"All right, boys!" Doctor Lynnton called to the stablemen, and waved away the horse, the attendants, the stable, the whole incident. "Thanks. Come on, Jordan—let's go up to the house and have a little drink before dinner."

"Oh, I'm afraid I'll have to————" Jordan began stiffly.

"You must have a wife or a mother or a—or someone who has spoiled you terribly," Leslie said. "You take teasing so hard."

"My sister," he found himself saying to his own intense astonishment. "I'm not married. My sister—I live with my sister."

"Oh well, that accounts for it. Why aren't you married, Jordan?"

"Now Leslie!" Doctor Lynnton remonstrated again.

He ignored this. "It seems strange to hear you call me Jordan." He pronounced it with a *u*, Jurden, Texas fashion. "Almost no one does. There's always been a Jordan in the family, but everyone calls me Bick." I'm talking too much, he told himself. What the hell does she care, whether there's always been a Jordan and they call me Bick.

"Bick Benedict," Leslie tried the sound of it. "No, I like your own name. Jordan Benedict. Why do they call you Bick?"

He began to feel really foolish. "Oh, when I was a little kid I suppose I couldn't say Benedict, the nearest I could manage was Bick, and it stuck as a nickname."

"Jordan," she said stubbornly. "You're staying to dinner. And the night. You can drive back to Washington tomorrow morning with Papa, he gets up at a ghastly hour and starts poking at people's insides before the world is awake."

"I came here to buy a horse," Bick announced rudely. "I won't go to any Hunt Ball."

Walking between the two men Leslie linked an arm into her father's arm, into Bick's. "I'll get up early and have breakfast with you two. There's Mama. We're late I suppose."

On the veranda steps stood Mrs. Lynnton and beside her a girl of sixteen or seventeen in men's pants—at least that was what Bick Benedict called them. Benedict was shocked. Even the professional rodeo girls wore full divided skirts in Texas. Even Joella Kilso who was champion woman bronco buster of the Southwest wore a buckskin skirt with fringed trimming and bright brass nailheads.

"Well, really," began Mrs. Lynnton with considerably less than storied Southern hospitality, "it's half past seven, dinner's at eight and you're not even———"

"Mama, Mr. Jordan Benedict from Texas. . . . Lacey—my sister Lacey."

Leslie performed the introductions at a clip which left her mother's complaint far behind. Mrs. Lynnton had made instant appraisal of this tall broadshouldered visitor in the ten-gallon hat and dismissed him as negligible.

"Are you the man who wants to buy My Mistake?" Lacey asked bluntly.

Mrs. Lynnton acknowledged his presence for the first time. "I hope so, before Lacey here kills herself riding her."

"No, Mr. Benedict's not buying her," Leslie said, without reason.

"Oh, yes ma'am, I am," Bick said with a great deal of drawl as always when angry. Too many damned bossy women around here, he thought. And he decided that Mrs. Lynnton looked like a longhorn with that lantern face, her hair in two sort of winged horns at the side, and her long lean wiry frame.

Doctor Lynnton waved a placating hand. "Let's not decide anything now. We'll have a drink and then we'll all clean up and see you downstairs at about eight, Jordan. Uh, Bick. Is that better?"

Stuck, he thought as he entered his room, but then instantly there came over him a sensation very strange—a mingling of peace and exhilaration. A large square high-ceilinged room, cool, quiet. Chintz curtains, flowers in a vase, a fire in the fireplace, a bathroom to himself, shaving things and sweet-smelling stuff in bottles in the bathroom, and big thick soft towels. Nothing like this at Reata in spite of the millions of acres and dozens of rooms and scores of servants and "hands."

Later in the evening when he mentioned the comfort of his room to Leslie she said flippantly, "Yes, who cares about the necessities, it's the luxuries that count. What if the dishpan does leak!"

Now he still could telephone Washington and have someone drive out to fetch him. What was the sense in staying? He'd made up his mind to buy the filly, if only (he told himself parenthetically) to show those women that they couldn't run him the way they ran Doctor Lynnton.

He stared at himself in the mirror, decided to bathe and shave, decided against it, the hell with it, dinner was at eight it was quarter to eight now, he couldn't make it if he wanted to. Whereupon he peeled off his clothes, jerked on the shower, shaved, cut himself, got into his clothes distastefully because they were the crumpled garments he had just kicked off, rushed downstairs to find no one there but Mrs. Lynnton in rustling silk doing something to chair cushions and looking surprisingly handsome. She greeted him politely, she looked at him fleetingly, the rumpled Texas tans the tan shoes that he had hurriedly wiped with a corner of the bath towel. Not only did she mentally dismiss him as an eligible or even a possible suitor for her daughter—she regarded him as a male nobody with whom she could relax cozily without pretense as one would in the company of a sympathetic servant or an old friend with whom one had nothing to gain and nothing to lose.

"You're from Nebraska, Mr. Beckwith?"

"Texas, ma'am. Uh—Benedict."

"Texas, really!" As though he had said Timbuctoo.

Old harpy. "You're from Ohio your daughter tells me."

"Well, we did live there at one time. But I'm a Virginian, my ancestors really settled Virginia, they were among the First Families."

"I've read about them," he said too dryly. "A very interesting, uh, type, some of them."

She looked at him sharply but his blue eyes seemed guileless, his smile winning. Here was someone a nobody, to whom she could unburden herself momentarily, a fresh receptacle. "My daughter Leslie makes fun of me, and so does the Doctor and even Lacey, for that matter, because I am proud of my ancestry. The Doctor calls me Mrs. Nickleby. Leslie's the worst. Daughters are a real problem, Mr. Uh. Of course Leigh wasn't. She's Lady Karfrey, you know."

"No, I didn't know."

"My, yes! She married Sir Alfred Karfrey, they live in England of course, he's a member of Parliament."

"Like our Congress," Bick said smoothly. I'm really being bitchy as a woman, he thought. But she had not heard, she heard nothing that she did not want to hear.

"Leslie could have married—well, anybody you might say. Goodness knows she's no beauty, skinny as a bird dog, and a slight cast in her left eye at times perhaps you've noticed, well, you'd think it would put men off her but they're bees around a honeypot. I don't know what it is, Doctor says Leslie has something that transcends beauty but I can't see it myself———"

Why, the old girl's jealous of her daughter, Bick said to himself.

"—and she has her nose in a book all day long and talks to the servants as if they were her equal—so does the Doctor for that matter—and she argues about what she calls democracy and human rights and stuff like that,

I declare I should think the men would run the other way at mention of her name————"

"I think she's fascinating," Bick Benedict heard himself saying, to his own astonishment. It was a word he had never used—certainly never in connection with a woman.

Mrs. Lynnton blinked a little as though coming out of a trance, it was plain that she had been talking to relieve her feelings, this man might as well have been, so far as she considered him of importance, an old uncle or a piece of furniture. She seemed even to resent his interruption as though he had committed an impertinence. She put this horse trader in his place. "So others say. Count Rorik. He'll be practically a king when his uncle dies. A principality they call it."

He was cursing himself for having stayed when suddenly, like a badly directed stage scene, there were voices on the stairs, in the hall, on the veranda, there were a dozen people in the room and introductions were being performed and trays were being passed. Sherry! I'll bet that's the old girl's doings. And there was Leslie, late but leisurely.

He looked at Leslie, he was startled by the rush of protective loyalty he felt toward her. She was wearing the disfiguring evening dress that was in vogue—the absurdly short skirt and loose hip-length waistline that so foreshortened the figure. Long slim legs, lovely shoulders, and now that she was rid of the white piqué stock and the rest of those stuffy riding clothes he saw how exquisitely her head was set on her throat and how, in some mysterious way, she was really a beauty in disguise. He couldn't make up his mind whether there really was a slight cast in her eye or whether her eyes were so large that there wasn't quite room enough for them in the socket. Another part of his mind was recalling that he had once seen an actress in New York—what was her name?—Ferguson, that was it—Elsie Ferguson. Her eyes had been like that, very large and liquid, not those stiff eyes that most women had, and there had been a little sort of quirk in one of them and he had been strongly attracted by this blemish.

Dinner. The colored man in white cotton gloves announced dinner. In later years Jordan Benedict sometimes referred to this evening as That Hell of an Evening When I First Met You.

6

ACROSS THE TABLE from him—across all those lighted candles and the flowers—were Leslie and that Rorik fellow still in the red coat. Only it looked dressier now and his hair very black above the red. Career man he'd been called. Bick disliked him for no reason. He was irritated by the way the man ate his dinner, using his knife and fork in the European fashion, a busy gathering of food with both utensils, a finicky little clatter of metal against china. He ate quickly, almost daintily, he talked and looked into Leslie's eyes very directly, and smiled. Since the war Washington was full of them, Bick thought, and scuffled his feet a little under the table; always hanging around the foreign embassies and legations. The food was very good. Wonderful, really. Run-down place, though. How could they afford it? Three daughters. Lady Karfrey, eh? Nuts to that!

The women did a great deal of talking, they were leading the conversation, especially that Leslie girl, it wasn't the formal sort of dinner-table talk that he had sometimes encountered in Washington on his infrequent business trips there. He rarely took active part in the Washington end of Texas affairs, that was his cousin Roady Benedict's business, that was why he had been sent to Washington. They were talking about everything from that crazy Scopes trial in Tennessee, with its monkey glands and its Bryan and its Darrow, to a book called *An American Tragedy* (which Bick hadn't read) to a play called *Desire Under the Elms* (which Bick hadn't seen). Bick Benedict ate his flavorsome duck and talked politely when necessary to the young woman on his right (whose name he hadn't caught) and the middle-aged woman on his left (whose name he hadn't caught).

Someone at the other end of the table must have asked Nicholas Rorik a question for now he paused in the sprightly businesss of the knife and fork, he raised his voice to carry down the line of dinner guests, and smiled deprecatingly and shrugged his shoulders as he replied in his very good Oxford English. "It isn't a large country as you know, it is a principality, my country. Our little kingdom, as you call it, is only—" he cast up his eyes ceilingward to juggle the figures into American terms—"it would be in your miles less than eight hundred square miles. Very small, as you consider size in this country."

"My goodness," said his questioner at the other end of the table, laughing a little and then turning to look at Jordan Benedict, "Texas is bigger than that, isn't it, Mr. Benedict!"

"Texas!" said Doctor Lynnton. "Why, Mr. Benedict's ranch is bigger than that. Sorry, Nicky. No offense."

"I've always heard these tall tales from Texas," said one of the men across the table—he, too, was wearing one of those red coats with a red face above it, "and now I'd like to have it right from the hor—right from headquarters, Mr. Benedict. Just how many acres have you got, or miles or whatever it is you folks reckon in? It's the biggest ranch in Texas, isn't it?"

Jordan Benedict never could accustom himself to the habit these Yankees had of asking a man how much land he had. Why, damit, it was the same as coming right out and asking a man how much money he had! How would that redcoat like it if he, Bick Benedict, were to shout across the table to ask him how much money he had in the bank?

"No," he said quietly, "it isn't the largest. It is one of the large ranches but there are others as large. One or two larger, up in the Panhandle and down in the brush country."

He felt that Leslie Lynnton was looking at him and he sensed that she understood his resentment though he didn't know how or why. That girl isn't only smart, he thought. She understands everything, that's why her eyes are so warm and lovely that's what her father meant when he said she's got something that transcends beauty.

"Yes," the fellow was saying persistently. "Yes, but how many acres, actually? I'd like to hear those figures really rolling out and know that it's authentic. I never could bring myself to believe them. A million? Is that right? A million acres?"

Jordan Benedict felt his face reddening. Still, a straight question like that, aimed at a man's head. You had to answer it or insult a man at your host's table. He had seen men killed for much less. There was a lull in the table talk. He looked squarely into Leslie's eyes, she smiled at him ever so faintly as a mother smiles at a shy child, in encouragement. He heard himself saying,

"Something over two million acres. Two million and a half, to be exact."

Doctor Lynnton nodded interestedly. "Yes, I remember my father saying something about it when I was a young fellow. It used to be four or five million acres, wasn't it? Years ago."

"Yes." God damn the man and his family and his friends.

"There you are, Nicky!" yelped the man who originally had asked the questions. "I guess that makes you look like a sharecropper." Nicky shrugged his shoulders again and spread his hands in deprecation and smiled at Leslie Lynnton beseechingly.

Mrs. Lynnton's head had been slightly turned away from the table to speak over her shoulder to a servant. She turned now to look at Jordan Benedict. It was a stunned look, the look of one who has heard but who rejects the words as incredible. She turned her head again automatically to speak to the servant, then again she faced forward with a jerk to stare at Jordan as though the sense of the words had just now penetrated. Her mouth was open before she began to speak.

"How many acres did you say, Mr. Benedict?"

"He said two and a half million acres, Mama," Leslie said with exquisite distinctness. "And you should see the greedy look on your face."

But Mrs. Lynnton was not one to be diverted from her quarry once she had the scent.

"Are there," she persisted, "any cities on the premises?"

Choking a little, "Why, yes ma'am, there are a few."

"Do you own those too?"

The company could no longer be contained. A roar went up. Bick Benedict's reply, "Not rightly own, no ma'am," was lost in the waves of laughter. Mrs. Lynnton turned her gaze upon her husband then. Her expression was one of the most bitter reproach and rage.

"Nobody owns a city," Bick persisted virtuously. Controller of every vote in the town of Benedict, and most of the county.

From across the table Leslie said, "How about Tammany?"

"Oh, now, Leslie!" pleaded a man seated beside Mrs. Lynnton. A New Yorker, Bick decided not very astutely. And anyway, what does a woman want to go and get mixed up in political talk for?

There followed, then, in that household between the hours of ten-thirty P.M. and seven A.M. three scenes which made up in variety what they may have lacked in dramatic quality.

At ten o'clock the dinner guests departed, bound for the Hunt Ball. Jordan Benedict declined politely to go, pleading no proper clothes and a very early Washington appointment. At ten-thirty Doctor Lynnton was in his own bedroom after a half hour's chat and a nightcap with Jordan Benedict. At ten-thirty Mrs. Lynnton opened fire.

"Well, Doctor Lynnton, I must say you seem to care very little about what becomes of your daughters!"

"What have the girls done now, Nancy?"

"It's you!" Then, at his look of amazement, "Bringing that Benedict here and never telling me a word about him. Not a syllable."

"Why, Nancy, he's a nice enough young fella. Texans are different. You can't judge a man by his hat. They're used to big open ways, lots of everything. He's a nice enough young fella."

"Nice! He said he owns two million acres of land! And more!"

"You're not going to hold that against him, are you?"

"Horace Lynnton, you know very well that there isn't a young man in Virginia, Washington, Maryland and the whole of Ohio she hasn't laughed at from the time she was thirteen. She's past twenty. I can't keep Lacey in pigtails forever waiting for Leslie to marry." She was becoming incoherent. "Look at her! She says I'm feudal. And I said to him right out that she was skinny as a bird dog and her eyes—how did I know he had millions of acres and everybody knew about him—you bring a man into the house and you never even . . . "

"But Lacey's only a kid and she isn't skinny she's over-plump if anything. What's she got to do with it?"

"Lacey! Who's talking about Lacey! Leslie! Leslie! For years she's been going on about how silly Washington society is and how she hates dinners and teas and calling cards and why can't things be big and real and American and here is this man with millions of land why it's an empire and you never even mentioned to me . . ."

At quarter of eleven Leslie Lynnton pleaded a crashing headache together with various other racking complications and left the Hunt Ball flat, returning to her home under the somewhat dazed escort of a bewildered young man who had long been a willing but unrewarded victim. She went straight to the library but seemed disappointed in what she found—or failed to find—there. But she made three silent trips between the library and her bedroom, her arms loaded each time with books of assorted sizes. These she plumped down on her bed and it was surrounded by these tomes that her sister Lacey in the room next door came upon her in a spirit of investigation, having seen her light and heard her moving about.

Lacey poked her head in at the door. "I thought it was burglars or a lover," she said.

Leslie glanced up from the book she was reading. "Well, it would have been nice to see you in either case. And where do you learn such talk!"

"What are you home for!"

"To read. About Texas."

"You mean you came home from the Hunt Ball just to have a read! About Texas!"

"Go along to bed," Leslie said. "There's a good child."

Lacey gave her a hard look. "Aha!" she said. "Likewise oho! Texas, huh?"

The Lynnton family knew what Leslie meant when she said she was going to have a read. Her bed in the old Virginia house was by no means the meager maiden couch upon which the unwed usually compose themselves to sleep. Leslie had seized upon a vast four-poster that had reposed for years in the jungleland of the attic. Originally it must have been meant for at least one pair of ancestors and a suckling infant. A vast plateau, as broad as it was long and as long as any six-foot Virginian could have wished, it stood, not with its headboard against the wall as is the custom of all well-behaved beds, but in the middle of the room for reasons that no one of the family could fathom and that Leslie never explained. The headboard soared almost to the ceiling. Above blazed a crystal chandelier, full blast, and on either side were lamps. All over the bed and in piles on the floor were books large and small, making a sort of stockade in the confines of which Leslie Lynnton had composed herself to read for hours. Books of history, encyclopedias, pamphlets, almanacs, even fiction. Leslie Lynnton read and as she read she twined and untwined a lock of hair between her fingers until tendrils curls and wisps stood up, medusa-like, all over her head.

Upon this spectacle Lacey gazed without astonishment.

"Oh, Leslie, are you in love with him!"

"Perhaps. Yes, I think so. He says Texas is different from any other state in the whole United States."

"Pooh! Everybody says that about their own state. That's what Papa says about Ohio and Mama about Virginia."

"Not like that. He talks as if it were a diffrent country altogether. A country all by itself that just happens to be in the middle of the United States."

"It isn't in the middle. It's way down near Mexico or something."

Leslie ignored this. "He calls it 'my country' when he means Texas. I asked him about that and he said all Texans—he says Texians—call their state their country and they even call their own ranches their country as if they were kings. I never was so interested in my life. Never. I've got all the books I could find in the library that might have something about Texas and Pa's files and the Congressional Records since way back and the encyclopedia and a lot of histories and *Your Southwest* and *How to Run a Ranch* and *Life of a Texas Ranch Wife* and *The Texas Rangers* and *Texas, a Description of Its Geographical, Social and Other Conditions with Special Reference to——*"

"Good night!" said Lacey, and closed the door firmly. Lacey awoke once during the night and heard the great clock in the downstairs hall strike three. Turning over drowsily she saw the thin line of light still grinning beneath Leslie's closed door.

Breakfast at the Lynntons' was a pleasant thing. The dining room itself was perhaps the friendliest room in that openhanded house. A noble old room, high-ceilinged, many-windowed. On a sunny day such as this it was no room for a woman who preferred to shun the early morning light. A brilliant bay at the south end led to a terrace and the haphazard garden. Inside shone mahogany and silver and crystal.

Bick Benedict, entering the room rather diffidently, noted that the napkins were neatly darned, the flower-patterned carpet threadbare. It's the luxuries that matter, Leslie had said. Who cares about the necessities.

Breakfast here was done in the English fashion, a movable feast. Doctor Lynnton was likely to breakfast at six and Lacey Lynnton at five or at ten, while other members of the family and assorted guests might appear between seven and eleven. On the long sideboard were the hot dishes cozily covered and freshly replenished from time to time but certainly the early risers had the best of it. Eggs, kippers, sausages. Hot biscuits toast muffins. Tea coffee jam honey. You helped yourself, you sat and you talked or you sat and ate if you had awakened grumpy or you sat and read your paper, the sun streamed in, the coffee was strong and hot, there was an air of leisure mingled with a pleasant bustle of coming and going.

Leslie Lynnton came in with a rush which she checked at once.

Early as she was, Doctor Lynnton and Bick Benedict were there before her. She looked very young and pale in the little blue dress with the white collars and cuffs, her black hair tied with a ribbon. She had had three hours of sleep.

"Hello!" she said. "Good morning!"

"Why Leslie!" said Doctor Lynnton.

She hurriedly blotted this out by saying, as she helped herself to coffee, "I almost always breakfast with Papa." She looked very straight at Bick Benedict and he at her. She saw in the morning light that his eyes were crinkled at the corners from sun and wind; he looked even taller and broader of shoulder there at breakfast in the sunny room.

"You're looking mighty pert, Miss Leslie," he said inadequately. "You don't look as if you'd been dancing all night."

She drank her entire cup of coffee, black, she set the cup down carefully in the saucer and sat a moment very still as though ignoring the little compliment, so that the two men as they regarded her so admiringly and thought of her, the one with the love and affection of many years, the other with an emotion that bewildered and exhilarated him, felt momentarily puzzled.

She made her decision. "I came home at quarter to eleven," she said quietly, "and I read about Texas until four this morning."

"Oh, Leslie!" groaned Doctor Lynnton. "Leave the poor boy to eat his breakfast in peace."

Bick Benedict was astonished and he did not believe her. He smiled rather patronizingly. "Well, what did you learn? It takes a lot of reading, Texas does."

"We really stole Texas, didn't we? I mean. Away from Mexico."

He jumped as if he had touched a live wire. His eyes were agate. He waited a moment before he trusted himself to speak. "I don't understand the joke," he finally said through stiff lips. He thought how many men had been killed in Texas for saying so much less than this thing that had been said to him.

"I'm not joking, Mr. Benedict. It's right there in the history books, isn't it? This Mr. Austin moved down there with two or three hundred families from the East, it says, and the Mexicans were polite and said they could settle and homestead if they wanted to, under the rule of Mexico. And the next thing you know they're claiming they want to free themselves from Mexico and they fight and take it. Really! How impolite. I don't mean to be rude, but really! Of course the Spanish explorers, and the French, that was different. There was nobody around and there they were tramping and riding across the hot desert in all those iron clothes, with steel helmets and plumes. They must have been terribly uncomfortable. Those Conquistadores—isn't it a lovely word!—Coronado and De Soto and Whatshisname De Vaca, poor dears, looking for the Seven Cities of Cibola like children on a treasure hunt. Still, they didn't actually grab the land away from anyone, the way we did. Of course there were the Indians, but perhaps they didn't count."

Doctor Lynnton glanced at Benedict. He was startled to see that the man was rigid with suppressed anger. The muscles of his jaw stood out hard and stiff. For a moment it was as though he would rise and leave the room. Or throw the cup in his hand. These Texans.

"Now now, Leslie," Doctor Lynnton murmured soothingly. "You mustn't talk like that to a Texan. They're touchy. They feel very strongly about their state." He smiled. "Their country, you might almost say. To some of them the United States is their second country. Isn't that so, Benedict?"

"Oh, but I didn't mean to be impolite!" Leslie said before Bick could voice his pent anger. "I was just talking impersonally—about history." She picked up her cup and saucer and came over and sat beside him, cozily, her elbow on the table, she leaned toward him, she peered into his face like an eager child. It was disconcerting, it was maddening, if she had been a man he would have hit her, he told himself. "It's all in the books, it's news to me, I just meant it's so fascinating. It's another world, it sounds so big and new and different. I love it. The cactus and the cowboys and the Alamo and the sky and the horses and the Mexicans and the freedom. It's really America, isn't it. I'm—I'm in love with it."

Bick Benedict's heart gave a lurch. Watch out, he said to himself. Rattlesnakes.

Women did not talk like that. Certainly Texas women didn't talk like that. Of course, in those two years he had spent at Harvard because the Benedict men always had a couple of years at Harvard so that no one could say they were provincial, he had met a few girls who had a lot of opinions of their own but they weren't popular girls, they weren't girls you saw at the football games or the prom. Well, if she wanted to talk about Texas he'd talk to her as if she were a man.

"I never saw anything as ignorant as you Easterners. All you know about American history is what's happened east of Philadelphia. Valley Forge and

Bunker Hill and Washington crossing the Delaware. The Delaware! Did you
ever hear of the Rio Grande! I'll bet they don't even teach about the Alamo
and San Jacinto in your schools.''

"No, they don't. Do they, Papa?'' Doctor Lynnton passed his hand over
his face with a gesture like that of brushing off cobwebs. But she went on
without waiting for his confirmation. "And anyway, we're not Easterners,
Mr. Benedict.'' With earnestness she had grown formal. "Not at all. Are
we, Papa?'' A rhetorical question, purely. "Tell him.''

"Hell no!'' said Horace Lynnton. "Ohioans are no Easterners. But now
don't you get into any fracas with a Texan, Leslie. They're touchier than
a hornet, didn't you know that? Besides, you came near being a Texan
yourself.''

"She did!'' Bick exclaimed in a surprisingly pleased tone of voice.

"Maybe you've forgotten, Leslie. I guess I haven't mentioned it since you
were a very little girl and you didn't pay much attention.''

He reached for a hot biscuit and split it and placed a great gob of butter
in the center of the upper half and on top of this he perched a large gobbet
of strawberry jam. He gazed admiringly at the brilliant gold and ruby picture
before he bit into it.

Leslie said, very low, with a concern more wifely than filial, "You know
not so much starch and sugar and fat.''

"I know,'' he agreed ruefully, as though speaking of something beyond
his powers of accomplishment. "My patients mind when I tell them but I
don't.'' And went on eating and talking with enjoyment. He looked at Bick,
genially. "My father was a doctor too, you know. Scotch-Irish stock. He
heard the talk about Texas when he was living in Ohio about 1870, before
I was born. When I was a kid I used to hear him say he went to Texas to
settle down there and grow with the country. He fell in love with it, like
Leslie here, before he ever laid eyes on it. Well sir, he stayed about six
months and worked up quite a practice, there weren't many doctors then
in Texas. He didn't mind the climate. The heat. And the northers. And the
dust. But he packed up and went back to Ohio. He said his digestion was
ruined for life in those six months. Fried steak. Fried potatoes. Fried bread.
Fried beans. Said that people who fried everything they ate, and fried it in
grease and cared as little about good food and knew as little about cooking
as the Texans, would take all of another hundred years to catch up with the
rest of the civilized world. No offense I hope, Jordan,'' He had a thin pink
curl of Virginia ham on his fork and now he used it to chase a few buttery
biscuit crumbs around his plate before dispatching it. He eyed the covered
dishes on the sideboard, caught Leslie's disapproving gaze and sat back with
a sigh of renunciation. "The Lynntons all set too much store by their palates,
I suppose. Leslie here would rather try a new recipe than a new dress.''

"You're worse than any of us,'' Leslie retorted. She turned to Bick.
"Everyone knows there's been a feud for years between Papa and Caroline
the cook about which can make the most delicate crème brûlé''

"What,'' inquired Bick Benedict, "is crème brûlé'' At sight of their
stricken faces he laughed, but not very heartily. "One thing you'll say for
us—we never bragged on our food. But I like it.'' Then, to his own surprise,
"Texas would be a good place for Virginia women. They're pampered and
spoiled out of all reason.''

"I'm not. Am I, Papa? But then, I'm not a Virginian.''

Horace Lynnton turned to look at his daughter with the appraising gaze
of one who is freshly curious. "Oh, you, Leslie. You were born out of your
time. You'd have been good in the Civil War, hiding slaves in the Under-

ground or, before that, pioneering, maybe, in a covered wagon crossing the prairie with an ox team."

Leslie, stirring her second cup of coffee, considered this and rejected it. "I wouldn't have liked it, except the freedom and no Washington society and all that nonsense. Nothing to fear except scalping by the Indians, no household worries except whether you'd find water on the way. It does sound rather lovely, doesn't it? But awfully uncomfortable. You've brought me up wrong, Papa. I love old silver and Maryland crabs and plenty of hot water day and night with bath salts, and one glass of very cold very dry champagne."

Bick Benedict waved an arm that dismissed silver, hot water, house, garden, champagne, and the entire Eastern seaboard.

"All this is decadent," he said. "Dying. Or good and dead."

"It isn't!" Leslie contested. "It's been sick, but now it's just coming back to life. If Lincoln had lived another two years. He had plans. The South would have been better after the Civil War instead of broken because a lot of ignorant greedy———"

"Well," Doctor Lynnton interrupted, very leisurely, and brushing the crumbs off his vest. "I won't have time for this, if the Civil War's going to be fought again."

Leslie looked directly into Bick's eyes. He thought, What's coming now? "Do you read Carlyle?"

"My God no!" Bick said.

Horace Lynnton stood up. "Look here, Leslie. It's all right to attack a Texan about Texas in the early morning but you can't batter a guest at breakfast with Carlyle."

"I don't know much about Carlyle," Bick said, and he, too stood up as Leslie rose, so that the three made a curiously electric group without actually being conscious that they were standing. The two young people faced each other. Their talk became disjointed like the dialogue in a bad English translation of a Chekhov play. "My Mistake. The filly, I mean. I've bought her. If you ever come to Texas, Miss Leslie."

Sadly, "I never will." Her eyes turned to the open door and the apple orchard beyond where the blossoming trees in their bouffant white skirts stood like ballet dancers a-tiptoe, row on row.

His eyes followed hers. "Those apple blossoms. You can smell them way in here."

"I read about those yellow blossoms on your trees—or are they shrubs? Are they sweet-smelling?"

"Retama?"

"Huisache. If that's the way it's pronounced."

"After the spring rains there are desert flowers. Miles of them, like a carpet."

"Then it is a desert, Texas?"

"No. You can grow anything. From grapefruit to wheat. Pretty soon there won't be anything you can't grow better in Texas." Then, to his own horror, he heard himself saying, "If it's freedom you want, come to Texas. No one there tells you what to do and how you have to do it. No calling cards there and young squirts in red coats. Cattle and prairie and horses and sun and sky and plenty of good plain———"

"Plenty of good plain cactus and ticks and drought," Doctor Lynnton interrupted good-naturedly. "And northers and snakes. You Texans!" He shook his head in wonderment. "Don't you think you ought to look at My Mistake again before we go? I don't think you ought to buy her unless you're dead sure. You'll have to watch out for that trick she has of doing fancy dance steps just when she's supposed to be getting near the post. Ten thousand dollars is a lot of money."

"I've paid double that for a good bull," Bick said, but not boastfully. Absently, as though this were something unimportant, to be dismissed for more pressing things. "Do you like it living here in Virginia?" he asked Leslie.

"Yes, I suppose so."

"Everything looks so little."

"Big doesn't necessarily mean better. Sunflowers aren't better than violets."

"How far west have you been?"

"Kansas City once, with Papa."

"Kansas City! That's east! And little. In Texas there's everything. There's no end to it."

"Perhaps too much of everything is as bad as too little. I suppose I'm used to everything being sort of cozy. I don't mean little and cramped. But sort of near me. Family and books and friends and the kitchen if I want to go out and try something new and Caroline doesn't mind."

Doctor Lynnton cleared his throat to remind them of his presence. They were weaving a pattern, warily, of which he was no part. "We'll have to be getting along, Bick," he said. "Unless you would like to stay on, we'd be happy to have you but I'm due at the hospital————"

"Good morning!" cried Mrs. Lynnton from the dining-room doorway in clear ringing tones. "Good morning, everybody." She looked straight at Bick. "Good morning, Lochinvar!"

Bick Benedict, rather red, stammered, "Uh—good—uh————"

"Don't mind Mama," Leslie said, not at all embarrassed. "She's been trying to marry me off for years. And anyway, Mama, if you're going to be geographical, Lochinvar came out of the West, not the Southwest. It wouldn't have scanned."

"Leslie reads too much," Mrs. Lynnton explained blandly. "Horace dear, fetch me a sliver of that ham, will you? For a young girl, I mean. But it's her only fault and you wouldn't really call it a fault. Leslie dear, if Mr. Benedict has finished breakfast don't you want to show him the stables?"

"He saw them yesterday, Mama. Besides, we've just quarreled in a polite way about Texas so it's no use your trying to palm me off on him. And anyway Mr. Benedict has three million acres and five hundred thousand cows or whatever they're called in Texas————"

"Head of cattle," Bick suggested, "and not quite five————"

"—head of cattle then. And hundreds of vaqueros and consequently he's engaged to marry the daughter of the owner of the adjoining ranch who, though comparatively poor, is beautiful and has only one million acres and fifteen thousand horses and two hundred thousand head of cattle and six hundred vaqueros."

"What is a vaquero?" Mrs. Lynnton demanded, dignified in defeat.

Jordan Benedict walked round the table to stand beside Leslie as though he were talking to her rather than to her mother. "A vaquero is a Mexican cowboy," he said crisply, with no trace of a drawl. "Did you ever hear the word buckaroo? That's what the old Texas pioneers made of vaquero, they couldn't get the hang of the Spanish word vaquero. You see—vaca, cow. Vaquero—fellow who tends cows."

"Is she pretty?" demanded Mrs. Lynnton, turning the knife in her wound.

Doctor Lynnton bent over his wife's chair and kissed her lightly on the cheek. "Good-bye, dear. Mr. Benedict and I are going now. I'm late."

Baffled, Mrs. Lynnton must still know the worst. "What, may I ask, is the name of the lucky young lady you are marrying, with all those cows?"

Then even Leslie was moved to protest. "Oh dear Mrs. Nickleby, that was just my little joke."

Bick Benedict just touched her hand with his forefinger. "It's more or less true—or was. My next-door neighbor does have a daughter—only a next-door neighbor in Texas is fifty miles away, usually. And he does have just about all that land and those horses and the cattle. And perhaps there was some idea of my marrying his daughter like the fellow in a book. But I'm not."

A radiance lighted Mrs. Lynnton's austere features. "Dear me, it all sounds so romantic. I never knew anyone from Texas before, it's very refreshing, of course it's quite a distance, Texas."

"It is a far piece, ma'am," Bick agreed, still looking at Leslie. "But when you get there you never want to live anywhere else."

"Yes," Mrs. Lynnton agreed happily, "with those new fast trains and all you can visit back East in no time at all. And you're going back tomorrow. Dear me, what a pity. I don't know when I've met any young man that seemed so much like one of the family."

7

AFTER THIRTY-SIX hours of travel the bride and bridegroom seemed to have set up miniature housekeeping in their drawing room on the Missouri Pacific's crack Sunshine Special. Books and papers and bundles and bags were heaped on couches and racks. A towering edifice of fruit in a basket, untouched, was turning brown under the hot blasts that poured through the screened window. A vast box of Maillard's candy, open on the couch, was coated with the fine sift of dust that filmed the little room. A bottle of bourbon clinked against a bottle of water in the wall bracket. Railroad folders and maps of Texas splashed their brilliant pinks and blues and orange and scarlet against the drab green of the car upholstery and the grim maroon of the woodwork. The door of the compartment adjoining the drawing room was open, and this was piled with a formidable array of luggage.

They had been traveling hours, days, yet Texas was not in sight. Bick Benedict did not appear eager for a glimpse of that fabulous commonwealth from which he had been three weeks absent. He lolled on the hot plush seat, the withering southwest blasts poured over him, the dust clogged his throat, the electric fan set the cinders to spinning more merrily in the stifling little room.

He had been bred on heat and dust. This was nothing.

He looked at Leslie and he was like a man fanned by ocean breezes, laved in the perfumes of fresh-cut meadows. But now and then when he leaned against the gritty cushion and shut his eyes his face muscles tensed, his fingers clenched, and it was obvious that his inner vision presented a picture less than idyllic.

The bride was reading a railroad timetable. Bick Benedict eyed her through narrowed lids. "I've married a bookworm." They both laughed as though the timeworn joke were new-minted.

It was incredible that any woman could appear as cool and fresh as she after thirty-six hours in the gritty luxury of a train drawing room. She seemed to have an unlimited supply of fresh blouses and just to watch her open a filmy handkerchief and to catch the scent that emanated from it as she shook out its white folds was a refreshment to the onlooker. She brushed her hair a great deal. She poured eau de cologne into the lavatory wash basin and bathed her wrists and her temples and the scent of this, too, pricked the grateful nostrils.

"I don't know how other brides feel on their honeymoon," she now said, "Mr. Benedict sir. But I'm having a lovely time."

"Well, thanks."

"It isn't only you. It's traveling. I love train-riding even if it's hot and dusty."

"If we'd had the private car as I wanted———"

"Private cars for two people are immoral. And anyway, they're dull."

"Well, thanks again."

"I'll bet you," said the bride, "that this minute, sight unseen, I know more about Texas than you do."

"Mrs. Benedict, if I may call you that, I am taking the filly known as My Mistake and the young woman formerly known as Leslie Lynnton, off the hands of Doctor and Mrs. Lynnton, respectively. The understanding was that the one can run and the other is intelligent as well as lovely. Perhaps one of you has got the wrong name."

"Leslie Benedict," she mused. "It isn't as pretty as Leslie Lynnton."

"But you're prettier. I don't say that I'm taking full credit. But you are."

"It's the fresh air," she said. "And the regular hours. Darling, will you let me know the minute we reach Texas?"

"Texas isn't exactly a secret."

"It's different from other states, isn't it? It looks different?"

He was seated opposite her on one of the grim settees. Now he leaned forward and clasped his hands between his knees and smiled up at her, so earnest so eager so alive. "You're a funny girl. You didn't marry me just for the trip to Texas, did you?"

"I won't say I didn't."

He laughed aloud then and held out his hand for hers and swung around so that he sat beside her on the seat that had been facing him. They looked at one another a moment, smiling, and then they became serious and silent.

The sound of the drawing-room door buzzer was like an electric shock. Bick Benedict passed a hand over his forehead and shouted, "Come in!" It was the dining-car steward, sallow and sleek and obsequious.

He purred. He bowed. "Parn me," he said. "But I figured you'd want to get your order in early, before the rush. You can just run your eye over the menu, but I have a couple of suggestions. Our last stop we took on some———"

"Oh, let's have dinner in the dining car," Leslie said. "With the rest of the world. Let's have olives—the big black ones—in a bowl of cracked ice with celery. And melons. And brook trout."

"Brook trout!" Bick protested doubtfully. "They don't have———"

"But we do," interrupted the steward with injured dignity. "I was just trying to tell Mrs. Benedict. We took them on at Baxter just for our special passengers."

It had been like that from the moment they had turned their faces toward the West. Passenger agents had come aboard at various stops for the sole purpose of inquiring about their comfort.

"They behave as if you were royalty," Leslie had said. "Do they always do that? Or just for brides and bridegrooms?"

"The Benedicts have been around these parts a long time," Bick explained. "And we travel a lot. And Reata beef travels a lot too. They're the really important passengers when it comes to railroad arithmetic."

It seemed to Leslie that the conductors, the stewards, the porters the station agents knew more about the members of the Benedict family of Texas—their names, habits, characteristics and whereabouts—than they knew about President Coolidge and his family in the White House.

The Pullman conductor, benign and spectacled, with all those stripes on his sleeve and the Elks charm and the little gold nugget dangling from his watch chain, was introduced with friendly formality.

"Leslie, I want you to know Mr. McCullough. The newest member of the family, Ed. Mrs. Benedict."

"Well, say, Bick! I heard, last trip up. Certainly pleased to make your acquaintance, Mrs. Benedict. This is great news. The girls are all fit to be tied, I bet. They had just about given him up, I guess. But say!" His tone was jocose, his manner almost paternal. He turned, beaming, to Bick. "Yessir, great news this is. How's Miz Maudie Lou? She come for the wedding? She hasn't ridden with us here lately. How's Miz Luz? Did she get over that nasty fall she took? How's Uncle Bawley? Bowie was riding with us last week, never let out a yip about the wedding, and prolly on his way to be best man. Awful closemouthed, Bowie is."

Leslie thought that her mother would have loved all this kowtowing on the part of railroad crew and officials. In those brief days before the hurried wedding Mrs. Lynnton had chanted her refrain endlessly.

"Jordan Benedict of the famous Benedict ranch in Texas, you know. Jordan Benedict Third. Everybody knows about the Benedict ranch. It's practically a kingdom. It's a kind of legend Doctor Lynnton says."

The Benedict family had not come to the wedding in great numbers. Bick's younger brother Bowie had come as best man and of course his cousin Roady in Washington and his sister Maudie Lou Placer and her husband Clint. But his older sister Luz, the one who kept house for him at the ranch, the one who never had married, caught the grippe or something at the last minute and couldn't come. Nor did Uncle Bawley, who practically never left his big untidy bachelor house from which he ran the five hundred thousand acres of the Holgado Division. Assorted aunts and uncles and cousins had not been urged to come. There had been no time, really.

The Virginia newspapers and the Washington society columns referred to it as a whirlwind courtship—a phrase that delighted Mrs. Lynnton. Rushed though she was with the wedding preparations, Mrs Lynnton snipped out all the newspaper clichés and pasted them in a Bride's Book—white leather with gold tooling—which she presented to Leslie and which, years later, Leslie's daughter Luz came upon with whoops of mirth at the knee-length skirts and the ear-hugging coiffures.

The lovely Leslie Lynnton. The dashing Texan. Virginia belle. Cattle King. Bick Benedict had battered down everyone's opposition to such haste.

"Wait for what!" he demanded of Leslie, of Doctor Lynnton of Mrs. Lynnton. "Now!" he insisted. "Now, while I'm here. Suppose I do go home and come back here again in a month—two months. What for!"

"Trousseau," Mrs. Lynnton insisted. "There are a million things a bride has to have, besides clothes. Linens and———"

"There are a million things at the ranch. There's everything anybody needs and no one there to use them—except my sister Luz. Boxes of stuff, barrels of them, closets stuffed with them. Fifty beds, and sheets for a hundred, and all the rest of it."

"My daughter Leslie will be married as befits a Lynnton of Virginia. And her clothes will be as carefully chosen as those of her sister Lady Karfrey."

But here Leslie took over. "Mama dear, you are talking like someone out of Jane Austen. Anyway, I'm not a Lynnton of Virginia. I just live here. I was born in Ohio, remember? And Texas isn't England."

"What has that to do with it?" Mrs. Lynnton demanded unreasonably.

"Nothing. Not a thing. For some reason Jordan wants us to be married next week. And he's here. And why not!"

"It's odd. People will talk."

Leslie linked her arm through Jordan's and together the two faced Nancy Lynnton. Horace Lynnton, never doubting the outcome, smoked a smoking pipe and surveyed the battle with interest at once paternal and professional. Long ago he had learned, a male surrounded by females, to take on the protective coloration of the absent-minded professor.

Somehow it filtered through to Mrs. Lynnton that it was now or never. She looked at her husband, so maddeningly noncommittal; at Leslie who somehow, suddenly, had taken on a baffling mixture of soft bloom and hard resolution; at Jordan Benedict a man of thirty bewildered and in love for the first time.

It had not been much of a wedding, as society weddings go. The striped trousers and cutaway coats knew about Bick Benedict, and seemed somewhat pale beside him, not only from chagrin but because they hadn't a century of Texas sun and dust and wind behind them for coloration. The girls said, "Oh, Leslie, he reminds me of Tom Mix a little, only blond of course."

Bick's sister Maudie Lou Placer turned out to be something of a bombshell. Very chic. She and Clint Placer arrived the morning of the wedding and departed immediately afterward, leaving a somewhat stricken Mrs. Lynnton to digest the utterances of the strangely resentful Maudie Lou.

She had given Mrs. Lynnton a grisly five minutes. That doughty lady, recognizing an adversary when she saw one, had said, "It's a pity they will have such a short honeymoon. Just ten days. It would have been nice if they could have gone to visit my daughter Lady Karfrey in England. But Jordan says he must get back to his ranch."

"His ranch!" Maudie Lou had echoed, and with a peculiarly nasty laugh. "It isn't his ranch."

Nancy Lynnton had turned white and faint. "What do you mean by that!"

"Well, it's no more his than mine or Luz's or Bowie's or Roady's for that matter. Bick runs it. Manages, with Luz of course. But we all own it. Though if he keeps on with————"

"Of course," said Mrs. Lynnton feebly. "So many millions of acres."

"Though if he keeps on the way he is," Maudie Lou concluded angrily, "putting all the profits back into the ranch and going on with his crazy breeding and fads and experiments there'll be nothing left for any of us pretty soon."

Bick's oldest sister Luz did not come to the wedding. "She brought me up, really," Bick had told Leslie. "She has been like a mother to me. She had to be. She's nineteen years older than I am. She looks like Great-grandma Benedict. She even tries to look like her. Once she got the old hoop skirts out of the attic and went out into the pasture and tried roping in that crazy outfit because the story goes that that's what Great-grandma Benedict did back in the late fifties. She does her hair like her, too. Two braids in a kind of crown on top of her head."

"Like pictures of Mrs. Lincoln," Leslie observed thoughtfully. "Luz. What an unusual name."

"It's Spanish. It means light."

When the actual week of the wedding arrived there was a telegram. Luz was ill with the grippe, she had a fever of one hundred and two. The doctor said she absolutely must not travel. . . .

Bick Benedict seemed perturbed by this out of all proportion to its importance, the Lynntons thought. An elderly sister is ill and can't come to the wedding. How sad. But in another way how convenient, Mrs. Lynnton thought privately. A middle-aged woman, a bedroom alone of course, the house was crowded. It would have added to the difficulties without contributing anything to the festivities.

Bick had talked a great deal about this older sister. "She's wonderful, really," he had said, as though someone had said she was not. "Right out of a Western movie, you'll think. She can do anything a cowboy can. The boys are all crazy about her, but they're scared of her too."

Doctor Horace Lynnton, in these past few years, had related to this favorite daughter of his some of the phenomena which had emerged in the trial practice of a rather new branch of therapeutics called psychiatry. He was using it to help some of the broken boys who sat staring into space in the corridors and rooms of the crowded veterans' hospitals in Washington, Maryland, Virginia. He had given Leslie books to read, he introduced her to the writings of the giants in this new and inexact science. "Our thoughts, our dreams, our entire lives are influenced by the unconscious," he explained.

Leslie had found this new instruction fascinating, she had accepted it with calm. "I suppose," she said thoughtfully, "that I've been in love with you all these years, Papa, and that's why I haven't married."

"Quite likely," Doctor Lynnton agreed. Then, with a wry smile, "I wouldn't try, if I were you, to explain this to your mother."

Now, with the wedding only three days distant, it was with a certain amused thoughtfulness that Leslie received the news of her future sister-in-law's sudden illness.

Bick said with excusable stiffness, "I don't see why you find this amusing."

"I didn't know I was looking amused Forgive me. I was thinking. You know it's just possible that your sister Luz is sick to order. Sometimes those things happen when people are upset. Papa says he often encounters cases like that."

"I suppose Luz got a hundred and two just to order. Is that what you mean?"

"Lots of mothers do."

"Luz isn't my mother. What's the matter with you, Leslie!"

"Wives, I mean."

"Look, Leslie, have you gone loco!"

"Big sisters sometimes think they're wives. Or mothers. And mothers do too, Papa says."

This somewhat confused utterance was a maddening climax for Bick.

"I think you must be sick yourself," he had said with a harshness unusual in a prospective bridegroom.

But certainly Bick Benedict had no cause for complaint once the furor of the wedding was past. His bride was ardent and lovely and incredibly understanding. Three days of their honeymoon were spent in New York where the tall Texan in the big white Stetson and the starry-eyed girl in bridal grey caused a turning of heads even on Manhattan's blasé Fifth Avenue. They had stayed at the Plaza.

He seemed, curiously enough, in no great hurry to start the journey home. Strangely, too, he seemed not to have a great deal of ready money. They went to the theatre, they ate well, they drove in the Park, they shopped a

little but there was none of the lavish moneyed carelessness that one would
expect from the possessor of millions of acres of land and hundreds of
thousands of cattle.

Not that Leslie expected or coveted the brilliant baubles with which the
Fifth Avenue windows were bedecked. But perhaps he felt that some sort
of explanation was called for.

"Cattle men don't have a lot of ready cash," he said not at all apologetically. "We put it back into the ranch. More beef cattle, better stock, experimenting with new breeds. A good bull can cost twenty thousand dollars."

The bride had her practical side. "He can bring in twenty thousand too,
can't he? If you sell him. Or his—uh—sons?"

"You don't sell a bull like that. You buy him."

At the unreasonableness of this she laughed. But then she said seriously
enough, "I hope you're not stingy by nature, Jordan darling. Because that's
very bad for you. We've never had any money but we've always been
lavish."

"Perhaps that's why."

"Why what? Oh. Just for that perhaps you'd better buy me something
very expensive. Not that I want it. But as a lesson to you. Not the price of
a bull but a calf, say."

Now, as they neared the end of their journey, the little luxury room on
the train grew hotter, hotter, became stifling, the electric fan paddled the
heat and slapped their face with it, the whole body was fevered with heat
and dust. Too, another kind of fever possessed Leslie, it was the fire of deep
interest and anticipation so that she quite ignored the physical discomfort
of the stuffy train.

"You can see miles!" she said. "Miles and miles and miles!" She had her
flushed face at the ineffectually screened window, like a child.

"It's sort of frightening, isn't it—like something that defies you to conquer
it? So huge. Why, we've been riding in it for days. And ugly, too, isn't it!
I thought it would be beautiful. Oh, now, don't be sulky. I'm not talking
about your ancestors or something, dearest. I'm being interested. And clin-
ical."

"Like your father."

"Yes, I suppose so. Oh, I'm so excited. Look! There at that little station
we're passing—that's a cowboy, isn't it, it must be, I was just feeling cheated
because I hadn't seen a single cowboy. Are they like that at the ranch, at
Reata?"

He eyed her with fond amusement. "Sometimes I think you're ten years
old and not real bright."

"I can't help it. Geography always excites me when it's new places, and
I love trains and being married to you, and seeing Texas. When your grandfather came here it was wilderness really, wasn't it? Imagine! What courage!"

"They were great old boys. Tough."

"No trees, except that little fluffy stuff, it's rather sweet. What's it called?
Is there some at the ranch?"

His smile was grim. "That little sweet fluffy stuff is the damnedest nuisance
in Texas. It's called mesquite and if you can find a way to get rid of it you'll
be the toast of Texas, sure enough."

As far as her eyes could see she beheld the American desert land which
once had waved knee-high with lush grasses. She had never seen the great
open plains and the prairies. It was endless, it was another world, bare vast
menacing to her Eastern eyes. Later she was to know the brilliant blurred
pattern of the spring flowers, she was to look for the first yellow blossoms

of the retama against the sky, the wild cherry and the heavy cream white of the Spanish dagger flower like vast camellias.

"How big is it, really? Not in figures, I can't understand figures, but tell me in a kind of picture."

This was home again, this was what he knew and loved. "Well, let's see now. How can I——Look, you know the way the map of the United States looks? Well, if you take all of New England—the whole of the New England states—and then add New York State and New Jersey and Pennsylvania and Ohio and Illinois, and put the whole thing together in one block, why, you'd have a state the size of Texas. That's how big it is." He was triumphant as though he himself had created this vast area in a godlike gesture.

It was late afternoon when their train arrived at Vientecito. "Here we are!" he said and peered out through the window to scan the platform and the vehicles beyond in the swirling dust.

"What's it mean? How do you pronounce it?"

"Vientecito? Means gentle breeze. We call it Viento for short. The wind blows all the time, nearly. The Spanish explorers arrived here way back in 1519 before you were born I think, honey. Alonso Alvarez de Pinedo, if you want to know in round numbers. You see I did go to school. He and his crowd swung around hereabouts and liked the layout and claimed it for king and Spain. But they didn't know enough to hang onto it." He pointed at some object. "There we are. But who's that!" A huge Packard. In the driver's seat was a stocky young Mexican with powerful shoulders. About twenty, Leslie thought; a square face a square brow, his hair like a brush growing thick thick and up from his forehead. He was very dark very quiet he did not smile.

There was no one else in the car. There was no one to meet them. The man got out of the car, he stood at the open door looking uncertainly at Bick. He did not glance at Leslie. Bick's face was cold with anger, there was a curious underlay of white beneath his deep-coated tan, his jaw muscle swelled as he set his teeth. The two men spoke in Spanish.

"What are you doing here? Where is Jett?"

"Señorita Luz said she needed him. She sent me in his place."

"You don't know about a car. Here. Pile these bags in the back. Where's the pickup? There are trunks."

"Nothing was said about sending the pickup."

Bick Benedict's lips were a straight thin line, his fists were clenched.

This phenomenon Leslie surveyed with lively interest and no alarm.

"Bick, you look bursting. I must learn Spanish."

The boy, very serious and dignified, was inexpertly piling suitcases into the rear baggage section. This accomplished, he was about to take the driver's seat. "Out!" barked Bick. The boy paused, turned. Bick gave him the baggage checks. In Spanish he said, "You will wait here. The pickup will be sent. It may be two hours it may be midnight. You will wait here."

The boy inclined his head. Leslie came toward him, she put out her hand. "I am Mrs. Benedict," she said. "What is your name?"

The dark eyes met hers. Then they swung like a startled child's to encounter Bick Benedict's ice-blue stare. The boy bent over her hand, he did not touch it, he bowed in a curiously formal gesture, his hand over his heart, like a courtier. His eyes were cast down. "What eyelashes!" Leslie said over her shoulder to Bick. "I wish I had them!"

"Dimodeo" the boy said in English. "I am called Dimodeo Rivas!"

"That's a beautiful name," Leslie said.

"Leslie! Get into the car, please. We're leaving." His voice was a command. She smiled at the boy, she turned leisurely, she was somewhat surprised to see her husband's face scowling from the driver's seat.

"Coming!" she called gaily. She looked about her as she came—at the railway station so Spanish with its Romanesque towers, its slim pillars and useless grillwork. The sun burned like a stabwound, the hot unceasing wind gave no relief. The dark faces of the station loungers were unlike the submissive masks of the Negroes she knew so well in Virginia. No green anywhere other than the grey-green of the cactus, spiked and stark. Dust dust dust, stinging in the wind. Nothing followed the look or pattern of the life she had left behind her.

"It's like Spain," she called to Bick. "I've never been in Spain but it's like it." She stood a moment by the car door, hesitant, waiting for Bick to leap out. He sat looking straight ahead. The boy Dimodeo ran to her, he opened the Packard's half-door, she placed her hand delicately on his arm. "Thank you, Dimodeo. Uh—gracias—uh—muchas gracias! There! I can speak Spanish too. How did I happen to remember that? Ouch!" As she settled herself on the hot leather seat. "Read it somewhere I suppose."

With a neck-cracking jerk the car leaped away. Never a timorous woman their speed now seemed to her to be maniacal. She glanced at her husband's hands on the wheel. Nothing could go wrong when hands like that were guiding your life. He was silent, his face set and stern. Well, she knew that when men looked like that you pretended not to notice and pretty soon they forgot all about it.

"How flat it is! And big. And the horizon is—well, there just isn't any it's so far away. I thought there would be lots of cows. I don't see any."

"Cows!" he said in a tone of utter rage.

She was, after all, still one of the tart-tongued Lynnton girls. "I don't see why you're so put out because that boy came instead of someone else. Or the family. After all, it's so far from the railroad."

"Far!" In that same furious tone. "It's only ninety miles."

She glanced at the speedometer. It pointed to eighty-five. Well, no wonder! At this rate they'd be home in an hour or so. Home. For an engulfing moment she had a monstrous feeling of being alone with a strange man in an unknown world—a world of dust and desert and heat and glare and some indefinable thing she never before had experienced. Maybe all brides feel like this, she thought. Suddenly wanting to go home to their mother and father and their own bed.

He was speaking again in a lower tone now, but a controlled anger vibrated beneath it. "We don't behave like that down here."

"Behave?"

"Making a fuss over that Mexican boy. We don't do that here in Texas."

"But this still is the United States, isn't it? You were being mean to him. What did he do?"

The speedometer leaped to ninety. "We have our own way of doing things. You're a Texan now. Please remember that."

"But I'm not anyone I wasn't. I'm myself. What's geography to do with it!"

"Texas isn't geography. It's history. It's a world in itself."

She said something far in advance of her day. "There is no world in itself."

"You've read too damn many books."

She began to laugh suddenly—a laugh of surprise and discovery. "We're quarreling! Jordan, we're having our first quarrel. Well, it's nice to get it over with before we reach—home."

To her horror then he brought his head down to his hands on the wheel, a gesture of utter contrition and one that might have killed them both. At her cry of alarm he straightened. His right hand reached over to cover her hands clasped so tightly in her fright. "My darling," he said. "My darling girl." Then, strangely, "We mustn't quarrel. We've got to stand together."

Against the brassy sky there rose like a mirage a vast edifice all towers and domes and balconies and porticoes and iron fretwork. In size and general architecture it somewhat resembled the palace known as the Alhambra, with a dash of the Missouri Pacific Railroad station which they had just left behind them.

"What's that! Is it—are we near the ranch, Jordan?"

"We've been on it the last eighty miles, practically ever since we got outside Viento. That's Reata. That's home."

"But you said it was a ranch! You said Reata was a ranch!"

8

AND THERE AHEAD of them was the town. The town of Benedict. A huge square-lettered sign said:

WELCOME TO BENEDICT!
pop. 4739

"Is that for us, Jordan? How sweet of them!"

"No, honey. It's just the Chamber of Commerce saying howdy to any visitors who come by."

"Oh. Well, it's all been so regal, and everyone has done so much forehead-bumping I thought—— Oh, look! Look, Jordan." They had flashed into town, they were streaking down the wide main street. "Please drive slower, darling. I want to see. What a wide street for such a little—I mean——"

"It's wide because it was a cattle trail. We used to drive thousands of head of cattle to market along this trail, way up to Kansas. That was long before this was a town. Just a huddle of shacks on the prairie."

Now the vast white mansion had vanished, obscured for the moment by the town with its Ranchers and Drovers Bank, its Red Front Grocery, its hardware store, garage, drugstore, lunch room. But even as they roared through the town Leslie felt herself in a strange exciting new land. Dark faces everywhere, but not like the ebony faces of the Virginia streets. These were Latin faces; fine-boned Spanish faces; darker heavier Mexican Indian faces. Even the store-front signs were exhilaratingly different. Leslie hugged herself and bounced a little in her seat, like a child. Boots and Saddles Hand Made. . . . Come to Hermoso for the Fat Stock Show. . . . Quarter Horses For Sale. What was a quarter horse? . . . A little sun-baked dry-goods store whose sign said BARATO. Bargain Sale. She knew enough Spanish for that, at least. Sallow women in black with little black shawls over their heads under the blasting sun. Dusty oleanders by the roadside. Big beef-fed men in wide-brimmed Stetsons and shirt sleeves and high-heeled boots that gave their feet a deceptive arched elegance. Dark little men squatting on their haunches at the street corners. Lean sunburned tall men propped up against store buildings, their stance a peculiar one; one foot on the ground, the opposite knee bent so that the other foot rested flat against the wall. Small houses baking, grassless, by the road. Dust-bitten houses grey as desert bones.

"What's that! What in the world is that!"

In the courthouse square facing the street was a monstrous plate-glass case as large as a sizable room made of thick transparent glass on all sides. Within this, staring moodily out at a modern world, stood a stuffed and mounted Longhorn steer. A huge animal, his horn-spread was easily nine feet from tip to tip. Wrinkled ancient horns like those of some mythical monster.

"You've just got to stop. I must see him."

"You'll have the rest of your life to see him."

"I can't believe it. A—a cow stuffed and put into a glass case on the street."

He touched her flushed cheek tenderly and laughed a little.

"You're in Texas, honey. Anyway, they have lions outside the New York Public Library, don't they?"

"But this is real."

"Everything's real in Texas."

"What's it for? Do they worship it, or something?"

"He's a Longhorn—the last of the Reata Longhorn herd. They roamed the range wild a hundred years ago. Now they're as extinct as the buffalo, or more. Way back in the days of the Spanish Missions in the 1600s the Spanish brought the first livestock with them. When the Missions were abandoned the stock was left behind and pretty soon there were thousands and thousands of head covering the whole country. Tough mean animals. Hoofs and horns and hide like iron and the meat like leather. That's what we used to call beef, not so many years ago. And now there's the last Longhorn a museum piece in a glass case."

"Who'd have thought a cow could be so romantic! What are they like now—the Reata cows? And where are they? I haven't seen any. I don't believe you really have any. You've dragged me down here under false pretenses."

He laughed wholeheartedly and the sound delighted her. She was not used to morose faces, the Virginia house had been a gay lighthearted place. "Oh, we've still got one or two," he said airily, "hiding out in the mesquite and around. Wait till you see the new breed. We've been ten years experimenting and I think now we've just about got it. We brought Herefords from England and bred them to the best of the native stock. And now I'm breeding the cream of that to the big Kashmirs. Oriental stock. They can take the heat and they've got a body oil that discourages ticks and fleas. The King ranch crowd and some of the other boys are experimenting with Brahmans but I'm the Kashmir Kid. Wait till you see some of those Kashmir-Hereford bulls. They look like a house on legs. There's never been anything like them in the world. In the world!"

His face was brilliant with life, the silent man of an hour ago was a young eager boy. Some deep inner instinct pinched her heart sharply. That is his real love, it said. Reata and its past and its future are his life. You are just an incident, you are a figure in a pattern you don't even understand.

Now the town was behind them, they were again in the open country. Again and again, in the past hour, she had seen pools of water in the road ahead. But once the spot was reached the pool had vanished and another glinted a hundred yards beyond the speeding car.

"The water. The little pools of water in the middle of the road. And then they're not there."

"A mirage. Texas is full of mirages."

She looked at him quickly, smiling, but his face was serious. He was merely stating a fact. Now again she saw the house, its great bulk against the brassy sky, its walls shimmering in the heat. She stared at it in a sort of panic but she asked quietly enough, "Did you build it?"

"The Big House. God, no! My father built it. He said he built it for Ma but I reckon he really built it to show the cotton crowd that he wasn't just a big high-powered cattle man. He wanted to show them that he was in high cotton too."

"High cotton?"

"Here in Texas the cotton rich always snooted the cattle rich. And now if this oil keeps coming into Texas the old cattle crowd will look down their noses at the oil upstarts. You know, like the old New York De Peysters snooting the Vanderbilts and the Vanderbilts cutting the Astors." He pointed with his left hand. "See that low greyish building about half a mile from the Big House? That's the old ranch house. That's where I was born. It's always been called the Main House."

She stared for a long minute at the low rambling outlines of the old house, so small and colorless in comparison with the magnificence and ornamentation of the great mansion. She leaned toward him gently, her arm pressed his arm. "I like it. It looks like a house to be born in." He was silent again. She glanced sidewise at him. "Who lives in it now? Your sister Luz, does she—will she live there?"

"Luz lives with me," he said. "With us. In the Big House. She's run it ever since Ma died twenty-five years ago." He laughed a short mirthless little laugh. "Some say she runs the ranch."

"It will all be strange to me at first. Of course at first I'll have to learn how things are done here. I hope she won't—mind."

"Hard to say what Luz will or won't mind. Let's just relax and be happy we're home."

She longed to say, But a wife runs her house, doesn't she? A wife wants to manage her own household and plan things and decide things and be alone with her husband. Some new wisdom told her to say nothing.

He was speaking again, rather hurriedly for him, as though he felt she must have certain knowledge squarely placed. "Texians are openhanded kind of folks you know, Leslie. Hospitable. Tell you something that maybe you don't know. Texas—the word, I mean—comes from the word Tejas, that's an Indian word that the old confederacy of Indian tribes used to use, and it means Friend."

"Nice," she murmured drowsily, for she was very weary. "Nice."

"So the Big House is usually full of folks. Every ranch is the same all through Texas, Panhandle to the Gulf. Folks drop in, sometimes two, sometimes ten, sometimes twenty. Feed 'em, bed 'em, mount 'em."

"People you don't even know!"

"Sometimes. Interested in ranching, or breeding, or feed crops. Open house. Old Waggoner was the same, and all of us. Tejas."

"My goodness! And I thought Virginians were hospitable!"

A turn of his wrist, the car ground to a halt before high iron gates. A man ran out of a little gatehouse and he seemed to bow as he ran. He opened the gates, he raised his hand in salute and his teeth flashed, his face was joyous with welcome.

"Bienvenido! Bienvenido, señor, señora!" A dusky skin, the face square, the features finely cut; an ageless face, perhaps forty perhaps sixty. He had limped a little as he ran, so that between the running and the bowing and the limping he had a hobgoblin aspect, but there was dignity, too, in his bearing, you saw pride in his face.

Bick Benedict raised a hand from the wheel in greeting. "Cómo estás, Arcadio!"

"Muy bien, gracias. Gracias!" He looked at Leslie, his hand went to his forehead, he saluted gravely, ceremoniously.

"Hello, Arcadio," Leslie called to him. She smiled and waved. As they moved on and the gates closed behind them she pinched her husband just a little nip. "Is that all right? Tell me if I do something wrong, darling. I feel as if I were in a foreign country. I'm not used to acting queenly."

"Don't be silly. This is Texas. Everything free and open. You're home."

"I shall simply burst if I don't ask questions. Darling, is his name really Arcadio, how enchanting, and why does he limp so terribly and is the gate always closed you said everything's free and open in Texas I don't mean to be critical I'm just so interested I can't wait till I write Papa————"

"It's really Arcadio, though I don't know why that's enchanting. He was just twelve when they put him in the corrida, and so was I. They gave us old horses to ride, we were only kids. One day when he was helping hold the herd his horse stumbled and fell on him, his right leg was pinned beneath it and then the horse's hoofs began to dig into him and tear him apart. His father was a ranchero but they were out on the range, there wasn't a doctor within fifty miles————"

"Poor little boy," she said. "Poor little man, limping and bobbing."

"You can't be sentimental on a ranch."

She thought, I don't even know what a corrida is.

Up the long drive. An old adobe building on this side. Another on that. Big square buildings, small squatted buildings. She longed to say what's that what's that what's that? Something restrained her.

Far off across the flat land she saw what seemed to be another town made up of toy houses huddled on the prairie.

"Do you remember that first night at dinner? When Mama asked if there were any cities on the premises? Is that another town—all those little houses way off there?"

"That? That's no town. That's just where some of the ranch help live— some of the married ones with families. Some of the vaqueros live there and a few of the rancheros. Most of the rancheros live out on the ranchitos, they're spread about ten or fifteen miles apart, of course."

"Of course," Leslie echoed solemnly. Then she giggled, what with nerves, travel-weariness, and some amusement. "Mr. Benedict, sir, your bride wouldn't know a vaquero from a ranchero when she saw one—if she ever saw one."

"You will." Then, as they made a sharp turn in the drive, "You're going to see a heap of vaqueros right now. Old Polo has put on a show for you."

They were approaching another gate—a wooden one, crossbarred—and a line of fence that stretched away endlessly. On the other side of the fence, facing them, were perhaps fifty men on horseback. They sat like bronze equestrian statues. Erect, vital, they made a dazzling frieze against prairie and sky. Their great hats shaded the dark ardent eyes. Their high-heeled boots were polished to a glitter; narrow, pointed, they fitted like a glove. Their saddles, their hatbands, their belts were hand-tooled. Their costumes lacked, perhaps, the silver, the silks, the embroidery, the braid, but in every basic item this was the uniform that the Mexican charro had worn three hundred years before and that every American cowboy all the way from Montana down to Arizona and Texas had copied from the Mexican.

On either side of the gate they made a single line, reined up side by side like cavalry on parade. Immobile they sat in their saddles, they did not smile, they did not raise a hand in greeting. Only their dark eyes spoke. At the gate, mounted on a splendid palomino, was a man of middle age, dark like the others but with an almost indefinable difference. Authority was in his bearing. Slim and small, he was a figure of striking elegance. Now his horse moved daintily forward with little mincing steps like those of a ballet dancer on her toes. The man swung low in his saddle and opened the gate, he drew up squarely then in the path of the car.

He spoke the greeting. "Viva el señor! Vivan los novios!"

From the men then, like a chant, "Viva el señor! Vivan los novios!"

She tweaked his coat sleeve. "Jordan, what's it mean—los novios? What do I do?"

But Bick Benedict nodded carelessly to the men, he raised a hand in greeting and gravely he spoke his thanks in the Spanish tongue. Then, out of the corner of his mouth, to Leslie, "They've put on a real show for you, honey. Welcome to the bridal couple. Say gracias, will you?"

She was enchanted, she opened the car door, she stepped to the fender and leaned far out. "Thank you!" she called, and her voice was warm and lovely with emotion. "Gracias! Gracias! Thank you for the beautiful welcome!"

"Don't overdo it please, Leslie."

"Can't I blow them a kiss! I'm in love with all of them."

"Come in and sit down. We're moving."

"Especially that beautiful café-au-lait Buffalo Bill."

"Polo's got ten grandchildren. He'd be shocked to his Mexican core."

"Why were they so stern and silent? They hardly looked at us."

"They saw you all right," he said as he shifted gears. "They'll tell their families everything you wore, what you said, how you look. The grapevine will carry it to every barrio, through the ranchitos out to the West Division where our Holgado ranch is, and south to Hermoso and up to La Piedra that's the North Division and over east to the———"

"But you told me to say thank you. I thought it was picturesque and wonderful. Did I do something wrong?"

"No. No. Perhaps you overdid it just a little."

"But you didn't marry me because I was like the girls you know in Texas. You'd have married one of those if you'd wanted your wife to behave like a Texan."

Behind them the thunder of hoofs on hard-baked clay. The sun flashed on stirrup and spur, was reflected dartingly in iron and silver. The horsemen spoke together softly as they rode, the one to the other very softly. Now the hoofbeats were like an echo.

"No está mal. Not bad."

"Sí, pero le faltan carnes. A little thin for my taste."

"Tuerta?"

"No, you fool. Her eyes are soft and dark like the eyes of a gentle heifer, but with spirit, too, in them. That little flaw in the eye it is a mark of beauty in a woman, very stirring to men."

Now the car made the last curve in the long drive and there they were at the foot of the great broad stone steps that led to the doorway of the house. She looked up at it. She had hoped that when they actually came upon it the whole thing would vanish miraculously like the mirages she had seen on the road. But now it was real enough, yet about it there hung a ghostly quality in spite of the blinding sun, in spite of the bulk of walls and columns and towers. No one came to the car, no one stood in the doorway, all was quiet, breathless, waiting, like the castle of the Sleeping Beauty. Nothing could be really sinister in sunlight, she said to herself. And aloud, "It's siesta time, isn't it? Just like in Ol' Virginny, though we never paid much attention to it."

He held out his hand to her, his hand was hard, was crushing. "Neither do we." He looked up at the house, together they began to mount the steps.

"Would it sound too sickening and coy if I asked you to carry me through the doorway, just for luck?" And she smiled. "Of course I'm a big girl———"

He stared at her incredulously, he saw that her lips were trembling. His hands were on her shoulders, he swung her around and picked her up in his arms as if she had been a child, and so up the steps, across the broad veranda and through the doorway, her arm about his neck, her cheek against his. He pretended to be panting as they came into the shade of the huge entrance hall, dim after the glare outside. They were laughing, and the sound echoed against the high grey walls. Her arm went more tightly about his neck, he still held her in his arms. He bent his head impetuously and they kissed long and silently.

Like a vast flue the great doors east and west drew the prevailing wind from the Mexican Gulf. "Oh, it's cool!" she said inadequately. He tipped her to her feet and she staggered a little and leaned against him and looked about her, blinking with the sudden change from glare to shade. Then she saw against the grey-white background the six flags of Texas, draped and brilliant in a burst of color upon the wall that faced them. The Spanish flag, the French flag, the Mexican flag, the flag of the Republic of Texas, the flag of the Confederacy, the flag of the United States of America.

No sound disturbed the utter silence of the enormous room. Yet Leslie had a feeling that on the other side of every door and wall there were ears listening, listening. They stood in the middle of the great hall like tourists, Leslie thought. Or like guests who have mistaken the time at which they were expected. "The flags," she said. "Against the wall like that. They're history, alive. They're so lovely. Gay like the flags in the cathedral at St. Denis."

"What's going on here !" yelled Bick. He clapped his hands. "Tomás! Vincente! Lupe! Petra!" Then, in a great bawl that topped all the rest, "Luz! Luz, what the hell is this! Come out here before I come and get you."

From nowhere there appeared a little plump woman. Until this moment Leslie had not been aware that she had pictured this older sister of Jordan's as a tall dark woman—swarthy, almost—with straight black hair and straight black brows. But this Luz who came toward them was a pink-cheeked bustling little body in a pink ruffled dress and a bright red hat. Thick plaits of grey-white hair and, in unexpected contrast, very black eyes that gave the effect of having been mistakenly placed in a face meant for blue eyes. Their hard brightness startled the beholder like sudden forked lightning in a sunny summer sky.

Her voice was shrill and high, she walked with a little clatter and rush of short steps, hers were the smallest feet Leslie had ever seen.

"Jurden! Stop that bawling like a calf's just been branded." Her manner was brisk, not to say hearty. She kissed her brother on the cheek, a mere peck. She came to Leslie. "Howdy, Miss Lynnton," said Luz Benedict. "Excuse my being late." An added flush suffused the pink rouged cheek.

Bick Benedict put one hand on his wife's shoulder. "Now Luz, don't you go roweling Leslie first thing. This is Mrs. Jordan Benedict, and don't you forget it."

9

"WE LOOKED FOR you a week ago," said Luz. She took Leslie's hand in a grip of steel and smiled up at her.

"But we didn't plan to come sooner," Leslie said. "What made you think we did?"

"I didn't figure Bick would stay away. All the spring work to be done. It's the worst time of the year to be away. The big spring roundup."

"But this is—was—our honeymoon!"

"No honeymoon's as important as roundup at Reata."

Leslie felt suddenly inadequate in an argument involving the relative importance of a honeymoon and a roundup. She was mildly amused to hear herself saying, "Yes, it must seem so to all but the two involved." She stood with her arm through Bick's, she turned to smile at him tenderly, she was startled to see that he apparently had heard none of this exchange, he was staring at the big doorway through which they had just entered. There was the sound of a motor in the drive.

"Jett!" yelled Bick, and released his arm with a jerk as he started toward the door. "Jett! Come on in here."

"Don't you want to see the house?" Luz said hurriedly. "Let me show you the house." She grasped Leslie's arm firmly.

"Yes. Yes, of course," said Leslie. "But I'll wait. I'd rather wait for my—for Jordan."

"Oh, Jordan and Jett are everlastingly jangling about something. Come on." It was plain that she was anxious to be off. The sound of the men's voices rose in argument. Leslie glimpsed this Jett Rink in the doorway now— a muscular young fellow with a curiously powerful bull-like neck and shoulders. He wore the dust-colored canvas and the high-heeled boots of the region, his big sweat-stained hat was pushed back from his forehead and you saw his damp dark curls. His attitude, his tone were belligerent. About twenty, Leslie decided. She decided, too, that he was an unpleasant young man.

"She wanted for him to go, not me. It was her doing. I don't like for Dimodeo to drive the big car any more'n you do. Ever time he does I got to spend two days patching her up."

"You'll do as I say."

"Tell that to Madama. How am I going to know what to do? Her hauling one way and you another. Tell me who's boss around here and I'll do like they say."

Leslie turned away, annoyed at the boy's hard insolence. Her eyes had become accustomed now to the dimness of the great hall. Through open double doors she glimpsed other rooms, they seemed as vast as this. She looked about her, interestedly. Luz Benedict had disappeared. Madama. The boy Jett had called her Madama. Funny, her going off like that.

Glancing about, she smiled as she thought of the first line of the letter she would write to her father tonight or tomorrow. Dear Papa, do you remember when I was about ten the time you took me to the Natural History Museum in New York? Well, that's where I'm living now, only it's been moved to Texas.

Everywhere on the walls were the mounted heads of deer, of buffalo, of catamounts, coyotes, mountain lions; the vicious tusked faces of javelina or wild hog, red fox, grey fox, and two sad-eyed Longhorns whose antlered spread and long morose muzzle dwarfed all the other masks. In the space not occupied by these mortuary mementos were large gold-framed paintings of cows (Herefords) of Longhorns (extinct) of sky and prairies and prairie and sky—of all that which the sun-tortured eye could see if it so much as peered through a crack in a window blind in this land of cattle and sun and sky and burning hot prairie.

Through the wide door at the rear she saw the patio and a glimpse of green, she walked toward it inhaling a deep breath as she walked, feeling suddenly shut in and stifling. As she went she said, aloud, socially, "Oh, how lovely, there's a terrace do let me see that," though there was no one to hear her. Oleanders in tubs stood disconsolately about, the white walls under the glare of the sun glared back gold at their tormentor. Leslie sank for a moment into one of the big wicker chairs and sprang up with a little screech. It was like sitting on a bed of red-hot coals. She began to know why Texans never sat out of doors, why they sought the dim shade of inner rooms.

She came back into the hall and stood there and now Bick joined her, he took her hand. "Leslie! I thought you'd gone upstairs with Luz."

"I was waiting for you."

"You must be hot and tired. Where's Luz?"

"She was very nice, she wanted to show me the house." Suddenly she had a horrible feeling that she was going to cry—she who so rarely wept even when a child. She raised her swimming eyes and looked at him. "I waited for you. I want my husband to show me his house."

"Of course, my darling, of course. Things have kind of gone loco around here while I've been gone. Luz can get the whole place in a———"

The tap-tap-tap of Luz Benedict's little feet sounded on the stone floor. "Oh, there you are, Bick! Going off and leaving this poor little bride of yours alone. She wouldn't come with me. Come on, Bick. You show her the house. I'll tag along."

Leslie was to become accustomed to the clatter of men's high-heeled boots on these tiled floors, and the clank and jingle of spurs and the creak of leather. Texas sounds. Everywhere the creak of leather. The staccato tap-tap of Luz Benedict's little heels were to stay in her mind long after they had ceased forever. She and Bick went hand in hand but Luz chattered and clattered close behind them. "And this is the big room and that there is the little sitting room and this is the library and this is the music room and over there is the dining room and that is the men's den."

And "How wonderful!" Leslie exclaimed. "How interesting!" as they walked through the dim vast rooms. Everything was on a gargantuan scale, as though the house had been built and furnished for a race of giants. Chairs were the size of couches, couches the size of beds. There were chairs of cowhide with fanciful backs fashioned from horns. Luz was displaying the monolithic rooms as a hostess guides a guest whose stay is so temporary that all must be crowded into a brief time.

Leslie was weary, warm, her face was burning, her eyes smarted. The three ascended the great stone stairway now. Leslie put a hand on the balustrade and it seemed damp to the touch. She was to learn many things about this pseudo-Spanish palace of stone and concrete and iron that was foreign to the Texas land and that had been rejected by it. The elements had turned upon it to destroy it. The battle was constant, day after day, summer and winter. In a norther the concrete would break out in a cold sweat. Patches of mold followed the spring rains. Fungi sprang up in dark places, shoes in closets were covered with a slippery white mildew. Plumbing rusted. There seemed forever to be a tap-tapping and clink-clinking as workmen busied themselves with leaky roof, sprung floor, cracked wall, burst pipe.

Fifty bedrooms Bick had said in his argument with Mrs. Lynnton. Leslie had assumed that this was a figure of speech. Now it seemed to her that there were acres of dull bare bedrooms with their neat utility beds and their drab utiliy chests of drawers and one armchair and one straight chair and a drab utility table and an electric light bulb in the middle of the ceiling. A hotel. A big, bare unattractive hotel with no guests. A terrible thought occurred to Leslie.

"Have they ever been filled—all these rooms?"

"My yes!" Luz shrilled happily. "And then some. Times we had 'em sleeping in cots out here in the hall. Sitting-room couches too. Bick, remember that time of the big rodeo in Viento, Kale Beebe blew in late and stepping a little high, laid down on the big tapestry sofa with his spurs on and must have been riding nightmares all night because in the morning the sofa was ribbons and the stuffing all over him like a store Santa Claus."

Luz clattered on down the hall, she pointed briskly to a big room whose door stood open. Two Mexican women and a man were bending over open suitcases which Leslie recognized as Jordan's.

"That's Bick's room," Luz said breezily. She marched on down the hall, turned right, turned left. "And this," she said, "is your room."

There was the fraction of a moment of utter silence. Then Leslie began to laugh. She laughed as helplessly as one does who has been under fearful strain and then Bick too was laughing, they laughed leaning against each other, the tears streaming with their laughter; they laughed as two people laugh who love each other and who have been apart in spirit and now suddenly are brought together again by the stupendous absurdity of the situation at which they are laughing. And oh! they whooped, and ugh! they groaned in a pain of combined laughter and relief.

The black eyes stared at them, the pink face was rigid with the resentment of one who does not share the joke.

Bick wiped his eyes, he patted Luz's shoulder. "Look, sis, Leslie and I are married. We're having these two big front connecting rooms where the breeze'll get us, one for a bedroom and one a kind of sitting room where we can sit and talk if we want to."

"Away from me, I suppose."

"Why no, honey, we don't mean————"

"Yes," said Leslie then, with terrible distinctness. "Away from anyone when we want to be. When we want to talk together." Then, at the look on the woman's face, "Not secrets, Luz. Just husband and wife talk." Poor dear, she doesn't know.

"Get Lupe and one of the other girls," Bick said hastily. "They'll fix us up. I hope those trunks get here. They could unpack while we're eating supper."

"Supper!" Leslie repeated rather faintly.

"Supper's at six," Luz announced firmly. "How'd you like a cup of coffee right now? I clean forgot, with Bick yapping at Jett."

"Oh, I'd love it. But could it be tea?"

"Tea!" Doubtfully.

"Or coffee, if it's—coffee will be wonderful." She realized now that she had vaguely envisaged a tea table on their arrival, with hot tea for the wise and a pitcher of cold lemonade for the foolish, and little thin sandwiches and a deceptively plain-looking pound cake. And decanters for the men. That was tea at the Lynntons' when you were hot and tired and thirsty at five or at six.

Bick now pressed a wall button. "That'll fetch somebody. Leslie, I'm going to take a look at the ruin that's gone on while I've been away. . . .

Now Luz, don't you get sore again. . . . The girls will help with your things, Leslie . . . I'll see you at supper. Anything you need, just tell Luz.''

He was gone. "Well now," said Luz, and settled herself in a chair, "the girls will fix you up in a jiffy. I hope you didn't bring too much fussy stuff. We're plain folks out here. I ain't got enough clothes to dust a fiddle.''

It came to Leslie with a shock that this woman was acting a part. Was purposely talking a kind of native lingo. The black eyes were darting here and there as the suitcases and bags were opened. Lupe had come in with a tray on which was coffee.

"I hope it won't spoil my dinner," Leslie said.

"Coffee never spoiled anything. Here in Texas everybody drinks coffee morning to night and night to morning.''

"It's the climate," Leslie thought suddenly, but thinking aloud. "That's it. Hot and flat and humid. They have to have it as a stimulant.''

"Nothing wrong with Texas climate I know of," Luz countered belligerently.

"No, no, I just meant—you know, the English drink a lot of tea. Uh—Bick told me you went to Wellesley when you were a girl.''

"Yes, the Benedict girls go to Wellesley for anyway two years and the boys to Harvard, but it never takes. I don't talk like college, do I?''

"Perhaps not. I don't know.''

"Where did you go? Vassar, I suppose. Or one of those places up on the Hudson.''

"No. In fact my sisters and I had the sketchiest kind of education. Papa didn't believe in separate schools for boys and girls. He said they were tribal vestigial.''

She felt better now that she had had the coffee. She had gulped it down, hot and strong. "That was lovely," she said. Lupe was taking things out of the bags. She was a dark silent woman in a shapeless clean dress of no definable color pattern or material. A covering. On her feet were soft shapeless black sandals. Her garments, her face, her hair were decent yet she gave a general effect of untidiness as though she had thrown on her clothes in a hurry and had not since had time to adjust them. Leslie was to grow accustomed to this look in the house servants, as to so much besides. The young girl Petra had joined the older woman. Now the clean bare room with its big white bed, its neat wooden chairs, its stark table burst suddenly into bloom like a spring garden released from winter. Lacy filmy silken things. Soft beribboned flowered things. Scent. Color.

"My!" Luz exclaimed inadequately. "Where you fixing to wear those?''

With a sinking heart Leslie thought of the trunks that were even now on the road from Vientecito—trunks crammed with more dresses, more chiffons, silks, laces. The woman Lupe and the girl Petra were not being very helpful. They caught up the scented silken things and gazed at them as a child would look at a toy, in wonderment. They held them and stroked them, making little crooning sounds of admiration and amazement. As they hung the garments in the inadequate closets they chattered to each other in Spanish, hard and fast, the sound of the consonants falling on the ear like hailstones on a tin roof. Leslie began to hate the filmy bits of lace and ribbon that Nancy Lynnton had insisted were the proper garments for a bride's trousseau, Texas or no Texas. Suddenly, too, she felt an unbearable weariness and lassitude. She wanted to be alone. More than anything in the world she wanted to be alone. It was not an urge merely, it was a necessity. For over two weeks now she had not had an hour, a moment alone. She longed to be alone in the big bright room and rid of the two chattering women, the little pink-frocked woman still wearing the red hat beneath which her tight round little pink face was like a baked apple bursting its skin.

"Do you know," she began haltingly, "it's the queerest thing but I feel so—so terribly tired. And sleepy, too. I can hardly————"

"Texas," Luz said triumphantly. "Lots of strangers from up North feel like that. Thin-blooded is what's wrong with them. Texas air is so rich you can nourish off it like it was food."

"That must be it. And everything so new and strange."

"Texas is different, all right. But you'll have to get the hang of it."

"Oh, I will. I'm going to love it. It's so big and new and different—as you say. I just thought if I could have a tiny nap before dinner—supper."

"Well, sure. You go right ahead."

"And a bath. That will be lovely."

Luz took charge. "Lupe! Un baño caliente."

"No. No thanks so much. I'll just take my time and perhaps sleep a little first and then have the bath, or perhaps the other way around. I don't know." She was growing incoherent with weariness.

"Go at once," Luz commanded the two women. Leslie caught the Spanish inmediato. "Cierra la puerta."

As they went Leslie remembered her two-word Spanish vocabulary. "Gracias! Muy gracias!"

They were gone. The door was closed. She stood with her back against it for a moment like a woman in a melodrama. Don't be silly. Where did you think you were going to live? Paris? This is all strange and wonderful and tomorrow you'll love it, but you're tired and tense. That's all that's wrong with you, Leslie Lynnton. Benedict.

A bath, that was what she wanted after all that grit and grime of the train journey and the dust of the drive. The immense tub was a man's tub, when she tried to relax in it her toes were six inches from the tub end. The immense towels were men's towels. It was as though no arrangements were made for the comfort of women in this man's world of Texas. Everything in the bathroom and the bedroom was good, utilitarian, and plain as a piece of canvas and as durable. Well, she argued to herself, this is a ranch, isn't it? You and your silly trousseau—what do you expect!

She went through the pleasant relaxing ritual of the bath, the powder, the lotions, the creams. Nancy Lynnton had made a warning din about cold cream. "That Texas climate is frightful for the complexion. Remember to use cold cream all the time, every minute, or your face will look like leather." Leslie had laughed at the mental picture of her face grinning socially through a mask of oily white cream. Still, it wasn't advice to be sneered at, she thought now as she patted the smooth stuff on cheeks and chin and was startled to see it vanish like water into thirsty earth. She put on a plain silk dressing gown, stood blinking a moment in the disordered bedroom and was reassured by the scent of the perfume that Leigh Karfrey had sent her from Paris, by the look of the pink bottles and jars ranged neatly on the grim bureau, by her own small frilled and lacy pillow, the satin mules, the peignoir flung across a chair, by all this fluff of feminine belongings that had turned the dour chamber into a woman's room.

She threw herself in a fine Gulf draft across the great double bed and was immediately asleep in spite of the strong coffee and the bewildering day.

She awoke to a bedlam of sound, she sat up terrified, her terror mounting as she stared about her at the unfamiliar room and did not know where she was or how she had got there. Now she remembered and now she translated the sounds that had shocked her into wakefulness as the clamor of metal on metal. A brazen gong was beating within the house. An iron-tongued bell was shattering the air outside. She sprang up, she ran a comb through her short clipped hair and arranged its waves tenderly over each cheek in the mode of the day. I don't care, she argued to herself, I'm going to put on a pretty tea gown for dinner, that's what they're for, I'm not going to dress in linsey-woolsey just because I live on a ranch, what's linsey-woolsey I wonder, anyway I'm going to dress as if I were having dinner with the family at home. At home. You are at home, you little fool. Hurry.

She put on the filmy tea gown with the lace fishtail in the back though it came just below her knees in the front. The clamor had ceased, the sound of the brazen gong had died away. Suddenly it was cooler—not actually chill but the fierce heat of the day was gone. She shivered a little standing there in her transparent chiffon gown, she wondered if perhaps she should have worn something heavier. They'll have a fire in the fireplace, she told herself, and a glass of sherry. Perhaps Jordan hadn't come in yet, that's why they rang that big bell outside. She went carefully to the hall and peered over the banisters. The vast hall below was empty but she heard the murmur of voices and now they were raised in something very near a shout. Here I am, Leslie Lynnton—Leslie Lynnton Benedict—tiptoeing around and peeking over stair rails like a schoolgirl afraid to go down to her first party. She stepped slowly down the great stone stairway in her slim pointed satin slippers with the brilliant buckles and the high heels. The javelinas and the jaguars and the buffalo glowered down upon her from the stairway and the hall, their lips curled back from their teeth in sneering distaste.

She stood a moment in the center of the hall. Then she followed the direction of the voices. Jordan and Luz Benedict were talking with considerable animation in the room that Luz had designated as the music room. Curiously, it was Luz who was standing in front of the fireplace facing the door and Jordan who was seated. Their voices were loud and, Leslie sensed, angry.

"Maudie's a hog for money," Luz was saying, "she wouldn't care if the ranch was put in sheep if she could get more out of it. And Placer—well—Placer! A pair of fools, but Maudie's the worst, because she knows better." At this somewhat ambiguous statement she saw Leslie in the doorway. "Well, come on in. Where's the party at? My!"

For one terrible instant Leslie sensed that her husband had momentarily forgotten that he was married, had forgotten that she was in the house, had forgotten that she existed.

Now he jumped up, he came to her and took her two hands in his and held her off to look at her. "You're prettier than a sunrise. Just look at her, Luz!"

She came closer to him. "I fell asleep."

"Don't I know it! I came up and there you were stretched across the bed, dead to the world, and the room looking as if a norther had struck it."

"Really! Really were you there while I was asleep?"

"I didn't have the heart to wake you, I sneaked out and washed up in the next room."

"You look kind of wonderful yourself," she said, and meant it though he wore boots, brown canvas pants and brush jacket, a brown shirt open at the throat. Luz was as she had been through the day. Leslie was relieved to see that she had taken off the red hat. Her hair was wound quaintly in neat slick braids like a crown round her head, just as Jordan Benedict once had described it.

No fire in the fireplace. No sherry. A concert grand piano dominated the room, it bore the Steinway stamp. "What a beautiful piano!" Leslie exclaimed. "I haven't seen one like that since I heard Paderewski play in

Washington years and years ago. Who plays? You, Luz?'' She opened the
lid, the keys were yellow, she ran a tentative handful of notes, it was badly
out of tune.

"The strings go to rusting," Luz said. "Bick plays a little and so do I, Ma
made us all take lessons, like it or not, but there's no time for piano playing
on a ranch.''

"Why not?'' Leslie inquired innocently.

"There's too much work to do.'' Luz, in spite of the baby-pink cheeks
and the plump comfortable body, seemed always to speak with belligerence.
Now the gong sounded again furiously from the dining room. "Come on,''
said Luz, "let's go eat.'' She led the way, scudding across the tiled floor.
The two followed slowly, his arm about her, her shoulder nestled in his
shoulder. The lace fishtail slithered after them, absurdly. From the upper
hall dark eyes watched it, wondering.

She pressed her cheek against his arm. "I'll have to learn to be a rancher's
wife. Look at me!'' She kicked up a satin-shod foot. "Ridiculous.''

"No it isn't. I love it. Don't change. There are too many ranchers around
here already.''

The great table would have seated twenty, it was covered with a white
tablecloth, a mammoth spread that could have been rigged as a sizable tent.
Down its middle, at five-foot intervals, were clustered little colonies of ketchup, bottles, chili sauce, vinegar, oil, salt, pepper, sugar bowl, cream
pitcher.

Luz took charge. "Bick sits there of course. You sit there. I sit here.''
The three huddled at one end of the table, Bick at the head. Places were
laid for ten.

Leslie sat down, she tucked her absurd chiffons about her, she shivered
a little in the damp air of the vast vaulted room through which the Gulf wind
blew a ceaseless stream. She eyed the empty places with their expectant
china and glass and silver. "Is there company?''

"No, thank goodness for once,'' Luz said. "But you never know on a
ranch whether there's going to be two or twenty. Folks stop by.''

Leslie smiled at Luz, at Bick. "We're like that at home. There's always
enough for sudden guests. But not quite twenty.''

Bick reached forward to cover her cool fingers with his big hand. "You're
cold! You must be starved. I remember now you hardly ate a bite at lunch.''

"I was so excited. I couldn't. We had just half an hour before time to
leave the train. But now I do feel kind of hollow and limp.''

Two Mexican girls came in, very quiet and neat in dark dresses and white
aprons, their feet slip-slapping in sandals. They carried platters and vegetable
dishes. There was steak—not the broiled steaks of the Eastern seaboard,
crisp on the outside, pink on the inside, juicy and tender and thick. These
were enormous fried slabs, flat, grey, served with a thick flour gravy. Mashed
potatoes. Canned Peas. Pickles. Huge soft rolls. Jelly. Canned peaches.
Chocolate cake. It was fundamental American food cooked and served at
its worst, without taste or imagination.

Wrestling, Leslie found that the steak once cut could not be chewed. She
felt her face flushing scarlet, she tried to swallow the leathery mass, it would
not go down, she choked a little, took a sip of cold water, chewed again
resolutely, swallowed with a final fearsome gulp and thought what a surprise
it would be for her stomach when the door opened and that rude mass of
rubber beef tumbled in. She ate her mashed potatoes, she ate her peas, she
worried the steak around her plate and tried not to think of little broilers
and strawberry meringue and lobster bisque and spoon bread. She looked
with wide bright eyes that still did not seem, somehow, to envision things

very well, at the clump of ketchup chili sauce vinegar and other condiments that served this particular corner of the long white expanse which spread like a roadway down the room.

"Doesn't she look lovely, Luz!" Bick was saying.

"Certainly does," Luz agreed, without enthusiasm. "I was just wondering where at she was fixing to wear all those party dresses."

"She's going to wear them for me, aren't you, Leslie? I'll feel like a maharajah. Run cattle all day and when I come in evenings there you'll be all satin and sweet."

"I was thinking of sending them all back home to Lacey," Leslie said, "and swapping them for her blue denims."

"Don't let Luz fool you, just because she goes around looking like an old daguerreotype. It's a pose of hers. Texas girls are mighty dressy. Wait till you see them, they go to Chicago and New York for their doodads."

Here Luz made a bewildering about-face. "They don't have to," she said spiritedly. "We've got plenty of stores right in Hermoso and Houston and Dallas and around."

"That's so," Bick agreed. "I heard that Neiman-Marcus dresses the cotton crowd up in Dallas now and the new oil rich. They say they've got stuff there makes Bergdorf and Saks in New York look like Indian trading posts."

Luz smiled a little secret smile. "You'll have a chance to see for yourself tomorrow."

Bick leaned forward. "Leslie's going out with me tomorrow. . . . There's a roomful of riding clothes here in the house, Leslie. All sizes all shapes."

"But won't my own things be here by then?"

"Well, yes. They're probably here now, unless Dimodeo and Jett Rink want the hides skinned off 'em. But your kind of riding clothes out on the range———"

Luz cut in. "The girls are coming. We've fixed up a real old-fashioned barbecue tomorrow noon. Out at Number Two."

"Call it off."

"Likely. With some of them on the way this minute from every which place. It's a welcome for the bride."

"How lovely!" Leslie said weakly. She was afraid to look at the fuming Bick.

"Damn it, Luz! Why don't you mind your own business! Leslie wants to see the ranch."

"She'll be seeing it on the way."

"I don't think she'd like a barbecue."

Leslie began to laugh a little hysterically. "If it's me you're talking about I'm right here. Remember? And of course I'd love a barbecue. It's like a picnic, isn't it? And cooking out of doors?"

Dinner was finished. Bick rose abruptly. "This is different."

"How?"

"Well—different. I know what you Virginians mean by a picnic. Chicken and ham and champagne cup and peach ice cream and a darky in a white coat to hand it around."

She went to him, she linked her arm through his, she looked up into his eyes. "But if that was the kind of picnic I wanted for the rest of my life I wouldn't be here, would I?"

The little clatter of Luz Benedict's heels, the high shrill voice. "Gill Dace is waiting on you, he phoned twice."

"Yes, I know. I'm going down now."

To her horror she heard herself cry out. "No. No, don't go away. Stay with me, Jordan. Don't leave me alone."

"Why honey, Luz is here."

"Where are you going? I'll go with you."

"You can't go down there in those clothes."

"Where is it?"

"Gill Dace is the vet. He's the man who doctors all the four-footed characters and there isn't a more important man on the ranch. I'll take you down someday soon." He kissed her lightly on the cheek, the friendly placating kiss of a husband of ten years' standing, whose thoughts are elsewhere. He was off down the hall and out into the twilight, she heard the sound of the car roaring down the road. She stood in the center of the great hall with the stuffed animal heads goggling down at her in her trailing tea gown. Luz was standing on the stairway waiting for her to ascend and as Leslie looked up at her it seemed to her weary and confused gaze that this face had in it much of the quality of those others eying her from the walls.

"I guess you'll find things different out here from what you're used to." Leslie managed a light gaiety. "I want it to be different."

"I suppose you're all tired out, traveling and all. You'll want to turn in quick, be all raring to go for tomorrow. The girls are wild to see you."

Solemnly they were ascending the stairs. Leslie heard herself making polite conversation and she began to feel very odd; light in the head and heavy in the legs. "Are they all nearby neighbors—the girls?"

Luz laughed a sharp little cackle. "Texas, anything less than a hundred miles is considered next door. Only real nearby one is Vashti Hake and she's better than sixty miles. The Hake ranch."

Leslie was tempted to ask if this Vashti Hake was the girl whom Jordan in spite of family pressure had not married. Better not. I'll know when I see her. Luz was still rattling on, Leslie forced herself to listen, standing there in the upper hall, a politely interested smile on her lips, the light glaring down on her tired eyes.

"Texas ranch folks, a lot of them, have gone to living in town and only come out to the ranch when they feel like it. The Hakes and us and two three more around are about the only ones left hereabouts who live on the place, summer and winter, day and night, the year around. Of the big countries, that is. Of course the Klebergs over to the King ranch they do too. There used to be a saying the Benedict men and the Hake and Beezer men, they were married to their ranches, any wife coming in would be only morganatic."

Leslie held out her hand. "Good night, Luz. You're right, I do seem to be awfully tired. I'll write to Mama and Papa and then I think I'll————" Her voice trailed off, emptily.

"Sure I can't help you with anything?"

"No. No really."

"Good night." The heels pounded down the hallways. Over her shoulder she tossed a final word. "I'll wait up have coffee with Bick like always."

Her trunks had come, the two women were slip-slapping about in her bedroom, the lights were blazing, it was horribly hot. They had hung away most of the gowns; the bureau drawers, open, showed neat rows of pink and blue and white, but a froth of lace and silk on chairs and bed testified to the inadequacy of the room's cupboards and chests and the fantastic unreality of Mrs. Lynnton's geographical knowledge.

Leslie, standing in the doorway, began to laugh for no reason at all and the two women, with quick Latin sympathy, laughed to keep her company so that an outsider coming upon the scene might have mistaken the moment for one of girlish merriment.

Leslie clapped a hand to her head. "I am very tired. Will you go away now. And take these things somewhere. Anywhere."

They were full of little murmurs and nods of understanding. "Sí sí sí! Dolor de cabeza. Rendida." They looked about the room rather wildly, they snatched up armfuls of delicate clothing, they bowed gravely. "Buenas noches, señora." They were gone, the slip-slip of their feet on the tiled floors. Silence in the great house.

From somewhere outside the hum of a stringed instrument—a guitar? A scent drifted in—a sweet dusty scent. The wind had not stopped blowing, she had hoped it would by nightfall. Hot winds made her nervous and irritable. I must ask Jordan if the wind always blows like this in Texas. Perhaps this was just a windy day. Tomorrow I'll take a walk. A nice long walk, I've been cooped up in that train for days and days.

There was a little glass-fronted bookcase and in it perhaps a dozen books leaning disconsolately against each other or fallen flat in zigzag disorder. She opened the glass door. A little pile of magazines, the *Cattleman's Gazette*. Webster's Unabridged Dictionary. *A Girl of the Limberlost. The Sheik. Wild Animals I Have Known.* The Texas Almanac for 1919. She closed the little glass door.

She went to the door and listened. Nothing. She went through the bedtime ritual of her adult life in Virginia; brushed her hair, washed and creamed her face, wiped it carefully and canceled the process by dusting it over with powder. Men, she had learned, found cold-creamed wives distasteful. She sat down at the little table-desk, she took from the drawer the stationery engraved with the reata, she thought, Lacey would love this.

Dear Papa and Mama and Lacey. She stared at this for a long time. I am camping out in a Spanish castle. But how did you go about writing a letter in which you thought one thing and wrote another?

When Bick came in an hour later she was still seated there with her pen in her hand drawing curlicues on the paper before her—the sheet of paper that said only Dear Papa and Mama and Lacey.

"You still up, honey!"

"It's only a little past ten—on my beautiful watch that my husband bought for me in New York."

The dusty clothes he had worn at dinner were a trifle dustier now and as he bent to kiss her there was a horsy smell that was not too unfamiliar to her Virginia background, nor too repugnant. But she made a little face. "Phew! You certainly have been down to see the vet."

"Gone about a month and you'd think I'd been away a year. Luz always gets the whole place to milling when I'm off." He paused at the door. "Coming?"

"Where?"

"I'm going down to have some coffee."

"Can't you have them bring it up here, all cozy? I don't think I'll have any. I'm dead for sleep, suddenly. Do you think it's the change in climate?"

"Sure. Texas air's too heady for you after that thin Virginia stuff. Texas air's so rich you can practically live off it."

"Darling, you Texans have a kind of folklore, haven't you?"

"Why, I don't know exactly. What———"

"Nothing. Uh—look, dear, I must order a lot of books from Brentano's in Washington."

"Oh, you won't do much reading out here."

"But I always read. I read a lot. It's like saying you won't do much breathing out here." Her tone was a trifle sharp for a bride.

"Here in Texas there's so much more to do. You won't have time to read."

"The house, you mean? Yes, I suppose there must be a lot to do, just running a big house like this."

"Oh, I didn't mean that. Luz runs the house."

"But Jordan! I mean—I'm quite good, you know. Really. I know about food and servants and furniture and I'm even a pretty good cook. I'd like to——"

"We'll let Luz tend to all that. She wouldn't like anyone else to run the house. She and old Uncle Bawley out at the Holgado Division they can't bear to have anybody mess in with their way of doing things."

"But I'm your wife!" Her sense of the ridiculous told her that she was talking like a woman in a melodrama. She began to laugh, rather helplessly. "Let's not be silly. This is my—this is our house, isn't it!"

"As long as we live and want it, honey. And you're going to be happy in it, and relax and have fun. You're going to love it down here, all the space in the world——"

"Space! Some of the happiest moments of my life have been spent in a telephone booth."

Bick pulled off his brush jacket and tossed it on a chair, he yawned a shade too carelessly and stretched his arms high above his great hard lean body. There was nothing amorous in the glance his bride bestowed upon this fine male frame. "I'm going down for a cup of coffee. Come on."

"Jordan Benedict, do you mean you're going downstairs to have your coffee!"

"I've got to talk to her anyway about something. We'll have to give her time. Luz is used to being the point, she'll have to have time to get used to being the drag."

"I don't know what you're talking about. I don't know what those words mean."

"That's so, you don't," he agreed genially. "In a roundup—you know what a roundup is—everybody knows what a roundup is—a man—on a horse of course—a man is posted one east one south one west. In a kind of triangle. The front man, the man at the front tip of the triangle, is the point. The other two men at the base of the triangle, at the rear end, they're the drag. Of course the swing men, they're stationed behind the point man they've got to swing in the herd when they scatter. You know we've got a saying here in Texas if you owe money or somebody is after you hot on your trail we say, 'He's right on your drag.' "

She flew to him, she twined her arms about him, the lace and silk and ribbons were crushed against his dusty boots his crumpled shirt. "You don't wish you had married a Texas girl, do you, Jordan? That Texas girl. Do you? Jordan!"

"You're the one I wanted to marry, the only one. Sweet. Wonderful."

"I'm frightened. For the first time in my life I'm frightened."

"Frightened of what, honey!"

"I don't know about all those things. Those Texas things."

"You will. You're just tired out. Look, I'll just run down and see——"

"Stay with me!"

"I'll be back in a minute. Come on down with me. Come on, Leslie, unless you're too tired."

"Yes, I am. I am too tired. I'll finish my letter and then I'll pop into bed. I think I never was so tired in my life."

She stood a moment after he was gone, listening to the sharp click-clack of the high-heeled boots on the hard floors. She went to the desk, she stared a moment at the words on the paper. Dear Papa and Mama and Lacey. She took up the pen and went on.

> I love it. Texas is so different and wonderful. Jordan's house is huge but then everything's big here. Luz, Jordan's sister, the one who was ill, is here with us and I know we're going to be great friends she's so refreshing. And all those picturesque vaqueros and the stuffed heads I must write you all about them when I'm feeling more rested after the long journey down.

She began to cry and the tears plopped on the sheet of paper and she quickly dried them with a blotter but they left a little raised spot anyway.

10

SHE AWOKE TO the most exquisite of morning smells—hot fresh coffee and baking bread. Piercing shafts of light stabbed the drawn window blinds. The wind again. The wind the wind hot and dry. Faraway shouts. The thud of horses' hoofs. And from somewhere below in the house the mumble of voices talking talking talking an endless flow of talk.

She glanced at the wedding-gift bedside clock, a charming bijou. It was six o'clock. Curiously enough she felt rested, refreshed. Bick was not beside her, he was not in the bathroom, he was nowhere to be seen or heard. In her slippers and robe she tiptoed into the hall. Then she remembered that this was her home, that she was mistress here. She ceased to tiptoe, her slipper heels clip-clapped on the stone floors like every Texan's. She leaned over the banister as she had done the night before and again she heard the little rustling and stirring near by, but when she turned she saw no one. So she called, very clearly, "Lupe! Petra! Tomás!"

And there was Lupe the silent one and behind her Petra, the younger one, less somber and secret. Buenos días, señora. Buenos días, señora. Buenos días Petra buenos días Lupe if this keeps on I'll be speaking Spanish in no time. On the little tray in Petra's hand was the ubiquitous coffee. The delicious aroma pricked the senses. Leslie drank the brew sweet and black and hot, two of the little cups that were the size of after-dinner cups in Virginia.

"Mmm! Delicious!" she said.

The two nodded violently, their faces broke into smiles, they seemed delighted out of all proportion. "Delicioso, sí! Delicioso!" And Leslie repeated delicioso after them and added a word to her Spanish vocabulary.

It was the nearest approach to friendliness that they had shown. She wondered about them a little. It was curious, their manner, not unfriendly but withdrawn even for a servant—strange, as though they wished to be as unnoticeable as possible. They moved silently, fluidly and with remarkable inefficiency. It was much as though children were trying to help and only succeeding in getting in the way.

But Leslie had decided that nothing would upset her today. A new day, a new home, a new life. Adventure and strangeness and novelty, that was what she always had wanted—freedom from convention and custom grown meaningless. And here it was.

She bathed, listening for Bick's returning footsteps. She dressed, one ear cocked. She decided on one of the plainer daytime frocks, a little silk, her mother had called this sort of dress. Anything inexpensive was "little"—a little dress, a little dressmaker, a little tailor, a little piece of jewelry. This little dress was of soft blue silk, quite simple. The white suede shoes with the smart blue kid tips and the not too high heels. There was a blue head-hugging hat to match—a cloche, it was called. She was hurrying now, she was listening for departing hoofbeats. But he wouldn't leave without seeing her.

When she had clattered downstairs there was no one about. The dining room, of course. There was the long table and the same islands of ketchup and chili sauce and vinegar and sugar and oil and cream. The tablecloth, she noticed, had lost the pristine freshness of the night before. She decided that she'd soon attend to that. Spotted tablecloths indeed!

Seated at the table were two men and a woman; the men in boots, canvas trousers and shirts, the woman in what, in Virginia, they called a wash dress. They were eating T-bone steaks with fried eggs on top; and grits and enormous rolls and there were big cups of coffee and large bowls of jams, yellow and purple and scarlet. The three glanced up from the business of eating and looked at her amiably as she entered.

"Howdy!" they said. "Howdy!" And went on eating.

So Texans actually did say howdy like that. She decided to try it herself but shied away from it at the moment of test and said "good morning" instead. "Isn't it a lovely morning!"

At this they again looked up from their plates but now they regarded her thoughtfully, their gaze more searching and direct.

One of the men—the older one—said, "You visiting from the East, ma'am? Kansas City or around?"

She hesitated a moment. She did not want to embarrass them. "I'm from Virginia. I'm Mrs. Benedict."

They seemed to find this in no way remarkable. "How-do!" said the young woman, a little more in the way of formality. "Howdy, ma'am," the men said. And the older one again took the lead. "Hodgins is my name. Clay Hodgins." He pointed with the tip of his knife. "My boy Gib and his wife Essie Lou. We're from up in Deaf Smith County, we been taking in the Fat Stock Show down to Hermoso."

Leslie had seated herself at an empty place at table, she leaned forward, her face alight with interest. "Why that sounds fascinating. I'd love to go to a fat stock show." And she meant it.

"Well, it's over, honey," the girl said.

A Mexican girl placed a platter before Leslie. On it was a slab of flat greyish steak that bore a nightmarish resemblance to its twin of the night before. Two fried eggs atop it glared at her with angry yellow eyes. Hot thick biscuits in a little baking crock, they bubbled a little with heat and butter. Coffee. Hurriedly Leslie poured the coffee, she regarded the three bright-eyed over the cup's steaming fragrance. "Tell me about it," she said. "Do they have to be fat—and how fat?"

They all laughed politely at that and she realized that they thought she was being humorous. The young man now spoke rather shyly in a charmingly soft musical voice, he blushed a little as he spoke. Leslie thought him most engaging. "We figured we'd best get an early start, we lit out of Hermoso three this morning it looked to be such a hot of a day down here, we figured to make three four hundred miles before daylight and we sure enough did."

"How nice," Leslie murmured inadequately.

Now the girl spoke up again, her voice was a shrill rasp after the man's low soft drawl. "We come away without what we went down after, mostly, though."

"What a pity," Leslie said. "What was that, do you mind telling me?"

"Appaloosas," the girl said.

Defeated in this, Leslie was girding herself for further enlightenment when the younger man unwittingly came to her rescue.

"You wouldn't believe, would you," he demanded, rather heatedly for one whose voiced indignation was so gentle and slow-spoken, "that they wasn't a bunch of appaloosas I'd cut up into horse meat! All we was looking for was five six real using horses that rein good and work a rope."

"Well, now," the older man ventured gently. "I wouldn't go so far's to say they wasn't some might have fitted in, but not what you'd call real outstanding individuals."

"So," the younger man concluded, ignoring this defense of the four-footed humans, "we said well, look, we're riding right by Bick Benedict's country we could easy drop in see what he can show and sure enough we got just what we come for, we could of saved ourselves a heap of time and trouble down to Hermoso."

"Yes, but," the girl protested, " had a real time for myself with the stores and the shows and all."

"Well," the man named Clay said, and rose from the table. "We got to be going along." Gib and Essie Lou pushed back their chairs. "Next time you come up to Deaf Smith you come and pay us a visit we'd sure be glad to see you, we're up there outside Umbarger. Course it's kind of wildish up there, not like here, and we only got a small place—couple hundred thousand acres—it ain't what you'd call a braggin' ranch—but it's all deeded, no lease land, and like I say to Gib and Essie Lou, it's home." He drew a long breath after this speech and glanced at the others in a kind of oratorical triumph.

"I'd love to," Leslie said. "Perhaps someday when my husband is out that way he'll take me along. I want to see every bit of Texas. Is it far?"

Gib considered this question a moment as though loath to be less than strictly accurate. "It's a far piece, yes ma'am. But then again, not too far. About eight hundred miles if you come right along————"

Taptaptap. Swift high-heeled boots. Luz Benedict. "Well, howdy!" she cried. "Sure nice to see you! When'd you blow in? You been treated right?"

"Sure have, ma'am."

"Hope you're aiming to stay awhile."

"That's mighty kind of you," Clay Hodgins said with great earnestness. "But we got to mosey along. You know how it is this time of year."

As they stood the men were enormously tall and quietly powerful and graceful, too, in a monolithic way, Leslie thought. The girl was rangy, she seemed to have too many bones around the elbows, the hips and the shoulders. Leslie, in her mind's eye, tried various dresses on the lank frame, did her hair over, corseted her, shod her, and gave it up. "Good-bye," she said. "Do drop in again soon."

The older man's face crinkled good-naturedly. "I wouldn't rightly promise soon, ma'am. Maybe a year from now we might be down this way, I wouldn't say for sure."

They clattered out, the men with their great hats in their great hands, their walk leisurely almost cautious, as though this were an unaccustomed form of locomotion.

The two women, left alone, regarded each other warily. "They're sweet," Leslie said. "Are they great friends of Jordan's—and yours?"

"Hodgins? Don't scarcely know 'em. They just dropped by. They got a little place up in the Panhandle."

"Little!"

"But they sure had a run of luck," Luz went on, resentment in her tone.

"They had a little bitty no account piece up near Luling and a gusher came in on their land last year, must bring in a million."

"A million gallons!" Leslie exclaimed, fascinated.

"Dollars."

"A million dollars in one year!"

Luz Benedict looked at her pityingly. "A million a month."

"How terrible!"

Luz ignored this. "My, you sure look dolled up in all that silk dress and citified shoes and all. You must of got up before breakfast to get all that on, as we say here."

Leslie laughed, but not very merrily. "I was just going to say that you look as fresh as if you'd slept twelve hours. But I heard you and Jordan— it was you, wasn't it?—talking at six this morning."

"Sure was. Bick and me, we have our coffee and talkee every morning of our lives at five, sit and talk and get things rounded up for the day. Any other way we'd never get a head start."

Leslie stood at the long table's edge, her smile sweet, her eyes steady. "I know. There must be such a lot to do on an enormous ranch like this. And this house. Now I'll be able to take a lot of the household duties off your hands. I thought we might have a little talk perhaps this morning————"

"Now don't you go getting yourself beat out." Luz sat smiling up at her from the chair into which she had dropped at the table. She poured herself a cup of coffee from the massive pot, she slopped a great dollop of cream into it and two heaping teaspoons of sugar. "You look real ganted I was saying to Bick. Not real strong. We want for you to get a little meat on your bones, and have a nice time."

Leslie felt the color rush into her face. Careful now, she heard her father's voice say. Slow now. This is new country for you, this is that Texas I told you about, remember? "That's so good of you, Luz. But I'm just naturally slim, we all are, but I'm really very strong and well. I'm never ill."

"Me too," Luz agreed, her manner all amiability. "Never sick a day in my life. Course you don't count being throwed by a horse and tromped by a mean————"

"But you were ill. You had the grippe and couldn't come to the wedding." And could have bitten her tongue for having yielded to an impulse so childish.

Luz laughed a great hearty guffaw. "That's so, I guess I didn't want to let on I remembered ever being sick. The Benedicts are that way, always bragging on their health. When Pa died he made us promise he wouldn't have any slow funeral, solemn and slow wasn't his way. I want for you to promise you'll gallop the horses all the way, Pa said, as if I was riding, and I will be. You never saw such a funeral, streaking down the highway and across the prairie to our family cemetery, the family and the boys and the chuck wagon and all, like he wanted it, all going like possessed, and we promised him we'd eat out there off the chuck wagon, his last roundup, and so we did. No automobiles, Pa said. Horses. The family and the vaqueros and the neighbors and half the county. It was better than a movie. Poor Pa."

Leslie was entranced. "All this is so new and exciting to me." She hesitated a moment. "I hope you won't mind if I seem a little strange at first, I've never been West before—really West, I mean. I'll soon learn Texas ways. And in a little while I'll be able to run the house too." She must know. It was unthinkable that she could go on like a guest in her husband's house. Better to settle things definitely and at once.

Luz had set her coffee cup down with a sharp clack. "The house runs itself, honey, with me giving it a little shove and a push now and again. I know how to handle the Mexicans, I been living with 'em all my life, and

my pa and ma and grampa and gramma before me. They'd be squatting on
their honkers all day if I didn't keep after them. Now you just run along and
enjoy yourself." She shoved back her chair with a grating sound.

She had boundless vitality. No, it wasn't vitality, Leslie decided. It was
energy. Luz bustled. She ran bounced hurried scurried. Energy was merely
motion, wearying to witness. True vitality was a deep inner strength that
sustained anyone who came in contact with it. Later, trying to describe her
to her father, Leslie said, "She makes you long to sit quietly in a low chair
in a dim peaceful! room with your eyes shut listening to nothing, not even
to a faraway string quartette."

Leslie stood very still in the middle of the big dining room with the hot
Gulf draft blowing through four doors. "I think I'll go up and attend to my
room—I mean put away————"

She was a little girl again, uncertain, talking to her domineering mother,
without the understanding and sustaining protection of her father.

Luz patted her shoulder as she trotted briskly by. "The girls'll have you
all fixed up by now and prob'ly know every hook and eye on every dress,
and every button and shoelace. But they never sweep the dust that's under
the bed."

"I'm going to take a walk," Leslie announced.

Luz turned at the door. "A what!"

"A nice long walk, perhaps into town and look around at things. Or
perhaps around the—the garden—the—to see the place and poke into some
of those quaint buildings————"

Luz came back into the room. Her round pink face looked sharp. "You
can't do that."

"Why not?"

"People don't walk in Texas. Only Mexicans. If you want to ride one of
the boys'll saddle you a nice gentled riding pony."

"I'll let you know," loftily. "I'll speak to my husband about it later in the
morning."

Luz laughed, a short little bark of a laugh. "Honey, if you think Bick's
got nothing to do only take people around the ranch. He's been away weeks
now, he's got to catch up if he's ever going to. Now honey, you just do
some sewing or something or reading, Bick says you're a great hand to read.
H'm?"

She bustled out of the room, click-clack click-clack. Leslie felt a surge of
murderous rage. She turned sharply and walked out of the room out of the
great front door through which she had been carried so gaily the day before.
She walked out into the blazing Texas morning.

She almost ran down the dusty roadway. The young fellow who had met
them at the Vientecito station was on his knees at the edge of a small lawn
of tough coarse grass. Through many years she was to see him thus coaxing
green growing things and brilliant colorful flowers to thrive in spite of the
withering sun and the Gulf winds that shriveled them with the heat and the
sudden icy northers that blasted them with the cold.

To see him was like encountering a friend, she was dizzy with the sudden
rush of gratitude as the boy's face lighted with recognition, his eyes his smile
became radiant.

"Hello!" she said. "Hello, Dimodeo!"

The boy rose from his knees in one graceful fluid motion, he bowed low.
"Señora. Buenos días señora."

"How far is it to the village?" At the blank look on his face, "You speak
English, Dimodeo. You understood me yesterday."

"Yes, señora, I speak English, certainly. I am only more in the way of Spanish. . . . Village?"

"Yes. The town. Benedict. How far is it to the town? I want to walk there."

"But you cannot walk to the town." He was genuinely shocked. He looked toward the house. "I will tell them the automobile. Or a horse. No, you are not dressed for riding. The automobile."

"No. I want to go alone and—and just look around and see things. I don't want to sit in an automobile. I'm sick of sitting and sitting and sitting, here's a million miles of land and doesn't anyone ever walk on it!"

"We walk," he said. "The Mexicans walk."

"Where is the schoolhouse? Yesterday we passed a schoolhouse. Down there. Is that the building? Down the road."

"It is the school. It is the school where the children go who live on Reata Ranch. The little ones. Until they are ten or twelve and can work well."

"How many?"

"Oh, many, señora. And many in other schools on other divisions."

She waved good-bye with a gaiety she did not feel, she trudged down the road in the blue silk dress and the white suede shoes. It was fearfully hot and dusty, she saw no one, nothing moved. She reached the schoolhouse, she sauntered past it and heard the drowsy bee-hum of children's voices. Abruptly she turned up the little path that led to the whitewashed adobe house. It looked very old and picturesque like pictures she had seen of missions built by the exploring Spanish priests centuries ago. Perhaps it had once been a mission, she thought.

There was a tiny whitewashed vestibule, surprisingly cool. She was to learn to appreciate the coolness of these thick-walled adobe buildings, she was to learn to stay through the day in the dim cool shelter of a house interior.

She knocked at the closed door. The humming and buzzing ceased abruptly. Silence like the listening silence of the upper hall at the Big House. She knocked again with some authority now. She had a feeling of exhilaration and discovery.

The door was opened by a woman of about thirty, a thin sallow woman in a drab dark dress. A fretful-looking woman with fine black eyes whose heavy brows met over her nose in a dark forbidding brush. She stood, the door open a few inches only, her hand on the doorknob.

"What do you want?" she said.

"I'm Mrs. Jordan Benedict," Leslie said, smiling. And extended her hand. "Perhaps I shouldn't disturb you. I was passing by and I couldn't resist dropping in————" The woman was staring at her so fixedly that Leslie was puzzled, then startled. "You are the schoolteacher, aren't you?"

"Yes."

Leslie decided not to be annoyed. This was, she told herself, a gauche girl who possibly was not accustomed to visitors during school hours. The woman was looking at her with the slow appraising stare of the Mexican girls, but she was not Mexican. She looked at Leslie's white shoes, dusty now; at the blue silk dress that now was a little damp with dark spots here and there. Leslie could feel tiny rivulets slithering wetly down her spine.

All very interesting and different and she was enjoying herself immensely. It was wonderful to say, "I am Mrs. Jordan Benedict." She said it again because she thought the woman had not understood. It was a shock to see a look of pure hate flick into the woman's eyes like the red darting flash of a snake's tongue. It came to Leslie that the teacher was actually barring her way.

"I just thought I'd drop in and see the children," she said then. "I'm out for a little walk."

"Walk!" the woman repeated after her as the others had done, as Luz and Dimodeo had done. It was becoming slightly annoying. Leslie took a firm step forward feeling suddenly tall and dignified and very important and for one dreadful moment she thought the woman was actually going to stop her.

"What is your name!"

"Cora. Cora Dart."

What was everyone so cross about? Leslie stepped rather too briskly into the room. A vast whitewashed room crammed with children. Children of from four to fifteen. Their eyes were fixed on her with a steady stare that combined to give the effect of a searchlight. Immediately Leslie was struck with the fanciful thought that the seated children made a pattern like that of a gigantic piano keyboard. The faces shaded from ivory to almost black, and the lighter ones seemed to occupy the front rows, the darker the back.

Cora Dart seemed to have recovered from the shock of a visitor, she placed a chair for Leslie and suddenly Leslie was frantic to be gone. The room was stifling, she felt unbearably drowsy, as though drugged.

"Go back to your work," Cora Dart said in English. "Go back to your work," she then said in Spanish. The battery of eyes turned briefly down to the desks, the next instant was lifted again.

"I won't stay, really," Leslie said hurriedly. She felt she should ask some intelligent questions, she remembered the way grownups used to behave when they had visited her childhood public school in Ohio. "Uh, are the pupils the children of people who work—who live on the ranch?" You know they are, how silly. She moved toward the door, she smiled at the children, feeling foolish, she smiled at the dour Miss Dart.

"Thank you so much, it is all so interesting, you must come up some afternoon after school or perhaps on a Saturday and have tea with me."

"Tea!" echoed Cora Dart as one would say opium.

Leslie's nightmarish feeling of being an interloper now drove her to the point of being unable to terminate a distasteful encounter.

"Or coffee," she corrected herself hastily. "Coffee I've learned seems to be the national drink of Texas—I mean they seem to prefer it here—uh— have you been teaching here a long time?"

"Too long for my own good," Cora Dart said with extraordinary venom. "They've had about a million teachers here, first and last."

"But that's too bad. I should think it would be upsetting for the children— the pupils."

The woman stared at her with the eyes of pure hate. "You'd better speak to your husband about that. Your husband is the person to speak to about that, Mrs. Jordan Benedict."

The woman's mad, Leslie thought as she turned abruptly to go. Stark staring mad, literally.

Outside again in the glaring heat Leslie glanced at her watch and incredulously saw that it now was ten minutes past nine. Her day was just beginning but she felt she had been up for many hours. She wondered where Jordan was, she longed to see him, she looked out and out toward the endless haze of prairie and sky. He was miles and miles off somewhere with those thousands and thousands of cows.

There was so much to learn, so much to see. She supposed she was what they called a tenderfoot, she realized now what a good and descriptive word this was. She wished that she felt more like moving briskly about and not so listless and inclined to lie down and sleep somewhere in the shade. The shade. May. May in Virginia. Cool and sunny in Virginia with a breeze from the Blue Ridge and the grass always richly green in the meadows and pastures, the apple blossoms all gone now but the late spring flowers bravely abloom. The Rivers of Virginia. Walking in the dust and glare of the Texas road, stubbornly, she thought of the Rivers of Virginia, the very sound of them was cool and fresh and clear as she said them over in a little murmur, it was like dipping her fingers in their limpid softness and laving her throbbing brow. The sound of them rippled and flowed. Shenandoah. Roanoke. Rappahannock. Potomac . . . And the flowers . . . Mountain laurel . . . Wisteria . . . Rhododendron . . . White alder . . . Wax myrtle . . . Trumpet flower . . . What were the rivers of Texas? Rio Grande. Nueces. Diablo. Brazos. Hot Spanish names. Don't be like that, silly.

She must have taken a wrong turning, what with the heat, the glare and her weariness, for she found herself off on a smaller rougher road lined with rows of shanties, small and tumble-down. Flimsier, even, than the Negro cabins she had seen so familiarly in Virginia. These were on stilts, there were no green or growing things about them. It was strange that there seemed to be no pleasant human hum of life from within these shacks.

A thin wailing sound. From within one of the hovels an infant crying. Leslie turned and looked about her. In her resentment and bewilderment she had come farther than she knew. There was the Big House shimmering in the heat, but it seemed terribly far away. She wondered if she should telephone and ask them to come for her. The thought of walking back under the blazing sun made her feel a little sick.

The Girls. Luz had said the Girls would be there early. A barbecue, a great hot red barbecue. Of course there wouldn't be a telephone in any of these crazy dwellings. But perhaps someone could be sent to fetch a car. . . . She followed the sound of the wailing infant, she ascended the rickety steps and knocked at the doorway hung with strips of flyspecked paper. The baby cried without ceasing—a high-pitched kitten-like mewing. She knocked again.

"Entre!" A woman's voice.

She brushed aside the paper strips, she entered the dark close-smelling room. For a moment, blinded by the transition from glaring sun to gloom, she could see nothing. She put her hand over her smarting eyes.

"I am Mrs. Benedict," she said to no one in particular.

"Sí, sí," said a woman's voice, low and soft, with a note of weakness in it. "Perdóneme. Pardon me that I do not rise. I am ill." This in Spanish. Miraculously, Leslie thought, she caught a word—two words—and translated their meaning. Perdóneme. Enferma. Now she looked about her. A woman on the bed in the little front room. A girl, really, black-haired, big-bosomed, her eyes bright with fever. The girl half sat up, she even essayed a little bow as she sat there in the disordered bed. "I have a fever," she said in Spanish. "Fiebre." Leslie nodded. The infant's shrill cry came from a tiny second room at the rear; the lean-to kitchen of the shack. This front room evidently was bedroom and sitting room. In one corner an altar, all pink crepe paper and bits of ribbon and gilt and paper flowers, with a gilt cross in the center and a bright pink and blue and scarlet picture of the Christ and the Madonna, gilt-framed.

Dimodeo had understood English, and spoken it. This girl must, surely. "I am so sorry. Is the baby ill?"

The girl nodded sadly. "He is ill because I am ill. My milk is not good."

"Well for heaven's sake!" Leslie said. "You just get a formula and feed him that." The girl said nothing. The child's wailing pulsed through the hot low room. Leslie went to him. He lay in a basket, very wet; dark mahogany beneath the brown skin, very angry. There was no water tap, no pump, no sink. He smelled badly. She took off his clothes, she found some water in a pitcher, she wiped him with a damp rag, the woman, bare-footed, came shakily across the sagging floor to hand her a diaper. "Go back to bed," Leslie said, and smiled at her a little ruefully. "I'm not very good at this, but it's better than having him so wet and—so wet." She diapered him inexpertly and he never stopped crying, looking up at her with great black swimming eyes. She felt like someone in a Victorian novel. Lady of the manse. How old-fashioned. She ought to have—what was it?—calf's-foot jelly, revolting stuff it must have been that they were always bringing in napkin-covered baskets for the defenseless poor. The floor of the little wood and adobe hut was broken so that you actually could see the earth over which it stood. Rats must come through those gaps, Leslie thought, looking at the squirming infant. Rats and mice and every sort of awful creeping thing.

She returned the child to the basket and his screams were shattering. The woman on the bed looked up at her submissively. Leslie felt helpless and somehow foolish.

"What is your name?"

"Deluvina."

"What does your husband do here—what is his work?" She wished she didn't sound like a social worker invading someone's decent privacy.

"He is Angel Obregon. He is vaquero." So this splintered shanty was the home of one of those splendid bronze gods on horseback. "He is vaquero. My father too and my father's father are vaquero here on Reata Ranch." She said this with enormous pride.

Leslie longed to ask what his wage was. She told herself this would be disloyal to Jordan. She must ask him.

There was the sound of a motorcar stopping outside, a horn brayed, quick steps on the broken wooden stairs.

"Miz Benedict!" called a man's voice. "Ma'am! Miz Luz says you come along home with me, they're waiting on you Madama says."

At the door stood Jett Rink. "You ain't supposed to be in there," he said. "Bick'll be mad as all hell. And Madama's fit to be tied."

1 1

SHE SAID NOTHING, she stood there, she looked at him, he stared at her, she thought, almost insolently. The eyes that were too small, very blue; the curiously damp-looking curls with one lock falling across the forehead. Those pagan goatlike young gods in the Greek pictures—that was it.

"I am Mrs. Benedict," she said needlessly and very formally.

"Well, sure." He waved a hand toward the car, a new Ford, dust-coated. "We'd better get moseying."

She was relieved to have been sent for, she welcomed the sight of the car. He had spoken of her husband as Bick. Coolly she said, "Did Mr. Benedict send you here for me?"

"No. She did."

Leslie stifled the impulse to say, haughtily, And who is she? She looked back at the woman on the bed. The child yelled. In silence she entered the car. Now she looked down at herself. The little blue silk was a mess. A great stain on her lap. The baby. Dust and perspiration. Her hair blown by the hot wind, her white shoes grey-brown. "How did you know I had gone into that place?"

He spun the wheel expertly, they leaped down the road. "Everybody knows everything anybody does around here, there's a saying you can't spit without she knows it."

Leslie decided that she must speak to Jordan about this oaf. He turned his head and stared at her with a quick bold glance.

"I watched you from the garage." He said gradge. "You ain't aiming to do much walking like that around here, are you?"

"Why not?"

"Right around the house it's all right, maybe, if you want to stir yourself afoot, but I wouldn't go to walking out on the road and cutting across prairie like you done."

"Why not?"

"Rattlers."

"Rattlers!" she repeated somewhat faintly.

"This time year it's beginning hot the rattlers start to stir around and come out when the sun is good and hot and they look for something good to eat hopping around. Shoes like yours," he glanced down at her soiled slippers and her silken ankles, "why they're liable to take a bite out of you by mistake."

"That's ridiculous!" she said. "You're trying to scare me."

"Might be. But anyway, you're too ganted to be loping around in the hot of the day, walking."

"Ganted ganted! What do you mean!" She had heard this word too often.

"Ganted. Thin."

"Whether I am thin or not is none of your business, boy."

"Sure ain't. But like I always say, the nearer the bone the sweeter the meat."

She was deciding whether to be really angry or merely amused at this cheeky lout when they approached the Big House and she saw a dozen cars clustered in the drive. Again she looked down at herself in dismay. The Girls.

"They mustn't see me. I look so awful. If I could change before they———"

He spun the wheel, he swung the car sharply around to the rear of the house. "You come on with me." They whirled past the kitchen and stopped at a blank wall that seemed part of the foundation. "Out." She climbed down, feeling like a conspirator and not liking it. Carefully, slowly he looked about him, then he reached high above his head and pressed at two corners the long bar that seemed part of the heavy ornamentation of this Spanish castle. She saw that the block was not wood but painted metal, and now part of the wall opened just enough to make entrance possible, and within she just glimpsed the outline of a spiral stairway and she heard the sound of water dripping ever so faintly.

He slid within, he held out his hard oil-stained hand.

"No!" she cried in panic, even while her reasoning mind told her that the whole situation was ridiculous was fantastic. She ran acrosss the paved court, into the kitchen, leaving behind her a row of staring dark servants' faces, into the vast dining room. From the hall there came the high shrill chatter of many feminine voices and she smelled the ever present coffee and the scent of it sickened her a little now. Someone was playing the piano and with power and authority. Brahms. Well, that was better. It needed tuning. She must remember to have it tuned. Leslie turned and looked about her.

There was, surely, a rear stairway hereabouts, somewhere. They mustn't see her looking like a drowned rat. Jordan Benedict's new wife.

From the doorway through which she had been peering came Luz Benedict's strident voice. "There she is now! Where're you getting to, Leslie? The Girls are here waiting on you."

Well, there's nothing you can do about it now, so face it and don't be silly. Stained silk, dusty shoes, flushed perspiring face, straggling hair, she advanced toward them smiling, toward the women who had been wondering about her these past weeks, whose topic of conversation and speculation she had almost exclusively been.

She smiled directly into the cluster of staring women's faces, she spread her hands in a little appealing gesture.

"Forgive me. I'm late. And I'm a sight. And I did so want to make a good first impression on all of you."

The staring faces relaxed, softened. The Girls moved toward her, she advanced toward them, her hands outstretched.

"Who was playing the Scherzo?"

"Adarene. That was Adarene Morey," the Girls said.

"Lovely. I'm going to have the piano————"

But Luz stepped between them and took over with the strict conventionality of the provincial mind.

"Meet Joella Beezer . . . Ila Rose Motten . . . Eula Jakes . . . Miz Wirt Tanner . . . Aurie Heldebrand . . . Fernie Kling . . . Miz Ray Jennings . . . Vashti Hake . . . Adarene Morey just married a month and come all the way down from Dallas just to meet you. Girls, this is Bick's wife—Leslie. That's a boy's name hereabouts, but she's Bick's legal wife just the same."

They clustered round her, their voices were high and shrill in welcome but there was, too, a genuineness about them, an eagerness and warmth. They were expensively and formally dressed in clothes that Leslie would consider city clothes. She wondered if she had expected a feminine version of the men's canvas and boots. Fringed antelope perhaps, and beadwork. They took her hand very formally, they said, for the most part, Howdy or Pleased to Meet You and she loved it. She behaved as though she were wearing the freshest of toilettes, the least shiny of noses. Of the group, two faces impressed themselves on her mind. There was Adarene Morey the Dallas bride—a plain quiet girl with intelligent understanding eyes and a queer knobby forehead and skimpy mouse-colored hair. It was she who had been playing the piano. Adarene. One of those names that sounded made up. The other girl had come forward almost timidly—the Girls had, in fact, given her a little push toward Leslie. A very fat girl with an alarmingly red face. She bulged above her clothes, her blue eyes were fixed on Leslie with something like anguish. The young woman grasped Leslie's hand in a terrible grip, she looked deep into Leslie's eyes with a look of pain and questioning.

"And your name—forgive me—I want to be sure I have you all clear in my memory————" Leslie said.

"I'm Vashti Hake—your nearest neighbor—our Place meets Bick's—yours————"

So this was the girl—this trembling mound of hurt pride and emotion.

"I hope we're going to be friends as well as neighbors." What a speech, Leslie! that inner voice said. Being mistress of the manor again, are you?

Above the chatter Luz Benedict's voice called to her. "Look what the Girls brought you!" She pointed to the great hall table on which stood bowls and platters and baskets. Mystified, Leslie stared at the offerings. A great bowl of chicken salad plastered with bright yellow mayonnaise. A plateau of chocolate cake. A saddle of venison. Jars of preserves. A ham. Homemade wine.

Dazed, Leslie surveyed these assorted edibles and wondered what she was supposed to do with them. Eat them, but how, when, why? The barbecue. The barbecue of course.

"How friendly of you! We'll take them to the Picnic, shall we?"

They appeared shocked at this. "It's a barbecue. You can't eat that at a barbecue."

Luz Benedict's voice again. "And time to start, too. Come on."

"But Luz, I've got to change my clothes. I look simply terrible."

"We haven't got time," Luz said firmly.

Serenely Leslie moved toward the stairway. 'You girls look so fresh and crisp. I can't go like this. I'd disgrace you."

"We're going," said Luz.

"I went for a walk," Leslie continued, as though she had not heard. She was ascending the stairs, smiling down on the others as she went.

"A walk!" they echoed incredulously as everyone else had done. She noted for the first time the feminine regional habit of making two syllables out of a one-syllable word. "A wo-uk!" they drawled.

"And I visited the school and when I came out I sort of got lost and then I heard a baby crying in one of the cabins and I went in to ask the way and the mother was sick and the baby was so wet and wretched and it was so hot and while I was changing it———" Ruefully she glanced down at herself. "I'll only be a minute. Does anyone want to come up to keep me company?"

In one concerted movement they surged up the stairs.

"Could we see your things? Could we?"

"Of course. But I didn't get much. Jordan and I were married in such a hurry."

The procession slowed, the heads turned as though moved on a single pivot to stare at Vashti Hake. The red anguished face became a rich purple. Equably Leslie went on, "Maybe my clothes aren't right for Texas. You've all got to tell me the right thing to do and the right thing to wear. Will you?" And she looked at Vashti Hake and she looked at Adarene Morey and she thought, Well, they will, at least. And impartially she smiled at all the rest. She was, in fact, rather fancying herself by now.

Though they were well dressed, if somewhat too elaborately for a noonday barbecue on the plains, it was obvious that East Coast fashions had not yet penetrated the Southwest. They watched her while she changed from the stained blue silk to a cream silk with a border of two shades of green. The skirt came to her knees, the neckline was known as the bateau, the whole as a sports costume. It was hideous to the point of being deforming but it was high fashion and over it the representatives of Dallas, Fort Worth, Hermoso, Vientecito, Corpus Christi, Kingsville, Houston and Benedict cooed and ohed and ahed. They rummaged clothes closets and held fragile garments up against their own ampler bosoms.

"Look Joella! This would be perfect on you with your hair and all. Black chiffon with bead things. What do you call those, Miz Benedict?"

"They're paillettes. And I'm called Leslie."

"Oh my! Lookit!" Her Virginia riding habit, the breeches of beige Bedford cord, the coat of tweed, the canary waistcoat. The silks. The pink jersey sweater blouse. The pajama negligee of satin and lamé. The blue-green chiffon over chartreuse yellow for evening.

"They're all too dressy, aren't they? For ranch life?"

"You'd be surprised," Adarene Morey reassured her. "We all dress like mad, we've got nothing else to do."

Luz's voice rasped her dissent. "You don't see me worrying where I'm going to wear chiffon and paillettes and fancy riding pants. I got plenty to do."

The Girls laughed tolerantly at that as at a family joke. "Oh, you, Luz. Everybody in Texas knows you'd rather work cattle than make love."

Leslie adjusted the cloche hat of green grosgrain ribbon, she gathered up the fresh white gloves. From her new white buckskin shoes to her brushed and shining hair she was immaculate again and eager for the day ahead. She faced the Girls, smiling and friendly. "It was dear of you to wait while I changed."

She had changed more than she knew, in their eyes. Downstairs, seeing her for the first time, they had thought, Well, he'd have done a heap better to take Vashti Hake, fat and all, instead of going way up to Virginia to bring him home a ganted cockeyed wife.

They were off now in a haze of dust, a clatter of talk, a procession of cars down the long road, then across the prairie itself, into draws, down rutted lanes, through sandy loam, the mesquite branches switching and clawing the cars as they lurched past.

The talk was of people Leslie did not know, of events and customs and ways of which she was ignorant. She listened and smiled and nodded. I like the plain one with the knobby forehead, she thought, and the fat one with the touching look in her eyes. Jordan. I'll see him at the barbecue, I can't wait to see him. I've scarcely seen him at all since yesterday, it's ridiculous.

"I love picnics," she said aloud. "We used to have them at home in Virginia, the very first warm spring day." She thought of the great hampers covered with white starched cloths; the delicate chicken, the salad of lobster, the bottles of wine, the fruit, Caroline's delectable cakes and perhaps a very special cheese that some epicurean patient had sent Doctor Lynnton from Baltimore or New York.

Sociably she turned to the girl seated next her. Eula, they called her. "Do you live near here?"

"Eighty miles?" said Eula, and her voice took the rising inflection, as though asking a question rather than answering it.

"And you came all that distance? What's the name of your town?"

"Forraje?" Eula ventured again with the rising inflection, tentatively, as though she would be the first to retract the name if her hearer did not approve.

Leslie began to speculate about the high shrill feminine voices, about the tentativeness, about the vague air of insecurity that touched these women. It was very hot, but she was having a fine time, it was all new and strange, she felt light and free and very very hungry after that early coffee and the emotional hours since then. Quietly, she listened to the talk. Horses, children, clothes, cooking, barbecues, bridge, coffee parties. Well, what's wrong with that, she demanded of herself.

Miraculously, as though divining her thoughts, Adarene Morey said, very low, beneath the crackle of high voices, "That's the way it is. You'll never hear a word of talk about books or music or sculpture or painting in Texas."

"But why?"

Adarene shrugged, helplessly. "I honest don't know. Maybe it's the climate. Or the distances. Or the money. Or something. They never speak of these things. They have a kind of contempt for them."

"Then what about you?"

"Oh I'm considered odd. But it's all right because the Moreys are old Texas cotton."

"What you two buzzing about, looking so sneaky!" bawled Ila Rose Motten.

They were stopping before another gate. There had been gates and gates and gates. There were miles of fence—hundreds of miles of fence it seemed to Leslie. They were forever stopping and someone was forever clambering out of the car, opening a gate, closing it after the procession of cars had passed, climbing in again.

"Let me do it," Leslie volunteered finally. "I'll have to learn sometime." But she was clumsy at it, there was a trick about it, the women laughed good-naturedly and Leslie joined them. "Well, you can't say I'm not trying to learn to be a Texan." Luz was in one of the other cars. Leslie wondered if it was that which made her feel gayer, younger, more free. There was a high-humored air about the whole jaunt as they bumped their way over the dusty roads, across what seemed to be endless prairie. And now a long low cluster of buildings squatted against the horizon.

"There we are," said Adarene Morey, and turned to smile at Leslie. "That's headquarters bunkhouse, in case you don't know. I guess you aren't really acquainted yet, are you? Reata's so big, even for Texas."

Vashti Hake in the front seat beside the driver had been markedly silent. "You certainly have got your best company manners on today," Eula Jakes called to her, "for a girl who generally never stops talking."

Vashti Hake turned in the seat and the anguished blue eyes fixed themselves on Leslie. "Some of the boys are going to be there," she announced.

This Leslie had taken for granted until now. "I hope Jordan will be, at any rate. I haven't seen him since—well, I haven't seen him today," she confessed.

This appeared to cheer Miss Hake. "There'll be others too," she announced mysteriously. Eula caught this challenge. "Vashti Hake, you got a new beau and haven't told any of us!"

"Old Eusebio?" Adarene inquired, laughing. Then, at Leslie's failure to comprehend, "Old Eusebio's the cook, he always does the barbecue at Reata, it's been going all night."

"I can hardly wait, I'm starved."

Now they drew up in the bare dusty space surrounding the bunkhouse. The sun glared upon the group standing near the long wooden table. Hopefully Leslie saw a little clump of mesquite pale green and cool-seeming but it was soon to prove deceptive. She was to learn there was little comfort or shade beneath this thin-leaved prairie shrub.

There was Jordan, not only in the boots and spurs and tans and Stetson but in chaps like a movie hero. As this leather god came toward her Leslie found herself running toward him, she had no other single thought in her mind but to be near him again. The Girls, Luz, the half dozen men who had hailed them as they drove up, the figure squatted in front of a red-hot fire on the ground, the Mexicans bent over a steaming hole near by—all vanished in a hot haze and she heard, unheeding, only a thin echo of their indulgent laughter as she stood on tiptoe to meet his kiss, her arms about his neck.

"You left without even good-bye."

"How do you know? You were sleeping in a tight little bunch as though nothing could wake you."

"I know, dearest. I was exhausted."

"I want you to meet some of the boys. I want to show you off, first chance I've had."

"I'm so happy. Stay near me."

He led her forward. "Boys, this is my wife Leslie. Leslie, Lucius Morey down from Dallas—you met Adarene. . . . Bale Clinch —you want to watch out for him he's running for Sheriff. . . . Ollie Whiteside . . . smartest lawyer around. Keeps us out of jail. . . . Pinky Snyth from the Hakes' place—say, Vashti, I hear your pa's sick and couldn't come.''

Vashti Hake looked at Jordan Benedict without replying. The plump rosy face flushed deeper, then paled ominously. Deliberately, and with a kind of awful dignity, this fat girl walked to the side of Pinky Snyth the little cow hand, so diminutive beside her, even in his high-heeled boots and towering Stetson. She took his hand in hers and as she spoke she abandoned the patois of of the Texan.

"Pa isn't sick. He's sulking. But he'll get over it. There's more than one bride and bridegroom here at this barbecue. Mott Snyth and I were married yesterday in Hermoso.''

A final glare at Jordan Benedict, a look that was a tragic mixture of wounded pride and pitiful defeat. The triumphant bride burst into tears, bent to bury her face in the bridegroom's inadequate shoulder.

A hubbub of cries and squeals, of guffaws and backslappings, of congratulations uttered too loudly and disapproval muttered sotto voce.

Vashti Hake had made her point, attention was centered on her now, Bick had kissed the bride's wet cheek and wrung the little man's surprisingly steel-strong hand. Together, happily unnoticed, he and Leslie were free to move about unhampered. Only Luz Benedict bustled up to them as they turned away from the shrill group. She glared at Leslie, she jerked her gaze toward Bick.

"You're the cause of this!''

"Fine,'' said Bick equably and patted Luz's shoulder. "Vashti should have been married five years ago, big bouncing girl like that.''

But nothing could disturb Leslie now. Here was Jordan, here was a day crowded with new sights, new sounds, fresh experiences. Vashti Hake and her little blue-eyed cowboy—they were part of the picture, touching, a little ridiculous. And this sinister spinster, this Luz Benedict with her plans and her frustrations—she was ridiculous too, and not to be taken seriously for a moment.

Leslie tucked her arm through Bick's. "Show me the bunkhouse. I've read about them all my life.''

He pressed her arm close. "Nothing much to see.'' It turned out that he was right. Cots, each covered with a thin grey-brown blanket. A bit of mirror stuck on the wall and their meager belongings ranged on shelves—a razor, a broken-toothed comb, a battered clock. Dust-caked boots on the floor, a saddle, a bit of rope, a leather strap. A guitar on an upended wooden box.

At the look on her face Bick laughed indulgently. "What did you expect to see?''

"Pistols. Poker chips. Silk garters. Silver spurs.''

"Serves you right for reading so much. Our boys aren't allowed to carry guns unless they're out on the range, and sometimes not even then. Or hunting, of course.''

She threw a final look over her shoulder at the bare, hot gritty little room. "Another girlish dream gone. Tell me, darling, how much are they paid, your vaqueros?''

"Oh, twenty a month—some of them thirty. The top hands. Plus mounts and found, of course.''

She stared in unbelief, she started to protest, thought better of it, was silent. It was high noon now, as they came again into the clearing the heat struck like a blow. Other than the bunkhouse the sole shelter was an open shed attached to the house. From the rafters hung strings of dried peppers and onions and herbs. There were strips of something dark and thick toward which she turned puzzled eyes until she realized that these were long hanks of beef drying in the sun and wind and dust while over them flowed a solid mass of flies. She turned her eyes away. She detained him, her hand on his arm.

"Jordan, was it pique? That sounds like a novel. I mean did that poor girl marry that little man because of you—and me?"

"I suppose so. But it had to be somebody. Think no more of it."

"Jordan, if you hadn't met me—if you hadn't happened to come out with Papa that evening to look at My Mistake—where is she, by the way?"

"She's in pasture, under a canopy for shade, and she asked for you this morning. We'll go see her this evening when this thing is over."

Having started she must go on. "But would you? Would you have married her even if you couldn't possibly have—I mean she is ever so nice but she isn't very attractive." She couldn't say, Would that sister of yours actually have deviled you into it, finally.

"Well, now, honey, while we're asking questions, would you have married that fellow in the pink coat?"

"Him—or someone. But you———"

"The girls are looking for you. The barbecue's about cooked, I guess."

She gave it up. As they walked toward the others she saw that the company had separated into two groups, male and female. The Girls were clustered near the table talking all together in high shrill voices. The men stood apart, bunched, low-voiced. Leslie thought the men looked strangely alike. Little Pinky Snyth was a miniature copy of the giants who towered above him. They all wore wide-brimmed hats of the same dust color, rolled at the brim; they wore the same khaki clothes, the same high-heeled boots, their strangely boyish faces were russet from sun and wind, their voices were soft and rather musical. Her arm through Bick's, she strolled with him toward the men's group. He disengaged his arm. "The girls are over there."

The dark shadowy figures of the Mexicans came and went. Some of these wore sombreros made of plaited straw and there was a strap of leather under the chin, very foreign-looking and somehow dramatic.

One of the women called to the grouped men, petulantly. "Now you boys come over and talk to us, I bet you're telling Pinky stories and they ain't fit to hear and we'd like to hear them. You come on, now, or we'll be real mad!" May-ud.

And when the men replied, speaking to the women, it seemed to Leslie that they changed their tone, it was as adults change when they speak to little children, coming down to their mental level.

The women were fair-skinned, without a trace of sun or windburn. She never had seen women so unrelaxed out of doors. She decided they must spend their days indoors, in the dim rooms. It was as though they regarded Nature as their enemy rather than as their fragrant soft-bosomed mother. Perhaps with good reason, Leslie reflected. There was no lolling on the cool fresh-smelling grass, for grass there was none. There was no lifting one's face to let the cool breeze blow gratefully over one, for the wind was the hot noonday Gulf wind.

Now the preparations for the meal were accelerated and she came forward interestedly to see and to learn.

In the center of the cleared circle, its perimeter neatly swept, was the red-hot bed of live wood coals on the ground. This was no ordinary picnic bonfire, this was a hard-shaped mound that must surely have been going for many hours. Leslie put the thought of the beef strips out of her mind and joined the women chirping and fluttering about the long wooden table.

Old Eusebio, squatting on his haunches before the fierce heat of the fire, was manipulating four cooking vessels at once. First, of course, there was the five-gallon pot of steaming coffee. Near by, on a crude tripod, was the vast skillet of beans. As Leslie watched, fascinated, Eusebio lifted the top off a still larger skillet and gave a stir to the mass of rice and tomato bubbling around chunks of beef. Chunks of beef. Leslie thought of the hanging strips with their crawling burden and decided against that luncheon dish. She was hungry in spite of the heat and the dust.

"Starving," she said sociably to Adarene Morey.

Adarene pointed to the pit near by about which three vaqueros were stooped. They were lifting something out of the hole in the ground and a delicious steam permeated the air. "They're taking out the barbecue. Here, have a piece of this. Have you ever eaten Mexican bread, it's delicious." They were all nibbling wedges of something crisp and stiff.

On the table were stacked disks a foot in circumference and thin-edged, they were piled a foot high and now Leslie saw the last of these being taken out of the third skillet and placed neatly on top of the stack. Adarene broke off a generous wedge from one of the crisp disks—the last one, still hot from the skillet—and Leslie munched it and found it rather flat-tasting and said it was delicious.

Adarene Morey moved closer, her voice was low in Leslie's ear. "Talk to Vashti Hake, go over and talk to her, will you?"

Leslie looked into the kind intelligent eyes. "Thank you, Adarene."

Adarene Morey's voice went on, very low. "The Hakes are old ranch family. Texas ranch girls don't marry cow hands much, no matter what the storybooks say."

Casually Leslie strolled over to where Vashti Hake stood smiling defiantly, surrounded by a little group of the Girls. They were drinking coffee again, before dinner, steaming tin cups of the hot brew. They wandered about in their pretty shoes and their delicate summer dresses.

"Now Pinky! You, Bick! It's a scandal the way you're neglecting your brides, I'm surprised they stay with you."

The little knot loosened somewhat to disclose a bottle and the tin cups. "We're drinking a toast to the brides. Any you girls like a splash of bourbon?"

Leslie slipped her hand into that of the moist and rumpled Vashti, she searched in her bewildered mind for the right thing to say—she, one of the quick-witted Lynnton girls. "Uh—it's wonderful to come to Texas a brandnew bride and find there's a bride even newer living on the next ranch."

The big bosom heaved: "Oh, I guess you and Bick won't have much time for me—and Mott."

"Oh, but we will. We brides must stick together, you know."

"I noticed you call Bick by his right name, Jordan. I do that too. I call my husband by his right name, Mott. Everybody else calls him Pinky but I think the way you do, it's more dignified to call your husband by a name isn't just a nickname everybody uses. A wife is something special."

"Oh, very special," Leslie said, "I couldn't agree more with———"

Floundering for an end to this speech Leslie was saved by the shout that went up as two vaqueros bore the steaming succulent treasure that had emerged from the hole in the ground. Leslie came forward with the group round the table. Tin plates. A clatter of steel cutlery. Leslie had known the fish dinners and clambakes of the Atlantic shore—the steaming pits from which emerged the juicy lobsters and clams and crabs and the sweet corn, all drenched with hot butter sprinkled with salt and pepper, the whole melting on the tongue, sweet and succulent beyond description.

These men were carrying a large sack, dark, wet, and steaming. This outer sack they deftly slit with sharp bright knives. Beneath it was another cloth, lighter and stained with juices. Still thus encased, the burden was carried to the table and placed on a great flat wooden board. They were crowded all round the table now, and in each hand was a wedge of the crisp thin bread.

The feast dish. Cloths that covered it were unrolled carefully, there floated from the juice-stained mound a mouth-watering aroma of rich roast meat. Leslie thought of her school days when the class had read Lamb's essay on roast pig, and how all the children's mouths—certainly her own—had watered at the description of the crackling savory meat.

The final layer of wrapping was removed. A little Vesuvius of steam wafted upward on the hot noonday air. There on the table was the mammoth head of an animal. It was the head complete. The hide—hair and the outer skin—had been removed, but all the parts remained, the eyes sunken somewhat in the sockets but still staring blindly out at the admiring world. The tongue lolled out of the open mouth and the teeth grinned at the Texans who were smiling down in anticipation. Collops of roast meat hung from cheeks and jowls.

"M-m-m-m!" cried the Girls.

"There's another down in the pit where this came from," shouted Pinky Snyth jovially. "Can't fool me. I saw it."

"We'll sure enough need it," Bale Clinch bellowed. "Appetites these girls have they're liable to leave us boys with nothing but the ears."

Curiously enough they stood as they ate. Deftly Eusebio jerked the tongue out, he sliced off the crown of the head, someone began to peel the smoking tongue and to cut it neatly on the wooden board. The hot spicy tidbits were placed on the pieces of thin crisp bread held out so eagerly and there arose little cries of gustatory pleasure.

"Here," Vashti said, and hospitably extended to her erstwhile rival a moist slice on a wedge of bread. "If you don't say this is about the best barbecue you ever ate."

"It's been eighteen hours cooking," Ollie Whiteside explained in his slow pontifical voice that was to stand him in such good stead when years later he attained his judgeship.

"How interesting," Leslie murmured faintly.

"Needs a sprinkle of salt," Vashti cautioned her.

Bick was regarding her with some anxiety and, she thought, a shade disapprovingly. Through her mind, as she smiled and accepted the food held out to her, went an argument founded on clear reasoning against instinct. You're being silly and narrow-minded. You've eaten cold sliced tongue, where did you think it came from—did you think it was born on a silver platter bordered with sprigs of watercress? After all, perhaps Texans wouldn't like the idea of lobsters and oysters and crabs, they're not very attractive either when they come up from the baking pit, with all those claws and tails and whiskers.

Bick was talking, he was explaining something to her. His low charming voice flowed over her soothingly. "This is the real Spanish-Mexican barbecue, Leslie. They despise what we Americans call a barbecue—meat roasted over coals. This pit-cooking is the real Mexican barbacoa. That's where we get the word."

"How fascinating," Leslie managed to murmur again. "Barbacoa."

"You see, we take a fresh calf's head and skin it and place it in a deep pit dug in the ground on a bed of hot mesquite coals. We wrap the head in clean white cloths and then tightly in canvas and down it goes the night before, and it cooks down there for eighteen hours————"

Now spoons were being used. With glad cries the Girls were dipping into the top of the head and removing spoonfuls of the soft gelid brains and placing them on fresh pieces of bread with a bit of salt sprinkled on top. Joella Beezer, a hearty matron, brought up an eye with her spoonful. Leslie turned away, she felt she was going to be very sick, she steeled herself, she turned back, she smiled, she felt a little cold dew on her upper lip and the lip itself was strangely stiff.

"Eat while it's hot!" Miz Wirt Tanner urged her. "They's plenty more."

"I'm not very hungry, really. Perhaps if I just had a little of the rice and some coffee. I'm not accustomed to the—the heat—yet."

"My gosh, this ain't hot. Wait till July!"

She ate. She drank. She talked. She laughed. She said delicious how do they make it the rice is so yes indeed we eat it in the East though we usually think of Virginia as the South but of course it must seem East to you there is a dish we sometimes calves' brains with a black butter sauce.

The second head was brought up from the pit, was eaten though perhaps without the gusto of the first. Replete, then, the little company wandered off and left the littered table to the vaqueros and to old Eusebio. "It was wonderful," Leslie said to him. Her new word came to mind. "Delicioso. Gracias." The old mummy face with the live-coal eyes bowed stately, accepting his due as a culinary artist.

She had not disgraced herself, she had not disgraced Jordan, she drew a long breath off achievement. She laughed and chatted, seated on a tree stump, feeling strangely lightheaded and cool in the blinding sun. One of the vaqueros at the table so recently deserted was pouring a full measure of molasses into a tin cup and now he sat spooning it up with relish, as though it were ice cream. In a corner under the open shed another of the Mexicans had got hold of the calf's head from which the company had so recently eaten. As she watched him he took a piece of bread and plunged his hand into the open top of the empty skull, he wiped the interior briskly round and round with the bit of bread, he brought the morsel up, dripping, and popped it into his eager open mouth.

Someone asked her a question, she turned her face up to the questioner, she smiled a stiff contortion of the mouth, she even arranged a reply of so in her mind, but it never was uttered. At that moment the bunkhouse tipped toward her, the sky rolled with it and the ground rose up in front of her and rapped her smartly on the head.

For the first time in her healthy twenty-odd years Leslie Lynnton had fainted dead away.

12

"NO," THE DOCTOR (hurriedly summoned from Benedict) said. "No, no sign of it I can see. Sun got to her, I'd say." The doctor from Benedict had worn boots and a Stetson and this had outraged Leslie's deep feeling for the medical profession, though she did not express her protest. She had shut her eyes and her mind against him, she had refused to answer his questions. "I feel perfectly well, really. I feel quite wonderful. It was just—Jordan— if you'll just———" She whispered in Bick's ear. "Make him go away. Please."

Very white she lay then in the big bare bedroom at Reata and Bick had sent for Doctor Tom Walker at Vientecito. When he came in Leslie knew it was all right. He was a small slight man, his suit his shoes his hat were the clothes she had been accustomed to see worn by middle-aged men in Virginia's hot weather—by her father. Rather rumpled linen stuff, pale in color, with neat white or blue shirt and small bow tie and easy comfortable black or tan oxfords. He placed the soft straw hat and the scuffed black bag on a table and came over to the bed. He did not take her hand he did not feel her pulse, he did not say "Well, how are we?" heartily. He just stood there, dabbing his forehead a little with a white handkerchief.

"How nice," said Leslie to her own astonishment. She had not in the least meant to say it, it had blurted itself out.

"I never will get used to this damned heat," Doctor Walker said. "I'll just go in and wash my hands. How are you, Bick? I heard you'd married. High time."

She heard the water and his hearty splashing and then he stood in the bathroom doorway wiping his hands briskly and talking casually.

"This climate's new to you, h'm?"

"Yes."

"It takes a while. I was saying to Bick downstairs. I'm from Tennessee myself but this is different. I wouldn't want to live anywhere else now, this is wonderful country but you have to get used to it and look at it the long view. Fifty years from now."

"Fifty years!" She did a simple problem in arithmetic. "I'll be seventy-three! Seventy-three!"

"That's a nice age. You'll see wonderful things in Texas when you're seventy-three."

"I won't care then."

"Yes you will. Especially if you've been part of it."

"You sound like my father," she said then.

He had finished wiping his hands, he folded the towel neatly, he came again to the bedside, relaxed and easy. Now he picked up her hand as it lay there so inert on the coverlet.

"And who is he?"

She watched his face intently. If he didn't know when she said it he was no good either, just like the other one. "He was intent on her pulse. "His name is Lynnton. Doctor Horace Lynnton."

There was one sign only, and she noted this because her eyes were so intent on his face. His eyes had widened, then the lids had dropped again over them. His hand was cool and steady on her wrist. He placed her hand gently on the coverlet, he smiled a little. The routine. The chest, the lungs, the back, the stomach, the heart, the belly.

"She'll be all right I think," he said turning to Bick Benedict standing so tensely at the bedside. "I'd say a temporary fatigue and a sort of—have you had a shock?"

"No."

"She's been fine," Bick said. "She's been wonderful until just today. When she fainted we thought—some of the women thought maybe————"

"Maybe next week you'll drive to my office where I can really examine you properly. You do that, will you?"

Doctor Tom Walker took out his pad and fountain pen, he began to write a prescription in a neat hand. He finished it, he capped the pen and he snapped his shabby black bag. He looked up at Bick, his glance went about the stark room with its incongruous drifts of silk and flashes of silver and crystal that bespoke her occupancy there. His eyes came to rest on her face.

"Horace Lynnton's daughter."

"Do you know him?"

"Do I know Horace Lynnton. It's like asking a private in the infantry if he knows the General of the Army."

She felt the tears, hot and stinging, in her eyes. "Thank you," she said inadequately. Then, "I'll write him you said that. No I won't. He'll think I'm ill."

"You're not," Doctor Walker said.

"What about it, Tom?" Bick asked. "What about it then? What made her faint and stay that way so long? She just wouldn't come to. I don't know how long. I guess I went kind of crazy I was so scared."

"Unconscious a long time, h'm?"

"The heat I suppose eh, Tom? It wasn't a really hot day but maybe if you're not used to it, and in the morning I hear she ran around a lot in the sun."

Luz, Leslie said to herself. She told him—she or someone. Told him what? It doesn't matter. I went for a walk.

Doctor Tom Walker was silent. Then he stood up and he had the air of one who has made a decision. "Fainting is a way of shutting out of your consciousness something you find repellent. In the old days ladies used to do it quite a bit. It was a kind of weapon. They don't use it so much nowadays because they're more free to rebel against what they don't like. This young lady doesn't look like the fainting kind to me."

Bick brushed this aside with some impatience. "Yes. Sure. But what do you advise now? What's the thing to do for Leslie?"

Tom Walker seemed to ponder this a moment. "Well, Bick, if I were married to this girl I guess I'd spend the rest of my life cherishing her—no, I'll give you the advice of a man of medicine, not a romantic. You see, all this is new to Mrs. Benedict."

"Leslie," she murmured rather drowsily from the bed. She was feeling strangely relaxed, suddenly, and lighthearted and understood.

"New to Leslie. Beginning marriage is an adjustment under the most simple of circumstances. But when you have to adjust to marriage and Texas at the same time! Well, that's quite a feat."

"Now Tom! You're talking to an old Texian, just aiming to rile me."

Doctor Walker shook his head then, hopelessly; he turned to Leslie. "Tell me, if you could do whatever you liked here what would you want to do?"

She sat up vigorously and pushed her hair back from her forehead. Her face was sparkling, animated. "I feel better. I feel wonderful. Do you mean exactly whatever I'd want to do forever—or for a week, perhaps?"

Doctor Walker, neatly packing his stethoscope, looked at Bick Benedict. "Let's start with a week."

Bick had been standing at the foot of the bed, his eyes intent on her. Now he came to the side of the bed and sat down and took Leslie's hand. Absent-mindedly he ran his thumb over the narrow band that was her wedding ring. "Hardly anybody in the world can do exactly as they please for a week."

"Why not! If no one else is hurt by it."

Then, simultaneously, as though rehearsed, the two men asked, "What do you want to do?"

The three laughed, tension snapped, the doctor's visit took on an air of coziness. Leslie smoothed the coverlet with her free hand, her face serious and thoughtful. She raised her eyes to the window and the brazen sky, she glanced at Doctor Tom Walker and then her eyes came to rest in Jordan Benedict's eyes.

"I want to go into the kitchen and cook two chickens—pan-roast them— a quick broil first to brown and then a slow oven. Delicious. In butter and a strip or two of bacon for flavor. I want to whip up a meringue. With strawberries on top. Are there strawberries in Texas? . . . I want to go to Benedict and walk in the town and look in the store windows and I want to see the side streets where people live in their houses. . . . I want to have the piano tuned. . . . I want to see the Alamo at San Antonio. . . . I want to learn to speak Spanish. . . . But most of all I want to go with you, Jordan—I want that more than anything—to go with you and see what you do. I promise not to bother you—just to have someone show me and let me see and learn about the ranch. . . . And I'd like to talk—I mean good talk with all kinds of people at dinner and after dinner . . . and books . . . and flowers in the house . . ."

Bick's brow was furrowed. "Look, Leslie honey. You'll do all these things in time. But why not just relax for a while and take things as they are. Don't you think so, Doc?"

The slight figure in the rumpled linen suit stood looking down at the two seated there on the bed, hand in hand and miles apart. Slowly he tore into small scraps the prescription he had so recently written, he gathered the bits neatly in his palm and, walking over to the desk, he let them sift slowly out of his fingers into the wastebasket. "I think Leslie's prescription is better than this one. I'd advise you to try it. . . . Well, I'll be getting along." He stooped for his bag. Then, without glancing over his shoulder he said, "Come on in, Miss Luz. The diagnosis has been made there's nothing wrong. Just a rush of ambition to the ego."

And there was Luz Benedict, not at all embarrassed at being caught. Doctor Tom looked at her, he quirked one eyebrow. "You weren't eavesdropping, were you, Madama?"

"There's no call to get personal, Tom Walker. I've got a right to know in my own house———"

"What a word—eavesdropping," Doctor Walker continued rumatively. "Eaves. Dropping. Hanging over the roof to the eaves' edge, to listen at the window. Or perhaps beneath the window where the eaves used to drip. Eaves dripping, perhaps it used to be. A word caught here and there, drip drip . . ."

"What in the world are you taking the stump about?" Luz demanded.

But now the three seemed again as unconscious of her presence as when she had been lurking, unseen, in the hall. "What do you think, Doc?" Bick Benedict asked again, worriedly.

"I'm a man of medicine. Are you asking me as a physician or as an average intelligent man with a wife and three children?"

"Both."

Tom Walker leaned against the doorway, his bag in his hand. "I'd say, as a man and a doctor, there's nothing Leslie wants to do that isn't good and proper and even mighty helpful and shows the right spirit in a young wife. She wants to go into her kitchen and cook. Well what's wrong with that! She wants to learn about her new home. She wants to see the sort of work her husband does, and how he does it. She wants to acquaint herself with the town in which her husband has lived all his life and in which she will spend the rest of her days. She wants to play the piano and talk about things of the mind and the emotions. She wants—what was that other thing?—oh, yes, she wants to learn something of the history of the most colorful and dramatic and ornery state in the United States of America. If there were more wives like that———"

"I run this house." Luz Benedict's voice was high and shrill. "Her house! Her kitchen! I should think anybody'd be glad to have all that responsibility taken off them. She can't even speak Spanish———"

"I forgot that one," Tom Walker put in, but she went on, unheeding.

"—they would make out that they don't understand English the way they do when they don't want to understand or do something. Whyn't you just relax," she demanded, turning directly to the girl, her voice taking on a wheedling note. "Bick and me, we just want for Leslie here to have a good time." She apparently was addressing Doctor Tom Walker but her eyes were on Leslie. "She ain't real strong, you can see that. And look at what happened at the barbecue, just toppling over like a person dropped dead." This last with a certain relish. "Poor delicate child, so ganted."

Leslie, sitting up in bed, seemed now to tower as she sat. She flung the bedclothes aside and swung her long legs in a decorous arc so that in one swooping movement she had got out of bed, was standing in her nightgown, had thrust her arms into her robe and was wrapping it about her with the air of one who buckles on a coat of mail.

"Luz Benedict," she said, very distinctly, "I'm not going to behave like Dora in *David Copperfield,* I'm not the crushed little bride in a Victorian novel, and you're not going to behave like a fantastic combination of Rosa Dartle and Aunt Betsey Trotwood———"

"We don't read Dickens in Texas," Doctor Tom interrupted.

"I don't want to take your place, Luz Benedict, but I won't have you take mine, either. I know I can't take over this huge house twenty-four hours after I've come into it. I don't want to, yet. But I won't be a guest in my husband's house, I won't pretend I've just dropped in for a meal like those people at breakfast yesterday—or was it today—I'm all mixed up, it seems days ago."

"You see," said Luz. Bick came to Leslie, he held her to him. "Leslie honey, you're tired and upset and you don't seem awfully strong———"

"Look here. Listen a minute." Tom Walker had an edge to his speech now, very unlike the soft casual tone of a few minutes earlier. "What are you trying to do? Break her down! Let me tell you something. This girl is as wiry as a steel spring and as indestructible. She's sound and strong and she'll bounce back when you two big high-blood-pressured people are wondering why you feel so tired after eating all that beef. You let her do as she rightly pleases." He picked up his bag again and turned toward the door, then he wheeled and turned back, his mouth smiling but his eyes serious. "And Luz, I've known you long enough to be sure that when you go in for that Texas homesy folksy lingo you sure got your kettle on fur somebody to git scalded. Honey." He made for the door, one hand held high in farewell. "Call me if you need me, any hour of the day or night." He was gone. Bick was after him. "Tom! How about a drink or a cup of coffee?"

And Tom Walker's voice from the stair well. "Next time, Bick. Lot of people to see, they think they'll feel better if I look at them, it's all in the mind." You heard the snort of his car in the drive.

The two women in the bedroom looked at each other. "That's all right," Luz said meaninglessly. Her usual high color was drained away now and Leslie found herself startled by this aspect, there seemed something sinister in the new white face.

Leslie said, "Let's have everything clear and open, Luz, and then there won't be these dreadful hidings and listening and little insinuations. I'm sorry if that sounds rude. I'm just trying to be honest."

"That's all right," Luz said again.

"I'm going to dress now. I feel just fine. It must be nearly dinner time. I'm going down to see what there is in that great enormous ice chest in that great enormous pantry and the one in the kitchen too, and wherever else there is one." At the look in Luz's face, "I think I'll go down right now, in my wrapper, and settle it. No steak."

13

BICK HAD SAID that night, "How about riding out with me after breakfast? Horses, I mean." Then, at her look of pure joy, "Yes, I know. But I start before daylight and it's a far piece down there. Dusty and noisy and hotter than today. Roundup."

"Roundup!" She repeated the word as though he had said Venice— lagoons—gondolas—music—love in the moonlight.

"It's tough going and you haven't felt so—yes, I know what Tom Walker said, you're all set to outlive me in a lot of coquettish black from Bergdorf's or Neiman's. But just the same today was a bad time."

"The barbecue," she murmured. "Not wishing to seem ungrateful, sir, but the barbecue."

"We'll eat from the chuck wagon. Rosendo's a good cook, I've ordered a special—no, I won't tell you. Anyway, no barbecued calves' heads. Jett'll drive you home when it gets too hot, I don't want you to ride back in the sun. He'll call for you with the car."

"Oh, Jordan, it sounds heavenly!"

"It isn't like the movies. Don't expect romance. What you'll see is rough."

She was happy. Even next morning when she wakened to the scent of strong coffee in the blackness and heard the murmur of faraway talk be- lowstairs she dismissed from her mind the sure knowledge that she was the subject of the conversation over the pre-breakfast coffee in the vast kitchen. Luz and Jordan. Luz talking, talking, Jordan placating. Buzzbuzzbuzz. Mumblemumblemumble. On and on. Defiantly she put on robe and slippers and slip-slapped down to the source of the sound. It led to the kitchen. There they sat at the kitchen table, Luz and Bick, elbows on the table, drinking their coffee before the first fingers of dawn had tapped at the windows. Through the years it continued to madden her that everyone in Texas rose before dawn, reason or no reason. Up early, to bed late, a vestigial custom left over from pioneer days, as useless now as the appendix.

"Good morning!" she cried and then thought, I sound like Mama. "Can I have—uh—I'm having a cup of coffee, too, before I dress."

Bick was in boots, canvas, shirt. "I was going to wake you when I got up. But I smelled Luz's coffee so I beat it downstairs first."

Leslie looked at Luz. She was dressed for riding. "I'll be dressed in a minute. Jordan and I are riding out to the roundup."

"I know."

"I thought we'd better begin to get acquainted. Honeymoons don't count, you're on your good behavior. Mm, lovely!" as she sipped her coffee. The Mexican servants were slipping into the kitchen, they made their morning greetings formally and respectfully, first to Jordan Benedict, the mighty male. Buenos días, señor. Buenos dias, señora. Buenos dias, madama. "Are my riding clothes going to be right?"

"You'd better let me give you a brush jacket," Bick said. "We go through mesquite some of the way. What's your hat?"

"Very informal. Just a little round-brimmed riding hat."

"That's no good. You'll be burned alive. Your face and the back of your neck. Luz, find her a jacket and a hat. . . . You know, all this stuff we wear in Texas isn't because it looks good in the movies."

So she rode in a haphazard costume made up of her own pants with glittering Eastern riding boots and high-necked shirt, a Texas brush jacket and a ten-gallon hat. The moon was still in the sky as the sun came up.

Moonlight and starlight and sunlight, and the dawn air cool and a little moist and the Gulf wind stirring only gently. "This is the best time of day," Leslie found herself saying. "That's why they get up early. Now I know. Just give me time and I'll learn."

"That's why. That, and habit, and a few million head of cattle in these parts to see to."

The Mexican boys stood with the horses in the dim cool morning. No sound as they came down the steps but the stamp of the waiting horses' hoofs. "I wish one of them would neigh."

"Why?"

"No reason. Except that it would make the whole thing perfect."

Luz did not see them off. As they rode away Leslie found herself going over in her mind anything she might have left in her room in the way of letters, notes, memoranda. Then she was ashamed of having allowed this suspicion to enter her mind.

It was hard riding, she was unaccustomed to this broad Western saddle, the mesquite was a hazard, their talk was disjointed. Leslie felt free and gay and new. To ride again was exhilarating after days of trains and hotels and automobiles. She was to see the purpose of these millions of acres, she was to be part of the everyday work of Reata Ranch and of every ranch in this gargantuan commonwealth. She began to sing out of sheer high spirits, whereupon her horse stopped.

"Why did he do that?"

"He's a cow pony. When the cattle were restless the boys used to sing to them. Just sitting in the saddle, singing sort of slow and gentle. It quieted them. They don't do it much any more. That was in the old days—my grandfather's day—when they drove the big herds overland. One of the old hands must have broken in that pony of yours."

"It's enough just to feel like singing. This is what I hoped it would be. I shan't do any fainting today, Jordan. My very own Jordan. That sounds silly to you but it doesn't to me."

"I didn't say it sounded silly."

"A whole new life, brand new, for me. Imagine!"

"Girls do have, don't they, when they marry"

"Leigh didn't. My sister Leigh."

"She married Karfrey, didn't she? And went to England to live? And he's a member of the English nobility. I should think that would have been———"

"But it wasn't. They live in Kent. In a house in the country in Kent. And people who live in a big comfortable house in Virginia have spent the last three hundred years trying to live like their English ancestors. When I visited her three years ago it was so much like Virginia, except that the English take their houses and gardens and clothes and horses more for granted. The cream was thicker, and the tweeds; and the carpets a little shabbier and the manners nicer and the women's voices higher——— Heh, wait a minute!"

"What?"

"The English women's voices. They're rather high and shrill. And the Texas women's voices are higher and shriller. English women have been regarded as sort of second-rate citizens for centuries. And Texas women seem to live in a kind of purdah. So they both talk in a high shrill way in order to get male attention."

"You're getting too much male attention at the moment, Mrs. Benedict. We'll get there by noon, at this rate."

"It's so wonderful to be talking to you alone like this. I thought I'd never have a chance to talk to you again."

They rode side by side now. "Have to be careful of gopher holes here. Your horse step into one of those he can throw you—or he can break a leg."

"Can't I wait for you so that we can ride back together when you're finished?"

"No, it'll be too hot then. And no telling when I'll be through. You'll see why after you've sat out in the sun for a few hours. Yesterday they nooned at the creek but today there'll be no shade. Jett will call for you and drive you home after lunch."

"Tell me about this Jett Rink."

"Jett's all right when he behaves himself. When he drinks he goes kind of crazy. I've fired him a dozen times but he always seems to turn up back at the ranch, one way or another. He's a kind of genius, Jett is."

"He is! Why, he just seemed to me a sullen loutish kind of boy. And sort of savage, too. I don't know. What do you mean, genius?"

"Oh, lots of ways. Machinery. Mechanics. There's nothing he can't fix, nothing he can't run that has an engine in it. That's invaluable around a modern ranch this size."

"You mean he's the only one?"

"One! There are dozens all over the place. But not like that locoed Rink. He's a wizard—when he's sober. But drunk or sober he doesn't belong on a ranch because you can't trust him with animals."

"How do you mean—trust him?"

"He's naturally mean with them. He abuses them. Kicks horses. Hits them over the head. I've seen him slam a calf right————"

"Don't! Don't tell me. I don't want to hear it. But why? That's what I want to know."

"He's got a grudge against the world."

"He sounds an exquisite escort for your bride."

"Don't you worry. I wouldn't let you drive back with him if I didn't know. He knows his place when it comes to the family. A funny thing, the girls are hot for him, even the Mexican girls and you know how strict their parents are with them."

"No, I don't know."

"That's so, you don't. Well, they are. Regular old Spanish stuff, even the poorest of them. The girls don't go out alone with boys, sometimes they hardly have a chance to speak to the man they marry until after they're married. At the Mexican dances their mothers sit on the side lines like the old Boston and New York dowagers before the stag line came in. You've got to see it. Not a peso to their names, the fathers are cotton pickers if they're lucky, and you'd think the girls were just out of some finishing school. Of course our boys—the Reata vaqueros—they wouldn't let Jett come within a mile of their girls."

They had long ago ceased really to ride. They were sitting on their horses and the horses were walking as sedately as though they were not descended from the Arab horses brought into the country by the Spaniards centuries earlier; as though they had never been broken and trained with a hackamore, a snaffle bit or a rope.

"He sounds irresponsible and sadistic," she said.

"He'll probably end up a billionaire—or in the electric chair," Bick predicted.

The nearer the bone the sweeter the meat. It floated to the surface of her consciousness, she thrust it back. "I suppose ranches are sadistic sort of places, aren't they? I mean they make you————"

"Ranches are full of life and death and birth, if that's what you mean. A

couple of hundred thousand of any living thing and you're likely to see some
pretty fundamental stuff going on.''

"I know. Give me time, darling. It's going to take me a while."

In silence they rode for a moment. Only the creak of leather, the faint
jingle of metal. Horses' hoofs on sun-baked earth. Texas sounds.

"Leslie, since we came home I've been up to my ears in work. Maybe
you've felt left out of things. Look, it's like this. I'm pulling one way—I
think it's the right way—and Luz and Maudie and Bowie and Roady and the
rest of them they're all pulling another. They want the money—all the money
they can get out of the ranch. And I want to put money back into the ranch.
It takes a lot. I want to raise and breed the best beef cattle in the world, I
want to experiment with new breeds and new grasses, I'm interested in the
same sort of thing that Kleberg's interested in on the big King ranch. Years
ago those fellows on the old XIT ranch had an inkling of the future but of
course they hadn't much technical knowledge, they didn't really know modern breeding or range rehabilitation. Neither did the old Matador crowd. All
the big operators. They used up the range and shipped the cattle and finished
them in the East and bred the old Longhorns to Herefords, Angus, Jersey,
Swiss—anything that didn't die right off from the ticks and the worms and
the heat. The only one of the family who's with me on the program I've
mapped out is Uncle Bawley up at the Holgado Division. Say, I've an idea
you'll be crazy about old Uncle Bawley. He's a character. Nearly seventy
but full of beans. We'll have to take a trip out there, you'll love it. It's high
country, the mountains————''

"Mountains! In Texas!"

"Sure mountains. There's everything in Texas. Mountains and forest and
rivers and desert and plains and valleys and heat and cold.''

"I know. You're in love with it.''

He reined his horse, he looked at her, his eyes full of pain. "Maybe it's
going to be hell for you down here. Maybe I shouldn't have brought you to
Texas.''

"It's a little late now. We're in it, darling. You didn't marry a Texas
belle.''

"You're on that again, h'm? I will say Luz tried to shoo off most of them
but she was hell-bent on my marrying Vashti and the reason was that one
end of the Hake ranch touches ours, it's like the old plot in the mellerdrama.''

"Jordan, did it ever strike you that Luz is a little—melodramatic herself?''

"Luz! She's just a bossy old maid who wants to be everybody's mother.
She feeds the world—or would if it came near her kitchen, she knows everybody's business and thinks she runs Reata.''

"And you.''

"Funny thing, you know years ago she was supposed to marry old Cliff
Hake. He wasn't old then, he was a handsome young heller, they tell me,
big beefy fellow, but she didn't want to go to the Double B to live, she
wanted to combine the two ranches and bring the whole thing under Reata.
Of course Cliff wouldn't hear of it and they split up. Would you believe it!''

"Yes, I'd believe it. And so you were to marry Vashti in her place, all
these years and years later. And now Vashti is married to that little pink
man all because of you. Or really because of Luz.''

"I meant to marry. Not Vashti, but I meant to marry, God knows there
were plenty of girls around. I'm saying that without meaning to be a stinker.
But I wasn't in love with any of them. Maybe you're right. Maybe I was in
love with cattle.''

"And power.''

"How do you mean—power?''

"Papa says————"

"You set great store by your father, don't you?"

"I suppose I was in love with him in my own way just as you————"

"I don't like that kind of talk. It's ugly."

"Why no, dear. I'm just talking—uh—scientifically."

"Women have no call to be scientific."

"Not even Madame Curie?"

"What the hell has she got to do with it!"

"Nothing. Everything."

"Half the time I don't know what you're talking about. I don't believe you do either."

"I do this time. I don't think Texas is free at all. Free, the way you said it was. I've been here two days and every natural thing I've said and done has been forbidden. I'm not reproaching you. I'm just stating a fact that astonishes me. Speaking to the employees as if they were human beings like myself. Wanting to wear pretty clothes in my home. Not liking to eat out of skulls. There are—I'm warning you—certain things I'm going to do, Luz or no Luz."

"Such as what?"

"I told you yesterday."

"I don't know that I can see my way clear to prettifying the house. Pa spent enough on that big pile and Ma never even lived to enjoy it. Anyway, the ranch comes first, every time, always. I put all the money I can scrape together into new projects. We're working on a new dozer for clearing the mesquite. If it works it's a human monster. We're setting up a testing station for grasses. Gill Dace and I are working on the new breed of cattle. The Herefords can't take this climate, they get the pinkeye and worms, and the fleas and worms together eat the calves alive. It cost me plenty to learn that. You should have heard the family at the last yearly meeting! You'd think I was embezzling the funds."

"Then why don't you let them do it?"

"It's for me to do. They're just a lot of money-eaters. Maudie Lou and that husband of hers, they like yachts. Yachts! For a girl born and brought up in Texas."

She gazed about her at the flat endless burning plain.

"Rebellion," she said.

But he went on, he seemed not to have heard. "If we can breed up just one animal that will start a new race of cows. The tough old Longhorns could stand the heat and the tick but their meat was like rawhide."

Still is, she thought privately.

"Wait till you see the Kashmirs! Humped like camels, grey-greenish velvet coats, there's an oil in their skins that repels the fleas. If we can combine the Hereford meat and the Shorthorn strength and the Kashmir resistance! I'm willing to spend the next twenty years of my life in bringing the perfect Kashmir bull to the perfect Hereford-Shorthorn cow and if I do it's going to be the most important mating, by God, since Adam and Eve."

"If that's what you want to do more than anything in the world why do you need millions of acres to do it in? A few thousand would do, wouldn't they? We could live in a six-room house and one car and no minions and be free. Free!" She stared about her. "How did you get all these millions of acres, anyway?"

"Never mind how we got it."

"I'm going to read up on it. There must be a book about it somewhere. In the Public Library at Benedict."

"There isn't a public library."

"Why not?"

"Oh, I don't know why not. You're worse than kid—why why whywhy! All the time. We bought the land. We got it through purchase—my grandfather did. A hundred years ago. We swapped for it. We got it through Spanish land grants. And using our brains. It was my father's and my grandfather's and it's going to be my son's————"

"No one in the whole United States has the right to own millions of acres of American land, I don't care how they came by it."

"You're completely ignorant of what you're talking about. In my grandfather's day there was enough range grass to support a steer on two acres of land. In another five years you did mighty well if you could feed a steer on six acres. Now there are whole sections—hundreds of miles of Texas range—that won't support even one steer to every sixty-five acres. Even on what we call good range it takes a full twenty acres to feed a steer. It's gone to desert. And the ranchers just spend their time hoping at the sky."

"What made it that way, if it was all right years ago? Where did the grass go?"

"I never saw any woman ask so many damn questions!"

"I just want to know, darling. How else am I going to learn about Texas?"

"Come on," he said abruptly. "Let's get riding. We're headed for a roundup. Remember? That's my business. That's the way I earn my living."

"Living! How about life! You just look upon life as an annoying interruption to ranching. I stole that. It was first said in another way by a French writer named Gide—or maybe it was Proust. Pretty soon I'll forget how to read."

"I told you what it was like down here. The first time I met you. Now you've seen the setup. You know what it is. Like it or not, this is it."

"Jordan, let's not—Jordan, I'm going to love it. It's just that————"

"Reata takes all my time. It always will. You'll be a neglected wife. Everything's against you—climate—people—family—customs. I know. I warned you." He looked at her, his eyes agonized, pleading. "I love you. I love you. I love you."

The two horses stood close, side by side, leather creaking on leather. They stood like good Texas cow horses while the man and woman strained toward each other there in the saddles, his knee against hers, his thigh against hers, his shoulder his lips on hers there in the brilliant wild endless Texas plain, in the early morning scent of the desert spring and the false coolness and the faint false green of the unavailing mesquite.

She looked at him as they drew apart slowly. At no time in her life, before or after this moment, was Leslie Lynnton so nearly beautiful. They sat a moment, withdrawn, like two figures on a too highly colored Remington calendar print.

"It's going to be wonderful," she said finally, "and terrible. I suppose we're in for a stormy future. I'm going to try to change you and you're going to be impatient when I don't melt into all this." She swept the vastness with her arm.

"I'll try not to be."

"Whoever said love conquers all was a fool. Because almost everything conquers love—or tries to."

The sun was up, full blast. Already it was growing hot. Bick gathered up his reins. "Yippee!" he yelled like a character in a Western movie. Without another word they streaked across the prairie mile on mile, they galloped into Number Two Camp to find it a welter of dust, thudding hoofs, color, bellowing, clamor.

"Stay here. Just here. This is Tomaso. He'll take care of you. If you get tired you can sit on top of the high fence there. You may be better there anyway. Too bad you didn't wear Texas boots, the heels hook in better. A million pairs at the house. Tomaso will look after you. I'll be back. Here, take this. You'll need it. Across your face.''

He tossed her his handkerchief and was off into the melee, a figure of steel and iron and muscle.

Cattle. So close-packed that it seemed you could walk on their backs for a mile—for miles as far as the eye could see. From the little sand hills, from the mesquite motts and the cactus came the living streams, a river here a river there, a river of moving flesh wherever the eye rested, and these sluggish lines were added to the great central pool until it became a Mississippi of cattle fed by its smaller tributaries. Little figures on horseback guided the course of these streams. Now Leslie understood, she saw now what Bick had meant when he had said, "She's been the point so long she can't get used to being the drag." These little figures on horseback formed a triangle, and there in front was the point and there at the rear ends the drag. To the east the west and the south these tiny dots on horseback moved the rivers of red and white Herefords, the torrents of cattle with the white clown faces and the pink-rimmed eyes. The bawling of the calves, the bellowing of the cows was earsplitting. Now it was almost impossible to see through the dense clouds of dust. The men wore handkerchiefs tied in a triangle before their faces so that only their eyes were free. Leslie took the big handkerchief that Jordan had tossed to her, she tied it so that her nose and mouth were covered, a Moslem woman in riding clothes. The animals moved close-packed. Curtain on curtain of dust, the men on horseback the men running about on foot were ghostly figures in a fog of dust. Their faces were stern and intent, the riders seemed not riders at all but centaurs part horse part man, swaying with the animals as though they were one body.

They rode headlong into the herd, they seemed not even to touch the reins, they swung slightly in the saddle as the horse wove in and out like a fluid thing. You saw how this weaving movement of man and horse separated the bawling calf from its mother, the high plaintive blatting becoming more anguished as the animal sought frantically to return to the seething mass. Wide-eyed, breathless, Leslie watched this ancient process, unchanged for centuries. These men leaped off their horses, threw the struggling calf and roped him, were on the horse again in a swift single leap and off into the surging herd. As they rode you heard them calling softly, tenderly, quieting the milling frantic sea of cattle. Woo woo woo vaca! Woo woo woo novillo. Woo vaca. Woo woo woo! Like a mother humming to her restless child.

To Leslie it was a legendary scene, incredibly remote from the world she had always known. A welter of noise, confusion; the stench of singeing hair and burned flesh. Perched on the corral fence with Tomaso as bodyguard, her heels hooked on a lower rail, she began slowly to comprehend that in this gigantic melee of rounding-up, separating, branding, castrating there was order; and in that order exquisite timing and actually a kind of art. Here, working with what seemed to her unbelievable courage and expertness, were men riding running leaping; wrestling with huge animals ten times their size; men slim heavy tall short young old bronze copper tan lemon black white. Here was a craft that had in it comedy and tragedy; that had endured for centuries and changed but little in those centuries.

Bick had said, just before he left her with Tomaso, "This is going to be pretty rough, Leslie. I don't want to see you keeling off that fence."

"I promise you I won't do that again. I'm a big girl now."

She saw Bick Benedict—her own husband Jordan Benedict, she told herself with mixed feelings of pride and resentment as she watched him—working in this inferno of heaving flesh and choking dust and noise and movement and daring and danger and brutal beauty. Working like any one of the vaqueros amidst hoofs and flanks and horns.

A ballet, she said to herself. A violent beautiful ballet of America.

Idiotically she turned to Tomaso. "Couldn't it be done some other way? Without all this danger and I mean not so many—thousands and thousands———"

"Yo no comprendo, señora," said Tomaso, sorrowfully.

She thought she recognized two or three of the men as among those who had been drawn up so proudly in line at the gates as she and Bick had entered Reata—when was it?—yesterday? The day before? A week a month ago? It seemed something far in the past. It was easy to recognize Polo with his air of authority, his unique elegance, the white teeth in that dark fine-boned face. This was, Leslie thought, a henchman such as a king would have. The night of their arrival she had happened to speak again of Polo and his dramatic vaqueros and Bick had said, "Old Polo's practically part of the family. When he was a boy he used to sleep outside my father's door."

Startled, she had said, "How do you mean—outside his door?"

"On the floor in the hall."

"Good heavens, why!"

"I don't know. They do. His son slept outside my door when I was a kid. For that matter, they still do, I suppose. Tomaso or one of the boys around the house."

"Now!" She was aghast.

"They're not there when I come in and they're gone when I get up. It's been going on for a century. I think it's pretty damned foolish, myself."

"Foolish! It's feudal! It's uncivi———"

"Now, now, honey!"

"Sorry."

"You should see the look on your face. I'd give anything to know what you're thinking, Yanqui."

"I was just reassuring myself by thinking of awfully American things. Like pork and beans. And Fourth of July. And Vermont. And pumpkin pie. And Fords. And Sunday school. And cocky Midwestern hired girls in Ohio, when I was a child."

"This is what I call American," he had said.

In a far corner out of the dust of battle old Rosendo had set up a tarpaulin, the chuck wagon was backed handily at its edge. The wind wafted the scent of his cooking to the scene of feverish activity but it was lost in the stench of the branding. Calves bawled, cows bellowed, men yelled, hoofs pounded, gates slammed, flesh burned, irons clanged, dust swirled, sun glared. Leslie Benedict clung to the fence rail and knew why Texans paid fifty dollars for great cool sheltering ten-gallon Stetson hats.

Up clattered Bick, his teeth gleaming startlingly white in his dust-grimed scarlet face.

"All right, honey?"

"Fine. I want to ask questions."

"I was afraid of that." He pulled his horse up beside her there at the fence. "Hungry?"

She wrinkled her nose. "No."

"You will be when you get to the camp. Old Rosendo's part Mexican part Negro part Indian, he's a real cook, we'd have him up at the house kitchen but he won't work indoors."

"What can he cook under that little pocket handkerchief of a tent?"

"You wait. You'll see."

"Everybody talks Spanish. Tell me, that's Polo, isn't it, who was so splendid and dressy to welcome us."

"Yes. Polo's caporal. Foreman."

"What's he doing? He and the others. It looks cruel but I suppose it isn't."

"Not if America wants to eat. They're roping. And branding. Only the foreman and the bosses and the best of the ropers do that. The others—the men who are throwing the calves—they're called tumbadores. It's a great trick, throwing a calf, there's less to it than meets the eye, really. It looks like a feat of strength but they're not really lifting those calves. You squeeze the calf's ear, it jumps, you pull him sideways and he falls flat on his right side with his left side up, ready for branding. Over there's the branding fire. And those fellows who run the brands, they're really specialists. Marcadores, they're called."

"Marcadores. A lovely word. For such a nasty job. What's it mean?"

"Figure it for yourself, really. Marcar means to mark—to stamp—to brand. Marcadores—markers, branders. It's tricky work. Those irons are red-hot. It's the Reata brand, of course. If they press too hard the calves get a burn sore. If they don't press hard enough the brand won't be clear. They're dehorning too, those other fellows."

"It seems horrible but perhaps it isn't. What are those boys doing? The ones with the sticks and the buckets?"

"They're atoleros. Atole—well, mush. They've got a kind of lime paste in those buckets, they have rags wrapped around those sticks and they smear the lime on the fresh burns to heal them. . . . Well, you wanted to come."

"Don't you worry about me. I'm tougher than I was yesterday. I'm a tough Texan. Go on."

He grinned. "Well, brace yourself. You won't like what comes next."

"The one who's doing something to their ears and————"

"And castrating the male calves. He's the capador. He castrates the males and that makes them steers. And he nicks a piece off the end of the left ear of male and female and sticks it in his pocket, and he marks the right ear with a hole and a slit, for identification. At the end of the day he adds up, and the number of pieces of ear in his pocket shows the number of calves we've branded."

"Jordan Benedict, I'll never eat roast beef again as long as I live."

"Oh, yes you will."

"Don't tell me that's what you've planned for lunch!"

"No. Rest easy. It's chicken and Rosendo's apple pie."

"It just may be I'll never eat *any*thing again. . . . Look, there's a darling little boy putting something in a bucket. Gathering up and putting—why, he can't be more than ten years old. What's he bringing to the fire in the bucket?"

Matter-of-factly Bick said, "That's little Bobby Dietz, his father is ranch boss on Number One."

"But what's he doing?"

"Well, you might as well have it straight, you'll be here the rest of your life. He's picking up the testicles of the castrated calves. The tumbadores roast them on the coals, they burst open and they eat them as you'd eat a roast oyster, they're very tasty really and the vaqueros think they make you potent and strong as a bull. They're considered quite a dainty. . . . Come on, honey, it's time for lunch. Here's Tomaso with your horse. And listen—there's Rosendo's bell."

"Why don't the men stop working? I should think they'd be famished."

"They'll eat after we've finished."

On their way to the dinner camp they passed the fire of hot embers and she averted her eyes and then forced herself to look, and to smile. And at Bick's call the little lad came running to their horses, he came shyly, a handsome boy with very blue eyes bluer in contrast with the sun-browned face.

"Hello, Bobby!"

"Howdy, Mr. Bick."

"Where's your father?"

"He went back there in the draw, he says there's a bunch there the boys missed."

"Does, eh?" Bick looked at Leslie. "This kid comes of good stuff. He'll make a wonderful hand when he grows up. What are you going to be when you get to be a man, Bobby? A cowboy?"

"I'm going to be a Ranger, and shoot people."

"Not me!"

"No. Bad people."

"Bobby, this is Mrs. Benedict. This is the new señora."

The deep blue eyes were turned on her like searchlights. "What she wearing them funny clothes for?"

Bick grinned. "She hasn't had time to get some Texas clothes."

And away they cantered from the little boy and his macabre task, but not so far after all, they were to discover twenty-five years later.

Though ten minutes before she had been repelled by the thought of any sort of food under any circumstances Leslie now found herself eating Rosendo's food with relish, not to say gusto. Having polished off chicken, string beans, apple pie and half a disk of skillet bread she inspected the chuck wagon with its orderly compartments for spices, flour, beans, rice, cutlery, tinware. She complimented the gifted Rosendo and was enchanted with the benign and wrinkled face beneath the vast straw sombrero. She felt well and buoyant of spirits.

"Let me stay this afternoon and come home with you. I'm not tired."

"Two more hours of sun and you'd wish you hadn't."

"I could steal a nap here under the canvas."

"Even a Mexican couldn't sleep under this canvas at noon."

In the burning sun the men were sitting on the ground scooping up their beans and red rice, spooning up molasses and wiping their plates with hunks of bread torn from the great disks stacked on the tent table. Certainly they seemed much less dramatic now squatting before their food, eating wordlessly and concentratedly like the animals they tended.

Sitting there with her husband under the scrap of unavailing canvas the gently bred girl was trying to arrange in her mind a pattern that would bring order into the kaleidoscope of these past three days.

Gropingly, as though thinking aloud, she said, "In Washington and in New York and in Chicago and Detroit and Columbus men get up and take a streetcar or a bus or an automobile and go to work in offices and shops and factories, they write things down, they push a lever, they go to a restaurant and eat lunch and come back to work and weigh something or add up something or sell something or dictate something, and they go home. And that is a day's work. But this!"

"Now what? What's the matter with this?"

"It's incredible, that's all. I can't believe that men earn their living this way. It's too difficult. Why, just look at Polo!"

"Where! What's the matter with him!"

"Nothing, darling. I just mean—look at him on his horse, he looks like a Spanish grandee. I've never seen a Spanish grandee but did Polo do all these circus stunts when he was a young man?"

"He sure enough did. Top hand. That's how he got to be caporal. He can still do them, and better than men half his age."

"How old is he?"

"Nobody knows. I doubt that he does himself. But he's getting too old for this job. And too old-fashioned. Would you believe he keeps his accounts in his head! Hours, wages, stock counts. They always tally, he's never been wrong, no one's ever been able to solve his system of mathematics, but it's infallible. It can't go on, though. I'll have to retire him and put in a modern system like that in the other divisions. I've humored him long enough. You ought to hear Maudie Lou and Bowie and the others on the subject!"

"Why don't they run the ranch, then?"

His head came up, his jaw set, his whole aspect changed as though he had been challenged. "I run this ranch. Don't make any mistake about that."

She looked at old Polo, seated so lightly on his beautiful horse. The vaqueros had finished their noonday meal, they were stretching and yawning, one of them took a mouthful of water from a tin cup and spat it out on the ground in some sort of primitive ablution.

"What will he do then?"

Bick was silent a moment. When he spoke he did not answer her question. "Polo put me on a horse when I was three. He taught us all to ride like the vaqueros, they're the best horsemen in the world, the Mexican cowboys, they're better than those Hungarians that used to show off in all that glitter at the Horse Show in New York. I used to hear my father say that by the time Luz was eight she could ride like a charro."

Charro. Charro? I can't ask questions every minute, I'll buy a Spanish dictionary.

"Dearest, do you work like this every day?"

"Well—no. No, I don't."

"I mean it's wonderful that you can do it, but it's ghastly rough and tough."

He actually blushed a little then beneath the russet burn, and he laughed rather sheepishly, like a boy. "Tell you the truth, honey, I was just showing off today in front of my girl. Like a kid chinning himself on the apple tree."

The men were mounting their horses, fresh horses she saw, from a great cluster of them she had not noticed until now, grazing against the horizon.

"New horses? Are they going to start all over again?"

"Sure, new horses. Or fresh, we'd say. Every Benedict vaquero has got at least ten horses. They've been changing right along, you just haven't noticed. They'll be riding about five different horses each, today. See that bunch of horses over there? That's called a remuda. They're what we call cutting horses. They're used to cut out certain animals from the herd. Trained for it. You don't even have to touch the reins half the time. Just sway your body and your horse will turn with your weight this way or that."

"Jordan! I forgot all about My Mistake. These two or three days have been so new and strange—different I mean. I forgot about My Mistake. Is she here? Where is she? Do you think she'll know me? My girl friend from home in Virginny. She brought us together. She introduced us. I'd never have met you without her. I love her."

"She's out in pasture. Very queenly, with a canvas shade on poles in one corner if she finds Texas too hot. A six-mile pasture, if you want to know. One of the boys has been exercising her a little every day to keep her in shape after the long trip down. I meant to tell you. Obregon there—over

there, that tall fellow in the straw hat—had her out yesterday he says she's
the finest little————"

"Oh, let me talk to him, will you? I'm homesick for her. Tonight when
you get back let's visit her. Or surely tomorrow. Will you? I'll have to write
Lacey all about her."

Summoned, the man came toward them. He was noticeably taller than the
average and very slim, with broad shoulders like the American cowboys
Leslie had seen in Western motion pictures. His skin was a deep copper
color and yet under the skin were freckles, an extraordinary thing. A chin
strap held the crimped straw sombrero. His hair was cut in little dandified
sideburns along his ears.

"Angel," Bick said as the man came toward them. "Angel Obregon."

"That's the husband of the woman with the baby! Tell him I know his
wife. Is he the one? If he has a new baby he is. Yesterday—but then you
don't know about it."

The man stood before them. Bick acknowledged his presence with his
charming smile and an openhanded gesture as he said, "Un minuto, Angel."
He went on speaking to Leslie, his manner leisurely. "The Mexican Ob-
regons stem from some long-ago Irishman named O'Brien. That's the story,
anyway. The Irish came in here in 1845, you know, section hands working
on the new railroad, and a lot of them married Mexican Indian girls. Look
at those shoulders. He inherited those from some pick-and-shovel grandfather named O'Brien. Three generations in Mexico made him an Obregon.
Look at the Irish freckles under the copper skin."

"Jordan, he can't like it—standing there while you talk about him as if
he were a—a—one of your bulls."

"He doesn't speak English. Look, Leslie, I'm not Simon Legree, you
know." He turned to the man. "The little filly you exercised yesterday,"
he said in Spanish, "is a great favorite of the señora. The horse is her own.
She has great feeling for the horse."

The man's face flashed into sudden radiance, he began to speak, the words
rolling out with a great drumming of Spanish Rs. "He says she is a miracle
of a horse, that she is swifter than any horse in Texas but she is not happy,
he says perhaps she longs for her home."

A little involuntary cry came from Leslie. "Oh, Jordan, I must see her.
She's homesick for Virginia. I want to put my arms around her neck and
comfort her."

"Yes," said Bick stiffly. Obregon was speaking again, his hat was in his
hand, he was speaking directly to Leslie in a flood of Spanish, the dark eyes
glowing down upon her.

Helplessly she smiled up at the ardent face, then she recalled the words
with which Tomaso had expressed his own inability to understand her, "No
comprendo," she said triumphantly.

Bick stood up. "He is thanking you for being so kind to his wife yesterday. He says you have worked a miracle, his wife is much improved, his
infant son—say what is all this, anyway! I can't have you messing around
with————"

But she sprang up, impulsively she laid her hand on the man's arm. "Oh,
I'm so glad. Tell her I'll be in to see her again, I'll bring her some delicious
things and something for the baby."

"The hell you will! . . . That is all, Obregon. To work now." The man
turned away, was off, he mounted his horse for the afternoon's work with
the others. The siesta was finished.

The man and woman stared at each other. "Not again," Leslie said.

He came close to her. "You just don't understand. There isn't a ranch in the whole Southwest looks after its people better than we do. But you don't know these people. They're full of superstitions and legends. They believe in the evil eye and witchcraft and every damn thing.''

"But he didn't say my eye was evil.''

"It was just luck he didn't. If the child or the girl had turned sicker instead of better it would have been because you looked at them. They've got a whole lingo about pregnant women and newborn babies and all that Mexican stuff. You just don't know, honey. Look, the Hake ranch uses some vaqueros. Ask Vashti next time you see her, if you think Luz and I are—feudal, wasn't it?''

A dot had been scurrying like a bug across the prairie. Now it came closer, it spun around in a spiral of dust, it stopped with a yip and a grinding of brakes. The calves ran bleating and scattering. The cattle leaped in terror, the horses reared, the vaqueros muttered imprecations. "Damn that lout!'' Bick said. "If he ever runs down one of those calves I'll beat him up myself.''

Jett Rink leaped out and yelled to the world in general, "You et?''

"Sí.''

"I ain't.''

He heaped a plate with beans stew rice bread and squatting on his haunches he ate the boiling-hot mess in the boiling-hot sun.

"You're late,'' Bick said.

"It ain't me. I had to catch that horse for Madama.''

"What horse?''

"That new one. My Mistake. She wanted to ride her.''

"She can't,'' Leslie cried, and there was outrage in her voice. "She can't! My Mistake's a race horse.''

"She's riding her,'' Jett said coolly, and heaped his plate again with the steaming stew. "She sure hated to put on that Western saddle, that little filly did. Took two of us to get it on her. But Madama, she could ride a bat outa hell.''

A trifle worriedly Bick said, "It's all right, Leslie. Luz can ride any four-legged thing.'' Abruptly he turned to Rink. "Eat your dinner and get going. I want Mrs. Benedict out of this heat.''

Jett shoveled the food into his mouth, he gulped and swallowed and wiped his face with his sleeve. He coughed and choked a little. He burst into laughter. "Wait till you see her.''

Bick turned back, stared. "See her! See who?''

"Madama. She's riding My Mistake way here. She darned near kept up with me in the car, there for a stretch.''

"You're crazy!''

"I ain't the one.'' Jett laughed again. "You know what else she done? She rigged herself out in a old hoop skirt she got out of the attic, she said her grammaw could ride and rope in a hoop skirt and by God she's got herself rigged out in that outfit, rope and all, and she's riding hell-bent this way, last I saw of her. I'm surprised she ain't here aready. Said not to tell you. Said she'd show you. Acted like she was mad at something, the way she does.''

Bick took off his hat and ran his hand over his hot wet forehead. His eyes searched the endless plain.

"Jordan, I want to stay. I want to wait till she comes. My Mistake isn't used to this terrible—to the sun and the brush and that heavy Western saddle. I want to see if she's all right.''

Almost harshly he said, "You'll go along with Jett. I'll tend to Luz. Alone. I'll have Angel ride My Mistake home.''

"But she'll have to rest first. My Mistake will have to rest. She isn't just a riding horse. A mile—two miles—three—but not this."

"I know a little about horses, honey. It'll be all right, I tell you. I'll send over to a line house—Dietz's place—and get some of Mrs. Dietz's riding stuff for Luz, take that damn masquerade off her. I'll send her home on a horse out of the remuda there. No, I'll put her on the horse you rode here. Gentle as a cow. That'll teach her."

"And when will you be home, Jordan?"

"Oh, God, how do I know! When my work's done."

Two million acres. He works like a cow hand. I've turned into a nagging wife asking her husband when he'll be home. But this is all crazy. Nobody can say it isn't crazy as a nightmare. Hoop skirts and race horses and old-maid sisters with twisted souls.

Her eyes followed Jordan's gaze out across the miles of open range, past the heaving backs of milling cattle and the figures of mounted horsemen. No moving thing dotted the landscape beyond.

Fifty feet away Jett Rink got up, tossed his empty tin plate and cup into the heap, wiped his mouth with the back of his hand.

Quietly Leslie said, "All right, Jordan." She came close to him, she saw the sharp white ridge of the jaw muscle beneath the sunburned skin. The blue eyes were flint-grey.

14

ALMOST GRATEFULLY SHE had sunk into the hot dusty front seat of the car. "I want to sit up front," she had said to Bick, "so that I can see everything on the way home."

Bick on his horse at the side of the car had leaned over and touched her hand. "We'll make a real Texian of you yet, honey. At that, I don't know any Texas woman who could take the heat and ruckus better than you did. Unless it's Luz."

"Nothing to see, up front, or back," Jett Rink said. But they were oblivious of him.

"I've had a marvelous morning. This was just what I meant. Yesterday, when that nice Doctor Tom asked me."

"You haven't seen anything. It'll take you years."

"I know. And we've got years. Isn't it lucky!"

Bick threw a quick glance around. He leaned far off his horse so that he was standing in one stirrup, his left hand on her shoulder, she leaned toward him he bent far forward into the car, and kissed her hard on the mouth. Instinctively she sensed or saw out of the corner of her eye that Jett Rink's foot moved to press the accelerator, then stopped, poised. She knew that he had suppressed a sudden murderous impulse to start the car with a swift leap while Jordan hung perilously half on the horse, half in the car.

Bick straightened, he turned in his saddle to look back at her as he rode away, his hand held high in farewell. He looked handsome and vital. Suddenly Jett pressed the accelerator hard and caught up with him.

"Look, Bick, can I take her around by the other way, the long back road? If she wants to see things, different things."

Bick looked down at them, hesitating. "Oh yes, Jordan," Leslie said. "If it's a different way."

Reluctantly he said, "Well, all right. But you, Jett, don't you get any big touring notions in that empty sheepherder's head of yours." He grinned.

"Put him in a car and he goes road-crazy. Last December he started out to take Cora Dart—that's the schoolteacher—to the fiesta in Viento. Ended up at the Cowboy Christmas Ball at Anson in Jones County, better than two thirds the way up across Texas."

Jett's grin was sour. "Sure. Vamos por la casa. That's me."

They stared hard at each other. It was, Leslie thought, as though they hated one another and yet there was a kind of understanding—almost a bond—between them.

Now they shot off at terrific speed over the vast bare terrain. But once the camp had dwindled in the distance they slowed down, Jett was driving at the merest horse-and-buggy jog.

"You want to go round Benedict way, seeing you didn't make it walking yesterday?"

"How did you know I started to walk to town?"

"Like I told you, everybody knows everything anybody does around here."

Enough of that. "Where is the road—the highway? You said you were taking the long road back."

"This here is it."

"But this is just a little wider than the one we took this morning with the horses. It isn't really a public road, is it?"

"No road. No road like that. I guess you don't know how big this outfit is. The roads around Reata are Reata. Anybody tries to cut across here that don't belong, why, they turn up missing. Anybody wants to drive from here to yonder, why they damn well got to go about a hundred miles out of their way to get there."

"Who says they must?"

"Bick Benedict, that's who says."

She decided not to pursue the subject with this strangely angry young man. His eyes actually were bulging a little and his mouth muscles were drawn back in a snarl like that of the stuffed catamount's head on the wall in the great hall. She began to regret the drive, she decided to ask no questions of this boor, since every utterance seemed to send him into a rage. They went along in silence, their speed now was frightening. He began to speak again, he spat out the words.

"How'd they come by it! Millions of acres. Who gets hold of millions of acres without they took it off somebody!"

Here at last was Leslie's chance to make use of that knowledge gained from books of Southwest lore over which she had so eagerly pored. She darted about in her mind for remembered facts, statistics.

"In those days Spanish land grants could be bought by anyone who had the money. It was just like a deal in real estate. The settlers bought it from———"

"Bought it—hell! Took it off a ignorant bunch of Mexicans didn't have the brains or guts to hang onto it. Lawyers come in and finagled around and lawsuits lasted a hundred years and by the time they got through the Americans had the land and the greasers was out on their ears."

"That's not true—at least, not always," Leslie retorted, a trifle surprised to find herself suddenly on the other side of the argument. "They often bought it and paid for it."

"Yeah. Five cents a acre. Say, you're Bick's wife, you ain't supposed to go against a Benedict."

"I would if I thought they were wrong."

"Look, someday I'm going to have more money than any Benedict ever laid hands on. Everybody in Texas is going to hear about me. I ain't sitting here sleeping with my eyes open. I'm going to be a millionaire and I ain't kidding. I'm going to have a million dollars. I'm going to have a billion. I'm going to have a zillion."

"That'll be nice," Leslie said soothingly. She really must talk to Jordan about him. He was dangerous. That movement of his foot toward the accelerator. But perhaps she had only imagined it.

"You're not exactly loyal to your employer, are you, Jett?" She saw his head turn on that thick pugnacious neck as he stared at her. She went on, lightly, conversationally, a polite half-smile of interest on her lips. "You talk so interestingly about other people's background. Tell me a little about your own, will you? Your childhood and your father and mother. Unless you'd rather not."

"Why wouldn't I!" he yelled belligerently. "They was here in Texas enough years ago to be rich, too, only they wasn't foxy. It sure tells good. Ma, she's been dead since I was about two years old, I don't remember her even, they was seven of us kids, I don't know where they're at, most of 'em. Pa, he went in one day around here with his gun to get him some birds for us kids to eat, I guess. Strictly not allowed. Private, those birds, and the air they fly in is private. He never come out. He never turned up again after he went in there with his gun."

"Maybe he went away. Sometimes people do that—they don't mean to but the responsibility is too much for them, their minds just————"

Now he turned squarely to look at her, his laugh was a short sharp yelp. "You sure got a lot to learn about Texas."

"I want to learn. I want to know about you and all the others on Reata."

"Yeh, well, we're all doing great. Me and all the others and the Mexicans specially. If they don't like it they can go back to Mexico and starve. I'm real petted. Bick, he give me a few acres out Viento way. Real lovely. You couldn't feed a three-legged calf off it."

"Jett, I find I'm more tired than I thought. I'd like to go straight home."

"You said you wanted to go see Benedict."

"I've changed my mind."

"Say, I didn't go for to make you mad. You asked me and I told you straight out. If you didn't want to know you got no call to ask me. You want everything prettified up, that's what's the matter with you."

Stunned, the impact of this truth silenced her. They tore along the landscape, it seemed to Leslie that movement was reversed in some nightmarish way and that it was the car that stood still, the flat glaring plain that whirled past them like a monotonous changeless cyclorama.

Far, far in the distance against the flat tin sky was etched the outline of Reata. "No!" she said to her own astnoishment. "No, let's not go home just yet."

"The town?"

"Yes."

"The other side of Benedict—that's why I come this way—is Nopal."

"What's that?"

"Nothing. Only Mexicans. It's Benedict only they call it Nopal like it's another town. It's like real Mexico, I don't guess there's two white people living there."

"White. You mean—but the Mexicans aren't————"

"They sure ain't white, for my money. Two Americans then. Maybe you like that better."

"Jordan told me—my husband told me that some of the Mexicans had been there—their families, I mean—hundreds of years. Haven't you read your Texas history! They were here long before you, or the Benedicts, or

Reata, or anything that's here now. They belong here. They're more American than you are!"

"God damn it to hell!" he yelled. "You—if you was a man I'd kill you for that." His foot jammed down hard on the floorboard, they were tearing crazily along the ribbon of road. We are going to be killed, she thought. We must surely be killed. She sat quietly while the past day—the past week—this past strange changeful month of her life marched in orderly array through her mind. It was like reviewing some sort of noisy over-colorful and crowded party from which she was about to take leave as decently as possible. I must go, she said to an imaginary hostess. It's been so interesting. Thanks for letting me come.

They entered a down-at-heel little town, they had flashed past a broken road sign that said NOPAL. The car slid and bumped to a jolting halt in front of the dusty little plaza. Leslie lurched forward, slammed back, brakes screeched, tires squealed. The boy looked at her. Blandly he said, "Nopal means a prickly-pear tree, it's a kind of cactus."

She began to laugh a little hysterically. Then she stopped abruptly and sat silent a moment, her hands covering her eyes. When she brought her hands down they were fists. She pretended to look about her, she was conquering an almost overwhelming impulse to hit hard that heavy-jowled young face with the hard blue eyes set so close together.

"Ain't you feeling good, ma'am? You like a drink or something, Miz Benedict?"

Furious, she said, "You drove like a maniac. If my husband knew you drove like that! You're out of your senses!"

"I didn't go for to scare you. That's the way we drive in Texas. Everybody."

"I'm going to get out and walk," she said.

"Sure," he said, humbly for him. "But whyn't you wait and drive around a little first, it's just a dump of a town, nothing to see. Anyway, you don't want to walk, do you, in them clothes? What you always wanting to walk for?"

She glanced down at herself. Riding pants made by a Washington tailor. She looked about her. The plaza, the streets were deserted except for a woman in black ascending the church steps, a black rebozo covering her head.

"I want to telephone."

"I bet they ain't a telephone in town only the priest's house and maybe one two places you wouldn't go into." He hesitated a moment. "Say, don't be sore, Miz Benedict. I get mad easy. Uh—don't get sore."

For a moment she thought he was going to blubber. Well, the boy was a lout and something of a brute, but here she was and being here it was silly not to see something of this bit of Mexico in the United States. Here was another civilization, a strange land within her own familiar land. Streets of shanties on stumps, or flat on the dirt ground. The dwellings pitted and seared and scoured by wind and sand and heat and sudden northers. Dusty oleanders like weeds by the roadside. Broken sidewalks, crazily leaning balconies, sagging porches.

They were moving now, slowly, inching their way around the little bare plaza with the paintless bandstand in the center. Yet there was something about the town—a kind of decayed beauty. The church stood richly facing the plaza, its limestone and brick and stained-glass windows in startling contrast to the rest of the dilapidated little town.

"That there's the church, they call it a cathedral, I got to laugh." Jett Rink had assumed the air of official—though scornful—guide. "They don't

do anything different from what they did a hundred years ago. Sundays you
know what they do? They walk. And Saturday night. The band plays and
they act like they never heard of America. The girls walk up on one side of
the walk in the park here, and the boys they walk down on the other side
and they ain't allowed to talk to each other. They just look at each other,
they can't talk alone, they say it's just like in Spain. . . . American! I got
to laugh."

A priest in his black strode across the plaza and disappeared within the
neat limestone house beside the church. A little velvet-eyed girl ran through
the quiet street, she glanced shyly at the car parked there at the plaza's
edge. A rickety cart trundled by, a cask on wheels, it was the cart that sold
water to the Mexican households in this dry land. . . . Dim wineshops. The
C.O.D. café. Garza's Place . . . Rutted roads of white shell . . . Dusty
footpaths leading to the church.

"They ain't changed, those dopes, the way they eat and live and all. They
make their cinches of horse manes, by hand, like they did a hundred years
ago, and reatas of rawhide and they got their own way of tanning buckskin.
They stick together and can't even talk English, half of 'em. Go around
solemn-looking on the outside, but boy! when they get together! Dancing
and singing their corridos telling about everything they do, like a bunch of
kids."

"People do that, you know. They cling together when they feel frightened
or unsafe."

EMILIO HAWKINS said a sign tacked crazily outside a grocery.

"There! Is that one of your two Americans?"

"Half-and-half."

A dapper figure emerged from Garza's Place. Glistening black hair, sideburns, a roving wet eye, brilliant yellow boots, an incongruous dark cloth
suit such as a businessman might wear in the North. His Stetson was smooth
and pale and fine.

"Hi, Fidel!" yelled Jett. "Hi, Coyote!"

The man bared his teeth and spat on the ground. Then he saw Leslie, he
stared and wet his lips and his great hat came off as he bent in a low bow
on the dusty street. He made as though to come toward them but Jett stepped
on the accelerator, they darted forward, Jett laughed a high sardonic laugh
of triumph.

"He seen you, he knew who you was, all right."

"What of it?"

"Nothing."

"What did you call him? Coyote? Is that his name? How queer."

"Ha, that's good—coyote a name! They call him Coyote, his name is
Fidel Gomez, he runs the Mexicans he's the richest man in town. He's got
a nice house—I'll show it to you—no 'dobe stuff but concrete whitewashed
and a tree in front and a bathroom and a dining-room set and a bedroom set
and a parlor set and a Chevy and he married the swellest-looking Mexican
girl in town, she was brought up real strict, she can't speak a word of English,
he keeps her dumb all right. Everybody in the county knows Gomez. He
makes out like he's the poor Mexicans' friend."

She glanced back. The man was still standing there gazing after them.
"I want you to turn around," she said. "I want to speak to him."

"Say, you can't do that."

"Turn around, boy."

"Bick'd give me hell if he found out. I ain't going to turn."

Suddenly she was trembling with anger. "You'll do as I say. You'll take me back to where that man is standing. Don't you dare to tell me what I can or can't do!''

He looked at her, a sidewise almost comical look of surprise.

"Okay. Está bien.'' He spun the wheel, he turned with a shrieking of rubber on shell and brought up before the man at the edge of the dusty footpath. Astonishment was plain on the man's face, his eyes his mouth were ovals of apprehension.

"How do you do, Mr. Gomez,'' said Leslie with a formality which the man did not seem to find absurd. "I am Mrs. Jordan Benedict.''

Again the man's hat was swept off with a gesture that belonged to another century. He bowed elaborately from the waist.

"La señora es muy simpática.''

"I am sorry. I don't speak Spanish.''

A gesture of his hand made nothing of this. "You need no language. Ma'am.'' The dark eyes rolled. "I say you are very charming.''

Well, perhaps Jett Rink had been right, after all. "Uh—I—I'm told you are a very important citizen here in Nopal. I am just having a look at your interesting little town.''

His glance at Jett Rink was pure venom. His mouth was smiling.

". . . muy bondadosa,'' he murmured.

"I will tell my husband we met.'' She sounded, she thought, like an exercise in a child's copybook. "Good-bye.''

Again the business with the hat. The bow. The baffled look. As before he stood looking after them as they drove off.

"But why do they call hm Coyote?'' She had to know.

"That's a name for hombres like him, it's a name the Mexicans call a chiseler, a crook. He lives off of them he sneaks them across the border from Mexico to work as pickers and then when they're here time he's through with them they don't have nothing left when they get through working in the Valley crops. And he rounds up the Mexican voters and does a lot of dirty jobs.''

"I can't listen to talk like that.''

"There you go again. You ask me, and then when I tell you you get sore.''

Primly she said only, "It's getting rather late. Drive me home now, please—but not as fast as you drove here.'' Suddenly she was tired with an overpowering weariness.

"What's the hurry?'' She did not reply. "You're grown up, ain't you? Your ma won't whup you when you get back, will she?'' As she still disdained to answer, "We're only about fifteen minutes from Benedict, you said you wanted to walk around there and there's something there I wanted to show you, you'll be mighty interested.''

"Some other time.''

He rounds up the voters and does a lot of dirty jobs. In silence they drove into the town of Benedict. She wondered now why she had found it so fascinating that day of her arrival. Three days ago. Perhaps now it seemed commonplace in contrast with the old-world town she had just glimpsed. She saw it now as a neat enough little Southwest town squatting there in the sun and dust of a late spring afternoon; living in its little heat-baked houses and selling its groceries over its decent counters and handing its tidily stacked bills out of the bank teller's window. Drinking its soda pop and Coca-Cola and eating its chili and enchiladas at the lunch counter and riding in its Ford.

"It's good and hot. You want to get out and walk, like you said?''

"No.''

"Nothing to see in Benedict. Viento, that's different, that's a town. Or Hermoso. You ever been to Hermoso?''

"No."

"Corpus Christi?"

"No."

"Houston? They got stores there bigger than New York."

Bigger. Biggest ranch. Biggest steer. Biggest houses. Biggest hat. Biggest state. A mania for bigness. What littleness did it hide? Her eyes were lacklustre as she now surveyed the main street and the side streets that ended in the open prairie. There were neat street signs here and she saw that the names had been nostalgically bestowed by people who long ago had crossed the endless plains all the weary way from the green moist Atlantic seaboard, from the woods and streams and fields of the Middle West. Ohio Street. Connecticut Avenue. Indiana Street. Iowa Street. Somewhere in their background, far back among the family photographs, was the inherited memory of Northern sounds and sights; the crunch of wagon wheels on snow, the crack of clapboards in sudden frost, rocking chairs on shady front porches, ancient wine glass elms dappling August streets.

Now they still lived like Northerners with the blood of the North in their veins. They lived against the climate in unconscious defiance of this tropical land. They built their houses with front porches on which they never could sit, with front yards forever grassless, they planted Northern trees that perished under the sun and drought, they planted lilacs and peonies and larkspur and roses and stock and lilies-of-the-valley and these died at birth. Arrogantly, in defiance of their Mexican compatriots, they wore Northern clothes, these good solid citizens, the men sweating in good cloth pants and coats, the women corseted, high-heeled, marcelled, hatted. We're the white Americans, we're the big men, we eat the beef and drink the bourbon, we don't take siestas, we don't feel the sun, the heat or the cold, the wind or the rain, we're Texans. So they drank gallons of coffee and stayed awake while the Mexican Americans quietly rested in the shade, their hats pulled down over their eyes; and the Negroes vanished from the streets.

So the big men strode the streets, red of face, shirt-sleeved, determined. Their kind had sprung from the Iowa farms, the barren New England fields, from Tennessee. Their ancestors had found the land too big, too lonely, it had filled them with a nameless fear and a sense of apartness, so they set out to conquer it and the people whose land it was. And these, too, they must overcome and keep conquered, they were a constant menace, they kept surging back to it. All right, let them work for us, let them work for a quarter a day till the work is done, then kick them back across the border where they belong.

"Hiya, Murch!"

"Howdy, Dub!"

So there it was, the neat little town, squatting in the sun and dust and trying to look like Emporia Kansas and Lucas Ohio. And Leslie Lynnton, with the romantic and terrible and gallant and bloody pages of a score of Texas history books fresh in her mind, thought of its violent past; it marched before her eyes. The Spanish conquistadores in their plumes and coats of mail marching through this wilderness. The savage Karankawa Indians. Coronado, seeking the fabulous Gran Quivira. Sieur de La Salle in the tiny ship *Amiable* wrecked in Matagorda Bay. Fort St. Louis on Garcitas Creek, a rude stockade with six little huts clustered about it. The Jesuit priests; the Spanish Missions, with their brown-robed sandaled monks living their orderly routine in this desert wilderness, and the bells in the chapel towers ringing across a thousand miles of nothing . . . Moses Austin, the middle-aged St. Louis banker who, by trying to establish three hundred American families in the Texas wilderness, thought to retrieve his fortune lost in the panic of 1819 . . . Stephen Austin, his son, the calm, the dignified, the elegant, and what was he doing in Texas, he sadly asked himself as he wrestled with his dead father's gigantic problem. . . . Sam Houston, the mysterious swashbuckling hero of a thousand tales. . . . Santa Anna the glib and tough and crooked little Mexican general . . . Bowie the lionhearted . . . Travis the war-minded . . . Davy Crockett the great fellow from Tennessee . . . the magnificent hopeless defense of the Alamo . . . Texas the Spanish . . . Texas the French . . . Texas the Mexican . . . Texas the Republic . . . Texas the Confederate . . . Texas the Commonwealth of the United States of America . . . Commonwealth . . . common wealth . . .

"Say, I bet you'd like to see what Ildefonso's making for you in there." She stared at Jett. "What? What did you say?"

"That there's Ildefonso's place, he makes leather stuff for Reata—boots and saddles and straps and every kind of leather on the place, he gets fifty dollars for a pair of boots and more. And he can get any amount for one of his real tooled saddles and that's what he's doing for you. Want to see it? Looka these boots I got on, I saved up ten months for them."

The smell of leather, rich and oily, came to you even before you entered the shop of Ildefonso Mezo. And there in the front of the shop was the ancient Mexican saddle tooled over all in an intricate pattern of flowers and serpents, the classic scrolls and leaves and patterns of ancient Spain and Mexico. Not an inch of it that was not embossed or embroidered, and stirrups pommel bridle reins shining with silver engraved in a hundred designs.

Jett Rink swaggered in, there was no one to be seen, he walked behind the glass case that held the boots of every size and degree of ornamentation— boots for a child of three, boots for a six-foot man, stitched and scrolled, high-heeled, pointed of toe. A whirring and a tapping and a clinking came from the long dim back room. "Hi, Ildefonso! Here's Miz Benedict come to see her new ridin' riggin'."

And here was Ildefonso Mezo, as much an artist of the leather of the Southwest as Cellini had been master of the silver-worker's craft in Italy. A little brown-faced man with bright black eyes and grizzled hair, and hands that might have been made of the leather which he artificed.

Standing before Leslie, the man bowed with the utmost formality. "Buenas tardes, señora. Entre. Ildefonso Mezo at your orders. I am honored."

What could she do, what could she say? "Gracias—uh—muchas gracias."

Then she laughed a little helplessly and Ildefonso laughed to keep her company and because he thought she was not so bad looking and because she was Señora Benedict.

"Show us the saddle," yelled Jett Rink. "And the boots and the belt and the whole outfit."

"It is still in the work. I must ask Señora Benedict to come to the workshop."

Leslie, standing before the sumptuous old Spanish saddle, was tracing its design with her forefinger, feeling the great weight of the leather encrusted with embossed silver. It seemed enough to weigh down a stalwart horse to say nothing of his burden of rider and accoutrements.

"But this one—first tell me about this one. Did they actually use this!"

"How else!" Ildefonso assured her. He was plainly enchanted by her interest. "I could show the señora silver horseshoes that were used, silver was nothing it was everywhere. The Spaniards came to Mexico and they found silver in the mines and they covered everything with silver—their clothes and their furnishings and their saddles and harnesses. Until the Spaniards came there were no horses in Mexico but soon the Mexicans became the most daring riders—more daring even than the Spaniards. And so they still are."

"Come on! Come on!" bawled Jett. "Okay, the Mexicans are big shots, show us that saddle you're cutting will you!"

Still smiling, but not mirthfully, Ildefonso shook his head. "Gato montés. Wildcat," he said. He led the way to the workroom doorway, he stood aside then so that Leslie should enter before him. Jett Rink swaggered after him. And now Ildefonso was the artist in his studio. Along the wall beneath the windows were the worktables and the dark heads were bent over these and the keen little tools made delicate intricate marks on leather yellow and brown and cream and tan and black. Wooden horses held saddles in every state of construction and ornamentation. Leather straps and belts hung in rows like curtains, there were boots in the making, reatas, hatbands, bridles, every manner of leather thing needed on the vast ranch.

Ildefonso led the way to his own worktable. And there were Leslie's saddle and her boots and her belt and her reata and her bridle and her hatband together with straps and thongs and coils of leather whose use she did not even know.

"Weeks!" Ildefonso assured her earnestly. "Weeks ago they were commanded. But work such as this needs many weeks. A pair of such boots alone they need many days. From Virginia weeks ago the señora's shoes was sent to me. You did not know."

So that was where the old brown boots had got to. Leslie looked at all this artfully tooled trousseau of leather, stamped and patterned so intricately by hand with the coils and twists of the Benedict brand. And between these twisted coils were her initials—her new initials squirming over everything: L L B. She looked at the heavy ornate saddle and she loathed it. In a museum, yes. Beautiful to look at. But to use? No. She liked all things neat and reticent. A well-made English saddle, so clean-cut and economical in its lines, had always seemed to her as lovely as a sonnet. She thought how shocked her sister Leigh Karfrey would be if ever she saw this; and Lacey, who looked upon a horse and a saddle as other girls regard a jewel of exquisite depth and cut. And My Mistake, that fleet and lovely lady, she must never be forced to carry this ornate waffle on her slim back.

Ildefonso Mezo looked at her, triumph in his eyes. Waiting.

Leslie overdid it. "It's—it's wonderful. It's magnificent. I've never seen anything like it." She decided to think of all the polysyllabic adjectives she knew and add an O at the end of them. "Magnifico! Uh—marvelous! Extraordinario!"

Ildefonso, under extreme emotion, then gratefully expressed himself in Spanish. "What you say is true, señora. This is no common work of art this is art of the highest kind in leather, in all of Texas there is no one who can do this work to equal Ildefonso."

She understood not a word but his meaning was unmistakable. She found herself falling into his own pattern of stilted English. "Sí," she agreed genially. "Sí sí sí. I shall go home now and thank my husband for all this. He told me nothing about it."

A look of horror transformed Ildefonso's beaming face.

"It was to be a surprise for the señora. How did you know if he did not tell you? I thought when you came in————"

She looked at Jett Rink.

Under her accusing gaze and Ildefonso's Jett's expression was one of utterly unconvincing innocence. "He don't tell me what he's doing, does he! Anybody can come into this here shop, can't they, and look around!"

Abruptly Leslie turned away.

"Thank you for letting me see the beautiful saddle, Ildefonso, and all the other—I must go now, I am very late."

Ildefonso bowed, his expression his manner were correct. But as she turned he managed to catch Jett's sleeve for just a second and his swarthy face was close to the ruddy hard-featured one. A whisper only. "Cochino. Piojo!"

"Spig," said Jett Rink briefly. And clattered out to the car on those high-heeled boots for which he had paid fifty dollars.

Leslie was already seated in the car, she was rather bored now with the whole business, she thought, Well, I suppose I've done something again that I shouldn't have. But what? Sight-seeing, driven by a kind of oafish hired man. What's wrong with that!

"Look," he began truculently, "I didn't know he was buying them like a surprise for you, how would I———"

"It doesn't concern you at all," Leslie said in her best Lynnton manner. "I am rather tired. It has been a long day. Thank you for showing me the little Mexican town. I would like to sit quietly now, and not talk."

Across the little town then, past the mournful steer in his glass case, out to where Reata could be seen hazily like a mirage shimmering in the heat against the flat Texan plain and the searing Texas sky.

I just drove around with this boy—around and around—because I didn't want to go back to the house. And to Luz. I didn't want to go back to my home. But that's terrible, not to want to go home even when you're as tired and hot and thirsty and stiff as I am. You can't go on behaving like this, you know, Leslie my girl, she told herself.

". . . girl like you before."

Jett Rink was saying something. She hadn't quite heard. He seemed to be driving very slowly, for him. "What? What did you say?"

The knuckles of his hands on the wheel showed white. "I says———" He cleared his throat. "—I says I never seen a girl—a woman—like you before. You sure are different."

She was rigid with resentment. Then she relaxed. Now don't be silly, this is an ignorant ranch hand, poor kid he's never been taught anything, he's never known anything but poverty. So now she laughed a prim little artificial laugh and said, "Yes, the East and the West are different here in the United States, even though we say we are one big family."

He faced straight ahead. "I ain't talking about no United States geography. I'm talking about you. I never seen a girl like you. You ain't afraid of nothing. I've seen a lot of women. I been going with Cora Dart—the teacher—since she give up hoping she could hook Bick. She's got education and all, but I never seen anybody like you, that's for sure."

They were nearing the gates now. She'd never need to be with him again. "Well, that's a very nice compliment, Jett. I'll tell my husband you said so."

Boldly, deliberately, he turned to face her. "No you won't," he jibed.

She turned her head away in disgust. How could Jordan have dreamed of letting her go about with this dirty little boy. If Jordan didn't know someone should tell him. She would.

There was quite a cluster of cars parked in the drive as she came up. She had not yet learned to distinguish the Reata cars from others. Horses, too. She wished that one of these could be Jordan's and that he might be home to greet her. But that was impossible. Still, it was after five, surprisingly enough. Late, really. She had been up and about twelve hours. Tired. She opened the car door, stepped out without a word or a backward glance. Slowly she ascended the steps. This was the first time she had walked alone up these imposing front steps. She enjoyed it, it gave her a sense of belonging. She glanced about her with a spacious feeling. She was after all coming home; tired and hot, she was coming home. Now she noticed a glass-doored gun cabinet just inside the doorway, vaguely she recalled having seen it before out of the tail of her eye and having perhaps subconsciously dismissed it as improbable. But there it was, a neat row of guns hanging handily behind the glass doors of the case, long-barreled and shining and ominous. One, curiously enough, was outside the case, leaning negligently against a panel.

This somehow annoyed her. Guns. Whoever heard of a woman having to enter her house past a row of guns! These weren't Indian days—pioneer scalping days. Don't forget to ask Jordan. Anyway, it was a relief to be back after the long difficult day. A bath and a change. And after all, guns in the hall are kind of romantic. They're probably the Texas version of front hall clutter, like our tennis racquets and golf clubs and fishing rods back home.

Quite a hubbub of voices from the big room. Jordan's voice. "Yoo-hoo!" she called and felt a great surge of happiness. He was there, he would be waiting for her.

Bick came swiftly toward her across the great hall, the light from the doorway was on him, she thought, Why, he looks sort of strange and wild.

"Where the hell have you been!"

"Been?" she echoed foolishly.

"Where the hell did you get to!"

"Why, darling, you look all hot and haggard. Is anything wrong?"

Now it was he who repeated. "Wrong!" he yelled.

"I had a lovely time seeing Texas, we went to Nopal, it's unbelievable, isn't it, it's like a foreign village————"

But he was shouting again. "Nopal! Nopal! That locoed drunken bum took you to Nopal! Leslie, Leslie!"

"But it's all right, Jordan. What's so terrible about that!"

There in the big living-room doorway she saw Vashti Snyth and Cora Dart, they became part of a confused and bewildering picture. "Why hello! How nice to see you," she began, very socially, and moved toward them. Over her shoulder she added, in the direction of the purpling Bick, "It was your idea to have him call for me."

She was embarrassed, she was angry, she was mystified. So she erred rather on the stately side. Her code condemned family exhibitions of temper. She went smiling to the two women in the doorway, she took Vashti's hand in greeting, she had to pick up the limp and unresponsive hand of the school-teacher but she managed it well enough. "D'you know, there's really more protocol in Texas than there is in Washington—or at the Court of St. James's for that matter. But I'll learn." She thought they were looking at her too strangely. "How nice to find you here. Uh, Miss Dart, I've had a wonderful idea; could you give me Spanish lessons—out of your school hours I mean— if you could————" Then she saw Luz. She was lying on the big couch in a curious stuffed-doll fashion, her mouth was open, her eyes were shut and her breathing was a snore, but more horrible than a snore.

Leslie turned her head then to stare at the two women watching her so intently. "What?"

"The horse," Vashti said inadequately.

Bick came up behind her, his face was a curious grey beneath the russet now, and rigid. "It's our fault. She wanted to go with us. My Mistake. She can ride anything. The Western saddle—the horse stepped in a gopher hole, deep."

"What is it?"

"Concussion. Or worse. Fracture, maybe."

"Doctor Tom. Doctor Tom Walker."

"He's here. He's telephoning."

"Hospital in Benedict."

"There is no hospital in Benedict."

"That other—that Viento place."

"No hospital in Viento."

Cora Dart spoke for the first time. "She's dying." As though she found satisfaction in saying it she repeated it. "Dying."

Hurriedly then Vashti became conversational. "He broke his leg, the horse. When he stumbled and threw her. Luz's head came up against a mesquite stump. They had to shoot him. Bick had to shoot him."

Crazily Leslie thought, My Mistake will never have to wear that silly saddle. That will teach you not to ride in hoop skirts, Luz Benedict.

"Look out!" yelled Vashti Snyth. "She's going to faint again. Bick!"

With a tremendous effort of will Leslie Benedict pulled the swirling world into steadiness. "Oh, no I'm not," she said. "I'm never going to faint again."

15

EVERYBODY CAME TO the funeral. Fortunately the actual basic Benedict family was small. A closed corporation. But Texas converged from every point of the compass. Friends, enemies, employees, business connections; ranchers, governors, vaqueros, merchants, senators, cowboys, millionaires, politicians, housewives. The President of the United States sent a message of condolence. There had been no such Texas funeral since the death of Jordan Benedict Second.

Luz Benedict had become a legendary figure though no one actually knew her in her deepest darkest depths except, oddly enough, outsiders such as Jett Rink and Cora Dart and Leslie Lynnton Benedict. Perhaps Doctor Tom Walker. Bick Benedict, her baby brother, knew her least of all; or if he knew, refused to face the knowledge. Bick Benedict, whom she had deviled and ruled and loved, whose life she had twisted and so nearly ruined; toward whom she had behaved like an adoring and possessive mother wife sister combined in one frustrated human being. The world of Texas knew her as the Benedict family matriarch. Sometimes they wondered why a patriarch, in the person of Uncle Bawley Benedict, ruler of the vast Holgado Division, and older than his niece by fifteen years, did not head the clan. To this the wise ones made answer.

"Bawley! Why, say, he wouldn't have it a gift. That ol' Bawley, he's a maverick. If he had his druthers he wouldn't see a Benedict one year's end to the next. He's smarter than any of 'em; than Bick, even. If he put his mind to it he could make the whole passel come up to the lick log. But he sets back like he's done for years, smiling and hushed, and lets Bick run Reata and Luz run Bick."

Everybody who was anybody in Texas came to the funeral. They came, not to mourn the violent exit of Miss Luz Benedict, spinster, aged fifty, but to pay tribute to a Texas institution known as the Benedicts of Reata Ranch. Almost a century of Texas was contained in the small and resentful arrangement of human clay now so strangely passive in the bronze and silver box.

Mortuary artifice had been powerless to erase entirely the furious frown that furrooowed her brow. The lips were unresigned, the jaw pugnacious. Luz Benedict, tricked by sly and sudden death, could almost be said to bristle

in her coffin. You, Death! You can't do this to me! This is Luz Benedict of
Reata, this is my house this is my ranch this is my Texas this is my world.

Familiar faces, bent over her for a last good-bye, could well say that she
looked natural. Power was depicted there, arrogance, and the Benedict will
to rule and triumph. You can't do this to me, I do as I please, all the Benedicts
do as they please, I am a Benedict of Reata I am Texas.

Every bedroom in the Big House was filled, guests were sleeping in the
bookless library, in the mute music room. Even the old unused adobe Main
House of family tradition—the house in which Bick Benedict and the Benedicts before him had been born—was opened now and aired and made
habitable for the funeral guests who swarmed from every corner of the vast
commonwealth and from most of the forty-seven other comparatively negligible states of the United States of America.

Privately the family thought how like Luz to inconvenience everyone in
the Benedict world and to make them do her bidding against their own plans
and inclinations. Here it was late spring and Maudie Lou Placer and her
polo-playing husband had been just about to sail for a summer in England
and Scotland and France. Roady Benedict had secretly sneaked a holiday
from his Washington job of looking after Texas interests and was game-
fishing in the luxurious wilds of the Benedict Canadian camp. Mr. and Mrs.
Bowie Benedict were knee-deep in the blue grass of their Kentucky racing
stables. Uncle Bawley was, as always, a lone eagle in his eyrie at the Holgado
Division spread amongst the mountains of the Trans-Pecos.

Assorted cousins of the first second and third degree were snatched from
their oysters Rockefeller at Antoine's in New Orleans, from their suites at
the Mark Hopkins in San Francisco, from their tennis in Long Island, from
the golf links of White Sulphur, and summoned to pay last homage to their
kinswoman.

Leslie moved from group to group, from room to room, from crowd to
crowd. Sometimes she did not try to identify herself, sometimes she said,
"I am Mrs. Benedict."

"Which Mrs. Benedict?"

"Jordan. Mrs. Jordan Benedict."

Mystified for a moment, they would stare. Then, "Oh, Bick! Bick's wife.
Well, say! I heard. Sure pleased to meet you."

"Do you live near here?"

"Milt K. Masters."

"Oh. Yes. I just wondered if you lived near Reata, Mr. Masters."

"Mr. Masters! Say, that's a good one. My name ain't Masters. My name's
Decker—Vern Decker."

"I thought you said————"

"That's the name of the town I live in, town of Milt K. Masters. Named
after the fella started it."

But she had not time then to ponder on what manner of man this Milt K.
Masters had been to wish to perpetuate himself by stamping his undistin-
guished name on a little Texas town.

"How interesting. Of course. Named after a man. Like Houston or Kingsville or—or Benedict, for that matter."

"Well now, it's just a little cow town but we think it's just about the best
little town in the whole state of Texas. Quite a piece from here, four five
hundred miles. You want to come down, pay a visit. How come you ain't
been, you and Bick? I take it real unfriendly."

"I've only been a few days in Texas."

A few days. It was with a feeling of unbelief that she heard herself saying
this. A few days since she had stepped off the train at Vientecito.

"Well, ma'am, you sure got a treat coming to you. You're going to get acquainted with the greatest state in the country. Yes ma'am, and I don't mean only size. I mean greatest everything. Crops. Cotton. Cattle. Horses. Folks."

"Do excuse me a moment, won't you? I think my husband is beckoning to me. He's just over there."

"Sure. Run right along. Say, it's pretty lucky Bick's got you now, keep him from being low-spirited. He's sure going to feel Miss Luz being gone. She was more like a mother to Bick than a sister."

She had telegraphed to Virginia the news of this family tragedy. Her father had offered to come to her, as she knew he would. Do you want us to come, his telegram had said, Mother and I can start immediately. Don't come, she had replied. It's such a journey the funeral is day after tomorrow I am well Jordan is well enough but terribly shocked how strange and terrible that it should have been My Mistake.

Her husband was a stranger whom she could not reach. She was someone living in his house. It seemed to her that there was no cousin so remote but he or she yet seemed closer to Jordan Benedict than his wife. He was sodden with grief and remorse. In his stunned mind was a confusion in which Luz and Leslie and My Mistake and the morning of the roundup and his years of deep and hidden resentment against this dominating woman were inextricably blended. Leslie tried to comfort him with her arms about him, with her intelligence, with her sympathy her love her understanding of this emotional shock whose impact he himself did not grasp.

For the hundredth time. "She just wanted to ride out to the roundup with us," he would say. "Why didn't she? Why didn't she come with us?" He wanted her to say it.

"We wanted to be alone. And that was right."

"If I hadn't bought My Mistake she'd be alive today."

Leslie decided on stern measures. "Yes, if you hadn't bought My Mistake your sister Luz would be alive today. And if Papa hadn't cured the ulcers of the horse's original owner he wouldn't have wanted to show his gratitude by giving Papa the horse. And if Wind Wings hadn't wandered into the wrong paddock, My Mistake never would have been born. If you want me to go on with this, if Papa hadn't been a surgeon, and if he hadn't married Mama and if I hadn't been their daughter—well, you can go back as far as you like, Jordan darling, if you really want to torture yourself."

She was shocked, she was in a way frightened, when she learned that by Jordan's orders Luz Benedict's saddle, her boots, her Stetson, her riding clothes and even the tragic hoop skirts of family tradition were to be left untouched in her bedroom as a shrine. How he must have hated her, Leslie thought. Guilt is an awful thing, it can destroy him, I won't let it.

So she went from group to group, from room to room, always with an eye on Bick. To anyone who had known her in the past it would have been amazing to see how she took charge of this vast household. The obsequies had assumed the proportions of a grim public ceremonial.

"We can put up another bed in this little sewing room. They can use the bath across the hall. . . . I know he will want to see you, he is resting just now he had no sleep last night. . . . A cake! How good of you I know it will be appreciated they are so busy in the kitchen. . . . You are Jordan's cousin Zora? Of course of course he often speaks of . . ."

The Girls were wonderful; and of the Girls Vashti Snyth and Adarene Morey were twin towers of strength and efficiency. They knew their Texas, they knew their Benedicts, they were the daughters and granddaughters and great-granddaughters of men and women who had wrestled and coped with every native manifestation from drought and rattlesnakes to Neiman-Marcus and bridge.

"I'll do it, Leslie. Just you sit down."

"I don't want to sit down. I can't."

"I know it. I don't mean really sit down. I mean let me do this and you make out like you're listening to all these people keep bawling at you, it'll take all the strength you got." This from the salty Vashti.

Adarene and Lucius Morey had arrived the day after Luz's death. They must have driven at ninety miles an hour, hour on hour, to make the distance. They entered the Big House, they took over. Servants. Food. Telegrams. Telephones. In a bedlam of big boots and big hats and big men and a cacophony of voices male and female these two seemed pure peace—Lucius Morey of the neat dark un-Texan suit and the neat dark un-Texan shoes and the shrewd blue eyes in the bland banker's face; Adarene of the plain countenance and the knobby forehead and the correct clothes and the direct gaze and the debunked mind.

The crowds streamed up the steps of the great front entrance, solemnly they Viewed the Remains, they swarmed in the dining room, the grounds, the drive, the outer road, the town of Benedict, the roads for miles around were alive with them. Arcadio at the gatehouse entrance could not limp fast enough to encompass the steady stream of visitors flowing through his portals. Three Mexican helpers were delegated as assistants. Besieged though they were, no one passed the gates who was not known to one or all of them, whether white black brown, from Fidel Gomez the Coyote of Nopal to the Governor with his aides, come all the way from Austin.

Bick met them all, his bloodshot eyes mutely questioning each mournful face as though hoping to find there the comforting answer to his self-reproach.

". . . Well say, Bick, I sure was throwed when I heard the news . . ."

". . . As representative of the Great Commonwealth of Texas I wish to extend in the name of my fellow citizens . . ."

". . . Mi estimado amigo, lo siento mucho . . ."

Leslie, with a scant week of Texas experience to guide her, moved among the mourners trying hard to remember Texas names, Texas faces, Texas customs. The Placers, that was easy; and Bowie and his wife and Roady and his wife and even a niece or two and a couple of nephews. But the others, millions of others. Let me remember . . . Uh, Mrs. Jennings . . . Somebody Beezer . . . Ila Something Motten . . . Mrs. Jakes . . . Kling.

Vashti Snyth insisted that food was the panacea for grief. She kept plucking at Bick's sleeve, she grasped Leslie's arm, she motioned in the direction of the dining room from which came a sustained clatter accompanied by rich and heavy scents.

"You got to eat if you're going to keep your strength up. How you going to expect to go through tomorrow if you don't eat! Leslie, Bick looks terrible. Bick, Leslie looks real ganted. Pa tried to get over and couldn't. He'll be next, mark my words. He's down sick, I ought to be there right now looking after him, he don't even beller at Mott any more, just lays there so pitiful, course he ain't been real rugged for a year and more, yesterday he said to me, Vashti, he said, it won't be long now, and when it comes you promise to put me away like I want to be put, no tie and my leather brush jacket. . . . Bick, whyn't you eat something, you look real peaked. Leslie, come on have a cup of coffee and a cake."

Adarene Morey came close to Leslie, her voice low in the midst of the clamor. "Relax. Bick's all right. It's good for him to have all these people around. Don't work so hard. Let them do the work. They're curious about you, you know. Even more than they are about seeing Luz, and how Bick behaves.''

"Why?"

"The Queen is dead. Long live the Queen! If she can take it."

"I can take it."

There was a stir at the doorway, there was an acceleration of sound. "What's that? Who's that?"

Uncle Bawley's arrival was something of an event. Uncle Bawley who kinged it alone in splendid squalor at the Holgado Division, Uncle Bawley who had ignored Bick's wedding except for the sending of a monolithic silver edifice that resembled a cenotaph. Its purpose, whether for use or ornament, Leslie—and even Mrs. Lynnton—never had been able to fathom.

Now, as he strode through the welter of relatives, guests, neighbors and officials, Leslie was shocked. His eyes were streaming with tears, they washed down his cheeks and dropped off his chin. This was all the more startling because Uncle Bawley towered even above these Texas men who seemed to fill the rooms to bursting with their great shoulders, their pyramidal necks, their leather-colored faces, their leather-colored clothes, their enormous hats, their high-heeled boots, their overpowering maleness.

Yet there was about this gigantic man a grace, an air of elegance. He was wearing a dark suit and black boots and Leslie's knowing eye was quick to see that these garments had been born of the needle and shears of a New York tailor or even perhaps of a London magician of men's clothes. They almost hid the slight bulge that, at nearly seventy, was just beginning to mar his waistline.

Leslie felt she could not bear to face this giant with the streaming eyes. Those eyes were a faded blue, and the lids crinkled so that lines, etched by the sun and the wind, radiated from them fanwise at the temples. She knew he had been a Ranger in his youth, with gun notches and all the rest of the fabulous fanfare that went with stories of pioneer Texas times. Even now, in spite of his city suit, he was startlingly like a figure in the romantic fables of the region.

He came across the room, threading his way toward Bick, making slow progress because of the outstretched hands and the spoken greetings, muted but hearty with affection. She knew that he had arrived and that he had refused to stay at the Big House or at the old Main House. He was quartered in one of the nearby line houses. Later, when she knew him better, she had remonstrated at his uncomfortable quarters. "You should be staying here, in the Big House."

"Me here! Like to choke to death living in this pile. Just as soon sleep in the Egyptian pyramids."

At a gesture from Bick he turned to face Leslie. His eyes narrowed, then widened.

There was no escaping him, his gaze was upon her and now as he came toward her Leslie was dismayed to see that he mopped his eyes with his handkerchief and she marveled that his features were so composed under this fountain of tears. He stood beside her, he took her hand in his and looked down at her from his towering height.

Inadequately Leslie murmured, "I know what she must have meant to you—your eldest niece. I am so terribly sorry for you and for Jordan and for———''

He dabbed at his eyes with his free hand. "Don't pay this no mind," he said, and his voice was gentle and low and almost caressing. "I ain't bawling. This is what they call an allergy. Took me better than forty years to find out about it."

"Allergy!" she repeated after him, stunned.

"That's right. I'm allergic to cattle. Makes my eyes water quarts."

She smiled wanly and dutifully, scenting one of these regional jokes she did not understand. She played up to it. "Tell me the rest."

"The smart new doctors found it out after I'd been snuffling and bawling around for forty years and better. All my life a cowman and the whole Benedict family first and last for a hundred years or nearly. And then a kid at Johns Hopkins finds out I'm allergic to cows."

Leslie was utterly fascinated. She forgot about Luz and mourning etiquette and bereaved relatives-by-marriage. Temporarily she even forgot about Jordan. With a hand tucked in Uncle Bawley's arm she maneuvered him toward a quiet corner of the vast room, away from the tight groups that seemed to prefer to stand in the center of the room, talking talking talking. A huge couch whose overstuffed arms were the size of an average chair was angled away from the room proper, by some mistaken whim of a decorator—or perhaps of Luz. One corner of this engulfed Leslie though she sat with one leg crossed under her.

"This is wonderful," she said, and looked up, up at his towering height. "I'm—well—I know now what my mother meant when she used to say I-haven't-sat-down-today."

"Nothing can beat you out quicker than a houseful of people come for a funeral, especially if they're choused up like this. And you're new to it here. Bad enough if you're a Texian." His shoulders relaxed against the back of the vast couch, his long legs sprawled across the polished floor, his feet turned toes up, slim and arched in the beautifully hand-tooled high-heeled black boots. Leslie regarded him with anticipatory relish.

"I must tell my father all about you. He'll be enchanted."

"Enchanted with me?"

"He's a doctor."

"He here?"

"No. No, he's home. I mean he's in Virginia where we—where he lives. He'll be so interested. Please tell me a little more about it. The allergy, I mean. And about you. Do you mind if I call you Uncle Bawley—though I must say it doesn't suit you."

"I'd just purely love for you to do that. Leslie? I don't know as that suits you either. Usual thing I go slow with Yankees using their given names. They're touchy."

"That's funny. I think Texans are touchy."

"They're just vain," Uncle Bawley said in his soft almost musing voice. "Vain as peacocks and always making out like they're modest. Acting all the time, most of them. Playing Texas."

She stared at him, fascinated, she broke into a laugh, then checked herself horrified. She inched her way across the hummocks of the couch so that she sat now just beside him and facing him her back to the room. "How refreshing you are! I hope you don't mind my saying that, Uncle Bawley. Jordan told me about you, but not enough. Why didn't you come to our wedding?"

"I never go to weddings. Waste of time. Person can get married a dozen times. Lots of folks do. Family like ours, know everybody in the state of Texas and around outside, why, you could spend your life going to weddings, white and Mexican. But a funeral, that's different. You only die once."

She lied politely. "You sent us a magnificent wedding present, even though you didn't come."

"Was it? I never did rightly know what they sent. I just wrote to Tiffany's and I said for them to send a silver piece looked like a wedding present ought to look."

"They did," Leslie murmured, wondering when the packing boxes containing all those wedding gifts would arrive from Virginia, and where she could possibly place Uncle Bawley's cenotaph even in this gargantuan house with its outsize rooms. Mischievously she decided to try a Texasism. "They sure did." Gently she led him back to the original fascinating subject. "You must find it very trying—the allergy I mean. In your—uh—business."

"It's mean as all hell, pardon me, but up in the high country where I live, mountainous and the air clear, why sometimes I hardly notice it. It all but stops except for a few weeks maybe in the hot of summer if we don't get the seasonal rains we should. Down here, though, in the brush, the minute I set foot it starts like a fountain. The dust and the wind and the cow claps and the hair hides all together they set these springs to working. If the folks around here was smart they'd pay me just to walk around sprinkling this brush country. Course the dust's the worst down here. That and the wind."

"The wind," she repeated after him. "The wind the wind. Doesn't it ever stop? Don't tell Jordan—but the wind makes me nervous. Blowing blowing day and night."

"Don't pay it no mind," he said soothingly. "Texas folks are all nervous and jumpy. Don't appear to be, being so big and high-powered, but they are. You notice they laugh a lot? Nervous people do, as a general rule. Easy laughers, but yet not what you'd call real gay by nature. Up in the Panhandle they're even jumpier than they are down here in the brush. Up there the wind blows all the time, never stops blowing, even the cattle are kind of loco up there. But where I live, in the Davis Mountains, it's just about perfect."

He took from his coat pocket a folded handkerchief, white and fine, and as he wiped his brimming lids Leslie caught the pricking scent of eau de cologne. She sniffed the tangy scent now and beamed upon her new-found relative. This giant of the leathery skin, the gentle voice, the fine linen, the glove-fitting boots, was something of a dandy.

Now he glanced at her, a sharp sidewise look. "Maybe you think it's funny, a cowman getting himself all smelled up pretty."

"No, I like it. I like fastidious men."

"It's made me a heap of trouble. First off, my real name's Baldwin—Baldwin Benedict—that's what they named me. Then along come this crying and that cinched it. I was Bawley Benedict."

"Oh, Uncle Bawley, I'm so sorry. What would you like me to call you?"

"That's all right, I'm used to it. But I had to fist-fight my way through school and college. The Mexicans hereabouts call me Ilorono—The Weepy. At Harvard I was fullback and heavyweight boxer just in self-defense. I was a heavier build then. Puppy fat. I like to wore out my knuckles proving I wasn't a sissy. I have to laugh when I think of it now."

"Harvard?"

"We all go a couple of years, didn't Bick tell you? And a trip to Europe young. The girls go to some school in the East." His tone, his diction took on a complete change. "Just to prove to the world and ourselves that we aren't provincial."

She leaned toward him. "Please don't think I'm rude. But you talk—I mean Harvard and Europe and everything—and just now you—but most of the time you talk—well, the only ones who don't are Jordan, and Maudie Lou. And now you—when you weren't looking."

"I know. Sometimes we forget to talk Texas."

"But Uncle Bawley, it's regional, isn't it? A kind of dialect just as the Boston people speak one way and the deep South another and the Middle Westerners another."

He had not mopped his eyes for a full five minutes, the tears had ceased to flow. "Partly. That's right. Down here it's a mixture of Spanish and Mexican and Nigrahs and French and German and folks from all over the whole country. It settled into a kind of jargon, but we play it up. Like when I was a young squirt visiting New York there was a girl named Anna Held a French actress. She was all the rage, milk baths and pearls and so on, by that time she could speak English as good as you and me, but there she was a-zissin' and a-zattin' because it was good publicity and cute. That's us. Mostly, we know better. But we talk Texas because it's good publicity and cute."

"Uncle Bawley," she said earnestly, "I love talking to you."

He blushed like a girl. "That's funny."

"Why?"

"I hardly ever talk to a woman. I got out of the habit. No women up to the Holgado Division, hardly, except two three of the section bosses live in the line houses with their wives and kids. But most of the cow hands are single, we don't use vaqueros up there, too near to the border. Course there's all the Mexican families in Montaraz, that's the town just outside the ranch."

The town outside the ranch. She smiled.

"What you smiling at?" he demanded. "What'd I say made you smile like that and kind of shake your head?"

"I just thought how very Texan. The town outside the ranch. Most people would say, the ranch outside the town, wouldn't they?"

"Maybe so. If it wasn't for Holgado there wouldn't be any town. Handful of Mexicans, maybe."

She hesitated a moment, but only a moment. The habit of wanting to know was too strong. "But didn't you ever marry? Why?"

"What girl would have a man who stands there bawling with tears running down his face while he's asking her to marry him!"

Leslie was staring at him, she was scurrying about in her mind, putting together bits and pieces as her years with her father had taught her to do. "Cows!"

"How's that?"

"Allergic to cows."

"That's right."

She was looking into his face with the most utter concentration. "Uncle Bawley, did you want to be a cowman? Did you want to be head of Holgado and a big Benedict rancher and all that?"

"Hell no, honey."

"What did you want to be?"

"Funny you should ask me that. I haven't thought about it in years. What I wanted to be was, I wanted to be a musician. Pianist." Leslie's head turned toward him as if it had been jerked on wires. But the big pink face was bland, almost dreamy. "There's always been music in the family, one way or another, but the minute it shows its head it gets stepped on."

"Uncle Bawley, do you mean you wanted the piano to be your career?"

"Well, I don't know's I looked at it square in the face, like that. But when I got to Europe I studied there with Levenov till they made me come home. Big rumpus, there was. The whole family. You'd thought I wanted to run a faro wheel or marry a Mexican. Young men were younger then, I guess, than they are now when they're young. Pa got after me. Bick's Pa too. My brother, named like Bick. Jordan. They got me out roping and branding and one thing another. Nothing spoils your hands quicker than that. For piano, I mean. Time they got through with me I was lucky if I could play chopsticks. About that time Brahms was just beginning to catch on, I was crazy about his—well, you know, you can't fool around with anything like that, I sat there at the piano looking at my fingers, it was like they were tied on with wires. That was when I quit.''

"Oh, Uncle Bawley dear!" She was terribly afraid she was going to cry. She looked down at his great sunburned hands, splotched with the vague brown spots of the aging.

He looked at her and smiled, his teeth were brownish and somewhat broken, the great round face was beginning to be a bit crumpled, he was a monumental structure he was almost three times Leslie's age, she wanted to take his hands in hers and press her lips to them as a mother comforts a child who has been hurt. He must have sensed something of this as he looked at her. Apologetically he hurried on. "How'd we get onto that! Well, there was Holgado to run and I was picked to run it. Now when I look back on it, it's kind of crazy. Benedicts and big Texas ranch folks, they act like they were royalty or something. Old-fashioned stuff." He leaned toward her. "Let me tell you something, Leslie. If your kids get a real notion they want to do something, you see to it they do it.''

"I will, Uncle Bawley. I promise I will.''

"You get Bick to bring you out to Holgado for a nice visit. In the spring it's real pretty. When the Spanish dagger is out. And summers, after the seasonal rains it's right green, places.''

"Is it a success? Does Jordan—do you and Jordan think it's successful?''

"Holgado! Why, say, it's the money-maker of the whole outfit. Even Maudie Lou and Placer and Bowie don't complain about its being unfinancial. Course I don't stock all the newfangled stuff Bick goes in for here at Reata. Not that I don't think Bick's a smart boy. There's nothing he don't know about a ranch—horn hide and hair.'' He smiled at her, a singularly sweet and childlike smile. "I ain't talked this much to a woman in years.''

"You're just fascinating," Leslie said. "You're wonderful. I love you.''

From behind her shoulder came Maudie Lou Placer's high hard voice, she was leaning a little over the back of the huge couch.

"There are people coming in all the time, they are asking for you, naturally. Elly Mae and I are doing all we can, and Roady and Lira of course, but Bick is worn out and it seems to me that you and Uncle Bawley—well———''

Leslie sprang up. "Oh, Maudie Lou, I am so sorry. I wasn't thinking.''

"Rilly!" said Maudie Lou in her best borrowed Eastern accent.

The big room was now so densely packed that just to elbow a way through it was a physical effort. Nowhere in all this vast desert could one find an oasis of peace and quiet. A clamor of talk here, a rumble of sound from the adjoining rooms and the great hall. The huge dining room was all too small. The modest twenty places habitually laid had swollen to sixty—seventy— and now there were three rows of tables and there was never a gap in the places. People drifted in as though it were a restaurant, they sat and ate and left and others took their places, the food flowed out of the kitchen an avalanche borne on a flood of coffee. The air was heavy with the odors of cooking, grey with cigarette smoke. A dozen—twenty—Mexicans manned the cooking and serving. Steaming plates platters bowls. Back and forth back and forth. Siéntese, señor . . . Traígame el café solo. . . . Crema. . . . Heh, Domingo! Traígame otro . . . Sí señor, sí señora.

The driveway swarmed with cars and horses, they stretched down the road and spilled over into the weed-grown space in front of the old Main House half a mile distant. There was, for the accommodation of house guests, quite a fleet of cars shuttling back and forth between the Big House and the Main House, like a bus service.

It was midafternoon, Leslie had eaten almost nothing that day. She looked at the great double doors of the parlor beyond—the doors so constantly opening and closing to admit the intimate hundreds to the room they called the parlor where the little angry woman lay in state. And she tried not to think of the heat and of the night and of the next day. And she wished with all her heart that the huge house and the well-meaning hordes that swarmed within it and without it, and the hundreds who served it, would vanish into the desert distance and that she could be alone with that Jordan Benedict she had met in Virginia, away from the noise and clamor and uproar of the endless spaces of Texas.

She made her way to Bick standing there near the doorway with a group of men. She slid her arm through his; she thought, He looks ghastly it's as if he had shrunk in his clothes.

"I've been talking to Uncle Bawley. He's marvelous."

"Yes. Uncle Bawley's great guy."

"Jordan, have you eaten anything?"

"Yes. I had some coffee."

"Coffee! You can't live on coffee. I haven't had anything either. Won't you come with me?"

Gently he took her hand from his arm, he shook his head. "One of the girls—Maudie Lou will go with you—Adarene—here's Adarene, right here." He turned back to the men.

And here was Adarene. "You look kind of funny," said Adarene. "Are you all right?"

Leslie clutched her arm. "Adarene, would they think it was queer if I just went up to rest in my own room a few minutes?"

"Of course not."

"Will you come with me?"

Guiltily they wormed their way through the crowded room, through the hall to the stairway up and down which people she never before had seen were purposefully tramping. It was like being in a museum on a free exhibition day. When she opened her own bedroom door would she find a score of strangers there, sprawled on chairs and bed?

"Here we are," said Adarene, and turned the doorknob. The door was locked. The two women stared at each other.

"Who?" demanded Leslie fiercely. "Who is in there?" She pounded on the door with her fist, her feeling of outrage was the accumulation of days. There was no sound from within.

"Shall I peek through the keyhole?" asked Adarene.

"Keyhole! My own room!"

"It's an enormous keyhole."

"Well———" Leslie faltered, and glanced apprehensively over her shoulder down the length of the long hall. There was Lupe coming swiftly and soundlessly toward them. In her hand was the cumbersome key that fitted the massive door. Her dark eyes were lively and understanding, she jerked her head meaningfully toward the swarming crowd. The key grated in the lock, she flung the door open, her eyes darted about the room as though someone might have crept through the keyhole.

"Entre, señora." She handed the key to Leslie and made a quick motion of the hand that advised locking the door from the inside. With another jerk of the head toward the babel below she vanished, closing the door behind her. The two women sensed that she waited a moment there outside until she heard the turn of the key.

"They're the ones who'll really mourn Luz," Adarene said. "Did you hear them last night?"

"No. Hear what?"

"The Mexicans will have their own mourning ceremonies for her. Lew and I could hear them last night, long after midnight down in the barrios, playing the guitar and singing her favorite songs. For weeks they'll be saying rosarios—evening prayers. And a lot of other mourning customs that are kind of weird, some of them."

"Because she was a Benedict? A kind of feudal custom?"

"No, not altogether. She was hard on them but she understood them— the older generation anyway—they respected her. She was the leading mare—the madrina. Of course they never called her that, but they knew. They always know. . . . Why don't you lie down and shut your eyes, rest a while? Maybe you can sleep."

"Adarene, dear good Adarene."

"Do you want Lupe to bring you a cup of tea?"

"Not now. Just to sit here away from the crowd."

Briskly Adarene said, "Anyway, it's given you a chance to meet the State of Texas. Ordinarily it would have taken a newcomer weeks and months and years. They're all here—large and small. Old Texas and new Texas. The cotton rich and the rotten rich and the big rich. Cattle, and the new oil crowd, and wheat and the Hermoso and Houston and Dallas big business bunch."

"I wish I knew half of what you know," Leslie said. "It would be better for Jordan."

"You were pretty vivacious over there talking to Uncle Bawley, weren't you?"

"I didn't realize."

"You're on exhibition. Uncle Bawley's never been known to talk as long as that to any woman. He's woman-shy."

"I didn't mean to be disrespectful to—to Luz. He was enormously interesting."

"Luz was a bitch and a holy terror and kind of crazy, too. Everybody knows that. But she was Luz Benedict. Madama."

"There's so much I don't understand."

"You'd have to be born here—around 1836."

"Adarene, are you happy here?"

"I wouldn't be happy living anywhere else. I've tried it. Texas is in my blood. I don't rightly know what it is—a kind of terrific vitality and movement."

"I get the feeling that they're playing wild West like kids in the back yard."

"Maybe. Some of the time. But it really still is the wild West—a good deal of it, with an overlay of automobiles and Bar-B-Que shacks and new houses with Greek columns and those new skyscrapers that my Lucius and Gabe Target and his crowd are running up. Skyscrapers out on the prairie where there's a million miles to spread out."

Leslie walked to the window and glanced out between the jalousies and closed her eyes and came back and sat at the edge of the bed. She smoothed the coverlet a bit with her hand, a little aimless gesture. Then she lay back and pressed her forearm over her eyes.

"I'm kind of scared."

"No wonder. You've had quite a week. But you'll get used to it. It's the ranch that's got you scared. I don't know why Bick keeps on living here the year round. I won't do it. We're ranchers too, you know. Everybody's got a ranch, big or little. But I won't live on it. It's all different. Or maybe I am. Even the cows are different. I'm not thirty but I can remember the Longhorns. Not many, but some. Now they're stocking grey velvet oriental monsters with slanting eyes and humps on their backs. Scare you. Scare anybody."

"Oh, Adarene————" Leslie began. There was a smart knock at the door. A series of them with determined knuckles. Leslie sat up, she smoothed her hair. The two women exchanged glances, Adarene's finger went to her lips.

Leslie stood up. "Maybe it's Jordan. . . . Who is it?" Aloud.

"Girls! Girls, can I come in?" Vashti.

"Damn!" said Adarene, under her breath; her eyebrows went up in rueful inquiry. Leslie nodded. And there, when the great key had been turned, was Vashti bouncing in with the over-eager uncertain look of a little girl who tags along unwanted by her playmates. Round red eager she glanced from Leslie to Adarene. "I saw you go up and then when you didn't come down I thought, well, they didn't just go to the lou all this while maybe there's something the matter is anything the matter?"

"Thank you, Vashti," Leslie said. "Nothing's wrong. I just felt I had to rest a minute."

Vashti threw her washed-blue eyes ceilingward in an effort at mental concentration. "Let's see now. How long is it since you and Bick were married? Wedding trip and all. Month, anyway—isn't it?"

"No," Leslie said. "I mean, yes, it's a month. But I'm tired because of what's happened, and so many people to meet."

"I guess," Vashti offered then, "you'll be glad when this all over."

Adarene Morey took charge. "Vashti, stop talking like a dope. Do people usually like to keep a funeral going on around the house!"

Vashti moved about the room humming gently to herself which was a habit she had—Leslie was later to learn—when she had a bit of gossip to impart. She meandered to the broad expanse of the dresser with its silver and crystal and scent and silk. She sniffed at the stopper of a fragrant flask of perfume, her head on one side like a wary plump bird, her eyes glancing corner-wise at Leslie.

"I guess Jett Rink will be too," she observed airily. "Glad."

Adarene Morey stood up. "Let's go down now, girls. If you feel rested, Leslie."

"What has Jett Rink to do with it?" Leslie asked, though instinct told her not to.

Vashti now assumed the air of an aggrieved little girl. "Well, I just meant what they're saying downstairs, the men and all."

"Vashti Hake!" Adarene said in sharp warning.

"Snyth," retorted Vashti in correction.

"All right. Hake or Snyth," Adarene went on, dropping into Texas patois in her indignation, "you've got no call to go eyeballing around picking up gossip don't concern you."

"I didn't pick it up. Mott told me." She melted in a fatuous smile. "That's the nicest thing about being married to Mott Snyth. He knows all the talk around, first off."

"I'll bet!" said Adarene with vigor.

"Adarene Morey, if you mean because Mott used to be a cow hand before he married me and cow hands are the talkingest men there is————"

"No, Vashti, I didn't mean anything like that. Pinky Snyth is no worse than all the other Texas men when it comes to gossiping."

Leslie felt there had been enough of this. "Will you two please tell me what you're talking about!"

"We-e-e-ll," Vashti began, with dreadful relish, "they're saying around it was Jett got Miss Luz to try riding My Mistake in the first place and it was him said he bet she could put on a hoop skirt like her grammaw and rope anything running in a roundup, and why didn't she do it and ride out just to show you————''

"Me!"

"Well, I'm just saying what they said he said, I don't know. So sure enough what does Luz do but go up to the attic trunks and get out that hoop skirt and a big old Western saddle with a horn like a hitching post. And the minute that horse felt that saddle and glimpsed that hoop skirt he was like possessed it took three to hold him and she hardly'd climbed on Mott said when he was off like a bat out of hell—that's what Mott said—and they're saying around that after Bick shot the horse that killed Luz, why, Gill noticed there was a kind of funny-looking spit, like, around the horse's mouth————''

"Gill?"

"The vet. The head vet. Gill Dace."

"Oh yes. Yes."

"So he noticed there was a funny-looking spit, like, around his mouth and so he made some tests in the lab and sure enough somebody must have given him something hopped him up, Gill said it was enough to hop up a whole herd of drought-starved Longhorns, let alone one horse."

Adarene Morey attempted to stay the flood. "That's just a lot of stable talk, I don't believe a word of it, anyway Jett Rink wouldn't dare."

She thought Leslie looked very odd, feeling around like that for the edge of the chair behind her before sinking down on it.

"He would so. He and Luz hated each other like poison and then when Cora told Luz about her and Jett, why, Luz said she'd turn them both off the ranch, you know the way she wanted to run everybody's business her own way and seemed she couldn't bear for anyone to get married, even if they had to, like Cora, look at the way she behaved about you and Bick————''

Leslie stood up very tall and straight. "Thanks so much for coming up with me, it was sweet of you. I'm going down now. Are you coming?"

"Sure," Vashti agreed briskly. "I just came up to see if I could help. The boys are saying Bick gave Jett ten minutes to get off the ranch and they say he's going to take that piece of land away from him he gave him that time old Rink turned up missing, but he can't do that because Jett was smart, he's got it down on paper it's his. They started a terrible fist fight only if Gill and those hadn't pulled them apart."

Leslie was moving toward the door, she proceeded rather grandly, giving the effect of wearing a long train which definitely was not in evidence. The key turned with a great clunk. She opened the door, "Petra!" she called above the din below. "Lupe!" She felt very strange and light in this new world of sound and movement and violence. It's because I've eaten nothing I suppose, she thought.

Aloud she said, "Vashti, when you were a little girl did they ever smack you good and hard?"

"My yes."

"Not hard enough," said Leslie.

Innocently, quite unruffled, Vashti prattled on. "Even now, sick as he is, times I think Pa'd like to slap me if he could, Pa's always bossing everybody around, he's always after Mott, saying Pinky do this way, Pinky do that way, just like Luz does—used to do. . . . It's sure going to be nice for you, Leslie, having the run of this big house and nobody to boss you around. . . . Ooh, look, they's hardly anybody in the dining room now, it must be getting late, I'm kind of hungry myself. It's funny, funerals make you hungry, I guess it's feeling so bad and worked up and all . . ."

But Leslie was not listening. She put her hand on Adarene Morey's arm. "Listen. Get hold of Lupe, will you? She'll be here in a minute, she's always materializing here in the upper hall. Tell her—here's the key—to bring here to my bedroom some cold chicken and a bowl of fresh fruit and a pot of hot coffee and some bourbon and ice and a quart of champagne—and if they haven't any champagne in this big damned arsenal I'll scream my head off."

"They have, honey."

"I'll be back. I'm going to get Jordan."

Downstairs she found him exactly as she had left him, a strangely shrunken giant surrounded by other giants who seemed to have gained in height and breadth in the half hour that had elapsed since last she saw them.

As always the men now assumed different faces as they turned toward her, a woman; the faces they would put on for conversation with a child.

"Well, Miz Benedict, you're holding up mighty well and so is old Bick here. It's sad occasions like this and how you stand up to'em shows what a person's made of. . . ."

She heard them, she replied only with that agreeable grimace which, very early in her Washington and Virginia social life, she had learned would pass for conversation in a pinch. She came close to Bick, she spoke very low in his ear. "Come with me, dear."

He shook his head. "No. I'm all right."

She faced the men. "Jordan is exhausted. He hasn't slept or eaten. I'm trying to have him rest before the evening—uh—" she had almost said the evening session—"before the evening." Appealingly she looked up into those big tan faces. "I feel quite faint myself—but that doesn't matter."

They rallied with a boom. "That's right, Bick, you go'long. . . . You got to think of yourself and the little girl here. . . . Times like this it's the ones are left behind got to keep up their stren'th and carry on. Now you mind the Missuz and go'long, now."

Toward the hall, toward the stairway, her hand on his arm. In the hall melee they encountered Uncle Bawley battling his way toward the open outer door. "Uncle Bawley! Where are you going?"

"See you all tomorrow." He dabbed at his eyes.

"But dinner. Have you had dinner?"

"I'm eating with Dietz over to the line house."

"Jordan's going upstairs to rest just a little while. You'll be back this evening?" She wished Jordan would say something.

Uncle Bawley shook his head, the teardrops flew right and left. "Crowds aggravate it. Anyway, I turn in at eight."

"Eight!"

"Up at four. See you tomorrow, Bick." He strode off. They were ascending the stairs when he came up behind them, he grasped Bick's arm, he jerked a thumb toward Leslie, he looked into Bick's face. "This girl is an unexceptional," he said earnestly. Was off down the stairs and out of the door.

Lupe had been partially efficient for once; the bowl of fruit was there, the bourbon, a bottle of champagne in a nest of ice.

"What's this?" Bick asked testily.

"This, darling, is what's known as food and drink, and the rest of it will be along in a minute. I hope."

The great brass sun was descending now in the vast tin sky, she opened the jalousies a little, she wished she could open the door so that the Gulf wind would meet the draft that funneled through the house, and at least move the air with a semblance of coolness.

Bick stumbled into the bathroom as Petra flung open the bedroom door without knocking, a habit that from the first moment Leslie had found maddening. Petra and Lupe carried trays, there was no table laid, Leslie cleared a space on the desk-table. She saw with utter dismay that the chicken she had envisaged as a platter of delicate cold slices in a nest of crisp green was a vast hot boiled fowl with gobbets of yellow fat marbling its skin, its huge thighs turned upward, steaming. There was a bowl of hot mashed potatoes and a wet greenish mass that looked like boiled beet tops. These bowls she picked up, one in each hand, and gave them to Petra and Lupe. "Take them. Take them away."

But they shook their heads, they placed the bowls again on the tray, Lupe, the older, spoke in Spanish as always, her voice low but vibrant with insistence. Leslie caught a familiar word or two—"patata . . . con carne . . . señor . . ." The señor likes potatoes always with his meat. All right. I'm being quite a clever girl, she thought, with my new Spanish. She smiled, she nodded, she urged them from the room. She busied herself with the trays.

The bathroom splashings and puffings had ceased. He emerged, his face seemed clearer, younger, the sagging lines were partly erased.

"What's this?" he asked as before, viewing the table with distaste.

"It's chicken," she said briskly. "I ordered it cold and they brought it hot. This is potato, I can't imagine why, and that's some sort of dreadful greens. And this is your wife. Remember?"

She came to him, she stood before him, she placed her cool slim hands on his cheeks. He bent his head and kissed her perfunctorily and walked away from her and seated himself in a chair by the window away from the food.

"A drink," she said. "You can have bourbon or you can have champagne, one or the other. You can't have both because one is grain and one is grape and they say you mustn't mix them. The French say so."

He looked down at his hands, he turned them over and inspected his palms as though expecting to find there something fresh and interesting. "The French, huh? They sure ought to know. You're hell-bent on civilizing me, aren't you?"

"Champagne I think," she said, and plunked ice into the glasses to cool them and gave the bottle a twirl. "Bourbon lasts longer but champagne's quicker. Open this, will you, dear?"

"Celebrating, aren't you?" he said, his eyes ugly.

I'm going to take over now, she told herself. I'm going to go right straight through, I'm going to jolt him out of this.

"No. I just wanted to make you eat a little and rest a little because if you don't you'll be ill. And because I love you. I wasn't thinking of Luz at the moment."

He passed his hand over his forehead and brought the hand down and wiped its palm on his handkerchief. "I didn't mean—I'm all mixed up today."

"But now you've brought it up, the truth is that it was Luz or us. And it is better that it was Luz."

He brought his head down to his two clasped hands. She came to him and knelt on the floor and put her hand on his shoulder.

"Jordan, after this is over and everything is quiet, Jordan darling, couldn't we close this house or just use it for guests or something—there are so many here all the time—couldn't we open the old house—the little Main House—and live in that, you and I?"

"Why? What for?" He had raised his head. He was listening.

"I like it. It's a house. I'd love to live in it."

He looked around the room now, she saw that his mind was looking at the rooms and rooms and rooms that made up this fantastic pile rearing its bulk on the plains. "What's the matter with this house?"

"It's like living in a big public institution. It's got everything but high stone walls and sentries. It's Alcatraz—without charm. And then those miserable shanties down there where the Mexicans live."

"I noticed your nigger cabins in the dear old South weren't so sumptuous."

"I know. But neither are the sumptuous old mansions sumptuous any more. The South has been busted for almost a century. And Texas is booming. Papa says that twenty-five years from now the cabins and the mansions will disappear in a new industrial————"

"Forget what Papa says."

"All right. Your father built this house. Do you feel sentimental about it?"

At last he was jolted out of his numbness. He stood up as though jerked to his feet. "I hate it. I've always hated it. Ma hated it too. The only person who likes it is—was—Luz." His head drooped again.

Now! she thought. "I want our son to be born in the little old house."

"Son!" he shouted.

"It's just bound to be a son. No real Benedict would consider anything but a male first child. And I want him to be born in the house where his father was born."

16

THE GIRLS SAID she ought to get away. "It's fierce here July and August, even for us Texians, and we're raised on it." Proudly they quoted astronomical Fahrenheit figures. "Your condition and all, Leslie."

"My condition's fine. Fine and normal. My adrenal glands are working like a pumping station, Doctor Tom says. I'm a mass of energy."

"Yes, but just you wait," they predicted darkly.

"I'll have to. Unless they've modernized that old nine months' schedule. It's odd, isn't it? but the heat seems to stimulate me in some crazy way. Jordan says I whirl so fast that he has to go out in the pasture and look at the big windmills to rest his eyes."

The Girls fancied the local custom of dropping in for coffee and conversation at ten or eleven in the morning. They arrived with their hair in pins, they sat they talked they drank gallons of coffee. Or they telephoned in the morning. They sat at the telephone and talked and drank coffee. These timewasting habits drove Leslie to quiet desperation.

Mr. and Mrs. Jordan Benedict were moving out of the Big House and into the old Main House. The County rocked with the news. Together Bick and Leslie were supervising the reconstruction of the ancient dwelling. But it was Leslie who majored in the project. Leslie had plans to redecorate and refurnish from eaves to root cellar. She whisked about all day with rainbow-hued swatches of cloth in wool silk canvas felt denim linen chintz dangling from her fingers, stuffing her handbags, pinned crazy-quilt-fashion to the front of her dress. She knew exactly what she wanted, her decisions were almost instantaneous, her taste unerring, but no one was safe from her happy plans. It was as though she were giving a huge party and wanted everyone to share in the entertainment.

"Do you think this blue is too deep? Too Mediterranean? I want it to be the color of the Texas sky. That washed grey-blue. . . . This pale yellow is just right against it, don't you think? The lemon-yellow of the huisache in the spring. . . . What a time I had finding this pale green, just the shade of the mesquite. Jordan says he's spent billions trying to blast the mesquite off Reata and now I'm bringing it into the house. . . . Is this the color of mountain pinks? I've never seen them but if Jordan takes me up to Holgado later perhaps they'll still . . ."

Bits of paper flapped in the wind. Daubs of paint waited for approval on newly plastered walls. Chairs chests tables beds appeared remained or vanished. Leslie carried notebooks and a six-foot metal measuring tape that sprang out at you like a snake, whirring and rattling. Her supercharged energies encompassed Spanish lessons as well. She had discovered in the town of Benedict a sad-eyed professorial man of middle age who worked in some obscure capacity at the Ranchers and Drovers Bank.

"Pure Spanish," Bick assured Leslie. "Oñate's got no Mexican in him. He's as Spanish as Alfonso and darned near dates back like a Habsburg, too. His people have been in Texas practically ever since North America cooled off."

Fascinated, Leslie asked, "How many millions of acres does he own? He looks so defeated, though."

"Not an acre."

"But why!"

"Oh, you're still that Why Girl. Uh, the Oñates sold their Spanish land grants a century ago."

"Mhm," she said musingly. She supplemented the Oñate hours with alternate lessons in the more colloquial Mexican-Spanish lessons given her by the new schoolteacher who now ruled in Cora Dart's place. "Señor Oñate's Castilian Spanish is all very nice in Madrid court circles but I notice that when I go lisping around the Mexicans don't know what I'm talking about. Though all you need to do, really, is to speak Texan."

"What d'you mean, Texan?"

"Even if you don't know a word of Spanish you can't talk to anyone on Reata—to anyone in Texas, for that matter—five minutes without using words borrowed from the Spanish. Or Mexican. How about Reata! Retama. Remuda. Corral. Ranchero . Stampede. Mesa. Canyon. Rodeo. Corral. Sombrero. Pinto. Bronco. Thousands of words."

"Well, naturally. Everybody knows that." He regarded her fondly. "You really feeling all right, Leslie?"

"Simply superb. And so do you." Yes, you, she thought. We're happy, normally naturally happy, because a woman named Luz Benedict is dead, and it's much healthier to admit it, but he won't or can't yet.

He laughed. "Me! Well, that's different. I'm not exactly uh———"

"Yes you are, in a way. Because you're in love with me and I'm in love with you. We're one. We're three in one, really. What you feel I feel, what I feel you feel, you're really as pregnant as I am."

"Say, honey, for a girl brought up the way you were you're pretty rough-talking, aren't you?"

"Rough? It's a biological fact that two people in love———"

"All right all right all right! Suits me fine. Say no more." His arms about her, his vital being engulfing her.

Leslie and Vashti now had a common bond. These first weeks of pregnancy were not, however, flattering to Vashti. The Hake glands did not adjust as skillfully as did the Lynnton. Panting and uncomfortable, Vashti eyed her enceinte neighbor with an expression as near resentment as her naturally placid features could convey.

"Lookit the way you look, and then me. It's made you pretty, almost, your complexion and eyes and all. I got spots and my hair is stringy no matter what I do with it, and you don't even show. I look seven months instead of seven weeks. Pa doesn't even believe that Pinky and I behaved right before we were married, he says."

"It's because I'm tall and skinny," Leslie assured her. "What you all call ganted. Never mind. We'll both look worse before we're better."

But Vashti, moist and lumpy, was a disconsolate heap in one of Leslie's bedroom chairs. She sipped her ubiquitous coffee. "It's all I can do to sit up, let alone run around the way you do. Run run run with all those samples and stuff. What do you want to go and live in the little Main House for anyway, honey? It looks like a bad old mill. All these lovely rooms here in the Big House, it's a palace. Compared to it that old Main House is a Mexican shack."

"Palaces have gone out. Like the people who used to live in them."

Jordan the erstwhile glum bridegroom, Jordan of the knotted brow and the tense jaw, relaxed in this atmosphere of bustle and change and anticipation. He laughed at her, fondly. "You're trying to make Texas over into Virginia, honey. Next thing you'll have me riding in one of those red coats and some big old bull will come along and tromp me to death."

"Why are you Texans so afraid of anything that's beautiful or moving! You're all still stamping around with a gun in one hand and a skillet in the other. You're still fighting Indians and Mexicans and orange soufflés. Give up. Adapt yourselves. They're here to stay."

He shook his head, hopelessly. "I should have known. That very first morning up there in Virginia when you came down to breakfast blinking like a lighthouse pretending you were wide awake and used to getting up early. Talking a streak about Texas. You'd never heard of it until you reached out and grabbed me."

"My knight in shining armor! Shining, that is, if I use enough Brillo."

Grinning he regarded her and his smile faded. "Do you know what? I think you need to get away. How would it be if you took a breather somewhere cool with Adarene, maybe, or Vashti?"

"Darling, you don't know very much about wives, do you? I don't want to go anywhere until I've finished the house. And when I do go I want to go with you."

"I'm up to here in work."

"You always will be. Me too—I hope. But I'd like to see lots of places. San Antonio and the Alamo that they're always talking about."

"I know. But hot there now."

"Just a day or two. And then we could go up to Uncle Bawley's in the lovely mountains. Mountains!"

"Girls aren't invited to Uncle Bawley's."

"This one is."

"No!"

"Yes! Remember he left two minutes after the funeral? He came over to me with his eyes streaming and said, 'Along about July you get Bick to bring you up to Holgado. No women as a general thing, but you're different.' I've never been so flattered. And some of those Washington boys weren't bad at it."

"In July it's likely to rain up there in Jeff Davis County."

"Oh, it's *that* Davis!"

"High up there at Holgado, a mile high some places, the nights are cool."

"It sounds heavenly! Jordan, can't we plan to go perhaps by midsummer? The house will be set and the ranch can run itself for a little while—all these millions of people on it, somebody must have some sense besides yourself. Anyway, I'm supposed to have whims now, and be humored."

Chip-chip clink-clink hammer-hammer went the tools of the workmen as they pierced the rocklike clay walls of the old Main House, transforming small dark rooms into luxurious bathrooms, adding servants' quarters, devising closet space, building the wide veranda that Leslie stubbornly insisted would be like an outdoor dwelling added to the house itself. "I won't sit indoors all day, like a cave dweller. And it will be cool, with this everlasting breeze, if we shade it and plant a sun-shield of trees, and lots of vines and have everything cool canvas in pale greens and pinks and blues. They do it in the tropics. Why not Texas!"

The old house had originally been built by slow hand labor, its stone and adobe walls were two feet thick, its window embrasures were cavernous, even the fierce shafts of the brush-country summer sun could not pierce this century-old fastness. It was cooler than the Big House ever had been.

Luz Benedict gone. Jett Rink gone. Cora Dart gone. Harmony. Peace. Home. The Big House became to Leslie as impersonal as the Vientecito depot. Guests came, went, it was like an hotel without a room clerk or a cashier's window. Sometimes—not often—Leslie found herself watching a doorway, listening for the quick tap-tap of scurrying boot heels, dreading to see the small vigorous figure, to hear the strident domineering voice dictating plans to the carpenters and painters. Leslie sensed that Bick, too, sometimes listened and held his breath. At such moments she would come to him and slip her arm through his and look up into his face. And she would say, as she had on her honeymoon, "I'm having a lovely time."

Almost fearfully he would bend his head to her lips. "Me too, honey."

"I feel as creative as Leonardo da Vinci, what with the baby going on inside and the house going up outside."

Her letters home were chatty and high-spirited. . . . I don't want to come back home for a visit now with my figure like a grampus and it's no good your coming here at this season it's howling roaring hot but somehow I don't mind I feel so very vital that I'm scared the baby will turn out to be an acrobat. . . . No Mama dearie don't send a complete layette from Best's there are really good shops here in Houston and Dallas and Hermoso though I haven't seen them yet, and even in Vientecito near by. . . . Besides, they have showers here, I don't mean Rain Showers I mean Baby Showers, the Girls give you Baby Showers and bring bootees and bibs and rattles and knitted gips. . . . Everything is different here you must see it. I am beginning to understand it a little. Some of it is wonderful and some of it is horrible, but perhaps that is true of any place—San Francisco California, or Chicago Illinois, or New York New York. But this isn't only an outer difference. You know how these things interest me, Papa. Your fault, I'm afraid. It's a difference that has to do with the spirit. Goodness, that looks awful on paper. So smug. . . . Doctor Tom says I can ride and walk and exercise as usual but no one walks. . . . We are going to a great Fiesta in Vientecito it's an annual thing, they never have bazaars or fairs or exhibitions in Texas it's always a Fiesta and everything's very Spanish or very Mexican or both and yet the real Mexicans aren't allowed to . . .

Not gradually, but quite suddenly, she felt that she belonged. She was part of the community. Her unabated curiosity about every aspect of Reata ranch life and the life of the town and the county and the far-flung state itself was a source of mingled amusement and irritation to Bick. He would greet her with a groan and, "Here's that Why Girl again," when she appeared at unexpected moments in unlikely places; when he and Gill Dace, the chief vet, were deep in some bovine experiment at the ranch lab; or in the midst of one of the rare sales of choice Benedict breeding bulls, attended by only the most serious and solvent stockbreeders within a radius of five hundred miles.

In the evening Bick would say, "Look, honey, what did you want to come down to the tent for! Hot and all that dust and yelling around. That's no place for a woman. In your condition."

"My condition's simply elegant and I don't even look out of drawing yet. Anyway, Luz used to take part in all that, didn't she?"

A muscle in his cheek twitched. "That was different."

"I'll never huddle in the harem and nibble poppy seed and sew a fine seam. You knew I was a nosy girl when you married me. I didn't deceive you, sir. From the first moment we met I couldn't have been more unpleasant."

"True, true," he murmured. "I only married you because I hoped I could slap you around and bully you into being my ideal little woman."

"Your mistake. You're stuck with it. Anyway, you know you're crazy about me."

Half in earnest, "Only your grosser side. That fine mind you inherited from your father is pretty damn repulsive. In a woman, that is."

"It'll come in handy when we're old gaffer and gammer."

Up and down the ranch. In and out of Benedict. The tradesmen and the townspeople recognized her and greeted her in open friendly Texas fashion. She drove her own car now, for short distances. The workings of the little town, the pattern of its life, of the county life, of the Texas way of living and thinking, began to open up before her observant eye and her keen absorbent mind.

"Jordan, what are those streams and streams of old broken-down trucks and Fords that go through town with loads of Mexicans? Men and women and boys and girls and even little children. Swarms of them."

"Workers."

"Workers at what?"

"Oh, depends on the time of year. Cotton pickers. And vegetables and fruit. In the Valley."

"Where do they come from?"

"If they're Mexicans they come from Mexico. Even a bright girl like you can figure that out."

"And when everything's picked where do they go?"

"Back to Mexico, most of them. A few sometimes hide out and stay, but they're usually rooted out and tossed back."

She tidied this in her orderly mind. Little bits and pieces marched obediently out of her memory's ranks and fell into proper place. *Coyote. Gomez. Fidel Gomez. Coyote. That's a name the Mexicans call a chiseler a crook. He lives off of them he sneaks them across the border from Mexico to work as pickers. . . . Time he's through with them they don't have nothing left when they get through working in the Valley crops. . . . And he rounds up the Mexican voters and does a lot of dirty jobs. . . .*

"Where do they live while they're here, with all those children and everything? What are they paid?"

"Leslie, for God's sake!"

"I just want to know, darling. This is all an everyday bore to you but I'm brand new, everything's different and strange to me. I can't help it. I am that way."

"I don't know. Very little. Couple of dollars. Whatever they're paid it's more than they'd get home in Mexico starving to death."

"Where do they live?"

"Camps. And don't you go near, they're a mass of dysentery and t.b. and every damn thing. You stay away. Hear me!"

"But if you know that why don't you stop it! Why don't you make them change it!"

"I'm no vegetable farmer, I'm no cotton grower. I'm a cowman. Remember?"

"What's that got to do with it! You're a Texan. You've been a great big rich powerful Texan for a hundred years. You're the one to fix it."

He shook his head. "No, thank you very much."

"Then I will."

"Leslie." His face was ominous, his eyes stared at her cold with actual dislike. "If you ever go near one of those dumps—if I ever hear of your mixing into this migratory mess————"

"What'll you do?"

"I swear to God I'll leave you."

"You can't leave Reata. And to get me out you'd have to tie me up and put me in a trunk or something. And I wouldn't stay put. I'd come back. I'll never leave you. I love you. Even when you glare at me like Simon Legree."

"And you'd look like Carrie Nation, barging around stuff that's none of your business. Fixing the world. We'll be the laughingstock of Texas if this keeps on. I've heard that women in your condition sometimes go kind of haywire but I never thought my wife would be one of them."

He clumped out of the room, she heard the high-heeled boots clattering down the hall, the slam of the door, horse's hoofs on sun-baked earth.

He's gone. Where? Not far. Gill Dace. The Dietzes'. Old Polo. Anyone who is part of this kingdom. If Luz were alive he'd be rushing to her, his mother-sister. And she'd tell him he's right, he's always right. Should I do that? You're a wife your uh individuality should be submerged in the I don't believe it I can't I must be myself or I am nothing and better dead. Now sit quietly here in the chair and think. What started this squabble that is one of a hundred we're always having and then we make up in bed. Then in a day or two or three we are bickering again. Bick bickering now pull yourself together don't be cute. What started this one? You wanted to know about those thousands of Mexicans piled into trucks like cattle where do they live while they are picking what do they earn but you must not know this is a state secret so many things are state secrets all the things I am interested in perhaps I am becoming a worthy bore like those Madam Chairmen Madams Chairman anyway those large ladies in uncompromising hats at Meetings with gavels and pitchers of ice water. Jett Rink. He's the boy who could whirl me out to one of those camps and tell me all about the pickers. Put that out of your mind. Well then who else because I've made up my mind I'm not going to sit home and drink coffee and talktalktalk and play bridge in a Southwest harem the rest of my life Jordan was really furious this time I suppose I really am a kind of nuisance to him my darling Jordan. It is still early morning who will drive with me? Vashti? No. The new schoolteacher that Miss Minty, no. Besides, she has to teach school don't be silly. Señor Oñate at the bank, no. I wish Adarene were here instead of way up in Dallas it would be wonderful with Adarene. Dimodeo could drive me or one of the men in the garage or the stables.

"I'll go alone," she said aloud. "Why not! Don't be a sissy. After all, the

Valley lies just the other side of Nopal, it won't take more than two or three hours, the whole thing, I'll be back in time for lunch.''

In her shining little car in her neat silk dress, exhilarated and slightly short of breath from excitement, she tooled along the wide bright road in the wide bright morning. Through Benedict, familiar now, past the fences and fences and fences that were still Reata, into the grey-white somnolent little town of Nopal. The office of Fidel Gomez. That was the thing. He was the one to take her to a camp. He brought them in in droves. Let him explain what it was that Jordan didn't want her to see.

In her smart white kid handbag she had her little pocket Spanish-English dictionary. *Spanish and English used in the Western Hemisphere,* the cover read. Then neatly, *Español e inglés* (why the small i, she wondered always) *del Hemisferio Occidental.* Fair enough, she said to herself happily. She was enjoying herself immensely, full of success.

The streets were strangely empty, as before. A woman in a black rebozo came toward her. The street boasted no sidewalk, there was only a dirt path. Leslie stopped her car, she waited, she leaned out and called in her stumbling Spanish, "Oficina Señor Fidel Gomez. Favor de—uh—decirme.''

The woman looked at her she looked away she muttered Yo no comprendo, she walked on. A man then. A small dark man with a resigned suffering face and greying hair in the black. Favor de decirme Oficina Señor Fidel Gomez? The man stopped dead, his eyes swiveled past her, he shrugged, he hurried swiftly on.

Well. What was the matter with everybody! Or what was the matter with her Spanish, more likely, she decided. Perhaps he didn't have an office. He had been hanging around outside that wineshop or whatever it was, that last time. Maybe that was the place. But Jordan wouldn't like that, her going there. She would just park outside and blow the horn. Up one dusty little street and down another. Bodega. There, that was it.

At the second blast of the horn, as though this were an accustomed form of summons, a figure leaned far out of the doorway and it was magically Fidel Gomez. Leslie decided not to try a lot of favor de this time.

"Come here, Mr. Gomez.'' Three faces appeared in the doorway peering behind Gomez' shoulder. With a nervous backward glance he came forward, removing his great Stetson passing his jeweled brown hand over his hair, placing the hat again on his head and again removing it as he stood at the door of the car. And as before she noted that his eyes were wide with apprehension.

No nonsense. "I am Mrs. Jordan Benedict. Remember?''

"Señora, can you ask———''

"Yes, well, I was talking to my husband this morning and I told him I wanted to see one of the camps—you know—where the Mexicans work— the pickers I mean. Where they live. So I drove over. Will you get in and we'll drive to one. You'll have to show me the way.''

He shook his head, smiling a little patiently as one would gently chide a child. "No, señora, you would not want to go there.''

"But I do. If you don't take me I'll go alone.''

"You cannot do that.''

"Don't tell me what I can or can't do! Is this the United States or isn't it!''

"Oh yes, señora,'' he assured her earnestly.

"Well, then, get in the car and we'll go.''

"I will first telephone. I will call your husband.''

Briskly, "He isn't home. He's—he's way out on the range or whatever you call it, somewhere. He left early this morning. Get in the car, Mr. Gomez.''

Fidel Gomez pointed to a large bright scarlet automobile blazing proudly under the rays of the Southwest sun. "My automobile is there."

"Oh. Well?"

"If you will permit I will drive before you and you will please to follow me. We will stop at my house if you will honor me and my wife. We will drink coffee."

"No! Really no. I can't. I don't drink much coffee————"

Very gravely, "It is ten o'clock. My wife will be honored. She will, of course, come with us."

She looked at him standing there, so bland so obsequious so immovable so—I never knew how to pronounce it, she thought, but the word is imperturbable. He bowed now, he entered his car and preceded her, a small solemn procession, down the street.

The Gomez house was a neat square white box. Mrs. Fidel Gomez was a neat square dark box. Mrs. Gomez spoke absolutely no English, the Coyote informed Leslie when she tried to assure Mrs. Gomez that coffee was not necessary and that Mrs. Gomez' presence on this expedition was not necessary.

"My wife is happy to accompany us," Fidel Gomez assured Leslie. "She is honored. She will come with us. First we will have coffee."

In Mrs. Gomez' round olive Latin-American face and in Mrs. Gomez' round black eyes Leslie detected a faint flash of Anglo-American wifely resentment. She then vanished briefly while Leslie, in a quiet fury, and the Coyote in a pattern of correct Mexican etiquette sat on the edges of their chairs and conversed. A parlor set in a large-patterned combination of plush and flowered stuff. A large bridal photograph, gold-framed. And in a corner the household altar with its gaily colored images and its paper flowers, its candles and incense burners and the cross.

"I am interested in everything that is Texas," Leslie babbled, feeling foolish. "And Mexican, of course. Whole families in those trucks. Even babies and old men and women. They can't work, can they? Children of seven or eight, they seemed. And quite old old people?"

"Excuse me," said the Coyote. "One moment only."

"It's no use your telephoning my husband. He's not there."

"Excuse me. One moment only."

When he returned, "What are they paid?" she asked, relentlessly.

Mrs. Gomez appeared, carrying a tray. She had changed from her neat house dress to a tight and formal black. The ritual proceeded. They drank the strong black sweet coffee eying one another over the cup's edge, crooking their little fingers, fuming and smiling. He is being correct, Leslie realized. He is following an absolutely correct plan of conduct for a coyote toward a Benedict. Click-click cup on saucer, sip-sip coffee on tongue, quack-quack voice on air. He is just trying to take up time for some reason. Jordan.

Abruptly she rose. "I am going now. If you wish to come with me, come. But you needn't. I can find a camp alone."

At a word from him Mrs. Gomez gathered the cups and in stately silence carried them away. A moment later the three stood facing the two cars by the roadside.

"Would you and Mrs. Gomez like to ride with me? Or . . . ?" She sensed there was some sort of protocol here.

The stiff and unconvincing smile still on his face. "It will be more comfortable for you if my wife and I we drive in my car to show the way. You will follow in your car. In that way————"

Uh-huh, she thought. He is not to be seen driving with the wife of Jordan Benedict. "Lovely," she said, matching smile for smile. "But I want to see a camp. No nonsense."

"Mrs. Benedict," he said. At least he's dropped the señora stuff, she noted.

Each in the burning-hot front seat of a car. Off. A mile, two three four. There was the Gomez hand flipping a stop signal at the left of the red car. And there was a desolate trampled piece of land by the roadside. And there were the broken camp shacks and the sheds; there were the crazy outhouses. A low-slung crawling dog, lean as a snake. No human thing moved in the camp.

Fidel Gomez came around the back of his car and stood at the door of Leslie's car as it stopped. He leaned an arm against the sill and smiled. "It is not worth to get out," he said. "There is no person there."

"Why not?"

"What is here is working, picking. The season here is near the end."

She looked at the barren field. No shade from the cruel sun.

"But I saw little children in those trucks and those old broken cars with the mattresses and the pots and pans. And old people."

"They are picking."

Sharply she jerked the brake, locked the car, dropped the keys neatly into her handbag. "I'm going to get out and see the place."

Her challenging eyes met his flat depthless black ones and in that instant she saw two little red points leap at the center of his pupils. Two little red devils, she told herself. How strange. I've never seen that before. She stepped out, shook her rumpled skirts, adjusted her hat. "Mrs. Gomez?"

She was almost relieved to notice that he no longer wore the smile. "My wife will sit in the automobile. She will wait."

She walked down into the roadside ditch and up the other side and into the smothering dust of the bare field. Now she saw that there were ragged small tents beyond the sagging sheds. She walked swiftly toward the nearest shed. She heard his footsteps just behind her. She peered into the splintered shelter. Empty. A mattress or two on the floor; blankets, too, spread there as though the sleepers had risen from them and left them as they were; some sagging collapsible beds. No one. Two or three rusty stoves, open and unlighted, stood incongruously in the open field. Here and there on the ground you saw the ashes of what had been an open fire.

"You see," came the voice of Fidel Gomez, always just behind her, "there is no one, they are all busily at work in their jobs. A good thing."

Now she heard a low murmur of talk. Gingerly, and feeling somehow embarrassed, she peered into one of the ragged pup tents. A woman lay on a mattress on the ground. Squatting on her haunches at the side of the mattress was an old woman. The two looked wordlessly, without a sign of resentment, at the chic silken figure that held aside the open tent flap.

"Oh, I'm so sorry. Please excuse me," Leslie murmured idiotically. And stood there, staring. Then, over her shoulder to Gomez, "There's someone here. Please tell them in Spanish I'm sorry to have—I mean intruding like this————" as if she had blundered, unbidden, into a formal dwelling.

"I speak English," said the girl on the mattress.

"Oh, how nice!" Leslie said. "Are you ill?"

"I have had a baby," the girl said.

"How lovely!" Leslie said.

"He is dead," the girl said.

Leslie took a step forward and let the tent flap fall, so that she stood within and Gomez outside. The heat under the canvas was stifling. "When?"

"Last night." Then, at the look in Leslie's eyes: "They took him away this morning, early, before my husband went to work, and the others."

"Let me help you. Let me——— Where is your home? Are you Mexican?"

"I am American," the girl said. Now Leslie, accustomed to the half-light of the tent, saw that the pinched and greyish face was that of a girl not more than seventeen. She felt her own face flaming scarlet. There! she said to herself. Take that!

"I have my car here. If you're able—could I somehow take you home? I'd be glad to help. You and your—mother?"

"My home is Rayo. Near the border. There is no one there. We are all here, working. This"—with a little gesture of formality—"is the mother of my husband."

"Working," Leslie repeated dully. She began to feel strange and unreal. Then, to her own horror, "Who?"

"All of us. Tomorrow I will work, or the next day. My husband and my brother and my husband's brother and my sister and my husband's mother."

She had to know. "How much? What do they pay you?" She heard a little stir outside the tent.

The girl did not seem to find the question offensive or even unusual, she answered with the docility of one who never has known privacy. "Together it is six dollars a week."

"Six!"

"Sometimes seven. Sometimes five."

"All?"

"Sure all."

Leslie opened her smart white handbag. Sick with shame at what she was doing. A crumpled little roll of bills there—ten—twenty—she didn't know. Miserably she stepped forward, she stooped and placed it on the mattress. "Please," she said in a small wretched voice. "For the baby. I—please don't mind."

The girl said nothing. The old woman said nothing. They looked at the money, their faces expressionless. Abruptly Leslie turned and stumbled through the tent flap into the blinding sunshine, she bumped into the man standing so close to the flap but she went on unheeding until a stench that was like a physical blow made her recoil. She opened her eyes. There were the open latrines, fly-covered, an abomination beneath the noonday sun.

The early morning quarrel, the drive, the hot sweet coffee, the shock, the heat, the stench now gathered themselves tightly together like a massive clenched fist to deal Mrs. Jordan Benedict an effective blow to the diaphragm. She was violently sick on the dust-covered scabland.

Delicately Fidel Gomez turned away.

17

No, HE HAD not come in at midday, they told her. But then, he rarely did. White and shaking she put herself to bed. No, no coffee, she said in her halting Spanish to Lupe; and put her hand quickly to her mouth. She lay there in the heat of the day, quivering a little now and then with an inexplicable chill. The sounds of the great house and of the outdoors came to her with curious remoteness as though filtered through a muffled transmitter. The hammering and clinking of tools wielded by the workmen busy with the remodeling of the Main House. Far-off voices from the Mexican quarters. Cars coming, going. As always there were guests here at the Big House, half the time she scarcely knew who they were, or what their purpose there. Hoofbeats. It was one of the sounds she loved. She dozed a little. Words drifted through a mist. I have had a baby. How lovely! He is dead. Leslie turned over on her elbow and began to cry, ceased to cry and fell asleep.

She awoke refreshed, she bathed, she dressed herself in one of her trousseau tea gowns, tried a dab of rouge, regarded herself critically in the mirror, decided that pallor was more effective for her purpose, even if less flattering, wiped off the rouge. She read and listened. She wrote a letter and listened. The crude clangor of the dinner gong. The voices of guests in the hall, the tap-tap of high-heeled boots. He had not come up and when she went downstairs, her head high her spirits low, he was not there. How do you do? Good evening. Howdy. Have you had an interesting day? Oklahoma! No, I haven't but of course I've heard so much about it. Yes, he usually is but he is so very busy at this time of year.

They sat at dinner, eleven in all, she could see the doorway and the great hall beyond but he did not come and she ate quite a surprising dinner and talked and listened and said I hope you will excuse me I have been a little not really ill but under the Texas weather. With a society laugh.

Back in her room she took up some sewing. She sat near the lamp and made small stitches. The Little Mother To Be. She hated sewing. She wadded up the stuff and tossed it aside, she took up her book but a slow hard hot kernel of anger was forming in her vitals. I really hate him, she said. I hate all of it. I loathe and despise it. She leaned back and looked straight ahead at nothing, her eyes wide and staring. She relaxed, slowly. She slept again, worn out by emotion and the heat.

When she awoke Bick was seated across the room. He was looking at her, his arms hanging loosely on either side, his legs sprawled. She was wide awake. In silence they stared at each other. Hammer hammer hammer. But the workmen had gone. It was her heart. She stood up. He stood up. They came together, they were not conscious of having walked or run or even moved. They were together. She could not be near enough. "Closer," she demanded insistently. "Closer closer."

Flushed and disheveled then she lay in his arms.

"That Gomez telephoned?"

"Yes."

"What's so terrible about it! What's so terrible about going to look at a Mexican work camp?"

"Sh! Never mind. I talked to Adarene."

"Here?"

"No, Dallas. I called her. She thinks you're due for a change. So do I. Let's go up to Holgado for a few days."

"Oh, Jordan! When?"

"Right away. Adarene said they could start tomorrow, if we can. But I said day after tomorrow."

Her disappointment was like a knife thrust. "Can't we go alone, just you and I? It would be so wonderful if we could go alone."

"It would. I know. But there are a lot of things I've got to talk to Lew about. Luz's will and a lot of things. He knows the whole family setup. And Vashti and Pinky are———"

"No no no! Please! Not the Snyths too!"

"It's ranch business, honey."

"I can't see why that's a reason for traveling in bunches, like a safari."

"Texans always do. It's a hangover, I reckon, from the old days when if they didn't stick together they'd be scalped by Indians or lose their way or get bitten by rattlesnakes."

"How are we going? A string of automobiles? Or perhaps all of us in big hats on palominos with old Polo in the lead like a Buffalo Bill Wild West parade."

"My bittersweet bride. I thought we'd drive as far as San Antonio—if you still insist on a day there, in the heat. The Moreys will come down from Dallas and meet us there. I don't want you to take a long trip by automobile. From there we'll go by train, a private car, San Antonio to Holgado."

"Like royalty."

"In the last fifty years that road has made enough off us to give us private parlor cars for shipping beef cattle, if we want it."

Before they slept she told him of her day at Nopal. It was cleansing to her, like a confessional, until he said, "But it's got nothing to do with us."

"But it has! It *is* us!"

Sadly, almost desperately, he said, "Are you going to keep on being like that? Are you always going to be like that?"

"Always," she said.

Bick at the wheel, Pinky and Vashti following in the car behind them, they started Texas fashion two days later in the dim starlit dawn. Into the hot old romantic city of San Antonio with its hot new commercial streets like the streets of any modern American city, North or South East or West. Leslie made no comment, she was crushed by disappointment. They passed the Plaza with its towering office buildings its busy bus station its crowds milling up and down the streets.

"Alamo," Bick said briefly, and pointed to a dust-colored building with its dust-colored wall.

"That." Her voice flat.

Ignoring the modern St. Anthony Hotel they went to the Menger because the Benedicts always stayed at the Menger. It was old Texas with its patio and its red plush and its double beds; its smell of bourbon and bay rum and old carpets and fried food and ancient dust; its tiled floor sounding to the tap of high-heeled boots and the clink of spurs.

"Well, that's more like it!" Leslie exclaimed, heartily. "I love it."

"You're pleased by the damnedest things," Bick said. "You turn up your nose at the Big House and here's this hotel filled like a museum with the same kind of Texas stuff———"

"That's different," she argued airily. "Who wants to live in a museum! Jordan, when we really move into the Main House let's not have a visitor stay overnight there, ever. It will be our house. They can stay at the Big House, I don't care who they are. Royalty or even Papa and Mama or Maudie Lou or any other Benedict."

"I've always heard about this Virginia hospitality," he jibed.

Vashti knocked at their door, you could hear her eager small-girl voice chattering with Pinky like a child at a party. In they bounced. Ten minutes later the Moreys arrived from Dallas. The bourbon emerged from suitcases, ice and glasses came tinkling down the corridor, Adarene, as quietly executive as a professional guide, took the plans in hand. Immediately the three men went into a small huddle. Bick made a large gesture. "Anything you girls say is all right with us."

"You look simply lovely, Leslie," Adarene said. Then, hurriedly, "You too, Vashti. Now girls, we've only got this one day and part of tomorrow, and it's awfully hot, even for San Antonio. Let's get organized. Though I don't think you two are ideally fixed for sight-seeing just now, I must say."

"Nonsense. We're full of demon energy," Leslie said. "The Alamo. That's the first thing."

But Adarene had made her plans more dramatically. "No, you've got to work up to the Alamo. The Missions come first."

"Now just a minute," Bick objected, emerging from the huddle. "Those Mission stairs. Leslie can't go climbing those. Every step is a foot high, they twist like a rope, it gets you in the thighs and the knees and the calf of the leg. I'm not going to have my son born with corkscrew legs."

"That's right," Vashti agreed. "I never will forget the first time I visited San Antonio, Pa brought me, I was fifteen. Everything in one day. I did all the Missions, one right after another. Concepción wasn't so hard, and then that cute little San Francisco de la—something—Espada I think. Anyway, couple others, and by the time I got to San José Mission I was beat, I didn't know about those twenty-three stairs built like a fan so you kind of meet yourself climbing up to the tower. Next day I was like somebody had their legs cut off and pinned back on with safety pins. They wouldn't hold me up. Crippled."

"I won't do them all," Leslie pleaded. "But I've got to see them and climb just one stairway. The San José one, Jordan?"

"Not the San José," firmly.

"It's sort of a novelty, being considered fragile."

Adarene eyed her thoughtfully. "I was just thinking. Maybe we should have gone right on up to Holgado."

"Stop hovering, dearies. Yes, it's hot. And I'm having a lovely time."

Lucius Morey, that strange mixture of Vermont and Texas, Lew the un-loquacious, in his dark business suit and his plain black shoes and neat white shirt and the incongruous Stetson hat, had sat silent while the talk eddied about him. The bland face, the keen light blue eyes now turned toward Leslie. He spoke in that nasal dry tone that they termed his Coolidge voice. "Leslie, you're a real fine girl," he said gravely.

Leslie did not share in the laugh that greeted this pronouncement. Just as gravely she said, "Thank you, Lucius. For the first time I feel sort of Texan, here in San Antonio."

"No wonder. This is where the whole thing began," Bick explained. "I don't mean the Spanish Missions and all that. This is the real beginning of Texas. This is where two old boys, flat broke and in their fifties, met up on the Plaza. One of them was the Baron de Bastrop and the other was old Moses Austin. This was San Antonio de Bexar in those days. And Americans were about as welcome in Texas then as——"

"As Mexicans are now," Leslie said.

"Texas history is real interesting," Vashti offered. "Only nobody knows anything about it only Texans. Easterners always yapping about Bunker Hill and Valley Forge and places like that, you'd think the Alamo and San Jacinto were some little fracas happened in Europe or someplace. Look how important they were! If it hadn't been for Sam Houston, and Bowie with that knife of his, and Davy Crockett and Travis, why, there wouldn't of been any Texas in the United States, can you imagine! No Texas!"

"Vashti, don't give any Texas lectures when Leslie's around," Bick advised her. "She began to bone up on Texas ten minutes after she met me. By now she knows so much Texas history she makes old Frank Dobie look like a damyankee."

"Let's get going," Pinky cautioned them. "Maybe Leslie knows more but Vash can outtalk any historian living *or* dead. Say, Bick, you ever tell Leslie about how Texas has got the right to split up if it has a mind to?"

"No," Leslie said, mystified. "Split up? How?"

"Oh, all right," Bick groaned. "They put it in the state constitution when

Texas joined the Union. She wouldn't join otherwise. It says Texas has the right to split itself into five separate states any time it wants to."

Leslie stared, unbelieving. "Like one of those bugs," she murmured, not very tactfully, "that reproduces by breaking off pieces of itself."

"If we ever do it," Lucius Morey reflected, "we'll have enough United States senators down here in the Southwest to run the whole damn country."

"Never will though," Adarene announced with definiteness. "Texas'll never split itself because if it did it wouldn't be able to say it was the biggest state, and being biggest is what we yell about most."

"Anyway, all five pieces would want to claim the Alamo for itself," Pinky concluded, "so I guess we're yoked for life."

"San Antonio's rigged for the tourist," Lucius Morey said, "but back of the bunco it's the real thing anyway, somehow. It's an old Spanish city real enough, with a flower in its hair and a guitar handy."

The narrow river meandered through the town like the stream of tourists, doubling on itself, turning up at unexpected places. Here in this ancient American city the brush-country Texan momentarily forgot about the miles of mesquite and the endless plain. Hermoso hadn't this look, or Houston or Dallas or Vientecito or Austin. Adobe huts two hundred years old crouched in the shadow of skyscrapers. Blood and bravery and beauty and terror and the glory of the human spirit were written in the history of these winding streets. They had been trails stamped out by the feet of conquistadores and of padres and the early Spanish settlers. And by the hoofs of the Castilian cattle brought in by the Spaniards in 1690. Their wild offspring, caught and bred again and again through the centuries to Longhorns Shorthorns Angus Hereford Brahmans Kashmirs, were to become the monolithic monsters who fed on the nutritious grasses of Reata Ranch.

Leslie bought a guidebook and a concise history of the city, modern and debunked. She walked about reading from these, one finger between the pages, her gaze going from book to object in approved tourist fashion.

"You can't do that!" the Texans protested, outraged.

"Mmm—San Antonio," mumbled Leslie. "Who named it San Antonio?"

The Texans stared at one another. "Uh————"

Her forefinger traced down the page. "Let's see . . . Don Domingo Teran de los Rios, with Father Damian Massanet and an escort of fifty soldiers . . . June 1691 . . . came upon ranchería of Payayas . . . What's a Payaya?"

"Indian tribe," Bick replied briskly.

"Wonderful word, isn't it?—all those ya-yas in it. I never heard of them."

Emboldened by Bick's success, "A branch of the Comanches, I believe," Lucius Morey ventured. "Mean-acting Indians, the Comanches were."

"Look, Leslie," Vashti objected. "This way we'll never get to show you anything. Why can't you just see things and not have to know about how they got there and everything."

But Leslie was reading again in a rather maddening mumble. ". . . The Indians called the village Yanaguana . . . "

She looked up, speculatively.

"Nobody knows nobody knows!" Adarene assured her.

" . . . uh . . . Father Massanet set up a cross . . . christened the place San Antonio in honor of St. Anthony of Padua. . . . In 1718 Don Martín de Alarcón and Fray Antonio de San Buenaventura Olivares with settlers monks and soldiers . . ."

She looked up from the book, her face alight. "Don Domingo de los Rios. Fray Antonio de San Buenaventura Oli———— I don't know why it makes me happy just to say all those words and to know about Payayas and those poor little fifty soldiers. But it does."

"It reads real pretty," Pinky agreed. "If there's one thing about San Antonio, it's history."

"Who's showing who Texas, that's what I want to know!" Vashti demanded, somewhat sulkily for her. "Indians. Who cares about Indians and soldiers and stuff! The Mexican quarter is real picturesque, they wear charro outfits and play guitars."

Leslie tucked the guidebook under her arm and turned to a passage she had marked in the modern volume. "Uh, San Antonio is the pecan-shelling center of the Southwest. The industry employs about twelve thousand Mexican workers in the Mexican Quarter . . . uh . . . average piecework wage for a 54-hour week is $1.56. . . ."

Gently Bick Benedict took the book from her hands and closed it. "How would you have liked it if I'd told you how Virginia————"

"But we stumble all around Europe with our noses in Baedekers. I don't see why we shouldn't know about our own sights." The tactful Adarene to the rescue.

Pinky settled it. "The Benedicts have been in these parts for about a hundred years now. Anybody around here see Bick Benedict with his face in a guidebook, he's liable to be run out of the state of Texas."

"Oh, my land let's get going." Vashti again.

So off they went to visit the musty little Missions with their tortuous stairs and Leslie produced her book again with its dry terse accounts of incredible deeds in which padres and Indians and Spanish grandees, slaughter and agriculture and sculpture and frescoes were fantastically mingled.

"The walls of Mission Concepción are forty-five inches thick," Leslie read. "Think of it! The Indians built them with almost no tools. And the monks." She read on. "Acanthus leaves . . . front facade . . . Renaissance influence of the Churrigueresque school of Spanish Baroque . . ."

"Oh, for heaven's sake, Leslie!"

They ate Mexican food to the strumming of the Mexicans' guitars on the Plaza. Spicy burning food. Tortillas. Enchiladas. Mole de guajolote.

"What's that?" Leslie asked.

"Terrific turkey thing," Bick explained. "It's the top Mexican dish. Turkey with a sauce made of—oh—chiles and ground almonds and all kinds of spices and chocolate————"

"Chocolate!"

The musicians in their charro clothes. Shadowy figures in and out of the dim arcades. A vendor's soft persuasive cry. Strange exotic smells. Leslie fell silent.

Bick touched her hand. "Come on back to us, honey. What are you thinking about way off there?"

She turned toward him gravely. "I was thinking of Boston."

"Boston!"

"I mean—it's a kind of wonderful country, isn't it? I mean—I was thinking about how it all hangs together somehow even when it's as different as—I was thinking about Boston because San Antonio and Boston are absolutely the most different—the Ritz Hotel in Boston. That cool green dining room with the long windows looking out on the Common. Those big elm-tree branches make a pattern against the glass. And those dowdy Boston women and the agreeable Boston men with their long English heads. And the lobster so sweet and fresh and tender and the heavy white linen and the waiters' beautiful clean white fingernails. And old Faneuil Hall." She stopped, she looked into their disapproving faces. Lamely, "I haven't explained very well. I just meant it's just a kind of wonderful country altogether I mean———'' Her voice trailed off into nothing.

She was noticeably silent in the Alamo. "I guess maybe you were oversold on it in the first place," Lucius Morey said. "All Yankees are. Anyway, the Alamo is a feeling, not a place."

All around the adobe walls swirled the life of a modern city. Big business streamed in and out of the department stores, in and out of the new post office, in and out of the bus station. The old tragic Alamo with its history of blood and bravery was a new Alamo, reconstructed within an inch of its life.

Picture postcards. Souvenirs. At a desk in the great grey stone hall sat a schoolteacherly woman in spectacles who eyed the visitor with detached severity. The figures moving about the dim room tiptoed as in a cathedral and their voices dropped to a whisper.

In the glass cases were the mementos. Proof of the mad glorious courage of a handful of men against a horde—men who had come to this Texas wilderness from Massachusetts and Tennessee, from Virginia and Louisiana and Connecticut. In the glass cases under lock and key were the famed long-rifles that had barked so hopelessly against the oncoming enemy. Neat and cold and quaint in their glass caskets the long-rifles lay now, with their ornamental brass eagles and their six-foot unavailing barrels. And there was the slashing knife of Bowie. Bowie, on his cot in the crumbling Alamo fortress, Bowie already dying of typhoid and pneumonia and exposure and alcohol, wielding the pistols and the knife from his cot bed until they ran him through with their bayonets and it was finished.

The letters under glass too—stiff formal letters written in extremity by desperate men. " . . .Your favour of the 11 Inst came safe to hand by the last mail and I will hasten to answer the contents."

He must indeed hasten, this Davy Crockett who wrote so politely, for he was soon to die for Texas—for this strange and vast and brutal land that he and the drunken ruined brave Bowie of the terrible knife and the glory-seeking Travis all fought for and died for, though they had perhaps little legal right to do either.

Tourists trailed through the garden, through the chapel, through the museum, whispering and pointing and staring. Young bridal couples, honeymooning. Middle-aged ranchers, their high-heeled boots clicking on the stone floors, their wives plumply corseted in city clothes. Leslie watched a stout dark-skinned Mexican with his wife and three small children. Their faces were impassive as they looked at the knives, the guns, the flags. They were neatly dressed in their best. The woman trailed a little behind the man, and stared and quieted the restless infant in her arms.

There at the far end of the dim room were the silk flags that had flown in sovereign authority over this violent and capricious state. Draped and festooned, they made a brilliant splash of color against the grey stone wall. The flag of ancient Spain. Of France. Of Mexico. Of the Republic of Texas. The Southern Confederacy. The United States of America. Two hundred and fifty years of violence of struggle, of unrest.

Leslie Benedict stood in the shadows of the great vaulted room, her head averted. "Don't mind me. Pretend you're not with me. I cry at parades, too, so don't mind me."

She stood there in the room that had become a sort of shrine to the arrogant swaggerng giant—Texas. Texas. Jett Rink. Jordan Benedict. Adarene Morey. Doctor Tom Walker. Angel Obregon. Pinky Snyth. Uncle Bawley. Vashti Hake. She stared at the festooned flags and the colors misted and became faces and the faces faded and the folds of the flags began to ripple strangely.

"Heh, you feeling funny, Leslie?" Bick, his arm around her shoulder, his eyes searching her face with concern.

"No. I'm feeling fine. The flags. I suppose I stared at them so long the colors made me dizzy."

"You've just about seen it all. How about going back to the hotel and getting a rest? Before we make the train."

"In just a little while. I want to see the pictures. Just the pictures, and then we'll go."

Oil paintings made vivid splashes of scarlet and blue and gold against the walls. Men in buckskin breeches. Men in battle. Men dying. Men attacking. Invariably there were the brave white Americans rising superior over the dark-skinned Mexicans. Even if they were about to die they fought on, facing their adversaries with fortitude and an expression of civilized superiority. The Mexican and his wife and children had finished gazing at the old guns and knives and battered mementos in the glass cases, and puzzling over the faded ink of Travis' desperate letters:

> Commandancy of Bexar,
> Feb. 23d. 3 o'clock P.M. 1836
>
> To Andrew Ponton, Judge, and Citizens of Gonzales:
>
> The enemy in large force is in sight. We want men and provisions. Send them to us. We have 150 men and are determined to defend the Alamo to the last. Give us assistance.
>
> W. B. Travis-Col, Commanding.

They were standing just beside Leslie now staring at the paintings in oil of those to whom the men and the provisions never came. Here in crude glowing colors were depicted the dark-skinned men in natty bright uniforms and the white-skinned men in the bloodstained shirts and the buckskins of the storied pioneer, and the dark men were hacking with knives and shooting with guns at the valiant white-faced men, and the faces of the one were ferocious and of the other agonized and brave. And which was right and which was wrong? Leslie asked herself. And which was aggressor and which defender?

Beside her the Mexican and his wife with the child in her arms and the two wide-eyed children gazed at the pictures and the oldest child—the boy—pointed and asked a question, puzzlement in his eyes and in his voice. And the man replied in Spanish, low-voiced.

"Better watch out, Bick!" Pinky said. "Your wife's got that look in her eye can't tear herself away from Bill Travis. Or is it Sam Houston?"

Bick laughed as he took Leslie's arm. "They were both great boys with the ladies. Which is it, Leslie? They're good and dead, so I don't have to mind too much."

Leslie turned as though she had not heard. "You were right about sight-seeing. I am rather tired."

"You take things too hard," said the practical Vashti. "What was it you were so upset about in there?"

"It could be so wonderful."

"What could? What could be so wonderful?"

"Texas."

"Texas! Listen at her! Texas *is* wonderful. Honestly, Leslie, sometimes I think you're real horrid, the way you talk."

Bick's arm was about his wife's shoulder. "It used to rile me too, Vashti, until I caught on. It's what they call impersonal observation."

Briskly Adarene Morey said, "Anyway, we've all had enough of Missions and Mexicans and mole de guajolote. I'll be glad to get on that train."

"When we're all settled on the train let's order something wonderful for supper," Vashti suggested as they walked down the Alamo garden path.

"Steaks," Pinky said.

"No!" the women shrieked.

Vashti's plump pink face took on the look of a misty-eyed dreamer. "What I'd love is regular train food you never get anywhere else, hardly. Chicken potpie with teensy onions in the cream gravy, and corn muffins and that salad with Roquefort cheese dressing and for dessert blueberry pie à la mode with chocolate ice cream."

"You all right, Leslie?" Adarene inquired anxiously, as her friend turned noticeably pale.

"I'm all right," said Leslie. "Holgado. Is it really cool?"

18

THE SPECIAL CAR had been docilely waiting for them on the siding at San Antonio, ready to be picked up by the crack express that hurtled across the continent to the Mexican border and beyond into Mexico itself. There was the porter welcoming them like an old family servitor. He knew who took charged water, who took branch water, who took it straight; the Benedicts and the Moreys and the Hakes apparently had been part of his railroad life for years. He greeted them like long-lost benefactors.

"Well, this is mighty nice," Lucius Morey said and sank into one of the great plushy seats with the air of one who has come home after a hard day's work.

Pinky tossed his big Stetson with an expert twirl so that it landed neatly in the overhead rack at a distance of twenty feet. "I haven't done so much walking since one time my horse died on me middle of the desert. I had to lug my old kack twenty miles afoot. Nothing beats you out like sight-seeing."

"That's right," Bick agreed. "I'd rather do a day's roundup than one more Mission."

The jaunt took on a holiday air. Everyone felt relaxed. Vashti bubbled. "Ooh, look, it's a brand-new car they've got it upholstered in blue isn't that cute I never saw blue before on a train it's always green . . ."

"George, we'll want a setup right away, plenty of ice . . ."

"That goes there and this goes here—no, the Benedict drawing room . . ."

"A menu from the dining car we'll eat right here . . . "

The three men then said "Phew!" and glanced toward the little pantry from which came the tinkle of ice and glass. A waiter in a cardboard-stiff white apron and jacket appeared with menus. "Tengo hambre," Pinky yelled. "Come on, amigos, let's get together on this. Vash! Girls!"

The three women emerged from their rooms along the corridor at the far end of the car. In some miraculous way heat and weariness had vanished. They were fresh and fragrant as peppermint patties.

Solemnly they sipped their highballs and scanned the list of dinner dishes "Six dinners to haul in from the galley back in the dining car," Pinky said. "So don't let's go hog-wild and order the works, it'll take from here to breakfast to get it."

There was a gate—a little crossbarred iron gate—that stretched across their car platform and separated it from the other cars. It was not locked, it folded back on itself like an accordion. Their private porter, full of his own importance, closed it opened it as he went back and forth on his errands. Now and then a stray passenger would drift in past the folding gate, thinking this was a public lounge car, he would see six people seated there talking and drinking and laughing, he would sink into one of the luxurious seats and look about him with an air of relief and calm. Slowly an uncertain look would come into his face, then puzzlement, then embarrassment. No one said anything, the deferential colored porter did not approach these people. They vanished, red-faced. One man came in, boots, Stetson, city clothes. He seated himself, then his face beamed with a smile of recognition. "Well, say, Bick, you old sonofagun! Pinky! Howdy, Pinky!"

"Hi!" the men said. "Howdy, Mel!"

He rose, he came toward them, then a certain something seemed to strike him, an apprehensive look came into the frank blue eyes. Deliberately he stood. Those crinkled eyes that had stared so many years across the endless plain now slowly encompassed the luxurious room on wheels, the strangely empty seats, the porter eying him with amused hostility from the far doorway; the neatness, the lack of piled-up luggage.

"Have a drink, Mel?" Bick called to him. "How about supper with us? Had your supper?"

"Well, say," Mel stammered, blushing like a boy. "I didn't go for to stomp in on your party. Excuse me!" He shook his head and raised his hand in a rather touching gesture of apology and farewell as he walked out of the car. You heard the little folding gate outside go clink and clank as it opened and closed.

Leslie felt guilty and embarrassed but no one else seemed to attach any importance to the coming and going of Mel or his fellow travelers.

Pinky said, "Mel still got that little bitty place up to San Angelo? About fifteen sections, ain't it?"

"Thereabouts. Ten twelve thousand-acre piece," Bick said. "Over-used his grass, and over-stocked. Going under, I'd say."

Pinky disposed of him. "That's the trouble with those little fellows. Feeders. They let the grassland run down and have to feed their young stock cake and then they wonder where the money goes."

"Cake!" said Leslie, scenting a Texas joke.

They laughed tolerantly, Bick laid a fond possessive hand on her knee. "Cake, Yankee, is feed—cottonseed cake. Concentrated cow feed and good and damned expensive."

"That's right," Pinky agreed virtuously—Pinky the erstwhile cow hand newly come into the prospect of two million acres. "Abuse the rangeland and what's happened to Texas the last half century! Couple inches of topsoil lost from millions of acres, that's what. Like to've wrecked the state."

"Why don't they make them put it back?" Leslie inquired.

A roar went up. Vashti Hake's shrill defense came to her through the uproar. "Never you mind, Leslie."

She could laugh with them, but she persisted. "Well, but why?"

Thoughtfully Bick stared out of the window at the hundreds—thousands—millions of acres of semi-arid land.

"Because man hasn't the trick of making earth—or maybe he just hasn't got the time. To build back a couple of inches of topsoil in Texas would take nature from eight hundred to four thousand years."

Fascinated, Leslie persisted. "Then why doesn't somebody teach them not to neglect the grassland in the first place?"

Vashti had been rummaging in a huge box of chocolates with which she had fortified herself against the rigors of the journey. She was eating a fondant-filled sweet and drinking a bourbon highball, a unique gustatory feat of which even Pinky disapproved. He offered mild protest. "Vash, chocolates and liquor don't go together, they don't set right. Anyway, all that supper'll be along any minute."

Vashti ignored this epicurean counsel. Through a mouthful of creamy fondant and a sip of the highball she still sounded brisk and emphatic.

"Teach hell! They got no right to go ranching on a little bitty old piece you couldn't run a goat on. They'd do better go to work for folks know how to run a real ranch. Like Pa. Or Bick. Or even the Moreys though they only run two three hundred thousand acres since they got to be city folks."

"No!" said Leslie, to her own surprise. "That isn't the way. That isn't a good way."

Vashti hooted good-naturedly. "Isn't the way! Listen at the Texian talking!"

It was not until twenty years later that Bob Dietz the agronomist spoke the words which Leslie now was too inexperienced to phrase.

"Reata" he said two decades later, "and the Hake ranch and all those overgrown giants are dated. A man who knows modern methods can make a success of four sections and not feed his stock a pound of hay or cake even in a drought season. But success or failure, a man who's running his own ranch is a man. But on a place like Reata he's a piece of machinery. And anyway, no man in a democracy should have the right to own millions of acres of land. That's foolish old feudal stuff."

Now, falteringly, Leslie tried to express her own half-formed observations. "I just mean I think it's better for a million men to own their own little farms than for one man to own a million——"

"Heh, hold on there!" Bick laughed. "You're talking about the husband of the woman I love."

"That's right, you want to watch out with that kind of talk," Vashti said. "Every single thing you say is repeated all over Texas inside of twenty-four hours."

Leslie smiled politely. "Now Vashti. I've been in Texas long enough to know you mean all over Reata."

"I mean all over Texas."

"Why?"

"Because you're Mrs. Bick Benedict. And a Yankee. And different. And Texas is like that. Next thing you know they'll be saying you're one of those Socialists."

"Pooh, you're just trying to scare me. I won't scare."

Bick leaned toward her, smiling, his eyes serious. "Texas," he said, "is a village—of about three hundred thousand square miles. There's more cattle in Texas than there are people. And Texas people are kind of lonesome people, they like a piece of news to chew on. You're news."

"In Ohio," Leslie said equably, "we three Lynnton girls always were considered slightly crazy, and even Virginia thinks we're odd. But Papa brought us up to think for ourselves and say what we thought."

"He sure did!" Bick said in full round tones.

"Papa!" Vashti yelled. "That's funny. My pa raised me up too."

"Well, they don't come any crazier than you do, Vash," Pinky stated reasonably.

"Of course Texas," Leslie went on, "is really very conventional, so that anyone who varies from the——"

"Conventional!" shouted the Texans in chorus.

Lew Morey, the mild-faced, raised a placating hand. "It's too hot to be arguing whether Texas is conventional or not."

"I kind of know what she means," Adarene Morey said. "I honestly do. But didn't you mean provincial instead of conventional, Leslie?"

"Never mind who means what," Bick interrupted irritably. "People have been wrangling about what Texas is and isn't for a hundred years and more. Let's talk about something else, will you!"

Smoothly Lucius Morey poured a conversational oil slick. "I'll bet anybody that in another ten years, the way the airplane business is booming since the war, you'll be flying up to Holgado inside an hour, instead of having to eat and sleep on a long train trip this way."

Pinky took a thoughtful sip of bourbon. "I don't know's I'd relish flying up to Holgado in all that mountain country. Too many hard clouds up around there, as the fellas used to say in the war."

Adarene Morey regarded her undramatic Lucius. "Lucius flew in the war," she said to Leslie. "You wouldn't think it to look at him, but he was an ace."

"Why wouldn't you think it to look at me!" her husband challenged her. "Mars kind of changed his face these last couple of wars. Used to be a big hairy fellow with whiskers. Now he's mostly a kid just about managed to have his first shave."

Leslie regarded the bland Morey with new interest. She was silent a moment. Then she swung her chair around away from the window view of the flat land skimming by in the early evening light. "You won't believe it! I've never asked Jordan what he was up to in the war. We've all wanted to forget it, I suppose. Jordan, did you win the Battle of the Marne single-handed?"

Vashti spoke quickly. Even Luz could not have sprung more alertly to his defense. "Some had to stay home and raise beef cattle so the soldiers could eat."

Thoughtlessly Leslie said, "Old men can raise beef cattle." Immediately she regretted it.

"If it hadn't of been for Texas," Vashti went on, "we probably wouldn't even have won the war."

"Well, now, Vash," Pinky drawled in mild remonstrance, "maybe that's a little bitty overspoken. But did seem every second one who got a medal was a Texan."

Leslie tried to cover the hurt. "I didn't mean—Jordan, I didn't mean———"

"That's all right," Bick said stiffly. "My father was a sick man. I was twenty-two. He died just a little after. I guess he figured it might be better in the end to raise a few hundred thousand head of beef cattle to feed the world than for me to kill a couple of Germans. Maybe he was wrong."

"Practically he was right," Leslie said quietly. "But for you he was wrong."

Now it was Adarene Morey who tried to guide the talk into impersonal paths. "Everything's changed since the war. I don't know. As if something was lost. Even old San Antonio is all changed."

"It'll be just one big flying field, the whole town, the way they're headed," Pinky predicted morosely. "We thought it was something big, time they put down Kelly Field. Now they're starting in on this new Randolph Field, they say it's going to set us back better than ten million dollars, just to lay it down. Keep on, pretty soon San Antonio can't see the sky for the wings."

"That's all right," Lew Morey said. "That's just Texas making sure they can't ever start another World War on us."

"Who'd be fool enough to start it!" scoffed Bick.

Clink-clank went the little iron gate. Quite a parade of starched white aprons and starched white coats and alert black faces beneath precarious trays. At the head of this procession, like a commanding officer, marched the dining-car steward (white). "Well, Mr. Benedict, it's mighty nice to have you traveling with us again. . . . Haven't seen you this way in a long time, Mr. Morey. . . . Miss Hake . . . uh . . ."

"I'm Mrs. Mott Snyth now. This is my husband Mr. Mott Snyth."

"Hope everything's going to suit you all right I tended to it myself personally if you find anything wrong why just send word, why, thanks now if you folks going to want breakfast it might be a good idea give us your order now, well, coffee anyway, I always say a cup of coffee first off and you can face anything. . . ."

It was not a gay meal. The little side tables had been hooked ingeniously into the wall, the couples sat two by two before the over-abundant food. Pitchers of cream, mounds of rolls, bowls of iced butter in the true tradition of North American waste. The repast finished, the six sat replete, somewhat uncomfortable, and silent. Even Vashti was strangely quiet.

"We're due in at daybreak," Bick said.

"Everything in Texas starts at daybreak," Adarene Morey complained. "Pioneer stuff." Leslie smiled at her across the aisle. Dear Adarene. Dear oasis.

Bick stood up, yawned, stretched, peered through a window at the Texas night. "I don't know how the rest of you folks feel but I'm all for letting the scenery go by until morning."

The Benedicts had the drawing room, the Moreys and the Snyths a compartment each. "Just roughing it," Pinky grinned. "But anyway it's better than on the ground like I've done a million times, with my saddle for a pillow."

Mumblemumble whisperwhisper! They all knew better than to talk aloud in those connecting cubicles.

"Jordan darling, I didn't mean it that way. I just remembered that we'd never talked about the war, I suddenly thought————"

Vashti expressed herself in whispers to Pinky. "Sometimes she says the meanest things and doesn't mean them, that I ever heard spoken."

Lucius Morey ran an investigating thumb over his chin as he stared at his reflection in the mirror of the little bedroom. "She'll be all right as soon as she gets the hang of Texas."

"She's all right now," Adarene retorted very sotto voce from the depths of her lower berth. "It's just Bick that never will be really in love with anything but Reata."

Next morning at dawn Leslie saw in the distance something that broke at last the limitless horizon. There, blue against the golden plain, were the mountains. She felt a lift, a lightness in the air. And there at the little station was Uncle Bawley towering yet blending into the landscape like the mountains themselves.

Leslie walked toward Uncle Bawley, she did not extend her hand to him she kept on walking and quite naturally walked into his arms and stayed there a moment with a feeling of having come home to someone she had known for a long long time.

"Well, there's something Holgado never saw before," Bick said.

"You better look alive, Bick!" Pinky yelled. "Uncle Bawley's going to cut you out!"

Bick grinned. "I've seen history made. Uncle Bawley with his arms around a girl."

"If I'd knowed it was so easy," Uncle Bawley said ruefully, "I'd of started earlier."

They piled into the waiting car, a glittering costly thing, elegant and sleek as Uncle Bawley's boots, but even the women recognized it as a model of vintage make.

Bick surveyed this conveyance, opulent and stuffy as a dowager in black satin. "You still pushing this ice wagon, Uncle Bawley!"

"I never drive the thing myself, I keep it for visiting royalty, like you folks. Nothing the matter with it, it sits there in the garage, the boys have to take it out and exercise it every week to keep it from going stale on me, like a horse."

Over the roads at a fearsome Texas speed. The air seemed a visible opalescent shimmer, there was about it a heady coolness, dry and bracing as a martini.

Leslie gazed about her. "I don't wish to seem too annoying, but I am going to take a number of very deep breaths." In the middle of one of these she stopped and pointed dramatically as they sped along. "They're real mountains!"

"What did you think they were? Cream puffs?" Bick said.

"I mean they're high. They're really mountains."

Bick produced statistics. "Baldy's over seven thousand feet. Sawtooth's almost eight. That right, Uncle Bawley?"

"Seven thousand nine hundred and ninety-eight," Uncle Bawley said. "Only reason I remember is I always wondered why the fella that measured it couldn't have throwed in the extra two feet, made it an even eight. Sounds higher that way. But no, he had to go and be honest."

Seen from the road as they approached it from a far distance Holgado seemed a village in itself, a collection of adobe houses, whitewashed, squatting on the plain. But presently the main house took on dimensions, sprawling like the old Main House at Benedict in a series of rooms and patios. Here were the offices, the bedrooms, the dining room, the big living room whose waxed and shining tiles were strewn with Mexican rugs and the skins of mountain lions.

Though here, as at Benedict, stuffed animal heads complete with horns manes fangs and ferocious eyes glared down from the walls upon the beholder, Leslie could regard them impersonally. They seemed to suit this house and region. They made a proper background for this giant in the canvas working clothes of a rancher.

"You have some coffee on the train?" Uncle Bawley asked. "Breakfast is ready any time you are. You folks probably want to go to your rooms first—you girls specially."

The thick-walled house was incredibly cool, no sunlight penetrated the deep window embrasures. Neat white bedrooms opened off a neat white gallery; neat white bathrooms, a haphazard Mexican chambermaid a precarious Mexican waitress, a neat black male cook in a very starched white apron and towering chef's cap.

"Well!" Leslie exclaimed coming into the cool dining room and feeling strangely fresh and gay considering the journey and the hour. "You pioneer Benedicts certainly rough it. What's that heavenly smell?"

"Ham and eggs and biscuits and steak and fried potatoes is my guess," Bick said, "if I know Uncle Bawley. And probably sausage and pancakes and maybe chicken."

"No, I mean an outside smell. I got it as I came along the veranda. A lovely scent, fresh and sweet."

"We had mountain showers," Uncle Bawley said. "That's the smell of

wet greasewood and piñón and grass, it's a nicer smell than any French
perfume.''

In came the steaming breakfast dishes in fantastic profusion, they were
ranged on the long side table against the dining-room wall.

''Oh, how lovely and lavish!'' Leslie said. ''That's the way we serve
breakfast at home.''

Vashti looked up from her plate. ''You do! For just you and Bick!''

''Oh. I meant at home in Virginia.'' A little too brightly she turned in
confusion to meet Uncle Bawley's eyes. ''Do you think it's the altitude
makes me feel so gay?''

''Let's say it's that and the company,'' Bick suggested. ''And maybe
Uncle Bawley's coffee, it's notorious, they say a pound to a cup is his rule.''

''No such thing, it only tastes like that because up here folks are already
pepped up with the air,'' Uncle Bawley said. ''Down in the brush country
you got to hop yourself up with coffee every few minutes to keep going.''

''By now, Leslie,'' Adarene Morey explained, ''you've probably noticed
that West Texans look down on East Texans, and South Texans think nothing
of the Panhandle crowd up north. Central Texas snoots the whole four
corners, and the only time they all get together is when an outsider belittles
the entire darned state.''

''That's right,'' Pinky agreed. ''Take like my maw, she used to pick on
all us kids, big and little, and we picked on each other, but let anybody
outside say a word against any of us, why we were one and indivisible.''

Blandly Lew Morey inquired, ''Bawley, you're going to show Leslie and
the girls your house, aren't you?''

''You well know I ain't.''

''But isn't this your house?'' Leslie asked.

''It's my house. But I don't live in it. I only visit here when I have
company.''

''But where . . . ?'' Startled, she stared at him.

He pointed past the veranda to an adobe house perched on a little rise a
hundred feet back from the main house. A rather shabby old structure, its
veranda slightly off plumb, its windows curtainless.

''That's the house I live in.''

''Oh, Uncle Bawley, do let me see it. You must have wonderful things
in it.''

A shout went up. Bewildered, Leslie looked from one to the other. ''Jordan, have I said something?''

''No, honey. I thought I'd told you that no woman has ever set foot in
Uncle Bawley's house, even to clean it.''

''Especially not to clean it,'' Uncle Bawley corrected.

''But I never saw a man who looked more spick-and-span than you, Uncle
Bawley,'' Leslie argued.

''Only from head to foot. Not underfoot.''

She looked at the old man, she marveled at the pain which old wounds
could continue to inflict.

It was more than five years later that Leslie finally saw this retreat in
which old Bawley Benedict nursed his loneliness and unfulfillment; this
welter of newspapers, saddles, boots, saddle soap, pipes, gourds, trophies,
pans, massive silver punch bowls, empty peach tins, time-stained copies of
the *Breeder's Gazette*. Five years later, when Jordy was four and Luz three
a female entered this sanctum. Leslie had taken the two children up to
Holgado for the cool air and the altitude. The three-year-old Luz was missing
one frantic afternoon. There was a galloping here and there by cowboys, a
calling and a searching before they came upon her. She had trotted off in

the absence of her Mexican nurse, she had made her way up the little hill
to Uncle Bawley's house, and there they found her flutterng and rummaging
ecstatically amongst the heaped-up scraps and piles of waste like a sparrow
in the dust of the road.

Now Leslie was never to forget these fist ten days at Holgado. The clear
lightness of the air exhilarated her after the humid heat of the Gulf coast
country. The mountain showers seemed to bring up from the earth a sweet
freshness, reticent but haunting.

"It smells like white freesias," Leslie said. "People are always making
a fuss about honeysuckle and roses and magnolias. Freesias have the most
exquisite scent of all."

"None of those around here," Uncle Bawley said, "and I don't know's
I'm familiar with that brand of flower. But we've got a blossom up here
comes out in the spring. It's called the Spanish dagger on account of the
sharp spikes of the plant, they can go into you like a stiletto. It's too late
now, they've gone by, but the flower is white-petaled and mighty sweet. To
my notion it's about the prettiest flower there is anywhere." He paused a
moment. "If you can liken a person to a flower, why, I'd say that's the one
you're most like."

This compliment delighted her, she repeated it to Bick that first evening
when, red-eyed and yawning, he came to their room where she already was
sitting up in bed, reading. The house was bookless except for a shelf of
technical volumes. These were ranged in the grim room that contained the
big glass-doored gun cabinets. Shining and sinister in their racks, these slim
black-barreled items of ranch household equipment did not appear anachronistic to anyone but Leslie.

The books turned out to be gnawed-looking volumes on Spanish land
grants in Texas. Intended as a baldly stated record of early land transactions
in the region, they actually were, quite unconsciously, a cloak-and-dagger
account of such skullduggery, adventure, and acquisitive ruthlessness as to
make the reader reject the whole as mythical. Settlers, pioneers, frontiersmen used cupidity against ignorance, turned land into cash and live men into
dead men with blithe ferocity. Leslie devoured them, fascinated, horrified.

"Jordan, what do you think? Uncle Bawley is turning into a ladies' man.
He told me about the Spanish dagger flower and he said he thought it was
the loveliest flower in the world. And then—pardon my pointing—he said
I was like the flower. How's that for a misogynist!"

"Uh-huh. He meant spikes and all, I suppose?"

Spiritedly she said, "I hope so. Who wants to be merely white and sweet,
like a blanc mange!"

The first evening after the very good dinner, and on each succeeding
evening, the four men gathered into the tightest of knots in one corner of
the great living room. Their talk was low-voiced but their tone had the timbre
of intensity. Occasionally a word wafted itself over to the somewhat looser
knot formed by the three semi-deserted women. Election . . . Commissioner . . . tax . . . district . . . oil . . . Congress . . . Gomez . . . precinct . . .

Vashti sometmes played a defeated game of solitaire through which she
chattered unceasingly. "Jack on the queen ten on the jack I hope it's a girl
because they're so cute to fix up with pink and hair ribbons where's that
nine for goodness' sakes but a course Pa and Mott they're yelling it's got
to be a boy whee there's that ol' nine————"

Adarene was doing a gros point chair tapestry, her basket of brilliant-hued
wools made a gay splash of color in the firelighted room. After three evenings

of this Leslie drifted casually across the room and sat down on the couch beside Bick.

Conversation ceased.

"Aren't you men being a bit too cozy?"

Bick's left ear, she noticed, was a brighter pink than usual. "This is ranch stuff, Leslie. Business."

"How fascinating! I'll listen. And learn a lot."

Lew Morey leaned toward her, he patted her knee in a strangely paternal gesture for a man of his years. "Now now you don't want to fret your head about such talk."

Suddenly she saw him clear. The bland almost expressionless face, unlined, quiet. There leaped into her mind a line she had read in a newspaper story about a frightfully rich oil man from the East. He had come to Oklahoma in the early oil days of that fantastic commonwealth, he had made his brisk millions, he had lost them almost as briskly. "They cleaned me," he had said in the newspaper account. "The still-faced men. They got to me."

The still-faced men. Bland. Nerveless. Quietly genial. Lucius Morey.

"We're fixing it so that you girls can have all those doodads you're always buying," Pinky Snyth explained, his rosy face creasing into a placating smile—a smile such as one would bestow upon an annoying and meddlesome brat. "All that stuff you're getting for that new house of yours. How d'you think poor ol' Bick's going to pay up for all that unless we figger out!"

The cow hand. The shrewd pink-cheeked curly-headed little gimlet. Turned cattle king.

Leslie settled back as for a long stay. "How right you are! I ought to know. Here I am, spending all that money without realizing how Jordan has to plan and—and devise—to get it. So now you just go on talking and I'll listen as quiet as a mouse—though I must say I think mice are awfully noisy, squeaking and scuttering around———"

Bick's voice was flat and hard. "This isn't only business. It's politics. Men's stuff."

"But darling, I was brought up on politics. You lads talk as if you hadn't heard that women have the vote. To us Washington was as next-door as Benedict is here. We were in and out like whippets. And Jordan, you know our house was crammed with political talk and career men and striped trousers and national and international what not. Go on. Talk. I love it."

They were absolutely dumb. Uncle Bawley broke the silence. "My, that's a pretty dress you're wearing, Leslie."

In disappointment she looked at him. "You too, Uncle Bawley!"

The gaze of the handsome old wreck of a giant met hers and to her amazement his faded blue eyes suddenly were deeply blue-black with the burning intensity of a young male in love.

Leslie stood up. She was furious she was confused. "You men ought to be wearing leopard skins and carrying clubs and living in caves. You date back a hundred thousand years. Politics! What's so dirty about your politics that I can't hear it! Gomez! Jett Rink! Gill Dace! And all of you. Smiling and conniving———"

Bick Benedict rose, he seemed to tower above her. "Leslie, you're not well———"

"I am well! I'm well in body and I'm well in mind. But mildew is going to set in. I can feel it. That slimy white sticky stuff that creeps into all the corners and closets down there unless you open the doors and windows and let the sun in."

Feeling rather triumphant though strangely shaky she walked across the room to where the two women sat like figures, she thought, in the fairy tale of the Sleeping Beauty. Vashti's right hand was suspended in mid-air, a playing card held in her fingers. Her mouth was open, her eyes very round. Adarene's needle was poised motionless above her embroidery frame.

"Boo!" said Leslie.

Uncle Bawley called across the room. "What do you girls say we have a sunrise breakfast tomorrow, ride up into the hills? And I'll cook."

Vashti's childlike squeal. "Ooh! I'd love it! Let's."

"Well, then, you girls better get your beauty sleep," Pinky said. "Or we won't be able to rout you out come daybreak."

Shrewishly Leslie called to him over her shoulder, "Yes, send the idiot children to bed so that you massive brains can talk in peace."

The men managed a tolerant laugh but Leslie hoped she detected in it a touch of malaise.

Adarene again began to ply her needle, in and out, in and out. She did not look up. "If you think anything you can say will make a dent in the tough hide of Texas."

"I'd like to crack their skulls together like coconut shells."

"I'm going to get me a snack before I go to bed," Vashti said.

Automatically Leslie rejected this. "After all that dinner!"

"I'm eating for two." Virtuously.

"At least," Adarene agreed. "Look, Leslie, just pay them no mind. It's the elections coming up this autumn. With Luz dead and Jett Rink off the place and that Fidel Gomez getting uppity they say, there are lots of important things to straighten out. I heard that Jett Rink was trying to make trouble with the ranch hands."

"What's that got to do with elections?"

Adarene took three or four careful stitches, the big needle went through the coarse stiff web of the material, pop pop pop. "You've never seen one of our elections, have you?"

"No. What about them?"

"Well, sometimes it gets sort of—uh—dramatic. The Mexican vote is pretty important."

"Isn't any vote important?"

"I suppose so. There are about four million whites in Texas. And about a million Mexicans."

"Whites. Mexicans. I never thought of Mexicans as—but if they vote they're citizens, aren't they?"

"Yes. Yes, of course. But———"

Vashti, slapping down the cards with the vehemence of one who is playing a losing game, was still mumbling maddeningly as she played. ". . . There! There's the deuce. . . . Come on now you ace. . . . Oh, damn!" Scrabbling the unobliging cards together she looked up, defeated. "It's real exciting at election. Regular old times, guns and all. They lock the gates and guard the fences, nobody can get out."

"Who can't?"

"Everybody. The Mexicans. The ranch hands."

"Vashti. Uh—look, Adarene. You two girls forget sometimes that I'm new to Texas. I love to know about things. Now. They lock the gates so that people can't get out at election time. Why?"

In a tone of elaborate patience, as one would speak to a backward child, Vashti said, "So they'll vote right of course, honey. So they won't go out and get mixed up with somebody'll tell 'em wrong. This way they vote like they're told to vote."

"Told by—who tells them?"

"Depends. Our place it's Pa and two three behind him. And now Pinky too, of course."

"Of course. And at Reata, who?"

Adarene rolled up her embroidery, her voice cut this interrogation. "How about a three-handed game of bridge if those mean men won't talk to us or play?" •

But Leslie leaned toward Vashti in utter concentration. "Who at Reata?"

"Oh goodness, I don't know, I don't pay much attention to men's stuff like elections and so on. Luz, she used to be the real boss. She sure was the point when it came to rounding up the Mexicans. Then there was Jett Rink, of course, drunk as a sheep election time but that always made him tougher and they were scared of him. And then Fidel Gomez around Nopal and Benedict, all the Mexicans there."

Adarene Morey stood up. "Girls, I think I'll go to bed, get my beauty sleep if we're going to get up before dawn. How about you, Vashti?"

"I ain't really sleepy. We slept so late this morning. Pinky never batted an eye till seven. I thought he was dead. It's this mountain air and all, I guess."

"Listen a minute, Vashti. What offices do they vote for? Local? State? National?"

"H'm? Oh. I don't know, rightly. Do you, Adarene? I don't pay any attention. Commissioners, I guess. Anyway, for around here. Of course everybody is tied up with the ranches, miles and miles around. Why, they wouldn't be alive if it wasn't for us, it's their living, hauling cattle, working cattle, supplies and stuff and all that goes with it. I don't know, don't ask *me,* Pinky says I'm a nitwit about stuff like that. Whyn't you ask Bick? Bick'll explain to you all about it. I'd like a sandwich or something, wouldn't you, girls? And a glass of milk and maybe some of that pie left over if there is any. Let's raid the icebox, maybe the boys will too."

Leslie glanced toward the four men at the far end of the room. Their heads were close together, their voices low, their shoulders hunched.

"No, I think I'll take Adarene's advice and go to bed. And read."

"You can take my movie magazine I bought in San Antonio, I'm through with it."

Adarene laid a hand lightly on Leslie's arm. "Stop looking like Lady Macbeth, honey. Take Texas the way Texas takes bourbon. Straight. It goes down easier."

"All I know is," Vashti now was prattling on, "Mott says less'n ten years from now about six men'll be running the whole of Texas. Gabe Target he says, and Ollie Whiteside if he gets Judge, and Lew and a course Bick and Pinky—Mott, I mean."

At ten o'clock Leslie, reading in bed, smelled the aroma of coffee, the state nightcap. The strong smell of the brew made her slightly queasy, she wished Bick would come in and open another window. She took deep grateful breaths of the cool sweet air. There was no sound. The men must be in the kitchen at the far end of the house. She resumed her reading of the naïve volume on Spanish land grants. She must have dozed a bit for suddenly Bick was in the room, he was pulling off his boots with a little grunt.

"Jordan! I must have dropped off like a dozy old lady. It's this heavenly air."

Bick Benedict did not reply. He regarded his bride with a hard and hostile eye. She looked very plain. Her habit of reading in bed through long night hours had made spectacles advisable and these were of the owlish horn-rimmed variety. The bare electric light bulb was glaring down on her face. As always, when emotionally disturbed or when reading absorbedly, she had wound and unwound tendrils of her hair so that now she presented a Medusa aspect. There was a small highlight of cold cream on one cheek. Finally, the slight cast that usually made more piquant the beauty of her eyes now was exaggerated under the strain of reading beneath the glaring white light.

Harsh unspoken words formed in Bick Benedict's mind as he went about the business of preparing for bed. So this was Leslie Lynnton the Virginia belle and beauty that he had split a gut to get. No Texas girl good enough, huh? Oh no!

She now removed her glasses and regarded him thoughtfully, tapping her teeth with her spectacle bows. She had closed her book, one finger inserted to keep her place. He's angry, she told herself, because I wanted to hear the talk. And I suppose I wasn't very polite. That cave-man stuff.

"This old book is fascinating, it's about Spanish land grants. It says in those days they measured by varas. Do you know what a vara is?"

He did not reply.

Mm. So you won't talk, eh? She went on then, equably. "They cut a switch off a tree—about a yard long, it says—and that's what they measured the land with. A vara's length. A switch's length. And then sometimes they measured by the wagon wheel, it says. They tied a red rag to a wheel spoke and walked behind the wagon and every time the red rag flashed round it was roughly fifteen feet. Isn't that sweet! No wonder people could have million-acre ranches—I mean————"

In his pajamas he was standing before the wall mirror running an investigating hand over his cheek. He regarded his own image intently. "Why, thanks," he said. "Can you tell me more about Texas? It's all so fascinating."

"Sorry about my cave-man speech, darling. I'll apologize tomorrow to the others, first thing."

"That's big of you." He came to the foot of the bed and stood glaring at her in anger. His diction was pure Harvard and hard-bitten. "You certainly distinguished yourself this evening."

"Sh! Jordan! They can hear every word in every room along this veranda."

"That's fine. And we heard every word you said in there too, tonight. Dirty politics! And we date back a hundred thousand years! Who the hell do you think you are! Joan of Arc or something! "

She held her breath as the words rang through the little stark white bedroom. They were holding their breath too, she thought, and hearing all this, there in those other little stark white bedrooms along the gallery. "I said I'm sorry about the name-calling. It was impolite. But in principle I was right."

"You come down here and try to tell us how to run the ranch! And the town! And the state! I swear to God I think you're crazy! Insulting my friends. I've stood it because of your—the way you feel just now. I'm through with that. You're my wife, you're Mrs. Jordan Benedict. When the hell are you going to settle down and behave like everybody else!"

She got out of bed then and stood facing him, the book still in her hand, pressed against the laces at her breast. "Never."

They stood glaring at each other. Automatically his hand came up. He stared down at it. Dropped it to his side.

"I almost hit you."

"I know. My darling."

"You're running around in your bare feet. Cold."

"It doesn't matter."

"Get back into bed."

Shivering she crept between the covers. He turned out the light.

Silence in the little room, silence in all the little rooms, silence in the dark fragrant Texas night so full of turmoil and unrest and conflict.

"Oh, Jordan, I wish we could live up here in the mountains. I wish we could stay up here and Uncle Bawley could run Reata. Couldn't he? Couldn't he?"

"Get this. If you can understand anything that isn't Virginia and pink coats and hunt dinners and Washington tea parties. Just get this. I run Reata. I run Holgado. I run the damn wet Humedo Division and Los Gatos too and a lot you've never heard of. Everything in them and on them is run by me. I run everything and everyone that has the Reata brand on it."

"Does that include me?"

"Dramatizing yourself, like a cheap movie." Silence again. He spoke, his resentment hung almost a palpable thing in the darkness. "Tired. The hardest kind of day's work doesn't wear me down like ten minutes of this goddamned wrangling. I'm not used to it."

"You're not used to marriage. . . . Jordan, who was it said that thing about power?"

"Oh, Christ! I don't know who said anything about power."

"Papa used to quote it. He said————"

"Papa Papa! Forget Papa, will you!"

She lay very still, concentrating. The cool still fragrant mountain night. Suddenly she sat bolt upright. Her low vibrant voice hung in the darkness. "Power corrupts. That's it. I can't remember who said it. An English statesman I think. He said power corrupts. And absolute power corrupts absolutely. Jordan."

But he did not hear her. He was asleep.

19

IT WAS DARKER than night when the Mexican maid brought the morning coffee to their room. But all Holgado was astir. Hoofbeats. The deep reverberations of powerful motor vehicles, the sound intensified on the thin mountain air. The hiss and drum of Spanish spoken along the corridors. The tap-tap of men's boot heels, the clink of spurs. The scampering feet of Mexican servitude—a sound that Leslie found irksome. "They don't walk. They run. On their heels. I should think it would shatter their gizzards." But the other Texas morning sounds she loved. . . . Sí sí señor . . . Momento señora . . . Las botas, sí . . . Hace mucho frío . . .

Bick emerged from the bathroom fully dressed. Tiptoeing. He peered toward her bed, the bathroom light behind him.

"I'm awake."

"Vashti's complaining about the cold."

"It's heaven."

Last night's quarrel was cast aside like a soiled garment discarded in the fresh new day. "If we're going to make that fool sunrise breakfast of Bawley's. Even you girls can't make the sun wait while you dress."

She threw aside the covers, sat a moment hugging her shoulders. "I'll be dressed in fifteen minutes. I must say I'd like sunrises just as well if they could run them later in the morning."

"I don't know—is this ride up the trail good for you now? How about you girls taking a car instead? We boys can get a head start riding."

"The first time I met you you bragged that your mother practically produced you on horseback."

"She was a Texan."

"Even for Texans the equipment is, I believe, standard."

He grinned. "See you later. I'm going down to the corral. I'll pick a gentled one for you."

She was still slim and almost boyish in her riding clothes. As she came along the veranda she could hear Uncle Bawley's voice from the direction of the dining room, there was a sharp edge to his usual tone of almost caressing gentleness. "No, I don't want any cook along, I'm going to do the cooking myself. How about a couple dozen those Mexican quail, I'll rig up an asador over the fire, they'll make good breakfast eating, with bacon."

Vashti and Adarene were not yet down. It was still dark, the lights shone everywhere about the place. In her hand she carried the book on Spanish land grants, she had finished it and now she would tuck it back into the sparse shelf in the gun room just off the patio. She opened the door, peered into the grim unlighted room, her hand groping for the electric switch. A sound, a little quick startled sound. She hesitated. Waited. Silence. But there was a sense of presence there, of a something that held its breath and waited. Oh, pooh, a mouse. Her fingers found the light, flicked it on.

A boy, dark ragged shaking, was flattened against the whitewashed wall, the palms of his hands were spread against it like one crucified, the emaciated body was trying to press into the wall itself. The black eyes, fixed in a frantic stare, became imploring as the eyelids relaxed a trifle and a caught breath lifted the rags on his breast. Before she darted out and shut the door, before she lifted her voice to call, in that split second her inner voice said, That was Fear you just saw that wasn't flesh and blood that was blind naked Fear in the form of a man. Then she called, a note of hysteria in her voice. "Uncle Bawley! Uncle Bawley! Uncle Bawley!"

He was there with incredible swiftness, speeded by the urgency in her voice, towering above her, his hands on her shoulders. "What's wrong! Leslie!"

"In there. There's a—there's somebody hiding in there."

He flung open the gun-room door. The boy was on the floor, a heap on the floor like a mop like a rag. Speaking in Spanish Uncle Bawley said, "Get up!" The boy did not move. Uncle Bawley picked him up as you would a wet dog, gingerly, by the neck and shoulders and half carried half dragged him along the floor to the patio.

"No," Leslie whispered. "No. Don't——"

"It's all right. Happens every day." Uncle Bawley looked enormous above the little heap of rags on the floor. "Nobody's going to hurt him. He's just a wetback."

"A what?"

"Wetback. Swum or waded the river between Mexico and here, must have walked a hundred miles and more."

Foolishly she stammered, "What river?"

"Now Leslie! Rio Grande of course. They do it all the time." Now he leaned over the boy, he spoke to him in Spanish, Leslie caught a word here and there. In Uncle Bawley's voice there was something that caused the bundle of rags to raise its head. Leslie's Spanish lessons bore fruit now. A familiar Spanish word, the inflection of Uncle Bawley's voice, her own instinct combined to give her the sense of what was being said. Come come, boy, stand up! You have waded the Rio Grande you have walked the long miles, that takes the courage of a man. Don't crouch there then like a dog.

No one will hurt you. Stand up! You are a man! He stirred the bundle with the toe of his shining boot.

The rags moved, the thing got to its feet, the face was a mask of abject terror and glimmering hope mingled. Seventeen, perhaps. A skeleton.

"How long have you been in there?"

"This morning only. I walked all night and the night before and the night before and before. By day I lay where I could, hiding."

"Food?"

The shoulders came up, the bony hands spread.

"Have you seen Immigration Officers or Rangers these past nights?"

"Once men passed near me as I lay in a ditch. I prayed I pressed deep into the ground I pushed myself into the desert I was the desert I prayed to the Miraculous Christ and to the Señor de Chalma and to the Virgin of Guadalupe and they heard and my prayers were answered."

"I bet," said Uncle Bawley.

The boy was still talking, a stream of words poured out in relief and hysteria and hope.

"Tell me," Leslie said. "I only catch a word here and there."

"It's nothing, Leslie. Happens all the time I tell you. About fifty sixty thousand of these wetbacks slip out of Mexico every year, swim or wade the Rio Grande where it's shallow, travel by night and hole up by day. The Border Patrol and the Immigration boys and Rangers and all, they can't keep all of them out. Sometimes they make it, a lot of 'em are caught and thrown back. Sometimes they're shot by mistake, sometimes they wander around and starve. This skin-and-bones says he's been eating rats."

"No!" She was stiff with horror.

"But he ought've come in with the regular Mexican labor lot. Thousands of them brought across legally here to Texas. Pick the cotton and the crops, fruit and vegetables in the Valley, and so on. He says he tried to make it, they were full up."

"I'm going to call Jordan."

Instantly Uncle Bawley raised his hand. "Nope. Jordan's against it. He'd call the Immigration boys come and get him."

"He wouldn't!"

Uncle Bawley glanced over his shoulder. "If Bick comes along now and sees the boy he'll turn him in. He's set against it I tell you."

She stared at him. "If I don't call Jordan what will you do?"

"Feed him give him some decent rags turn him loose tonight."

She stared now at the boy, the black eyes were fixed on her, they shifted then to the great booted towering figure. "Do that," she said. "Do that." Her lips felt stiff.

Uncle Bawley turned to the boy. He spoke again in Spanish, he pointed to his own shabby house on the hillock behind the main ranch house. "Has anyone else seen you?" The boy shook his head. "That house. Run there now. No. Wait. I'll take you."

Leslie stood in the patio. She watched the two quickly ascend the little slope, Uncle Bawley's huge bulk just behind the shadowy figure, screening him. She stood there, waiting, peering into the dark. She was there, outlined against the patio light, when Uncle Bawley emerged and joined her.

"What you getting upset about, Leslie? Immigration fellas come along looking for hide-outs the way they sometimes do, why, they wouldn't dast go near my house up there, they well know nobody's allowed, I'd take their jobs away from them if they did."

She was completely bewildered. She thought, What a statement! "I'm so mixed up," she stammered.

"What you so upset about, Leslie?" In that soft strangely musical voice. "He's mostly Mexican Indian, that boy, he's used to traveling hundreds of miles afoot." A tiny door in a corner of her memory opened and a handful of words flashed out. Walk! You can't walk. Nobody walks in Texas, only the Mexicans. "Anyway," Uncle Bawley went on, "he'll have a regular fiesta today, sleep in a corner all day up there, I'll fetch him up coffee now and a lot of good grub, give him pants and a shirt and shoes—he'll sell the shoes first off———"

"How do you know Jordan would have turned him back! I don't believe it. He isn't like that. In the Valley . . . I saw . . . there's a horrid man called Gomez . . ."

He came to her, his great hand on her shoulder, he looked down at her. "Now now Leslie girl, nothing to go to bawling about, just another Mexican Indian coming back to Tejas, you might almost say. It's only that Bick's made a rule against it here at Holgado, so near the border, and all over Reata. And he's right. Texas can't take in all of Mexico's misfits. It's illegal, it makes big trouble. If they come in with the seasonal labor migration, that's different that's in the law. Haul 'em in, pay 'em a couple of dollars, haul 'em back, well and good. But a kid crawls in, starving like that one, I pay Bick no mind. Only let's keep this just between us, you and me. H'm?"

"Yes, Uncle Bawley. I wish I could get it all straight in my mind. They use them. Cheap. And then throw them back, like old rags. A century of it but it's never really worked out right, has it?"

Evasively, "Where's the rest of the boys and girls, I wonder, haven't heard a peep out of the Moreys or the———" His voice trailed off. He faced Leslie squarely. "Strictly speaking—which hardly anybody does—why, what with picking the cotton and the fruit and now the Valley is all planted with vegetables, a big new industry, and the old railroad building days and all, why you might say the whole of Texas was built on the backs of boys like that one. On the bent backs of Mexicans. Don't let on to Bick I said that."

Through her tears she looked up at him and the blur wiped the lines from the face, the little sag from the shoulders. With a gesture utterly unpremeditated, wanton, overpowering, she threw her arms about his neck she brought the fine old head down to hers, she kissed him full on the lips, long hard lasting.

Horrified. "Forgive me. What is the matter with me! Uncle Bawley!"

He stood a moment, his arms hanging at his sides. "My, that was nice," he said quietly. "But you ever get a notion to do that again, Leslie, I'll turn you over my knee and spank you good. Hear me."

"Yes, Uncle Bawley."

Vashti's voice high and shrill from the direction of the guest rooms. "Adarene! Leslie! Where's everybody got to!"

Uncle Bawley turned and walked into the house.

Adarene's voice, "I'm coming. We overslept."

Pinky skipping along the gallery toward the patio. "Now Vash, don't you go to eating before breakfast."

"Why don't we get going, then! I'm starved."

"All right. Cup of coffee."

Fifteen minutes later they clattered out in the cool scented darkness, Bick keeping close to Leslie. Adarene sat very straight in the saddle. "Rides like a Yankee," Lucius Morey commented. "Adarene never got over that school she went to, up the Hudson."

Vashti, an imposing mound of flesh looming ahead in the first faint dawn, rode cowboy fashion, one vast hip slipped to the side, one arm hanging loose or waving in the air, she kept up with the men and greeted the dawn like a Comanche on the warpath. The hills loomed grey then brown then rose then burst into scarlet. The plains, green and gold, ran to meet them.

"Oh, Jordan!"

"Not bad, huh?"

"The light, the curious light. Not like anything in America. It's Egypt—with the Alps thrown in."

"Egypt and Alps hell! It's Texas."

A streak of gold-beige, like a flash of smoky sunlight, shot across the nearby brush and vanished behind a hillock.

"Antelope," said Bick.

He was riding at Leslie's left, Uncle Bawley was at her right. "Uncle Bawley, you told me that there are more cattle than people in Texas," Leslie said. "But I never see any. Look. Miles and miles and miles, but not a four-footed thing."

"They like the brush," Uncle Bawley explained. "And the quiet places away from the roads and highways. Maybe the old wild Longhorn strain ain't all bred out of them. Like me."

"And cowboys. Where do you keep them? I saw more cowboys in the movies at home. Those strong silent handsome males were all over the place—in the pictures. My sister Lacey writes and asks me————"

"Strong silent clabbermouths! Cow hands talk all the time, they're lonely people, they'll talk to anybody. If they can't talk they sing to themselves or to the cows."

"Movies!" scoffed Bick. "Movies and those rodeos at Madison Square Garden and around, they give people the impression that a cow hand goes out and throws a steer every morning before breakfast, just for exercise. It's a technique, like any other profession, you have to have a gift for it, you have to spend years learning it, it's something you have to have handed down from father to son. I did, and my father did, and my son's going to."

"That's right," said Uncle Bawley. "They write to Bick all the time, and they write to me and the big ranches around, college kids that want to be cowboys. They say they can ride a horse, they ride on the farm in Vermont or Kansas or someplace, and they ride in Central Park in New York, they say they want to learn to be cowboys. Well, say, I wouldn't have them free, they ain't worth picking up off the ground after the horse has threw them."

Suddenly, "Look, Leslie," Bick said, and pointed to a small herd gloomily regarding the riders from the range fence.

Leslie stared at the animals, they returned her stare glumly, hunched near the fence, their shaggy heads and bald faces, their humped backs and short-haired hides giving them the aspect of monsters in a nightmare. "What are they! They're frightening!"

"Now, Bick, don't you go making me out a fool, front of Leslie."

Bick was laughing, and the riders ahead were pointing and grinning back at Uncle Bawley. "They're called cattlo. Tell her, Bawley."

Ruefully Uncle Bawley eyed the weird creatures so mournfully returning his gaze as the little cavalcade rode by. "That's right—cattlo. It's a word made up out of cattle and buffalo and that's what those critters are, they're bred up out of cattle and buffalo, bred years back to see if we couldn't fetch something the heat and the ticks wouldn't get to."

"You got something sure enough," Bick grinned.

"I don't know's they're much meaner-looking than those critters you're talking so big about, Herefords bred to those old humpy sloe-eyed beasts you're always yapping about. Kashmirs! And Brahmans. Camels with an underslung chassis, that's what they are. Cows with humps on their backs. It ain't in nature!''

But Bick laughed as he rode along. "Just you wait, Bawley, you're going to see a breed that'll make cattle history before Gill Dace and I finish with them.''

Pinky turned in his saddle to shout back to them. "I never heard so much talking a-horseback in my whole life. Who ever heard of talking riding!''

"It's me," Leslie called to him. "I have to talk to them riding because it's the only time they ever sit down.''

"I'll go along ahead," Uncle Bawley said, "get a fire going and the skillet on." He was off with a clatter and a whoosh. The other horses tried to follow but the big man on the powerful horse outdistanced them.

"That horse of Bawley's," Bick explained, as he eyed Leslie with some concern after their spurt of sudden speed, "is the fastest thing in Jeff Davis County and maybe in Texas. For riding, that is. And look at the build of him! A regular galon for size.''

"He'd have to be huge to carry around that mountain of a man. Uh, sorry, dear, but I feel a question coming on. Galon? What's a galon?''

As they jogged along with the rose of sunrise reflected in their faces, "Well, let's see. I just used the word unconsciously. The Mexicans call a big horse a galon, it's a horse they used to have for hauling, not for riding. Before machinery did the work. They say that in the war for Texas Independence the Mexicans would hear the American teamsters yelling at those big square pudding-footed horses going through the Texas sand and mud and clay, hauling the heavy stuff of war. The teamsters would yell to the horses, 'G'long! G'long!' Get along, get along, see? So the Mexicans thought a heavy horse was a galon.''

"True?''

"True enough. Anyway, it's fun telling you tall Texas tales. You always look like a little girl who's hearing Cinderella for the first time.''

"Antelopes and galons and cattlos and sunrise and quail for breakfast———''

"And me.''

"And you.''

"And Vashti.''

"Jordan, we're quite near the Mexican border, aren't we?''

"Not far.''

"If we were to meet a wetback now—just one poor miserable Mexican wetback—what would you do?''

"Dear little Yankee, do you think wetbacks go dripping along the road in daylight carrying a printed sign that says I Am a Wetback?''

"No, but if you did see one, there in the ditch, hiding. What would you do? Would you pass him by, would you help him, would you turn him in?''

"You know what happens to little girls who play with matches, don't you? They get burned.''

"Oh, Jordan, I'm just trying to get things straight in my mind. It's all so new to me and some of it's fascinating and some of it's horrible. Labor, almost like slaves, but that's legal. Wetbacks, but that isn't legal. You all use the Mexican vote in Benedict and the whole county———''

"Uh-huh. Like your Negro vote in the South.''

"Yes, but that doesn't make it right.''

"Honey, if I'd known you were going to turn into a Do-Gooder I'd have married any nice comfortable Texas girl and damned well let you wrestle with Red Coat and his dandy little Principality. I'll bet you'd have had a fine time straightening out the Labor Situation in the Schleppenhausen or wherever it is he rules. . . . Come on, they're all miles ahead of us. Let's really ride before they send back a search party for us."

Clattering down the main road, then off on a dirt side road and up the narrow trail with the smoke of Uncle Bawley's fire pointing the way and the scent of Uncle Bawley's coffee and quail and bacon. He was squatting Mexican fashion in front of the fire of mesquite, the plump quail were roasting on an improvised spit and the bacon was slowly sizzling in the pan. The others already were sipping burning-hot black coffee as they stood about the fire.

"Mm, smells divine!" Leslie said.

"Let me warn you, Yankee," Bick said. "Before you begin to complain. Texas quail are tough as golf balls."

"Let me help, Uncle Bawley," Leslie offered. "I'll baste them. That'll make them tender."

"He'll never let you," Vashti said. "Uncle Bawley is a real batch, he likes to do things his own way. Texas way."

"No different from anybody else," Uncle Bawley argued. "Cooking over an open fire is cooking over an open fire, no matter where." He was lifting the crisp strips of dripping bacon out of the pan as they curled and sizzled, he looked about him for an absorbent receptacle on which to place them to drain until the quail should be golden brown. His wandering gaze—the eye of the practiced rancher and camper—fell on a nearby clop of old sun-dried cow dung; porous, dehydrated as a sponge or a blotter. Delicately, methodically, he placed the first strip of bacon, and the second and third, on top of this natural draining surface. "No different from anybody else," Uncle Bawley repeated. "Texans aren't, only maybe some little ways."

Leslie began to laugh, peal after peal, helplessly. The others stared at her, surprised, vaguely resentful but scrupulously polite.

20

THE BOY WAS named Jordan. Jordan Benedict Fourth. Like royalty. Leslie had objected to no avail. It became Jordy for short in order not to confuse him with his father, Jordan Third.

"Yes, I know there's been a Jordan in the family for a century. Jordan First Second Third and now Fourth. But remember what happened to all those dynasty boys? Those Ptolemys and the Louis lads and the Charleses?"

"What would you call him?"

"David."

"David! What David?"

"The boy with the slingshot. The one who killed the giant Goliath."

"That's a nice bloodthirsty idea."

Bick Benedict's happiness was touching to see. "But he's no Benedict," Bick said, regarding the black-haired dark-eyed morsel. "He's his mother's son. I've been canceled out of the whole transaction."

"You're just disappointed because he didn't turn out to be that perfect Hereford-Kashmir bull calf you've been trying to produce."

A month later Vashti Hake Snyth presented Pinky with twin daughters. Mercifully, old Cliff Hake had died just before the birth of the twins. The mammoth matron made no secret of her disappointment. "In a way I'm glad Pa went before the twins came. He was mad enough when I was born. They say he wouldn't speak to Ma for a month after. He'd prolly have disinherited me, seeing these, or shot Mott for a Texas traitor."

She named the plump girl babies Yula Belle and Lula Belle. As they grew in length and width and attained young girlhood they were fated to be known to the undazzled swains for five hundred miles in every direction as the Cow Belles.

Vashti's plan for at least one of these stolid morsels was confided with her usual subtlety to Bick and Leslie.

"Your Jordy'll have to marry one of 'em, stands to reason. No crawling out of it this time, with two of them waiting."

"Both or nothing," Bick said.

To Bick Leslie said, not altogether humorously, "Vashti as my Jordy's mother-in-law! I'd send him to Tibet, rather, and have him brought up a lama in a lamasery."

"Don't you worry. Jordan Benedict Fourth is going to be a tough Texas cowman. Nobody'll have to tell him where to head in. He'll take care of himself."

Jordy Benedict was scarcely a month old when his father gave him his first reata, his boots, his Stetson his saddle, all initialed all stamped with the Reata Ranch brand. As he outgrew the tiny boots expressly made for him fresh ones were ordered, exquisitely soft bits of leather fashioned by the hands of the craftsman Ildefonso Mezo. When the boy was two years old Ildefonso had taken the baby foot in his brown sensitive hand. He saw that it was not high-arched like the feet of a century of booted Benedicts. Hesitantly, frowning a little, the boy's small foot in his palm, he looked up at Bick Benedict.

"Plana." He ran a finger over the instep. "Flat. This is more the foot of a dancer."

"Dancer!" yelled Bick.

"This is not the foot of a jinete. It is not a foot for the stirrup."

"It damned well will be."

At three, arrayed in full cowboy regalia, the boy had been lifted to the horse's back. Bick himself had set him there, had placed the reins in the baby fingers, had remained alongside, mounted on his own horse while Leslie stood by tense with fear. The child had sat a moment in frozen silence, his eyes wide, his mouth an open oval of terror. Suddenly he broke, he began to slip off the saddle, he screamed to be taken down. Down! Down!

Bick was disgusted. "I rode before I could walk."

"He's only a baby," Leslie said, her arms about the screaming child.

"When I was his age I yelled to be put on a horse, not taken off. If they didn't put me on I began to climb up his legs or tail or something. Ask anybody. Ask Polo."

"All right, that was very cute, but that was you. This is another person. Maybe he just doesn't like horses. Maybe he doesn't like riding. Maybe he's a walker like his mother."

"He's a Benedict and I'm going to make a horseman out of him if I have to tie him to do it."

"You've been playing God so long you think you run the world."

"I run the part of it that's mine."

"He's not yours. He's yours and mine. And not even ours. He's himself. Suppose he doesn't like sitting in the saddle from morning to night! If there's something else he wants to do I won't care if he can't tell a horse from a cow. There are important things in the world outside Reata. Outside Benedict. Even outside Texas!"

"Not to me."

"I think you actually mean that."

"Damn right I do."

But this came later. Just now the boy was seven months old. Leslie longed to have her father see him; to show him to her mother and her friends. She began to plan a Virginia visit. "It's been almost a year and a half. I can hardly believe it. Jordy'll be all grown up before they see him."

"Why don't they all come here for a visit?" Bick suggested.

"I wrote them. But Papa can't get away just now. Lacey's got a beau who isn't safe to leave she says. Mama alone . . . ?"

"You're right." Hastily.

"I feel so—I don't know—kind of listless and no appetite and this morning———" She stopped, struck by a sudden shattering suspicion.

Doctor Tom had made the suspicion a reality. "No!" Leslie, appalled, had rejected the diagnosis. "I can't! Jordy's only seven months old!"

"Everything grows fast in Texas."

"I won't! There'll be only—let's see—nine—sixteen months between them. I won't!"

"You're a healthy young woman. It'll be all right, Leslie. If this one's a girl you'll have a nice start toward a real family, all in about two years." Doctor Tom regarded her with keen kind eyes. "It's better this way. Something—two somethings—real and important to tie you to Texas."

Bick had been startled, then hilarious and definitely pleased with himself. "I'll consent to a girl this time, just to show you I'm no pasha."

Half laughing half crying, "I'm like one of the Mexican brides. I haven't even had a chance to wear my trousseau dresses. They'll be museum pieces."

"Give them to the Mexican girls around the house."

"Mama would sue." A terrible thought struck her. "Now I can't go home."

"Next year then, honey. In triumph. With two babies. Don't forget to show them to that duke or whatever he was, in the pink coat. I'll bet he couldn't have———"

"Oh, I wouldn't be so sure. He seemed to me quite a talented young man." She felt irritable, restless, trapped. "I wish I could dress up and sit at a restaurant table and hear some music. And even dance, perhaps. I look awful. My skin is like a crocodile's. I hear that dresses are longer and waistlines shorter and the boyish bob is out. I feel like a squaw."

"I can't get away for a long trip now. Anyway, you don't feel up to it. Tell you what, let's run down to Viento and stay at the Hake for a couple of days."

"Hake. If it's anything like———"

"It's quite a hotel. Music and the Seville Room and hostesses and a gold-and-marble lobby, all new. Didn't I ever tell you about the Hake? Besides, this is Fiesta week down there."

"Crowded."

"We'll be all right. We keep a big suite at the Hake the year round. It's quite a story. Old Cliff Hake built the hotel to spite the Jaggers outfit at the old Lone Star House. He was staying at the Lone Star and he got good and boiled one night and thought he was back in the old days fifty years ago. He ran out of his own liquor and forgot all about Texas being dry, began shooting up the Coffee Shoppe, poor old maverick, and then he shot his way into the lobby, there was a Baptist Bible Society Convention going on———"

"Oh, Jordan, you're making this up!"

"Ask Vashti. Ask anybody. After that they wouldn't give him a room at the Lone Star. Old Cliff was so mad he said he'd build a new modern hotel that would put the old Lone Star out of business and he sure did. The night of the opening he and Vashti led the grand march in the ballroom, you had to dress in Spanish costume, the invitations said Frontier Fiesta, Cliff was drunk as an owl and Vashti wasn't exactly cold sober. Well, guests began playing hide-and-seek behind those new marble pillars in the lobby, dodging bullets.''

"Poor little man,'' said Leslie. "Living in a day that is gone.''

Bick stared. "I wouldn't put it exactly that way. Cliff was modern as the next one.''

The Vientecito trip was quite a success. Leslie was amazed at the natural beauty of the thriving little city, perched as it was on the high bluff overlooking Vientecito Bay and the Gulf of Mexico beyond.

"It's dazzling!'' she exclaimed as she and Bick drove along the miles of waterfront. "In any other country in the world it would be a Riviera, with casinos and beaches and restaurants and all that dreadful stuff. Miles and miles and miles of waterfront! Jordan, let's get out and walk. Really walk.''

"Walk! What for?''

"What does anybody walk for!''

"I never could figure out.''

The long promenade was strangely deserted, even the Fiesta crowds only drove briskly by, staring at the brilliant expanse of rolling waters as at some strange and unapproachable phenomenon of nature. Boats bobbed at the piers, sails glinted against the horizon. The man and woman walked alone, two figures against the background of sky and water, no other living thing moved except the swooping gulls and an occasional Mexican fisherman sitting hunched over his crude pole at the edge of the breakwater. The wind blew, it whipped you along if you went with it or buffeted you if you went against it, there was none of the exhilarating salty tang of ocean air.

Leslie drew in a few experimental deep breaths. Nothing happened. "Had enough?'' Bick asked.

"Why doesn't it make me feel terrific?''

"Uh—how would you like to go out in one of the boats? I always keep a boat here and so does Roady. And there's the speed boat too, if you want to hit it up.''

"Boat. Oh, I think boats aren't the thing for me just now————''

The bright thriving city was in gala dress. Plump matrons in fringed silk shawls and high combs and mantillas, mahogany giants in costumes that were an impartial mixture of late Texas and early buccaneer thronged the streets, the Hake lobby. Mexican food was dispensed at street corners, signs worded in Spanish proclaimed this attraction or that, there was a gigantic parade which Bick and Leslie and an assortment of unexpected guests (true to the state custom) watched from the windows of the big Benedict suite. Float after float rumbled past, bunting-draped flower-festooned; Spanish costumes, Mexican costumes; charro costumes, vaquero costumes, señoritas, ruffled long-skirted dancers, grandees, pirates, conquistadores, toreros, Spanish music, Mexican music; Miss Charlene "Cookie'' Tacker, voted Queen of this year's Fiesta, held royal court atop a vast moving platform transformed for the occasion from its prosaic everyday aspect as Baumer's Trucking and Hauling vehicle. Men and women in satins and sombreros astride creamy palominos. The horses, glinting in the sun, looked like mythical creatures in a child's fairy tale. Skittish quarter horses prancing and sidling. False ferocious mustaches and beards, grandees in goatees.

"You all right, Leslie?''

"I'm wonderful.''

"You don't want to get all tired out. Maybe you'd better go in and rest for a while. Lie down. This'll be going on for hours.''

"I love it. After it's finished—later—let's go down in the lobby. I want to look at all the people."

"An awful jam down there. We'd better have dinner served up here."

"Oh, no! No! I want to have it in the restaurant. It's—it's kind of stimulating to be in a crowd again. People, lots and lots of people."

"Pretty rough down there. . . . All right all right. I'll reserve a table. I hope. But it's late."

"Never too late for a Benedict," the dining-room telephone assured him.

The parade the music the clamor the crowds streamed and blared and shouted on and on in the street below. At last, baffled, Leslie asked her question. "But where are the Mexicans? It's all about Spain and Mexico and old Texas. Where are they? All the people in the parade and even on the streets are what you call—well—Anglo."

"Uh—oh, they have a celebration of their own another day—a real Mexican Fiesta over in the Mexican part of town."

"Mexican Americans who live here in Vientecito?"

" Well, sure."

"I suppose Coronado and all those conquistadores you're always naming everything after were one hundred percent white Protestant Americans."

"You going to start all that again? Come on now, this is Fiesta, Yankee. No fair crabbing."

The hotel lobby fascinated her. Vast, marble-columned, it was, architecturally, a blend of Roman bath and Byzantine bordello. Gigantic men in boots and ten-gallon hats lolled in the stupendous leather chairs amongst the mottled marble and the potted palms. The Mexican bellboys, slim and elegant in their tight uniforms, agile as eels, were in startling contrast with the monolithic men whose bags they carried, whose errands they ran.

Clearing a path ahead of her, battling his way through the lobby mob . . . Hi, Bick! . . . Bick, you old maverick, where you been all these . . . Howdy, Bick! Say, I'd like for you to meet my wife she's right over there. . . . What you doing in this stampede! . . .

A corner in a far end of the room near a pillar and beneath a gigantic palm. The assistant manager magically produced a chair. Here you are, Mrs. Benedict, right in the middle of the roundup. You want to look out, Bick, she don't get tromped the way they're milling around today.

Bick was puzzled. "It doesn't seem like you, Leslie, wanting to get into the middle of a mob like this."

"I know. I suppose I'm hungry for people. Crowds of people. Once in a while it's sort of exhilarating."

"Will you be all right here for a minute? I'll just butter up those people in the dining room so we'll have a decent table. The Beezers are here, they're going to eat with us, and the Caldwells and Jim and Mamie Hatton—you met the Hattons, remember? At Len's?"

"Yes, of course." Brightly. Hattons?

The clamor was tremendous. She enjoyed it. She seemed to draw in through her skin and her senses a kind of vitality from the sheer strength and high spirits that flowed from these sun-soaked beef-fed people. Quietly she sat in her corner in her pretty trousseau dress, a bit snug for her now, and watched the surge and flow of these pseudo-Spanish and mock-Mexican Texans in their Fiesta finery.

"Howdy, Miz Benedict."

Jett Rink in his good Stetson and his good handmade boots and his clean canvas clothes. "Jett!"

"Yes ma'am. I watched for you to come down. I knew you had to,

sometime. I heard you was here. And I was across the street watching the
parade, I seen you—saw you—at the window.''

Seen you saw you. The schoolteacher wife. "How are you, Jett?"

"Good."

"And your wife? I hear you married Miss Dart, the schoolteacher."

"Not now we ain't. That's all busted up."

She glanced past him toward the dining-room doorway. Jordan would be
furious if he found her talking to this boy. She turned her head away. But
he stood there before her, staring at her.

"I'm running a rig now. Ain't you heard? I'm the works, driller and tool
dresser and grease monkey all rolled in one."

"Grease monkey?" She couldn't resist the question.

"On the oil rig. We're drilling on my own piece, me and my uncle and
little brother. Starting to, that is."

She rose. "That's splendid. Good-bye."

"Huh?" He glanced over his shoulder. "Say, I know Bick's got his kettle
on for me, I ain't aiming to meet up with him—yet." He turned his hard
relentless gaze upon her, those hot narrow eyes set so close together bored
into her eyes. They traveled slowly down her face to her mouth and rested
there a moment, then down to her throat, her breast. "I been wanting to see
you," he said, almost humbly.

She brushed past him, she began to push her way through the throng.

"I'll be seeing you again," Jett Rink said. It was not a casual farewell.
It was a threat.

The crowd closed in on her. She was elbowed this way and that. A hand
gripped her arm. "Leslie! I told you to stay till I came back for you."
Jordan's dear face full of concern for her.

"I didn't like it there. Hot."

"The folks are waiting for us. Let's have dinner early, before the big
mob."

The Seville Room maître d'hôtel turned out to be a headwaitress, brightly
blonde and dressed as Carmen. Her kind care-worn face beamed a genuine
welcome. "Hiyah! Right this way, honey." In the same breath she speeded
a parting guest. "Come back quick!" Her flounced skirts bobbed energetically as she skipped ahead of Jordan and Leslie. And there were the Beezers
and the Hattons and the Caldwells, brimming with friendship and warm
hospitality. The men had brown paper parcels under their arms, and these
they now somewhat sheepishly brought forth as bottles. Carmen hovered
solicitously, she beckoned and a Mexican bus boy brought ice and glasses
and water.

"Where at's your castanets, Carrie?" Ed Beezer inquired.

"Never you mind," Carmen retorted inadequately, her anxious eye on
the doorway even as she bent over their table.

"Pay him no mind, Carrie," Joella Beezer said kindly. "How's your little
girl?"

Carmen momentarily forgot the doorway guests. "Little! Say, you ought
to see her! Taller than me, she's singing in the choir of the First Baptist now,
and taking vocal."

"Well, you got a right to be real proud!"

Bick looked at Leslie. "Well, you asked for it." His hand sought hers.
"I love it," she said. She dropped her voice. "I love you."

Carmen, guileless as milk, bustled off to greet the Fiesta diners that now
thronged the doorway. Her voice rang above the blare of the big band on
the platform at the far end of the room. "Hiyah! Howdy! Sure nice to see
you. Right this way, honey!"

Well, Mexican food is the thing tonight, sure enough, they decided. Not as good here as it is in a real Mexican joint, but good enough. What d'you say we start with enchiladas? . . .

Heartburn. "I think a steak for Leslie here," Bick said. "Steak all right, Leslie?"

"Fine," Leslie said. "Perfect."

The band broke into the measured beat of a tango. Gourds chattered, drums pounded. The little dancing floor in the center of the dining room suddenly was asquirm with posturing figures in mantillas and silks and boleros. Handsome Texas males. Blooming Texas matrons. Dazzlingly pretty Texas girls with their strangely boyish six-foot beaux. The aroma of coffee, the smell of hot spicy food. No dark faces other than those of the Mexican bus boys moving silently from table to table.

Ed Beezer challenged Leslie's wide-eyed interest in the colorful clamorous room. "I bet you never saw anything like this up North, Miz Benedict. You'd never believe you were in the United States, would you?"

"Never," Leslie said. "Never."

21

EVEN BICK CONCEDED that the girl, from the moment of her birth, was completely a Benedict. She was fair as her brother Jordy was dark, sunny as he was somber. "Well, that's more like it!" Bick exulted. "Too bad we can't switch them around, but anyway now we're really coming through with the strain." With a cautious caressing forefinger he traced a path down the fragile pink face from brow to chin.

"Luz. H'm? We'll call her Luz."

"No!" Leslie cried. "We've never even mentioned that among the names we've———"

"Yes, but she looks it, though. All that yellow hair and blue eyes and look at that skin! Luz Benedict. Luz. It means light."

"Not Luz. Not that."

"What then?"

"You'd think I was some sort of prize cow that has her calf taken away from her after she's produced it."

"Wrong. Cows feed their calves."

"Oh, all right, if that's the only language you understand. And if it's light you want we'll name her Claire. Not Luz. Never Luz."

"Nothing to get so upset about, honey. You just don't like Benedict names, that's all. You were dead against Jordan too, remember?"

"This is different. I can't bear it."

"All right. I'll be big about it." His arms about the woman and the child, his cheek against Leslie's. He laughed a short grudging laugh of confession. "I guess I'm so set up about these two kids—two new Benedicts for Reata— I won't admit anybody else has a right to them. Even their mother. My darling girl. My two darling girls. . . . All right then. Your turn this time. If Claire is what you want then it'll be Claire."

But he fell into the habit of calling her Luz. Just a kind of nickname, he said. And in time the child and everyone who knew her forgot that she ever had had another name. Only Leslie remembered. Even she, in time, became accustomed to the use of the name she hated. The child was Luz to the hundreds on Reata, Luz at school, Luz to her friends. She herself forgot the name of Claire and signed herself Luz Benedict. At school in the East she explained, "I was named for my aunt, Luz Benedict. You ought to hear the stories about her! A real Grade B Western movie type."

The County began to approve of Leslie. In a limited way. Mrs. Jordan Benedict—you know—Bick Benedict's wife. Yes, she took to Texas like a heifer to cake. You wouldn't hardly know she wasn't a Texian born, only a little ways. Two children, boy and girl.

Now she longed for a glimpse of her family; for Virginia, for a taste of the easy graceful life of her girlhood. "This is your home. But you talk as if you were homesick," Bick said.

"I suppose I am. I suppose I will be until I see it again."

"It's going to feel mighty funny to me, end of the day, no kids no wife."

"It will be fine for both of us. We've been together every day every night since the day we were married."

"Isn't that good?"

"It'll be better after a few weeks apart."

"All right, all right. Tell you what, I'll come up and call for you. I'll have to go to Washington anyway about that time. That's what I'll do. Otherwise you'd probably never come back to this poor old beat-up cow hand."

Though they spoke lightly they were both terribly in earnest. This was more than a little visit with the family back home in Virginia. This was a long look around. This was a separation in spirit as well as body. These two terribly dissimilar people would not admit even to themselves that they were about to take a cool detached look at the brief tale of their married years, and a long speculative look at the years that stretched ahead.

In the spring she made the trip to Virginia, traveling true to Benedict tradition in a private car with two Mexican nursemaids; Petra her own maid; a welter of trunks, boxes, bags, small luggage; and gifts ranging from a complete Western riding outfit for Lacey including saddle boots hat, to crates of Valley grapefruit and bushels of paper-shell pecans.

Leslie was in a state of chills and fever as the Southwest receded, then the Midwest was left behind and the train approached the Eastern seaboard. Her father. The lovely rambling old shabby house. Lacey. Apple trees in bloom. Rich green grass in the meadows. Her mother. In exactly that order of her longing. Jordy and Luz were dressed within an inch of their lives hours before they reached their destination, managed to ruin this effect, were undressed, dressed again. The safari wound its way out of the train to the station platform in such a brouhaha of squeals shrieks chatter laughter tears Spanish English and Southern sweet talk that Leslie only tardily became aware of the actual presence of her sister Leigh, Lady Karfrey, here in the flesh in Virginia instead of being a voice on the overseas telephone from England.

"Leigh!" Her surprise was less than completely joyous. She looked about her. "Is Alfred with you?" She hoped not, she wanted only her own dear family for this homecoming.

"He's joining me in a few weeks. Leslie, he's mad to see Texas."

"To see Texas!" Leslie repeated with sinking heart. Then, hastily, "He wouldn't like it."

But there was no time now to go into this. Jordy and Luz were being kissed, exclaimed over, thoroughly disorganized. Howling, they were carried off by their Mexican nurses who conversed in a torrent of Spanish to the Lynntons' Negro servants. With the miraculous rapport of the minorities they understood each other.

Mrs. Lynnton said, "Leslie! Your skin!" She said, "Leslie! Your hair!" She said, "Leslie Lynnton, that's one of your old trousseau dresses. Well,

I should think the wife of a husband with three million acres would be able———"

"Only two and a half, Mama."

Lady Karfrey said, "You travel like an East Indian maharanee. I thought Texas was a republic or a democracy or something. Do all Texans travel with a retinue?"

"Only a few."

Lacey looked at her gift of the massive Western saddle, the hand-tooled boots, belt, reata, as one would gaze upon an exhibit of prehistoric tribal utensils. The saddle especially fascinated her. "It looks like a rocking chair. And all that carving! It weighs tons, doesn't it? . . . What a pommel! Goodness, look at it miles high, what do they use it for—flying the Texas flag?"

Doctor Horace Lynnton said, "Well, Leslie."

It was she who threw her arms about him and held him close as if he were a child. "Oh, Papa!" He looked so much older than she had remembered him, so much frailer, so much paler and more stooped. "Oh, Papa, you aren't—have you been well?"

"You've been looking at seven-foot beef eaters for two years, all Eastern men will look like albino dwarfs to you."

He held her off and regarded her with the eyes of a loving father and a great physician. Then he nodded his head as at the conclusion of a satisfactory diagnosis. "You've come through it all right. Some scar tissue. But in the main a triumph."

"Through what?" snapped Lady Karfrey. "One would think she'd been to the wars and back." Leigh Lynnton Karfrey of the tart tongue had always been tinged with the jealousy of the first-born for the next in years. "What has your darling daughter been through that's so terrible!"

"Through the first years of marriage. Two children in two years. And Texas. It makes any mere warrior look like a sissy." Doctor Horace rolled a non-existent pill between thumb and forefinger, an elderly habit that Leslie had never heretofore noticed in him.

In a haze of sentimental remembrance Leslie walked through the lovely and beloved old house. The drawing room. How faded the curtains were. Her old bedroom so tidy now, with the bed head pushed against the wall. It all looked shabbier than she had so longingly pictured it in these past nostalgic years. And smaller. There was the apple orchard in bloom. With the new vision of one who has seen a vast domain equipped with every modern mechanical device she noted that the trees badly needed spraying and pruning and mulching. There in Virginia and Washington and Maryland were the boys and girls—men and women now—with whom she had spent her carefree girlhood and the more serious years of young womanhood during the war. Now they welcomed her with all manner of festivities. Cocktail parties. Hunt balls. Dinner parties. Teas. Receptions. Luncheons. Presidential, ambassadorial, senatorial affairs, quite splendid and formal. Local society affairs, quite the opposite.

"But Leslie, you can't go to all these things in those clothes!" Even Lacey, of the erstwhile overalls, was scornful of Leslie's dated gowns. "The new things are way below the knees, and some evening dresses are almost to the floor."

Mrs. Lynnton took her daughter in hand. "It's bad enough to have Leigh home for the first time in ten years looking like a frump. But she does it purposely. She tries to out-English the English. They've always been dowdy, God knows, but since the war they've made a religion of it. Leigh's brought along enough scratchy old tweeds for daytime and moth-eaten old portieres for evening to make a British county wardrobe."

"But Mama, you know perfectly well Jordy was born almost on the dot of nine months. I had hardly time to change from my traveling suit to a negligee when I found I was pregnant."

"Don't be common, Leslie."

"Well—uh————" Leslie indulged in a noncommittal grin. "Then just as I'd got myself pulled together and thought I'd go to Hermoso or Dallas on a dress-buying spree————"

"Dallas!"

"You'd be surprised. So then it was Luz. And here I am."

"Well, Washington's no place for shopping, heaven knows, but it will have to do. You can't go to Washington dinners looking as if you were dressed for a hoe-down."

There was a great deal of talk about a catastrophe called the Crash, and a long-lasting condition known as the Depression. This, it seemed, was an emotional as well as a financial condition. People dated things from it as they once used the war as a basis for time computation. Before the war. During the war. After the war. Now they said, "No, we haven't had one since the Depression. . . . I used to but that was before the Depression. . . . He's been like that ever since the Depression."

She was having a dazzling time of it. Old friends, new clothes, delicious food; gaiety, amusing talk; girlhood beaux who had not found consolation in her absence. Surprisingly, they all seemed to have learned quite a lot about Texas. Modern Texas.

"How did you know that!" Leslie would exclaim when someone referred airily to the vast Hake or Beezer or Waggoner or King or Benedict ranches; or to Neiman-Marcus in Dallas or the newest skyscraper in Houston.

"Everybody knows about Texas," they said. "It's getting to be the fashion. Pretty soon Texans won't even have to brag any more."

A newly met acquaintance at a Washington dinner might say, "I know you're from Texas, Mrs. Benedict. Well, of course we've all heard of the fabulous goings-on down there. Exaggerated, I suppose?"

"No. Understated."

If he happened to be a somewhat stuffy newcomer he would smile uncertainly, scenting a note of sarcasm. Reassured by Leslie's earnest gaze, he would go on. "But I suppose the Depression has hit you folks down there just as it has everyone else. Wall Street has a long reach."

"No one ever complains about the Depression down there. I don't think it has touched them. Us. When I left Texas everything seemed as booming as always. If anything, a little more so."

Her warm and charming smile took some of the edge off this. But the man would glare and then sigh as he drank a mouthful of pleasant dinner wine. "If I were twenty years younger I'd go down there and start all over again."

After the first two weeks her nostalgic longing was satisfied. She took to visiting Caroline in the kitchen in quest of that gifted woman's somewhat haphazard recipes. "Yes, but just how much sugar, Caroline?" Or flour or baking powder or butter or lemon. "It's delicious when you make it, but what are the quantities?"

"A body cain't be so businessified about how much this and how much that, Miss Leslie. I just th'ow in."

Mrs. Lynnton said, "You didn't come up here to fuss around in the kitchen. If your cook isn't suitable why don't you send her away?"

"My cook is a he. Not bad. I've tried to teach him a lot of Virginia recipes. But the Mexicans aren't very gifted with our kind of cooking."

"A Mexican cook! No wonder your skin looks blotchy. Chili and red peppers and all sorts of strange hot spices. Deathly!"

"Reata food is now considered epicurean. Most of Texas prefers beef cut hot off the steer and flung into the frying pan."

When at last she encountered Nicky Rorik the conversation and the emotions in which they became involved were something of a shock to both of them. Safely Mrs. Jordan Benedict, mother of two. The Pink Coat was at the point of marrying an attractive rather prim girl of Pittsburgh derivation whose grandfather (not at all hale at the moment) possessed one of the four greatest fortunes in the Western Hemisphere.

Leslie and Nicky relaxed comfortably and had a real talk.

"According to the storybooks," Leslie said, "I ought to find you pallid and what-did-I-see-in-him. But my goodness you're attractive, Nicky!"

"If I were to tell you what I feel about you this minute you would leave me sitting here. Leslie."

"It's pleasant to know that we both had such good taste. We were almost in love in a nice—or maybe not so nice—kind of way."

"And then along came that enormous Texan."

"Not so enormous, really, when he's stacked up against his native state. Anyway, it wouldn't have done. No money in the Lynnton family—if you don't mind my putting it crudely. Is she terribly rich?"

"Fantastic."

"And very nice, I hear.",

"She is a little like you. A carbon copy, fourth perhaps and not sharp and clear like the original. But like."

"Your country will be grateful to you. And to her."

It was all very reassuring. She wondered if she could possibly tell Jordan. No, of course not. Still, it would be pleasant to think about later, perhaps, when she was older and the children had the measles and Jordan was even more matter-of-fact than usual.

Lady Karfrey was proving something of a problem. As the time for Sir Alfred's arrival was now a matter of days she attacked the business at hand with her usual ferocity, possessed as she was of a drive equal to Leslie's but with none of Leslie's charm.

"I've been studying up on your Texas, Leslie. I must say you don't seem to talk much about it."

"I didn't think you'd be particularly interested," Leslie countered faintly.

"Of course I am—as we're going down I hope. Now tell me, what do you do down there? For society, I mean. I know it's a ranch, and millions of miles. But what do you *do?* I mean—concerts plays clubs gardening politics committees? House guests?"

"Uh, no gardening, dearie. Don't confuse the Texas climate with Kent, England. But house guests, yes. Hordes of house guests."

"That will be stimulating. But what do you *do?* All that land and all those cows. You don't just sit and look at it."

"Well—uh—people visit, sort of. And everybody drinks a lot of coffee."

"Coffee!"

"Oh, my poor darling girl!" moaned Mrs. Lynnton, who was sitting over the breakfast crumbs with her two daughters.

"Poor me eye!" Leslie said briskly, to her own surprise.

Lady Karfrey now moved in for the kill. "Alfred always has been fascinated by Texas, he's mad to have a look at it. His grandfather, you know, had an interest in that vast thing that went bust in the 1870s, wasn't it? Called the T. and P. Whatever that means."

"Texas and Pacific Railroad." Horace Lynnton now spoke from the corner of the veranda off the dining room where he had been smoking his pipe, viewing the Virginia sky through the falling apple blossoms, and listening to the acquired English accent of his least favorite and eldest daughter. "It went bust through Jay Cooke and those big Wall Street boys in the panic of 1873. A lot of English had money in it. The railroad was to service the big ranches that the English were supposed to buy."

Speculatively Leslie surveyed her formidable sister. "Just imagine if it hadn't failed, Leigh. You'd have been the Texan in the Lynnton family. Though I don't know how you'd have met Alfred."

"Let's talk about our visit. When would it be convenient for you?"

"Leigh, we'd love to have you, of course. But I don't know that you'd like it, really. Alfred isn't used to—he'd find it too terribly hot after the cool English———"

"Nothing's too hot for the English," Leigh Karfrey stated with great definiteness. "Or too cold. Remember India. And Hudson's Bay. And all that. They just put on a topee or long woolen underwear as the case may be, and thrive. They always have."

"But you can be frying under the sun at noon and freezing an hour later in a sudden norther. Texas is like that."

"It sounds absolutely Alfred's cup of tea," said Lady Karfrey.

Leslie tried to imagine Sir Alfred at Reata. A chubby little Englishman with a somewhat falsetto speaking voice and a mottled magenta coloring. He doted on good food, had a name as a collector of antiques and bibelots. Christie's and Fortnum and Mason's were always sending him special notices.

"Besides," Leslie said deliberately, "I don't know when I'm going back."

There was the silence that follows indrawn breaths. When she had recovered, "Just what does that mean!" demanded Mrs. Lynnton.

"Benedict's in Washington, isn't he, next week, that is?" Lady Karfrey marshaled her facts. "He's calling for you, isn't he? To take you and the children back? You said."

"That was the plan."

"Was!" shrilled Mrs. Lynnton.

Doctor Horace Lynnton stood framed in the veranda doorway. "Want to take a little walk with your old pa, Leslie? I've hardly seen you or talked to you since you came. Really, I mean. And now this talk of going back home." Wordlessly she joined him, she tucked her hand in his arm, close, as they descended the broad shallow steps to the garden. Horace Lynnton's voice, louder than necessary, came clearly to the undeceived ears of his wife and eldest daughter. "I've been at the hospital every day, you're at some party every night. Next thing I know you'll be gone. Why don't you stay until you're really ready to———"

"Well!" said Leigh Karfrey to her mother. "What do you make of that!"

The somewhat stooped elderly man and the blooming young woman walked close together through the garden, through the orchard, across the meadow and into the woods as lovers would have walked, seeing nothing with the conscious eye. Silent.

When Doctor Lynnton broke the silence it was as though he were continuing a spoken conversation. "Of course it's something no one can decide for you. But if you feel like talking about it a little."

"Oh, Papa. I'm so confused."

"You don't love him?"

"That's the terrible part of it. I do. Not only that, I'm in love with him. More than when I married him."

"But he seems to me to have a first-rate mind, too. Not only smart but aware and civilized. And amusing, too, I thought. Amusing is very important after the first years."

She thought of her mother. Not amusing. She pressed his arm. "Yes, he's all those things. But he's got that blind spot. Papa, he and I don't see alike about a single thing—except unimportant things. Handsome intelligent sexy ambitious successful vital amusing tender tough. Everything."

"But———"

"Power-mad. Dictator. His thoughts and energies and emotions are bounded by the farthest fence on the remotest inch of Reata Ranch. He's not unkind to people. Around, I mean. But to him they're only important in relation to the ranch, his life, Texas. He'll never change."

"No, we don't change."

"We?"

"Dedicated men. Men primarily in love with their work. Like Bick. And me." As she stared at him, peered into his face open-mouthed, like a child: "Leslie, your mother talked the same way. Poor girl, she's had a thin enough time of it too all these years while I've been pouring myself into the laboratories and hospitals. She's had what was left, and it wasn't much. It was unreasonable of me to expect her to understand. So I took it out on you girls. I tried to make you conscious of the world. Your mother never changed. But neither did I."

"Jordan will never change. I know that now."

"No. But you're forgetting something."

"What?"

"The world will. It's changing at a rate that takes my breath away. Everything has speeded up like those terrific engines they've invented these past few years. Faster and faster, nearer and nearer. Your Bick won't change—nor you—but your children will take another big step. Enormous step, probably. Some call it revolution but it's evolution, really. Sometimes slow sometimes fast, horrible to be caught in it helpless. But no matter how appalled you are by what you see down there in that strange chunk of the United States, still, you're interested. Aren't you?"

"Fascinated. But rebelling most of the time."

"What could be more exciting! As long as you're fascinated and as long as you keep on fighting the things you think are wrong, you're living. It isn't the evil people in the world who do the most harm. It's the sweet do-nothings that can destroy us. Dolce far niente. That's the thing to avoid in this terrible and wonderful world. Gangrene. The sweet sickening smell of rotting flesh."

Bick Benedict, when he arrived, seemed by his very buoyance to make all this talk mere academic babble. He was a mass of charm and high spirits. Virile handsome actually boyish, Leslie thought she never had seen him so pleased with himself and the world. His arms about her, Jordy and Luz flung themselves at him. In the first flush of their reunion she thought it was herself and the children that gave him this vibrating aura of well-being and elation. But she began to detect something within himself that was the source of this bubbling.

Surveying him with a wifely gaze, "What makes you so full of beans? This glitter in your eye can't be just wife and children."

"Purely spiritual, honey. It's just the result of all that high-minded talk down there in Washington. They've voted to continue the twenty-seven percent tax allowance on oil. Clear."

"But you haven't any oil. Have you? You've always said you hated the stinking oil wells."

"That's right."

"I don't understand."

"But I'm right petted on oil—off my land. I don't mind others having it because from now on the whole world is going to be yelling for oil. Texas is booming. The rest of the country is flat.''

"Is that good?"

"Only good enough to make us the richest state in the whole country. We're a country within a country."

"Again!"

"Oil and beef and cotton. You can't stop it, you can't top it." He breathed deeply, for a moment she thought she saw a strained look in his eye. He gazed around and about the Virginia landscape and he laughed. "God, it looks little! The fields. And the sky. Are you ready to come back with your old man, honey?"

"Jordan, I'm no different from what I was when I left."

"I don't want you different. We Texians like a little vinegar on our greens. Gives it flavor. Come on, let's go home."

22

ON THE JOURNEY homeward Leslie said, "If you had told me, on our honeymoon, that the next time we made this trip I'd be traveling with you and masses of our children and hundreds of nurses and millions of bags and bottles and toys and stuff!"

"You'd have made it anyway."

"You're so pleased with yourself I think this is the time to tell you that Leigh meant it when she said she and Karfrey want to visit Reata."

"Why not!" Bick demanded, largely. "Penned up on that little island all their lives! Do'em good to have to hunt for the horizon. Anyway, it'll be worth it just to see Karfrey in a ten-gallon hat."

"I wish Papa and Mama would come down at the same time. And Lacey too. Just to take the curse off the Karfreys."

His well-being encompassed this without a sign of strain. "That's a fine idea. Folks down here are beginning to think you're an orphan. Look, I'm going to send them all a telegram at the next stop."

Down they came to Reata, the lot of them.

"Do you mean to tell me," demanded Mrs. Lynnton, "that I am not going to be allowed to sleep under the same roof with my daughter and my grandchildren!"

"Mama dear, you're staying in the Big House because there isn't room here in our house. You'd go simply crazy here, and I don't like to shush the children. Over there it's bigger and quieter and more restful for you."

"Restful! The place is full of utter strangers stamping and jingling through the halls all hours of the day and night. Nobody even knows who they are. I asked one of those Mexican girls. She just shook her head and jabbered something in Spanish. Spanish!"

"They're business acquaintances of Jordan. People he has to see. Or they come to see the ranch. They come from everywhere."

"What are you running? A hotel! God knows we're hospitable in Virginia. But this!"

"Mama, this isn't just a ranch. It's a scientific laboratory too. And a kind of show place for the whole ranching world. Reata and the King ranch and the Hakes' Double B and a few others are sort of famous, you know. People come to see and learn. Jordan loves it. He's breeding a new kind of cattle."

"If God had meant to have men create new cattle He'd have given them the job in the first place, with all He had to do."

The family visitors adapted themselves to the climate, the environment and the customs with astonishing ease. Lacey was off on a horse from morning until night, she was more at home in the stables than the house. The vaqueros adopted her as one of themselves, they explained in Spanish and she understood in English. Even old Polo demonstrated to her the value of the new breed of fleet-footed creatures whose swift quarter-mile spurting powers were invaluable in the roundup and on the range. Quarter horses, they were called.

Mrs. Lynnton took alarm. She sought out Bick. "Lacey spends all her time with those Mexican men, no one knows where she is the day through and half the night. I've spoken and spoken to Horace about it but he's as bad as she is."

Bick grinned, he pretended to misunderstand. "No! You mean the Doctor's galloping around on quarter horses!"

"You know perfectly well he's down at that laboratory of yours with that vet, or poking into the wretched shacks around here, looking for local diseases, they're worse than any slave quarters in the old Virginia days I can tell you."

He could not be angry with her, actually, though he thought privately that he would like nothing better than to drive her out to really good rattlesnake country some hot bright afternoon.

Reata was a country in itself to which each visitor could adapt according to his or her own taste. Luxury or hardship, leisure or work. Lacey ate her midday meal out on the range with the vaqueros. In the evening she reported on her day, to the horror of Mrs. Lynnton.

"For lunch we had some rather awful stuff looked like entrails. And beans of course. Don't they ever tire of beans!"

Mischievously Bick said, "I must ask the boys to fix you up with a tasty dish of magueys."

"Magueys?"

"It's quite a Mexican delicacy. White maguey worms fried crisp. Elegant eating."

A squawking sound from Mrs. Lynnton. Sir Alfred took a more world-wise view. "Why not? All foreigners eat certain beastly messes. Look at the French with their snails!"

"True, true," agreed Horace Lynnton. "And is there anything more repulsive-looking than a succulent Baltimore soft-shell crab? Or, for that matter, a nicely aged English plover's egg or a properly disintegrated woodcock."

Lacey, full of her day's doings, rattled on. "I rode miles and miles today and ended up at the Dietzes' place, that little Bobby Dietz is the smartest little boy I ever saw. Not smarty smart like Eastern kids but wise smart. He knows about soil and cattle and feed and horses. The Dietzes say they're going to send him to Texas U., but he says he wants the husbandry course at Cornell. If he were ten years older I'd ditch my beau and marry him. What a kid! . . . Look, Bick, there was a fellow in the camp today he came rushing in sort of wild-looking and covered with grease and driving the worst broken-down Ford I ever saw. He gulped down his lunch red hot though I must say the Mexican boys didn't seem very glad to see him. When he found out who I was he was really rather nervy. I mean not like the cowboys and vaqueros I've met, I think he'd been drinking. He wanted to know all about you, Leslie."

Bick stopped her. "What was his name?"

"Something that sounded like Jeb———"

Bick pushed back his chair and stood up. "By God I've told them that if he ever sets foot on my land they're to shoot him."

Lacey giggled a little at this. "Yes, they told him—at least I gathered they told him——— Do you know I can understand quite a lot of Spanish now———"

"Oh, they told him."

"And he just said sort of 'pffft!' as if he were spitting through his teeth— he was, really—and jabbered something I couldn't get in Spanish, I must say it didn't sound too complimentary———"

"Now Jordan," Leslie said quietly. "Sit down and finish your dinner."

"I've finished. Excuse me, folks. I've got some business to tend to." You heard him a moment later talking on his office telephone, the Spanish words drumming.

Leslie pretended to make nothing of this. "Ranch business again. Oh dear! And we're having the most lovely dessert."

"I'm awfully sorry, Leslie," Lacey said. "I was just talking, I didn't dream there was anything important about this really crummy-looking man."

Mrs. Lynnton eyed her youngest daughter disapprovingly. "Lacey, how many times have I told you not to chatter? Men don't like women who talk so much."

At the shout of laughter that went up she looked about her in vague surprise.

After dinner Doctor Horace took Leslie aside. "Tell me something about this fellow Lacey was talking about. I don't like to see a big full-blooded man like Bick go as white as that."

"When Jordan's sister died I didn't write you and Mama all the queer details because you'd have been upset. I was. Horribly. I don't yet quite understand the whole gruesome business."

She told him, speaking rapidly and very low, meanwhile smiling and nodding reassuringly across the room at her mother. "What are you two whispering about?" that lady demanded. As Leslie talked and her father listened she began to feel strangely relieved as from a burden. "You see, he's just an ignorant crude lout. But tough. He has some sort of crazy plan in his head, I suppose. But I can't understand," she concluded, "why Jordan takes him so seriously. He's nothing, really."

"Nobody's nothing," Doctor Lynnton said. "You can't cancel out any living human being. Sometimes they surprise you. This boy has a deep grudge. Not only against Bick, I'd say, but against the world. If he's strong enough and carries it long enough he might do quite a lot of damage."

"I don't see how. He never can touch us, that's sure."

Doctor Lynnton, during this visit, covered a great deal of scientific ground so unobtrusively that he seemed scarcely to move at all. He ambled. He spoke to everyone he encountered—vaqueros, merchants, servants, ranchers, any Mexicans within reach. He himself talked little, they seemed always to hold forth while he listened and nodded his head gently and said I see I see. His conduct was, in a more orderly and intensified way, based on the pattern his daughter had followed when first she had come, a stranger, to Texas.

"Well, Papa," Leslie said, at the end of the first week, "do you get the idea?"

"Somewhat. Somewhat. Very complicated, beneath the surface. But fascinating beyond my expectations. This is a civilization psychologically different from any other part of the United States. The South is a problem, certainly; and the Eastern seaboard. The West Coast is faced with its peculiar difficulties, and even the Middle West isn't as serene as it seems. But this! Bigness can be a curse, you know, too. Texas is very big. Reata is very big. Your Bick is very powerful. People in big empty places are likely to behave very much as the gods did on Olympus. There's a phrase for that—one of those nice descriptive American sayings. 'Throwing your weight around,' we say.''

The visitors met and were entertained by the neighbors for hundreds of miles around. "Con Layditch telephoned,'' Bick would announce casually, "wants us all to come over, they've finished their new house, they're having a barbecue and square dance to celebrate.'' At an anguished look from Leslie, "No, honey. Steaks.''

The visitors would find themselves whirled two hundred miles for dinner.

"All these foreigners,'' Sir Alfred remarked as they scudded through the little towns, as they watched the vaqueros at roundup, as they were served their food. "These Mexicans everywhere. I should think they'd be quite a problem, what?''

"Yes,'' Doctor Horace agreed. "And imagine the problem we were to them when we came swarming in a hundred years ago. We were the foreigners then.''

"Room enough for everybody now, I must say,'' Mrs. Lynnton announced, looking about her largely. "Miles and miles and miles of nothing. Scares you. Makes me want to holler.''

Doctor Horace pounced on this. "It does!'' Thoughtfully.

Leslie had dreaded the inevitable meeting between Vashti Snyth and Lady Karfrey. They came together with a clashing of broadswords. After the first encounter Leslie found herself defending the people and customs she herself had so recently criticized.

"Vashti is a college graduate. She's traveled quite a lot in Europe. They go East every year. She speaks French very well.''

"It hasn't touched her,'' Lady Karfrey asserted. "She's a Texas national monument like the Alamo or that cow you showed us in the glass case in the village. Neither college nor Europe or time or tide will ever change her. I hope.''

Conversations between Vashti Snyth and Leigh Karfrey were brisk and bristling.

"My, I should think it would feel wonderful for you to get where you can really draw your breath,'' Vashti said with that tactlessness which was, perversely enough, a rather endearing quality in her. "That little bitty old England, you can't take a good long walk without you fall over the cliffs into the ocean. I liked to choke to death there in all that cramped-up fog. And then the mutton. Mutton! My.''

"You imported all our beautiful English Herefords. And immediately they arrived they fell heir to your cattle diseases—pink eye, and ticks, and worms!''

"We're trying to breed out all the Hereford strain in our stock. We don't really need to haul anything in here. We got everything. We got cattle in plenty. And cotton. And wool and mules and grapefruit and horses and wheat and turkeys. And Mott, my husband, says we got sulphur and coal and copper and lead and a thing called helium—I don't rightly know what that is, but anyway it's good stuff to have around—and lumber he says and limestone and vegetables in the Valley, and pecans. And a course all this oil now. We got just everything in Texas.''

Lady Karfrey cleared her throat.

"I have been gathering a few facts, dear Mrs. Snyth, since I arrived in your state. Everything you say is true.''

"Sure it's true," repeated the unsuspecting Vashti.

"As you say, of all the states Texas is first in cotton—but last in pellagra control. First in beef—and forty-fifth in infant mortality. First in wool—and thirty-eighth in its school system. First in mules—and forty-seventh in library service. First in turkeys—and its rural church facilities are deplorable. First in oil—and your hospitals are practically non-exis———"

Magenta surged into Vashti's indignant face. "I been in England. I never saw such poor runty beat-up looking people in my born days as you got in what you call the East End. And poor teeth and bad complexions, drinking tea all the time and nobody in the whole country gets milk and oranges and he says the roast beef of old England is a non-existent, Mott says."

Strangely enough it was Karfrey, the Englishman, who said, "How right you are, Mrs. Snyth. But then you must remember that you could put all of England down in one corner of Texas and never find it, really."

Mrs. Lynnton, in her own insecure way, struggled for a foothold of understanding. The food, the storerooms, the swarms of servants inside and out, the vastness, the lavish scale on which the Big House and the Main House were run, bewildered and irritated her.

"When I get back home I'm going to send Mitty down. You remember Mitty, Caroline's daughter? She's every bit as good a cook now as Caroline and in some ways better."

"No, Mama. It wouldn't do."

"You owe it to your children. I saw Jordy yesterday with that weird little Mexican girl he's always playing with, they were both eating tortillas as if it were bread and butter."

"So it is, in a way."

The visiting Lynntons and Karfreys usually drove over from the Big House before dinner there to lounge in comparative coolness on the Main House veranda. There were always tall iced drinks, the Gulf breeze filtered through vines and screens, the voices of the children came pleasantly from the far end of the veranda. It was the most relaxed hour of the day, it was the time Leslie liked best. Bick was always at his most charming. Lacey was full of her day's doings. Her father and mother had learned to accept for her this strange life of hardship and fantastic luxury. The Karfreys were frankly having the time of their lives.

"Besides," Leslie now said, continuing her conversation with her mother, "that weird little Mexican girl isn't a girl at all. She's a boy."

Mrs. Lynnton turned to stare at the distant children.

"I don't believe it."

Bick called to them. "Jordy! Angel! Ven acá!"

The two came reluctantly, Jordy to stand at his mother's side, her hand on his shoulder; the other child stopping short of the group. Weird, Nancy Lynnton had said. Now the group of adults gazed at the dark small Mexican child and the child stared back at them poised lightly, like a tiny fawn, as though ready to dart off at a sound, a hostile glance. Fawnlike three-cornered eyes, due to a slight lift or pinch in the center of the upper eyelid. The little figure was bony of shank, flat of chest, the hands strong and big-boned sticking out of the stuff of the sleeves. A small boy's hands, a small boy's legs, a small boy's chest and eyes; and the bones of the alert face and the well-shaped head were those of a boy. But the dress with its Mexican ruffles and its petticoats and the red hair ribbons—all this was the garb of a girl. And the long black hair was neatly brushed and braided, it shone with brushing and with unguents, unlike the thick careless locks of other small Mexican ranch children.

"This is Angel Obregon," Leslie said, and smiled at the boy, "the son of Angel Obregon, who is a vaquero here at Reata." And she held out her hand to him as she spoke, as though to draw him to her side with Jordy, her own son. But the boy only looked at her and did not move.

In her halting Spanish Leslie said, "Won't you say good evening, Angel? Buenas tardes, señoras. Señores."

"Señores come first in Spanish, honey," Bick reminded her.

Now Angel's black eyes were strangely sparked with determination, the baby jaw was set with fierce effort. The lips opened, the whole face took on animation and purpose. "Good . . . even . . . ing . . . sirrrs . . . good . . . even . . . ing . . . madamas." In a triumph of stumbling English. Then, with a shriek of hysterical laughter he was off. Jordy, too, broke away, the two could be heard down the veranda howling at the splendid joke.

"Well, if that don't take the rag off the bush!" Bick exclaimed. "The little muchacho has learned English off of Jordy!"

"Splendid!" observed Doctor Horace. "It's beginning to work."

It was obvious that Leigh Karfrey was busy taking mental notes on the Habits and Dress of the Mexican Child in Texas. Mrs. Lynnton was quivering with disapproval.

"Leslie Lynnton, will you tell me the reason for dressing a child like that! Day after day, playing with Jordy!"

"I suppose it does seem queer," Leslie agreed. "We're used to it."

"Tell them," Bick urged her. "It's quite a story."

Leslie took a little fortifying sip of the cool drink in her hand. "Mm, let's see. Well, that very first day after I arrived in Texas, a bride———"

"And what a bride!" Bick muttered, ambiguously.

"—I started out for a morning walk, in my youth and innocence. To see the sights."

"Dear me!" said Doctor Horace.

"Finally I began to feel like a wanderer dying of thirst in the desert and I stumbled into one of the Mexican houses. I'd heard a baby crying there. The woman was in bed, ill. It was her baby, crying. The baby was little Angel there. Not a word of English. But I understood her, sort of, just the same. We've become great friends since then. And later I learned about her and her baby. She'd been married almost three years and no baby which for a Mexican girl is practically a disgrace. She was ill a good deal but finally this child was expected. They knew what had caused all the trouble, of course. One night Angel had left his hat on the bed and everyone knows that is bad luck. So Deluvina, the wife, had paid for special masses and she had taken herb medicines and the midwife had massaged her and on the Tree of Petitions she had hung a little cradle made of bits of mesquite wood and in it she had put a tiny doll dressed as a girl baby because she thought they were being punished for wanting only a boy all these years. She prayed morning and night and in between. And she promised God that she would be humbly grateful for girl or boy, and that in either case its hair would be tended and brushed and anointed and when it was a foot long it would be cut off and given as a thank offering to God. You can't know what that means. Mexican girls don't cut their hair. It is their glory. The child's name was to be Angelina. And Angelina was born, and she was a boy. But the promise had been made to God by Deluvina and by Angel Obregon kneeling before the altar. They named him Angel after his father. They let his hair grow and Angel was dressed as a girl and his hair was always tied with a red ribbon as you've seen it and washed and brushed and anointed for it belonged to God. Other Mexican children might have piojos in their hair, but not Angel. His grandmother's chief duty is to keep it brushed and shining.

And when it is a foot long there will be a great celebration and Angel's hair will be cut off by the priest and placed as an offering on the shrine. Then they will put Angel in pants and take away his skirts.''

"Well I never!" exclaimed the outraged Mrs. Lynnton.

"Barbaric!" said Lady Karfrey.

"By that time," Doctor Horace mused, "he'll be so confused as to be incoherent. Or such a tough guy, in self-defense, that Reata Ranch can't hold him."

Sir Alfred was casting an eye toward the dining room. "Dinner any second now," Leslie assured him. "Will anyone have another drink?"

"Do you think," Nancy Lynnton demanded, "that this child is a fit playmate for Jordy!"

"Don't let those skirts worry you," Bick assured her. "This kid's a tough hombre. In fact, I wish Jordy had some of his stuff. His father Angel Obregon used to be my sidekick when I was a kid. And his father's father taught me roping—he and old Polo. Even today old Angel is the best mangana thrower on Reata. In Texas, for that matter."

"This could be wonderful," Doctor Horace mused aloud. "Maybe someday it will be."

But no one consciously heard him or heeded him, except Leslie.

"Mangana?" inquired Sir Alfred, abandoning hopes for immediate dinner.

"To throw the mangana you have to be a brush roper. And roping in the brush is trickier than roping in the open. For the mangana the animal is running and the roper is standing still. The loop turns over in the air and it catches the animal high around the front legs so's not to break the leg between the brisket————"

But now there was the sputter and cough of an engine in the drive. A grease-spattered Ford with flapping fenders came to a stop with a shrill squeal of old brakes and seared tires.

Jett Rink sprang out. His face was grotesque with smears of dark grease and his damp bacchanalian locks hung in tendrils over his forehead. He leaped from the car and began to run as he landed, without a pause, and he limped a little as he ran.

He came on, he opened the door of the screened veranda, he stood before the company in his dirt and grease, his eyes shining wildly. They stared at him in shocked suspense, relaxed as they were against the cushions, glasses in hand. Leslie thought, Now he is really crazy something terrible is going to happen. Jordan. The man stood, his legs wide apart as though braced against the world, the black calloused hands with the fingers curiously widespread as they hung, his teeth white in the grotesquely smeared face. He stared at Bick with those pale blue-white eyes and there was in them the glitter of terrible triumph.

Bick did not even rise from his chair. Very quietly, sitting there, he said, "Get out."

Jett Rink spoke four words only. His voice was low and husky with emotion.

"My well come in."

"Get out of here."

Now the words shot geyser-swift out of Jett Rink's mouth like the earth-pent oil his labors had just released.

"Everybody said I had a duster. You thought ol' Spindletop and Burk-burnett and Mexia and those, they was all the oil there was. They ain't, I'm here to tell you. It's here. It's right here. I got the laugh on you."

Now it was plain the man was drunk, the eyes were bloodshot, you could smell the raw liquor on the heavy hot air of the shadowy veranda.

Bick leaned forward slightly his muscles tensed; and still the others sat staring at the man.

"My well come in big and there's more and bigger. They's oil under here. They's oil here on Reata and someday I'm going to pay you a million dollars or five million or ten and you'll take it because you'll need the money. I'm going to have more money than you ever saw—you and the rest of the stinkin' sons of bitches of Benedicts!"

Now, rather wearily, Bick stood up, he said, "Leslie, honey, you and the girls go along indoors."

Leslie stood up, neatly folding the bit of sewing in her hands. But she did not go.

"Go along home now, Jett," she said. "It's nice you've struck oil. Go along now." As she would have spoken to a stray that had run in on the place, man or animal.

He looked at her, lurching a little with weariness or drink or both, his legs wide apart like one who walks the deck of a ship. Then, with the swiftness with which he always moved, the man came over to her, he reached out and just jerked ever so lightly with a grimed hand one end of the soft little bow that finished the neckline of her silk dress. He tweaked the piece of silk with a gesture that would have been insolent even in an intimate and an equal.

"My, you look pretty, Leslie," he said. "You sure look good enough to eat."

Bick's first blow struck him squarely in the jaw but Jett Rink's monolithic head scarcely went back with it. Bick hit him again, Jett dodged slightly and the blow landed full on his mouth and a little blood trickled down his chin and he twisted his mouth as though he were eating and she thought he was going to spit out the blood full at Bick, but he laughed only and did not even lift his hand to wipe the blood away.

"My, you're techy, Bick," he said. "You're techy as a cook."

Karfrey came forward, and Horace Lynnton. And now Jett Rink turned as though to go, grinning, and Bick rushed to grapple with him. He had reached the screen door. Bick was on him. Jett Rink's knee went sharply back and then drove forward like a piston and struck Bick squarely on the groin. Bick grunted. Doubled. Even as they caught Bick and dragged him to a chair Doctor Horace's hands were moving expertly over him.

Jett Rink had leaped into the battered car, had spun it like a crazy toy, was off in a cloud of dust.

23

"No!" Bick commanded, fuming among his pillows. "Keep Roady away and Bowie, too. Get Bawley on the telephone."

Uncle Bawley had come down from Holgado in a swift overnight journey. Now he sat in Bick's bedroom, and for once it was the Lynntons, not the Benedicts, who held conclave: Doctor Horace, Mrs. Lynnton, Leslie.

"Soft!" Uncle Bawley declared, his gentle voice soothing the sting of the words. "That's what's chousing up this world. Everybody's turned soft. Pulled your gun and shot him, Bick, you'd saved youself a heap of trouble. But no, you let him give you the knee and stroll off."

"He didn't stroll. He ran." Leslie to her husband's defense. "Jordan hit him twice hard enough to fell a steer. It was like hitting a stone wall."

"Drunk. No use hitting a fella who's crazy drunk. He don't feel a thing."

Doctor Horace nodded in agreement. "An anesthetic, alcohol."

Mildly chiding, Uncle Bawley went on. "Shot him, the whole state would have been beholden to you. A loco umbry like Rink gets hold of oil and money, why, he's liable to want to be Governor of Texas. Or worse. What started you wrassling with a polecat like Jett in the first place?"

Propped up against his pillows, his eyes flint-grey with fury, Bick's legs threshed between the sheets. "He came up to Leslie and put his filthy stinking hand on her."

"No!" shouted Uncle Bawley.

"Yes!" Bick yelled.

"Bick's first blow was pure reflex," Doctor Horace observed. "Straight to the jaw."

"Bick well knows Rink's got a jaw like a jackass and besides he don't fight fair. Belt him in the ba—I mean, hit him below the belt, and first. That's the only kind of fighting he understands. Now you can't do a thing. Not a thing."

"Why not!" Mrs. Lynnton demanded. "Why not, I'd like to know! We saw it, all of us. You can call Leigh and Alfred. They'll tell you. And Lacey."

"Bring 'em on!" Bick shouted, glaring. "Bring everybody! Call in the house help. Call in the county!"

Leslie, seated at the bedside, leaned toward him, gently she placed her hand on his waving arm. "Now darling, you know perfectly well no one saw except my own family."

"Mexican servants hear everything and see everything and know everything that goes on. They get it through their pores or something. And what about that skunk! I suppose he isn't talking."

"Psychopath," Doctor Horace murmured. "Actually, of course, this Rink should be confined for treatment. Potentially dangerous."

Uncle Bawley rose, a commanding figure in the room now so charged with conflicting emotions. "Look how it sounds. Rink's fired from the ranch a few years back, he marries the schoolteacher he's got into trouble—pardon me, Miz Lynnton ma'am—and he don't seem to hold a grudge he starts wildcatting for oil with no money and no crew and no sense on his own little piece of no-account land Bick gave him long ago, deeded. And by God, what does he do, he hits oil. So he jumps into his junkheap car to tell his old boss Bick about his good luck he's struck oil on the piece Bick gave him time his father turned up missing." At a growl from the man in the bed—"Well, now, Bick, I'm just telling it the way it would sound, told. And this young fella spills his good news and his old boss throws him out and wallops him in the jaw front of everybody. That'd go good in a court of law."

"I wasn't thinking of the law," Bick said, sullenly.

"Furthermore," Uncle Bawley went on, "look what I heard this morning. Just on the way from Viento to here. I heard Rink's got hold of leases on pieces around. No-account land that's prolly rotten with oil."

With a mighty gesture Bick threw the covers aside. "I'm going to get up. What am I! Du Barry! Vamoose, ladies, as they say in the Westerns, unless you want to see a really fine physique in the raw."

Leslie glanced quickly at her father but he only smiled approvingly. "That's fine, Bick. You're all right."

"Sure Bick's all right," Uncle Bawley agreed, but the eyes that searched Bick's face were doubtful. "He took worse than that many a time when he was Harvard tackle."

"That's right," Doctor Horace agreed, too genially.

"Where's the kids?" Uncle Bawley demanded. "I want to look at something fresh and pretty. No offense, ladies. But this kind of ruckus makes me sick, nothing clean-cut about it. The good old days we'd of————"

"These are the good new days, Uncle Bawley."

"Maybe. Say, Leslie, where at's Jordy and Luz? Kids kept separate from grownups nowdays, like they were a different kind of animal. Mix 'em up they learn quicker, it's good for them."

"They're waiting for you, dying to see you. I told them first thing this morning, it was a mistake, they were so excited they hardly ate a mouthful."

"I suppose old Polo's got Jordy up on a horse roping a steer every morning before breakfast."

Leslie tucked her arm through his as they walked toward the veranda. "Jordy doesn't like riding. He isn't even interested in horses, much."

"No!"

"I sometimes think perhaps he's a little like you—when you were a child, Uncle Bawley."

"Poor little maverick."

"Luz is the rancher and cowboy. Do you know what that baby did! She somehow got hold of Jordy's riding things—his boots and rope and hat and all—she wriggled into the outfit every which way and there she was wobbling around in high heels and the pants wrong side to, and the Stetson down over her ears. I've never heard Jordan laugh like that."

"Luz, h'm?" He glanced, a quick sidewise look, at Leslie. "She sounds like she's taking after—uh, she bossy too?"

"Well, independent."

"And Bick, he's hell-bent on breaking Jordy in already, I bet."

"Yes."

"There's a difference between breaking in and just plain breaking."

"Somebody will have to help me. Later."

"I'm good for another fifteen eighteen years—maybe twenty. Hard cash and a pretty good brain. Neither of 'em going to go soft on me even time I'm ninety unless the United States and me both are hit to hell."

"Uncle Bawley." She looked up at him. "Thanks, Uncle Bawley."

"Well, I guess I'll go hunt up the kids."

"I'll be with you in a minute. I want to talk to Papa."

"Yes," he said, as though in answer to an unspoken question. "I'd do that."

Alone with her father in Bick's office she put it to him squarely. "Why did you put him to bed?"

"Shock," Doctor Lynnton said, his manner very easy. "And it was the best place for a man as crazy mad as Bick was. Take away a man's pants and he can't go far."

"I don't think that was your real reason." They stood facing each other, the man benign, controlled; the woman determined to hear what she feared. Between them the resemblance was startling. "I don't believe you. If you don't tell me I'll send for Doctor Tom."

Horace Lynnton seated himself at Bick's desk, he motioned his daughter to a chair. Suddenly they were no longer merely father and daughter, they were physician and patient. Leslie's steady eyes did not leave his face.

"That young savage didn't do Bick any real physical harm. Uncomfortable, though, a terrific dirty blow like that." He was looking down at his own square blunt-fingered hands spread out on the desk top. "Later, after we'd brought him round and put him to bed, I thought I'd give him a real going over while I was about it. Of course I didn't have the proper equipment."

"Well?"

"Did he ever complain—that is, does he ever get short of breath?"

"No. At least I haven't noticed it if———"

Now he looked up and full into his daughter's eyes. "It's a thing that has to do with the heart. Now wait a minute. It isn't the heart itself. That's a perfectly sound muscle, I'd say. But the big artery that feeds it."

She looked down at her own hands gripped tightly in her lap.

"What do we do now?"

"Nothing. And don't look so serious. I don't believe I'd even say anything to him, just now. Apprehension is sometimes worse than the disease. If you could manage to have him not quite so active, not galloping hundreds of miles on those horses, up before dawn, running this empire singlehanded."

"He loves it more than anything or anyone. It's his life."

"It's his life."

"He can't do things halfway. It's always extremes. A rage one minute, angelic the next."

"Rages are bad for him."

"He's only like that when he's crossed in something he wants to do."

"From what I've learned about your Bick these past days, roaming around this enormous place, I've gathered that Bick's father ruled him—and the ranch—like an emperor. Then this sister Luz took his father's place and his mother's too. She must have been a real top sergeant. Now I gather the rest of the family are at odds with him. He's interested in experiment and they're interested in income."

"He'll never change, Papa. You might as well ask the Gulf wind to be quiet, or a norther tearing in from the sky. What shall I do!"

"Twenty years from now, when he's pushing those middle fifties, make him rein in. Now it's a matter of not taking things so emotionally and not doing everything himself. Why doesn't he go out on the range occasionally in a car instead of on a horse? I see others doing it."

"Yes, he's modern about everything but himself. He's an engine. He's a power plant. He's a dynamo."

"So is the heart."

"I'll never know a moment's peace again."

"Yes you will. Human beings can adapt to almost anything. Just hold onto his coat sleeve now and then, if he's going too fast. Leslie, I'll tell him if you want me to."

"He'd only go faster, in defiance. He is like that."

When the family left Reata—the Lynntons and the Karfreys to the east, Uncle Bawley to the west—a new peace seemed to settle down upon the Main House, upon the ranch, even upon the town of Benedict. Nancy Lynnton, departing, had flung a final shower of admonition at her daughter. " . . . and watch that cook he'll poison you yet . . . hardly more than a baby and putting him on that huge horse . . . get a good rich skin cream and pat it in night and morning . . . children . . . Mexicans . . . sun . . . wind . . . dust . . . "

"Mama's marvelous," Leslie remarked, feeling strangely gay and released. "In those last ten minutes she covered everything in the heavens and the earth beneath."

"Families are fine," Bick announced. "But they should be exposed to each other one member at a time. That goes for my family too, so don't get your feathers up."

"But Jordan, I couldn't agree with you more. It was wonderful to have them and to see them here————"

"And to see them go."

For the first time since her coming to Texas she felt something that was almost contentment. She had seen her old home and her friends in Virginia;

her family had seen her new home. There, she thought. That's that. Now then. Jordan. Jordy. Luz.

Suddenly, as she looked at herself in the mirror there in the intimate quiet of their room—the guests gone, the children asleep, the world their own—she had a disquieting thought. She turned to stare at her husband.

"Jordan! We're the older generation, aren't we? Suddenly."

"Not me," he said firmly. "Maybe you, old girl."

"No, but I mean it. Jordy and Luz are the next generation we're always talking about. How did that happen? What's become of ours? We were the next generation until just a minute ago."

"It's always the next generation. I never could understand why they were always the generation that mattered—the next generation. They're always supposed to be better or smarter or more important. And we're supposed to sacrifice for them. So perhaps you're right, we are the older generation all of a sudden. Gosh! And I was feeling right romantic a minute ago."

"Jordan, would you sacrifice for Jordy? And Luz?"

"Sacrifice what?"

"Anything. Beginning with life itself."

"Let's not get dramatic, honey. I've had a hard day in the salt mines."

"But I mean. Just suppose—for example, I mean—that Jordy should want to do something different, be something beside a Benedict of Reata. What would you say to that?"

"Jordy's going to be a cowman. I'm not going to live forever."

"Yes, but suppose when he's eighteen or twenty he says he wants to be—oh, an engineer or a poet or a doctor or President of the United States or an actor or a lawyer."

"Well, he won't be."

"You don't mean you'd try to stop him, like a father out of Samuel Butler!"

"Who?"

"*The Way of All Flesh*—oh, never mind that—I mean you wouldn't actually stop him!"

"The hell I wouldn't."

24

JORDY GREW TALL and slim. Jordy grew handsome and shy. Jordy was possessed of quiet charm and looked like his mother and walked in the footsteps of his father and loathed the daily deadly grinding business of roping and branding and castrating and feeding and breeding and line-riding and fence-building and dipping and shipping.

"I want you to know everything," Bick said again and again. "A Benedict ought to be able to do anything on Reata that any hand can do, white or Mexican. I could, at your age. Maybe as a kid I wasn't as good as the older men. But good enough. That's the way I was brought up."

In the choking dust the boy learned to cut out a calf a cow a steer from the vast herd. He would ride in amongst the bellowing animals, he handled his cutting horse with dexterity, zigzagging this way that way in pursuit of the desired quarry. Bick, mounted on his own horse, would stand watching near by, immobile as an equestrian statue.

"Get that white-faced boneyard. How did an esqueleto like that get in . . . That runty red there . . ." Grudgingly, at the end of a long burning day of grinding work he might say, "You did pretty well, son."

"Thanks, Papa." The boy did not raise his eyelids to look at his father. Leslie always said those long silky lashes were wasted on a boy. "Thanks, Papa." He looked down at his leather-bitten hands.

Leslie called Bick's attention to a little defect in speech that somehow seemed more pronounced as the boy grew older. At first it had seemed a childish trick, rather endearing. "Jordan, have you noticed that Jordy stutters quite a lot? Especially when he's upset."

"He'll outgrow it."

"But it's worse than it was. A real stammer."

"Lots of kids do that. Their ideas come faster than they can talk."

"Jordy isn't really a little boy any more. And Luz wears lipstick as automatically as levis. Let's face it. They're almost grownups."

No one needed to say do-this do-that to Luz. She had taken to horses as other little girls demand dolls and lollipops. By the time she was twelve she could cling like a cat to an unsaddled horse's back. Riding low she could stay plastered to the side of a quarter horse running through the brush, a wilderness of thorns and branches, the twining arms of one mesquite interlocked with the arms of the next and the next so that they formed a bristling barrier.

Bick's admonitions to his daughter were the reverse of the orders he issued to his son. "You're not to ride alone in the brush. Hear me! . . . Keep away from that stallion, you crazy!"

Now her physical resemblance to her father was startling. The sunburned blond hair, the blue eyes that gazed unsquinting almost straight into the glaring sun. She stood as he stood, she spoke with his inflections. Headstrong. Direct. Somewhat insensitive. When the Snyth twins, arrayed in identical pink, were bound for this or that festivity, Luz, in pants and shirt, would be down in the corral or sprawled, grease-grimed, over a balky Ford.

"Luz, the Snyth twins have been on the telephone for hours. They say you promised to pick them up. Scrape that grease off and hustle into your clothes. It's a seventy-mile drive it'll take you at least————"

"Why don't they take themselves! I'm tired of those cowbelles hanging around my neck."

The Reata vaqueros worshiped the girl. In the non-Mexican line-house families she was as accustomed as their own members, she was as likely to be found eating with them as at home. To the Dietz family she was as casual as one of their own sons or daughters. From Bob Dietz, eleven years her senior, she unconsciously received a fundamental education in the sciences embracing soil, seeding, feeding, breeding. During his summer vacations from Texas University and, later, from Cornell, he worked as a matter of course on Reata. Whenever he permitted her Luz rode with him or drove with him, a wide-eyed child in pigtails, her mind absorbent as a thirsty desert plant. She was twelve. Fourteen. Fifteen.

Leslie took this up with her husband. "Jordan, Luz spends all her time with that Dietz boy."

"I wish Jordy did. Bob Dietz knows more about modern ranching than any man on the place. Of course, some of his ideas are cuckoo. I'm all for modern methods but some of this stuff they give them at college!"

"Yes, but I mean Luz isn't a child any more. Bob's a nice boy, and smart————"

"I'll tell you how smart I think he is. Someday that kid's going to be General Manager of Reata unless Jordy pulls up his socks and gets going. That would be a fine thing, wouldn't it! A Benedict just a kind of figurehead on Reata."

"I'm talking about Luz. She's down at the corral or galloping around with Bob Dietz the minute he's home."

Bick waggled his head in admiration. "Gill Dace says she knows more about the stock than his boys do. He says the first time he used that fifty-thousand-dollar Kashmir bull on the new prize heifer Luz was down there telling him about the advantages of artificial insemination."

"Oh, Jordan!"

"This is Reata, honey. Luz knows by this time that the stork doesn't bring our calves."

"Oh well, she'll be going away to school next year."

Luz, the outspoken, ranging the countryside in the saddle or at the wheel, came home with bits and pieces of gossip and information which she dispensed perhaps not as artlessly as one might think. Mealtime frequently was enlivened by her free-association chatter.

"They say Aunt Luz was always trying to keep people from getting married, she couldn't bear the thought. . . . Papa, they say when you brought Mama home you were more scared than if you'd been a horse thief. They say Aunt Luz took to her bed with a fever so she wouldn't have to go to the wedding when you were married, and she actually did have a fever, isn't it wonderful! Of course in those days they didn't understand about psychosomatic illness. And they say———"

"Hold on! Who's this They?" Bick demanded.

"Oh, around. I forget who."

"Well, you just forget all the rest of it then, will you! The whole driveling pack of lies."

She would regard her father with the disconcerting gaze of the young and merciless. "Is it true, Bick honeh, that every woman in Texas tried to get you? They say there wasn't a prize catch like you since before Sam Houston got married."

"I'm sure it's true," Leslie agreed briskly. "It took me two whole days to land him. And in Virginia that's considered overtime."

"They say there was a schoolteacher named Cora Dart at the ranch school and there was some hanky-panky going on between her and you, Papa, and then———"

Angrily, "Who's been telling you this stuff?"

"I don't remember. Somebody at the Beezers' barbecue. I wish people were as romantic as that now. It sounds like a movie. They said Cora Dart tried like everything to marry you. She's the one that crazy Jett Rink married and divorced, isn't she? The first one. And when Papa married you Cora Dart took up with this horrible Jett—you should just hear the stories about *him!*—and when Aunt Luz learned what was going on she said Cora Dart would have to leave. And then she got killed. Aunt Luz, I mean, and they say Aunt Luz was really in love with Jett Rink herself even if she was old enough to be his mother, really it all sounds so fascinating and uncouth I just wish———"

The hot red of fury suffused Bick's face.

"Now Jordan!" came Leslie's voice, cool and calm. "Now Jordan, don't get upset over nonsense. You know it's not good for—for anyone."

Like twin scenes in a somewhat clumsy comedy the boy and the girl privately confided each in the parent who was sympathetic.

"Look, Mama," Jordy said, "I wish you'd speak to Papa."

"You're a big hulking boy now, Jordy. Isn't it time you did your own speaking? And time you stopped this calling us Papa and Mama?"

"He says that's what he called his parents. When it comes to human beings everything has got to be done around here just as it was a hundred years ago. Reata without end, amen! Of course cattle that's different. It's no good my trying to talk to him. He acts as if I were ten years old and feeble-minded."

Jordy's entire aspect changed when he talked to his mother. He was a man, assertive, rebellious, almost confident. In his father's company he dwindled to a timorous hesitant boy.

"What is it you want me to speak to him about?"

"Harvard. That's part of the old pattern. But it happens that that's what I want to do more than anything in the world."

"You do!"

"Yes. But not for his reason. They've got the best pre-med course in the country. And after that I want Columbia University P. and S."

"Now wait a minute. Being a doctor's daughter I know pre-med means—"

"That's right. Pre-medical. Biology chemistry physics. And Columbia's Physicians and Surgeons has got it all over the others. Besides, the New York hospitals give you a better chance at material than any city in the world except maybe London."

She stared at him. "You want to be a doctor."

"I'm going to be."

"Oh, Jordy! Your grandpa will be so happy to know————"

"Yeh, that's fine, but I don't want to slide along on his reputation. He's in all the encyclopedias and medical books and everybody knows about him. Horace Lynnton's grandson, he'd better be good. I don't want that. When I'm through I want to work right here in Texas. A Mexican with tuberculosis here hasn't got a chance. There's a Doctor Guerra in Vientecito, he's got a clinic I'd give anything to————"

"Your father takes the most wonderful care of the people on Reata. You know that. Free medical attention and all that."

"Uh-huh. The cattle too."

"Your father probably will be delighted. You'll have use for all that medical knowledge right here on Reata."

"I don't want to use it here on Reata. I want to be free to work where I want to work."

She knew she must tell him. "Jordy, your father isn't as strong as he seems. It's a heart thing. The arteries that feed it————"

"Yes, I know."

"You do!"

"I've learned a lot about the human body down at the lab with Gill and out on the range doctoring the stock with him and the boys. It isn't the same, of course. But there are quite a few hearts and lungs and livers and lights in a Reata herd."

"Your father expects you to take his place someday." She must know if he was strong enough to reject this.

He stood up. "I'd die for Papa if it was a quick choice between his life and mine. But I won't live for him."

"He won't consent to it, Jordy. Even if we're both for it."

He saw, then, that she was with him. The boy's brooding face came alive. "I haven't any money, Jordy. You know how it is on Reata. Millions, but nobody's got ready cash."

"Don't I know it!" Jordy agreed ruefully.

Quietly she said, "Uncle Bawley will do it if your father won't."

"Old Bawley! What makes you think so?"

"He will. I know."

Luz used the more direct approach in her talk with her father.

"I'm not going to Wellesley."

"What does your mother say to that?"

"She doesn't know."

"The Benedict girls always go to Wellesley."

"No girlie school for this one."

"Oh, I suppose Yale, huh? Or maybe Harvard with Jordy." He laughed at his own joke, not very heartily.

"You're warm. Cornell."

"You're crazy."

"You go to college to learn something. Cornell has got the really scientific husbandry course."

"You've got a little-girl crush on Bob Dietz. If he took a course in dressmaking in Paris that's probably what you'd want to do all of a sudden."

She faced him angrily. "You wouldn't say that to Jordy."

"Your mother says you've concentrated too much on cows already. She thinks a year or so in one of those schools in Switzerland."

Elaborately casual, Bick and Leslie approached the subject, each testing the other. Until almost eleven that night he had been working in his office that adjoined the Main House dining room. Now it was time for that last cup of coffee in the Texas coffee ritual. Leslie had brought the tray to him and she had said, "Jordan, all this coffee so late at night, it can't be good for you, anyway you don't get enough sleep, up at———" when she stopped. She put the tray down on his desk, he leaned back in his chair and looked up at her.

"What's the matter?"

"It just came to me that I was saying something I've said five thousand times. I must be getting old."

"If it weren't so late at night I'd make you a hell of a gallant speech about that, honey. But anyway I realized today we've got a couple of grown-up kids."

"Just today?"

"Know what Luz said? Of course she's too young to know what she really wants. But she said she won't go to Wellesley or even to that school in Switzerland you're so stuck on."

"What then?"

"Says—get this—says she wants to go to Cornell and take the husbandry course."

"No!" But even as she uttered this monosyllable of rejection she thought, Well, perhaps we can make a bargain. Perhaps now is the time to tell him.

"We've hatched a couple of odd fledglings, darling. Jordy says he wants to be a doctor."

Bick shrugged this off. "Over my dead body."

"I feel the same about Luz."

Almost warily they eyed each other like fighters in their corners.

"Anyway, Jordy's going to start his first year at Harvard, just as we always have."

"Don't you think that's a sort of outworn family tradition now? Unless he's going to learn something really valuable and practical? You Benedict boys were sent East for—what was it?—a polish. Jordy doesn't need it."

"He's going."

"It takes seven years of medical school to learn to be a doctor."

"Now look here, Leslie, I don't want to hear any more of that."

"It might be a good idea if Luz skipped Wellesley and went to Switzerland right off. She could use a swipe of polish, if you ask me."

"They're both too young to know what they're doing. One thing's sure. Jordy's going to run Reata. He's got to learn."

Jordy learned. He rode magnificently. He spent days and nights and weeks and months out on the range with the vaqueros, sleeping as they slept, eating as they ate. Old Polo's family became as much a part of Jordy's life as his own. Old Polo taught him from his rich store of knowledge acquired through the centuries before the Anglo-Saxon had set foot on this hot brilliant land. Polo's wrinkled wife gave Jordy strange unguents and weird brews to use when he had a cold or a fever (Leslie threw these out); Polo's handsome daughter-in-law fed him hot spicy Mexican dishes; Polo's pretty little grand-daughter, Juana, one of a brood of eight, gazed at him adoringly, managing demurely to convey with her eyes that which a proper young Mexican girl must not express in words.

Old Polo, the caporal, deposed now but refusing to admit his downfall, hovered over Jordy like a benevolent despot. He still sat his palomino, a storybook king of vaqueros. The Benedict vaqueros still addressed him as Caporal, though Angel Obregon now reigned in his place, and young Angel, seeming one with his horse like a centaur, galloped at his father's side.

Young Jordy in the saddle and Bick mounted near by, with Polo on his miraculous quarter horse that he had trained to work reinless, guided only by a pressure of the knee or by the weight of the rider's body thrown from this side to that. In the lean brown hands that looked so fragile and that yet were so strong was the rope that obeyed his every wish like a sentient thing, whirling, leaping, performing figures in mid-air.

"The media cabeza," Bick called to Jordy. "The half head. Now watch Polo. The loop will catch the bull behind one ear and horn and in front of the other and then under the jaw. All at once. That's a mean-acting bull."

Out would go the rope, snakelike, curving, looping. The huge animal was stopped dead in his tracks.

"Maravilloso! Rebueno!" Jordy shouted.

"Shut up, Jordy. You telling Polo he's good!"

"Yes, but did you notice his hands?"

"Hands! What do you suppose he uses———"

"I mean—" sotto voce—"the old boy's got a little tremor, see, in the right hand, but when it came to throwing the rope he controlled it. That's pretty terrific."

"This isn't a diagnosis, this is roping, for God's sake what's the matter with you!"

But Bick's heart lurched within him in pride as he saw the boy thus mounted; in his cream-white Stetson and the shirt and the buckskin chaps; the rather sallow pointed face, the dark eyes ardent beneath the great rolling hatbrim. Leslie's eyes.

The lazo remolineado. The piale. The mangana. These were tricks used for expert roping in the brush. "Keep close to the horse's mane when you ride in the brush," Polo counseled him. "Where his head can go you can go."

Roping in the open range was less hazardous. "Not so many motions," Polo would warn him. "Leave all that to the city cowboys, to the brave ones who rope the skinny cows in the rodeo in New York. The motions are pretty, but you scare the cattle."

Young Angel Obregon, shorn now of his long black braids, needed no such instruction. Of the two inevitable reactions to his childhood years of petticoat servitude he had chosen the tough one. He rode as one of his charro ancestors. At sixteen he was a swaggerer, a chain smoker, the despair of his father Angel and his mother Deluvina. At seventeen he spurned Reata with all its years of Obregon family loyalty. He took a job as bellboy at the Hake in Vientecito and on his visits to the ranch he swaggered the streets of Benedict in sideburns, fifty-dollar boots, silk shirt, his hair pomaded to the lustre of black oilcloth. He and his friends affected a bastard dialect made up of Mexican jargon, American slang, Spanish patois. His talk was of cars and girls. He did not speak of an automobile as a coche but as a carro. A battery was not an acumulador but a batería. A truck was Hispanicized as a troca. A girl was a güisa—a chick. The Reata vaqueros said of him, in Spanish, "He's trying to change the color of his eyes to blue." Young Angel ran with the bonche.

His father, Angel Obregon the Caporal, his mother Deluvina, were by turns furious and sad at this metamorphosis. He was a disgrace to the raza—the proud race of Mexican people. They were ashamed. They spoke to the padre about him. To old Polo. Even to the patrón, Bick Benedict.

Almost tearfully Angel Obregon said, "He is a good boy, Angel. It is as if some bruja, some evil witch, had him under a spell. He is without respect for the things of life."

Thoughtfully Bick agreed. "I don't know what's the matter with the kids today. They're all alike." He hesitated a moment. But it was a temptation to talk to someone who felt as he did—someone to whom Reata was life, was the world. "My son doesn't have the real feeling about Reata." They were speaking in Spanish. Bick looked at this man whose blood for generations had gone into Reata. He wanted Angel to dispute his statement, he wanted him to say, no, you are wrong, he is a sincere Benedict, the type genuino. But instead Angel now nodded in sorrowful agreement.

Curiously enough, the friendship of the two boys had endured. On Angel's rare visits home he and Jordy discarded the pretense they wore in the presence of their parents. They heard each other in understanding.

"Vaquero with twenny or twenny-five dollars a month," Angel said, and laughed scornfully. "Sometimes I earn that in two days at the Hake if there's a big poker game on in one of the rooms, or a drinking bunch, and I'm on duty. Vaquero like my father and his father and his father, not me! I want to marry with Marita Rivas, Dimodeo Rivas' daughter. But I don't want my kid to be vaquero, and his kid and his kid. Now who does that is a borlo.'

Jordy said, "My father is always experimenting to get better beef. The perfect all meat all tenderloin heatproof tickproof beef animal. That's good, that's swell. But I want to do that with people, not animals. T.b.-proof Mexican-Americans, that would be even better."

On parting Angel no longer said, "Adiós!" He used the Mexican slang of the city. "Ay te watcho!" I'll be seeing you.

Bick Benedict decided that the time had come for action. He would have a talk with Bob Dietz, the kid was finished at Cornell, he'd speak to him now. He planned not to make a casual thing of it, a mere chat about a job if he happened to meet the boy out on the range or in the lab or the corral. This would be a serious talk. He called the Dietz telephone at supper time.

"Bob? . . . Bick Benedict. . . . Bob, I want to talk to you about something important. Jump into your car and come over here about eight."

But Bob Dietz, it seemed, was going to a Grange meeting. Somewhat nettled, Bick said oh, the hell with that, you can go to a Grange meeting another time, this is important.

"I'm sorry," Bob said, "but I'm the speaker there this evening. I'm scheduled to talk on soil and crop rotation. I'll be glad to come tomorrow if that's all right with you."

"You turned into a dirt farmer or something?" Bick jeered.

"Just about," Bob Dietz said genially. "Tomorrow okay then?"

Bob arrived before eight. Bick in his office heard his voice and Luz's laugh from the direction of the veranda, they seemed to have a lot to say to each other, though Luz did most of the talking, there was the slower deeper undercurrent of Bob's voice with a curiously vibrant tone in it. Frowning, Bick came to the door. "Bob! Come on in here. I'm waiting for you."

"Oh. I thought I was a little early."

Bick preceded him into the office, he motioned him to a chair, he sat back and looked at the young fellow, he thought, Golly that's a handsome hunk of kid. There was rather an elaborate silence during which Bob Dietz did not seem ill at ease.

"You wondering why I sent for you, I suppose."

"Why, no, Mr. Benedict. Not especially."

"You'd better be. I've got something pretty important to say to you." There was another silence. Bob Dietz did not squirm or shuffle his feet or cough. Bick thought he never had seen such clear eyes. The whites were blue, like a baby's. Healthy young bull. "I've been watching you pretty close these last few years. Ever since you were a little kid. It took me a while to get over the idea that you were ten years old, two front teeth out, the kid that used to run around fetching for the tumbadores at branding." He laughed.

Bob Dietz laughed too, politely. "I thought I was pretty smart," he said.

"Well, you were right. You are. Now I'm going to come to the point. Reata may have dropped a million acres or so in the last fifty years, but it's bigger than ever in more important ways. Our breeding and feeding program is something I needn't tell you about. You know. This isn't just a ranch any more, it's a great big industrial plant, and run like one. It takes experts. I know about you—well say, I ought to—and I've checked up on you at Cornell. And what they say there is pretty hot."

Bob Dietz looked mildly pleased. He said nothing.

"I'm not getting any younger—that's what my wife calls a cliché————" Bick was a trifle startled to see Bob Dietz grin at this. "Anyway ten years from now this is going to be too much for me even with Jordy taking over a lot of it. I want to start you in now. From what I know about you, I'm not making a mistake. Soil. Irrigation. Breeding. Feeding. Crops. You know the works. My plan is, you start in next spring. I've got a ten-year plan and then another ten-year plan, and so on. Say, the Russians haven't got anything on us at Reata, huh? At the end of ten years you'll be General Manager around here—under me and Jordy. At the end of another ten years—well, anyway, you're fixed for life. And good. Now don't tell me any more, when I call up, about how you have to go to a Grange meeting. Got it?"

"I think so, Mr. Benedict."

"You'll want to go home and talk this over with your folks. You ought to. So I don't expect you to say anything just now. You go along home and mull this over and we'll talk about it again, say, day after tomorrow, that's Wednesday."

"I know now," Bob Dietz said. "I couldn't do it."

"Couldn't do what?"

"A ten-year plan—a twenty-year plan—the rest of my life on Reata, like my father. I want a place of my own."

"You crazy kid! A place of your own. Do you imagine you'll ever have a ranch like Reata!"

"Oh, no sir! I wouldn't want it. I wouldn't have it for a gift. Heh, that doesn't sound good. I know the terrific stuff you've done here. I want a little piece of land of my own for experimentation. Never anything big. That's the whole point. Big stuff is old stuff now."

"Is that so!" Bick was stunned with anger, he could feel something pinching his chest, little pains like jabs. "So big is old-fashioned now, huh?"

"I didn't mean to be—I didn't go to make you mad, Mr. Benedict. I just mean that here in Texas maybe we've got into the habit of confusing bigness with greatness. They're not the same. Big. And great. Why at Cornell, in lab, they say there's a bunch of scientists here in the United States working on a thing so little you can't see it—a thing called the atom. It's a kind of secret but they say if they make it work—and I hope they can't—it could destroy the whole world, the whole big world just like that. Bang."

As he left Luz must have been waiting to see him go. Sitting in his office, stunned, furious, Bick heard them talking and laughing together again. Then their voices grew fainter. To his own surprise he rushed out to stop them like a father in a movie comedy.

They were just stepping into Bob Dietz's car.

"Luz! Where you going!" Bick yelled.

"Down to Smitty's for a Coke."

"You stay home!" But they were off down the drive in the cool darkness.

Leslie appeared from somewhere, she slipped her hand into his arm, she leaned against his shoulder. "Luz is almost a grown-up, darling. Girls of her age don't have to ask permission to go down to Smitty's for a Coke."

25

"SOMEDAY," TEXAS PREDICTED, wagging its head in disapproval, but grinning too, "someday that locoed Jett Rink is agoing to go too far. There's a limit to shenanigans, even his."

The Spanish conquistadores had searched in vain for the fabled Golden Cities of the New World. They had died on the plains, their bones had rotted deep in the desert and the cactus and the mesquite and the dagger flower grew green above them, their thorns like miniature swords commemorating the long-rusted steel of the dead men. And now here were the Golden Cities at last, magically sprung up like a mirage.

There were in these cities a thousand men like Jett Rink and yet unlike except for their sudden millions. Other men might conduct their lives outrageously but Jett Rink had become a living legend. Here was a twentieth-century Paul Bunyan striding the oil-soaked earth in hundred-dollar boots. His striding was done at the controls of an airplane or at the wheel of a Cadillac or on a golden palomino with tail and mane of silver.

A fabric made up of truth and myth was hung about his swaggering shoulders. Wherever men gathered to talk together there was a fresh tale to tell which they savored even while they resented it.

"Did you hear about that trip of his, hunting there back of Laredo? Seems him and that Yerb Packer were in that hunting shack Jett's got there. They were eating in the kitchen—you know Jett—drinking more than eating I reckon, and with this and that they got to quarreling and then to fighting. They was clawing and gouging like a couple of catamounts, blood running down their faces, their clothes half tore off. Well, Yerb clouts Jett a real sock and Jett he reaches out on the shelf there for a big bottle of some kind of fluid like it kills bugs and you pour it down the sink and plumbing and so on. It's got acid in it or something. Anyway, he fetches Yerb a crack over the head with it, the bottle busts and the stuff pours all over Yerb, liked to burned the hide right off him, they say he'll be months . . . "

" . . . You know that hospital for old Vets of the World War, a bunch of them been sitting around there for years now, poor lunks, went in maybe when they were twenty after the war, thinking they'd be out cured, and now they're forty and more, some of them, and never will be out. Well, anyway, somebody sent over a bunch of free tickets for the football game. So the bus took some of them that was well enough to go to the game. But along about the middle of the game a mean norther blew up, rain and cold, and quite a few folks skedaddled for home. This one old fella he gets soaked, he wasn't feeling too good to begin with, a artificial leg and all. So he leaves, he starts heading down the road toward the car park, he figures somebody will sure pick him up and give him a lift back to the hospital. Well, along behind comes Jett in his Caddy he's got those strong-arm guys always riding with him. Jett's driving though, you know how he is, he'd been liquoring up to keep warm. You know the way he drives, even sober a hunderd miles is crawling to him. This lame old vet don't hear him coming or maybe Jett don't see him in the thick rain, he misses him by an inch. Well, the vet gives a quick jump, just barely saves himself and falls down a course with that leg and all, but he scrambles up and shakes his fist at Jett like a fella in a play and he lets out a line of language even Jett Rink couldn't do better. Jett gets an earful of this and what does he do he gets out with those guys with him and they beat up this old cripple, they hit him around the head and all, they say he's lost his hearing. I hear Jett paid out quite a hunk afterwards but just the same what I say is someday Jett Rink's agoing to go too far."

"What became of that first woman he married? Schoolteacher, wasn't she? Imagine!"

"Oh, that was a million years ago. He's had two others since then. Maybe three. I haven't kept track. Second one was a secretary of his, must have had something big on him."

"They say when he's really good and drunk he talks about that wife of Bick Benedict."

"He's a dirty liar! She's straight as they come. Too straight. They say a regular do-gooder. From up North, she is. But straight."

Sometimes he strode, very late, into one of the big city shops—Neiman's or Opper's or Gulick's—when they were about to close for the day. He liked to inconvenience them, he felt deep power-satisfaction in compelling the saleswomen or department heads to stay on after hours, serving him, Jett Rink. He liked his little joke, too. He would extend his hard paw to shake hands with a saleswoman of middle age, perhaps, with a soignée blue-grey coiffure and a disillusioned eye. As her thin hard-working hand met his she would recoil with a squawk of terror. In the great palm of his hand he had concealed a neat chunky steel-cold revolver.

As he lolled in the brocade bower that was a fitting room they would spread for his selection furs silks jewels.

"This looks like you, Mr. Rink," they would say, fluffing out the misty folds of a cobweb garment. Frequently they were summoned to bring their wares to one of his ranches and there these would be displayed for him, an oriental potentate in redface. A mink coat. A sapphire. A vicuña topcoat for himself or a special hunting rifle with a new trick.

SOCIETY
By Gloria Ann Wicker

Mrs. Jordan Benedict and daughter Luz are Hermoso visitors and shoppers this week. While in the city they are stopping at the Tejas Hotel. Miss Luz Benedict will spend a year or more at a select girls' school in Switzerland. There are other more interesting rumors which have not yet been confirmed.

Luz read this aloud to her mother as they sat at breakfast in their sitting room at the Tejas. "What rumors, I wonder. And just how interesting. It sounds so tantalizing. No girl ever had a duller summer."

"Reata's always good for a rumor," Leslie said, "when there's no news. Come on, dear, let's get started or we'll never cover this list."

"It's too hot, anyway. Why can't we wait and get it all in New York next month?"

"I like the idea of shopping for ski pants in Texas when the temperature's one hundred."

Gulick's opulent windows reflected the firm's disdain for such whims as temperature time or place. Hot or cold, autumn was just around the corner. Gulick's window displays were aimed at those Texans who early armed themselves for a holiday in New York in California in Florida Europe Chicago or even that Yankeetown Dallas. The lure of one window was too much even for shoppers like Leslie and Luz, bent on sterner stuffs. Wordlessly they stopped to gaze at it. Luxurious though every article was, each had the chaste quality of utter perfection.

The window held a woman's complete evening toilette. Nothing more. A fabulous fur wrap. A satin-and-tulle gown. Diamond necklace. A bracelet of clumped jewels. Long soft gloves flung carelessly on the floor like thick cream spilled on carpet. Cobwebs of lingerie. Wisps of chiffon hosiery. Fragile slippers. Jewel-encrusted handbag.

"Mm," said Luz.

"Nice," Leslie said.

As they stood there a hand slid through the arm of each, separating the two women. "Like it?" said a man's voice. "I'll buy the whole window for you, Leslie."

Leslie stared into Jett Rink's face.

Instinctively she jerked her arm to free it. His hand held it inescapably. He was scarcely taller than she, his eyes were level with hers, his face was close, the eyes intent, bloodshot. He was smiling. Now, still holding the arms of the two women locked beneath his arms, an iron hand pressed tightly against each hand on his shoulder, he turned his head slowly on that short thick neck to stare at the girl.

"You're Luz. I'm Jett Rink, Luz."

"Yes. I've seen pictures of you. Look, do you mind, you're just a little too hearty, you're hurting me."

"Luz. A hell of a thing to do to a pretty girl like you, name her after that old bitch."

The arms of both women jerked to be free. He held them. He turned again to Leslie. "Am I hurting you too, Leslie?"

She thought, clearly. On Sonoro Street in Hermoso in front of Gulick's. Nothing must happen. Nothing to disgrace Jordan and the children. She spoke quietly as she always had spoken in the past to the violent boy, now a more violent man.

"I'm not going to wrestle with you on the street. Take your hand away."

He swung them around as if in a dance, one on each side. "Would you wrestle in the car?" At the curb was an incredibly long bright blue car. A man sat at the wheel, another stood at the rear door. "Come on, girls. Let's take a ride."

It was unbelievable it was monstrous. For the first time she knew fear. He propelled them across the sidewalk.

"No!" Leslie cried. Faces of passers-by turned toward them, uncertainly.

Luz's free left hand was a fist. Now she actually twisted round to aim at his face but he jerked his head back, and he laughed a great roaring laugh and the passers-by, reassured, went on their way grinning at the little playful scuffle. "I'm not going to hurt you. Don't make such a fuss." He and the man standing at the car door half lifted half pulled them into the deep roomy rear seat, Jett between them. The door slammed, the man whirled into the front seat with the driver, the car shot into traffic.

Her voice rather high, like a little girl's, Luz said, "What is this, anyway! Let's get out, Mama."

Leslie looked at the monolithic faces of the two men in the front seat. "If you hurt Luz," Leslie said, her voice low and even, "you know perfectly well that no bodyguards can keep him from killing you." At the absurdity of this melodramatic statement she began to laugh somewhat hysterically.

"There you!" Jett turned triumphantly to Luz. "Your ma knows I was just fooling, I saw in the paper where you girls were in town and I been wanting to have a little talk with your ma. I been stuck on your ma for years. Did you know that?"

"I think you're a goon," Luz shouted.

Jett's voice took on an aggrieved tone. "There you go. Comes to a Benedict, no matter what I do, it's wrong. I was just kidding around. I watched for you to come out of the Tejas. And then over to Gulick's and standing there looking in the window like a couple of little stenographers or something. Say, you don't have to tell me," he went on, easily, conversationally. "I know Bick's pinched for money all the time, that big damn fool place he thinks he runs. I'd buy you the whole Gulick setup, Leslie, the whole ten floors and everything in it, if you say the word. I'm sick of buying stuff for myself. At first I got a bang out of it, but not any more. Look at this coat! I got a topcoat like it, too. Vicuña. Feel! Soft as a baby's bottom. Looka this watch." He thrust out his great hairy wrist. "It does everything but bake a cake. This Caddy's a special body and armored, thirty thousand dollars."

"What are we going to do, Mama?" Luz said. Her voice now was as quiet as her mother's had been, but its undernote was tremulous.

"It's all right, dearest," Leslie said, "It's his idea of a joke."

"I ain't joking, Leslie. I got to talk to you. Like I said."

The man seated at the right, in front, picked up a sort of telephone receiver that was one of a battery of contrivances attached to the dashboard. He spoke into it with mechanical clarity and conciseness. "Passing corner of Viña and Caballero. . . . Three minutes. . . . Past corner Viña and Caballero. . . . Two and three quarter minutes."

Their speed never slowed, a huge building like a warehouse loomed ahead, a ten-foot metal fence enclosed it. The car approached this at terrific pace, in that instant before what seemed an inevitable crash the gates swung sharply open, the car tore through without diminishing speed, the gates swung shut, the huge car stopped with a shriek of brakes. The man in front got out. He stood at the car door. Jett Rink was scribbling a note, holding the pad up close to his chest as he wrote. He tore it off, the man at the door took it. "You call them yourself. And tell them it's got to be there within a half an hour or no dice. . . . Now then, girlies, I want to talk to your ma, Luz. Do you want to sit here in the car while we go and sit on the bench there in the shade? Or do you want to sit there and we'll stay in the car."

Curiously, it was Luz who now took over. "We'll both get out or we'll both stay in. Or I'll begin to scream and while it probably won't do any good in this place I'll scream and scream and scream until———"

"Oh, all right." Wearily, as though agreeing to the whim of an unreasonable child. "It's hot, no matter where you sit. You go on over there, other side of the entrance. Your ma and I'll sit on that bench here, have our little talk. Either you girls want a Coke or something cold to drink?''

Leslie looked up at the blank windows of the building. "What is this place?''

"It's nothing only a warehouse where I keep stuff, valuable stuff. I got places like this all around. First I was going to drive you out to the ranch, I got a place about an hour out. But a lot of folks out there all the time, visiting and all, I figured you wouldn't like that. I wouldn't want to do anything you wouldn't like—you and the kid.''

She glanced at him but his face was serious. "I thought you were drunk. But you're not, are you?''

"I ain't had a drop for two days. Minute I knew you was in town I quit, I knew I wanted a clear head and sometimes I get fuzzy when I take a couple. I'm stone cold sober.''

Slim, almost boyish seated there beside her in his neat expensive clothes, a blue shirt, a polka-dotted tie.

"Such silly behavior. You've scared Luz to death, she didn't know you when you were a greasy kid on Reata. What is it? You want me to help you make friends again with Bick, or something like that, I suppose.''

"You suppose. You suppose I don't know you're smarter than that! You're the only really smart girl I ever knew. And that ain't all. Not. Quite. All.'' He had been smoking a cigarette. Now he tossed it away. "Look. I been crazy about you all these years. You know that well and good.'' He was talking carefully and reasonably as one would present a business argument or a political credo. "I tried everything to get shut of it. I had all the kinds there is. I even been married three four times. Did you know that?''

"I've never thought about it at all.''

"Why do you suppose I done that—did that?''

"Some men do. It's an unadult trait. It means they've never really grown up.''

He dropped his tone of calm reasoning. The little twin dots of red flicked into the close-set hooded eyes. He leaned toward her. "I got to get shut of it. It's making me sick. Look at this.'' He held out his hand. "Look at that! Shakes like that all the time.''

"That's alcohol and shot nerves and fear.''

"Leslie. Leslie. Come with me. Leslie.''

Equably, and quite conversationally as though exchanging chitchat with a friend. "I'm really quite an old lady now, you know. You just think you're still talking to that rather attractive girl who came, a bride, to Reata. . . . It's very hot here, Jett.''

"Anything you'd want. Anything in the world. He wouldn't care. He don't care about anything only Reata.''

She stood up. "All right, Luz!'' she called. "We're going now.''

He grasped her arm. "I'll go after Bick and you and your two kids. I swear to God I will. I'll never let up on all of you.''

"You've been seeing too many Western movies.''

She moved toward the car. The man sat up at the wheel. The second man came down the steps and toward the car.

"I ain't going,'' Jett said. "Luz, you sit up front there with him. Leslie, you get in the back here. You too, Dent'. You call back here for me in ten minutes.''

He stood there a moment in the brilliant sun.

"I'll do like I said,'' Jett called softly to Leslie, through the window.

"Where to?'' asked the driver.

"Gulick's,'' Leslie said airily. "We have a great deal of shopping to do.''

"No. Please." Luz did not look round. "I'd like to go to the hotel first. For a minute. I forgot something."

"Tejas," Leslie said then.

The gates opened.

Down the street. In traffic against traffic in and out in sickening suicidal zigzags. He has told them to kill us this way, Leslie thought. Then, reasonably, No, they'd be killed too, so probably not. They stopped at the Tejas entrance. They were in the lobby, they were in the elevator, they were in their rooms.

"I'm going to call up Papa."

"I wouldn't," Leslie said. "Not until we've talked a little first."

Luz was crying, quietly, her eyes wide open and the tears sliding unwiped down her face. "I was scared. I kept thinking I'd do something terrific and brave, but I was scared."

"So was I, dear."

Luz wiped her face now, she stood staring at her mother as at some new arresting object. "I think it's the most romantic thing I ever heard of! And I think he's kind of cute."

"Don't say that."

"But I do. I've heard a lot about him and I never believed it, but it's true. He's a kind of modern version of the old buccaneer type like Grampa and Great-grampa Benedict. They were tough, too, in a different way, of course, land swiping and probably a lot of hanky-panky with the Mexican girls. I must say Jett Rink's windup was an anticlimax, though. I expected rape at the very least————"

"You're being silly, Luz. This man is a twisted————"

"The Snyth twins say he's the fashion now, he's so tough he's considered chic. I must say I'm impressed with you, Mama, being the secret passion of that hard-boiled . . ." She had gone into her bedroom, her voice trailed off, then came up sharply: " . . . what in the world is all this! Mom! Come here!"

Boxes. Boxes and boxes and boxes. Stacked on beds and chairs. The smart distinctive blue-and-white striped Gulick boxes.

Miss Luz Benedict, the address slips read. Miss Luz Benedict. Miss Luz Benedict. Miss Luz Benedict.

She yanked at the cords. She opened a box. Another. Another. The fabulous fur wrap. The satin and tulle evening dress. The necklace. The slippers . . . The window.

" . . . Gulick?" Leslie at the telephone. "I want to talk to Mrs. Bakefield. Mrs. Bakefield's office. . . . This is Mrs. Jordan Benedict. . . . Mrs. Bakefield? Yes, Mrs. Jordan Benedict. There has been a mistake. We just came in—the Tejas—and there are a million packages that don't belong to us. It is just some terrible mistake. . . . Oh, Mrs. Bakefield! He must have seen some sort of mention in the newspaper. . . . No . . . Oh no, she doesn't even know him . . . I hear he is very—well—eccentric now and then. . . . Just send for them . . . yes . . . now . . ."

26

A BENEDICT FAMILY meeting—a Benedict Big Business Powwow—was in progress. But this was not the regular annual Benedict family business assemblage. This was an unscheduled meeting called by the outraged members of the clan. For the first time in a quarter of a century the Big House was cleared of all outside guests. Only the family occupied the bedrooms, clattered down the halls, ate at the long table in the dining room. But the house was well filled for they had come, down to the last and least voting member. The thick walls seemed bursting with the strain of temper and fury within.

They sat in the vast main living room that had been planned to accommodate formal occasions such as this—funerals, weddings, family conclaves. A handsome lot they were, too; tall, fit, their eyes clear their skins fresh with carefully planned exercise and expensive proteins and vitamins.

Uncle Bawley, oldest member of the clan, was presiding but no one paid the slightest attention to him. In appearance he was extraordinarily unchanged with the years except for the white shock of hair above the mahogany face. These meetings were ordinarily conducted with parliamentary exactitude, everyone polite and gruesomely patient in spite of the emotions always seething beneath the ceremonial behavior. But now the great chamber vibrated with heat and hate and contention. Parliamentary procedure was thrown to the Gulf winds. Uncle Bawley's gavel (mesquite, and too soft a wood for the quelling of Benedict brawls) rapped in vain for order.

Bick Benedict stood facing them all, and Bick Benedict shouted. "I won't have it. We're doing all right without oil. I won't have it stinking up my ranch."

"Your ranch!" yelled a dozen Benedicts. Then, variously, "That's good! Did you hear that! You're managing this place and getting your extra cut for it. Your ranch!" New York Chicago Buffalo California Florida Massachusetts Benedicts.

Leslie, sitting by, an outsider, thought, Oh dear this is so bad for him I wish they'd go home or why don't they stay here and try running it for a change, the Horrors.

One of the more arrogant of the Benedicts, who dwelt on the East Coast, now dropped all pretense of courtesy.

"Just come down off it, will you, Bick? And face it. You've got delusions of grandeur. You're big stuff, I know, among the local Texas boys. But we happen to have an interest in this concern. And we've got the right to say by vote whether we want or don't want a little matter of five or ten million a year—and probably a lot more—a whole lot more later—divided up amongst us. I don't know about the rest of you boys and girls, but me, I could use a little extra pin money like that."

Stubbornly facing the lot of them, his face white beneath the tan, and set in new deep lines, Bick repeated stubbornly the words he had used over and over again as though they presented a truth that made all argument useless. "Reata is a cattle ranch. It's been a cattle ranch for a hundred years."

"That's just fine," drawled an unsentimental Benedict. "And there used to be thirteen states in the Union and the covered wagon was considered hot stuff."

The laugh that now went up encouraged Maudie Placer to sink a deft dart. "And please don't quote that story about old Pappy Waggoner when he was drilling for water and they brought in all that oil on his North Texas place. Quote. 'Damn it, cattle can't drink that stuff.' Unquote."

Now Leslie saw with a sinking heart that the grey-white in Bick's face was changing to scarlet. "Do you people know who wants the lease? Do you know who wants the rights?"

"Yes, Teacher, we do. It's the Azabache Oil Company and a mighty pretty little outfit it is, too. I'm real petted on it."

"I'll bet you are. You've been away from Texas so long you've forgotten your Spanish. D'you know what Azabache means! It's Spanish for jet, if you want to know. And it doesn't mean just jet for black oil. It's jet for Jett

Rink. Jett—Azabache. He controls most of it. Well, by God, I won't have Jett Rink owning any piece of my country here on Reata————''

"Hold on there! Just—a—minute. You've got a pick on Jett Rink, you've had it for years. Some little personal feud. Who cares!''

"I tell you you'll all care if he gets a toe in here.''

"All right all right. He's a mean umbry. Everybody knows that. We don't want to love him. We just want a nice thick slice of that billion he's got stashed away.''

"He's got nothing but a lot of paper. He's in over his head. Everybody knows that Gabe Target could sell him down the river tomorrow if he wanted to.''

Now Uncle Bawley forsook Rules of Order. "That's right, Jurden!'' he bellowed—he who never had called his nephew anything but Bick. "Don't you let'em ride you!''

"The law!'' shouted a Benedict.

"How about Pa's will!'' Bick countered. "And Grampa's! You going to fight those too?''

"You bet we are. We're going to fight them for years if we have to. We don't care what the will says. There wasn't any oil on Reata or anywhere near it when Pa's will was made. We'll get every lawyer in New York and Chicago and Houston and Hermoso and Corpus Christi and Austin and Vientecito————''

Uncle Bawley threw his mesquite gavel across the room and brought his massive fist down on the table with a crash and a succession of crashes that silenced even the shouting Benedicts.

"Stop this bellering I say or I'll arrest the lot of you and I can do it. I'm a State Ranger and I'm supposed to keep law and order and I'm agoing to. . . . Sit down! . . . Now then. I'm sorry, Jurden, but we got to put this to a vote. And what the vote says, goes. That's the law. That's the rule of this family and always has been. . . . Roady, pass those slips. . . . Bowie, you'll collect. . . . You all get out your big gold fountain pens and I hope they leak all over you for a bunch of stampeding maverick Benedicts. Now vote!''

The vote stood two to twenty-five. That night Uncle Bawley took off for Holgado and the high clear mountain air. Within three days there was not one Benedict left in the cavernous walls of the Big House.

Leslie Benedict found herself in the fantastic position of a wife who tries to convince her husband that a few million dollars cannot injure him.

"You'll go on with your own work just the same. Better. It won't affect the actual ranch. You'll be free of their complaints now.''

"Rink.'' Bitterness twisted his mouth as he spoke the name. "Jett Rink owning rights to Reata.''

"He doesn't. He just holds a lease on a tiny bit of it. Besides you've told me yourself the Azabache Company isn't only Jett Rink. It's a lot of other people. Some of them are people you know well.''

"He controls it.''

"You'll never need to deal with him. Think of the things you can do now!'' She paused a moment. "I don't mean only the things you're interested in. They're wonderful but I mean—couldn't we use some of it maybe for things like—necessary things, I mean, like new houses for the ranch people and perhaps the start of a decent hospital and even a school where they're not separated—a school that isn't just Mexican or just———— Oh, Jordan, how exciting that would be!''

He was not listening, he did not even consciously hear her.

"Nobody's ever set foot on Benedict land except to produce better stock and more of it. You're not a Texan. You're not a Benedict. You don't understand.''

"I'm not a Texan and I'm not a Benedict except by marriage. I do understand because I love you. It embarrasses you to hear me say that after all these years. I'm trying to tell you that if there's got to be all that crazy money then use some of it for the good of the world. And I don't mean only your world. Reata.''

"Uh-huh. You won't be so smug when you see Benedict swarming with a pack of greasy tool dressers and drillers and swampers and truckers. It's going to be hell. Pinky Snyth was talking about it last night. Vashti's leased a piece of the Double B to Azabache.''

"Well, there you are! You needn't feel so upset.''

"The whole country's going to stink of oil. Do you know what else Pinky said! He and Vashti are talking of building in town—Viento or even Hermoso—moving to town and the family only coming out to the ranch week ends and holidays. Like some damned Long Island setup.''

"Vashti might like that. I'm sure the twins would.''

"Yes. Maybe you would too. H'm? Nice slick house in town? Azalea garden, nice little back yard, people in for cocktails and Patroness of the Hermoso Symphony and the Little Theatre in the Round—Square—Zigzag— or whatever the goddamned fashion is. We could use these two three million acres for picnic grounds and so on.''

"Jordan my darling. Jordan. Don't be like that.''

She hesitated a moment. She took a deep breath. Now for it. "You know, we don't exactly have to have millions of acres in order to live—you and the children and I. It's killing you—I mean it's too much. Why can't we have a few thousand acres—how Texas that sounds! But anyway—why can't we have a ranch of our own, smallish, where you could breed your own wonderful————''

The blue eyes were agate. "I've lived on Reata all my life. I'm going to live here till I die. Nothing on it is going to change.''

"Everything in the world changes every minute.''

"Reata's just going to improve. Not change.''

So now the stink of oil hung heavy in the Texas air. It penetrated the houses the gardens the motorcars the trains passing through towns and cities. It hung over the plains the desert the range; the Mexican shacks the Negro cabins. It haunted Reata. Giant rigs straddled the Gulf of Mexico waters. Platoons of metal and wood marched like Martians down the coast across the plateaus through the brush country. Only when you were soaring in an airplane fifteen thousand feet above the oil-soaked earth were your nostrils free of it. Azabache oil money poured into Reata. Reata produced two commodities for which the whole world was screaming. Beef. Oil. Beef. Oil. Only steel was lacking. Too bad we haven't got steel, Texas said. But then, after that Sunday morning in December even the voice of the most voracious was somewhat quieted.

With terrible suddenness young male faces vanished from the streets of Benedict. White faces black faces brown faces. Bob Dietz was off. The kids in the Red Front Market. The Beezer boys. High. Low. Rich. Poor. The Mexican boys around Garza's in Nopal and the slim sleek boys at the Hake in Viento and even the shifting population that moved with the crops and the seasons—all, all became units in a new world of canvas. Texas was used to khaki-colored clothes, but these garments were not the tan canvas and the high-heeled boots and the brush jackets of the range and plains. This was khaki with a difference.

Young Jordy Benedict at Harvard was summoned home to Reata.

"You're needed here on Reata," Bick said tersely. "Beef to feed the world. That's the important thing."

"I can't stay here now."

"Yes you will. Any one of ten million kids can sit at a desk in Washington. Or shoot a German. Producing beef here on Reata is the constructive patriotic thing for you to do. You're just being hysterical."

"I'll go back to school. Or I'll be drafted. I won't stay here."

"No draft board will take you. I can fix that all right anywhere. And I won't send you a cent if you go back to Harvard."

The two men were talking in Bick's office. The boy quiet, pale. The older man glaring, red-faced. Casually, Leslie strolled in and sat down.

Brusquely Bick said, "We're talking."

"I'm listening. I've been listening outside the door so I may as well come in." Jordy glanced at her and smiled a little. It made a startling change in the somber young face. "Jordy, you look more like your Grandpa Lynnton every day."

As if this were a cue Jordy relaxed in his chair, his eyes as he looked at his father now were steady. "When I'm through at Harvard I'm going on to Columbia P. and S."

"P. and S.?" Bick repeated dully.

"Physicians and Surgeons. School. We need doctors as much as beef. That's why I'm going on instead of in. I haven't used any of the money you've sent me all this time. And thanks, Papa. Your money is all in the bank there in Boston, waiting for you. I couldn't use it because you didn't know about me."

Bick Benedict turned with a curiously slow movement of his head to look at his wife. "Then you must have been sending him your money."

"Jordan dear, don't go on like a father in a melodrama. I haven't any money. You know that. Everyone on Reata is short of money except the cows."

"Who then?" He stood up. "Who then!" A dreadful suspicion showed in his face. "Not . . . !"

She came to him. "It's Uncle Bawley. And I asked him. So don't blame him for it."

Slowly he said, "That old turtle." Then, "The three of you, huh?"

Jordy stood up. "Papa, you know I never was any good around here. I never will be. Any man on Reata can do the job better than I ever could."

"That's right," Jordan said. "You never were any good. You never will be. You're all alike, you kids today, white and Mexican, you or Angel Obregon. No damn good."

"Angel's fine," Leslie said matter-of-factly. "I saw him today in Benedict, he looked wonderful in his uniform. Jordy, Angel's going to be married Tuesday. Did you know that?"

"Yes. I'm staying for the wedding."

"Oh, you're staying for the wedding?" Bick repeated, cruelly mimicking his son just a little, even to the stammer. "Well that's big of you! That's a concession to Reata, all right." He turned the cold contemptuous eyes on Leslie. "You've been years at this. Twenty years. Satisfied?"

Her tone her manner were as matter-of-fact and good-natured as his aspect was tragic. "Watch that arithmetic. Jordy going to be twenty-one pretty soon."

Bick had been standing. Now he sat again rather heavily at his desk. He did not look at them. "That's right. We were going to have a party. Big party."

"Not in wartime, Jordan."

He looked up at his son. "I hadn't forgotten, it just slipped my mind.
You'll be coming into your Reata shares. You don't mind living off Reata
even if you don't want to live on it, huh?"

Quietly Jordy said, "They'll see me through. I've thought about that. I've
got as much right to them as Roady's kids, or Bowie's or Aunt Maudie's."

Bick Benedict picked up a sheaf of papers on his desk, shuffled them, put
them down. "Doctor, h'm? New York, I suppose."

"Now Jordan!" Leslie protested. "You know Jordy loves Texas as much
as you do. In another way, perhaps."

"You counting on putting old Doctor Tom out of business, maybe."

"I think I'm going to have a chance to work with Guerra in Vientecito
when the war's over. If he's lucky enough to come back in one piece."

"Guerra! You don't mean—why, he's———"

"Rubén Guerra. His practice is all Mexican, of course. Uh—look. There's
something else I'd like to talk to you and Mama about. I'm afraid you won't
like this either."

"I've had about enough for just now," Bick said, and turned back to his
desk and the aimless shuffling of papers. "Tell your life plans to your buddies,
why don't you! Doctor Guerra———"

"He's busy in Europe just now."

"Well, Angel Obregon. Or Polo." He was racked with bitterness and
disappointment.

"All right, Papa. I will."

27

YOUNG ANGEL OBREGON did indeed look fine in his uniform. Uniforms were
nothing novel to Angel after his tenure in the skin-tight mess jacket and the
slim pants, the braid and gold buttons of the Hake Hotel bellboy. But this
uniform he wore with a difference. His movements about the vast marble
columns of the Hake lobby had been devious and slithering as a seal's. Now,
in the plain khaki of a private, he swaggered. Months of camp training had
filled him out, he was broader in the shoulder, bigger across the chest. He
always had had, like his forebears, the slim flanks and the small waist of the
horseman.

"One of those Pacific places," he said. "I bet. That's where they're
shipping all us Mex—all us Latin Americans, they say we're used to the hot
clmate, they're nuts. Vince Castenado came home with malaria, he says it's
all jungle."

Half of Benedict and practically all of Nopal were invited to the wedding.
Angel was marrying Marita Rivas, one of the daughters of Dimodeo. A
middle-aged husband and father now, Dimodeo Rivas, head of the clipping,
snipping, nurturing, spraying, watering, planting group of men who tended
the flowers, the precarious lawns, the rare transplanted trees, the walks the
roads, the new swimming pool—the whole of the landscaping around the Big
House and the Main House.

Of course young Angel had furnished the trousseau according to custom.
The importance of Marita's marriage would be gauged by the display of her
gowns and her bridal dress, at the boda—the wedding feast.

"We'll have to go," Bick said heavily, grumpily. "Angel's son. It wouldn't
look right if we didn't. I'm only going because of his father."

"Why Jordan, I wouldn't miss it! Angel! He was the first Reata baby I
saw. The morning after I came here. He wet all over one of my trousseau

dresses. And now we'll see the trousseau dresses he's got for his bride. I have to laugh when I think of those long black braids he used to wear."

"You don't see him wearing any hair ribbons now."

Everyone was there, from the Benedicts of Reata to Fidel Gomez the coyote from Nopal. Fidel was a personage now, he no longer needed to bother about exploiting his own people. Fidel Gomez, too, had been touched by the magic wand of the good fairy, Oil. His run-down patch of mesquite land outside Nopal now hummed and thumped with the activities of the men and machinery that brought the rich black liquid out of the earth.

There was the bridal ceremony, full of pomp and ritual, and the bride in white satin with pearl beads and wax orange blossoms. The dress was later to be hung properly in the best room for all to see, and never to be worn again. A high platform had been built outside Dimodeo's house. After the church ceremony the bride appeared on this in each of the seven dresses of her bridal trousseau, so that all should see what a fine and openhanded husband her Angel Obregon was. The girls eyed her with envy and the men looked at her and at the proud Angel and thought, Well, a lot of good those dresses and that pretty little chavala will do you when you are sweating in the islands of the South Pacific. What a tontería! But Marita walked proudly along the platform.

Leslie had seen all this before at many ranch weddings but she was as gay and exhilarated as though she never before had known the ceremony of the boda.

"This is the kind of thing I love about Texas. Everyone here and everyone happy and everyone neighbors. It's perfect." She squeezed Bick's arm, she smiled, she met a hundred outstretched hands.

"They'd be a hell of a lot better off if they'd save their dough and get married quietly now in wartime," Bick said. "But they're all the same. Marita'll be pregnant tomorrow and have her first in nine months flat."

"Like me," said Leslie, "darling. When we were married."

Young Angel had had a few drinks of tequila. "Fix 'em over there quick, and I come home to Marita and a little Angel—only we don't call him Angel, that is a no-good name for a man."

The tables were spread out of doors, long planks on wooden standards, and there was vast eating and drnking, and laughing and talking and the singing of corridos especially written for the occasion, telling of Angel's prowess and potency and Marita's beauty and accomplishments, and the blissful future that lay ahead of them. Luzita, away at school, would have loved it, Leslie reflected. She would write her all about it. Just look at Jordy. He seemed to be having a wonderful time, not shy and withheld as he so often was. She called Bick's attention to Jordy.

"Look at Jordy! He's having a high time. I was afraid he'd feel—uh—that he would be upset, seeing Angel in uniform. Going, I mean, so soon. But look at him!"

"Mm." Bick stared down the long table at his son seated next to a pretty young Mexican girl and looking into her eyes. "He's being a shade too gallant, isn't he, to that little what's-her-name—Polo's granddaughter isn't it?"

"Don't be feudal. She's a decent nice little girl and her name is Juana. Jordy's being polite and she loves it."

A fine feast. Barbecued beef and beans. The great wedding caque was the favorite feast cake called color de rosa. It was made of a dough tinted with pink vegetable coloring, or colored with red crepe paper soaked in water, the water mixed with the cake dough, very tasty. There was pan de polvo, little round cakes with a hole in the middle, shaped with the hand, delectably sugary and grainy. There were buñuelos, rolled paper-thin and big as the big frying pan in which they had hissed in deep fat. Delicious with the strong hot coffee. There was beer, there was tequila, there was mescal. A real boda, and no mistake.

So Angel and Marita looked deeply into each other's eyes, and danced, and behaved like proper young Mexicans newly married. Everyone drank to Angel's return, unharmed, to Benedict. No one knew that Angel would return from the South Pacific, sure enough, landing in California after the close of the great Second World War, and coming straight back to Benedict. But he came home as bits and shreds of cloth and bone in a box. He came home a hero, his picture was in the papers, he had proved himself a tough hombre sure enough there in those faraway sweating islands. So tough that they had given him the highest honor a tough hombre can have—the Congressional Medal of Honor. The citation had been quite interesting. Private First Class Angel Obregon . . . conspicuous gallantry and intrepidity, above and beyond the call of duty . . . undaunted . . . miraculously reaching the position . . . climbed to the top . . . heroic conduct . . . saved the lives of many comrades . . . overwhelming odds . . .

It made fine reading. And the widowed Marita and old Angel Obregon and his wife and his ancient grandmother all knew that there must be a funeral befitting the conduct of the bits that lay heaped in the flag-draped box. But the undertaker in Benedict—Funeral Director he now was called—said that naturally he could not handle the funeral of a Mexican. Old Angel, a man of spirit, said that his son was an American; and that there had been Mexicans in Texas when Christopher Columbus landed on the continent of North America. But the Funeral Director—Waldo Shute his name was—big fellow—said Angel should take the box to Nopal, why not? Someone—there were people who said it might have been Leslie Benedict—thought this was not quite right. Talk got around, it reached a busy man who was President of the United States of America way up north in Washington, D.C. So he had the flag-draped box, weary now of its travels, brought to Washington and buried in the cemetery reserved for great heroes, at Arlington. Marita wished that it could have been nearer Benedict, so that she might visit her husband's grave. But she was content, really. And she had named the infant Angel, after all, in spite of the other Angel's objections that day of the wedding.

None of this the guests could know now as they laughed and danced and ate and sang, and the small children screeched and ran and darted under the tables and gobbled bits of cake.

The music of the guitarras grew louder, more resonant. "Come along home now, honey," Bick said. "We can go now. I've had enough of this and so have you."

He rose from the crowded table, and Leslie with him. Angel, the bridegroom, and Marita, the bride, seeing their guests of honor about to leave, started toward them in smiling farewell.

It was then that Jordy Benedict stood up, too, and to the amazement of the wedding guests he put his arm about the girl Juana's shoulder. He was very pale and his dark eyes seemed enormous.

He spoke formally in Spanish. "Ladies and gentlemen! My mother and my father! Friends! I have not spoken until now because I did not want to intrude on the festivities of this wedding of my friends Angel Obregon and Marita Rivas. But now I can tell you that yesterday morning Juana and I were married in the rectory of the Church of the Immaculate Conception in Nopal. We are husband and wife."

He spoke without his usual stammer. No one noticed this. Though perhaps somewhere in his mother's stunned mind it registered.

28

SPRAWLED COMFORTABLY ON a veranda chair, Bick was deep in talk with Judge Whiteside and Gabe Target and Pinky Snyth and Uncle Bawley. Cattle, oil, politics were the primary subjects of discussion as always in a group of Texas males. Wars and the end of wars; nations and the fall of nations; human lives and the shattering of human lives; all these were secondary.

"My family and I live just the way we've always lived here at Reata. All that black grease in the far lot," Bick said contemptuously, "hasn't made a mite of difference. Plainer, in fact. Look at the Big House where I was brought up compared to this little shack."

"That's right," Pinky Snyth agreed. A gleam of malice danced in the seemingly guileless, blue eyes. "Just like in the old-timey days, that's you, Bick. Nature is all. God sure was good to you Benedicts to hand you a seventy-five-foot reinforced concrete swimming pool set down in the brush right in your own front yard."

Bick good-humoredly joined in the laughter. "Well, now, it's a health measure. Leslie's in and out like a seal. And the young folks. We'd have had that pool in time, oil or no oil."

Gabe Target was a realist. "Like hell you would! That twenty-seven and a half percent exemption on oil fetched all the little knicknacks around your country here like swimming pools and airplanes and Caddys and whole herds of fifty-thousand-dollar critters. And that goes for the rest of the state, too."

"Depreciation," Pinky Snyth mused. "It's wonderful."

Judge Whiteside spoke pontifically. "One of the finest laws ever passed in Washington, that oil-well depreciation."

There was the sound of light laughter from the shadow of the vines at the rear of the veranda. The heads of the five men turned sharply. "That you, Leslie?" Bick called.

Her voice, a lovely sound, came to them though they could not see her. "I get starved for male conversation. I'm in the harem section pretending not to be here."

"Whyn't you move down here where we can look at your pretty face, not only hear you," suggested that ancient charmer, Uncle Bawley.

She came out of the vine shadows then and stood a moment, waving them back to their chairs. "No, I'm not staying. Relax. I was just wondering about depreciation in first-class brains. My father, for example. He's way over seventy now, he's given his life to saving other men's lives. He's a weary old gentleman now, and not well. What about depreciation exemption there?"

Gabe Target, bland and benevolent, undertook to clear this feminine unreason. "Oil is a commodity, and valuable. How you going to measure the value of a man's brains!"

"By his record." Her voice was crisp now. "When a country considers oil more important than the spirit of man, it's a lost country."

"Now Leslie." Bick's tone was fond, but a trifle irritated too. "Get down off that stump. Someday a short-tempered Texian is going to take a shot at you."

"All right. I'm off." Her voice was gay but her eyes were serious.

"Where you going, hot of the day like this?" Pinky asked.

"Stay here," Uncle Bawley pleaded. "It rests my eyes just to look at you."

"Gentlemen, I'll tell you this privately," Bick announced, "old Bawley's always been in love with my wife."

"Who hasn't!" The heavily gallant judge Whiteside.

Straight and slim as she had been more than twenty years ago. A misting of white in the abundant black of her hair. "I wish I didn't have to go, but I've promised. Luz and I are driving Juana and little Jordan over to Bob Dietz's new place. Bob's got a new lamb to show Jordan, he's never seen a lamb."

"All these Jordans around here," Gabe Target said, "I should think you'd get mixed up."

"His name isn't really Jordan, you know. Jordy and Juana named him Polo, after his grandfather. But Jordan began to call him Jordan———" Laughing, she gave it up.

"Dietz's place," Bick said, and shuffled his feet a little. "That's a far piece for the kid to go, day like this."

"He's tough."

Bick's frown cleared and he wagged his head. "He sure is. I sat him up front of me on my horse yesterday, just to see what he'd do, and when I took him down he began to bellow to be put back up again. Kicked me."

"Well, real Mexican———" Pinky began. Then he stopped abruptly.

Brightly, but looking them over with a clear cool gaze, Leslie said her polite farewells. "I'll be back by six. You know the way Luz drives. Won't you all stay for supper? And tell me what you've talked about while I'm away. If you dare. Just what are you five evil men up to now, I wonder. And don't you know you'll have to pay for it in the end?"

She vanished into the house. The five men looked at each other.

"Leslie's always been real sharp talking," Judge Whiteside said, and his tone was not altogether admiring.

Uneasily Bick dismissed the criticism. "Leslie doesn't mean it. When she gets going I just come back at her with some mild questions about the South and Tammany in New York and a few things like that."

The men sat quietly a moment. Reata Ranch sounds came to them on the hot Gulf wind—humming metallic sounds now, different from the sounds of a quarter century ago. The men pondered this, too, as they sat seemingly relaxed but actually tense with a kind of terrible Texas tenseness born of the fierce sun and the diet of beef and the runaway pace of prosperity.

"Don't hardly ever hear a horse nowdays," Gabe Target observed.

"Do when I'm moving around," Bick said.

Pinky eyed him keenly. "Thought you didn't gallop around as much as you used to."

"Leslie's always after me to take it easy, but I pay it no mind."

"Everything and everybody taking it easy now," Gabe Target mused. "Reach in the deep freeze for food. Lunch counter right in your own kitchen like a café—pie, coffee, sandwiches. Bump gates, touch 'em with the nose of your car, out they open and bingo they close. Bulldozers. Stingers. Jeeps. Planes in the back lot like Fords."

"My twins," Pinky said, "they went zooming down to Houston yesterday, and back—slacks and their hair in curlers—said they had to get them some lobsters, they had the girls coming for a card party they'd set their hearts on these lobsters Luggen's store just flew in special from up in Maine. They thought nothing of the trip, three four hundred miles each way, like running to the corner grocery."

Uncle Bawley often sat with his eyes shut, listening. His fingers tapped a tuneless rhythm on the chair arm. Now he opened his crepey lids and surveyed the younger men. "Oil! What do folks use it for! In the war they were flying around shooting up towns of women and children. Now it's lobsters from Maine. Got to have lobsters. And streaking hell-bent in automobiles a hundred miles an hour, going nowheres, killing people like chickens by the roadside. Pushing ships across the ocean in four five days. There hasn't been a really good boatload of folks since the *Mayflower* crowd.''

"You don't get around enough, Bawley," Gabe Target argued. "Look what it's done for the state! Look what it's done for Houston and Dallas and Hermoso and Corpus and a hundred more. Look at the people there!''

"Yep. Look at 'em. The girls all got three mink coats and no place to wear 'em. And emeralds the size of avocados. The menfolks, they got Cadillacs like locomotives and planes the size of ocean liners, and their offices done up in teakwood and cork and plexiglas. And what happens! The women get bored and go to raising pretty flowers for prize shows like their grammaws did and the men go back to raising cattle just like their grampappies did a long time ago. Next thing you know mustard greens and corn bread'll be fashionable amongst 'em, instead of bragging about how they eat at the Pavilion Café and the Twenty-One Club when they go to New York. My opinion, they're tired of everything, and everybody's kind of tired of them. They made the full circle."

"Well, anyway, Uncle Bawley," Pinky Snyth protested, grinning, "you can't object to the breed of beef cattle that oil money has raised up here on Reata."

"Can," declared Uncle Bawley. "And do. I was thinking yesterday in that big tent Bick set up there, selling off bulls and steers. All out of that big black bull Othello, scares you to see him, a black Kashmir bull with all those greeny-white cows it's miscegenation. Priced fifty thousand dollars, he is."

"Sixty," Bick said. And he thought, Oh, shut up for God's sake will you, Uncle Bawley, I'm tired and edgy.

"Fifty—sixty—when you get up into those figgers for a he-cow what's the difference! Like Jett Rink's holdings. Has he got a thousand million or only a hundred million? What's the diff? It ain't money any more, it's zeros. There they stood, those critters in the auction tent, solid square, low-slung like a Mack truck, legs just stumps, all beef and more of it in all the right places than any beef animal that ever was bred up on this earth."

"Yes, well now look, Uncle Bawley———" Bick interrupted.

"—And it put me in mind of the fat women in the circus," the old man continued, unheeding. "Fattest Woman on Earth, the fella says, hollering about how big she is. And sure enough, there she sets, enormous, she's all female, she's got more of everything in the right places than any woman on earth. But who the hell wants her!"

A yelp went up. Even Bick, annoyed though he was, joined in the laughter. "You'll eat those words along with that steak we're going to have tonight for dinner."

"Don't know's I will, at that. Looking at two three those animals yesterday that you keep aspecial for family feeding. Looked like a string of freight cars standing there. One of them had laid down with his legs kind of splayed out instead of doubled under and by golly it couldn't get up. They finally had to buckle on ropes and chains and straps and haul the thing up standing. I've et steaks off those behemoths. They've had the flavor bred right out of them."

"Tell you what, Uncle Bawley," Pinky suggested. "Maybe one the boys'll go out rustle up an old Longhorn that's been hiding somewhere in the brush these past fifty years. Leslie'll have you a good old-time leather steak cut off of that.''

The calm low tones of Gabe Target's voice undercut the talk and laughter. The cold grey eyes grew opaque, expressionless. ''Now boys, this is very pleasant, sitting here gabbing and joshing in the hot of the day. But I'm due back home tonight, and this isn't what I came down for. You want to state your situation, Bick? Not that we don't know it. But just between us, off the record, cut down to bare bones.''

Bick Benedict hunched forward, his hands clasped in front of him between his knees, his arms resting on his thighs. ''Here it is, straight. We didn't realize, when we let out the oil leases, how many oil workers were going to swarm in on Reata. There's a mob of them. I've got nothing against them, big husky fellows, work hard and spend their money. They know they have to keep away from me and I keep away from them. Well. At first it was work and sleep and eat and live in those shacks just anyhow, for them. But now the whole outfit has sort of shaken down, they've brought in their wives and kids and so on. At first they stuffed their houses with refrigerators and radios and gadgets. But now they've got together in a bunch called The Better Living Association.''

''Better living!'' snorted judge Whiteside.

''How many of them?'' Gabe Target did not waste energy on emotions.

''Oh, good many hundreds by now. Swarming all over the town and county.''

''Dissident votes,'' Pinky Snyth announced, like a checker of lists. ''Right in this precinct.''

''They're yelling all over the district they want what they call decent schools for their kids and a hospital for the sick and injured and so on, and homes for their families. And the oil property—about a hundred and fifty thousand acres of it—is in my precinct here. In the town of Benedict. If they vote—and they will—and carry it—and they will the way it stands now—they don't want my—the old Commissioner. They want him voted out and a new Commissioner in. There'll be a new tax rate on every acre of land hereabouts. That tax on a couple of million acres can just about cripple Reata. They win, and it'll spread to your Double B, Pinky. And you know it.''

He unclasped his hands, threw them open, palms up. The lines in his forehead were deep, the eyes strained and bloodshot. Pinky Snyth, looking at him, thought irrelevantly, Vashti's right, like she said Bick's letting Reata eat him up alive.

Judge Whiteside cleared his throat. ''You talked to the Azabache crowd about this, Bick?''

''What do they care! It doesn't affect them. They said Jett Rink heard of it, he laughed his crazy fat head off.''

Silence. The hot wind rustling the vine leaves. The drum of a powerful motor somewhere far off on the prairie. One of the nearby workboys calling in Mexican-Spanish to another busy at the pool. The five men sat eying each other. Waiting.

Smoothly, benevolently, Gabe Target broke the silence. ''Well now, Bick, we don't want anything that isn't perfectly legal and aboveboard, of course.''

''Course,'' the four echoed, and their eyes never left his face.

Silence again, brief, breathless. ''I suggest—and of course I'd want the sound legal opinion of our good friend the Judge here—I suggest a very simple feasible plan, Bick. Now first I'd like to ask you a couple questions. You don't need to answer if you don't see fit. But my little plan kind of depends on the answers.''

Goddamned old pompous fool, Bick's inner voice yelled. Aloud, "All right, Chief. Shoot."

"Plainly speaking, the County Commisioner's your man. That right?"

"Right."

"The Mexicans on your place—vaqueros and so on—they vote right?"

"They vote—right."

"All of them?"

"Yes."

"I heard some of the younger Mexican fellas since the war's over they've come home and haven't settled down right, they've been rabble-rousing, shooting their mouths off, getting together saying they're American citizens without rights and that kind of stuff. They want to be called Latin Americans, not Mexicans any more. I hear they're getting up organizations, the boys who fought in the war, and so on. Spreading all over, they say. Got some fancy names for their outfits with America in it to show how American they are."

"Well?"

"Can you handle them?"

"I can handle them. Always have. They'll quiet down."

"The full vote is needed to carry your candidate. Am I correct? Without it, he's out?"

"Out."

Gabe Target's eyes were flat disks of steel sunk in the caverns below his fatherly brow. "Well, my boy, you don't want a crowded big noisy city sprung up around this beautiful Reata———"

"As fair a piece of Nature's bounty," Judge Whiteside intoned, by now somewhat piqued at finding himself shorn of his accustomed curls of peroration, "as there is anywhere in this Great Commonwealth, and I may say, anywhere—North America, South America, the uncharted wastes of Asia———"

"If you think Asia's uncharted, Judge, after this last war," Pinky Snyth interrupted somewhat pertly, "you better get set for a shock to your nervous system."

"Boys, boys!" Gabe Target's kindly chiding tones like those of a gentle schoolmaster.

Bick held his temper by an effort. "Let's just hear Gabe out, will you? This is pretty important. I know a few millions don't matter much any more in Texas. But Reata matters to me more than anything in the world."

Pinky thought, By gosh he means it. More than anything in the world.

But Gabe was talking in that quiet reasonable voice so that everything he said sounded plausible and right and somehow beneficent.

"That's a mighty fine sentiment, son, and it does you credit as a real Benedict and Texian. Now then. These boys in the big oil outfits—and I don't doubt they're good fine boys, though maybe mistaken some ways— they ought to have their own town. They've earned it. Hard-working boys. And keep Benedict the way it is, population and layout and nice little town government and all. And taxes. The same. Just have the precinct lines rearranged and the town line set to where it was before oil. B.O. There's a big enough population sprung up there outside to make a fine little town of their own, the oil crowd and their wives and all. Get 'em incorporated, all fair and aboveboard—before they know where they're at. Town line. Board. Commissioner. Everything in good order. They could call the town— for example, if they were so minded—Azabache. Or town of Jett Rink. And leave him build the schools they're bawling for, and the hospitals and the city hall and the gymnasiums and pave the streets and put in the water. And let Jett Rink pay the taxes.''

Silence. Gabe Target's eyelids came down over the flinty eyes, giving him that aspect of benevolence again.

Finally Bick spoke. ''You really think it can be done?''

''Judge Whiteside here will bear me out I think. Won't you, Judge? Bick wants to know if it can be done.''

Judge Whiteside cleared his throat. His voice had the finality of one who is the Law. ''It's as good as done this minute. You can forget it.''

''Little drink would go good,'' Pinky suggested.

Everything had been conducted in the approved fashion. Like the concocting of a well-made Texas barbecue sandwich. The preliminary conversational chitchat was the blandly buttered under slice of bread. Then the quick hot spiced filling of meat and burning sauce. And now the layer of pleasant aimless talk again. The top slice of bread.

Bick reached for the little bell on the table at his side. Almost before its tinkle had died away on the hot restless air the two Mexican girls appeared, one with the tray of bourbon and ice and water, the other with the coffee.

Solemnly the men drank, the talk was more desultory now, their voices as always low, pleasant, almost musical. Gabe looked at Bick Benedict, he thought the man's russet coloring was now like a lacquer over a foundation of grey. ''Bick, how's Jordy working out as a doctor?''

Bick hesitated a moment before answering. When he spoke it was with a wry lightness. ''Oh, you know young folks today. Jordy takes after Leslie's side of the family, more. Her father.''

Blunderingly, Judge Whiteside must satisfy his own curiosity, now that Gabe Target had inserted the entering wedge in a topic that the Benedicts' social circle considered closed to discussion. ''I suppose this Guerra's office he's in—I suppose Jordy's starting off using the Mexicans like a clinic, more. For experience—observation—so forth.''

Bick did not reply.

''I can't get the right of it,'' the Judge persisted. A thick unctuous layer of virtue was spread to conceal his sadism. ''Only son and all. Where's his feeling about Reata! To say nothing of his pa and ma!''

The little crooked smile on Bick's lips did not deceive the four keen-eyed men. ''Oh well, Judge, you can't tie a kid to a horse. His talents lie another way, that's all. I'll make out. I'm not quite through—yet.''

Judge Whiteside blustered reassuringly. ''You! Why, Bick boy, you're good for another fifty years hard riding. Look at old Bawley here! A thousand, ain't you, Bawley! And spry as a gopher.''

Gabe Target's cool measured tones cut through this persiflage.

''Bick, you ought to get you a good smart solid young fella, now the war's over, knows stock and range and feed and all. Modern —'' hastily—''like yourself. Train him into manager to do the routine hard over-all work. College type but with his feet on the ground. And I mean Texas ground.''

Pinky Snyth spoke up. ''That's Bob Dietz. Say, I tried my best to steal him off you, Bick, years ago to work the Double B. He wasn't hardly more than a kid then. Wouldn't come.''

Bick's gaze went out and out, past the veranda and screening, on and on to the distant line where the dome of the sky met the golden-tan curve of the earth. ''I offered him the job. He wasn't interested. He as much as said I was old-fashioned. Said this was the time for pioneering in advanced range management techniques. That's what he said. Said he was interested in ranching as a way of life for the many, and not to make big money. He said people who wanted big money ought to try the stock market or the oil industry or most anything but agriculture and stock."

A stunned silence followed this recital of heresy.

Judge Whiteside cleared his throat. "I don't aim to appear nosy, but I heard around that this Dietz and your Luz were running together a good deal. Dietz isn't invited to parties and places, but a lot in her plane and his car and hamburger joints talking, and so on."

Bick shrugged in an effort at carelessness, but his brow was thunderous. "Oh, kid stuff. Dietz is smart enough, but he's one of those know-it-all kids. Luz is a real rancher, she'll talk to anybody who'll teach her something new. The Dietz kid—or anybody."

"He's no kid," Uncle Bawley announced, suddenly awake, wide-eyed. "He's getting along."

The guffaw that this brought forth lightened the heavy resentment of Bick's tone. "Well, anyway, this ancient Bob Dietz, he says the big ranch is doomed. The feudal system he calls it. That's you and me, Pinky. Says that with artificial insemination and modern long-term reseeding, pretty soon you won't need to feed your stock a pound of hay or cake. You'd think to hear him talk he was the one first discovered Lehman's love grass and yellow bluestem and sideoats grama and blue grama and all. He's got a piece about twenty sections now, down near the Valley, he calls it a trial range unit, he says he———"

"How about water?" scoffed Judge Whiteside. "He got water fixed to eat out of his hand too?"

"Oh sure. He says no reason why water can't be harnessed and led across the continent. In the future. Says the Tennessee Valley showed us a little something. Says they'll find a way to take the salt out of salt water and hitch the whole Gulf of Mexico to Texas. That's in the future too. He says."

"If they ever get water into Texas," Gabe Target said, "God knows what'll happen."

"I'll tell you what," Uncle Bawley announced in his gentle musing voice. "The youngsters will cut Reata into pie slices and raise up a steer to the acre."

29

EVEN AFTER ALL these years Leslie Benedict always felt a distinct shock as she came out of the dim cool rooms of the Main House to meet the full blast of the Texas sun. The Big House hummed with air conditioners but here at the Main House the family relied on the massive old walls for protection. Leslie often had suggested a cooling unit for Bick's bedroom but he said he'd as soon sleep with a woman who snored as that thing. He even refused to have one in his office.

"Let the barbecue shacks have them," he said, "and the Houston and Hermoso zillionaires, and Neiman-Marcus and the Hake Hotel. I was brought up on Texas heat. Sun and sweat have made Texas."

Luz said, pertly, that he was beginning to sound like Uncle Bawley.

Now Luz and Leslie in the front seat, Juana and little Jordan in the back, the four were off for Bob Dietz's ranch in the Valley.

Leslie cast an anxious eye toward the child. "It'll be cooler as soon as we begin to move."

"And we're really going to move," Luz threatened as she released the brake and they were off.

"Now Luz, no stunts. It's two hours out and two back, even at your speed. . . . Juana, you don't think it's going to be too much for Polo, do you?"

Juana glanced down at the child beside her. "He loves it. He was so excited this morning he wouldn't eat his breakfast." Juana's English was spoken with precision. Her voice was soft and low and leisurely, unlike the strident tone of many Mexican-American women. Old Polo stemmed from Spanish blood and his granddaughter's skin had a creamy pallor, the dark eyes were soft and the black hair was fine and abundant. About her throat she always wore a strand of pearls that Leslie had given her—Benedict family pearls—and the luminous quality of these seemed reflected in her skin. But the child Polo had the café-au-lait coloring of his Mexican grand-mother and great-grandmother; and their Mexican hair and eyes.

Now the car rounded the curve in the long driveway and passed the Big House. Three or four people were descending the broad stone steps and there were cars waiting in the drive. Almost automatically Leslie bowed and waved and smiled, though she knew only vaguely who the guests were this week or this particular day.

"It seems to me," Luz remarked, "that our visiting strangers get stranger and stranger. Who's that lot?"

"I don't know, really. Not very important. Two of the boys have been delegated to take them around. But next week!"

"I hear it's a king and queen. Doesn't it sound silly!"

"Yes, poor darlings. And a swarm of other people. It's a weird list. Somebody must have slipped up on it—Jordan's secretary or somebody. They can't all be interested in cattle."

"Who?"

"You won't believe it, even for Reata. Uh, let's see—there's a prize fighter and a Russian dancer and a South American Ambassador. And a movie queen who's bought a ranch in California and wants to stock it. And her husband. I don't remember who else. And I'm afraid your Aunt Maudie and your Aunt Leigh are descending."

"I may suddenly be called away."

"Now Luz! Anyway, they're all invited to that big thing at Jett Rink's new airport."

"Oh, that! I may hop over for a look at it but I wouldn't be found dead at the idiotic howling dinner."

"Your father would like you just to show up, and Jordy, too, and all of us."

"That's ridiculous! What for?"

"Because everybody is going to be there, and if we stay away it will look queer. Anyway, there's a political reason of some kind. He doesn't like it any better than you do. But Roady asked specially that we all go—you and Jordy and Maudie———"

"Me!" asked the child's eager voice from the back seat.

Leslie turned, she held out her hand to the child and smiled at him. "No, you don't have to be political, my darling. Not yet."

The child looked at her solemnly, the great dark eyes almost mournful. "I'm hungry."

"There!" Juana said. "Because you didn't eat your breakfast."

"I want my breakfast now."

"Listen, Snooks," Luz called to the child, "wait till we get out of Benedict and past Nopal."

"But I'm hungry."

"In a little minute, mi vida," Juana said to the child. "Near the Valley where it is quiet. You will have milk and we will drink coffee. And we will have lunch at Bob Dietz's house.''

"And I will see a baby lamb!''

They had whirled through the streets of Benedict. The old main street had become a business section that branched in all directions. Plate-glass windows reflected, glitter for glitter, the dazzling aluminum and white enamel objects within. Vast refrigerators, protean washing machines, the most acquisitive of vacuum cleaners. There were three five-and-dime stores and the dime had burgeoned into a dollar. All day long in these stores mechanical music droned a whining tune sung by a bereft crooner. Why do you make me feel so blue? he complained. Don't you want me as I want you? Mexican women with four small children, the woman always pregnant, wandered up and down the crowded aisles, fingering the gaudy wares piled in tempting profusion. The children touched everything with slim caressing dark fingers. Plastic things, paper things, rayon things. Gadgets. Pink panties marked 59 cents. Machine embroidery on these depicted a lewdly winking yellow sun with He Loves Me stitched in pink and blue around its rays.

The leather shop of Ildefonso Mezo was little more than tourist bait now, for Ildefonso was long gone. Tourists from Iowa and New York and Missouri stopped to buy stitched high-heeled cowboy boots in which their offspring hobbled back into the waiting family car.

The moth-eaten Longhorn steer still stood in his glass case morosely staring out at the procession of motorcars streaming along the road which in his lifetime had known only the quick clatter of horses' hoofs and the bellow and shuffle and thud of moving cattle.

As the Benedict car flashed through the town and out Leslie's quick glance darted this way and that. "How it changes! Almost from day to day. You should have seen it when I came here a bride, before any of you were born.''

"Well, I hope so, madam!'' Luz exclaimed virtuously.

"That first week! I'll never forget it. I rejected just about everything— except your father. The—the vaqueros' horrible little shacks were worse than the Negro cabins in my Virginia. Texas food was steak and the steak was sole leather.''

"Still is,'' Luz observed.

"But not at our house. And there are all those modern houses in the barrios now. And they're talking about a new hospital here in Benedict and a new school.''

Juana's voice was very low, for the child had fallen asleep against his mother's side. "The school for the Latin American children is a disgrace.''

Leslie turned in her seat to face her daughter-in-law there at the rear of the car with her lovely sleeping child. "I know, Juana darling. We must keep on working.''

Their speed on this flat endless road would have been terrifying to anyone not a Texan. Past the fine new house of Fidel Gomez in Nopal. Fidel Gomez, wallowing in oil, scarcely bothered now to manage the business of bringing the Mexican migratory workers, men women and children, into the Valley for the seasonal crop picking at twenty-five cents an hour.

Nopal was changing, too. TORTILLA FACTORY a sign read in the town where once the pat-pat of women's hands had sounded from every little dwelling. The dry-goods store was a department store now, it boasted a plate-glass expanse of its own and in the window a large printed sign announced LADY CASTLEMERE SHEETS! ADVERTISED IN LIFE! And staring into the window a black-garbed Mexican woman with four children tugging at her skirts, and it was plain to see that she never had lain between such sheets, nor would; and that Life as she knew it had always been lower case.

There were motion picture theatres offering Westerns. *Border Bad Man*. *Wagon Wheels West*. Coals to Newcastle, Leslie thought as the great car swept through the small towns and out again into the open road.

"There isn't any open road any more," she announced. "Just the other day I read that a hundred years ago—less than a hundred—Congress voted money for camels to be sent to Texas. They came from Syria and Alexandria and Constantinople with the camel drivers, to be used in the United States Army. Imagine some Texas pioneer woman looking out of the door of her little shack and suddenly seeing a camel chewing its cud in the open prairie under the Texas stars."

"I want to see a camel!" little Polo demanded.

"The camel has gone away, my pet. Look at that enormous thing with all those aluminum chimneys or whatever they are. Acres of it."

"Lexanese plant," Luz said.

"They couldn't have run it up overnight. But I don't remember having seen it before. I must get about more. I'll turn into a homebody if I'm not careful."

"If you weren't so stubborn about letting me take you up in the little plane," Luz reminded her, "you'd see the world."

"You and Jordy don't really see the world. You've learned your geography from planes. You think the world is little blocks and squares with bugs wriggling over them. To you Tennessee is a red and pink checkerboard, and Louisiana is a smear of purple and black. And the Mississippi is a yellow line slithering through it all. I don't think you ever really see anything from the angle of the ground. What with horses and planes and cars you never set foot to earth."

"Bob says you forgot to teach me to walk. But anyway, what I see from the air is mighty pretty, missy. Which is more than you can say down here."

"Tell me, what's Bob's new house like? Is it attractive?"

"Attractive as a box car. You could put the whole thing in our pantry."

"Modern pioneer, h'm?"

"You and Pa are a little worried about Bob Dietz, aren't you?"

"Well, no, not worried. I think he's a wonderful young man. I don't suppose you plan to marry every man who interests you."

"No. Only one. Bob and I have talked about it. He says he wouldn't marry any girl who has Reata hung around her neck." The girl's voice was even and her eyes were on the road ahead but something intangible asked mutely for guidance.

"Your Aunt Luz, that you were named after, thought that Reata was more important than marriage." Luz said nothing. They drove on in silence. Luz just turned her head, then, to glance at her mother, and again her eyes came back to the road. In a tone of somewhat dry reminiscence Leslie went on. "She was in love with Cliff Hake—that was Vashti Snyth's father—and he was in love with her. But he wouldn't come to live at Reata and she wouldn't go to live at the Double B, and they wouldn't throw the two ranches into one. So she lived at Reata an old maid. And died there."

"I'm still young," Luz said, her voice airy, "even if I am over twenty. Young in spirit, that's me. . . . I danced with Jett Rink the other night."

"No, Luz!"

"It was only for a minute or two. He was drunk but not violent. It was last week when I went to Houston for the party. We were having dinner at the Shamrock, Glenn McCarthy came into the Emerald Room with a bunch of Big Boys and Jett Rink was one of them. He looked quite handsome in a Mississippi Gaylord Ravenal kind of way. He had the nerve to come up

to our table and ask me to dance. I decided it would be better to try it than
to risk his going into one of his slugging matches with one of our men.''

"What did he say?''

''Sort of babbled. Still mad at the Benedicts but not you and not me, as
nearly as I could gather. A lot about you. And then he suggested it would
be nice if I'd marry him. What an ape!''

''I'm hungry!'' Polo was wide awake now.

Leslie turned to reassure him. ''All right, my precious. We'll stop somewhere.''

''I want my breakfast,'' the boy demanded.

Luz called back to him, ''Sweetie, there's a kind of monotony about your
conversation. Juana, there's a nice clean new place about a mile further on.
Bob and I stopped there for a sandwich the other night. They toast them.
Quite good. I could do with a Coke, myself.''

There were a dozen cars outside the little roadside lunch room. A radio
whined. Trucks and passenger cars and jeeps mingled affably in the parking
place. ''You go along in,'' Luz said. ''I'll park away from these bloodthirsty
trucks.'' Leslie took the boy's hand in hers as he walked with his uncertain
staggering steps. He looked proudly up into her face. She loved the feel of
the velvety morsel in her palm. ''Now, my pet. We'll all have something
good, but not much because Bob Dietz will want us to eat lunch at his house,
he won't like it if we're not hungry.''

''Won't he let me see the little lamb?''

''Oh yes, he'll let you see the lamb. Now then. Up the little step.''

A coffee counter. Metal tables with chairs upholstered in scarlet imitation
leather. A harassed middle-aged woman behind the counter, a red-faced
shirt-sleeved man behind the cash register; a waitress wiping a table top with
a damp cloth. Truck drivers at the coffee counter, women and children eating
at the tables.

They stood a moment, Leslie, Juana, the child, in the bright steamy room
with its odors of coffee and fried food. ''That table in the corner,'' Juana
suggested. ''Perhaps there is a high chair for you, mi vida.''

''I don't want a high chair, I am a big boy.''

They sat down. ''What's keeping Luz?'' Leslie said, and tucked in a paper
napkin at Polo's neck which he at once removed.

''We don't serve Mexicans here.''

They did not at first hear. Or, if they heard, the words did not penetrate
their consciousness. So now the man came from behind the cash register
and moved toward them. His voice was louder now. ''We don't serve Mexicans here.''

Leslie Benedict stared around the room, but the man was looking at her
and at Juana and at Polo. Leslie was frowning a little, as though puzzled.
''What?''

''You heard me.'' He jerked a thumb toward the doorway. ''Out.'' The
men drinking coffee at the counter and the people at the nearby tables looked
at the two women and the child. They kept on eating and drinking, though
they looked at them and glanced with sliding sidewise glances at each other.

Leslie rose. Juana stood, too, and the child wriggled off the chair and ran
to his mother's side. ''You can't be talking to me!'' Leslie said.

''I sure can. I'm talking to all of you. Our rule here is no Mexicans served
and I don't want no ruckus. So—out!''

The worried-looking woman behind the lunch counter said, ''Now Floyd,
don't you go getting techy again. They ain't doing nothing.''

Leslie felt her lips strangely stiff. She said, ''You must—be out of your
mind.''

"Who you talking to!" the man yelled.

Luz came blithely in, she stared a moment at the little group on whose faces was written burning anger; at the openmouthed men and women at the counter and tables.

"Heh, what's going on here!" she said.

The man glanced at the golden-haired blue-eyed girl, he pointed a finger at the two women and the child, but Leslie spoke before he could repeat the words.

"This man won't serve us. He says he won't serve Mexicans."

Even the jaws at the counter had ceased champing now.

The scarlet surged up into Luz's face, her eyes were a blazing blue. Leslie thought, with some little portion of her brain that was not numb, Why she looks exactly—but exactly—like Jordan when he is furious.

"You son of a bitch!" said Miss Luz Benedict.

The man advanced toward her.

"Floyd!" barked the woman behind the counter.

"Git!" shouted the man then. "You and your greasers." And he gave Polo a little shove so that he lurched forward and stumbled and Luz caught him.

Luz reverted then to childhood. "I'll tell my father! He'll kill you! Do you know who my father is! He's————"

"No! No, Luz! No name. Come."

As they went they heard, through the open doorway, the voices of the man and woman raised again in dispute.

"You crazy, Floyd! Only the kid and his ma was cholos, not the others."

"Aw, the old one was, black hair and sallow, you can't fool me."

Leslie put a hand through Juana's arm, she took the child's hand in hers. "Come, children. Sh! Don't cry!"

"That is a bad man," Polo said through his sobs.

"Yes, darling."

"I am hungry I want my breakfast."

They were climbing into the car now. "Grandma will sit back here with you. That man didn't have nice milk to drink. Luz will get out at the next place and she'll get you a bottle of milk and some crackers and you can drink the milk through a straw as we ride along and you can see the little lamb all the sooner. Won't that be fun!"

30

SHE HAD THEIR promise. All the way to Bob Dietz's ranch and all the way back they had argued. But in the end Luz and Juana had promised.

"Please," Leslie had implored them, "please not until after that horrible Jett Rink party is over. Please Luz, please Juana, don't tell your father don't tell Jordy don't tell Bob until after that. You know they'd do something—something hasty, it would get into the papers, it would be all over the state. All those guests at the Big House, and a thousand people going to the party. There'll be publicity enough. Please just wait until next week, then we'll all talk about it quietly, together."

"Quietly!" shouted Luz. "I'm going to tell Bob the minute we hit the house. He'll kill that baboon."

"Luz, I promise you it won't be left like this. I promise. But it can't be now. This is the wrong time. It's got to be handled through proper channels, carefully. Your father and Gabe and Judge Whiteside.''

"Judge Whiteside!" Luz scoffed. "That belly-crawler!"

Quietly Leslie said, "We're furious because of what that ignorant bigot did. But we all know this has been going on for years and years. It's always happened to other people. Now it's happened to us. The Benedicts of Reata. So we're screaming.''

"All right," Luz snapped, "then let's hit it.''

"Yes. But not now. Please. Not just now. It's the worst possible time to make a public fuss.''

And deep inside her a taunting voice said, Oh, so now you're doing it too, h'm? After twenty-five years of nagging and preaching and being so superior you're evading too. Infected. Afraid to speak up and act and defy. Hit the rattlesnake before it strikes again. Tell them now, tell them now, what does it matter about the silly guests and the ranch and the oil and the banquet and the talk and the state? It's the world that matters.

At six that evening Bick Benedict, sprawled on the couch in their bedroom, regarded his wife with the fond disillusioned gaze of the husband who is conditioned to seeing cold cream applied to the wind-burned feminine face.

"What the hell went on down there at Bob Dietz's?" he inquired. "You girls came home as sore-acting as if you'd been scalped by Karankawas. Juana looked as if she'd been crying and Luz stamped past me without speaking. Just glared. Did the two girls quarrel or something? What the hell went on down there, anyway?''

"Nothing," Leslie replied. "Just tired, I guess.''

"Uh-huh. All right, keep your girlish secrets. You don't look so good yourself, by the way.''

Leslie continued to pat the cold cream on her cheeks. "Thanks, chum. There's nothing like a little flattery to set a girl up before dinner.''

"The boys decided not to stay. Except Uncle Bawley. He's not going back to Holgado until tomorrow.''

"Did you finish your business? That private business you were all so cagey about?''

"Uh, yes. Yes.''

"I thought you all looked as guilty as kids who were going to rob an orchard. Did it turn out all right?''

"Fine. Fine.''

"What was it all about?''

"Oh, nothing you'd be interested in, honey. Town business. Elections coming up. Stuff like that.''

Tell him now, the Voice said. Tell him his wife and his daughter and his daughter-in-law and his grandson were kicked out of a roadside diner and it's his fault and your fault and the fault of every man and woman like you. But she only said, aloud, "We brought the little lamb back with us in the car. Bob gave it to Polo.''

"You trying to make a sheep man out of a Benedict! Don't let that get around the cow country.''

"He insists on keeping it in a box in his bedroom. Juana's having quite a time.''

He laughed like a boy at his mental picture of this. Then he fell silent. When he spoke he was serious, he was urgent. "Leslie, I wish they could live here at Reata. Not only little visits like this, but stay. Do you think they might? The kid loves it here.''

"Of course he does. He thinks it's heaven. Wouldn't any child who'd lived in a three-room New York apartment while his father went to school?''

"Speak to Juana about it, will you? Maybe if Jordy sees how happy she and the boy are here he'll leave Vientecito and give up that stinking clinic, settle down here at Reata where he belongs."

Agreeably, quite as though she did not know that what he suggested was hopeless, she seemed to fall in with his plan. "Wouldn't that be lovely! I'll speak to Juana tomorrow."

He sighed with a sort of deep satisfaction as if the impossible were already accomplished. "Let's have a little drink up here before I have to go down and start arguing again with Uncle Bawley." After she had given the order, "What's Dietz's place like?"

"Compact as a hairbrush. You wouldn't know it was Texas. Everything planned to the last inch like a problem in physics. It's planted right up to the front door, I expected to see grass growing in the house."

"Did, huh? See his stock?"

"Yes. Some. It looked—what's that word?—thrifty. Bob said it was solid beef cattle, he wasn't going in for collectors' items."

"Snotty kid."

"Let's be fair. Bob's more than that. Jordan, maybe this boy has got hold of something so fundamental that it's enormous."

"You sound as if you'd been talking to your daughter Luz. I want to know what you think of him."

"Bob's a fine man. And more than just smart. For the rest, perhaps he's just a le-e-etle bit too earnest for my taste, and not enough humor. But maybe that's the mark of future greatness. Great men are usually pretty stuffy. Except you."

The Mexican girl came in with the tray and placed it on the table beside him. Bick opened the bourbon, cocked an eyebrow at Leslie, she nodded.

"That's mighty pretty talk, missy." But he was not smiling. "Look. Is she going to marry him?"

"I don't know. Neither does she. He won't marry Reata. I'm sure of that. Not even if he has to lose Luz. And he's crazy about her. But not that crazy."

He put down his glass. "Heh, wait a minute! This is where we came in, isn't it?"

"Sort of. We talked a little about her Aunt Luz today. I told her about Luz and Cliff Hake—before he was old Cliff Hake."

He got up and began to stride about the room. "Oh, you did, eh?"

"Yes. I thought she might be interested to know what happens to a woman, sometimes, if she doesn't marry because of some unimportant thing like a ranch, for example."

"She doesn't want to marry that dirt farmer. Anyway, she isn't going to. Not if I can help it."

"Twentieth century. Remember?"

Moodily he stared at her. "Oh, let's forget it. I'm tired. This has been a stinker of a day."

Instantly she was alert. "What happened?"

"Nothing. Everything. After the boys left I sat there talking to Bawley a while. He looked like an old hundred-year turtle, mopping his eyes and mumbling. I love the old goof but he sure can drive you crazy. Talking. He thinks he's one of the Prophets or something now, the way he talks."

"But what did he say that upset you?"

"Nothing. Nothing that made sense, that is. It was just the whole stinking day. I got to thinking about this damned Rink shindig next week. Bawley said he wouldn't be seen dead there, oil or no oil. And to tell you the truth I'd rather be shot than go."

"That's wonderful! We won't go."

His shoulders slumped. "We've got to. Because everybody's going. If we stay away we'll be the only outfit for a thousand miles around that isn't there. Everybody's going and nobody wants to—nobody that is anybody. Stay away and we'd be more marked than if we went to the party naked. . . . To think that that cochino could make decent people do anything they don't want to do!"

"He can't. We don't have to go." She faced him squarely, hairbrush in hand, she gesticulated with it as she spoke. "You keep on doing—we keep on doing things we're really opposed to. You just can't keep on doing things against your feelings and principles."

Belligerently, "You don't say! What things?"

"You've just said it. This hideous kowtowing to a thing like Jett Rink. But that isn't so important. It's a thousand other things. Oil. And the ranch. And the Mexicans. The bigotry. The things that can happen to decent people. It's going to catch up with you. It's taken a hundred years and maybe it'll take another hundred. But it will catch up with you. With everybody. It always does."

"Go join a club," he said wearily, and turned away from her and threw himself again on the couch, his boots scuffling the silken coverlet.

She came over to him and sat beside him. "Bick, do you feel ill?"

He stared at her. "You called me Bick."

"Did I?"

"Why?"

"I don't know, Jordan. I didn't know I had."

"You've never called me that before. Never. Everybody else did, but you've never called me anything but my name, since the day we met. Say, that's kind of funny. Maybe it means you've kind of finished with your husband Jordan."

She sank down against him, her cheek against his, her arm across his breast. "Jordan's my husband, darling. Bick's my friend."

"Tell your friend to get the hell out of my wife's bedroom." But he was not smiling. He lay inert, unresponsive to her. After a moment he began to talk, disjointedly, as though unwillingly admitting the doubts and fears that for months had been piling up against the door of his consciousness. "I guess it's kind of got me . . . the Boys this afternoon screwing around . . . and the whole damned oil crowd . . . it's like any dirty boom town now, Benedict is. . . . And on top of everything Jordy turning out a no-good maverick. . . . Oh well, no real Benedict, anyway. . . . Doctor Jordan Benedict! Can you imagine! Down in Spigtown with the greasers in Vientecito, a shingle on the door right along with a fellow named Guerra. . . . Juana and the kid . . . Juana's all right she's a decent girl she's Jordy's wife Jordy Benedict's wife and the kid looks like a real cholo . . ."

"Darling, don't say things like that! They're terrible. They're wrong. You don't know how wrong. You'll be sorry."

"Yeh, well I know this much. Things are getting away from me. Kind of slipping from under me, like a loose saddle. I swear to God I sometimes feel like a failure. Bick Benedict a failure. The whole Benedict family a failure."

She sat up very straight, she took his inert hand in hers, his brown iron hand, and held it close to her. "Jordan, how strange that you should say that just today!"

"Today?"

"Because today was kind of difficult for me too, in some ways. And I thought, as we were driving along toward home—Luz and Juana and little Jordan and I—I thought to myself, well, maybe Jordan and I and all the others behind us have been failures, in a way. In a way, darling. In a way that has nothing to do with ranches and oil and millions and Rinks and Whitesides and Kashmirs. And then I thought about our Jordan and our Luz and I said to myself, well, after a hundred years it looks as if the Benedict family is going to be a real success at last.''

As he turned, half startled half resentful, to stare at her, the man saw for just that moment a curious transformation in the face of this middle-aged woman. The lines that the years had wrought were wiped away by a magic hand, and there shone there the look of purity, of hope and of eager expectancy that the face of the young girl had worn when she had come, twenty-five years ago, a bride to Texas.